THE VERONA LEGACY

THE VERONA LEGACY

THE COMPLETE SERIES

L A COTTON

Published by Delesty Books

Verona Legacy: The Complete Series

Edited by Andie M Long
Cover designed by The Pretty Little Design Co.

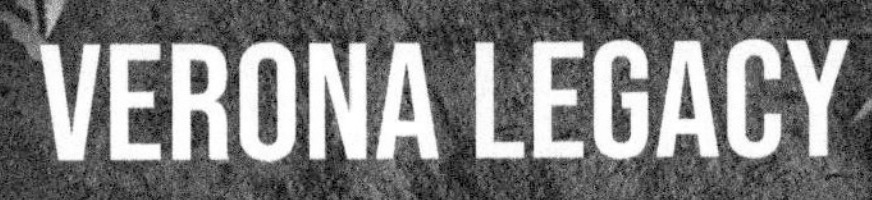

Angel of Tears
A Verona Legacy Prequel Story

Prince of Hearts
Nicco & Arianne's Duet Book #1

King of Souls
Nicco & Arianne's Duet Book #2

Villain of Secrets
A Verona Legacy Story

Savior of Regrets
A Verona Legacy Story

Thief of Virtues
A Verona Legacy Novella

Knight of Sins
A Verona Legacy Short Story

ANGEL OF TEARS
A VERONA LEGACY PREQUEL STORY

ONE

MATTEO

"SORRY I'M LATE." I jogged over to my cousins, running a hand through my hair. Fat drops of rain sprayed everywhere. A storm was blowing in, a river of water already gushing down the street.

"Let me guess, Bella giving you shit again?" Enzo asked.

"Nah, she had some homework..."

"You're a good brother, Matt." Nicco clapped me on the back. "Come on, let's get this over with."

We slipped past the two burly men guarding the door and entered the club. No one batted an eyelid except the bartender, who waved us over. DiMarco's wasn't the kind of place they let just anyone through the door.

"Would you get a load of that?" Enzo let out a low whistle, flicking his head to the circular stage in the center of the room. The girl flicked long, wavy dark hair off her shoulder as she shimmied around the pole, working her body into angles that should have been impossible.

"We're not here to play." Nicco cut Enzo with a hard look. "Keep your dick in your pants, capisci?"

"Yeah, yeah. But it doesn't hurt to look." He smirked.

He was right. She was hard *not* to look at, her body slim and toned. Legs that went on for miles. But it was her face, the way it was obscured by a filigree eye mask, that really piqued my interest. I wanted to know who she was... and what she was hiding.

Forcing myself to look away, I rolled my shoulders back. This wasn't a guys' night out, it was business, and I knew better than to let myself be distracted by a piece of hot ass.

I needed to keep my head in the game.

We all did.

Nicco led us across the room, pausing at the end of the bar. "Is Zander in?" he asked the bartender.

"Back there." The guy flicked his head to the black door framed by dark purple velvet curtains. The whole place was opulent, as if guys came here with their fat wallets and seedy desires for the décor. I snorted.

Nicco pulled back the curtain and disappeared into the dark abyss. "What?" Someone grunted. "Oh, shit. Nicco, my man, I didn't realize it was you."

"Zander," my cousin replied coolly. "We're here to collect."

Zander sat back in his leather chair and ran a hand over his jaw. "About that..."

"No excuses." Nicco slid his hand inside his jacket. "You and I both know we're not leaving here without what you owe..."

The temperature in the room dropped. Niccolò Marchetti might only have been nineteen like me and Enzo, but age was just a number when you were the son of the boss.

Zander stared up at him as if he were weighing up his options, which was pretty fucking ironic since he had none.

You either paid up or you paid the price.

In our business, it was that fucking simple.

"Don't keep me waiting," Nicco ground out. Enzo twitched at his other side, no doubt itching for a fight. He was my cousin, my brother in all the ways that counted, but he was a loose fucking cannon. Me, I preferred it when things went smoothly, and we avoided bloodshed.

My father said it was my weakness. That I was a soft touch. I guess he had a point. Being a soldier for the Marchetti family required a certain level of detachment, the ability to do whatever it took to protect and uphold the family name.

Zander let out a frustrated breath, letting us know how unwelcome we were. "You're a real fucking piece of work, you know that, Marchetti?"

"What the fuck did you just say?" Enzo shot forward. "Do you know who you're talking to?"

"Enzo," Nicco warned, pulling him back. He stepped forward, power exuding from him. We were all bound to this life, whether we wanted it or not. But for Nicco, it was different. One day, he would be the head of the family. The boss. The guy with all the power. And I knew him well enough to know he had yet to make his peace with the legacy bestowed upon him.

"You dare to disrespect me?"

Zander stood up, meeting Nicco's stare, defiance rolling off him.

"You moved into our territory, that was on you. You knew the deal; you knew what it meant. We let you do business here and you pay. You're. Fucking. Due."

Zander tsked, tugging at his collar. "Yeah, yeah, Marchetti, I know the deal." He walked over to a giant painting on the wall, ran his finger along the edge, and pulled it away, revealing a safe hidden in the brick wall. Once he had the envelope, he closed it again, repositioned the painting and stalked toward Nicco. "Nice doing business with you, kid." He thrust the envelope at Nicco's chest.

A low growl vibrated from Enzo, but before he could intervene, Nicco whipped out his pistol and jammed it against Zander's forehead. "Get your dirty fucking hands off me." Tension crackled through the air.

"Whoa, easy there, Nicco." The blood drained from the cocky fucker's face. "It's all good, we're all friends..."

"Does it look like we're friends?" Nicco gritted out, slowly forcing Zander backward. "You pay your dues just like everyone else. Got it?"

"Yeah, yeah, man, of course. I was just—"

"Mouthing off like a little bitch?" Enzo said, grabbing the envelope off him.

Nicco finally withdrew his pistol, shoving it back in the holster strapped to his body. But his expression remained dark.

He didn't like Zander DiMarco. None of us did. But business was business and his legitimate chain of strip clubs in and around Providence, Verona County, and Pawtucket made the family a good chunk of change in exchange for protection.

"Look, let's start over. Stay. Have a drink; on the house of course." He slicked back his hair. "And if you want a dance, something a little extra, just say the word."

Enzo's eyes flared. Dirty bastard couldn't keep his dick in his pants for longer than a couple of hours. My thoughts went to the girl out front, the dancer.

What was it about her?

"See something you like out there?" Zander threw me a knowing smile.

"We didn't come here to relax," Nicco interjected.

"Of course. But stay for one drink. Let me reassure you that we can continue to make good business together."

Nicco's brow quirked up and Enzo smirked. Like this fucker had any choice in the matter. You didn't renege on a deal with the Marchetti.

Unless you wanted to end up in a body bag.

"One drink." Nicco gave Zander a sharp nod.

We all filed out of Zander's office and reentered the main room. There was a new girl riding the pole. All bottled-blonde and fake tits, she didn't do a damn thing for me. But Enzo looked hungry for more than just a dance.

We each took a seat at the bar. "Shaun, see to my guys here, okay?" Zander clasped Nicco on the shoulder. "Whatever they want, on the house. Gentleman, I'll leave you in good hands."

"See you next month." Nicco cut him with a hard look.

Zander gave a small nod before strolling away as if he hadn't just come close to getting his brains blown out.

"Remind me why your old man thought it would be a good idea to bring in someone like DiMarco?" Enzo grumbled.

"His chain of clubs brings in good money, you know that."

"The guy is a complete asshole."

"You're not wrong there." Nicco let out a heavy sigh, propping himself back against the bar.

"Did you see the way he almost shit himself when you pulled your piece out on him?"

"Enzo." I shook my head discreetly.

Nicco didn't enjoy pulling rank, and I knew things weighed heavily on his shoulders.

"Gentlemen." The bartender slid a tray of drinks our way. I wasn't sure I'd ever get used to someone calling me a gentleman. I was nineteen; we all were. Yet, we'd seen more than most kids our age.

Lived more.

Less than a year ago, before we were officially initiated into the family, things were different. Our lives were our own to some degree. Now we were nothing but puppets, slaves to the cause.

Enzo lived for it. The power and control. The violence. He took after his old man, Uncle Vincenzo, in that respect. Nicco was different though. He went through the motions, exacting his father's orders because it was expected. But despite his misgivings about it all, he was good at his job.

We all took a glass. I swirled the contents around, watching as the amber liquid sloshed up the sides. We weren't old enough to legally drink, but age was nothing but a number, and once a Marchetti man turned eighteen he took his role in the family. That's always how it had been, always how it would be.

"To family," Nicco said, catching my eye, and I knew his words held a double meaning.

The family business would always come first.

It had to.

But our families—my sister, and Nicco's sister—were our driving force.

Everything we did was to keep them safe, to give them the life they deserved.

A life I hoped, one day, would one see Arabella far far away from Verona County.

"It's looking bad out there," Shaun said as we stood up and thanked him for the drinks. "Be safe guys."

"Thanks." I pulled out my wallet and threw down a fifty.

"Fuck, I need to get laid," Enzo said as we passed the podium where another dancer was working the pole. "We heading to L'Anello's?"

"Not tonight. I promised Bailey I'd hang out," Nicco said.

"You do realize you're not his fucking babysitter, don't you?" Enzo grumbled as we exited the club. Shaun wasn't wrong, the storm had arrived. Rain hammered down on the roof of the club, the wind howling like a pack of hungry wolves.

"He's a good kid," Nicco replied.

"Yeah, yeah. Why don't we pick him up and take him with us? Who knows, maybe we can get him his first blow job?"

"He's fifteen, E."

"Like you weren't getting your dick sucked in ninth grade." He shot me with a knowing grin, and I rolled my eyes.

"My truck is in the next block over," I said. "I'll see you guys tomorrow."

Nicco nodded, while Enzo held out his hand. We bumped fists before I hiked up the collar on my jacket and jogged across the street. The place was deserted, but it was hardly surprising given how bad the storm had gotten. So when I reached my truck and heard a scream, my blood ran cold. I froze, straining to hear against the rain and wind wreaking havoc around me.

Nothing.

Shaking off the initial alarm I'd felt, I curled my hand around the door handle.

"Help! Somebody, help me."

My spine went rigid. There was no mistaking the noise this time. Spinning around, I searched the street for any signs of trouble.

"Please, don't—"

My boots ate up the sidewalk puddles as I tried to locate the noise. A momentary reprieve in the wind gave me a chance to listen.

"No, no!"

Bingo.

I charged down the street and cut down a darkened alley. The rain was relentless, lashing down, making it hard to see. But there was something up ahead in the shadows. My eyes narrowed, trying to understand what I was seeing.

"Fuck," I breathed as murky image in front of me finally became clear.

And then I charged forward.

TWO

CAITLIN

"DON'T, PLEASE." I tried to fight off the monstrous guy as his fingers wrapped around my arm, biting into my skin. He shoved me hard against the wall, sending the air *whooshing* from my lungs, pain radiating through my shoulder.

"Hold still, bitch," he spat, his rancid breath washing over me. I fought the urge to retch.

"Help! Somebody, help me." My cries were lost in the wind as it howled down the alley.

"I saw you tonight, riding that pole like a fucking pro. Well, I've got something you can ride right here." He roughly grabbed my hand and shoved it down to his crotch.

This time I did retch, tears rolling down my cheeks. "Please, don't—"

"Get the fuck off her," a voice yelled.

Relief washed over me. Someone was here. Thank God.

"Fuck off, asshole." The guy's grip on my arm tightened. My jacket was drenched, rivulets of water running down my back and breasts.

"I said," the guy was ripped away from me, "get the fuck off her."

I stumbled away, watching as my savior grabbed the guy by his collar and yanked him closer. "You like beating on women?"

"Who the fuck are you?" He spat. "She's good for it. Fucking cock tease."

He didn't get another word out. My savior slammed his head into the guy's nose, sending him flying backward.

"Motherfucker." A pained groan filled the air.

"You want me to call the police on this piece of shit?" He glanced over at me, his expression murderous. But he didn't scare me. There was a softness in his eyes that drew me in, and somehow, I knew this dark angel wouldn't hurt me.

"N- no." The last thing I needed was the police turning up, asking questions.

"You get the fuck out of here and don't look back, you hear me?" He shoved the guy hard, letting him land in a big puddle.

"Okay, chill, man." The guy held his hands up, then scrambled to his hands and knees, blood pouring from his nose, turning the rain beneath him ruby red.

We watched him clamber to his feet and then skulk away into the shadows.

"Are you okay?"

"Thank you," I said through chattering teeth.

"Shit, you're cold. Do you have a car around here?"

"No," I sniffled, tears streaming down my cheeks. "I was walking home."

"Walking..." He let out a strained breath. "I have my truck right around the corner. I can take you to wherever you want to go, or I can call you a cab and wait with you if you'd prefer that?"

I dipped my hand in my purse feeling for the can of mace and my cell phone. A crack of thunder rumbled overhead followed by a flash of lightning.

"Fuck," the guy whistled. "It's getting bad out here. Come on." He held out his hand as if it were the most normal thing in the world.

In my line of work, it wasn't.

Tentatively, I slid my palm into his. We were both soaked to the bone, the rain showing no signs of letting up. "I'm Matteo," he said.

"Caitlin."

"Nice to meet you, Caitlin. Now let's get you home before you freeze to death."

The truck was warm by the time Matteo pulled up outside my apartment building, but I was still like a drowned rat.

"This is me."

"Are you sure you're okay? Is there someone you want to call? Friend? Boyfriend?" He turned off the engine. Another bolt of lightning lit up the sky, startling me.

"No boyfriend," I whispered, peering up at the sky. It had been a long time since I'd seen a storm this bad. "Jesus," the word spilled from my lips as thunder crashed overhead.

"Not a fan of storms?"

"Something like that," I mumbled.

Damn Gisele. She'd been my ride home, but had gotten held up. So I'd decided to walk. It wasn't anything I hadn't done before. Tears welled in the corners of my eyes as the reality of what could have happened sank into me.

"Hey, don't cry." Matteo touched my arm, and our eyes met. "You're safe now."

Nodding, I averted my eyes, trying to swallow the rest of the tears.

"Tell you what," he said. "Why don't I walk you up to your apartment, make sure you get in okay?"

My eyes flicked to his, and he smiled. "I don't bite, I promise."

Matteo seemed so different to the men I encountered at the club with their wandering hands, fat wallets, and indecent morals.

"Only if you're sure."

His eyes lit up. "Of course. It's really getting wild out there. Let me come around and open your door, okay?"

After battling against the force of the wind, he managed to climb out. Seconds later, my door opened. "We'll have to make a run for it." To my surprise, Matteo had taken off his jacket to use as a shield. I slipped out of the truck and buried myself into his side, and we took off toward the building.

"Holy crap, that was intense," I said the second we reached the doors. Matteo frowned, and I knew what he probably saw. I didn't exactly live in The Four Seasons. But I earned every square inch of the small apartment I called home.

"After you." He pulled open the door and I slipped past him. My sneakers were ruined, water squelching every time I walked.

Matteo followed me to the first floor. "This is me," I said, just as the strip lighting flickered overhead. "Do you want to come inside and get dried off?"

Our eyes met, and I felt shy all of a sudden, which was ridiculous given the fact I spent five nights a week stripping in front of complete strangers.

The whole sky lit up again as a fork of lightning struck right above us.

"Yeah, okay." He gave me an uneasy smile. "If you're sure?"

I fought a smile. Maybe I wasn't the only one afraid of the storm?

Unlocking my door, I pushed it open and moved inside. Matteo followed, closing the door behind him.

"Fuck, it's bad out there." He peeled the wet t-shirt away from his body, revealing a smooth slab of stomach. His eyes caught mine and his brow went up.

Crap. Busted.

Flushed, I spun around and went straight to the small kitchenette, peeling off my soggy jacket and dumping it in the sink. "I'm going to change into something a little less wet."

The second the words left my lips I realized my mistake. Matteo's eyes darkened as he chuckled.

"Okay, I'll be... uh..." I hurried into the hall leading to the bathroom and bedroom. "Feel free to dry your stuff on the radiator," I called. "I'll grab you some towels."

"Thanks," he replied.

What was I doing?

I knew better than to invite a stranger into my home.

But he saved you.

Heading into the bathroom, I flicked the switch and gasped when I saw my reflection in the mirror. My hair was a wet matted mess, and my face was streaked with ugly black lines. I looked like I'd been dragged out of a swamp. Shedding my wet, soggy clothes, I dumped them in the tub, and slipped into my big fluffy robe. Grabbing a flannel, I ran it under the hot faucet, and began cleaning my face. It wasn't much of an improvement, but it would have to do. Next, I towel dried my hair and piled it in a messy bun on top of my head.

After grabbing a bunch of towels off the rack, I went back into the living room, pausing at the sight of Matteo standing there shirtless. "H- hi," I choked out.

God, he was beautiful. All hard lines and defined muscle. Tattoos decorated his skin, curving over one of his pecs and around his shoulder.

"Are they for me?" he asked, nodding to the towels, and my cheeks burned.

"Yes. Sorry, I just... nice tattoos."

God, kill me now.

"Do I make you nervous?"

"I'm just not used to having guys in my apartment," I stuttered over the words.

"I find that hard to believe, Caitlin." His face paled. "Shit, I didn't mean... that came out *all* wrong."

I chuckled. "How old are you?"

"Nineteen, why?"

"It doesn't matter." I hadn't expected him to say that. He seemed so sure of himself, so together for someone who wasn't even old enough to buy liquor in a bar.

The lights flickered, another crack of thunder booming outside, making me flinch.

"You really don't like storms, huh?"

"We all have our fears, right?" I gave him a weak smile. "Dry off and I'll make us some hot cocoa?"

"Sounds good." Matteo took the towels from me. He had a body carved of sin and painted with ink, but his eyes were kind and his smile genuine.

It was a refreshing change from the men I usually encountered. Men who always wanted something more than polite conversation.

I left him to dry off while I went and changed into some leggings and my favorite oversized *Tinkerbell* t-shirt.

"Nice." Matteo chuckled, pointing at my chest.

Feeling myself grow hot, I hurried to the kitchen to make the hot chocolate. "Marshmallows?" I asked over my shoulder.

"Is there another way to—"

A blood curdling shriek tore from my lungs as the power went out, sparks and fire exploding outside the window.

"Relax, relax." Matteo rushed over to me, wrapping me into his arms. Thank God, he'd put his t-shirt back on. "It's just the storm."

It didn't look like the storm, it looked like Armageddon had arrived.

He guided me over to the windows, the only light the silvery hue of the moon outside. "See, just a power pole. But it looks like it blew the entire block." He was right, everything was steeped in darkness. "Do you have candles?"

I nodded, my heart still like a runaway train in my chest. "They're in the cabinet over there."

"Okay, how about you stay here," Matteo gently pushed me toward my small couch, "and I'll light some candles?"

"I can do it." The tremble to my words betrayed me.

"Look, I'm here, so let me help. It's the least I can do."

Matteo wasted no time locating the candles and setting them up around the apartment. By the time he was done there was a warm amber glow flickering around the room, and my heart no longer felt like it was going to explode.

"Jesus," I said. "I'm not usually like this."

"Like what?" He frowned, bringing me a steamy mug of hot cocoa. I took it from him, our hands brushing. Sparks danced over my skin, sending a shiver racing up my spine.

"A damsel in distress."

"Jesus Christ," he let out a strained breath. "You were attacked. I'd expect you to be on edge."

"But I wasn't, because you arrived." I smiled at him, an overwhelming sense of gratitude washing over me.

But it was deeper than that.

All my life I'd been controlled and manipulated. As sad as it was to admit it, the man in the alley was just another in a long list of points in my life I'd rather forget. But I knew I would never forget tonight. Because for the first time ever, someone saved me.

Matteo saved me.

And he was here, asking for nothing in return.

He stared back at me, his warm blue eyes searching for something.

What, I didn't know.

Then Matteo tilted his head to one said and said the strangest thing to me, "Do I know you?"

THREE

MATTEO

SHE LOOKED FAMILIAR. I traced my eyes over the soft features of her face, lingering on the curve of her neck. Her milky white skin contrasting with the pile of deep red hair gathered on her head. There was a smattering of freckles dotted over her nose and her lips were full and soft and totally kissable.

Caitlin was fucking beautiful.

Get your head out of the gutter, Bellatoni. It wasn't appropriate to think about her in such a way after her ordeal tonight. Not to mention the fact she was terrified of the storm.

When I'd seen that stronzo with his hands on her petite body, I'd almost lost it. Images of Arabella had flashed through my mind. I didn't like to spill blood often, but for the women in my life, there wasn't much I wouldn't do.

Family was *everything* to me.

Seeing the fear in Caitlin's eyes, hearing her screams, seeing the tears roll down her cheeks, had reached something deep inside and taken hold. Truth was, before she even invited me inside, I'd already made the decision to camp out in the truck right outside her building. Just to be sure. Part of me wondered if I should have called the cops, or better yet, called some of our guys to come and deal with the piece of shit.

I knew Enzo would give me shit for it—hell, probably Nicco too—but I knew I wouldn't rest without knowing she was okay.

"Do I know you?" The words spilled from my lips.

Caitlin's brows knitted as she slid a hand up the side of her neck. "Providence is a big place, but I suppose our paths could have crossed." She gave me a tentative smile.

"Actually, I hail from Verona County."

"Oh." It was strange. There was a disappointed edge to her words that conflicted against the relief in her eyes.

"You said you were walking home from work?"

"Yes, I... uh, wait tables. It's not exactly glamorous, but it pays the bills."

"What's the name of the place?"

"Stella's."

"Doesn't ring a bell." I didn't know Providence well, but I'd been around enough to know some of the local haunts.

"What brings you this way?" Caitlin placed her mug down, tucking her legs underneath her. The storm continued beating down on the building, but I was too caught up in her to even notice. There was something about her. "What?" she asked, staring up at me through long lashes.

"You're beautiful." Her eyes widened with fear. "Shit, I'm sorry. That was a dumb thing to say." I raked a hand through my hair. It was still damp beneath my fingers. "I'm not trying to hit on you, that's not what this is. I just... Jesus, I should stop talking."

Enzo would have a field day watching me stumble over my words like this. But you usually didn't need words to get the attention of chicks at L'Anello's or a campus party. There was a line of girls ready and waiting to dance on the dark side, to have their shot at taming one of the Marchetti men. But they were nothing more than warm bodies and willing bed mates. I'd never found a single girl I wanted to get close to; to spend time lying in the dark just talking with...

Until now.

"It's okay." She chuckled, the soft sound like music to my ears. "I know it's late, but are you hungry? I mean if you don't have anywhere to be?"

As if on cue my stomach rumbled. "I never turn down the offer of food. It's the Italian in me."

"I did wonder." Caitlin got up and I followed her to the small kitchenette, taking a seat at one of the stools. "You have a slight accent."

"I'm fourth generation American-Italian. My mom's great-grandfather moved here in the late nineteenth century. What about you?"

"Irish-American. Didn't the red hair and pale complexion give it away?" She began rummaging around in her refrigerator, the inside light illuminating her face.

"Eyes."

"Excuse me?" Caitlin looked over at me and I smiled.

"Bingo. They're green."

With a little shake of her head, she continued her forage. "I have eggs, spinach, some questionable looking cheese, tomatoes, or leftovers from lunch."

"We could always order in?"

"And make some poor delivery person drive in this weather?" She looked disappointed.

"Relax, I'm joking. Omelet sounds good or eggs over easy with spinach and cheese."

"A man after my own heart." Caitlin set about gathering the ingredients, and heating oil in a small frying pan. "So, Matteo..."

"Bellatoni." Part of me wondered if I should have given her my real name, but Bellatoni was non-descript enough. Marchetti on the other hand...

"Matteo Bellatoni. Tell me about you. Are you in college?"

"I'll be a sophomore at Montague University in the fall."

"Isn't that the super elite school in Verona County?"

"It's just a college, Tink."

"Tink?" She glanced after me over her shoulder, lips parted, expression playful. It was like watching a flower slowly bloom.

And I loved it.

"Would you prefer I call you fairy?" I fought a grin.

Caitlin left the spinach and eggs cooking while she pulled out a plate and some silverware. "Are you sure you don't need to be somewhere?"

The rain and wind battered the side of her apartment and I pressed my lips into a thin line. "It's getting dangerous out there. Besides, I would never leave a pretty girl home alone during a storm."

"You're so different," she whispered.

"I am?" It was a weird thing to say.

"Yeah, at the diner... a lot of the guys are assholes."

"How old you, Caitlin?" There was a vulnerability about her, a softness I couldn't quite put my finger on, but it was there.

"I turned twenty last month."

"How long have you been living here?" I glanced around the small apartment. It was small and tidy, but tired. The paint job needed redoing and the door to the building was barely hanging on its hinges. The neighborhood seemed okay, except for the fucker in the alley.

"Since last summer," she replied.

"And before that?"

Something changed, and Caitlin's walls went up. I didn't want to push, but I was desperate to know all her secrets.

It was fucking weird.

She was a stranger, and yet, I felt completely at ease with her.

"You want to sit here or on the couch?"

"Wherever you normally sit."

"Couch it is," she said, sliding me a plate of food.

We got situated in the living room, and I wasted no time tucking into the eggs. "Damn, that's good."

"It's kind of hard to screw up."

"Oh, I wouldn't be so sure." I smiled, thinking of all the times me and Bella tried to help Mamma in the kitchen when we were younger.

"So how do you like college?"

"It's okay I guess."

"Isn't it supposed to be some life altering experience?"

It was. But when you were there with an ulterior motive, it was kind of hard to embrace the college life.

"You didn't want to go?" I asked Caitlin. Her eyes dropped to her plate and I knew I'd hit a nerve.

"It wasn't really on the cards for me. Who knows? Maybe one day, if I save enough money, I'll get to do night classes or something. I've always wanted to dance."

"You dance?"

"I used to." Her smile fell. "Had high hopes of one day making a living out of it, but it wasn't to be."

"There's always time," I said.

"I guess. Are you finished?" She nodded to the empty plate.

"Yeah, thank you."

Taking it from me, she asked, "When do you think they'll get the power fixed?"

"Tomorrow once the storm passes." Caitlin's eyes fluttered closed, a visible shudder rippling through her. "Hey, I can stay... I mean, I don't want to overstep, but I'm in no hurry to go."

"I can't ask you to do that. I'm an adult. I should be able to survive a storm." She rolled her pretty green eyes.

"Ask me," the words rolled off my tongue.

"I..." She hesitated, indecision flickering in her eyes. Another crack of lightning lit up the apartment and she flinched. "Okay, will you stay, please?"

"I would love to stay."

"Pineapple on pizza, yes or no?"

"What kind of question is that?" I grimaced. "No. There is never an excuse for fruit on a pizza."

"You do know tomato is a fruit, right?" Caitlin laughed. She'd been doing that since I said I would stay.

"That's an exception. The *only* exception." I grinned. "My turn. Guys with tattoos, yes or no?"

"Hmm." She pressed a finger to her lips. I don't think I'd ever been more jealous of an appendage. "That depends... If it's something tasteful that has sentimental value then sure, I can get on board. But if it's something brash and showy like I don't know, a skull or eagle for example, then it's a no from me."

My eyes almost bugged, but realization dawned on me. "Were you checking me out earlier?" I smirked.

Heat crept into her neck and ran into her cheeks. "Busted. But if it's any consolation, I really like your tattoos."

Well, shit, if she didn't just steal the air from my lungs.

Something was happening.

Maybe it was the storm or the fact I'd saved her, or maybe it was the hot cocoa and spinach and eggs, but Caitlin was exactly the kind of girl I could see myself falling for one day.

She was funny and unafraid to call me out on my bullshit. She was beautiful —*so fucking beautiful*—and she had this vulnerability that made me want to protect her.

"The beach or the city?"

"Neither. I'm a homebody," I said. "There is nothing more I like than to spend Sundays with my family, with good food and laughter. Sounds kind of dumb, huh?"

"Not at all." She gave me a weak smile. "It's sounds kind of perfect actually. Family is important to you, isn't it?"

"Absolutely. My mom and my sister are my whole world."

"They're lucky to have you." Sadness etched into her expression.

"What about your family? What are they like?"

"I haven't spoken to them in almost two years."

"Shit, Caitlin, I'm sorry." She looked so lost, I wanted to pull her into my arms and comfort her. But it wasn't my job.

Not yet. The thought came out of left field.

"It's okay. I've made my peace with it." She smiled again, but it didn't reach her eyes. "There's this saying I love, 'it's not about waiting for the storm to pass, it's about learning to dance in the rain', I try to remember that."

"Do you want to talk about it?" I sensed there was a story there.

"I'd rather not."

"Okay. Well, the night is still young." It really wasn't, but I didn't want to say goodnight yet. "Do you have a pack of cards?"

"Yes, I think I have one lying around somewhere." She got up and went over to the kitchenette, rummaging through one of the drawers. "Bingo."

"Excellent." I grinned over at her. "How do you feel about strip poker?"

FOUR

CAITLIN

"YOU WANT TO PLAY *STRIP* POKER?" My cheeks flamed. Matteo was the perfect distraction. Apart from the odd crack of lightning, I'd barely noticed the storm raging on outside. He was funny and sweet, and he had this smile that made me feel at complete ease.

"I'm joking." He frowned. "It was a joke."

"Oh, okay."

"I mean, I'm down if you are..." Matteo flashed me a blinding smile. "Or we could just play Truth Blackjack."

"Truth Blackjack? That's not a thing." I rolled my eyes.

"Sure, it is. We'll take it in turns to deal. Win the hand and you get to ask a question and the other person has to answer. Lose and the dealer gets to ask the question. If you pass, you have to do a dare."

"I think I prefer the sound of strip poker."

His eyes flashed with something. I didn't want to believe it was lust because that presented all kinds of problems.

But I couldn't deny a tiny part of me wished it was.

Matteo was a like a breath of fresh air compared to most of the guys I came across in my life. He was selfless and kind and it was obvious how much he cared about his family. It almost made me wish I was braver. Made me wish I had the confidence to do something impulsive like lean over and kiss him.

But sex changed things.

And I didn't want to ruin a single second of my finite time with the man who had saved me tonight.

Because despite his age, I didn't doubt Matteo was all man.

"Okay, rack 'em up," I said. "Actually, hold that thought." I got up and hurried to the refrigerator. Sure enough, there was a couple bottles of beer stowed inside the door rack.

"I have supplies." Waving them in the air, I returned and got comfortable on the couch.

"Now we're talking." Matteo uncapped them both, offering me one. "Cheers." We clinked the bottles and Matteo took a long pull before placing it down to shuffle the cards.

"I'll deal first. You know the rules?"

"I know the rules."

He dished me two cards and I peeked at them before flipping them over and putting them down in front of me. Matteo gave himself two cards and left one unturned. "It's your call."

"Hit," I said confidently. Matteo flipped the next card.

"Six. The lady has twenty."

"The *lady* can speak for herself." I smirked, taking a gulp of beer. "Stand."

"The lady stands." He turned his second card. "The dealer has sixteen."

"Oh, you're going down," I teased.

"I'll take my chances." He got ready to turn another card off the pack. "And he's bust. Dammit."

"Yes! My question."

"Go easy on me."

"What are you doing in Providence?"

He studied me, running a hand over his rugged face. "Ah shit, Tink." I gave him a pointed look, and he grumbled, "Visiting some old friends?"

It sounded more like a question than it did an answer.

"Old friends? That's very open of you. Is it the truth?"

"Are you accusing me of being a liar?"

"I'm just trying to figure out what kind of guy is walking the streets of a small neighborhood in Providence late at night."

"The nice kind?" He smirked.

"Touché. I'll accept your vague answer, this time." I tipped my bottle at him. "But next time, I want details."

"Okay, let's go."

I took the pack from him, dealing him two cards and myself two, flipping one. Matteo flipped an Ace first. "Come to Daddy," he chuckled, flipping a picture card next. "Blackjack!"

"No freakin' way!" I turned my second card, giving me fifteen. I pulled a third card off the top of the pack and mumbled, "Bust."

"Okay." Matteo rubbed his hands together. "Let me think..." He scratched his jaw, silence stretching out before us.

"The storm will be over if you don't hurry."

"You should never rush perfection." His brow quirked up.

"Well, okay then." I smiled. I couldn't help it. His grin was infectious.

"I'm ready. Schoolgirl crush?"

My brows pinched. "I gotta say, I'm a little disappointed."

"Just hear me out, okay? What's your answer?"

"I don't know."

"Come on, everyone had a crush in high school."

"Justin Bieber, maybe?" High school was a time in my life I preferred not to think about, but I didn't want to tell him that.

"The Beebs?" Matteo stared at me like I'd grown a second head. "Really?

"Hey, you asked. Besides, he was cute."

"Well it totally ruined my plan."

"Tell me..."

"Nah, I'll wait for another opportune moment." He dealt us both a new hand. "It's looking like my hand." A smug grin played on his lips.

"I'll be the judge of that." I laid out my two tens and shot him a grin of my own.

"You have got to be shitting me. It's okay, there's still a good chance that I have..." He flipped his card. "Twenty-one, yes! That'd be another question to me. How many times have you thought about kissing me tonight?"

My cheeks burned as I inhaled a surprise breath. "I haven't—"

"No?" He pouted. "Too bad."

"Why, have you thought about kissing me?"

"Nah-ah! He wagged his finger. "It's not your turn to ask questions. But it is your turn to deal." Matteo handed me the deck, our fingers brushing. He let his hand linger, sparks of electricity shooting up my arm. Our eyes collided, the air crackling around us.

Overwhelmed, I averted my gaze and cleared my throat. "Let's see what we have," my voice trembled. Suddenly, it felt like the stakes were higher, and I didn't know how to feel about that. I liked Matteo, but he was a stranger.

He saved you. He had. But it wasn't a valid reason to throw myself at him.

Was it?

It had been so long since I had been treated right by a guy, I'd almost forgotten what good honest company felt like. I didn't want to jinx that—no matter how much Matteo affected me.

I turned a nine, watching as Matteo laid out a nine and eight. "What'll it be?" I asked.

"Hmm, stand."

"You sure?"

"I'm sure." He nodded.

"Okay then. I have a two, that makes eleven. I'm going again." I pulled a nine. "Bingo! The lady has twenty. *My* question."

"Do your worst."

"How many times have you thought about kissing *me* tonight?"

"You went there." He inhaled a sharp breath, his eyes locked on mine.

"I went there."

"I don't want to lie," he swallowed, "but I also don't want to send you running for the hills, so I'm going to pass."

"You know that means I get to challenge you to a dare, right?"

"I live for dares." He smirked.

"I want you... I mean, I *dare* you ... to kiss me." The words spilled from my lips before I could stop them.

I wanted him to kiss me.

God, I wanted it so much.

Consequences be damned.

Matteo's eyes grew to saucers. "For real?"

"I mean, yeah, all in the name of the game, of course."

"Of course." He edged closer, his eyes fixed on my mouth. My breath caught as he leaned in, a soft moan escaping from my lips when his hand glided up the side of my neck. I could feel the scratch of his stubble against my skin; the warmth of his breath fanning my face. Then his lips were on mine. A featherlight touch at first, as if he was scared I might disappear at any second.

"Is this okay?" he asked, and I nodded. "Thank fuck, because I've wanted to do this since the second we walked into your apartment."

Matteo let his fingers tangle in my hair as he swept his tongue into my mouth. He tasted like mint and fine whisky. Everything about him was so refined. From his soft leather jacket, to his sleek pickup truck that looked more expensive than any car I'd ever ridden in. I sensed Matteo came from money.

And I, did not.

In fact, everything I owned was right here in my small apartment.

"Okay," he eased back, "where did you go just now?"

"Sorry." I blushed, letting my fingers twist into his t-shirt. It was still damp, but it only served to mold to his broad shoulders more.

"You're not feeling it, I get it." He started to move away, but I pulled him closer.

"That's not it at all. I just... Who are you, Matteo Bellatoni?"

"I'm just a guy," he whispered. "A guy who really *really* wants to kiss you."

I closed the distance, brushing my lips over his. "I think I'd like that."

He cupped my face and fixed his mouth over mine. This time there was no trace of uncertainty for either of us as our tongues tangled. Heat coiled deep in my tummy as I moved closer. Matteo sensed my urgency, pulling me onto his lap, letting my legs fall on either side of his.

"Jesus, Caitlin," he breathed, his words a flutter over my lips. "You're so fucking sexy. But I need you to know this wasn't my plan. I'm not that kind of guy."

I eased back, smiling. "Well that's probably a good thing then, because I'm not that kind of girl." *But with you, I might be.*

I dived back in, kissing him with everything that I had. Matteo groaned, his body hard beneath me. I felt the hard outline of his arousal press into me. But I didn't flinch. I imagined things. Dirty, sensual things.

One of his hands gripped the back of my neck, pulling gently to reveal the expanse of my neck and collarbone to him. "I want to taste you," he said. "I want to paint every inch of your skin with my tongue."

Oh my.

His lips met my throat in a gentle caress, but it wasn't enough. Something told me it would never be enough with him.

The overwhelming thought startled me. I let my hands slide into his hair, anchoring him to me. The second his tongue swiped along the column of my neck, I was a goner.

I'd never wanted to give myself to another.

Until this moment.

It was a powerful thought, if not a little disarming. I barely knew Matteo. But I felt more at ease with him than I ever had before.

He took his time painting my skin. Sucking and nibbling and kissing. My soft moans became a gentle undercurrent to the storm outside. One of his hands trailed down my spine. Clamping it around my hip, he pulled me down on him while he ground into me. A wildfire swept through me as we rocked against each other, hands touching, mouths searching.

"Shit, Tink," he choked out. "If you don't stop, I'm going to finish in my pants like a twelve-year-old at a wet t-shirt contest."

I chuckled, burying my face in his shoulder. "I guess we kinda got carried away."

Matteo slid his hand against my cheek, coaxing me to look at him. "I guess we did."

He eyes were dark and hooded, simmering with hunger. But it didn't scare me.

"I might be a gentleman," he said thickly, "but I'm no saint, Cait. So you need to tell me now if I need to apply the brakes."

Did I want him to stop?

The rational, logical... *safe* answer, was yes.

But I'd spent my whole life living with my wings clipped. Tonight, I didn't want to be that girl, I wanted to be free.

I wanted to choose for myself.

Standing, I held out my hand. My body trembled as Matteo stared up at me. "You sure?" He stood up, bumping his chest against mine.

"I am."

He swept a strand of hair off my face, staring at me with such intensity, I felt winded. "I don't know what's happening here," he said. "But I'm so fucking relieved the universe decided to lead me down that alley tonight."

I flinched at the memory. "Cait, look at me."

Matteo didn't ask if I minded him calling me Cait, but it sounded so natural rolling off his tongue, I didn't correct him.

My eyes peeked open and he smiled. “There she is. We don’t have to do anything you don’t want to do,” he said.

“I want this,” I replied. “I want you.”

FIVE

MATTEO

FUCK.

What was I doing?

I didn't mean for any of this to happen... but one thing led to another, and another, and before I knew it, I was standing in Caitlin's small bedroom, stripping the Tinkerbell t-shirt from her slender body. She chuckled when it caught on her messy bun, sliding her hands over mine to help me pull it off.

"Come here." I tried to keep my eyes on hers, as I gently unraveled the ponytail holder and her dark red waves cascaded down her back and over her shoulders.

Fuck me.

She was stunning.

Heat flooded her cheeks as she watched me watch her. I couldn't resist letting my eyes trace over her collarbone, following the hollow of her chest down between her two perfect tits. Jesus. My dick strained painfully against my jeans. She was every man's wet dream come true, and I was the lucky sonofabitch who got to call her mine for the night.

And then what? A little voice whispered. I didn't want to think what happened when the storm passed and the sun came up. Moments like this were rare and you had to grab them with both hands and make the most of them. Even if I never saw Caitlin again, if this was nothing but one amazing night, I would make sure it was one to remember.

She lowered her eyes and gazed up at me through dark, thick lashes. Her green eyes were mesmerizing, the color of the wet moss that grew on the banks of the Blackstone River.

"Christ, Tink," I said. "Are you real?"

She gingerly took my hand, pressing it to her sternum. "Does this feel real to you?"

I swallowed hard, the flutter of her heartbeat thrumming beneath my fingers. Caitlin laughed softly. "Your turn," she said, raising a brow.

I didn't need asking twice.

Pulling my t-shirt off, I made quick work of unbuttoning my jeans and pushing them down my hips, stepping out of them. Her gaze dropped to my black boxer briefs, her lips forming an *O*.

"You got me worked up on the couch." It was my turn to chuckle. She continued her perusal, reaching out to trace the tattoos covering my breastbone and wrapping around my shoulder. "They're beautiful."

"*You're* beautiful." Hooking an arm around her waist, I dragged her closer. Caitlin's hand looped around my shoulders. She had to crane her neck to look at me since I was a good few inches taller than her. My hand stroked her hip, smoothing over the swell of her skin. She was all soft lines and toned muscle, the lingering shape of her dancer's body evident.

"Do you still dance?" I asked.

I felt her tense. It was obviously a sore subject.

"Hey." Brushing my nose over hers, I kissed her. "We don't have to talk about it."

"I think I'm done talking." Caitlin stepped backward, pulling me with her. I watched through glazed eyes as she sat on the bed and elegantly moved up the mattress until she was laid out before me in nothing but a black, lacy pair of panties.

"Look at you," I drawled, hardly able to believe this was happening.

She was perfect. Smooth long legs, dancer's legs. I could imagine her gliding across a stage with sheer grace and beauty. Dropping one knee to the bed, I reached for her, wrapping my hand around her ankle, sweeping it up her leg.

Caitlin trembled, moaning softly at my touch. "Why does this feel so good?" She sounded blissed out already and I'd barely even gotten started.

"Eyes, Cait," I said, and she locked her bright greens right on me. Watching with heated curiosity as I crawled between her legs, brushing my fingers along the soft flesh of her thighs.

"Can I?" My hand hovered at the elastic of her panties. She nodded, and I gently inched them off her hips, dropping back to pull them off.

The second I covered her body with mine, I knew this wasn't just some random night with a stranger. I hooked her legs around my hip, grinding into her. I still had my boxer briefs on, but her heat felt incredible, her body desperately trying to pull me inside.

"God, Matteo, it feels..."

"Yeah, Tink, I know." I dipped a hand between us, strumming her clit a couple of times before sinking a finger deep inside her.

"Oh God," she moaned, clinging onto my shoulders. "That feels incredible."

I chuckled against the hollow of her throat. "You haven't felt anything yet." I wanted her wet and ready, writhing beneath me. I wanted to feel her shatter and scream my name. And then I wanted to bury myself inside this beautiful red-haired angel.

She arched against me, riding my hand as I added another digit. My thumb went to work on her clit, rolling slow torturous circles that had Caitlin gasping for breath.

"More," she cried as I licked and suckled her neck. "Yes, just like that."

I rose above her, watching as she began to fall. Her hands were curled in the sheet, her body shaking, and her skin damp with sweat.

"Give me your eyes, Cait." I worked her faster, hooking my fingers deep inside her and rubbing the spot I hoped would send her flying off the edge.

"Matteo!" My name echoed around the room as she tried to catch her breath. I leaned down, kissing her.

"Don't move," I instructed. Climbing off her, I discarded my boxers and grabbed a condom from my wallet.

"Are you always so prepared?" Caitlin watched me, her head resting on one fist, her red hair tumbling over her like a fiery waterfall.

"Oh, I'm a real Boy Scout." I smirked as I tore open the wrapper. Stroking myself a couple times, I rolled on the latex and sat on the side of the bed. "Do you trust me?"

She bit down on her bottom lip, nodding.

"Come here." I curled a finger and Caitlin followed, sliding over my lap.

"You're full of surprises, Mr. Bellatoni."

But I was too focused on her body, the way her perfect tits brushed up against my chest. Curving a hand over her hip, I helped Caitlin line up. "Ready?"

She didn't wait, sinking down on me without warning. "Fuuuuck," I groaned. She felt incredible. Intense pleasure shot down my spine as she gripped my dick.

"It feels so deep."

"You good?" I gathered her hair off her shoulder and wrapped it around my hand, clutching the base of her neck. She gave me a reassuring nod and I ground out, "Ride me, Tink."

She started moving, sliding up and down my length like she was born to do it. It was so fucking erotic watching her, eyes glazed, and lips parted. Those small little moans that kept falling from her pink kissable lips.

"Wrap your legs around me." I needed her closer, tighter.

I needed *more*.

Caitlin made easy work of it. She was so fucking flexible, my mind started going to all the positions I could have her in. But I couldn't move right now. I couldn't think about anything but the intense sensations as she gripped and released me, over and over.

Letting go of her hair, I let my hands go to her hips, giving myself leverage to thrust up as she rolled down, until we were rocking in perfect harmony.

"Oh my god," she cried, "I'm almost there."

Yeah, me too. I tried to focus, to tell myself to slow down. I wanted to savor this, to imprint this moment to memory. But it felt too good.

She felt too fucking good.

"Go faster, baby," I murmured against her lips, delving my tongue into her mouth.

Caitlin picked up the pace, and her body began to shudder, her walls rippling around my dick.

"Oh yeah," I choked out. "Fuck, baby. I'm gonna... Fuck."

Blinding white pleasure crashed over me, Caitlin's spent body melting against me. I dropped onto the mattress, taking her with me, covering her face with kisses. "That was..."

"Tell me about it," she chuckled. "I can't believe we just did that."

"Believe it," I replied. "And get ready for round two in about fifteen minutes. I just need to catch my breath first."

"Again?" Her eyes went wide.

"Hell yeah," I glanced over at the window. "The storm hasn't passed yet." And I hadn't had my fill of her yet.

I wondered if I ever would.

"Until the storm passes?" Her eyes danced with mischief and the promise of dirty, dirty things.

Pulling her face down to mine, I grinned. "Until the storm passes."

Sunlight hit my eyes as I opened them. "Whoa." I went to pull an arm over my face, but realized there was a very naked, very beautiful girl in my arms.

Sweet Jesus, last night had been real.

Somewhere this morning, during my pleasure ridden dreams, I'd felt sure Caitlin was nothing more than a figment of my imagination. Nothing on Earth could feel that good. But there she was, asleep in the curve of my arm, a faint smile tracing her lips. I hoped she was dreaming of me. Remembering how intense it had been between us, how fucking real.

I'd never felt anything like it. After the first time, our bodies didn't need any assistance. They came together like two pieces of the same puzzle. Her stamina was impressive, and she'd let me love her long into the early hours of the morning, until my muscles ached, and her eyes were heavy with sleep.

"Hey, Tink," I said gently. "I kind of need my arm back."

"Huh?" She murmured. "Oh, hey."

"Good morning." I dropped a kiss on her head. "I need to..." My eyes flicked to the door.

"You need to go?" She bolted up. "Oh God, I'm sorry."

"Relax." I frowned. "I just need to use your bathroom."

"Oh." She blushed. It reminded me of all the ways I'd made her blush last night. I already wanted to it again.

But we'd agreed one night.

One perfect storm.

"I'll be back," I said, my voice thick with regret. I already knew I didn't want this to be over.

I wanted more.

More kisses.

More silly card games.

Just more of her.

Grabbing my boxers, I slipped them on, pretending not to notice Caitlin watching me. Her eyes followed as I slipped out of the room and across the hall into her small bathroom. Everything about the apartment was small. But it was neat and tidy and had that feeling of being cared for.

It suited her.

After washing up, I found some toothpaste and gave my teeth a quick finger brush. The bedroom was quiet when I peeked my head around the door, and sure enough Caitlin was sleeping soundly.

With a smile, I tiptoed down the hall to the kitchenette and checked the refrigerator. She'd been right last night—there wasn't much. But there was bread on the counter and a few eggs left in the carton.

Caitlin had given me an amazing night last night; the least I could do was make her breakfast in bed.

SIX

CAITLIN

THE NEXT TIME I opened my eyes, it was to the smell of coffee and the crackle of fried eggs. Smiling to myself, I sat up and yawned. My body ached, but in the most delicious way.

Matteo has been insatiable. He was such a skilled lover. It was a surprise given how gentlemanly he'd been up to getting me in the bedroom.

I smothered a grin. I still couldn't believe I'd done that. Dared him to kiss me. Asked him for more.

What had I been thinking?

I didn't regret it though. I couldn't. It had been perfect.

He was perfect.

The perfect distraction.

I pulled on a clean nightshirt and some clean panties and padded into the hallway. Matteo was busy at the stove, humming a tune while he poked and prodded the eggs.

"What did those eggs ever do to you?" I said around a smile.

He looked good in my kitchenette, standing there shirtless, cooking for me.

A little too good.

"Well, I was going to surprise you with breakfast in bed." He glanced over his shoulder, his muscles rippling. Matteo's body was a sculpted work of art.

"You didn't have to do that."

His eyes flashed to mine, dark and searching. "I know I didn't have to. I wanted to. Sit and I'll get your coffee."

"Wow, a girl could get used to this." The words rolled off my lips before I could stop them.

Thankfully, Matteo ignored my little slip, saving us both the awkward conversation about what happened after he left to return to Verona County, and I went on with my life here in Providence.

He served me coffee before pushing a plate toward me. "Something tells me you'll be hungry this morning." His eyes twinkled.

"Oh, I see how it is. The storm passes and the real Matteo Bellatoni comes out." We shared a secretive smile. A smile full of stolen touches and sighs of pleasure. "I hope no one back home missed you last night."

"They know I'm safe. I do need to get back soon though." Regret washed over him.

"That's okay. I'm so grateful for... *everything*." The words almost got stuck, and Matteo smothered a rumble of laughter.

"It was some night, huh?"

"It was." God, he gave me that smile again, and I felt myself melt.

I worried it was branded on me.

That *he* was branded on me.

But our time together was finite, and all good things had to come to an end.

"This is really good," I said as I tucked into my breakfast.

"You sound surprised."

"Not surprised. More like... impressed."

"I can cook. It's in my blood."

"It must be nice, having a big family."

"It's the best." He smiled, cleaning off his plate. "But having so many cousins and aunts and uncles means there isn't much privacy. Everyone's always all up in your business, wanting to know everything."

"At least they care." Pain coiled around my heart.

"Shit, I'm sorry. I didn't—"

"No, not at all. You should never feel ashamed for having a family that loves you. You're incredibly lucky."

Something passed over his face, but before I could ask what was on his mind, his cell phone vibrated. Matteo quickly read the message, letting out a frustrated breath. "I hate to cut this short, but I need make tracks. Family emergency."

"Oh no. I hope everything's okay?"

"It will be, but I need to get home." He stood and sadness snaked through me.

I didn't want to say goodbye. I didn't want to let him go. Because I knew once he walked out the door, all I would have were hazy memories and lingering touches. And eventually, time would take them.

"Thank you," I said as we reached the door. "Last night was unexpected in the best kind of way."

"Shit, Cait." His hand brushed my cheek. "I'm not ready to say goodbye."

"We both agreed until the storm passes."

"Yeah, but it can be more. Maybe it can—"

"Matteo." I pressed my hands against his chest, leaning up to kiss the corner of his mouth. "Moments like this, what we shared last night, are rare. Like shooting stars. They burn bright, but don't last. Yet, if you are ever lucky enough to see one, you can bet you'll never forget it."

He buried his hand in my hair, pulling my face to his. Our lips met in an earth-shattering kiss. It wasn't just goodbye; it was Matteo's attempt on branding himself on my soul.

What he didn't realize was, he already had.

"Let me have your number?" he said, touching his head to mine.

"Matteo..."

"Please." The desperation in his voice squeezed at my heart.

"Do you believe in fate?" I asked him.

"I like to think there's a higher purpose, sure."

"Well I believe that sometimes people come into your life when you need them most. I needed you last night, Matteo. You prevented something terrible from happening to me and you gave me something so beautiful in return. And I'll never forget it."

I'll never forget you.

"So that's it? You're going to break my heart?" He gave me a playful smile, but there was something hauntingly sincere about his words.

"Who knows?" I said over the lump in my throat. "Maybe our paths will meet again one day."

"Until the next storm?" A spark of hope glittered in his eyes.

"Until the next storm."

I watched him leave my building and climb into his truck. He glanced up, but I knew he couldn't see me.

And it was for the best.

A guy like Matteo would soon move on. He had options. He had the whole world at his feet. Eventually, he would meet a beautiful girl who could be everything he needed, and he would forget about his night with me.

But I would never forget.

I would remember the guy who made me feel worthy.

The guy who showed me how good it could be.

I would forever remember how brightly we'd burned.

PRINCE OF HEARTS
ARIANNE & NICCO'S STORY: PART ONE

For never was a story of more woe than this of Juliet and her Romeo

~ William Shakespeare

ONE

ARIANNE

"OH MY GOD, can you believe it?" Nora sighed as she flopped back onto her bed, the one she'd claimed within two seconds of arriving in our dorm room. "We're here. We're really here. I never dreamed your father would actually go through with it."

"Don't jinx it," I said, half-teasing as I began unpacking my small suitcase. "There's still time for him to change his mind."

My best friend shot up, glaring at me. "Why would you say such a thing?"

"Chill, Nor, I'm just kidding. Mom made him promise he wouldn't do anything stupid. Besides, orientation is almost over. If he was going to rescind his offer, he'd have done it by now."

I did another sweep of the room. It wasn't much. Two single beds pushed up against opposite beige walls, matching nightstands separating them. Two desks, one closet, and a small bathroom with a shower. It was clean and tidy and in one of the two girls only dorms on campus. It could have been a hovel for all I cared.

Because to me, it was freedom.

"Have you decided what you're going to wear?"

"Huh?" I blinked over at Nora and she blew out an exasperated breath.

"Please tell me you haven't forgotten. Your date with Scott?" Her eyes grew to saucers as she watched me.

"Ugh. That." I melted back into the pillows, pulling one free and burying my face in the soft feathers.

"One of the hottest guys at MU asks you out and you're acting like it's a chore?"

I mumbled some incoherent response, but then my bed dipped and Nora's fingers were prying the pillow away from my face. "Ari, talk to me."

"I..." The words dried on the tip of my tongue.

She was right. All I'd wanted was my freedom. A chance to be a normal eighteen-year-old girl. To experience all the things other girls my age got to experience. "I don't feel anything with Scott."

"And?" She looked like I'd just spoken in the mother tongue to her.

"Nor, come on, you know what I mean. There's nothing there. No spark or butterflies. Scott looks at me and I feel... nothing." Even with my virtually nonexistent experience with guys, I knew that's not how it was supposed to be.

Her eyes rolled dramatically. "You have spent far too much time reading those romance books of yours. Real life isn't like that. It's messy and ugly and most of the time it hurts like a bitch. No one is saying you have to marry the guy; it's a date. Go, have fun, make out in the back of his car. Be a *normal* teenager."

But that was just it; I wasn't a normal teenager. Not even close. I was daughter of Roberto Capizola, Verona County's most successful businessmen. Heir to the Capizola fortune. Up until starting Montague University, I had spent the last five years living under lock and key at my father's orders. If it wasn't for the fact my older—and overprotective—cousin Tristan was a senior here; and Nora, my best friend since forever, had agreed to room with me; I would be stuck studying online courses from the safety—or as I liked to call it, prison—of my bedroom.

"Look." She shifted further onto my bed, crossing her legs in front of her. "Scott is Tristan's best friend, right? He's practically Capizola certified. He's safe. You need to see this for what it is."

"And what would that be?" I raised my eyebrow and she giggled.

"A practice date. A test drive. You're eighteen, Ari, and you've never even been kissed."

"I've kissed a guy before."

She frowned. "Your father or Tristan does not count."

"I..." My mouth hung open, but I had nothing. She was right. I didn't make a habit of kissing guys for the sake of it. And when the only guys you ever got to be around were all family friends, it was kind of a non-starter.

"This is a good thing," she smiled, "I promise."

"Okay, fine." It was just one date.

What could possibly go wrong?

"Problem with your chicken?" Scott asked before shoveling another spoonful of spaghetti into his mouth.

"No, I'm good," I said, glancing around Amalfi's, a cute little Italian place in the city overlooking the river. It was one of my favorite restaurants despite not seeing the inside of the place for almost five years.

"You must be relieved to finally be at MU."

"What's that supposed to mean?" The defensive edge to my voice surprised me. Scott was no stranger to how sheltered I'd been growing up. But there was something in his tone I didn't like.

"Lighten up, A—"

"Lina," I hissed, my eyes darting wildly around the restaurant.

"Geez, relax. We're in the city. No one is—"

"Scott..." I warned.

"Fine, fine. I didn't mean anything." He held up his hands. "I'm just saying, it must be a relief to finally have some freedom."

"It's only been a day." A strangled laugh spilled from my lips as I placed my silverware down gently on the plate. I'd barely touched the food, but my stomach was a giant ball of nerves.

Scott had been nothing but a gentleman, opening doors and helping me into my chair, complimenting me on how pretty I looked, but his touch was a little overfamiliar, his gaze a little too intense.

It didn't feel like a test run, it felt like something else entirely.

"You know," he said, his voice dropping an octave, "I've been trying to get your father to let me take you out for almost two years."

"You have?" I blurted out, feeling heat creep into my cheeks.

"Lina, come on." He gave me an easy smile, relaxing back in his chair. "How long have we known each other? If you failed to read between the lines all those times I hung out at the house, I seriously need to brush up on my charm."

"I..." Nothing. I had nothing.

Scott was one of the few people allowed over to the house, usually accompanied by my cousin. There had been family parties and gatherings, or sometimes they came over to get away from campus and hang out at the pool or use the fully equipped gym. Of course, I'd caught him watching me, I wasn't blind. Too often his baby blue eyes would linger in my direction. But I'd never acknowledged it because it was Scott. He might not have been family but he sure felt like it.

My eyes darted around the restaurant again. I was so used to being kept at home, walking around the city freely was... disarming. No one paid me any attention though, probably because they had no idea who I was. Father had made every effort to keep me out of the public eye since I was thirteen.

I suppressed a shudder.

"You're safe here with me," Scott added, as if he could hear my thoughts. "You know that, right? He leaned over and covered my hand with his. "I would never let anything hurt you, Lina."

Nodding, I offered him a polite smile. His words, meant to comfort, only served as a reminder that my life would never be normal. I could attend college and try to blend in, but I would always be Arianne Carmen Lina Capizola.

I would always be my father's daughter.

“It’s getting late and I’m kind of tired.” I yelled over the music. Scott leaned closer and my back hit the wall.

“What’d you say?” His mouth almost brushed my ear.

“It’s late, and I’m tired.” I said, but he only grinned back, closing the distance, skimming his lips over mine. Pressing further into the wall I tried to avoid his advances, using my hands to gently push him away.

“I want to leave, now, Scott.”

He had been bearable at the restaurant, gentlemanly even if a little smarmy, but since we arrived at the party, something had changed. He was still attentive, making sure I had a drink, hovering at my side. But his attention was elsewhere.

“Already?” He pouted, big blue eyes glittering at me.

I rolled back my shoulders and nodded. “I’m really tired.”

For a second, a flash of irritation twisted his features, but it melted away as he took my hand and led me through the sea of bodies. Guys hollered at him and girls watched us. But I was used to it. Occasionally, Papá had allowed me to visit Tristan at college, and a couple of times he’d brought me and Nora to a campus party. In secret, of course, and with the promise that we were nothing more than family friends. Tristan was kind of a big deal. A Capizola *and* the star quarterback for the Montague Knights. And Scott was his second. His best friend and teammate; his brother in all the ways that counted.

I knew most girls would have felt special; walking hand-in-hand with Scott Fascini, but there was nothing there. Not even the flicker of possibility. I just wasn’t attracted to him. He was a good-looking guy in that All-American way, inheriting his mother’s genes instead of his father’s Italian coloring. But I didn’t want to settle. I wanted to hold out for someone special. Maybe that made me naïve or a dreamer, but my life had never been my own. So this—my kisses, my body, my first time—it would be mine.

On my terms.

“Where to, bellissima?” Scott said as we reached his Porsche, and I glanced up, narrowing my eyes at him.

“Are you drunk?” I started mentally recalling how many drinks I’d seen him with. One at dinner, two maybe. But he’d drunk water at the party, or so he’d told me.

“Worried about me? That’s cute.” He hugged me into his side but I shucked out of his hold.

“Maybe I should drive?”

“No fucking chance. Do you have any idea how much this car is worth?” He smirked and something about the glint in his eye had me on high alert.

“Fine. I’ll call Tristan to come—”

“Fine, you can drive. No need to bust my balls, *Lina*,” he grumbled as he slipped the keys into my hand. This date was rapidly going downhill and I made a mental note to remind Nora never to railroad me into this again.

Inside his car, the air was thick, hostile, and from Scott's clumsy movements, I knew he was more than a little buzzed. But it was only a ten-minute drive to the other side of campus where I planned to leave his car and let him walk his sorry ass back to the frat house on the edge of campus that he shared with Tristan and their football player friends.

Silence lingered between us until his hand slid over my knee and up my thigh. I froze, my fingers clenching around the wheel. "Scott," I warned. "What are you doing?"

He laughed. Deep and smooth. The kind of laugh most girls would melt into a puddle to have aimed in their direction. But I was cranky and so over this date.

"Come on, Ari, don't be such a tease. I've been waiting for this a long time."

My eyes flashed to his as I turned for my dorm building, relief flooding me when it came into sight. "I'm going to park at my dorm," I said, ignoring his hand still smoothing over my thigh. Thank God for pantyhose. "You can get it tomorrow or something."

"Yeah," he slurred. "Whatever you want, babe."

I found a spot and parked up. The building was bathed in shadows with no signs of anyone coming or going. Slowly, I turned to him and smiled. "Thank you for a lovely evening. I'll see you—"

"Whoa, so eager to leave?" Scott's brows quirked up as his hand continued his exploration of my leg. I slid my hand over his and encircled his wrist.

"Scott, I said stop."

Confusion creased his face but then he was smirking, leaning in closer. Forcing me to wiggle closer to the door. "Come on, dolcezza." His fingers grazed my chin, tilting my face up. "I'll make it good for you."

"Make what good—" His mouth crashed down on mine, stealing my words, and the air from my lungs. Fear bolted through me as I struggled to understand what was happening. I mean, I knew what was happening, but why?

Why was Scott, my cousin's best friend and a guy my father adored, doing this?

"Scott," I breathed out, but it was a mistake. His tongue slipped past my lips, invading my mouth until I gagged. I curled my hands into fists, slamming them into his chest, trying to stop him. But he was big. All broad shoulders and thick muscle. And I was small. Slender and delicate and weak.

He fumbled between us and the seat swung back. I shrieked into his mouth but then he was there, covering my body, clawing at my hose. My skirt. My thighs.

"I'm going to make you feel so good, Arianne," he whispered, grinding into me. Bile rushed up my throat when I felt his erection pressing into my thigh.

Oh God.

This was happening.

Scott Fascini, a guy I'd known for most of my life, was going to steal the one thing I'd promised I would never give without giving my heart first.

"Shit, babe, you taste so good." He dragged his tongue over my jaw. My neck.

The curve of my chest. His fingers ripped through the crotch of my hose, finding the soft material of my panties. *No, no, no*, the silent plea got stuck in my throat as he hooked the material aside and began touching me. I grappled desperately with his shirt, trying to get leverage, something, *anything*, to get him off me. My hand traced the door and I found the handle, yanking.

The door swung open, fresh air blasting my face. Scott started pulling away, muttering under his breath, but I didn't wait around to hear his pleas. Using all my might, I rammed my knee into his dick. He recoiled in pain, grunting and cussing. It was enough for me to clamber out from beneath him and haul myself out of the car. I landed with a thud, the asphalt scraping my hands and knees, pain shooting through me. But there was no time to see the damage. I took off, sprinting across the lawn, tears streaming down my face, skirt hitched up around my waist, torn hose clinging around my legs.

The dorm was right there. But I cut left, running away from the building.

Away from Scott.

"Cazzo!" he yelled, although it was more like a roar. I didn't look back though. I just kept running, feet pounding the sidewalk, heart hammering in my chest. The feel of his fingers still on my skin.

The sound of laughter made me pause, my eyes darting around for somewhere to hide. I ducked around a building—the library, I think—and dropped to my hands and knees, dragging desperate breaths into my burning lungs.

"What the...?" My eyes snapped over in the direction of the voice. Two guys were hidden in the shadows at the end of the alley. "Hey, are you okay?" One slowly approached me and I threw up my hands, scrambling away.

"Whoa," he said, holding out his hands. "I'm not going to hurt you. I just want to check..." He stepped into the light. "Oh shit, Nicco, I think she's hurt."

"Please, I just need..." The words stuck in my throat as the other guy came fully into view. His hard eyes swept down my tattered form and flashed with an indecipherable emotion.

"Do we need to call campus security?"

"No, no," I cried, my hand still warning them not to come any closer. "I just need..."

What?

What did I need?

I couldn't go back to the dorm. Not with Scott still there. And Nora. Oh God, she'd lose her shit if she ever found out about this. But it was Scott Fascini for Christ's sake. His family was almost as powerful as my father. And it was my word against his.

"What should we do?" It was the younger guy who spoke and the other guy—Nicco, he'd called him—dragged a hand over his jaw, his eyes still set firmly on me.

"A guy do this to you?" He flicked his head to my skirt and I tried to smooth it out.

"It doesn't matter. I just need..."

"What? What do you need?" He inched closer and I sucked in a sharp breath. I was one second from falling apart in front of two complete strangers; the weight of what happened—what *almost* happened—sinking into my bones, but something in his voice grounded me.

And I clung to it.

"I need to get out of here. Just until I can figure things out."

"Bailey, I need your car."

"Come on, Nicco, shouldn't we at least call someone? She's pretty messed up."

"Bailey," he ground out and the younger guy relented, handing him his keys. "You good to ride my bike back?"

"For real?" The kid's eyes sparkled and Nicco smirked.

"If there's even so much as a scratch on her..." He let the warning hang in the air.

"You have my word." Bailey turned to me and offered me a weak smile. And then he was gone, swallowed by the shadows.

"Are you sure there isn't someone you want me to call?"

My eyes went wide as realization dawned on me. "My purse," I gasped. "It must have..." I swallowed the words, panic filling me.

"Must have what?"

"When I... ran... I must have dropped it somewhere. My cell phone was in there." Tears began streaming down my face again.

"Come on." Nicco ran a hand down his face. "Let's get you out of here and then we'll figure out the rest."

TWO

NICCO

"WHAT'S YOUR NAME?" I asked the girl curled up on Bailey's seat. She hadn't uttered a word since I led her to his Camaro. Or when I'd asked her if there was somewhere she wanted to go. She had completely closed down on me and I didn't know what the fuck to do with that.

The silence was deafening. Then, after what felt like an eternity, a whisper of a voice said, "Lina."

"I'm Nicco." I gave her a sideways glance. "The young guy you met back there, he's my cousin Bailey. Good kid."

"He seemed nice." She shifted, rolling her scraped knees toward me. "Thank you, for doing this. I- I didn't know what else to do."

I gave her a tight nod and settled my eyes back on the road, but I couldn't fight the urge to keep glancing over at her. The rips in her hose. The grazes on her knees. It had taken everything in me not to grab her by the shoulders and demand she tell me who did this to her. But she'd been like a skittish animal. All wild eyes and uncontrollable sobs. I didn't want to scare her any more than she already was.

"Where are we going?" Lina stretched her legs out, hissing with pain, and sat straighter.

"Is there somewhere I can take you?"

"No, I just... I'm not ready to go back yet."

"You live on campus?"

"Yes. I just moved into Donatello House. I'm a freshman."

Jesus. She'd been in MU less than a week. She didn't look the type to draw unwanted attention, and my blood boiled at the idea of someone hurting her. But I couldn't babysit her all night.

"Are you sure there isn't someone I can call?" My eyes slid to hers and she gave me a weak smile, shaking her head.

"I just need a minute." Her body was trembling, mascara streaked down her cheeks.

Rapping my fingers gently against the wheel, I waited. Nervous energy rippled off her, filling the car. I knew I was in way over my head, but I couldn't leave her now. "I can walk you back to your dorm, make sure—"

"N- no," she rushed out. "I can't go back there... Not yet."

"Listen, I'll make you a deal. I know a place we can get you cleaned up and then I'll drive you to wherever you want to go, okay?"

Her eyes grew wild, her whole demeanor jumpy, so I added, "No strings, I promise."

A beat passed.

And another.

Then eventually, she choked out, "Okay."

I breathed a sigh of relief when I finally pulled into the empty driveway. Even when I didn't intend on going into the main house, Aunt Francesca liked to venture out to my apartment above the garage to fuss over me.

"Where are we?" Lina sat forward, rubbing her eyes and I stole another quick glance at her. It was impossible not to.

"My place."

The air shifted as she sucked in a sharp breath. "Your place? Just how old are you?"

"Nineteen. Relax. I live in the apartment above my uncle's garage."

"When you said you knew a place, I assumed you meant a Wendy's or something." She flashed me an uncertain smile and my chest tightened.

"We don't have to..." My eyes flicked to the stairs around the side of the building.

"I could really use a drink and somewhere to clean up." My pinched brows must have said it all because she quickly added, "Water, I could use a glass of water."

Quiet laughter rumbled in my chest. "Come on." I climbed out and went around to the passenger side, opening the door for her. She mistook my action for an offer of chivalry and reached out for me, her slim fingers finding my hand.

Fuck.

What the fuck was I doing?

"I... uh..." Jerking away, I thrust my hands in my pocket. "We should go inside." My eyes darted around the place, met with nothing but the shadowy figures of the surrounding red leaf Maple trees. Lina hesitated, folding in on herself. I hadn't noticed how small she was before, but now we stood here, me looming over her, my six-foot-one stature seemed almost giant like.

Lina stuck close behind me as we walked to my apartment. Last year, I'd had a place on campus but it was bad enough being in class, let alone being in dorms. And since my family's place was across the river, it had been the excuse I needed to move into the apartment above my uncle's shop.

"It isn't much," I said, pushing the door open and flipping the switch. The dim lighting cast shadows off the walls as we stepped inside. "There's a bathroom back there," I flicked my head to the hall toward the rear of the apartment, "if you want to clean up?"

Lina's eyes swept around the place. It wasn't much: an open-plan kitchen and living area with a small hall off it, leading to the bathroom and bedroom. There was a charcoal sectional pushed up against one wall, facing a modest flat screen. The refrigerator usually housed an assortment of leftovers, courtesy of my aunt. It wasn't a warm and inviting space, but it was mine, which was more than enough.

"Thank you," her soft voice cut through the silence like a blade, and Lina took off toward the hall.

The vibration of my cell startled me, and I dug it out of my pocket.

Is she okay?

I smiled. Bailey was too fucking good for this life.

I'm way out of my league here.

I should have never brought her here. But the desperation in her eyes had called to something deep inside me—something I thought I'd buried a long time ago.

Want me to come over?

No, I don't think we should crowd her.

What do you think happened to her?

. . .

My fist clenched until my knuckles whitened.

Nothing good.

I wasn't a saint. I'd done some god-awful things in my short lifetime. Things no kid should ever see. But if my less than conventional upbringing had taught me one thing, it was that even in the bowels of hell there still existed a thin line of what a person was or wasn't willing to do.

And I'd promised myself a long time ago, never to lay an unwanted hand on a woman.

Movement caught my attention and I turned to find Lina standing there, arms still wrapped around herself like a protective shield. My gaze immediately went to her legs. She'd taken off her hose and cleaned up her scraped knees, but I barely saw the cuts; all I saw was inches upon inches of smooth olive skin.

Get a grip, Marchetti. She isn't a plaything, she's a damsel.

"Want to talk about it?" I found myself asking. Mainly because if I knew who was responsible for the skittish look in her eyes, I could make the piece of shit pay.

"N- no," she croaked out.

"If someone hurt you, Lina, I—" I stopped myself. This wasn't my mess to fix, not this time. I had enough problems circling me, like piranhas waiting for the perfect moment to strike.

"I'm fine. I just needed to get away."

"Here." Grabbing a bottle of water from the refrigerator, I slowly approached her. Lina took it from me, our fingers brushing. My brows drew together as sparks shot up my arm.

What the fuck?

I inched back, dragging a hand through my hair. My blood boiled and my skin itched, and I knew sleep wouldn't come easy tonight.

It rarely did.

Not unless I found a way to expend some of the tension currently radiating through me.

"Are you okay?" Lina stared up at me and I fought a chuckle. As I suspected, she had no idea, no fucking clue who I was and what I was capable of. It was probably a good thing too. She'd already suffered enough trauma for one night without discovering her knight-in-shining-armor was in fact nothing more than the devil in sheep's clothing.

"I'm good. Are you sure I can't take you somewhere?"

"I don't have anywhere else to go." There was something so fucking sad about the way she said the words, I found myself wanting to know more.

Who was she?

What had happened tonight?

Why did she come with me, a stranger, instead of seeking help elsewhere?

"Then you should call someone. A friend? Roommate?"

"I lost my cell, remember." Sadness edged into her dark-brown eyes. "When he..." Lina trembled as she pressed her lips together.

Anger zipped up my spine. Some fucker had done this to her. Hurt her. Put his hands on her. Scared her enough to run.

It seemed fucking ironic that she'd ended up where me and Bailey just happened to be meeting.

"Here, you can borrow mine." I held it out, but she just stared at it like it was contagious.

"I'm fine, really. Besides, it's late." She stood taller, letting one hand glide to her neck. "If it's not too much trouble, I should be getting back. My roommate will be worried about me."

Lina wasn't looking at me. In fact, she was looking anywhere but at me.

"Reality finally crashing down around you?"

"Excuse me?" Her eyes flashed to mine.

"It's sinking in?" I asked. "Whatever happened to make you run? The fact you agreed to get in a car with a total stranger and are now standing in his apartment with no cell phone or no way out." I was being a dick, but her sudden change of heart had caught me off guard.

"You're right, I'm being rude." She pulled herself taller, eyes fierce on mine. "I really do appreciate everything you've done for me, Nicco. It's just late and I'm tired. I want to go back to my dorm and forget this whole night ever happened."

She was too calm, too fucking composed for someone who was almost nearly... shit. I didn't have any idea about what had gone down. I'd just taken one look at the girl with holes in her hose and tears in her eyes and acted.

But Lina was giving me a get out of jail free card, and I needed to take it. I wasn't the savior she wanted or needed. Even if I did want to find whoever was responsible for hurting her and make him bleed.

"Come on," I grabbed my keys, "I'll take you back."

"Thank you, Nicco, truly." She smiled, a real honest-to-God smile that hit me right in the chest. Jesus, I needed to get laid. Or fight.

Maybe even both.

By the time we pulled up outside Donatello House, it was almost one thirty. I cut the engine and ran my hands around the wheel. I didn't mind driving Bailey's car, but I preferred my bike. The feel of the wind whipping around my face, the rumble of the engine beneath me.

The freedom.

Lina had been quiet on the ride over, her head pressed against the glass, the rise and fall of her chest gentle. Not that I'd been watching her or anything. At one point, I'd even wondered if she had fallen asleep, but the second we turned into campus, her body tensed, her hands wringing in her lap.

"You okay?" I asked.

"I will be." She gave a little sigh, hesitating.

"I can walk you to the door, make sure you get in okay?"

"No, really, it's fine. I just... I didn't ever imagine the night would end up here."

"You should talk to someone."

"It's complicated," she whispered, her gaze darting away from me. Silence crackled between us. The urge to demand she tell me what happened burning through me.

"Lina, look at me." My tone was hard; harder than I meant it to be. But she responded, lifting her face slowly to mine. "No one has the right to put their hands on you, not if you don't want it. Remember that."

"You're a good guy, Nicco." She leaned over, pressing a soft kiss to my cheek. I went rigid.

I didn't move.

Didn't breathe as her lips lingered there, just for a second.

"I, uh..." Lina finally pulled away, "I should go. Thanks again."

Nodding, I watched her climb out of the car. I could still feel her lips on my skin, the warmth of her breath. There was either something very wrong with me or she had magical voodoo powers because I wanted nothing more than to run from the car, pull her into my arms, and kiss her the way a girl like her deserved to be kissed.

But what the fuck did I know about girls like her? Girls so sweet and pure and innocent that when they looked at you, you wanted to drown in their light.

Nothing.

I knew nothing.

It's why I didn't get out of the car. Why I watched, like a creeper in the shadows, as she slipped into her dorm building.

It's why five minutes later, when she had disappeared and everything had gone quiet again, I was still sitting there.

A strangled laugh spilled from my lips, yanking me back to reality with an almighty *thud*. I was losing my fucking mind, and all over some girl. A girl who didn't belong with a guy like me.

Putting the car into reverse, I spun a U-turn and took off. It was late but the night was still young.

And I needed to burn off some energy.

"Didn't expect to see you here tonight." My cousin and one of my best friends, Enzo, stalked toward me.

"It's been a weird-ass night. Figured I'd drop by and see who's on the roster."

My eyes flicked to the ring where two guys were pounding the crap out of each other. People hollered and whooped with every crunch of bone, every grunt of pain. The smell of blood and sweat lingered heavy in the air, calling to the restlessness inside me.

Enzo's brows knitted. "Bailey causing you shit again?"

"Bailey's a good kid."

"He's a fucking liability." My cousin took a pull on his beer, staring out at the crowd.

"He's family."

"I'm fucking family, and yet I don't see you running to fix my problems every five seconds."

"You know I've got your back." My eyes slid to his, narrowing.

"So what's his issue this time?"

"It wasn't Bailey, it was..."

Enzo inclined his head, studying me in that cold, calculated way of his. "What the fuck is up with you?"

"There was this girl." I blew out a long breath, scrubbing a hand over my jaw.

"A girl? What girl?" he hissed the words.

"Hey, Nicco, you weren't—"

Enzo cut off our other cousin, Matteo, who wore an easy just-got-fucked smile as he breezed up to us. "Nicco was just telling me all about the girl that has him twisted up in knots."

"She doesn't..." I glowered at Enzo. "It wasn't like that. She was running from someone. Me and Bailey just happened to be there."

"Running from someone?" Matteo clarified.

"Fuck, I don't know. Her hose were all ripped and her knees were scraped."

"Didn't you call campus security?"

"She didn't want us to, asked us to get her out of there."

"Don't tell me you did it?" Enzo clucked his tongue.

"What was I supposed to do, leave her there? She was terrified. She's a freshman."

"Not your fucking problem." He shrugged.

"You're a heartless bastard, E," Matteo said, his lips thinned with disapproval. "Where d'you take her?"

"To my place."

Matteo nodded. He was the best of us. Enzo was cold and cruel. He used girls for sex and then cast them aside like they were nothing. Sometimes I wondered if the guy even had a heart. But he was loyal. So fucking loyal. The kind of guy you wanted by your side when things went to shit. Matteo was different. There was still some good left inside him. Maybe it was his mother and sister's influence. He had people to remind him how to be kind and compassionate. He had people who loved him.

Enzo was dark as night and Matteo was a hint of sunshine on a rainy day.

And me?

I was fucking numb.

Stuck in purgatory, awaiting the day fate finally claimed my soul.

"Have you lost your fucking mind?" Enzo glared over at me. "You took a complete stranger back to your apartment?"

"I didn't know what else to do." The lie soured on my tongue. The truth a huge knot in my stomach.

Because my cousin was right.

There were a hundred other things I could have done with Lina. I could have dragged her ass to campus security or let Bailey take her somewhere. I could have taken her to to a late-night drive thru and gotten her a soda and something to eat and then washed my hands of her.

But I hadn't.

I'd taken one look into those terrified pools of dark honey and wanted to comfort her.

It was disarming, the way she had completely bewitched me.

Not to mention completely out of character.

"Nicco, my man." Jimmy, the owner of L'Anello's, strolled over to us.

"Hey, Jimmy." I shook his hand. "How's the roster looking?"

A slow smirk tugged at his lips. "Better now you're here. Want me to find you a spot?"

"Nicco, this isn't a good idea," Matteo whispered.

"Yeah." I stepped forward, stretching my neck from side to side, a blast of adrenaline shooting through me. "Set it up."

I swear dollar signs flashed in his eyes. "The regulars have been asking when the Prince of Hearts is going to make an appearance again."

"Not that bullshit again," I mumbled.

"Heartless Prince didn't have the same ring to it." Deep laughter rumbled in Jimmy's chest.

"Fuck off, old man," I growled. "Before I change my mind."

Jimmy winked before disappearing into the crowd.

"Prince of fucking Hearts my ass." Enzo slammed his beer down.

"You're just jealous you didn't get a stage name." Matteo smothered a grin.

"It's bullshit," our cousin grumbled.

"It's just a nickname." A stupid nickname Jimmy had given me the first time I'd ever stepped into the ring when I was a cocky sixteen-year-old. I didn't need a name; everyone already knew who I was. But the people liked a show and Jimmy liked busting my balls.

He caught my eye across the basement and gave me a thumbs up. "That's my cue," I said to my friends. My brothers in all the ways that counted.

"You have nothing to prove," Matteo said. "Tell him, Enzo. Tell him he doesn't need to do this."

"Like he'll listen."

"It's cute you care." I flashed Matteo a smug smirk. "But I need to do this."

"You could just call up Rayna and get her to come over." Enzo suggested.

And on any other night I would have.

But not tonight.

Tonight I needed to hurt.

I needed to hurt until it all went away.

Until *she* went away.

THREE

ARIANNE

"HOLY CRAP." My eyes widened at the sight of Nora staring down at me. "Creeper much?"

"Sorry, it's just I have a meeting at ten and you were out for the count. Since you didn't get home before I was asleep, I wanted to..." She let the words hang between us.

"You wanted to know all the gory details." I sucked in a shaky breath, my fingers curling around the sheet.

"Ari, what is it?" Concern flooded her expression. "What happened?"

I sat up, pressing my back into the pillows. "Everything was fine. I mean, I didn't feel the spark or anything, but Scott was polite. After dinner he took me to this party and things went downhill from there."

"Downhill how?" She frowned.

"I wanted to leave. He was buzzed, so I drove his car and then he..." The words lodged in my throat as I remembered his fingers clawing at my thighs, his hot breath on my face.

"Ari?" Nora's voice cracked. "What did he do?"

"N- nothing," I breathed, forcing down the memories of his fingers clawing at my skin. "I managed to get out before he could..."

"I'll kill him." She leaped up. "I'll fucking kill him."

"Nora, calm down."

"Calm down?" Her eyes almost bugged out. "Oh, I'll calm down. After I've called your dad and told—"

"No." I shot to my knees, wincing as my tender skin brushed the sheet, and scrambled off the bed. "You can't call my father."

"I most certainly can," she seethed.

"Nora, think about it. Scott is as good as family. He's Tristan's best friend. And I'm nobody."

Her brow quirked up at that. "You're not nobody."

"I know that and you know that, but to everyone here I'm just another freshman at Montague. Besides, if my father thinks for a second that I'm in danger he'll yank me out of here quicker than I can say no." If he even believed me. In his eyes, Scott was a good man. An upstanding member of society.

"So what did you do?"

"I... I managed to get away and came straight here." I flinched. The lies were stacking up around me.

I don't know why I felt so guilting lying to Nicco about my name last night. After all, it was only what everyone else believed. I was here under false pretenses, a condition to my father agreeing my enrolment at MU. I was too precious, too important, to be here under my true identity. So for all intents and purposes, I was Lina Rossi, a friend of the Capizola.

I didn't want to lie. It wasn't in my nature. But some lies were worth it.

Some lies meant my freedom.

I'd spent so long locked away on my family's estate. Lonely days spent watching the world beyond from the window seat in my bedroom. When I was a young girl, I'd often dreamed of a handsome prince coming to rescue me; to steal me away from my prison. Nora said it was the romantic in me, but when you had so much time to daydream, reading became an escape. I was no longer a prisoner though. I finally had some freedom and I was not about to let Scott Fascini, or anyone else for that matter, ruin it for me.

Nora regarded me, some of her anger ebbing away. "You're right, it'll be the excuse he needs to end your college experience before it's even started." She flopped down on her bed defeated. "But what are you going to do about Scott?"

"Nothing." I swallowed the bile rushing up my throat. "I'm going to do nothing. Tristan and Scott are seniors. They're going to be busy with the football team and classes. I can avoid him easily enough."

"I still don't like it, Ari. He tried to..." Guilt flashed in her eyes.

"This is not your fault. Hopefully Scott will realize I'm not the kind of girl who wants to fool around in the back of his car and turn his attention elsewhere."

"I heard he was hooking up with Carmen Medina over the summer."

"See, maybe they'll start up again." I could hope. Carmen and Scott had history. Messy, colorful history. She was also a family friend, but I'd never really gotten to know her. Like most of the people in my life, I knew them. I knew all about their lives and their families, but they didn't really know me.

They weren't allowed to know me.

I was the girl looking in, always on the periphery but never in the spotlight.

Just then, a knock at the door startled us. Nora frowned, glancing back at it.

"Expecting someone?" I shook my head, and she went over to it, peering through the peephole. "You have got to be freakin' kidding me."

"Who is it?"

"Scott," she half-whispered, half-snarled.

"Let me." I steeled myself, grabbing a hoodie and slipping it over my thin pajama top.

"Are you sure? I don't like this." My best friend gnawed her thumb while glancing between me and the door.

"It's fine. Maybe he came to apologize."

Taking a deep breath, I opened the door and stared right at the guy I'd known almost as long as Nora. "Scott," I said flatly.

"Hey, Lina. I just wanted to bring this by, you left it in my car last night." He thrust my purse at me, and my eyes narrowed.

"That's all you came by for?" Anger rippled up my spine. He was acting as if nothing had happened. Smiling at me in that easy way of his.

"Did you need something else?" He turned the tables on me, the faintest smirk lifting the corner of his mouth.

"Nope, I think I'm good."

His eyes went to my chest and I yanked the zipper up higher, suppressing a shudder.

"I guess I'll see you around then. Welcome to MU." He gave me wicked smirk before spinning on his heel and walking away as if he hadn't tried to force himself on me last night.

As if it had all been a dream.

But I was wide awake and I had the scraped knees to prove it.

"What the hell was that?" Nora asked as I closed the door, clutching the purse to my chest, anger radiating through every inch of me.

How dare he.

How dare he act as if nothing had happened.

"He knows I won't say anything."

Nora made a hacking sound low in her throat. "Tristan would—"

"Would he?" I arched a brow. "You know as well as I do, the two of them are practically Montague royalty." Scott didn't apologize because he didn't need to apologize. He was used to girls falling at his feet. Acknowledging my rejection would be a huge dent in his reputation. Besides, nobody would ever believe I turned him down.

"This is bullshit, you know that, right?" God, I loved Nora. She was exactly the girl I needed in my corner if I was going to survive MU. I'd been so excited about coming here, about escaping my four-walled prison. I'd underestimated just how difficult it would be being no one.

"Don't worry about me," I gave her a weak smile, "I can handle it."

I had to.

Because the alternative, telling my father, was not an option. Not now. Not ever.

A look of pride washed over her. "Damn right, you can. Just wait, Ari, you'll see. This year is going to be epic. Starting with the party tonight."

"Party?" My stomach dipped. "I'm not sure—"

"Oh, hell no," she grinned, "We missed all of orientation. So no excuses. We are doing this and we are going to have fun. It's long overdue."

Fun.

I rolled the word around on my tongue. It was unfamiliar. Full of possibilities and promise.

It was my life now.

And Nora was right, it was long overdue.

Montague campus was beautiful. A mishmash of Gothic architecture and limestone buildings were scattered among a canvas of red leaf Maple and Oak trees. Perfectly tended lawns and evergreens filled the open spaces. But the showstopper was the Saint Lawrence Chapel, standing proud at the heart of the campus, with its pointed arches and intricate bell tower.

"Seeing it never gets old." Nora let out a little sigh of contentment. Being here was as much a blessing for her as it was me. Nora's family, the Abato, had served my family for generations. Her father was my father's driver, and her mother was our housekeeper. They lived in the cottage on our estate. Outside of immediate family, Nora and her brother, Giovanni, had been my only playmates growing up. We'd spent our summers exploring the grounds, discovering new ways to sneak beyond the perimeters. It helped there was a stream at the back of our property that flowed into the Blackstone River. We used to go down there and try to catch fish or dip our toes into the icy cold water.

I never saw Nora as anything less than me and she never looked at me as anything more than her. We were best friends. And when my mother finally convinced my father to let me attend Montague University, I think they were both relieved I wanted Nora by my side.

Of course, as a benefactor of the college, Roberto Capizola was able to pull enough strings to not only secure Nora's place at MU, but to make sure his daughter and her best friend were allocated a shared dorm room.

"Are you hungry?" Nora turned to me.

"I could eat. Maybe we can try out the coffee shop?"

"You read my mind." She hooked her arm through mine as we walked toward the Student Union. "How are you feeling about classes?"

"Nervous. I haven't sat in a class for a long time."

"Like I've told you a hundred times before, you really didn't miss much." Nora flashed me a smile. "I can't believe we only have one class together." She tucked her head onto my shoulder.

"You'll live," I chuckled. "I can't wait for Introduction to Philosophy with Professor Mandrake. He's one of the best in his field."

"And this is why we only have one class together. I like answers to my questions."

"Because the Sociology of Fame is so much better." I rolled my eyes.

"To each their own."

"Indeed." Our laughter filled the air and I took a moment to appreciate this moment. Me. Nora. A wealth of possibilities before us. So maybe I couldn't truly be myself here, but I could still soak up the fresh air; the knowledge that, for the first time in my life, I was free.

"What?" Nora pulled away to look at me, her brows knitting together.

"Nothing." My lip quirked.

"You're finally getting it, huh?"

I gave her a small nod, understanding passing between us.

"Come on," she said, taking my hand. "I might be your much poorer friend but I think I can afford to buy you coffee."

We entered the coffee shop only to be met with a sea of students. "Wow," Nora breathed. "It's... busy."

"It's fine." My eyes scanned the room for a table. "I'll find a seat while you order?"

"Sure." She joined the line while I stood there, rooted to the spot. There were so many people. Friends talking over one another, trying to hold court. Couples kissing over pastries and lattes.

Taking a deep breath, I focused on the task at hand when a deep voice said, "Lina, is that you?"

I found Tristan across the room, sitting in among a group of people. Football players, if their jerseys were anything to go by. He waved me over and I jolted into action.

"It *is* you." He stood up, waiting for me to reach their table. "Everyone, this is my friend Lina Rossi. Lina, this is everyone."

God he was good at this. The lies. The façade.

A grumble of hellos rang out around me while I lifted my hand in a small wave. I recognized a few of the guys—Tristan's teammates—the girls not so much. One eyed me up and down as she pulled my cousin back down beside her.

"I'm Sofia."

"Lina."

Her eyes narrowed. "Freshman?"

I nodded, aware everyone was watching our icy exchange. "Oh you might know Emilia," she tipped her head to the pretty girl beside her, "She's a freshman too."

"Are you the same Lina, Scott took out last night?" Emilia asked, jealousy glittering in her eyes.

Heat flooded my cheeks. "I..."

"Put your claws away, Em." Scott appeared, slightly breathless. He ran a hand through his dirty blond hair and flashed me an easy smile. "Lina is a friend," he said without missing a beat, "I wanted to help her settle in."

"I bet you did." Sofia and her friends snickered.

"Back off, babe." Tristan glared at her. "Lina's family are good people." He shot me a knowing wink.

No one else spoke. But I was hardly surprised. It wasn't the first time I'd seen my cousin exert his position as my father's favorite eldest nephew.

"Let me get you something to drink?" he asked, his eyes silently asking me more.

Was I okay?

Did I need anything?

"Nora's in line."

"Nora and Lina?" Sofia's perfectly plucked brow mocked me. "Cute."

Emilia smothered a snicker, and I wanted the ground to open up and swallow me whole.

"Don't be a bitch, babe."

Sofia ignored Tristan's warning though, pressing herself closer to his side to whisper something in his ear. My cousin released a strained breath, desire clouding his eyes.

I'd watched enough men to know when they were drunk, angry, or in this case, turned on. I already disliked the beautiful girl at his side, but I couldn't deny I envied the way she handled my cousin. How she used her female prowess to command his attention and distract him from the situation at hand.

Me.

"I'll catch up with you later," I said, excusing myself before Tristan could argue. Scott caught my eye as I turned to find a table but I didn't linger.

I had nothing to say to him.

Nothing good, anyway.

A couple got up, leaving an empty table. I slid onto the soft leather couch and searched for Nora in the line. She was finally being served, thank goodness. Seeing Tristan and Scott had set me on edge. Or maybe it was Sofia and Emilia's reaction to me. Whatever it was, my good mood was slowly dissipating.

"Here we go, one caramel latte, extra cream."

"You're the best." I gave her a warm smile as she placed the tall glass down in front of me.

"I see shitface is here."

"Nora!" I almost choked on my latte.

"What? He deserves it. Who's the girl?" She discreetly glanced over in their direction.

"That would be Sofia, Tristan's latest fling." My cousin was a playboy. But it was okay for him. He wasn't the heir to the Capizola empire.

I was.

He got to play football and attend college. To date pretty girls and get drunk at parties. He got to have the life that should have been mine. And while I loved him like a brother; a small part of me also hated him for it.

"If she thinks he'll keep her around, she's sorely mistaken."

I shrugged. "They want to tame him." And they always failed.

"I don't get it," Nora mumbled, "the whole taming a bad boy thing."

"That's because you don't read romance." My brows waggled.

"Oh, please. Don't tell me you buy into the whole notion?"

"I don't know." Sitting back, I ran my finger around the glass. "There's something poetic about the tortured hero and the girl who saves his soul." Dark intense eyes filled my head.

Nicco's eyes.

He was brooding and mysterious enough to rival any of the heroes of my favorite romance novels.

"You need to get out more."

"Hey!" I protested and Nora poked her tongue out, laughter shaking her shoulders.

"It'd be one way to stick it to your dad. Can you imagine if you went home with someone like..." Her eyes roved the coffee shop, landing on two guys over by the display counter. "Him."

As if he heard her, one of the guys glanced our way, his cold stare sending a shiver up my spine.

"Sweet baby Jesus, he's looking over here."

That was one way to describe it. He wasn't looking at us. He was glaring with such intensity, the air left my lungs.

"Too dark and broody for me." Nora broke the strange stand-off between us and the stranger.

I blinked at her. "Yeah, he's a whole other level. Anyway, it's not like I can actually date," I grumbled. Letting me come to MU was one thing but if my father found out I was dating, I shuddered to think.

"You can do anything now," Nora said around a mischievous smirk. "You just have to get creative."

"Like the party tonight?"

"Exactly. Now, you keep out of trouble while I go to this meeting. I'll catch you later, and then we can let loose." Her smirk morphed into a grin, and I couldn't help but wonder what I was getting myself into.

"It's loud," I yelled over the music. The beat pulsed through me, making me feel a little dizzy. Or maybe it was the drink Nora had insisted we have. Clutching the red cup like it was an anchor, I followed her through the sea of bodies.

"Of course it's loud, it's a party." Nora swayed her hips. My best friend was amped, looking every bit the college freshman out for a good time. I'd raised a brow earlier, when she'd stepped out of our shared bathroom wearing the skintight dress that dipped low in the back and sculpted to her ample curves. But then I'd checked myself, remembering this wasn't only my college experience, it was Nora's too. One she never thought she'd get to have. It didn't stop me reaching for something more modest though. After my altercation with Scott last night, the idea of wearing anything less than jeans and a sheer blouse was simply not an option. I'd let Nora curl my hair though. It hung around my face in soft waves, barely touching the nape of my neck.

I loved it.

"Oh, I love this song." Nora grabbed my hand, pulling me toward the makeshift dance floor. Downing the rest of her drink, she discarded the cup and began shaking and rolling her hips, hands weaving patterns in the air. "Come on," she mouthed, as I stood there. A fish out of water.

It was a just a party.

I'd been to them before. But then Tristan had kept us in his sights. He hadn't let us drink, or dance with guys.

But Tristan wasn't here now.

"Come on, please." My best friend crooked her finger.

"Fine," I mouthed, looking for a place to dispose of my drink. Spotting a table, I made a beeline for it only to be cut off by two guys. They didn't see me, too busy looking at something on one of their cell phones.

"Hmm, excuse me..." I croaked, trying to move around them.

"Hold up, pretty thing," a gravelly voice said, and I looked up to find two vaguely familiar eyes pinning me to the spot.

"Leave it, Enzo," the other one said, pocketing his phone and finally giving me his attention. "Lina?" A strange expression passed over his face.

It was him.

The guy from last night.

"Hello, Nicco." I smiled, a strange sensation taking root in my chest.

"You two know each other?" Disbelief dripped from the other guy's words.

"We, uh... we have a mutual friend."

We did?

I gave him a questioning look, but Nicco averted his eyes. "Come on, man," he grumbled, "this party sucks. Let's go hang out at L'Anello's."

"Fuck yeah, the pussy is better there anyway."

My lips parted on a gasp as my hand drifted to my neck. Nicco lifted his eyes to mine, and I was ensnared. A beat passed, the air crackling between us.

"It's nice to—" I started, but Enzo roped an arm around Nicco's shoulder and led him away.

No goodbye.

No, how are you.

Nothing.

Dejection pulsed through me.

"Hey, what's up?" Nora nudged my shoulder. "Was that the guy from the coffee shop earlier?" She flicked her head to where Nicco and his friend had disappeared into the stream of people coming and going.

"I... was it?"

"It looked like him. Hard to forget that face. Mind, his friend wasn't too bad either."

"Hussy," I replied, trying to deflect her question, and give myself chance to catch my breath.

To try to understand what the hell had just happened.

"Hey, it's college and I am more than ready to experiment."

"Weren't you the one telling me earlier dark and broody wasn't your thing?"

"It's not, but that doesn't mean I don't want to sample the goods before I make a final decision."

"Who are you and what have you done with Nora Abato?"

"I'm young, free, and single, and ready to mingle." Her laughter was infectious, her mood like sunshine on a summer's day. I wanted to bask in it. To let her happiness blot out the dark corners of my mind.

I wanted to forget.

About Scott.

About my father's expectations and the future that awaited me.

About the weird connection I felt between me and Nicco.

Who was I kidding? There was nothing between me and Nicco. He was just in the right place at the right time.

So why had he lied to his friend about me?

And why every time I closed my eyes, did I see his face?

FOUR

NICCO

SHE WAS THERE.

Lina.

I had been so surprised to see her at the party, I'd totally froze. Well, that and I didn't want Enzo to figure out she was the girl from last night.

"Hey, what's gotten into you? You seem jumpy?"

I glanced back at the house. "Maybe we should stick around. Just in case trouble blows up."

What the fuck was I saying?

"Trouble? It's a college party. Those guys couldn't find trouble if it yanked down their pants and attached itself to their dicks."

My eyes narrowed.

She was still in there.

Why the fuck was she in there after what happened last night?

"You sure you're okay? You're acting weird."

"Just restless."

"Still? I would have thought taking it out on Domenico last night would have loosened you up. He was a mess."

I inspected my knuckles, relishing the sting of pain as I clenched and unclenched them, watching the tender skin stretch and contract over bruised bone. Enzo was right. I had gone to town on Dom, and it had helped. Until I'd found myself staring into dark honey eyes again.

The bleep of Enzo's cell phone cut through my thoughts. "It's Matteo," he said. "He's going to meet us at L'Anello's."

My expression fell and Enzo scoffed. "You're not coming to L'Anello's, are you?" His icy glare burned through me.

"You go. Tell Matt I said hey. I'll catch you tomorrow."

"You're going back in there?" He flicked his head to the house.

"Nah, man." I gave him an easy smile, playing down my strange mood. "I'm going to ride, clear my head."

"Yeah, okay, whatever." Enzo shrugged, letting out an exasperated breath. "Don't do anything I wouldn't," were his parting words as he cut across the street to his car.

He never parked his car with the rest of the cars. It was his most prized possession, that and an 1886 original Saw Handle Derringer. Enzo had three great loves in his life: restored cars, hot women, and collector's edition weapons.

I headed for my bike and waited. When the taillights of his GTO disappeared in the distance, I circled back to the house, pulled up the hood on my jacket, and slipped inside. The place was crammed full of drunken students looking to let loose and get it on. Bodies writhed together in the middle of the room, touching and kissing. The air was thick with lust and longing.

It didn't take me long to find her.

Lina and her friend were right where I'd left her only minutes earlier. Only now, they had a group of guys circling, like a pack of wolves moving in for the kill. I lingered near the wall, in the shadows, watching as Lina tried to evade some asshole with bad taste in clothes and even worse taste in hairstyles. Her friend wasn't playing so hard to get, letting one of the guys pull her in for a dance. Next thing you know, he had his tongue down her throat. Lina's eyes went wide as she stood there completely out of her depth. Douchebag attempted to move in on her again, crowding her into a darkened corner of the room.

Before I could stop myself, I stalked over to them, roughly fisting the back of his shirt. "You need to leave, now," I growled.

He swung around, indignation burning in his eyes. "Who the fuck do you..." he choked over the words, the blood draining from his face as I cut him with a deadly look. "Yeah, I... uh... sorry, man." He almost tripped over himself trying to get out of there, not sparing Lina a backward glance.

"What was that?" Lina was in my face, glaring at me.

"That was me saving your ass, again."

She rolled her eyes. "I had it handled."

"Looks like you did, Bambolina," the word spilled from my lips without warning.

"Doll?" Her eyes flashed with irritation. "You can't call me that."

"Just did." I shrugged. It wasn't a word I'd ever really used before, but it fitted her to perfection. She was small and dainty, with perfect skin and lips, and eyes that were too big for her face.

The fact she was pissed at my impromptu nickname only made it sweeter.

"What do you want, Nicco?" She let out a heavy sigh, looking over my shoulder to check on her friend.

"You need to be more careful," I said, a strange sense of possessiveness snaking through me.

"I need to be more... wow. So you think what happened last night was my fault?" Disappointment edged into her expression and my chest tightened.

"That's not what I meant." What the fuck did I mean? She wasn't mine. I had no right to charge in here like a bull and tell her how to live her life.

A couple of guys barreled past us, forcing me closer to Lina. Her breath caught as my hand shot out to the wall beside her head.

"Why didn't you tell your friend how we know each other?" she asked.

"Did you tell your friend about me?"

Lina's lips pressed into a flat line as she gave me a little shake of her head.

Yeah, Bambolina, didn't think so.

"So I'm your dirty little secret too?"

"Don't do that." Disapproval clouded her eyes.

"Do what?" I leaned in, unable to resist the way she smelled. Like cotton-candy with a hint of vanilla. "What am I doing, Bambolina?"

She craned her neck to look at me. "Playing with me. I'm not a toy."

"No, you're not." *You're so much more than that.*

I felt it in my soul.

Lina was trouble.

A distraction I didn't want... *or need.*

Yet, here I was, in the middle of a college party, caging her against the wall, lecturing her on staying safe, as if it was my God given right to protect her.

Squeezing my eyes shut, I inhaled a shaky breath, trying to get some clarity on the situation. Only to open them and find Lina staring back at me. Jesus, the way she looked at me... it completely disarmed me. Made me want things.

Things I could never have.

"I need to go," I said.

"Go?" she balked, looking at me like I'd lost my fucking mind.

It occurred to me that maybe I had.

"This, us, it's a bad idea."

Her eyes grew to saucers. "There's an us now?"

"I... fuck, no... I just meant..."

"Nicco." She smiled, tucking a loose curl behind her ears. "It's okay, I like you too."

"You shouldn't."

Her expression fell. "I see."

"I'm not the good guy here, Lina, I'm..." I rubbed a hand over my face. "Complicated."

"Said every guy ever." Her soft laughter was like a bolt of lightning straight to my hardened heart.

"If I ask you to go back to your dorm, will you?"

"And leave Nora?" She grimaced. "Not going to happen."

"Please?" The corner of my mouth lifted.

"It's just a party. I think I can handle it."

I let my gaze fall down her body. If her outfit was an attempt at demure, she'd failed. The denim molded to her hips like a second skin, and her blouse, while long-sleeved, was sheer enough to draw my eyes to the outline of her bra. When I finally finished my perusal, and lazily dragged my eyes back to her face, she was flushed and I was sporting a semi.

"Do you have any idea how fucking good you look?"

"I..." Lina swallowed. Something told me she didn't. She wasn't here to catch some guy's attention. If I had to put my money on it, the only reason she was here was for her friend.

"I'm taking you home," I said.

"W- what?"

"You can go get your friend or I can pick you up and throw you over my shoulder. Your choice, Bambolina, but we are leaving." I had no plans to make her leave with me, but it was impossible to resist playing with her. Earning me another one of her starry-eyed expressions.

My brow rose. "I'm waiting."

She gave a little huff, rolling her eyes, before slipping around me and making a beeline for her friend. Lina didn't mess around, yanking the girl's arm, causing her to break the kiss. They had a heated conversation, both their gazes flicking to me on more than one occasion. Then Lina walked back to me.

"She doesn't want to leave; apparently Kaiden plans to show her a very good time later." Her eyes rolled.

I smirked. I couldn't help it.

"Is that so?" I scratched my jaw. "Okay, come on." Grabbing Lina's hand, ignoring the jolt of electricity, I went straight over to her friend.

"I'm taking her home," I said. "You should come with us."

"But Kaiden wants to—"

"Yeah," I cut her off, glaring hard at the guy plastered to her side. "What *does* Kaiden want?"

His eyes narrowed and then widened with realization. "Shit, man, I didn't know you knew Nora."

"I don't. But she's my... she's Lina's friend, and I know Lina. So listen up and listen good. You get her home in one piece. If I hear you put so much as a finger wrong, I will—"

"Whoa." He threw his hands up. "I'm not a total dick. I'll look out for her."

"You'd better." My jaw clenched.

"You're going with him?" Nora asked Lina, who stood beside me, her eyes dancing between the three of us.

"I think so. The party isn't really my thing. But stay, have fun with Kaiden." She settled her eyes on him. "Hurt her and I'll kill you."

"Fuck," he breathed through a strained smile. "The three of you are intense."

"Relax, I have a can of mace in my purse. We're all good here. Go." Nora wasn't looking at me, she had her eyes fixed right on her friend and they said, 'don't do anything I wouldn't'.

"I'll see you later." Lina said, leaning over to give her friend a hug.

"Tomorrow." Nora chuckled. "I'll see you tomorrow. Don't wait up."

Fuck, what the hell had I gotten myself into? Lina was hard to get a read on, but her friend was something else entirely.

"I'm watching you, Kai." I jabbed my finger in the guy's face.

"It's Kaiden," he stuttered.

"Whatever, we're out." My hand tightened around Lina's as I led her through the crush of bodies. I knew I'd just made a statement, at least in front of Nora and Kaiden. But the semester hadn't officially started and everyone else was too wasted or high to pay us any real attention.

I could take her home, make sure she was safe, and then move on with my life.

"I can't believe she's staying with that guy," Lina said as soon as we stepped outside.

"Why did you come tonight?"

"Nora wanted to. She wants us to have all these college experiences."

"Is it so surprising she's in there with him then?"

"I guess not, no." Lina dropped her gaze. And something inside me twisted. She wasn't supposed to cower, she was supposed to stand tall.

I didn't know her, not really. But I knew enough to know she wasn't like most girls at the party. She had class. An alluring naïveté that was a rare find these days.

Bottom line, Lina was special.

I felt it.

I didn't want to, but I did.

"What?" she asked, and I realized she was looking at me again and I was staring at her like a fucking idiot.

"Nothing, come on." Taking Lina's hand again, I guided her to where my bike was parked. Releasing her, I grabbed the helmet and held it out.

"You want me to ride on that death trap?"

My mouth twisted. "I'll go slow."

"No. No way."

"You want the full college experience, right? Well hop on, Bambolina."

"Nicco, I'm not sure—"

"Look," I ran a hand through my hair. "It's almost a mile walk back to your dorm or we can ride my bike."

Her eyes drank it in, running over the polished frame up to the handlebars. I'd restored every inch of her in my uncle's shop; she was my pride and joy.

And I'd never had a girl on the back.

"Okay." She took a deep breath, a small twinkle in her eye. "But promise not to go too fast."

"I promise. Here." I helped Lina get the helmet on. "It suits you." *A little too much,* I swallowed the words.

Swinging a leg over my bike, I got situated and glanced back at Lina. "Slide on behind me."

She looked so fucking adorable, standing there, gawking at me.

"Any day now," I teased, fighting a smirk.

Gingerly, Lina climbed on, careful not to press too closely to me. But I hooked an arm behind me and snagged her hip, pulling her as close as possible. Her breath hitched, and my heart did a somersault. Okay, so maybe this was a bad idea. She felt too good; her thighs hugging me... her hands pressed flat against my stomach.

Fuck.

I hadn't expected her to fist my t-shirt. To hold on as if she never intended to let go.

And I really didn't expect to like it so damn much.

I kicked the starter and the bike rumbled to life beneath us. Lina let out a little shriek of excitement as I took off down the road. I wasn't lying earlier when I'd told Enzo I wanted to ride, to clear my head. But now I had Lina on the back of my bike, I imagined taking the road out of town and hitting the highway. Miles and miles of open road. Just me. My bike.

And my girl.

Lina wasn't mine though, even if part of me wanted her to be. Something deep inside me already felt tethered to her. Protective and possessive. It didn't make any sense. None of it. And it wasn't like I could act on it. She was too good for a guy like me.

Somewhere around halfway to her dorm, she pressed her cheek against my back, gripping me tighter. I almost felt disappointed when we finally rolled into the small parking lot behind Donatello House. I hadn't gone around front to avoid drawing any unnecessary attention. I cut the engine and heavy silence filled the space between us.

"Wow, that was... wow." Lina climbed off the bike and pulled off the helmet, shaking out her curls. "I had no idea it could be so invigorating." A slow smile broke over her face. "You'll have to take me on a proper ride sometime. I mean... if you want." Embarrassment stained her cheeks, and I chuckled. I was pretty sure there was a joke in there somewhere, but I didn't want to ruin the moment.

"You look good on my bike," I said.

And that I fucking meant.

"Thanks for the ride."

I tucked the helmet into my chest and gave her a small nod. "You should go inside." My eyes flicked beyond her to the door.

"I think I'll have to go around front."

"Your key operates both doors."

"Oh, okay." Lina rocked on her kitten heeled boots. I couldn't resist letting my eyes sweep down her body again. She was everything I could never have.

Everything I'd never wanted.

Until now.

I swallowed, lifting my gaze to hers. "Go on."

"Goodnight, Nicco." Lina smiled.

"Goodnight."

She didn't move. Her eyes didn't leave me even for a second. Slowly, she walked over to me and slid her hand against my face. "Thank you, for coming to my rescue again." There was a playful lilt in her voice.

"Anytime, Bambolina." I smirked but it was wiped away when Lina leaned in, her lips brushing my cheek. She hesitated just for a second, but it was enough for me to turn my head and let my lips slide against hers.

Rookie. Fucking. Mistake.

The moment I tasted her, everything shifted. All I could think about now was pulling her down on my bike and devouring her. She tasted too good. Too tempting.

She tasted like my fucking downfall.

"Nicco." My name was a whisper against my lips as I ran my tongue against the seam of her mouth. My hand slid into Lina's hair, anchoring her to me as I kissed her deeper, harder. Her body shuddered, a soft sigh getting lost between us. I wanted to paint her skin with my lips, brand every inch of her. This wasn't even a real kiss. It was fleeting and cautious. But I already knew I wanted more.

I wanted everything this girl—this *stranger*—had to give.

"What are you doing?" she whispered when I paused, my lips hovering over the corner of her mouth. "Nicco, what are—"

I jerked back as if I'd been struck by lightning. "You should go, Lina. I'll wait until you're inside."

"I see." Her lips thinned as she stepped back, putting a thousand miles between us, the invisible tether between us almost snapping. "Well, I guess I'll be going then." She didn't hesitate this time. Lina walked away from me with her head held high, without so much as a backward glance.

It was no less than I deserved, but it hurt all the same.

I wanted her.

I wanted Lina the way I'd never wanted another girl before. But I couldn't be that guy. I couldn't give her hearts and flowers and romance.

I couldn't be the prince she deserved, because my life wasn't a fairytale.

It was the stuff nightmares were made of.

FIVE

ARIANNE

"GOOD NIGHT?" I peeked over at Nora as she slipped into our dorm room wearing an oversized MU hoodie and her shoes from the night before.

"Oh. My. God. The best." She flopped down on the bed, arms stretched out by her sides, a dreamy expression plastered on her face. "I think I'm in love."

"With Kaiden?"

"With his tongue. Seriously, Ari, he did this thing—"

"Whoa, too much information." My cheeks heated, my stomach clenching. "You stayed over?"

"He brought me breakfast in bed. Can you believe that?"

"That's... nice." At least, it seemed like a nice thing to do. It wasn't like I had experience. I'd barely even been kissed.

Nicco kissed you.

Technically, I'd kissed him first, but still, I could vividly remember the way his lips felt against mine. The roughness of his day-old stubble against my soft skin. The way tingles had zipped through me, firing off in all directions. It was imprinted on my mind.

He was imprinted on my mind.

Unfortunately, the look of regret as he'd jerked away from me was also imprinted there.

One thing was certain though, Nicco gave me whiplash.

"Ari?"

"Sorry, what?"

"I was telling you all about Kaiden and you're over there, lost in your own thoughts. Wouldn't happen to be thinking about a certain brooding hotty who practically dragged you out of the party, would you?" Nora pushed up on her elbows, grinning at me.

"Who, Nicco?"

"Oh, he has a name. Nicco, you say? Funny because the two of you looked far too close to be new acquaintances, and yet I've heard nothing about a guy called Nicco. Spill."

"There's nothing to spill, not really. He helped me out… the other night."

"The other night?" Her brows pinched. "But we've only been here two nights… no," she gasped. "He helped you out with the Scott situation? But you said you came straight here."

"It was confusing."

"I can see why you'd be confused over a guy who looks like he does."

"Nora!"

"What? The guy was hot. If tall, dark, and brooding is your thing, which it obviously is."

"He's very bossy."

"So what happened after you left the party?"

"He gave me a ride… on his motorcycle."

"Sweet baby Jesus, he's got a bike? That just upped his hotness by at least ten."

"You have a scale of hotness?"

"Not important." Nora rolled her eyes, sitting up fully. "So did anything else happen?"

Everything and nothing, I wanted to say.

The kiss had been unlike anything I'd ever experienced. But then, Nicco had pulled away like a bucket of ice-cold water had been dumped all over him. It left a sour taste in my mouth. He felt the chemistry between us, I was almost certain he did. But he was hesitant. And I couldn't help but wonder if I was the problem.

"Ari…" Her brow rose.

"We kissed."

"Thank God," she shrieked with delight.

"Seriously?"

"Oh, come on. Nicco is totally into you and you'd be a fool to not want to sample the goods."

"You make it sound so crass."

"It's only sex, Ari. Everyone does it."

"Yeah, but I want my first time to be right."

"I hate to disappoint you, but first times are usually a huge let down. All the fumbling and awkward condom conversation, not to mention it's usually over in less than five minutes."

"At least you've had sex." She'd gotten all the teenage rites of passage stolen from me: homecoming, first kisses, first base, prom, the party after prom… *sex* at the party after prom.

"It'll happen. We're in college now, the world is your oyster." She gave me a warm smile. "Hey, who knows, maybe *Nicco* will be willing to pop your cherry."

"Stop, just stop." I picked up a pillow and threw it at her. Nora caught it, falling back onto the mattress in a fit of laughter.

"Okay, I'm sorry," she finally calmed down. "So what do we know about him?"

"He's a sophomore."

"And?"

"He rides a motorcycle and has a cousin named Bailey. Oh, and his best friend is the guy from the coffee shop."

"The guy from earlier, with the intense eyes and tats? No freaking way."

I nodded.

"What is he studying?"

"I don't know." Okay, so maybe I didn't know much about Nicco at all.

"Well, he's someone. Didn't you see the way Kaiden almost peed his pants when Nicco warned him to behave?"

"You didn't ask?"

"We didn't exactly talk much." Nora smirked.

"Will you see him again?"

"Who, Kaiden? Maybe." She shrugged. "The sex was good, but I don't want to tie myself down. It's only fall semester. What about you? Will *you* see *Nicco* again?"

That was the million-dollar question. After his strange dismissal last night, I wasn't sure he'd seek me out again. But something deep inside me felt like our paths would cross again eventually.

And I couldn't deny part of me hoped they did sooner rather than later.

By the time Monday morning rolled around, I'd almost forgotten about the kiss with Nicco.

Almost.

I found myself looking for him, hoping to catch a glimpse as I walked from building to building, class to class. Nora teased me about him constantly over text. She even asked me if I wanted her to text Kaiden and snoop, but I told her if she dared, I'd call Gio and tell him all about his baby sister's freshman *activities*. He might have been off pursuing his dream of becoming the next great football player, on an all-expenses paid scholarship to the University of Pennsylvania, but he was fiercely protective of Nora. Protective enough that he wouldn't hesitate to drop everything and drive back to Verona County if he thought Nora was in trouble.

It was lunchtime when I finally saw him. I'd arranged to meet Nora in the food court, where I found her flirting with yet another guy.

"There you are," I said, approaching them. "I almost didn't see you for all the *people*." I shot her a knowing look before sliding my eyes to the guy. "Hi, I'm Lina."

"Dan. I'll catch you tomorrow?" he asked Nora and she nodded. "See ya."

He left and I turned to her. "Another guy? You work fast."

"Oh stop, we were talking."

"I heard you can catch all kinds of disgusting things from *talking*."

"So you didn't spot hotty the second you got here?"

"I..." My eyes flicked over to where he sat with Enzo and some other people, my brows crinkling when I noticed the girl sitting a little too closely to him.

My stomach sank.

"They look friendly." Nora linked her arm through mine, guiding me toward the pasta counter.

"He can talk to whoever he likes."

"Mmm-hmm." My best friend was too busy eyeing today's selection.

I risked peeking over at him again, only this time, he was looking right back. His intense gaze pinned me to the spot. Our connection was severed though when Enzo nudged his ribs. He cast a dark look in my direction before commanding the attention of everyone at their table.

Releasing a heavy sigh, I picked some lunch and followed Nora to the service counter. Once we had paid, we found an empty table. Montague had an impressive food court; something more fitting for a shopping mall. But it was no surprise really, given the college's very private, very elite status. Montague University was built with old money.

Old Italian money.

Founded by the original settlers during the first wave of Italian immigrants who arrived in New England during the late eighteen hundreds, MU was on the cusp of celebrating its Centennial.

Celebrations my father and mother had a personal hand in planning.

"You're sitting at the wrong table." Sofia, the girl from the coffee shop, glared down at us.

"Excuse me?" Nora rolled back her shoulders. "I didn't see a sign that said it was taken."

"Well," Sofia flicked her hair off her shoulder, shooting her girlfriends a smug look. I noticed Emilia glaring at me as if I'd stolen her favorite toy. "I'm telling you now, we sit here."

"Come on, Nora, it isn't worth it." I grabbed my tray to get up, but Nora slammed her hand down on top of it.

"We're not moving, Lina. If they want to sit here, there's plenty of room." Her eyes went to the empty chairs.

I might have spent the last few years locked away from the world, but I knew girls like Sofia and Emilia. They were self-absorbed and spoiled and had claws sharper than any lion.

"Nora," I whisper-hissed, shrinking into my seat as people around us began to stare.

"Ladies," Tristan appeared out of nowhere, slinging his arm over Sofia's shoulder. "What did we miss?"

"Oh, nothing." Sofia smiled sweetly. "We were just telling Lina and her friend that this is our table."

He snorted. "Seriously, babe?"

"What?" She pouted. "We always sit here. Everyone knows that."

"So let's all sit then," he shrugged, "there's enough space." Chairs scraped and people stared as Tristan and his friends began to sit down. Emilia shot around the table to take the seat at Scott's side, smirking at me as if she'd won this round.

"What do you possibly see in her?" Nora grumbled beneath her breath.

"She gives great head." Tristan grinned, leaning over to high five Scott and their friend. Sofia acted mildly offended, swatting his chest. But her anger quickly melted away as my cousin began kissing her.

"Disgusting," Nora said what we were both thinking.

"So, Lina, how is your first day of classes going?" Sofia asked me, her voice saccharine sweet. The table fell quiet, watching the two us."

"Babe, lay off—"

"It's just a question, Tristan, lighten up."

He threw me an apologetic glance. If Tristan made a big deal out of standing up for me, it would look suspect, something I couldn't afford.

"It's fine," I said. "Classes are good, thank you."

I felt Scott staring at me, and I hated that Tristan wasn't the only one who knew the truth. It wasn't like I wanted to deceive people about who I was, but my parents agreed that it was for the best initially. At least, until I'd settled in. If people knew I was Roberto Capizola's daughter, heir to the Capizola empire, things could turn sour for me pretty quickly. Even with Tristan's protection.

"What about you, Nora? How is your college experience shaping up so far?"

"What the hell is that supposed to mean?" Nora stiffened.

"I heard you've been making yourself at home, if you know what I mean." Sofia snickered, and Scott and his friend followed suit.

"Something you want to say?"

"Guys talk, especially in the locker room."

"You mean Kaiden..." Her teeth ground together. "What an asshole."

"Watch your back with that one," Scott added, "he's known to get a little handsy. If you know what I'm saying." His gaze found mine again, a smug expression on his face.

A deep shudder worked through me as I averted my gaze. Thankfully, Sofia chose that moment to steal the limelight. "Oh, is that the time," she said. "I need to go. Girls." They got up, lingering while she made moon eyes at my cousin.

"See you after practice?" Tristan asked her.

"Maybe, if you're lucky."

"Will I see you after practice, Scott?" Emilia made no attempt at hiding the lust in her eyes as she flipped long golden hair off her shoulder.

"I... uh... sure, maybe." His eyes found mine as he stumbled over the words.

She gave him a placated smile and took off after her friends.

"Sorry about them," Tristan said the second they were out of earshot. "I can talk to Sofia, maybe explain—"

"Please," it came out a low groan, "don't make things any harder for me than they need to be."

"Yeah, you're right." He let out an exasperated breath. "I think you made a good impression the other night," Tristan whispered out the corner of his mouth. "He hasn't stopped talking about you."

I went rigid, curling my hand around the chair. "We're just friends."

He chuckled. "You know he wants to be more than friends, right? It's time to grow up and live in the real world."

A frown crossed my expression. "What is that supposed to mean?"

"Nothing." He let out an exasperated breath. "It means nothing. Just give Scott a chance, yeah? Who knows, the two of you could become the golden couple of MU before the year's out."

"How about you lay off my girl, Capizola?" Nora arched a brow at him. "We've barely been here three days."

"I'm done," I announced, breaking the strange tension that had descended over the five of us. "Nora?"

"Yeah." She got up. "It's a little too crowded."

"Watch your back, Rossi," Tristan called after me. He was joking, I knew that, but after what happened with Scott, and the fact my cousin knew nothing about it, things between us felt wrong.

"Who the hell do they think they are?" Nora hissed as we emptied our trays and headed out of the food court.

"The elite of MU." I rolled my eyes.

"Did you see Sofia's friend practically drooling over Scott? If only she knew..."

"Whatever. If she wants him, she's welcome to him." Because one thing was for sure, I had no intention of going out with Scott Fascini ever again.

We reached the doors, but I hesitated, glancing over my shoulder to where Nicco and his friends were sitting. Enzo was staring right at me, his eyes sharp and cold.

But Nicco was gone.

"Welcome to Introduction to Philosophy, I'm Professor Mandrake. If you're in the wrong class, please leave now."

A chorus of snickers rang out around me. After a quick trip to the restrooms, I'd arrived with seconds to spare, sliding into an empty seat in the back row. It was the perfect spot to blend in. The professor got straight to it, scrawling the topics for this semester on the whiteboard while students tapped out notes on their iPads and phones. I preferred the old-fashioned method, decorating a fresh page in my notepad with words like philosophy of mind, moral philosophy, metaphysics, and epistemology.

"For the next couple of weeks, we'll be looking in depth at free will. Reading is chapters one and two of your textbooks." Someone slid onto the seat beside me. I peeked over at them, my heart skipping a beat when I realized it was Nicco.

"Hi," he mouthed.

"Hmm hi," I whispered, feeling myself get hot all over.

He gave the professor his full attention, but I caught a hint of a smirk tugging the corner of his mouth.

For the next twenty minutes, I sat there, barely breathing, trying to think about anything other than the feel of Nicco's lips ghosting over mine. By the time the professor asked us to introduce ourselves to the person on our right, I felt ready to combust.

"I guess we're partners," Nicco said, giving nothing away. He twisted his broad shoulders to mine, leaning in slightly. The black t-shirt he wore displayed his muscular arms

My breath caught again.

"Intro to Philosophy? I thought you were a sophomore?" And this was a freshman class.

He regarded me long and hard, inching closer. "How do you know Capizola?"

"Excuse me?"

"Tristan Capizola. How. Do. You. Know. Him?"

"Are you kidding me? Who *doesn't* know him?" I schooled my expression, ignoring the storm sweeping through me.

"I saw you today, at lunch."

"Then you saw his girlfriend giving us crap over *their* table. I guess he felt bad or something because we were already sitting there and she was making a scene."

"So you don't know him?"

"Sure I do. My parents know his mom. But we're hardly friends, if that's what you're asking." The lie rolled off my tongue too easily.

"And Fascini, is he a friend too?"

"Are you jealous?" I deflected his question, a funny sensation washing over me.

"Jealous?" Nicco said through gritted teeth. "Of Capizola and Fascini, please."

The air had turned thick making it hard to breathe. "We should answer the questions." I tried to steer the conversation to safer shores, but Nicco was staring at me with such intensity I couldn't think straight. His gaze darkened as his eyes dropped to my mouth, lingering there.

I felt lightheaded; disarmed by his proximity. I'd never felt such a strong reaction to anything or *anyone* before. It was like I could feel him. Feel him undressing me with his eyes. Touching me with his fingertips.

Professor Mandrake's voice cut through the air, startling me. Nicco let out a quiet chuckle, shifting his attention back upfront. It was my first philosophy class, and I'd already failed the first task. If I had any hopes of staying on course, I couldn't partner with Nicco. He was too distracting.

Too intense.

Too *everything.*

"This week I want you to ponder this, 'men make their own history, but they do not make it as they please'." I scribbled down the famous Marx quote. "I expect you to come to our next class armed with ideas, people. This is, after all, philosophy." Professor Mandrake excused the class, and everyone began to gather their things. It was only then I noticed Nicco had nothing with him. No notebook, no phone or iPad... not even a bag.

"Do you have a photographic memory or something?" I asked him, standing up and slinging my backpack over my shoulder.

"Or something." He tapped a finger to his temple. "See you around, Bambolina." Nicco ducked into the aisle and disappeared into the stream of bodies filing out of the room before I could even form a reply.

It was that moment I realized Nicco was like a storm. He swept in without warning and disappeared just as quickly, with no regard for the wreckage left behind.

I didn't want to be wrecked by him. But much like the storm, sometimes it was impossible to escape. You just had to batten down the hatches and hope you survived.

I was walking back to Donatello House when my cell phone rang. "Hello, Mamma."

"Ciao, cucciola," she replied. "So how is it? Tell me everything."

"It's... college, Mamma." I chuckled. "I just got done with classes."

"My baby at college, I can hardly believe it. The house isn't the same without you."

"I'm sure you're finding ways to keep busy." Gabriella Capizola was a force to be reckoned with. Strong and opinionated, there was never any doubt she wasn't cut out to be a trophy wife. Of course, my father humored her, and together they had become one of Verona County's most influential couples. It was hardly surprising, considering the Capizola were one of the founding families of our small slice of Rhode Island.

My father's grandfather and his father before that, had worked tirelessly to build a life for themselves after emigrating from Italy in the late eighteen-hundreds. Through hard work and a lot of blood, sweat, and tears, they had laid the foundations to pave the way for my grandfather to become one of the most successful men in the State. Property development, real estate, business, he had held a broad portfolio. A portfolio that all got handed down to my father when my grandfather died.

Capizola was a name people revered. A name that commanded respect.

For me though, it was a life sentence.

"How is he holding up?" I asked.

"Billy has only had to refuse to drive him out there twice. I'd call that a success."

"It's been three days."

"A lifetime to your father," Mamma said. "You're his most precious possession, Arianne."

Possession.

It sounded sweet rolling off my mother's tongue, but it felt wrong; reducing me to a thing rather than a person with feelings and hopes and dreams of her own.

I knew he meant well.

They both did.

It was just too heavy a burden to shoulder at times.

"Tristan is here. Scott too." I suppressed a shudder. "And Nora is extra sassy since we arrived. I'm fine, Mamma. I promise."

"Oh, I know, Principessa. Just promise me you'll keep your wits about you."

"I promise."

"Good. Will you be home over the weekend?"

"I'm not sure yet. Nora is taking our freshman experience quite serious."

"I'm glad she's there with you."

"Me too."

"Oh, silly me, I forgot to ask how your date with Scott went?"

"You know about that?" Incredulity lingered in my voice.

"Of course we know. Scott asked your father's permission."

"To take me out? That seems a little much, Mamma." My eyes rolled.

"He's a traditionalist like your father. I think it's sweet."

"I'm not sure we're compatible."

Her soft laughter filled the line. "It was one date, Arianne. These things take time. Give it a chance."

"I don't want to give it a chance." I stopped outside my building.

"Your father approves of Scott, he's practically family. The Fascini are good people."

"Okay, Mamma, what's going on? First Tristan, now you. Why the sudden interest in mine and Scott's relationship?" Or lack thereof.

"You know, I was talking to Suzanna just the other day about the Centennial Gala. It's set to be a big affair." She launched into a blow by blow account of the planning, of which my mother and Scott's mother were both on the committee. Eventually, Nora caught up with me and I made my excuses to end the conversation.

It wasn't until we said goodbye and I hung up, I realized she never answered my question.

SIX

NICCO

"NICCO, MY MAN, WHAT'S UP?"

"Hey, Darius." I tipped my head at the short stocky guy behind the counter, while Enzo and Matteo checked out the place.

"Is it that time of the month already?" he gave me a toothy smile.

"Sure is. You good for it?"

"Ain't missed a payment yet. I'll be right back." He disappeared through the door.

"What is all this shit?" Enzo grunted, holding up some weird-ass dish.

"It's a pawn shop, cous. One man's trash is another man's treasure."

"Wrong kind of pawn if you ask me." Enzo smirked over at Matteo. "Is it me, or does this take longer every month?"

"Relax, E," I said. "You know Capizola is applying pressure."

"Right, boys." Darius reappeared with a brown envelope. "I'm good for most of it but I need a little time—"

"Darius," I let out an exasperated breath. "You know the deal. My father lets you trade your harder to find items out of the store, and in return he expects a cut of the profits."

"I know, Nicco, I know. It's just Capizola is turning up the heat. Had his Suits come around the place again the other day, offering to help me shift some of my stock. Said I could move to one of his fancy stores over in the city."

"You really think they're going to let you sell this shit over there?"

"Enzo," I warned. Darius was a proud man. The last thing we needed was Enzo showing disrespect to his business; his legitimate one, anyway.

"Yeah, yeah." My cousin waved me off, stalking out of the store.

"It's got to be the full amount, Darius. I can't be going back to the boss short."

"Just a couple of days, Nicco. Please. Trade ain't what it used to be around here."

Matteo caught my eye, shaking his head. He knew the deal. We both did. If you gave an inch, people like Darius would take a mile. His pawn shop might have fallen on hard times but his side business dealing in counterfeit goods and providing high-interest loans to people in and around La Riva and Romany Square was booming.

"Go check the safe again, D." I peeled back one side of my jacket, flashing him my pistol. "You're only what? Two or three hundred short? I'm sure you can dig deep and find it."

Panic flooded his expression. "Come on, Nicco, we're friends, aren't we? I just need a—"

"Don't make this any harder than it needs to be, D." My hand slid into my jacket. "Go get the cash or I can make you get it."

"Shit, yeah. Okay." He ran a hand through his thinning hair.

"What's his deal?" Matteo drummed his fingers on the counter as we waited.

"Fuck knows." I didn't doubt Capizola had sent his guys to rattle local business owners. He wanted people scared, ready to offer them false promises and pipe dreams about a better life across the river.

But guys like Darius would use any excuse to try and shirk from paying up.

He reappeared a couple minutes later and slapped the envelope down. "It's all there, you can count it."

"I trust you, D." I shoved it into my inside pocket. "Same time next month."

"Yeah, yeah. Maybe ask your old man what he plans to do about Capizola. This shit is getting out of control, Nicco. I heard Horatio's place got torched, destroyed half his stock. There are rumors circulating Capizola is prepared to use any means necessary to get people to sell up."

"Is that so?" I raised a brow. "Well you can spread the word that La Riva, Romany Square, and everything west of the river still belongs to Antonio Marchetti."

"So why the fuck isn't the boss doing anything about it?" Darius glared at me.

"Nice doing business with you, D," I said, cutting the conversation short before shit got out of control. "See you next month."

Matteo followed me out of the store. "It's like they think Uncle Toni can just have him taken out. It's Roberto Capizola for fuck's sake. A hit like that would bring all kinds of heat."

"Exactly," I snapped. "But Capizola knows that. It's why he's putting pressure on local businesses because he knows my father's hands are tied."

"It's bullshit, is what it is." Enzo strolled over to us.

"Yeah, well, it's only going to get a whole lot worse before it gets better." The vibration of my cell phone caught my attention. I pulled it out and scanned the incoming text.

"We're needed at the house," I said.

"Uncle Toni?" Matteo asked, and I nodded.

"Who else."

"What do you think he wants?"

"Beats me," I said to Enzo as we piled into his fully restored Pontiac GTO. "You know how it is. When the boss calls, we come running."

Matteo ducked into the backseat, his knees digging into my back. "You need to get a bigger car." I eyed Enzo and he smirked. It was his international language for fuck you.

"Maybe he's got another job for us."

"We don't know what he wants yet," I grumbled.

But gut instinct told me it wouldn't be anything good.

The ride back to our neighborhood was about fifteen minutes, enough time for Enzo to tell us about the threeway he'd had the other night.

"I'm surprised your dick hasn't fallen off," I said. "Too much fucking use."

"More like too many diseases."

"Fuck you, Bellatoni, I wrap that shit every time."

"That's what she said."

"What's up with you, Nicco? I heard you snuck into Mandrake's class today?"

"Philosophy?" Enzo balked, his questioning gaze burning into the side of my face.

Fuck.

I ran a brisk hand over my head, hoping to deflect Matteo's question, but he was like a dog with a bone.

They both were.

"Just wanted to remind him we're here, watching."

"I thought he settled things with Uncle Toni?"

"He did." I shrugged, trying to act indifferent. Mandrake had paid the debt he'd run up at one of my father's gambling circuits fair and square, but it wasn't the first time we'd watched someone to make sure they didn't become a persistent problem.

"Going against the old man's orders?" Enzo chuckled. "It's like you have a death wish or something."

"Lay off it, Enzo. Those business classes are as boring as fuck."

"And philosophy is better? That shit is senseless."

"Full of hot booksmart girls though, am I right?" Matteo grinned at me through the rear-view mirror, pushing his messy dirty-blond hair out of his eyes. "Maybe I'll come next time, scope out the potential pus—"

"Do you two think with anything other than your dicks?"

"Since when *didn't* you think with yours?" Enzo's brow rose.

"I just... fuck, I don't know."

I did know, and she had eyes the color of honey.

"You've been tense the whole weekend. You need to either fight it out of you or fuck it out. And you already kicked Dom's ass, so I guess we all know the answer you're looking for. Just call up Rayna and make it right." His hand tightened around the wheel as we crossed the bridge separating Verona City with La Riva.

"Just drive, yeah. I've heard enough of your bullshit for today." I leaned back against the leather headrest, watching the city roll by. The landscape changed the further you moved out toward La Riva. The houses were smaller, with worn paintwork and overgrown lawns. Tired and forgotten, it wasn't a bad neighborhood, but it wasn't in the same league as its flashier more upmarket counterpart over the river.

Enzo navigated the streets with ease. We grew up here. Played on the very blocks we passed. La Riva was our home. Every childhood memory, the good and bad and sometimes the downright ugly. It was in our blood.

And it was my legacy.

While Roberto Capizola and his holier than thou Suits in the city controlled the three biggest towns in Verona County—Roccaforte, University Hill, and Verona City—my father owned the streets of La Riva, and Romany Square, and refused to give them up to the man he hated more than anything.

It was fucking ironic that Capizola was trying to make life difficult for my father because of his *associations*, when the very money that got old Rob to where he was today was stained with the blood of his enemies.

That's partly why I'd been so taken aback to see Tristan Capizola, Roberto's eldest nephew, hanging around Lina. He was a sneaky sonofabitch who enjoyed flashing his family's name around. Everyone knew he wanted to fill his uncle's shoes one day, to take over the family business; but unlucky for him, Roberto already had an heir.

A daughter.

Not that anyone had seen her in years. Roberto apparently kept her locked away on their estate in Roccaforte. There were even rumors circulating she was dead. I didn't believe that. I believed Capizola was a smart man. A man who, just because he'd renounced his family's tainted history, hadn't forgotten what it meant to have enemies. A man like Roberto Capizola was untouchable; he had too many friends in high places, was in the public eye too much. But his family, his daughter wasn't.

The sight of my childhood home silenced my thoughts. I always had mixed feelings about coming back here. Ever since my mother left five years ago, it felt empty. It was one of the reasons I'd so easily agreed to go to MU. College wasn't my choice, not when my life was already mapped out before me. But if it meant being out of this house, of pretending just for a little while that my life was my own, then I'd take it.

The other thing tethering me here, besides obligation and loyalty, was currently running down the driveway in a blur of wild curls and soft laughter.

"Jesus, you're going to have to beat them off with a stick when she's older."

"She's almost seventeen," I reminded Matteo.

"Still, that girl has trouble written all over her."

"You're not actually checking out my sister—my *baby* sister?"

"The fuck I am, she's my cousin," he ground out. "I'm just saying, I have eyes, and she's a looker. Takes after your mom."

"Way to go, man," Enzo snickered. "First Alessia and now his mom."

"You know that's not what I mean. Shit, Nicco, you know I wouldn't—"

"Relax, I know. Just don't go talking about my sister like that again, okay?" The thought of my sister ending up with someone like Matteo or Enzo made me want to tear my fucking hair out. She was too good. Too fucking pure. She was all my mom while I was every bit my father. It was a burden I would gladly carry if it meant I could shelter her from this life.

Enzo killed the engine and we climbed out. I'd barely even gotten my feet on the ground when Alessia leaped into my arms. "Nicco," she breathed, "I missed you."

"Nice to see you too, Sia." Enzo chuckled, kicking the gravel with his boot. "Is my dad here?"

"Yeah, he's inside. Uncle Michele too."

He shot me a serious look. If Uncle Vincenzo and Matteo's father, Michele, were here too then it was as a good as a family meeting.

"How's school?" I asked Alessia, tucking her into my side as we approached the house.

"It's okay, I guess." She gave a small shrug.

"Sia, it's junior year. You need to learn to let loose and have fun. But not too much fun," I quickly added. "No guys. Definitely no guys until you're eighteen."

Or never, if I had anything to say about it.

"Relax, big brother, it's not like anyone wants to date me anyway."

"What the fuck does that mean?" I pulled Alessia in front of me, holding her at arm's length. "Any guy would be lucky to have you."

Her eyes darted to the ground.

"Sia, talk to me," I said softly.

She slowly lifted her face to mine and what I saw there gutted me. "I'm a Marchetti, Nicco.

"So?" Being a Marchetti in high school had never been a problem for me. Guys looked the other way and girls all wanted a piece of me. The three of us—me, Enzo, and Matteo—had ruled the halls at high school.

"It was different for you. You're a guy. It earns you a certain level of respect. Not for me though, it makes me untouchable," her voice trailed off.

"Someone said something to you, Sia?" Matteo inched closer. "Because if they have—"

"*That*, that's the problem." She didn't sound angry, just resigned, and it was like a vice around my heart. "No guy will even look twice at me because of who my brother is. Who my family is."

"Screw them," Matteo said, and I frowned at him. That was supposed to be my line. But then, he had a younger sister too, so I guess he knew how to handle this kind of thing. "If a guy is intimidated by the fact you're a Marchetti then he doesn't deserve you."

"Thanks, Matt." Alessia gave him a coy smile. "Maybe I need to find someone older. A college—"

"*Do not* finish that sentence," I growled.

Enzo chuckled darkly from the porch. "Told ya." He motioned swinging a bat. I flipped him off.

"Come on, we don't want to keep daddy dearest waiting." He didn't like tardiness.

And I had a feeling the day was already about take a turn without getting berated by my old man for being late.

"Hang out with me for a little while later?" Alessia asked.

"You know it." I gave her a warm smile before following my friends into the house to find out whatever awaited us.

We found my father and uncles in the den. It was my father's office/meeting room/room where he liked to entertain. And until a little over a year ago, it had been strictly off limits to me and my cousins. But ever since graduating high school, we'd been officially initiated into the family. A deep shudder worked down my spine, remembering exactly what we'd done that night. But it what was it was. The world was a dog eat dog place, and we all had our parts to play.

Mine just so happened to be the only son to Antonio Marchetti, boss of Dominion, or as it was called among outsiders: The New England Mafia. With his cousin, Alonso Marchetti, running the Boston faction, my father, with my uncles at his side, and a string of cousins, extended family, and associates in the ranks, owned and controlled various businesses in and around Verona County. Most were legitimate, providing a smokescreen for racketeering, money laundering, and gambling.

Verona County was built and founded on mafia money. The very foundations it stood on were tainted with blood and deceit. But people were happy to turn a blind eye to what went on around them, to forget their less than holy roots, if it meant they got to drive around in their posh cars, wearing their expensive fucking suits and clothes, eating rich people's food and sipping bottles of champagne that cost enough to feed a third world country.

"Niccolò, boys, get in here. Have a drink." My father motioned to Genevieve, the housekeeper, although I was pretty sure her duties far extended servicing just the household chores.

I sucked in a harsh breath. My father had aged well. His eyes still sparkled with the Marchetti charm and he still had a head full of dark unruly hair. He also kept physically fit thanks to many hours spent at my uncle Mario's gym. But he was my father, and I knew him better than anyone. I saw what others didn't see—the extra crows feet around his eyes, the dark cloud circling him.

My father was tired. Worn down by life. And although I knew he would never admit it, I suspected he still suffered with a broken heart. Which was fucking ironic since he was the reason my mother fled.

Enzo and Matteo accepted a glass of whisky each, but I refrained, opting for water instead, preferring to keep my wits about me. "What's going on?" I asked, pulling out the various envelopes of cash and throwing them down on the table. Michele got up to collect them, depositing them in my father's safe. They'd count the cash later before cleaning it.

All I wanted to do was get down to business. The sooner we were done, the sooner I could spend some time with Alessia and then get the hell out of here.

"How is college?" Uncle Vincenzo asked, relaxing back in the big leather chair. "Plenty of fresh pussy?" One of his thick brows rose suggestively.

"Really, old man?" Enzo scowled. "If Nonna heard you—"

"You should know by now, son, what happens inside these four walls, stays inside these four walls." He chuckled as if we didn't all know just how important the code of silence was. "So, how is it, really? Have you managed to bed any—"

"Enzo," my father scolded his younger brother. "We haven't come here to talk about your son's sex life. Although, kid, I gotta say it, remember to wrap that shit. The last thing we need is some girl getting knocked up with Marchetti seed."

"Jesus," I muttered under my breath.

"A-fucking-men to that." Uncle Vincenzo lifted his glass before necking the contents.

"Thanks, Gen, you're excused. If we need anything, I'll be sure to call."

The housekeeper nodded, before scurrying out of the room. She couldn't have been much older than me. Far too young to be underneath my father but he wasn't exactly the type of man you told no.

"How's things in that department?" Uncle Michele flicked his head to the door.

"It's not serious," my father said quietly, loosening his tie as his eyes slid to mine.

"Don't look at me. Whatever you do in your spare time is your business."

"Niccolò, do you have to be—"

"Are we ever going to get to the point of this meeting?" I grumbled.

"You're right." My father's expression hardened. "There's been an interesting development with Capizola."

"Tommy finally found some dirt on him?"

Tommy, one of our best, most trusted investigators had been watching Roberto for years. Trying to find enough dirt to knock Capizola off his pedestal. But so far, he'd come up with nothing but a few parking tickets and planning regulation violations.

"Not exactly. But we think we might know where his daughter is."

We all sat straighter. "She's alive?" Matteo asked.

"You didn't really believe she was dead?" I asked around a smirk. He was so fucking gullible sometimes.

"No one has seen her for the best part of five years." He shrugged. "I figured perhaps she was pushing up daisies and her old man wanted to keep up pretenses."

He had a point. In a world where money and power were everything, for someone like Capizola, having a living heir was vital.

I knew that first-hand.

"So, where is she?" I turned my focus back to my father.

"We think she's attending Montague University this year."

"What?" I balked. "No way he'd send her there." He had too many enemies watching him, waiting for the opportune moment to strike.

"Obviously we don't think he's sent her there under her true identity."

"Hiding her in plain sight... makes sense." Enzo said. "And it wouldn't be hard. No one has seen her in years. I doubt she still looks like a child."

"You think the intel is good?" I asked my father, and he nodded.

"Tristan will know her. They're cousins, and Roberto treats him like a son. He's the key. Get to him and you'll get to her."

"Yeah, but let's be real here, it's not like he'll be parading her around campus." Enzo snorted. "It won't be someone in his circle, that's way too obvious."

"Get to her to do what exactly?" Matteo asked.

"Son," Michele grumbled, throwing my father an apologetic look. Matteo straddled the fine line between wanting to embrace the life and wanting more. Unlike Enzo, he wasn't inherently angry, and unlike me, he wasn't permanently numb.

Until her. My mind flickered to Lina. Wondering what she was doing right now this second. I wanted her so fucking much. On the back of my bike. In my bed. Underneath me.

I wanted her any way I could fucking get her, but it wouldn't be fair, to either of us, for me to pull her into this world.

A world where we were talking about using an innocent girl to get to her father.

"If we have to spell it out to you, Matt, then you're not the sons we raised." My father's words lingered in the air, heavy and laced with meaning.

Beside me, Matteo shifted uncomfortably. I narrowed my eyes, hardly surprised my father wanted us to handle this. It was, after all, why we were at MU. Not only did it give the illusion of our family wanting a more legitimate future, it placed us somewhere where we could have our ear to the ground. Kids talked. Especially kids so drunk and high on college life. But a year into college, and our intel was lacking to say the least. My father and our uncles didn't seem too concerned. Taking down Roberto Capizola was the endgame. As long as we kept up pretenses, attended classes, and brought in some cash from our on and off campus ventures, they were happy enough.

"We'll handle it," Enzo said. "When we figure out who she is, how far can we take it?"

The air rippled with dark energy as my father ran his finger around his glass of whisky. "Whatever it takes to make her break. She's the missing piece of the puzzle. Get to her and we'll have the leverage we need to get the upper hand," my father's voice dropped an octave. "I've watched Capizola bleed his redeemed soul bullshit all across Verona. He wants La Riva, then he'd better be prepared to take it from my bloody broken fingers because this is our home and I won't go down without a fight."

The men raised their glasses, toasting their plan. Enzo joined them, always too thirsty, too eager, to get his hands dirty. Matteo was a mask of uncertainty, but he clinked his glass with the others, nonetheless.

Everyone looked at me expectantly. One day, I'd sit here in my father's chair, calling the shots and toasting *my* plan. It was a future I'd never asked for. A future I didn't want. I didn't want the responsibility or the power. Getting my hands dirty, fine. I could do that. I could swallow the orders and see them through. I could even handle being a capo and having my own crew. But I didn't want to be the person making the big decisions.

"Niccolò." Antonio Marchetti didn't like to be kept waiting. His hard, assessing gaze on mine, I lifted my glass and gave him a sharp nod.

I might not have wanted this life.

But it was mine regardless.

Because no one walked away from the family except in a body bag.

Especially not the only son of the boss.

SEVEN

ARIANNE

I DIDN'T SEE Nicco for the rest of the week. It was almost as if he'd disappeared off the face of the earth. He wasn't in Professor Mandrake's class, and I didn't see him and his friends in the food court, or around campus.

If it wasn't for the lingering memory of his lips against mine, I would have thought he was a figment of my imagination. But nothing that good could be made up.

Could it?

"You're looking for him again, aren't you?" Nora asked as we walked back to our dorm building.

"Who?" I played dumb.

"Oh hush, you're so looking for hotty. Not that I blame you."

"I haven't seen him all week. That's weird, right?"

"He's a guy. They're all fucking weird." Nora wore college life well. She'd always been a free spirit but living on my father's estate had clipped her wings to some degree. Since we'd arrived at MU though, I'd watched her blossom.

"Did you decide what to wear to the party tonight?"

"About that..."

She ground to a halt and ducked in front of me, fixing her eyes right on me. "Oh no, I don't like that tone."

"It's just, I'm not sure parties are my thing." When Nora had mentioned the masquerade party at my cousin's frat house, I'd given her non-committal maybe. I probably should have told her no, but she'd been so excited. I didn't want to drag her down, I wanted Nora to have the full college experience... I just wasn't sure it was what *I* wanted.

No, I was more interested in the flyer I'd gotten from the Student Community Action Committee. They were looking for volunteers to help at the local shelter. I'd spent so long cut off from the real world, locked away in my ivory tower, there was something that called to me about helping others. I'd never wanted for anything in life, I never would. I was born into a life of money and privilege. But it didn't mean I took it for granted. If my father had taught me anything, it was that the higher we found ourselves, the more humbly we should walk. He worked hard, made a lot of money, and yes, he lived a life of privilege, but he also gave to those less fortunate. He donated to charity and contributed his time to non-profits.

I wanted to follow in *those* footsteps, the ones he trod that made a real difference.

"I think I'm going to do it," I said, feeling a sense of rightness wash over me.

"Yeah, you'll come?" Nora's eyes lit up and I immediately felt a pang of guilt.

"No, I... uh, I meant volunteer with the SCA."

"The student action thing?"

I nodded. "They need volunteers to help at the shelter."

"That's great, Lina, but do you need to go right now?"

"Well, no."

"So you'll come? I know shitface will be there but it's a masquerade party, we'll blend. Besides, he'll no doubt have a harem all wanting to get on his dick."

"Nora!"

"What?" She hooked her arm through mine, "you know I'm not wrong."

"No, but you're so..."

"Liberated?" She snuggled close to me. "I feel it, Lina. Like I can really be myself here, you know?"

"I'm happy you're happy," I said. We reached the door and Nora released me to dig out her keycard. I noticed a guy over by the corner of the building, pretending not to watch us. He looked familiar. I'd seen him around campus a few times, always alone, always waiting for something, or someone.

Huh.

Strange.

Nora fumbled with the key, drawing my attention. "I can never get the stupid thing to—"

"Here." I took it from her and gently pressed it against the pad. The door clicked open. "Just needed a magic touch."

She rolled her eyes, pushing open the door and slipping inside. I went to follow her but paused at the last second. There was something else about him, a gentle nagging in the back of my head.

Then it hit me.

It was the guy Nicco had been with the night I'd fled from Scott. His cousin. What was his name? Ba... Bailey! Yes, that was it. He'd been in the alley. It was his car Nicco had driven me in.

My eyes shifted to the corner of the building, but Bailey was gone.

And I was beginning to think I was losing my mind.

Nora had picked out the gaudiest, most over the top, Columbine Venetian masks she could possibly find. I was almost relieved no one would be able to recognize me; they were that bad. But she assured me it was what everyone would be wearing. Apparently, she'd met a guy who had the inside scoop. I just hoped he wasn't on the football team with Tristan and Scott because that would be all kinds of awkward.

"He's a sophomore so he doesn't exactly hang with them," she clarified. "But he is on the team."

"Seriously? I don't like this. I don't like it at all."

"What would you rather be doing? Reading one of your smutty romance novels in your flannel pajamas, eating your bodyweight in Twizzlers?"

My mouth opened and then snapped shut. "You know I'm right. You blew off going home for the weekend for a reason. So let's make the most of it. If the party sucks, we'll leave. And I promise to stay by your side tonight."

"Until you see the first hot guy and decide he's better company."

"If I recall correctly, you left me with Kaiden when hotty decided to drag you out of there."

The mention of Nicco had my stomach flipping. Maybe I'd see him tonight at the party. Who was I kidding? I couldn't imagine Nicco and his friends at a football team party. He didn't seem to like my cousin much. Not that I blamed him. Tristan didn't just fit into the elite of Montague, he *was* the elite. The king of the kids who walked around flashing their trust funds and family connections. I'd noticed it more and more throughout the week. The cliques and socialite groups versus the outsiders and kids who hovered on the fringe of everyone else. I hadn't realized college would be so much like high school. But then MU wasn't like most colleges. It was very insular; deeply rooted in Italian history and culture. It was no surprise it was the first-choice college for Italian-American families in and around New England to send their kids.

Not to mention, it was extremely expensive. You either got accepted to come here because you had money, and lots of it, or you had an excellent academic standing and received one of the very coveted, very rare scholarships.

"Okay, ready?" Nora asked me as we reached the frat house. It was on the edge of campus, steeped in red leaf Maples and lit up like The White House. Of course, my cousin would live here. It wasn't really a frat house at all, since MU didn't subscribe to the ethos of Greek letter organizations, but the name had stuck. I guess it made a kind of sense considering most of the football team lived here and with the amount of parties they had.

People littered the front lawn, disguised in their own gaudy masks. At least Nora's friend had gotten it right and we didn't stand out like sore thumbs.

"Come on". She grabbed my hand and pulled me toward the door.

"Passphrase?" A guy wearing a red and black Harlequin mask said.

"Passphrase?" I whispered to Nora. But I should have known she'd come prepared. She leaned up, cupping her hands around his ear. A sloppy grin broke over his face and he stepped back, granting us entrance.

"So what was it?" I asked.

"Carpe vinum."

I sifted through my very limited knowledge of Latin. "Seize the wine? How very original."

Nora chuckled. "I guess no one knew the Latin for beer and cheap liquor."

There wasn't a familiar face in sight, but there were plenty of Voltos and Gattos, Pantalones and Scaramouches. We blended in with ease, and I immediately felt some of the tension ebb away from my shoulders.

"See, I told you we wouldn't stand out." Nora pushed her way to the makeshift bar and got us two drinks. I waited for her to sniff the contents. "It's punch." She took a sip. "Sweet with a bitter aftertaste but it isn't bad."

"I think I'll pass," I said, pushing my cup at her.

"Suit yourself."

"At least the football team are wearing their jerseys." I wouldn't have to worry about Scott creeping up on me. He was the last person I wanted to see. But part of me also didn't want to hide, to give him any kind of satisfaction.

"Exactly," Nora nodded, downing the rest of her drink. "It's perfect. We're incognito which means we can dance the night away and not have to worry about Tristan or Scott. The night is ours." She made a sweeping motion with her arm and I smothered a laugh.

"You're crazy."

"Certifiable." Nora grinned. "But you love me."

"I do. I wouldn't be here otherwise."

Just then, one of my favorite songs blasted through the house and even I couldn't deny the hum of excitement coursing through my veins. Nora was right; no one here knew me. I was just another faceless person in the crowd. I could relax and let my hair down.

I could do this.

I could be a normal teenager enjoying a college party.

Moving around Nora, I grabbed a drink and knocked it back in one.

"Whoa, girl." My best friend laughed. "What's gotten into you?"

Grabbing her hand, I smiled. A real genuine smile, and said, "Let's dance."

We danced and drank and danced some more. After three or four cups of punch, I switched to water. I had a nice buzz, but I didn't want to get drunk; not in a houseful of Tristan and Scott's football player friends. A couple of guys had tried to dance with us, but Nora had quickly sent them on their way. It was loud, the air thick with the cloying smell of sweat and liquor. But it was fun. I was having fun. More fun than I'd had in a really long time.

"I told you this was a good idea," Nora yelled over the music, a sloppy grin plastered on her face. Her mask hid her eyes, but I knew they would be glassy with the effects of all the punch. Unlike me, Nora had opted not to switch to water. But she deserved this, we both did.

"Okay," I conceded. "I can admit it. This is fun."

"I knew it." She fist pumped the air. "I knew you had it in you." Her eyes flicked over to a tall guy wearing a Pierrot mask. There was no mistaking that his eyes, although barely visible, were locked on my best friend. He crooked a finger at her, taking a step forward.

"It's okay," I said, too exhilarated to spoil her fun. "You can go dance with him." She bit her lip, glancing between us. "Nora, it's—"

The words died on my tongue as strong arms looped around my waist. I went rigid, the air evaporating from my lungs. Nora's mouth fell open, then curved into a knowing smile.

"I'll be right over there." She mouthed, tipping her head to where the Pierrot guy was waiting.

"I missed you." Nicco's voice sent shivers rolling up my spine. I wanted to turn around, to look into his eyes to make sure it was really him. But I didn't want to break the spell. His body was hard behind mine, his hands splayed possessively on my hips as he rocked us to the sultry beat.

I rested my head back against his shoulder and asked, "How did you know it was me?"

He also wore a simple Pierrot mask painted with black and golds. His lips ghosted over mine. "I would know you anywhere, Bambolina."

"Where have you been all week?"

"Later," he said cryptically. "For now, come with me."

Nicco took my hand, leading me away from the party. He seemed to know the layout of the house, turning down a long hallway that grew darker and darker, quieter and quieter.

"Where are we going?" I whispered, my heart crashing violently against my ribcage.

I'd missed Nicco. All week I'd searched for him. It made no rational sense, but whenever I had walked into a room, I found myself looking for him. Hoping to catch even a glimpse. I knew people would say I had a crush. A silly schoolgirl crush on the elusive mysterious bad boy who had saved me. But there was more to it. I felt tethered to Nicco. Inexplicably linked to him. Maybe it was because he'd been so gentle with me that night, but I couldn't stop thinking about him. He was under my skin and now he was here, leading me to God only knew where.

It didn't matter though.

I would have gladly followed him into the depths of Hell just to savor the moment.

We reached what I presumed was the back of the house. I could see a large yard beyond the window, a huge pool, and a bunch of chairs situated around a grill. Nicco let go of my hand and tried a door to our left. Sticking his head inside, he whispered, "All clear."

"All clear for—"

He pulled me inside, pushing my body up against the wall. A sliver of moonlight poured in through the window, illuminating the profile of his mask as he stared down at me.

I swallowed hard, the air crackling with anticipation. "Nicco..." My hands reached for him, trembling fingers curling into his black sweater. It molded to his chest, his muscular biceps. My tongue darted out, wetting my lips. I was suddenly so thirsty, my body hot and needy and restless.

Maybe it was the liquor.

Or maybe it's the fact you're in a dark room, alone, with Nicco.

"Jesus, Lina..." He sounded in pain, his words strained and so full of desperation, I wanted to fix it. To ease whatever burden was weighing on him.

"What... what is it?"

He leaned in, brushing his nose across my mine, setting off a hundred butterflies in my tummy, their wings flapping wildly. And then he slowly untied my mask and slipped it off, hanging it on the door handle, before pushing his own up over his head.

"Do you have any idea what you do to me?" His mouth moved to my ear, his voice low and gravelly... and seductive. "I can't get you out of my head. I want to know where you are, what you're doing, who you're with... you're in here." He grabbed one of my hands and pressed it to his temple, his eyes pinning me to the spot.

"Has Bailey been following me? I saw him the other night and I'm sure I've seen him around campus. Did you..." I swallowed the words. What was I saying? Nicco hadn't asked Bailey to follow me. It was ridiculous. And yet, his mouth curved into a wicked smirk.

"He was supposed to be discreet."

"So he is following me?"

"I prefer to think of it as looking out for you."

"But why? I don't understand."

"I feel this irrational need to protect you, Bambolina, and I had to go out of town for a few days to take care of some... personal things."

"So you sent Bailey to watch over me? Isn't he like a kid? Doesn't he have school?" My mind was reeling.

"It doesn't matter. All that matters is that you're safe."

I didn't understand. He was talking like I was in danger. But he didn't know the truth, he couldn't possibly know the truth.

Guilt snaked through me. Something was happening between us. Like a runaway train, it was unstoppable and unpredictable, hurtling toward the unknown.

And nothing could stop it.

Nicco deserved to know the truth. Before we went any further, he deserved to know who I really was. But when I tried to say the words, they wouldn't form. Because I was scared. Soul achingly scared of losing this—the inexplicable connection between us. I felt it, twisting and tightening, anchoring us together.

Nora had been with guys. She'd dated here and there. Told me all about the butterflies and toe-curling kisses. But she'd never once described anything that came close to what I felt right now, in this second. I looked into Nicco's eyes and I felt... *home*.

Was that even possible?

I'd read enough romance novels, watched enough films, to be familiar with the concept of soul mates; of that one person in the whole world meant for you, and you alone. But it was nothing more than a romantic notion penned by the greats: Shakespeare, Wilde, and Beckett.

It wasn't real life.

"Tell me what you're thinking," he breathed the words against the corner of my mouth.

"Do you believe in fate, Nicco?" I asked.

"Until I met you, I didn't." His finger trailed down my neck, eliciting a soft moan from me. My head dropped against the wall with a gentle *thud*, every inch of my skin vibrating. "What is it that Mandrake said? Men make their own history, but they do not make it as they please."

"What does that mean?"

"It means, I shouldn't kiss you," Nicco whispered, his words a gentle caress over my skin. "It means, I should walk out of this room and never look back. It means, I should do the right thing and walk away from you, Lina. That's what it means."

"But..." my voice quivered, betraying me.

"But I never claimed to be good." He let out a steady breath. "I'm not your prince, Bambolina."

"I see you, Nicco. I see the good in you. And I want—"

I didn't get the rest of my words out. Nicco's mouth crashed down on mine, hard and bruising and demanding. I gasped against his lips, trying to keep up. Trying to stay afloat as I drowned in him. His tongue sliding against mine; his fingers in my hair; his strong, hot body caging me against the wall. My hands ran up his chest, curving over his broad shoulders as he kissed me harder, deeper. Kissing me with a fierce desperation and need that made my knees weak and my body tremble.

"Jesus, Lina, you taste like heaven." He pressed even closer, grinding his hips again at an angle that made me boneless. I could feel him, feel his hard length nudging up against my core as I rocked and writhed, desperate to feel him *there*. Desperate for him to ease the ache building inside me.

Gathering my hair off my face, Nicco pulled away to look at me. My skin was burning, my body a tight bundle of nerves. "You like that?" he asked, and I bit down on my lip, nodding.

"Fuck," he swallowed hard before diving at my mouth again, claiming me. Branding me with every kiss and nibble, stroke and nip. Nicco continued to rock into me, one of his hands dropping to my thigh, hitching my leg around his waist. His pace was slow at first. Teasing and torturous. But he quickly built a rhythm that had me soaring into uncharted heights. I moaned his name, moaned for more.

More.

More.

Nicco cursed: my name, some Italian I couldn't decipher. But he didn't stop. Our bodies were joined in every way possible considering we were both still fully clothed. "Something's happening," I moaned, barely aware of what I was saying. All I knew was it felt good, *too good*, as he ground against me. "More, Nicco, I need..."

His hand dived between us, disappearing underneath my skirt and finding the soft flesh between my thighs. He hooked my panties to one side and thrust a finger up inside me without warning. It stung, but the sharp stab of pain was quickly erased as I bucked against him, riding the waves of pleasure crashing over me.

"Oh God," I chanted over and over as Nicco's finger and thumb found the perfect rhythm, working me into a breathless frenzy. I'd never been touched like this before, not even by myself. It was... everything.

And then it wasn't.

Nicco tore away from me, touching his forehead to mine. "Tell me that wasn't what I think it was?" He ground out, the words raw.

"W- what do you mean?"

"Tell me that wasn't the first time you've been touched... like *that*."

"I... What does it matter?" My breath was ragged, my chest heaving.

"Fuck." His fist slammed against the wall beside my head, the sound reverberating through me, erasing the blissed-out feeling enveloping me.

"Nicco, it's okay." I leaned into him, trying to kiss him. But he jerked back, narrowing his eyes at me.

"I have to go," he said.

"What?" I frowned, my heart beating erratically in my chest. I couldn't think, let alone process what he was saying.

"I wasn't supposed to do that."

"Kiss me?"

"Among other things." The corner of his mouth turned downward as he inched back, leaving me cold and vulnerable. I hiked my skirt down, smoothing out the crinkled material, the icy fingers of reality clawing at my throat as realization dawned on me as to what had just happened.

What was happening right now?

"I wanted you to touch me," I said, trying to fix things. I'd been so happy, and now everything was ruined. "I liked it. You don't need to feel guilty just because I'm a..." I choked over the word. The truth.

His eyes darkened, shame glittering there. And my heart withered in my chest.

"Lina, I'm sorry. I should—"

"Go, you should go." My expression hardened as I forced down the tears threatening to fall. I'd given Nicco something special. Something I'd never given to another, and he couldn't get away from me fast enough.

"It isn't what you think," his voice cracked, "I just..."

"It's fine, I understand," I said, flatly. "You can go now."

"Bambolina, please." He took a step toward me, but I dodged his advance, wrapping my arms tightly around my waist. "Fine," he said through gritted teeth. "But this isn't over."

I stared at him, willing for him to go. I didn't want to fall apart in front of Nicco. Not after what had just happened. He gave me one last lingering look before slipping out of the room.

Taking a piece of my wounded heart with him.

EIGHT

NICCO

BAILEY FOUND me down the hall from where I'd left Lina. I hadn't meant to kiss her, to touch her like that. But she called to me. Her body, her smile, every-fucking-thing about her.

She was my own personal siren's call, and I was too weak to resist.

But a virgin?

Fucking hell.

I realized the second I pressed my finger inside her. She was tight despite how wet she was, and her body had tensed, though only for a split second. But it was enough for me to know the truth.

The fact she'd trusted me enough to touch her so intimately made my heart soar. But I had no right. None. Not when I wasn't here for her.

It had almost killed me not being on campus all week, not seeing her in class or across the food court, but after our family meeting, my old man had gotten a call from Boston. My Uncle Alonso was having problems with his hot-headed son, Dane. He decided to send me, Enzo, and Matteo to deal with it. We'd spent three days babysitting the kid to keep him out of the clutches of a rival gang, while Alonso and his guys took care of the threat.

"We've got a problem," my cousin said, hands jammed deep in his pockets. Bailey was a good kid, loyal and willing. But he was also lost. It's why I'd taken him under my wing.

"Yeah?" I said. "Let me guess. Enzo's struggling to keep his dick in his pants?"

Bailey snickered. "He's with her friend. The wild one." I'd tasked Bailey with watching Lina while I was gone. He was supposed to be in school, but he was going through some stuff. I figured it was better for him to be busy than skipping class and getting into all kinds of trouble he didn't need to be bringing to my aunt and uncle's doorstep.

"Nora? Fuck." When I'd left Enzo dancing with her, I hadn't considered he'd try to fuck her. But then, he didn't know who she really was. He thought I was looking to let off a little steam before we did what we came here to do. Not to mention, the second my eyes found Lina across the room, everything else had faded into the background.

She was the flame and I was the moth who couldn't seem to stay away, even if she burned me to nothing but ash and dust.

"Where are they?"

"Bathroom. First floor."

Shit. He wasn't supposed to be lurking around the house. We could be spotted. Even with our Pierrot disguises.

"And Matt?"

"He's watching the target."

My lip curved. "You've always wanted to say that, haven't you?"

Bailey stood taller, puffing out his chest. "Fuck, yeah. Can I come with you, when you... ya know?"

"Not tonight, kid. You stick with Lina, okay?"

"Nicco, come on. I can help. I can—"

"She's important to me. I need you to stick with her, okay? Text me the second she leaves."

His dejected expression morphed into fierce determination as he gave me a sharp nod. "I won't let anyone touch her."

"I know you won't."

I slid my mask back in place and walked down the hall. I wasn't supposed to know the layout of Capizola's house, but I made it my business to know. The three of us had snuck in here in freshman year and scoped out the place. We knew every entrance, exit, and hidey hole. It's how I knew exactly where to find Enzo.

Taking the stairs two at a time, I knocked on the bathroom door. "Fuck off, we're busy," his growl echoed through the wall.

I could have done the decent thing and told him it was me. I could have pulled rank and told him to get his sorry ass out of there. But I wasn't feeling very decent, not after how I'd ended things with Lina. So I dug my wallet out of my pocket, taking out a credit card and a metal toothpick. In less than thirty seconds, I'd cracked the lock. Quietly opening the door, I peeked inside.

"Oh yeah, just like that." Enzo guided Nora's face to his dick. Her hand was wrapped around the base, stroking him, her lips parted with anticipation. It was one of the weirdest things I'd ever seen, given they were both still wearing their masks.

"We need to go," I said without warning.

"Nicco, fuck," he hissed, jerking his dick away and stuffing it back into his pants. Nora stumbled backward, landing clean on her ass.

"What the hell?" She glared at me. I couldn't see it, but I felt it from behind her mask.

"Sorry to interrupt, but I need to borrow him. And something tells me you'd only regret it in the morning." My hard gaze shifted to Enzo. "Let's go, now."

"Yeah, yeah," he grumbled, raking a hand through his hair as he took one last look at Nora and then followed me outside.

"What the fuck was that?" I asked.

"Like you haven't been balls deep inside that girl. I saw the two of you sneak off. Who is she?"

"Not the point." I ignored his question. "You were supposed to be keeping an eye on the place. Not getting your dick sucked."

"Relax, Matt is—"

"Doing his fucking job." I stomped off down the hall. I needed to get a grip.

"Hey," Enzo caught up to me, grabbing my shoulder, "I'm sorry, okay? She was rubbing her tight little body all over me and I got carried away."

"One day, your dick is going to land you in a whole heap of trouble." My brow rose. "Try to keep it in your pants, we have work to do."

He gave me a wicked smirk, rubbing his hands together. "Ooh, I love it when you talk dirty to me."

"You're a strange fucking guy. You know that, right?"

"Never claimed to be anything else." He ran his hand down his slacks and I knew he was feeling the hunting knife strapped to his thigh.

"Keep a cool head, okay?" I warned him. "This is a recon mission."

Tonight wasn't about doing any serious damage; it was about sending a message. About getting the confirmation we needed.

I only hoped the guy at my side remembered that.

We found Matteo downstairs in the open-plan kitchen. It ran the whole width of the house with French doors leading to the yard. There was a big island in the middle with black and chrome stools around it. Stools currently occupied by half-naked girls wearing various masks while they watched Tristan and his closest friends neck shooter after shooter.

Our cousin pushed off the wall and approached us, wearing an identical Pierrot mask to ours. "Football players are pussies," he said, sipping his beer.

"Tell us something we didn't already know," Enzo grumbled, snorting as one of Tristan's friends puked all over himself. Everyone cheered, whooping like the guy hadn't just barfed everywhere. It was fucking embarrassing.

"Your guy know what he needs to do?" I asked Matt and he nodded.

"Just say the word."

I glanced over at Tristan again. His arm was slung around someone, the two of them laughing. He was such a smug fucker. I was itching to knock him off his throne. But that wasn't our order, not yet.

"Now."

Matteo nodded to someone. Three seconds later, the word 'fight' rang out and all hell broke loose. Bodies jostled past us all trying to get a look at whatever was going down. We moved closer to Tristan who was still laughing and joking with his friends.

"Man, you should come see this," someone yelled, and another couple of guys left him, rushing to the chaos unfolding at the far end of the kitchen.

"Don't fucking trash the house," Tristan slurred, clearly buzzed. He staggered over to the counter and dumped his cup. He was all alone now. We circled him like wolves. Something crashed, glass shattering, and people gasped, grunts of pain following.

"What's with the freaky as fuck mask?" Tristan asked Enzo who was closest to him. "You need something?"

"Yeah, I need something." Enzo roughly grabbed him. Tristan started to protest but Matt was there to silence him. I yanked open the back door, keeping one eye on the crowd, and we herded him out the back door.

We didn't stop, dragging his drunk ass all the way to the workshop at the bottom of the yard. The inky night cloaked us, our dark outfits blending into the shadows.

Inside, Enzo shoved him hard. Tristan stumbled back, his mask slipping off his face. "What the fuck is this?"

"We need to talk," I said.

"Marchetti? Is that you, because when my uncle hears..."

"Do you hear that?" I asked my friends. "The coglione is going run crying to his uncle." Enzo snorted, while Matteo dragged a chair to the middle of the room. "Sit," I commanded.

"Cazzo si—"

Enzo was on him in a second. Fisting him by the shirt, he maneuvered Tristan onto the chair. His fist clenched at his side, his body shaking with rage.

"Walk away, E."

Enzo hesitated but finally withdrew. We all knew the drill—no names, no prints, no faces. It's why we'd added gloves to our outfits. Tristan knew exactly who we were, but he'd have zero proof and without proof he couldn't come after us.

Not unless he wanted to start an all-out war, and he and his uncle knew we didn't play fair. Unlike their family who, these days, preferred to solve their problems with vast quantities of cash, we had a more hands-on approach.

"My uncle—"

"Your uncle isn't going to do shit." I crouched down to his eye-level while Matteo worked on restraining Tristan's hands behind his back. He barely resisted which told me all I needed to know.

He knew he was outnumbered, and he knew this was one fight he couldn't win.

"You think good old Uncle Roberto wants to bring *this* to his doorstep, to tarnish his perfectly good reputation with the likes of us. Nah," I chuckled darkly, "your uncle is smarter than that. Question is, are you?"

"Fuck you, Marchetti." He seethed, his nostrils flaring.

"You know we would have been on the same side, right? If history had written itself the way it should have, we'd be family right now."

Tristan spat at me, "Vai a farti fottere!"

Before I could stop myself, I backhanded him. His head snapped back, a loud grunt of pain filling the air. I pulled a tissue from my pocket and cleaned myself off.

"You think you're so much better than us. We know your uncle isn't as squeaky clean as he claims to be. It's only time... But that's not why we're here," I stood up. "We know she's here."

Tristan didn't flinch. He remained perfectly still, perfectly calm.

Too fucking calm.

"Did you hear?" I asked. "We know the Capizola heir is here."

Tristan stared straight ahead, giving nothing away.

"You don't want to help us? Fine." Giving Matt the signal he pulled another chair around to the front of Tristan before untying one of his hands.

"I heard it's a big year for the Knights. You have a real shot at the championship. It would be a shame if their star player finds himself suddenly injured."

Enzo stalked closer, the hammer in his hand slowly coming into view. Tristan's eyes went wide. I grabbed his wrist and flattened his palm against the chair. He was a big guy, ripped from all the hours of conditioning and football drills. But the effects of the liquor were working in our favor. Besides, fear was a powerful motivator.

Enzo handed me the hammer and I stared down at Tristan. "What?" he spat. "You want me to point her out to you? Have you lost your fucking mind?" He laughed bitterly. "Do your worst, Marchetti. I have nothing to say to you. I'm not a rat and I'm not scared of anything you try to do to me." His eyes narrowed but I saw the flicker of fear. "Do your worst. I still won't talk."

A slow smile tugged at my lips. Tristan was deflecting, but what he didn't realize was he'd already given me everything I needed. His silence was an admission of the truth. She was here.

The Capizola heir was here on campus.

All we needed to do was find her.

I lifted the hammer and slammed it down, his cries echoing around us.

"See you around, Capizola," I returned the hammer to its rightful place and left Enzo and Matteo to deal with Tristan while I went to get some air.

I read Enzo's text before pocketing my cell phone. They had knocked Tristan out, cleaned up the workshop, and dumped his body in the yard. It would be as if we'd never been there. He was going to wake up with one hell of a headache and in a shitload of pain. He was lucky I only smashed his pinky finger.

Bailey appeared at the end of the alley and whistled. I jogged toward him. "She left right after the fight broke out. Her friend wasn't feeling good, so they walked home. I've been watching the building ever since. She's been sitting out there for about ten minutes."

"Any sign of anyone else?"

He shook his head. "It's just her. I know she's the girl from the other night, Nicco, but *who* is she?"

Mine, the word echoed through me.

"Thanks, kid." I ignored his question. "Now go straight home. I'll be calling Aunt Francesca to check you got there, okay?"

"Nic," he started to protest but my stern glare made him swallow the words. "Fine, I'll head straight home. See you Sunday for family dinner?"

"You know it." I clapped him on the shoulder. "Now go."

He ducked out of the alley and melted into the shadows. MU had plenty of lampposts lining the sidewalks and paths, but the overgrown trees provided enough cover that if you didn't want someone to see you, or for campus security to catch you up to no good, you only had to learn the blackspots.

Pulling up my hood, I slipped out from between the two buildings and followed the short path toward Donatello House. Lina was right where Bailey had said she would be, sitting on the bench outside the building, watching the stars.

"It's a beautiful night," I said from the shadows.

"Nicco?" She glanced around, searching for me. When her eyes landed on me standing by the corner of the building, she stood up. "What do you want?"

"Ahh, Bambolina." I let out a weary sigh. "That is a loaded question."

"Humor me." Lina took a step closer. The moonlight danced off the soft features of her face.

Jesus, she was so fucking beautiful.

"I want to kiss you." I inched toward her, unable to resist the magnetic pull I felt whenever I was around her. "I want to finish what we started earlier. I want to feel you beneath me, hear you cry my name."

I want to make you mine.

"You couldn't get away from me fast enough earlier." Her confused gaze cut me like a thousand tiny blades over my skin.

"It's not what you think," I said, moving closer still. Lina mirrored my movements until we were standing in front of each other.

Until she was close enough to touch.

"What's happening to us, Nicco?" she whispered. "Why do I feel like this?"

"What do you feel like?" I brushed the hair off her neck. She had a thick hoodie pulled over her body, but I was still able to stroke the skin beneath her ear. Lina's eyes drifted closed as she inhaled a shaky breath.

"I look for you when you're not there. I feel you when you're close. I can't get you out of my head." Her eyes opened again, fixing on mine. She smiled and it was like a bolt of lightning to my heart.

This girl.

This innocent sweet girl was ruining me.

"Is it always like this?" she asked, leaning into my touch.

"Is what always like this?" I curved my hand around the nape of her neck, pulling us further into the shadows. No one from the main path would be able to see us now.

"When you like someone. Is it always so intense?"

"You like me, Bambolina?" Her confession shouldn't have affected me as much as it did.

"It feels like... *more.*" Her cheeks flushed and Lina dropped her gaze.

"Hey." I slid my finger under her chin, tilting her face back to mine. "Don't ever shy away from me."

"You're right, I'm a... virgin." She swallowed. "I have no experience with guys, at all, and you're so... *you*."

The corner of my mouth kicked up. "I think there's a compliment in there somewhere." I leaned in, brushing my mouth over hers. It was only supposed to be a moment of reassurance, but Lina fisted my sweater, anchoring us together as she flicked her tongue over the seam of my mouth.

"Lina, that's not why I came, not tonight." I gently eased away from her.

"I see. Is it not the same for you?" She was so curious about the world, so fucking naïve.

What the fuck was I doing?

Silence stretched out before us, our eyes saying all the things we couldn't. Then she surprised me by leaning in and kissing the corner of my mouth. "I know you feel it, Nicco. You want to protect me, and I get it, I do. It's the chivalrous thing to do. But maybe I don't want protecting; maybe I just want to let go and feel."

I pulled us further into the shadows, pressing her body flush with mine. What I really wanted was to spin her around and cage her against the wall while I showed her exactly what I felt. But I didn't want to scare her, and I didn't want to take more than I deserved. So instead, I kissed her. I let my hand dip underneath her hoodie and tank top and trail up the warm skin of her stomach while our tongues stroked together in slow, lazy licks. Lina's soft moans had a direct line to my dick, already painfully hard inside my pants.

"I feel it," I said, dragging my lips over her jaw and down her neck. "I look for you," I repeated her words back to her. "I feel you when you're close. And I want to make you mine in every way possible. But..."

"No." Lina pulled back, sliding a single finger against my lips. "No buts. We say goodnight here and then tomorrow night, you can pick me up and take me out on a real date, and we can get to know each other."

I hesitated and Lina's hopeful expression fell. "You don't want—"

"Yes," the word rolled off my tongue. "I do. I just need some time to arrange something."

"Nicco, I don't need anything lavish."

"I know but you deserve it. Give me a few days, please." I knew the perfect place to take her, but it required a favor, and those didn't happen overnight.

"A few days, okay."

"You won't regret it, I promise."

Even if I was going to hell for it.

NINE

ARIANNE

"YOU'RE DOING IT AGAIN," Nora said as she forked some spaghetti into her mouth.

"No, I'm not." I glared at her.

"Yes, you are. If you'd have just gotten his cell phone number like a normal person, I wouldn't have to survive you searching for him every five seconds."

"I'm not... okay, maybe just a little. But there's something romantic about it, don't you think?"

"It's the twenty-first century, Lina. We have cell phones for a reason."

"Why do we have cell phones?" Tristan approached us. My eyes immediately went to the bandage around his hand.

"What happened?"

"Oh, this." He shrugged, cradling it against his body. "Drunken accident. It's nothing."

"Can you still play?" I knew how important the team was to Tristan.

"Yeah, it'll take a little more than an accident to keep me away. I didn't see you Saturday?"

"Oh, we were there," Nora said, smothering a laugh. I stamped my foot down on hers under the table and she swallowed a yelp.

"It was a masquerade party, we were incognito."

Tristan gave us a funny look. "So long as you had fun."

"We did." Nora grinned. "It was very, *very* enlightening, wasn't it, Lina?"

I glared at her, trying to get her to shut up. I didn't want Tristan to know about Nicco, not yet. Not since the two of them seemed to dislike each other. My cousin's frown grew. "Are you sure everything's okay?"

"Why wouldn't it be?" I smiled.

"Just be careful, okay? I've got to go but I'll be watching." His serious expression melted away replaced with mischief. Before I could protest, Tristan left.

"What the hell was that?" I snapped at Nora who exploded into a fit of laughter.

"You should see your face."

"It's not funny. I don't want Tristan to know about this yet. If he does..." My heart sank. Being with Nicco was exhilarating. New and exciting. I felt alive every time he looked at me.

I didn't want to lose that.

"Relax," Nora said. "Tristan thinks you're far too sweet and innocent to be cavorting with the likes of your brooding hotty."

"You make it sound so dirty."

"Lina, you let him—"

"Okay." I clapped a hand over her mouth. "Enough of that." My cheeks burned at the memory of how I'd let him touch me up against that wall in Tristan's house. "It's almost time for class. Nicco might..." I stopped myself. I didn't want to get my hopes up that Nicco would show up in Professor Mandrake's class.

But it was too late.

I was already there—already hoping.

"Just remember," Nora said. "Guys like Nicco are... they're usually experienced and not the settling down type. I don't want you to get hurt."

"I won't," I said with complete conviction.

Because Nicco wouldn't hurt me.

I don't know how I knew; I just did.

Nicco didn't show up to Intro to Philosophy though. I didn't see him the next day either. But when I woke up Wednesday morning, Nora was standing over me, her eyes sparkling.

"Apparently the building isn't as secure as the brochure said." She thrust an envelope at me. "Found this pushed under the door."

I snatched it off her, greedily tearing it open. "Lina," I started, and she shot me a disapproving look. "I'll tell him, I will." I just didn't know when.

"Well, don't keep a girl waiting, what does it say?"

"Tomorrow night at seven. I'll be waiting in the rear parking lot. Wear something warm and comfortable. Nicco."

"That's it? He went to all the trouble of sneaking into the building for *that*."

"I think it's sweet." I read it again, my heart galloping in my chest.

"Those books of yours have a lot to answer for," she grumbled. "Now I have to survive two more days of you swooning over three little sentences."

"You're only jealous." My lips curved, and Nora leaped onto my bed, letting out a dreamy sigh.

"You're absolutely right. Now give that here so we can dissect every word."

Our laughter filled the room as my best friend launched into a detailed analysis of where he could be possibly taking me. But it didn't matter.

All that mattered was that Nicco had kept his promise.

"Are you nervous?" Nora asked me. She was sprawled out on her bed, still nursing a hangover from last night. She'd gone out with Dan, her new *friend*. Apparently there had been wine. And sex. Lots and lots of wine-induced sex.

"A little. He's very... intense."

"Yeah, just like his friend," she murmured.

"That's the third time this week you've grumbled something about Enzo." I laid out my outfit choices on my bed and went to her side. "Come on, spill. What happened between the two of you last weekend at the party?"

She'd been tight-lipped about it, and I hadn't wanted to push. But maybe she needed a little nudge after all.

"Ugh." Nora grabbed a pillow and stuffed it over her face. "I don't want to talk about it."

"Hey." I snatched it away and perched on the end of her bed. "You made me talk."

"I almost... you know." Nora's eyes widened.

"Slept with him?"

"In a bathroom in a frat house? Really, Ari, you think I'm that—"

"No judgment." I held up my hands.

"I almost gave him a blow job, okay?" She slapped a hand over her eyes. "We didn't even talk or make out and I almost..."

"He is kind of hot, in that dark and brooding bad boy way." And completely terrifying, but I didn't add that. Enzo was too intimidating for me. But Nora wasn't like me. She had balls and spirit, and strangely, I could picture the two of them together.

"It's college, freshman year. You're allowed to sow your... well, that."

Nora chuckled. "You're too good to me." She reached for my hand, tangling our fingers together. "Just promise me, whatever happens this year, we won't let any guys come between us."

"Are you kidding me? You're my person, Nora, you always will be."

"Ditto. Now what did you decide to wear for your date?" She beamed.

"Well, he said to dress warmly and comfortably, so I was going to stick with jeans, a sweater, and my boots."

"Hmm, it could work. But I think I might have something..." She sat up, observing the clothes scattered over my bed. "I have an idea." Nora stood up, a mischievous glint in her eye.

"I don't want to be overdressed."

"Oh hush, it's a date; you want to look irresistible. That's the point."

"Right," I grumbled, already half-regretting letting her help.

"Okay. I think I've got it." Nora dumped a pile of clothes in my arms. "Try them on and we'll go from there."

"Nora..."

"Ari, trust me. Nicco won't be able to keep his hands off you."

Well, when she put it like that... maybe I did need her help.

At three minutes past seven, Nora finally let me out of the room. She'd insisted I play it cool, saying it was my womanly right to make Nicco wait a couple of minutes. It seemed unnecessary to me, but all my reservations melted away when I reached the back door and saw him sitting there on his motorcycle.

"Sei bellissima," the words formed on Nicco's lips as he approached me. "Hey." He dipped his head, pressing a kiss to my cheek.

"Hi." Wings beat furiously in my stomach. "Are we taking your bike?"

"If that's okay?"

"I'd like that." I gave him a tentative smile.

"Let me." Nicco put his helmet on me, making sure it was secure. His eyes lingered on me, dark and intense and swirling with desire. "You look beautiful, Lina."

Guilt flashed through me, but I forced it down. He didn't know my true identity yet, but I was still me.

I was still the same girl inside.

Nicco swung his leg over the bike and got situated before motioning for me to get on. "Hold on tight," he said over his shoulder as my hands slid around his hard stomach, his leather jacket cool beneath my fingers.

One of his hands slid down my leg, squeezing gently before he kicked the starter making the bike rumble beneath us. We hadn't even moved yet, and anticipation already trickled through me.

"Ready?" Nicco asked and I nodded against his back. He sped off, the *whoosh* of air taking my breath away. He didn't take the main road out of the campus; instead, taking a smaller road behind the administration building. I clung to him, anchoring my body around his as we left campus behind us and whizzed through the streets of University Hill. It was already dusk, the sun disappearing behind a bank of fluffy white clouds. It was beautiful. The soft material of my pantyhose felt warm and snug around my legs, despite the skirt Nora had insisted I wear bunching around my thighs. Seeing the flare in Nicco's eyes when he'd watched me walk out of Donatello House was worth it. He'd looked at me like he wanted to devour me right there in the small parking lot.

A thrill shot through me.

Nicco kept going, taking the road out of town, toward Providence. After another fifteen minutes, he finally eased off the gas, taking a turn down a dark narrow road. I could just make out a fence perimeter, separating the road from perfectly tended lawns. It looked like a golf course, the natural mounds just visible.

Eventually, we rolled to a stop and Nicco cut the engine. I shimmied off the back of the bike, waiting for him. Electricity crackled between us as he removed my helmet and stroked his fingers through my hair, taming the loose curls Nora had taken her time to style.

"I've never had a girl on the back of my bike before."

Warmth spread through me at his words. I didn't doubt there had been other girls in his life, probably lots of them, but I had one of his firsts. And I liked it.

I liked it a whole lot.

"What is this place?"

"Blackstone Country Club, but don't worry we're not heading inside." Nicco smirked as he took my hand and pulled me toward the perimeter fence.

"Are you sure we should be sneaking inside?"

"Don't you trust me?" He closed the space between us, gazing down at me.

"I do." I swallowed.

"Come on."

We walked a little way down the perimeter before Nicco stopped and yanked back a piece of broken fencing. "In you go." His eyes lit up with playfulness.

I slipped through the gap with ease, careful not to snag my hose on any of the brambles on the other side. Nicco followed, wrapping his arm around my waist and pulling me against his solid chest. His warm breath hit my neck before being replaced with his lips, sending shivers rippling through me. "I could spend my life kissing you and it still wouldn't be enough."

Oh my.

Nicco took my hand again, pulling me further around the perimeter. I could just make out the clubhouse in the distance, with people milling around inside. We stayed out of sight, on the other side of the golf course, until we reached a lake surrounded by Maple trees on one side, its vast surface twinkling under the moonlight.

"It's so beautiful," I said, letting out a little sigh.

"Wait here, okay?" Nicco dropped a kiss on my head and then disappeared into the shadows. Another figure appeared and the two of them talked in hushed voices. The guy's eyes darted to me and he smiled before giving Nicco a knowing look and then handing him a brown bag. He disappeared again and Nicco came back to me, taking my hand once more.

We walked a little further, the trees now surrounding us, until we burst through a clearing to where the trees met the water's edge.

"This is... wow." There was a picnic blanket laid out and a candle lantern flickering, casting golden shadows off the water.

"I wanted you all to myself." His big strong arms wrapped around me from behind again, as we stood there, looking out at the water.

"I can't believe you did all this for me. It's beautiful."

"You're beautiful." He pressed a soft kiss to my neck. "You make me want to be better, Lina. To be more."

Nicco's words hung over us. I didn't know what to say. Everything was so overwhelming.

He was overwhelming.

In the best possible way, and I was already becoming addicted.

"Are you hungry?" he finally broke the silence that had descended.

"I could eat." My stomach grumbled with approval.

Nicco led me to the blanket and we sat down. "Milo is a good friend. He had the chef make my favorite. I hope you like it." He pulled out two containers, two forks, and napkins.

"Is that Bistecca alla Florentina?" The rich smell of meat filled the air.

"You've never tasted it like this." Nicco jammed the fork into the container and brought it to my lips. "Open."

I closed my mouth around the fork, flavor exploding on my tongue. "Mmm," I groaned. "So good."

Nicco's eyes widened, his jaw clenched.

"Sorry." Embarrassment stained my cheeks.

"I'm only jealous," he said quietly.

"Jealous?"

"Yeah, of that fork."

"Oh... *oh!*" I turned a shade darker, the sound of Nicco's laughter sinking into me.

"Come on, eat up. There's dessert too."

"Tiramisu?" I asked, hopeful.

"You'll have to wait and find out." There was a glint in his eyes that made my tummy tighten.

Nicco was right, the food was to die for. The Florentine steak and the pasta, even the bread was delectable.

"This is so good," I mumbled, wiping the corner of my mouth with a napkin. Nicco watched me intently, his eyes dark and sparkling with lust. My tummy clenched. "Tell me about you, your family..."

"What do you want to know?"

Everything. I wanted to know everything. But something told me Nicco kept his cards close to his chest. Something I could empathize with.

"Do you have any siblings?" I asked.

"A sister. Alessia. She's a junior in high school and a total pain in the ass."

"I always wanted a brother or a sister."

"It's just you?"

I nodded. "Although Nora is like a sister to me. I've known her forever. We grew up together."

"How are you liking MU so far? Is it everything you thought it would be?"

Guilt snaked through me, but I forced it down. I didn't want to let anything ruin this. Not even the secrets I kept.

"Classes are fine. I mean, I like learning. But I didn't expect it to be so..." My gaze dropped to the blanket.

"Lina?" Nicco's voice coaxed me to look at him. "What is it?"

"Do you ever feel like you don't fit in?" My eyes widened. I hadn't meant to say the words, but Nicco made it so easy. I wanted to tell him everything—confess my deepest, darkest secrets. I wanted him to know me.

The *real* me.

When he didn't reply, the silence between us thick and heavy, I backtracked. "Ignore me, I'm just nervous, and when I'm nervous, I ramble."

His hand reached out, brushing my jaw, tilting my face to his. "You don't need to be nervous with me, Bambolina. Ever."

I melted at his words, the way he touched me like I was the most precious thing in the world.

"I want to know everything about you," I blurted out.

Nicco chuckled, "We have time," he said. "But first have dessert."

Nicco's eyes darkened, hooded with desire as he pulled out another container. He shucked out of his leather jacket and rolled it up, placing it behind me. My breath caught as his hand ran up my stomach, pressing gently against my breastbone. "Lie down, Lina," he commanded.

I dropped back on my elbows, unable to take my eyes off him as he straddled my outstretched legs. When his fingers toyed with the buttons on my tight-fitting blouse, I realized now why Nora had been so insistent I wear it. One after one Nicco popped open the buttons revealing my black lacy bra to him. Picking up the last container, he flipped the lid and dipped his finger inside.

"Now where shall we start?" His eyes ran over my body. They lingered on my breasts, trailing ever so slowly up my neck until they locked on my heated gaze. Nicco leaned in, painting my lips with Tiramisu before capturing my mouth and licking them clean. "Hmm, my favorite," he breathed against my skin.

My body trembled beneath him, a coiled spring of nerves. He knew I was inexperienced, and yet, he didn't touch me with hesitation. He touched me with confidence and skill.

Nicco touched me in a way that made me want to give him everything.

His finger dived back into the container but this time he trailed the dessert all over my chest, taking his time to lick it away. "You taste so fucking good," he rasped. My fingers buried deep into his hair, scraping his scalp as he teased the curve of my breast.

"Do I not get to try dessert?" I asked, surprised at the confidence in my voice.

Nicco lifted his head, smiling. "You only have to ask, Bambolina." Sitting up, he dipped his two fingers into the dessert container this time, before bringing them to my lips. My tongue darted out, tasting the sticky sweet goodness, but it wasn't enough. I sucked his fingers into my mouth, imagining it was something else entirely.

"Fuck," he hissed, watching me through hooded eyes. But Nicco didn't watch for long. He pulled his hand away, capturing my lips in a bruising kiss. His body came down hard on top of mine, our hands touching and teasing as he kissed me into submission.

When he finally pulled away, I was high on the taste of him; a quivering ball of nerves.

"Nicco, I want—"

"Ssh, Bambolina, I know what you need." He rolled to one side of me, peppering my lips, my jaw and neck, with tiny kisses while one hand slipped to the hem of my skirt. Nicco carefully inched my hose down my legs, the cool air brushing against my skin. A shiver rolled through me, but then warm fingers were touching me, setting me alight.

"You're so wet for me." Nicco dipped two fingers inside me, stretching me. I couldn't breathe, I felt so good. So... full. It felt even better than the other night. Then he circled my clit with his thumb, and everything grew more intense, the world closing in around me.

"Nicco, I can't..."

"Just feel it," he breathed against my lips. "Feel what I do to you." He hooked his fingers inside me, rubbing deeper. My back arched off the blanket as my body began to quiver.

Nicco kissed me, his tongue mimicking the way his fingers glided in and out of me. It was so erotic, I wanted to watch him. But I could barely keep my eyes open, intense waves of pleasure building deep inside me.

"More," I cried. "More, Nicco."

"Ti voglio," he mumbled before tearing away from me.

"Nicco?" I pushed up onto my elbows, breathless and dizzy. He smirked at me as he kneeled between my legs and inched my hose further down.

Then he was there, flattening his tongue against me and making me cry out his name. He added a finger, licking and sucking, stroking some magical place inside me that set off an explosion of stars behind my eyes.

"I'll never eat tiramisu again without thinking of you like this, sprawled out before me, looking like an angel." Heat burned in his gaze as he stared up at me.

"I don't know many angels who let boys do that to them." Soft laughter bubbled in my chest as I slowly caught my breath. Nicco pressed a final kiss to my inner thigh before straightening my hose.

"Better?"

"Much." I smiled. Nicco made me reckless. Impulsive and uninhibited. But I loved it. He made me feel so special and desired.

I was going to tell him.

When he took me back to my dorm, before we said goodnight, I was going to come clean. Because I was falling for Nicco, and I didn't want to start whatever this was, what I hoped it would become, based on lies.

I only hoped he understood.

"Hey, what is it?" His hand curled around my neck, drawing me close to him. I buried my face in his chest, letting him kiss my head.

"Thank you, for tonight. It was everything."

"You're everything, Lina. Sei più bella di un angelo." He eased back to kiss me. Soft and tender and the perfect end to a perfect first date.

"It's late," he said, "I should get you back before your crazy roommate sends out a search party."

"Hey, Nora isn't crazy, she's just... determined to soak up college life."

"I shouldn't have said that." Nicco held out his hand, helping me up. "She's good for you."

"She is. Although I think she has a thing for your friend, Enzo."

Nicco paled. "That's not a good idea."

"Nora can handle him."

"I love Enzo like a brother, but trust me when I say Nora is better off forgetting all about him, okay?" He sounded so serious all I could do was nod.

"Hey, shouldn't we clean up?" I asked, realizing he was pulling me back toward the hole in the fence.

"Milo will handle it," he said. "He owes me."

Owed him?

I couldn't imagine what kind of debt he possibly had to repay that required him to clean up after us.

When we reached Nicco's bike, I grabbed his hand before he reached for the helmet. If I didn't say this now, I never would.

"When we get back to the dorm, can we talk? It's nothing bad. There's just something I want to tell you before we... well, before this, us," I stumbled over the words. "Before we go any further."

"You can tell me anything." He lifted my hand, kissing my knuckles. "Come on, let's get you back."

Nicco helped me secure the helmet and we got situated on the bike. He didn't need to tell me to hold on this time, my arms locked around his waist and I tucked myself into his leather jacket.

The night hadn't even ended yet and I was already thinking about our next date. And the one after that. Because Nicco wasn't only buried under my skin.

He was imprinting himself on my heart.

TEN

NICCO

I HAD the biggest grin on my face the whole ride back to MU. Not to mention the taste of Lina still on my tongue. Jesus, watching her come like that had been everything. I'd wanted to take her right there on the picnic blanket, under the stars. But she deserved more. She deserved flowers and a romantic dinner and all that stuff. Stuff I'd never even imagined doing.

But I wanted to do it with her.

My hand covered Lina's as I slowed to a stop behind her dorm building. I already wanted to kiss her again, to slide my tongue against hers and never come up for air. There was so much still left to say though. Things I had to eventually tell her, but I was too lost in the moment with her.

Lina climbed off the back of my bike, slipping the helmet off and hanging it on the bars. I hooked an arm around her waist, pulling her in close. Her hands went around my neck as she leaned down and kissed me. I loved it when she took the lead; the way she peppered tiny kisses over my lips, down my jaw. The soft uncertain flick of her tongue against mine.

"Come on," I said, finally breaking away, knowing that if she carried on, I wouldn't be able to resist taking it further. "I'll walk you to the door."

It was a risk, but she was worth it. Being with Lina made me feel invincible. Like I could take on the world and win.

We walked hand-in-hand to the back door, but there was an out of service notice. "Guess we'll have to go around front," she said, leaning up to kiss me again.

We stumbled against the wall, all teeth and tongue and soft laughter. My heart was a constant drum in my chest, adrenaline coursing through my veins. I felt like an addict flying high off their last hit, and I never wanted it to end.

"What did you want to tell me?" I whispered against her lips, letting my hands drift to her ass and pressing her closer.

"In a minute," she murmured, "I want to make the most of this." Lina curled herself around me as I found the strength to walk us around the side of the building.

"I can barely keep my hands off you."

"So don't." She laughed and it was so fucking pure and real, I wanted to bottle it and keep it for a rainy day.

We kissed and kissed and kissed some more. Until someone cleared their throat. "Arianne?"

Lina went rigid in my arms. "Tristan?" She turned slowly to where Tristan Capizola stood glaring at us.

No, not us.

Me.

My spine stiffened. What the fuck was going on?

"Papá?" Lina croaked.

I hadn't noticed the man at Tristan's side. But I saw him now. Expensive suit. Polished shoes. Smooth beard and sharp, assessing gaze.

"Papá?" I choked out, the truth barreling into me like a runaway train.

"Gosh." Lina stepped out of my hold, smiling up at me with guilt shining in her eyes. "This isn't how I wanted you to find out."

Taking a step back, I motioned a hand at Roberto Capizola and his... *daughter.*

The word lodged in my throat.

Fuck.

How could I have missed it?

"You're... you're Arianne Capizola?"

"Surprise." Lina... no, Arianne said.

"Arianne, please come over here," her father commanded.

"Papá, I know this is probably going to sound crazy, but I want you meet my... Nicco. We've been hanging out and well, I... hmm." She tucked a curl behind her ears, shooting me a coy look. "I like him a lot."

"Niccolò Marchetti, this is a surprise." Roberto enunciated every letter. "How is your father?"

My fist clenched at my side as I stared down at the man who thought he held our future in his hands.

"Papá," Arianne whispered, looking between us. "You know Nicco?"

The hopeful look on her face sliced me open.

"His father is an old friend. You should probably say goodbye to him now, mio tesoro. We have much to discuss."

My cell vibrated in my pocket, but I couldn't move. I couldn't get past the part where Lina, *my Lina*, was Arianne Capizola, daughter of Roberto Capizola, and the girl who was the key to everything.

Arianne bounced over to me, her expression so full of relief I felt gutted. "I take it this was what you want to talk to me about?" My voice was tight.

"I'm sorry I didn't tell you, but Papá thought it would be safer—"

"You should go to him."

Her brows knitted, her expression melting away. "Is everything okay? You look like you've seen a ghost."

"I'm fine." I jammed my hands in my pockets to stop myself from touching her.

I'd known from the second I met her, that Lina didn't belong in my world. But I never anticipated we were enemies on opposite sides of a long and bitter feud between our families. And from the way she was staring up at me starry-eyed and full of lust, she had no idea.

This was a fucking shitshow and there was nothing I could say or do to fix it.

Arianne wasn't mine to have.

She never was.

"Okay," she said hesitantly. "Will I see you tomorrow?"

"Lina ... I mean, Ari—"

"It's one of my middle names, you can still call me Lina. Or Bambolina." She stared up at me with a megawatt smile. "I'll dream of you."

"Arianne," her father said again.

"Coming, I'm coming." Leaning up, she pressed a single kiss to my cheek. I sucked in a harsh breath, my heart cracking clean in two.

I wouldn't ever get to feel this again.

I'd never get to hold her in my arms and kiss her.

Roberto would yank her out of MU and lock her away where no one could get to her. Where *I* couldn't get to her.

And then he'd come for me.

"Goodbye, Bambolina," I steeled myself, locking away every single thing I felt for her, watching as she walked over to her father and Tristan.

"Let's go inside where we can talk." Roberto roped his arm around Arianne's shoulder and led her toward the dorm building, his eyes fixed on me the whole time. Burning with hatred. "Tristan, see that Niccolò gets off okay. And then join us inside please."

"It would be my pleasure Uncle." The fucker smirked at me.

Arianne glanced back, giving me a small wave. I wanted to go after her; to steal her right out from under him and take her far far away from here.

She was mine.

I felt it deep in my soul.

Lina belonged to me. But Lina wasn't Lina at all, she was Arianne Capizola.

If only you'd paid more attention. But it had been too easy to fall for her. Her smile and innocence. Her beauty and warmth. I'd been so wrapped up in Lina, in the idea of her, I dropped my guard. I'd seen her with Tristan, even asked how she knew him.

But I hadn't wanted to see what was right in front of me.

It was too late though. Arianne had disappeared inside the building. Leaving me outside with Tristan.

"Did you fuck her?" he snarled. "Did you touch my cousin with your dirty fucking Marchetti hands?" He stalked toward me, a splint restraining his pinky finger and the one beside it.

"How's the finger?" I mocked as he drew nearer. My cell vibrated again, but there was no time to check it or text for help. Tristan was coming for me and from the glint in his eye, he was out for blood.

And the worst of it was, I couldn't blame him. If our roles were reserved, I'd want blood too.

"You should have made sure to do both hands. Because I only need one good hand to put you on your ass, Marchetti."

"Take your best shot." I drew to my full height. I could take him. Years of fighting at my uncle's gym and then moving to the underground circuit at L'Anello's meant I could take guys twice my size. But he was Arianne's cousin. Her family.

And even after everything that had just gone down, I didn't want to hurt her.

I couldn't.

"I'm not going to fight you, Tristan," I said keeping my voice even.

"Pussy." He spat, circling me.

"I didn't know. I had no idea who she was. She told me her name was Lina for fuck's sake." I held my hands up in defense.

"You think I believe anything you say?"

"It's the truth." I dragged a hand down my face. "I didn't know."

"You'll pay for this. You know that, right? You'll pay for tainting her. For ever looking twice at her." He was almost on me now.

The fighter in me wanted to attack, to unleash all the anger and surprise and bitterness I felt at the universe for giving me something as good as Lina and then ripping her away from me.

"You don't want to do this, Tristan," I said, flicking my gaze to the dorm building. Arianne was in there, her father no doubt painting me as the devil in disguise.

I rubbed the heel of my palm against my forehead.

"Don't tell me you actually feel something for her?" Tristan laughed bitterly. "Holy shit, you do. You like her." He taunted me. "What did you think, Marchetti? That you and her were going to ride off in the sunset together? She lied to you, and I'd put money on the fact you haven't been entirely honest with her either."

"Fuck you. You don't know anything about us."

"I know she'll never be yours. I know that once she finds out exactly who you are, she'll never want anything else to do with you. Arianne is better than you. She'll always be better than you. You're nothing, Marchetti, nothing but—"

I snapped. My fist flew toward Tristan's face, but he saw it coming, dodging to the side. "Motherfucker," he roared, his fist barreling toward me. I tried to move, tried to duck out of the way. But it was too late. He clipped me right in the chin, sending my head snapping backward. Pain exploded through my jaw as I went down, my head cracking against the pavement.

And then everything went black.

"Here," Bailey threw a bag of frozen corn at me. "It's the best I could do."

"Gee, thanks." I pressed it to my jaw, hissing at the blast of icy pain.

"He got you good, huh?"

"I wasn't about to fight him." Although I was quickly beginning to regret that. Tristan was a smug fucker. This would only bolster his ego.

"So your girl is the Capizola princess? That's some bad fucking luck."

"Hey, language," I snapped, and heavy silence settled between us.

Bailey had found me a few minutes after Tristan had laid me out. He'd managed to get me up on my feet and onto the back of my bike while he drove us back to my aunt's.

"I keep playing it over in my mind, trying to figure out what I missed..."

"But you only saw her."

"Yeah," I let out a weary sigh. "I only saw her."

The kid was too smart for his own good. But he was right. The second I'd seen her in the alley, scared and disheveled, something shifted inside me. I'd wanted to protect her. To make her smile and keep her safe.

I'd wanted her.

Plain and simple.

And the more time I spent around her, the more I wanted to make her mine.

"Now what happens?"

"Lina..." My heart clenched. "I mean Arianne, will probably be yanked out of college and Roberto will come after me for touching his daughter."

"You really think he'd risk war over her?"

I would.

Deep down, part of me knew I'd risk it all for her. It made no fucking sense, but I felt it.

She was mine.

Even if she wasn't.

"You're falling in love with her?" Bailey asked, but I found no judgment in his eyes.

"Nah, I don't know how to love." A wall slammed down over me. "It's probably better this way. She deserves someone who can give her all the things I'll never be able to." Like safety and security and a normal future.

"Don't sell yourself short, Nicco. You love Alessia, Enzo and Matteo... me. You love my parents too and your other aunts and uncles."

"You're family, of course I fucking love you."

"So fight for her," he said as if it was that simple.

"There are things at play even I don't understand, Bay. The history between our families goes back to the beginning, right back to the birth of Verona County. And me and Arianne are on opposite sides of the line. Nothing will ever change that."

"Maybe this is a chance to fix things," he added. "Maybe this is a chance to reunite the families."

Strangled laughter rumbled in my chest. This wouldn't fix things; it would only make them a hundred times worse. If my father found out I'd been mooning after the Capizola heir, he would cut off my balls and feed them to me.

My feelings for Arianne might have been soul deep, but his hatred for her father, her family, ran deeper. It was ingrained in the very fiber of his being, coursing through his blood.

"You need to keep this to yourself. Can you do that?" I asked my cousin, and he nodded. Until I figured out what the hell to do, no one else could find out the truth.

"Now hand me that bottle of whisky. I need to dull this pain." My jaw stung like a bitch, but it wasn't the only part of me hurting.

I snatched the bottle from him, unscrewed the cap and took a huge gulp. The liquor burned my throat but distracted me from the deep sting every time I opened my mouth. Grabbing my cell, I re-read Enzo's messages. He'd been on Tristan watch when he'd seen Roberto Capizola's black SUV pull up outside of the football team's house.

While I'd been licking tiramisu off Arianne's body, he'd been doing his job just like I'd told him to. He'd followed them as far as the library but then got ruffled by security. He knew something was going down, he just hadn't gotten close enough to learn what.

It was a small mercy, but the universe obviously hadn't completely sided against me.

I typed out a quick reply, letting him know to take it easy for the rest of the night. Enzo was as loyal as they came, but once he found out about my betrayal, I didn't know how he'd react. He hated the Capizola with a fire not even I possessed. So the fact I'd been, albeit unknowingly, fooling around with one would be a giant hurdle in our friendship. Matteo would side with me, his loyalty was unwavering. But Enzo could pick the family over me, and that would be a problem.

What the fuck was I saying?

My loyalty was to my family, it had to be. I had Alessia to think of, her future and safety. Arianne was just a girl. I'd get over her. The fact she was the enemy should have been motivation enough. All I needed to do was call up Rayna or any of the other girls chomping at the bit to get on my dick and fuck her right out of my system.

She's not just a girl, and you know it.

I let out a weary sigh and my fingers tightened around the neck of the bottle as I took another swallow.

"Maybe that's not such a good idea," Bailey said, eying the bottle.

"Do you have a better idea? Because right now it's either get shitfaced on whisky or drive over to her dorm building and..." I mashed my lips together. Going there wouldn't help things, not tonight. I needed to think. I needed to figure out a way forward that didn't end up with Arianne hurt. But first I needed to forget. I needed the gaping hole in my chest to heal. I needed to be so drunk I couldn't do something stupid.

Something I would regret.

Something that would end up with me behind bars, or worse, with a bullet between my eyes.

ELEVEN

ARIANNE

"MR. CAPIZOLA," Nora rubbed her eyes. "This is a surprise." She glanced from me to him and back again, silently asking me what the hell was going on.

I gave her a little shrug.

"Can we, hmm, get you something to drink?"

"No, that's quite alright. But I would like to speak with Arianne alone, if that's not too much to ask."

"Of course not." She wrung her hands. "I can go hang out downstairs in the common room."

"Nora, you don't need to—"

"Thank you, Nora," my father interjected, "that would be much appreciated."

My brows drew together. He was acting weird, sending tingles zipping up my spine. I'd been so surprised to see my father and Tristan standing there, so embarrassed. No doubt he had questions about Nicco, about the nature of our relationship. But in a strange way, I was also glad the truth was out. Now I didn't have to pretend anymore.

Deep down, I'm sure all my father wanted was for me to be happy.

Safe and happy and loved.

Three words I felt every time Nicco looked at me. Even if it was far too soon to be feeling such things.

So why did I feel like everything was about to change?

"I'd like Nora to stay," I blurted out, suddenly feeling out of my depth, panic swelling in my chest. "Please, Papá."

"Arianne, this does not—"

"*Please*," I said, reaching for Nora's hand. The happiness I'd felt only minutes earlier was rapidly diminishing. Something was wrong, I felt it.

I'd been so blinded by my amazing date with Nicco, I hadn't assumed my father was here for anything besides a social visit. But it was late on a Thursday night and he hadn't called ahead.

It made no sense.

Nora slid her fingers between mine and squeezed, giving me the strength to ask, "What's going on, Papá? Why are you here?"

"Very well, this will affect Nora too. Please," he motioned to our beds. "Let's sit."

Nora and I plopped down on her bed while my father took one of the desk chairs. Just then, the door swung open and Tristan entered the room. He met my father's gaze and gave him a sharp nod.

"Tristan?" I asked, my voice quivering. "What happened? Where's Nicco?"

"He took off." There was something in his voice, but my father cleared his throat, commanding my attention.

"It has come to my attention that you are no longer safe here."

"Safe?" I choked out. "What do you mean, I'm not safe? I haven't even been here two weeks. I don't understand. Did something happen?"

"How long have you been seeing the Marchetti boy?"

"Nicco, Papá, his name is Nicco. And it all happened quite suddenly. He's been—"

"Have you been intimate with him?"

"Wh- what?" Embarrassment stained my cheeks.

"Mr. Capizola," Nora interrupted. "I don't think that's really an appropriate question to ask in front—"

"Answer the question, mio tesoro."

"N- no," I lied, indignation burning through me. What right did he have to ask me that? In front of Nora and Tristan no less.

"No." I collected myself. "I'm still..."

"Good, that's very good indeed." His shoulders visibly relaxed.

What the hell was happening?

My father had always been curt, but he had never been so cold with me before. Everything he'd ever done, although overbearing and over the top, was out of love. I'd never doubted that.

Until now.

"You are no longer to see Niccolò Marchetti."

The words rattled around my head. I didn't understand what he was saying.

"I'm sorry to do this to you, Arianne," he went on. "I am, but you need to pack your things immediately. We leave tonight."

"Leave?" I leaped up, tears streaming down my face. "I'm not leaving. I'm not going to stop seeing Nicco. He makes me happy. He makes me feel... *normal*. You said—"

"I said you could remain here as long as you were safe." My father stood, smoothing a hand through his beard. "You are no longer safe."

"What does that even mean? Does someone want to hurt me? Who?" I cried, tears burning the backs of my eyes. "I've done everything you asked of me. I've barely even talked to anyone except Nora and..."

"Marchetti?" My cousin ground out, a look of disgust washing over him.

"Tristan?" I said softly. "Tell me what's going on. What does Nicco have to do with any of this?"

"She should know," he said to my father, clenching his fist. I noticed it looked sore, the skin around his knuckles red and angry.

"Tristan," he warned. "Now is not the—"

"What did you do?" It came out shrill, the pieces of the puzzle shifting and changing, slowly slotting into place. But I was still missing too many vital parts to make any sense of it. "What did you do to Nicco?"

"Nothing he didn't deserve." Tristan shot up, glaring down at me.

"You bastard," I yelled, fists clenched at my sides, my heart crashing violently against my chest.

"Whoa, there." Nora flanked my side. "I think everyone should just calm down. Mr. Capizola, what is this all about? Is Arianne in immediate danger?"

His eyes clouded with indecision.

"I want to stay here," I said, finally finding my voice. "At least for tonight. This is my life, *my life,* Papá, and I'm not sure I want to go anywhere with either of you until you tell me what the hell is going on."

"Arianne," my father tsked. "Must you be so difficult?"

"Difficult? You think this is me being difficult? You kept me locked away at home for five years. Five. Years. Papá. I was so excited to come here, to finally be a normal teenage girl, and you want to rip that away from me. Because I'm in danger. But you won't tell me why. Well, I'm sorry, but that doesn't work for me." I ripped my hand from Nora's, planting it on my hip.

He couldn't do this.

He couldn't take away college, my freedom... *Nicco.*

I'd only just found him; I couldn't just forget about him.

I wouldn't.

"You're one of the most powerful men in Verona County, in the State." My eyes narrowed at him. "Surely you can make sure it's safe for me to stay here?"

Tristan's expression softened but it was too late. If he'd even laid so much as a finger on Nicco, we were done. "She has a point, Uncle. I'm here, Scott too. You know we wouldn't let anyone hurt her."

Nora tensed beside me and I quickly shot her a look that said, 'please don't say anything'.

"I'll leave two men."

"Bodyguards?" Disbelief coated my words. "That's not what I—"

"It's this or you can pack a bag and come straight home with me."

"Fine." I folded my arms over my chest, wondering how we'd gotten here.

Less than an hour ago, I'd been floating on clouds, wrapped in Nicco's arms, falling so deeply into him I never wanted to come back to reality.

And now... now, they talked about him like he was the enemy and we were at war.

I didn't understand any of it.

All I knew is that my heart was splintering in my chest, and I wasn't going anywhere, not tonight.

"Very well." Father buttoned his jacket. "But Arianne, this isn't permanent. You are my daughter and I will always do whatever it takes to keep you safe. Do you understand that? Take the night to calm down and we'll pick this up again tomorrow."

I didn't trust myself to speak, so I gave him a tight-lipped nod. He came to me, pressing a single kiss to the top of my head. "Mio tesoro, you have grown into such a strong young lady. But don't let yourself be fooled by things as fickle as love. We are Capizola, Principessa. It's time you started to act like one."

Nora's eyes burned into the side of my head as I watched my father walk out of our room as if he hadn't just tipped my world on its axis.

Tristan lingered, his eyes glittering with apology. "Ari, I tried to buy you more time, but I didn't realize you were—"

"Don't 'Ari' me," I sneered. "Look me in the eye and tell me you didn't hurt him, Tristan. Look me in the eye and tell me."

"I'm sorry," he whispered, "But there are things you don't know, cousin. So much history you don't... fuck."

"You need to leave," Nora said, wrapping her arm around me. "Now."

"Yeah, okay." Tristan's gaze lingered on me, but I couldn't look at him. "But you can't hide from this forever, Arianne. This is your destiny. Whether you like it or not."

My cousin stalked out of the room, closing the door behind him.

And I crumpled into my friend's arms, wondering when life had gotten so complicated.

"Here." Nora handed me a cup of hot cocoa. "How do you feel now?"

"Are the Muscle Twins still standing guard outside my room?"

She went to the peephole and took a look. "Yep."

"Well then, that was all real, and I didn't dream it. So I guess you could say I feel angry, betrayed, confused, disappointed... does that work for you?"

Nora gave me a weak smile. "I'm proud of you."

"Proud of me?"

"Hell yeah. You didn't just pack a bag and dutifully follow your father back home. You stood your ground."

"He told me nothing, Nora. Nothing. All that talk about MU not being safe and forbidding me from seeing Nicco again. What the hell was that? And Tristan..."

"You really think he hurt Nicco?"

"Didn't you see his hand? Something went down." The knot in my stomach tightened.

"Can't you text him?"

"I... I don't have his number..." My voice trailed off.

"You didn't get it tonight? Ari, come on..."

"I realize how stupid it sounds, but he never asked me and I didn't want to... God, Nora, have I been fooling myself this whole time? Is Nicco somehow related to the threat my father was talking about? You should have seen how shocked they were to see me with him. I've seen my father angry plenty of times, but I've never seen him like that."

"What did they say his name is? Marchetti?"

"Yes, why?"

"Marchetti... it sounds familiar. I'm sure I've heard it before. Come on, let's Google him."

"Google him? I don't know if—"

"Ari, they're keeping something from you. And I know hotty came in and swept you off your feet and had you so starry-eyed you failed to get any of the important details from him, like his surname and phone number, but it's time you found out the truth. Don't you think?"

I placed down the mug and let out a heavy sigh. She was right. I'd been too naïve, too wrapped up in how Nicco made me feel to worry about how little I really knew about him.

"Okay." I joined her on her bed. Nora fired up her laptop and we sat back against the headboard.

"Niccolò Marchetti." She entered his name into the search bar and hit enter. "Student at MU, tell us something we don't already know. No hits on social media. No images. Oh wait, what's this?"

She clicked one of the links and the article loaded. "Son of Antonio Marchetti, boss of Dominion, the organized crime syndicate operating out of La Riva, Verona County. The Marchetti have a long and colorful history in Verona that dates back to the original founding families..."

"Crime syndicate?" I whispered. "As in the... *mafia*? But that's—"

"Oh my god," Nora gasped. "That's where I've heard the name before. Giovanni used to tell me these stories about how Verona County was founded. Your great-great-grandfather Tommaso Capizola emigrated here in the late eighteen-hundreds. He and his best friend built a life for themselves. Giovanni made them out to be these larger-than-life characters who built this illegal empire, but I always thought he was exaggerating. Your father is the most law-abiding man I know, but maybe there's more to it?"

I'd heard the stories, knew all about my family's legacy of being the founders of Verona County, but I'd never heard Nora's version. "What are you saying? That my father's great-grandfather's best friend was a Marchetti?"

She nodded slowly. "I think so."

Leaning in, I studied the article. "Dominion," I said, typing the word into the search bar followed by Verona County.

"Holy shit," Nora let out a shaky breath as we poured over article after article linking the Marchetti name to a string of offences. "They're mobsters," she said. "Real life Italian mobsters."

"It's not..." I inhaled sharply. "It can't be true. Nicco is—"

"Prince of Dominion." Nora pointed to the screen. "He's next in line to take over Dominion. At least now we know why your father and Tristan freaked the hell out when they caught you making out with him."

"Nora..." A heavy weight settled over me.

"Sorry, just trying to lighten the mood."

I didn't appreciate her humor, not right now. Not when everything I thought I knew was being obliterated. My family hadn't built their success on the foundations of hard work and determination; they had ridden the coattails of their mobster ancestors. Nicco wasn't just a mysterious bad boy with a good heart; he was the only son of New England's mafia boss.

He was everything I wasn't.

"Ari?" Nora rushed out as I slumped back against the pillows, the air sucked clean from my lungs.

"What am I going to do?" I sobbed, my heart breaking for the boy who had made me feel alive and the girl he'd pulled from her shell.

It made some sense now; Nicco's constant torment over being with me. The way he always referred to himself as being no good for me.

But even though I knew the truth, and I knew there was still a lot more to the story to uncover, I couldn't forget how Nicco made me feel. The way he'd handled me with such love and affection. It wasn't something you could fake, was it?

"I can feel my heart breaking," I cried into my hands, the pain overwhelming. "Was it real? Was any of it real?"

"Ssh," Nora stroked my hair. "We'll figure it out, Ari. I promise we'll figure it out."

But I wasn't sure of anything anymore.

All I'd wanted was a normal life. Then I'd met Nicco, and it was like being in a fairytale. My very own prince to chase away the monsters and protect my heart. But it was all a lie.

The truth was much worse.

The truth was my life had just become a living nightmare.

One I didn't know how I would survive.

Sleep didn't come easy.

I tossed and turned all night, replaying the events of the night over in my head. At one point, I'd given up hope of falling to sleep and began searching the internet for more information about Nicco's family, hoping, *praying*, that Nora was wrong.

Niccolò Marchetti wasn't the son of a mafia boss.

He couldn't be.

Yet, deep down, I knew the truth. What had he really told me about himself?

Nothing.

And foolishly, I hadn't asked. I'd been so enamored with him, so set on keeping my own secret, I hadn't stopped to consider he was keeping devastating secrets of his own.

"Hey, are you awake?" Nora's voice was thick with sleep. She'd managed to drop off sometime around one, after I'd soaked her pajama top with tears.

"I couldn't sleep," I replied, rolling onto my side and pulling the covers higher. "I wanted it to all be a dream."

"But it's not," she said, sadness heavy in her words.

"It's not."

"So I guess his best friend, Enzo, is also... you know."

"I don't know. I don't know anything anymore."

"You're falling for him, aren't you?"

"I..." The words stuck in my throat. "It's crazy, right? You can't fall for someone you hardly know."

"You can if it's written in the stars."

I chuckled bitterly at that. "Nothing about me and Nicco is written in the stars, Nor. He's a criminal. You read the articles. Murder. Intimidation. Racketeering. Fraud. It all leads back to Dominion."

"Not all people choose to be bad, Ari, some have no choice. You won't know Nicco's story until you ask him."

"Ask him?" I gawked at her. "You really think he's going to want to speak to me now he knows who I am?" Silence lingered between us, and then I whispered, "I found something..."

"What?" She pushed up onto her elbows.

"I couldn't sleep, so I did some more digging. One of my father's companies is trying to get permission to redevelop La Riva."

"But that's Marchetti territory." We'd learned that during our late-night internet search.

I nodded slowly, my stomach churning. "Antonio Marchetti refuses to give up the land."

"You think that has something to do with the bad blood between them?"

"It's a start." Although I had a feeling it went much deeper than that.

"What are you going to do?"

"I'm going to go and see my father."

She bolted upright. "Ari, I'm not sure that's a good idea. If you antagonize him, he might make you return home."

I swung my legs over the edge of the bed and sat up. "I can't spend my life being his dutiful, docile daughter. I spent my entire teenage years locked away in the house. I want to know why."

Nora mirrored my position, pushing her feet into fluffy gray slippers. "So I guess we're going home this weekend after all?"

"You'll come with me?"

"As if you even need to ask."

"Thank you." I smiled.

"You think the Muscle Twins will drive us there?"

"There's only one way to find out. But before I face my father, I need breakfast."

"Are you sure?" Her brow rose. "Maybe we should—"

"It's college, Nora. What could possibly happen to me here? Besides, it's not like we'll be alone." My gaze flicked to the door. I was used to seeing my mother and father being flanked by bodyguards. Even Nora's dad, Billy, was trained in close protection. It was all part and parcel of working for Verona County's wealthiest family.

"I think we should get drive-thru on route."

"Nor, come on. It's just breakfast."

"I get it." She gave me a weak smile. "You're feeling defiant and you want to fight back. I would too. But we still don't know all the facts."

"Fine," I conceded. "We can get drive-thru."

She was right. I did feel defiant. It burned through me, swirling with anger and frustration. I wanted answers.

I wanted the truth.

Even if I didn't like it.

In less than half an hour, we were both washed and dressed, staring at the door as if it led to some unknown world. "Are you sure about this?" Nora asked me.

"It's the only way. I want answers. I deserve answers, Nor. And my father has them."

"I like you like this." She smiled. "All feisty and strong."

"Oh, I don't know about that." Inside, my heart was battered and bruised. But my father was a formidable man and I didn't want to give him even an ounce of ammunition. He needed to see I was an adult now. A young woman capable of handling the truth.

"You've got this, Ari. *We've* got this. Come on." She yanked the door open and stepped out into the hall. The two bodyguards stood to attention, focusing their narrowed gazes on me.

"Miss Capizola. Your father has requested—"

"I need you to drive me home," I said.

They shared a glance. "Mr. Capizola would prefer it if—"

Clearing my throat, I took a deep breath and said, "What are your names?"

"I'm Luis, and my partner here is Nixon."

"Well, Luis, you can either drive me home or we'll make our own way."

"Very well," he said. "The car is out front."

Of course it was. I rolled my eyes at Nora who chuckled. A couple of girls were walking down the hall toward us, their eyes widening at the sight of me and Nora being escorted by Luis and Nixon. But I let their whispers of curiosity roll off my shoulders. They were the least of my problems right now.

"I know things are a mess right now." Nora leaned in close. "But you can't deny there's something kind of cool about this." She motioned to Luis.

Trust her to find this exciting. Giving her a little shake of my head, we followed our escorts out of the dorm building and toward the sleek black SUV.

"At least everyone already left for class and we don't have an audience," Nora murmured.

She was right, there was no one around. No one except...

"Bailey," I breathed, spotting him at the corner of the building, hiding between the wall and a huge Maple tree.

"Bailey?" Nora whispered.

"Yeah, Nicco's cousin." Hope blossomed in my chest. "I have to go talk to him."

"Hmm, hate to break it to you, but they're never going to let you go over there. Let me handle this, okay?"

My brows pinched as I glanced over at Bailey again. I needed to talk to him. I needed to know Nicco was okay.

"Okay, but what are you going to—"

"Oh, crap," Nora announced, jerking to a stop. "I need to go grab something from the apartment."

"Miss Abato, we really need to be going."

"You stay with Ari in the car. I'll be two minutes."

"Nixon." Luis motioned to him. "Go with her."

"No, *no!* It's... girl's stuff. Highly embarrassing. As if being escorted out of the building by two burly bodyguards isn't embarrassing enough," she grumbled. "I'll be two minutes. In and out, you'll see. Go get Ari in the car, she's the important one here."

Luis yanked open the door and motioned for me to get inside.

"Hurry," I called after Nora as she hurried back toward the building. I had no idea how she planned on getting Bailey's attention without alerting Luis and Nixon, but my best friend was full of surprises.

The atmosphere inside the SUV was tense. Luis discreetly talked over his radio while Nixon kept his eye trained on the building. Bailey was right there, and it killed me not being able to go to him.

A minute passed, and another. Nixon started to grumble. "It's been long enough, I'm going to—"

"She got her period," I blurted out.

"I... uh, right." He ran a hand down his face while I fought a smile.

Another five minutes passed, and even I was starting to get worried. But then I saw her jogging toward the SUV. The door swung open and she climbed inside. "All better, sorry it took me so long."

"Please buckle up," Luis said, putting the car into drive.

"What did he say?" I whispered, keeping one eye on the rear-view mirror.

"Not here." Nora shook her head.

"Nor, please..."

I needed to know something, *anything*.

She reached out and grabbed my hand, keeping her face upfront. "He's okay," she mouthed, anger flaring in her eyes. "But you were right, Tristan did hurt him."

My heart sank. "Oh God." Tears welled in my eyes and I desperately tried to blink them away.

"Ssh, it's going to be okay, Ari."

But nothing about this was okay.

Not a single thing.

TWELVE

NICCO

"NICCOLÒ, what on earth happened to your face?" Aunt Francesca reached for me, cooing as she smoothed her fingers over my jaw.

"Leave the boy alone, amore mio." Uncle Joe ushered her away from me, narrowing his eyes on my bruised face.

"Should I be worried?"

"Nicco met a girl. Isn't that right, cous?" Bailey breezed into the room, smirking in my direction.

"Fuck you," I mouthed over my uncle's shoulder. He flipped me off, earning him a slap upside the head.

"No swearing at my table. Now get washed up and sit. This food isn't going to eat itself."

"Smells good, Auntie," I said, dropping into one of the chairs. My head hurt like a motherfucker and my stomach was tender, but I knew if I missed breakfast, my aunt would come looking for me. Besides, there wasn't much her eggs and bacon couldn't fix.

"So, tell me about this girl." She placed their final bowl down on the table and took her seat. "What's her name? Does she go to Montague?"

"There is no girl. Bailey is just busting my balls." I levelled him with a hard look.

"Well, it wouldn't hurt you to think about settling down. You're almost twenty, and with so much... responsibility on your shoulders."

"Fran," my uncle warned. "Let the boy be. He's here to get away from all that nonsense."

Heavy silence settled over us. Unlike Matteo's father who had worked his way up the ranks before marrying into the family and becoming one of my father's captains, Uncle Joe had wanted nothing to do with it. Aunt Francesca's mother had been my grandfather Francesco's sister, and like her daughter, she had been allowed to marry a man with no ties to the family.

The Romano weren't really my aunt and uncle in the traditional sense of the word, but they were family in all the ways that mattered.

"Bailey, would you like to say grace?"

My cousin grumbled but nodded all the same. We all linked hands and waited while he said thanks. When he was done, Uncle Joe served for my aunt and then himself, handing me the spoon.

"How are classes?" he asked.

"Dull." I admitted. "I'd rather be in the workshop helping you or down at the gym."

"An education will serve you well, Niccolò." He gave me a knowing look. We all knew why I was attending MU; we just didn't talk about it. It was the way of the life—the code of silence, or as we called it omertá.

"You need to hurry if you're going to make your classes today," she said.

"Actually, I'm heading down to the gym," I said, wiping my mouth with the napkin. "I need to burn off some steam."

And beat the shit out of something, or someone.

"I'm going to tag along," Bailey said, "if that's okay?"

"What about school?" His mom shrieked. "You need to make an effort, Son. Please."

"I can't be there, not right now." He slid his fingers into his hair, tugging the ends. "I'll go Monday, I promise."

Aunt Francesca let out an exasperated breath. "Okay, you stay out of that ring, ragazzo mio."

"Yes, Mamma."

"I'll keep an eye on him."

"Such a good boy," she crooned, leaning over to pat my hand. "Now eat. You know I like a clean plate."

"I have something for you," my cousin said the second we climbed into his car.

"Is it a magical wand to fix this fucking shitshow?"

"It's better."

That piqued my interest as I glanced over at him. "Here." He rummaged in his pocket and pulled out a scrap of paper, pressing it into my hand.

I smoothed it out. "It's a phone number."

"Not just any number, *her* number."

My muscles tensed. All night I'd thought about Arianne, and if I hadn't been thinking about her, I'd dreamed of her.

She was the Capizola heir.

The girl my father wanted to use as leverage against Roberto.

But she was also the girl who had reached into my chest and ripped out my heart, holding it in the palm of her hands.

"How did you get this?" My teeth ground together.

"I went back over there last night."

"You what?" I barked.

"Relax, nobody saw me. Anyway, they never left. Roberto posted two of his men at her dorm, but she stayed. I went back this morning to case the joint. And guess who I saw just before they were about leave?"

"Arianne," I breathed. Just saying her name hurt. Tore my chest open that little bit more until I was sure I was bleeding out all over Bailey's car.

"You spoke to her?" I asked.

"No, her roommate managed to shake Capizola's guys. She told me to give you this and I quote, 'tell him if he meant any of it to fucking call her'. She's feisty that one."

I stared down at the digits. This was my link to her. All I had to do was dig out my cell and call her.

"What are you waiting for?" Bailey asked after a few seconds.

"I need to figure shit out first."

"Nic, just call her, man. You want to. I know you do."

Dragging a hand through my hair, I let out a long breath. "You don't know anything, kid. Just drive."

He cussed me out in Italian but didn't say any more. What was there to say? No amount of his mom's home-cooking was going to fix this.

We pulled into the dusty parking lot of Uncle Mario's gym ten minutes later. He was my father's second cousin, but it was tradition to call our elder relatives uncle. It was in the heart of La Riva on the corner of one of the commercial blocks.

I spotted Enzo's Pontiac immediately. He'd been blowing up my cell about Roberto Capizola being on campus last night, but I hadn't had the energy to get into it with him.

Besides, I still hadn't decided what to tell him.

We climbed out of Bailey's car, and I grabbed my bag out of the trunk.

"Nicco," a couple of guys greeted us as we entered the building.

Hard Knocks smelled like a sweat pit, but there was something comforting about the stale air, and the grunts and groans echoing off the walls.

"We need to talk," Enzo stalked over to me the second he noticed me.

"Not now." I dumped my bag down on a bench and peeled the t-shirt off my body. "Tape," I said to no one in particular and Bailey handed me a roll of tape. I began fixing it around my knuckles, pulling it tight enough to protect my skin but not enough to prevent movement.

"Yo, Russo," I yelled over to the trainer working the ring. "I want in."

"Killian's paid for a full hour." He motioned to the guy jabbing the air in the center.

"I'll fight him," the beefed-up guy said, slowing his movements and walking over to the ropes.

"You don't want to do that, my man." Russo let out a low whistle. "That there is Niccolò Marchetti."

Recognition flared in the guy's eyes. "I'm in, if he is."

"It's your funeral." Russo mumbled, pulling up one of the ropes and beckoning me over. I kicked off my sneakers and climbed barefoot into the ring. I liked to feel the canvas beneath my feet, the vibrations through my body.

"I've heard of you, kid." The guy smirked. "I gotta say, I'm not impressed so far." His scrutinizing gaze looked me over.

Stretching my neck from side to side, I rolled my shoulders, bouncing on the balls of my feet. Usually, I warmed up before getting in the ring with someone. But I didn't want to go easy today. I wanted to hit. To hurt. I wanted to feel every-fucking-thing.

"Kick his sorry ass, cous," Bailey called out. The rest of the guys in the gym had stopped their workouts and moved closer, all ready to watch me go head to head with Killian.

"I'm going to put you on your ass, kid."

"Bring it on." I banged my fists together. The air crackled around us, thick with anticipation.

"You sure about this, Nicco?" Russo gritted through his teeth as he got into position.

"Just call it," I said.

"Okay then." He shoved his arm between us. "Keep it clean. No shots below the waist, no holding, tripping, or kicking. If I see any teeth or cheap shots, you're out, got it?"

I nodded, my hard eyes fixed on Killian. I'd never seen him around before. Didn't know his strengths or weaknesses, but I didn't need to know. All I saw was a target. Someone to take out all my frustration and anger on. Adrenaline pumped through me.

"You're mine, pretty boy," he taunted, dancing on his feet.

I raised a brow. "We'll see."

"Fight," Russo's voice rang out like a shotgun firing. I dropped back, anticipating his move. Sure enough, he came at me like a bull out of a gate, fists swinging.

Staying light on my feet, I dodged a right hook and came up ready with a counter upper cut. My fist made contact, Killian's head snapping back as his pained grunts filled the air. He staggered back, but I didn't give him time to shake it off. I was on him. Fast and hard, hitting him blow after blow.

"Get him good, Nicco," someone yelled, their words drowned out by the roar of blood in between my ears.

"Easy, Marchetti." Russo forced himself between us, letting Killian catch his breath. His brow was split open, a trickle of blood snaking down his face.

"Still ready to put me on my ass?" Now I was taunting him. But I felt pumped, molten lava running through my veins, spurring me on. I wasn't even close to soothing the beast raging inside me.

"Let's go, brutto stronzo." I chuckled darkly, bouncing on the balls of my feet.

He barged Russo out of the way and lunged for me, his clumsy punch colliding with my shoulder. A sharp blast of pain ricocheted through me but it barely registered. Pain was good. Pain reminded me I was alive. It drowned out all the other shit weighing me down.

"Figlio di puttana," Killian grumbled, diving for me again as I ducked and dodged his advances. His wrapped knuckles grazed my cheek a couple of times, crushing into the soft tissue between my ribs. But it was nothing I couldn't handle.

"Finish him, Nicco," Enzo yelled.

But I had no plans to end it too quickly. I was still too wound up.

I advanced, crowding Killian against the ropes, landing punch after punch. Face, chest, ribs, it didn't matter. So long as my fist kept finding body parts, there was no stopping me. He went down on his knee, desperately trying to block his face.

"Nicco, relax," someone shouted. But I couldn't stop. My knuckles rained down hellfire on him until I could see nothing but mangled skin, blood, and fresh bruises.

"Easy boy." Strong arms grabbed me from behind, tearing me away from Killian. "Go walk it off." Russo gave me a hard shove to the opposite side of the ring where Enzo and Bailey were watching me, concern etched deep into their frowns.

"What?" I snapped, climbing out of the ring and grabbing a bottle of water. I drank it down, pouring the rest over my head. Icy cold water ran in rivulets down my chest, cooling my temperature and my mood.

Glancing back, I took in the state of Killian. He looked like he'd been jumped by four or five men.

"Fuck," I cussed under my breath. Guilt flashed through me, but I shook it off. He'd challenged me, acting like he could take me. It wasn't my fault if he caught me at a bad fucking time.

"If you wanted to kill the guy," Enzo said, falling in step beside me as I headed for the locker room. "You almost succeeded."

"He knew what he was getting into."

"Did he?" My best friend's eyes burned into the side of my face. "What the fuck has gotten into you? Is this about Capizola because we need to—"

"Not now, yeah." I brushed him off. "I need to get cleaned up."

Enzo slammed his hand against the lockers, cutting me off. "Talk to me, cous. What's going on with you?"

I finally met his questioning glare. "Let me shower and then we'll talk, okay?"

He gave me a sharp nod, removing his hand. "I'll call Matteo."

"It's Friday. You know he drives Arabella to school today and takes his mom for breakfast."

"Business comes first."

And that was the problem. Enzo was too devoted to the life. It gave him purpose, made him feel like he belonged. I wanted to believe it was because he'd never had a mom growing up, but part of me thought it might just be the way he was wired.

"Okay," I conceded. "Tell him to meet us at Carluccio's in an hour."

"An hour?" Enzo balked.

"Family is important too. Let him eat with his mother and then he can come meet us. I need some time under the hot jets anyway."

"You mean you need a post-fight release." He smirked and I flipped him off. "I'm sure Rayna would come over and help you with that."

"Me and Rayna are done." I grabbed my shit and started toward the shower blocks.

"Does she know that?" he called after me and I flipped him off again over my shoulder. Rayna hadn't been on my radar ever since I met Arianne.

I stripped out of my sweats and stepped in the shower, turning on the jets. The hot water soothed my tender muscles. It wasn't long before my hand slipped down to my rock-hard dick. Enzo was right; usually after a fight I needed another kind of release. But the only person I wanted was the one person I couldn't have.

My hand gripped the base of my shaft, stroking up and down as I pictured Arianne's face, her big honey eyes staring up at me as she came all over my tongue.

Fuck. How was I just supposed to walk away? It wasn't just a physical attraction I felt toward her, it was deep inside me.

She was inside me.

My palm flattened against the tiles, keeping me upright as I worked my hand harder, faster, chasing the release I so desperately needed. I imagined her on knees before me. Teasing me with her tongue, looking up at me through her thick lashes. Giving me another one of her firsts.

Jesus.

I couldn't let her go. There was too much I wanted to show her, to experience with her. I wanted to make her mine in every way possible until we were bound together in a way nothing and no one could sever.

Bailey was right all along.

I had to fight for her.

I had to.

Because not fighting for her felt like giving up on part of my soul. A part I'd never get back.

The bottom line was, meeting Arianne had changed me, and I wasn't sure I could go back to before.

I just had to figure out how the hell to balance what I wanted to do with what I should, while keeping everyone I cared about safe.

Matteo was waiting for us when we got to Carluccio's diner. He looked up from the booth and saluted. "What's up?" he asked the second he slid in opposite us.

"Nicco broke a guy's face at Hard Knocks."

"What's new?" Matteo gave me a wolfish grin.

"This was different," Enzo replied coolly. "He was out to ki—"

"So maybe I got a little carried away." I shrugged, grabbing a menu. "The guy will live."

I'd stuck around after my shower to make sure he was okay. Russo wanted to take him to the local medical center to get one of the cuts above his eye looked at, but Killian didn't want the fuss. Probably didn't want to admit a nineteen-year-old guy had kicked his ass.

"Where were you last night? I thought this one,"—Matteo flicked his head toward Enzo—"was going to lose his shit when we spotted Capizola's SUV on campus."

"I was busy." I signaled for the server.

"Usual?" she asked.

"I'll just take a basket of fries and a chocolate shake, please. Enzo?"

"Yeah, usual please, Trina." He leaned forward. "I almost had her. You said he'd lead us right to her and he would have if it wasn't for that fucker Johnny getting in the way."

"Security Johnny?"

"Yeah, he thought I was acting suspiciously. Well, I guess I was, but he didn't realize it was me until it was too late. He'd already called for backup. I lost Capizola heading toward the library. That road only leads to three other buildings."

"The Administration Building or the girls only dorms," Matteo added. "So she most likely lives in either Donatello or Bembo House?"

"It doesn't matter, he knows we know," I said, sinking back against the leather bench. "Tristan must have tipped him off."

Fuck.

I needed to tell them.

I needed to just come clean and tell them.

But I couldn't get the words out over the giant lump in my throat. If I told them, there was no going back.

The scrap of paper Bailey had given me burned in my pocket. I needed to hear her voice, to know she was okay. Maybe Arianne had some idea about how we minimized the impact of this bomb that had been dropped on us.

Unlikely. I smothered an exasperated breath. She'd been in the dark as much as I had. I'd seen the flash of surprise in her eyes when her father indicated he knew me.

We were both pawns. Her unknowing. Me unwilling. Both of us bound by our family's legacies.

"What the fuck are we supposed to do now?" Enzo grumbled, clearly pissed about the turn of events. "He's probably already whisked her back to Castle Capizola and locked her away in the tower."

"Maybe, maybe not. There's a reason he sent her here in the first place, a piece of the puzzle we haven't figured out. Why now? After all these years? Roberto is no fool." I went on, trying to keep the focus on Roberto and not his daughter. "He must have known we would find out eventually, so what changed? That's what we need to figure out."

"You know your old man is going to lose his shit when he hears about this?"

I levelled Enzo with a hard look. "Which is why we won't tell him anything until we have more information. We know she's enrolled at MU; we know she's staying in either Donatella or Bembo House; and we know Roberto paid her a visit last night. Now we just have to see how it plays out."

"It's a big risk," Enzo said. "We could have let her slip through our fingers before we—"

The server appeared with our drinks. "Here you go." She placed them down. "Your food will be along shortly. Anything else I can get you?" Her eyes raked over Matteo, lingering on the tattoos snaking down his neck and disappearing under his tight black t-shirt.

"We're good," Enzo grunted, and she scurried off.

"Do you have to be such an asshole?" Matteo rolled his eyes.

"She was practically foaming at the mouth."

"Just because she wasn't ready to climb on your dick." He clapped Enzo on the back. "You're losing your touch, cous."

"Oh yeah? You don't think I could get her to follow me into the restroom and drop to her knees?"

"Seriously," Matteo balked. "What the fuck is wrong with you? It's Trina, we've known her for years."

"And yet, you still haven't done shit about it."

He shrugged. "She's not my type."

"They never are."

"Enzo," I warned.

"Yeah, yeah." The air cooled between the three of us.

"Let's eat and then figure shit out."

"Fine by me," Enzo muttered.

"Yeah, whatever, Nic, it isn't like I just ate a big meal or anything."

"Porca puttana!" My hand slammed down on the table, rattling the salt and pepper shakers. "You two are driving me in-fucking-sane. Knock it off, capito?"

They both stared at me as if I'd lost my mind.

And I was beginning to think that maybe they were right.

THIRTEEN

ARIANNE

"BREATHE," Nora whispered as we sat in the kitchen, waiting for my father.

We'd arrived at the house almost an hour ago, only to discover he was unavailable, and my mother was in the city at her appointment with her personal trainer.

So we waited.

Nora's mother, Sara, prepared a spread of breakfast items for us, despite us both telling her we weren't hungry. But it was Mrs. Abato's way of smothering the tension. She'd taken one look at my tight expression and decided to start cooking.

After all, food fixed everything.

"I'm sure he will be along soon," she said, cleaning away the dishes.

"Mamma, let me help." Nora stood up and began helping, but her mother waved her off. Mrs. Abato served our family proudly, she always had, but she wanted more for her daughter. It was the thing I admired most about her. She raised Nora to be limitless, to want more than a life of servitude, despite their family's ties to my family. My father agreeing to finance Nora's time at MU with me was like a dream come true. She would get a first-rate education, life experience outside of my family's estate and connections, and the opportunity to make a future of her own.

I loved my best friend, but I also envied her.

Her wings would only continue to grow, to beat harder, taking her to unknown heights.

My wings were clipped.

My future decided.

One day the Capizola empire would be mine, whether I wanted it or not.

The air shifted and I glanced over my shoulder to see Luis and Nixon step into the room, followed by my father. "Arianne," he said around a smile. "This is a surprise."

"Papá." I stood up and went to him, letting him wrap me in his arms.

"Thank you, Luis, Nixon. You may leave us."

"Can I get you anything, Mr. Capizola?" Nora's mother asked, wiping her hands down her apron.

"No, thank you, Sara, all I request is some privacy with my daughter."

"Of course. Nora, come, cucciola."

Nora shot me a questioning look, but I nodded. "I'll see you in a little while, okay?"

She offered me a tight-lipped smile before following her mother out of the kitchen.

"We should go into my study," my father motioned for me to go ahead.

"Very well." We walked down the long hall in silence. We lived in a Victorian style house, nestled among three acres of land in the most easterly point of Verona County, where the boundary line met Providence County. It was full of character with its steep gabled roof, asymmetrical windows, and wraparound porch. I had fond memories of playing in and around the house, exploring the vast grounds. What I hadn't realized back then, when I was just a child, was that it would one day become my prison. A beautiful, sprawling prison with a huge library and many sitting rooms. We even had a sizeable indoor pool. Then there was the kitchen, one of my favorite rooms in the entire house. It was warm and homely, and overlooked the luscious green lawns and many Maple trees, and it smelled constantly of Mrs. Abato's home cooking.

It was home and I'd loved it. But somewhere along the way, I began to resent it too.

We entered my father's study and he closed the door. I hovered, my stomach a tight ball of nerves. I'd felt so determined to demand answers earlier, but now I was here, staring at the man who had only ever done everything in his power to protect me and provide for me, and words failed me.

"Is there something you want to say, Arianne?" He sat down in his leather chair.

I'd spent so many hours in here as a child. Sitting at his feet playing while he worked. He would lift me onto his knee and tell me all about his projects. Plans to make Verona County thrive. I'd listen raptly as my father talked so passionately about making a future for the younger generation.

For *me.*

But now I looked at him and no longer saw that man.

I saw a liar.

"Arianne, mio tesoro, sit, please." He gave me a warm smile.

"How do you know Nicco's father?" I blurted out.

"Antonio Marchetti is a businessman much like myself." Father loosened his tie but didn't flinch.

"Businessman? What kind of business? The legitimate kind, like you?" My brow rose.

"He's not entirely legitimate, no."

"Is it true you want to redevelop La Riva? The Marchetti neighborhood?"

He stroked his beard, a flash of surprise in his eyes.

"Is that how you know him? Or is it because our families used to be friends?"

Now his brows furrowed. "How did you—"

"It's called the internet, Papá."

"There is so much you don't understand."

"A lot you've kept from me, you mean."

"Principessa," he sighed. "Don't you trust me?"

"Why don't you want me to see Nicco anymore?"

I wanted to hear him say the words.

I *needed* him to say them.

"Arianne, mio tesoro." His eyes pleaded with me.

"Tell me." I inhaled a shaky breath. "Tell me the truth, Papá. I need you to tell me the truth."

He pinched the bridge of his nose, letting out a long sigh. When his resigned gaze met mine, I steeled myself for whatever bomb he was about to drop.

"You know our family moved here in the late eighteen-hundreds. Well, my father's great grandfather, Tommaso Capizola, was one of the first men to arrive here with his best friend, Luca Marchetti. They wanted to escape the oppression in Italy and make a better life for themselves, but it wasn't easy. Settling in La Riva, although it was called something different back then, they turned their hand to anything that could make them a dollar or two. The Marchetti had ties to the mafia, and with the introduction of the statewide Prohibition Law, it wasn't long before Luca saw an opportunity to make a quick buck bootlegging.

"By the late twenties, the population of La Riva had grown, spilling into new townships: Romany Square and Roccaforte. Luca and Tommaso were a force to be reckoned with, and many of the Italian families arriving in New England gravitated to them. In order to expand their control, Tommaso moved across the river and Luca remained in La Riva. Then in the early thirties, they petitioned the State for secession from Providence County to form a new county."

My brows furrowed. He was giving me an in-depth history lesson but still omitting crucial facts.

Releasing a frustrated breath, I finally asked the question on the tip of my tongue. "Was Tommaso Capizola a mobster, Papá?"

The blood drained from his face, his fist curling against his polished mahogany desk. "Just how much did you research?" His brow rose.

"Enough."

The temperature cooled as he inhaled a long-ragged breath.

"Papá, I deserve the truth."

"The truth." It came out bitter. "I have spent my entire life trying to protect you from the truth, Arianne. Things you didn't need to know, that you still don't need to know."

"What really happened when I was thirteen?"

I remembered the day like it was yesterday. It was the end of the school day and Nora and I were walking to the car when suddenly, we were surrounded by my father's men. They ushered us into a different vehicle and took off at lightning speed. I'd been too scared to even ask what was happening, but Nora had kicked up a storm, demanding they tell us. Of course, they hadn't. They had simply delivered us into the awaiting arms of my parents, and Nora's mother. Father told me that my school was no longer safe, that there had been some kind of security breach. A fellow student had threatened to hurt me, and my father didn't want to risk my safety.

It was the last day I ever stepped foot into school.

Nora was transferred to the public high school in Roccaforte, and we never spoke about it again. My parents just wanted to keep me safe. I still had the best education, the best teachers and classes; I just had them all from the safety of our home.

"An attempt was made on your life." He said every word with precision, as if he couldn't take any chance of me misinterpreting them.

"An attempt on my life?" A shiver zipped down my spine. "You mean someone tried to... *kill* me?"

He nodded, a grim expression washing over him. "I thought you were safe at that out of county private school. It was off the radar. I didn't think he'd find you."

"Antonio Marchetti?" I staggered back, crumpling into the chair. "Antonio Marchetti tried to kill me?"

"We think he gave the order, yes."

"So you don't know for certain it was him?" A tiny seed of hope took root in my chest. Maybe this was all some big misunderstanding. Nicco's father didn't want me dead. It made zero sense. "It could have been—"

"The likelihood is that Antonio Marchetti called in the hit."

"H- hit?"

I'd seen all shades of my father's expressions, but I'd never seen him look so devastated as he did now.

"I'm sorry, mio tesoro. All I ever wanted was to protect you. You were safe here. Nothing could touch you."

He wasn't wrong there; our estate was like Fort Knox. But there was still something I didn't understand.

"What happened, Papá, between our family and the Marchetti?"

"That is a whole other story entirely," he said with an air of sadness.

"I have time. Besides, I think I've earned it."

"Figlia mia, so much like your mother." He ran a brisk hand over his face. "I guess you might as well know the full story. It all started with a woman, Arianne. My father's great-aunt, Josefina..."

Nora found me in my bedroom. I was sitting in the window, lost in my thoughts, looking out over the lawns that led down to the stream. "Ari," she said quietly. "Can I come in?"

"Sure."

"Your father said I might find you up here. Is everything—"

"He told me." My heart clenched. "He told me everything."

My best friend joined me on the seat. "It's true? About Nicco's family?"

I nodded. "My grandfather's aunt, Josefina, was promised to Nicco's grandfather's uncle, Emilio. They were to be married, but Emilio loved another, Josefina's brother's fiancée Elena. They ran off together. Josefina was devastated. My great-great-grandfather, Tommaso, too. But where her brother's pain turned to hatred, Josefina's turned to grief, and, eventually, she took her own life. Tommaso never recovered. It caused a huge rift between him and Luca Marchetti that spilled down the families. But it all came to a head when he finally tracked down Emilio and ordered his son to avenge Josefina and kill him."

"Holy crap," Nora breathed, her eyes alight with a strange mix of intrigue and horror. "What happened then?"

"Emilio's brother wanted vengeance, but Luca and Tommaso came to a truce. They knew any further bloodshed would greatly diminish their power. So they agreed to split the county. Tommaso Capizola would take the east side of the river: Roccaforte, the city, and what we now know as University Hill. And Luca took everything west of the river: Romany Square and La Riva.

"Tommaso died shortly after that, and Alfredo became head of the family. He carried so many demons over losing the love of his life and killing his best friend, that he wanted out of the life. Gradually, he started to clean up the family businesses, moving into legitimate ventures. His empire went from strength to strength while Luca's remaining son, Marco Marchetti, and his son, Francesco, Nicco's grandfather, positioned themselves as the mafia stronghold of Rhode Island."

It was strange. I'd been so shocked hearing my father recount the story, the real truth behind my family, and Nicco's. But telling Nora, I felt like a weight had been lifted.

"So your hotty really is a mafia prince?"

"It should matter, shouldn't it? Our history is painted with so much blood and hatred. I should run from Nicco and never look back. But..."

"But you can't." Nora smiled sadly.

"I don't think I can," I admitted. "It's like I feel him, in here." I touched a hand to my heart.

Just then, my cell phone vibrated, cutting the tension like a knife. I snatched it off the desk and scanned the message.

I shouldn't be writing this. I shouldn't even be thinking about texting you, and yet, here I am. Tell me what I'm supposed to do here, Bambolina. Tell me how I'm supposed to fix this?

I stared at Nicco's text, tears welling in my eyes. Nora tried to peek, but I covered my phone, holding it against my chest.

"That bad, huh?" Nora moved in closer, resting a hand on my arm.

"Tell me we're not doomed," I said. "Tell me there's a way for us to figure this out?"

"You're not doomed." Her voice was full of fake enthusiasm. "Feel better?"

"Not even a little." A fat tear rolled down my cheek.

"Hey, hey, no tears. He texted you. That's a good sign, Ari."

"Is it?" A weary sigh spilled from my lips. "Maybe we should make a clean break. My father will never let me see him again and his father wants me—" I swallowed the words.

"Wants what, Ari? What aren't you telling me?"

"My father thinks Antonio Marchetti tried to have me killed five years ago."

"HE WHAT?" She leaped up. "*That's* why you had to leave school? Sonofabi—"

"Nora..."

She held up a finger. "Let me have my moment, I deserve that much. I knew there was a whole history book's worth of bad blood between your families, but I didn't realize... dead." Her eyes grew to saucers. "He wants you *dead*."

"Maybe. Maybe not. But at least now I know my father wasn't irrationally overprotective." A weak smile tugged at my lips.

"This changes things, Ari. You have to know that? What if..." She mashed her lips together, but it was too late, I saw the guilt in my best friend's eyes. "What if this is all part of his father's master plan?"

My eyes fluttered closed as pain washed over me. "No," I whispered. "It's not possible."

It couldn't be.

What I felt was real. Every stolen glance and secret touch. Every kiss and fleeting moment. The connection between us wasn't a trick or game. Some cruel scheme to lure me into his father's claws. Nicco would never do that to me.

He wouldn't.

What do you really know about him, an unwelcome voice whispered.

"He wouldn't," I said, reading his text over again.

Before I could stop myself, my fingers flew over the screen.

. . .

I need to see you.

"What the hell, Ari?" Nora peered over, this time seeing every letter.

"I need to see him. I need to look him in the eye and see the truth."

"Hmm, in case you haven't noticed, we're in your house in the middle of your very fortified, very well protected estate. It's not like he can just stroll up and knock on the door. Besides, maybe you should give this some more thought. I'm worried about you." The panic in her expression faded.

"I can't explain it, Nora, but what I feel toward Nicco is..."

"He's your first crush, not to mention the fact he helped you that night. It's no surprise you feel a strong attachment to him. But everything is different now."

Everything was different.

I knew the soft brush of his lips, the gentle caress of his fingers. I knew the taste of his tongue and the way his heart beat like thousands of wild horses galloping across open fields. But it was all the little things too. Not to mention the tether I felt every time he was around.

Nicco and I were bound.

It defied all logic, disregarded all rational thought, and made me sound like a lovesick puppy. But I knew.

Deep in my soul, I knew Nicco was mine.

As much as I was his.

"I need to go back to Montague," I said with complete conviction.

"Have you lost your goddamn mind? Your father is never going to allow it, not now."

"Have you lost your balls?" I clapped a hand over my mouth, surprised by my words.

Nora stared at me in complete shock; her wide eyed at me, and me wide eyed at her. Then slowly, her mask cracked as laughter bubbled from her chest. She flung her arms around my neck, her hysteria wrapping me up in nothing but love and comfort. "You're right," she said. "You're totally right. What do you need from me?"

I pulled back to look at her and said without hesitation, "I need you to help me convince my father to let me go back to MU."

FOURTEEN

NICCO

"SPILL," Matteo said as he drove us back to my aunt's. My cell phone rested against my thigh; my fingers curled so tightly around the damn thing that I was surprised the screen didn't crack.

"Huh?"

"Whatever's on your mind, spill."

Where did I even begin?

I shouldn't have texted Arianne, but I had, and now she wanted to see me. She knew we were enemies, pitted on different sides, and yet, she *still* wanted to see me.

For all I knew, it could have been a trap. Some mindfuck scheme laid down by her father to teach me a lesson.

"It's her, isn't it? The girl you saved that night."

"I didn't save—"

"You know what I mean." He gave me some serious side-eye. "I know you, cous, and you haven't been the same since that night. All this anger and frustration, it's her."

"When the fuck did you get so intuitive?"

Matteo shrugged. "I pay attention."

I nodded, bending my leg to rest my foot against the glove compartment.

"So spill," he repeated. "I'm not going to give you shit like Enzo or tease you like our uncles. I'm here, Nicco, one hundred percent."

"You wouldn't believe me if I told you."

"Try me."

"Something happened that first night, Matt. I can't even... fuck, I feel like such a pussy saying this."

"You fell hard."

"Yeah, cous, I did. It's like I took one look into her scared honey brown eyes and drowned. I wanted to hunt down the motherfucker who hurt her and make him pay, but more than that, I wanted to protect her and make sure it never happened again."

"You think it made all the shit with your mom come back to the surface?"

I inhaled a sharp breath. "Maybe. I don't know. But there was something about her... something I couldn't forget."

"So... what happened?"

"I followed her."

"Let me guess, Intro to Philosophy?" The corner of his mouth kicked up.

"Yeah."

"Jesus, cous, she must have you tied up in knots to get you to sit through one of Mandrake's classes."

It had been worth it, though.

So fucking worth it to watch her eyes sparkle as the professor talked about free will and determinism. Watch how her breath had caught every time I inched closer, our legs brushing underneath the desks. I loved seeing how I affected her. Because, dammit, if she didn't affect me too.

"I took her to Blackstone Country Club; we made out under the fucking stars."

"You really are the Prince of Hearts." He punched my shoulder, chuckling.

"Fuck off with that bullshit."

"Relax, I'm only busting your balls. You really like her, don't you? So what's the problem?"

"She's..." The words stuck in my throat.

"Nicco, come on, cous." Matteo shifted, easing off the gas as he turned onto my aunt's street. "It can't be that bad."

"Oh, it's about as bad as it can get... She's... fuck. She's Arianne Capizola."

His foot slammed on the brake, sending me flying forward. My hand shot out just in time to break my fall against the dash. "Jesus, Matteo," I gritted out.

"Sorry, I just... Capizola. She's the *Capizola* princess?"

I jammed my fingers into my hair, scraping my scalp, and nodded slowly.

"Fuck," he exhaled.

Fuck, indeed.

Before I went into any more detail, I gave Matteo a chance to pick his jaw up off the floor. Bailey joined us in my apartment, and the three of us sat around, drinking beer, avoiding the huge fucking honey-eyed elephant in the room.

"Arianne Capizola, that's some bad fucking luck," Matteo said. "It's like fate thought you deserved to be dry-fucked in the ass."

"Whoa, dude," Bailey fake retched. "Bad fucking visual."

"Language," we both yelled at him.

"Just exactly how far have you two..." Matteo's brow lifted. "You know."

"Not *that* far."

"So Roberto Capizola won't be coming around to chop off your dick just yet."

"Oh, I wouldn't be so sure about that." I tipped my head back, letting my eyes drift closed, trying my best not to picture her. "What the fuck am I supposed to do here?"

"Have you spoken to her since?" Bailey asked.

I met his knowing gaze. "I texted her."

"And?" His eyes lit up. I knew the kid was rooting for us. I didn't get it. Hell, I didn't get any of this, but it was nice having him in my corner.

"She wants to see me."

"Of course she wants to fucking see you. It's probably a trap."

My eyes shifted to Matteo. "You think I don't know that."

"So what will you do?"

"I don't know yet."

"Enzo can't know," Matteo added. "Not yet, not until you've figured shit out."

"I know." The thought of lying to my best friend, a guy I trusted with my life, didn't sit well with me. But while I knew he'd take a bullet for me; I also knew he'd try to protect me from myself if that's what it took to make sure the family came out unscathed.

"Well, whatever you need from me, just say the word."

"Just like that?"

"Just like that." Matteo shifted forward, clasping his hands between his legs. "I'm loyal to *you*, Nicco, you should know that by now. I trust you and I trust your judgment. And if Arianne is the girl for you, then that extends to her. Besides, the idea of hurting an innocent... it doesn't sit right with me."

"Thanks, cous, I appreciate that. More than you know."

"Hey, me too," Bailey added. "I trust you too. And I've already been looking out for her."

"I know you have, kid. And I appreciate it."

"So you're going to meet her?"

"Yeah, I am."

Because I had to know. I had to know if everything I'd felt with Arianne was real.

I had to know if she wanted to fight for us too.

Turns out, I didn't have to figure out how to get to her. About thirty minutes after arriving at my place, Arianne had texted me. She was coming back to MU and she wanted to meet me. Tonight. That's how I found myself, hiding in the shadows, staring up at Arianne's window.

"Are you sure about this?" Bailey whispered.

"Nope, but do you have a better plan?"

"Okay," Matteo jogged beside us and inhaled a ragged breath. "The guy is all set."

"And he won't talk?"

"He's trustworthy."

"How much did you pay him?" I asked.

"Enough. Tell me the plan again."

"Your guy will turn up out front, demanding to see Nora. She'll come down and the two of them will get into it, keeping Capizola's guys on her. I'll climb the fire escape and slip into Ari's room."

"And if there's a bodyguard in there with her?"

"There isn't." I checked my cell phone again. Arianne and Nora had persuaded Roberto to let them return to MU under the watchful eye of her cousin, and a small army of his men. She'd concocted the entire plan. All I had to do was provide the distraction, in the form of Matteo's guy, and scale the fifteen-foot wall to her window balcony.

"You heavy?" Matteo asked me, and I nodded, feeling the weight of my pistol beneath my hoodie. "You get so much as a whiff of it being a set up and you give the signal, okay? I mean it, Nicco. I know you're in deep with her, but she's not worth getting sent down."

Another nod and I inched out of the shadows, waiting for her text. Two seconds later, my cell vibrated. I quickly scanned the message and jogged over to the wall. The building was fitted with fire escape ladders that made climbing to Arianne's window easy. Within a couple of minutes, I'd pulled myself over her small balcony. My knuckle rapped gently against the glass. She appeared, relief sparkling in her eyes as she opened the window and waited for me to climb inside. I immediately did a quick sweep of the room.

"You really thought I'd set you up?" There was a trace of hurt in her voice.

"Not you, your father."

"I am not my father, Nicco," she said, defiance burning in her eyes. "Just like you're not yours."

"But I'm not good, Arianne. I might not be my father, but I'm no saint either."

"Have you ever… killed anyone?" The words spilled from her lips. Before I could answer, she added, "Wait, I don't want to know."

"Bambolina…" I drew in a harsh breath as I stepped forward, drawn to her light. Her beauty.

"Oh my god, your face." Guilt swirled in her eyes. "I'm so sorry—"

"Don't you dare apologize for him."

"Does it hurt?" Arianne winced, reaching for me.

"I've had worse."

"Still, I hate that he did that to you. I had an interesting conversation with my father yesterday. He told me things... things about my family I didn't know. Things about you and your family. I keep telling myself it should matter...." She stared up at me, her eyes glittering with so much emotion I felt winded.

"But?" I whispered, stepping closer still.

"But I'm not sure it does. Everything I thought I knew about my family, my life... my legacy, it's all a lie."

"Some lies protect us."

"You're right." Arianne's lips curved into a sad smile. "Sometimes the truth is too much to bear."

"I would never hurt you." I reached out, tucking a strand of hair behind her ears.

"But you hurt other people? Men? Your enemies?"

"Men make their own history, but they do not make it as they please," I repeated the quote Mandrake had spoken in his first class. "I was born into this life, Ari, just as you were born into yours. It doesn't mean I like the hand I've been dealt, but it is mine nonetheless."

She slid her hands up my chest, pressing her head to them, and breathed in a gentle sigh. Everything else faded away. My arms hooked around her waist, anchoring us together.

This wasn't a trap.

Arianne was here with me because she felt it too.

Because she couldn't forget either.

"Our fathers will never agree to this," she whispered, finally giving me her eyes again.

"I can't give you up," I leaned down, brushing my lips over hers. "I won't."

Arianne's fingers curled into my hoodie, clawing at me with the same desperation I felt coursing through my veins. "He wants me dead."

The words echoed through my skull, and I jerked away, staring down at her. "What did you say?"

"Five years ago, I was at school; a private school out of state. It was just a normal day, until it wasn't. My father told me there had been a security breach, that another student had wanted to hurt me. That was the last day I ever set foot in school."

"I don't understand... What does that have to do with my father?"

Arianne looked at me with so much pain and regret, I felt my chest crack wide open. It hurt worse than any man's fist crunching against my ribs. "He ordered a hit on me, Nicco."

"No..." It rolled off my lips, piercing the air like a gunshot.

My father was many things. Cold. Calculating. Callous. But he would never—

"Five years ago?" Realization slammed into me. "When exactly?" I grabbed her shoulders. "When did it happen?"

"I..." Sadness washed over Arianne. "It was right before the holidays. I remember because we'd been practicing for the annual talent contest and I didn't get to perform."

I tore away from her, trying to do the math as I paced the room. But I already knew the answer, the truth rattling around my head.

"Nicco?" Arianne watched me as I slowed to a stop, dragging a hand over my face. "What is it? What's wrong?"

"My mother walked out five years ago. Gone, just like that. She left a note that she couldn't do it anymore. She could no longer stand at my father's side. She left us... and I think it might have something to do with you."

Nothing about my mother's disappearance made sense. Like most wives in the family, she'd stood by my father through thick and thin, through the good and bad, the endless string of goomars. But through it all she'd kept her dignity. And above all, she'd been a doting mother to me and Alessia.

Growing up, my father had a short fuse and a quick backhand. I'd watched countless times as he took his frustrations and anger out on her. As I got older, I defended her with my growing body. But she never once wavered in her loyalty, her vows, remaining steadfast at his side.

Until one day, she didn't.

It came out of the blue for my father. He had mellowed somewhat over time as Alessia and I got older. He was more attentive to her, showering her with gifts and affection. But when he sat us down, and told us she was gone, part of me wasn't surprised. I was relieved. Watching your father beat your mother until her pained cries filled the house was something I never wanted to witness again. It was ironic that a man of so much honor could be so cruel and violent.

"I- I don't understand." Arianne reached for me, the brush of her slim fingers sending shocks zipping through me. My head hung low and I looked at her, strands of my hair falling over my eyes. I'd never really talked to anyone about that day. About being a fourteen-year-old boy being told that your mother was gone. Alessia took it the hardest. She was only eleven and our mamma had been her world. She felt betrayed. Unable to understand how any mother could abandon her children like that.

"I want to tell you everything," I confessed, inching closer. Close enough that I could drop my chin on Arianne's head and tuck her into the hard lines of my body. "I can't explain it, but I want to bare my soul to you, Bambolina. But it's unfair of me to ask you to walk this life with me. A life where our families will never agree to us being together. A life filled with darkness when you deserve nothing but light."

She craned her neck to look at me. "Nicco." My name was a prayer on her lips. "I have spent the last five years bending to the will of others, to the will of my father. But I am no longer a child." Her palm rested against my face. "I choose you, Niccolò Marchetti. I choose us."

Leaning down, I fixed my mouth over hers. The second our lips touched, I felt it. Felt a sense of peace wash over me. Arianne was my sanctuary. She was the other half of my soul. Even if I walked away from her, I knew we would always find a way back together.

But I wasn't walking away.

Not now.

Not ever.

It would only be a matter of time before Arianne's identity was discovered, and then she wouldn't be safe, with or without me by her side. I'd stood by so many times when my father hurt my mother, I'd promised myself I would never do it again.

I'd promised *her* I would never do it again.

Maybe Arianne was my redemption? My shot at righting all my wrongs. I would never be a good guy. My soul was too black and dirty for that.

But I could be good... for her.

Arianne pushed up on her tiptoes, pressing her body closer to mine. My hands slipped down to the backs of her thighs, hoisting her against me. Her legs wrapped around my waist.

"I want you," she whispered. "More than I have ever wanted anything in my life."

"I am yours, Bambolina." I touched my head to hers, barely breaking the kiss. "I am yours and I will do whatever it takes to keep you safe, okay? But you have to trust me. You have to trust me, Arianne. No matter what happens, what you hear or see, you have to trust that whatever I do, whatever I say, it's to protect you. To keep you safe."

She nodded, tears spilling down her cheeks. "I trust you, I do. Just promise me we'll get through this. Promise me, we'll find a way to be together."

"I promise." I kissed her hard, pushing my tongue deep into her mouth, stroking it against hers. I wanted more. I wanted to lie her down on her bed and worship every inch of her skin. I wanted to take each one of her firsts and make them mine.

I wanted it all.

Her heart.

Her body.

Her soul.

But Capizola's men were right on the other side of the door. And I couldn't protect her if I was locked up behind bars, or worse, dead.

"I have to go now," I said, slowly lowering her to the floor. Arianne resisted, hugging me tighter. Her quiet sobs cutting me to the bone. "Ssh, Bambolina, don't cry." Cupping her face, I swiped the tears away with my thumb. "I'll figure this out, I promise. I just need time."

"Time." She nodded, swallowing her tears like the strong brave girl I knew she could be. "When will I see you again?"

"Soon. I'll text you." I started moving toward the window, but Arianne caught my wrist, leaping into my arms and kissing me again. My laughter was lost in the taste of her lips, her tongue moving against mine.

"This, us, it's real," she said against my mouth. "Tell me it's real, Nicco."

"It's real, Bambolina." I smoothed a hand over her head, pressing a final kiss to her forehead. Arianne watched as I climbed out of the window, the longing in her eyes matching my own as we silently said everything we hadn't been brave enough to say out loud.

I had to force myself to break the connection, hopping over the balcony and dropping onto the fire escape ladder. It groaned with my weight, the sound piercing the air. I held my breath, tucking my body against the wall. But nobody came.

Once my feet were firmly back on the ground, I jogged over to Bailey and Matteo, disappearing into the shadows.

"Thank fuck it wasn't a trap," Matteo said. "What happened?"

Bailey snickered. "Take a good guess."

"Hey." I gave him a pointed look. "We're... okay."

"Okay? You just risked everything to know the two of you are... *okay*?" Matteo smirked.

"Fuck off." This was awkward. How did I even begin to explain what I felt for her? That already, I felt like a part of me was missing.

"Relax," my cousin said after a beat. "I'm just busting your balls. I'm happy for you, cous." He clapped me on the back. "What's the plan now?"

"I don't know, but I found out something else."

"Yeah?"

"Yeah." Anger boiled beneath my skin. "My father tried to have her killed."

"What the fuck?" Even in the darkness, I could see the blood drain from Matteo's face.

"And that's not all," I said, my fists clenched at my sides. "I think that's why my mom left."

FIFTEEN

ARIANNE

"IS THIS REALLY NECESSARY?" I levelled Luis with a frustrated look.

"It's Mr. Capizola's orders I'm afraid."

"And what about if she has to pee?" Nora smothered a snicker.

"One of us must be with you at all times."

My brow rose and Luis shook his head. "Of course, you can visit the bathroom on your own. But make no mistake, Miss Capizola, we will be right outside."

"This is ridiculous." I grabbed Nora's hand and yanked her down the hall.

"It's not his fault, Ari," she said, shooting him an apologetic glance.

"I know, I'm just so... so annoyed."

"What did you really expect? He let you return after telling you that Antonio Marchetti,"—she stopped herself, waiting for a couple of girls to pass—"tried to, you know."

"But do they have to be so obvious?" Nixon was waiting at the end of the hall while Luis trailed behind us. There was no mistaking they were here to protect me. I'd heard the whispers as we made our way out of Donatello House, and I knew it wouldn't take long for the entire campus to learn that Arianne Capizola was in fact... me.

Over the weekend, it had seemed like a small price to pay to return here and be closer to Nicco. But in the harsh light of day, I'd realized the life of secrecy I once resented so much, was now looking like a walk in the park compared to this. People stopped in their tracks as we passed them. Gawking at me like I'd grown a second head. A faint rumble of whispers followed us, their speculations brushing up against me, making me bristle.

"Everyone's looking," I breathed, clutching Nora's hand tighter.

"You need to own this, Ari. You're Arianne freakin' Capizola for Christ's sake. Don't you dare cower."

Her words sank into me, making me stand taller. I *was* Arianne Capizola, and I could do this. Until Tristan and Scott swaggered over to us.

"Ladies," Scott said around a smug grin.

"What is this?" I refused to look at him, focusing only on my cousin.

"Your father didn't tell you?" There was a brief flash of guilt in his eyes. "We're here to chaperone you to class."

"Hate to break it to you," Nora said. "But I think you're two bodyguards too late."

Tristan gave Luis a sharp nod and they dropped back.

"What the hell is going on?" I leaned in closer to Tristan, my teeth clenched behind my lips.

"Relax, cous. I thought you'd prefer it this way. Luis and Nixon will be around, but at least this way you won't feel so suffocated."

"Don't be so sure about that," I grumbled.

"Arianne," he let out a heavy sigh. "Work with me here."

"Work with you?" I seethed. "You expect me to—"

"Ari." Nora squeezed my hand. "He's right. Let's get to class and figure the rest out later."

"That's the most sensible thing ever to come out of your mouth, Abato." Scott grinned.

"Fuck you, Fascini." She mouthed back.

"Okay, okay, this isn't doing anything but drawing more attention." Tristan ran a hand over his mouth. "The cat is out of the bag now. Soon everyone will know Arianne Capizola is on campus and your life will be—"

"Save me the lecture." I barged past Tristan and took off toward the building.

"Ari, wait." He snagged my wrist, catching up to me. "I'm sorry, okay? I was just following orders."

"Like you were just following orders when you failed to tell me the real truth of our family's legacy?"

His lips pressed into a thin line, his silence all the admission of guilt I needed.

"Whatever, *cousin*. You hurt him, Tristan. You hurt someone I—" I swallowed the words.

"Hurt someone you what?" His eyes narrowed at me.

"It doesn't matter. It's over." My stomach knotted. "Nicco is—"

"The enemy. He's the *enemy*, Ari. You need to remember that."

"I get it. My life has been flipped sideways; I don't need you making it worse."

"Jesus..." He blew out an exasperated breath. "Come here." Tristan pulled me into his arms and I went willingly. He had to believe Nicco was no one to me. Even if it did physically hurt me to pretend.

"I know you probably don't believe me, but I am sorry," he whispered into my hair.

I pulled back and gave him a weak smile. "Yeah," I sighed. "Me too."

His smile grew, and I knew then that my cousin didn't really know me at all. He didn't hear the lie behind my words. See the guilt glitter in my eyes. He truly believed I was the dutiful, docile daughter I had always been.

And that was something I could never forgive.

It didn't take long for news to travel. By the time lunchtime rolled around and we headed for the food court, people had begun to step aside to let me pass them. It was disconcerting to say the least.

"It's like you're freaking Moses or something."

"Moses?" I asked.

"Yeah, parting the seas."

I rolled my eyes at that. "Hopefully it'll pass soon."

"Not likely. You just went from being no one to someone..." Nora's voice drowned out when I found Enzo glaring at me. He was standing by the entrance to the food court, his icy stare burning into me.

"Ari, I said what do you... oh. *Oh.*" Nora exhaled, slipping closer to me. "He looks like you just killed his favorite puppy and he's plotting all the ways to get his slow and ever so painful revenge."

She wasn't wrong.

I kept my eyes ahead, ignoring him as we entered the busy food court. Silence descended over the room. It happened like a wave. Gentle at first, a few people nearest us, and then the table closest to them. But quickly it spilled over to the rest of the tables, until everyone was looking.

"Okay, then. Shall we...?" Nora's hand slid down my arm, grabbing my hand. "Together?"

"Together." Head held high, I tried my best to block it all out as we went to our favorite counter. Luis and Nixon stayed close, failing to blend in at all. Not that two immaculately dressed bodyguards ever could.

"Arianne?"

I turned to find Tristan's friend Sofia hovering. "Yes?"

"I just wanted to say, I didn't know... I mean, I thought I kind of recognized you, but I didn't..." She fumbled over the words and Nora snickered beside me. "Well, I guess what I wanted to say was, I'm sorry. And welcome to MU. If I can help with anything..."

"I think we're good." Nora stepped forward. "But thanks for the offer, Cynthia."

"Uh, Sofia, my name is Sof ... aaaand you already know that. I guess, I'll just be..." She spun on her heel and took off toward her friends. Emilia's mouth hung open as if she couldn't believe what had just happened. But then she trained her eyes on me, narrowing them, her expression drenched with jealousy.

"God, that felt good."

"Really, Nor?"

"What? She deserved it. Now she knows her place and we can move on with life."

It sounded great in principle. But I wasn't sure anything would ever be the same again. Then I felt him.

Nicco.

"What is it?" Nora asked, her brows furrowed with concern as I stood there, holding my tray, frozen in place.

"Nicco," his name left my lips in a single breath. I didn't look over my shoulder. I didn't have to.

"He's sitting with Enzo and their friends."

"What are you getting?" I asked, trying to act normal. Trying to resist the urge to abandon my lunch and run to him and ask him to take me far away from here.

But I'd made him a promise, and I intended on keeping it.

"The Asian noodles look good." Nora played along.

"They do." I gave my order to the server and thanked her. As she handed me the bowl, she said, "Is it true? Are you Roberto Capizola's daughter?"

Even the servers had heard the news? I didn't know what to do with that.

"I am."

Wonder filled her crinkled eyes. "Wow, that's... Sorry, I'm being rude." Her cheeks flamed. "It's just... I always wondered what happened to you."

My brows furrowed. "You know my family?"

"I used to serve your father when he was a student here. Such a wonderful young man, so generous and gracious. I always hoped to meet his daughter one day."

"What's your name?"

"Lili."

"It's nice to meet you, Lili."

The woman smiled at me as if I'd just given her the greatest gift in life. "You ignore the rest of them."

Luis moved closer, his proximity irritating me. "Is there a problem?" I asked.

"Nothing to report." His reply was clipped.

"Please don't tell me you're concerned about Lili being a threat?" I whisper-hissed at him. Thankfully, Nora had engaged the women in which dish to get.

"Miss Capi—"

"Arianne. My name is Arianne, and I get it, you're here on my father's orders. But this isn't working for me, Luis. It's college, my life. You need to back off."

"Yes, Mis..." He cleared his throat. "Arianne. I'll be right over there." He joined Nixon, the two of them talking in their usual hushed tones.

"Ready?" I asked Nora, and she nodded.

"Don't be a stranger, Arianne," Lili said.

"Thank you."

Nora went first, weaving through the tables of curious stares and veiled whispers. She chose the table we'd sat at last week. We had no sooner sat down when Tristan and Scott appeared with even more friends in tow.

"What's good?" My cousin dropped down beside me and slung his arm over the back of my chair.

"You, sitting elsewhere?" Nora snickered.

"I have something you can sit on," one of Tristan's friends jammed his hand under the table, grabbing his crotch. The guys all exploded with laughter, but it quickly died down when Tristan glared at them.

"Don't mind them," he said. "Their default setting is asshole."

"Baciami il culo," one of the guys grumbled, flipping my cousin off.

"So what are your plans tonight?"

"There are no plans. We'll probably just do some reading and hang out at the dorm."

"You should come over to the house and hang out."

"That's a joke, right?"

"Ari, cut me some slack. It isn't party central all the time, and I know Scott would like to—"

"Tristan, how many times do I have to say it? There is no me and Scott."

"Because of him." His eyes slid over to where Nicco was sitting, and I felt the anger radiating off my cousin. Thankfully, Nicco wasn't looking at us, but he had been.

I'd felt him.

"This has nothing to do with Nicco."

"So come over later. We have a movie room. We can watch whatever you want. Most of the guys will be out. It'll be fun."

Panic flooded me. Was this a test? Had my father asked him to watch me? To make sure I didn't try to see Nicco?

My fist clenched against my jeans as I said, "We could come over for a little while."

Nora caught my eye and mouthed, "What the hell?"

"That's great, Ari. You won't regret it, I promise."

"On one condition, Tristan," I added, erasing his smile. "You stop with the me and Scott stuff, okay?"

"Sure, I can do that. I'm just happy we'll get to hang out. It's long overdue."

My cell phone vibrated, startling me. Tristan roped his arm around my neck and pulled me in, kissing my cheek. "I need food." He left and the other guys followed.

"What the hell was that?" Nora wasted no time, but I was too busy digging out my cell phone, my heart catapulting into my mouth when I saw Nicco's number.

. . .

What was that about?

God, I wanted so desperately to look at him. To stare into his eyes and tell him it was nothing more than me playing a part.

It's nothing, don't worry.

I will always worry about you. Every second of every day.

"Ari," Nora whispered, and I looked up to find some of the guys returning to our table. Shoving my cell into my lap, I typed as quickly as I could.

I am yours and I will do whatever it takes to keep you safe, okay? But you have to trust me. Trust me, Nicco. No matter what happens: what you hear, what you see, you have to trust that I only do it to protect you.

He'd said something similar to me last night. But his words worked both ways. I wasn't the only one who needed protecting. I didn't doubt Tristan and my father would hurt Nicco again if they believed I was still seeing him. Which is why they needed to believe it was over. That he was no one to me. Which is why I had to play Tristan's games.

Another text came through.

I trust you.

Relief sank into me. I could do this.

We could do this.

Because the alternative, a world where I was forbidden from seeing Nicco, wasn't a world I wanted to live in.

"At least it's not full of football players," Nora whispered as we stepped into my cousin's house.

"You guys want a beer? Don't feel like you need to stand guard all night." Tristan grinned at Luis and Nixon. "She's safe here."

"You know our orders, Mr. Capizola."

"Yeah, yeah, my uncle is a stickler for orders. But it's my house. No one is getting in or out without me knowing about it. Besides, you can protect her and still relax. Have a beer, grab a seat, fai come se fossi a casa tua. We'll be right down the hall in the movie room. Ladies." Tristan swept his arm in an arc. "This way."

The smell of fresh popcorn drifted down the hall as we followed him. Nora hadn't wanted to come, but she understood why I had to and decided she couldn't let me suffer alone.

"You came," Scott said the second we stepped foot into the room.

"Fascini, I'd say it's a pleasure," Nora quipped. "But it's really not."

"Bite me, Abato."

"Guys," Tristan groaned. "Can we try to not kill each other before the movie starts?"

It seemed like he really was trying. Away from all his friends, out from under the spotlight, Tristan wasn't a bad guy. He just enjoyed playing to a crowd. He liked status and power and money, and somewhere along the way, the cousin I'd grown up with had transformed into a man I barely recognized.

Part of me missed him, but part of me also knew we'd become different people.

"What movie do you want to watch?"

"Anything," I said, taking the seat furthest away from Scott. His heavy gaze lingered on the side of my face, but I refused to look at him. I could do this—sit here and watch a movie with him—but I wasn't about to pretend we were friends.

"Has your father talked to you about the Centennial Gala yet?" he asked.

Tristan clucked his tongue, levelling his best friend with a hard look.

"What?" Scott said. "It was only a question."

"No, he hasn't actually. Why?"

"It doesn't matter," Tristan replied. "The popcorn is getting cold."

He was deflecting, and I didn't like it. I made a mental note to ask my father about it.

Nora snagged a blanket off the back off the couch and shuffled closer to me, throwing it over our laps. "You might have to physically restrain me," she whispered through a tight-lipped smile, and I fought a snicker. Scott deserved her wrath, but he wasn't worth it.

"Get in line," I mouthed and we shared a secret smile.

"What are you two whispering about?" Tristan asked, grabbing the television remote and settling back into one of the chairs.

"Oh, nothing," Nora said. "So what are we watching?"

"I figured we'd stick to something safe. *Avengers Assemble.* Remember, Ari? It was one of your favorites growing up."

"I was ten, Tristan. I had a crazy crush on Chris Hemsworth."

The movie started and silence fell over the four of us. It was strange, sitting here with Tristan and Scott, in their frat house, pretending we were all friends. It felt fake. Like we were all waiting to see who would break out of character first.

Nora leaned over and grabbed one of the bowls of popcorn, shoving a handful in her mouth. "Might as well make the most of it," she grumbled, offering me the bowl.

I wasn't hungry—being around Scott was enough to kill my appetite—but I took a handful. It was a distraction. Something to stop me saying something I might later regret.

Two hours later, the film was finished and Nora didn't wait a second longer to make our excuse to leave.

"This has been nice and all," she gave Tristan a saccharine sweet smile. "But I have a thing and I need Ari's opinion."

"Thing?" Scott drawled. "Is that code for some freaky sex move?"

"Nora's right, we should go. But thanks for... the popcorn."

"Come on, cous, stay, hang out." Tristan leaped up. "I'm pretty sure we have some wine coolers in the refrigerator."

"Maybe another time." When hell froze over.

"Sure, okay. Let me walk you out." Tristan led the way, but the second he stepped into the hall, Luis and Nixon stood to attention. "Arianne and Nora would like to return to their dorm."

"Arianne and Nora can speak for themselves." I reminded my cousin. He ran a brisk hand over his head, amusement dancing in his eyes.

"You've changed," he said.

"So have you."

Something passed between us, but I couldn't quite figure out if it was a mutual feeling of respect or resentment. Maybe a mix of both.

"I need to pee," Nora announced.

"Back down the hall, last door on the left."

"I'll be two minutes," she said to me.

"Go, I'll be fine."

No sooner had she disappeared, did Tristan move toward the door with Luis and Nixon. The three of them were discussing something, talking so quietly I could barely make out anything they were saying.

"This game you're playing is cute." Scott stepped up beside me, his proximity setting my teeth on edge.

"Game?"

"You're not fooling anyone, princess, especially me." His warm breath hit the back of my neck, sending a deep shudder rolling through me.

"I have no idea what you're talking about." I hissed, refusing to look at him. But Scott stepped closer, his hard chest brushing up against my shoulder.

"It's okay," he drawled. "I enjoy the chase."

My body began to tremble. Anger. Fear. It swirled inside me like a vortex.

"Please get away from me," I ground out, keeping my eyes on Tristan, willing him to look over at us. But he and Luis were deep in conversation.

"Sorry I took so—"

Scott darted away from me and I released the breath I'd been holding. "There you are." I turned to Nora who was looking at me funny. She flicked her eyes to Scott who pretended to be checking his cell phone, and back to me.

"We should go," I said.

Tristan and my bodyguards fell into silence as we reached them. I raised a brow. "Is there a problem?"

"No problem." Tristan slung his arm around my shoulder. "Thank you for coming. I know you're still pissed at me but we're still family, Arianne. Us Capizola need to stick together."

Nora let out an exasperated breath and slipped around us, pulling the door open. "Goodnight, Tristan," I said, following her and Luis outside.

"Okay." Nora shuffled close beside me. "What do you think your cousin is up to?"

"You caught that, huh?" I glanced to Luis, and then Nixon, who was following behind us.

"I know he's family, Ari," she lowered her voice to a whisper, "but I don't trust him."

I didn't either.

Not anymore.

The vibration of my cell phone startled me, and I dug it out of my pocket.

I need to see you.

You can't risk it.

I would risk anything for you.

Nicco...

Bambolina, I need to see you. Don't make me beg...

"Is it...?"

I silenced Nora with a hard look. There were too many people listening. People loyal to my father.

. . .

We're just walking back to our dorm.

I know.

My eyes went wide as I searched the surrounding area. It was dark though, long leafy shadows dancing over the sidewalk winding through campus.

I can't see you.

It should have felt all kinds of creepy that Nicco was watching me, but it didn't.

Then you're not looking hard enough.

I smothered a smile, walking taller, knowing that Nicco was out there somewhere.

"Oh, you have it so bad." Nora smirked. "I guess you'll be wanting me to make myself scarce when we get back to the dorm?"

"I don't know, we shouldn't..."

"But we both know you will. Just promise me you'll be careful, okay?"

"Where will you go?" I mouthed, keeping one eye on Luis. But he was too focused on our surroundings.

"I'm not against making a booty call."

"Kaiden?"

She shrugged. "Or Dan."

"Hussy."

"Hey, Lu," she called, and Luis glanced over his shoulder. "I'm going out. Is that a problem?"

"I'll let Maurice know."

"Maurice?"

"He's assigned to you."

"I have my own bodyguard?"

"He's on your assignment, yes."

"Cool. But you should probably tell Maurice he might want to bring earplugs."

I quickly typed out a reply to Nicco.

. . .

Nora's going out. I'll be all alone.

His response was instant.

Leave the window open.

SIXTEEN

NICCO

I WAITED.

Almost an hour had passed since I'd seen Arianne enter her building, flanked by her bodyguards. She walked with such poise and grace. Her entire world had been flipped upside down, and yet; my brave, strong girl carried herself with confidence.

She carried herself like her father.

I wondered if she realized how similar they were, minus the fact her father was a scheming traitorous asshole.

Arianne hadn't texted me again. It was possible she had fallen asleep. But then her slender shadow appeared at the window, her eyes searching the tree line below for me. Pulling up my hood, I ducked into the darkness and followed the path to the building. I knew MU campus well enough to know every blackspot in the security cameras, every place to hide and remain out of sight.

Climbing the fire escape with ease, I pulled myself onto her balcony. Arianne had disappeared, but the window was open, the curtains billowing in the gentle breeze.

"You came," she whispered.

"You thought I wouldn't?" Stepping into the room, my eyes landed on her sitting on the edge of her bed in nothing but an oversized MU t-shirt.

Fuck.

I swallowed.

"It's been an hour." She looked up at me through her thick lashes, a playful smile tipping the corner of her mouth.

"Were you waiting for me?" I dragged a thumb over my bottom lip as I stalked toward her. Dropping to my knees, I ran my hands up her legs, ankles to thighs. A soft moan slipped from her lips.

"Nicco..."

"Does Fascini have a thing for you?"

She reared back, eyes fixed on mine. "Why would you say that?"

"I've seen the way he watches you, Bambolina." And I fucking hated it. "What were you doing at their house?"

"Tristan wanted us to hang out."

"With the football team?" My brow rose, anger simmering in my veins. I'd almost lost it when I'd watched them disappear into the house. I wasn't supposed to be following her, but after her text at lunch, about doing whatever it took to protect me, I found myself texting Bailey. Between us, we'd watched Arianne all day.

"No, it was just me, Nora, Tristan, and..."

Her gaze dropped to the floor. I slid a finger underneath her chin and forced her to look at me.

"And?"

"And Scott."

"He wants you."

"Well, he can't have me," she said with fierce conviction.

"Yeah, and why is that?"

"Because I'm yours."

"Damn right, you are." My hand slid up Ari's body, my fingers splaying across one side of her neck as I kissed her hard. She looped her arms around my neck, her legs hooking around my waist, anchoring us together.

"I want you, Nicco," she murmured against my lips.

Jesus. She was testing my patience.

"Not here, not like this,"—my eyes flicked the door—"with your bodyguard right outside."

"You don't want to?" Arianne's expression fell.

"I do. So much. See what you do to me." Grabbing one of her hands, I pulled it down between us, letting her feel how hard I was. "When I finally make you mine in every way possible, I don't want to worry about who might hear you scream my name".

"Oh." The cutest blush worked its way up her neck and flooded her cheeks.

"I didn't come here for that, not tonight. I came to make sure you were okay." *I needed to see you were okay.*

"Because you were jealous." A faint smirk tugged at her lips.

"I will always be jealous where you're concerned. You think it doesn't kill me knowing I can't be the one to stand at your side?"

"Nicco, I didn't..." She fisted my hoodie, letting out a resigned sigh. "It hurts me too."

"I know, Bambolina, I know." I crushed Arianne into my arms. The sound of her soft sobs gutted me. I wanted to tell her everything would be okay, to reassure her I had a plan. But the truth was, I had no fucking idea how I was going to fix this. There was too much history between our families, too much hate.

"Come here." I stood up, taking Arianne with me, cradling her body against mine. Walking around to the side of the bed, I managed to pull back the covers and lie her down.

"You're leaving, already?"

"I'm not going anywhere." I kicked off my boots. "Scoot over." I laid down beside her and wrapped my arm around Arianne, pulling her close.

"This is nice," she whispered.

"I've never done this before," I confessed.

"You've never snuggled? That's kind of sad."

"I've snuggled. Alessia and my mom. But I've never snuggled with a girl."

"So I'm your first?" Arianne gazed up at me, a goofy smile plastered on her face. "I like that. I like that I get some of your firsts too."

"Tell me something..."

"Anything," she replied.

"Was it Scott who hurt you?"

"Wh- what? No... no, Nicco."

"You're sure?" I narrowed my eyes. "Because the way he looks at you..."

Ari moved onto her knees, cupping my face in her hands. "It wasn't Scott. It was nobody. Just a guy I stupidly agreed to go out with. Forget about him, Nicco. Please."

"The idea of someone touching you, Arianne, of putting their hands on you. It makes me murderous."

"Ssh." She leaned in, kissing my jaw. "Don't talk like that." Her lips brushed mine, but I curved my hand around the back of her neck, holding her still.

"I would kill for you, Arianne. That's who I am. I might not like everything about my life, my legacy, but this life, the codes I am bound to, run through my blood."

"I... I understand." Her voice quivered.

"This... us, it's not fleeting for me. I'm not going to decide in a week or a month I no longer want you." I smoothed my thumb down her cheek. "If you want out, now is the time to tell me."

"You'd let me walk away?" Surprise clung to her words.

"You could try."

"But you just said..."

"Just because you want to walk away, doesn't mean I won't do everything in my power to win you back. You're mine, Arianne Carmen Lina Capizola. Forever."

"Forever... that's a big promise to make."

"Does it scare you?"

"What?"

"To know that you're mine. To know that I already love you completely. Heart, body, and soul."

"Nicco..." Her eyes fluttered closed as she drew in a shaky breath.

"I don't need to hear it back." I kissed the end of her nose. "Not yet. But you need to know this is not a game to me. It's real, Arianne. And nothing or no one is ever going to take you from me."

Fixing my mouth over hers, I sealed my promise with a kiss. Our tongues met in deep unhurried strokes that reverberated through me. Ari took me by surprise, sliding her leg over mine and settling above me.

"Bambolina, are you trying to kill me?"

"Ssh." She kissed me again. "Stop talking and just let go and feel."

Oh, she was a clever girl, constantly throwing my own words back at me. But I didn't stop her, I couldn't. She felt too fucking good, grinding down on me. Riding me, even if there were layers and layers between us.

My hands dipped under her t-shirt, running over her warm, smooth skin. "We should stop..." The words held no meaning as I slowly dragged the material up her body. Arianne lifted her arms and let me pull it over her head.

"You're right, we should definitely stop." Her hands went to my hoodie, curling around the hem. I sat up, helping her yank it off. Her eyes drank me in, roaming over my tattoos, the tiny white scars littering my skin. Her fingers followed, ghosting over every blemish.

"What's this one?" Her thumb brushed a larger scar running beneath my last rib.

"Stab wound," I admitted. There was so much I couldn't tell her: family business, secrets that I would take to the grave, but I wanted to give her the parts of me I could.

"This one?" She shuffled back, giving her more space to lean down and inspect my chest.

"Brass knuckles, split my skin clean open."

Arianne winced, but didn't stop her exploration. "And this one?" Her fingers hovered precariously close to the button of my jeans.

"What are you doing, Bambolina?"

She worked the button free without hesitation. "I want to touch you."

I hissed as her hand dipped inside, grazing the tip of my dick. "If anyone catches me in here with you..."

"You could be inside me, instead."

"Jesus, Arianne." My heart crashed violently in my chest as she continued stroking me as if she was born to do it.

"This is a bad idea," I rasped. It was pointless though. I was weak against her touch. How good her hand felt wrapped around me.

"I want to taste you," she whispered.

"Ari, you don't have to..." But she was already slipping down the bed, working my jeans off my hips. My fingers slid into her hair, involuntarily guiding her parted lips forward.

"What do I do?" she asked.

"Whatever you want."

Arianne took her time, flicking her tongue over the head and running it down my shaft. She was cautious at first, taking an inch into her mouth, sucking and licking, tasting and teasing. But her confidence grew with my moans of encouragement.

"Jesus, you feel... Fuck." The words got stuck as she took me further into her mouth, her hand pumping me hard and fast.

"Bambolina," I tugged her hair gently. "I'm going to come."

She reached for my hand, tangling our fingers together, keeping her lips firmly around me. My body began to tremble, a familiar tingling building at the bottom of my spine.

"Ari, fuck... that's... Jesus." I clenched down as pleasure shot through me. Arianne's soft laughter filled the air as she sat up, flushed and starry-eyed. "That was fun," she said with a hint of pride as she licked her lips.

"You are amazing." I leaned up to kiss her, but someone banged on the door.

"Arianne?" A deep voice rumbled.

"Crap." She scrambled off the bed. "You should go. He'll want to see me, to know I'm okay."

My hoodie landed on my head as she began pulling her own t-shirt back on. It would have been enough to kill my post-blow job high if it wasn't for the fact she looked so adorable.

"Come here." I stood up, hooking my finger in her belt loop.

"Nicco, this is serious. You need to—"

"Arianne?" Another knock.

"I'm just changing, Luis. I'll be right there."

"You need to go." She gazed up at me.

"And I will. But not before I do this." I claimed her lips in a deep kiss, tasting myself on her tongue. I'd never been into all that before, but with her it was different.

Everything was.

"You taste so fucking good." I buried my hands into her hair, kissing her again. "Maybe I should come all over your body so I can lick it off."

"Nicco, God..." It was a breathy sigh.

I walked us backward to the window, refusing to break the kiss. But eventually, she pressed her hands against my chest and tore away. "I do too, you know."

"Yeah, and what's that?"

"I love you, Niccolò Marchetti." Arianne pressed a single kiss to my lips. "But if Luis storms in here and finds you, I will never forgive you. So please, go."

I smirked, and she frowned. "What?"

"Until next time, Bambolina."

Before she could reply, I ducked out of the window and hurled myself over the balcony. My body slammed against the ladders, but it was nothing I couldn't handle.

Arianne had that effect on me.

She made me feel invincible.

Made me feel like I could fly.
She was everything I never knew I needed.
And she was mine.

I didn't make it back to my apartment. After I left Arianne, my father had called telling me to get straight over to L'Anello's. You didn't tell the boss no, so that's how I found myself standing outside the club a little after midnight, waiting for Enzo and Matteo to show up.

My cousin's headlights lit up in the distance, and I climbed off my bike, waiting. He pulled up right outside and killed the engine. "What's happening?" he asked the second he climbed out of the car.

"Jimmy called my old man, said some guys were causing trouble."

"So, why couldn't Jimmy's guys handle it?"

"Because it's the guy from the other night, the one I fought at Hard Knocks."

"You're shitting me?" Enzo fell into step beside me as we entered the club.

"Seems he didn't get the message the first time around."

"So what's the plan?"

"The plan is to make sure he leaves here tonight knowing not to come around here again."

Matteo let out a long yawn.

"I'm sorry," I said, "are we keeping you awake?"

"Shit, sorry, Nic. I stayed up to help Arabella with her homework, that shit is enough to send anyone to sleep."

"You know you could hire her a tutor, you have the money," Enzo suggested.

"I know, but she likes me to help her and I don't mind. She's my kid sister. Someone's got to look out for her."

"It's a good thing you do, cous." I clapped him on the back. "Everyone stay cool, okay? I don't want this to become something bigger than it needs to be."

The second we stepped foot into the place, heads turned and a low rumble of whispers followed us as we moved deeper into the club.

"Hey, fellas," one of the servers greeted us. "I think Jimmy's expecting you downstairs."

"Thanks, Cassandra." Matteo flashed her a smile.

"Anytime, baby. You know, you should call me, you have my number."

"Another time," he mumbled. "Duty calls." Matteo ducked ahead of us, and Enzo snickered.

"Don't be a dick," I warned. "And whatever you do down there, do not lose your cool. Capisci?"

We took the dimly lit hall toward the back of the building where Jimmy ran the fight ring. It was a lucrative venture with monthly fight nights bringing in anywhere between ten to twenty-five grand.

Enzo shifted beside me, slipping his hand inside his jacket, and I knew he was either feeling for his pistol or one of his many blades.

"E, chill."

"I'm chill," he mumbled. "I just like to be prepared."

The reinforced steel door loomed up ahead. Matteo banged on it twice and the peephole opened. The guy took one look at us and opened up. "Nicco." He gave me a nod. "Been waiting for you to get here. Guy over there says you owe him."

"I don't owe anyone anything, Bobby, you know that."

"Told him as much. But the asshole refused to leave before he got an audience with you."

"Don't worry, I'll handle it."

Jimmy was busy over near the ring, no doubt taking bets for the next fight. He was a trusted associate; not of the bloodline, but someone who had worked with the family for most of his life. He was as loyal as they came. Killian was at the bar, surrounded by a few guys as big and tatted up as him. A couple of them wore leather cuts depicting a biker gang operating out of Providence.

Just what we needed, a biker gang in Marchetti territory.

"Shit, cous, he brought back up." Enzo was like a livewire beside me, itching for a fight. Matteo was quiet, no doubt contemplating all the ways this could go in our favor, or not.

And me?

I only had eyes for the guy whose face I'd already rearranged once.

He spotted me approaching and pushed his friends aside to stand and greet me. "You owe me, kid," he said.

"I already put you on your ass once, old man. I'm surprised you want to go a second round."

The room had fallen quiet, everyone watching as we went head to head.

"Cazzo sí!" he grunted but I ignored him.

"I see you brought some friends." I looked each of them over. "Did you tell them who I am?"

Confusion crinkled their faces. "What's he talking about, Kill?" one of them asked.

Enzo snorted beside me. "Oh, you didn't, did you? You let them come here without giving them all the information."

"Fuck you," Killian spat, and Enzo lurched forward. My arm flew out, blocking him.

"You want a rematch, is that it?" I narrowed my eyes at Killian.

"I want my pound of flesh, kid, sure."

"Too bad. I'm not looking to break a sweat tonight. Do yourself a favor and go back to whatever hole you crawled out of. You're no longer welcome here. Jimmy, show the guy the door." I spun on my heel but didn't get very far. A heavy hand landed on my shoulder yanking me back. A collective gasp filled the air as my hand went inside my jacket and I pulled out my pistol. Releasing the safety, I whipped around and pointed it straight at Killian.

"You dare to touch me?"

"Whoa." His hands went up, the blood draining from his face. "Easy, kid. I didn't mean no harm."

Stepping forward, I pushed the barrel of the pistol into his forehead, watching as beads of sweat rolled down his face. "Who am I?"

"W- what?" he stuttered.

"Who. Am. I?" I seethed, Matteo and Enzo at my side, staring down Killian's guys. Jimmy's guys had closed in too, forming a semi-circle around us.

"Nic..." his voice quivered. "Niccolò Marchetti."

A couple of his guys grumbled. "You brought us here to start shit with a Marchetti? Antonio Marchetti's son?"

"What the fuck did you think we were coming for?" Killian hissed. "This is La Riva, it's Marchetti territory."

He had a point. I raised a brow at his friends.

"Hey, man, we got no beef with you or your family." One of them stepped forward, hands up in surrender. "Killian said—"

"I think we've all established *Killian* needs to learn to keep his fucking mouth shut," Enzo said.

"Is he a member of your MC?" I asked.

"Hell no, but he is family. I can see we made a bad judgment call coming here. The Providence Phantoms have no beef with you."

"You should probably leave then." My eyes flicked to the door.

"What will you do with him?" They hesitated, glancing between me and their friend.

Killian was still sweating on the end of my pistol.

"Nothing less than he deserves." I pressed the barrel harder, angling it downward so he had no choice but to drop to his knees. "Who am I?" I repeated my question from earlier.

"Niccolò Marchetti," he rushed out.

"Wrong answer. Who am I?"

He began trembling; a grown ass man cowering in front of me like a small child.

"I am your worst fucking nightmare. Step foot in La Riva again and I'll put a bullet between your eyes, you feel me?"

"I- I feel you... please, don't hurt me. Don't—" I smashed the butt of my pistol against his face, sending him flying backward. His friends hauled him up and dragged him out of the room.

"What?" I asked Enzo who was staring at me.

"You should have at least shot him in the kneecap. Fucker deserved it."

"We're not all as trigger happy as you." Besides, I was a capo. A captain. One of my father's third-in-command. I couldn't just shoot a guy in cold blood in front of a room full of people. It wasn't how we operated.

It wasn't how *I* operated.

Fear commanded respect just as much as action when you carried a name like Marchetti. Hopefully Killian would heed my warning and never set foot in La Riva again.

Because if he did, I'd have to make good on my promise.

"Nicely handled." Jimmy came over and clapped me on the shoulder.

"Yeah, well, we'll see." I tucked my pistol back in its holster. "Hopefully he won't come sniffing around here again."

Jimmy led us over to the bar. "Three of our finest, Darla. You boys okay if I go take care of business?"

"Sure thing, Jimmy." Enzo shook his hand, and the old man disappeared.

"Here you go, on the house." The server placed down three glasses of Bourbon. "Nice to see you again, Enzo." She let her heavily made up eyes rake over his body, earning her a wicked smirk from my cousin.

"Looking good, Darl," he drawled.

Matteo rolled his eyes, leaning back against the bar, watching as Jimmy got the next fight underway.

"Hey, Nicco."

My eyes shuttered as I rubbed my temples. "Rayna," I said, slowly turning to find her standing there.

"It's been a while." She smiled coyly.

"Yeah."

"You didn't call." A crestfallen expression slid over her face.

"What was the point?"

She inhaled a shaky breath. "Can we maybe go somewhere and talk?"

Rayna looked good in tight-fitting jeans and a black oversized sweater that hung off one shoulder. Her dark hair hung in waves down her back framing her face. But she no longer set my body on fire the way she once had.

"I don't think so, Ray," I said. "Not tonight."

"So that's it? You're really throwing away everything—"

I stepped into her personal space, narrowing my eyes. "This is not the time or the place."

"So come, talk with me". She curled her hand around my arm as if she owned me. "I missed you, Nicco. I missed us."

There had been a time when I saw myself and Rayna being more than bed partners. She'd grown up in the life. Knew more than most girls. Knew what it meant for someone like me.

Rayna made it easy. She didn't ask questions or dig for dirt. But I never fell hard for her. Not the way I had for Arianne. Being with Rayna had been like a warm, spring day; comfortable and easy, requiring little effort. But being with Arianne was like the sun. Intense and hot and if you got too close you were bound to get burned. But it was a risk you would gladly take just to say you'd been in its orbit.

I removed Rayna's hand, dropping it at her side. "It's done," I said, devoid of emotion. "We're done."

Surprise flashed in her eyes, but she didn't stick around, storming off in a huff.

"Have you lost your damn mind?" Enzo grumbled. "Rayna just offered it up to you on a silver platter and you turned her down?"

"Have you forgotten, she slept with some coglione while I was seeing her?"

"You weren't exclusive though."

"It doesn't matter," I replied, not wanting to get into it with him. "It's done."

"She's got you all tied up in knots, cous; it's not healthy."

"What did you just say?" My hand clenched into a fist. Surely, he didn't mean...

"Now that the Capizola princess is walking around campus like she owns the fucking place. I can't say that I blame you."

"Oh... that. Yeah, it's a problem." I ran a hand through my hair, shooting Matteo a silent cry for help.

"If you ask me, she's innocent in all of this," he said. "I mean, he kept her locked away for years. Imagine how she must feel. It doesn't feel right using her as leverage."

"It is what it is." Enzo shrugged. "The way I see it, we're at war, and innocent people always get caught in the crossfire. That's how it goes."

I snatched up my glass and downed it in one. "I need to ride. I'll catch you guys tomorrow."

"But, Nicco, we should talk about—"

Enzo's words melted into silence as I walked away from them.

I needed air, before I said something I would live to regret.

SEVENTEEN

ARIANNE

THREE DAYS PASSED.

I didn't see Nicco much. There were no late-night visits, and he didn't appear in Mandrake's class again. Instead, I had to survive on stolen glances across the food court and a few heated text messages. I felt him though. Felt his eyes follow me around campus. Sometimes I was sure I could feel him nearby, but when I searched for him, I never caught so much as a glimpse.

"You're restless," Nora said as we entered the food hall. It was Friday and I was looking forward to the weekend. At least then I could avoid my classmates and their curious stares. It had gotten somewhat easier to walk into a room and have everyone look, whisper, and point, but I was more than ready for a break from feeling like an exhibit at the zoo.

"That's weird," Nora stared at her cell phone. "Mamma said, 'see you over the weekend'. I haven't—"

My cell phone began ringing. I dug it out my purse and sighed. "It's my mother. Hello."

"Arianne, figlia mia, how is it?"

"It's college, Mamma. It has its moments."

"But you're okay?" she went on. "I've been so worried."

"Luis and Nixon never let me out of their sight. And if I'm not being guarded by them, it's Tristan. I'm quite safe."

"Good, that's good. If anything were to happen to you..."

"Nothing is going to happen." I rolled my eyes at Nora who smirked.

"Suzanna is coming over tomorrow and we thought it might be nice if you joined us."

"Me, but why?"

"We're discussing the final preparations of the Centennial Gala, and well, your opinion would mean a great deal to us."

"It would?"

"Of course. Besides, it's time you start embracing your role within the family, Arianne."

"Fine, I'll be there." She let out a small shriek of approval, but I quickly moved on. "There was something I wanted to talk to you about actually. I've signed up to help at the local shelter. But I'm worried father will—"

"Oh what a wonderful idea. I'll handle your father. You should probably talk to the coordinator and shelter staff about your... situation though. If you're going to have Luis and Nixon with you it might be intimidating for some of their clients."

"You're right. I didn't think of that. I'll call them later."

"Oh, I'm so proud of you. You have such a big heart, Arianne. You're going to do wonderful things. I can feel it in my bones."

"We'll see you tomorrow then."

"We?" It was her turn to sound confused.

"Yeah, Nora will be coming with me."

"Oh, yes, of course. I'm sure she'd like to see her parents. Until tomorrow."

"So I gather we're going home for the weekend?" Nora asked the second I hung up.

"She wants me to help her and Suzanna Fascini with the final preparations for the Gala."

"Oh fun... not." Nora piled some salad onto her plate. "Have you spoken to him?"

I glanced around to check for eavesdroppers. "Only through text. After the other night..."

"Yeah, that was a close call. You can't be reckless, Ari. Not with the Muscle Twins watching your every move."

"I know." I hadn't intended to let things go so far the other night with Nicco. But every moment with him felt finite, like we were racing against the clock. I wanted to soak up every second, experience everything I could before things came crashing down around us.

We paid for our lunch and headed for our usual table. Tristan, Scott, and their friends were already there. Sofia was too but without her usual group of girlfriends. *Thank God.* I wasn't in the mood to deal with Emilia's death stare.

"Cous," Tristan pulled a chair free for me. I dropped onto it, smothering a chuckle when Nora made a big scene of pulling out her own chair.

"And they say chivalry is dead." She glared at my cousin.

"Act like a woman and maybe you'll be treated like one." Scott grinned across the table, high fiving his friend.

"Don't be such a dick, Scott," Sofia scolded him. "It's the twenty-first century. If a girl wants to enjoy sex, she should damn well be entitled to."

Nora frowned at me, and I shrugged. "Thanks," she said to Sofia. "I think."

"I'm not a total bitch. Besides, Scott thinks he can do or say whatever he wants and I'm tired of his shit."

Suddenly, I saw Sofia in a whole new light. "Something we can agree on," I whispered.

"Hey, I heard that," Scott protested.

"Good, maybe you'll heed our words." My eyes locked on his, saying all the things I wish I had the freedom to say aloud.

"Yeah, whatever. I'm going to get some more dessert." He stalked off and the tension lifted.

"Babe," Tristan said to Sofia. "Must you poke the bear?"

"Oh, come on, Tristan, you know he's a liability. He practically forced himself on Emil—" My cousin cut her dead, kissing her hard. Sofia melted against him, letting out a little sigh.

"Eww, gross," Nora exclaimed but I was replaying Sofia's words over in my head. Had he tried to hurt Emilia the way he'd tried to hurt me?

Someone needed to know about him, but like my own, the Fascini were a powerful family.

Frustration welled inside me. What was the point of being Arianne Capizola, heir to the Capizola fortune, if I couldn't use my voice for good? To bring entitled rich assholes like Scott to justice. Of course I wasn't the first girl he'd hurt. Guys like him took what they wanted, when they wanted, with little thought to the consequences, because society taught them there were no consequences.

"What are you thinking?" Nora leaned in. "I know that look and you're scheming."

"He can't get away with it," I said feeling a sense of determination wash over me. "I don't know how yet, or even when, but he has to pay, Nor. He has to—"

"Yeah, I think they add an herb or something. It's really tasty. Here." She forked some salad leaves on her fork and offered it to me, discreetly flicking her eyes to where Scott was approaching the table.

"No, I'm good thanks," I mumbled.

I had a fire in my belly.

Scott Fascini would pay.

One way or another, he would pay.

"Arianne, it's so lovely to see you," Suzanna Fascini embraced me, kissing each cheek before holding me at arm's length. "Such a beautiful girl. Tell me, how is college treating you? I hope that son of mine has made you feel right at home."

"I... uh... Scott has been very... welcoming." I chewed the inside of my cheek.

"Good, that's good to hear. He thinks very highly of you, Arianne."

"Hello, Mrs. Fascini, I'm Nora Abato." She stepped forward. "You probably don't remember me."

"Nora, of course. How rude of me. It's lovely to see you again. Will you be joining us or—"

"Actually," my mother appeared, "Nora is spending the day with her mother."

"I am?" Nora frowned.

"Indeed. I've arranged a day out for the two of you at my favorite spa."

"Oh, wow, Mrs. Capizola, that is... wow." Nora glanced at me, but I had nothing. Suzanna was acting like me and Scott were a couple and my mother seemed off.

And ever since we'd turned into the estate, dread had snaked through me and taken root in my stomach.

"I guess I'll see you later?" Nora's voice pulled me from my thoughts. "You'll be okay?"

"Of course she'll be okay," my mother laughed. "We have quite the day of planning ahead of us."

I gave my best friend a tight-lipped smile and watched as she doubled back and left the house.

"Come, let's sit on the terrace. It's such a lovely morning."

She and Suzanna chatted while we trailed through the house. I noticed Mrs. Abato had prepared quite the spread for us. Fresh fruit and pastries, finger sandwiches and crudités. My stomach grumbled and both women chuckled.

"You need to eat more, mia cara. Italian men like a little something to hold onto. At least, Mike does." Suzanna cackled, the sound like nails down a chalkboard. I shuddered, suppressing the urge to gag.

Mom sat down and opened her planner. "Ah yes, outfits."

"I thought we were here to talk about the final preparations?"

"Choosing the perfect dress *is* the final preparation." Suzanna smiled at me.

I was clearly missing something. I thought they wanted my opinion about decorations and entertainment. Not dresses.

"I'm sorry. I'm not sure I understand."

"The theme is a traditional venetian carnival. So we were thinking something big and bold." My mother pulled out a page and slid it across the table to me.

"Wow, they are... something." The gaudy rococo and baroque inspired gowns were all very *Mary Antoinette* and nothing like the simple dress I'd planned to wear.

"You need to make a statement," Suzanna said.

"I do?"

"Well, of course dear. You and Scott will be the—"

"What Suzanna is trying to say, sweetheart, is that this is a perfect opportunity to make a statement."

I frowned, still not following. "Is there something going on I should know about?" I asked.

Mom let out an exasperated breath, as if my cluelessness frustrated her. "Our families need to show a united front, Arianne, now more than ever."

"And Scott and I figure into that how exactly?"

"You are the future of Capizola Holdings," Suzanna chimed in, "and Scott is set to become a partner in Fascini and Associates as soon as he graduates. Separately we are powerful, but together we could be unstoppable."

"Mamma?" I felt the ground shift beneath my feet.

"Scott is a good man, sweetheart, and he has always had a soft spot for you. Your coupling makes sense."

"Our coupling?" I choked over the words. "You can't actually be serious? You want me to date him because it's good for business?"

"Well, we had hoped you would find your way together naturally once you started MU, but I can see that isn't the case." Her lips thinned with disapproval.

"Unbelievable." I stood up.

"Arianne, what are you—"

"I need a minute. Please excuse me." I made a beeline for the house, anger coursing through me like wildfire.

My mother hadn't summoned me here for a planning meeting.

It was an ambush.

A tag team effort to get me to agree to date Scott.

Luis followed me down the hall, quiet and brooding behind me. "Really, in my own house?" I threw over my shoulder.

"It's for your own—"

"Protection." I sneered. "Wow, just wow." Reaching the staircase, I gripped the rail. "Are you going to stand guard outside my door too?"

His silence told me all I needed to know.

"Very well then." Taking two steps at a time, I stomped up the stairs and hurried down the hall to my door. Slamming the door gave me an ounce of satisfaction but it didn't last. I was furious, anger trembling inside me like a powerful storm. It was bad enough I'd spent five years of my life locked away on the estate, now I was being forced to date Scott, a sexual predator, all because it was good for business.

A frustrated cry spilled from my lips as I ran to the window, curling up on the seat. I pressed my head against the cool glass. Retrieving my cell phone from my pocket, I texted Nicco.

How do you do it?

He texted straight back.

Do what?

. . .

Carry the burden of your family legacy? Be who they expect you to be?

Nicco's number flashed across the screen, and I hit answer. "Did something happen?" he asked, his words a low rumble that reverberated deep inside me.

"It's nothing..." The sound of his voice settled me. "I just hate this. All the lies and secrets. I don't know who or what to believe. Nothing makes sense anymore."

"Bambolina," he sighed, so guttural and full of emotion. I pressed my palm against the glass and closed my eyes, imagining he was right there. "Talk to me, Arianne."

"I'm fine. Just my mother and her friend and their meddling ways. It's been an overwhelming morning."

"I wish I could take you away from there; just you, me, and the open road."

"Where would we go?" My lips curved.

"Anywhere. Maybe drive down the coast to New York, head to Long Island. Somewhere no one will find us."

"I like the sound of that."

The silence was deafening as we both allowed ourselves to fall into the dream. Me and Nicco and a world that didn't want to tear us apart.

"I should go," he finally said. Three little words that yanked me back to reality with a resounding *thud*.

"Okay," I whispered.

"You'll be okay?"

"I will."

"I love you, Arianne Carmen Lina Capizola. Don't ever forget that." He hung up abruptly and part of me wondered where he was and who he was with.

Calling me was a risk. Texting each other was too. But I couldn't not speak to him. Not when our messages back and forth made the days bearable until the next time we got to see each other.

A knock at my door startled me from my thoughts. "Hello?" I called out.

"Arianne, it's me."

"Come in."

My mother slipped into the room, closing the door behind her. "Figlia mia, is everything okay?"

"Really, Mamma?"

"I'm sorry, okay. I didn't mean for this morning to feel like an ambush."

"Well, it did. You know I don't like Scott in that way, and yet, you're still pushing for me to give him a chance. He's not the golden boy everyone makes him out to be, you know?"

"Oh, I don't doubt that." She gave me a wistful smile. "Scott is entitled and power hungry and used to getting what he wants. Men like that aren't used to being told no."

"Well, perhaps he should get used to it."

"In an ideal world, you're right. But this isn't the real world."

"So that excuses his behavior?"

"Oh, Arianne. You are so wise beyond your years." She moved closer, leaning over to brush a stray hair from my face. "But you also have so much to learn about the world. A man like Scott needs a good woman by his side. Someone strong and good, to whisper in his ear and keep him on the right track."

"And you want that person to be me?"

Her expression turned sad. "It is not my decision to make."

"You mean Papá—"

"Your father only wants what is best for you."

"Did he tell you?"

"Tell me what?" A frown crinkled my mother's eyes.

"That I know the truth about our family. Our legacy."

She sucked in a harsh breath, mumbling, "Porco miseria! He didn't, no."

"I didn't think so." She'd said nothing to me of it. Part of me even wondered if she knew the whole story, but sitting here, listening to her talking about a woman's duty and how men like Scott needed a strong woman by their side, it occurred to me that perhaps she wasn't as clued in as she considered herself to be.

Tears pricked my eyes as everything came crashing down on top of me.

"What is it, figlia mia? What's wrong?"

Mashing my lips together, I shook my head gently.

"Arianne, sweetheart. Whatever it is, whatever is wrong, you can tell me."

I wanted so badly to tell her. To offload my secret on someone. But I couldn't risk it.

Could I?

"Talk to me. I'm your mother. You can trust me, whatever it is."

"I love another, Mamma." The words poured out, tears rolling down my cheeks.

"W- what?" Fear simmered in her eyes. "But who?"

"Niccolò Marchetti."

All the blood drained from her face. "M- Marchetti? No, no, Arianne, it cannot be..."

"It's true, Mamma. I love him and he loves me."

"Does your father know?"

"He knew I was seeing him, yes."

"And now?"

"He thinks it's over."

"Good, this is good." She grabbed my hands in hers. "You must never see that boy again. Do you understand? If your father ever found out..."

"Why are you saying this, Mamma? I love him. I thought you'd understand."

It was a mistake telling her. I realized that now. She didn't look happy or relieved or even surprised. She wore a mask of terror.

"It must end. Immediately. There is too much blood, too much pain between our families to repair history. What is done is done. Promise me you will end it. Promise me, Arianne."

"I promise." The words killed a tiny piece of my heart. But only for the lie I'd told. For nothing would keep me from Nicco. Not my father, nor my mother's fearful expression. Not Tristan, or Scott's interest in me.

Nothing.

People had spent my entire life lying to me.

Maybe it was my turn to repay the favor.

The Verona County Transitions Initiative was based in Romany Square. It was technically Marchetti territory, but the director, Manny, had reassured my father personally that I would be safe. I didn't know the details of their conversation; I didn't want to. I was just relieved to be here, helping.

Having my best friend by my side only made it better.

"You know, this is pretty awesome," Nora said, as she laid out another tray of biscuits. Manny had set us up at the tea and coffee table. On Sunday's the center provided people all over Verona County the chance to get a warm meal and hot drink with a side of non-judgmental conversation. Permanent staff were trained in a broad spectrum of skills including: advice and guidance, counselling, therapy, and crisis management, and all volunteers had to undergo an induction session, which we'd completed before our shift started this morning, and then had access to a rolling program of training sessions.

"So you didn't tell him yet?" Nora asked as we waited for Manny to open the doors. It was almost twelve and they expected a full house. Luis and Nixon had strict orders to stay outside of the building unless absolutely necessary. I knew my mother probably had a hand in making it happen.

I tried not to think about whether it was because she genuinely wanted me to experience life, or because she felt guilty after yesterday.

"It doesn't feel right telling him over text message."

My father expected me to attend the Centennial Gala whether I wanted to or not. If I didn't go, I risked him growing suspicious over Nicco; and if I did go, I risked hurting the guy who had stolen my heart.

The answer, no matter how hard, was simple.

I had to protect Nicco.

"You should just rip that Band-Aid clean off. Text him, let him cool down, then try to see him. He's going to lose his—"

"Nor," I hissed, shooting a smile at one of the other volunteers.

Manny had agreed it was safer for everyone if I was here under a false identity. So once again, I was Lina Rossi; not that I expected anyone to ask my name. By all accounts, people came for the free food and company.

The doors opened and people began flooding in. Nora stood beside me, wearing an eager smile. I didn't realize how fulfilling serving strangers tea and coffee could be until I'd gotten through fifty cups and endless carafes of tea and coffee. Some people made small talk, commenting on how refreshing it was to see two new faces, while others offered only a meek smile before they swiped a biscuit or two and moved on.

"That was fun," Nora exclaimed, wiping her hands on a VCTI-branded towel.

"Don't get too excited just yet," a volunteer named Brent said. "The rush doesn't really start until later."

"R- rush?" Nora choked out. "You mean that *wasn't* the rush."

Brent chuckled. "Welcome to Sunday's at the VCTI. You might want to restock those trays while it's quiet." He nodded to the empty silver trays laid out in front of Nora.

"I can go," I said. "I need to use the bathroom anyway."

I left Nora and Brent talking while I made my way into the back. There was a small staff room with a bathroom attached. I quickly grabbed my purse and slipped inside, locking the door behind me.

I had two texts. One from my mother, checking to see how it was going; and one from Nicco.

How is it?

I typed a reply, unable to fight the smile forming on my lips.

Great. I feel so... useful. Is that silly?

Of course not. I'm proud of you.

Guilt flashed through me. Nora was right. I needed to tell him. I needed to rip off the Band-Aid and just tell him. He would understand.

Actually, there's something I need to talk to you about...

Why do I not like the sound of this?

. . .

I'd barely started to type a reply when my phone blared to life. "Hey," I whispered.

"What's wrong?" His words were clipped, only tightening the knot in my stomach.

"I... uh, well you know it's the Centennial Gala in a couple of weeks? My mamma and her friend are on the planning committee and they thought it would be nice if I went with Scott Fascini... as his date." The words spilled out in a single breath.

"What the fuck did you just say?"

"Nicco, please, you have to understand. If I say no—"

"Meet me out back in ten minutes."

"Nicco, I can't just sneak off. I'm at work." It might have been voluntary work, but it was still important to me, and I wanted to do a good job. "Besides, Luis and Nixon are here. If they see—"

"Out back in ten, Arianne. I mean it." The anger in his voice startled me. I knew Nicco had a darker side, one he rarely let me see.

"I'm only doing this for—" The line went dead. I quickly typed another message.

I know you hate him. I'm not particularly fond of him either, but if I don't do this, my father will only get suspicious. You have to understand the predicament I'm in, Nicco. It's just a stupid gala. A few hours. I'll probably barely see Scott. He'll get drunk and find some poor unassuming girl to hit on. You have nothing to worry about. Nothing. I promise.

The lies were piling up around me. But I had to try to reassure him. Because if Nicco ever found out the truth... a deep shudder rolled through me. It didn't bear thinking about.

He didn't text back, but I couldn't stay locked in the bathroom forever. So I brushed myself off, and went in search of more biscuits, hoping Nicco would read my text and trust that I knew what I was doing.

Even if I barely knew myself.

EIGHTEEN

NICCO

SCOTT FUCKING FASCINI.

The second Arianne had said his name, I saw red. It was a good thing I was in my Uncle Joe's garage and not with the guys, because there would have been no disguising my anger.

I think the fact that, deep down, I knew she was right only made it ten times worse.

She had to go as his date.

His girl.

When every single piece of her belonged to me.

Just the idea of him putting his hands on her made me murderous. I'd seen the way he watched her around campus, like a predator stalking its prey. It gave me the creeps, not to mention made me want to rearrange his face.

I'd stormed out of the garage, climbed on my bike, and spun out of there before I could even consider the consequences. I needed to see her, now. Luckily for me, we did business with a few places on the same block as the VCTI, so I knew the building well. Well enough, I was aware of the back entrance used for deliveries. I parked down the street, careful not to draw too much attention to myself, pulled up my hood, and headed for the VCTI. I spotted one of Capizola's men standing point outside. Ducking into the alley between the building and the adjoining store, I followed it around back and hid behind two dumpsters, waiting. Arianne had sent me a long-ass message trying to explain, but I didn't need words, I needed to look into her eyes and know this was nothing more than another one of her father's attempts to control her.

Time ticked by. I counted the seconds and then the minutes. I counted the number of bricks on the wall, the number of places I'd kissed Arianne, and all the places I was yet to kiss. I counted anything to stop me from storming into the VCTI and forcing her to leave with me. Despite every cell in my body wanting to do things my way, I knew Arianne already had enough people trying to control her. She didn't need me to become another.

Another five minutes went by and there was still no sign of her. Maybe I'd been too harsh, too quick to lose my temper. I dug my cell phone out, ready to text her again, when the big steel door swung open. Arianne stood there, two huge trash bags slung behind her. She stepped gingerly out of the door and headed straight for the dumpsters. I allowed myself a minute to look at her. She looked so focused, so determined. The corner of my mouth lifted. She was fucking beautiful, even taking out the trash.

"I know you're out here," she said. "I felt you the second I opened the door."

Stepping out from my hiding spot, I held up my hands. "You got me."

She dropped the bags and ran at me, slamming her hands into my chest. "Don't ever hang up on me again." Her eyes were wild as she glared up at me.

"Jesus, Bambolina." I rubbed my breastbone. She was feisty when she was angry, but she was also a lot stronger than I gave her credit for. "Let me guess, your old man had you take self-defense lessons?"

"Something like that," she mumbled, stepping back to put some distance between us. "I'm sorry I hit you."

"I'm sorry I hung up on you. Was that our first fight?" She didn't answer so I crooked my finger at her." Come here."

Arianne fell into my arms, and I pulled us behind the dumpster, giving us a sliver of privacy. "Look at me," I said, gliding my hand to her jaw. She looked up through damp lashes.

"I know you don't want me to go, but I have no choice, Nicco. Not if I want to protect you."

"You have a choice, Arianne; you always have a choice."

"You think I want to go with him? I can't stand him." Her expression darkened. "But my father has it into his head that it's good for business, whatever the hell that means."

"And you're okay with that? You're okay with being his pawn?" The words came out harsher than I intended and I immediately regretted it when Arianne flinched.

"We're all pawns really." She gave a small shrug. "This is no different."

I hooked my arm around her waist and spun us around so I could crowd her against the wall. My hand pressed the brick beside her head as I leaned in. "You can't seriously expect me to stand by and do nothing while you're out there, on a date, with him?"

"Nicco, please..."

"Please what? Give you my blessing that I'm okay with this? I will *never* be okay with this." My voice shook. "What if he wants to dance? To touch you right here." I smoothed my hand over the curve of her hip, and her breath hitched.

"What if he leans in to kiss you, right here." My lips gently sucked the skin beneath her ear. "What if, at the end of the night, he expects more than just a kiss? What then?"

"What would you have me do?" Arianne fisted my hoodie, her big honey eyes pleading with me. "If I don't go, it looks suspicious."

"Fake a stomach flu. Say you have to study. Say *anything*. But don't go." *I'm begging you.*

Arianne's eyes squeezed shut, a rogue tear slipping down her cheek. I swiped it away, feeling like a royal dick. But I couldn't bear it. I couldn't bear the thought of her on his arm, laughing and smiling at him.

Even if it was all an act.

She opened her eyes, staring at me with such intensity I felt it all the way down to my soul. "It's all pretend, Nicco. An act. I feel nothing for Scott, *nothing*."

"You're going to do it, aren't you?" Disbelief coated my words. "Regardless of what I say, you've already made your decision?" I staggered back, pain crushing my chest.

"Nicco, please. It's the only way to appease my father."

"And if our roles were reversed? If it was me about to take out another girl. To make her believe my act? You'd be okay with that?"

Her eyes flared with jealousy. "I'd trust you knew what you were doing. Even if I didn't like it."

"I see." A wall slammed up between us. I was too pissed to listen to any more. Even though part of me knew she had no choice; the other part, the dominant possessive alpha inside me, refused to accept it. Refused to understand why she wasn't going to stand her ground on this, why she was going to be the good little princess and do what daddy dearest said.

It was fucking bullshit.

Heavy silence hung over us. Thick and suffocating.

"Say something," she whispered.

"There's nothing left to say, we're done here."

"D- done?" That single word gutted me. I should have corrected her. Right then, I should have told her I just needed time to process everything; that once I'd cooled off, we'd talk.

But I didn't.

Instead, I left her standing there, wondering if we were over before we ever got started, and walked away.

"Nicco." Alessia ran toward me, her long hair cascading over her shoulders like a golden river. "I didn't know you were stopping by."

"Can't I come see my sister on a whim?" I hooked my arm around her waist, guiding her back toward the house. I was here on business, after being summoned by my father. But Alessia didn't need to know that. Besides, after leaving things so shitty with Arianne, some quality time with my sister was exactly what I needed.

"I've been helping Genevieve prepare dinner. Will you stay?"

"Sure, kid."

She rolled her eyes at me. "You're like three years older than me, Nicco."

"Yeah, but I'm a guy, and you'll always be my *baby* sister."

"Bite me." Alessia poked out her tongue and took off down the hall toward the smell of rich tomato sauce.

"Nicco," Genevieve greeted me, giving me a tentative smile. "We weren't expecting you. I'll set an extra place."

"Don't go to any trouble," I said.

"Oh, it's no trouble. I'm sure your father will be happy you're joining us." My brow quirked up and heat flooded her cheeks. "I'm sorry. I didn't mean—"

"Relax, it's all good." Her position within the house was blurred. She cared about my father, that much was obvious, and I was pretty certain he cared too. He just didn't care enough to promote her from housekeeper to lady of the house. I think, deep down, he still hoped that one day Mom would return. When we all knew she wouldn't.

She had escaped a life I never would.

"It smells good, Sia."

"Genevieve has been teaching me."

"You're too kind, mia cara." They shared a warm smile.

It hadn't been easy leaving Alessia here, with my father. But she adored him, and he doted on her. Besides, it wasn't like I could take her with me. So it made me breathe a little easier knowing she had Genevieve. Matteo's mom also came over a lot, and although they were in different grades; Arabella, his sister, and Alessia went to the same school.

My sister had people. She was surrounded by family who loved her. Aunts and uncles and cousins. So even though it brought back too many bad memories being in this house, I knew it was the right place for her to be.

"Is he around?" I asked Genevieve but it was my sister who answered.

"He's in his study... waiting for you." She cut me with a knowing look.

"Busted." My lip curved.

"You're lucky I love you, Niccolò." Alessia smiled, before turning her attention to the pan of bubbling sauce.

I grabbed a beer from the refrigerator before heading down the hall to find my father. "Come in," he called before I'd even rapped my knuckles against the door.

I ducked inside, taking a seat on the long couch pushed up against the wall. He was busy at his desk.

"What's eating you?" he grumbled.

"Nothing."

"Don't give me that bullshit." He clicked his tongue. "I can feel the tension rolling off you. What did Enzo do to piss you off this time?"

I chuckled. "You're barking up the wrong tree, old man."

"Hey, less of the 'old man' talk, kid. I've still got some good years left in me yet." One of his thick dark brows rose as he looked over at me. "You're dragging on this job; why?"

Jesus. Trust my father to cut straight to the point.

"It's complicated."

"Did you go after the cousin?"

I nodded. "Tristan confirmed she was on campus. Of course he didn't say anything else."

"So..."

"He went running back to his uncle and told him we knew."

"Fuck, Niccolò." He slammed his hand down.

"She's still on campus but she has protection. Around the clock bodyguards. They never let her out of their sight. I'm not sure she's the—"

"She's the key, Son. It has to be her." Relaxing back in his chair, my father ran a hand down his face.

"You'd really hurt an innocent girl to get leverage over Capizola?"

His expression darkened. "Don't tell me you're turning soft like Matteo? She's a means to an end, Niccolò. I'm not expecting you to seriously harm her, just scare her a little. Enough to make Roberto know we're serious."

My hand curled against my thigh as I searched his face for any hint of the truth. I wanted so badly to ask him about five years ago. To confront him about what Arianne had told me. But if I did, it would out us, and possibly put her in more danger.

So I pressed my lips together, forcing the question down.

"Is there something you need to tell me, Son?"

Yes, I wanted to yell.

"You need to trust me to handle this," I said. "It's going to take time—"

"We don't have time. Capizola has issued another petition to the court. He's obsessed with tearing down La Riva and replacing it with some fancy mall and expensive housing. He wants to turn it into a replica of Roccaforte. This is my home, Son. *Our* home. Our great-grandfathers shook on it and now he wants to piss all over that."

"What does Stefan say?"

Stefan was my father's consigliere, his advisor and trusted friend. He was out of town right now, helping Alonso up in Boston deal with something.

"He thinks we should start paying off the right people."

"He really thinks the court will rule in Roberto's favor?"

"Capizola has as many officials on his books as we do." A guttural growl tore from my father's throat. "He can't take La Riva. If he does, we might as well give him Romany Square because it'll only be time before he comes for that too. The girl is the lucky break we need. Don't fuck this up, Niccolò. I'm counting on you."

I gave him a curt nod. What else could I do? My father believed I would do whatever it took to protect the family, and Arianne believed I would do whatever it took to protect her. And I was in the middle wondering how the fuck to make both happen without everything imploding.

"You staying to eat?" My father asked, changing the subject.

"I told Alessia I would."

"Good, it's about time you came around more. I know things have been hard on you, Niccolò. But you're a capo now. You need to start—"

"Spare me the lecture. I know what my responsibilities are."

"Son, please..." He let out a weary sigh. "I can't change the past, but I'm here, and I'm trying to be better. Alessia is—"

"My sister needs her father, I know that." But I hadn't needed him in a long time.

"You remind me so much of her." Sadness filled his eyes. "Her tenacity—"

"Don't," I said quietly, my body vibrating with frustration. "I'm going to call the guys, see if they want to come over." Rising from the couch, I walked toward the door.

"Niccolò, one day this will all be yours. Whether you want it or not, it will be yours. Just remember, Son, heavy is the head that wears the crown."

I glanced back at my father, his eyes saying all the things he would probably never say. There was so much pain and regret and shame in his wistful stare. I knew what he meant; I knew he was trying to tell me that sometimes the life was too much. It was too easy for a man, despite all his honor and good intentions, to get pulled into the less honorable side of the life. He became quick tempered with those he loved, those he had to continually keep secrets from. He found comfort in the arms of countless goomars, women who were not his wife. And above all, he lost a part of himself.

All in the name of Dominion.

Dominion flowed through our blood, and he was right.

One day, it would be mine.

NINETEEN

ARIANNE

"I THINK I'm going to throw up." I pressed a hand to my stomach, trying to ease the ball of nerves.

"Well, you sure look the part." Nora let out a low whistle as she appraised my dress. It had taken us almost thirty minutes to get me into the damn thing. But even I couldn't deny the handiwork was stunning. The emerald green rococo style gown cinched impossibly tight at my waist, the bodice embroidered with fine gold lace detailing. It flowed over my hips into a full skirt that kissed the floor.

"I look ridiculous." I picked up the layers of material and swished them around my legs.

"You look stunning. Me on the other hand..." Nora glanced down at her own dress, her lip curling. "I look like your much poorer, much uglier cousin."

"Oh hush, you look beautiful." Her dress was simpler in style, one panel of black velvet fitted and flared around her curves with long sleeves that billowed around her wrists. Nora had taken her time curling her hair before styling mine into an intricate updo woven through with diamantes. Suzanna had sent me a necklace she requested I wear, a family heirloom apparently. It was a big gaudy black onyx teardrop pendant that hung in between my ample cleavage, all thanks to the corset bodice. I didn't want to wear it, but I knew better than to risk offending her.

Tonight was about playing a part and appeasing the parents.

"Any word from Nicco?"

"A couple of texts here and there." My chest constricted, and, this time, it wasn't the corset's fault.

Ever since that day, almost two weeks ago outside the VCTI, when Nicco walked away from me, things had been different between us. He'd texted me an apology, reassuring me he understood. But part of him had withdrawn. I felt it, felt the tether between us fade a little.

He was hurting and there was nothing I could do to fix it. Because I had to do this. If I wanted to keep our secret, I had to attend the gala with Scott.

"He'll come around," my best friend said, squeezing my arm.

"I have to get through tonight, then I'll worry about Nicco."

When he'd uttered the words, 'we're done here' my mind had instantly gone to a bad place. A place where Nicco was no longer mine. But I'd quickly realized it was nothing more than his defense mechanism. Nicco liked to be in control, but he couldn't control this.

We were puppets in a game with rules and expectations we couldn't just ignore.

"Okay." Nora leaned in, swiping some gloss over my lips. I blotted them together and forced a smile. "Ready?" she asked.

"As I'll ever be."

The sooner we left, the sooner the night would be over.

Nora opened the door, helping me navigate my dress through the narrow opening. Luis and Nixon stood to attention, and I was sure I caught a flash of emotion in Luis' expression. "Arianne," he said, stepping forward and crooking his elbow. "Mr. Fascini is waiting downstairs with the car. May I?"

I slid my arm through his, letting him escort me down the hall. We took the elevator as it was a little tricky to navigate the stairs in my dress, but there wasn't room for Nora and Nixon, so they took the stairs.

Heavy silence hung over us, the seconds ticking by painfully slowly. Luis shifted beside me, clearing his throat. "Is there something you want to say?" I asked, craning my neck to look at him.

"I serve your father, but as my mark, my loyalty is with you." I was about to ask what he meant when the doors pinged open. "Ready?" he asked, and I nodded.

But the second my eyes landed on Scott, smirking at me through the glass doors like the cat who got the cream, I wanted to turn around and run back inside.

You can do this. I rolled back my shoulders, steeling myself. Nora clutched my hand, squeezing gently, offering me her strength. Which was good because something told me I was going to need all the strength I could get if I was going to survive the night ahead.

The Montague Auditorium had been transformed into an exuberant Venetian Carnival. Masked dancers and acrobats greeted us, some eating fire, others hanging from silk ropes suspended from the ceiling. I had no idea how my mother and Suzanna, and the rest of the planning committee, had pulled off something like this, but when money was no object, the sky was the limit.

Scott kept his hand on my arm, leading me through the arch of gold and black balloons. He'd showered me with compliments on the short ride over. We could have just as easily walked, but Scott demanded an entrance, and so an entrance he got. Nora's date Dan, a guy from one of her classes, had greeted her at the steps, looking drool worthy in his tuxedo and plain black Columbine mask. Nora had opted for no mask after my mother and Suzanna requested I didn't conceal myself. I was to be visible—on display.

The noise crescendoed as we entered the inner auditorium. The seats had been cleared to make room for huge circular tables laid out in two sweeping arcs around the stage and dance floor.

"Wow," I breathed, my heart pounding in my chest. I'd never seen anything quite like it.

"This is just the beginning," Scott said, finally unhooking my arm from his. "I'll get us some drinks. Don't go anywhere."

"I wouldn't dream of it." It came out saccharine sweet.

Nora joined me as I stood taking it all in. People glanced my way, doing a double take when they realized it was me. The Capizola heir. But their stares no longer concerned me.

"Your mom sure knows how to throw a party."

"Just a shame she has terrible choice in dates."

We shared a snicker, falling silent as the woman in question breezed over to us. "Girls, aren't you a sight for sore eyes. Bellissima, you look stunning."

"Thank you, Mamma."

"And Scott? He liked the dress?"

I ignored that. "Is Papá here?"

"He's working the room. You know your father, always on the clock." She smiled brightly. "He's hoping to raise a substantial amount for the trust with the silent auction."

The Capizola Charities Trust, was one of my father's many passion projects, bettering the lives of those less fortunate.

"Oh my, Scott, look at you, so handsome."

"Mrs. Capizola." He turned on the charm, taking her hand and kissing it. "It's good to see you again."

She giggled. My mother actually giggled. Nora fake-gagged quietly beside me. "Please, call me Gabriella." She patted his cheek like they were old friends.

I didn't like it. I didn't like it at all.

I was beginning to think Scott possessed some magical qualities that blinded people to his creeper status.

"Well, enjoy the party, won't you?" She brushed a curl from my face. "So beautiful. I'll see you later, okay?"

"Goodbye, Mamma." I watched her walk away, a strange tugging sensation in my stomach.

I put it down to the guy beside me. Scott was oblivious to my disdain at being here with him; that or he just didn't care.

"To us." He lifted his glass and waited. Reluctantly, I clinked my champagne flute against his. "To friends," I enunciated, holding his stare.

"We'll see about that." He winked.

"Excuse me, I need to visit the ladies' room."

"Do you want me to come with?" Nora asked, but I shook my head. "You should stay with Dan." He looked a little out of his depth. "I'll only be a few minutes."

Luis followed me as I wove through the sea of bodies. Some girls wore dresses like mine: big, ostentatious gowns that blended in with the decor. Others had opted for sexy and seductive over authenticity and style. I spotted Sofia and my cousin. She made a beeline for me, her lips parted as her wide-eyed gaze swept down my dress.

"Holy shit, Ari, you look... wow." She leaned in to kiss my cheeks. Somewhere over the last two weeks we had become friends. Or at least, she no longer treated me like a social leper. I still wasn't entirely comfortable with her touchy-feely approach, but her dislike of Scott made her an ally in my eyes. Unfortunately, Sofia's change of attitude hadn't extended to Emilia, who still looked at me like I was the competition. I wanted to talk to her, to ask if Scott had tried to hurt her too, but I didn't know how to approach someone who spent most of their time burning holes into the side of my face.

"Cousin." Tristan kissed my cheeks. "You look amazing."

"Thanks. I'm actually trying to find the bathroom. Do you know—"

"See those doors over there." Sofia pointed across the room. "Straight through there. It's like maze back there so don't get lost."

"I'm sure I can manage. See you both later." I grabbed my skirt and took off. Luis kept close behind me, but I didn't mind. Not when there were so many people.

I burst through the doors, relieved to find the hall empty. "I'll wait right here," Luis declared. "The ladies' restroom is down the hall on the right. There's only one way in and out, so you'll be safe."

I gave him an appreciative nod, hardly surprised he knew the layout of the place. "I won't be long."

"Take all the time you need."

My brows crinkled. Luis seemed different. I didn't want to make assumptions, but he seemed concerned. Obviously not concerned about my safety, because I knew he and his partners working the Gala tonight wouldn't let anything happen to me. But he was acting fatherly, almost like he cared about me.

I moved down the hall, slipping through the archway marked 'Ladies restrooms' and went inside a stall. It wasn't easy navigating through the many layers of skirts, but I eventually managed. After flushing, I headed back out to wash my hands, almost jumping out of my skin when I came face to face with a figure all in black wearing a Pierrot mask.

"You didn't reply to my text," Nicco said.

"What are you doing here?" I didn't know whether to throw my arms around his neck or slap him upside the head. "You can't be here, Nicco."

He snagged my wrist, pushing off his mask, and pulled me into him. "I missed you too, Bambolina." His words settled the fire inside my tummy, and I melted against him.

I'd been so dead set on seeing tonight through, I hadn't allowed myself time to think about the consequences. About how Nicco must be feeling about me being here with Scott.

"Tell me you're still mine," he whispered against my ear, nibbling the skin there. Desire shot through me as I clung onto him.

"Nicco, you have to go before someone sees—"

"Ssh, amore mio. I needed to see you. I needed to know we were okay."

"Where have you been?" I slammed my hands into his chest, my resolve slowly cracking and crumbling. "Two weeks, Nicco; it's been two weeks."

"It's complicated. But I'm trying to figure it out, I promise." He curved his hand around my neck and drew me closer, fixing his mouth over mine. Nicco kissed me with such intensity I couldn't breathe. I couldn't do anything except give in to him.

"Jesus, Arianne," he breathed against my lips. "You look incredible."

"I feel completely ridiculous." My eyes dropped down, but I noticed he wasn't looking at my dress, he was staring right at my chest.

I cleared my throat, smirking when he looked at me and swallowed hard. "If he so much as lays a single finger on—"

"It's not going to happen, I promise. I'm here for my mother and father, that's it."

Nicco's jaw clenched as he warred with himself. I knew he probably wanted to confront Scott, to stake his claim on me. But his hands were tied, just as mine were.

"You really should go."

"Okay." He let out a resigned sigh. "Just promise me you'll stick close to Nora and your bodyguard, okay?"

"Is something going on?" I frowned. There was something in his voice, an urgency that had alarm bells ringing.

"Everything is fine." He kissed my head again, lingering. "You should go first."

"Wait, how did you know I was here?"

"I am always watching you, Bambolina, even when you think I'm not. Now go."

We shared a last look as Nicco backed away, breaking our physical connection.

"I love you," I mouthed, before slipping out of the restroom. I couldn't stay to hear him say it back, because although I was trying so hard to be strong, inside I felt weak.

Inside, I felt on the verge of begging him to get me out of here.

"Ladies and gentlemen, alumni, and friends," my father's voice rang out across the room. "It is my honor to welcome you here tonight, in the stunning Montague Auditorium, to celebrate the University's Centennial. My family has a deep history with our great county and it is thanks to my forefathers that you stand here now, in this institution of such academic greatness and achievement, shaping the lives and minds of so many of our children."

A chorus of applause filled the room. Scott stood beside me, nodding and clapping much like every other person gathered here. I couldn't help but feel betrayed. My father presented an air of such integrity and humility, but it was all a front. Hiding a history he'd worked hard to keep buried.

It was bullshit, and I was so over it.

"You need to smile," Nora whispered through gritted teeth, nodding to where my mother stood at my father's side, frowning in my direction. Suzanna and Mike Fascini flanked his other side, the four of them donning nothing but smiles and solidarity as my father held the audience in the palm of his hand.

"You need to relax, babe," Scott leaned in, his lips almost brushing my ear. I jerked away, swishing the loose curls around my face at him.

"Behave," Nora mouthed. Her date, Dan, had relaxed somewhat since Scott had been keeping his drink full. No one seemed to mind that a lot of the people here were under twenty-one. Champagne flowed freely and there was a bar for beer and other drinks. I, on the other hand, had refused his last three attempts to get me a refill.

My father's voice became a monotonous drone as he talked about regeneration and building a secure future for all of Verona County. My thoughts drifted to Nicco and the future. I wanted to believe we had one, but standing here, at Scott's side, with our parents watching on, it was hard to see a way over the obstacles stacked in front of us.

I searched the crowd for any signs of his familiar Pierrot mask, but it was impossible to see in the sea of faceless bodies.

Suddenly, a wave of exhaustion rolled through me and I swayed on my feet, grabbing Scott's arm. He glanced down at me, frowning. I forced a smile, waving him off.

"Hey, are you okay?" Nora asked me.

"Just tired and I can barely breathe in this dress."

Thankfully, my father chose that moment to wrap up his speech. The crowd broke into another round of raucous applause.

"What's wrong?" Scott asked.

"I just felt a little light-headed, I'm fine now."

His eyes narrowed. "You sure?"

But there wasn't time to answer as our parents swooped in on us, showering us with affection and compliments. "Arianne, mia cara, whatever is the matter?"

"She's feeling a little overwhelmed." Scott addressed the four of them, answering for me as if it was his God-given right.

"Is this true, mio tesoro?" My father stepped forward to inspect me.

"I'm fine." I pushed his hand away. "I think the dress is a little too tight."

"You should get some fresh air," Suzanna suggested. "Scott, why don't you take—"

"Actually, Mamma, Papá," I said feeling another strange wave of exhaustion crash over me. "I don't feel so well." My eyes fluttered closed as I reached out to steady myself.

"Ari," Nora's voice edged into my thoughts as I blinked at the six pairs of concerned eyes watching me.

"I think I should take her home," Nora said.

"I've got it, Aba... Nora," Scott interjected, wrapping an arm around me.

"Sweetheart," my mother pressed her hand against my cheek. "Scott will take good care of you; isn't that right?"

"Of course, Gabriella. I'll see to it that she gets back to her dorm room."

"I'm fine." I tried to brush him off, but Scott was already leading me away from them. "Scott," I hissed but it came out more of a pleading cry. "Just stop for a second."

I needed to catch my breath.

Thankfully, as we exited the main auditoria, Luis caught up with us. "Arianne?" He silently asked me what was wrong.

"I- I don't feel so good." My limbs were getting heavier. "Can you please take me back to Donatello House?"

Scott didn't protest but he didn't release me either, keeping his arm wrapped firmly around me. People were looking, their curious stares no doubt working overtime. I'd arrived with Scott, now I was leaving with him. I could only imagine what conclusions they were drawing, ready to spread around the gossip mill on Monday morning.

I just hoped Nicco wasn't out there, watching this.

Watching me.

Luis moved away, whispering into his radio.

"Arianne?" Nora called after me and I turned to see my friend come running through the doors. "Are you okay?"

"I'm fine." I pursed my lips. "I think I just needed some air."

"You're sure?" Concern glittered in her eyes. "I left Dan chatting to your father. He looked terrified."

"You should probably go save him. Luis and Nixon are going to take me back to the dorm. Stay, have fun. One of us should."

"What about..." She glared in Scott's direction.

He flipped her off, chuckling to himself.

"Scott is going to do the right thing. See that I get home okay and then leave," I said loud enough for him and Luis to hear me.

I knew he wouldn't walk away yet, just as I knew my parents had seen a golden opportunity to let him be my knight-in-shining-armor. Just as I also knew I had to find a way to put an end to this charade. For Nicco's sanity, and my own.

Nora hugged me. "Are you sure? I can come back with you?"

"It's fine," I said. "I promise. I have Luis and Nixon with me."

"Okay, don't wait up." She kissed me, before picking up the skirt of her dress and hurrying back inside.

"Alone at last." Scott stepped closer.

"Really?" I quirked a brow.

He smirked but didn't reply as he ushered me toward the main doors. "Nixon is bringing the car around." Luis stepped up beside me, but my father's deep voice said, "Actually, Luis, let Scott take her."

"Of course, sir." Scott stood taller, shooting me a knowing smirk.

"Papá." I turned toward my father, frowning. "I would prefer it if Luis and Nix—"

"Don't make things difficult, mio tesoro." He cupped my face, brushing his thumb over my cheek. "Scott will take good care of you, and who knows, maybe you'll get chance to talk."

"Talk." My brows knitted. "I'm not sure..."

"Come on, Arianne." Scott took my elbow. "We should get going. I'll take good care of her, sir."

"I know you will, Scott."

"Mr. Capizola," Luis cleared his throat. "Perhaps it would better if I drove them—"

"You can follow in a second car," I heard my father say as Scott led me out of the building. "Give the two of them some space. They have much to discuss."

"But, sir..." Luis' voice trailed off as he met my gaze, a flash of concern passing over him. But then the door swung closed and he was gone.

At least the fresh air cleared some of the fogginess in my head.

"Miss Capizola," Nixon said, approaching me as I made my way down the steps. I had been relieved to be heading back to the dorm, wanting nothing more than to get out of this dress and into something more comfortable. Something that didn't make it feel like I was fighting for every breath. But now, it was turning into a nightmare. I didn't want Scott to accompany me, not without Luis or Nixon.

"Where's Luis?" Nixon asked.

"He's—"

"Inside, talking to the boss." Scott held out his palm. "You can hand over the keys and go bring the second car around. I've got this."

Storming off toward the car, I clenched my teeth, anger and frustration rippling through me. I climbed inside, pulling my skirt in behind me, and slammed the door. Scott climbed in a few seconds later. "Shall we?"

"You're enjoying this, aren't you?" My head spun again and I sucked in a harsh breath.

"Everything okay over there?"

"It's this dress, it's... it doesn't matter." I looked out of the window, relieved when I saw Luis and Nixon on the steps, watching after our car. They would follow behind us and they would make sure Scott left after walking me to my room.

"You need to learn how to relax, princess."

"Can we *not* do this?" I snapped, rubbing my head as another wave of exhaustion crashed over me. It was more intense this time, a heaviness pulling me down. "I think something is wrong." I cried, my body and mind splintering apart as I began to fall. Strong arms caught me, "Just let go," a voice said. "I've got you."

"Nicco?" My lips formed his name, hoping, *praying*, he was here to fix this. Something was wrong. I didn't feel right. Locked away in my own thoughts, unable to move.

"I've got you," someone whispered as the world shifted again.

I felt weightless.

Free.

And then I felt nothing.

"N- Nicco?" I peeked an eye open, wincing as I waited for everything to stop spinning. "What are you—"

"I knew it," Scott growled, roughly grabbing my hair. My head snapped backward, a garbled cry spilling from my lips as I tried to make sense of my surroundings. It was dark. So dark I could barely see him. But a sliver of moonlight shone down on the devil, illuminating his features—monstrous eyes, evil smirk—as he moved above me. Fear pinned me in place, dropping to the bulge in his slacks.

No.

Oh God no.

I willed myself to move, to do something, *anything*, but I was paralyzed.

"Have you given it up to him? Did you let him fuck you like a little whore?" He backhanded me so hard my teeth clattered. Pain exploded along my cheekbone, tears burning the backs of my eyes.

"W- why are you doing this?" Everything still felt hazy as if I hadn't quite woken up, frozen somewhere between a nightmare and reality. "What did you do to me?"

"Such a good little princess, only drinking one glass of champagne. I wanted to do this the good old-fashioned way. Get you wasted and then fuck the daddy's little princess right out of you, but I had to get... creative."

"D- drugged me..." My head rolled back as I fought against whatever sedative he'd given me. "Where's... Luis? Nixon?"

"No one's coming." He trailed a finger down my neck, toying with the sweetheart neckline of the corset. "We're all alone and I can take what's mine, finally."

"Stop, p- please stop."

He backhanded me again, pain exploding behind my eyes. I cried out, the sound drowned out by his maniacal laughter. "I'm going to have so much fun with you. I had hoped you'd be more... willing but this will work just as well." Scott cocked his head, staring down at me like I was a science project he couldn't quite figure out, as he ground himself against me. "I've never had a girl tell me no before. Well, not after enough drinks."

Bile rushed up my throat.

"My father will—"

"What?" Scott leaned down, pressing his lips to the corner of my mouth. "What will good old Roberto do? He practically handed you over on a silver platter. You think he's going to believe anything you say? He needs me. He needs my family. This, you and me, it *is* happening. The sooner you get on board with that, the better." His fingers dipped into the tight corset and he began clawing at my breasts.

"Stop, you're hurting me." I tried to lift a hand to fight him off, but my muscles were heavy like lead.

"Let's see what you're hiding up here shall we?" He yanked up the skirt before shoving his hand into the layers of material. It was foolish to think they would provide any protection against him, but I couldn't help the pang of disappointment that hit me when his greedy fingers met the soft flesh of my thighs.

"Bingo." He chuckled darkly, pinching and pawing at my legs, moving higher and higher until he grazed my panties. "Lace," he crooned. "For me? You shouldn't have."

"D- don't, please." I tried to force my knees together, to do anything to keep him out. But Scott was strong, his careless touch like sandpaper against my skin. Tears began leaking from my eyes.

"Beg me to stop," he taunted against my lips. "Go on. Beg."

I pressed my lips together in defiance. He could hurt me, touch me against my will, but he would not break me. I refused to give him that power.

"Oh, you want to play it like that? We'll see how long you last." He bit down on my lip, splitting the skin. Blood trickled into my mouth, painting his lips red as he grinned at me. "By the time I'm done with you, that fucker Marchetti won't ever want to touch you again."

I tried to turn away from him, to smother my tears as his fingers tore through the last of my defenses and pushed inside me. A pained cry bubbled up my throat, but I refused to give him the satisfaction. Scott could take everything from me, but I would give him nothing in return.

"I'll make you want it," he drawled, licking my face, tonguing my mouth.

I went into myself, deep into a place where Scott couldn't reach me, until my body became nothing more than an empty vessel. He felt the shift, grew frustrated at my unresponsiveness. He rubbed harder, kissed me deeper. Yanking down the corset, ripping the material wide open, he bit my breasts, desperately trying to elicit a response.

But I gave him nothing.

"Fucking bitch," he spat at me, wrapping his fingers around my neck and squeezing until I thought I might pass out. "I'm going to fucking destroy you, and when I'm done, when he no longer wants you and you come crawling back to me, I'll make you beg for more."

He snapped open his belt and shoved down his slacks over his hips. I knew then; I wasn't going to make it out of this unscathed. Scott intended on taking everything from me.

My body.

A piece of my soul.

And my virginity.

It was the one thing I'd been determined to give on my terms, and he was going to take that away from me.

Something in me snapped.

I couldn't do it.

I couldn't *not* fight.

With everything I had left, an almighty roar tore from my throat as I thrashed against him, trying desperately to gain leverage. Scott was stronger than me, but he wasn't expecting me to fight. He lost his footing and slipped off the bed, "Cazzo!"

I tried to pull myself up, but he was too quick, too overpowering. I bucked and kicked, screamed until my lungs burned and blood pounded between my ears. But in the end, I failed.

Scott backhanded me so hard, my vision blurred and I felt myself slip under again.

But not before I felt him move above me.

Not before I felt him tear through my innocence and rip out a piece of my soul in the process.

Not before I cried, "Nicco, forgive me."

I dreamed of voices. Angry voices arguing about a girl.

"She needs a hospital. I'm taking her—"

"N- Nicco?" the girl cried out.

"She needs him. I don't care what you say. I'm taking her to him."

"Now you hang on a second, kid. She's my responsibility. I should never have let her—"

"What... what did you do?"

"Nothing, I... fuck. We should call her parents."

"We both know that isn't going to help her. Not tonight. Something about all this doesn't add up."

"Nicco, where are you?" the girl murmured.

"Shit, she's waking up. Your choice. Are you going to let me help—"

"Fine, *fine!* But so help me God, you better know what you're doing."

Silence followed...

The feeling of weightlessness.

Flashes of pain and agony.

Of complete helplessness.

"Nicco?" the girl cried out again.

"Ssh, Arianne. I got you. I got you."

Arianne?

That couldn't be right.

I was Arianne.

Which meant this wasn't a dream at all.

It was my worst nightmare come true.

TWENTY

NICCO

THE LOUD KNOCK STARTLED ME. I jumped off the couch and hurried to the door, yanking it open. "Bailey?"

He looked pale, eyes wild and lip quivering as he croaked out, "It's Arianne."

My spine stiffened. "What happened?"

He tipped his head to his car and I saw her. Shoving past him, I jogged down the stairs and pulled open the door. "No," the single word cracked open my chest. "No, no, no..." Pain like I'd never experienced welled in my chest, clenching my heart like a fucking vice.

Arianne, my sweet innocent Arianne, was lying across the back seat, her dress torn, blood dried on her lip and down her chin. A red welt was streaked across her cheek, the skin sore and tender. Her dress was all wrong, the material ripped and twisted at her thighs, stained with patches of red.

No.

No!

I squeezed my eyes shut, trying to swallow down the acid rushing up my throat.

"N- Nicco," she murmured, barely conscious, her eyes closed as she hugged something.

Fuck.

It was a hoodie.

One of *my* hoodies.

I felt Bailey step up beside me. "What the fuck happened?" I growled, feeling myself unravel.

It was obvious what had gone down, but I needed to hear him say the words.

I needed confirmation before I drove back to MU and put a bullet through Fascini's skull.

"After we got rumbled and you and the guys split, I stayed around."

"You were watching her?" My eyes slid to his, although it physically pained me to take my attention off Arianne.

"Yeah. I couldn't just leave her, ya know?"

I don't know what I'd done to deserve this kid, but he was as loyal as fuck. Even if he did have a serious issue with following orders.

"She left with him. Her security detail followed behind, but when I got to the dorm something didn't feel right. One of her bodyguards was standing guard outside the building, but he looked... I don't know. Pissed. So I stuck around. Douchebag eventually left, and I snuck in through the back door and went up to her room. I can't explain it, Nic, but I just knew something wasn't right. Her bodyguard must have felt it too because when I got there, he was there too. And I took one look at his face and knew... I didn't even have to go inside her room."

My fists clenched at my side, agony and anger swirling inside my chest like a vortex. "And Fascini?" I gritted out.

"He was long gone. The bodyguard wanted to call her parents and we almost got into it, but in the end, he knew I was right. He knew I had to get her out of there."

Clamping my hand on his shoulder, I squeezed. "You made the right call, thank you."

"She's hurt pretty badly," he whispered. "She might need a doctor."

Fuck, he was right. She needed medical attention, someone to make sure he hadn't done any internal damage. I exhaled a steady breath, trying to rein in the emotion bubbling inside me. "I have to take her to my father."

"But Nicco—"

"I know. I know, Bay, but this changes everything." Arianne needed help. She needed proper care and attention. My father could get her that, off the record. He could also make sure everything was logged appropriately should we need to use it as evidence for the future.

Not that the legal route was an option for a piece of shit like Fascini. He didn't deserve jail time, he deserved a slow and painful death.

And he'd sealed his fate, the second he'd laid a hand on my girl.

"Can you drive?' I asked Bailey, and he nodded, running a hand down his face.

"Let's go, before someone sees us." I closed the back door and went around to the other side, gently easing into the back seat of his Camaro. Careful not to hurt Arianne, I lifted her head, cradling it in my lap and brushed the hair from her face.

"N- Nicco?" Her eyes fluttered open. "Is that you?"

"Ssh, Bambolina. I've got you. Everything is going to be okay now."

Bailey got into the car and fired up the engine. "You sure about this?" His eyes met mine in the rear-view mirror. "We can take her to my mom."

"No, it has to be my father." He was the only one who could protect her now.

Bailey nodded, reversing out of the parking lot and taking off toward the smaller road out of campus. I dug around in my jean pocket and pulled out my cell phone.

"Niccolò," my father answered on the second ring. "Is it done?"

"We have a problem," I said. "I need you to call Doc and tell him to meet me at the house in fifteen minutes."

"Should I be worried?"

"I'll explain everything when I get there." Hanging up, I dropped my head back against the seat rest. Arianne was out cold, gentle sobs still racking her body. There was every chance she was in shock.

"Bailey," I choked out, feeling my grip on reality waver.

"Yeah, cous?"

"Hurry."

We beat the doctor. Bailey pulled into the driveway and cut the engine. "What do you need?"

"Go on ahead and make sure my sister stays in her room. She doesn't need to see this."

"And Uncle Toni?"

"Let me deal with him."

"Maybe we should call Matteo, strength in numbers?"

"No," I said. "Not yet." The fewer people who knew for now, the better.

Bailey got out of the car and headed toward the house. I gingerly ran my fingers through Arianne's hair. "Amore mio," I whispered, "can you hear me?"

"Nicco?" She began to move but cried out. "It... it hurts."

I swallowed down the tears of anger burning my throat and opened the door. "I'm going to carry you inside, okay?"

"D- don't leave me."

"I won't, I promise."

Arianne wasn't only in shock, she was barely conscious. There was a likely explanation. One I didn't want to consider.

That motherfucker had drugged her.

I inched her fragile body out of the car and hoisted her into my arms. The front door swung open and my father came bounding down the steps, his eyes widening at the sight of the lifeless girl in my arms.

"Tell me you didn't—" A feral growl rumbled in my chest, and my father paled. "I'm sorry, Son. I should have known better. Who is she?" he asked, flanking my side as we approached the house.

"Not now, later. Is Doc on his way?"

"Should be here any minute. Want me to have Genevieve prepare the guest room?"

"I'm taking her to my room. When he gets here, send him straight up." Arianne stirred in my arms.

"Niccolò, wait." His hand landed on my shoulder and I paused, glancing back at him. "What happened here, Son? Talk to me?"

"I'll tell you everything once I've made sure she's okay."

Genevieve appeared in the hall, and gasped. "I'm sorry, I didn't—"

"Gen, help my boy, okay?"

"Of course, Anton..." she hesitated. "Mr. Marchetti. I'll get some water and towels."

It wasn't Genevieve's first rodeo. She'd been around my family for long enough to know the drill. Except it wasn't usually half-conscious girls in beautiful ball gowns; it was men in blood-soaked shirts.

"Please bring them to my room," I said, moving toward the stairs.

"Bailey?" my father asked.

"Distracting Alessia."

He nodded. "Go see to her, but then you and I need to sit down."

I didn't stick around, taking the stairs two at a time. It had been almost eighteen months since I'd lived here but my room was the same. Same charcoal bedding and gray curtains. But it didn't *feel* the same.

I lay Arianne down on the middle of my bed, tucking a pillow underneath her head. Her hand reached for me as her eyes flickered open again. "Nicco." It was a whimper.

"I'm right here."

Calm settled over her again, as if my presence soothed her. Genevieve knocked, before peeking inside. "How is she?"

"Honestly, I have no idea."

"She was... attacked?"

I nodded, unable to speak over the lump in my throat.

"What can I do?" she asked.

"Will you stay with her, when the doctor gets here? I'm not sure... I can't be here when he..." Fuck. My vision blurred as a wave of emotion crashed over me.

"Niccolò." Genevieve touched my arm. "You care about her." It wasn't a question, so I didn't offer an answer. "I'll stay with her; you have my word."

"Thank you."

I heard voices downstairs, the familiar Italian lilt of our family doctor. He was used to attending to emergencies; used to patching up stab wounds and bullet holes. He'd stitched nearly every scar on my body. But I doubted he'd ever dealt with something like this.

Footsteps sounded on the stairs and then my father's voice drifted into the room. "Niccolò, Doc's here."

"Come in," I said moving to the door.

Genevieve moved to Arianne's side and I knew she was in safe hands. I wanted to stay, to be right there while the doctor checked her over, but I wasn't sure I was strong enough to see... I pushed the thoughts down.

I greeted my father and Doc. His gaze went over my shoulder and he muttered, "Dio santo! She might need a hospital."

"No," I snapped. "No hospitals. If you need specialist supplies, I'll have someone go get them. But she stays here."

"Okay, Nicco. I'll examine her and see what we're dealing with."

"Thank you." I let him enter, watching as he snapped on some plastic gloves and approached the bed.

"Come on, Son. Come share a drink with me." My father walked off, and I followed, knowing no amount of liquor could fix this.

"Who is she?"

Three little words I'd dreaded ever since the day I realized I couldn't walk away from Arianne, seemed so insignificant now. She was lying upstairs drugged and beaten, assaulted and broken, and everything else no longer seemed important.

"Arianne Capizola," I said, meeting my father's hard glare with my own.

"I'm sorry, you need to repeat yourself, Niccolò, because it sounded like you just told me the Capizola heir is upstairs in your bed. And I know you're not that fucking stupid, boy."

"It's her."

He flexed his hand, the one curved around his glass of bourbon. I was hardly surprised when the glass whizzed past my face, shattering against the wall behind me. "Tell me you haven't fallen for her? Look me in the eye and tell me, that you haven't gotten into bed with the enemy."

"She is *not* the enemy. I know you think she's the way to Roberto, but she isn't." I kept my voice calm and controlled. "They're using her too. I don't know all the pieces of the puzzle yet, but he's using his own daughter to align himself with Fascini. We're missing something, but I'm telling you, she is not the enemy here."

My father collapsed back in his chair, scrubbing his jaw. Anger simmered in his eyes. He was pissed and I didn't blame him. After all, I'd played him. I'd put Arianne first over the family.

In our line of work, I'd committed the ultimate betrayal.

"What happened, Niccolò? And I want the truth, Son. Not the version of events you want me to know. The truth. Whatever you say in the next five minutes will determine your punishment."

I flinched at the severity in his tone. But as long as Arianne was safe, I could handle whatever he decided.

So I told him.

For the next ten minutes, I told my father everything that had happened over the last few weeks. From finding Arianne that first night, to sneaking her out to the country club, discovering her true identity, right up to the moment Bailey turned up at my door tonight.

"Jesus, Niccolò, of all the girls on campus, it had to be her."

"I know it doesn't matter, but I want you to know I never planned for this to happen."

He regarded me, disappointment clouding his eyes. "Do you love her?"

"More than I have ever loved anything else," I said without hesitation.

"Cazzo, Niccolò! And this Scott Fascini, what do we know about him?"

"I have Tommy looking into it. His family is wealthy. They own several businesses in and around the county. Capizola Holdings, and Fascini and Associates, are set to sign a multi-million deal to support Roberto's redevelopment plans for the west side of the river.

"Arianne's parents have been pushing for her to date Scott. I think they think it's good for business. But the guy is a real piece of work. I'm almost certain it was him who attacked her the first night I met her. If I'm right, Arianne was adamant she didn't want to go to security, and I'm betting she never told her parents. Which means she must know they'd have a hard time believing her." It was the only thing that made sense.

"Jesus Christ," my father let out a low whistle.

"You saw what he did to her." I clenched my fist against my thigh. "I had to bring her here. I had to."

"We'll deal with that later. Who knows she's here?"

"Me, Bailey, you, Genevieve, and Doc."

"Okay, let's keep it that way. See what Doc has to say. I'll make a few calls, see what I can find out about the name Fascini."

"Shit, the bodyguard; he knows Bailey took her."

"You think he'll tell Capizola?"

"I'm not sure. Bailey seemed to think he's on her side..."

"Which might mean we can use him. If Roberto finds out his daughter is missing, the clock starts ticking before he points his finger in our direction."

"Bailey can get to her friend. Maybe she can buy us some time?"

"Set it up. But for the love of God, Niccolò, make sure that kid doesn't end up in the wrong hands."

"He can handle it." I knew he'd do it if I asked him.

"Get out of here." My father grabbed the telephone. But I paused at the door and glanced back at him.

"Why are you doing this? Helping her?"

"Because despite what you think of me, Son, I took one look at that girl in your arms and saw Alessia. The thought of someone ever doing that to my little girl..." Pain filled his expression. "And because maybe this can benefit both of us."

"What do you mean?" I wasn't sure I liked where this was heading.

"I take it you've already decided you'll do whatever it takes to protect her?"

I nodded.

"Maybe there's a way for you to keep the girl and for us to use her as leverage over Roberto."

Of course he would see it like that. I should have known.

My jaw ticked.

"Don't look at me like that, Niccolò. You brought this upon us. *You*. You had to know the second you decided to bring her here that you were hand delivering me the leverage we need to get Roberto to back off."

He was right.

Of course he was fucking right.

Still, it made it no easier to swallow.

"I won't let you hurt her," I said defiantly.

"And I would expect no less. She is your woman, your heart, you should protect her with your life. But do not forget, love blinds us. It makes us weak. There will come a day when you have to make a choice; the family or your heart, and it is a choice I do not envy."

Arianne.

My choice would always be Arianne.

But could I really sacrifice everything? My family. Alessia and Bailey. Matteo and Enzo. My aunts and uncles.

Even my father.

Could I condemn Arianne to a life bound to a mafioso who had broken the cardinal code of honor?

"I can see you have a lot to consider. Go be with your girl. I'll make some calls."

"Thank you." I left his study and closed the door, dropping my head against the wood. When Bailey had turned up at my door and said Arianne's name, all I could think about was getting to her, protecting her. I didn't stop to consider the consequences because all I saw was her.

But my father was right. I had set into motion a chain of events there was no stopping now.

A chain of events I didn't know if either of us was ready for.

A chain of events, we might not survive.

I quietly knocked on the door. It cracked open and Genevieve smiled at me. "She's been asking for you." She pulled open the door to reveal Arianne propped up in my bed, talking in hushed tones to the doctor.

"Nicco," she breathed, tears pricking her eyes.

I went to her side, sitting on the edge and taking her hand in mine. "How are you feeling?

"A little groggy and sore." Her gaze dropped, but I gently tipped her chin back.

"You're safe now."

"Niccolò, if I might have a word outside?"

"Sure, Doc. I'll be right back, okay?"

"Promise?" Fear clouded Arianne's eyes.

"I promise. Genevieve will be right here."

"Of course." She nodded, moving to the other side of the bed.

"I'll stop by tomorrow to check on you, okay, Arianne?" Doc said.

"Thank you, for everything."

He gave her a warm smile before leaving the room. I followed him into the hall, closing the door behind me. "How is she?"

"Miss Rossi," his brow rose with doubt. But he knew the drill; he wouldn't ask questions. "Is strong. It's likely she was given a sedative leading up to the assault. I have given her fluids and treated several minor cuts. She informed me that she was a virgin so I have also taken blood samples to run a full work up as she can't remember if her attacker wore a condom."

My eyes shuttered, my fist barreling toward the wall. Pain splintered through my wrist and up my arm.

"Nicco..."

"Sorry, Doc," I drew in a sharp breath, cradling my hand against my body. "Carry on."

"Very well. Since Miss Rossi is not on birth control, I have also issued her with the emergency contraceptive pill. I would like to stop by tomorrow and document any new bruises. She has some faint bruising around her throat which suggests—"

"I don't need the specifics," I ground out," I just need to know if she's going to be okay."

"Like I said, she's strong. After some fluids and painkillers she already seemed much brighter. But Niccolò, this type of thing affects everyone differently. The physical scars will heal, but the emotional scars may take more time." His expression turned grim. "I have taken photographic evidence and swabs. I assume you'll want me to analyze and record those?"

I nodded, too choked up to reply.

"Go be with her, the rest can wait until tomorrow." He squeezed my shoulder.

"Thanks, Doc, I appreciate it."

He took off down the hall, and I went back into my bedroom. Arianne and Genevieve were talking but her eyes immediately locked on mine.

"I'll leave you both. If you need anything..."

"Thank you." I offered Genevieve a weak smile, and she left us, tension filling the room.

"I'm sorry," Arianne sobbed. "I'm so, so sorry."

I rushed to her side, dropping to the side of the bed and gathering her in my arms. "You have nothing to be sorry for, amore mio."

"B- but I wanted it to be you. I wanted to give you all my firsts, Nicco. Every single one."

My heart stopped as pain obliterated me. "*Never* think like that." I cupped Arianne's face gently in my hands and gazed down at her. "You're safe and you're here, it's enough."

"But—"

"Ssh." I kissed the corner of her mouth, careful not to touch the split in the pillow of her bottom lip.

"It feels like a dream, like I wasn't really there."

"Do you want to talk about it?"

"Not yet." Her lips quivered but she didn't cry. "I would like a bath though. The doctor said that would be okay if I felt up to it."

"A bath? I think I can do that." Dropping a kiss on Arianne's head, I stood up. "Will you be okay if I..." I flicked my head to the adjoining bathroom door.

"I'll be okay." She gave me a small smile. My strong girl putting on a brave face even in the direst of circumstances. Being around Arianne grounded me, forced the beast living inside me back into its cage.

"Give me five minutes, okay?"

She nodded, and I disappeared into the bathroom, turning on the faucets of the corner tub before searching for some bath salts. Or maybe salt wasn't a good idea. Shit, I didn't know the first thing about any of this crap.

Searching through the cabinet, I settled on a bottle of lavender and chamomile bath soak, adding a couple of drops to the water. Bubbles began to froth, a floral aroma filling the air. I grabbed some towels from the rack and hooked them beside the tub.

When I went back into the room, Arianne was already trying to get out of bed. I went to her side, wrapping my arm around her waist and taking her weight. "Okay?" I asked and she nodded, pain etched into her expression.

She was wrapped in a fluffy robe, but I could see the faint bruises Doc had told me about. "Don't look at me like that, please," Arianne's voice cracked.

"Sorry." I swallowed. "It's just hard seeing you like this."

"I'm still the same person, Nicco."

Jesus. My body trembled, white hot fury pulsing through me, as I led her into the bathroom. But I knew I needed to be strong for her.

"Can you get undressed if I give you some privacy?"

"No," she blurted out. "Stay, please." Arianne reached for me, threading our fingers together. "I need you."

Slowly, I pushed the robe off her shoulders, gently inching down her arms. Her breath hitched a couple of times, but Arianne was otherwise quiet. She wore nothing underneath, the doctor no doubt collected her underwear and dress for evidence, or as we usually called it, leverage.

I tried to keep my eyes on her face, to ignore the bite mark on the curve of her breast, or the one further down.

"Nicco," she whispered, palming my cheek. "Don't let him in here with us."

"How do you do it?" I asked, feeling so far out of my depth I was drowning.

"You're here. With you by my side, I can do anything." She leaned in, touching her head to mine. I breathed her in, letting her words sink into me.

"I'm so sorry," I whispered. "I should have never left the gala." Not that I'd had much choice with her father's security men breathing down our necks all night.

"Stop," Arianne brushed her lips over mine, but I pulled away.

"Come on, I'll help you in." I took her elbow, guiding her into the tub. Arianne let out a little hiss as her body disappeared under the water. "Too hot?" I asked.

"It's nice. Soothing. I'm just a little... sore."

The word was like a glacier between us. I didn't want this to be about me, about how it affected me, but I didn't know how to control all the thoughts slamming into me.

I leaned down, turning off the faucets and perched on the edge of the tub. "Do you want me to go?"

"Do you want to go?"

"You know I don't."

"Good." She smiled, relaxing back against the tub. "So this is where you grew up? You know, I've thought a lot about seeing this side of your life. I hoped it would be under different circumstances." A beat passed as she swished the water around her body. "Your father knows I'm here?"

"He does. But don't worry about that right now. You're safe, and that's all that matters. Bailey has gone back to MU to find Nora. He's going to buy us some time while we figure out what to do."

"I'm not going back," she said with an air of defiance.

"We'll talk about that later."

Arianne pressed her lips together, silence settling over us. When she was done soaking, I helped her out of the tub and wrapped her in a fluffy white towel. Scooping her up against my chest, I walked into the bedroom and laid her on the bed.

"You should get some rest," I said.

"Lie with me."

My body went rigid.

"Nicco, please..."

Kicking off my boots, I went around and lay on the other side of the bed. Arianne nestled into my side, slipping her hand under my hoodie. "Bambolina, stop." I gently pushed her away. She stared up at me with those big honey eyes of hers, cheeks flushed and lips parted.

"I want this, Nicco. I *need* this." It wasn't the pain in her voice that surprised me, it was the strength. The conviction.

Arianne truly believed she wanted this.

Wanted me.

After everything she'd been through.

"You don't know what you're saying," I whispered, the words raw against my throat.

"I do." She wiggled closer, kissing my neck, dragging her tongue up my neck. Jesus, it felt so good.

But it was wrong.

Everything about this was fucking wrong.

"Amore mio, stop. *Stop*." This time she jerked back of her own volition.

"You don't want me?" Hurt flashed across her expression. "But I thought—"

"I want you," I admitted. I wanted her more than my next breath. But not here, not like this. "You're hurting and you're confused..."

"Confused?" She gasped, inching away from me. "I'm not confused. Nothing about what he did to me is confusing. I remember it, you know? It's hazy but it's there. His weight pressed against me. The feeling of the air being squeezed from my lungs while he..."

Anger radiated through me. Unbridled blistering anger. Scott Fascini was a dead man. Maybe not tomorrow or the day after that. But he would pay. I wanted to watch him bleed. I wanted to stand over him while he begged for his life.

Anything else was simply not an option.

"Ari—" I reached for her, but her hand shot out, keeping me at a distance.

"He raped me, Nicco. He took the one thing I promised myself would be given to the person of my choosing, on my terms. He took that from me." Tears streamed down her face, but I'd never seen Arianne look fiercer. "And I can never get it back. But I can do this. I can choose to give myself to you, Nicco. I choose *you*."

Her resolve began to slip, desperation clinging to every word. "I choose you, so please, *please* don't take this away from me too. I want you. I want you to show me how it's supposed to be. I want you to make me feel good."

I ran a hand down my face. I'd wanted Arianne ever since I'd laid eyes on her and fighting the urge to make her mine hadn't been easy. But I'd done it. I'd done it because I knew giving in would only complicate things in a way she wasn't ready for.

Yet here she was, offering herself to me. Begging for me to erase her memory of that sick fuck Fascini.

"Nicco." Arianne pressed closer, her hands going to my chest again. Her touch was corrosive, slowly decimating my walls. Walls I'd spent my whole life building. She leaned over, her lips ghosting over my jaw, the corner of my mouth. My body trembled with need. To take what she was offering. To do the right thing.

To be the better man.

But I wasn't a good man. I was Niccolò Marchetti, son of the devil, prince of hell.

Ari though, she was an angel. Pure and good. She was everything I wasn't. Everything I could never be.

Yet, she wanted me.

She'd *chosen* me.

Or maybe it was never a choice. I'd never much believed in fate or destiny. My family, like most Italian-American families living in Verona County, were Catholic. But I'd seen too much, experienced too much to have the unwavering faith so many of my elders had.

"I want you to do this, please." Her voice smashed through the last line of my defenses.

How could I deny this girl?

This strong courageous woman before me, with nothing but hope in her heart and desire in her eyes.

The answer was, I couldn't.

But tonight, I would.

I had to.

Because she needed me to make that decision for her.

"Sleep, Bambolina." I pulled her into my side, feeling the fight leave her fragile body. "We have time. We have all the time in the world."

Arianne didn't answer and I knew she'd fallen asleep.

And I hoped peace would find her there.

TWENTY-ONE

ARIANNE

I WOKE WITH A START, memories of the night before slamming into me one after another. I sat up, wincing in agony.

"Can I get you anything?"

My eyes darted to the corner of the room, landing on a petite girl with familiar eyes. "Oh, I'm sorry. I'm Alessia."

"Nicco's sister," I breathed.

"One and the same." She gave me a warm smile. "You must be the other important woman in his life."

My brows bunched together. "Arianne. My name is Arianne."

"I'm sorry... for what happened to you."

"He told you?" I pulled the covers higher, feeling the need to shield myself. I wasn't offended he'd told her, just surprised.

"Oh no, he doesn't think I'm old enough or strong enough to know stuff like that... whatever." She shrugged. "I'm pretty good at finding my way into places I shouldn't. Is it true, you're Roberto Capizola's daughter?"

I nodded. What did it matter who knew my true identity now?

Everything was different this morning.

I was different.

Scott had taken something from me, something I wouldn't ever get back. But it was more than that—he'd killed a part of me.

The truth was, Scott had changed me.

In ways I knew I didn't fully understand yet.

Tears pricked my eyes, but I would not cry. Not in front of this sweet girl trying to... distract me?

The sound of raised voices drifted into the room. "What is that?" I asked.

"That would be the aftermath of you." Alessia smiled again but this time it was sad and full of sympathy. "My cousins, Enzo and Matteo, got here a while ago. They've been like this ever since."

Enzo.

If he was here, he knew about me. It was the only explanation for all the yelling.

"I have to go down there," I said, throwing back the cover. Every muscle in my body protested, pain radiating in places I didn't even know could hurt.

"You should probably stay here," Nicco's sister warned. "He wouldn't want you to witness..." she paused, "*that.*"

"It sounds like they're going to kill each other."

"It wouldn't be the first time. You have met my brother and his friends, right?"

"I..." Had no idea how to answer that. The Nicco I had fallen in love with was kind and attentive, but I knew he had another, darker side. One he'd tried to conceal from me.

Someone yelled a string of Italian cuss words. It was quickly followed by a loud crashing noise.

"And I'm supposed to pretend none of this happens." Alessia curled a strand of hair around her finger.

"I don't suppose you have any clothes I could borrow?" We looked to be similar sizes.

"For real, you're going down there?"

"I need to see Nicco."

"Okay, then. But don't say I didn't warn you." Alessia got up. "I'll get you something to wear. And while we're at it, you might want to do something with your hair."

I touched a hand to the untamed curls. "That bad, huh?" Laughter bubbled out of me, and it felt good, and strangely cathartic.

Last night had been the single worst night of my life. But then Nicco had taken care of me and I'd fallen to sleep wrapped in his arms, and I knew I would be okay. Because while Scott had taken something from me, he hadn't managed to touch the most important thing—my heart.

That belonged to Nicco.

Always.

"For the record," Alessia paused at the door, "Nicco has never brought a girl home before." She walked away as if her words meant nothing. When in fact, they meant everything.

I smiled to myself.

Scott might have left me bruised and bitten and bloody. But he had failed to break my spirit, and that felt like a small victory.

"Do I pass?" I asked Alessia twenty minutes later. She'd had to help me get dressed in the end. It had been an awkward moment I didn't want to relive anytime soon, but I'd never felt so grateful to have a stranger around to help me.

"You'll do." Her lips curved. "I should probably warn you; it isn't looking great down there. Enzo looks murderous and Nicco is like a caged animal."

"Not quite the Sunday morning I had planned..."

"Life has a funny way of playing with us."

"Thank you, Alessia. I don't know what I would have done this morning if I'd have woken up alone."

"My brother would have turned up eventually."

I didn't doubt it, but in a way, I was glad it had been Alessia and not Nicco. I could still remember the way he had rejected me last night. My head knew he was only doing the right and honorable thing, but my heart didn't quite agree. And part of me couldn't help but worry if he would see me differently in the harsh light of day.

I forced down the thoughts. There were more pressing issues. Like stopping him and Enzo from killing one another.

"Ready?" Alessia held out her hand and I slid my palm against hers. With every step, the voices grew louder, until we were standing outside a door downstairs. "You don't have to do this." She whispered, squeezing my hand. "No one expects you to get involved."

"I need to see him." I nodded resolutely, despite the band of wild horses galloping in my chest.

"Here goes nothing." Alessia let out a little sigh as she opened the door and stepped inside. I followed her, waiting for the men to notice me. But they were too busy arguing. Nicco and Matteo sat on the couch, while the man I presumed to be his father sat behind the desk, and Enzo paced. There was no sign of Bailey.

"This is bullshit," Enzo ground out. "We need to hand her back to—"

"Arianne." Nicco leaped up, staring at me with surprise. "What are you—"

"Did you honestly think she'd sleep through this?" Alessia raised a brow.

"I... shit, I'm sorry." He slowly approached me, his concerned gaze running over my face. "Bambolina..." It was a pained whisper.

"I'm okay," I said, answering his silent question.

He reached for me, brushing the hair from my face. "You need to rest."

"I slept for hours. I needed to see you."

"Niccolò," his father commanded, and I moved around Nicco to come face to face with Antonio Marchetti.

"Thank you," I said without hesitation. "For letting me stay here."

He nodded, his cool expression giving nothing away. "I'm afraid you caught us at a bad moment, Miss Capizola."

"I didn't mean to interrupt. But I had to see Nicco."

"You have got to be fucking kidding me," Enzo spat, disdain rolling off him. "Are we really going to sit here and act like this is okay? She's the Capizola heir, for fuck's sake. If he gets even so much as a scent of her being here, we might as well leave town now."

"Lorenzo," Antonio warned. "Miss Capizola is our guest. It would do you well to remember your manners."

"Uncle, I mean no disrespect, but only a few weeks ago, we were planning—"

"Enzo, *enough*!" He slammed down his hand against the polished wood. "Alessia, go and find Genevieve please. Make yourself useful."

"But, Papá—"

"Alessia..."

"Fine." She huffed. "But one day, you're going to have to accept I'm old enough to understand what this life means." Alessia fled from the room, slamming the door behind her.

"Please, sit," Antonio said, motioning to the couch. Matteo shuffled along, giving me a tentative smile as Nicco guided me over to it. We sat down.

"You've landed us in quite the predicament, Miss Capizola. I would like to hear your version of events, if that's not too much to ask?"

Nicco started to protest, but I covered his knee with my hand, squeezing gently. "I know you hate my family, sir," my voice quivered. "But I am not my father. In fact, I'm not sure I even want to call him my father right now."

"Arianne, you don't have to do this," Nicco whispered.

"Yes, I do." I met Antonio's heavy stare again. "Until recently, I wasn't even aware of our families' history. I knew nothing of my father trying to acquire La Riva for redevelopment. And I knew nothing of the Marchetti."

"Impossible," Enzo gritted out.

"It's the truth. I have spent the last five years of my life sheltered from the truth, from the world beyond my family's estate. I never questioned it, until now." My gaze slid to Nicco.

"What happened last night?" his father asked.

"No," Nicco went as white as a sheet.

My body was trembling, the memories demanding attention. The feel of his hands around my throat. His weight above me. The way he clawed at my skin. I suppressed a shudder and forced myself to take a calming breath. "Scott Fascini, the son of my father's prospective business partner, drugged and raped me."

Matteo sucked in a sharp breath beside me while Antonio looked on, his lips twisting in disgust. But it was Enzo who surprised me the most.

"Porca troia," he mumbled under his breath, clenching a fist against his thigh. "He did that?" He flicked his head to my face. I knew I looked a mess; the red welts although faded some, still visible. Not to mention the finger marks around my throat and the cut in my bottom lip.

"And worse," I confessed.

It was Nicco's turn to cuss. "Enough. That's enough. She's not on trial here."

"You're right, Son, she isn't. But if we are going to help Miss Capizola, we need to know the full story."

Just then, there was a knock at the door. "Come in," Antonio called, and the woman from last night slipped inside. She wore a simple white blouse and black pants.

"Genevieve," he said curtly.

"I'm sorry to interrupt, but Bailey just arrived and he's not alone."

"What the hell has he gone and done now?" Enzo grumbled.

"Nicco, go deal with him please."

"Me, but—"

"Now, Niccolò."

"I'll be right back, okay." He brushed his hand over mine before taking off after Genevieve.

The tension in the room doubled. Enzo was glaring at me, his cold assessing gaze like razorblades across my skin. Antonio let out a breath as if he was about to speak, but instead settled back in his chair again.

The silence stretched on.

My heart beat like a drum against my rib cage.

So when the door swung open and I saw Nora and Luis standing behind Nicco, I almost cried out in relief. "Thank God." My best friend rushed over to me, wrapping me into her arms. I winced and she immediately withdrew "Crap, I'm sorry."

"It's fine."

"Nothing about this is fine. I'll kill him. I'll skin him alive, chop off his dick, and feed it to him, that disgusting piece of—"

Antonio cleared his throat and Nora slowly peeked over at him. "Hmm, sorry."

Enzo snorted, and the tension in the room ebbed away.

"Arianne." Luis stepped forward and I went to him. "I am so sorry. I will never forgive myself."

"It's not your fault." I hugged him tight.

"And you are?" Antonio's voice rang out.

"Luis, sir. Luis Vitelli, Arianne's bodyguard."

"I see. You were there last night?"

Luis' expression turned dark as he nodded. "I was at the building, but Mr. Capizola had requested that I give Arianne and Mr. Fascini space to... *talk*."

"Talk?" Enzo sneered. "Seems that fuck Fascini is unaware of the meaning of the word talk."

"Enzo," Nicco sighed.

"You're lucky I'm still standing here. All this time you've been seeing her, a Capizola. The enemy." He pushed off the wall and stalked closer. "You lied to me, cous, over a fucking girl."

"We've been over this." Nicco put himself between me and Enzo. Luis tried to move around me too, but I stood my ground. Refusing to be pushed aside by these men.

"I am not my father," I repeated, locking my eyes on Enzo. His nostrils flared, anger and betrayal swirling around him like a vortex.

"This isn't a game, little girl. It's a fucking war. We make a wrong move and people get hurt. People die. Are you ready for that? Are you ready to watch the people you care about get hurt? Are you ready to—"

"You need to back off, Enzo. I'm warning you." Nicco growled the words, the air shifting around us, crackling with anticipation.

"Uncle Toni," Matteo interjected. "Maybe you should—"

"Leave them be." He dismissed him. "She needs to see this."

"You betrayed me." Enzo lunged for Nicco, clipping his face with a resounding crack. Nicco managed to elbow his best friend and the two them circled each other.

"You need to stand down. I'm warning you, E."

"Stand down? I need to knock some fucking sense into your thick skull, cous. She's the enemy. You're in bed with the enemy."

"Vaffanculo!" Nicco ground out, throwing up his hands in surrender.

"She is in the middle of this, Niccolò," Antonio interjected. "Whether you like it or not. The question is, is she strong enough to handle it?"

Everyone looked at me. I felt their stares burning into my face as I looked ahead. I didn't have all the answers. I was barely holding myself together, my body broken and sore. But if I showed even an ounce of weakness, I knew Nicco's father would use it against me.

Maybe even send me back into the arms of my father.

Stepping around Nicco, I looked to Enzo and then Antonio. "I am not my father," I said again. "He betrayed me. He lied and kept his secrets to protect me, but then handed me over to Scott Fascini like I was nothing but a prize to be coveted. I am not going back there. I- I can't. I'd rather die." The words echoed around my skull. I hadn't intended to say them, wasn't sure I even meant them, but I needed Nicco's father to understand I wasn't just a pawn in this game.

"I love your son, Mr. Marchetti. I choose him. Always."

What was I saying?

Antonio Marchetti didn't care about me; he'd tried to have me killed when I was just a young girl.

He probably couldn't wait to dangle me in front of my father as leverage.

Oh God...

Nora rushed to my side as I swayed on my feet. "Ari," she cried.

But it was too late.

Everything was crashing down around me. The temporary strength I'd found, crumbling like sand beneath rain. Nicco flanked my other side, his arm wrapping around my waist, taking my weight. Luis moved up behind me.

We'd drawn an invisible line in the sand. But I didn't expect Matteo to cross it and stand beside Nicco.

"Well, well, isn't this interesting." Antonio folded his hands on the desk and leaned forward. "Lorenzo, care to throw in your position?"

"I'm still deciding." He'd moved back to the far wall, arms folded over his chest, a purple shadow forming around his eye. Nicco hadn't come off unscathed either, a small cut along his brow and some swelling around his lip.

"I'm taking Arianne back up to my room." he said quietly. "And then we will settle this." Nicco cut Enzo with an icy look, before scooping me into his arms and carrying me out of the room.

"How are you feeling?" Nicco stroked my hand. He'd carried me back to his room and insisted I stay put until the doctor arrived to check on me.

"A little tired."

"What were you thinking, coming down there and confronting my father?"

"I wanted to see you."

He inhaled a harsh breath. "This is a delicate situation. If anything happened to you... because of me, I would never forgive myself." Pain edged into his expression.

I sat up, cupping his face. "I meant everything I said. I choose you, Nicco."

"You do not know what you're saying."

"How can you say that to me, after everything?" Tears pooled in my eyes. "I love you. It doesn't even begin to come close to how I feel about you. You are my life."

"Ti voglio sempre al mio fianco," he whispered. "Do you know what it means?"

I could pick out a word or two, but I hadn't grown up speaking fluent Italian like a lot of Italian-American families living in Verona County.

Nicco leaned in, brushing his nose over mine. "It means, I want you by my side, always. Sei tutto per me, Arianne Carmen Lina Capizola."

"You're everything to me too." Our lips met in a gentle caress. "I was so worried you might feel... differently about me."

"Bambolina, I love you. You are my life. Nothing will ever change that." His eyes burned with a fierce possessiveness. It wrapped around me like a warm blanket. "But the road ahead of us is not simple, you have to know that. This life, the family, it isn't a choice. I can't walk away, Arianne. If we do this, if you meant what you said, by choosing me, it means you're choosing this life. And I should be a better man, I shouldn't let you make that choice."

"It's done," I said. "I won't take it back, Nicco. Not now, not ever. I wasn't sure I meant it downstairs, but I know I did. I don't want to live in a world without you, Niccolò Marchetti. I won't."

A knock at the door broke our connection. Nicco let out a weary sigh. "Yes?"

It opened and Antonio appeared. "Niccolò, I would like to speak with Miss Capizola, alone. If that's okay?"

"Arianne?" Nicco asked me and I nodded.

"Come in, Mr. Marchetti."

"I'll be right outside, okay?" Nicco dropped a kiss on my head, moving past his father.

"The guys are waiting for you. I think Miss Abato would also like to talk to you. She's an interesting one, isn't she?"

I smothered a chuckle, dreading to think what Nora had possibly been saying to Antonio. Nicco left us, and Antonio took the chair beside the bed. The family resemblance was stark: same dark eyes and strong jaw. The Marchetti men had eyes that could look straight through you.

"It would seem you have bewitched my son, Miss—"

"Please, call me Arianne."

"Very well". He gave me a small nod. "I haven't seen Nicco care the way he cares for you with anyone except Alessia. When his mother left, it affected him far more than he has ever acknowledged. This life, it demands a man to harden his heart, Arianne. It doesn't mean we don't feel; quite the contrary. Sometimes we feel so deeply that it can be suffocating. But it's different for mafioso. We are men of honor, bound to the code of omertà. Do you know what that means?"

"Yes, sir. It's a code of silence."

"At its most basic definition, yes. But it is so much more than that. It means family first. And I'm not talking about family in the traditional sense." He gave me a pointed look. "Life with Niccolò will be difficult. There will be times he cannot talk to you, times when he disappears and he cannot tell you where he is. You will read things in the papers, see things on the news. But you can never ask. That is the code of omertà and I have seen it ruin more relationships than you can count."

He glanced away, lost in his own thoughts. "It cost me my wife, Arianne. The love of my life. So you see, while I commend your unwavering faith to stand at my son's side, you should know that loving Niccolò is a life sentence your heart probably won't survive."

"And if I still choose Nicco? If I choose to stand at his side?"

"Then I hope you are ready for hellfire to rain down on you both. Because your father won't just roll over and accept this. He will fight, Arianne. He might have renounced his roots, his blood, but it is still inside him. And when he does come, we will have no choice but to retaliate. It will be war."

"You know," I said. "You're not at all what I expected."

"No?" His brow rose. "And what did you expect?"

"Well, for someone who gave the order to have a young girl murdered, I expected someone more... monstrous."

Antonio's eyes clouded with surprise, but he didn't flinch. "A monster has many disguises, Arianne. You would do well to remember that."

"So you're not denying it? You did order a hit on me?"

"Does Nicco know about this?" He ignored my question.

"I told him what my father told me, yes."

"Very well. I need to speak with my son. Please excuse me."

"That's it? No apology? No explanation? I spent five years of my life in solitude because of you, Mr. Marchetti, I think I deserve to know why."

"And you will, all in good time." He rose, smoothing down his jacket. "Doc should be here soon. If you need anything, I'll have Genevieve see to you."

I dropped my head back on the pillow. If I thought Nicco was a lot, his father was something else entirely.

And I couldn't help but think there were still pieces of the puzzle yet to reveal themselves.

TWENTY-TWO

NICCO

"YOU REALLY LOVE HER?" Enzo looked at me like he no longer recognized me. It stung but I knew I deserved it.

"I do, cous. I know it's not what you want to hear, but she's it for me."

"Jesus," he let out a low whistle. "The Capizola heir. I knew there was something about her. I just didn't realize it was because you were bang—"

I levelled him with a hard look, and he threw up his hands. "My bad. I'm still pissed at you, probably will be for a good while yet, but even I can't deny what that fucker did to her makes my blood boil."

"Is she okay, really?" Matteo asked. He was still sitting on the couch. Luis and Nora had gone up to say goodbye to Arianne. They were going to buy us some time until we figured out what the fuck to do next.

"I think she's holding on by a thread."

"She's strong," he said. "I've never seen anyone stand up to a roomful of guys like that before. Let alone Marchetti men."

He had a point. She had been fierce if not a little reckless.

There was a knock at the door and Luis poked his head inside. "She's sleeping."

Thank fuck. At least if she was asleep, she wasn't causing trouble.

"I thought you should know her mother called Nora while we were up there."

"Did Arianne talk to her?"

He nodded, slipping further into the room. "Turns out Fascini went back to the party last night after..." Luis drew in a harsh breath. "He told them Arianne had gotten sick on him and was so embarrassed she kicked him out. He reassured them he would check on her today."

"Motherfucker," I roared, my jaw clenched impossibly tight.

"Easy, cous." Matteo stood up. "What else did the mom say?"

"She asked Ari if she needed anything. Nora grabbed the phone at that point and said Arianne had made a dash for the bathroom, adding it was probably best she stayed away until whatever it was had passed. It should buy you some time."

I gave him an appreciative nod. "What about Roberto? Has he been in touch?"

"He texted me earlier requesting I stay put until anything changes."

"And what about your partner? Is he going to be a problem?"

"I'll handle Nixon."

"Okay, so we have the rest of the day and tonight if we're lucky. But we need to figure out what happens next. Arianne has already said she won't go back to the dorm." Not that I wanted her anywhere near that place. Not after what he did to her there, in her own goddamn room.

Anger flared inside me and I rubbed my temples, trying to rein in the urge to go after him.

"Hey, you okay?" Enzo asked me with a concerned expression. I gave him a tight nod, forcing myself to take a deep breath.

"I'll speak to Nora," Luis said. "We may have an idea."

"Can we trust her?"

"Who, Nora?" Luis balked. "She loves Arianne more than anything. You don't need to doubt that girl's loyalty one bit."

"Okay," I said, "and thank you. For everything. It makes things a little easier knowing she has someone on their side watching over her."

Luis held my stare with his own. My father had already ordered his tech guy to run a background check on Luis Vitelli. He was squeaky clean, except for his current employer being Roberto Capizola. But Luis wasn't mafioso, he didn't operate under the same codes as we did. He was hired help. And hired help usually had a price. Turns out, finding Arianne after Scott's attack was enough to turn him.

"You have my number," I said. "If anything changes, use it."

With a final nod, Luis disappeared out of the room.

"I like him," Matteo declared.

"You like everyone."

"I only like you sometimes."

Enzo flipped him off, then his expression darkened. "So what the fuck do we do now?"

"You two go find Alessia and try to smooth things over. I need to speak with my father."

"Babysit? You want us to baby—"

"Come on, E." Matteo fought a grin. "We can put an ice pack on your face. It might improve things a little."

The two of them jostled each other out of the study. I dropped onto the couch and let out a long breath. Things were moving too fast; the pieces of the puzzle multiplying by the second. Arianne was safe, for now. But it still left the issue of what we were going to do when tomorrow rolled around.

"Niccolò." My father entered their room, closing the door behind him. "I learned some interesting things after speaking to Arianne."

Shit.

His eyes fixed on me, dark and assessing.

"She told you," I breathed.

"And yet, you said nothing. Why?"

"Because I knew it would reveal our secret and I didn't want to put her in harm's way."

"That must have been very difficult for you."

"Finding out my father, a man I thought I could trust, ordered a hit on a *child* and subsequently drove my mother away, was fucking difficult. But I managed." Bitterness coated my words.

"Watch your tongue, boy." His tone was scathing. Antonio Marchetti might have been my father, but he was still the boss. And you never disrespected the boss. "You know," he went on, "I always wondered what drove Roberto to hide his heir away." His fingers tapped the desk.

"Wait a minute." I digested his words. "You mean you didn't order the hit?"

"Niccolò," he sighed. "I am many things, but I am not a child murderer. You believed her? You really thought I could—"

"The timelines fit." Confusion and guilt slithered through me. "Mom left right after it happened."

"I see." He was quiet for a second, contemplative. "It would appear there are things happening not even I understand. But I promise you, Niccolò, I did not order that hit on Arianne."

"But if you didn't, who did?"

"That is what I intend on finding out."

Jesus, we couldn't catch a break. The revelations just kept on coming.

"But Mom—"

"Coincidence, or there might be another explanation." His brows furrowed. "We have more pressing issues to deal with right now though."

"Like how we keep Arianne safe without starting a war?"

His lips pressed into a grim line. "Exactly. Go be with your girl, she needs you. I'll consult Vincenzo and Michele, get their input."

"Do you think that's a good idea?"

"Niccolò, they are your uncles. My capos. I trust them with my life. And now, we must trust them with Arianne's life. I suspect Vincenzo won't like it. But Michele will be on our side."

"So *we're* on the same side?" I wanted to be one hundred percent sure.

"Son, even if you tried to walk away from that girl, something tells me she would find a way to glue herself to your side. She has made her choice. And you made yours the second you brought her here. Whether I like it or not, she's one of us now."

"Thank you." Relief sank into me. I hadn't realized how much I needed him to say the words until they were out there, hanging between us.

He gave me a tight nod. "We still need a plan. And you should prepare yourself for the fact that she might have to return to her family, at least until we can figure out our next move. But Arianne has my protection, I give you my word."

I got up, going to the door, but his voice gave me pause. "There's still the issue of Scott Fascini. He'll get what's coming to him, Niccolò, but until we know more about his family, you are to stay away from him. That's an order. Understand?"

I pressed my lips together, anger vibrating through me.

"Niccolò, you are not to go anywhere near Fascini, do you understand?"

"I'll try." It wasn't what he wanted to hear, but it was the best I could do for now.

Fascini had hurt Arianne. Stolen her innocence. He deserved nothing less than my hands around his throat squeezing the air from his lungs.

I would have my pound of flesh.

It was only a matter of time.

"This all looks amazing," Arianne said. The second she'd smelled Genevieve's cooking, she had wanted to come downstairs. I couldn't deny her. She seemed lighter somehow. Like a weight had been lifted since our conversation this morning. Doc had stopped by to see her again and was happy with her progress.

"Alessia made pie," Genevieve said over her shoulder. "I have a feeling it's going to be her best yet."

My sister beamed, standing two inches taller, and guilt coiled around my heart. I'd left her. As soon as I'd been able to, I'd moved out and abandoned her. Yet, she'd never blamed me. She never made me feel anything less than her brother, her protector.

It was more than I deserved.

"Nicco?" Arianne's hand curled into my sweater. "What's wrong?"

"Nothing." I dropped a kiss on the end of her nose. "Everything's fine."

Alessia caught my eye and frowned. She was too perceptive for a sixteen-year-old. I should have known she wouldn't stay put last night, or this morning. She was a perpetual thorn in my side, but I loved her dearly. Everything I did, everything I would do in the future was to secure her future. To make life safe for her.

Only now I had two lives to think about.

Sliding my arm around Arianne's chest, I pulled her back against me. She let out a soft sigh, completely at ease in my family's kitchen. Alessia had already taken to her, eager to know everything there was to know about Arianne and her life at MU. Matteo, although quiet, had sided with her without question. Even Enzo was slowly coming around to her. She'd completely bewitched my friends and family. And more and more, it was beginning to feel like Arianne Capizola belonged here, at my side.

"You two are so adorable," my sister crooned.

Enzo snorted, rolling his eyes at us.

"Maybe you and Nora could finish what you started?" Arianne said, smothering a giggle.

He stood up and glared at her. "I need some air."

Me and Matteo chuckled. Enzo didn't date. He barely talked to the girls he hooked up with. He and Nora were complete opposites, but then I knew firsthand that sometimes opposites attracted.

"You shouldn't push his buttons." I whispered against the shell of Arianne's ear. She shivered, tilting her head to one side. I couldn't resist flicking my tongue over her pulse point, pressing my lips there.

"You should probably close your eyes, Sia."

"Screw you, Matteo," Alessia shrieked. "I'm sixteen. I know what sex is. I'm practically the only junior *not* doing it."

My head whipped up as I stared at her. "What did you just say?"

"Nicco." Arianne squeezed my arm.

"She's sixteen." I protested. "She shouldn't be talking about sex."

"Almost seventeen." Alessia glared back, and Genevieve laughed.

"This is nice," she said wistfully.

"It won't be nice when I lock my sister in her room for the next year."

Arianne stiffened and I cussed under my breath. "Sorry, that was insensitive."

"It's okay. Nicco's right though, Alessia. You should wait. So many girls rush to have sex and they regret it. Wait for someone who deserves you, someone who will treat you right." There was no missing the sadness in her voice.

Pain flashed through me.

"Crap, Ari," my sister rushed out. "I'm sorry. I didn't..."

"It's fine, I'm okay."

"You're nothing short of amazing, Bambolina," I breathed against her neck.

"That," Alessia added, a goofy smile plastered on her face. "I want what you guys have."

"I can't argue with that." If Alessia found someone who loved her even half as much as I loved Arianne, she would be a lucky girl. But he'd still have to pass the brother-test first.

My father joined us and the six of us ate. He even hooked his arm around Genevieve and pulled her down onto his lap, feeding her generous amounts of chicken. Her laughter filled the kitchen, but she quickly grew quiet, blushing profusely, when they realized we were all watching. "I should go check the pie," she said, excusing herself.

"What?" my father barked, smoothing a hand over his hair.

"Nothing, old man." I smirked.

Something was changing between us. He'd sided with me and Arianne, it was more than I could have hoped for.

My cell phone vibrated, and I dug it out of my pocket. "What is it?" Arianne asked as I read the incoming message.

"Nothing," I tried to school my expression. "I need to go make a call."

"Nicco..."

"Welcome to my world," Alessia grumbled, shoveling another piece of chicken into her mouth.

"Be right back."

Enzo caught my eye, but I shook my head. Until I knew more, there was no use in causing a panic. As soon as I was out of earshot, I called Luis.

"Nicco?"

"Yeah. What's going on?"

"He's here. Turned up about five minutes ago. Strolled into the building like he owned the damn place. He's demanding to see Arianne."

"Fuck." I pressed the heel of my palm against my head. "Is Nora..."

"She's in their room, packing some stuff. She doesn't want to stay here either."

"Can you get rid of him?"

"I can try but he's going to ask questions if he realizes she's not here. Leave it with me. I'll see what I can do."

"Keep me updated." I hung up and let out a weary sigh. This was a problem. If Scott learned Arianne wasn't in her dorm room, he would sound the alarm and our temporary cover would be blown.

I walked back into the kitchen, but Arianne wasn't in her seat. Matteo flicked his head to the back door, where I found my girl on her cell phone. She looked over at me, her face as white as a sheet and nodded. "Tomorrow, yes, Papá. I'll see you then."

So much for buying us time.

The clock had officially run out.

"Hey," Arianne smiled over at me. "It's going to be okay." I didn't respond and she pressed closer to me, sliding her palm along my face. We were sitting in the yard with Alessia and the guys, drinking beers and listening to Enzo and Matteo's stories about growing up in La Riva. The stories we could tell the girls anyway. I'd wanted to take her up to my room but Arianne wanted to hang. So here we were... hanging.

"Nicco," she smiled up at me, "we knew this might happen."

She was right.

Fuck. Of course she was right. Roberto would want to see his daughter eventually. I just thought we had more time. I thought we would have a plan in place before she had to go anywhere near MU again.

As it was Roberto had summoned her to his estate. It was a small mercy he hadn't wanted to visit her at the dorm, but it meant we couldn't tail her past his estate's perimeter.

"Tell me again," I said.

"Cous, we've been over this—"

"Tell me again." I touched my head to Arianne's, ignoring Matteo's heavy stare. "Please."

"We'll meet Luis and Nora just outside University Hill. Then he'll drive us to my father's estate. I'm going to tell him that a guy Nora has been seeing is starting to get a little intense and that we want to move out of Donatello House." Her eyes shuttered as she drew in a shaky breath.

"Hey," I said, brushing my thumb over hers. "I'm right here."

"I know." Two dark pools of honey settled on me.

"And if your father pushes to know who the guy is?"

"Nora will get upset and say she let it go too far. I'll add that since everyone knows who I am now, I would prefer to live off campus anyway."

"You think he'll buy it?"

"We'd be living in one of his buildings with round the clock security. Of course he'll buy it." She smiled weakly.

"Okay... and if he brings up the gala?"

"I'll affirm Scott's story. He drove me back to the dorm, walked me to the door and I got sick. I was embarrassed and told him to leave."

My jaw muscle flexed. "Okay. Luis will be there, and we'll be close by. If you need me—"

"Nicco." Arianne ghosted her fingers over my face, lingering on my lips. She leaned in, almost kissing me. "We knew our fairytale wouldn't last."

"Our fairytale?"

"Yeah, my prince whisking me off to his castle to protect me."

"Prince, huh?" I chuckled at the irony. She still didn't know everything about me. She didn't know what they called me at L'Anello's. I'd tell her.

I'd tell her everything one day.

Once we got through this.

The next morning rolled around too quickly. I'd barely slept, unable to take my eyes off the sleeping angel beside me. It had been torture being so close to Arianne and not being able to touch her. Thankfully, she was exhausted and was out like a light the second her head hit the pillow. She needed to rest, to heal. She needed all her strength for whatever today would bring.

We met Luis and Nora in a parking lot just outside University Hill. Arianne dashed from the car, running straight to Nora, the two of them hugging. I caught Enzo watching, a strange expression on his face. He saw me and I smirked, earning me a, "fuck off."

Luis strolled over, offering me his hand. "How is she?"

"She's strong but I'm worried about what will happen."

"I won't leave her side, you have my word. It's likely Scott tipped off Roberto. There's no way he could know Arianne wasn't in her room, but he wasn't happy Nora wouldn't let him see her. Told me to 'go fuck myself' on his way out. The kid is unhinged." His eyes flicked over to the girls. "I wouldn't put it past him to try to hurt her again."

"He's a problem," I said. "But don't worry about Fascini. Your job here is to keep eyes on Arianne. Always her, okay?" Luis nodded. "Do you think Roberto will buy their story?"

"It could work. I know Mrs. Capizola had to push hard to get him to agree to let her live on campus. He would have preferred her to commute or stay in one of his buildings."

"Any idea which one he'll put them in?" The more we could anticipate, the better.

"La Stella is a real possibility. It's close to the campus and smaller than some of his other buildings. La Luna or L'Aquila are both in that vicinity, but L'Aquila is popular with young single professionals working in the city. I don't think he'd put the girls there."

"Okay. E." I beckoned him over. "I want you to find out everything you can about two of Capizola's buildings: La Stella and La Luna."

"Seriously?" His brow shot up. "You're putting me on research duty?"

"Do I need to repeat myself?"

"No, *boss*." Sarcasm dripped from his words.

"Is he going to be a problem?" Luis whispered as Enzo walked away.

"You worry about Capizola and let me handle my guys. Did you sort things with your partner?"

"He wasn't looking to get on the wrong side of Capizola, so with my advice he's taking an extended leave of absence. Roberto trusts me with Arianne. He trusts that I'll call for back up if I think we need it. I have a couple of other guys on the team I trust, if it comes to that."

"What do you think Capizola's end game is, with Arianne and Fascini?"

"It's hard to tell. Mike Fascini is an elusive man, I can't get a good read on him, but the pressure seems to be coming from him for the relationship to move forward between his son and Ari."

"Okay, I've got my guy looking into them. The second he finds anything, he'll let me know. Arianne," I called over to her. She untangled herself from Nora's arms and came to me without hesitation. I pulled her into my chest, burying my hand deep into her hair. "Luis will be right there, okay? If something doesn't feel right, excuse yourself, find Luis and he'll bring you straight to me."

She eased back to gaze up at me, tears glossing her eyes. "Don't cry." My voice cracked. "I couldn't bear it."

"I'm so angry at him, Nicco. He might as well have given Scott permission to..." Arianne swallowed, her eyes fluttering closed.

"Bambolina, look at me." My thumb smoothed over her cheek. "I won't let him hurt you again, I promise."

Her resolve began to crack so I kissed her, pouring everything I felt into each touch, every stroke of my tongue, until her gentle sobs subsided turning into soft moans.

"Niccolò," she breathed.

Someone cleared their throat, probably Enzo, the cocky fucker.

"You should go. Remember, stick to the story, and I'll talk to you later, okay?"

Arianne nodded, drying her eyes. My cousins flanked my side as Luis led her over to Nora and guided them both into his SUV.

"She's strong," Matteo said. "She'll be okay."

"And if she isn't?" Enzo had to say the one thing I didn't want to think about. I glared hard at him, but I found no malice there. In fact, if anything, he looked as worried as I felt.

"She's strong enough," I said through clenched teeth.

She had to be.

TWENTY-THREE

ARIANNE

"MIA CARA, ARE YOU FEELING BETTER?"

"I'm okay." I clutched the scarf around my neck. Alessia had thought it would be a good idea to conceal the faint bruises around my throat. Thankfully, with a little concealer and make up, the marks on my face and the split in my lip were barely visible now.

"Where is Nora?"

"She headed to the cottage to see her parents. Actually, I was hoping to talk to you and Papá about something."

"It would seem we all have much to discuss then." My father appeared at the end of the hall. "Come, let us move to the sitting room."

"Scott was really quite worried about you," my mother started as we followed my father down the hall. "Did he stop by to check on you earlier?"

"Gabriella," my father grunted, and she fell silent.

I hated this.

Hated that I no longer trusted my father or his motivations. He'd always been so dead set on protecting me, on keeping me safe, but now when I looked at him all I felt was betrayal.

We sat around the ornate coffee table while my mother poured us some tea. My father had taken the chair opposite me so there was no avoiding his sharp, assessing eyes.

"I spoke to Scott earlier, mio tesoro. He seemed concerned that you wouldn't let him in to see you."

"Papá, he told you what happened last night? I was so embarrassed, and I still felt a little unwell. I asked Nora to tell him I wasn't feeling up to visitors."

"Arianne, must you make it so difficult for him? He cares about you."

"I am sorry, Papá. His affections are too much. I'm not ready for..."

"Roberto". My mother laid a hand on his thigh. "This is all new to her. We are perhaps rushing something that needs more time. A more subtle approach."

"What do you mean, rushing something? What something, Mamma?"

"Oh, Arianne, my sweet girl. You are a young woman now. You must have... desires. Scott can show you the world. He will court you, woo you to your heart's content."

"Woo me? Really, Mamma?" I balked. If only she knew what Scott liked to do to innocent girls in the dark, I'm sure she would be horrified. But I couldn't risk telling them. Not yet. Not when my father seemed so set on making it work between us.

"Arianne," my father clipped out. "He is not an ogre. He will cherish you, mio tesoro. That is all a father wants for his daughter."

"What about what I want?" Tears pricked my eyes as I tried desperately to stay strong. "I feel nothing with Scott. It isn't romantic, it's hard work. We have nothing in common, and he..."

"He what, Arianne? Tell us?" Concern flashed in my mother's gaze.

"He is much more experienced than I am. He expects things... things I am not ready for."

My mother glanced at my father, and a seed of hope unfurled in my stomach. Maybe she would understand. Maybe she would tell my father it was too much to expect me to be with someone I didn't love.

But a mask of indifference slid over my father's face, as he let out an exasperated breath. "He is good stock, Arianne; everything you could hope to find in a partner. Scott is a man of honor, of traditions. He would never seek to harm you."

But he already has, I wanted to scream. Instead, I steeled myself, biting back the tears threatening to fall.

"It is too much, Papá," I croaked.

"You just need to give him a chance, Arianne. Spend time together, get to know each other. I'm sure you will see you have much in common. These things don't come overnight, they take time and effort. You'll see."

He was wrong though.

When it was right, when someone was meant to be yours, it did happen fast. It happened so fast you didn't see it coming. Before you knew it, your life was entwined with theirs, the fabric of your souls inexplicably woven together. As if Fate herself had willed it.

"Scott would like to take you out tomorrow night. I've told him you are looking forward to it."

"I see." Anger vibrated inside me. So much so, my hands began to tremble. I stuffed them under my thighs and took a calming breath. "Is that all?"

"You had something you wished to discuss with us?"

"I did." I inhaled a deep breath. It was now or never. "Nora has found herself in a difficult situation. There is a guy... he hasn't hurt her or anything like that, but he's becoming a bit of nuisance—"

"Give me his name and I'll have security deal with him."

"Nora doesn't want that, Papá. You see she feels responsible. She gave him the wrong impression and now he's infatuated with her. It's quite sad really. He's always hanging around the dorm building though. So we were thinking, we'd like to move off-campus."

"Off-campus?" My father sounded suspicious.

I nodded. "Honestly, now everyone knows who I am, the attention is stifling. We spend all our free time in the dorm, like prisoners. And now Nora has gained an unwanted admirer, it just all feels like too much."

"Sweetheart," my mother said. "Did something else happen? That's a big request, Arianne. You know how hard I worked to get your father to agree to let you live on campus."

"I know, I do, and I'm so thankful for the experience. But honestly, it's not all I thought it would be. I think we'd be much happier in an apartment off-campus. Just the two of us." I glanced at my father, trying to read his expression. "I think I'd feel safer too."

His eyes softened and I knew I had him. My father, despite some of his decisions of late, still wanted me safe. "Arianne, I would feel much more comfortable talking to campus security about this and smoothing this—"

"I'll give Scott a chance," I blurted out. "If you let us move off-campus, I'll try and be more open minded to the idea of us."

His shoulders sagged as he regarded me with a mix of uncertainty and pride. "You are more like me than I give you credit for."

"So is that a yes, can we leave the dorm?"

"I'll need a little time to sort—"

"No," I said a little too hastily. Shifting on the couch, I smoothed out my blouse and smiled at my parents. "Nora doesn't want to stay there anymore... there's a little more to it. But that is her story to tell, not mine, and I'd appreciate it if you didn't railroad her into telling you."

My father shot forward. "Arianne, if Nora was hurt—"

"She wasn't, I promise. But we'd prefer to be out of there sooner rather than later."

"When did you get so grown up?" He grumbled. "Okay, I can make some calls. There are a couple of apartment buildings near the campus that could work. If I can't set it up today, you can stay here tonight." He gave me a look that said it wasn't up for discussion. "Are you certain you don't want to tell me what really happened?"

Even if I did, you wouldn't believe me.

"Like I said, it's not my story to tell." The lies came easier now. I barely felt even a sliver of guilt.

My father was wrong though, I hadn't grown up.

I'd changed.

I no longer looked to my parents for approval or validation, and I wasn't happy living a life with my wings clipped.

I wanted more.

I *deserved* more.

I deserved once in a lifetime, fated-in-the-stars, love.

The kind of love I'd found with Nicco.

He might have been my enemy by name, but our souls were the same.

And I would tell a thousand lies if it meant protecting him and the love we shared.

"Very well, I'll make some calls. You and your mother should spend some time together. She can perhaps regale you with stories of how I won her heart. It wasn't an easy task."

"Ruffiano!" My mother waved him off, smiling at him with such adoration it made my heart ache.

My father left, closing the door behind him. I released a garbled breath.

"Oh, mia cara, come here." She patted the couch and I went to her. The second she wrapped her arm around me, I crumbled. "Oh, sweetheart. What is it? What's wrong?"

The tears wouldn't stop. I'd tried so hard to remain impassive during the conversation with my father. I'd underestimated how hard it would be to keep up the façade with my mother. The woman who was supposed to love me unconditionally.

She cupped my face gently in her hands, coaxing me to look at her. "Arianne, I am your mother. You can tell me anything."

"Can I?"

She blanched, pain glittering in her eyes. "You think you cannot trust me?"

"I- I don't know what to think any more."

"Sweetheart, you are my flesh and blood. Is this about Scott?"

I nodded.

"Did something happen? Earlier, when you were talking to your father, I sensed..." she trailed off.

Slowly I unknotted the scarf at my neck and eased it off. My mother gasped, her eyes homing in on the bruises. "I didn't get sick on Scott, Mamma. He... he drugged me, and he forced himself on me."

"No, no, no. What are you saying, Arianne?"

"He raped me." The word came out a garbled cry as my mother wrapped me into her arms again, crying with me.

"What am I going to do, Mamma? You heard Papá. He is determined that I give Scott a chance. Should I tell—"

"No, Arianne," she rushed out. "You cannot tell him. No good can come from him knowing. He will not..." My mother cussed, something she rarely did.

"He won't change his mind," I finished, my worst nightmare coming true. "He'll still make me go along with this, won't he?"

"Oh, sweetheart. This is not what I wanted for you. But I don't know how to protect you from this."

"Nicco," I whispered. "Nicco will protect me."

"You're still seeing the Marchetti boy...? Of course you are." She gave me a weak smile. "Arianne, do you understand what will happen if your father finds out?"

"I don't care, Mamma. I love him. We have a plan."

Her eyes shuttered as she murmured something under her breath again. She looked so defeated, so helpless. But then her expression hardened, and she nodded. "Okay, okay. Tell me what I can do."

We ended up staying the night. By the time my father came to find me it was late and Nora was already asleep. I hadn't wanted to spend a second longer than necessary there, but I couldn't give my father any more reasons to be suspicious than he already had. The good news was he had found an empty two-bed apartment in one of his developments in University Hill. We could move in immediately.

"I can't believe he bought it," Nora whispered as Luis drove us back to the dorm. I didn't want to ever return there but we needed to pack up our things. My mother had begged me to consider staying at the house, but the truth was, I wanted space from my father.

"Have you texted Nicco?" she asked, and I nodded.

"This is him now." I scanned his reply.

I'll be watching. Stay safe. I love you.

I showed Nora and she swooned, sinking against the seat. "He's so alpha; it's a total turn on."

"Nora..." My cheeks flamed.

"You know," her expression turned serious, "We haven't really talked about what happened, with you know who."

"I refuse to let what he did define me," I said.

"And that's commendable, it is. But maybe you should talk to someone about it, a professional."

"Like a shrink?"

"Or a therapist, yes. Someone who can give you a safe space to come to terms with it."

"I don't want to keep reliving it." I folded in on myself, as if wrapping my arms around my waist would keep out the memories.

"And I get that, I do. But you need to deal with it, especially if you're going to have to see him again."

I didn't want to think about what I'd promised my father, not now. I'd said the words to appease him, to get what I needed from him. I hadn't considered what would happen when I actually had to go out with Scott.

I'd done what needed to be done at that precise moment.

"I'll figure it out."

"Nicco is going to lose his shit," she whispered.

"Which is why we're not going to mention it yet." I gave her a pointed look.

"My lips are sealed." She mimicked throwing away a key.

I love you too xo

I hit send and pocketed my cell phone. Nicco would be close by. It wasn't ideal, but it was enough.

It had to be.

We pulled into campus less than ten minutes later, the knot in my stomach so tight I wasn't sure I could do this.

"Hey," Nora said, noticing how quiet I'd become. "You don't have to come inside. Me and Luis can get everything."

"No," I said. "I need to do this. I need to..." Silent tears flowed down my face. "I just need a minute. You two make a start. I'll wait here."

"I can call someone to come and take care of it," Luis said. "We have enough guys—"

"No, no more security."

He nodded as I clutched my cell phone to my chest. I needed Nicco. But I couldn't ask that of him. Not here, where people might see us.

"Go. I'm fine."

Luis looked uncertain but I gave him a weak smile. "Nothing is going to happen to me." He knew the threat from the Marchetti no longer existed. I was one of them now. Not by blood or name, but because the boss' son loved me. Besides, Nicco would be close by. I knew he wouldn't be able to let me out of his sight, not even now.

Reluctantly, Luis and Nora climbed out of the SUV and disappeared inside the building. Less than five minutes later, they reappeared with more bags than they could carry. Luis loaded them in the truck while Nora yanked open the door. "I can get your things. You don't have to do this."

"I do," I said, sliding out of the SUV.

Nora linked her arm with mine as we walked inside. A few girls were hanging around the common room but paid us little attention. Of course, I knew they were probably texting their friends a blow by blow account of our visit. I wondered if they would believe my story if I told them—if they would side with the mysterious Capizola heir, or believe the football playing, rich, entitled guy who had hurt me? He was one of MU's most eligible bachelors. Girls wanted to date him and guys wanted to be him. Would they turn on their prince or believe his lies?

I knew the answer.

It's the very reason I hadn't told my father. He was too blinded by Scott's shiny reputation, by his stupid business deal with Mike Fascini, to see the truth. Even if he saw the truth, I wasn't sure he wanted to hear it.

My heart sank.

With every step, my body began to tremble. Details of that night were hazy like a dream. But you didn't wake up from a dream with bruises littered over your body and dried blood staining your skin.

"Are you sure you're up to this?" Nora whispered.

"I'm fine." I swallowed the lie.

We reached the door to our room. Luis opened it and went first. I took a deep breath and stepped inside. It looked the same, but it didn't feel the same. A deep shudder rolled through me. Nora stayed glued to my side as I stood there, letting the memories of that night wash over me.

"I have most of my stuff. I'll make a start on yours." Nora squeezed my hand before leaving my side and making a start on gathering up my belongings. Luis helped her fill the small suitcase and the couple of duffel bags they had brought up. But I was paralyzed.

A knock at the window startled me and Luis grumbled beneath his breath. "What in the hell?" He stalked over to the window, pulling back the curtain, but I already knew who he'd find.

"Nicco," I breathed, inching forward. He climbed inside, his eyes landing on mine. I ran to him, flinging myself into his arms. He caught me, pressing one hand against the small of my back, fitting us together like two pieces of a puzzle.

"You're here, you're here," I cried, locking my arms around his neck.

"Ssh, Bambolina. Don't cry."

"Marchetti," Luis said, his tone full of warning.

"I had to," Nicco replied over my shoulder.

"I can't say I blame you."

"We'll give the two of you some space," Nora said.

I felt them leave, heard the door click shut behind them, but I didn't leave the comfort of Nicco's arms. I couldn't.

"Shit, Arianne," it was a low grumble. "You shouldn't be here."

"I had to." I fisted his hoodie. "I had to show myself he doesn't have power over me."

I knew it didn't really make sense, but by coming back here, it felt like I was sticking it to Scott.

"He'll pay, amore mio." Nicco slid his fingers under my jaw and tilted my face. "One day, he will pay, I promise."

He kissed me, his tongue licking the seam of my mouth, demanding entrance. It wasn't a hot intense kiss like so many of them were. It was a gentle caress, full of healing and acceptance. It was Nicco's way of telling me that no matter what Scott had done to me, I was still his.

Irrevocably and inexplicably his.

He tucked a strand of hair behind my ear, touching his lips to my forehead. "You okay?" I nodded. "Good. I already have Enzo working on La Stella. Your father has it locked down pretty tight, but we might have something."

"Okay." I hesitated. Now was as good a time as any to tell him about the trade-off I'd made with my father. But as I stared into his dark eyes, shining with so much love and possessiveness, I couldn't do it.

I couldn't ruin this perfectly imperfect moment.

There was a gentle knock at the door and Nora stuck her head inside. "We should probably go."

"She's right." Nicco kissed my hair. "We'll follow behind, okay?"

"I'll see you soon?"

"Nothing will keep me away, not even one of your father's fortified buildings." Nicco smirked. "Now go." He released me, inching back into the shadows. Luis and Nora grabbed the final bags. There were still some things we hadn't packed, but nothing that couldn't wait. I glanced one last time at my bed, suppressing a violent shudder.

"Arianne?" Nora said quietly. "Are you ready?"

"I am." I followed her out of the room.

What had started as my freedom had slowly unraveled into a nightmare. But in the midst of all the pain and confusion, I had found Nicco.

And for that, I would never be sorry.

"All set?" Luis glanced at me through the rear-view mirror, and I nodded. But he had barely fired up the engine when Scott appeared, his eyes narrowed with anger.

"Get out of the car, Arianne." He slammed his hands on the hood of the car. Luis climbed out to confront him.

"He's crazy," Nora said, hitting the lock on the door. "Batshit crazy".

"Arianne," he yelled around Luis who was trying to calm him down. "We need to speak, baby. Just get out of the car and we can talk."

Lights went on in windows as people began to look outside and see what all the commotion was.

"Is he trying to cause a scene?"

"Touch me again, Vitelli," Scott growled, "and you and me will have a problem."

Without thinking, my hand curled around the handle.

"Oh, hell no," Nora mumbled. "You are not seriously considering going out there?"

"What choice do I have? If Nicco sees him..."

"Crap." She unbuckled herself. "I'm coming too."

"Just try and keep calm, okay?"

"Calm? If he so much as touches you, I'm calling the cops."

"Nora..."

"Fine. But I don't like this, Ari. I don't like it one bit."

Steeling myself, I climbed out of the SUV and marched around to Scott and Luis. He instantly stepped away from my bodyguard, focusing solely on me. "What is this bullshit, Ari? You're moving out?"

"There was an incident," I said, schooling my expression.

"An incident?" he sneered.

"Yes, a guy Nora has been seeing became a little too interested. Turns out he couldn't take no for an answer."

"Is that right?" Scott's eyes flared as he scrubbed his jaw. He took a step toward me and I inched back. "You think you can run from me, is that it?"

"I'm not running from anyone." I rolled my shoulders back, refusing to show even an ounce of fear. "We'll be staying at one of my father's buildings. I'm sure he already gave you the details."

"What game are you playing, Arianne?" His voice was a low growl as he stalked closer.

"I have no idea what you're talking about. Now if you'll excuse me, we need to get going." I began to shuffle away but his voice gave me pause.

"Does he know?" Scott called after me. My muscles locked up, my breathing ragged. "Does Marchetti know how I took the one thing he wanted but can never have?"

I turned slowly, unable to fight the tears any longer. "Why are you doing this?"

He stalked toward me again, caging me against the SUV, his nostrils flared, eyes narrowed dangerously. "Because you're mine. Because that tight little body of yours is mine. You think you're too good for me? Better than me?" Spittle flew everywhere. "I'm going to enjoy watching you break."

Nora gasped somewhere to the side of me and then I saw him. Nicco standing over by the tree line. He looked deadly, his eyes trained right on Scott.

Scott glanced over his shoulder and snarled, "You shouldn't be here." He grabbed me, his hand digging roughly into my hip as he pulled me around to face Nicco.

"Take your hands off Arianne," he said.

"Excuse me? Didn't you get the memo, Marchetti? She's mine. Her pussy... Fuck, man, she was so tight. So—"

"I'm not going to tell you again, Fascini. Get your hands off her." Dark energy rolled off Nicco, his pupils blown and jaw clenched so tight it looked painful.

"Nicco..." I begged, silently trying to tell him to go. To leave before this got any worse.

I felt Luis approach. Nicco glanced at me. Telling me something.

And then all hell broke loose.

Luis grabbed my hand, yanking me free of Scott just as Nicco crashed into him. The two of them began fighting, fists flying and bone crunching. Nora rushed to my side, pulling me clear of them.

"Do something," I cried. "Someone do something." But Luis didn't move, staying by our side while he let Nicco and Scott battle for dominance. Scott was big, broad, and muscular from hours of conditioning on the football field, but Nicco was quick and deadly.

"You're a dead man, Marchetti," Scott grunted, throwing his fist straight into Nicco's face. But it only spurred Nicco on. He slammed his body into Scott's, the two of them falling hard to the ground. Nicco dived on top of him, raining his fists down blow after blow, sickening crack after sickening crack.

"Luis," I yelled but Tristan appeared out of nowhere, diving for Nicco.

"Fuck, man, you're going to kill him. Stop, Marchetti, just—" Nicco slammed his elbow into my cousin's face and Tristan staggered back. He lost his footing and fell backward, cracking his head on the asphalt.

Nora rushed to his side. People had begun to swarm around the building now. "Ari," fear clung to every syllable, the world going from underneath my feet as she pulled her hand from beneath my cousin's head, her fingers coated with sticky red blood.

"Oh God, Luis."

Luis jumped into action, hauling Nicco off Scott. He was like a wild thing, fist clenched and bloody, eyes blacker than the depths of hell. "You need to go. Get the fuck out of here before the authorities show up."

Nicco's eyes finally found mine, my Nicco slowly resurfacing. "Arianne?" he choked out.

"Go," I mouthed. "Please, go."

Sirens wailed in the distance, the reality of what had just happened crashing down around me.

Scott lay groaning, his face a mangled mess, while Tristan's body was still and unmoving, a pool of dark red blood spreading around him.

"Go," I whispered, pain splintering my soul apart.

Nicco's gaze lingered, saying everything he couldn't say.

He was sorry.

He loved me.

He didn't know how to fix this.

And as quickly as he'd appeared, he was gone.

TWENTY-FOUR

NICCO

"WHAT THE FUCK WERE YOU THINKING?" Enzo growled as we tore out of the campus via the back road.

"I wasn't thinking." Flexing my knuckles, pain zipped up my hand and into my wrist. I was pretty sure I'd broken something, maybe a metacarpal or two. But it was worth it.

Worth it to feel Fascini's bone smash under my fist, hear him cuss in agony.

But I hadn't meant to hurt Tristan. Fuck. He hadn't looked good lying there, blood surrounding him like a red halo.

Fuck. Fuck. Fuck.

I slammed my good hand against the dash. I'd screwed up. I should never have gone after Fascini, but the second he'd crowded Arianne against the side of the SUV, I saw red.

"Uncle Toni is going to shit a brick when he finds out."

"I'll deal with him. It's Arianne I'm worried about. She shouldn't have to go anywhere near that piece of shit."

"I know, cous. But you know it's not that simple."

"Motherfucker," I roared, emotion spilling out of me. I slumped back against the leather seat, Arianne's broken expression imprinted on my mind as she'd told me to go.

She knew.

Arianne knew I'd fucked up, and yet, she'd still tried to protect me.

Jesus. There was no coming back from this.

Just then, my cell phone vibrated. "Luis?" I barked.

"It's not good news. Tristan is unresponsive. They're taking him to Verona

County Hospital. Roberto is meeting us there. I have orders to take Arianne and Nora straight there. Fascini is being taken in for monitoring, but by the time the EMT's got done with him, he was up and cussing me out, so I think he'll live."

I murmured under my breath.

"How is she?"

"How do you think she is?" His tone was harsh.

"I deserve that."

"Nicco, I didn't mean... Arianne is strong," he whispered, and I knew she must be within earshot. "But she's not strong enough for the hellfire her father is about to rain down. You just changed the game, Marchetti. I hope you realize that." Luis drew in a harsh breath. "But honestly, I can't say that I blame you. I wanted to kill him with my bare hands too."

"I didn't know it was Tristan until it was too late. It was an accident," I said, knowing it wouldn't matter. Roberto's nephew was being whizzed to the hospital because of me. Because I'd let Fascini get the better of me.

Because I'd fucked up.

"Tell her I'm sorry."

"You should probably tell her yourself. I'll keep you updated." He ended the call, but he might as well have shot me at point blank range.

Because he was right.

The game had just changed again.

And I only had myself to blame.

"Nicco, what happened?" Alessia ran down the drive, smothering me with attention. "I heard Daddy yelling and then he smashed something."

"Guess the cat is out the bag," Enzo grumbled, heading for the house. "It was nice knowing you, cous," he called over his shoulder, before disappearing inside.

"Is Arianne okay? Where is she?"

"She's fine. I could do with some TLC though." I held up my busted hand.

"Oh, brother, tell me you didn't do anything stupid."

"I messed up, Sia. I really messed up."

"Was it because of Arianne?"

I nodded, and my sister touched my cheek. "Then it was worth it."

I only wished my father would see it like that.

We entered the house and Alessia went to grab the supplies. I knew I probably needed an X-ray but it would have to wait.

"Niccolò," the anger in my father's voice shook the house.

"Good luck with that," Enzo said.

Alessia reappeared with the first aid kit, but I waved her off. "It can wait. Go find Enzo something to eat or drink."

"But..."

"Sia," I warned, and she skulked off.

I made my way to my father's study. He was sitting behind his desk, his hand curled into a tight fist. "Tell me you didn't nearly kill Fascini when I ordered you not to go anywhere near him."

"How did you find out?"

"One of your Uncle Vincenzo's guys picked up the call when it came in over the scanner."

"I fucked up. I know that. But you didn't hear what he was saying about her, the way he was intimidating her."

"Damn it, Niccolò. Do you have any idea what you've done?"

"I didn't mean to hurt Tristan. He took me by surprise and I elbow—"

"Tristan? What the fuck does he have to do with this?"

"He got hurt," I said. "It was an accident but it's bad. They're blue-lighting him to County Hospital."

"Maledizione! This is all we need." My father breathed heavily through his nose. "I found out something about Fascini."

"You did?"

"Tommy called."

My spine stiffened. Tommy was supposed to call me with any updates, which meant if he'd gone around me and straight to my father, it was bad.

Real fucking bad.

"Tommy couldn't turn anything up on Mike Fascini. His businesses seemed kosher, his investment portfolio all above board. So he started digging deeper and found something interesting."

"What?" I raked a hand through my hair, wondering how much more bad news I could take.

"You ever heard me mention the name Ricci growing up?"

"It doesn't ring a bell."

"That's because it isn't a name we talk about much anymore." He let out a heavy sigh, leaning back in his chair. "Remember the stories I used to tell you about why there is so much bad blood between us and the Capizola?"

I nodded. We all knew the story. It was ingrained into us from a young age. My father's great-grandfather, and Roberto's great-grandfather, had wanted to unite our families and make them strong. But Luca Marchetti's son, Emilio, didn't fulfil his promise to marry Tommaso Capizola's daughter. Instead, he ran off into the sunset with her brother's fiancée, setting off a chain of events which tore the families apart.

"When Emilio ran off with Elena, it didn't only end the union of the Marchetti and Capizola. It severed our ties to the Ricci too."

"Ricci?"

"Emilio ran off with Elena Ricci. She was promised to Alfredo Capizola. It wasn't just a union of love, it was union of strength, arranged by their fathers, to bring the Ricci family into the fold."

"Okay, but what does any of this have to do with Fascini?"

"Turns out Mike Fascini hasn't always been a Fascini. It is, in fact, his mother's surname. His father took her name when they married. His father's actual name is Ricci."

"So you're saying the Fascini aren't Fascini at all? They're Ricci? I don't understand."

"Me neither, Son. Me neither. It could be pure coincidence, but instinct tells me it's not. The Fascini have positioned themselves right in the center of Robert Capizola's business. Which puts them right at the center of our business. I've been around long enough to know if something seems off then it probably is. Tommy's going to dig deeper, let me know what he finds. But this shit you pulled tonight, that is a big fucking problem, Niccolò."

"I'll make it right." I didn't know how yet, but I would.

"I'm sending you to Boston."

"What?" I shot forward. "You can't—"

He slammed his hand down, making the table shake. "I can, goddamn it, and I will. I might be your father, Niccolò, but I'm still the boss, and you will follow me on this. Go to Boston, lay low, and let me figure out how to smooth this over. When Capizola finds out you're responsible for this, he's going to want your head on a silver fucking platter."

"But Ari—"

"Arianne got you into this mess. Jesus, Niccolò, you need to think with your head here. You can't protect her if you're locked away or pushing up daisies. Go to Boston, let me see what Tommy can dig up. And trust me to try and clean up this mess you've made."

"If anything happens to her..." Fuck, I couldn't bear it.

"She's under my protection. I gave you my word. I'll figure it out."

"I love her. I love her so fucking much."

"I know you do, Son. But look at your ancestors, learn from them. Love almost destroyed this family once before. Don't let it destroy you too. Go to Boston and lay low until I can get a handle on this thing."

"I won't lose her," I said with absolute conviction. Losing Arianne was not an option, in this lifetime or the next.

My father leaned forward, levelling me with a hard look, but I was certain I saw a flash of regret there too. "Let's hope you don't have to."

He wanted me to leave first thing. But there was no way I was leaving without seeing Arianne first. She'd spent all night at the hospital, waiting for news of Tristan. He'd suffered a traumatic brain injury, and doctors had induced a coma due to swelling around his brain. There was a certain irony in the fact that I'd wanted to kill Scott, to watch his life drain from his eyes with my bare hands tight around his neck, but Tristan was the one lying in a hospital bed.

Even though I didn't like the guy, I knew if I could take back that moment, I would. I'd played it over and over in my head, but I couldn't rewrite history. If he didn't wake up or the damage to his brain turned out to be too extensive, that was all on me.

It was my elbow.

My blow to his face.

My. Fucking. Fault.

Sure, I couldn't have known he would fall and crack his head, but if I'd have only reacted differently.

Arianne didn't blame me. She'd told me again and again over text. It didn't ease the guilt snaking through my chest though. I'd spent all night awake in my childhood bedroom at the request of my father. I think he expected the police to show up and wanted me close by just in case they did. But no one came. Dawn broke and with it the reality that, by dusk, I would be gone.

I hadn't plucked up the courage to tell Arianne yet. Her world had been obliterated again, and I didn't want to add to her worries. But I had to tell her eventually. Instead, I called Luis and asked him to have Nora call me. There was something I needed from her, from them both.

It was my last request before I left Verona County.

Before I left Arianne.

"You look like shit," Enzo said as I dragged my sorry ass into the kitchen. "It's true then, you're leaving?"

"Leaving?" Alessia gasped.

I shot Enzo an irritated look before turning to find my sister standing there, her eyes full of worry and betrayal. "It's only temporary," I said.

"You can't leave." Her lip quivered. "I need you. Ari needs you."

Inching forward, I opened my arms. But she jerked back. "You can't go, Nicco. I don't care what happened last night. We need you." Big fat tears began to trickle down her face. I pulled her into my arms and held her tight.

"Enzo and Matteo will look out for you. Bailey too. And I'll be back before you know it." I hated lying to her, but it was better than admitting the truth.

I had no idea when it would be safe for me to return. If Roberto and Fascini pressed charges, I would be a wanted man. And if they didn't, it would be because they intended on dealing with me in a different way entirely. Roberto Capizola might have been a straitlaced, law abiding citizen, but he had enough money to make things happen and then make the paper trail disappear. And if Fascini was somehow related to the original Ricci, who knew what his family's real motivation was for being here.

The thought of leaving my sister and Arianne was almost too much to bear. I was supposed to be here to protect them.

"What will I do without you?" She sobbed into my chest, the sound gutting me.

"Ssh, Sia. You have to be strong, okay? You're a Marchetti, and it's time to act like one."

"You're right." My sister eased away, steeling her expression. "If you let anything happen to you,"—she slammed her hands into my chest—"I swear to God, Nicco. I will never forgive you."

Enzo chuckled. "You have nothing to worry about. We'll look out for her."

"Like you aren't going to miss me." I tried to lighten the mood, but his expression darkened.

"Nothing about this is right, you know?"

"My father is right. If I stay... I can't do that to you all. If I go, at least you stand a shot of figuring out a way to take Roberto and Fascini down."

Then I could return. I could be with Arianne and we could get a shot at our happily-ever-after.

Who the fuck was I kidding?

Happy endings didn't exist in my world.

But she deserved one.

Arianne deserved the sun, the moon, and all the stars. And I was determined to try to figure out a way to give them to her.

Even if it killed me.

TWENTY-FIVE

ARIANNE

"ARI," Nora nudged my side and I jerked awake. Not that I was really sleeping. Exhaustion weighed heavily in my bones, but true sleep wouldn't come. I was too plagued with nightmares. Scott's breath as he taunted me and Nicco, the feel of his fingers splayed possessively on my hip. The way Nicco had unleashed his darker side, the side I'd been sheltered from, to rain fire and fury down on Scott's face. Tristan's lifeless body, his blood smeared on Nora's hands.

Oh God, the blood.

For a split second, I had thought he was dead. Killed by the one I loved more than anything else in the world.

It was an accident. I knew that. A tragic turn of events. But I also knew it wouldn't matter to my father. He'd raised Tristan as good as his own. My Aunt Miriam was a single mother, Tristan's father long gone before she ever gave birth.

Nicco might as well have hurt me, that's how hard it had hit my father.

He stood in the door, his expression cold, grief seeping from every inch of him. "I'd like to speak to my daughter alone," he said.

Nora got up and squeezed my hand. "I'll be right outside."

At least twelve hours had passed since they brought Tristan to the hospital. A sleepless night of waiting and worrying. Even the first light of morning had brought no solace. Tristan was stable but he was in a coma while they gave his brain time to heal. Until they woke him, doctors were unable to comment on the severity of his injuries.

"You have created quite the mess, mia cara."

Not 'mio tesoro'.

His voice sounded so cold, so clinical.

"It was an accident, Papá. You have to believe me. Nicco never meant—"

"*Do not* speak his name in front of me. That boy is nothing but trouble. I told you to stay away from him. I told you and yet you disobeyed me, and now Tristan is..." He swallowed, his Adam's apple pressing roughly against his throat.

"It was accident," I repeated, as if it mattered. As if the fact Nicco hadn't meant to hurt Tristan changed anything.

"And what about Scott? Was he an accident too? He's black and blue, Arianne. Did your boyfriend's fist just slip into Scott's face?" He was furious, his anger permeating the air like a dark storm on the horizon. "What on earth were you thinking?"

"I love him, Papá. I love Nicco," I cried.

"Love?" He sneered. "That monster cannot love; his blood does not allow it. Scott is—"

"Scott is a monster." My body shook with the force of my words. "He hurt me, Papá. He... he forced himself on me."

"Don't be ridiculous, Arianne. Scott told me what really happened the night of the gala. He told me things moved too fast for you and you lashed out."

"He said that?" Of course he had. Why did I expect anything less? "I told him no, Papá. I told him no and he still—"

"*Basta!*" The vein in his neck throbbed. "You will not speak ill of Scott again. Do you understand me? He is a good man from a good family."

"But, Papá..." Tears streaked down my cheeks, my eyes sore and puffy.

"Niccolò Marchetti is done. His father might have friends in high places, but I am Roberto Capizola. I'll throw everything I have at him to make sure he never sees the light of day again."

"You wouldn't..." Fear gripped me like a vice.

"When will you learn, Arianne. I will always do what is best for you. Always."

"You mean you'll always do what is best for you and your business!" I spat the words, but my father had already turned on his heel, reaching for the door handle.

"If you do this," I said quietly. "I'll expose Scott for what he really is. A sexual predator who can't take no for an answer."

My father turned slowly, his expression darkening. "Are you threatening me, figlia mia?"

"I have proof. Evidence of what he did to me. If you press charges against Nicco, I'll release it to the police. I'm pretty sure I'm not the first girl on campus he's attacked. I could persuade others to testify." I narrowed my eyes, nervous energy vibrating through me. "It'll be a huge scandal. It'll ruin their family name. Their reputation."

"Evidence?" He choked over the word. "But he said it was a misunderstanding."

"He lied. I have the bruises to prove it."

"Are you saying that he... he *raped* you?"

"Did you not hear anything I just told you?" I shrieked. "You chose to put your business deal first. Nothing you do is to protect me; it's all to progress the company. To better you."

"Arianne, mio tesoro." The blood drained from his face. "That is not—"

"Don't." I stabbed my finger into the air. "Don't you dare backtrack. You weren't interested in hearing my side of the story until I told you I had evidence. So here's my deal, *father*. Drop the charges against Nicco, and I won't release the evidence to the police or go public with my story."

"Scott and his father will never agree to those terms. They want blood, Arianne. Nicco's blood."

"Well you need to convince them then, because I'm not playing around. If Nicco isn't cleared of all charges, then you'll find out exactly the lengths I'm prepared to go to for the people I love."

My father stared at me as if he no longer recognized me. It was fitting really. The man I once worshipped had turned out to be a man I didn't know, and the daughter he adored had turned out to be a girl he didn't know at all.

"Who are you, mio tesoro?" Sadness edged into his expression as he stared at me.

"You mean you don't recognize me, Papá?" I stood taller, knowing there was no going back now. I'd made my choice, picked my side. "I am Arianne Capizola. I am my father's daughter."

Our new apartment was a small two-bed in one of my father's buildings situated in the heart of University Hill. La Stella boasted a fully equipped gym and heated swimming pool and was located on a busy block that had a coffee shop, Chinese takeout, general store, and laundromat.

"Ooh, fancy," Nora said dropping her bags on the floor and scanning the room.

"I just want to sleep," I groaned. My father had finally given us permission to leave the hospital.

"At least we don't have to go to class today. I might go see my parents later." Nora glanced at Luis who was busy checking the place over. "After what happened to Tristan, I feel like I need to hug them, ya know?"

"I'm not sure I want to go back home yet." I'd had enough of my father for one day.

"I can arrange to have Maurice take Nora to the estate. I will stay here with you."

"Thank you, Luis," I said. "For everything."

He gave me a swift nod. "I'm going to introduce myself to security and check in with the team. If you need me just buzz." He stepped out of the apartment, leaving us to it.

"How are you feeling?" Nora asked.

"Like my head went through a meat grinder."

"Tristan will come out of this okay. He's too big and annoying to let something as little as a bump to the head keep him down."

I forced a weak smile. I knew she meant well, but the joke was lost on me. "I'm not sure me and my father can come back from this," I whispered, dropping onto the couch.

"But you said he seemed shocked when you said there was evidence."

"If anything, that only makes it worse. Like my word wasn't enough." I swallowed down the tears burning my throat. "I'm not sure I can ever forgive him, Nor."

"And that's okay. He hurt you, Ari. It's understandable. But maybe he can come through for you when he talks to Scott and his dad?"

"Yeah, maybe."

"Have you spoken to Nicco?"

"He's making arrangements in case my father can't talk Scott and his dad out of dropping the charges. Whatever that means."

"Does it bother you that he's got this whole other life that you'll never truly be a part of?"

"It should," I confessed. "But if you love someone, really love them, you have to accept all the little parts of them, don't you? Even the ones you might not fully understand."

"What do you think about Enzo?" Nora changed the subject. "I can't figure him out. I mean he's so freakin' hot and he's big... *down there*."

"Nora!" I covered my ears, smothering a giggle.

"Oh come on, we're freshman at college. This is what life is supposed to be about. I came eye-to-eye with that thing and let me tell you, it's a monster."

"Stop. Oh God, make it stop." I tried to slap my hand over her mouth, but she peeled my fingers away.

"At least ten inches. Can you imagine? And he's so muscled and angry. I bet he's a real—"

"You can't go there, not with him."

"What, why? You've got yourself your very own mafioso, seems only fair I get one too." She smirked.

"He's not like Nicco, Nor. Enzo is... well, he's something else entirely."

"Yeah." She sighed, flouncing back against the couch. "You're probably right. I always pick the jerks."

"You'll find someone, just give it time."

"Made you laugh though, didn't I?" She peeked over at me and we shared a smile.

"I don't know what I'd have done without you through all this."

"Probably something very stupid. Now let's go take the tour of our new place. I think we deserve it." Nora grabbed my hand and pulled me up. "Ready?"

I wasn't, but what choice did I have? Life went on whether you wanted it to or not. You just had to figure out how to put one foot in front of the other and keep going.

"Ari." Someone gently shook me, but the pull of sleep was too much to resist. "Ari, I'm leaving. Maurice is here to drive me home. I'll call you later to let you know when I'll be back. Enjoy your evening." Nora's voice grew louder, the hint of amusement in her words rousing me awake.

"Nor, what's going on?" I murmured.

"Nothing." She smothered a snicker.

My eyes flew open. "Nora Hildi Abato, what did you do?"

"Me? Nothing. I've got to go, love you." She moved to the door. We'd finally chosen our rooms after pulling straws earlier. I drew the smaller room at the end of the hall with its own bathroom, while she drew the bigger one next to the master bathroom. I'd barely gotten fresh sheets on the bed when I'd fallen on top of it and succumbed to sleep.

"See you later." I waved her off, snuggling back down under the covers.

"Oh, and Ari," she called. "You might want to wear something less... bed chic." The door clicked shut and I bolted upright. What the hell did she mean? Unless...

I scrambled off the bed to check my cell phone, and sure enough there was a text from Nicco.

Six thirty. Be ready xo

My heart swelled. He was coming here. I don't know how he'd found a way inside, but I didn't care. Until I checked the time and realized I only had forty-five minutes to get ready.

I leaped into action, stumbling against the dresser, cussing under my breath as pain shot through me.

"Arianne?" Luis called.

"I'm okay," I replied, rubbing my hipbone. "I'm going to take a shower."

A deep rumble of laughter drifted down the hall, but there was no time to dwell. Nicco was coming here, and I looked like I'd been dragged through a hedge backward.

Thirty-minutes later, I had scrubbed and primped, cleansed and styled to within an inch of my life. I'd opted to wear a floaty dress that scooped low at the chest and hit just above the knee. It was feminine and light and clung to my curves when I walked. My makeup was subtle, and my hair fell into thick waves around my face. The girl in the mirror looked lovesick; her eyes glittering and skin radiant. But it was more than that. I just needed to see him, to know we were okay.

I needed Nicco in a way that terrified me.

When I entered the living room, Luis cleared his throat, sitting straighter. "Arianne, you look... beautiful."

"Thank you."

"Nicco is a very lucky man."

"Thank you for everything that you've done for us. I'll never forget it."

He stood up, nodding. "I'll go and make the arrangements."

"He's not putting you or himself at risk, coming here?"

"Let us handle all that. You just enjoy your evening. Lord only knows, you've earned it."

The butterflies in my stomach multiplied and I gently pressed a hand there, trying to calm myself. Luis disappeared out of the apartment leaving me alone. I checked my cell phone, hoping to see a message from my father. There was nothing, so I typed out a quick message to him.

Anything?

He replied straight away.

These things take time, Arianne.

Nicco doesn't have time.

Be patient, mio tesoro, please.

Make this right, Papá. I'm begging you.

I will do my best.

It would have to do for now. It was almost six thirty. I hovered nervously by the counter, waiting. After what seemed like a lifetime, the door swung open and Nicco was standing there looking every bit the dark and dangerous mafioso I knew him to be.

Our eyes met, relief and possessiveness swirling in his depths.

My breath caught as I drank him in. It was like seeing him for the first time all over again. Without a second thought, I ran to him, flinging my arms around his shoulders. "Nicco," My resolve cracked with that single word, all the pain, confusion, and anger of the last few days spilling out of me.

"I'm so fucking sorry," he said, cupping the back of my neck and holding me.

"Sorry?" I eased back to look at him. "But what are you—"

"For Tristan. I never meant to hurt him." His eyes shuttered, pain rippling off him.

"Ssh." I pressed a finger to his lips. "It was an accident, and maybe it makes me a selfish, horrible person, but I don't want to think about Scott or Tristan or my father right now." Something stirred inside me.

Nicco was here.

He was here, for me.

"Say something," I said, feeling the heat of Nicco's gaze drift over me.

"You look... Fuck, Bambolina. I had every intention of coming here and doing this right. But all I can think about is carrying you into your bedroom and undressing you."

Desire flooded me, my stomach coiling tight. "Yes, please," I whispered.

God, I wanted this man.

I wanted him more than I'd ever wanted anything in life.

More than freedom.

More than the truth.

More than I needed my next breath.

"I brought dinner." He held up a brown bag, a rich aroma filling the apartment.

"Dinner can wait," I took it from his hands and placed it on the counter. "I need you, Nicco."

I need to know this is real.

"Amore mio, there is no rush. We have time." Nicco stared down at me with such love and affection I could hardly breathe.

I ran my hands up his black shirt. He'd rolled the sleeves up at the elbows and left it tucked out of his black dress slacks. I'd never seen Nicco look so smart. So devastatingly handsome.

"See something you like?" He lowered his face to mine, a faint smirk tugging at the corner of his mouth.

"You are so handsome." My fingers drifted over the profile of his face, lingering on his lips. Nicco's eyes shuttered as he inhaled deeply, the air crackling around us. "Do you feel that?" I asked.

"I feel it." He gulped, sliding one of his hands against mine, interlocking our fingers. "God, Arianne, the things I want to do to you."

"I want it all. Every single thing."

"You don't know what you're asking." He touched his head to mine, his breaths coming in ragged bursts.

"You. That's all I want." My mouth chased my fingers away, kissing him softly. But then Nicco scooped me up in his arms, making me shriek in surprise. He carried me down the hall, pausing at Nora's bedroom door.

"Next one," I smiled, wrapping my arms around his neck.

Nicco kicked open the door and entered my room. "I haven't had time to decorate yet," I said, "but the bed is pretty comfortable."

His eyes darkened with lust as he stalked over to the bed, lowering me down like I was precious goods. "Are you sure?" he asked.

I pressed a hand to Nicco's cheek, my skin tingling with anticipation. "I have never been more certain of anything."

I'd gone to so much effort to look pretty for him, taken my time choosing the perfect dress. But it didn't matter. Nicco always looked at me like I was the most beautiful girl on the planet. It was both exhilarating and intimidating, knowing that he—Niccolò Marchetti, mafia prince—wanted me.

He straightened, letting his hands fall to his shirt, slowly unbuttoning it. I watched with rapt fascination as more of his skin was revealed. My eyes greedily tracing over the planes of his abs, lingering on the perfect V disappearing into his slacks.

"Hungry, love?" he whispered, letting his shirt fall to the floor.

I wasn't hungry, I was ravenous. Confidence stirred inside me, and I rose onto my knees, sliding my hands down my body, curling my fingers around the hem of my dress. Nicco was as still as a statue, the rise and fall of his chest quickening, as he watched me drag the material slowly up my waist.

"Sei bellissima." It was a low growl in his throat as he took a step forward. "May I?" He finally reached me, dropping to his knees at the end of the bed. I nodded, removing my hands, shivering when Nicco's fingers replaced them, brushing my thighs. He grabbed the material, working the dress up my body, stealing my breath as he pressed his lips to my navel.

My hands slid into his hair as he travelled up my stomach, kissing and licking. Nicco broke away to pull the dress over my head, and then he was kissing me, sweeping me up in his storm. I clung to him, breathless and quivering, and he'd barely even touched me yet.

"Nicco," it was a breathy moan. A plea.

I needed more.

So. Much. More.

He changed direction, trailing his lips up the slope of my neck, nipping the skin beneath my ear. In one swift motion, he picked me up, hitching my legs around his waist, and lay me down. His eyes darkened as they found the faint bruises still tarnishing my breasts and the swell of my hips. My breath hitched, waiting to see what he would do. Whether it would be too much for him. But they didn't deter Nicco.

Dipping his head, Nicco took his time kissing each one, replacing every lingering memory of pain with nothing but pure pleasure. When he reached my thighs, he pulled my body to the edge of the bed and removed my panties. A shiver rolled up my spine as he flattened his tongue against me, sucking my clit into his mouth. I bucked beneath him, pulling on his hair as he worshipped me.

Feasted on me.

"You taste like heaven," he drawled, slipping a finger inside me. "Okay?" Nicco asked, and I nodded, waiting for the discomfort to pass. He kissed my inner thigh, sucking gently, turning the lingering pain to sheer pleasure as he curled his finger enough to hit the spot deep inside me that made me shatter into a thousand pieces.

I was soaring, floating away on a cloud of ecstasy.

But then Nicco climbed my body, staring down at me with nothing but hunger. His hooded gaze grounded me. Anchored me to the moment. "Voglio fare l'amore con te," he leaned in, whispering the words against my lips.

"My Italian is a little rusty," I admitted.

Nicco smiled, giving me a little shake of his head. "I said, I want to make love to you, Arianne. So much..." He brushed the hair from my face, staring right into my soul.

"Yes."

I was stripped bare to him, but it was so much more than skin on skin.

It was two hearts beating as one.

Two souls uniting.

Swallowing, Nicco stood up, digging his wallet out of his pocket. He pulled out a foil wrapper and placed it down on the bed beside me, before unbuttoning his slacks and pushing them and his boxer briefs clean off. My tongue darted out, licking my lips. His body was a sculpted piece of art. All hard lines and carved muscle. But it was his scars that made him beautiful; a permanent reminder of how fragile life was. Of how important it was to make the most of moments like this.

Intense. Overwhelming. Magical moments.

"If I do anything you don't like, anything that hurts, I need you to tell me, okay?" He kneeled on the bed, wrapping a hand around his hard length and stroking himself. I wanted to lean up and taste him again, but I couldn't move. Frozen in place by the nervous energy zipping through me.

Nicco covered my body with his, careful not to put his full weight on me. Dipping his hand between us, he gently worked a finger inside me.

"Oh..." I gasped, trembling at the intimate position. It felt so much more than before, his dark gaze pinning me in place, unyielding. I was lost to him, completely at his mercy as he touched me, his thumb circling my clit in slow motion. It was too much, too sensitive.

Yet, at the same time, it wasn't enough.

"Nicco," I breathed. "You, I need you."

His eyes turned as black as night. Nicco kissed me, easing off me to roll on the condom. Then he was there, nudged up against me. "I love you, Arianne. Never forget that." With one smooth glide, Nicco was inside me.

"Okay?" he asked, brushing his nose over mine, giving my body a chance to adjust.

I nodded, too overcome with emotion to speak. He was everywhere. Inside my body, my heart, my soul.

"I'll take it slow."

"No." I gripped his arm, arching my back. It made him slip deeper, and we both groaned. He buried his face in my neck, and I knew he was holding back. "I don't want you to treat me like glass, Nicco."

After a second, he began to move. Slow at first. Nicco kissed me deeply, mirroring the way his hips rolled against mine in measured torturous strokes.

My fingers curled into the sheets as sensation hit me from every direction. I'd always known being with Nicco would be everything. But I hadn't expected to be so consumed by him. Every thrust, every dig of his fingers, the graze of his teeth against my collarbone. I felt it all.

Interlinking our fingers, Nicco pressed our hands beside my head as he rocked harder, deeper. His kisses grew hungry, dirty. He licked and nipped and gently bit my breasts, flicking his tongue over my nipple, chasing away the sting with tender kisses. My hips began to rock, desperate and searching.

"More," I panted. "I need more."

"You feel so good," Nicco rasped against the hollow of my throat, my body stretched out beneath him. He flattened himself to me, changing the angle, reaching some place deep inside that made my breath catch. "I don't ever want this to end, amore mio."

I didn't either.

I wanted to lose myself in him, to drown in his dark waters and never come up for air.

"Arianne…" Nicco was drowning too. I felt it. Felt him ready to shatter. "Fuck, I can't…"

"It's okay," I murmured against his lips, kissing him as hard as I could, lifting my hips to meet his. My body began to tremble as intense waves of pleasure crashed over me. "Oh God…" I cried, clinging to Nicco's body as he stilled above me, groaning my name.

Silence wrapped around us like a bubble as Nicco stared down at me with so much love and longing in his eyes, I felt weightless. "You are everything to me, Arianne. Sei la mia metá. No matter what happens, I will love you until the day I die."

Brushing my fingers against his jaw, I smiled. "Everything is going to work out, Nicco, you'll see."

It had to.

Because Nicco was right.

What we had wasn't fleeting. It was soul deep.

Written in the stars.

It was the kind of love they told stories about.

I woke with a smile, reaching out to feel the hard planes of Nicco's body. Only to be met with cold silken sheets.

"Nicco?" His name was like a prayer on my lips. Everything about last night had been perfect. From the way he'd dressed up smart for me, to the delicious meal we'd had to reheat and eat wrapped in bed sheets, to the way he'd worshipped every inch of my skin throughout the night.

I'd never wanted it to end—desperately fought sleep as my sated body slowly succumbed to the pull of exhaustion. The only thing that could have made it any better was waking in his arms, safe and cherished and loved.

"Nicco?" I called again as if I expected him to materialize in front of my eyes. There was no sign of him. No clothes strewn over the floor or sound of running water to signify he was taking a shower.

Nothing.

I swung my legs over the edge of the bed and sat up, rubbing the sleep from my eyes. He wouldn't have just left me. Not without an explanation.

Then I caught it.

A note.

A small scrap of paper propped up against a glass on my dresser. Dread filled me, every step toward it like wading through quicksand.

Bambolina,

I love you more than words can say.

Wait for me, please.

Until we meet again,

Nicco xo

"What the...?" I hurriedly read the words again, trying to understand their meaning, trying to read between the lines of a note that otherwise sounded a lot like goodbye. I rushed over to the nightstand and snatched up my cell phone, dialing my father's number.

"Arianne." That one word told me all I needed to know.

Something had happened.

"What did you do?" I ground out, my hands trembling with anger.

"Luis will drive you to the house. I'll see you soon." Then he whispered, "Perdonami, figlia mia."

I hung up, collapsing on the bed in a heap of frustration. Grabbing my pillow, I screamed.

"Ari?" Nora rushed into my room. "What is it? What happened?"

"He's gone," I cried. "Nicco is gone."

"Oh, Ari." She sat by my side, wrapping an arm around me. "I'm sure there's a good explanation."

"Did you know?"

"That he planned to leave? Of course I didn't. I'd hoped everything would work out, just like you." She squeezed me tighter.

"I'm going to call him." I called Nicco's number, but it rang out.

"Try texting him."

My fingers flew over the screen as I typed a message. But no reply came. Nicco wasn't answering. That, or he was ignoring me.

"I need to go to see my father." I shrugged out of Nora's hold and began pulling on clean clothes.

"Maybe we should think this through. I'm sure there's an explanation—"

"He's behind this," I snapped. "When I called him just now it was like he was expecting my call and he'd said something... Perdonami, figlia mia."

"Forgive me? He said that?" she asked, and I nodded.

"He promised me he would try to fix this. He promised."

"Well then," Nora said, standing. "Let's go get you some answers."

In the end, I told Nora to go to class. She'd wanted to come with me, but I needed to do this alone. Well, I wasn't totally alone. Luis was with me.

We entered the house together, the quiet bang of the door closing behind us like gunfire echoing through me. Nora's mom greeted us. "Oh, mia cara, come." She enveloped me in her arms. "Tristan is a strong boy; he will pull through this."

"Thank you," I said. "Is my father—"

"He and his visitors are waiting in his office."

Visitors?

I frowned, glancing up at Luis. "Will you come with me?"

"Of course." He motioned for me to lead the way.

Something felt off but I couldn't put my finger on it. All I knew was that something had happened between last night and this morning for Nicco to up and leave me.

I knocked gently on my father's office door and he said, "Come in."

The second I stepped inside, the ground went from under me. Luis pressed close behind me, giving me the strength I needed to face Scott Fascini and his father.

"Arianne, how lovely to see you," Mr. Fascini smiled revealing a set of perfectly white teeth.

"What, no greeting for me?" Scott sneered. His face was a mess; a patchwork of cuts and bruises and tender spots.

"Scott," I said politely. "Mr. Fascini. This is a surprise." I turned my attention to my father. "What is this, Papá?"

"Sit, Arianne, we have much to discuss," he commanded. No explanation, no gentle request.

Nothing.

"I think I'll stand." I rolled back my shoulders, facing the three of them. Steeling myself for whatever bomb was about to drop now.

"Very well," my father said, his expression devoid of emotion.

Who was this man?

Because it certainly wasn't my father.

"There is something we need to tell you," he started, shifting uncomfortably in his chair. "Something that may come as quite a shock."

Fear gripped me, my breath catching in my throat as he looked at me with such regret, apology glittering in his eyes. "What did you do?" I asked, my voice quivering.

And then he delivered the words that would flip my world upside down forever.

TWENTY-SIX

NICCO

I WAITED until I was twenty miles clear of Verona County to pull over. Dust sprayed up around my bike as it came to a halt. Ripping off the helmet, I inhaled a lungful of air, hoping it might ease the tightness in my chest.

I'd done a lot of fucked up things in my lifetime, but none had felt more wrong than leaving Arianne under the cover of darkness. She'd fallen asleep almost immediately after she had given herself to me so completely. It had been the best fucking moment of my life, loving her, being joined as close as two people could possibly get. I'd lain there for hours, stroking her skin, watching her sleep.

It was perfect.

A single moment in time I wanted to freeze-frame in case we never got another moment like it.

It had almost killed me, finally slipping out of the bed and getting dressed. She'd stirred, my name falling from her lips in a soft murmur. She must have been dreaming of me. The thought had made me both smile and die inside. For when she woke and realized I was gone, I knew her love for me would slowly turn to hatred.

One day, I knew she would understand, but in the harsh light of day, Arianne would only see that I had abandoned her after what should have been the best night of her life.

Fuck.

I was a bastard.

Yet, I'd had no choice. To stay and see her this morning would have been torture, and there was only so much pain a man could take before he surrendered. I knew if I told her, if I looked her in the eye and said goodbye, I would never let her go. I would either stay and face the consequences of my actions, or I would risk it all and take her with me.

So I left in the night like the coward I was.

Digging out my cell phone, I expected to see numerous missed calls and text messages from Arianne.

I didn't expect to see Luis' name.

My heart crashed against my rib cage as I opened his message, silently praying that it wasn't about Arianne, that she hadn't done something reckless in the wake of finding me gone. But it was worse.

So much worse.

I stared at the message, reading the words over and over, willing it to be wrong. I had done what he said. I had left Verona County to keep Arianne safe, to protect her.

So Luis' message had to be wrong.

Because there was no way in hell Roberto Capizola would agree for his daughter to marry the piece of shit who stole her innocence and covered her body in bites and bruises.

Yet that's exactly what the message said.

You'd better tell your father to work quickly, because I don't know what game Roberto is playing but I brought Arianne to the house to confront him, and Scott and his father were here. Roberto announced he had agreed to their engagement... are you hearing this bullshit, Marchetti?!

Your girl is promised to that piece of shit.

I hope you have a plan because come her nineteenth birthday, they are set to be married.

KING OF SOULS
ARIANNE & NICCO'S STORY: PART TWO

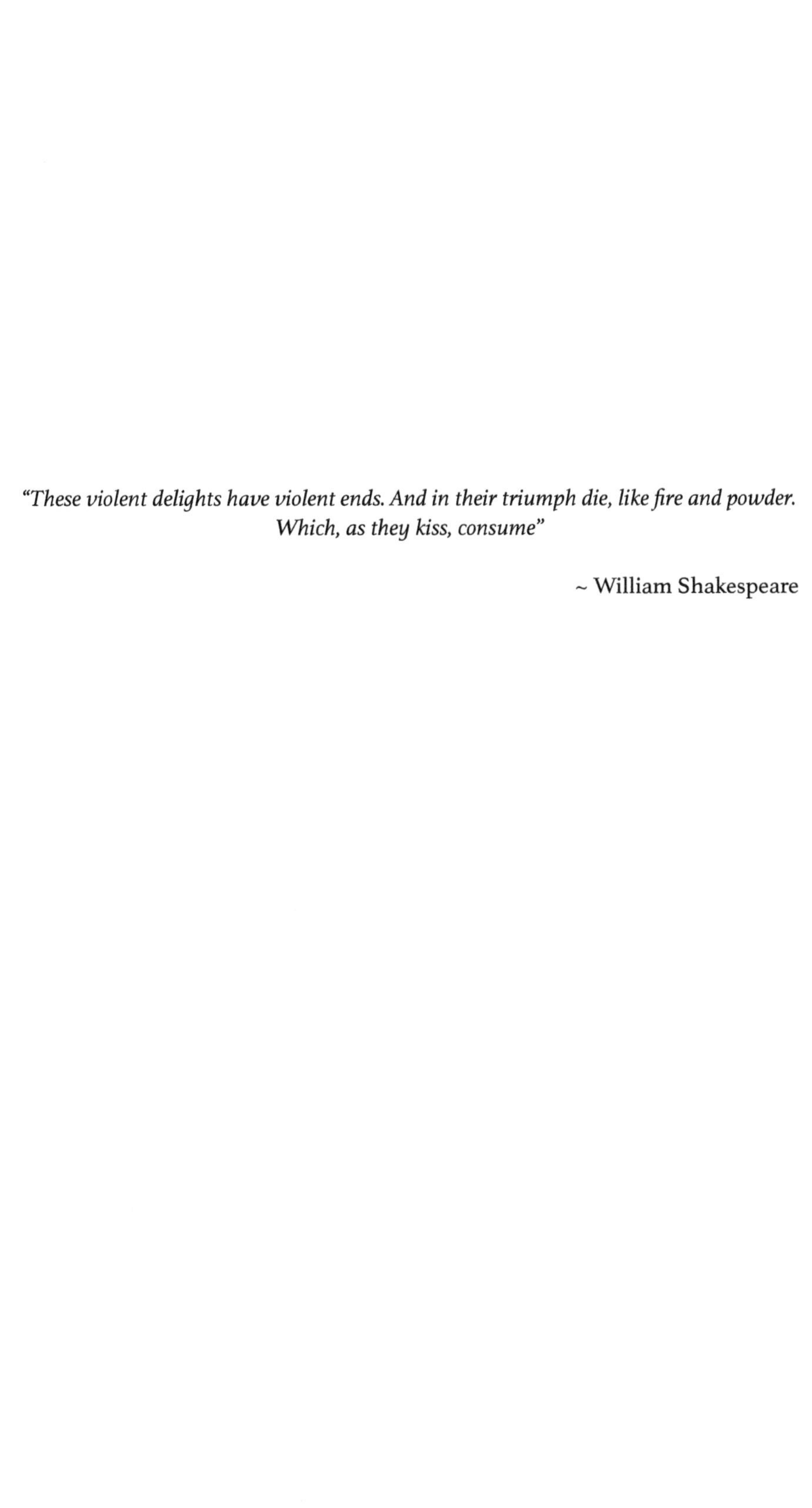

"These violent delights have violent ends. And in their triumph die, like fire and powder. Which, as they kiss, consume"

~ William Shakespeare

ONE

NICCO

"COME ON, Nicco, is that all you've got?" Dane came at me, his fists swinging and teeth snarling. He was a cocky little fucker. Reckless and impulsive with impressive strength for a seventeen-year-old.

He reminded me of myself when I was his age.

"Keep talking shit, kid, and you're going down." I jabbed my finger at him.

"Is that a threat? Because I'm shaking in my fucking boots." His friends snickered, fist bumping and high-fiving as if the result was inevitable.

A couple of the older guys caught my eye and smirked. They knew how it was. They knew Dane was one hit from getting his ass handed to him.

The truth was though, I needed this. I needed to feel his sloppy fists curled against my ribs. The flash of pain as he clipped my jaw. I needed the deep burn radiating through every one of my muscles.

I needed it all.

He came at me again, but this time I anticipated his move, ramming my fist into his stomach.

"*Oomph*." He went down like a sack of bricks.

"Stay down, kid," I said, running a hand down my face. Sweat coated my skin and my knuckles were split open again, the new skin not hardy enough to withstand the impromptu sparring session with my cousin.

"I almost had you." He grinned up at me, blood trickling down his mouth as he did so. I held out my hand, and he grasped it so I could help pull him up. Dane staggered to his feet, shaking his head. "Next time, your ass is mine, Marchetti."

"Yeah, yeah, keep talking, kid." I ruffled his hair before shoving him toward his friends.

Grabbing a towel, I dried myself off. "Looking good out there," Benny said, approaching me. He was one of my uncle's capos. A typical southie who had worked his way up the ranks to become a made man.

"Yeah, well, I've got a ton of anger to work off."

He handed me a bottle of water and I uncapped it, chugging the thing down.

"I smell trouble with a broad." My expression fell and he cussed under his breath. "Shit, Nic, that bad?"

Inhaling a ragged breath, I rubbed my jaw. "Just how much did Uncle Al tell you?" My brow rose.

"He said you needed to come lay low until the dust settled."

Until the dust settled...

It was going to take a lot more than the dust settling to fix this.

I hesitated. The less people who knew the truth about Arianne, the better, but word would get out eventually. Besides, I really needed to talk to someone because it was killing me. Every second that I was here, and she was back in Verona County, destroyed another piece of my soul.

"Come on, I think I have some of the good stuff laying around here. You can tell me all about her over a drink." His big hand landed on my shoulder and squeezed.

I didn't get out to Boston much. Uncle Alonso and his guys handled business here, just like my father and our guys handled business in Rhode Island. But Benny was as good as family. Whatever I confided in him tonight would be between us. Capo to capo. Man to man.

I looked at him and grimaced, feeling the fight ebb away. The clench of my jaw mirroring the ache in my chest. "You'd better make mine a double."

"Thanks, Lyra," Benny said to the server, letting his eyes linger on her ass as she sauntered off. She was dressed the same as every other woman in Opals, in very little.

It was one of my Uncle Al's clubs in South Boston. I would have preferred to go somewhere quieter, but Benny's gym was right around the corner and he had some business to attend to here, so I went with the flow.

Checking my cell for the hundredth time today, I tapped my foot against the stool. Despite going a few rounds with Dane at the gym, restless energy still vibrated through me. I knew the only thing that would settle me was the one the thing I couldn't have.

Not right now at least.

Arianne.

I could vividly picture her big, honey eyes. Her soft, full lips. Her irresistible smile.

My sweet, strong, compassionate Bambolina.

Fuck, I missed her.

It hadn't even been twenty-four hours since I left Verona County. Since I walked away from the only woman I would ever want.

The woman who held my heart in the palm of her hands to do with as she pleased.

I was here for her. To keep her safe until my father discovered a way to fix my mess. But nothing about it felt right.

Not a single fucking thing.

"Easy, Nicco." Benny pushed a glass of scotch toward me. I unclenched my fist, curling my fingers around the glass. "Now tell me about this girl of yours."

"I don't even know where to start," I admitted, flicking my weary gaze to his.

"Al hinted that she was forbidden fruit." He gave me a knowing look. Benny was at least twenty years my senior, as were many of the capos in Dominion. Age was but a number when you were the son of the boss though.

I ran my thumb around the rim of the glass, trying to focus on something —*anything*—except the shitstorm brewing.

"Loving her could start a war." My voice wavered.

"That bad, huh?" There was a teasing edge to his words. "She must be some broad."

"She's..." *Everything*, the word teetered on the tip of my tongue.

"It takes a strong woman to stand by a mafioso's side, Nicco. And you're so young..." I cut him with a hard gaze and he smirked, a deep rumble of laughter shaking his shoulders. "All I'm saying is, are you sure she's the one? Because from the sounds of it, ain't no coming back from this. And the family has enjoyed a certain amount of peace for the past two decades."

"That's what we're calling it?" My brow rose. "So what was that bullshit with Dane a few weeks back?"

"The kid's a hothead. Wades into a situation all guns blazing. Like we weren't all the same at his age."

I knew what he was saying, but Dane should have known better. Uncle Alonso might have been second in the chain of command, but he was still the head of the family in Boston. One day that responsibility would fall to Dane. He would be Alonso... and I would be my father.

And if Dane was going to hold the power one day, he needed to learn how to respect it.

Bringing the glass to my lips, I knocked back the scotch in one. The burn was sharp, but I didn't flinch.

I couldn't resist digging my cell phone out of my pocket again and checking for any messages.

"You could call her, you know."

"She's pissed at me."

"When ain't a broad pissed at her guy?"

"I left her." I'd just upped and left without saying goodbye. But I'd known if I woke her, if I held her and kissed her, that I would never let her go.

Arianne was having a hard time understanding that though, refusing to take any of my calls or respond to my texts.

I didn't blame her.

I couldn't.

Not when I was the one who pulled her willingly into this world, into my life.

I should have walked away. The second I found out her true identity, I should have walked away and never looked back.

But how did you walk away from something so vital as the other half of your soul?

The answer was, you didn't.

You couldn't.

Leaving Arianne, forcing myself to deny our connection, would have killed me.

Over time, it would have killed us both.

She wasn't just some girl. A fleeting crush. Arianne Capizola was my heart. The better part of me.

She was the woman I was going to spend my life with.

I let out a long breath.

If only it were that simple.

"A wise man once said," Benny said, pulling me from my thoughts, "love keeps no record of wrongs. If she is half the woman you claim her to be, she will come around."

"Niccolò, Benny, there you two are." Uncle Alonso joined us at the bar. "Where is that hothead son of mine?"

"Nicco taught him a lesson in the ring."

Alonso chuckled. "I hope you put him on his ass enough times to drill the message into his thick skull?"

"He's not a bad kid," I said. He reminded me a little of Bailey. Misguided and confused about his place in the world. But unlike Bailey, Dane didn't have any problem throwing his weight around.

"I'll talk to him again," I said. It had only been a few weeks since me, Enzo, and Matteo had driven out to keep Dane from the clutches of one of the gangs operating out of Boston. Alonso and my father felt that perhaps I could reach him, since I was only a couple of years his senior.

"That kid will be the death of me. He turns eighteen next year." Alonso shuddered. "And then what the fuck am I going to do with him? He's lucky the Diablos didn't put a bullet through his brain for that little stunt he pulled." He drained his drink, wiping his mouth with the back of his hand.

"The Diablos don't want any trouble," I said. When we'd sat down with their leader, Manny Perez, he'd been clear he didn't want war. But he did want compensation for Dane's attempt at moving in on the Diablos' territory in and around Roxbury. A compensation my uncle had reluctantly agreed to in order to save his son's life.

"Yeah, well, it's created a problem we didn't need."

"Sounds like Dane isn't the only kid causing trouble." Benny smirked at me, clapping me on the back.

"Vai a farti fottere," I growled, my blood itching for another fight. "It wasn't like I planned on any of this."

"Relax, Nicco, I'm busting your balls. What better reason to go to war than over love?"

"Benito," Alonso hissed, motioning for his capo to leave.

"I'll see you around, Nic." Benny took off.

"Excuse Benny. He is one of my most trusted men, but he is a fool."

I smirked at that. "It's okay. I know people won't understand my reasons."

"The Capizola heir." He let out a strained breath, rubbing his neatly trimmed beard. "Antonio must have blown a fuse when he found out."

"If it wasn't for the fact she was..." I swallowed the words, pain squeezing my heart like a vise. Seeing Arianne hurt like that, the blood and bruises, it made me murderous. It made me want to drive back to Verona County and make Scott Fascini pay for his sins.

"He told me she was hurt." I nodded. "We are all guilty of losing our cool now and again, but to defile a young girl so brutally..."

The words hung between us, only fueling the anger swelling inside me. It was like a fire, sweeping through me, threatening to scorch me to nothing but ash and bone.

"It is a rare thing to find what you have found, Niccolò." Alonso's hand landed on my shoulder, heavy yet reassuring. "But don't let it consume you. I have seen many a man driven to madness by love."

"You sound like my father," I said.

A smirk tugged at the corner of his mouth. "Antonio is a wise man. It would do you well to listen to him."

"I'm here, aren't I?"

His smooth chuckle washed over me, easing some of the storm raging in my chest.

"The Family must always come first, Niccolò. It is the burden we bear."

My eyes flashed to his. I'd never heard one of my uncles refer to this life as a burden before. Being mafioso was in our blood. Ingrained on our souls. You entered this life alive and you left dead. There was no other way.

I raised a brow and he chuckled again. "We all have stories, son. But some of us prefer to keep them close to our chest."

"I keep thinking it would be easier not to love her... to let her go, instead of binding her to this life." A life of secrets and heartache.

"You truly think you could do it?"

"No." My hand curled into a fist once more. "And I hate myself for it."

"Antonio has filled me in on the details and it sounds like her life was decided long before your paths crossed, the same way your life was decided. Setting her free is not the answer here."

"So I fight?"

"You fight. This thing is bigger than you and Arianne, Niccolò. It is a broken history demanding to be righted. The Capizola and Marchetti were always supposed to be united."

It wasn't the first time someone had suggested it, but I couldn't see past the war heading our way.

And to think I'd trusted him.

I'd trusted Roberto to do the right thing and be the father Arianne deserved. But instead he'd deceived me. He'd played me like a fool, and I'd left.

I'd fucking left her there and now she was... engaged to that piece of shit Fascini.

My knuckles turned white as they clenched the glass again.

"Niccolò." Concern coated Alonso's words. "You will get through this. We are Marchetti. It is what we do."

I gave him a sharp nod. It was all I could do, while the inferno raging inside me burned hotter and hotter. It was my duty to protect her. To shield her from harm and keep the monsters at bay. Yet, here I was. Banished to some far away land unable to reach her.

My head knew it was the right call, knew it was the only option. But my heart... my foolish fickle heart was quick to forget the vows I'd taken, the responsibility that lay squarely on my shoulders.

I wasn't just a capo in the family, I was my father's son.

The Marchetti Prince.

I had an entire legacy to uphold.

A legacy that would one day see me crowned King.

But every King needed his Queen...

Didn't he?

TWO

ARIANNE

"HOW ARE YOU FEELING?" Nora handed me the mug of coffee and sat down beside me.

We were in our new apartment. The one I'd convinced my father to let us move into.

My gaze was fixed on the hall and beyond that my bedroom. The same bedroom Nicco had made love to me in, less than forty-eight hours ago.

He'd loved me... and then he'd left me.

And now I was bereft, lost at sea without an anchor.

Nicco was gone.

And he'd taken my heart with him.

"I still can't believe he left." I ran my thumbs around the mug.

"He had no choice, Ari. I know it hurts, but it would have hurt a damn sight worse if you'd had to watch him be dragged away in handcuffs; or worse, a body bag."

A violent shudder ripped through me as I smothered a whimper.

"Sorry, I didn't mean—"

"No, you're right. It's not so much that's he's gone, it's that he didn't tell me himself, face to face." If I'd have known it was the last night I was going to get with him, I would have savored every second. I would have begged him to make love to me over and over again.

I would have imprinted every touch, every kiss, and sigh to memory.

"You should talk to him."

My chest tightened, my hand drifting there, as if the pain were physical. It sure felt like it. My heart felt bruised and battered.

"I know, I just... what am I supposed to say to him? He's gone, Nor." And I was stuck here, living my worst nightmare.

Tristan was still in a coma. My father had betrayed me in the worst possible way. And I was promised to Scott Fascini. The guy who had drugged me and stolen the one thing that had never been his to take.

Tears pricked the corners of my eyes as I pushed down the hazy memories. Cruel touches and dirty words. He'd tainted me. Beaten and bruised me. But I hadn't let him take my heart.

He could *never* have that, for it belonged to another.

It belonged to Nicco.

He knew about the engagement. Luis, my bodyguard, had told him the second we'd left my father's estate. I had been too numb to function. Too blind-sided to do anything but quietly sob the whole ride back to University Hill.

My father had promised... he'd promised to fix things.

And he'd lied.

After Nicco had beaten Scott, and accidentally hurt Tristan, I'd made a deal with my father. A deal he had broken the second my back was turned.

Anger skittered up my spine. I'd eventually confided in my father, revealed to him just exactly the type of guy Scott really was, and he'd *still* betrayed me.

Roberto Capizola had picked a side and now he might as well be dead to me.

"Ari, look at me." Nora shuffled closer, covering my hand with hers. "I know everything looks dismal now, but you'll get through this, I know you will. Antonio is working on it, and you have me, and Luis, and your mom. We'll figure it out. But I'm begging you, call Nicco. You need to talk about everything."

I gave her a slight nod. She was right. It was a conversation Nicco and I needed to have. But how did you tell the man you loved that you were promised to another? That you were expected to court him and spend time with him and—

I stopped myself.

"Now is as good a time as any." Nora handed me my cell phone. I stared at it like it was a grenade. "Take it," she urged, and I slid my trembling fingers around it.

"I'll give you some privacy."

"Thank you," I whispered, blood ringing in my ears.

Nora offered me an encouraging smile before disappearing down the hall toward our bedrooms. The apartment was only small, but it was light and airy and untainted with painful memories.

All except one.

Waking yesterday morning to find Nicco gone, reading his goodbye note, had broken something inside me. I'd thought we would face the coming storm together, but now he was there, and I was here, and like a mountain too steep to climb, Scott was wedged right in between us.

Inhaling a deep breath, I found his number and hit dial.

"Arianne?" My name was a whispered prayer that cracked my heart wide open.

"Hello, Nicco."

"Thank fuck," he breathed. "I've been so worried. Are you okay? Where are you? Is Luis there? Tell me everything."

I smiled; I couldn't help it. Nicco's protectiveness was something I would never tire of.

"I'm at the apartment with Nora. Luis is right outside. He doesn't let me out of his sight. Not that we've been far. We didn't go to classes again today. Not after..."

"Perdonami, Bambolina. I didn't want to leave like that. I didn't want to run like a coward. But I knew if I didn't... I knew if I stayed and tried to explain everything, then I wouldn't be strong enough to leave you."

"You hurt me, Nicco, you hurt me so much." Pain coiled around my heart as I swallowed the tears threatening to fall. "My father betrayed me. He said he'd fix it, he said—"

"He betrayed us both."

I gasped. "What do you mean?"

"He contacted me, before I came to the apartment. He said that there were things at play I didn't understand and that he needed some time. He asked me to let him handle it and lie low."

"He said that?" I can hardly believe what he's telling me.

"My father had already ordered me to go to Boston and lie low. So I told your father I would disappear as long as he gave me his word you would be safe."

"It doesn't make any sense. When he summoned me to the house, Mike Fascini was there with..." I can't say his name, but I know Nicco knows who I'm talking about from his sharp intake of breath.

Tears pooled in my eyes as I lost the fight to smother my heartache.

"Ssh, you don't need to say the words, Bambolina. Luis told me everything."

A garbled cry spilled from my lips. "I'm sorry. I'm so sorry."

"Don't cry." His voice wavered. "Please, don't cry. Nothing can come between us, Arianne, I need you to know that. It doesn't matter what your father says or what that piece of shit Fascini does... nothing can come between us. Not a damn thing. Il mio cuore è tuo."

I wanted to believe him. I wanted to believe him so badly. But Nicco wasn't here. He wouldn't be there tomorrow at school or tomorrow night when Scott came to pick me up for our date.

I flinched.

Just the very idea of Scott being anywhere near me made my skin crawl. But I could see no way out. Scott was out for blood—Nicco's blood. There was no telling what lengths he would go to. I couldn't risk that.

I wouldn't.

"Bambolina, say something..."

"How's Boston?"

Nicco's chuckle filled the line. It was like a balm to my broken heart, filling some of the cracks. "Boston is okay. Although my cousin Dane took an ass-beating earlier."

"You were fighting?"

"I do that sometimes..." he said warily. "It relaxes me."

"Fighting relaxes you?" I blurted out, disbelief coating my words. "What else don't I know about you, Niccolò Marchetti?"

It was a loaded question.

I'd fallen hard and fast where Nicco was concerned, which meant we were learning about each other as we went.

"Nothing important." I heard the smile in his voice. "You know my heart, Bambolina. You know my soul."

The honesty in his words twisted my insides. "I don't know if I can do this," I whispered.

There was a beat of silence, and then Nicco let out a strained breath. "You are so strong, Arianne. You can do this, I know you can."

"But what if he expects..." The unspoken words hung between us like a glacier.

My father and Mike Fascini expected me to date Scott... they expected us to behave like a couple, despite the official engagement announcement being kept under wraps for now.

My father expected me to be alone with him after he'd.... I pushed the thoughts down, swallowing the bile clawing its way up my throat. I couldn't go there. Whatever Scott had done to me in the past, I had to find a way to turn it into strength to help me survive this.

"Luis is working on it," Nicco said.

"What does that mean? What's going—"

"Bambolina, listen to me. You are not alone. I know it feels that way, but our friends, our allies, will do all they can to keep you safe. Just promise me you'll stay strong..." He hesitated, his silence deafening. "Promise me you'll fight."

"I promise." My voice trembled involuntarily. I wanted to be strong. I wanted to face the future with defiance in my heart and fury in my veins. But the truth was, I was scared.

I was scared of what would happen.

Of what I would become.

A rumble of voices filled the line, and Nicco said, "I have to go. But I'll call you soon, okay?"

"Okay." Pain was woven into every syllable.

Talking to Nicco wasn't enough. I needed to see him. To feel his arms wrapped around me, his breath fanning my face.

"I love you Bambolina. Sei tutto per me."

"I love you too," I whispered as I hung up, pain burying itself further into the cracks in my heart.

"Ari?" Nora came rushing into the room, crushing me into her slender arms as I sobbed. "Ssh, it's going to be okay. I promise."

But people kept making promises and they kept breaking them.

My father. My mother. Scott... Nicco.

People called me the Capizola heir. The kids at Montague looked at me like that meant something; something to revere and envy.

Being the Capizola heir didn't make me powerful though.

It made me a pawn.

A pawn in a game for which I didn't understand the rules.

A game I was currently losing.

The next morning didn't bring any signs of hope. Luis knocked early to inform me my father expected me to resume classes. Nora said it was a good thing—getting back to normal.

But nothing about my life felt normal anymore.

I went through the motions: showering and dressing, combing my hair and letting it hang in gentle waves around my face. I didn't bother with make-up.

Nora made coffee and heated some waffles, but I wasn't hungry. The pit in my stomach didn't want food, it wanted answers. It wanted a solution to the mess I'd found myself in.

The door opened and Luis appeared. "All set?"

I nodded, feeling the claws of uncertainty tighten around my throat.

"Nora, the car is downstairs," he said. "Could you give me and Arianne a few seconds alone?"

"Of course." She grabbed her bag and came over to me. "You've got this." Nora squeezed my hand gently before disappearing out of the apartment.

Luis closed the door and stepped further into the room. "How are you feeling?"

"Numb."

"I'll be right there," his expression softened, "every step of the way."

"And when I go tonight. Will you be there also?"

Luis' nostrils flared, but he didn't flinch. He was good at his job, able to present a calm and composed front at all times. He'd tricked my father, lied to his very face. It made me wonder if he could also lie to me.

"You can trust me," he said, as if he had heard my thoughts. "I won't let that piece of shit hurt you again. I promise."

I released a small sigh.

More promises.

Promises meant nothing when you were dealing with men like Scott Fascini and my father. Men who manipulated and lied and twisted the truth to their ends.

I'd learned that the hard way.

"Have you spoken to my father?"

Luis' expression morphed into anger. "He called me this morning."

"Did he say anything?"

"Nothing. But something doesn't add up. He's a ruthless man, Ari, but I can't believe he would hand you over to Fascini unless he thought he was doing it to protect you."

"Protect himself more like," I mumbled, indignation burning through me, betrayal and deceit lying heavy in my chest.

"Your father is many things, Ari, but he is not a monster. I have worked for him since before you were born, and everything he has ever done was to protect you."

"How can you defend him after he...?" The words got stuck over the lump in my throat. I took a deep breath, forcing myself to calm down, but my body trembled with anger. "He handed me over to Scott like I was nothing more than a possession. I told him what Scott did to me. I looked him in the eye and told him he..." I glanced away, refusing to let Luis see me break.

"I know," he exhaled a strained breath. "But there has to be more to it. There has to."

Slowly, I lifted my glassy eyes to my bodyguard. "So tell me, Luis, what am I supposed to do?"

"You are the Capizola heir, Arianne. You raise your head high and refuse to cower. Sometimes we don't realize how strong we truly are until we are faced with our greatest weakness. Try to remember that," he said around a half-smile. "Now come on, you don't want to be late for class."

I scoffed as he ushered me out of the apartment.

Being tardy was the least of my problems.

"Everyone's staring," I said to Nora as we made our way to the food court.

"They're just curious."

"Curious?" My brow rose. "*That's* what we're calling it?"

She rolled her eyes, dragging me toward the doors. I didn't want to be here. Everyone knew about Tristan. Everyone thought they knew the events that unfolded that fateful night, but they didn't know the truth.

They couldn't.

So I'd spent all morning trying to ignore the constant buzz of whispers and rumors.

"Arianne?" I stilled at the sound of Sofia's voice. Slowly, I turned to meet her tear-filled gaze. "Is there any news?"

I shook my head.

She smothered a garbled cry with her hand. "I tried to visit, but they said it's family only." Her eyes pleaded with me, as if she somehow thought I had the answer.

I didn't.

"Roberto would prefer to keep things private for now," Nora answered for me. "But I'm sure he'll let you know once Tristan is accepting visitors."

She smothered another whimper. "I know we weren't serious... but I care about him, I care about him a lot."

"I'm sorry," I said.

"Oh, Ari." Sofia threw her arms around me, hugging me tight. "If you need anything..."

"Thank you."

She stepped back, finally composing herself. "I should go. But I meant what I said... I'm always here."

As soon as she was gone, Nora let out a low whistle. "That was..."

"Don't." I made my way to the salad bar. I still couldn't bear the thought of food, but I knew I needed to eat.

"Have you seen you know who at all?"

"You can say their names, Nor."

"Can I? I don't know the rules of espionage."

My brows knitted as I met her amused gaze. "Seriously?"

"Made you smile though, didn't it?"

"Fine," I relented. "You made me smile."

Nora leaned in closer, filling her own plate. "I know things are bad right now, but we have to find flickers of light in the dark."

"We do, do we?"

"Yep. Besides, I was hoping to get another good look at Enzo's—"

I clapped a hand over her mouth. "Keep those thoughts to yourself."

"Prude."

"Hussy."

"But you love me." She grinned.

I couldn't argue with that. Nora was my best friend. My confidante.

She was the sister I'd never had.

And I was going to need her more than ever if I was going to make it through the next few months.

THREE

NICCO

"YOU LOOK LIKE SHIT," Dane said as I traipsed into the kitchen.

Alonso roared with laughter. "Couldn't keep up with me and Benny."

I grumbled, rubbing the back of my neck. I didn't let myself drink a lot; I didn't like the feeling of losing control. But after speaking with Arianne yesterday, I'd been a mess. I wanted to fight, to hit and hurt. But my uncle knew I was in no state to get in the ring so instead, he'd invited Benny over, pulled out his best bottle of scotch, and the three of us had sat around the fire pit out back drinking and talking until well into the early hours.

"Niccolò," my Aunt Maria came over and kissed my cheek. "There's coffee in the pot and I'm making pancakes."

My stomach turned. "I think I'm good with coffee."

Alonso and Dane snickered. "Shouldn't you be at school?" I asked my cousin.

"Yes, he should." Maria shot her son a meaningful look.

"But, Mamma—"

"No buts, Polpetto. It's senior year, and you will graduate. Tell him, Alonso."

"Ma, don't call me that," he grumbled.

"Your mother's right. Go to school and try to learn something. And stay out of trouble."

Dane mumbled something under his breath as he tucked into a pancake drenched in syrup.

"Not sweet enough already?" I flicked my gaze to the sticky mess covering his plate.

"Fuck you," he mouthed around a smirk.

Laughter rumbled in my chest. Dane was a strange mix of Enzo and Matteo. He had Matteo's humor but Enzo's temper. It made him unpredictable and reckless and I didn't doubt he was going to cause my uncle a few more headaches before he turned eighteen.

I helped myself to coffee and moved over to the window. My uncle's house was a big corner plot overlooking South Boston's shoreline. He'd bought it a few years back for Maria who wanted to move out of the brick rows in the heart of the neighborhood. It was ostentatious and came with a hefty price tag, but Maria was his wife, his woman, and she had my uncle wrapped around her pinky finger.

My thoughts drifted to Arianne; icy fingers of regret clenching around my heart. She would be heading for class soon. I knew because Luis had already texted me to tell me of their plans. He might have been on Roberto's payroll, but I trusted him. I trusted him to do right by Arianne.

My pocket started vibrating and I pulled out my cell, surprised to see my father's name. "I'm going to take this outside," I said to my uncle and aunt before slipping out on the deck.

"Niccolò."

"Old man," I teased.

"Watch your tongue, boy."

"How's... everything?"

"Tommy is working round the clock to dig for dirt on Mike Fascini, and I have Stefan helping him."

"Did they find anything yet?"

"Aside from the fact he might be a ghost from the past coming back to haunt us, no." He let out a heavy sigh. "How's Boston?"

"It's not home."

A beat passed and then my father said, "I know, Son. I know. But you need to stay put. The last thing we need is to go to war before we've got all the facts."

My hand clenched around the rail. "He promised her to him. He fucking handed her over to that piece of shit as if she's nothing more than a—"

"Niccolò," my father's tone was sharp. "You need to keep your head. We can't have another incident."

I winced at that. "Tristan was an accident."

"I know that and you know that, but he's in a coma for fuck's sake, Son. Roberto has every right to want retribution for that."

"He was on our side," I said. "He was going to buy us some time with the Fascini."

"Was he? Or was he just trying to get you out of the picture?"

"Something doesn't add up." I released a frustrated breath. "Arianne told him about the evidence, told him she had proof that Fascini..." The words drowned in my anger, my body vibrating with unspent energy.

"You need to calm down, Son. Letting your anger get the better of you will do nobody any good."

My teeth ground together behind my lips as I pressed them into a thin line. I would never forget seeing Arianne broken and bruised in the back of Bailey's car.

"Niccolò, listen to me. You cannot lose yourself to this. Do you hear me? You're up there in Boston while your woman has to stand strong and play her part. If she can do it, then by God, you have to—"

"I know." I expelled a long breath, forcing my muscles to relax.

My father was right. I couldn't afford to drown in anger and rage. It wouldn't help me, and it certainly wouldn't help Arianne. I just felt so useless being exiled here, so powerless.

"Tell me what to do." My voice cracked, my pain filling the silence that followed.

"You stay strong and you wait. You are Marchetti, Niccolò. We don't cower to our enemies and we certainly don't run."

I scoffed at that because I had run. I was hiding out in Boston while he tried to get a handle on things.

"I know what you're thinking," he said as if he could hear my thoughts, "but we need to handle this the right way. If she's as important to you—"

"She is," I snapped.

"I know, Son." He let out a resigned sigh. "I know. That girl... she has a way of bewitching even the coldest of hearts. Arianne is as good as family now. I give you my word I'll do everything within my power to make sure she doesn't get hurt again. But you need to trust me."

"I trust you," I ground out. "That isn't the problem." I just didn't trust that piece of shit Fascini. He'd already hurt Arianne twice before. What was stopping him from doing it again?

"She has her bodyguard. And I'm putting a guy on them."

"Who?"

"Niccolò." His tone was harsher. "Trust me to do my job. We have time. You said Arianne's birthday isn't until February. That gives us enough time to figure out how best to play this. If we go in all guns blazing it could jeopardize everything, Son. And we can't risk that, I won't. La famiglia prima di tutto." He let out a heavy sigh. "I'll call as soon as I have more."

"Okay." The word weighed heavily on me.

He was right. So long as I was in Boston and he was there, I had to trust he could handle things.

It didn't mean I had to like it though.

I spent the day with Benny and a couple of his guys, collecting pizzo. It wasn't ideal, but it was better than sitting in my uncle's house, dwelling.

"Heads up, Nic," Felix said as we approached the dingy bar. "We usually don't walk away from this place without getting our hands a little dirty."

My spine stiffened, my senses going on high alert. It looked like bad news. The flickering neon sign was busted, reading hooters instead of Shooters, and the door had seen better days. But it only seemed to amuse Benny as we ducked inside.

Some bluesy track spilled out of a jukebox in the corner of the room and a few guys sat around drinking beer and playing cards.

"Benny." One of them gave him a sharp nod.

Felix and Dimitri fanned out, one of them hovering by the door, the other moving to the door to the restrooms. One hand casually rested inside their jacket, their expressions void of emotion. The temperature in the bar cooled significantly.

The group of guys drinking seemed unaffected though, going about their game of poker as if it was just business as usual. And it probably was. People involved with the Family knew the score. They knew that at least once a month guys like me and Benny would come around to collect. Sometimes they paid for protection, sometimes they paid to do business on Marchetti territory, and sometimes they paid because they had a debt to the Family. Either way, when the date came you paid up.

And if you didn't... well, that was a whole other story.

"Yo, Gino, you back there?" Benny called out. He was standing at another doorway, this one concealed by a heavy black curtain. There was some shuffling and cussing and then a muscled guy appeared wearing a white wifebeater, tattoos snaking up his arm and around his neck.

"What the fuck, Benny? You can't cut a guy a little slack?"

I smirked. It was always the same with these coglioni. They knew the order of things, yet nine times out of ten they tried to wiggle out of paying up.

"You know, Gino, I thought you'd get a fucking clue by now."

A couple of the guys at the table glanced over, and Felix inched forward. I felt for my own piece but Benny shot me a look that said, 'we've got this'.

"Gino," a petite woman appeared, grinding to a halt when she spotted us. "Oh, hey, Benny. Gino didn't say you were coming around."

"Seems Gino has a little problem keeping a check on the date."

"Let me get you guys a drink?" She added, "Maybe something to eat?"

"For fuck's sake, Jen, they don't want a drink."

"Actually, I could take a drink." Benny glanced over at me. "What about you, Nic? You want a drink?"

I shrugged. I wasn't here to play games; I was here to distract myself.

"Sure thing, Benny, let me see to you guys." She started moving around the bar, but Gino's hand shot out grabbing her wrist. "Go out back and fucking stay there."

"Don't be that way, baby." She smiled, but it didn't reach her eyes. "We have guests. We should show them a proper Shooters welcome."

He leaned into her space, pressing his face up against hers. I lunged forward, but Benny's hand shot out. Anger simmered in my veins. She was half his size and Gino was staring at her as if she was the devil incarnate.

"I said get in the fucking back, puttana."

"Gino." She laughed, but it was strangled. "Please, we have guests." Her eyes pleaded with him, but it only made his nostrils flare.

She went to move around him, but he grabbed her wrist again, and pain etched into her expression. "Okay, I'm going... I'm going, stop making a scene."

Gino muttered to himself as she disappeared through the curtain. "Fucking broad doesn't know when to keep her mouth shut."

Benny sucked in a harsh breath. "You kiss your mother with that mouth?"

"Fuck my mother. Stupid whore didn't know her place either."

"Nice to see you keeping it classy, Gino," Felix deadpanned, his expression tight with contempt as he pulled to his full height.

"We came here to do business, not to shoot the shit, so can we move this along?" Benny raised a brow.

"More like came here to fuck me in the ass."

"I hate to break it to you, stronzo," Felix barked out a laugh. "But you're not my type."

Gino grunted, pulling out a money tin. The group of guys seated at the table paid him no attention as he pulled out a chain from around his neck and unlocked it. "It's been a slow month."

"Tell it to someone who cares." Benny smirked, advancing on the bar. "Make sure it's all there," he ordered.

"Yeah, yeah, keep your hair on."

I tsked under my breath. The guy was a real piece of work, and he was grating on my last nerve.

"Here you go." He shoved a fat envelope at Benny. "Now get the fuck out my bar."

"Tut tut, Gino. That temper of yours is going to get you into trouble one day." Benny tapped him on the cheek before heading for the door. I followed, letting my eyes run over each of the guys sitting at the table. They were obviously regulars, but I couldn't decide if they were Gino's guys or just indifferent patrons.

Felix and Dimitri exited the bar first, with me and Benny coming up behind. I'd just reached the door, when I heard Gino's raised voice. A cry pierced the air followed by a loud grunt and more muffled cries. I glanced back, but Benny's large hand landed on my shoulder.

"Leave it be, Nicco. We got what we came for."

But I saw red when I heard another faint whimper. Shrugging off Benny, I turned around and stormed through the bar. I came face to face with one of the guys as he leaped up. "I wouldn't go back there if I were you."

My hand went inside my jacket, flashing him the butt of my pistol. "You going to stop me?"

"Have at him, man." He held up his hands and stepped aside.

I ignored Benny's calls, fueled by nothing but anger and rage. She was still crying, her quiet sobs bleeding into me, turning my blood to molten lava.

"Get your fucking hands off her," I growled as I burst through the curtain. It was a small office and right there against the desk, Gino had his woman cowering, a bruise already forming around her eye.

"What the fuck?" he spat. "You don't get to come in here and tell me how to handle my shit."

"Apologize, now."

"Vaffanculo!"

I didn't give him another chance. I descended on him in a blur of fists and fury, relishing the crunch of my knuckles against his cheek, the soft tissue of his throat. He went down like a sack of bricks, blood trickling from his eye, grunts of pain spilling from his dirty fucking mouth. But I didn't stop… I couldn't.

"Don't hurt him, please…" The woman cried and I wanted to shake some goddamn sense into her. But I knew how it went. I knew how these women made excuses for their boyfriends and husbands. How they became so blinded to the cycle of abuse that they only ever had a list of excuses.

My chest heaved as I crouched down, grabbing him by his collar and yanking him forward. "Touch her again and next time it won't be my fists you have to worry about."

"Who the fuck do you think you are?" Spittle sprayed into the air as he tried to compose himself.

"Your worst fucking nightmare."

"Niccolò," Benny's voice cut through the tension. "We need to go."

"N- Niccolò?" The guy stuttered, confusion clouding his eyes. But then they grew wide as realization dawned. "Marchetti? Niccolò Marchetti?"

I didn't answer.

Shoving him hard, I stood up and smoothed down my jacket. "You should find a guy who treats you right," I said to the woman who was still sniffling.

"I- I love him."

Benny caught my eye and flicked his head to the main bar. I ducked out of there and walked out of the place as if I hadn't just lost my cool.

"What the fuck was that?" Benny asked the second we hit the sidewalk.

"Just letting off some steam."

"Jesus, Nic, you're supposed to be laying low."

"He going to be a problem?" I flicked my head to the dingy bar.

"Nah, I'll handle it. But maybe you should stay at the house. You're a fucking liability."

He wasn't wrong. But I'd heard that woman's cries and all I heard was my mom and father arguing, his raised voice, her soft whimpers. All I'd seen was Arianne's broken and bruised body all over again. And then Alessia. My sweet, innocent sister with a faceless man, a man leveraging his power over her.

"It triggered some stuff," I confessed.

"You don't say." He clapped me on the back. "For a second there, I was worried we'd be adding clean up to our daily roster."

"It's been a long time coming if you ask me," Felix added. "Gino is a real piece of work. It isn't the first time I've seen Jenny black and blue and it probably won't be the last."

"You're right," I said around a grimace. "I probably shouldn't come around here again."

FOUR

ARIANNE

MY HANDS SHOOK as I finished putting the final touches to my hair. Nora had helped me style it off my face in messy bun, with stray waves framing my face. It was relaxed yet elegant.

The total opposite of how I felt.

My stomach was a tight knot and my chest felt like it was in a vise, but I had to do this.

"Ari?" Nora called, her head appearing around the door. "Are you almost... Oh my, you look beautiful." There was a tightness to her words that had me inhaling a shaky breath.

"He'll be here soon."

Emotion slammed into me like a tsunami, and I reached out for the dresser to steady myself.

"Hey," Nora rushed to my side. "Everything's going to be okay. It's just dinner. Luis said—"

"Just give me a second". Eyes screwed shut, I took three deep, cleansing breaths. I could do this.

I had to do this.

What other choice did I have?

If I didn't play my part—if I didn't paste on a smile and pretend to at least tolerate Scott—I might never get to see Nicco again.

"Okay." My eyes flickered open, my fingers curling around the edge of the dresser. "I'm ready."

It felt like preparing for battle, only my words were a weapon and my heart was the battlefield.

"Luis will be there the entire time."

"I know." I brushed a curl from my face and forced a weak smile.

Luis was to act as our chaperone. It was all part of my father's latest arrangement with Mike Fascini. Scott would court me—take me out for dinner, to business parties, family events—but our relationship would remain innocent until our wedding night.

Wedding night.

I still couldn't believe they wanted me to marry him.

My father said it was to protect me, but his words meant little considering he'd handed me over to my rapist as if I was a prized cow.

I followed Nora into the living area. Luis was waiting, his expression grim.

"Your father wishes to speak with you." He held out his cell phone and I let out a heavy sigh. Taking it, I pressed it to my ear and waited.

"Figlia mia?"

"Father."

"Mio tesoro, please... there are things you do not understand. Things I am trying to protect you from. This arrangement is the safest option for you right now."

"Very well," I clipped out. "Was there something else? Or are you just calling to wish me a nice evening with my *fiancé*?"

He sucked in a harsh breath, cussing under his breath. "Everything I do, I do for you. One day, you will realize that."

"I will never forgive you for this," I seethed. "For handing me over to the man who..." I swallowed the words. Saying them gave them credence. It gave Scott power. And I refused to allow that. I refused to let him taint the memories I had of Nicco loving me.

He could have my company, my time, and even my hand in marriage, but he couldn't have my heart.

Never my heart.

"Arianne, please try to understand—"

"Then tell me the truth. Tell me what this is all about..."

"I can't, not yet." He let out a frustrated breath.

"Then goodbye, Father." I hung up and held out the cell to Luis. He took it, failing to hide his disapproval. But I knew it wasn't aimed at me, rather at the man I no longer called Papá.

"I'll be right there," Luis said, "every step of the way."

I gave him a sharp nod and waited for him to open the door. Scott might have held a certain amount of power over my life now, but I refused to give him my obedience. I would find pleasure in the small opportunities for dissension.

Starting with meeting him downstairs at his car.

But as Luis pulled open the door, I froze, hatred boiling my blood.

"Arianne, so early." He smirked, and I pressed my lips together, swallowing the hundred things I really wanted to say to him.

"We thought it would be less—"

"Yeah, yeah, you can save the excuses." He dismissed Luis, stepping closer. "Flowers, for the lady." Scott winked, handing me the bouquet of roses. I stared at them as if he was offering me his heart, carved from his chest, bloody and still beating in his fingers.

"Thank you," I almost choked over the words. Reluctantly taking the flowers from his hands, I doubled back only to find Nora standing there, tears and anger in her eyes.

"Burn them for all I care," I thrust them at her and she snickered.

"Ari..." Concern glittered in her eyes.

"I'll be okay. I promise."

Steeling myself, I spun around and made my way out of the apartment, not bothering to stop for Scott. He stumbled after me, his dark chuckle making my spine stiffen.

"The harder you push, the sweeter it'll be when you finally give in." He grabbed my arm, lacing it with his. I glared up at him. Anger vibrated through me, but Luis cleared his throat, moving around us to open the door.

"You'll follow in the SUV," Scott barked as if he had the power to give orders.

"Not part of the deal. I go where Arianne goes." Luis cut him with a hard look, but Scott didn't relent, the two of them locked in a silent battle of wills.

"We can always call Roberto or your father and settle this?"

"You ride in the back," Scott conceded, guiding me over to his sports car. It was so pretentious and full of bad memories. A shiver worked its way through me as he pulled open the door and pressed his hand to the small of my back. "Remember how much fun we had the last time we were in here?"

I ducked around him and slipped into the car, forcing myself to breathe. The familiar smell of the leather hit me, overwhelming me.

This was all a game to him.

A sick twisted game in which Scott wanted me afraid and cowering. But he was forgetting one thing. When a wild animal was cornered it either surrendered or fought—and I wasn't about to cower to Scott Fascini, regardless of how much he tried to disarm me.

My fingers curled into the soft leather seat as I forced myself to slow my breathing. My senses were on high alert. For as much as I wanted to forget, I could remember every detail about the last time I was in this car. That fateful night had been the catalyst for a chain of events I couldn't have imagined even in my wildest dreams. A chain of events that had flipped my world on its head in so many ways.

The car doors slammed as Luis and Scott climbed inside.

"Well, isn't this cozy?" he sneered. "Maybe I should have made the reservation for three?"

Luis smothered a snort. "Just drive," he grumbled.

"I think you'll really like the restaurant I picked." Scott's hand landed on my knee, my body tensing. He smirked over at me. The grin of a predator tracking its prey. But I wouldn't be his victim again.

I refused.

My hand slid over his, my fingers slipping into the spaces between.

"See," he said. "That wasn't so difficult—"

I wrenched his index finger back, his pained grunt filling the car. "Fucking bitch."

Flashing him my own smirk, I said, "Who, me?"

"That's really how you want to play it?" His brows furrowed, his voice a low growl. "Because you should know, my fiancée, I never lose."

Sorrento's was a seafood lover's paradise. Nestled in one of the quaint streets of the city, it was a decadent fusion of Italy and America. I'd only been here once, when I was a child. But my parents had a monthly reservation. Anyone who was anyone in Verona County did. So I was hardly surprised that Scott had managed to get us a table.

"Mr. Fascini," the Maître D said, "we have your regular table ready and waiting."

"Thank you, Carlo." Scott urged me forward, his hand pressing the small of my back in a possessive display of ownership.

I hated it.

I hated everything about this.

Knowing Luis was close by gave me some sense of comfort, but did little to ease the tight knot in my stomach.

"Wine?"

"A bottle of champagne please, we're celebrating." Scott barely acknowledged the Maître D, keeping his eyes fixed firmly on my face.

"Of course, Mr. Fascini, I'll have someone bring it right out." He scurried away.

"Alone at last." Scott relaxed back in his chair, making no attempt to hide the way his eyes lazily appraised my body. I'd opted for black pants and a chiffon blouse. It was demure yet elegant. Date worthy but safe. If I'd have had my way, I would have worn a burlap sack, but as Nora reminded me, I needed to play my part. At least until someone figured out how to get me the hell out of this nightmare.

It would have been so easy to run; to get up and never look back. I could flee to Boston and Nicco and I could disappear across country. But he had responsibilities. He had a whole legacy weighing on his shoulders, not to mention Alessia and his cousins. I couldn't ask that of him.

Besides, Verona was my home. Nora was here. My mom... My life.

Running felt like surrender, and I refused to cower. Not to Scott, not to my father, not to this game I didn't fully understand yet.

"Has your father talked to you about the party?"

"Party?" Dread snaked up my spine.

"The engagement party, of course. Well, at least it will be once they announce it."

Just then, the server arrived with our champagne. I wasted no time holding out my glass. "Thank you," I muttered, downing it in one. The bubbles fizzed all the way down and I covered my mouth with a hand.

Scott chuckled. "My fiancée just found out some exciting news."

"Oh, well congratulations." The server offered to refill my glass, but I declined. I needed to keep my wits about me, not succumb to the tempting distraction of alcohol.

"You should have another." Scott motioned to the bottle on ice. "Loosen up a little."

"I think I should probably stick to water."

"Spoilsport," he drawled. "I went to see Tristan today. The doctors said he could wake any day."

Pain coiled around my heart. Me and my cousin might not have always seen eye to eye, but he was still my family, my blood. I didn't want him to die.

"I hope he does."

"At least Marchetti is gone. He's lucky he isn't rotting in a cell like he deserves for what he did to Tristan." Scott said the words as if it negated his responsibility for what happened that night. If he hadn't provoked Nicco we wouldn't be sitting here right now.

Oh, who was I kidding?

I didn't know how things would have turned out because it was abundantly clear that my life was not my own. I was but a puppet and my puppet master was a man who wore many faces.

Father.

Traitor.

Sinner.

Liar.

Roberto Capizola was a man I could no longer trust. A man who spoke of protecting me and putting me first, but who locked me away in our house for five years to save me from the truth.

My father was not a good man.

My legacy was not built on the blood, sweat, and tears of an honest past. It was built on lies and secrets and a dark past he didn't think I was strong enough to know about.

I grabbed the bottle of champagne and refilled my glass.

"Are you ready to order?" The server reappeared, looking a little sheepish. Scott straightened and folded his hands on the table.

"I'd like my usual, hold the sauce with extra greens please."

"Very good, Mr. Fascini. And for the lady?"

Before I could get out the first word, Scott said, "She'll have the same, thank you."

The server gave him a tight nod and started walking away, but indignation burned through me. “Excuse me,” I called after him grabbing one of the leather-bound menus. “Actually, I’d like a garden salad with a side order of the shrimp.”

“Excellent choice.” He gave me a small smile before hurrying away.

“I’m quite capable of ordering my own meal.”

“You want to be independent,” Scott relaxed in his chair again, “I can dig that. But you know, Arianne, you need to get used to being taken care of.”

“I’m not looking to be somebody’s arm candy, Scott.” His name vibrated through me.

His lip curled with amusement. “You have so much to learn about the world, Bellissima.”

“Do not call me that,” I seethed, my fingers curling around the edge of my seat.

“Our union will make our families strong. It will make us a force to be reckoned with. The Capizola and the Fascini.” Something flickered in his eyes. “You and me, it's happening, baby. So you can either get on board with that, or you can fight me at every turn. Either way, I’m going to enjoy the ride.”

The champagne washed in my stomach, and I swallowed the acid rushing up my throat. Scott wasn’t going to make this easy. He was going to push and taunt me at every turn.

He picked up his glass and inspected it, his eyes catching me through the polished crystal. “I am counting down the days until I can have you again.”

I sucked in a harsh breath. I couldn’t do this. I couldn’t sit and listen to his sick and twisted words. “Excuse me, I need to go to the bathroom.” Gingerly, I stood and grabbed my purse. Luis immediately caught my eye and moved into position to follow me. I hurried toward the back of the room and slipped into the ladies’ restroom.

There was a knock and Luis’ gruff voice followed. “Arianne? Are you okay?”

“Just a minute.” My voice cracked, as I fought desperately to keep the tears at bay. I’d foolishly thought that if I didn’t give Scott power over me, he couldn’t hurt me.

I was wrong.

People like Scott—*men* like Scott—didn’t wait to be given power, they took it. He wouldn’t stop his tirade until he won. Until he had me broken at his feet, begging him to stop.

“Arianne, I’m coming in.” Luis cracked the door open and ducked inside. “What is it, what’s wrong?”

“He—” An ugly sob tore from my throat as my body trembled with frustration and pain.

“Ssh.” My bodyguard wrapped me into his arms, holding me. “He’s just trying to get a reaction from you.”

I eased back to look at him. “Well, it’s working.” Luis handed me a tissue and I dabbed the corner of my eyes. “I don’t think I can do this.”

“You can.” He gave me a sad smile. “You must.”

I glanced away. In that moment, I didn't want to fight. I didn't want to stand tall and refuse to let the likes of Scott Fascini and my father walk all over me.

I wanted to run.

I wanted to beg Luis to take me far away from Verona County and never look back.

"Arianne, look at me," he let out a strained breath. Slowly, I lifted my tear-stained eyes to his. "You are one of the strongest people I know. You are kind and compassionate and you have such a big heart. Don't let him take that from you. Don't let that piece of shit win."

"O- okay. I'm okay." I slipped out of his hold and went over to the mirror, drying my eyes. "Can I have a minute?"

Luis hesitated, but after a beat, he nodded, leaving me alone.

Digging my cell phone out of my purse, I opened my messages.

Tell me something good.

It pinged straightaway, making my mouth curve into a half-smile.

I love you.

Another message came straight through.

Is everything okay?

It will be. I love you too.

Emotion clogged my throat as I awaited his reply. God, I wanted to see Nicco. To bury myself in his arms and breathe him in.

Be strong, Bambolina. Be strong for me. For us.

FIVE

NICCO

"IS THAT HER?" Dane asked me as we sat out back with a beer. The flames from the fire pit licked high into the inky night's sky, the crackle hypnotic.

"Yeah," I said tightly, dropping my cell on the arm of the chair.

"What's she like?"

"You really want to know?"

"I can't ever imagine meeting a chick who knocks me on my ass, humor me."

"Arianne is..." I released a small breath. "She's like no one else I've ever met."

"And you had no idea that she was... you know. The enemy." He whispered the words as if they were forbidden.

"None." My chest tightened. "Do you really think I would have...?" I stopped myself. To suggest a world without Arianne seemed impossible.

I knew what Dane thought, what all of my uncles and the guys thought. They didn't understand how I could fall so hard and fast for a girl I barely knew. Hell, even I didn't understand it. But I was done questioning it. Fate had entwined our paths that night, and I wouldn't have wanted it any other way.

Before Arianne, I had been numb; a reluctant prince wearing a crown too heavy. My only priority was the Family and fulfilling my duty. But meeting Arianne was like taking my first breath. She smiled and all the stars came out to take notice. And something inside me had come to life. I wanted to protect her. Stand by her side. I wanted to bind myself to her with permanence and loyalty and love.

I wanted things with her I had no right to want as a nineteen-year-old mafioso. A mafioso who would one day be head of the Family.

"It's rough, man," Dane let out a low whistle before taking a long pull on his beer. "The one girl you want is the only girl you can't have."

My eyes cut to his, but I found no arrogance there, just mild curiosity. Dane was still green, skirting on the fringe of the Family before he turned eighteen, graduated high school, and took his role under his father's rule.

We were the future.

Our fathers' legacies.

But it was something no one could prepare you for.

"Maybe I'll get to meet her one day. Show her I'm the better looking Marchetti." He waggled his brows and I threw my bottle cap at his head. Dane batted it away, laughter rumbling in his chest.

"Not a fucking chance."

He shrugged. "It's not like I don't already have options."

"Options?" My brow rose. Cocky fucker.

"Like you, Enzo, and Matteo didn't screw around in high school. Enzo is one of the biggest players I've ever met. That guy is—"

"Don't ever let him hear you say that shit." The vibrations of my cell phone demanded my attention and I picked it up.

They're at some fancy place in the city. Luis is with them.

Good. Stay on them.

I hit send, unsure whether to feel relieved or more anxious. I hadn't even had to ask Bailey to keep an eye on Arianne, he'd offered. I didn't want to drag him any deeper into the shit between me, Fascini, and Roberto, but something told me he wouldn't listen anyway. And the truth was, I needed to have eyes on her, eyes I trusted with my life.

"Everything okay?" Dane asked, and I nodded. "You sure don't look like everything's okay. You can talk to me, you know. We're family. One day we're going to be running everything, together."

I didn't ever let myself look too far into the future, not when it was mapped out before me. But things were different now.

I was different.

"I'm trying to see a way through this, but I'm not going to lie, kid, it's real fucking hard."

"Hey, less of the kid. You're like two years older than me."

"Three."

"Yeah, yeah, whatever." He waved me off. "You know your old man will fix it. Uncle Toni isn't going to let some Suit piss all over him and the Family."

"You know the history between the Marchetti and the Capizola?"

He gave me a half-shrug. "I know all I need to know. They went one way, we went the other, now we're on opposite sides of the line."

I smirked. The kid sure had a way with words. "Something like that." I scrubbed my jaw. "The point is, we've got history." And history had a funny way of repeating itself.

Dane grumbled to himself. He was still young. He didn't understand the finesse required when handling certain situations. Roberto Capizola and Mike Fascini weren't just your everyday guys. They had power, money... they had connections. If we were going to finally go up against them, we needed to have an airtight plan. Because when you went to war people got hurt.

People died.

"I just hate knowing that she's there... with him. If he hurts her again..." Pure rage exploded in my veins. My body shook, my teeth grinding violently behind my lips.

I wanted to kill Scott Fascini.

I *would* kill him.

One day, when he was least expecting it, I would watch the life drain from his eyes and feel nothing but satisfaction.

"Shit, Nicco, you're a better guy than me. Some dude ever touched a girl I was seeing, I'd tear his dick off his body and feed it to him."

I smiled at that. I couldn't help it. "Trust me when I say, he'll get what's coming to him."

One way or another, Scott Fascini would pay.

Silence settled over us as we stared at the roaring fire. Boston was worlds apart from La Riva. My thoughts drifted to Enzo and Matteo and what they would be doing right now. Part of me wondered if Matt would be able to keep our hot-headed cousin out of trouble. I'd asked them both to keep an eye on Alessia. I wanted to ask them to watch over Arianne, but Enzo was still coming to terms with everything, and I knew he intimidated her. So Bailey seemed like the better option, for now. We all needed to lie low, to let the dust settle. Roberto Capizola might have double crossed me, but he'd obviously pulled some strings because I was still breathing and as far as I was aware, there had been no comeback on the Family yet.

Everything was quiet.

The calm before the unstoppable storm.

I'd beaten the crap out of Scott and put Tristan Capizola in a coma. You didn't just walk away from that.

"What's it like?" Dane finally broke the silence. "Being a capo? Being out there, working for the Family?"

Dane was a tall kid. He had broad shoulders and a trim waist, and it was obvious he worked out. But right there, with the glow of the fire dancing across his face, he looked like a little kid, scared and fascinated in equal measure.

"It is what it is." I ran my thumb around the bottle neck. "Being Marchetti means family, it means putting the Family above all else. It means being prepared to fight... to hurt... to *die* for Dominion."

"Your initiation..." His voice was quiet, a trace of uncertainty there. "What did you have to do?"

"You know what it entails." All men born into the Family did.

"Yeah but hearing about it and knowing it are different things."

I tipped my head to the sky, letting out a strained breath. I didn't think about that night often. The night me, Enzo, and Matteo were formally initiated. But I could still remember it as if it were yesterday.

They said your first kill changed you; well mine had tattooed itself on my soul, a blood-stained shadow that would never fade.

"Come," my father beckoned us into the dimly lit room. I felt like a complete idiot in the all-black outfit. The floor was cold beneath my feet as I led my cousins—my two best friends in the whole world—to the table where my father stood.

I knew the drill; I'd heard enough stories about the making ceremony growing up around the boss.

"Niccolò, Lorenzo, Matteo, the time has come." He motioned for us to approach the table. The flames from the candelabras flickered wildly, casting shadows around the room. A half-circle of my father's most trusted men stood around him. I spotted my uncle Michele, and Enzo's father, my Uncle Vincenzo. They all looked the same in their slacks and dress shirts, their hair neat and tidy, expressions like stone. It was no surprise; they knew what was to come.

They knew what we'd have to do.

Enzo and Matteo stood quietly, flanking each of my sides. As son of the boss, they knew I would be called first.

"Niccolò Luca, how do you arrive here tonight?" My father lifted the small dagger, light bouncing off its blade. A shiver ran up my spine. This day has been inevitable for me from the moment I took my first breath. It was in my blood.

It was my legacy.

"I come ready to take the oath," I repeated the words I always knew I'd one day say.

My father motioned for me to give him my hand. I lay it palm open facing up, as he began. "Niccolò Luca, tonight you are reborn. The blood that flows through your veins is Marchetti blood," he jabbed the tip of the knife into my finger, but I did not flinch, "the blood of Dominion. It means you will put first the Family above all else. You will answer the call of the Family above all else. And you will defend the Family above all else. Do you understand?"

"I do."

He pinched my finger, letting the beads of blood drip onto the card of the saint. "Swear on the saint that you will carry the secrets of the Family always."

"I swear."

My father took a lighter and ignited a corner of the card, dropping it into the palm of my hand. "As she burns so too does your soul. When the flames die, you are reborn."

The card turned to nothing but smoke and ash in my hand. I didn't know how I'd feel, finally taking my place in the Family, but as I stood there, I felt the ties snake through me, binding me to a life I'd never asked for.

A life I had to embrace anyway.

I loved my family. I loved my father, my uncles, and my elders. But to take this oath, to swear Omertà, was to sacrifice my freedom.

The flames died out as my father's large hand landed on my shoulder. He leaned in kissing my cheek. "La famiglia prima di tutto."

I stepped aside, letting Enzo take my place. He repeated the same ceremony, Matteo going last. My father's men descended on us, clapping us on the back and welcoming us to the Family. But it was all a formality. For the night was only just beginning. It wasn't enough to take the oath and swear on the saint though. You had to prove your allegiance.

"Let us eat," my father declared, moving to the long table set up behind us. "Tonight, we welcome my son and my nephews into the fold. Tonight, they become real men."

My eyes lowered to Dane. He was watching me, curiosity and fear glittering in his eyes.

You should be scared.

"Enjoy senior year," I said. "Make the most of the time you have left to be a kid. Because once you take the oath..."

I took a long pull on my beer, trying to wash down the lump in my throat.

"It's all good." Nervous laughter vibrated in Dane's chest. "I'm ready," he added.

"We're all ready," I said quietly. "Until the time comes." Until they forced a gun into your bloodied trembling fist and told you to pull the trigger.

Another vibration of my cell jolted me from the dark memory. "I need to take this," I said, standing.

"Sure thing, man. I'll catch you tomorrow."

"Is she okay?" I asked the second I was out of earshot.

"She's...." Luis let out an exasperated breath. "This shit is messed up, Marchetti. Fascini is acting like he didn't..." I heard him swallow the words.

"Did he—"

"No, no. He's said a few things and sat there with that fucking smug smirk on his face. But for the most part, he's been like a well-behaved dog."

"Where is she now?"

"He ran into some friends. They're all at the bar talking."

"You can still see them?"

"I won't let them out of my sight.... You know it would be so easy." Silence fell over the line. "So fucking easy to put a bullet between his eyes. I could do it, I could—"

"No." The words cracked my chest open. "We need to know exactly what we're dealing with first." If Scott and his father were somehow related to the

Ricci, we needed to know. Ending Scott—no matter how much I wanted that—had to wait. We had to see this thing through.

"How are you holding up?"

Luis' question caught me off guard. I ran a hand down my face, feeling my days old stubble beneath my fingers.

"This isn't about me," I ground out, unable to disguise the quiver in my voice. "It's about Arianne."

So long as she was okay, I would be okay.

"That girl must have balls of steel to do what she's done tonight. But I gotta say, Marchetti, I don't trust him. Even if Roberto has managed to negotiate a celibacy agreement, he's a monster. I see it every time he looks at her. He's playing by the rules now but I'm not sure how long he'll be able to curb his hunger."

I bristled, my eyes shuttering at his words. "Just stay on her. I need you to stay on her every fucking second."

"I will. I'll check in when we're back at the apartment."

"Thank you."

Luis hung up but I was still staring at the screen long after he was gone. I couldn't see past the red mist descending in my vision. Nothing about this felt right.

Not one single fucking thing.

SIX

ARIANNE

"I WANT TO LEAVE," I said through gritted teeth, forcing a smile so that Scott's friends didn't think I was rude.

I didn't care what they thought but I also didn't want to draw any attention to myself.

"Come on, baby," Scott crooned. "Just a little while—"

"You can either take me home, or I'll have Luis call for a car." He was bound to have a car nearby, just in case.

Scott laughed nervously, his gaze flicking to the couple we had spent the last hour chatting with at the bar. "Don't make a scene, Ari. Dale and Kayla are good friends. Just one more drink and then we'll go."

"You enjoy that drink." I slid off the stool, gently nudging him out of the way. "I'm leaving."

I couldn't breathe. Between the constant fake smiles and forced laughter, the rubber band around my chest had grown tighter and tighter. If I didn't get some fresh air soon, I was either going to faint, or say or do something I might live to regret.

"Is everything okay?" Dale asked.

Peering around Scott's shoulder I mustered a weak smile. "Actually, I'm not feeling so good. I think we're going to call it a night." I slipped my purse underneath my arm and tucked a stray curl behind my ear.

"Already? The night is still young. Scott was just getting to the good part."

I had to force myself not to roll my eyes. Scott hadn't stopped talking. As the evening went on, it became more and more apparent he loved the sound of his own voice. Dale had asked him about his injuries, and Scott had jumped at the chance to tell them about the night he had defended my honor against the infamous Niccolò Marchetti, who almost killed him and my cousin.

And I'd sat there silent, pretending that reliving that night wasn't like a thousand tiny blades cutting away at my skin.

"Darling, if Arianna says she needs to go, leave them be."

"It's Arianne." I almost bared my teeth at Kayla. She wasn't trying to help me out. She was trying to belittle me, the way she had the entire night. But jealousy was a powerful motivator, and I hadn't missed the way she'd made moon eyes at Scott ever since we joined them at the bar.

She obviously didn't see the monster beneath the expensive clothes and wolfish grin.

"Oh, silly me." She splayed a perfectly manicured hand on Dale's stomach, her eyes half-lidded with lust as she let them run over Scott's chest. His lip curled in a knowing smirk, causing a deep shudder to roll through me. They were being so blatant.

It was disgusting.

"Perhaps, you should stay?" I suggested. "I'm sure Layla would like that."

Dale started choking as his girlfriend narrowed her eyes at me. Scott merely chuckled, grabbing my hand in his. "Jealous, love?"

I pressed my lips into a thin line.

Breathe. Just breathe.

"It's such an unattractive quality, don't you think?" Kayla sneered.

"Now, now ladies." Dale let out a strained laugh. "Let's put the claws away. Rest assured, Ari, this one knows who she belongs to." Kayla yelped and I could only assume Dale had pinched or smacked her butt.

"Well, it was nice to meet you." I started to pull away from Scott, silently praying he wouldn't fight me on it.

"I'm sure we'll be seeing you again." Dale winked, a knowing glint in his eye.

Oh God, did he know? Had Scott already told him about the engagement?

"Enjoy the rest of your night," I said, not sticking around to hear Scott's parting words. I needed to get out of here.

Now.

Luis approached me, silently asking me if I was okay. I pursued my lips, nodding. "Come on," he said. "Let's get you home." Luis pulled open the door just as Scott caught up with us.

"Vitelli, you can drive." He thrust his keys at Luis.

"Maybe I should call for a car?"

"Worried you can't handle her?"

Luis' expression tightened. "I'll drive. But you need to figure out how you're going to get home from La Stella."

"Maybe I'll stay over?" Scott smirked in my direction.

I didn't dignify his suggestion with an answer, slipping past him and leaving the restaurant. The cool air instantly hit me, and I inhaled a deep breath in a desperate attempt to temper the storm raging inside me.

"You need to learn your place." Scott moved beside me, placing his hand on the small of my back. The intimate action was like a knife to the stomach. "Dale Manzello is a good friend and a respected businessman. It wouldn't hurt you to show a little respect."

"Like Kayla was showing you so much respect?" I all but spat the words.

"Careful, Principessa, I might mistake your venom for jealousy."

I swallowed a groan.

"This is fun." Scott dipped his head to my ear, his touch growing firmer. "It's going to be so fucking sweet watching you kneel at my feet."

My fingers curled into fists so tight my nails began to cut my skin.

"The car." Luis cleared his throat and I used the moment to my advantage, stepping away from Scott and toward my bodyguard.

"Thank you," I said as he opened the passenger side door. But Scott cut across my body, preventing my access.

"I think Ari and I will sit in the back, together." His hand brushed my waist, lingering on the curve of my butt. "After all, we have so much reacquainting to do." He leaned in, his breath hitting my face, his mouth so close I could almost taste the whisky on his tongue.

My vision began to blur, a crippling wave of nausea crashing over me.

"Arianne," someone yelled as I reached out for something—anything. But it was too late. The world began to tilt, the black abyss swallowing me whole.

"Arianne?" Luis' concerned expression filled my vision. "Meno male!"

"W- what happened?"

"You fainted." He crouched down beside me. We were still on the sidewalk, a crowd of people gathered around all wearing similar expressions of concern.

"Here," someone thrust a bottle of water at me. "You should drink something until the EMTs arrive."

"EM—no." I lifted a hand, swaying slightly as everything started to spin again. "I'm fine, thank you."

"Arianne, baby, thank God." Scott burst through the crowd. "I was worried sick."

"Luis." I clutched my bodyguard's arm, confusion muddying my thoughts. "I want to go home," I whispered.

"The car should be here any second."

"Now hang on a minute." Scott began to interject, but Luis straightened to his full height and the two of them had a silent conversation while a kind-faced woman gently patted my hand.

"Is it the baby?"

"Excuse me?" I sat upright.

"Oh, I'm so sorry." Guilt flashed in her eyes. "I thought... early pregnancy knocked me off my feet more times than I can count."

"I'm not pregnant." I suppressed a shudder.

"Did you eat?"

"I'm fine. I just got a little overwhelmed."

She nodded, offering me a sympathetic smile. "Your fiancé was so concerned. It really was very sweet. And your uncle, he seemed—"

"Uncle?"

"Is he not—"

"Arianne." Luis loomed over us. "The car is here."

"What about Scott?" His name was like ash on my tongue.

"I've made arrangements for him to get home safely. Come on." Luis offered me his hand and I accepted, letting him pull me off the floor and onto my feet. "You good?"

"I think so." Embarrassment burned through me, but it was nothing compared to the memory of Scott's hand on the curve of my waist, his mouth dangerously close to mine.

I felt him watching, his stare heavy and thunderous. Glancing back, I met his eyes and held his stare. Scott was pissed, it was written all over his face. But it was more than that. There was a possessiveness in his narrowed gaze that made my body tremble. He truly believed I was his. And despite my resolve not to let him get to me, I couldn't deny I was terrified about the lengths he would go to, to make sure I remained so.

Luis led me to the sleek, black SUV and opened the door. I climbed inside, surprised when he followed me.

"Everything good?" The driver asked. I recognized him. He was the security guy who usually stayed with Nora.

"Just drive," Luis said gruffly.

"Are you okay?" I asked, peeking over at him.

"Shit, Arianne. That's supposed to be my line."

"I'm okay. I think I just..."

"It triggered you."

"What?"

"Something Scott said or did. I think it triggered you."

I curled my hands over the edge of the cool leather seat. "He wanted me to get in the car and it was like I couldn't breathe. I couldn't—" A garbled cry spilled from my lips.

"Hey, you're okay." Luis shuffled closer, pulling me into his arms. "You're okay."

Fisting his shirt, I sobbed quietly into his chest. Maybe he was right. Maybe Scott had triggered something. Despite everything being so raw, I had tried my hardest to switch off the memories. I refused to give them power over me. But the scars were real, and they did have power over me.

He had power over me.

I needed to accept that.

I needed to accept it, then find a way to wield it.

"You need me to call Nicco?" Luis whispered and I shot up.

"No, you can't tell him." If he knew what had happened... I didn't want to think about what he might do.

"Ari," Luis exhaled a strained breath. "I'm not sure we should keep this from him."

"Please, promise me. You can't tell him, Luis. Nicco needs to stay in Boston."

His expression softened. "Okay. But if it happens again... maybe you should see a doctor?"

"I don't need a doctor." I needed a miracle.

"I'm just saying, maybe talking to someone will help."

"I just got overwhelmed. It won't happen again."

"Ari—"

"I'm fine, Luis." I waved him off. "I just need to rest."

"Then rest. I won't let anything happen to you."

At his reassuring words, my eyes fluttered shut and I let myself drift, desperately wanting to believe him.

"Are you sure?" Nora asked the next morning, over coffee and pancakes.

"I need the distraction. I can't stay here all day, hiding. It'll drive me stir crazy."

"I get that but after last night..."

"Last night was... well, I don't really know what last night was. But I'm fine today. I can do this. I need to do this."

She gave me a knowing look. I'd seen it before. It was usually right before she delivered me some truth bomb.

"He raped you, Ari. Scott slipped you something and then he... *hurt* you." She took a shuddering breath. "I admire your strength. I admire the fact you want to face this head on and not let him hold the power. But I also think Luis is right, you need to give yourself space to deal with this. You need help, babe. Professional help. Maybe you should give yourself some time—"

"Time?" I shot up out of my seat, coffee spilling everywhere. "I don't need time. I need Nicco. I need for my father not to be a lying manipulative asshole. And I need to not be a pawn in some game I'm still not sure I even understand. Talking to some doctor or shrink isn't going to give me any of that. It isn't going to fix this nightmare I've found myself in.

"He gave me to Scott, Nor. My own father handed me over like a baton, and I'm terrified that if I don't comply, if I don't follow the rules, something bad will happen." Because a tiny part of me had to believe there was more to this, that my father wasn't as cruel and callous as he seemed.

Angry tears streamed down my cheeks as I inhaled a ragged breath. "So no, I don't want to talk. I don't want to try to explore my feelings about what happened. I want to carry on as normal and pretend that I still have the power to make choices about my own life. I want to pretend that I'm not just waiting for the next bomb to drop. I want—"

Nora rushed over, pulling me into her arms. "I'm sorry, I'm so fucking sorry. Whatever you need, I'm here. I just... I was so worried when Luis texted to tell me what happened."

"He did that?" I pulled back, swallowing the lump in my throat.

"He cares about you, Ari. We both do." She smiled weakly. "He also told me you made him promise not to tell Nicco."

"He can't know, Nor." Pain splintered through me. "He just can't."

"That's not... yeah, okay."

"I just need to be more aware of my emotions around Scott. He deliberately pushed my buttons most of the night. He wants to see me crack."

"Piece of shit," she sneered. "I can't wait for the day he gets what's coming to him."

"Nora." I wanted Scott to pay, I did. But I wasn't sure I wanted Nicco to spill any more blood.

Not for me.

She shrugged. "He deserves everything he has coming. I won't apologize for that."

"Who are you right now?"

"A girl who would do anything for her best friend."

"You're a little scary," I admitted around a weak smile.

"I just... God, he makes my blood boil. And don't even get me started on your dad."

"My life was never my own, I realize that now. I will always and forever be the Capizola heir."

"No. No way. I refuse to accept that." Nora shook her head. "You are so much more, Arianne. You are kind and compassionate and humble. And strong... you're so fucking strong. And what you've found with Nicco is rare. It's worth fighting for. It's worth hurting for.

"Nicco and his father will come through, babe. I don't doubt that. Because family is everything to Antonio, and you are everything to Nicco. So we'll do it. We'll keep on pretending everything is fine while we figure this out."

"Thank you," I breathed, relief spreading through me. Maybe one day, I would stop and take stock of everything that happened to me. But today was not that day.

It couldn't be.

Because if I stopped, my control on things would slip. And if I slipped, if I lowered my guard for even a second, that's when Scott would strike.

If I'd learned anything since arriving at Montague it was that the good guys weren't always good, and the bad guys weren't always bad.

"Okay, let's go," she said, "We can stop at the coffee shop on the way."

"We already ate."

Nora shrugged. "I can always make room for a blueberry muffin. Luis," she called, and he slipped into the room. "We're going to walk to the coffee shop and then head downtown."

"It's a nice morning for it." He gave her a tight nod, his gaze flicking to mine. "How are you?"

"I'm okay, thank you."

He nodded again.

I had just grabbed my bag when my cell started ringing. "Mia cara," Mom's voice filled the line. "How are you? How was...?" She trailed off.

"It was okay." Nora caught my eye and gave me a reassuring smile. "Something happened though. I fainted."

"Oh gosh, Arianne." She smothered a cry. "I am so sorry, sweetheart. I wish things were different, I wish I could... But your father, he's withdrawn. He won't even talk to me about it. Something is happening, but I don't know how to—"

"It's okay, Mamma." It wasn't but I couldn't do this. I couldn't carry her guilt as well. "I'm just about to go out with Nora. Can we talk later?"

"Of course. Your father has asked... he wants you to come to the estate later to talk about the..." She inhaled a shaky breath. "There are arrangements to make, for the party."

The permanent knot in my stomach tightened. "Very well," I said flatly. "I will see you later."

"Wait," she rushed out. "I love you, figlia mia. I love you so much. And we'll get through this, I promise."

I mumbled goodbye and hung up.

"Everything okay?" Nora asked from the door.

"My father has summoned me. He wants to see me at the estate later."

Her expression faltered. "Did she say why?"

"The party..."

"Oh."

"Arianne?" Luis appeared over Nora's shoulder. The second his eyes landed on me he paled. "What is it?"

"Nothing."

Nothing I said right now would change anything. Not unless I asked him to take me away from here. And I couldn't do that to Nora or my mom, despite her misguided loyalty to my father.

For now, I was stuck here.

So I did the only thing within my power.

I held my head high, steeled myself, and said, "Let's go."

SEVEN

NICCO

I PADDED INTO MY ROOM, shutting the door behind me. It had been a long fucking day. My aunt had tried to keep me company, but I was like a bear with a sore head. Only four days in exile and I was already starting to feel like a caged animal.

My father had no updates. Tommy, our investigator, and Stefan, the Family's consigliere, were working around the clock to dig up dirt on Mike Fascini, but there was nothing new to report. And to make matters worse, Arianne had texted earlier to say she needed to talk to me.

Dropping onto the bed, I ran a hand through my hair. It was still damp from my workout. Dane and Uncle Alonso had a fully equipped gym in the house, so I'd spent a couple of hours burning off some steam. But it wasn't enough. Restless energy coursed through my veins like lava. The whole time, I'd only been able to picture that fucker with his hands on Arianne.

My girl.

My life.

Luis had said everything had gone fine; that after dinner and drinks with Fascini's friends, he had driven Arianne home and called Scott a cab. But my mind was the enemy, working against me to concoct all kinds of nightmarish endings.

And now she wanted to talk to me about something.

I was ready to detonate.

My cell started vibrating and I scooped it up, bringing it to my ear. "Nicco?" Her voice was small, and my chest tightened.

"Bambolina."

A beat passed.

Another.

Neither of us spoke but the silence was deafening. This was our life now. Pained silence and bittersweet memories.

"How are you?" Arianne finally spoke.

"I thought it would be okay. I thought I'd come here, and knowing you were safe would be enough... but it's killing me. It's only been four days and it's killing me."

"I know," she whispered. "I looked for you today. I wandered around downtown with Nora, expecting you to appear. What are we going to do, Nicco? How are we going to survive this?"

Letting myself fall backward, I inhaled a shuddering breath. "We keep going, Bambolina. We have to keep going."

"I..." Arianne hesitated.

"What is it, amore mio?"

"My father wants to see me tonight... It's about the party."

My blood boiled. "Do you know when it is?"

"Soon, I think."

I rubbed my temples. I wanted to comfort her, to tell her everything was going to be okay. But I couldn't find the words.

The thought of Arianne being paraded in front of everyone, introduced as Scott's fiancée, tore me up inside.

She wasn't his.

She would *never* be his.

Yet, he was there, and I was here and there wasn't a damn thing I could do about it.

"There's still time. Your birthday isn't until February. That's still five months away. My father will have a plan before then. He will—"

"Nicco, stop. Please. I don't want to keep doing this. It hurts too much."

"Bambolina," I breathed, her pain palpable even over the phone.

"Just talk to me, tell me about your day."

"There isn't much to tell," I confessed.

"Humor me."

"I had breakfast with my aunt, uncle, and Dane this morning. Then when he finally left to meet his friends, I helped my aunt around the house, then—"

"Wait, you did chores?"

I chuckled. "Surprised?"

"A little." I heard the smile in her answer. "I can't imagine big bad Niccolò Marchetti helping with the dishes."

"You think I'm big and bad?" The corner of my mouth tipped. I liked hearing Arianne like this: playful and happy.

"Well, aren't you?"

"Sometimes," I lowered my voice. "When I need to be."

There was a beat of silence, the slight ruffle of material. “What are you doing?” I asked.

“My towel slipped.”

Heat flooded me, zipping straight to my dick. “Don’t tell me you just got out of the shower?”

“Well, yeah...”

“Fuck, Bambolina. Do you have any idea how crazy that drives me, knowing you’re there, naked—”

“I’m not naked, I have a towel wrapped around me.” Arianne’s soft laughter was music to my ears, but it only fueled the blood pumping through me.

“I wish I was there.” It came out strained.

“Why?” Her voice was barely a whisper. “What would you do?”

“You really want to know?”

I waited with bated breath, my heart crashing against my ribcage. I hadn’t planned on this, but I’d take it. I’d take anything I could get where Arianne was concerned.

“Yes, I want to imagine you’re here, Nicco. I want to imagine you touching me.”

“I’m right there, trailing my lips all over your damp skin. Can you feel it, can you feel my kisses?”

“Y- yes.” It was a soft moan.

“Are you alone?”

“Yes, Luis is out in the hall.”

Thank fuck.

“Do you trust me?”

“You know I do.”

“Lie down on your bed.” There was a brief pause. “Good?” I asked.

“Good.” Her voice was thick with desire.

“Undo your towel, Bambolina.” I heard the slight hitch in her breath. “Now trail your hand down your stomach slowly.”

“It tickles.”

“It’s supposed to.” I smiled. Jesus, I wanted to be there. I wanted to worship her. “I can picture you lying there. The swell of your breasts, the soft curve of your hips. I want to trace my tongue over every single inch of you until you beg me for more.”

“God, I want that... so much.” Her voice was breathy.

“See how good you feel?”

“Hmm-mm.”

I was rock solid, my dick pulsing with need. Without hesitation, I worked my shorts down my hips and slid my hand around my shaft, stroking myself. I let out a long hiss.

“Nicco?”

“Touch yourself, Arianne. Imagine it’s my fingers, my lips. Remember how it was when I took you to the Country Club?”

"It feels so good," she smothered a moan, inhaling a shaky breath.

"What does it feel like? Tell me..." I jacked myself harder, thrusting up into my hand, imagining it was her.

"It's soft and warm... and wet."

"Jesus, Bambolina. I wish it was me. I wish I was buried deep inside of you."

"Yes... yes." Her cries were my undoing, beads of sweat trailing down my abs as I chased my release.

"Are you close?" I groaned the words.

"It feels good... but it's not like when you touch me," she admitted.

"I'm right there, Arianne. I can hear your tiny moans, feel the way your body trembles beneath me. Come for me, Bambolina, I need you to come for me."

A tingling sensation started at the base of my spine as I let myself drown in memories of Arianne. The way it had felt when I'd made love to her. It had been the single most intense experience of my life. Two bodies fitting as one, two souls binding together.

"Nicco, oh God..." she cried. "I'm going to..."

"That's it, amore mio. Let go. Just let go.... fuck." White hot pleasure shot down my spine as I jerked into my hand. My chest heaved with exertion, my body spent and sated.

"You still there?" I asked, grabbing a tissue off the nightstand and cleaning myself up.

There was a slight pause, and then she said, "I can't believe we just did that."

"I want to do everything with you, Arianne. I want to give you everything."

"Can I ask you something?" The hesitation in her voice had my attention.

"Anything."

"Do your feelings for me ever scare you?"

"Every second of every day. I wasn't lying when I said I knew that if I stayed that morning, I wouldn't have been able to say goodbye to you. I would have betrayed everything I am... for you."

"I keep thinking about running away. Just the two of us. Going somewhere no one knows us. But then I think of Nora and my mom and Alessia and your family, and I know we can't do it."

Silence followed. Thick, ominous silence. Then Arianne let out a small sigh. "It isn't supposed to be this hard, is it?"

Fuck. Her words gutted me. Slid into me like a jagged knife and tore up my insides.

"Arianne—"

"Don't," she let out a soft sigh. "It's okay. I didn't mean to ruin the moment."

"Bambolina, never think like that. Not with me. I want all your moments. The happy ones, the sad too. Even the angry, frustrated ones. I won't lie to you and say that I know how this will all work out. But I will tell you that I will always love you, Arianne. And I will always fight for you, no matter what. I promise.

"Ti amo più oggi di ieri ma meno di domani," I whispered.

“I love you too. I should probably go and get ready. Luis wants to leave soon.”

“Okay. Text me later?”

“I will. Bye, Nicco.” She hung up, the sudden loss like a bucket of ice water.

I got cleaned up and found some clean sweats, before grabbing my cell phone again.

“Niccolò?” My father answered on the first ring.

“Any word from Tommy?”

“I was going to call you. He’s on his way to Boston.”

“He is?” Dread snaked through me.

“It was as I suspected. Mike Fascini is, in fact, son of Michael Ricci. He and his wife, Miranda Fascini, came from Vermont in the seventies. Tommy found records of a living relative in Montpelier.”

“So you really think Mike and Scott are Elena Ricci’s descendants?”

“It’s too much of a coincidence, Son. The Ricci were going to be brought into the Family. When Elena and Emilio fled it bought great shame to her family, and they left Verona County. They never returned and it was always assumed that after Emilio’s death, Elena killed herself. But what if she didn’t... what if she escaped with Emilio’s child?”

“Hold up, are you saying that Scott Fascini is really a Marchetti?”

“It’s a possibility, Son. Tommy hit a few snags with the records, so he’s going straight to the source and I want you to go with him.”

“You want me to go to Vermont?”

“It’ll keep you busy. Besides, Tommy could use the back up.”

“Do I get any choice in the matter?” Vermont was a four-hour ride North. Another four hours away from Arianne. I didn’t like it, but from my father’s heavy sigh, I knew it was non-negotiable. “Fine, I’ll go.”

“Good, he’ll be there in less than an hour.”

“There’s a party,” I said. “An engagement party.”

“I know, Son.”

“You do?”

“I told you I’d keep my eye on Arianne, and I intend on keeping that promise. But we have to tread carefully if we want to avoid war.”

“Then tell me how to do this? Tell me how to sit here, while her father gives her to the piece of shit who...” I couldn’t say it.

“I understand your pain, Niccolò, but you have to keep your mind on the bigger picture. The Family must come first. Always. Arianne is your woman now, which means she has my protection. But we must get to the bottom of this thing with Fascini.”

“I understand.” I forced the words out. He kept talking about the Family and responsibility, but my head and heart were divided.

“Good. Go to Vermont and get answers and then we can figure out how to proceed." There was a pause and then he sighed. "Porca miseria. Your sister is outside hovering. Alessia, get in here,” he grumbled.

I heard her voice in the background. "Sorry, Daddy. I swear I wasn't eavesdropping."

I smiled. She was too smart for her own good sometimes.

"I'll speak to you soon." There was some muffled noise and then my sister's voice filled the line.

"Nicco?"

"Hey, Sia."

"How are you? How's Boston? Tell me everything."

"Whoa, take a breath."

"Sorry." She chuckled. "I was just waiting for Dad to leave."

"Sia?" My spine went rigid.

"So... I was thinking..." I didn't like the hesitation in her voice. "What if I invited Arianne to hang out? Maybe that would help."

My heart swelled. "Shit, Sia, that's what you wanted to talk about?"

"Well, yeah. You didn't think I really give a shit ab—"

"Language!"

"Chill, big brother. I like Arianne and I keep thinking about what she's having to do... he hurt her, Nicco, he hurt and—"

"I know," I let out a pained breath, "I know."

"But maybe if I offered to hang out with her, she'd know she wasn't alone. Not that she's alone, I know she has Nora, and she seems cool and all, but I thought—"

"You're worried about her."

A beat passed and then my sister whispered, "Yeah, I am."

"Leave it with me."

I didn't want to put Alessia at risk any more than I wanted to put Arianne at risk. But maybe she was right—maybe Arianne would feel better knowing someone close to me was there for her.

"For real?"

"For real," I chuckled. "But no theatrics, Sia. I mean it. This is a delicate situation. The last thing I need is you causing more harm than good."

"I'll behave, I swear. I just want to be there for her. And it isn't like I have a ton of girlfriends to hang out with."

"You have Arabella."

"Yeah but Bella is family. It's different."

I hated that Alessia found it hard to make friends. All I ever wanted was for her to flourish. But high school hadn't been kind to my sister. Her circle was small, and she struggled to trust people.

Not Arianne though.

She'd welcomed her into the fold with open arms and a big smile. Not that I was surprised. My Bambolina had that effect on people. She'd done the impossible, and even managed to weave my father under her spell.

"I'm going to give Arianne your cell phone number, okay?"

Alessia's muted shrieks of excitement told me all I needed to know. She saw Arianne as one of us now.

And it meant everything to me.

"I need to go. But stay safe and I'll talk to you soon, okay?"

"Okay, and thank you, Nicco."

"What for?" My brow knitted.

"For trusting me with her. I know how much she means to you, so thank you."

"Shit, Sia, you're my family. My blood. Of course I trust you."

"Well, it means a lot. It's not always easy being your sister..."

"I know." I released a heavy sigh, the weight of her words like a noose around my neck. "I know. I love you."

"Love you, too. Bye, Nicco." She hung up.

Before I could talk myself out of it, I pulled up Arianne's number and started typing.

Alessia wants to know if you want to hang out. I thought it might be nice for my two favorite girls to get to know each other better. I'm going to forward you her number. I love you. Always.

I hit sent and then forwarded my sister's number. Arianne replied straightaway.

I would love that. Do you think it would be okay though? I don't want to get her into trouble.

My lip curved. They were almost as bad as each other.

Leave it with me. I'm sure Luis can think of something. I have to leave Boston for a little while. I don't want you to worry but it's important. I'll call you when I can.

This is one of those times... isn't it?

My brows furrowed as I read her text.

What times?

. . .

Your father warned me that you would have to do things, things you couldn't tell me about... even if I asked.

Are you asking?

Blood roared between my ears. Everything had happened so fast, I hadn't had time to explain things to Arianne. There was still so much she didn't know, things she didn't understand.

No. All I'm asking is that you come back to me.

I exhaled a long breath. I don't know what I'd done to deserve Arianne, but I was so fucking lucky to have her in my corner.

I will. Nothing will keep me away. Not even death.

EIGHT

ARIANNE

"OH, SWEETHEART." Mom gently grabbed my shoulders, letting her eyes run over my face. "You're okay?"

"I'm fine, Mamma. Is Father—"

"He's in the living room with Mike and Suzanna Fascini."

"They're here?" I blanched.

"I didn't know, I swear, baby." She gave me a sad smile. "He isn't telling me anything."

"Is Scott here?" The quiver in my voice betrayed me.

"He's not. There was a team thing he needed to attend to."

Well that was something. Perhaps I would survive a meeting with my father, and the Fascini without fainting.

"Luis, it's nice to see you again." Mom's gaze went to my bodyguard.

"Mrs. Capizola," he replied with complete indifference, giving nothing away.

"Please, call me Gabriella." She laced her arm through mine. "Last night, Scott... he didn't—"

"No, Mamma."

"Thank God," she breathed. "I was worried sick. Your father was quite clear that you are not to consummate the marriage until your wedding night, but I don't trust them, Arianne. I don't trust any of them anymore."

My brows pinched as I inhaled a deep breath.

"What is it, mia cara?"

I pulled her to one side, putting some space between us and Luis. The estate was well protected. If anything, there seemed to be extra security as we'd entered the estate. My father's team were usually like ghosts. They made their presence known but you rarely saw them. Not tonight though.

Tonight, I'd noticed the extra men posted outside the house and at the gate house.

"I need you to stop, Mamma."

"St- stop? Whatever do you mean?"

"You were happy to go along with all this until you learned the truth about Scott. You wanted me to date him."

"Arianne, that's not—"

"Don't lie to me. You were on his side." Tears pricked the corners of my eyes, but I would not cry.

"You're right." Regret glittered in her gaze, her face pale with shame. "I was blinded by my loyalty to your father, to our family's reputation. But know that it was born out of love, Arianne."

"How can you say that? I'm eighteen, Mamma. I've never dated, never experienced life outside these four walls, and you wanted to shackle me to that monster."

"Sweetheart, that's not—"

"We should join them. I wouldn't want to anger Father." I brushed past her and moved down the hall, fighting the urge to apologize to her.

Luis moved behind me, letting me have some space. It was ironic that I felt more comforted by his presence these days than I did my own parents'.

"There you are, mio tesoro." My father stood the second I stepped foot in the room.

"Father." I didn't move toward him. "Mr. and Mrs. Fascini."

"Please, Arianne." Suzanna stepped forward. "We are going to be family soon enough." She grabbed my shoulders and planted a kiss on each cheek.

"Suzanna, let the girl breathe. Arianne," Mr. Fascini addressed me. "It's good to see you again. You too, Gabriella."

I hadn't realized my mom had entered the room, but I didn't acknowledge her. Instead, I pressed my lips together, forcing myself to nod. Mike Fascini was a real piece of work, to stand there and pretend everything was okay when he knew... he knew the kind of monster his son was. Yet he did nothing.

Not a damn thing.

"We have much to discuss; sit." He motioned to the leather couch as if it was his home, as if he was the one in control.

It occurred to me that maybe he was.

I sat down like the dutiful, docile daughter I'd once been. Defiance burned inside me like a wildfire, simmering in my blood and making my breaths come in short, shallow bursts.

Mike Fascini was like his son. Handsome. Charming. Sporting a smile that lured you in. But I wasn't fooled. Expensive suits and good looks didn't mean much in a world where money talked, and people were nothing but pawns.

"I have reserved the Michelangelo Suite at the Gold Star Hotel for next Saturday."

"That soon?" I choked out.

"We are keen to share the happy news," Mr. Fascini said. "Isn't that right, Roberto?"

Something passed between the two men, something that had a shiver rolling up my spine.

My father cleared his throat. "Indeed. Mike and Suzanna are handling the entire thing. Isn't that kind of them?"

"I think it's lovely," Mom said, patting my knee. I didn't miss the slight tremble of her hand.

"The invitations have already been sent. One-hundred and twenty of Verona County's most influential people will gather to witness the union of our two great families."

"I'm sure it will be quite the celebration." My father smiled but it didn't reach his eyes. In fact, he looked utterly defeated.

I wanted to see into his mind. To know why he was doing this.

"I have arranged extra security." Mr. Fascini's cold gaze flicked to mine. "Just in case."

"I'm sure that won't be necessary," my father added. "Arianne knows what's at stake."

"Yes, well, we can't be too careful. Nicco Marchetti is out there somewhere... I'm sure we'd all feel much safer knowing the party is well protected."

"Of course, Mike." Mom smoothed the hair from her face. "Have you decided upon a color? A theme? Is there a certain style Arianne should wear?"

"It will be a black-tie dinner," Suzanna beamed. "So break out those cocktail dresses and diamonds."

"I have just the dress." The two of them launched into a separate conversation about dresses and table centerpieces while I sat there, silent and suffocated, a storm brewing inside me.

Luis stood by the door, rigid and poised. He caught my eye, offering me a small nod of encouragement.

"Arianne?"

"Hmm, sorry?" I blinked over at my father and Mr. Fascini.

"Mike was just asking how your evening with Scott went last night?"

"It was fine, thank you." The lie wrapped around my heart, squeezing until it hurt.

"You'll have to excuse my son, Arianne. He can come on a little strong, but it's only because he likes you so much. He has been waiting a long time for this."

A violent shudder ripped through me. "He was quite the gentleman." The words almost choked me.

"I'm glad to hear it." Mr. Fascini picked up his glass and raised it slightly before knocking down the amber liquid.

I slid my gaze to my father. Guilt and pain were etched into his expression.

And I was glad. I was glad he had to sit here and pretend too. Because why should I be the only one paying the price?

"We have arranged for you to arrive together," Mr. Fascini said. "We think it will really make a statement. Then we'll eat, and after the meal, I'll make a toast to Capizola Holdings and Fascini and Associates becoming partners in more ways than one." He sat back against the soft leather couch, pulling his ankle across his knee. He was the epitome of a man in control; a man holding all the chips.

"We know this has all come as quite the shock, Arianne," Suzanna said, her smile wide and honest. She was like the girls at college. Girls blinded by the Fascini name: the money, the status and power, and good genes. "But in our world, couplings like this are good business."

"Hmm." I pursed my lips, smothering a groan.

"It's just a shame Scott couldn't make it tonight," she went on. "I'm sure he would have liked to be here to reassure you that everything will be fine."

Just then Mr. Fascini's cell phone started ringing. He dug it out of his pocket and frowned. "I need to take this, excuse me." He disappeared out of the room.

"It's a lovely evening. Perhaps a nightcap on the terrace?" Mom asked Suzanna.

"That sounds like a wonderful idea." The two of them left, leaving me and my father alone.

"Figlia mia —"

"Don't," I hissed.

"Arianne, please understand..."

"I will never understand. You lied to me, Father. You *betrayed* me."

"There are things... things you don't know. Things you can't yet know. But I'm begging you, please trust me."

Staring him dead in the eye, I didn't flinch as I said, "My trust in you died the day you sold me off to the Fascini."

"Arianne, please. I only want to keep you safe."

"Safe?" I seethed through gritted teeth. "Scott raped me... he drugged me and he raped me." My body trembled with anger. "So tell me, Father, how on earth is giving me to him, keeping me safe?"

The blood drained from his face as he let out a pained sigh. "You have to trust me. I know I don't deserve it... I know I have failed you, but I need for you to—"

"Business, it never sleeps." Mr. Fascini came back into the room. He stopped, glancing between the two of us. "Is everything okay?"

"Perfectly fine." My father's lips thinned.

"Arianne?" Mr. Fascini raised a brow.

"Arianne is in agreement with all the plans, Mike."

"I'm glad we're all on the same page." His cold, hard gaze landed on my father again. Something was passing between them once more.

A silent warning.

An unspoken threat.

"Let's join the women out on the terrace," my father suggested. He stood up, smoothing a hand over his jaw. He didn't look at me.

Maybe he couldn't.

But I saw him.

I saw his mask of guilt.

And I was almost certain I saw a single tear roll down his cheek.

I was eating my lunch the next day, when my phone rang with an unknown number. "Ari?" Someone said down the line softly.

"Matteo?" My eyes widened as I recognized his voice.

"Tonight, six-thirty, be ready."

"What are you—"

"Just be ready." He ended the call. I quickly texted Alessia.

Do you know anything about tonight?

It pinged straight back.

I just got a text from Matteo. They must have figured something out. See you later?

Can't wait.

"What has you smiling?" Nora sat beside me.

"I think we're hanging with Alessia tonight."

"They managed to figure something out?"

"I guess so." I shrugged. When I'd texted Alessia to say I would love to hang out, she told me to sit tight and let the guys figure it out. It wasn't like Niccolò Marchetti's sister could just turn up at the apartment building and ask to see me. We had to be discreet. We had to make sure my father and the Fascini didn't find out about it.

"Do you think Enzo will be there?"

"Do you want Enzo to be there?" I threw back at her.

Nora chuckled, her lips curving into a smirk. "Well he hasn't been around much, and he is quite pretty to look at."

"He isn't pretty, Nor. He's terrifying."

"Oh, I don't know about that."

"Nicco said—"

"Yeah, yeah, I know what Nicco said. It's not like I want to marry the guy. I just think he'd be a good time between the sheets... or up against the wall... or over the—"

I clapped a hand over her mouth, drowning out the words. Words I did not need or want to hear. "Are you done?"

"I'm done," she murmured against my palm, and I pulled it away.

"Anyway, I thought you and Dan were a thing?"

"We're casual. I don't have time for anything serious."

"Are those your words, or his?"

"We don't all fall madly in love with the first guy we meet." She laughed but I didn't join her. "Shit, Ari, I'm joking. It's a joke. I'm just saying most of us will never have what you and Nicco share."

"Do you think I'm fooling myself?"

"What? *No!* Nicco loves you, babe. He'd go to war for you. Do you have any idea how lucky you are?"

"Sometimes I don't feel so lucky... I feel doomed."

She grabbed my hand and pulled it onto her lap. "You say you're doomed, but the way I see it, what you and Nicco could have, it gives you something to fight for. Imagine if you'd never met him, imagine if he hadn't saved you that night... you would be miserable, alone, and still engaged to Scott."

"Why is this happening to me, Nora?" I tried so hard to fight the tears building, but it was impossible to ignore the emotion rising inside me.

"I'm not a religious person, Ari, you know that. But I do believe in fate. I believe that everything we experience, everything we survive, shapes us into the person we're supposed to be.

"This is your battle to fight, babe. Own it."

"You're getting good at this." I sniffled, drying my eyes on my jacket sleeve.

"Yeah, and what's that?"

"Always knowing the right thing to say."

"Oh, I don't know," she smiled, "I still have plenty of impropriety in me. Want to hear some more?"

"I think I've heard enough for one day."

"Too bad. I had this dream the other night, about Enzo and his monster di—"

My hand shot out, smothering her words. I was always grateful for one of Nora's pep talks. But if I had to hear about Enzo's monster dick again this century, it would be too soon.

"Good job today," Brent said as we tidied up the last of the chairs. The VCTI had hosted a drop in this afternoon.

Being here, with people less fortunate than myself, put things into perspective. I'd gotten lost in their stories of hopelessness and loneliness, swept away in their candid experiences of life on the streets. The VCTI was a safe space for so many, a lifeline. And I was thankful to have a small part in that.

"What are your plans for the rest of the evening?" he asked.

"Oh, she's with me." Nora appeared from the back room. "I got your purse, all set?"

"I think so." I gave Brent a smile. "Are we okay to go?"

"Absolutely. We'll see you both again soon?"

"Definitely."

"Enjoy your evening." He called after us as we slipped out into the inky night.

"Everything good?" Luis shot to attention, and I smothered a grin. He was always so uptight. I couldn't help but wonder if he regretted taking my side in all of this.

"Yep."

"Come on then." He ushered us to the car. The driver nodded but I didn't recognize him.

"Luis?" I asked, hesitating.

"This is Jay," he replied.

"Hey, Jay." Nora slipped around me and climbed inside. "I'm Arianne's best one, Nora."

He didn't reply.

Luis leaned in. "It's okay, you can trust him. He's a friend."

My brows furrowed. Surely, he didn't mean what I thought he meant.

"You mean he's—"

Luis silenced me with a knowing look. "We need more eyes and ears. This is a good thing, I promise."

"Okay." I got inside.

"So what's the plan?" Nora asked the second Luis hopped into the passenger side.

"You'll see," he said cryptically.

Nora caught my eye and waggled her brows. Trust her to be excited by the prospect of an adventure. I couldn't find it in myself to share her enthusiasm. Because although I was excited to be seeing Alessia, I didn't want to put her at risk.

"Hey, don't do that." Nora frowned, grabbing my hand. "Don't always assume the worst. Everything's going to be fine. You'll see."

We took the road out of Romany Square toward La Riva. My heart beat wildly in my chest as I watched the landscape change, but we didn't stop. The new guy kept driving, taking the road toward Providence, until the familiar landscape of Nicco's neighborhood became nothing but trees and shadows.

After ten minutes, we turned off the main road, taking a dirt track to nowhere. The dense canopy of trees made everything eerie; their dark, twisted fingers scratching against the windows and roof of the vehicle. Eventually, the thicket started to clear, giving way to a cabin.

"What is this place?" I asked no one in particular, as my eyes strained against the darkness.

"You'll see."

The SUV rolled to a stop alongside a truck, and Luis unclipped his belt. "Wait here." He climbed out and made his way toward the cabin. After a couple of seconds, the door opened, and Matteo stepped onto the porch. My shoulders sagged with relief.

They discussed something before making their way back to us. Luis yanked open the door and Nora wasted no time getting out. I hesitated though.

Matteo stuck his head inside. "Going to sit in here all night?"

Pressing my lips together, I shook my head. Matteo chuckled, offering me his hand. "Come on, I don't bite." He helped me out.

"What is this place?" I asked.

"It's a family hideaway. We have a few places like this in and around Verona County. We should go inside. I know there's someone dying to see you."

I didn't get chance to respond. A whirlwind of blonde flew out of the cabin and down the steps. "You're here," Alessia shrieked, launching herself into my arms. I hugged her back, laughing softly.

"I've been so worried," she whispered.

"One rule, Sia," a deep voice said. My gaze lifted to find Enzo in the door, cold glare right on me. "Stay in the damn cabin."

"Lighten up, E, we're safe out here." Alessia poked her tongue out at him but Enzo was no longer looking at her. He was staring right at Nora.

"You didn't say she was bringing her."

"I have a name, douchebag." She marched right up to him, shouldered past him and slipped into the cabin.

"What?" Matteo chuckled, clearly amused. "You didn't have to come."

"Yeah," Enzo growled. "I did." He spun around and disappeared inside.

"This should be fun." Laughter rumbled in Matteo's chest. "Come on, we'll give you the tour."

Alessia pressed herself into my side. "I'm so glad you're here."

It should have felt weird or overfamiliar, but it didn't. It felt nice.

It felt right.

It felt like something was shifting, like I had finally found my place.

"We'll be right outside." Luis gave me a reassuring nod. "This place is off the grid, but we've got it covered. You're safe here."

"He's not wrong," Matteo added. "We won't let anything happen to you, Arianne, I promise."

"Yeah, you're one of us now." Alessia smiled. "And we protect our own."

NINE

NICCO

"HOW DO you do this day in, day out?" I asked Tommy, drumming my fingers against my thigh.

We'd been at it all day. Staking out the address he'd found. It was tedious fucking work, but Tommy seemed to like it.

"I like the solitude... and I like people-watching."

Yeah, that wasn't creepy at all.

"I don't see why we can't just go knock on the door and talk to her."

Elizabeth Monroe.

Seventy-five-year-old widow. Born and raised in Montpelier, Vermont. But she hadn't always been a Monroe. She had, in fact, been born Elizabeth Ricci, and was Mike Fascini's auntie. The only remaining Ricci in Vermont according to Tommy's findings.

"Hey, who's that?" I flicked my head to the young girl entering the house. She looked to be my age, maybe a couple years younger.

Tommy ran his hand down the notebook, flipped a page and jabbed his finger at the thing. "She has a granddaughter. Charlotte Monroe. It could be her."

"A granddaughter? You didn't say anything about family."

"It's just her and Charlotte. She's a freshman at the college in Burlington." He shrugged, lighting up a smoke.

"Do you mind?" I raised a brow. "Those things will kill ya."

"I already got a one-way ticket to hell, kid. Might as well enjoy the ride." He took a long drag, cracked the window and exhaled the smoke outside.

I cracked my own window, breathing in some fresh air. It was a little after six.

Arianne would have finished her shift at the VCTI which meant Luis was driving her and Nora out to the cabin to meet Alessia.

God, I wanted to be there. I wanted to see her so fucking badly. But instead, I was stuck here with Tommy, breathing in his secondhand smoke and staking out an old woman's house.

"She hasn't left the house all day. She isn't a threat," I said, growing impatient.

"She isn't a threat, but we don't know that Fascini hasn't got eyes on her."

"You said Michael Fascini left Vermont before Mike was born."

"According to records, they arrived in Verona County in the seventies. But we still can't take any chances."

Letting out a frustrated breath, I raked a hand through my hair. "So what? We're going to just sit here all night?" It had already been hours.

"We wait for the girl to leave, then you go in."

"Me?"

"It's gotta be you, Nicco. Look at me, I'm not exactly grandma friendly."

Tommy had a point. The ugly jagged scar that ran from his left eye down to his jaw gave him a permanently angry expression. Which was ironic given that he was one of the best people I knew. But if Elizabeth Monroe saw Tommy standing on her doorstep, chances were, he wasn't going to get an invitation inside.

"Everything I dug up suggests Elizabeth and her brother were estranged. But the paper trail doesn't always paint the whole picture."

The door opened and the girl appeared. Elizabeth hovered in the door. She looked frail for seventy-five. They hugged and the girl kissed her grandma's cheeks before taking off down the sidewalk.

"Okay, you're up. You ready for this?"

"Talking to an old lady?" It was a piece of cake compared to some of the stuff we had to do.

"You packing? Just in case."

"Seriously?"

"If I've learned anything working for the Family, it's that you can never be too sure, about anyone or anything. I'll be close by." Tommy gave me a nod, and I slipped out of the car.

Cutting across the street, I jammed my hands in my pockets. The sun was just beginning to disappear on the horizon, dusk blanketing the neighborhood. I had no idea what I was going to say but the need to know the truth—to uncover the details of what led us to this point—sat heavy on my chest.

She lived in a small bungalow, a far cry from the huge place the Fascini owned in Roccaforte. Climbing the porch, I rapped my knuckles against the outer door. Nervous energy reverberated through me, which was fucking stupid. I didn't know this woman. She was no one to me.

No one.

And yet, she was.

If things had been different, she would have been family.

Maybe not by blood but her brother would have been.

It was some screwed-up shit.

A shuffle behind the door demanded my attention and then it cracked open, the fly screen separating us. "Yes?"

"Mrs. Monroe?"

"Who's asking?" she said in a soft Italian accent.

"My name is Niccolò. Niccolò Marchetti." I was already going against Tommy's advice, but something compelled me to the speak the truth.

"Marchetti, you say." She narrowed her eyes, her skin crinkled and tired. "I haven't heard that name in a very long time."

"I was hoping you can help me, Ma'am."

"Let me guess, that nephew of mine is causing all kinds of trouble?"

My spine stiffened.

She knew.

The old lady knew why I was here.

"I've been waiting for one of you to show up, you know. Didn't think it would take this long. You alone? Actually," she held up a finger. "Don't answer that. I know how you people work. Come on inside."

Elizabeth opened her door and stepped aside. I opened the screen and followed her inside. "I hope you like tea," she called. "I just made a fresh pot."

"Tea's fine."

"Well go on through there and take a seat, I'll just be a second." She motioned to the living room. It was a modest room, full of work furniture, every available surface littered with trinkets and photographs. I spotted the girl from earlier, her granddaughter, in most of them. But it was the one on the mantle above the fireplace that caught my eye. It was like staring at an older version of Scott Fascini. Same square jawline, same cocksure smirk. Except the photograph was an old faded black and white print.

"That's my brother, Michael." Elizabeth placed down a tray of tea and moved beside me, plucking the silver-framed photo off the shelf. "But you already know that, don't you?" She gave me a knowing glance. "Come, sit. I'm sure we have much to talk about.

"You keep talking like you've been waiting for this. I expected you to be more..."

"Unwilling to talk? No, I have been waiting for this moment to arrive. The past always catches up with you eventually, does it not? I am an old lady now, so I make every second count. Is he... dead?" Elizabeth deadpanned as she poured the tea.

"You didn't know?" According to Tommy, Michael Fascini had died almost twenty years ago.

"I haven't seen or heard from Michael since the day he left Vermont on his crusade."

"Crusade?"

"I'll never forget the day he found out the truth. Our mom never talked about his father growing up. We knew we had different fathers, but it didn't matter, not to me. I idolized my big brother. Even as a young boy he was strong and loyal. He doted on our mom something fierce. I think it's the reason she never found anyone else, because she feared what Michael would do.

"I was seven when she finally told him. Michael had just turned eleven. I remember because it was a bad winter and we were snowed in for days. He'd been asking more and more questions about his father and I guess she felt it was time he knew the truth."

Elizabeth gazed out at nothing, her eyes clouded with the pain of the past. "Everything was different after that. Michael became obsessed with learning all about the Marchetti and Capizola. He became withdrawn, started fighting and getting into trouble at school. Mom was beside herself. I knew she regretted telling him the truth, but it was too late."

"She told you what had happened too?"

"Not at first, no. They both kept some things to themselves. But when she got sick, she confessed everything. How she and Emilio had sparked the chain of events that led you to be sitting here today."

"Your nephew has threatened someone I care about."

She let out a heavy sigh. "I had hoped he would break the cycle."

"You knew? You knew he would come after us?"

"You have to understand, Nicco... may I call you Nicco?" I nodded and she smiled. "Our mother fled to Vermont with nothing but the clothes on her back. When Michael discovered the truth about his father, and his murder, it left a mark on his soul. A mark that, as he grew, festered into something bigger. Something malevolent. When he met Miranda, I had hoped she would be able to bring him out of the darkness. And for a little while, she did. But when they announced their move to Verona County, I knew what he was doing.

"I begged him not to go. Miranda was pregnant and she didn't know the whole story. She thought he wanted to make a better life for them. I could have told her... I should have told, but I still hoped..."

I let out a strained breath.

It was true.

It was all true.

Mike Fascini was Elena Ricci and Emilio Marchetti's grandson. He was my grandfather's cousin.

He was my family.

"Nicco?"

"Y- yeah?" I scrubbed my jaw, trying to wrap my head around everything.

"Just tell me, has Michael Junior hurt anyone?"

"Not yet, no. But his son—"

"A son? He has a son?"

"You didn't know?"

"I did not. My granddaughter is all I have left."

"What about your husband's family?"

"Kenny, God rest his soul, was an only child. There is only me and Charlotte left. Her parents, my daughter and son-in-law, they died in a car accident a few years ago."

"She lives with you?"

"She did." The old woman smiled fondly. "She recently moved to Burlington for college. I've made my peace with the past, Niccolò, but Michael never could. I knew him moving to Verona County would mean only one thing. I'm just sorry to hear his thirst for revenge has been passed down to Mike Junior."

"So it is about revenge?" I sat forward, clasping my hands between my legs. Elizabeth had been an open book. I didn't know what I'd expected when she opened the door, but it wasn't this.

"I can't claim to know what my nephew thinks or why he does the things he does. But I knew my brother. I looked into his eyes and saw the secrets of his soul. And that man was fueled by grief and rage. The Ricci were supposed to be one of the great families of Verona County. Instead, we became nothing. What lengths would you go to for the woman who gave you life, Niccolò?"

"My mother is gone," I said flatly, feeling pain snake around my heart.

"I'm sorry to hear that. Do you have siblings?"

I nodded. "A sister."

"And what lengths would you go to in order to protect her? To right any wrong befallen on her? I don't justify my brother's actions, but I can understand them. His father was murdered because he loved the wrong woman. I understand your ways, your code... but love knows no bounds, Nicco. It doesn't adhere to codes or laws or morals... sometimes it just is."

I couldn't argue with her.

I had fallen hopelessly in love with Arianne. Even after I discovered her true identity, I couldn't stop myself. Our souls were bound. And I couldn't help but think history was reliving itself. Only this time, it wasn't a Ricci and Marchetti breaking the rules.

"What is it?" Elizabeth asked.

"Do you understand why I came here?"

"For answers... for the truth."

"And do you know what I have to do with this information? What it means?"

"I do." Her expression softened. "Like I said, Nicco, I have long made peace with things. But it was different for Michael. Our mother gave him her name to protect him. But it only fed his obsession for vengeance. My brother wanted only one thing in life, Niccolò."

"Yeah? And what's that?"

"To take everything from the people who took everything from our mother." She looked me dead in the eye, and for the first time since coming here, I felt the invisible line between us. "To make the Marchetti and Capizola pay."

"That's some heavy shit, kid," Tommy said as we sat in the bar. "So Fascini is like your distant cousin?"

"Something like that." I ran my thumb around the neck of the bottle.

Tommy wanted to break out the hard liquor, but I knew if I let myself indulge, it would be a one-way street to doing or saying something I would regret.

He was family.

Marchetti blood flowed through Scott's veins.

It didn't change a thing.

And yet, it changed every-fucking-thing.

The sins of our forefathers had led us to this point, and now, it seemed we were the ones paying the price.

"Do you think he knows?"

"Who, Scott?" My jaw clenched, his name like acid on my tongue. "He has to, doesn't he? No one can be that twisted without some serious trauma in their lives."

Tommy shrugged, draining his beer. He slammed it down on the table and let out a heavy sigh. "Some people are just messed up. Maybe he knows, maybe he doesn't, maybe it's just in his blood... but he's the enemy, Nicco. Don't forget that."

"Forget... you think I could ever forget what he did to Arianne?" I seethed. "I will never forget." It was imprinted on my mind, engraved on every fiber of my being.

"Good." Tommy nodded. "A shitstorm is coming. I've known men like Mike Fascini in my lifetime. Men so blinded by the need for vengeance that it destroys who they are. He won't stop. There's only one way this thing ends."

He was right.

Michael Fascini had moved his family to Verona County with one sole purpose in mind: to destroy Arianne's family.

To destroy *my* family.

Even Elizabeth had resigned herself to the outcome.

The Fascini had positioned themselves as one of Verona's most powerful and influential families. The legal union of Scott and Arianne, and the business merger with Capizola Holdings would give them the resources, money, and power to destroy Roberto from the inside before going after the Marchetti.

"Why now?" I blurted out.

"Now is as good a time as any. As far as I'm aware, the Fascini aren't an organized group. It's just Mike and was just his father before that. But he's set himself up as the perfect Trojan Horse."

"Something doesn't add up. There are other ways to make the Family suffer. Other ways to make the Capizola suffer." The pieces were there but I couldn't make them fit.

"Maybe Michael tried and failed? Maybe he realized he couldn't do it alone?"

"Wait..." The pieces started moving, zipping around my head until they began to slow down, fitting together like a map.

Until everything zeroed in and became crystal clear.

"I don't like that look," Tommy said, his brows bunched together.

"I think I know," the words came out a strangled whisper. "I think I know what happened."

TEN

ARIANNE

"THIS PLACE IS INCREDIBLE," I said, getting comfortable on the huge soft sectional dividing the open plan living space.

There was a big real fire, the crackle of flames and smell of charred wood filling the air. It was rustic and homey and unlike anywhere I'd ever been before.

"Yeah, it's really something." Nora tracked Enzo's movements as he pulled Matteo out of earshot.

"Don't worry about them," Alessia said. "I'm so glad you're here. Both of you." She smiled at Nora. "I don't get to do this much, hang out with girlfriends."

"What about your friends at school?" Nora asked.

"School is... it's not always easy. Those three had it easy being Marchetti. But it isn't the same for us girls. Guys stay away because they're scared, and girls usually want to use us as a steppingstone to get to the guys."

"I'm sorry."

"Don't be." She shrugged. "It could be worse. If you two are sticking around," her eyes went to her cousins, "you could at least make yourselves useful."

Enzo's eyes narrowed dangerously. "Don't push your luck, Sia."

"Relax, E." Matteo slapped him on the back. "We're here now, we might as well kick back." He moved over to the kitchen and yanked open the refrigerator. "Bingo."

"This is bullshit." Enzo dropped onto one of the armchairs and pulled a blunt out of his pocket.

"Why did you come if you didn't want to be here?" I asked.

His eyes snapped to mine, hard and assessing. "You're Nicco's girl. And he's our..." Enzo pressed his lips into a thin line.

"What my cousin is trying to say is that you're important to Nicco and Nicco is important to them." Alessia flicked her gaze to Enzo. "Would it kill you be nice, E?"

He grumbled something before putting the blunt between his lips and lighting the end. The bitter scent lingered in the air, but no one seemed to mind.

"What are you hiding back there?" Nora got up and went over to Matteo. "I'll take one of those." She plucked a beer from his hands.

"You're not old enough." He teased.

"And you are?" She raised a brow.

"Touché."

"Ari, babe, there's beer or soda?"

"I'll take a soda," I replied, "please."

"I'll take a beer," Alessia said.

"No," her cousins barked in unison, and I smothered a chuckle.

"Are they always like this?"

"Worse." She rolled her eyes. "I'm surprised they haven't been trailing after you around campus."

"Actually, I haven't seen them around at all," Nora said.

Matteo glanced around Enzo who shook his head.

"What?" I asked noticing the two of them acting cagey.

"Just because you can't see us doesn't mean we're not around." Matteo uncapped his beer and took a long pull, but I didn't miss the guilt shining in his eyes.

"So you have been around?" I narrowed my eyes. "Why haven't we seen you?"

"Nicco thought it would make things easier on you if we kept a low profile."

"That makes sense, I guess." My chest tightened. The gossip mill was hot with rumors about the fight, about Tristan being in the hospital, and Nicco's sudden disappearance.

"Jeez, if I'd have known we were going to talk about this stuff all night, I wouldn't have bothered." Alessia grinned at me.

"Sorry. It's just been a lot to process."

"I know. But you're here and you're safe and I really hoped we could have some good old-fashioned girls' fun."

Enzo groaned, running a hand through his dark hair.

"You got a problem with that?" Alessia huffed.

"If it's going to be like the time you and Bella tried to braid my hair then yeah, I've got a fucking problem with it."

"Come on, E," Matteo added, "that shit was funny."

"Maybe you like getting your nails painted and hair braided but it's not exactly my kind of thing."

"You really did that to them?" Nora couldn't contain her amusement.

"We were like twelve. Nicco let me practice putting lip gloss on him."

Enzo scoffed. "We held him down and let you go at him."

Alessia rolled her eyes at him. "Your point?"

"You had him wrapped around your little finger." Matteo shifted in the chair. "And then you grew boobs."

"Gross!"

"What? It's the truth. Having a younger sister, knowing what I know about the world, it's enough to send me to an early grave."

"My older brother used to say he had two main jobs in the world," Nora said. "Making me smile and breaking the legs of any guy who ever hurt me."

Tension crackled in the air as she glanced over at Enzo who was focused solely on the wisps of smoke rising off his blunt.

"Sounds like my kind of guy," Matteo tipped the neck of his bottle at her. "What say you, Enzo?"

He grumbled again.

"Did your brother go to MU?"

"He's at UPenn, chasing dreams of pro-football, fame, and fortune."

"Enzo has a decent throwing arm."

"Fuck this, I need some air." Enzo got up and stalked to the door beyond the kitchen.

"Did you have to bring him?" Alessia grumbled. "He's so—"

"Miserable?" Nora smirked.

"That's cute." Matteo narrowed his eyes at her. "Pretending you don't care."

"I don't."

"We'll see." He got up. "Can I trust the three of you while I'm gone?"

Alessia glared at him, and his shoulders shook with quiet laughter. "I'll be back." He took off after Enzo.

"Thank God. I thought they were never going to leave."

"Leave? But Matteo said—"

"Relax. They won't go anywhere. There's a fire pit out back, some benches. It's pretty cool."

Nora looked longingly at the door.

"Down, girl," I chuckled.

"Wait a second, you and... *Enzo*?" Alessia balked. "I did not see that one coming. Have the two of you, ya know?"

"What?" Nora feigned surprise. "No. *No*!"

"But she wants to." I grinned.

"Word of warning, my cousin doesn't date. Hell, I'm not even sure he hooks up with girls in the traditional sense of the word. Enzo is... complicated."

"What's his story anyway?" Nora kicked her legs up and stretched out over the chair, making herself at home.

Alessia folded her legs up in front of her. "My Uncle Vincenzo, Enzo's dad, well he's kind of a hard ass. It was just the two of them growing up. My mom practically helped raise him. But then she..." Alessia swallowed and I reached over, grabbing her hand and squeezing gently.

"It was different for Nicco and Matteo. They had a strong female influence. They had sisters. But Enzo... he only had himself."

"That's kind of sad." Nora's eyes flicked to the door again, a look of longing there.

"Yeah. It hardened him for sure. His dad has always enjoyed bouncing from woman to woman, and I guess Enzo is the same. A lot of the men in the Family don't settle down."

"You make it sound so normal."

"It is normal, to me, at least. Our family has strong ideals when it suits them. Take me for example; you think any guy is ever going to be good enough in Nicco's eyes? Or my father's?"

"That's... rough." Nora grimaced.

"It's bullshit. They make out that their women are the most precious thing in the world but then most of them are screwing around with goomars or using them as a punching bag."

My heart sank, and I snatched my hand back, clutching the cushion in my lap.

"Shit, Ari, I didn't mean... Nicco would never do that to you. Not after what happened with our mom." Alessia gave me a weak smile. "I should probably stop talking now. Tonight was supposed to reassure you, not send you running for the hills."

"I'm not going anywhere." I smiled back. "What was she like?"

"The best. She was just a good person, you know? She was always feeding a house full of people. Loved to take care of everyone. And my brother, he doted on her."

She dropped her gaze, pretending to pick her nails. "I love my daddy, but he's a mean drunk with a short fuse. He thinks I don't know about the bruises. About all the nights Mom spent crying herself to sleep. But I see things. They think I don't, but I do. I always have."

"I'm sorry."

"Don't be." Her shoulders lifted in a half-shrug as she met my gaze again. "It could be worse. In this life, it could always be worse. But I never saw it coming. One day, Mom was there, the strong resilient woman she'd always been, and the next... she was gone."

"Do you know where she went?"

"She just vanished. Wherever she is, she doesn't want to be found." Sadness clung to Alessia's words.

I didn't know what it was like to lose a parent, but I did know what it was like to have your world ripped apart, to discover everything you thought you knew was a lie.

"I hated her for a long time, but I've made my peace with it."

Her expression said otherwise, but I didn't push. Alessia was still young. She still had to find her way in the world.

I'd felt the same when I'd arrived at MU, but everything was different now.

I was different.

The vibrations of my cell phone startled me. "It's Nicco," I said, digging it from my pocket.

"What does it say?" Alessia sat straighter, peering over to try to see. I pulled it closer to my chest.

Nora chuckled. "Trust me, you don't wanna know."

"Nor!" I shrieked, the same time Alessia grumbled, "Ew, gross. That's my brother."

Waving them both off, I read the text.

Found out some things today. We need to talk, but I want to do it in person.

You can't come back here. It isn't safe.

I know. That's why I'm going to arrange for Luis to bring you to me. But we can't tell anyone else.

"Ari, what is it?" Nora asked.

I hesitated. I knew better than most people that secrets and lies only led to heartache. Even if you thought you were protecting someone, even if they were told out of love.

I have to tell Nora. I won't lie to her.

Fine. But only Nora.

When?

Tomorrow. I'll set it up. I love you, Bambolina. Be safe and say hello to Alessia for me.

"Nicco says hey."

"Tell him he should come home soon."

"I wish he could." My heart ached.

"How is your cousin... Tristan, right?"

"There's no change. His condition is stable, and doctors say it could be any day now. It's just a waiting game."

"God, I'm so sorry." She clutched her throat. "I can't even imagine what that must be like... if it was Nicco..."

"But it wasn't." I gave her a tight smile. "And what happened was just a terrible accident."

"I really hope he gets better."

"Yeah, me too."

Tristan, despite his serious lack in judgment, was still family. I didn't want him to die. I wanted him to wake up and realize the truth about my father, about Scott.

I wanted him to do the right thing.

"Wow, we really know how to party, huh?" Nora said around a smile.

"Oh, I don't know," I glanced between her and Alessia. "This is nice."

"Yeah." Alessia beamed. "It is."

We stayed at the cabin for hours, talking and laughing. Matteo and Enzo eventually joined us, although Enzo had worn a scowl for most of the night. Luis and Jay drove us back to University Hill. Nora was half asleep by the time we made our way up to the apartment.

"I'll see you in the morning," she murmured, staggering toward her room.

"I'm making hot cocoa if you want to join me?" I said to Luis as he hovered in the doorway.

"Aren't you tired?"

"I haven't been sleeping well," I admitted.

"Nightmares?" He looked concerned.

"My demons don't haunt me in my sleep, Luis."

They were real.

Circling me like hungry piranhas waiting for their moment to strike.

"I wouldn't say no to a cocoa." He came inside and closed the door.

It was late, and I probably should have gone to bed given that I needed to return to classes tomorrow, but there was too much on my mind to switch off.

After making us each a mug of cocoa, sprinkling marshmallows on mine, I went to Luis. He'd made himself comfortable on the end of our couch. "Here you go," I said, handing him the mug.

"Thank you. Did you enjoy tonight?"

I sat at the opposite end of the couch, curling my body into the soft fabric. "Alessia is a sweetheart and Matteo seems nice. I still haven't made my mind up about Enzo."

"He's hardened. Most guys are in this life."

"You speak like you have experience?"

"Just because your family decided to walk a different path doesn't mean we don't get our hands dirty." His smile turned grim.

"What does that mean?"

I'd seen my father's true colors, but was Luis right? Was the entire Capizola empire built on lies and scandal?

"Monsters wear many faces, Arianne. Your father set out to take back La Riva and Romany Square from the Marchetti, but it was never his to take."

I stared into my cocoa, watching the marshmallows bubble and melt. "Is that why you're helping me? Because you don't agree with my father's ideals? You're his most trusted security guard."

Luis twisted his body toward me, letting out a long sigh. "I'm helping you because it's the right thing to do. Because no child should have to pay for the sins of their forefathers. This fight, the bad blood between the Marchetti and Capizola isn't yours to bear, Arianne. And what Fascini did to you... I will never forgive myself. It happened on my watch. I want to believe your father didn't know what Scott would do that night, but he knew *something* would happen." His words shook with anger.

"I never had children. My ex-wife and I, we tried. Tried for years. But it wasn't meant to be. So watching you grow, witnessing the young woman you have become, everything you have endured, I guess it spoke to me. To that part of me never fulfilled. I have served your father for the better part of twenty years, Arianne. But I serve you now. And if that means I serve the Marchetti, then so be it."

"What will happen if my father finds out?"

A dark shadow passed over his face. "Let's hope it does not come to that." He took a sip of his cocoa. "I didn't want to say anything, but I'm not sure I'll be able to get any sleep if I don't. Meeting Nicco tomorrow is a risk, Arianne. One I'm not sure you should be taking yet."

"I have to go."

"I know." He rubbed his jaw. "But if I'm going to protect you, that means being honest with you. And I think it's a bad idea."

"You don't want to take me?"

"I didn't say that. But there's a reason Nicco left Verona County. If Mike or Scott find out..."

"They won't. We'll make sure they don't."

I was going, even if Luis didn't take me.

I needed to see Nicco, more than I needed my next breath. Every second without him here, I slipped further under the deep waters I'd found myself in.

He gave me a sharp nod. Disapproval glittered in his eyes, but Luis didn't protest any further. "I'll make the arrangements. You'll need a cover story. Something I can feed to your father, something that will keep Scott off your back."

"I won't have to worry about Scott. He'll be at practice with the team, they have a big game coming up. He'll be distracted with that."

"That makes things easier."

"Nora has invited her friend Dan over tomorrow evening, so I'll make myself scarce in my room studying." I gave him a pointed look.

"Very well. I'll get our story straight with the rest of the team."

"Thank you, for everything. I don't know what I'd do if it wasn't for you and Nora."

"Something tells me you'd survive. You have great strength, Arianne. Never forget that. I know things feel desperate now, that you can't see a way out, but you always have a choice. It's just figuring out which battles to fight."

"I won't marry him."

I'd rather die.

"I have no intention of ever letting you walk down the aisle toward that asshole. But Antonio needs time to figure out a plan. Your father has always managed to keep his hands clean, but I think we can only assume Mike Fascini will go to any lengths to get what he wants."

"Do you know what he has on my father, Luis?"

My bodyguard liked to talk in riddles, but riddles didn't help my predicament.

"I have my suspicions."

I raised a brow. "Are you going to share them with me?"

"Will it change anything?"

Silence fell over us. "No, it won't." The truth was like a knife to the heart. "He made his choice. And I made mine."

Luis placed down his mug and stood. "You should get some sleep, it's late."

"You're probably right."

"I'll handover with the night shift and get some shut eye. See you in the morning, okay?"

I nodded. "Okay. Goodnight, Luis."

He gave me a tight smile, his mask of indifference sliding back into place as he resumed bodyguard mode and headed for the door.

But he paused at the last second, glancing back. "It won't always be like this, Arianne. Sometimes the bad things that happen in our lives set us on the path to the best things that will ever happen to us. Try and hold onto that."

I wanted to believe him.

But something told me the worst was yet to come.

ELEVEN

NICCO

SHE WAS LATE.

Arianne was supposed to meet me at the motel on the edge of Blue Hills Reservation, twenty minutes ago. But there was still no sign of her.

I'd almost worn out the spongy carpet pacing back and forth, waiting for the black SUV to roll into the parking lot. I'd been tempted to ask Uncle Alonso for the keys to one of his places, but it was already risky asking Arianne here. So I'd kept it vague. The glint in his eye as I'd told him I would be gone all night was all the sign I needed that he knew exactly where I was going. He didn't try to stop me though, because he knew he couldn't.

I needed to see her.

I needed to hold Arianne as I told her everything I'd learned after talking to Elizabeth Monroe. But it was more than that. I needed to know she was okay. I needed to look her in the eye and *see* it.

I was just about to call Luis when I spotted their car. "Thank fuck," I breathed, yanking open the door.

Luis climbed out and scanned the parking lot. I'd already done a sweep of the area. Twice. Watching Arianne step out of the vehicle had the tension in my shoulders melting away. She spotted me and ran. She ran all the way until she launched herself into my awaiting arms.

"Nicco." My name was a prayer on her lips. But it was me who wanted to fall to my knees and worship her.

"You're okay." I cupped the back of her head, cradling her body against mine. "You're okay."

"I've missed you." Arianne craned her neck to look at me. "I've missed you so much."

"I know, Bambolina. I know." Dipping my head, I brushed my lips over hers. Once. Twice. Letting myself memorize their shape, reacquaint with their taste. But it was Arianne who took control, fitting her body against mine like a missing puzzle piece and deepening the kiss. Her tongue slipped between my lips, searching for my own.

Luis cleared his throat. I liked the man, I did, but right then, in that moment, I wanted him to disappear.

"We should talk," he said, when I made no effort to break the kiss.

Arianne had fisted my sweater, anchoring us together. "Bambolina," I breathed against her mouth, gently tugging her hand away. "Give me a second."

She smiled up at me, her cheeks flushed, and lips swollen.

"Go inside." I flicked my head to our room. "I'll be right there, I promise."

"Okay." Arianne hesitated, letting out a small sigh as she stole another kiss before disappearing inside.

I pulled the door shut and stepped toward Luis. "You swept the area?" he asked me.

I nodded. "It's clean. No one knows I'm out here, not even my uncle."

"Nicco," he frowned, "that's a big risk."

"She's worth it".

"You said you found something in Vermont."

"I did. But we shouldn't talk out here. You were on Roberto's security detail when someone tried to get to Arianne at the school?"

"I was."

"I need you to talk to this guy." I handed him Tommy's nondescript card. "He's expecting your call."

"We can trust him?"

"We can. I got you a room." Fishing the second card out of my pocket, I gave it to Luis. "Didn't know if you'd want it, but it's yours."

"I'm going to set up on watch, but thanks, I appreciate it. You should probably go see to her, she's getting impatient." He handed me her overnight bag.

I glanced back just in time to see the curtain twitch. "I will." My lips curved. "But first, I need to know... how is she? Really?"

"It's been less than a week. Ask me again in a month." Luis' expression hardened. He cared for Arianne, that much was obvious. But part of me sensed he disagreed with how we were handling things.

"Go, be with her. We can talk tomorrow."

"Call me if there's any problems," I said, slowly backing up toward the door.

"Same goes for you."

I watched him double back to the SUV, before entering the room. There was nothing special about it: it had four walls, a small bathroom, a queen-sized bed, and a few other pieces of furniture. But it could have been a hovel for all I cared.

Because sitting there, on the edge of the bed, was the girl who held my heart in the palm of her hands.

"Bambolina." It fell from my lips on a whispered sigh, as I dropped the bag.

Arianne got up and came to me, pressing her hand against my cheek. "I can't believe you're here."

Inhaling a ragged breath, I drew her into my chest, holding her. "I had to see you."

"I know." She laid her palms on my chest, staring up at me with so much emotion, I felt winded.

I brushed a stray hair from her face, tracing the lines of her face. Arianne's breath hitched as I let my fingers glide down the slope of her neck. "Kiss me."

She complied, pushing up on her tiptoes and giving me her lips. I cupped her face with two hands, sweeping my tongue into her mouth, tangling it with her own. She tasted like love and promise.

She tasted like home.

"Nicco," she moaned softly, fitting herself closer. I kept kissing her. Peppering her face with tiny desperate kisses, licking and nibbling the skin beneath her ear. I wanted to paint every inch of her with my lips, brand her with my touch. The need to have her burned through me, a wildfire no amount of water could douse.

"God, Bambolina. I want you, I want you so fucking much."

Her hands slipped to the hem of my sweater, dipping underneath and finding my warm skin. Arianne explored my stomach, my abs and chest. Taking her time to trace every hard ridge and taut dip. "I've missed you so much," she breathed the words against the corner of my mouth. Her voice was thick with lust and want.

"I want to lie you down on the bed, strip the clothes from your body and make you mine in every way possible."

"Yes," she moaned, her hands dropping to the waistband of my jeans. "Make love to me, Nicco."

I snagged her wrist, holding it between us as I lowered my face to hers, staring into her honey-brown eyes. "We have time."

I didn't ask her here for this, no matter how badly I wanted her. We needed to talk. Arianne needed to understand the situation. But she was staring at me with such intensity, I wasn't sure I was strong enough to resist.

"Nicco, what it is?" Her eyes clouded with uncertainty.

I cupped her face, brushing my thumb over her cheek. "It shouldn't be like this. You deserve so much, Arianne, you don't deserve this." Guilt snaked through me, coiling around my heart as my eyes shuttered on a harsh breath.

"Nicco," Arianne smoothed her fingers over my jaw. "Look at me."

I opened my eyes and she smiled. God, her smile. It was enough to bring me to my knees.

"My life has never been my own, I realize that now. I have been groomed for a life I never asked for, a life I don't want. I thought going to MU was the start of my freedom, the start of me choosing my own path."

A tear slipped down her face and I swiped it away with my thumb.

"But it was all a lie. Until you. I choose you, Nicco. I choose a life... with you."

I leaned down, touching my head to hers. "There was never a choice where you were concerned."

I knew that now.

Something had changed in me that night Arianne stumbled across me and Bailey in the alley. I'd wanted to protect her, to make sure nothing ever hurt her again. And those feelings had only grown the more time I spent with her, turning into something primal, something soul-deep.

Something I couldn't fight even if I tried.

"We should talk, come on." I took Arianne's hand and led her to the bed. "I'm sorry about the room. I know it's not what you're used to."

"You think I care about that?" She sat down and kicked off her boots before crawling onto the bed and sitting against the headboard. It creaked and moaned as I joined Arianne, slipping my arm around her shoulder and pulling her into my side.

"I didn't think this through."

"Meeting me?"

"Meeting you at some dive motel." In a room that had no couch or chairs for us to sit on.

"It's not that bad." She peeked up at me. "What's really going on in that head of yours?"

"The truth?"

"Always."

"I'm having a hard time thinking about anything except getting you naked right now."

Heat flared in her eyes. "I'm right here."

A low groan bubbled in my throat. "I'm trying to do the right thing, Bambolina."

"And I love you for it." She shrugged out of my hold and moved around me.

"What are you doing, amore mio?"

"Making it easier for you." I felt her body tremble as she straddled my legs. My hands went to her waist, guiding her over me. "Is this okay?" Her voice was thick, and her pupils were blown with lust.

"More than okay." I curved a hand around the back of her neck and kissed her. Slow deep licks. "But you won't tempt me, Bambolina. We need to talk."

Disappointment etched into her expression, and I chuckled. "We have time."

"Do we though? Because it feels like the clock is already running out."

"Arianne," I breathed, pain slicing me open.

"It's okay. You said we needed to talk, so talk." My eyes narrowed, but she added, "I'm okay. You're here, that's all that matters."

"I found out some things."

"I'm listening..."

Fuck. How was I supposed to tell her this? After everything she'd already been through.

"Nicco, talk to me. Whatever it is, we'll get through it."

I guided Arianne's face to mine, inhaling a deep breath. "I think I know who ordered the hit against you."

"It really wasn't your father?"

I shook my head. "I think it was Mike Fascini."

Arianne frowned. But her confusion quickly turned to something else. Her gaze widened, fear swirling in her big brown eyes. "You think he... tried to have me killed?" She choked out the words.

"I met his aunt. That's where I went yesterday."

"What else she did say?"

"She wasn't surprised that Mike is trying start something. She knew, she fucking knew her brother moved to Verona County to come after us."

"Her brother?"

"Yeah, Mike's father. He died a long time ago. But I guess the damage was done."

"It doesn't make any sense... why would he want..." Arianne shuddered.

"Have you ever heard the name Ricci?"

"It isn't familiar, why?"

"There's a lot you don't know about our history, Bambolina."

My strong brave girl laid her palm against my cheek and gave me a sad smile. "So tell me."

I told Arianne everything. She already knew about Emilio Marchetti and Elena Ricci and their betrayal. But I told her how Alfredo Capizola hunted them down and killed Emilio. I told her how the Ricci fled Verona County and became an unspoken name among our families.

"I can't believe it," she sighed, the sound making my heart ache. The last thing I ever wanted was to cause Arianne any pain. But with every revelation came a new hurt.

"Scott's your... cousin."

"*Distant* cousin." That fucker might have had Marchetti blood in his veins, but he would never be family.

"Do you think he knows?"

"Does it matter?" My brow quirked up.

"No, I guess not. Why did you tell me?"

"Because..." I pulled her closer, putting us nose to nose. "You need to understand the severity of the situation. Scott and his dad are out for blood. They want to bring down our families. I think the hit on you was a way to incite war between the Marchetti and Capizola. If it had been... successful..." I barely got the words out over the lump in my throat. "Your father would have demanded revenge."

Arianne scoffed. "You don't know that. He doesn't care about me."

"He does, Bambolina. In his own messed up way, I think he thinks he's protecting you."

"By promising me to the family who wants to see us fall?"

"But what if he doesn't know the truth? Think about it... If he suspected my father was behind the hit, maybe he turned to the Fascini to strengthen his position. Fascini and Associates are well connected. Together, Mike and your father would be a force to be reckoned with."

"So what's his endgame? If Mike Fascini is really who you say he is, then where is all this leading?"

It was the one thing I still hadn't figured out. There were other ways to get revenge. Anyone with enough money could pay for someone to disappear or be taken out. They could make it look like an accident, a tragedy no one would question.

"Maybe he doesn't want to get his hands dirty," I said.

"Or maybe he has some bigger plan we still don't know about." Arianne let out a weary sigh.

"Hey." I kissed the corner of her mouth. "This doesn't change anything. I won't let anything happen to you."

"I'm engaged to Scott, Nicco. They want me to *marry* him."

Every muscle in my body tensed. "You will never be his," I ground out.

Arianne was mine.

"This," I pressed my hand against her breastbone, right where her heart lay. "Is mine. One day, when all this is over, I'll make you mine, Bambolina. You'll be my wife. My queen. Do you understand that?"

Her bottom lip quivered as she gazed up at me with tear-stained eyes. "Tell me you understand that," I said, desperation clinging to every word.

"I'm scared, Nicco." Silent tears streaked down her cheeks, and my heart broke for the girl who had already faced so much. "When I was at the restaurant with him... he went out of his way to make me uncomfortable, to let me know that he's the one in control."

"Did he... touch you?" My voice shook with anger. Luis had told me everything was fine, that Scott had kept his hands to himself. But I sensed it wasn't the full story.

"Not like that, no. But something happened..."

Red mist began to descend over me, my grip on Arianne's waist tightening. "I need you to move, Bambolina."

"Nicco, don't—"

"I'm okay," I said, "but I need space. Please..." My voice cracked.

Arianne crawled off my lap, pressing herself against the headboard and folding in on herself while I stood up, pacing the room like a caged animal.

"This is why I didn't want to tell you," she whispered.

"What did he do?"

"It wasn't anything really." Her eyes drifted past me as if admitting this to me was a burden too big to bear. "I wanted to leave. He wanted to stay. But I told him I was leaving. We got outside to the car and he told Luis he could drive. He got in my space and brushed my waist, that's all. But it felt so possessive, so intimate. Everything came rushing back to me. It was like this giant wave just hit me." She finally lifted her eyes to mine again. "Luis thinks I had a panic attack. I passed out."

"Fuck." My fist shot out, crashing against the solid wall. Pain ricocheted through my knuckles and down my wrist, burning like a motherfucker.

"*Nicco!*" Arianne clambered off the bed and rushed to my side.

"Wait." I held up my other hand to stop her. A dark angry storm was raging through me. I wanted to hit something, to hurt and bleed.

I needed it.

Dark rivulets of blood seeped over my hand, but I barely felt it. I was too wired. Too hungry for the kill.

"Let me take a look at it." Arianne stepped forward and I jerked back, like a caged animal being riled.

"Nicco, it's me. It's only me." She had me cornered with no way out. My body trembled violently as I desperately tried to hold on to my frayed rope of control.

"Nicco..." Arianne brushed the hair from my face. My head hung low, my shoulders hunched and tight. I wanted to kill him. I wanted to hunt him down and kill him with my bare hands.

"Come back to me." She gently lifted my busted hand and inspected the damage. "It needs cleaning. Let me see what there is." Arianne left me and went into the bathroom. When she came back, she had a small first aid kit. "I found it in the cabinet. Sit." Her gaze went to the bed, but I remained rigid.

"I need to stand."

"Okay. Hold still." She worked in silence, cleaning me up and bandaging my hand. My pulse began to slow, the tightness in my chest easing.

It was her.

Her touch, her calmness.

"I'm sorry," I choked out.

Arianne took my face in her hands and looked right at me. God, I wanted to drown in the dark pools of honey. "Talk to me."

"I want to kill him... I should have killed him."

"So why didn't you?"

It was the last thing I expected her to say, but I knew this wasn't about her, it was about me.

"It's not that simple," I released a heavy sigh. "If I'd have killed him... it would start something we might not be able to finish. I can't do that to the Family, to you."

She nodded, dropping one of her hands to mine and lacing them together. "I hate Scott for what he did to me. I hate him so much that sometimes I wish you had done it." Arianne took a shuddering breath. "But I want a life with you. I want a future. I can't have that if you're behind bars... or worse."

"If he hurts you again, I can't promise I won't do it."

Something flashed in her eyes, but before I could decipher it, Arianne kissed me. "I don't want to talk any more, Nicco. I want you to love me. I want you to make me forget about the monsters."

"Bambolina... You deserve—"

"Don't tell me what I deserve. I can choose my own path, Nicco. And it's you. Don't you see that? It's—"

My mouth crashed down on hers, swallowing her words. She was right. I didn't want to be another man in her life taking away her right to choose. I wanted her by my side, as my equal. As the better half of me.

"I'm not sure I can be gentle," I murmured against her lips.

I was too wound up to go slow.

Arianne gripped my jaw and eased back slightly, staring at me with nothing but love and lust. "Then don't."

TWELVE

ARIANNE

NICCO LOOKED ready to devour me.

Hunger simmered in his hooded eyes as they lingered on my lips. "Do you have any idea of how beautiful you are?" His words wrapped around me like a warm blanket.

When it was just the two of us, it was easy to forget everything else.

To get lost in him.

My hands went to the hem of his sweater, and I felt him shudder as I pulled the material up his body. Nicco took control, yanking it over his head. Reaching for him, I ghosted my fingers over the faded scars. There were so many. So many stories, so much pain. But every mark was a part of him. It made Nicco who he was. Fiercely protective and doggedly loyal. Nicco might have been mafioso but he loved with everything that he was, and I still couldn't believe I got to call him mine.

No words passed between us as he pushed the jacket from my shoulders. He worked on the buttons of my blouse next, popping each one with measured precision. His fingers traced the curve of my breasts, toying over the lace shell of my bra. "Sei bellissima."

My breath caught when his fingers found the waistband of my pants. Nicco only had eyes for me as he gently pushed the soft material off my hips, letting it pool at my feet in a silky puddle. He ran his hands down my spine, smoothing them over the swell of my hips. "I will never tire of this." It came out a rough whisper.

Without warning, Nicco picked me up, my startled shrieks filling the room. "Wrap your legs around me," he commanded, moving us in the direction of the bed.

His skin felt incredible against mine and I pressed myself closer, needing this moment with him.

Nicco stopped at the edge of the bed. I was curled around him, unwilling to ever let go. He nudged his nose against mine, inhaling a deep breath. A beat passed, delicious anticipation crackling around us. We'd only had one night together. This time felt different, like so much more. When our lips met it felt like a silent promise to everything that we were.

Everything that we wanted.

The world fell away around me as Nicco lowered me to the bed. He stood before me, strong and handsome; a dark angel put on the Earth to love me, and me alone. But there was a glint in his eye. A flash of something that had me sucking in a shaky breath.

Nicco popped the button on his jeans before dropping to his knees. His hair fell over his eyes so I couldn't see him, but I could feel him. Feel every kiss as he explored my skin, touching and tasting. He branded me with his tongue, swirling it in my navel before dragging down, down, *down*.

"Oh God," I breathed as he nibbled at the lace covering me.

"These need to go." He eased back and worked them off my hips and down my legs. Nicco gave me no warning as he dived for me, licking and sucking me into complete submission. It felt incredible, the warmth of his breath against the coolness of his tongue.

"You taste like heaven," he murmured against my damp skin. "I want to watch you fall, Bambolina. Eyes on me."

I pushed up on my elbows, gazing at him through lust-drunk eyes. "It feels so good," I breathed, my body shuddering.

Nicco watched me as he slowly worked two fingers inside me and curled them upwards.

"Oh my..." The words got stuck in my throat as he lowered his head and worked me with tongue and fingers in perfect synchrony.

"Come for me, Bambolina."

His words sent me flying off the edge. My head fell back as I screamed his name, intense waves of pleasure crashing over me. Nicco stood, pushing his jeans and boxers down his legs. I watched with rapt fascination as he stroked himself. He was long and hard and so perfect it hurt to look at him.

"See what you do to me, amore mio." His words were rough with need as he stalked toward me, kneeling on the edge of the bed. "You're mine, Arianne Carmen Lina Capizola. Nothing will ever change that." He crawled up my body until we were one.

"Yours," I whispered against his lips, hitching my legs around his waist.

Nicco thrust inside me in one smooth stroke, filling me so completely I couldn't breathe. I knew he was holding back; knew he was walking a fine line between being in control and losing it. But I didn't want him to be gentle with me. I wanted all of him. The good, the bad, and all the broken pieces. I wanted the mafia prince, the knight-in-shining-armor, the fighter, and the lover.

Simply put, I just wanted him.

Every last piece.

Tangling our hands together, Nicco pressed them at the side of my head while the other slipped to my thigh, hooking my leg higher, letting him go deeper. Harder. He kissed me like it was our first and last time together, like he wouldn't ever get enough. Our tongues danced a slow erotic dance as he rocked into me with breathtaking restraint.

"Nicco, I'm not glass. I won't break." I nipped his jaw, arching my back to meet his measured strokes.

"I don't want to hurt you."

"You won't," I breathed. "I want you. All of you." My hand slipped down his body, pressing him against me. He groaned into the crook of my neck, his pace quickening.

"You feel so good, Bambolina."

"But you need more," I said, raking my fingers over his skull.

He stilled, gazing down at me in awe. "Are you sure?"

Dragging my bottom lip between my teeth, I bit down gently, nodding.

"Hold on." Nicco moved my hands to his shoulders and rolled us without warning. My cheeks flamed at our new position. But I didn't need to worry, not with the way he was looking at me. Like I was the most precious thing on Earth.

Nicco sat up, crushing my breasts against his chest. "It'll be deep like this."

"It's okay."

His hands went to my hair as he kissed me. My body tingled with sensation, my stomach coiling tight as he moved one of my hands to his erection. I lifted myself a little, letting him guide himself beneath me and then I sank down. Slowly. Completely. Our breathy moans filled the space between us, but then he was kissing me, rocking into me. It was different. Deeper. More intense. It was like I could feel him everywhere. He curved his hand around the back of my neck and tugged gently, dropping his mouth to my collarbone, sucking the skin there.

"It feels... God..." I swallowed a moan. Everything was heightened like this, pure pleasure coursing through my veins. Nicco licked and sucked a path down to the curve of my breasts, teasing one of my nipples. I cried out, but his tongue replaced his teeth, soothing the sting.

"Perfection," he murmured against my damp skin, kissing a trail back up to my mouth.

Our bodies rocked faster... harder... *deeper*. Until our moans were a song. A rising cacophony of little sighs and breathy gasps. Nicco held me tighter, fitting our bodies so closely I didn't know where I ended, and he began. It was like he wanted to crawl inside and become a part of me.

He already was though.

His soul already entwined with mine.

"Fuck, Bambolina. Nothing," he gathered the hair off my face and pressed a kiss to the underside of my jaw, "will ever feel as good as this."

"I'm close," I panted, my body trembling.

"Together," he murmured, kissing me so intensely I felt myself begin to fall. But Nicco was there to catch me as we came together, the rise and fall of our chests quick, the beat of our hearts hard.

"I can't promise that things won't get worse before they get better..." Nicco met my heavy-lidded gaze. "But I promise I'll be waiting at the end."

I nodded, too choked up to reply. In our bubble, I felt safe. I felt safe and loved and cherished. But out there, without him by my side, I felt lost. Adrift without an anchor.

Nicco pulled us down onto the bed and pulled the sheet over our bodies. He held me, his fingers dancing along the curve of my waist as the silence crashed down around us.

"What are you thinking?" I leaned up to look at him. He looked so good. His hair was ruffled and damp, while his eyes glowed with possessiveness and love.

"Everything... and nothing."

"Sounds complicated." I shrieked as he rolled me underneath him.

"I'm wondering how I'm supposed to leave you tomorrow. How the fuck am I supposed to let you go back there, to him? Tell me, Bambolina, tell me how?" Pain edged into his words, making my heart ache.

I lifted a hand to his cheek and gave him a sad smile. "You just do, Nicco. This is bigger than us, you said so yourself."

He grabbed my hand and kissed my palm. "I know, Bambolina. Are you tired? Hungry? I could order something..."

"Nicco, stop." My arm looped around his neck, drawing his face to mine. "I have everything I need right here." I kissed him, running my tongue along the seam of his mouth and teasing him. Nicco took control, deepening the kiss and stealing my breath. Heat pooled low in my stomach and I felt Nicco hard and ready against my thigh.

"Again?" His intense gaze pinned me to the spot.

Suppressing a coy smile, I nodded.

"Jesus, Arianne." He dropped his hand between us, finding my center. I gasped as he pushed a finger inside me. "You'll be the death of me."

I pulled him closer, until we were nose to nose. "I can think of worse ways to go." My lips curved against his.

"I love you, Arianne. With everything that I am."

"Show me," I moaned already feeling the waves of ecstasy rise inside me.

He gazed at me, his eyes looking right into my soul as he whispered, "Senza di te la mia vita non vale niente."

I lifted my face into the stream of sunlight. It warmed my skin, coaxing my spent muscles from their slumber.

"Good morning." My lips curved as I reached out for Nicco, only to be met by cold empty sheets. "Nicco?" I sat up, pushing wild curls from my face.

The room was quiet. Still. I pushed back the covers and found a clean t-shirt and panties from my overnight bag. Pulling back the curtains, I scanned the parking lot, but it was as empty and still as our room. Dejection swarmed my chest. Nicco wouldn't just leave me, he wouldn't. Not again.

Not after everything.

Panic flooded me. What if something had happened...? What if—

The door handle rattled, and I froze, my heart beating wildly in my chest. I clutched my cell phone ready to call Luis.

"Morning. I have coffee."

"Nicco," I cried.

"What's wrong?" Nicco paled. "Oh, you thought I'd left, didn't you?" His head hung low, guilt swirling in his dark eyes.

"I... I didn't..."

"Hey, come here." He placed the coffee and brown paper bag down on the table and stalked toward me. "I'm sorry, I didn't think." Nicco pulled me into his arms and I went willingly, falling against his solid chest.

"I don't know what I thought." I buried my face in the crook of his neck.

"Bambolina, look at me." His fingers slid under my jaw and tilted my face up to meet his. "I won't ever do that to you again." Nicco seared me with his gaze.

"I know."

I did know.

But the deep sense of dread I'd felt when I woke up to an empty bed had been real. A natural reaction to everything I'd been through over the last few weeks.

"I was awake early, and you looked so peaceful. I didn't want to wake you." His arm looped around me, as he swayed us gently. "I have coffee and donuts."

"A man after my own heart." I smiled. "When do we have to leave?"

"We have time," he said, pulling me over to the bed. But I didn't let go and we tumbled in a tangle of limbs and laughter. Nicco gazed down at me, brushing the hair from my face. "I wish we had more time."

"Me too." The pit in my stomach was back. "Is Luis okay?"

"He's fine. Although I don't think he got much sleep."

"He stayed up all night?" My brows furrowed.

"He just wants to make sure you're safe." Nicco brushed his nose over mine, stealing a kiss.

"I need to brush my teeth." I pressed my palms into his chest, giggling when he began to pepper tiny kisses down the slope of my neck.

His soft laughter washed over me. "You think I care?"

Nudging him off me, I sat up. Nicco stood and fetched the coffee and donuts. "Breakfast, amore mio?"

"And after breakfast?" My heart sank at the thought of leaving Nicco. I was grateful for our night together, but it wasn't enough.

Not when I wanted forever.

"After breakfast, I'm going to carry you into the ridiculously small bathroom, strip the clothes from your body, and wash every inch of your skin, just so I can dirty you up again."

Oh my.

My stomach clenched. "Suddenly, I'm not feeling very hungry for coffee and donuts," I admitted.

"Eat, Bambolina. You need your strength." He gave me a pointed look, offering me the paper bag.

"Fine, but you know my mom always says a moment on the lips is a lifetime on the hips."

"Hush," Nicco said. "You're perfect just the way you are."

"Which is why eating donuts for breakfast isn't a good idea." I fought a smile. This was so nice. So normal.

"Hey," he leaned in, brushing my cheek, "don't do that." He must have noticed my expression fall. "We have time."

But it wasn't enough.

It would *never* be enough.

After breakfast, Nicco had made good on his promise to dirty me up. He'd loved me in the shower and again on the bed before finally succumbing to Luis' insistence that we had to leave.

Our time had run out.

"Everything good?" Nicco asked Luis as we stepped outside. He took my bag, offering us both a reassuring nod.

"We need to get back though before anyone suspects anything. I'll give the two of you a minute." Luis headed for the SUV.

"Don't cry, Bambolina." Nicco swiped the tears rolling down my cheeks.

"I'm trying to be strong," I replied. "I just hate this."

"I know." He cupped the back of my head, drawing me close. "I do too. But hopefully, it won't be for much longer. Now we know who Mike Fascini really is, we can make plans."

"What does that mean though?" My voice cracked, my heart already in tatters.

"It means we do whatever is necessary to find a way out of this."

"Okay," I conceded because what else could I do? Nicco didn't have a magic answer.

There was no answer.

"You can do this, Arianne. I know you can."

"It's easy for you to say, you're not the one—" I swallowed the words. I didn't want to argue. Not after such a perfect night. "You'll go back to Boston?"

"I will." Nicco looked gutted, guilt etched into the lines of his face. But it was more than his expression. It swirled around us, thick and heavy and suffocating.

"So I guess this is goodbye." A fresh wave of tears threatened to fall, but I swallowed them down.

"I love you, amore mio. Remember that." Nicco held me tighter. "You have to remember that."

"Arianne," Luis called from the car.

"I should go," I whispered, pain flooding my chest.

"This isn't goodbye, Bambolina."

It sure felt like it.

Nicco kissed me. Hard and bruising, not caring we had an audience of one. By the time he brushed a final kiss over my lips, I was breathless and nowhere near satisfied.

"Go," he barked roughly. "Before I ask you to come with me."

I walked away, forcing myself to put one foot in front of the other, until I reached Luis.

"Ready?" he asked.

I nodded, unable to speak. Glancing over my shoulder, I mouthed, "I love you," before climbing into the car, hoping he wouldn't hear the sound of my heart breaking or my tears falling.

THIRTEEN

NICCO

WATCHING Arianne climb into the SUV was one of the hardest things I'd ever done. After their car disappeared, I didn't stick around. I grabbed my bag and hopped on my bike, the familiar rumble of the engine beneath me settling my soul.

Arianne was going back to that monster.

It wasn't right.

But it was the only choice we had right now.

Mike Fascini wasn't just some guy—he was a man out for vengeance. Arianne was right, we needed to know his endgame.

The wedding—not that I ever planned on letting her actually marry that fucker—wasn't for another four months. It would make Arianne a Fascini, and the business merger would give Mike access to Roberto's empire. But what then?

He wanted to bring down the Marchetti. To destroy the Capizola from the inside out. But I was still missing some vital pieces of the puzzle.

One thing was for sure, if Mike was behind the failed hit on Arianne, and my money was on it being him, it meant he wasn't afraid to get his hands dirty. He wasn't afraid to murder a girl in cold blood to better his cause, which meant he was prepared to go to any lengths to get what he wanted, making him a dangerous man.

Far more dangerous than we'd first anticipated.

Blue Hills Reservation disappeared behind me as the Boston skyline came into view. I needed to speak to my father. We needed a plan. Arianne was safe for now, but what happened when Scott decided he was done playing nice?

I was biding my time. Playing by the rules and upholding the code of the

Family. But if he so much as touched a hair on Arianne's head again, I wouldn't be held responsible for my actions.

Because an attack against Arianne, was an attack against me.

And an attack against me, was an attack against the Family.

I just had to make my father and his men see that.

When I arrived back at my uncle's house, I was greeted with the sight of Matteo's truck and one of my father's cars.

Nervous anticipation skated up my spine as I parked up and went inside. Haughty laughter filled the air, the familiar cadence of my father and Uncle Alonso ringing in my ears.

"Niccolò, so good of you to join us." My father cast me a knowing look. "Sit, eat. Maria was good enough to prepare a feast." He motioned to the table of food.

Just then, the back door swung open and my cousins filed in.

"Nicco." Matteo came straight over, pulling me in for a guy hug. "It's good to see you."

"You too."

"Cous." Enzo tipped his chin, his expression as cool as his greeting. He still wasn't over everything. And part of me didn't blame him. But it didn't change anything.

I was with Arianne now.

She was in my life, whether he liked it or not.

"Niccolò," Uncle Vincenzo pulled out a chair and beckoned me over. "Come, we have much to talk about."

"After we eat."

"Hell yeah," Dane piped up, dropping into a chair and loading his plate with ridiculous amounts of food.

"Where's your fucking manners, kid?"

"Can we drop the kid, already?" Dane growled at his father.

"Do you want Nicco to put you on your ass again? Because it can be arranged. In fact, now Matteo and Enzo are here, maybe I'll have the three of them teach you a thing or two."

Enzo snickered, and Dane discreetly flipped him off. He really was a cocky little fucker. I might have enjoyed sparring with him, even putting him on his ass a time or two, but given half a chance, Enzo would annihilate him.

"I'm sure we can arrange something," my cousin said, his brows drawn together.

Dane swallowed his mouthful of pancake and stuttered out, "Name the time and place."

"Oof, the kid's got balls, I'll give him that." Vincenzo roared with laughter, slamming his big hand down on the table, making the plates and dishes clink and rattle.

"He needs to learn his fucking place." Uncle Alonso glowered at his son, but Dane remained unaffected as he continued tucking into his breakfast.

"This is unexpected," I said, raising a brow toward my father. He huffed under his breath, draining his coffee.

"We'll talk after we eat."

He was pissed.

Probably because I'd gone to Arianne before calling him. But I couldn't turn back time and even if I could, I wouldn't have changed anything.

Arianne deserved to know the truth about Mike Fascini.

She deserved to know exactly what she was tangled up in.

"Well, would you look at this." Aunt Maria breezed into the room looking every bit the underboss's wife. "It's been a long time since I had this many men in my kitchen." She ran a hand over her husband's shoulder, dropping a kiss on his head.

"You're looking good, Maria."

"Thanks, Toni. Now if you all don't mind, I'm going to steal that son of mine away and make sure he actually makes it to school today. Dane." She motioned for him.

"But, Mamma..."

"You should listen to your mother, kid." Uncle Michele said.

"This is bullshit," Dane grumbled as he stood. "I can handle whatever is going down."

"That's what they all say until a pile of shit lands at their feet." Uncle Al scoffed. "Get out of here, kid. And stay the fuck out of trouble."

Maria nudged Dane out of the kitchen, and a couple of seconds later, the front door opened and then shut.

"He's going to send me to an early grave."

"He's a good kid, Al," my father offered. "Young and eager. He's hungry for it."

"Too fucking hungry if you ask me."

"He just wants to do right by you, by the Family." My father's hard gaze snapped to mine. "It's not a bad thing."

"It's good to see you, Toni. Real good. Now what's this all about?" My uncle sat back in his chair, glancing between me and my father.

"Ask Niccolò."

"You want to do this now?" I asked him.

"Now is as good a time as any, Son."

I ran a hand down my face. I hadn't expected them to come here, let alone to have to trust them all with this. But they were my family.

The Family.

I was supposed to be able to trust each and every one of them with my life. But trusting them with my life, also meant trusting them with Arianne's life.

"Niccolò..."

I stared at the men seated around the table. The men closest to me. My father, my cousins, and uncles. I couldn't carry this burden alone, and yet, to share it with them...

"Niccolò," my father rasped. "We are waiting."

"We found something out, Tommy and me," I said.

"Well, spit it out, Nic," Uncle Vincenzo scarfed down another pastry, wiping his hands on a napkin.

"Mike Fascini is Elena Ricci's grandson."

Silence enveloped us. Thick and heavy with the sins of our past.

"What the fuck did you just say?" Vincenzo sat forward, his thick fingers curved around the table edge.

"You heard him, Vin," my father said. "He speaks the truth."

"Ricci? Minchia! It is not possible."

"Elena Ricci?" Matteo balked. "As in the very reason we're all in this mess in the first place?"

"I had hoped for a different outcome," my father sighed, "but the reality is, Mike Fascini is in fact, Marchetti."

"Bull. Shit," Enzo spat, standing. No one batted an eye though, it was typical Enzo. When things went to shit, he started to pace the room like a caged tiger. "That fuck isn't one of us."

"Of course he's not one of us," Uncle Michele scoffed. "But if what Niccolò says is true, then it is far more complicated than any of us realized."

"It's true, I talked with his aunt."

"His aunt? The fuck, Nicco?"

I glanced at my father and he nodded. "Me and Tommy drove out to Vermont. It's where Elena fled to after Alfredo..." I didn't need to say the words, we all knew the story. "She had Emilio's child, a son. Michael. When he married, he took his wife's name to become Michael Fascini."

"That is some fucked up shit," Enzo let out a low whistle.

"You knew about this?" Uncle Vincenzo glanced at my father.

"I had my suspicions."

"Fuck," he breathed, running a hand over his stubbled jaw.

"There's more," I said. "I think Mike Fascini was behind the hit on Arianne five years ago. I don't have hard proof yet, but my gut tells me I'm right."

"It makes sense," my father agreed. "Take her out and pin it on us."

My stomach sank while my uncles all nodded. Talking about the failed hit on Arianne was like being gutted with a jagged blade.

"But it failed," Uncle Al said.

"It did." It came out tight. "So now he's working a different angle. Tommy thinks he's positioning himself as a Trojan Horse."

"It's smart. Move in on Capizola's empire first and then come after us."

"He's working alone?"

I gave Uncle Michele a curt nod. "We think so. There's no evidence of him having anyone outside his personal security and his team at Fascini and Associates."

Enzo loomed over us, his eyes narrowed to dangerous slits. "Let's just take him out. He's one man. End him and we end all this bullshit."

A chill rippled through the air at his words. "Lorenzo," my father let out a weary sigh. "We can't just take him out. He's one of the most influential men in the county."

"I'm with my son, Toni. Mike Fascini is a thorn in the Family's side. Taking him out makes sense."

My father clucked his tongue. "Always so quick to turn to bloodshed. We have to look at the bigger picture here. The girl is—"

"The girl is a fucking liability." Uncle Vincenzo gritted out. "I'm sorry, Nicco, I am, but she's going to be our downfall if we're not careful."

I shot up out of my chair. "She is not up for debate."

"She's a dime a dozen, kid. Of all the pussy on Earth, you had to go fall for the fucking Capizola heir."

"Don't you fucking talk about her like that," I ground out, my fists clenched at my sides.

"Niccolò, Vin means no disrespect, do you?"

"Come on, Toni. He's your capo, your son... he knew what he was doing—"

"*Basta*!" My father slammed his fist down on the table. "We did not come here to argue about Arianne. Niccolò has made his choice. She is his woman now. Which means she is as good as family. Besides, she's the only leverage we have right now."

"Fucking unbelievable," I seethed under my breath.

"Watch your mouth, Son. I might be on your side, but your uncle has a point." His brows pinched as he released a strained breath. I knew the responsibility he bore sat heavy on his shoulders. Just as I knew it would one day be mine.

"Roberto is well connected, as is Mike Fascini. We can't just take him out. Not until we know his endgame."

"I think it's pretty obvious what the endgame is, Toni." Vincenzo snorted with disapproval.

"We need more time." My lips thinned as I ran a hand through my hair.

"Time gives him the upper hand, Nicco. We need to strike now, while we have the element of surprise."

"Vincenzo," my father hissed. "This isn't helping. We can't go after Fascini until we know he doesn't have a failsafe. If we take him out, what's to say he doesn't have something set up to take us all down? When we finally cut off the head of his operation, I want to make sure another two don't grow back in its place. I will not risk everything on what ifs and maybes.

"The Marchetti have as much claim on Verona County as the Capizola. I will not bend and I will not run. But I will not rush in all guns blazing to pacify your blood lust."

My uncle's mouth twisted in disgust. I hadn't witnessed my father pull rank often, but whenever he did, it always rubbed my uncle the wrong way. Unlike Uncle Michele who sat quietly. He wasn't a soft touch like Matteo, but he was the calm to Vincenzo's storm.

"So we play their games? We might as well bend over and let them fuck us in the—"

"Vin," Uncle Michele shook his head, gently drumming his fingers on the table. "We take Toni's lead on this. He's right, it's a delicate situation and until we're sure Mike Fascini can be dealt with without kicking up a storm, we should sit tight."

"And the girl?"

"Her name is Arianne," I barked, feeling a lick of fury trickle down my spine. My uncle was pushing me. But what he probably didn't realize was, where Arianne was concerned, I would always push back.

Or maybe he did.

Maybe this was all part of his plan to demonstrate to my father that I was in over my head.

"I need some air," I said.

"Niccolò..." My father let out a resigned sigh. "Go, we'll talk later."

I didn't need telling twice.

I stormed out of there and didn't look back.

"I'd forgotten how fancy this place was." Matteo dropped down onto one of the luxurious gray rattan, egg-shaped chairs.

"It's a far cry from La Riva, that's for sure," I grumbled.

"Yeah, but La Riva is home."

"It is."

"Talk to me, Nic."

"When I saw her last night, all I could think about was taking her far away from here, from Verona County. I wanted to do it." My eyes lifted to his. "I wanted to do it and never look back. What kind of guy does that make me?"

"You love her," he said as if it was the simplest thing in the world.

"Yeah, but I also love Alessia. You and Enzo... Bailey." Running a hand down my face, I let out a frustrated breath.

"I know you do. But it's not the same. You found your person, man. The girl who makes you want more. There's nothing wrong with that."

My eyes narrowed, scrutinizing Matteo. He'd always been different to me and Enzo. Softer around the edges with a big heart. That's not to say he didn't carry out his duties, he did. He understood what it meant to be mafioso. We all did.

"What's going on with you?"

"Me?" His brows knitted.

"Yeah, something's off with you lately." Now that I thought about it, he'd been off since the semester started. But I'd been too distracted by a honey-eyed angel to give it much thought.

Until now.

"Nothing's up." He sat forward, leaning on his fists.

"You can't kid a kidder, Matt. Spill."

"I met someone."

"You met someone? What the fuck? When did you...?" I was confused. Matteo didn't date. None of us did.

At least, I hadn't, pre-Arianne.

"Remember that job we did over the summer, up in Providence?"

"Zander's club?"

He nodded. Zander DiMarco ran a chain of clubs in and around Providence, Verona County, and Pawtucket. Dominion provided him with protection in return for a good chunk of change. We'd been up there over the summer to collect pizzo and the fucker had caused a scene. So much so, my father handed future collections to Uncle Michele and his guys instead.

"I'm not sure I'm following..." I said. It had been weeks ago, and he'd not said a single word about it.

"I stayed in Providence that night. There was a storm, remember?" I nodded, it had been a big one. "Well, I ran into this girl. One thing led to another and we..."

"You hooked up with some girl in Providence and never mentioned it?"

He paled. "It sounds completely stupid, but we had this connection. It was... Nic, it was amazing. But she ghosted me."

"No shit." I rubbed my jaw. "You really liked her?"

"She was... fuck, we just clicked. And the sex, I swear I died and went to Heaven. But I got the impression she wasn't telling me the whole story and you know I wasn't entirely truthful with her."

"So why are you telling me now?"

"Because I guess I thought you'd understand. Because I look at you and Arianne and I want that. I really fucking want that."

"You should call her."

"I already told you, she blocked my number."

"Well then, you should drive up there and go see her."

"Nah, man. I can't..."

"Why the fuck not?"

"It could never work. I'm here, she's in Providence. It was just one night."

But it wasn't. I saw it in his eyes, the slight downturn of his mouth.

Matteo had it bad, and I'd been too self-absorbed to notice.

"I'm sorry."

"You don't have anything to apologize for." He raked a hand through his dirty blond hair. "I didn't tell you and you're not a mind reader. Besides, you've been a little preoccupied."

Still, it didn't ease the guilt snaking through me.

"Look at us." I sank back in the chair.

"Yeah, who'd have thought it." He chuckled but it came out strangled. "I know the Family comes first, Nic... but family is important too. I know Uncle Vin gave you a hard time in there, but it's only because he doesn't get it. He doesn't understand what it's like."

Did Matteo?

Could he?

Most of the time, I didn't even understand what Arianne and I shared.

"I'm not sure he'll ever understand," I admitted.

Matteo gave me a sympathetic nod. "Then I guess, you'll just have to make him."

FOURTEEN

ARIANNE

"TRISTAN?" I rushed to the side of his bed, hardly able to fight the tears pooling in my eyes.

Tristan was awake.

"Hey, Cous," he smiled but it didn't quite reach his eyes.

"I'm so happy you're awake." Grabbing his hand, I squeezed it. "God, Tristan, I—"

"There she is."

My spine stiffened at the sound of Scott's voice. "I didn't realize you were here," I clipped out.

"Don't sweat it, baby." He roped his arm around my shoulder with complete ownership. "We can tell Tristan the good news now you're here."

My cousin frowned.

"Go on," Scott chuckled, "tell him."

I met his insistence with silence. I would never utter those words.

"We're engaged," he practically sang the words.

"Shit, Ari, for real?" Tristan grinned. "I knew he was going to pop the question, but I didn't think—"

"He didn't ask me."

"Say what?" Tristan's brows furrowed as he glanced between me and Scott. "But you just said—"

"Semantics." Scott shrugged. "After the accident things moved a little quicker than we expected. But it'll be official come next weekend."

"What's next weekend?"

"Our engagement party. Isn't that right, babe?"

I glowered at Scott, praying he'd drop the façade for just a second. I was here to see Tristan, nothing more.

"Why do I get the feeling you're not telling me everything?" Tristan's eyes bore into mine until I averted my gaze. I didn't want to do this, not here. Not with Scott right beside me.

Shrugging out of Scott's grip, I took Tristan's hand and squeezed gently. "The important thing is that you're awake."

"I still can't believe I'm out for the season. Senior fucking year." He all but growled the words.

"I'm so sorry," I choked out.

"Yeah, that makes two of us. Marchetti, is he—"

"Gone," Scott rushed out. "Won't show his face in Verona County again anytime soon if he knows what's good for him." I felt Scott drilling holes into the side of my head, but I didn't acknowledge him. I was too busy trying not to fall apart.

"What do you remember about that night?" Scott asked my cousin.

"I don't know, man. It's all a little hazy. The two of you were fighting..."

"He came at me out of nowhere. I was talking to Arianne and he just attacked me."

I smothered a whimper. That's not how it happened at all. Nicco was defending me, he was protecting me. But I knew the truth would only fall on deaf ears so long as Scott was here. He and Tristan were best friends, and there was no love lost between my cousin and Nicco.

"First he breaks your finger and then he comes after me. The guy is a psycho—"

"What did you say?" I finally looked at Scott.

"Which bit?" He smirked.

He knew exactly which bit I was talking about, but he was going to make me repeat myself.

"He broke Tristan's finger?"

"You didn't know?" His smirk twisted into a devious grin. "At the party a few weeks back."

"He really did that?" I asked my cousin who nodded.

"He and his guys grabbed me and dragged me out to the workshop. Fucker took a hammer to my finger." My stomach washed with disbelief.

"He didn't... he wouldn't..."

"It's only what I've been trying to tell you, baby. Niccolò Marchetti is a monster."

"But why would he do that?"

I knew he and Tristan didn't see eye to eye, but breaking his finger? It made no sense.

"Why do you think?" My cousin said coolly. "Because he wanted information. He wanted to know if my cousin, the Capizola heir, was really attending MU." Tristan didn't sound mad this time... he sounded resigned.

I didn't know what to feel.

I knew Nicco wasn't inherently good; he was a mafia prince for God's sake. I'd watched as he'd beaten Scott to a bloody pulp and then lashed out at Tristan in a fit of rage. But underneath the mafioso was someone who was fiercely protective of those he loved, loyal to a fault. So not knowing what he'd previously done to my cousin felt like a betrayal somehow.

"What's wrong, baby?" Scott trailed his fingers down my shoulder. "Finally realized the kind of person Marchetti really is?"

I didn't look at him, but I felt his disapproval, heard the smirk in his words.

"Lay off her, jackass," Tristan said, throwing me a sympathetic glance.

A seed of hope took root in my chest. Maybe my cousin wasn't gone after all.

"I'm so happy you're awake," I said again, as if that erased the awkward conversation of the last few minutes. "Has the doctor said anything about when you might be able to leave the hospital?"

"They need to run a few more tests, keep an eye on my vitals for a couple of days."

"Excellent news," Scott said. "You might be able to make the engagement party."

Suppressing a shudder, my eyes fluttered closed. When I opened them again, Tristan was watching me, his lips pressed into a thin line. I gave him a weak smile, and his gaze narrowed. He sensed something was wrong, but he didn't ask.

"The team is in good hands," Scott launched into an update about the Montague Knights and I let my thoughts drift.

There had been plenty of opportunities for Nicco to tell me about him hurting Tristan.

Yet, he hadn't.

My cousin said it was when Nicco was seeking information on the Capizola heir. He didn't know it was me back then, and I couldn't help but wonder if it would have changed the outcome if he had.

Nicco lived by a code, I knew that. He was groomed for a life I would never understand. But it didn't make me love him any less. Just as him discovering I was the Capizola heir didn't make him love me any less.

Our fate was decided the second I came across him and Bailey in that dark alley.

Nicco saved me that night.

I just hadn't banked on him setting me free too.

"Okay, Tristan." A nurse breezed into the room. "You need to get some rest."

"I guess that's our cue," Scott said. "Take it easy, man, and we'll see you soon." The two of them fist bumped.

Tristan squeezed my hand. "We'll talk soon."

I gave him a small nod. "Bye."

Hurrying from the room, I didn't wait for Scott to escort me. But my attempt to escape was futile. He caught up to me and snagged my hand in his. "Anyone would think you're trying to get away from me."

"I am," I snapped.

"Tut tut, Principessa, you need to learn some respect. I am your fiancé. Your betrothed. Soon enough, I'll be the one in your bed, the one between your legs."

Bile rushed up my throat, making my eyes water. Defiance burned inside me. "I will never be yours," I spat the words at him.

It was a mistake.

Scott tightened his hold on my hand and forcefully marched me into the stairwell. It was quiet in there, even less busy than the hall we'd just left. He pushed me up against the wall, curving his hand around my throat. "Say it again."

"I'll never be yours." My eyes narrowed with hatred.

"You think you get a say in the matter?" Scott leaned in, inhaling deeply, running his nose along the slope of my neck in a way that had me swallowing a fresh wave of tears and vomit.

"I will be inside you again, and you will want it. You will fucking beg me after I'm through with you."

"Get your hands off me," my voice shook, betraying me.

"What are you going to do, baby?" He licked my skin. "Scream? Because you know it'll only get me more—"

The door on the level below opened and voices filled the stairway. I used the moment to shoulder Scott out of the way and keep walking. His dark chuckle rolled off my shoulders, sending a shiver up my spine.

"The clock's ticking, Arianne."

I marched down the stairs and into the hospital foyer. Luis shot up the second he saw me. "Arianne, what is it?"

"Nothing, can we please go?"

He'd stayed down here to give me space. Of course, I hadn't anticipated Scott being here or him being crazy enough to try something in the hospital.

I wouldn't make that mistake again.

"Vitelli, fancy seeing you here." Scott strolled up to us wearing his usual smug smirk.

Luis glared at him before glancing to me. "Are you sure everything is okay?"

"Everything's fine." The words almost choked me.

"We had some things to discuss," Scott said. "But I think she got the message."

It took everything in me not to reply. I swallowed the words. I wanted to fight him, but I had to choose my battles carefully because I would need my armor in the coming weeks.

"Come on." Luis laid a gentle hand on my shoulder. "The car is waiting."

"What, no goodbye?" Scott pouted.

I walked away from him with my head held high. Scott could push me and taunt me, but I wouldn't let him break me.

I wouldn't.

As soon as we were clear of the hospital, Luis grabbed my hand. "What happened?"

"Just Scott being his usual creepy self."

"Did he do something?"

"It doesn't matter." I shrugged him off, fighting the tears threatening to fall.

"Arianne, it matters. If he's—"

"If he's what?" I hissed. "He holds all the cards and he knows it."

"Your father negotiated—"

"My father isn't in control here, they are. So no, I'm not okay. But I have to be. Because if I give Scott so much as an inch, he'll take everything from me, and I can't let him do that again, I won't."

"I won't leave your side again. I knew I should have—"

"Luis, this isn't your fault. We were in the hospital. You weren't to know Scott was here."

"Maybe we need to know."

"What do you mean?"

"Maybe we should start having him tailed."

I rolled my eyes. "If you think that'll help." I didn't, but I could see Luis wanted to do something, anything, to try to fix this.

"I'm going to speak to Roberto again, maybe he can—"

"No, you can't. We can't trust that he won't go to Mike with this, and if he does..." God only knew where that would land me.

My father was not an ally.

He was a pawn.

"I can handle Scott."

"You shouldn't have to deal with that piece of shit."

"You're right, I shouldn't. But what choice do I have?"

Indecision flickered in his eyes and then he leaned in and said, "I want you to carry something."

"What?" I gasped. Surely, I'd heard him wrong.

"Just a switchblade. Something discreet. You have self-defense training. I know your father made you take lessons after the attempt at the school."

"Luis, I'm not sure..."

"I know we need to bide our time, but you shouldn't be around that monster without some way of protecting yourself."

But a knife?

I didn't know what to think about that.

"It's only for self-defense and it would make me feel a damn sight better."

"Fine," I conceded.

"I'll arrange it and spend some time showing you how to—"

"I think I get it." A shudder ripped through me. "Can we go now?" Between my visit with Nicco and then Tristan, I was emotionally spent.

"As you wish." Luis guided me over to the SUV, holding the door as I climbed inside. Scott was still standing there, staring in my direction. His eyes saying a hundred things I didn't want to see.

There was no escape.

No way out.

I was his.

And he fully intended on making me realize that.

It was easy to avoid Scott at school. We shared none of the same classes, and he was a god on campus. Worshipped by the masses, it gave me a break from him while he soaked up their adoration. It should have made me feel a little better.

It didn't.

I was restless.

I missed Nicco. Despite all the questions I had about Tristan. About what happened between them. Then there was the fact I felt like I was waiting.

Waiting for Scott to make his next move.

"Ari?"

"Sorry?" I blinked over at Nora. It was Wednesday and we'd had to concede and eat lunch in the food court because of rain. But we managed to find a seating area away from everyone else. Away from the football team and their groupies.

"I said, what's up with that?" She flicked her head over to where Scott was sitting with his teammates. A girl was looming over them, her hands planted on her hips. Even from a distance, I could tell she was pissed.

"Is that Emilia?"

"Yep," I replied, watching as Emilia jabbed her finger into Scott's face.

"Man, she's really giving him what for."

Scott looked up at her, smirking. Laughter shook his shoulders as she continued her tirade. Emilia stormed off, rubbing at her eyes.

"I've got to go." I grabbed my bag and stood up.

"Go? But we only just got here." Nora stared at me like I'd lost my mind, and maybe I had.

"I'll see you later, okay? Feel free to eat mine." I nodded to my tray of untouched food.

"Should I come?"

"No, it's fine. Luis will be with me." He nodded before I took off across the food court, careful to avoid Scott and his friends.

"Emilia, wait up," I called to her retreating form.

"What?" She stopped, turning on her heel. "Oh, it's you."

"Can we talk?"

"What could we possibly have to say to one another?"

"Please?"

"Fine, five minutes. Come on." She motioned to the pergola beyond the doors. It was one of five dotted around the lawn. The rain beat down on us as we hurried to it. Luis stayed close but didn't follow us underneath the shelter.

"You have four minutes, forty seconds left," she sneered.

"Emilia, please..."

"I love him." She sighed. "I'm in love with him."

"You don't love him." She couldn't. He was a monster.

"How do you know what the hell I feel? He was mine before you came along and—" She smashed her lips together, shaking her head.

"Trust me, I wish things were different. I don't want Scott. I don't want any of this."

Emilia's brows furrowed as she studied me. "He told me you know? Taunted me about your engagement."

My heart skipped a beat. If she knew, others might. *Everyone will know soon enough*. I let out a weary sigh.

"Listen to yourself. Scott isn't a good person, he isn't..." Inhaling deeply, I chose my next words carefully. "Has Scott ever hurt you, Emilia? Made you do something you didn't want?"

"He would never... I love him. We were going to be happy together. We were going to..." Her bottom lip trembled, and I saw the realization in her eyes. Scott had hurt her; she just hadn't separated fantasy from reality yet. Maybe it was her coping mechanism, or maybe it was her way of making sense of everything, or maybe she really did love him.

But it didn't change the fact that Scott was a monster.

"You can do so much better," I said.

"Please." She rolled her eyes, indignation glittering in them. "Next to Tristan, Scott is the most eligible bachelor in MU. And he was mine." Her frown turned to a glower.

"I am not your enemy, Emilia. But I could be your ally."

"What the hell does that mean? You're engaged to him... you're going to be his wife, and you're what? Plotting some crazy revenge plan? I don't need to listen to this. Just stay away from me, okay? I don't know what you think you know, but you're wrong." Emilia started edging toward the steps.

"Just think about it, please."

If there were other girls like me and Emilia, maybe we could go to the authorities. They might be able to cover up one case, but if there were numerous someone would have to take it seriously, wouldn't they?

But my hopes were quickly dashed.

"You can't go up against a family like the Fascini," Emilia said with deep resignation. "You should remember that."

Emilia avoided me after that. The same way I continued to avoid Scott. Thursday morning rolled around, and I was almost able to trick myself into thinking I was just a normal girl living with her best friend and attending classes.

But I wasn't normal.

I was stuck in purgatory.

Living a nightmare.

I spent my time counting down the hours and minutes until my next message off Nicco. Like an addict waiting for their next high, I stalked my cell phone, desperate to hear the ping or feel the familiar vibration.

It was his words, his messages of love, that got me through the days.

It was bittersweet though. I knew I needed to ask him about hurting Tristan, but there was never a right time. He was in Boston, and I was here, and it wasn't a conversation I wanted to have over the phone. I needed to look him in the eyes when I asked him, to see his expression.

Then there was the small matter that with every passing day, it was a step closer to the engagement party. Mom had already sent across three dresses for me to choose from. I was to coordinate with Scott which meant when I had picked a dress, I needed to inform him so he could wear the matching tie.

But informing him meant talking to him. And talking to him meant listening to him. So I'd asked Luis to pass on the message. I could have texted him myself, but it felt like a small victory to defy him.

Until I went into the living room and saw him sitting on our couch.

"If this is what you look like first thing in the morning, I'm going to be a lucky, lucky guy." He openly appraised my body, letting his hungry gaze linger on my bare legs. I was wearing an oversized MU t-shirt that finished mid-thigh.

"What are you doing here?" I wrapped an arm around my waist.

"Is that anyway to greet your fiancé? I just stopped by to bring you something for Saturday. I have extra practice today and a game tomorrow." He got up and stalked toward me. Slow, sure steps, like he owned the apartment and everything in it.

Including me.

Dipping his hand inside his jacket, he pulled out a rectangular shaped jewelry box. He flipped the lid revealing a diamond necklace. It was stunning. A delicate rope of sparkle and elegance.

I instantly hated it.

"It's too much."

"You're my fiancée, Arianne. There's plenty more where this came from." He went to take it from the box, but I laid my hand on his.

"I'll wear it Saturday." If he tried to put that thing on me now, I feared I might break.

"Very well." He snapped the lid shut and placed it on the counter beside me. "You should wear the silver dress."

"How do you—never mind."

He studied me, his sharp gaze searching my face, for what I didn't know. "I know that we didn't get off on the right foot, but it's only because you drive me fucking crazy." Scott reached out, tucking a loose strand of hair behind my ear. "We could be so good together."

My body began to tremble with indignation. Did he really think anything he could say would fix everything?

He was more deluded than I thought.

"You should go," I said, backing away ever so slightly. He was being weird, and it was unnerving.

"Yeah. But wear the diamonds and the dress. I'll see you Saturday."

Dread slithered through me, resting heavy in my stomach.

The seconds ticked by, the silence awkward and suffocating. I half-expected for Scott to make a move, to make some crude comment or try to intimidate me. But he didn't. He let out a long breath before offering me a sharp nod and leaving.

Luis rushed into the room a couple of minutes later to find me standing in the same position. "Arianne, what happened?"

"He was here."

"That sly fucker," he seethed. "I got a call there was a problem in the underground parking lot. He must have called it in to sneak up here. Did he—"

"No. He was... it was weird."

"Weird how?" Luis drew closer.

"He was almost... normal."

He smothered a grunt. "Tell me exactly what he said."

"He bought me this." I handed Luis the jewelry box. "Told me to wear it Saturday with the silver dress."

"That's all he said?"

I nodded.

"This is all a game to him." His jaw clenched. "He wanted to show us he still holds the power. I'm going to increase security here. Make sure he doesn't slip through again."

"Okay," I murmured, still rooted to the spot.

There was something about Scott's visit that bothered me, and I was beginning to think nothing would keep him away from me. He knew every trick, every blind spot.

I could handle the dirty mouthed monster who enjoyed making me cringe and cower. But cool, calm, composed Scott was a different beast entirely.

He was changing the rules. Trying to disarm me.

And I was terrified it was working.

FIFTEEN

NICCO

"HOW ARE YOU?"

Silence filled the line. It was Saturday, the morning of the party. I wanted to call Arianne and reassure her that everything was going to be okay.

I'd wanted to do it all week.

But I couldn't find the words. And maybe I was growing paranoid, but she'd been off with me all week.

We still talked and texted. She told me all about her day and I told her about the monotonous routine of mine. But Arianne was distant, a lingering sadness in her voice I couldn't quite put my finger on.

It was eating me up inside.

Picking on every insecurity I had about our relationship, our future.

She hated Fascini, I didn't doubt that. My sweet Bambolina talked about him with such disdain I didn't once question her feelings toward him.

But *something* had changed.

I couldn't help wonder if it was the physical distance between us. If what we were asking her to do was too much. Luis kept an eye on her and checked in with me. But it wasn't enough. After another week apart, with no light at the end of the tunnel, I was beginning to lose faith.

Maybe Arianne was too.

"Amore mio?" I whispered. "Talk to me."

"I can't believe it's today," she finally replied, easing some of the tightness in my chest. "I lay awake all night wishing things could be different... wishing I was just a normal girl. But my life will never be normal." Her resigned sigh cut me to the bone. My girl was giving up. She was slipping through my fingers and I didn't know what the fuck to do about it.

If I went to her...

I couldn't. My father had given me strict instructions to stay in Boston. He'd given even stricter instructions to Uncle Alonso to make sure I didn't do anything reckless.

He didn't trust me where Arianne was concerned, and maybe he was right.

Because as I clutched the phone in my hand, waiting for Arianne's next words, all I could think about was driving back to Verona County.

"I only want to love you, Bambolina. With all that I am."

"I know," she took a shuddering breath. "And I want to be strong, I do. But I can't help but think tonight will change everything."

Fuck.

This was killing me.

Arianne had crawled into my soul, entwined herself with my DNA. If she hurt, I hurt. If she bled, I bled. If she cried, my soul wept with her.

"There's something else, isn't there?" I asked. "Something you're not telling me."

"How do you...?" She stopped herself.

"Whatever it is, you can tell me." My body shook violently. If Fascini had hurt... no, Luis would have told me.

"Are you having second thoughts... about us?" I barely choked out the words over the lump in my throat.

"What? *No*! It isn't like that. I love you, Nicco. There is no undoing that."

"So what is it, Bambolina? Tell me, please. You have to tell me."

Her silence was deafening.

"Arianne, please..."

"Tristan, he's awake."

"He is?" Relief flooded me. "That's good, isn't it?" I knew Arianne cared for her cousin, and I would never wish to inflict pain on her. So Tristan being awake could only be a good thing.

Yet she didn't sound pleased about it.

"I saw him at the hospital. Scott was there, he said some things... things about you."

My muscles locked up. "What things?" I tried to keep my voice even, but I couldn't disguise the trace of panic.

"I didn't want to talk about this over the phone, but I need to know... Did you hurt Tristan, Nicco? *Before* the accident?"

She knew.

That fucker had told her.

I hadn't purposefully kept it from her. Everything had just happened so fast, and now here we were.

"I should have told you," I said.

"So it's true? You broke his finger."

"It was before I knew the truth about you."

She inhaled a sharp breath. "I see."

"Bambolina, please. You know who I am. What I do."

"There's knowing it, and *knowing* it, Nicco."

"What do you want me to say?" The words came out raw.

This was who I was.

I couldn't change my legacy.

Just as Arianne couldn't change hers.

I was Marchetti. The Family came first. It would always come first unless I decided to walk away and bind us to a life in exile. It would be Emilio Marchetti and Elena Ricci all over again.

"Nothing," she breathed. "There's nothing to say. I just wish I knew. I wish Scott hadn't used the truth against me like that. I felt stupid."

"You're not stupid, Bambolina."

"No?" she seethed. "So tell me why I feel like this? I am sick and tired of having my life dictated to me by men. The only person who seems to understand that is Luis." Arianne laughed but it was bitter and strangled. Nothing like the sweet soft melody that usually spilled from her lips.

"He gave me a knife, you know. I've been practicing with him."

"He what?" My hand curled into a tight fist. Luis had never said a word during our check-ins.

"He said I should be able to protect myself."

"Bambolina, you're safe... I know it doesn't feel like it, but we're not going to let anything happen to you." Even as I said the words, I wasn't sure I believed them anymore.

This wasn't only about Arianne.

It was bigger than her, than me.

Than us.

"You're not here, Nicco." Her ragged words were like a slap to the face. "You don't get to reassure me of my safety when you're not here."

"That's not fair."

"None of this is..."

"Why do I feel like we're having our first fight?"

She let out another sigh. "I should go. I'm meeting my mother and Suzanna Fascini for facials." The lack of emotion in her voice concerned me.

I knew it was taking its toll on Arianne, but she seemed so defeated.

"I love you, Arianne Carmen Lina Capizola. You just need to hold on for a little longer. Can you do that?" *For me?* I swallowed that thought. Arianne was already pissed at me; I didn't want to add fuel to the fire.

But I needed her to fight just a little longer.

"Bambolina, please..." I added.

"I should go. I'll talk to you soon." Arianne hung up without warning.

I let out a guttural roar, launching my phone across the room. Luckily, it missed the wall, landing with a *thud* on the spongy carpet. My cell phone was my only way of keeping in contact with Arianne. If I didn't have that, I had nothing.

Every day spent away from her was another day my soul ached. Another day the ties binding us weakened. I knew enough of this life to know that it required sacrifice. It required men to offer up a piece of their soul, to put the Family above all else.

But most men didn't find a love like ours.

It transcended familial obligation and rational thought. It lived inside me, woven into the very fiber of my being.

I feared if I didn't fight for Arianne; if I couldn't be the guy she deserved, there would be nothing of me left to serve the Family.

Because without her I was not whole.

I spent the day hanging at the house, helping my aunt. She reminded me so much of my mom, her presence brought me an unexpected comfort. Aunt Maria didn't have a housekeeper, she liked to get her hands dirty. But it was more than that, she respected my need for space, letting me help her in comfortable silence or mindless conversation.

When we were done in the kitchen, she came over to me and took my face in her small hands. "Such a good boy, Nicco. Arianne is lucky to have you."

"Is she?" My brows drew together.

"You love her, no?" I nodded. "And you would do anything make her happy? To keep her safe?"

"You know I would."

"Well, then. Stop with the pity party. You are Niccolò Marchetti." She gave me a knowing wink and tapped my cheek. "I think I heard your cell phone vibrating. You should go check it. It could be her."

I'd left it in my room to avoid checking it every five seconds.

Aunt Maria went to leave, but I called out to her at the last second. "Are you happy?"

She stopped and gave me a warm smile. "We get one life, Nicco. Love, family, and good food, what else is there?"

"The other stuff... it doesn't bother you?"

"Of course it does, but I made my choice. Just like Arianne has made hers." Her eyes twinkled with love. "Life is short. Too short to live with regrets." She disappeared into the hall, leaving me with my thoughts.

Taking her advice, I grabbed a beer from the refrigerator and went up to my room. I'd taken the smallest guest room, not wanting to be a burden. It also afforded me my own bathroom and no neighbors.

My cell was flashing, planting a seed of hope in my chest. But it was quickly dashed when I saw Enzo's name.

"Hey," he said. "I've been trying to get a hold of you."

"I was helping Aunt Maria."

"You're turning into a domesticated pussy."

"Fuck off. They were good enough to take me in, the least I could do is help out. What's up?"

"I was just calling to see how you are..." He let the words hang.

"You mean you're calling to check up on me." Irritation rippled through me.

"Uncle Toni is worried; we all are."

"I'm here, aren't I?" I gritted out.

"Yeah, and it's the right thing to do," he hesitated, "I just thought that with it being the party and all, you might..."

"You thought I'd do something stupid like get on my bike and turn up there?"

The thought had crossed my mind. In fact, I'd thought of nothing else all week.

"You need to stay away and let us handle it. Promise me, Cous."

"What would you do? Tell me what you'd do if it was the girl you loved?"

He snorted. "Un-fucking-likely."

"You'll meet her. One day you'll meet the girl who puts you on your ass and I'll be there to watch, loving every second." The words came out bitter. Enzo didn't get it. Just like his old man didn't get it. It was foolish to think otherwise.

"I didn't call to fight, Nicco." He let out a small sigh. "I called because I'm concerned. I know it's hard on you. But Uncle Toni, my dad, and Michele are trying to figure out the best course of action."

"That doesn't involve taking out Mike Fascini?" Bitterness clung to my words.

"You're still pissed over that?"

"I'm pissed that you still don't have my back." I was picking a fight, but I couldn't help myself. I needed the outlet. I needed to get all this shit off my chest and Enzo was the unlucky bastard who was my verbal punching bag.

"That's bullshit and you know it. I have your back. I've always had your fucking back." He spat the words. "But since she came along you can't see straight. The Family comes first. Some piece of ass doesn't change that."

"I didn't ask for this, you know. I didn't go out looking for her. She barged into my life and knocked me on my ass before I even knew what was happening. You think I don't know she complicates everything? You think I don't ask myself every day if it would be easier for the both of us to just let her go?" My voice rose, my chest heaving with the weight of the words.

"Nic, that's not—"

"Loving her is killing me, E. It's fucking killing me. But not loving her, trying to walk away... there'll be nothing left of me to give." I drew in a shaky breath, feeling the weight of my words—the weight of being separated from Arianne—push down on my chest. "She's inside me, man. And I know you don't get it. I know there are so many layers of ice around your heart that you can't put yourself in my shoes and understand... but if I lose Arianne, if we can't find a way to make this work... you might as well drive out here and put a bullet between my eyes. Because she is it for me. There is no life without her. It's that simple."

Silence hung between us. "Fuck, Nicco."

"Yeah," I breathed. "One day you'll understand."

"I wouldn't bet on that. But I'm beginning to get it. I don't understand, maybe I never will. But I get it. I just don't want you to do something you can't come back from. You have to trust your father to get the job done."

"And if he doesn't?" A violent shiver ripped through me.

"He will. He knows what's at stake, maybe better than anyone."

"What's that supposed to mean?"

"He lost your mom. I know things between them weren't always easy, but he loved her. Aunt Lucia was the center of his universe. He wasn't the same after she left."

Enzo was right.

My father wasn't the same after Mom left. But he'd held it together because he had responsibilities. He had a family who needed him, and an organization that looked to him for leadership.

I let out a heavy sigh, the fight ebbing out of my system. "I know things haven't been right between us since Arianne," I said. "But you're my best friend, E. My brother in all the ways that matter."

"Don't go getting all emotional on me. You know I'll always have your back. But I'm not Matteo, Nic. I never will be. I won't always tell you what you want to hear. But I will always give it to you straight."

"And I love you for it."

"Fuck off with that shit. She's turning you into a soft touch."

"Maybe you and Nora should hook up and once this thing with Fascini is over we can all double date." A small smile tugged my lips. The chance to tease Enzo was too hard to resist.

He made some garbled choking sound, and I gave a haughty laugh. "Something tells me she could handle a guy like you."

"No one can handle a guy like me."

He had a point.

"But seriously, Cous, are you okay?"

"I'm not going to do anything stupid, if that's what you mean."

"Just sit tight. We've got tonight covered, and Vitelli will be with your girl. He won't let her out of his sight."

That wasn't the problem, not tonight.

"It should be me," I whispered.

I should have been the one at her side, the one claiming her as mine in front of all those people.

A beat passed and then Enzo let out a long sigh. "Who knows, if everything goes to plan, one day it could be."

SIXTEEN

ARIANNE

"READY?" Luis asked me.

Glancing at myself in the mirror on the wall, I nodded. My hair was braided in a crown atop of my head, soft tousles falling around my face. My eyes were smoky, and my lips were a deep shade of red. The diamonds Scott had given me hung like a noose around my neck. I'd almost decided against wearing them. But in the end, I'd snatched it from the box and asked Luis to fasten it for me.

Tonight, I would play my part. I would hang on his arm like the dutiful, docile fiancée I would never be, and I would do it all wearing a secretive smile.

"As I'll ever be." I grabbed my clutch purse and tucked it under my arm. We were, in fact, all staying at the Gold Star Hotel tonight, but Mike Fascini had insisted Scott and I arrive together in the limousine he had arranged for us.

"You look beautiful, Ari," he said, yanking open the door.

I felt beautiful. The dress wrapped around my body like a silky second skin, kissing the floor as I walked. But the night was already tainted.

We made our way downstairs together, fifteen minutes earlier than planned. I refused to have Scott arrive at the door again with flowers, not when he was offering me something much more sinister.

When we reached the foyer, Luis clutched his sleeve, whispering something into the hidden mic. I was used to his discreet communications now. What had once felt like an intrusion on my life was now something I took for granted.

Luis was my shadow, my guardian angel, and I felt safer knowing he was there.

"Do you think I made a mistake?" I asked him.

He glanced down at me, his brow raised. "It is not for me to tell you how to live your life, Arianne."

"I know." I gave him a polite nod. "But I value your opinion."

"I think..." He hesitated, disapproval swirling in his eyes, but then the corner of his mouth tipped. "I don't blame you for wanting to defy him."

"But you don't think I should poke the beast?"

"You must choose your battles wisely."

A sleek, black limousine pulled up outside the building and Luis crooked his arm. "Shall we?"

I laced my arm with his, letting him lead me outside. The driver stepped from the car and came around to open the back door. Scott stepped out, his eyes instantly going to my dress. "I thought I told you wear the silver one."

"I preferred the emerald."

His eyes burned with indignation. "My parents will be disappointed you chose to disobey me."

"I'm sure they'll get over it," I said.

"I'll be up front." Luis released my arm and waited for me to climb inside. Scott followed, crowding me to the far side of the long leather seat. The car door slammed shut, reverberating through my skull.

"Is this how it's always going to be?" Scott glowered at me. "I ask you to do something and you go out of your way to defy me?"

"I wore the necklace." I flashed him a twisted smile.

"You're feisty, I'll give you that much." Scott toyed with one of the strands of my hair, twisting it around his finger. I had no choice but to lean closer unless I wanted the pinch of pain to worsen.

"I just can't decide if I like it or not." He moved away, surprising me. "Champagne? We are celebrating after all."

"You think I'd ever trust you with my drink again?"

"That was... a means to an end."

Bile clawed my throat. He spoke about it so candidly. So callously. As if that night hadn't been the single most horrific night of my life. I glanced away, giving myself a moment to catch my breath.

"Suit yourself." I heard him pop the cork and pour himself a glass. When I finally lifted my eyes to his again, Scott was watching me.

"What?" I clipped out.

"For as much as I wanted you to wear the silver dress, that looks really fucking good on you." He rubbed his jaw, letting his eyes linger on the low-cut neckline. Then a slow smirk tugged at his mouth. "Good thing I came prepared." Scott leaned over to the counter running along one side of the interior and pulled out a small drawer.

My heart sank at the emerald tie wrapped in his fingers.

"You think I don't know you, Arianne, but I do." His eyes narrowed as he undid his silver tie and replaced it with the one to match my dress.

My eyes closed as I suppressed a shudder. Something was different tonight.

Maybe it was the fact I'd defied him by choosing a different dress or maybe it was the small blade strapped to my right thigh, but despite his attempt to disarm me, I no longer felt weak in his presence.

I felt strong.

Confidence coursed through me. A new sense of strength. Scott had already hurt me in the worst possible way, anything else he tried to throw at me was nothing I couldn't handle.

"I didn't wear it for you."

"No." He leaned in closer again. "But I'm going to pretend you did. I'm going to pretend you picked it out just for me." His fingers painted a trail along my arm, the emerald tie taunting me. "I have something for you. My father wanted me to wait until later, but I want to walk in there with you on my arm and my ring on your finger." His words dripped with possessiveness.

Scott pulled a small ring box out of his jacket and presented it to me. "I had it sized." He flipped the lid and removed it from its pillowed casing.

My hand trembled as he took my hand and gently slid the engagement band over my finger. It felt heavy. Unfamiliar and wrong.

It felt like he was stealing another one of my firsts.

"You're mine now, Principessa." His touch lingered, his gaze dark and hungry. My breath caught, nervous energy zipping through me. Scott was going to try to kiss me; it was there in his piercing gaze.

Thankfully, Luis chose that exact moment to lower the screen. "We're almost here. Your father has confirmed everyone is inside. You'll make your entrance and be seated for the meal."

Like I could possibly eat with the giant knot in my stomach.

"Are you ready?" Scott asked around a sly smile. He was loving every second of this, but I refused to show any sign of fear.

Not tonight.

"I am," I said, steeling myself for the night ahead.

The door opened and Scott climbed out, offering me his hand. I took it, squeezing a little harder than was acceptable. "Nice grip," he teased.

I smoothed my dress out and glanced up at the impressive hotel. There was security posted everywhere. I'd expected it to be well-manned, but I hadn't expected such a show of force.

"Tonight, is going to be a night to remember." His breath was warm on my face. I sidestepped him, narrowing my eyes.

There was something in his inflection. A veiled threat that had alarm bells ringing in my head. But what bombshell could he possibly drop on me that was any worse than his father officially announcing our engagement?

There wasn't.

Which meant Scott was just trying to get under my skin.

I would go to the party, eat and drink, and smile in all the right places. I would stand at his side and let them believe the lie. And then I would retreat to my room where, in the cover of darkness, I would allow myself a moment to break.

This time, when he touched the small of my back and pressed his body up close behind mine, I didn't panic. I simply held my head high, rolled back my shoulders, and took a deep breath.

I could do this.

I would do this.

Because I was Arianne Capizola. I was my father's daughter.

And tonight, I would bow for no one.

The Gold Star Hotel was an opulent place decked out in rich gold and warm beige. But the Michelangelo Suite was the showstopper. A huge room with high ceilings and floor-to-ceiling sash windows, it overlooked a perfectly trimmed lawn leading to a small lake. Two identical crystal chandeliers hung over the round tables. The chairs were wrapped in beige and gold bows and each table had a candelabra centerpiece woven with fresh gold-tinted roses. It was ostentatious. A dinner fit for a king.

And exactly the kind of thing I'd expected.

"You're shaking," Scott said as we stepped into the room. No one paid us much attention at first but then the whispers started.

"There you are." Mike Fascini spotted us and made his way over.

"Son, you're looking very smart, and Arianne..." He gave me the once over before he leaned in to whisper, "My son is a very lucky man. Shall we?"

Mike motioned to the table at the front of the room. I spotted my parents and Suzanna Fascini, and Nora and her date, Dan. It felt like everyone was watching. Maybe they were. I didn't let my gaze waver to check. I kept focused on Nora who was giving me a reassuring smile, her knowing gaze silently saying, 'you've got this'.

"Mio tesoro." My father stood, coming around to greet us. He took my face in his hands, gazing at me with such reverie I felt winded. "You look..." He swallowed hard, almost choking over the words.

It gave me an odd sense of satisfaction to see him so uncomfortable.

That makes two of us, Father. I gently shrugged out of his hold and bypassed him to reach my mother.

"Arianne, mia cara. The dress is perfection on you." She gave me a sly wink and I frowned. Did she know Scott had requested I wear the silver dress?

I got my answer when Suzanna Fascini greeted me. "Arianne, you look amazing. Did the silver dress not fit well?" She cocked a brow.

"I preferred the emerald." I shot her a saccharine smile before taking my seat. Unfortunately, we were seated male, female, male, female, so I wasn't directly next to Nora. But Dan was between us and she wasted no time sliding her hand over his lap to gently squeeze mine.

"Are you okay?" She mouthed, and I nodded.

Scott took his seat beside me just as Mike Fascini took to the stage. He unclipped the mic from its stand. "Good evening, everyone," his voice echoed through the grand room. "It's so endearing to see so many of our friends and colleagues gathered for a night of celebration. But before we get to all that, eat, drink, and enjoy good company. Cheers." He lifted his glass and the room repeated the word back at him.

An army of servers burst from a swing door carrying trays of appetizers, the rich smell of tomato and garlic filling the air.

"Wine?" Scott gently brushed my arm. The knot in my stomach twisted.

I glanced to Nora and she held up her own, reassuring me it was safe.

But I couldn't do it. I couldn't let him pour me a drink.

Laying my hand on Dan's arm, I smiled up at him. "Could you pour me a glass of the red, please?"

"Hmm, sure." His brows knitted as he glanced between me and Scott, who was still holding a bottle.

"Thank you." I lifted my glass toward Scott. "I'm good, thanks."

He snarled, his heavy hand landing on my thigh beneath the table. I went rigid, forcing myself to breathe. "Don't play games with me, not tonight." He whispered out of the side of his mouth.

"Get your hands off me." I pushed him away, resisting the urge to break his finger.

A plate of food was placed in front of me and I thanked the server. It looked delicious. Tomato and basil bruschetta with a balsamic jus. But my appetite was back in my apartment.

"You should eat," Scott said. "We have a long night ahead."

I caught it again. The hint of warning in his voice. The slight inflection of arrogance, as if he knew something I didn't.

Refusing to play his games, I kept my gaze ahead. My mother caught my eye and smiled. She looked stunning in her Italian designer one-shoulder drape gown. It was a deep blue, a perfect match to the sapphire and diamond pendant she wore. Suzanna was in an equally beautiful gown with her hair styled in a complex updo.

At some point during the first course, Scott rested his arm along the back of my chair, his fingers dancing precariously close to my skin. If I sat straighter, putting more space between us, he shifted closer. It was a battle of the wills, neither of us prepared to lose.

"Everything okay with your food, Arianne?" Mike asked across the table. I placed down my silverware and forced a smile. I'd picked at the entrée, moving it around my plate to give the appearance of having eaten some.

"I'm saving myself for dessert."

He chuckled. "You have a sweet tooth? You'll be right at home with Scott then. He's a huge fan of dessert. Growing up he couldn't get enough of Suzanna's cannoli and tiramisu."

Pain lanced my chest. Scott and tiramisu didn't belong in the same sentence together, not when that word reminded me so much of Nicco.

"Arianne, what is it?" My father's baritone voice reverberated through me.

"Nothing." I grabbed my wine glass and drank it down. "I'm fine."

"She's just a little nervous I suspect," Suzanna said. "It's to be expected."

"You need to relax, baby," Scott raised his voice slightly, enough that the nearby tables had to have heard him and roped his arm around my neck. "I've told you, everything is going to be fine."

Everything inside me screamed at him to get his hands off me but I swallowed it down. I couldn't cause a scene, not here. Not in the middle of this godforsaken dinner with Verona County's elite.

Grabbing his hand in mine, I removed it from my neck and placed it back in his lap. "And I've told you, I'm fine."

"You're going to have to watch that one," Mike laughed. "She's feisty."

"Don't I know it," Scott murmured under his breath.

The servers began collecting our plates, giving me a moments reprieve.

"Why don't you go see if you can get us a proper drink?" Nora suggested to Dan.

"But, babe, they have table ser—"

"There's a bar over there."

He finally took the hint and got up. Nora wasted no time sliding into her date's empty chair. "Are you okay?" she whispered.

My eyes flicked to my parents and the Fascini. They were deep in conversation and Scott was busy texting someone.

"I'm fine."

"It would be okay if you're not. It's kind of intense."

"I'll be okay. I bet Dan thinks he's entered The Twilight Zone." I let out a quiet sigh.

"After the Centenary Gala I think he knows the score where your dad is concerned."

"Abato," Scott leaned around me. "So nice of you to join us."

"I was invited, asshole," she sneered.

"Yeah, because I suggested it."

"You? Un-fucking-likely."

"Truth." His shoulders lifted in a small shrug. "I didn't want Arianne to feel out of her depth."

"How very thoughtful of you," I mocked, fighting the urge to roll my eyes.

"Fuck this, I'm going to take a piss." He got up and strolled away from the table.

"God, he's a vile asshole."

"Tell me about it. He's trying so hard to push my buttons."

Nora grabbed my hand. "And you're doing so well not rising to him. Nice little dig with the dress by the way. How'd he take it?"

"Tried to pretend he didn't mind, but it irritated him."

"Good, he deserves it, trying to tell you what to wear. Who the hell does he think he is?"

"My fiancé apparently." Bitterness clung to every syllable.

Her expression fell. "Shit, Ari, I'm sorry."

"Don't be. I'll never marry him. I'd rather—" I stopped myself.

"Don't ever say that," she gasped, concern glittering in her eyes. "It won't come to that," she whispered the next words. "Nicco would never allow it."

My breath hitched at the mention of his name and she frowned. "What is it?"

"We had an argument earlier. I said some things..."

"What things?"

"It doesn't matter." It did. But I didn't want to relive the conversation. I'd been frustrated and hurting, and I'd taken it out on him.

"Are you—"

Dan chose that moment to return, looming down over us. "I got us doubles; something tells me we're going to need it."

"My kind of guy." Nora shuffled back to her own seat and accepted the drink from him.

"I didn't get you anything, Ari, sorry, I didn't—"

"It's okay." For as much as a strong drink would no doubt settle some of my nerves, I couldn't afford to drop the ball.

Not tonight.

SEVENTEEN

NICCO

I COULDN'T DO IT.

I couldn't sit in my uncle's house knowing that she was at some flashy hotel being paraded around as his fiancée.

After our heated conversation this morning, I'd tried texting her. I'd even called again, but Arianne was freezing me out. It hurt. It hurt so fucking much that when I stormed out of the house and fired up my bike, I told myself I wouldn't go there. Told myself that I just needed to ride and clear my head. But before I knew it, the roads grew familiar... until I was in Roccaforte, the Gold Star Hotel looming in the distance like a neon fucking sign put there to taunt me.

She was in there with him.

My Arianne.

My strong, brave Arianne.

I found somewhere to park and threw my leg over the bike and just stood there. Staring at the place like it was a mirage in a scorched desert. You knew you shouldn't... but you just couldn't help yourself fall for the illusion.

It was a bad decision.

A moment of weakness that could land me in a whole heap of trouble.

But in that moment, I didn't care.

I didn't care I was defying my father's direct order, risking everything just to be near her.

Before I could stop myself, I started towards the hotel, keeping to the shadows. My hooded jacket afforded me some disguise, but I knew Roberto and Fascini's security guys would have been told to keep an eye out for any signs of me or my guys.

Part of me wondered if Fascini was banking on me showing up. That maybe this was all an intricate trap laid to ensnare me, and I was walking willingly into it.

But I had to see Arianne.

After our fight this morning, I needed to see her. I needed to look her in the eyes and know we were okay, that we could survive this.

As I drew closer to the Gold Star, I pressed closer to the rows of storefronts, careful not to draw too much attention to myself. It was heavily guarded, numerous security men posted on the entrance and beyond the glass doors. There was no way I was walking through the front door, but I knew there were multiple entrances. The hotel overlooked vast lawns that ran down to a private lake, that was my best option. It would give me a perfect vantage point of the Michelangelo Suite. I could watch, I could make sure she was okay, and then I could slip away like a ghost.

It shouldn't have been so easy. I'd walked right into the gardens, scaled a wall, and found the perfect place to watch from.

It all seemed very dull; dinner followed dessert. I could just make out Arianne as she sat quietly wedged between Fascini and Nora's date. There were security guys posted at every window, and the door was heavily guarded. But I wasn't going inside. Watching was enough.

At least, that's what I kept telling myself.

A crunch sounded behind me and I shot up, glancing around. My eyes strained against the darkness, my heart thudding against my ribcage. If anyone caught me out here—

"Enzo?" I frowned.

"You couldn't just do as you were fucking told, could you?"

"How did you...?"

"I know you, Nic. I knew you wouldn't be able to stay away. Just took me a while to find you."

"I had to come."

"You shouldn't have."

"I know." I looked back at the hotel. People had begun moving around while the servers worked quickly to clear away empty plates and dirty glasses. Arianne and Nora were huddled close. God, she looked fucking amazing. The emerald green dress accentuated her soft curves to perfection.

A low growl formed in my throat as I watched Scott loop his arm around her waist and guide her toward a group of people as if he owned her.

"Easy, Cous." Enzo's hand clamped down on my shoulder. "You need to relax."

"Relax?" I snapped. "She's in there with another guy. The same guy who..." The words soured on my tongue as I swallowed them down.

"I know but you need to keep your head. You shouldn't be here. If anyone were to see you that would be a shitshow of epic proportions. She's okay. You can see that. It sucks, I know it does. But she's okay."

She looked okay, smiling to the group as Scott made introductions. His hand remained possessively on her waist. I wanted to tear it from his body and beat him with it.

I wanted to watch that fucker bleed out and beg for his life. The need to hurt him never went away, it lingered under the surface. A sleeping beast waiting for its moment to strike.

"You need to go." His grip tightened, trying to guide me away from the cover of the large white oak tree. But I couldn't look away. Mike Fascini and his wife joined them, laughing and joking like they were old friends.

Like they were family.

The thought gutted me.

"Nicco, you need to—"

"I need to see her," I rushed out, slipping out of his hold, and taking a step forward. But Enzo grabbed me from behind and yanked me backward.

"What the fuck are you thinking?"

I spun around and met his thunderous expression. "I can't just stand by. It's killing me."

"Now is not the time. You're already risking everything by being here."

"I need to see her."

"Nicco, listen to me." He gave me a pointed look. "You need to get on your bike and get the fuck back to Boston before Fascini realizes you're here."

"No, I need to see her."

"Porca miseria!" he grumbled. "It's not like I can walk in there and get her out here."

"No, but Nora or Luis might be able to help." I dug out my cell and thrust it at him.

"You're serious?" His eyes bugged, glittering with disapproval.

"I just need five minutes." It would never be enough, but it would settle my soul until the next time I saw her.

"You've fucking lost your mind."

I didn't deny it.

I felt unstable.

Lost.

Like I was drowning in dark angry waters, being pulled under by the riptide.

"Wait here." Enzo glared at me. "I mean it, Nicco. You don't move a fucking muscle. If Vitelli says it's a no go, it's a no go. Do you hear me?"

All I could manage was a tight nod. I was too busy overanalyzing Arianne's every move. The way she stood close but not too close to Fascini. The smile that didn't quite reach her eyes.

Enzo gave me one last look before ducking out of the tree line. I wanted to go after him, to be the one calling Nora or Luis, and going to Arianne. But despite my evident lack of restraint, I didn't have an immediate death wish.

The minutes ticked by painfully slowly as I waited. People had begun to sit again as the servers went from table to table refilling glasses. I'd lost sight of Arianne.

Nervous energy vibrated through me as I rocked on the balls of my feet, desperate to see any sign of her.

But she didn't appear.

Enzo did.

"We need to move, now," he barked, beckoning me from the shadows.

I jogged over to him, following him around the side of the building to a small terrace area.

"Five minutes," he said. "I mean it, Nic. A second longer and I'll personally drag you from this place and kick your ass all the way back to Boston."

"You couldn't take me," I quipped back.

"Don't push me," he growled.

A door opened and Luis appeared. He shot me an irritated look. Apparently, Enzo wasn't the only one pissed at me. But none of it mattered when Arianne appeared.

"Bambolina." I rushed over to her, running my eyes over every inch of her body. "Thank fuck."

"Nicco," she sighed. "What are you doing here?"

"I had to see you. I had to know you're okay."

"You can't be here."

"Ssh." I brushed the hair from her face, moving in closer until I could smell the sweet notes of her perfume.

"Nicco." She fisted my jacket. "You shouldn't have come here."

My eyes snapped open, my brows pinched with confusion. "What do you—"

"It's not safe. If anyone were to see you..."

"They won't. After our conversation this morning... I couldn't just leave things like that." I ran my nose along Arianne's cheek, breathing her in. She shivered at my touch and the possessive part of me rejoiced at knowing I still affected her so viscerally.

I wound one hand around her neck, holding her against me. "You look so beautiful, Bambolina. I saw you... with him. Talking to his parents."

"I'm playing a part, Nicco. That's all this is." She stepped back but I snagged her hand, noticing the glint of light hit her finger.

"Is that... Fuck." I breathed through my nose, trying to rein in the tsunami of emotion crashing over me.

She was wearing a ring.

A huge diamond engagement ring.

His ring.

I was going to puke.

"Nicco, it's just for show." Arianne was the one clutching me now, her wild eyes pleading with me to calm down.

"He put his fucking ring on you?" A chill ran through me.

"Ssh," she moved closer, crowding me against the wall. "Don't do this, please. Not here, not now. It's all for show. An act. You knew what tonight was about."

"Did he get down on one knee and profess his love for you?" I sneered.

Arianne blanched, jerking back as if my words had slapped her in the face. "That isn't fair, and you know it."

"Shit, I'm sorry. I just... it blindsided me, okay. I hate knowing he's in there with his hands all over you."

"I don't exactly enjoy it." Tears pricked the corner of her eyes but my strong Bambolina forced them down.

"I know. Come here." I looped my arms around her waist and dropped my chin on her head. "You really do look beautiful, Bambolina. And I'm sorry you're having to do this. All of it."

"All I keep thinking is he's stolen another of my firsts... and I hate him so much for it."

I eased back to look at her, my spine rigid.

"You should go." She smiled weakly.

"How am I supposed to let you go back in there?"

"You just do." Arianne gave me a small shrug. She took another step back, our hands lingering between us.

"He can have your firsts," I said quietly, "but your forever... that belongs to me."

Arianne hesitated before throwing herself at me. I caught her and stumbled back with her in my arms.

"Kiss me," she breathed. "Kiss me like it's your ring I'm wearing."

Our lips met in an urgent collision of tongues and teeth. Arianne poured all her pain and frustration into every stroke and I greedily welcomed it. Her body fit against mine and our hands roamed and explored as we fell headfirst into the kiss.

I wanted forever with her.

I wanted the fairytale.

I might have been a mafia king-in-waiting, but I was nothing without my queen. And I didn't want to rule if I couldn't have her by my side.

It was that simple.

By the time I pulled away, Arianne was flushed, and her lips were swollen. Desire shone in her eyes and she looked ravished. But I couldn't find it in me to care. Because when she went back inside, when she went back to that fucker, she would be able to taste me.

And she would know exactly who she belonged to.

"Happy now?" Enzo gave me a hard shove toward my bike. "That was a close call."

"Yeah, yeah, save it for somebody who cares."

"That's just it though, Cous. You should fucking care. And I'm not talking about just the Family. What do you think that would have done to Ari tonight if Fascini's guys had found you? You're not thinking straight."

"She's wearing his ring, E." I scrubbed my jaw in frustration. "Am I supposed to just pretend this isn't happening?"

"You're supposed to trust your old man to get the job done."

My lips thinned. He had a point, and I hated it.

"Look, it's done." He let out a heavy sigh. "You saw her. Now you need to leave and stay your ass in Boston."

"Will you tell him?"

"What do you think?" He gave me a pointed look. "As long as you promise not to pull this shit again it stays between us, okay?"

"Thanks, I appreciate it."

"I know you think I don't get it, and maybe I don't, but I know you, Nicco. Nothing will ever change that."

I climbed on my bike, pulling on my helmet.

"Go straight home."

I nodded. I didn't want to lie to him, but there was somewhere else I needed to go first, and I knew he wouldn't agree.

"Did you get a glance of Nora tonight?" I asked, changing the subject. "She looked smokin' hot." I'd seen her through the window.

"Fuck you," he gritted out.

Laughter rumbled in my chest as I kicked the starter and gave him a nod before pulling into the street. The ride to County Memorial was only ten minutes. It was exactly what I needed to clear my head after seeing the ring on Arianne's finger.

I still couldn't believe it. It made perfect sense, they were engaged after all, but my mind couldn't make sense of it. Probably because my soul had already claimed her as his. So to see another guy lay claim to her went against everything I felt.

By the time I pulled into the hospital parking lot, the weight on my chest had eased a little. Arianne was mine. Something as materialistic as a ring didn't change that. But she'd looked so right standing at that fuck's side, his parents smiling at them like everything about the situation made sense.

I climbed off my bike and hung the helmet on the handlebars. This was another bad idea, but I needed to see Tristan.

Enzo was right, Arianne was changing me. Things that shouldn't have mattered before, did now. Like looking into the eyes of a guy I almost killed and asking for forgiveness.

The parking lot was empty as I crossed over to the main entrance. County Memorial was lit up against the inky backdrop, a sign that hospitals never slept.

But I found the place quiet inside. Still, they probably didn't take too kindly to random people walking the halls at night.

Taking the stairwell to the second floor, I checked the hall before ducking out of the door. I knew Tristan was up there, but I didn't know where. The nurses station loomed up ahead, manned by a lone woman. I waited a few minutes, hoping she would be called away.

When she finally got up and disappeared down the hall, I took my chance, jogging up to the station and checking the huge whiteboard.

"Gotcha," I whispered, making a mental note of Tristan's room number. It was only a couple of doors behind me.

I'd half-expected there to be security, but the hall was empty. Pressing my face against the glass, I glanced inside, and sure enough, Tristan lay sleeping soundly.

Guilt flashed through me. I'd done this. I'd put him here. But he was okay.

He was going to be okay.

I grabbed the handle and gently opened the door. It barely made a sound as I slipped inside. Moonlight streamed through the blinds, casting shadows off the walls, illuminating Tristan's profile. I stuck to the corner of the room, hiding in the darkness.

I wasn't supposed to be here. But I needed to fix things.

I needed him to know I never meant to hurt him that night when I'd snapped. Now I was standing here though, I didn't know what the fuck to say.

So I started with the truth.

"I didn't mean to fall in love with her," I said to the silence. "It just happened. It wasn't some grand plan to mess with your family. She wasn't a game, never to me. I just took one look at her that night and something snapped into place."

I let my head fall back against the wall as I inhaled a ragged breath. It was late. Mike Fascini had probably made the announcement. The engagement was probably official.

Pain squeezed my heart like a vise.

"She wouldn't want me to tell you this, but you should know. As the person who is like a brother to her, you should know that he raped her. The night of the Centenary Gala, he slipped something in her drink and raped her." Tears burned the backs of my eyes. "And now she's there, at the party with him. Your uncle and his father are parading them around like a happy couple... it's messed up. This whole fucking thing is messed up.

"We weren't ever supposed to be enemies, you know." I let out a long breath. "We were supposed to be family. If history had played out the way it was supposed to, we wouldn't even be here."

Tristan shifted in his sleep, the rustle of stiff linen piercing the silence. I froze, holding my breath until he settled.

"I shouldn't be here. I don't know why I came... but everything is different now. All I want is to protect her. To put an end to all of this. But I don't know how. I don't know how to save her."

I inched closer, staring down at him. "I never meant to hurt you that night. I didn't even realize it was you until it was too late. If Arianne is going to survive this thing with Fascini she's going to need all the allies she can get. So I guess I'm not only here to apologize, I'm here to beg you to do right by her. To step up and be the cousin she needs you to be. And to promise me that if something happens to me, you'll be there to look out for her."

I was met with nothing but silence.

This was stupid.

Tristan was out cold, and I might as well have been talking to a corpse. But it wasn't like I could wake him. He'd take one look at me standing in his hospital room and call for security.

Defeated, I headed for the door. My fingers wrapped around the handle and pulled gently just as a whisper carried in the air.

"You have my word."

I glanced back, expecting to find Tristan glaring at me. But he wasn't.

And maybe I really was losing my mind.

EIGHTEEN

ARIANNE

"SO… WHAT DID HE SAY?" Nora whispered as we made our way back to our seats.

"Not here." I smiled, trying to give the illusion of everything being fine.

Everything was not fine.

Nicco was here.

Or, at least, he had been.

I hoped he was far away now, out of the reach of my father's and Mike Fascini's men.

He shouldn't have come.

Yet my heart was so relieved to see him standing there on that terrace.

"There you are." Scott rose from his chair and pulled mine back slightly. "You almost missed the most important part of the night." He smirked.

It was late and I was tired.

Tired of keeping up pretenses and putting on a smile.

All I wanted was to retire to my room, lock the door, and wash the games and fakeness off my skin. But first, Mike had to make his grand speech.

He was already on the stage, microphone in hand, a glass of champagne on the shaker table beside him. The servers were busy moving from table to table, replacing wine glasses with flutes, filling them with Dom Perignon for the toast.

Once we were all in our seats, Mike gave our table a nod and the room ushered into thick silence. "Some of you may be unaware but I have roots in Verona County. My family was here in the beginning and they will be here as we move into a new future. A prosperous future full of opportunity and growth. Together, with Capizola Holdings, Fascini and Associates will become a household name in the redevelopment of our great county. Get up here, Roberto." He beckoned for my father to join him.

He kissed my mother on the cheek, the two of them sharing a long, lingering look.

What was I missing?

The pieces of the puzzle were right there in front of me, but I still couldn't see them all.

My father climbed the steps to the stage and shook Mike's hand.

"I invited you all here tonight," he went on, "to celebrate the partnership between our two great families. But some of you may have noticed by now, that it isn't the only thing we're celebrating." His eyes found mine, dark and full of wicked intent. "My son, Scott, has asked Arianne Capizola for her hand in marriage and she said yes."

A low rumble of whispers trickled around the room. "This union will not only cement our business relationship, but it will unite our families. So I'd like you all to raise your glasses and toast the happy couple with me. To Scott and Arianne."

The words reverberated through my skull as Scott slipped his arm around me and pulled me close. "You're mine now, Principessa," he breathed, his words sending a violent shiver skittering up my spine.

"Before we continue with the celebrations, I would just like to say to you, Arianne, we look forward to officially welcoming you to our family. I don't know about Roberto, but I can't think of a better way to celebrate Thanksgiving than watching our children take their vows. Now please, the night is still young, and the drinks are still flowing. I hope to see you all up on the dance floor before we say goodnight."

Applause and cheers filled the room as the light dimmed. But I didn't move.

I couldn't.

Scott's eyes drilled into the side of my face as Nora cussed under her breath.

Thanksgiving.

He'd said Thanksgiving.

That was only weeks away.

"You knew." My gaze slid to Scott.

He wore an arrogant smirk. "I told you tonight was going to be special."

I shoved my chair back with such force, it almost toppled over.

"Arianne, sweetheart?" The color drained from Mom's face.

"I'm fine." The band around my chest tightened, stealing the air from my lungs. "I just need to freshen up."

I marched out of there with my head held high, nodding and smiling at the wave of congratulations offered from faceless guests.

I could barely breathe, let alone engage in conversation.

Thanksgiving.

"Arianne, wait up." Nora caught up with me just as I stepped out into the hall, but I didn't stop. "Wait, just wait." She snagged my wrist and I conceded.

"Thanksgiving," I hissed.

"They really know how to ruin a girl's night, huh?"

"I need you to do me a favor."

"Anything..."

"I need you to go back in there and cover for me."

"Ari..." Her lips pursed.

"I'm only going up to my room. I need some space."

"You're sure?"

"Yeah, Luis will be with me." I glanced over at him and he nodded.

"Here," she handed me my clutch purse, "you forgot this."

"Thank you."

Nora pulled me in for a hug. "I know this is another blow, but it's just a game. They're just trying to keep the upper hand."

Nodding stiffly, I took a deep breath and met her eyes. "You should go before anyone comes looking."

"Okay, and for what it's worth, I'm so fucking sorry." She hurried back inside leaving me with Luis.

He came toward me, his brows drawn with concern. "They know," he said.

"So it would seem." We walked over to the elevator and waited.

"I'll let the Marchetti know."

I nodded. The doors pinged open and we stepped inside.

"It's a kink in the road but it doesn't change anything."

I released an exasperated breath. "I'm going to my room. I don't want you to let anyone inside, okay?"

"Arianne, maybe I—"

"Please, Luis. I need this."

"Very well," he said around a tight expression. "I'll make sure you have your space."

Good.

For the first time since all this happened, I felt out of control. Wild. I felt like a caged animal pushed to its limit.

And I was terrified that if I found myself cornered, I would do something reckless.

Something I couldn't undo.

My suite in the hotel looked like a storm had blown through it.

The second the door had closed behind me, I had unleashed all my anger and frustration. Clothes lay scattered around the floor; my dress was in a crinkled heap on the bed and the pillow was stained with mascara and tears.

But I felt better.

I felt calmer somehow.

True to his word, Luis had kept any potential visitors at bay. Nora had texted me to say the party was in full swing, detracting from my absence. Everyone thought I was sick.

But Scott and my family knew the truth. And they afforded me a moment to myself. I guess I should have been grateful, but it was the least they could do given the bombshell Mike had dropped tonight.

Thanksgiving.

They wanted me to marry the man who had raped me, stolen my innocence, and hurt me in inexcusable ways, in less than two months' time.

Luis was right. The likely explanation for the sudden change in plans was that Mike Fascini knew that Nicco and his father had discovered the truth about Elena Ricci.

I grabbed the glass off the nightstand and threw it across the room, the sound of my screams piercing the silence. It hit the wall, shattering into a thousand pieces.

"Arianne?" A knock sounded on the door.

"I'm fine, Luis. I just... I broke a glass."

"Maybe I should—"

"I said I'm fine," I yelled.

He didn't reply.

Pulling a pillow into my chest, I curled into a ball and laid down. I wanted to be stronger, to be down there putting on a brave face. But I was scared that if I did, and Scott said something to me, I would snap.

In here, I was safe.

They were safe from me.

Because I felt different. Dark volatile energy coursed through me, making my skin vibrate and my body hum.

I wanted to hurt him.

I wanted to hurt his father.

I wanted to make them both pay for what they'd taken from me. What they continued to take.

The last thought I had was of Scott on his knees, begging me for forgiveness, begging me for his life, before everything went black.

I woke startled.

Fear wrapped around me as I lay frozen on the bed. "Luis?" I called out.

Where was I?

It all came rushing back like a tidal wave.

The party.

Mike's announcement.

Me fleeing to my hotel room.

I lay listening for any sound but there was nothing.

Sitting up, I pushed the wild curls from my eyes. I was a mess. Dressed only in my underwear, my hair all over the place, and no doubt with makeup streaked down my face, I was thankful I couldn't see my reflection in the darkness.

Swinging my legs over the edge of the bed, I fumbled to find my cell phone. It was almost two-thirty. The party would be over by now, guests sleeping peacefully in their expensive suites. Nora would be with Dan, curled up in his arms. Dropping my cell back on the nightstand, I reached for the lamp switch but a noise in the corner of the room caught my attention. My eyes strained, my heart beating furiously in my chest.

"What did I tell you, baby?" Scott's voice had me paralyzed. He leaned forward, appearing from the black abyss like the Devil himself. "If you push, I will always push harder."

I flicked on the light, and my eyes widened at the sight of the gun in his hand.

"What are you doing here, Scott? Where's Luis?"

"He's around."

Bile rushed up my throat as I choked out, "You shouldn't be here."

"Like Marchetti shouldn't have been here earlier? Like he shouldn't have been snooping around in Vermont?" He got up and stalked toward me, rubbing the pistol against his head like it was a comb. "I don't know how many times I have to say this but you. Are. Mine."

I pulled my legs up, shuffling back onto the bed but Scott was quicker. His hand shot out, grabbing my ankle and yanking me toward him.

"Don't, please..." I couldn't let this happen, not again. "My father will—"

"You think your old man gets a say in any of this? I am untouchable. My father has enough lawyers and cops in his pocket to protect me. I could fuck you right here and cut you up into tiny little pieces and no one would do a thing about it."

Waves of nausea rolled through me.

"You're mine, Arianne." He leaned down, running his hands up my bare thighs, the overpowering stench of liquor on his breath. "Look at you, all laid out like this. Anyone would think you were waiting for me. Waiting for your fiancé to come and dirty you up."

My hand *cracked* against his cheek, and Scott staggered back. "Fucking bitch." He grabbed me by the hair, pain shooting through my skull, and threw me down on the floor. I tried to crawl away from him, but it was futile.

Scott rounded me like a predator stalking its prey. "You look good on your knees." He waved the pistol in the air, pointing it at me. "I think we should have a little fun, don't you?"

"Fuck you," I seethed.

I wasn't going to beg for mercy.

Maybe if I made him mad enough, he would shoot me and end this sick game I wanted no part of.

"Hmm," he chuckled darkly. "Kitty grew claws." He shot forward, pressing the gun to my forehead. "Move."

My body shook, silent tears streaming down my face. I didn't want to die. But I didn't want to be his toy, not again.

He kept the gun trained on me as he sat back in the chair, fumbling with his belt. His zipper went next and then he pulled his erection free, stroking himself roughly.

I dry heaved into my hand.

"You get me so hard, Principessa. You have no idea of the things I want to do to you."

"If you touch me, Nicco will kill you."

He stopped, his eyes darkening to two obsidian slits. "Marchetti is a dead man walking. In fact, I think I might serve up his head on a silver platter for you as a wedding gift. Would you like that?"

"You're nothing but a monster."

Scott slid off the chair, dropping to his knees. His erection brushed my stomach and I retched again, But then he grabbed my throat, cutting off my airway.

He pressed the gun to my lips. "Suck it."

I smashed them together, determined not to let him break me.

But he squeezed my windpipe harder forcing me to gasp for breath. Using my desperation to his advantage, he shoved the barrel of the pistol into my mouth. He was pleasuring himself. Moving the pistol in and out as he jerked himself off. All while silent hot tears streamed down my face.

I didn't understand what had happened to make him this way.

He wasn't only a monster.

He was depraved.

Grabbing my hand, he pushed it to his hard length, making me topple slightly, forcing the pistol further between my lips until I couldn't breathe.

"Fuck yeah," he groaned, thrusting his hips wildly.

He yanked the pistol free, grabbing my hair again and forcing my head down to his crotch. I sucked in big greedy lungfuls of air.

"You're going to put those pretty lips around me and suck."

I thrashed against him but then the click of the safety pierced the air and I froze.

"Do it."

I was on all fours, his hand forcing my head in place. Frantically, I searched the floor for something, *anything*, I could use to hurt him.

Then I felt it.

The soft leather knife holster Luis had given me. It was empty, the knife must have scattered when I'd thrown it.

"I'll count to five, Arianne. Don't make me get to zero, because you won't like what happens."

Oh God.

My eyes burned as I held myself in place, desperately trying to pat the floor for the knife without giving myself away.

"Five... four... three..." I couldn't find it, my fingers meeting nothing but soft carpet. "Two..." I stretched my hand further, praying to some higher power to help me.

"On—"

My fingertips met the smooth hilt of knife.

"Time's up." He almost sounded disappointed.

"Wait," I said, lifting my head slowly. Scott narrowed his eyes. "Not like this, please..."

His brow quirked up. If he glanced down to the left, he would see my hand, see me trying to reach for the knife.

"Sit in the chair," I said trying my best to hide the quiver to my voice.

"Okay," he said, "I'll play. But you'd better fucking make it worth my while."

Scott lifted himself into the chair, keeping his legs wide, his hand wrapped proudly around his length.

Everything about him made my skin crawl.

But there was no other way.

I scooched forward on my knees, sliding one hand up his thigh letting it drift precariously close to his erection. Scott groaned, sinking back in the chair. It was enough for me to grab the blade.

His hand went to my hair, yanking me closer. "Now, Arianne. I won't ask—"

I slammed the knife into his thigh. Scott let out a grunt of pain. "You fucking bitch." He shot forward to lunge for me, but I collapsed back out of his reach, grabbing the first thing I could find and swinging it at him.

The lamp crashed against Scott's head with a sickening *thud*. Scott groaned, falling back into the chair, blood trickling from the cut above his eye.

Clambering to my feet, I grabbed my phone and a hotel robe, wrapping the soft fluffy material around my body, and I ran from the room.

"Arianne?" Luis looked gutted as he appeared around the corner of the hall, flushed and breathless.

"We need to go, now."

"What did you do?" He glanced to my room.

"I... the knife..."

"Is he dead?"

I shook my head. Luis hesitated; his eyes fixed on the door. I knew what he was thinking. It was the same thing I was thinking. It would be so easy to go back in there and finish the job.

"He has a gun," I whispered, my body racked with fear.

"Shit, okay. Come on, we should get you out of here. I'll radio for some of our guys to deal with him."

Luis wrapped his arm around me and led me down the hall. We didn't take the elevator, slipping into the stairwell instead.

"What happened?" he asked as we hurried down the stairs.

"I woke up and he was there, in my room. I asked where you were and—"

"I heard something in the stairwell, so I went to check it out." His jaw clenched. "He got the jump on me and knocked me out."

"He had a gun and tried to..." I swallowed a fresh wave of tears. "I found the knife you gave me and stabbed him. I couldn't let him do that to me again. I just couldn't."

"You did the right thing." Luis glanced down at me. "But you know what this means?"

"I can't go back." I trembled.

"No, you can't." He pulled his cell from his pocket and typed out a text. It pinged two seconds later, and he read the message. "Okay, come on. Keep your head down and don't stop for anyone, okay?"

Luis opened the door and checked the coast was clear before beckoning for me to join him. We weren't in the main foyer; it was a side entrance used for guests only. Luis fished a keycard out of his pocket and pressed it against the keypad. The door clicked open and we exited onto the street. A car pulled up alongside us and someone climbed out.

"Enzo?" I blinked sure my eyes were deceiving me.

"We need to go, now." He and Luis shared a concerned look.

"Go, Enzo will keep you safe."

"Wait." Panic rose in my voice. "You're not coming with us?"

"I need to go back and make sure he doesn't do anything stupid. Consider it damage control."

"But he has a gun..."

"Vitelli can handle himself." Enzo wrapped an arm around my shoulder and guided me toward the car. The gesture was so unlike him, I didn't resist.

"I'll see you soon, okay?" Luis offered me a warm smile, but it didn't reach his eyes.

Everything had changed tonight.

And it was all my fault.

"I'm sorry I couldn't do it," I called over my shoulder.

He frowned. "It's okay, we always knew it might come to this."

I had no idea what he meant, but Enzo didn't give me chance to ask. He pushed me into the car and slammed the door, going around to the driver's side.

Enzo climbed in. "You okay?" he asked coolly.

"Not really." I leaned my head against the cool glass, trying to make sense of the last few hours. "But I will be."

What other choice did I have?

NINETEEN

NICCO

MY EYES SNAPPED OPEN, the blare of my cell phone like a siren in the night. "What the hell?" I mumbled, trying to locate it. "Yeah?"

"Nicco?" Enzo sounded distant.

I shot upright. "What happened?"

"It's Ari, she's... fuck, man. It's messed up."

"Is she okay?" A bolt of fear shot through me, my hands trembling as I gripped the phone tighter.

"She's okay. I brought her out to the cabin."

"Okay, I'm on my way."

"Be careful." He inhaled a ragged breath. "Fascini knew you were at the hotel, so there's every chance he's watching your movements. If you're being tailed, you can't lead them here."

He was right.

The cabin was off the grid. A family hideaway few people knew about.

"I'll take precautions." My words shook. "Can I talk to her?"

"She's sleeping."

"Okay, I'll see you soon." I inhaled a ragged breath. "And E?"

"Yeah?"

"Thank you."

After waking my uncle and explaining the situation to him, I packed a bag, grabbed my keys and fired up my bike. The ride to the cabin should have only been an hour, but if Enzo was right and I was being watched then I needed to take a different route.

It was the middle of the night, the roads deserted. But it worked in my favor. I'd barely made it out of Boston, when I realized I was being tailed.

The black SUV kept its distance, but when I pulled off the interstate and took the state highway, and it followed, gut instinct told me it was more than just coincidence. I didn't gun the engine. I kept a steady pace, trying to figure out how best to let things play out.

If I tried to shake them and failed, I could be leading them straight to Arianne, which wasn't an option. But if I tried to take them on, I could end up hurt ... or worse. I had no fucking idea if they were here on Mike Fascini's orders or his son's. Not that it mattered. Either way, I was the enemy in their eyes. Just as they were the enemy in mine.

I pulled over at a rest stop just on the outskirts of Rhode Island. Ahead of them by a couple of minutes, I climbed off my bike and scanned the area. There was a small brick building signposted 'restroom' and a couple of vending machines, but not much else in the way of places to hide. Slipping around the building, I pulled out my pistol and waited.

The SUV rolled to a stop. I couldn't see it, but I heard the doors open, heard heavy boots hit the gravel. There were two of them. One would have been easier, but it didn't matter.

No one was going to keep me from getting to Arianne.

Neither of them spoke, probably hoping to sneak up on me in the restroom while I went about my business. Once I heard them both enter the building, I tiptoed back around and silently slipped inside.

"He's not here," one of them said.

"He's got to be. Check—"

The shot rang out, one of the guys hitting the floor like a sack of bricks.

"Motherfucker," the other guy roared but I cocked my pistol right at him.

"Don't. Move."

He lifted up his hands, edging backward.

"Who sent you?"

His lips pressed into a thin line, but I wasn't looking to play games. Lowering my aim, I pulled the trigger and he went down on his knee, blood trickling from the hole in his leg. "Who. Sent. You?"

"Fascini."

"No shit," I grumbled. "Mike Fascini?"

"N- no. The son. Crazy sonofabitch that one."

My brow quirked up. "What were your orders?"

The blood drained from his face as he whimpered in pain. "Please man, don't kill me. I got—"

I stormed forward, pressing the barrel right against his head. "What. Were. Your. Fucking. Orders?"

"Tail you and make sure you didn't make it back to Verona."

Scott really was a crazy motherfucker.

"Look, man, I- I was just doing—"

The second shot hit him right between the eyes.

It should have bothered me, killing a man in cold blood. It wasn't something I ever relished, but this was different. This was about Arianne, about keeping her safe.

Doubling back to my bike, I didn't spare a second glance as I kicked the starter and sped off in the direction of the cabin.

In the direction of the girl I would kill for.

Thirty minutes later, I pulled up to the cabin. It was almost five thirty in the morning, the first signs of sunrise breaking on the horizon. I climbed off my bike hardly surprised when the door opened, and Enzo appeared. "You good?" he asked.

"I will be. Is she inside?" I shouldered past him.

"Hold up a minute. What happened?"

My eyes locked on his and I let out a heavy sigh. "You were right."

"About the tail?"

"Yeah."

"But you handled it?"

I knew what he was asking me. With a deep frown, I nodded.

"Hey, you did what you had to do." He squeezed my shoulder.

"Where is she?"

"In the first room. I wanted her close by."

"Thank you."

"Go see her and then we'll talk."

I took off down the hall. I hadn't been out here in a while, but everything about the place was still familiar. The door to Arianne's room was ajar and I slipped inside quietly. She looked so peaceful asleep in the middle of the queen-size bed, wrapped in a fluffy white robe. I moved closer, my mind darting in a hundred different directions. He'd hurt her again, that much was obvious. But it was hard to imagine right now while she seemed so at peace.

Leaning down, I brushed her cheek. Arianne murmured nestling further into the covers. But she didn't wake.

"I love you, Bambolina," I whispered.

Her hand was curled around the sheets, the ring on full display. Carefully, I eased her finger straight and slipped it off, placing it on the nightstand beside the bed. It didn't belong on her, but Arianne could choose what to do with it.

With one last lingering look, I left the room and went to find Enzo.

"Everything okay?" he asked as I joined him in the main room.

"She's sleeping. I didn't have the heart to wake her."

"It was a fucking shitshow by all accounts." His expression turned grim.

"What the fuck happened?" I dropped down into the chair opposite him.

"After you left, Luis called me, said he was worried about Scott's demeanor."

"Worried how?"

"Said he had a gut feeling."

"So I stuck around. Stayed in the shadows, watching. Nothing seemed out of the ordinary, but I stayed. Was half-asleep in my car when he called again." His expression morphed into one of disgust. "He said she—"

There was a knock at the door and my hand instantly went inside my jacket to my pistol.

"Relax," Enzo shot up, "it's Vitelli." He went and opened it, letting Luis inside. "I was just getting to the good part," he said to Arianne's bodyguard as if the last few hours had bonded them somehow.

"I'm sorry," Luis said, sitting on the end of the couch. "I shouldn't have let him get the drop on me like that."

"What happened?"

"Does he know?" he asked Enzo.

My best friend shook his head.

"Know what?"

"The wedding... Mike announced a new date. Thanksgiving weekend."

"That's a joke... you're joking, right?" That was less than two months away.

"I wish I were." A dark shadow passed over his face. "Fascini knows you went to Vermont."

"Fuck."

"Yeah, fuck." Enzo ran a hand down his face.

"But we have bigger problems right now." The two of them shared another look.

"Will someone just tell me what the fuck happened?" I was growing inpatient.

"Arianne left the party after he made the announcement. I think it was too much for her. She didn't want any visitors, so I posted myself outside. Everything was fine, then around two I heard something in the stairwell. I went to check it out and Scott jumped me, knocked me clean out. He managed to slip the guy we had on his room, and must have gotten an extra keycard for her room and slipped inside..." He cleared his throat clearly uncomfortable with whatever it was he needed to tell me.

"Arianne woke up and he held a gun to her head and tried to force her to..."

"He didn't just hold a gun to her head," Enzo snapped. "He made her suck the fucking thing while he got off. Your girl showed him though, drove a knife right through his thigh and knocked him out with a lamp."

"He did that?" The air was sucked clean from my lungs. It was bad enough he'd already hurt her, but to hold a gun to her head and force her to—

I swallowed the rush of bile up my throat. "Did he...?"

"No. She says he didn't touch her."

"Where is he now?"

"I stayed behind and woke up both sets of parents to let them deal with that piece of shit. Roberto was concerned and wanted to see Arianne, but I told him over my dead body."

"Nice," Enzo snorted. "You sure no one followed you out here?"

"I'm good at my job. I know how to stay off the radar." Luis almost looked offended at Enzo's words.

"I want him dead." I leaped up. "I want his head on a silver fucking platter." The red mist swallowed me whole until I could see nothing but Fascini's lifeless bloody body at my feet.

"You need to calm down." Enzo hovered on the fringe of my consciousness.

"No, what I need is to see that fucker bleed."

"Nicco?" Arianne's voice rose above the blood roaring between my ears. I turned slowly to meet her weary gaze. Her eyes were red and swollen, her face streaked with mascara. "You're here," she said shakily.

"I'm here." I went to her, falling to my knees and burying my face in her robe. I didn't care that we had an audience. In that moment, all I cared about was that she was here, and she was safe.

"Nicco." Arianne slid her hand against my cheek, coaxing my face to hers. "I'm okay."

But she wasn't.

She couldn't be.

"It's early and I'm still tired, come to bed with me." She tugged the collar of my jacket. I clambered to my feet, glancing over my shoulder.

"Go," Enzo said. "We've got your back."

I nodded, mutual understanding passing between us.

Arianne led me to our room, closing the door behind me. "I'm so fucking sorry." My voice cracked.

"Ssh," she whispered, pushing my jacket from my shoulders. Her hands went to the hem of my sweater next. I helped her work it off my body before unbuttoning my jeans and kicking them off. Arianne stood before me, drinking me in with her big, honey-brown eyes. "You're really here."

"I am." And I didn't plan on ever leaving her again.

Whatever Mike Fascini had up his sleeve we would face together.

She unbelted the fluffy robe and pushed it off her body. "Lie with me?"

I didn't need asking twice. I scooped Arianne up in my arms and laid her down on the bed. "Are you sure you're okay?"

"I am now." She leaned up, pressing a tender kiss to the corner of my mouth. "But I'm tired. I'm so tired, Nicco."

"It's okay." I climbed in beside her and rolled her onto her side away from me, tucking her into my chest. "I'm right here." My lips touched her shoulder, lingering, as a violent shudder rolled through me.

"Promise you'll be here when I wake up?"

"I promise."

Her body sagged against me as if she needed to hear the words before she could allow herself to relax. But I couldn't close my eyes, because if I did, I knew the nightmares would come. So I held her close and listened to the sound of her gentle breathing and tiny sighs.

Arianne never should have been there tonight. But she was right, she had been forced to play a part because of the men in her life who pulled the strings.

I wouldn't let it happen again.

If Fascini wanted war, I'd meet him on the battlefield. I'd fight with all that I had, if it meant protecting her from the likes of Scott and his father.

I'd always known my life in the Family was tenuous. I respected the Omertà; respected the codes we lived by, but Arianne was my woman.

My life.

And to put the Family above her was a betrayal to my soul.

A betrayal to the future I hoped we'd one day have.

I must have dropped off, because when I woke up the bed was empty, and I had a kink in my neck. Sitting up, I stretched out my muscles before pulling on my jeans and going in search of Arianne.

The last place I expected to find her was at the cooktop making breakfast for Luis and Enzo.

"You look like shit," my cousin said around a smirk.

I flipped him off, going to Arianne. Wrapping an arm around her waist, I pulled her against my chest and tucked my chin into her shoulder. "I missed you."

"You were sleeping. I didn't want to wake you."

"You should have." She tilted her face up to mine and I stole a kiss.

"I needed to do something. Luis went out for supplies so I could make breakfast."

"What time is it?"

"A little after ten."

"Any word?" I asked Luis.

"Roberto has been blowing up my cell, but I haven't responded yet. Figured we need to get our stories straight."

"What about you?" My eyes went to Enzo.

"You think I'm going to be the one to break it to Uncle Toni that we stole the Capizola heir *again*? Yeah, not happening."

"I'll talk to him." I ran a hand down my face, reluctantly pulling myself from Arianne.

"Are you hungry?" She seemed so content standing there, as if it was just a normal Sunday morning.

It wasn't.

Luis was right.

We needed to get our stories straight and figure out what came next. There was no way Arianne was going back to that piece of shit, but if she didn't... Well, it had the potential to pull the trigger on everything, and we were still in the dark about Fascini's endgame.

Catching Luis' gaze, I beckoned for him to follow me outside. "Stay with her," I ordered Enzo and he gave me a two-fingered salute.

"Tell me everything."

Luis closed the door behind him and joined me on the porch.

"Fascini is pulling all the strings. Roberto swears he didn't know about them bringing the wedding date forward."

"What do you think Mike has on him?"

"I don't know, but whatever it is, it's big. I've known Roberto a long time, Nicco. I have only known him as scared as this one other time and that was the failed hit on Arianne."

"You think Fascini has threatened to hurt Arianne again?"

"Not Arianne. She's the key. Think about it, she's the future of Capizola Holdings. They need her to get rightful and legal access to his empire."

"So if not Arianne... her mom?"

"Aside from Tristan, she's the second most important person in his life."

"Fuck." I raked a hand down my face. The bombshells just kept coming.

If Luis was right, and Arianne didn't go back, she could potentially be sentencing her mother to death.

"It's a mess, Nicco. But you know you can't send her back there, not now. He shoved a fucking gun in her mouth and—"

"Don't, just don't," I gritted out as my fist ground against the wooden railing. I wanted to fuck something up. Preferably that psychopath's face. "He needs to be dealt with."

"She won't let you do that. She won't want his blood on your hands."

"Do you have an alternative?" Because we were running out of options.

Luis' cell started ringing and he pulled it out of his pocket.

"Roberto?" I asked.

"No." He frowned. "But I need to take this."

"I'll be inside."

He nodded, stepping off the porch and heading for the SUV.

I went back inside, smiling when I saw Enzo helping Arianne find plates. Leaning against the door jamb I watched them. Enzo still looked like a cold-hearted bastard, but the fact he was here told me all I needed to know.

He was warming to her.

"Are you going to stand there all day?" His brow rose as he glowered at me.

"Put me to work."

"Actually, we're almost done. Take a seat and breakfast will be served." Arianne flashed me a warm smile, making my insides weak.

"Where's Vitelli?"

"Taking a call."

"Problem?" Enzo mouthed.

"I don't think so." I took a seat at the breakfast counter. My stomach grumbled at the smell of freshly cooked bacon and pancakes. "This looks great, Bambolina."

Arianne smiled as she served us each a plateful of food. "This is nice," she said, taking the stool beside me.

"When are you going to call Uncle Toni?" Enzo asked.

"We have time."

I needed this.

She needed this.

We'd spent our entire relationship fighting fires, I think we'd earned one morning.

"Nora texted me." Arianne cut into a pancake, pushing it around her plate.

I held my breath, expecting her to deliver another bombshell. "And?"

"She says hi."

"You told her?" Enzo groaned.

"No, I didn't tell her, but she's not stupid. She knows there's only one place I'd be if I'm not at the hotel or the apartment."

"You can't tell her," I said thickly. "Not yet."

"I know. She knows I'm safe, that's all that matters."

"I'm proud of you." Curving my hand around the back of her neck, I drew Arianne toward me, brushing my lips over hers.

"I keep thinking I should have killed him. If I'd have done it then this would be over..." She shuddered, dropping her silverware onto the plate.

"Hey, you did the right thing." She didn't deserve to have his blood on her hands.

"But I could have..."

"Nah," Enzo said, surprising us both. "You don't want to carry that kind of burden. You did what you needed to do to protect yourself, that's what matters. You leave the rest to us."

The protective edge in his voice soothed something inside me. I needed to know Arianne had people. If things went to shit and I got caught in the crossfire, I needed to know she was protected.

We ate in comfortable silence after that. Arianne seemed lighter by the time we were done. "I'll clean up," she said, but I batted her hand away from my plate.

"Me and Enzo can handle the dishes. You go get a shower."

"You two are going to do the dishes?" She wagged a finger between us.

"Don't look at me, Princess," Enzo teased. "I'm not—"

"Grab the towel," I barked at him. "You can dry."

Arianne's laughter lingered as she left us to it.

"You are so fucking whipped, I feel like I need to check for your balls."

"You just haven't met the right girl yet."

"If it turns me into... *this*." He pointed at me. "Then count me out."

My lip curved. "Thanks for looking out for her."

"She's family."

"She is."

"Well then, it's that simple. I might not always agree with you, Cous, but we protect our own." His words hit me square in the chest.

The fact he felt that way meant everything to me.

"But do me a favor, yeah, and keep your PDA's to a minimum."

"You just had to go and ruin it, didn't you?" I chuckled as we got to the dishes.

Before long, we had the kitchen looking brand new.

"Luis has been gone a while," Enzo said. "What do you think he's doing?"

"He said he had to take care of something." I shrugged, glancing down the hall where the bathroom was.

"You really trust him, don't you?"

"Yeah." I met my cousin's hard gaze. "I do."

"I hope you're right about this."

"I am."

I had to be. Because I'd entrusted him with Arianne's life. And if he betrayed me... it would not end well for him.

TWENTY

ARIANNE

"I STILL CAN'T BELIEVE he did that," Nora gasped. "I mean, I can... but shit, Ari. He's a real piece of work."

"I got away, that's all that matters." I tucked my legs up beneath me. Nicco was outside on the phone to his father, and Enzo was busy off doing whatever Enzo did.

"He's sick in the head, it's the only explanation."

"He's a monster." I shuddered at the memory of Scott manhandling me in the hotel room. The way he'd shoved the gun into my mouth and—

"Babe?"

"Sorry, I just..." *Breathe. Just breathe.*

"He can't hurt you now."

"I know, but it doesn't change anything, not really."

Scott was deranged. The soulless look in his eyes as he'd attacked me would forever be imprinted to my memory. If I hadn't found the knife... I couldn't even think about it.

"They'll figure it out."

My eyes flicked to the window. I was so relieved Nicco was here. I didn't want us to be apart, not again. But I knew it wasn't as simple as him being back. Not until things were settled with Mike Fascini and my father.

"Tell me about your night with Dan," I changed the subject, "how's that going?"

"He's nice enough."

"Nor, come on. He's a sweetheart. He got dressed up in a tux and came to the party for you."

"I know, it isn't him," she let out a frustrated sigh, "it's me. There's just something missing. He doesn't set my world on fire."

"Maybe you just need to give it time?" Dan was solid. He attended classes, held open doors, and bought her coffee. "You said the sex was good."

"The sex is good, it's just not... life changing."

I chuckled. "They're some high expectations you have there."

"I know, I know. You think I'm squandering a good thing. But I don't want to settle, babe. I want epic love, like you and Nicco."

Just then, Nicco came back into the cabin. He smiled at me, his eyes so full of love and possessiveness it made my heart skip a beat.

"He's there isn't he?" I heard the amusement in Nora's words.

"Yeah, he's back."

"Well, tell him I say hey. And tell him he'd better keep you safe. You're precious goods."

"I will. I'll talk to you soon."

"Damn right you will." She hung up and I placed my cell on the coffee table.

"Nora says hi." Nicco's brows furrowed and I let out a weary sigh. "I didn't tell her where we are. I promised you I wouldn't."

"I know, I'm sorry." He came around the sectional and sat beside me. "I just wish it wasn't like this."

"It is what it is."

"Bambolina." Nicco pressed his palm against my cheek and I leaned into his touch.

"What did your father say?"

He stiffened.

"That bad, huh?"

"He'll come around."

I sensed Nicco didn't want to talk about it, so I changed the subject. "Where is everyone?" Luis had been gone since before breakfast and Enzo was still nowhere to be seen.

"Luis had to go take care of something and Enzo has gone to pick up some supplies."

"What supplies?"

"Well, if we're going to be here awhile, we need clothes, food, toiletries."

"So that's the plan? To stay here?" I took his hand in mine and brought it to my lips, kissing his fingers.

"For now. It's safe here. You're safe."

"And we're alone?" Heat pooled low in my stomach.

"We are. But, Bambolina, I don't want to—"

"Ssh." I brushed my lips over his. "Stop talking." My arms wound around Nicco's neck as I pulled myself onto his lap, letting my legs fall to either side of his.

"Enzo could return at any second." He eased back to look at me.

"So take me to bed then."

His eyes darkened, a pained groan rumbling in his chest. "You're sure?"

I nodded.

I needed him, I needed him to erase all the memories of last night.

Nicco gripped me tightly and stood, carrying me down the hall. When we were inside our room, he kicked the door shut behind us and moved me to the bed. "I'll never let you go again," he murmured against my lips, trailing kisses along my jaw and down the slope of my neck.

"That feels so good."

But it wasn't enough.

I needed more.

I needed everything he had to give me.

Slowly, Nicco lowered me to the floor, my body sliding down his, making me whimper with need. "Tell me what you want, Bambolina?" He brushed the hair off my neck and kissed my collarbone, gently raking his teeth against the sensitive skin there. A shiver ran through me as I tilted my head to give him better access.

"You," I breathed. "I want you, Nicco."

"You have me, amore mio. Heart, body, and soul." He paused, gazing at me with complete reverie.

"Nicco?"

Snapping from his trance, he dipped his hand under my t-shirt. His warm fingers danced up my spine, higher and higher until the material was bunched around my chest. His hands kept going, and I lifted my arms letting him slide it off me.

"On the bed," he ordered, and I laid back, moving into the middle of the giant mattress. Nicco grabbed the hem of his black t-shirt, and pulled it clean off his body. My mouth watered at the sight of him, cut abs and taut, tanned muscle stretched over broad shoulders. He was a sculpted work of art.

And he was all mine.

Reaching out, Nicco brushed his hand along my ankle, his featherlight touch sending shivers skittering up my spine. He dropped to his knees, gently yanking me closer to him. Laughter spilled from my lips but quickly died as he toyed with the waistband of the boy shorts Enzo had found for me to wear. Nicco didn't break eye contact with me as he inched them over my hips and down my legs. His gaze was dark and intense.

Hungry.

He looked ready to devour me, turning my blood to molten lava.

Splaying a hand on my stomach, Nicco dipped his head and took a long, greedy swipe. I bucked against him, overwhelmed at the sensations. "Relax, Bambolina," he rasped. "I got you."

My head fell back as he began sucking and licking me. He slid two fingers inside me, curling them and rubbing until I was a quivering breathless mess beneath him.

"Nicco, it's..." My breath caught as his teeth teased the sensitive skin and his lips painted letters of love over my body.

"You taste like Heaven." His tongue circled my clit as he slowly worked me with his fingers. I shivered and moaned, arching into him, desperate for more.

"I will never let him touch you again," Nicco murmured the words against my core, making my breath catch.

"Oh my god..." I slid my fingers in his hair, gripping on tight as my body began to tremble, teetering on the edge of ecstasy. "Nicco..." His name was a prayer on my lips as I shattered around him.

He kissed my inner thigh before standing and sliding his boxers off his legs. Crawling up my body, he covered me until we were nothing but a tangle of limbs and love, skin and sweet nothings.

"I will kill him for ever looking twice at you, Bambolina." A storm swirled in Nicco's eyes as he stared down at me. His jaw was set, his breathing shallow.

"Nicco," I gasped, "don't say such a thing."

He took my hand, pressing it against his chest. "This is who I am, Arianne. My heart beats for you, and I am done being the nice guy where you're concerned." Dipping his head, he ran his nose along my jaw, ghosting a kiss over my lips. "I will do whatever it takes to protect you. Even if it means ending him."

A shudder racked through me. I didn't like hearing Nicco talk like this, but he was right. This was who he was. How could I deny this part of him when I loved the other parts so deeply?

"I know." I wound my hands around his neck, pulling him closer. "I love you, Niccolò Marchetti, all of you."

I felt the tension leave his body. Nicco needed this. He needed my acceptance.

No words were spoken as he hitched my thigh around his hip and sank into me with one smooth glide. "Fuck, Bambolina..." His voice was thick with desire. I ran my tongue along the seam of his mouth, desperate for more. More kisses, more sensation, just *more* of him.

Nicco rocked into me in a torturous rhythm; slow measured strokes that made it difficult to breathe. He was everywhere, his lips on my neck, his tongue and teeth marking my skin, his hard body caging me to the bed, loving me. Filling me so completely I was drowning in him.

"Mine," he whispered into my ear, rocking harder. Deeper. "Sei mia."

I clung to him as he pushed me closer to the edge. Being with Nicco was like being in the eye of a storm. Wild and reckless and unpredictable but awe inspiring, nonetheless.

The way we loved, the way our bodies came together as one, it was more than just lust. More than love. It was transcendent.

It was Fate working her will, binding two lives together until not even death could part them.

It should have terrified me.

It didn't.

With Nicco I felt whole. I felt home. I couldn't explain it, couldn't even really understand it, it just was.

"I love you," I breathed, grabbing his jaw and kissing him hungrily. Desperately. "I love you so much."

"Sei il più grande amore della mia vita."

Our skin was damp, our moans breathy. Nicco hitched my legs higher, grinding against me in the most delicious way. It created the perfect friction, making my stomach coil tight and my toes curl into the soft sheets.

"Come for me, Bambolina." He kissed me, swallowing my moans as waves of pleasure rippled through me.

My body shuddered, but he didn't stop. His pace was relentless, as if he was trying to imprint himself on my soul.

Maybe he didn't realize he was already there.

Branded on my heart.

Etched into the very fiber of my soul.

"It's okay," I dug my fingers in his hair, peppering tiny kisses over his face. "You can let go now."

A low growl built in his throat as he came inside me. His eyes were almost black, his expression lost.

"Nicco," I whispered against his mouth. "Come back to me."

He blinked, his expression softening. "You're okay." His voice cracked.

"I'm okay." I laid my palm on his cheek. "I'm right here."

Nicco's body began to tremble as he dropped his face to the crook of my shoulder. "I can't lose you," he murmured against my damp skin. "I can never lose you, Arianne."

"You won't," I whispered.

You won't.

After taking a shower together, we found Enzo in the main room.

"Don't mind me," he grunted, shoving a handful of chips into his mouth.

"We were just—"

He silenced Nicco with a knowing look. I smothered a giggle, burying myself into Nicco's side. "I'm hungry," I murmured.

"I'm not surprised." Enzo smirked.

"Watch it," Nicco jabbed a finger at his cousin.

"Where's Matteo?" I asked, slipping out of Nicco's arm and going over to the refrigerator.

"He's helping hold down the fort back home."

"What does that mean exactly?"

"Does she always ask this many questions?" Enzo raised a brow, and Nicco chuckled.

"Thanks for doing that..." the two of them fell into conversation, but I tried not to eavesdrop.

All that mattered was I was here with Nicco.

We could figure out the rest, together.

I checked the refrigerator for supplies and pulled out ingredients to make sandwiches. "You two hungry?" I called.

"Is the sky blue?" Enzo shot back and I poked my tongue out at him. He acted like the big bad wolf, but I was slowly figuring out he wasn't a bad guy. He was just guarded, layers of ice frozen around his heart.

"Are you always so smug?"

His brows drew together. "Watch it, Principessa. Just because you're Nicco's girl doesn't mean I won't—"

The box of eggs clattered to the floor, cracking in a pile of sticky yolk.

"Arianne?" Nicco rushed over to my side. "What is it?"

"Nothing." I inhaled a deep breath. "I just..."

"Something triggered you." Enzo came over, his eyes narrowed at me. "He called you that, didn't he?"

I nodded, forcing down the tears burning the backs of my eyes. "Sorry, I didn't—"

"Don't ever apologize for that fucker. I'm sorry." His expression softened. "I didn't know, or I wouldn't have..."

"It's not your fault. Sometimes I'm fine then other times, someone says something, or I remember something, and it's like I freeze."

"Come here." Nicco wrapped me in his arms.

"I'm okay, I promise." I hated that Scott still had control over me, but I knew you didn't just forget the kind of trauma he'd put me through.

"Nicco?" He was trembling again. I eased back, peeking up at him.

"Why don't you come sit down," Enzo said, gently taking my arm. "Give him a second to cool off."

He pulled me away, but my eyes remained on Nicco. His fists were clenched impossibly tight, and I could feel the anger rolling off him. It was like a storm cloud circling him. Dark and angry, and ready to unleash its destruction at any moment.

I sat down, flinching at the sound of Nicco's fist colliding with the counter.

"Should we do something?" I asked Enzo. He gave me a sympathetic look before going back to Nicco. He spoke in a low voice, making it difficult for me to hear. But I caught the odd word.

Calm down...

L'Anello's...

She needs you...

"What's L'Anello's?" I asked, trying to break the heavy silence.

Enzo glanced over at me, running a hand through his hair. "Somewhere you'll never go."

"E," Nicco sighed. "Don't."

"Fine. Have it your way." The two of them shared a look. "It's a bar. We... hang out there sometimes."

"A bar?" Suspicion clung to my words. I knew I wasn't supposed to ask questions and I knew even if I did, they weren't supposed to tell me anything. But I wanted to know as much as possible.

"Remember how I told you I fight sometimes? To burn off steam?" Nicco came over to the sectional and sat down.

"I remember."

"L'Anello's is where I fight sometimes."

"You fight in a bar?"

"The bar is a front for... other things."

"I see." My stomach twisted. "Are you good?"

"Jesus," Enzo muttered under his breath, casting Nicco a dark look. But he only had eyes for me.

"I'm pretty good, yeah."

"Okay."

Enzo snorted. "Nic just tells you he's a good fighter and all you've got to say is okay?"

I shrugged. "What else do you want me to say?"

"Nothing, I'm just surprised is all. I'm starting to wonder when any of this will freak you out."

"Oh, I'm pretty freaked out." I let out a strangled laugh. "But I also love Nicco and when you love someone you don't get to pick and choose the parts you want."

He studied me. "Yeah, I'm starting to see that." He moved over to the window, pulling back the curtains. "It looks like Luis is back. About fucking time."

I curled into Nicco's side, letting out a contented sigh.

"What the hell?" Enzo yanked open the door and Nicco moved me off him to stand.

"What is it?" Strolling over to his cousin, he peered over his shoulder.

"What did you do?" Enzo growled. I couldn't see him, but he didn't sound happy.

I got up, gingerly going to them, coming to an abrupt halt when I saw what Enzo and Nicco were looking at.

They weren't looking at Luis at all. It was the person standing beside him.

"Tristan?" I gasped, hardly able to believe my eyes.

He wasn't in the hospital anymore.

He was here.

And he looked as nauseous as I felt.

TWENTY-ONE

NICCO

"TRISTAN?" Arianne slipped between me and Enzo and hurried down the steps to greet her cousin.

"A word?" I tipped my chin to Luis. Enzo stepped aside to let him past.

"What the fuck were you thinking?"

"Relax—"

"Relax?" Enzo seethed. "You brought the fucking enemy into our safe house. I knew we couldn't trust you, Vitelli, motherfucking—"

"E," I cut him off.

"Look," Luis said. "I knew if I gave you a heads up you would fight me on this. Tristan has intel; he might be able to help. I met him off the highway, we dumped his car, and I blindfolded him, so he doesn't know where we are. It's safe, I promise."

Enzo made a hacking sound and I jabbed him in the ribs. "You did all that?" I asked Luis.

"I covered my tracks, yeah. I'm not stupid. I know what's at stake and I don't want Arianne in harm's way anymore than you. But you're going to want to hear what he has to say."

I gave him a tight nod. He had a point. Everything he'd done up until now made him trustworthy, but bringing Tristan here still felt like a big risk.

Luis doubled back to go outside. Enzo leaned in and kept his voice low. "I don't like this, Nic."

"You don't have to like it. But maybe Luis is right, maybe he does have good intel." Lord only knew we needed it. Tommy and Stefan were still yet to dig up anything useful on Mike Fascini, and my old man wasn't exactly over the moon when I told him me and Arianne were here. But he knew I wouldn't relent again. He hadn't even bothered to try to order me back to Boston.

I wasn't going.

I'd stay in the cabin for now, but if it came to it, I would return home and face any consequences.

"We can't trust him, he's Fascini's best friend," Enzo spat the words, "or have you forgotten that?"

My mind went to two nights ago when I'd stood in the hospital room, confessing my deepest, darkest sins to Tristan. I'd assumed he was asleep... but I wasn't sure now.

"Let's just hear him out."

Enzo pursed his lips, disapproval glittering in his eyes. "You hear him out. I'm going to take a drive around the perimeter, make sure Vitelli definitely covered his tracks."

"You're sure?"

"I think it's for the best. I'm not sure I can be held responsible for my actions if I have to sit and listen to any of Capizola's bullshit."

"Okay, but don't be too long."

Enzo stalked out of the cabin just as Arianne and Tristan came inside.

"I know this is as awkward as fuck," Tristan stepped forward, raking a hand through his hair. He looked pale, his eyes sunken and ringed with dark circles.

Guilt flooded me, but it didn't override the need to protect Arianne. My hand slid inside my jacket and before giving it a second thought, I whipped out my pistol, pressing it right against his temple.

"Nicco!" Arianne shrieked and Luis moved to her side, gently holding her back.

But Tristan didn't flinch. His hands went slowly up at his sides. "I swear, Marchetti, I'm here to help that's all."

"How can I trust you?"

"You can't." He inhaled a ragged breath. "You're just going to have to take a leap of faith. She's my cousin, she's family. Surely you can appreciate that."

Family meant everything to me, but to people like Tristan, people like Roberto Capizola and Mike Fascini, even family could be pawns. They'd proved that more than once.

We were locked in an impasse. I didn't want to trust him—everything inside me screamed at me not to trust him—but we needed allies.

We needed answers.

And he was one person who could possibly give them to us.

"I'm sorry," the words were out of me before I could stop them. I pulled my pistol away and engaged the safety, shoving it back in the waistband of my jeans.

"You don't need to apologize," he said. "I think once is enough, don't you?" His expression turned smug.

So he had been awake the other night.

I didn't know whether to be relieved or embarrassed.

"Let's sit." I walked over to the sectional. Arianne sat down beside me, sliding her hand into mine. She cast me a concerned look.

"I had to," I whispered.

"I know." She gave me a sad smile.

Tristan and Luis took the chairs opposite. Silence stretched out before us. Thick and heavy with the secrets of our past. Tense with the reality of our current predicament.

"I should probably start," Tristan said. "I got discharged from hospital yesterday."

"I didn't know." Arianne sat a little straighter.

"Mom picked me up and I crashed.

"I headed over to the estate this morning, hoping to catch Uncle Roberto. I wanted to talk to him about some things..." His eyes flicked from Arianne to mine. "I knew something was wrong the second I got there."

"You saw my father?"

He gave Arianne a sharp nod. "He was beside himself. I've never seen anything like it. Aunt Gabriella was trying to console him, but he got so angry. He trashed his office. That's when she told me everything."

Arianne stiffened. "H- how much?"

"Everything."

"Oh." She pressed closer to me.

"I want you to know I'm on your side, Ari. I didn't know..." He let out a weary sigh. "If I'd have known what he would do, I would never have pushed the relationship. I didn't—"

"Stop, just stop." She breathed. "You said I needed to grow up and live in the real world. You said it was my destiny whether I liked it or not. You said that."

"Fuck, I know, but I didn't think it meant *this*. You were supposed to date, fall in love, and get engaged." He paled. "It wasn't supposed to be like this, I swear."

"But you knew about my father's plans for me and Scott. You knew, and you never said a word."

"Shit, Ari. I know it sounds bad when you say it like that, but this is your legacy. You are the Capizola heir, one day the entire empire will be yours. Scott was my best friend. I thought you would be a great match. I thought it made good business sense. That's just how it is in this life."

"He's a monster."

Shame filled Tristan's eyes. "I realize that now. He's always been... intense. But I didn't know he would..." He swallowed hard, rubbing his jaw as if the words were just too painful to say.

"He raped me, Tristan. He slipped something into my drink at the Gala and raped me." Arianne's voice shook, but it was nothing compared to the rage boiling beneath my skin.

"You never said anything. You never—"

"Would it have mattered?" Her voice cracked. "I tried to tell my father and he acted like I was making a big deal about nothing. He downplayed my being raped because it didn't fit into his business plans." Bitterness clung to her words, but Arianne didn't cower. She didn't cry or whimper. She sat tall, her eyes locked on her cousin, on her family, as she purged her thoughts.

"He deserves your wrath," Tristan buried his face in his hands, scraping his fingers through his hair, "We both do. But the second I found out the truth, I called Luis."

"Is this true?"

Arianne's bodyguard nodded.

"You are my family, Ari, my blood. Scott hurt you which means he hurt me. I knew he could be a little forward. But I didn't know... I swear. Either way, I'm done. He's no one to me now."

"Just like that?" I scoffed. "Sounds too fucking convenient to me."

Tristan met my icy stare. He deserved some credit. Few people faced off with me like that. "We've all made mistakes, man. But Scott... he's obsessed with her. Uncle Roberto knows she isn't safe."

"So why the fuck did he promise her to that piece of shit?"

Tristan let out a heavy sigh, but it was Arianne who spoke. "I don't know that I can trust you again. You were on his side, Tristan."

"I appreciate that, and I know I don't deserve a second chance." He gave her a sad smile. "But I'd like the chance to earn it back."

She gave him a small nod,

"Okay." He sagged back into the chair. "So I always knew Uncle Roberto wanted to secure your future. After Antonio Marchetti tried to have you—"

"It wasn't Antonio," Arianne said.

"What?" Tristan's eyes almost bugged. "But it had to be. Uncle Roberto said—"

"She's telling the truth," I added. "It was Mike Fascini. We think he did it to try to set my father up and incite war between our families. When it failed, we think he decided to try another approach."

Tristan's brow drew together. "That doesn't make any sense. Why would he do that?"

"Because there's something else," I said. "Something we only recently found out."

"Go on..."

"What do you know of the name Ricci?"

"Ricci? As in Elena Ricci? The girl who betrayed our family and ran off with Emilio Marchetti?"

I nodded. "Mike is Elena's grandson."

"Cazzo!" His eyes went wide. "So this is what? Some sick attempt at righting history?"

"Michael Fascini, Mike's father, never got over what happened. According to his aunt, he became obsessed with getting vengeance. He moved to Verona County in the seventies with the sole purpose of getting even. When he died, Mike took over the reins and here we are."

"So Mike's the puppet master? It makes sense." He scrubbed his jaw before fixing his eyes on Arianne. "I know your father doesn't seem like he has your best interests at heart, Ari, but he loves you."

"He has a funny way of showing it."

"But if Mike has been pulling the strings all along, maybe he didn't have a choice."

The thought had occurred to me, but it still didn't excuse Roberto's actions.

"Do you think Scott knows the truth?" Tristan asked.

"We don't know. If he does, he risked everything last night and his father is likely to be pissed. If he wants to keep his hands clean, he needs Capizola Holdings and Arianne was his insurance policy."

"Hold on a second." Arianne grabbed my arm. "You think I'm a bargaining chip?"

I twisted my body around to look at her. "It's possible Mike threatened to harm you again unless your father complied, yes."

"I- I don't know what to say." The blood had completely drained from Tristan's face. "I came here ready to offer to talk to Uncle Roberto, to make him see sense. I didn't realize… fuck. What are we going to do?"

"We?" I raised a brow.

"I'm here, aren't I? I want to help."

"You need to buy us some time while we figure out our next move. Arianne cannot go back now, no matter what happens."

"Agreed." Tristan gave me a sharp nod. "But what about my uncle and aunt? If Mike wants Capizola Holdings, there are other ways to make it happen."

"I guess you need to make sure that doesn't happen. Arianne is my priority, and until we can be sure Fascini doesn't have a failsafe we can't touch him." He was one of the most prominent men in Verona County. If he turned up dead or missing, it would raise questions.

Questions that could lead back to the Family.

"What's it going to require to take him down?" For the first time since he'd arrived, I saw the fight in Tristan's eyes. He might not have been ready to bury the hatred between our families, but he was here for Arianne. And right now, that's all that mattered.

"If we want to avoid bloodshed, we need to be able to pin something on him. Something that will make sure he never sees the light of day again." He deserved to rot in Hell for what he'd done to Arianne. But a six by four cell would do all the same.

It all started with him, and it would end with him.

"And Scott?"

"He's mine," I ground out, feeling the familiar lick of fury skate up my spine.

"We have the evidence, Nicco." Arianne tugged my arm. "We can take it to the authorities."

Tristan caught my eye. He gave me an imperceptible nod, and I knew what he was telling me.

Scott was a dead man walking.

"Nicco?" Arianne spoke more forcefully this time, and I gave her my attention.

"It's okay, Bambolina. I'm okay." I pulled her into my side and kissed the top of her head.

I didn't want to lie to her.

But she didn't need to know that I wouldn't rest until I'd had my pound of Scott Fascini's flesh.

After we hatched a tentative plan, Tristan and Luis left.

Tristan would return home and try to find out everything he could about the nature of Mike Fascini's plan. He would also try and buy some time. Our enemy had become a turncoat. It was a risk, but it was better than doing nothing.

"You're quiet," I said to Arianne. She was reading a book she'd found on one of the shelves. Except, she hadn't turned a page in almost ten minutes, so she was either a really slow reader or she was using the book as a distraction.

I leaned over and snagged it from her hands.

"Hey," she protested. "I was reading that."

I gave her a pointed look and she let out a weary sigh. "Fine, you caught me."

"It's okay to need some space. If you want me to leave—"

"What? No!" She sat up. "I just... Do you think I should forgive Tristan?"

"That is not my decision to make."

"They both let me down, Nicco. When I needed them, my father and Tristan let me down."

"I know, Bambolina. Come here." I pulled her into my side. "You are so strong. It's okay to not want to forgive easily. But don't let your resentment fester. Eventually, there will come a day when you must decide to forgive or forget. But know that I'll be right here by your side and I'll support whatever decision you make, okay?"

She gave me the faintest of nods before kissing me. "Thank you," she whispered. "For everything."

"It is me who should be thanking you. You make the world a brighter place, Arianne."

Emotion swirled in her eyes as she suppressed a smile. "Tell me about L'Anello's." She cleared her throat. "About what you do there."

"You really want to know this stuff?"

"I want to know everything, but I know there will always be things you can't share with me. So all I ask is that you share the pieces you can."

"Fighting helps me burn off steam. I guess you could say it's a way to fight my demons."

She tensed. "But you could get hurt."

"Sometimes I want to hurt. It helps remind me that I'm alive."

"I'm not sure I understand."

"You're not the only one who has spent their life caged, Bambolina. I didn't ask for this life, it was decided for me. And I've made my peace with that, I have. But sometimes... sometimes I need to push back."

"So fighting is your way of retaining some control?"

"I guess you could say that."

"I don't like the idea of you getting hurt." Arianne leaned closer, brushing her nose along mine.

"It comes with the territory."

"What will life be like, for us, I mean?" Her voice wavered. "Will I be expected to stay at home and raise a houseful of babies?"

Laughter bubbled in my chest. "While that image does all kinds of crazy things to me," I grinned, my heart so fucking full I wanted to drag her to the bedroom and make a start, "I will always support your dreams, Arianne."

I wasn't my father. I didn't intend on ruling my household with an iron fist. I wanted Arianne to flourish. I wanted her to be happy.

"I think I want to help people, like at the VCTI."

"You have a big heart."

"But babies," she whispered against the corner of my mouth, "you want that one day?"

"I want everything with you, amore mio. But we're young, we have time."

Arianne was quiet but the contented sigh that spilled from her lips gave me reassurance she wasn't stewing on our conversation.

"I was thinking," she said after a couple of minutes. "Can Alessia come visit?"

"I'm not sure that's a good idea. The fewer people coming to and from the cabin, the better. At least, for now."

"Okay."

"You're not going to fight me on it?"

"I trust you Nicco." She smiled. "I trust you to keep me safe."

"It's all I want," I replied, ghosting my lips over hers.

Until my very last breath.

TWENTY-TWO

ARIANNE

"HMM, MORNING." I snuggled closer to Nicco. He was still asleep, strands of hair falling over his eyes a little.

I watched him, smiling to myself at how perfect the moment was. Because this time, I wouldn't have to say goodbye.

After Enzo had left us, we'd spent the night curled up on the sectional watching movies. Luis had stayed, but he'd made himself scarce.

I loved it out here, away from everything and everyone, where we could be together without judgment or scrutiny.

I knew it wasn't real. I knew our bubble would soon come to an end. But I intended on savoring every second we had together.

"I can feel you staring," Nicco murmured, his voice thick with sleep.

"That's because I *am* staring." I painted circles on his chest, ghosting my fingers over his scars.

He snagged my wrist, bringing my hand to his lips, sending a shiver up my spine. "Good morning, Bambolina."

"Good morning."

"I could get used to this," he shifted onto his back, fixing his stormy eyes on mine.

"I was thinking the same thing. It's so peaceful out here."

"We'd have to get rid of the bodyguard though." His mouth curved with amusement.

"And change the locks. I wouldn't want Enzo strolling in at any given time." Dipping my head, I brushed my lips over his. "I need a girl's minute and then I'll make some coffee."

"Okay."

I climbed out of bed and pulled on Nicco's oversized MU t-shirt. Enzo had bought us some extra clothes, but I was going to need my own things if we stayed here for any length of time.

It was strange.

I knew I was supposed to be worrying about everything: classes and my volunteer work at the VCTI, but it all seemed so insignificant given the circumstances.

After visiting the bathroom, I quickly brushed my teeth before heading for the kitchenette. Luis was already up and dressed, reading a newspaper.

"Good morning," I said. "Coffee?"

"I wouldn't say no to another." He slid his mug toward me. "Did you sleep okay?"

"I did, thank you. What about you?"

"I got a couple of hours."

"We're safe out here, Luis."

He smiled. "Old habits die hard, I guess. Is Nicco—"

"Right here." He padded into the kitchen, stealing my breath. He'd pulled on some sweats but left his t-shirt off, the hard lines of his body rippling and flexing.

Nicco's body was a sculpted work of art. Tanned skin pulled taut over cut muscles, broad shoulders and a narrowed waist that was defined by the delicious V disappearing into his sweatpants.

Luis cleared his throat, casting me an amused glance before giving Nicco a nod. "Morning."

"Everything okay?"

"Everything's quiet."

"Good." Nicco advanced on me, curving his hand around my neck and pressing his lips to my head. "I'm going to take a quick shower. You'll be okay?"

It was my turn to nod.

Once he'd disappeared, I joined Luis at the table. "I'm sorry you have to be here."

"I thought we were past all that?" He gave me a pointed look. "I'm here because I want to be here, Ari. You know, you seem different."

"It's him..." My eyes went to the hall where Nicco had gone. "I know you probably think we're too young and foolish..." I stopped myself. Luis didn't want to hear this.

He covered my hand with his. "Quite the contrary. I think what the two of you have found is quite remarkable. That man would die for you."

"I'd rather he didn't." I forced a smile, my stomach clenching at his words. "Can I ask you something?"

"Anything."

"Do you think my father is being blackmailed or threatened by Mike Fascini?"

"I think it's the most likely scenario, yes."

"But before all this happened, when I first started MU, what do you think my father was thinking then?"

"I can't answer that, Arianne. You know as well as I do your father is a determined and successful man who cares deeply for his family. I think he probably genuinely thought he was doing a good thing. By promising you to Scott, he was securing your future and absolving you of the full burden of one day running Capizola Holdings. I think part of him just wanted to see you cared for and looked after."

"But I'm eighteen. He could have waited."

"I think the likelihood is Mike Fascini has always been pulling the strings and whispering in his ear. Your father is a driven man, Arianne. The opportunity to merge with Fascini and Associates was too good to pass up. But the lines between business and family got blurred along the way."

I scoffed at that, and Luis squeezed my hand. "Hey, I'm not trying to excuse his actions. He has made a lot of mistakes, nothing will change that."

"Do you think he knows who Mike Fascini really is?"

"If he doesn't, he will soon enough."

I pondered on that thought. If my father didn't know, did it change anything?

I didn't have all the answers. Not yet. All I knew, was that in my heart, I felt betrayed. He was supposed to be the man I could trust with anything, the man who would move mountains for me.

He'd let me down too many times to just brush his infractions under the rug.

I finished my coffee before going to the refrigerator. "Are you hungry?"

"I wouldn't turn down the offer of breakfast." Luis gave me a rare smile. "If you're sure you don't mind?"

"I don't see anyone else here to cook, do you? Besides, it'll keep me busy."

And I could really do with that right now.

After breakfast, Enzo returned.

But he wasn't alone.

Nicco's father, his uncles, and Matteo filed into the cabin, filling the room with their somber expressions and larger than life presence.

"Ari," Matteo came over and hugged me, taking me by surprise. "I'm glad you're okay," he whispered.

"Arianne," Antonio said, giving me a nod. He was conflicted, his stormy eyes at war with the faint smile he wore.

"Miss Capizola." One of the other men stepped forward. "I am Michele, Matteo's father. It is nice to finally meet you."

"Hello."

"Vincenzo," Enzo's dad said coolly. He reminded me so much of his son, only scarier. If Enzo was cold, Vincenzo was a glacier. Disapproval radiated from him and I inched closer to Luis' side.

"Niccolò, perhaps Arianne would enjoy a walk. I'm sure Vitelli can—"

"She stays."

"Son, that is not an option."

"It's okay," I stepped forward and laid a hand on Nicco's arm. "I wanted to call Nora and my mom anyway. I'll give you all some space."

He looked at me, his brows drawn tight with uncertainty. "I'll be fine," I urged. "Go talk with your family."

"You stay," he said to Luis who stiffened.

"Are you—"

"You stay."

I went to leave but Nicco snagged my hand, drawing me back to him. "We won't be long." He cupped my face, leaning down to kiss me. My cheeks burned. Everyone was watching. His father, his cousins and uncles, the most important people in his life. Yet he kissed me like I yielded the real power over him.

It was heady.

Overwhelming.

It was everything.

"Go," he murmured quietly against my lips, "before I throw them all out and drag you back to our bed."

I couldn't hide my smile as I left them and went to our bedroom. Closing the door behind me, I grabbed my cell phone off the dresser and flopped onto the bed. I wanted to call Nora, but my mom had been bombarding me with texts since the party, so I decided to deal with her first.

"Mamma?"

"Arianne, thank God. I've been so worried."

"Luis told Father I was safe, no?"

"Yes, but it didn't stop me worrying after what Scott did—"

"I'm okay, Mamma, I'm okay."

"You're safe?"

I smiled dryly. I couldn't help it. She acted like an overly concerned parent, but she had been so willing to force my relationship with Scott before she discovered what a monster he was.

"Where are you?"

"You know I can't tell you that."

"Oh, figlia mia, everything is such a mess."

"Have you spoken to Tristan?"

"I have. He's trying to speak some sense into your father. He's beside himself, sweetheart."

Too little too late.

"You could come home, to the estate. We can keep you safe."

"I can't," I let out a weary sigh. "I won't."

"No." I heard the sadness in her voice. "I don't suppose you will."

"Have you spoken to Suzanna?"

"Not a word since the morning after the party. Once we found out what had happened, your father ushered me back to the estate."

"It isn't safe for you there, Mamma. You could be in danger. Is there somewhere you can go?"

"Whatever are you talking about?"

"Mike. He isn't who he says he is. You can't trust him."

"What do you know that you aren't telling me?"

I hesitated. "Just be careful, okay?"

"I will. Your father has extra security around the house. He's become very paranoid of late."

"You need to try to talk to him, Mamma."

"I'm not sure I can get through to him anymore."

"But maybe if Tristan is there too, maybe the two of you can make him see sense."

"I will try." A beat passed and then she said, "This isn't what I wanted for you, Arianne. I hope you know that."

"I know, Mamma."

But the truth was, I didn't know anything anymore. Not where my family were concerned. There were so many secrets and lies, it was impossible to sort the truth from the falsities.

"I have to go," I rushed out, suddenly overwhelmed.

"What should I tell your father?"

"Tell him, I'm not going back. I won't." Not while Scott was roaming free and Mike Fascini was still pulling the strings.

"Okay. I love you, sweetheart." She let out a small sigh. "Be safe."

"Bye, Mamma."

I hung up, swallowing down the tears burning my throat. But I didn't dwell on our conversation. Instead, I dialed my best friend's number. She answered on the third ring.

"Hey," Nora said. "How is it being secreted away with your handsome bodyguard and hot mafioso boyfriend?"

"Nor," I let out a strained chuckle.

"Please, you're in hiding with your guy... it sounds like heaven if you ask me."

"Have you forgotten why?"

"No, Ari. God no. But when life hands you lemons and all that."

"You're crazy." A faint smile traced my lips.

"And you love me. So what's up?"

"Antonio and Nicco's uncles just got here," I kept my voice low. I could only make out the rumble of their voices beyond the bedroom. It all sounded very fraught, but I couldn't distinguish words.

It was probably for the best.

"Wait a second, they're having a business meeting, right now?"

"I guess so."

"You have to go listen."

"Nora!"

"You're telling me you're not curious what they're," she lowered her voice, "talking about?"

"It doesn't matter. I would never—"

"They could be making decisions that affect you."

"Nicco will tell me."

"Will he? They live by a code, babe. Secrets. Lies. Cover ups. It's the mafia way." She was so flippant about this stuff.

"You've been watching too much TV."

"You know I'm right."

"Maybe, but I'm not about to go eavesdrop on them. It's... wrong."

"You say that like any of this is right."

What Nicco and I felt for each other was right.

No one would ever persuade me otherwise.

"What do you think they're—"

"Nora, seriously?"

She chuckled. "I should be there. I'd get us some answers."

"How are classes?" I changed the subject.

"Dull. It's not the same without you. The apartment is so empty, and Maurice isn't half as interesting as Luis."

"You could always ask Dan to keep you company."

"I think I have decided Dan and I are more compatible as friends."

"That's a shame."

"Not really. He's busy with the team, and I'm... well, I'm not really feeling it."

"Well as long as you're not throwing away a shot at something good for a certain brooding mafioso?"

"Enzo, really? Please, I have some dignity." The lilt in her voice suggested otherwise, but I didn't argue. We had bigger problems at hand.

A beat passed, and then Nora whispered, "When do you think you might be able to come back?"

"I don't know." My heart ached. We'd never really spent any time apart. Even when we'd lived on my father's estate, she was only ever a stone's throw away in her family's cottage.

"Okay, well, stay safe. That's all that matters right now."

"You be careful too. Scott is still—"

"He wouldn't dare try anything with me," she scoffed. "Besides, Maurice follows me around like my shadow."

I hoped she was right.

"I'll text you later, okay?" she said.

"Okay. Bye."

We hung up just as I heard raised voices coming from the living room. Tiptoeing to the far wall, I pressed my ear against the wood. I didn't want to eavesdrop, I didn't want to be that girl, but Nora had planted a seed. And I couldn't deny part of me wondered what was happening.

"No," I heard Nicco say. "No fucking way."

"Niccolò," Antonio clucked his tongue, "you need to..." His words were swallowed.

"Porca miseria!" I couldn't figure out who that was, possibly Enzo or his father.

"... to our advantage."

"I won't do it." Nicco sounded irritated. Something crashed and then a door slammed, reverberating through the cabin.

I stumbled back, regretting my decision to listen. A couple of seconds later, there was a knock at my door. "Arianne," Luis said.

"Come in."

He slipped inside and closed the door. "How much of that did you hear?"

"Not a lot."

He gave me a pointed look, and I let out a defeated sigh. "I heard the odd word. Is everything okay?"

"Things got a little fraught, but everything will be okay. Antonio and his brothers just left."

"So I can go see Nicco?"

"Umm..." His expression fell.

"Luis?"

"He's..."

I shouldered past him and went into the main room. "Nicco?"

"Hey Ari," Matteo looked sheepish, rubbing a hand through his hair and down his neck.

"Where is he?"

"I... uh... he's..." His eyes went to the door. I took off, yanking it open, catching Nicco about to take off on his bike.

"Nicco?" I called.

His body slumped back on the bike, his head hung low. I inched closer, sensing his torment. "Nicco, look at me."

"I need a minute." His voice was raw.

"You're leaving?" I rounded the bike.

"No, I would never... I just need..." He inhaled a ragged breath. "I'm sorry."

"I don't want you to be sorry. I want you to talk to me. What happened?"

His eyes shuttered and he exhaled a shaky breath. "Please don't ask me that, anything but that."

The need to know what had happened burned through me but Nicco was hurting and all I wanted to do was make it better.

"Will you come inside with me?"

"I need to ride, Bambolina. I need... space."

"From me?" Pain squeezed my heart.

"Not you, never you. I just... this is how I deal with things."

"So I'll come." I went to climb on the back of his bike, but Nicco hooked me round the waist, pulling me into him. "It's not safe."

"Then it's not safe for you either." I pressed my hand to his cheek, narrowing my eyes as I spoke my next words. "Come inside, Nicco. I won't ask again."

Pulling away, I marched back into the cabin and sat down on the sectional.

"Everything okay?" Matteo asked me.

"We'll see." I rested my chin on my fists, mindlessly counting the seconds.

If Nicco didn't come back, I didn't know what I would do. But if we were going to be together, if we were going to get through this, he had to realize he couldn't just take off every time the going got tough. He might not have been able to tell me everything, but he could *be* with me.

He could turn to me for comfort.

I glanced at the door, waiting for him to walk through it.

"Ari, maybe you should—"

"Don't," I groaned.

"It's not you, you have to know that. This is killing him."

"It's not exactly easy for me either." I met Matteo's sympathetic gaze.

"I know. Trust me, I know. But Nicco is used to being in control. He's used to—"

I didn't need to turn around to see Nicco, I felt him, the tether between us pulling taut.

"I'll give you two a minute." Matteo got up and left the cabin.

The air crackled between us, thick and oppressive. "Do you want to talk about it?" I said, breaking the heavy silence.

"I just want to be with you, Bambolina. Is that okay?"

I nodded, scared that if I spoke, we would lose this moment.

Nicco had relented.

Instead of running away to clear his head, he'd turned to me.

It felt like a turning point.

"I'm here, Nicco. Whatever you need, I'm here."

He finally moved, standing over me. His body vibrated with anger; I could feel it permeate the air. Sliding my hand in his, I stood. "What do you need?"

Nicco's jaw clenched impossibly tight. "Di te, Bambolina, I only need you." He curved his arm around my waist, pulling me close. I slid my palms up his chest, leaning up to kiss him.

"You have me," I breathed, "always."

TWENTY-THREE

NICCO

WE SPENT the rest of the day in bed. Matteo and Luis made themselves scarce. There was a fire pit around the back of the cabin. Arianne wanted to check it out, but I'd told her it wasn't safe.

I didn't want to share her, not yet.

Not after earlier.

I hadn't wanted to take off, but after seeing my father and my uncles, I'd needed air. What I'd really needed was to fight, but I couldn't do that, so I'd hopped on my bike with only one thing in mind.

Me and the open road.

Then Arianne had appeared.

I'd seen the disappointment in her eyes; it cut me like tiny daggers. But it was no more than I deserved.

I couldn't tell her the truth, not yet. And the secrets and lies were beginning to feel like a burden too heavy to carry.

When the sun began to sink behind the tree line, Matteo, Enzo, and Luis all returned to the cabin, this time with pizza.

"You seem better," Enzo said as the two of us found some plates and napkins.

"I'm okay." We shared a silent look.

My eyes flicked to Arianne, who immediately averted her gaze. I knew she wanted to know what had happened earlier, but so far she was respecting our privacy.

We joined them, and together we enjoyed an evening eating pizza and drinking beer with her bodyguard and my best friends. Between the food, easy conversation, and laughter it was easy to pretend there wasn't a shitshow happening around us.

"That was so good." She licked the grease off her fingers, and a low growl built in my chest when I noticed Enzo and Matteo watching her. They both chuckled, and I flipped them off.

Luis had been quiet, happy to listen to us regale Arianne with stories of our childhood. But when his cell phone vibrated for the fifth time, Enzo grumbled. "Are you going to get that?"

"It's Roberto." Luis' eyes flashed to me. "He wants Arianne to reply to his messages."

"I have nothing to say to him," she said.

Arianne had left her cell in the bedroom all day.

"If you need to talk—"

"I said I have nothing to say to him." Irritation laced her words.

"It's okay." I squeezed her knee. "Luis will handle it." I shot him a pointed look, and Luis clambered to his feet, disappearing down the hall.

Tristan was buying us time. Mike Fascini knew about Scott's latest attack. He knew Luis had taken Arianne to a safe place. As far as we were aware, Roberto had told him Arianne needed some space. But he wasn't a fool. Eventually, he would piece together that I was with her, that we were planning to make our move against him.

"Are you two staying?" she asked Matteo and Enzo.

"Yeah, we're going to crash here."

"What about classes?"

"It's all about keeping up pretenses, but maybe after all this, we won't need to —" Matteo elbowed Enzo in the ribs.

"Let me guess, you guys aren't supposed to talk about it." Arianne's expression fell.

"I'm sorry." I brushed my lips over her forehead.

"It's late," she let out a small sigh, "we should probably get some sleep."

"Like you'll be doing any of that," Enzo snorted.

I swiped a bottle cap off the table and threw it at his head. "Watch your mouth."

"I'll clean up first." Arianne got up but I grabbed her hand.

"They can handle it." I glared at my cousins. "We'll see you in the morning."

Guiding Arianne down the hall, we fell into the bedroom in a tangle of kisses and soft moans. "I feel bad," she breathed against my lips.

"What for?"

"Because they're stuck here while we..." Her cheeks flamed.

"They get it."

"Do they?"

"Enzo not so much but Matteo understands."

"What do you—"

"Bambolina?" I advanced on Arianne, not stopping until she was caged between my body and the wall.

"Yes?" She looked at me through her lashes.

"Stop talking."

"Why?" Her lips curved and I lowered my head, capturing them in a bruising kiss.

"Because, amore mio, I'm going to strip the clothes from your body, lay you down, and worship every single inch of you."

"Oh." She blushed.

"Still want to talk?" I cocked a brow.

Arianne shook her head. "I'll be quiet now."

"Good." Kissing the corner of her mouth, I whispered, "The only word I want to hear falling from your lips while we're in this room is my name."

The next morning, I left Arianne sleeping and went to find my cousins. They were already dressed, tucking into a stack of pancakes.

"Smells good," I said to Matteo.

"Hey, what makes you think he cooked them?" Enzo asked, and I frowned at him.

"When was the last time you cooked?"

"I cook."

"Dialing for pizza is not cooking."

He flipped me off. "Where's Arianne?"

"Sleeping."

"Did you wear her out?"

"Watch it." I jabbed my finger at him. "Any news?"

"Nothing to report," Matteo said, passing me a plate.

"Perhaps you need to think about what your old man—"

"Not. Happening," I growled.

"Okay, okay." Enzo's hands shot up. "Forget I said anything."

"We wait and see what Tristan finds out before we make any decisions."

"He needs putting down. He orchestrated the hit on Arianne when she was just a kid, Nicco. And then he let his son—"

"She's not strong enough." Arianne wasn't ready to enter our world, not really. I wanted to shield her from it for as long as possible.

"You're going to have to choose eventually." Enzo let out an exasperated sigh.

"He's right, Cous," Matteo added. "You might have to make the decision for her."

"I need more time. She needs more time."

"I hope you know what you're doing, man." Enzo got up and stalked out of the cabin. It was becoming a regular pattern with us. But at least we weren't solving our problems with fists these days.

"I know you want to do the right thing, but in our life, doing the right thing means something different in their world." Matteo gave me a pointed look.

"Their world?"

"Arianne, Nora, even Roberto. They live by a different moral code to us. I know you know that."

"I won't give her up."

I wouldn't give her up for anything.

"I know. I'm not saying you have to let her go. I'm just saying that you might have to make the hard decisions to keep her conscience clean."

I ran a hand down my face, letting out a strained breath. But Matteo wasn't done.

"If he was here right now, if Fascini walked in here, what would you do?"

My eyes narrowed to slits, anger reverberating through me. "You know."

"So, is Mike really any different? He wants to destroy us, Nic. He wants to take Capizola Holdings first and then come after us. He is the enemy."

"You think I don't know that?" I seethed, my fist clenched at my side. "It's *all* I think about."

It would be so easy to take them both out. We had several guys on the books who could do it. Hell, I could probably do it.

"We still don't know if he has a backup plan."

"Even if he does, it's nothing we can't find a way around. You're stalling."

He was right, I was stalling.

Because I wanted something better for Arianne. I wanted to be able to give her things, things I might not ever be able to provide.

"This is who you are, Nic. If she's going to be with you, you both have to accept that." Matteo clapped me on the back. "That girl loves you, more than she probably should. You're Niccolò Marchetti, Prince of fucking Hearts. You don't cower and you certainly don't shy away from making the hard decisions."

He left me with my thoughts.

I didn't want to be Arianne's prince. I wanted to be her king. The king of her heart.

The king of her soul.

But I was still holding back. I was trying to divide myself between Niccolò Marchetti, son of the boss, and Nicco Marchetti the guy in love with a girl.

Matteo and Enzo were right.

I couldn't be both.

There was no escaping my fate.

And yet, I still wanted to protect her from the inevitable.

I spent the day agonizing over my father's visit. He wanted to move against Mike sooner rather than later. But he knew what Arianne meant to me. He knew he risked losing me if anything was to happen to her.

But in the end, my torment was all for nothing.

Tristan arrived with news, and it wasn't what we'd hoped to hear.

"Mike has given my father until the weekend to bring Arianne back." He cast his bloodshot eyes to the quiet girl beside me. "I'm so sorry."

"Or what?" Luis barked.

"Or he's going to..." The color drained from Tristan's face. "Kill Uncle Roberto."

"What?" Arianne leaped up, her body trembling. "You're lying... he can't—"

"It's true. Uncle Roberto insisted I didn't tell you. But this isn't a game. Mike Fascini isn't playing around this time."

I grabbed Arianne's hand, gently coaxing her back down onto the couch. "How did he issue the threat?"

"There was a package. A letter and..." He ran a hand through his hair.

"Tristan," I urged.

"A flash drive. It contained live feeds of the entire estate."

"He bugged the house?"

He nodded.

"Fuck." Mike Fascini was more organized than we first thought.

"My uncle's study, the kitchen ... the bedrooms. He has enough to bring down Capizola Holdings at the press of a button."

Arianne clapped a hand over her mouth, smothering a gasp.

"He won't do it. He wants everything Roberto has. He's just trying to show him he holds all the cards."

"Maybe my parents can leave... maybe they can—"

"It won't change anything." I squeezed Arianne's hand in mine. "Mike Fascini has gone too far now. He doesn't care which way it ends, just that he holds all the power."

"I'll go back then. I'll go back and maybe you can—oh God."

"Bambolina, look at me." Cupping Arianne's face, I brushed her cheek. "You can't go back. Not now. It isn't only Mike we have to worry about, it's Scott too. He's unstable." And there wasn't a chance in hell he was getting within two feet of Arianne.

"He's my father, Nicco, I can't just let him..." Arianne let out a garbled cry and I pulled her into my arms, holding the back of her head as she sobbed gently.

"You know what has to be done." Tristan gave me a hard look.

"What?" Arianne eased back, gulping down her tears as she smoothed the hair from her eyes. "What has to be done?" She glanced from me to Tristan and back again.

I inhaled a ragged breath and whispered, "Mike Fascini has to die."

"D- die?" she choked out, edging away from me.

Her reaction stung but I'd expected no less. This was the ugly side of my world. The dark and tainted part I'd hoped never to share with her.

"As in you're going to *kill* him? That's... you can't..."

"If it means keeping you safe, I'll do whatever it takes."

"But killing a man?"

"Bambolina." I gave her a sad smile. "I have done much worse."

"It doesn't have to be you. It can be someone else, anyone else." Her voice rose as tears streamed down her face.

"It doesn't matter if it's me or if it's someone else. This is who I am."

"Okay," Luis said, standing. "Perhaps we should give the two of you some space."

But Arianne didn't look like she wanted space from them, she looked like she wanted space... from me.

"You two stay, I'll go." The words almost choked me. "I could do with some air."

"Nicco," she cried, and I lifted my eyes to hers. But nothing else came out.

She didn't ask me to stay...

She didn't say anything.

"Take your time." I gave him a stiff nod. "I won't go far."

I walked out of the cabin and didn't look back.

Because I knew if I did, I would break.

And a prince with a broken kingdom couldn't protect his queen.

When I finally got back to the cabin, it was dark. I slipped inside with a heavy heart. What would Arianne say? Would she want me to leave and never return?

I braced myself but found only Luis and Tristan in the main room.

"She's sleeping," Luis said. "How are you?"

"It's not me I'm worried about." I sat down and my eyes flicked to the long hall leading to our bedroom.

"It's been a lot for her to process."

"That's what worries me. How much more of this can she take?"

"Don't underestimate her," Luis said.

"What about you, what do you make of all this?" I asked Tristan.

"Honestly, I haven't got a fucking clue what to say. I knew, man. I knew my uncle planned to marry her off to that piece of shit. It cuts me up inside knowing I never saw his true colors until now."

My brow arched. "Arianne spoke like he'd hurt other girls before."

"He's known to be a little forward when he's had a drink, yeah. But he never—fuck, you think there are others?"

"Maybe. But not like Arianne. What he did to her at the hotel..." My spine stiffened.

"How do you do it?"

"Do what?" I asked Tristan.

"I want to kill him with my bare hands for ever hurting her, so I can't imagine how you must be feeling."

I didn't answer. I couldn't verbalize the things I wanted to do to that fucker.

"Do you think she'll come around?"

"Eventually." Tristan's brows pinched. "She hates Roberto right now, but he's her family, her blood. She would never want harm to come to him. That's not who she is."

"So we agree then? This is the only option?" The two of them nodded. "I'll need to call my father and make arrangements."

"You think he'll help?" Tristan asked.

"I know he will. He always knew this was how it would go. You can't negotiate with men like Fascini."

"And after... what happens then?"

I could read between the lines. He wanted to know what happened after Mike was gone.

"I love Arianne and I want a life with her. If she still wants me, I guess we'll be family one day."

He gave me a slight nod. "My uncle will be in the debt of the Marchetti; he won't like that."

"Not my problem."

I was doing this for Arianne.

To protect her.

"I'll talk to him again, try to explain that we have a plan."

I shrugged. "Do whatever you got to do, but just know, I will always put Arianne first. Always."

"Noted." He ran a hand over his jaw. "You know, Marchetti, we might not have always seen eye to eye, but I'm glad she's had you through all of this."

Standing, I narrowed my eyes at him. We were done here. I wasn't looking for his approval or even his gratitude. He hadn't been there when she'd needed him, too busy playing king of the campus at MU.

"Yeah, well she should have had you too." The words spilled out, but I didn't regret them. I couldn't. "Scott was your best friend, your guy. What happened between Arianne and him... some of that's on you."

"Shit, Marchetti, you think I don't know that? You think I don't lie awake at night thinking how different things might have been if I'd have been more clued in?

"Look, I can't change what happened but I'm here and I'm trying to do right by her now. I won't stand in your way. You love her and fuck knows she's made it abundantly clear she loves you."

I smirked.

As if he could actually come between us.

Arianne was a part of me now.

As much as I was a part of her.

TWENTY-FOUR

ARIANNE

I DREAMED OF DEATH. Of blood and screams, guns and fists.

I dreamed of Mike Fascini beaten and bloody on the ground, a ruby red halo around him, the life gone from his eyes. And standing above him, like a dark angel, was Nicco.

Startled, I clutched the sheet to my body, willing my heart to slow down.

"What is it?" Nicco asked, pressing his lips to my shoulder.

"Just a nightmare, go back to sleep."

He let out a quiet sigh, but soon slipped back under. But I couldn't sleep, not after the nightmare.

They wanted to kill Mike Fascini.

Perhaps it shouldn't have bothered me. The man was the villain of our story; hellbent on revenge and willing to do whatever it took to see our families fall. But I couldn't help but think there had to be another way. A way that didn't require his life in return for my father's freedom.

For *my* freedom.

Nicco seemed dead set on making me understand that this was his life, that his soul was already tainted.

I didn't doubt it.

But I still wanted to keep it as clean as possible.

Maybe it was a foolish notion, to think it mattered.

It did matter though.

To me, it mattered.

Mike and Scott deserved to pay for their sins, they deserved to feel everything slip through their fingers and fall away.

But death?

My conscience wasn't ready to accept that this was how it had to be.

"Do you wish you had never met me?" Nicco whispered against my skin.

"No. Never." My heart ached at the very idea of it. "But I do wish things could be different. I wish that I was just a girl and you were just a boy."

Nicco looped his arm tighter, tucking me against the hard lines of his body. "I love you with everything that I am. I hope you know that, Bambolina. I hope it's enough."

"I do. It is." I laid my hand over his. "But there must be another way."

"There isn't..."

"It isn't fair."

"Life isn't fair, Arianne. It's cold and cruel and painful. But there are sparks of light in the dark. You are my spark, amore mio. Your brightness outshines the darkness in my soul." He lifted his chin to rest in the curve of where my shoulder met my neck.

"I don't want it to be like this, Nicco."

"Sometimes we must make the hard choices, Bambolina. That's all we are at the end of the day; a chain of decisions, some good, some bad."

I thought back to that night in the alley. If Scott hadn't tried to hurt me, I wouldn't have run. And if I'd never run, I might have never met Nicco.

Scott's bad choice led me here. It was the catalyst of a series of events that had forever changed me. Yet, I still had faith in humanity, in people choosing to do the right thing. The morally just thing.

I closed my eyes and inhaled a shaky breath. There had to be another way.

There had to.

Nicco was gone when I woke up. He'd left a note in his wake. Four little words that eased the knot in my stomach.

I'll see you later.

When I finally dragged myself into the living room, Luis confirmed what I already knew. Nicco had gone to see his father. I felt conflicted. On the one hand, I knew he was trying to protect me from what was to come. But on the other, it seemed cowardly.

"This is the right move, Arianne," Luis said over his coffee.

"Is it?"

"He tried to kill you. That is not a man you want to negotiate with."

"But to murder him?" Bile washed in my stomach.

"I know this is hard for you."

"You don't know anything," I snapped. "I have been lied to and used and... *raped*. Maybe death should befall Mike Fascini. But it feels like the easy way out for him. He deserves to rot in Hell for his crimes."

He'd orchestrated everything.

The failed hit on me when I was younger.

The business merger with my father.

The engagement.

The wedding.

The engagement.

A plan slowly began to take shape in my mind. Mike Fascini had positioned himself as someone of worth to my father. That was something I could exploit.

Something I could use.

"Arianne?" Luis asked as I stared off into the distance.

Blinking, I let my eyes drift to his. "I need you to do something for me."

"Why do I not like the sound of this?"

"I need you to take me to see Antonio."

"Are you out of your mind?" His eyes were the size of saucers.

Quite possibly. But I didn't tell him that.

"I know Nicco has gone there to make arrangements." The word soured on my tongue. "But I need to talk to him."

"I'll call Nicco. We can get Antonio to come here."

"It can't wait." Now that the seed was planted, I knew what I had to do.

"Ari, I'm not sure—"

"I'm going. Whether you help me or not, I'm doing this, Luis. I have sat by letting these... these men trample all over my life, but I won't sit idly by while a man is murdered in cold blood. Mike Fascini deserves to be punished. But this is not the way."

His expression turned grim. "It is their way."

"Will you take me or not?"

"You really want to do this? It isn't safe..."

I glared at him. This was happening. I wouldn't rest until he delivered me to Antonio's house.

"Fine," he grumbled, disapproval etched into his expression. "I'll take you."

"Thank you."

Antonio Marchetti might have been the boss of Dominion, but he was a businessman at heart.

And I had an offer he needed to hear.

We pulled up outside the Marchetti house an hour later. Luis had been quiet the entire ride. He didn't approve of me being here. But it was too late now.

The door flung open and Enzo appeared. "What the fuck?" He marched to the car, yanking open my door. "What the fuck are you thinking?"

"I need to see Antonio."

"You shouldn't be here."

Indignation trickled up my spine. I climbed out and met Enzo's glare with my own. "Well, I'm here now, and I'm not leaving until I speak with Antonio."

"Nicco is going to lose his shit when he realizes you're here. And you." Enzo jabbed his finger at Luis. "You had one fucking job. Keep her at the cabin."

"She was going to find her way here with or without me." His eyes settled on me. "She can be quite stubborn."

"You don't say."

I didn't wait for them to approach the house. Slipping inside, I followed the sound of Antonio and Nicco's voices, finding them in the same room I'd found them in the morning after the gala.

Taking a deep breath, I knocked on the door.

"What?" Antonio barked.

Pushing open the door, I stepped inside.

"Arianne?" Nicco blanched.

"Well, if this isn't a surprise." Antonio glowered at me, sliding his eyes to his son.

"What are you doing here?" Nicco rushed over to my side.

"I need to talk to your father."

"You should have called me."

"So you could talk me out of it?" My lips pursed.

"Niccolò, what is this all about?"

"I'm sorry to just barge in here like this, but Nicco had no idea I planned to come here. I didn't until I woke up," I said, meeting Antonio's cloudy eyes. "But I need to speak to you, Mr. Marchetti. Urgently."

"Please, Arianne, call me Antonio." He relaxed back in his chair. "Well, I am waiting..."

"Actually, I'd like to speak to you... alone."

Nicco let out a low groan. I peeked over at him. He looked confused, betrayal glittering in his eyes.

But I needed to do this.

"Very well. Niccolò, leave us."

"Wait a minute," he shot forward, "maybe I should—"

"Niccolò! Arianne has asked for privacy, and she shall get it. Wait outside."

"Why?" Nicco asked, the hurt in his eyes almost too much to bear.

"I had to."

He stalked out of the room, and guilt snaked through me. But I would worry about Nicco later. Right now, I needed to talk with his father.

"It would seem I underestimated you, Arianne," he said. "Please, sit."

I took one of the leather chairs. "I am sorry for just turning up like this, but I couldn't just stand by. Mike Fascini and his son deserve to be punished, Mr. Mar—Antonio. But murder?"

"In our line of work, we prefer the term execution." He was so matter of fact it made my chest constrict. "Mike Fascini plotted against my family, Arianne. I'm sure you can understand I can't just let that go unpunished. He has directly threatened you, and now your father." He steepled his fingers. "Can I ask you something?"

I nodded.

"Would you rather sacrifice yourself to save Roberto?"

"No, that's not—"

"Sometimes we must make hard choices."

"That's what Nicco said."

"This life doesn't come easy for Niccolò. I suppose, in part, I am to blame for that. He blames me for his mother leaving. He blames me for a lot of things. And his blame isn't misplaced. I have done things, Arianne. Despicable things. But it is who I am. Just as you sit before me now as who you are."

"Is there another way?"

Antonio's brows morphed into a scowl. "Another way?"

"To deal with the Fascini. You are a well-connected man, you have the evidence of what Scott did to me, surely there is a way to take that to the authorities..."

"There is always another way, Arianne, but it doesn't mean it is the right way."

"I don't want anyone to die."

"Death is inevitable." He stroked his jaw, studying me, as if I was puzzle he was trying to solve.

"I want them to pay, I do. But not like this."

"You know, there are people who might think you should be sitting here thanking me. I am, after all, offering to save your father. My enemy."

"But you're not doing it for me, are you? You're doing it for you. For the Family. Kill two birds with one stone."

"Explain."

"If you get rid of the Fascini, it leaves my father in your debt. You can use that as leverage to ensure he doesn't come after La Riva. If Fascini is gone, my father's position is weakened. And the Marchetti come out on top."

"Interesting." His eyes twinkled.

"What is?"

"You're more like your father than anyone gives you credit for."

"Whether I like it or not, I am my father's daughter. And I am here to negotiate."

He sat forward; hands folded on the desk. "I'm listening."

"What if you didn't have my family in your debt but as a partner?"

"I'm not sure you are in any position to make that offer, Arianne."

"My father's life hangs in the balance and one day, Capizola Holdings will be mine. I think I'm exactly the person to make such an offer." My brow raised.

"Your terms?"

"Figure out another way to take down the Fascini. You said it's possible. If you can guarantee no one will get hurt, I'll make you a silent partner."

"Your father will never agree to those terms."

"It's not his decision to make." My voice shook. "We both know he's indebted to you either way."

"It's ballsy, I'll give you that. Our families are on opposite sides of morality. Bringing us together—"

"Is righting history."

"This won't change who we are, Arianne. It won't change who Niccolò is. Do you understand that?"

"I know." My voice was small. "I'm not a fool. I know what you do. I know what your family does. But this is different. This is personal. And I'm not sure I can carry the burden of murder."

"Say I was to consider your offer; I'd need reassurances."

"I give you my word. After the Fascini are dealt with, I'll have my father's legal team draw up all the necessary paperwork." My father would listen, he'd have no choice.

Not after Antonio saved his life.

Besides, he owed me.

My father owed it to me to let me have this.

"I appreciate your tenacity, Arianne. But it is all just words and paper. These things are easily broken."

My stomach sank. This was my Ace card, my final plea. If Antonio didn't take it... I didn't know what would become of me and Nicco.

"I'm sorry," I kept my voice even. "I'm not sure I understand. I can try to have the paperwork drawn up sooner, but we're running out of time. Mike is going to kill my father, Antonio. He's going to—"

He silenced me with his hand. "My son is prepared to kill for you, to *die* for you, Arianne... What are you prepared to do for my son?"

I frowned.

What did he mean?

"I love Nicco, I would do whatever I could to protect him."

"I'm glad to hear that." His lip curved, a dark expression crossing his face. It sent a shiver rippling through me. "The bonds of marriage are sacred in our world. They bind together two people far more than any promise."

Marriage?

"You want me to *marry* Nicco?"

"Mike Fascini might be blinded by his thirst for vengeance, Arianne, but he knew what he was doing convincing Roberto to promise you to his son. One day you will be the Queen of the Capizola empire and your child will be the heir. Fascini knew this. He knew if you gave Scott a child, the Ricci bloodline would supersede the Capizola line."

"I'm not... that doesn't..." It was crazy talk, yet, deep down, I knew he spoke the truth.

"My son loves you, Arianne. He has chosen you as his woman. One day, he will ask for your hand in marriage. It is inevitable. I am not asking anything of you that isn't already written in your destiny."

Antonio's eyes narrowed as he watched my reaction. I realized then, it was a test.

He was testing me.

I didn't belong in their world. I was too pure, too righteous. He wanted to know how far I would go to prove my loyalty to Nicco.

To his family.

Staring him right in the eye, I gave him a small nod. "I'll do it. Do this one thing for me. Save my father, and I'll marry Nicco."

"You will?" Antonio looked oddly relieved.

"Like you said, I love your son, Antonio. I look into the future and see a life with him. So yes, I'll marry him." My body hummed with nervous anticipation, with the idea of binding my life with Nicco's so definitively.

"Do you want to tell him, or should I?"

"Let me talk to him first."

He nodded. "As you wish. But, Arianne, you should know he might not like this. Niccolò has never taken well to following orders, especially my orders."

But this was different.

This was me giving myself to him completely.

Heart.

Body.

Soul.

And in marriage.

"Nicco?" I entered the kitchen and he looked up. His expression was crestfallen, tugging at my heart strings.

"You shouldn't have come here, Arianne."

"Yes, I should." I walked over to him, stopping just out of touching distance. "Can we talk? Somewhere private?"

His eyes swirled with uncertainty. I'd driven a wedge between us by coming here, and I knew he felt betrayed. But there was no going back now, only forward.

"Please," I added.

He pressed his palms against the counter and stood up. "Okay, come on."

It stung when he didn't take my hand, but I took a shuddering breath and followed him out of the back door to the fire pit where we'd once sat with his cousins and Alessia.

That night seemed so long ago, when it was only a couple of weeks. I was different now.

We both were.

But the truth was, I'd never felt stronger.

I no longer had to sit around and let other people determine my fate, I could carve my own path.

I just needed Nicco to see that.

He sat down in one of the lawn chairs and I did the same. The air was cool between us, and not only from the frigid fall temperatures.

"What did you offer him?" Nicco didn't look at me, his eyes staring off into the distance.

"How did you—"

His gaze finally shifted to mine, filled with so much intensity my breath caught. "I know you, Arianne. I think I knew last night that you wouldn't let it rest. So what did you offer him?"

"We negotiated," I said calmly, fighting every instinct to go to him and beg him to understand. "I offered to make him a partner in Capizola Holdings if he'll hand the Fascini to the authorities."

"And he accepted?" His eyes narrowed, dark and menacing. A shiver skated up my spine.

"He has terms of his own."

He scoffed. "Of course he does."

"I love you Nicco, and I want a life with you. I know who you are. I know what it means to be in your world, but I'm not ready to..." I swallowed the words. "I can't just give up my morality. I can't."

"So you decided to make a deal with the Devil?"

"That's not..." I pressed my lips together. Nicco had a point. "I can't really explain it. All I know is in my heart of hearts, I couldn't turn a blind eye to this. Maybe it makes me a fool or naive, maybe it makes me unworthy of your love, but this world has proved itself to me as a dark place. You said I was the light. I'm not ready to give that up."

Taking me by surprise, Nicco stood and came to me, falling to his knees before me. "You are the light, Bambolina, but it doesn't change the fact Fascini needs to pay for his crimes."

"I know." I brushed the hair from his eyes. "But there is always a choice."

"What did he want from you, Arianne?" Defeat washed over him.

"Nothing I wouldn't have one day given anyway." Leaning down, I cupped his face, touching my head to his. "He wants my name, Nicco. He wants us to marry."

TWENTY-FIVE

NICCO

"NO," the word was out of my mouth before I could stop it.

Arianne paled, jerking away from me, leaving me cold and desolate.

"No?" She cried. "But I thought... you don't want me?"

"Not like this." *Never* like this.

I wanted our future to be born out of love, not obligation.

"But it solves everything," she said unable to disguise the pain in her voice. "Your father will help make sure Mike and Scott pay for their crimes, my father's life will be saved, and we'll be together."

"You don't know what you're saying," I ground out.

I wanted a life with Arianne, a future. But she deserved more than... than *this*. She deserved an engagement and a bridal shower. She deserved to enjoy all the planning and lead up to her wedding day.

She deserved so much more than a last-minute wedding arranged as part of a business transaction.

"Your father said you wouldn't be happy." Sadness laced her words. "But I thought... I'm just trying to do the right thing." A soft sigh escaped her lips. "Is the idea of marrying me so unappealing to you?"

"Bambolina, that's not..." I inhaled a sharp breath. "This is not how I want it to be."

I wanted to put this all behind us and enjoy being a couple. I didn't want her to rush headfirst into something she wasn't ready for.

Something *we* weren't ready for.

"I know what I want, Nicco," Arianne's expression fell as if she could hear my thoughts and sense my torment. "Did I imagine I'd be married at eighteen? No, I didn't. But I also didn't imagine that I'd meet someone like you. I didn't imagine that everything I thought I knew would turn out to be a lie."

Frustration laced her words. "Nothing about this is what I'd ever imagined, but here we are. I love you, I love you so much..." Silent tears trickled down her cheeks but I was paralyzed, unable to reach for her.

My father had said all along that Arianne could be the leverage he needed over Roberto, and he had gotten his wish.

It didn't matter if Arianne thought the choice was hers. I knew the truth.

I would always know the truth.

And one day, it would drive a wedge between us.

"Nicco, please, say something."

"I need to talk to my father." I stood, running a hand over my jaw.

"It is already done." Panic overwhelmed her voice. "I made my decision. I don't understand why you're fighting me on this?" Defiance burned in her eyes. "Unless you don't want—"

"Bambolina, stop." I curved my hand around her neck, holding her close to me. "I love you, but I don't want you to do something you'll one day regret." Something she might one day resent me for.

"This will unite our families, Nicco." She eased back to look at me. "It will right things."

The sincerity in her gaze almost killed me. But you couldn't just rewrite a bitter history with a wedding—a wedding born out of business.

"Don't you see," I said, angling her face to mine. "You are just replacing one cage for another."

"No, that's not what this is. I'm choosing this, I'm choosing you. I want this, Nicco. I want you." Her bottom lip quivered. "I thought you felt the same about me. I thought—"

I pressed a hard kiss to her forehead, silencing her. "I need to speak with my father. I'll be back soon." Pulling away, I didn't look at her.

I couldn't.

Because if I did, I was worried I might say something I would regret. Something I couldn't ever take back.

Something that might destroy us both.

"Ahh, Niccolò, did Arianne tell you the happy news?" My father smirked, only provoking the storm inside me to rage harder.

"What the fuck were you thinking?" I seethed.

"Watch your tongue, boy." His eyes narrowed. "Arianne came to me with an offer and I saw an opportunity. You should be thanking me. This will make her your wife. It will bind your life with hers permanently."

"It shouldn't be like this." I shook my head.

"What you would you have me do, Son? Deny your woman and execute

Fascini? Make her hate me and resent you? She's not ready to have blood on her hands; you know I speak the truth."

I did.

But it didn't make it any easier to swallow.

"Arianne is strong," he went on. "She has proved that. I have no doubt she will make you a fine wife, Niccolò."

"It wasn't supposed to be like this," I looked at my father, silently pleading for him to fix this. But there was no magical solution.

He was right.

If he took out Fascini, Arianne would never forgive him. Forgive herself.

Maybe even me.

Or if he handed him over to the authorities and became a partner in Capizola Holdings like Arianne wanted, things might be okay for a while. But over time, Roberto would grow bitter and Arianne could end up resenting my family all the same.

And I couldn't let go of the fairytale she deserved.

"You love her, no?" he asked me.

"You know I do. More than I ever thought I could love another."

"Then perhaps it is time you trusted her." My father's expression softened. "Arianne has spent years having her choices removed. Now she is free, and she has chosen. I lost your mother because I couldn't see past my own proclivities, Niccolò. She was a good woman. Strong and loyal and beautiful. God, she was so beautiful." He stared off into the distance, shame washing over him.

It was a strange thing, watching Antonio Marchetti acknowledge his mistakes, watching him mourn for the woman he'd let slip through his fingers.

"Don't do something you'll regret, Son," my father offered me a sad smile. "That girl is everything I could wish for my son. I see so much of your mother in her, it scares me. But it also gives me hope. Hope that you will get a chance to right my wrongs."

Was he right?

Was I focusing on the wrong thing here?

Arianne seemed so certain, so sure of her love for me. But part of me couldn't accept that. It couldn't fathom that a girl like Arianne Carmen Lina Capizola could love a guy like me.

I kept pondering what Arianne deserved, but maybe the issue wasn't her.

It was me.

What *I* deserved.

What *I* was worthy of.

"Look, I know this isn't how you wanted things to go. But life doesn't always go to plan, Niccolò. Sometimes opportunities arise when you least expect them. If the outcome is the same does it really matter what path you took to get there?" He ran a hand over his jaw. "I cannot give you what you most desire, I cannot free you from this life. But I can give you this."

My body shook with anger, frustration, and uncertainty. I was Niccolò

Marchetti. Nothing would ever change that. But a life with Arianne by my side would make it all worth it.

"You know I'm right, Son."

I stared at my father, giving him a sharp nod. I still didn't know what I felt. I was too wired, too volatile.

"Go calm down," he ordered. "And then talk to her. She needs to know you support this, Niccolò. She needs to know you support her."

I didn't go to Arianne.

I sent Alessia instead, asking her to keep my girl company. My father was right, I needed to calm down. Which meant, I needed space and time. But I did text Arianne.

I promise I'm not running. I just need to figure out some things.

Her one word reply had almost gutted me.

Okay.

But when I came back, I wanted to be clearheaded and present. I wanted to be everything she deserved.

A whistle pierced the air, and I saw Enzo waiting over by his car. "So what happened?"

"Not here." I yanked open the door and ducked inside.

Enzo got in and fired up the engine. "Where's Arianne?"

"Inside with Alessia." Leaning back against the headrest, I let out a weary sigh. "I just needed some space."

"That bad, huh?" Enzo backed out of the driveway and pulled onto the street.

"She came here to bargain with him."

"She's got balls, Cous, I'll give her that. Let me guess, she asked Uncle Toni to spare that piece of shit?"

"Yeah, she wants to let the law handle it."

Enzo scoffed. It wasn't how we usually got shit done. We had our own code, our own justice system. If you betrayed or screwed over the Family, you were dealt with swiftly.

And Mike Fascini had attempted what no other person ever had.

"She's not cut out for this life."

"It's a good thing I'm not asking her to initiate into the family then, isn't it?" Sarcasm dripped from my words.

"Yeah, but you know what I mean. She'll never understand this life, she'll never understand what you do. What we do."

"She's agreed to marry me," I confessed "that's what they negotiated."

"What the fuck?" The car swerved as Enzo's eyes snapped to mine.

"Watch the road," I hissed.

"You can't just drop something like that on me and expect me to keep cool. Marriage... he wants you to *marry* her? Has he lost his fucking mind?"

"Nice, E. Real nice."

"Sorry, I didn't mean... But you're both young. Like really young. Marriage is a huge deal. It's—"

"A life sentence?" I could see that's what he wanted to say. "I love her. I love her so fucking much."

"I sense a 'but' in there..." He cast me a sideways glance.

"It shouldn't be like this. I don't want her to be obligated to marry me to save her father, to save that fucking monster."

My pulse spiked again, but I forced myself to take a breath. I was supposed to be calming down, not getting even more worked up.

"What do you want, Nic?" There was no trace of mocking in his voice, just mild curiosity.

"Her, I just want her."

"So maybe you have your answer. Maybe you just need to accept your fate and go with it."

I glanced out of the window. It was dark, only the headlights of passing cars and streetlamps lighting the way. My mind drifted to Arianne. To how she made me feel every time she touched me, the way my heart galloped in my chest whenever her big brown eyes found mine across a room.

She was my anchor.

My North star in the endless night sky.

And although our time together had been relatively short, I couldn't imagine life without her.

I didn't want to.

"What's going on in that head of yours?" Enzo's voice penetrated my thoughts.

"I know what to do," I rushed out, a sense of peace washing over me.

"So we're not heading to my place?"

"Change of plan. Can we stop by Matteo's?" Officially, he lived with Enzo in their apartment on the edge of Romany Square and University Hill. But more often than not, he stayed with his family at their house in La Riva.

I dug my cell out of my pocket.

"You're calling him?"

"No. Luis."

"Okay..." He frowned. "Going to share your plan with me?"

"I will, once we get to Matteo's."

"What are you up to, Nicco?"

A smile spread over my face. "You'll see."

Almost three hours later, Matteo looked up from his cell phone and said, "They're on their way."

My heart was beating so hard I felt a little lightheaded.

"You okay, Cous?" Enzo clapped me on the back. "You don't look so good."

"I'm fine," I mumbled, taking a long pull on my beer.

We were back at the cabin. I didn't want to do this there. Not with my father, Alessia, and Genevieve hanging around.

Arianne and I needed to talk, and I wanted total privacy when we did.

"You sure you don't want us to stay?" Enzo asked, and I shook my head.

"I've got this."

"Yeah, you do." Matteo grinned. He turned to the overhead cabinets and found three glasses, setting them down in front of us. "Is there any of the good stuff lying around here?" He went over to my father's drinks cabinet. "Bingo." Snatching up a bottle of scotch, he brought it over and poured us each a glass.

"I'm driving," Enzo reminded him.

"One won't hurt. This deserves a toast."

He gave Matteo a sharp nod, accepting a glass. I took mine, swirling the amber liquid around the sides.

Maybe it would settle my nerves.

"To the best cousins, the best friends, a guy could ever have. I love you guys," Matteo said clutching his own glass. "To friendship, family, and the future. Salute."

"Salute." We clinked our glasses with his, downing our drinks in one.

"Shit, that's strong," he spluttered.

"You need to grow some fucking balls." Enzo clapped him on the back.

"Being a cold-hearted bastard does not mean you have big balls." Matteo flipped him off and the two of them started jostling and punching one another.

"Knock it off," I ordered. "You two need to get going."

"We should probably stick around—"

"Now," I said, narrowing my eyes at them.

"Come on, E. Nic's right. We should make tracks."

"Call us after?" Enzo met my stare, concern shining in his icy gaze.

"I'll text."

He rolled his eyes. "Whatever, just let us know, okay?"

"Like he needs to." Matteo smirked.

"Goodbye." I tipped my chin to the door. I appreciated their support, but I wanted a couple of minutes to myself before Arianne got here.

There would be no going back after tonight.

I watched my friends leave. Watched as the headlights of Luis' SUV appeared in the distance. I watched him roll to a stop and climb out, opening Arianne's door.

I watched her climb out, a look of trepidation on her face. "Nicco?" she said, confusion clouding her eyes. "What is it?"

"Will you come inside with me?" I asked, holding out my hand.

Luis caught my eye over her shoulder and gave me a curt nod before climbing back into the SUV. Arianne glanced back. "He's leaving?"

"I wanted to be alone with you." I gently tugged her hand. "Come inside and we can talk."

"Nicco, you're scaring me."

"You have nothing to fear, I promise." I pulled her closer, brushing her cheek. "Do you trust me?"

"You know I do." She gave me a tentative smile.

"Then come inside, Bambolina." I led her to the cabin, my body trembling with anticipation.

"You're shaking," she said, glancing up at me.

"I'll be okay in a second. Go on inside..."

Arianne gingerly made her way up the steps. "Nicco," she gasped when she stepped inside. "What did you do?"

"Every girl deserves their fairytale," I said, wrapping my hand around her waist and pulling her back against me. Dipping my head, I brushed the shell of her ear and said, "I'm sorry."

But they wouldn't be the most important words I said to her tonight.

Not by a long shot.

TWENTY-SIX

ARIANNE

THE CABIN HAD BEEN TRANSFORMED into something out of a fairytale. Twinkle lights hung from the wooden beams, casting a flickering glow around the room. The open fire crackled, filling the room with its smoky scent, and vases of white roses littered the table and breakfast counter. It was so beautiful; I was overwhelmed with emotion.

Nicco walked us forward, keeping his chin tucked into the crook of my neck. "Do you like it?" he whispered.

"I love it. But I don't understand..."

"Sit." Nicco moved around me, guiding me over to one of the armchairs.

My heart was in my mouth as he dropped to one knee in front of me. "Oh my god," I breathed, clapping a hand over my mouth. My body trembled, blood roaring between my ears. "Nicco."

"Just give me a minute." He popped the collar on his dress shirt. It was then I realized how smart he looked. The black material molded to his shoulders, and he'd rolled up the sleeves to his elbows, revealing his strong forearms.

"You're all dressed up." I smiled.

"Well, yeah, this is a special occasion."

My hands went to his face, as I leaned down.

"God, I love you," he murmured against my lips. But Nicco didn't kiss me. He pulled away gently. "You're distracting me."

"Sorry." My cheeks burned, but he looked so good down on one knee, his eyes burning with nothing but love and adoration. "Okay," I sat up, "go on."

He took a shuddering breath. "If someone had told me four months ago, that I would have been here right now... I would have laughed in their face. I wasn't interested in a relationship. I knew what this life meant for me and, honestly, I wasn't sure I would ever want to drag a girl into that. And then I met you.

"That night I saw you in the alley, my first instinct was to let Bailey deal with you. And then I looked at you, *really* looked at you, and something snapped into place. I wanted to wipe the tears from your face. I wanted to pick you up and keep you safe. That feeling only grew the more time I spent around you."

Nicco took my hand in his, brushing his thumb across my skin. "It was disarming, Bambolina. You disarmed me. But I couldn't get enough of you. You consumed my thoughts and haunted my dreams."

"Nicco..." My breath caught, my heart beating wildly in my chest.

"Your inner strength never ceases to amaze me. Your compassion and big heart. Even when you found out who I really was, you didn't run. You love without limits, Arianne. And I will spend my life trying to be worthy of you." He slipped his hand into his pocket and pulled out a small velvet pouch. "I didn't have much time, so consider this a stand-in until I can get you something new."

The world fell away as Nicco emptied out the simple band into his palm. He discarded the pouch and took my left hand in his. "Arianne Carmen Lina Capizola, you are my heart, my soul, and my future. I don't want to do this thing called life without you." Nicco moved the band to my ring finger. "I want you by my side, always. So will you do me the honor of being my wife?"

"Yes," I cried as he slid the band on. "I love you." Flinging my arms around Nicco's neck, I threw myself at him. He caught me, his laughter and my happy tears filling the space between us.

"Sei la mia anima gemella." He cupped the back of my neck. "The future Mrs. Arianne Marchetti."

"I like the sound of that."

Nicco brushed his lips over mine, sealing the moment with a kiss.

I would be his.

In heart, body, soul, and name.

Nicco pulled me to my feet, peppering my face with kisses. "I'm sorry I acted like an asshole earlier. I was just so shocked that you would do such a thing with no consideration for everything you deserve."

"I only want you."

"I know that now." He took my hand, pressing a kiss to my knuckles, the embedded diamonds of the ring glittering in the light.

"It's beautiful."

"It's a family heirloom of sorts. My Aunt Marcella, Matteo's mom, had it. It was my nonna's. As soon as it's safe I'll take you to pick something—"

"No," I said, already feeling possessive over it. "I love it." The fact it was a family heirloom only made it all the more special.

"You're sure about this?"

My head almost bobbed off my neck in agreement and I smiled so hard it made my cheeks ache.

"Give me a second." He dropped a kiss to my head and left me standing there while he went over to the kitchen. There was a bottle of champagne on ice, two glasses waiting for us.

"You've thought of everything."

"I had a little help." Nicco uncorked the bottle and poured us each a glass. I went to him, accepting a glass.

"To us."

"To us." I clinked my glass with his. His eyes never left my face as I took a sip of bubbly.

"You are so beautiful, amore mio."

I held out my hand, admiring the ring. It was the last thing I had expected when I'd turned up at Antonio's house.

"What are you thinking?" Nicco asked me.

"I'm so happy... earlier, at the house, I thought that perhaps you were having second thoughts about us."

"It was never about not wanting you, Bambolina. I just didn't want you to make such a big decision out of obligation. Our love isn't a bargaining chip. Our future isn't leverage. You are not some possession to be traded." He spoke with such vehemence it took my breath away.

"What changed your mind?"

"My father, Enzo... *you*." He took the glass from my hand and placed it down on the counter. "You own me, Arianne. I am yours, in this life and the next."

Startling me, Nicco bent down and slid his hand under my legs, picking me up and cradling me against his chest. "What are you doing?" I shrieked, laughter spilling from my lips.

"You'll see."

He carried me into the bedroom, and a sweet aroma flooded my senses. "What is—" I spotted the container on the nightstand.

"Tell me that's not what I think it is." My stomach clenched.

"I called in a favor." Nicco lay me down on the bed. His eyes were dark and hooded as he trailed them over my body. He looked like a man starved, and I knew the tiramisu from the Blackstone Country Club wasn't the only thing on the menu tonight.

I woke to sounds of birds chirping. Nicco's arm was slung possessively over my hip, his body pressed impossibly close to mine. My lips curved at the memories of the night before.

He'd proposed.

Niccolò Marchetti, mafia prince, Prince of Hearts, had gotten down on one knee and promised me forever.

I was floating on clouds so high I didn't ever want to come down.

After carrying me into our bedroom, Nicco had loved me with words and his body. It had been everything, being one with him.

My fiancé.

Uncurling my hands from the sheet, I admired his grandmother's ring. Nicco's fingers ran down my arm, curving around my wrist. "It looks good on you," he murmured, his voice thick with sleep.

"I still can't believe it," I choked out over the lump in my throat. "It's like waking up from the best dream."

"Believe it, Bambolina. Soon enough, I will stand before all our family and friends and declare you mine." Nicco tugged me onto my back and leaned over me. "No regrets?"

"No regrets." Laying my hand against his cheek, I leaned up to kiss him. "I love you, always."

His eyes shuttered, as if my admission was almost too much to bear.

"Nicco, look at me." They opened slowly. "I want this. It's time to rewrite history."

I truly believed I'd met Nicco for a reason. It wasn't coincidence he was there, in the alley, that night.

It was fate.

"I will never let another soul hurt you. You know that, right?"

"I know. What do you think your uncles will say?" I wasn't stupid, I knew Antonio didn't usually solve their problems this way.

"It doesn't matter. My father is the boss. What he says, goes."

"But they won't be happy?" My stomach twisted.

"Uncle Vincenzo is blood thirsty. He'll be disappointed." I winced at Nicco's honest words. "Uncle Michele has a softer approach. He'll be more understanding. But either way, the deal you struck with my father will give the Family a better foothold in Verona County."

"And my father? What will happen to him?"

"I guess that all depends on Roberto."

"He'll come around," I said quietly.

He had no choice.

And if he didn't, well, I was sure Antonio would handle my father.

Nicco lowered his face to mine, kissing me deeply. I could still taste the lingering sweetness of the tiramisu on his tongue. I would never be able to eat that dessert again without thinking about Nicco licking it off the most intimate parts of my body.

"Are you hungry, Love?" he whispered against my mouth.

"I—"

My eyes jerked to the door at the sound of something banging. "What is that?"

"Stay here." Nicco darted off the bed and pulled on his boxers before grabbing his gun from the nightstand. I'd never seen him brandish a weapon before. But this was who he was, who I'd promised myself to.

"Nicco," I whisper-hissed as he crept closer to the door. "Maybe we should—"

"Ssh," he mouthed, reaching for the door handle. I clutched the sheets around my body, fear trickling down my spine.

Quietly, Nicco opened the door and slipped into the cabin. I leaned over, grabbing my cell phone ready to call Luis. But then I heard voices. Laughter. Pushing back the sheets, I climbed out of bed and pulled on some clothes. My heart galloped in my chest as I left the bedroom and moved down the hall toward the main room.

"You have some explaining to do." Nora made a beeline for me. "I knew you were here, I frickin' knew it. But we'll get to that later. Let me see it." She beckoned for my hand, but I was still standing there, gawking at her. "What did you do to my girl, Marchetti? I think you broke her."

"I... what are you doing here?" My brows drew together.

"We thought you might want to celebrate." Enzo gave me a pointed look.

"You did this?"

"And this?" Alessia peeked out from behind Matteo. "Congratulations." She came over to me, and her and Nora swooned over my ring.

"I can't believe you're both here." It was the perfect way to round off a perfect night.

"Group hug," Matteo shouted, bounding over and wrapping his huge arms around the three of us.

"Uh, Matt, you smell of bacon grease."

"Well, yeah, someone had to go and pick up breakfast."

"There's breakfast?" I asked, hopeful. There hadn't been much time to eat last night.

"We got extra." Matteo kept his arm around my shoulder, guiding me over to the breakfast counter.

"Only because you eat like a fucking pig," Enzo grumbled.

"I see you're as delightful than ever," Nora shot back.

"Shut up and eat, Abato."

"Hey, remember that time when she almost ate your—"

"*Matteo*!" Nicco cut him with a harsh look.

"Yeah, yeah, I'll behave. But seriously though, you two, congratulations."

"I can't believe we'll be sisters." Alessia beamed. "Can I be bridesmaid?"

"Me too," Nora added.

"Hmm, we haven't gotten that far." I glanced at Nicco and he smiled.

"Well, for what it's worth, I think you're both fucking crazy," Enzo said as he and Matteo unpacked the breakfast containers. "But if you're happy then I guess that's all that matters."

"Thanks, I think. You didn't invite Luis?" I glanced around, half expecting him to appear at any second.

"He's with Tristan, they're..." Matteo glanced at Nicco and he nodded. "They're with your father."

Silence fell over the six of us. Here we were celebrating, but there was still a difficult uncertain path ahead.

"Nope. Not happening." Nora declared. "This is a celebration breakfast. So less moping and more celebrating."

"Thank you," I mouthed at her and she nodded, pride glittering in her eyes.

"One good thing about weddings... bachelor party." Matteo smirked.

A low grumble spilled from my lips and all heads turned to me.

"Did Ari just growl?" His eyes were the size of saucers.

"I'm just hungry." I averted my eyes, heat burning my cheeks.

"She did, she growled." Amusement laced Enzo's words.

"Yeah, only because she knows what happens at such things," Sia replied. "Remember Uncle Sil? His bachelor party was wild."

"How the hell do you know what happened at Uncle Sil's party?" Nicco arched his brow at his sister.

"I hear things. Aunt Dru made him sleep on the couch for a—"

"Okay, Sia." Nicco clapped his hand over her mouth. "I think we get the picture." He shot me a pleading glance.

"Let the guys have their fun, I say." Nora stabbed her fork into a stack of pancakes. "While the men are away, the girls will play."

"I don't think that's how the saying goes," Matteo said, and she shrugged.

"It is in my world. I'm thinking a stripper, massages, the full works."

Nicco had gone as white as a sheet and I smothered a chuckle.

"Oh, I'm sorry." Nora offered him a saccharine smile. "Did you think we were all going to sit around and braid each other's hair and have pillow fights while you're off getting lap dances and drinking your body weight in liquor?"

"More like sharpen each other's claws," Enzo murmured.

"Careful, E, I bite too." She bared her teeth at him.

"You know you two just need to get it out of your system, right?" Alessia took a bite of bacon.

"Huh?" Nora frowned while Enzo sat deathly still.

"The tension between the two of you." She wagged a finger between my best friend and her cousin.

"Fuck that," Enzo gritted out.

"The feeling is mutual," Nora hissed.

"Okay, why doesn't everyone just take a breath?" I suggested. I was too happy to let their bickering spoil my moment.

"Ari's right," Matteo said. "We're here to celebrate." He grabbed a glass of orange juice and thrust it in the air. To Nicco and his fiancée, Arianne. May your life be filled with happiness, love, and lots and lots of hot newlywed sex."

After breakfast Nicco asked to talk to me.

"What is it?" I said as he led me away from our friends.

"I'm going to go back with the guys to see my father."

"You're leaving?" My heart clenched but I knew it would be like this sometimes. There were still things to take care of.

"Only for a little while. We need to figure out a plan. The sooner it happens," he cupped my face, "the sooner we can get on with our lives."

"Okay." I covered his hand with mine, turning my face slightly to kiss his palm. "Be safe."

"Always. Luis is on his way back. I think Tristan is with him."

"Maybe you should be gone before they get here," I smiled.

"I'm not scared of Tristan, Bambolina."

"I know." We'd moved closer, our lips almost brushing.

"You're mine now," he whispered. "Nothing can ever change that." The sheer possessiveness in his voice made my heart swell.

My hands twisted into his t-shirt. "Don't be too long."

"I promise. I think there's still some tiramisu left in the refrigerator."

My tummy clenched. "Nicco, you can't say things like that to me in public." I breathed, glancing to where our friends sat, as his lips painted a warm trail to the shell of my ear.

"But you taste so damn good."

"Vitelli is here," Enzo called. "We should go."

"I'll be back soon." Nicco pressed a kiss to my head before taking my hand and leading me back to our friends.

"Come on, Sia, let's go." Enzo's cold gaze went to where Nora and Alessia were sitting on the couch.

Nicco's sister pouted. "I could stay."

"Not. Happening. You're lucky we brought you here as it is."

"Fine." She hugged Nora before coming over to me. "I'm so happy for you."

"Thank you." We hugged, Alessia hanging on for dear life. There was something so pure about her easy acceptance. It only reaffirmed the feeling that I'd finally found my place.

Nora laced her arm through mine as we followed them out of the cabin. Nicco lingered at Matteo's truck, locking eyes with mine.

"Damn, Ari. Where can I get me one of those?"

"Hush." I nudged her with my shoulder.

Luis' SUV appeared down the track, rolling to a stop next to the truck. Luis and Tristan climbed out, stopping to talk to Nicco. My breath caught as I watched my cousin extend his hand to him.

"Well, I'll be damned." Nora squealed with delight as Nicco took it.

The two of them glanced over at us before Nicco pulled away and climbed into the truck.

Tristan approached us, a faint smirk tugging at his mouth. "Sounds like you have some explaining to do..." His eyes went to the band on my finger.

"We should probably talk, yes."

"Fuck, talking." He pulled me into his arms. "You've got balls of steel, Ari."

"I didn't do anything, not really."

"Like hell you didn't. You brokered a deal with Antonio Marchetti and went and got yourself engaged by all accounts."

"I did what I had to."

Tristan eased back to look at me. "But you're happy, right? You want this?"

I nodded, fighting a smile. "I know we're young and I know a lot of people won't understand—"

"Screw what anyone else thinks. All I care is that you're happy and you're safe."

"Have you seen the way he looks at her?" Nora scoffed. "Ari's safety should be the least of your concerns."

Tristan's eyes narrowed, a trace of hurt there. Or maybe it was guilt.

"Yeah," he said, "I'm starting to get that."

TWENTY-SEVEN

NICCO

WHEN WE ARRIVED BACK at my father's house, I half-expected to find my uncles there, ready to toast my news. But the house was quiet when we entered.

"Ah, Nicco." Genevieve rounded the corner. "I hear congratulations are in order."

"You know?" My eyes narrowed.

"Don't sound so surprised, Niccolò," my father moved beside her, squeezing her shoulder, "Genevieve is practically family."

I raised a brow at that.

"Sia, can I borrow you, in the kitchen?" she asked my sister, no doubt sensing the tension rippling in the air.

"Sure thing. I'll see you later." Alessia kissed my cheek before taking off after Genevieve.

"Niccolò, my office." My father turned on his heel and took off down the hall.

"Why do I get the feeling I'm in trouble?"

"Nah," Enzo smirked. "He probably just wants to give you the father/son talk and remind you of the three golden rules."

"Three golden rules?" Matteo frowned.

"Birth control, birth control, birth control."

Shaking my head, I flicked my head in the direction of the kitchen. "Go hang out, I'll be back soon."

Matteo clapped me on the back. "Everything's going to work out," he said.

I wanted to believe him.

Proposing to Arianne, hearing the word *yes* spill from her lips, then sliding my nonna's ring onto her finger, had been one of the most terrifying and best moments of my life.

But our struggle wasn't over yet.

It wouldn't be until Fascini and his piece of shit son were no longer a threat.

"Come in," my father demanded. I slipped inside, closing the door behind me. "How is Arianne?"

"She's fine."

"A toast." He moved to his drinks cabinet and pulled out a bottle of his finest scotch, pouring us both a glass. "Here."

I accepted it.

"I am glad you came to your senses, Niccolò. It is the right move for the Family as well as for your future."

Taking a seat, I glanced up at him, confusion clouding my eyes.

"This job, it can be a lonely life. I look back and realize how much time I wasted. How much I took for granted. Do not repeat my mistakes, Son. When you first brought her here, and I saw the way you looked at her, I was concerned she would be your weakness. But now I see that she can be your strength. Love gives you something to fight for, something to lose. Arianne will anchor you, Son.

"To family." He lifted his glass and I mirrored his action.

"To family. What happens now?" I asked.

"Tommy is waiting for my word to make the tip off to our friend down at the local PD. Michele's guys are handling Fascini's legal team."

One of Uncle Michele's guys, Johnny Morello, was our go-to fixer. With a penchant for extortion and coercion, he rarely failed to secure people's silence or compliance.

"And Uncle Vin?"

"I have ordered him to sit tight. He doesn't like it but the last thing we need is him barreling in all guns blazing."

"He needs to get on board with me and Arianne," I said, pressing my lips together.

"And he will. You're his nephew, my son. One day you'll be the boss. He'll get over it. Besides, once your ring is on her finger, she's family too. She'll be Marchetti."

Fuck.

My heart flipped violently in my chest.

I liked the sound of that.

"Are you sure this is going to work?"

Fascini wasn't stupid. He had to have his bases covered in case his cover was blown—reassurance policies, the best lawyers money could buy, not to mention his squeaky-clean business reputation.

Even if Johnny got to his most trusted inner circle... we couldn't guarantee Fascini wouldn't worm his way out. To the outside eye, Mike Fascini was an upstanding member of society. But everyone had secrets. You just had to know where to look and how to exploit them.

My father regarded me and scoffed, "Niccolò, have some faith. This will work. Mike Fascini and that son of his will pay. No one messes with the Marchetti and gets away with it." His hand tightened around his glass. "No one."

I gave him a small nod.

"I have to ask though, Niccolò. Are you sure you don't want that piece of shit taken care of for what he did to Arianne? She would never have to know. I can arrange for it to happen discreetly. Make it look like a suicide."

A bolt of anger rippled through me. "He lives. It's what she wants." No matter how much it pained me to say the words.

My father rubbed his jaw. "You are a stronger man than I. Either way, he will never get within a foot of Arianne again."

It was enough.

It had to be.

"It could be a few days before everything is in place. We keep this between us, do you understand?"

"I know the drill."

"There is something else..."

I went rigid.

Of course there was.

"She will need to return to her father's estate until it is done."

"No fucking way." I lunged forward.

"Nicco, hear me out, Son. We can't risk Fascini discovering our plan. There is also the small matter of Roberto sitting tight. She needs to talk to him."

"She can call him—"

"This is how it has to be. She will be safe. The estate is heavily guarded, and Luis will be there with her. Right now, we need to make sure everything falls into place."

"Then I'm going. I won't leave her again. I promised her." I'd promised myself.

My father's hand slammed down on the table. "Niccolò, I am not asking you. I am telling you, this is the way it has to be. The end is in sight, Son. Do not lose your cool now. She'll be safe there."

"If anything... *anything* happens to her, I will hold you personally responsible."

"I would expect no less. But she will be safe. Knowing she's back at her father's estate will appease Fascini until we make our move."

I didn't like it.

I didn't like it at all.

But what choice did I have?

Arianne had made her deal with the Devil and now we had no choice but to see it through.

My father let out a heavy sigh. "You should go be with her. I'm sure you have much to discuss. She doesn't need to leave immediately. Take the night, she can leave in the morning. And then you stay put at the cabin. Do you understand me?"

The urge to defy him burned inside me. But this wasn't only about me.

It was about Arianne.

"I understand."

"Good." He gave me a swift nod. "It won't be for too long, and then you can look to the future."

"About that... Do you have stipulations for the wedding?"

"Once Fascini has been dealt with, I imagine Roberto will need some time to adjust to our new... arrangement. But I would prefer we handled matters sooner rather than later."

I winced at his crass words. This was my life he was talking about. Mine and Arianne's future.

Our wedding.

But he wasn't my father right now, he was the boss.

"There is much to think about. Where you'll have the ceremony, a honeymoon," his lip curved, "where you'll live, make a home for yourselves."

I sank back in the chair, letting out a heavy sigh.

"It's happening fast." His expression softened. "I understand that."

"Do you?" It came out harsher than I intended.

"You are my son. Arianne is to be my daughter-in-law. You will want for nothing. Just say the word and you will have everything you want."

"I need to talk to her."

He gave me a sharp nod. "Of course. Go be with her. I can handle things here."

"You'll keep me in the loop?"

I didn't like taking a back seat, not where Scott was concerned, but Arianne needed me. And truth be told, I couldn't trust myself to do the right thing where he was concerned.

"Of course. You can trust me on this, Son, you have my word."

Draining the rest of my drink, I stood up and placed it on my father's desk. He let me get to the door before he stopped me.

"Niccolò," he said. "One day you will understand what it means to sit in this chair. But I have faith in you. And I have faith that Arianne is strong enough to stand at your side. This is your legacy... and now it is hers. And maybe it was always supposed to be this way."

Enzo gave me a ride back to the cabin. Arianne and Tristan were deep in conversation when I walked through the room. Luis caught my attention though, motioning for me to meet him in the kitchen.

"How did it go?" he asked.

"My father will handle it."

"And Roberto?"

"Tomorrow, I need you to take Arianne back to her father's estate and keep her there until this is all over."

"She's not going to like that, but it makes sense. Antonio wants Fascini to believe Roberto is complying."

I nodded, glancing over at her and Tristan. She caught my eye, smiling. God, that smile. "You stay with her at all times. If anything, and I mean *anything* feels off, you get her out of there."

"I will protect her with my life."

"I know you will."

"You know, I never imagined I would grow up to call a Marchetti a friend, but you're a good guy, Nicco, and I am happy for you both. Truly."

"Thanks. Can you take Tristan home and make yourself scarce tonight?"

"Of course. I'll come by first thing for her."

"What's happening?"

I sucked in a harsh breath, turning to find Arianne staring at us. "You're not supposed to be listening, Bambolina."

"Did something happen?"

"My father feels it would be best if you return to your father's estate while he takes care of things."

"When?" She was a picture of composure.

"Tomorrow morning."

"Good."

"Good?" I frowned.

"I should probably speak to my father face to face. It is long overdue."

"Come here." Pulling her into my arms, I held her tight. She'd changed so much in just a few weeks. Arianne was no longer the shy naive girl I'd met in that alley, but a strong woman who refused to bend to the will of the men in her life.

I was so fucking proud of her.

So in awe of who she was... and who she would continue to become.

Arianne commanded the respect of those around her, but she didn't do it with fear. She did it with humility and compassion.

"Luis will be with you."

"And I'll be around," Tristan said, approaching the three of us. His eyes locked on mine, mutual understanding passing between us.

"It's okay," Arianne said. "I'm okay. This is going to work. It has to. And then," she gazed up at me, "we get to put all this behind us."

"Is your mom okay?" I asked the second Arianne stepped into the room. After Luis and Tristan had left, she'd wanted to call her mother ahead of tomorrow.

"I didn't tell her everything, just that I'd be back tomorrow."

Done adding firewood to the open flames, I stepped back, holding out my hand for her.

"What is all this?" Her eyes went to the pillows on the rug, the strawberries and champagne on the coffee table.

"This is our last night together." My voice cracked.

"It's only for a little while." Arianne pressed her hands to my chest. "And then, when it's over, we have forever."

"Now that," I slid my arm around her back and dipped her, pressing my lips to the hollow of her throat, "I like the sound of."

Her soft laughter rose above the crackle of the fire and the quiet background music playing out through the Bluetooth speaker on the sideboard. "Do you know what kind of wedding you would like?" I pulled her back up to me.

"Honestly, I don't care as long as you're waiting for me at the end of the aisle."

"I thought all girls imagined their wedding day?"

"I'm not all girls, Nicco."

"No, you're not. My father asked us where we'd like to live... have you thought about that?"

Her lips parted on a small gasp, and I knew then, she hadn't.

"It's okay," I said. "We have time to figure it all out."

"It all happened fast, huh?"

"Does that scare you?"

Arianne shook her head. "It should, I know that. But when I think of sharing my life with you... it feels right."

My hand glided up her spine, pressing her closer to me. "Because it is right, Bambolina. I have never been surer about anything than I am about my love for you."

"Maybe somewhere in the middle. University Hill or the city. I'd like to be close to Nora." Her dreamy expression fell. "Oh God, Nora—"

"Will be fine." I kissed her forehead. "She just wants you to be happy."

"I know. I just feel bad. College was supposed to be this big adventure, the start of our freedom..."

"You can still have a life, Bambolina. I will never clip your wings, Arianne." I brushed my lips over hers. "I only want to make you happy."

"You do; so, so much." She deepened the kiss, sweeping her tongue into my mouth and tangling it with mine.

Need pulsed through me, and I picked Arianne up. She wrapped her legs around me as I dropped to my knees gently, before lying her down on the soft rug. "Are you hungry?"

I plucked a strawberry from the container and hovered it over her pink swollen lips. "Open, Bambolina."

Her mouth parted letting me feed the fruit to her. "Hmm," she moaned. "It's good."

I pulled it away and juice spilled over her chin. Dipping my head, I licked the trail of sticky sweet nectar away.

"Nicco." My name was a whispered plea on her lips.

"Tell me what you want, amore mio?"

"You." She twisted her fingers into my sweater, dragging me closer "I want you."

"You have me."

Possession flared in her eyes, making my chest swell. "Then show me," she uttered.

And I did.

All night long.

TWENTY-EIGHT

ARIANNE

"HOW ARE YOU FEELING?" Luis asked as we rolled to a stop at the gatehouse. The guard took one look at us and waved us through.

"I'm okay," I said, staring out at my father's estate. The place that had once been my childhood playground no longer felt like home. Instead, it was a lingering memory, faded by time.

"The last time I was here, my father sat me down in front of Mike and Scott and told me I was promised to him. I'll never forgive him for that."

"And I don't blame you."

"But?"

Luis drove up the winding driveway and came to a stop next to my father's town car. "People make mistakes, Arianne, but it doesn't mean their mistakes should define them."

"You're a good man, Luis. But I need time." And even then, it might not be enough to forgive my father.

"I try." He gave me a wistful smile. "Ready?"

I inhaled a deep breath and squared my shoulders. "As I'll ever be."

He climbed out, coming around to open my door.

"Arianne, sweetheart." My mother came running from the house, wrapping me into her slim arms with such force the air *whooshed* from my lungs. "I've been so worried." She held me at arm's length.

"I'm okay."

Her gaze narrowed. "You seem different." She studied me.

"We should probably talk. Where is my father?"

"He's in the sunroom. Since Mike's... warning," the word came out strangled, "he rarely leaves."

"You know about that?" My father had been shutting her out, so I was a little taken aback to find out she knew.

"He finally broke down and told me everything. But don't worry, sweetheart, he's going to fix it."

I grimaced. She was still blinded by my father's empty promises, and it made my heart ache. "We should go inside." I glanced to the security men posted either side of the door.

Luis followed us into the house, moving ahead of me, no doubt as a precaution. Restless energy flowed through me, making my stomach vibrate. Since discovering the camera feeds into the house, my father's men had swept the place and eradicated them all. But I knew Luis and Nicco still had concerns. It was probably why my father was in the sunroom. It was one of the few rooms that hadn't been bugged.

"Father," I said, stepping inside.

The formidable Roberto Capizola was a mess. Dark circles ringed his eyes and his attire was unkempt. He reminded me of some of the clients at the VCTI; people who didn't have the luxury of a hot shower and fresh clothes.

"Arianne, mio tesoro. You are safe."

"No thanks to you." My voice was flat.

My mother inhaled a shaky breath. "Arianne, that isn't—"

"Fair, Mamma? None of this is. But it doesn't matter." I moved to one of the soft leather couches. "Everything will be taken care of soon enough."

"Whatever do you mean?"

"She means... she sold me out." My father's voice held a trace of disappointment.

"I did what is best. You made a deal with the Devil. With the man who tried to kill me and start a war between you and the Marchetti. When that didn't work, he turned to more legitimate options. He wanted to control you, to use you… and you let him." Indignation raced through my veins.

"Roberto?" My mother's mouth hung open as if she couldn't believe it.

"Oh, he didn't tell you?" She'd implied she knew everything, but I should have known he would still keep secrets from her. "It wasn't Antonio Marchetti who tried to kill me, Mamma, it was Mike."

"No," she gasped, "that's not—"

"It is true." He hung his head in shame. "Mike wants to destroy me, to destroy us."

"I did what you could not," I said. "I went to Antonio and asked for his help."

His eyes slid to mine, burning with contempt. "That man is—"

"Willing to save your life."

"At a cost?" he scoffed. "I would rather..." My father swallowed the words.

"Die?" My brow raised. "Nobody is going to die. Antonio is willing to hand

Mike and Scott over to the authorities and in exchange he will become your partner."

"Absolutely not!" He shot up.

"It is done. I am the Capizola heir. I am eighteen now. One day your empire will be mine."

"I won't do it. I won't just hand over the business to that... that criminal."

"That *criminal* took me in after Scott, the man you wanted me to marry, raped me. He promised me protection when my own father wouldn't believe my words. That man is going to one day be my father-in-law. So yes, Father, you will do this. Otherwise, I will be dead to you."

"Arianne!" My mother's face went as white as a sheet, but I kept my attention on my father.

"I am marrying Nicco. You can either get on board with it, or not."

"You cannot trust them..." he murmured, scrubbing a hand over his face.

"Trust is earned, Father. And Nicco and his father have done a damn sight more to earn my trust than you ever have."

Devastation etched into his expression, but he needed to hear this. He needed to understand how deeply his betrayal had hurt me.

My eyes stung with unshed tears, but I would not cry.

Not today.

Not in front of the man who had broken my heart one too many times.

"I may never forgive you, but this is a start to you righting your wrongs."

He slumped down in the chair, a pained whimper leaving his lips. "I guess I don't really have a choice, do I?"

"No, Father." I looked at the man I'd once worshipped. The man I thought could do no wrong.

We were like strangers now.

Two people bound together by nothing more than blood and bad memories.

"You do not."

There was a knock at my door. "Come in," I called.

"It's only me." Mom slipped into my room. Although it didn't really feel like my room anymore.

"I just wanted to check and see how you are?"

"I'll be glad when this is all over," I admitted.

"I still can't believe..." She took a shuddering breath, moving to the chair in the corner of the room. "You must hate us."

"I don't..." I let out a weary sigh. "It isn't hatred I feel, Mamma. I just don't understand how we ended up here."

"I find myself asking that same question a lot lately." Her lips quivered as she inhaled a shaky breath. "Your father has always been overprotective, but he had his reasons. And then after the attempt on your life at the school... well, he changed after that. Became obsessed with protecting you. Despite all your father's faults, his actions came from a place of love, Arianne."

"I can't forget... I won't. What Scott did to me... it changed me, Mamma."

"Oh, sweetheart, I know. I know it will take time."

"It will take more than time. They say sons are born in their father's image. Well, I am my father's daughter. If he taught me anything, it's that everything comes at a price. This is mine."

"You're so young though. I knew things between you and Nicco were serious, but marriage, mia cara? That's very... permanent."

"You married Father when you were barely twenty and you were more than willing to give me away to Scott. You weren't worried about my age then, Mamma." Disbelief coated my words.

"Arianne, please..." She inhaled a shaky breath. "You're right, you father and I were young, but we had been together for almost four years by then." She gave me a weak smile and it wasn't lost on me that she'd chosen to ignore my dig about Scott. "This is all so new... and he's—"

"Mafioso?"

She flinched.

"Nicco would give his life for mine. Do you understand that? He would risk everything... for me."

"I know, but—"

"No, Mamma. I am eighteen. I can make my own decisions, and I choose him. I choose Nicco."

Nothing would come between us. Not my father, my mother, or his family.

"You need to talk to him." I lifted my chin in defiance. "You need to make him understand that this is happening. It would make everything a lot smoother if he gets on board."

"Very well." She gave me a small nod and stood. "I will let you get some rest."

I waited until she was almost out of the door. "Mamma?"

"Yes, sweetheart?" Her voice was laced with sadness and regret.

"I would really like it if you were at the wedding. Father should be there too, but I'll understand it if he'd prefer not to come."

"I will speak to him," she said.

They were my parents. To not have them there felt wrong. But they had to decide what they could live with, just as I'd had to decide.

And if they couldn't come to terms with me marrying Nicco, then I wouldn't beg.

After spending the rest of the afternoon and evening in the fragile sanctuary of my bedroom, I'd fallen into a restless sleep. I didn't want to be here, but I knew it was the only way, for now.

I showered, taking my time to wash away the lingering pain of yesterday's meeting with my father. When I went back into my room, my cell phone was ringing. My heart swelled at Nicco's name flashing across the screen.

"Bambolina, how are you?" he asked.

"I hate it here," I confessed. "I hate him, Nicco. For everything he's done, for everything he's put me through..." A whimper escaped me, but I steeled myself. We were so close now. So close to putting all this behind us. Antonio and his men would make sure Mike Fascini was no longer a threat, and Nicco and I would be married.

"Amore mio, what is it?"

"I hate him, I do. Yet, I can't help but feel sorry for him."

"He is your father; you can love him and hate him at the same time."

"I guess you're right. Part of me knows that deep down he probably had my interests at heart, but then I think about everything Scott has put me through and I..." My body trembled with pain, with the sting of betrayal.

Nicco hissed under his breath. "I should have killed him."

"No, Nicco," I rushed out. "I don't want you to carry that burden. Not for me." They had the evidence of what he'd done to me. It would be enough to seal his fate. Scott would follow his father to rot inside a prison cell, and I would be safe.

"When are you going to realize, Bambolina? I would do anything for you." The intensity behind Nicco's words made my breath catch. "I love you more than anything. The thought of him hurting you..."

"He can't hurt me anymore. He'll get what's coming to him, Nicco." I had to believe that.

"You are too good for this life, too pure." His torment crackled over the line. "I fear I am a selfish bastard for tethering you to my side."

"It is not your choice to make."

"These violent delights have violent ends..." he whispered the words.

"You're quoting Shakespeare at me?" I chuckled, but it came out strained.

Nicco was quiet, brooding. I knew he didn't agree with the deal I'd made with his father, and part of me wondered if I was foolish to think it could all end peacefully. But I had to believe that after everything we'd been through, we deserved this. We deserved to walk into the future with our hands unbloodied and our consciences clean.

I knew life with Nicco would mean skirting the line between light and dark, good and bad. But this was different. I didn't want this—what Scott had done—to come between us anymore than it already had.

When I didn't reply, Nicco let out a heavy sigh. "I would die for you Arianne." His voice was a low growl, "never forget that."

A shudder worked through me. "Then I would die with you." Because I didn't want to live in a world without him.

"Bambolina..."

"No, Nicco. You don't get to say stuff like that to me without expecting a reply. If something happens to you..." I couldn't say the words.

"Nothing is going to happen to me. You made the deal with my father. He will keep his word."

"I just want to put all this behind us. I wish you were here." With Nicco's arms around me, I felt strong. I felt like we could weather any storm.

"Soon, amore mio. Soon."

TWENTY-NINE

NICCO

I SNATCHED up my phone and rushed out, "Yes?"

"Niccolò," my father's gruff voice replied. "Everything is in place. Our friend down at the local PD will hit the Fascini this evening, when they are least expecting it."

A potent mix of relief and anger flooded me.

"Son?"

"I..." I dragged a hand through my hair. "That's good."

"I know it is not what you had hoped for." There was a distinctive lilt in his voice. "But this is a good outcome, for Arianne. For the Family."

"I know, I just..." Fuck, I wanted Scott to pay for his sins. I wanted to watch him bleed, knowing that I would spend my life loving the girl he would never get to hurt again.

"Be strong, figlio mio. Soon this will all be over, and you and Arianne will be able to get on with your lives."

"It doesn't feel right," I murmured. "Arianne is mine to protect, mine to..." The words died on my lips.

"Don't make the same mistakes I did, Niccolò. Don't let your need for vengeance eat away at your soul, not when you have something to live for. Arianne is safe, she is strong, and she will make you a good wife."

His words were like a fist around my heart. I wanted the happy ending, I did. But letting Scott live, it felt like a giant fucking mistake.

"What happened to taking him out and making it look like an accident?" I threw his words back at him, and he chuckled.

"The offer still stands, but I know you won't do it. Because that would be a heavier burden to carry. Arianne wants justice, Niccolò. She wants to believe that the authorities will do the right thing. She is not ready to accept that our world is—"

"Don't, just don't." Pain splintered me in two.

"Let me handle it, Son. Trust me to do this for you. For you both." I gave him a sharp nod even though he couldn't see me. "I know you're probably going out of your mind, so I'm sending you a distraction. Sit tight. It will soon all be over."

Just then, the familiar rumble of Enzo's GTO caught my attention. "They're here?" I asked him.

"You shouldn't be alone, Niccolò. They are your cousins, your brothers, be with them. I'll talk to you when it is done."

We hung up and I went outside.

"We brought supplies," Matteo called, waving two bottles of scotch in his hands.

Enzo tipped his chin at me as he approached carrying a pack of beer. "You good?"

"What do you think?"

He roped his arm around my neck and pulled me back toward the cabin. "I think we need to get lit and fuck some shit up."

Usually, I would have told him to rein it in.

But not today.

Today I needed my friends.

I needed to forget.

"It's the right call," Matteo said later, as we sat around the fire pit, drinking beer and shooting the shit.

"Like fuck it is." Enzo slammed his beer down on the arm of his chair. "That sick fucker deserves to bleed."

"Ari—"

"She doesn't get it, Matt. She doesn't understand this life."

"E," I warned. I had enough anger zipping through me without him making it worse.

"He raped her, Nic. And as if that wasn't enough, he took a gun and pushed it into her mouth and—"

"Don't," it came out a low growl.

I was losing myself, my thin rope of control fraying.

"You should be angry," he went on. "You should be fucking—"

"Enzo," Matteo glanced precariously between us, "this isn't helping."

"No, let him talk," I seethed, my eyes growing thin. "Let him tell us what he really thinks."

"You don't have the balls," he sneered. "You're letting her call all the shots.

You're Niccolò fucking Marchetti and you're out here, hiding like a little punk ass—"

I shot up out of the chair, fists clenched at my sides. "Say that again."

Enzo stood up, his cool gaze trained right on me. "You heard me." He stepped up to me, the air crackling with anticipation. "You don't have the ball—"

I wound my arm back and let my fist fly at his face. Enzo jerked back, my knuckles clipping his jaw.

"Come on, guys." Matteo was out of his chair too. "This isn't what Uncle Toni had in mind."

But it was too late.

Enzo had pushed me too far. He'd unleashed my inner beast and there was no going back until it had its pound of flesh.

My cousin rubbed his jaw, smirking at me. "You really want to do this?"

I shrugged. "Scared you can't take me?"

Matteo let out a mumble of disapproval, but Enzo and I only had eyes for each other. He watched me, his jaw set and eyes narrowed, as I shucked out of my jacket and threw it on the chair.

It had been too long since I fought, *really* fought. I'd been too preoccupied with Arianne, and I couldn't deny that she settled me. When we were together, it was easy to get lost in her, to bathe in her light. But sitting here, staring into the flames as they licked the night's sky, I'd succumbed to the darkness again.

And Enzo knew it.

He fucking knew where my head was at and he pushed me anyway.

He came at me like a bull out of the gates, wrapping his bulky arms around me and tackling me to the ground. We landed with a *thud*, the air sucking clean from my lungs. I slammed my shoulder into his, leveraging my weight and we rolled. Enzo glared up at me, and the fucker grinned. He actually grinned.

"Something funny?" My brow raised.

"You need this. I'm happy to oblige. Don't punk out on me now."

"So this is for my benefit?"

He shrugged. "Maybe I have some stuff to work off too."

"You two are fucking crazy," Matteo grumbled from over by the fire.

"I don't—

Enzo thrashed beneath me, bucking me off, and I clambered to my feet, circling him as he stood. Adrenaline raced through my veins as I studied my cousin. Enzo was a decent fighter, quick on his feet and unpredictable, but he'd underestimated one thing.

I was a man walking a razor's edge; fueled by love and tormented by the need for vengeance.

I rushed at him, sending a sharp uppercut to his jaw. His head snapped back, his grunts of pain filling the air. "I'll give you that one." He spat a mouthful of blood at my feet.

Strangled laughter rumbled in my chest. I felt wild, consumed by anger, and shackled by love. I wanted to protect Arianne, to worship and cherish her. But part of me also wanted to deliver Scott's head on a platter, to paint Verona red with his blood.

"Imagine I'm him," Enzo taunted. "Imagine it was me who hurt her. Me who—"

I lunged again, but Enzo anticipated my move, ducking to the left and deflecting my fist with a right hook of his own. Pain exploded in my cheek, but I relished the burn. I soaked it up, letting it feed the fire raging inside me.

"Seriously, guys, maybe we should just—"

We ignored Matteo's pleas. It was on, no holding back. Enzo wanted me to imagine he was Scott? Then he needed to be prepared to be torn limb from limb.

A shiver rolled through me as I cracked my neck. Enzo's eyes grew to thin slits, his lip twisting into a smirk. "There he is, the Prince of fucking Hearts. Time to show me what you got."

I stepped forward; fists ready... I wouldn't just show him.

I'd annihilate him.

"Pleased with yourself?" Matteo handed me an ice-cold compress before throwing one at Enzo.

"Watch it, fucker," he grumbled. He was slouched on the couch, his lip swollen and eye split wide open.

I had my fair share of injuries: split knuckles, a bruised rib or two, not to mention the ugly purple bruise around my left eye. But despite the persistent throb of pain radiating through me, I felt better. Lighter somehow.

Enzo had taunted me because he knew I couldn't just sit and do nothing.

And it had worked.

"I don't know about E," I said, glancing over at him. "But I feel great."

He smirked, flipping me off. "You swing like a girl."

"Tell that to the split in your lip."

"It worked though, didn't it?"

"Yeah," my voice grew thick, "it did." I held his glare, silently telling him how much I appreciated it.

"I'll always have your back." He gave me a sharp nod.

"You've lost your fucking mind." Matteo blew out a long breath.

"We can't all be lovers like you, Matt." Enzo nursed his jaw. "Some of us need to fight. We need it to hurt."

"You almost killed each other."

"Nah, I barely scratched the surface," I chuckled.

"Fuck you, Cous." Enzo shoved his arms behind his head, wincing in pain. "I almost had you."

My shoulders relaxed, the tension ebbing away. I hadn't realized how much I'd needed this until Enzo's fist collided with my face.

Fighting had always been my outlet, the way I'd dealt with my demons. But Arianne was changing me, molding me into something new, something more.

"Do you think it's done?" Enzo asked.

"He'll call when it is." It was almost nine, the sun long disappeared behind the tree line.

"Shit, I would have paid to see that fucker dragged away in a cop car. Smug asshole won't know what's hit him."

I grabbed my cell phone and opened my messages. I hadn't replied to Arianne's earlier message, I'd been too busy breaking my cousin's face.

Are you okay?

Her reply came straight through.

I am. Are you? I was getting worried.

Me and Enzo were working through some things...

What things?

I smiled at that. My sweet Bambolina always asking questions.

Just working off some steam.

You were fighting?

It's not what you think...

So tell me, what is it?

I know this is what you want, Bambolina, but I really wanted to make that piece of shit pay for ever laying a hand on you.

. . .

I waited for her reply, my heart crashing against my chest.

I know, and I'm sorry I took that from you, I am. But I couldn't do it, Nicco. I couldn't stand by and watch you lose yourself.

Slipping off the stool, I turned to my cousins and said, "I'll be back."

"Tell Ari we said hey." I heard the amusement in Matteo's voice, and I flipped him off over my shoulder.

I knew they thought I was whipped. That Arianne held my balls—and heart—in the palm of her hand.

But I didn't care.

All I cared about was her.

Doing right by her.

That's why I was sitting here, following orders like the dutiful son—for her. Not for my father or the Family.

Only her.

Inside our bedroom, I closed the door and sat on the edge of the bed before dialing her number.

"Nicco?"

"I needed to hear your voice," I confessed, running a hand over my head.

"Are you hurt?"

"You have such little faith in me, Bambolina?" My lips curved.

"I don't like the idea of you fighting with your cousin." Her voice was small, uncertain, but there was also a trace of disapproval there.

"It's not how you think. He was... helping me."

"Because you need to fight."

"Sometimes, yes."

"Because of me?"

I wanted to tell her no, that my demons were my own. But the truth was, I didn't want to lie.

"Nicco?"

"I want to kill him, Arianne. I want to take my gun and blow his brains out. He deserves no less."

"But don't you see, killing him won't change anything, and if you do it, I might lose you." A beat passed, the blood pounding between my ears. "I can't ever lose you."

"You won't. I'm right here."

"I know you don't understand it, Nicco. But this is just something I needed to do. One day, I hope you'll see that."

"Bambolina..." I breathed through the onslaught of emotion crashing over me. I was a mafia prince, torn between wanting to avenge the girl I loved, and honor her wishes.

The decision had been taken out of my hands, but I knew if I asked my father, he could make it happen. But I also knew that it still wouldn't be good enough. I wanted it to be my hands stealing the air from his lungs as I squeezed his throat. My pistol poised against the small circle of skin between his eyes.

Just then another call came through and I checked the screen.

"Nicco, what is it?"

"My father is calling, I need to go. But I'll call you later, okay?"

"Okay." I heard her sigh deeply and the sound almost splintered me in two.

"It won't be long now, I promise. Hold on for me, okay? I need you to hold on just for a little bit more."

"I love you."

"I love you too." *More then you'll ever know.*

I ended the call and hit answer, striding out of the bedroom toward my cousins. "Is it done?" I asked the second I heard my father's breath.

"It is."

Thank fuck. Relief spread through me. But I quickly realized he didn't sound pleased.

"What happened?"

Enzo and Matteo shot upright, their eyes asking me a hundred questions I didn't yet have the answers too.

"Mike Fascini was taken into police custody. He's down at the local station now."

"And Scott?" My skin vibrated.

"He got away. I don't have all the facts yet, but it looks like he managed to escape."

"You're joking right? That's a joke?"

"I wish it were, Son." Disappointment lingered in his voice.

"You promised me... you fucking promised—"

"I know, I know." He let out a heavy sigh, and I could imagine his dark expression. "I don't know what happened, Niccolò, but I will find out. And I won't rest until we find him. Okay?"

Fuck.

He was still out there.

Scott was out there, and Arianne was—

"I have to go to her."

"I know, Son. Go be with your woman. I'll call you when I have an update."

Enzo and Matteo were both standing now, concern glittering in their eyes.

"We're going to her?" Matteo asked, and I nodded.

"Scott escaped. That fucker managed to get away."

"Fuck," Enzo muttered. "What do you need?"

"We need to go to Arianne, now."

She wasn't safe.

As long as Scott was out there somewhere, she wasn't safe.

Luis met us at the gatehouse. His expression said it all; he was as pissed about Scott evading arrest as the rest of us.

"What the hell happened?" he ground out as I got out of the car to greet him.

"We don't know yet. Have you told Arianne?"

"No, but she knows something is wrong."

"Okay," I let out a small breath.

"Come on, she's inside. Let him through, Harlen." He motioned to the security guard. He glowered at us, but the gates began to recede.

"Don't mind him." Luis gripped my shoulder. "He knows what's at stake. They all do."

"You're a good man, Vitelli."

Luis gave me a firm nod. "I'll meet you back at the house. I want to do a perimeter sweep and talk to all the guards."

"Fucking hell," Enzo said as I climbed back into the car. "This place is like the White House."

He wasn't wrong. The Capizola estate was huge, and right in the center, stood the house with its grand balconies and alabaster pillars flanking the entrance.

"Is that...?" Enzo started to growl.

"Relax." I levelled him with a hard look. "Roberto knows the deal. He might be a piece of shit, but Arianne is still his daughter. He'll want her safe."

He snorted at that, and I knew what he was thinking. Roberto had practically handed Arianne over to Scott and the Fascini, gift-wrapped with a bow.

Anger trickled up my spine, but I shook it off. I wasn't here for Roberto; I was here for his daughter.

The car rolled to a stop, and we all climbed out.

"You," Roberto seethed, his eyes alight with contempt.

"Watch it, old man." Enzo stepped forward, but a voice gave us pause.

"Nicco?" Arianne flew down the steps and didn't stop until she was in my arms, her face buried in my chest.

"Ssh, Bambolina." I held her tight. Roberto caught my eye, a strange expression passing over his face.

"Something's wrong." Arianne eased back, craning her neck to look at me. "What is it? Tell me."

I stared down into honey eyes that had captured my soul and never given it back and whispered the two little words that had the power to push me into the darkness. "Scott escaped."

Her body tensed, her grip on my jacket tightening. "He got away?"

I nodded, watching her expression. But she didn't break. My strong Bambolina steeled herself and inhaled a sharp breath. "It's okay," she said calmly. "You'll find him."

"And if we don't?" someone asked.

"Scott would be a fool to try anything now." Her eyes never left mine, and then she said nine little words that spun my world. "He knows Nicco would kill him if he did."

"I..."

"It's okay." She leaned up, ghosting her fingers across my jaw. Her warmth seeped into me, wrapping around me and taking hold. "Scott is gone, he can't hurt me anymore."

She was too calm.

Too composed.

Enzo glanced at me, arching his brow.

"We need to stay here for now," I said. "Wait for word from my father. He has his men looking for Scott right now. If he's still in Verona, we'll find him."

Arianne took my hand and started moving toward the door. But Roberto stepped forward. "Figlia mia, I'm not sure—"

"Don't," she seethed. "Niccolò is my fiancé, Father. He is here to protect me. To protect us. You are going to make him welcome or you can go retire to your study." Her eyes bore into his until Roberto dipped his head and nodded.

"Please," he almost choked over the word, "join us."

Enzo looked impressed. Matteo grinned. And me? I stared at Arianne with nothing but love and pride for the woman she'd become.

When I'd first met her, she was so unsure and uncertain of her place in the world. But now, standing here, she was strong. And brave. So fucking brave.

She was no longer a pawn in a game she didn't understand.

She was the Queen.

My Queen.

And I was going to spend my life showing her.

THIRTY

ARIANNE

ONE MONTH LATER...

"Holy crap, babe, you look..." Nora fanned her face. "Tears, I have actual tears. Quick someone hand me a paper towel."

Genevieve grabbed a box of tissues and thrust it at Nora. "No crying. We can't have anyone spoiling Ari's make up. Sei bella come il sole." Her expression softened as she took me in.

"My brother is going to freak." Alessia caught my hand in hers.

"Oh, I don't know about that, Sia. The two of you will steal the show."

They looked flawless in their pale lilac dresses. With a halter-style top that scooped low in the front and back, the silk flowed over their hips and skimmed the floor. Their hair had been braided to one side and pulled into an intricate bun, woven with flowers matching the Baby's Breath and Larkspur of my bridal posy.

"Okay," Genevieve held out a tissue for me. "Blot and then I think we're done."

I did as she instructed, leaving a smudge of lipstick behind.

"Ready?" Nora helped me off the stool I'd spent the last hour sitting on while Nora and Genevieve took care of my makeup and hair.

Nicco had wanted to pay someone, but I didn't want any fuss. Besides, there was something special about sharing this moment with my best friend, my soon to be sister-in-law, and Genevieve. I hadn't quite distinguished her place in my life yet, but she had become a fast friend over the last few weeks, the two of us bonding over the Marchetti men in our lives. I wasn't sure if it was official, but I had it on good authority she was Antonio's date for the wedding.

I let her fuss over my dress, smoothing out the lace tail and arranging the long veil over my hair. Finally, they stepped back to look at me.

"Oh my god," Alessia breathed.

Nora had tears collecting in the corners of her eyes as she smiled at me. "You look amazing."

The door creaked behind me, but I didn't move for fear of ruining my hair.

"Sorry I'm late," Mom's voice filtered into our room.

The Blackstone Country Club had gone above and beyond to accommodate us on such short notice, but I wasn't surprised. I was quickly learning that being a Marchetti carried weight. They had transformed the place into something fit for a princess.

"Oh my... Arianne, sweetheart." Tears filled her eyes. "You look..."

"Thank you." My body vibrated with nervous energy.

"That boy has nothing to worry about." I frowned and she chuckled. "Nicco needed some final words of encouragement." A knowing smile played on her lips.

"You spoke to him?" My head whipped up.

"Hair, watch the hair," Nora scolded.

"Oops, sorry." I shot her an apologetic look before turning to my mother once again. "You saw him? Is he—"

"Fine, just some last-minute jitters. Tristan, Matteo, and Enzo are in the bar with him."

"The bar?" I groaned. "I hope someone is supervising them."

I'd witnessed the aftermath of the bachelor party. Nicco had ruined my favorite pair of sneakers after puking all over them before declaring his undying love for me and then passing out on the bathroom floor.

"Don't worry, Enzo is still in the doghouse for letting him get so drunk." Alessia gave me a wink.

"Ready?" Nora had positioned herself in between me and the mirror.

"No," my mom shrieked. "It is bad luck for a bride to see herself before the groom."

I rolled my eyes. After everything we'd been through to get here, I wasn't about to let a little Italian superstition worry me.

Moving over to the full-length ornate mirror in the corner of the room, I inhaled a deep breath.

"Wait," Genevieve said. "At least remove a shoe first."

"A shoe?" Nora balked.

"For luck," my mom added.

"Fine, take it." I lifted my foot and let Alessia slip off my ivory silk heeled pump.

"Ready?" Nora had moved in front of me, blocking my view.

"As I'll ever be." My heart was beating wildly in my chest but the second she stepped out of the way, and I saw myself, it stopped.

"I look—"

"Beautiful, sweetheart." Mom grabbed my hand, coming into the mirror's view.

My skin was glowing, my eyes wide with wonder and anticipation. But it was the dress that took my breath away. Layers of sheer lace gathered at my waist and fell around my body like a delicate waterfall. The batwing sleeves gave the illusion I was wearing a cape, but when I turned around and glanced over my shoulder, I saw the dress cut into a deep V. It ended at the bottom of my spine and flowed into a line of pearl buttons. It was simple yet beautiful, sexy yet demure.

It was perfect.

"I love it." I'd known the second I'd laid eyes on it; it was the one. I hadn't even tried any others. We found each other and it was meant to be.

Just like Nicco and me.

"Okay, now all that's left is your something borrowed and something blue." Nora approached me, a small silver and sapphire hair pin. She leaned over me, sliding it into my hair. Before flinging an ivory and lace garter at me.

"Nora!" My cheeks flushed

"What? It's tradition. Tell her." She looked to my mom and Genevieve who nodded.

"La giarrettiera." Genevieve winked.

"Thank you." I choked out over the lump in my throat.

"And something new." Alessia approached me next, a small jewelry box in her hand. "Nicco wanted me to give this to you." She flipped the lid, revealing a silver bangle. "Can I?"

I nodded, desperately fighting the emotion swelling inside me.

"It's says, 'tu mi completi'."

"You complete me," my mom sighed. "So romantic. My turn." She advanced toward me. "You can't walk down the aisle without your something old. It was my mother's, and hers before that." She lifted the small butterfly brooch and slid it into place on my dress. "Vola in alto, farfella mia."

Fly free, my butterfly.

"Mom..."

She wiped at her eyes. "I'm sorry, for everything. But today, this is your day, Arianne."

"Damn right," Nora added, cutting the heavy tension. "And Nicco is going to die when he sees you."

"Hopefully he won't," strained laughter spilled from my lips, "I kind of like having him around."

We were currently living in the apartment in my father's building. Nora had officially moved back to the dorms, but unofficially, she still stayed over a lot. I think we both knew once today was over, everything would change, so we were clinging onto each other for as long as possible. Nicco didn't seem to mind. In fact, more often than not, it was his idea to invite her over. Sometimes Matteo came too. Alessia even stopped by on the odd occasion. But never Enzo.

"We have five minutes before Allegra shows up and starts barking orders."

Allegra was the wedding coordinator, but Nora liked to call her Bitchzilla.

"Be nice," I said. "It's her job."

Genevieve ushered the girls over to the door, arming them with their posies. Nora would walk in first with Tristan, and Alessia would follow with Matteo. Then I would enter while Enzo waited upfront with Nicco.

God, I couldn't wait to see him. It felt like it had been days when it had been a little under twenty-four hours.

"Did he come?" I asked my mother, but her grim expression told me all I needed to know.

"He loves you very much, Arianne, but this has been hard on him."

"He made his choice." I stuffed down my feelings toward my father for another time.

Nothing would ruin today.

I'd made my choice just as he had made his.

"You should know he loves you very much, Arianne, we both do. Gosh, sweetheart, this is it. The first day of the rest of your life. Are you absolutely sure this is what you want?"

"I have never been more certain of anything."

She gave me a small nod.

"It is showtime," Allegra's voice rang out down the hall. "Grazie a Dio, you look sensational. Niccolò is going to stop breathing."

"Can we please stop with all the death jokes?" I gave her a tight smile.

"You remember your walk, no?"

I nodded.

"One, two, together. One, two, together... We keep our heads up and our eyes forward."

Nora caught my eye and pulled a face.

I smothered a laugh. "I think we've got it," I said, trying to placate Allegra who took her job very seriously.

"Of course you have got it." She clapped her hands together, sending my heart into a tailspin. "Let's go get your man." Allegra marched out of the room in the same whirlwind she'd arrived in.

"She's really something," Nora chuckled as we met at the door. I inhaled a shaky breath and she frowned. "Nervous?"

"Yes, and excited." There were a hundred butterflies in my stomach. "I just want to get to him."

"I'm so proud of you, Ari." She air-kissed my cheek. "Now let's go get your guy."

The Blackstone Suite was filled with one hundred of our closest friends and family. Really, they were mostly Nicco's aunts and uncles, but I'd been shown more love and acceptance from these people in the last month than I had my whole life.

I spotted Michele and his wife, Marcella; Matteo's sister, Arabella, beside them. The Boston family sat behind. Dane must have felt us standing beyond the door because he glanced over his shoulder, offering me a cheeky wink. He was trouble, that much was obvious, and I was relieved not to have to worry about him going after Nora. She might have enjoyed her newfound freedom, but she had boundaries, and Dane was still in high school.

Besides, the second the doors opened, and she took Tristan's arm, she had the attention of almost every guy in the room. Including Enzo.

"Ready?" Luis approached me. He looked mighty fine in his sleek black three-piece.

"I am." He crooked his elbow and I laced my arm through his.

"You look beautiful, Arianne. Every father should see their daughter take their wedding vows... I'm sure he will regret this day for the rest of his life."

"He made his choice."

"Well, his loss is my gain. It is an honor to accompany you down the aisle. Shall we?" We moved into place, waiting for the pianist and cellist to start the entrance music. The soft notes of Christina Perri's *A Thousand Years* filled the room and everyone turned to watch as Luis walked me slowly down the aisle.

I felt their stares, heard their sighs of approval, and whispers of judgment. But they all fell away the second my eyes found Nicco. His gaze grew, shining with pure and unconditional love as he drank me in. I wanted to run to him, to rush into his arms and declare myself his for all eternity. But I knew Allegra was watching, ready to intervene if anything went off script.

With every step closer, my heart beat harder, until I felt sure it would explode in my chest. We finally reached the officiant, and Nicco stepped towards us.

"Bambolina, you look..." the words died on his lips, but I saw the intention in his heated gaze, and color bloomed in my cheeks.

Luis laid my hand in Nicco's before dipping his head to kiss my cheek. "This is your moment, Ari. You deserve it." He backed away and we turned to face the officiant.

"Welcome, family, friends, and loved ones," he began. "We are gathered here today in the presence of God, to unite Arianne and Niccolò in holy matrimony. Marriage is a gift, given to us so that we might experience the joys of unconditional love with a lifelong partner..."

Nicco squeezed my hand, and I peeked over at him. He looked devastatingly handsome. The sharp, black three-piece molded to his broad shoulders and tapered in at his waist. His eyes were dark, swirling with possessiveness. But it was his smile that knocked the air from my lungs. He looked so happy.

He looked... *free*.

The officiant took a deep breath, smiling at the both of us. "Niccolò, do you take Arianne to be your wedded wife, to live together after God's ordinance in the holy estate of matrimony? Do you promise to love her, comfort her, honor and keep her, in sickness and in health, and forsaking all others, remain faithful to her as long as you both shall live?"

"I do."

My heart beat so hard, I inhaled a shaky breath.

"And Arianne, do you take Niccolò to be your wedded husband, to live together after God's ordinance in the holy estate of matrimony? Do you promise to love him, comfort him, honor and keep him, in sickness and in health, and forsaking all others, remain faithful to him as long as you both shall live?"

"I do."

He nodded with approval before looking out to the crowd behind us. "Who gives Arianne to be married to Niccolò?"

"I do," my father's voice rang out clear across the room, and my head whipped around.

He walked toward us, his eyes filled with pride and regret. "Sorry I'm late." He looked at me. "Mio tesoro." It came out choked. "Sei bellissima."

Tears welled in my eyes, but I forced them down. "You're here?"

"I am." My father turned his focus on Nicco. "Take good care of her, Son."

"I will." They shared a lingering look before he took the empty seat next to my mother.

She beamed at me, and a sense of rightness washed over me. I hadn't mourned my father's absence, but him coming here, being here to witness this, gave me hope for the future.

As the officiant continued, I was too lost in my thoughts to hear his words. Lost in a daydream of dark-haired babies with brown eyes, of laughter and happiness, and a home filled with love.

It wasn't until Nicco squeezed my hand again, I realized they were waiting for me.

"Sorry," I whispered.

"It's time for the wedding vows. Niccolò, you're first. Repeat after me...

I Niccolò Luca Marchetti take thee, Arianne Carmen Lina Capizola,
to be my wedded wife,
to have and to hold,
from this day forward,
for better, for worse,
for richer, for poorer,
in sickness and in health,
to love and to cherish,
till death do us part.
This is my solemn vow.

. . .

"Now Arianne..."

I, Arianne Carmen Lina Capizola take thee, Niccolò Luca Marchetti,
to be my wedded husband,
to have and to hold,
from this day forward,
for better, for worse,
for richer, for poorer,
in sickness and in health,
to love and to cherish,
till death do us part.
This is my solemn vow.

"And now the exchanging of the rings." The officiant called Enzo forward. "The ring is symbolic, it is without beginning and without end. I believe this exchange of rings not only reminds us of the unending love you have for each other, but also reflects the eternal love God has for each of you. May I have the token of the groom's love for Arianne?" He turned to Enzo who offered up a small velvet pouch.

"Niccolò, repeat after me..."

This ring I give in token and pledge, as a sign of my love and devotion. With this ring, I thee wed.

Nicco slid the band onto my trembling finger, his touch lingering as if he wanted to savor the moment.

"And now may I have the token of the bride's love for Niccolò?" Enzo handed the officiant Nicco's wedding band and he offered it to me.

This ring I give in token and pledge, as a sign of my love and devotion. With this ring, I thee wed.

I pushed the plain gold band onto Nicco's finger. The officiant placed our hands atop of one another's and took them in his. "Niccolò and Arianne, since you have consented together in holy matrimony, and have pledged yourselves to each other by your solemn vows and by the giving of rings, and have declared your commitment of love before God and these witnesses, I now pronounce you husband and wife in the name of the Father and the Son and the Holy Spirit. Those whom God hath joined together, let no man separate." He smiled. "Niccolò you may kiss your bride."

Nicco turned to me and moved in, pressing his palm against my cheek. "Ti amo più oggi di ieri ma meno di domani." His lips brushed mine, but I fisted his jacket, pulling him closer and deepening the kiss.

This man was mine, just as I was his, and I wanted the world to know.

People began to cheer, but it was the officiant who cleared his throat. I buried my face in Nicco's shoulder.

"It's okay, my wife." Nicco coaxed me out. "We have time." His eyes glittered with promise. And I knew he was right.

We did have time.

We had all the time in the world.

"Ladies and gentlemen," the officiant's voice rose over the *thud* of my heart, "it is my privilege to introduce to you for the very first time, Mr. and Mrs. Marchetti."

"You know, Nicco is a good guy, but I think you picked the wrong Marchetti."

"Nice, Dane, real nice." Enzo approached us. "Don't let him hear you say that. He already beat your ass once, but he'll do it again."

"I can take him," Dane scoffed.

"Keep telling yourself that, kid. And lay off the liquor before your old man realizes you're drunk."

"I'm not drunk..." He swayed on his feet. "I'm just happy."

"Yeah, yeah." Enzo clapped him on the back and gave him a gentle shove toward where Arabella and Bailey were sitting. "Go hang out at the kiddie table."

"He's a sweet kid."

"He's trouble." Enzo smirked. "You okay?"

"I'm good." I smiled. "Just resting my feet." I kicked up my dress to reveal my lack of shoes.

"That's just... weird." He jammed his hands in his pockets, his eyes fixated on the dance floor.

"You could go dance with her you know?" I said. I didn't really like the idea of Enzo with my best friend, but the tension between them was undeniable. Only I couldn't decide if they were harboring sheer hatred or burning lust.

"I don't dance."

"Matteo seems to have no problem." He spun Nora around like a rag doll, the two of them laughing and smiling.

"I'm pretty sure the bride isn't supposed to be hiding in the shadows, watching as everyone else enjoys her big day." He cast me a sideways glance.

"I'm not hiding, I'm just... taking a breather."

The Marchetti family was big. Full of loud characters and overbearing women. Nicco had spent the first hour of the evening introducing me to the people I had yet to meet. Everyone was sweet enough, but it was exhausting, and I needed to catch my breath.

"I spent the last five years of my life locked away on my father's estate, this is a lot."

"Welcome to the crazy. And everyone loves Nicco. He really is the Prince of Hearts."

I could see that, watching as he moved from table to table to greet people and check they had all they needed.

"They already look at him like he's..." The words died on my lips.

"The boss?" Enzo's brow went up, and I nodded. "You're not going to break my boy's heart, are you? Because you were just starting to grow on me, Ari. I'd hate to have to—"

"I'm growing on you?"

"Yeah, like a bad rash."

"Hey." I jabbed him in the ribs.

"Seriously, though. You have nothing to worry about. You're his Principessa now. And one day, you'll be Queen. There is a line of Marchetti men who would take a bullet for you."

There was a time such words would have instilled fear into my heart, but not anymore.

"Including you?"

"Yeah." His expression turned serious. "Maybe even me."

A beat passed and then I asked the question that I'd tried so hard to ignore.

"Do you think Scott will come back?"

"If he knows what's good for him then he'll stay far far away from Verona County. But if he does rear his ugly fucking head again, we'll be ready."

A shudder worked through me. It had been a little over a month since Mike Fascini was arrested and Scott escaped. Antonio's men had searched high and low for him. After a couple of weeks, they decided he had left. Everyone was still on high alert, but life finally felt like it was returning to normal.

Well, as normal as you could get after marrying into one of the biggest crime families in New England.

"Hogging my wife, E?" Nicco found us. He came around to my side and cupped the back of my neck, kissing me deeply.

"I'm standing right here," Enzo grumbled.

"I know." Nicco smirked. "I'm hoping if I make you uncomfortable enough, you'll leave me alone with my wife."

"She has a name, you know?"

"I do. Arianne Carmen Lina Marchetti. Mrs. Marchetti." He kissed the end of my nose. "My wife."

"You're drunk." Curling my hands into his lapels, I leaned in. I could smell the whisky on his breath.

"I had one or two."

"So long as you don't end up like you did at your bachelor party." My eyes shifted to Enzo and he straightened.

"That's my cue to go." He left us alone.

"Will you ever forgive me for that?"

"I loved those sneakers." I pouted.

"And I love you." Nicco fit his body between my legs, careful not to rumple my dress. "I missed you."

"I just needed five minutes."

"You're not having fun?"

"No, I am. Today has been perfect. Your family are just... intense."

His brows pinched. "Has someone said some—"

"Everyone has been very welcoming. I just..."

"It's too much." Dejection washed over him as his eyes dropped to the floor.

"Nicco, look at me." I slid my fingers under his jaw. "It's perfect. I couldn't have asked for anything more. But you have to understand, I'm not from a big family. Sometimes I'm going to need space to catch my breath. That's all it is."

"You're sure?"

I nodded. "I love you, Niccolò Luca Marchetti."

He kissed me, hardly able to contain his grin. "Not as much as I love you, my wife."

THIRTY-ONE

NICCO

I WATCHED Arianne as she danced with Nora and my sister. Genevieve and Arabella and some of the aunts had formed a circle around them, cheering and whistling.

"She looks good out there." My father joined me at the bar.

"So does Genevieve." I gave him a pointed look and he let out a hearty laugh.

"She's..."

"More than just the housekeeper?"

"Yeah, Son. I think she is." He dragged a hand over his face. "Do you think it's too soon after—"

"Everyone deserves a shot at happiness. Just promise me things will be different this time. Alessia loves that woman. If you hurt her, I'm not sure she'll ever forgive you."

"Niccolò, I'm not that man anymore."

I gave him an understanding nod.

"It has been a good day, Son. Arianne is glowing." He was about to say something else when a figure stepped up to us.

"May I?" Roberto motioned between us.

"I have to say it, I didn't expect to see you here."

"You're not the only one." Arianne's father was clearly uncomfortable. "But she's my daughter, my blood. And I owe her. I owe more than I fear I will ever be able to repay."

"We all make mistakes, Capizola," my father grunted. "It's what makes us human."

"Thank you." His lips pursed as if the words pained him. And maybe they did. You didn't just bury a century's worth of bad blood.

"You protected my daughter where I couldn't," Roberto went on. "And you saved my life. I will be forever in your debt."

My father regarded him. "That girl is special, and I will treat her as if she is one of my own. But it will never change the fact that she is Capizola." He held out his hand. "I am willing to work for a better future. The future our forefathers wanted us to have."

Roberto stared at my father's hand as if it was contagious. But after a beat, he took it. "To the future." They shared a long look before Arianne's father blinked as if he couldn't believe what had just happened.

"Excuse me, I need to find my wife before she embarrasses herself."

"That was unexpected," I said to my father as Roberto walked away.

"He's finally realized some things are more important than business." He laid a hand on my shoulder and squeezed. "I'm proud of you, Niccolò. Of the boy you were and the man you'll become."

And with that, he walked away.

"So how does it feel then?" Matteo asked me sometime later when the party was in full swing.

I dragged my eyes away from Arianne. "Huh?"

"Being hitched?"

"Fucking amazing," I said around a grin.

"Jesus, you're whipped." Enzo dropped down into a chair with another glass of liquor. As the night went on, his mood had become increasingly dark. I suspected it had something to do with the fact Nora had spent the last hour dancing with Dane.

"She won't go there," I said. "He's still in high school."

"I don't know what the fuck you're talking about," he grumbled.

"No? So you won't care that he's making a mov—"

His head snapped over to the dance floor, murder in his eyes. Matteo bellowed with laughter. "Oh, man. You have it bad."

"Fuck off. I don't even like her. She's... annoying."

"You just need to get her out of your system." Matteo smirked.

But there was something in Enzo's eyes. Something that looked a lot like fear.

"Whatever you do, don't screw her over. She's Arianne's best friend."

"You can rest easy," he grumbled. "I'm not going there."

"Good to know." I fought a knowing smile.

"Are you worried Fascini might show his face again?" He changed the subject.

"I'm not unworried. But our friends down at the local PD have an APB out on him and we've got our guys on it too. He'd be a fool to try anything."

But he was always there, lurking in the back of my mind. Arianne had taken his disappearance better than I anticipated. But if I wasn't with her, Luis and Jay were. We had eyes on her at all times, and they had eyes on them. That motherfucker wouldn't get within ten feet of her without me knowing.

"Don't let that piece of shit ruin your day. You're married, man." Matteo raised his glass at me. "It's a good day."

He was right. It was a good day.

The best day of my life.

As if she heard my thoughts, Arianne found me across the dance floor and crooked her finger.

"I think your bride wants a dance," Matteo chuckled. "Go get her, tiger."

I undid my cuffs and pushed my sleeves up.

"Oh shit, he means business," Enzo teased and I flipped him off.

The circle of women parted as I made my way towards them. We'd already had our first dance but that was before the drinks had flowed. I wasn't worried about Allegra's steely gaze now, unlike earlier when she'd been dead set on giving us the perfectly timed day. The celebration was well under way and I wanted nothing more than to pull Arianne into my arms and claim her in front of everyone.

Which is exactly what I did.

Our lips met in a passionate kiss as I held her body flush to mine.

"Hi," she breathed, breaking away to look at me.

"Hi yourself." I leaned over her, kissing her again.

"Nicco, everyone is watching."

"Let them watch. You're mine now, Bambolina. Ti amerò per sempre, fino alla morte." She slid her hands up my chest as I twirled us around to the music. "Have you enjoyed your day?"

Arianne's lips curved. "It has been perfect."

"Allegra did us proud." I ran my nose over hers. I couldn't get enough of her.

My attraction to Arianne had always been intense, but when I'd seen her appear down the aisle, it was like seeing her for the first time. Her eyes sparkled with so much love and happiness it made my heart stop. And her dress... It was sheer perfection as if it were made to fit her body. But despite how good it looked, I couldn't wait to peel her out of it later.

The very thought had my blood running hot.

"When do you think we can leave?"

"It's still early, we can't just—"

"I want you, Mrs. Marchetti. I need you more than I need my next breath."

She flushed, staring up at me through hooded eyes. "Soon."

"Room for a little one?" Nora's arms went around us both as she wiggled between us.

"Me too," Alessia called, joining the huddle. Matteo and Dane were next, then Arabella and Bailey. Enzo hovered on the periphery until I beckoned him over and he reluctantly joined the fray.

"Only for you," he mouthed.

"Thank you."

Watching them surround us, witnessing their smiles and laughter, the joy radiating from everyone, it was the best feeling.

I'd spent so long at war with myself, with my destiny. But my father was right.

Love didn't make you weak, it made you strong.

And I had everything I needed right here.

Good friends.

A loving family.

And the other half to my soul.

My wife.

Sunlight streamed down on me as I peeked open an eye. Arianne was curled up into my side, snoring gently, the sheet pulled up around her naked body. Hazy memories filled my mind of stripping her out of her dress and making love to her on the bed, and again in the walk-in shower. There wasn't a single inch of her skin I hadn't teased and tasted, branded with my lips.

My dick stirred to life, rubbing against the curve of her ass.

"Hmm," she murmured. "Is that a gun in your pocket or are you just happy to see me?"

Laughter rumbled in my chest as I hooked my arm around her waist and dragged her body closer. "Good morning, Wife." I nipped her shoulder.

"Good morning, Husband." She tilted her head, giving me her mouth. I kissed her, slow lazy licks of my tongue that had me desperate for more.

"How are you feeling?"

We'd barely slept, too lost in one another.

"I feel—"

A loud knock at the door sounded. "If that's Enzo, I will strangle him."

"It could be important. You should go see who it is."

"Okay, but don't move. I'm going to send them on their way and then come back and finish what we started."

"We started something?" Her eyes finally opened, heavy lidded with sleep.

"Don't. Move."

"So bossy." Arianne laughed softly as I climbed out of bed and pulled on my dress slacks.

The bridal suite at the Country Club was secreted away at the back of the property. One entrance in and out, with a balcony overlooking the lake and golf course. A balcony I had hoped to enjoy this morning with Arianne, when they delivered us our champagne breakfast.

"What?" I yanked open the door to be met with Enzo's pale face. "What happened?"

"It's Nora—"

"Nora?" Arianne gasped and I winced.

"I thought I told you to stay put, Bambolina?" I slipped my arm around Arianne's shoulder and drew her into my side.

"Did you hurt her?"

"What? *No*!" Enzo balked. "She's gone."

"Gone? What the fuck do you mean, she's gone?"

"I... we..." He inhaled a ragged breath. "After you called it a night, we stayed up drinking. One thing led to another and I ended up in her room. But when I woke up this morning, she was gone."

"Maybe she didn't want to do the awkward morning after?" Enzo wasn't exactly known for his bedside manner.

"That's what I thought, but all her shit is still in the room." He held out a cell phone.

"That's Nora's," Arianne whispered, taking it from him.

"Is there any sign of forced entry? A fight?"

"Nothing."

"You were there the whole night?" I asked him because nothing about this made sense.

He nodded. "But I think I passed out. Things got pretty wild... Fuck." Enzo dragged a hand through his hair. "I told her security guy to take a hike. I had my gun and knife right there."

"N- no." Arianne dug her fingers into my side. "You think she was... *taken*?"

"It had to be him." Enzo looked murderous. "I'll kill, I'll fucking—"

"Calm down." I levelled him with a hard look. "We don't know what happened yet. There might be a perfectly reasonable explanation." I knew he was most likely right, but I didn't want to worry Arianne unnecessarily.

"Have you raised the alarm with anyone else?" I asked.

"No, I came straight here."

"Call Luis. Go room to room. We search the entire place."

"Got it." He hesitated before settling his stormy gaze on Arianne. "I didn't know... I swear, I didn't think—"

She stepped forward, laying a hand on his arm. "It's not your fault. But please, find her." A shudder ripped through Arianne and I pulled her into my arms.

"Go." I mouthed to Enzo. "And keep me updated."

He gave me a stiff nod and took off down the hall.

"You really think Scott did something?" Arianne stared up at me with glassy eyes.

"It could be something or it could be nothing. For all we know, Nora freaked and is in Alessia's or her parents' room right now sleeping it off."

"Yeah, maybe." She gave me a weak smile.

"Let's get dressed and then we'll go look, okay?"

"Okay."

Anger zipped up my spine, threatening to take hold. This was supposed to be the first day of the rest of our lives and that fucker Scott Fascini had found a way to ruin it.

You don't know it's definitely him yet.

But my gut instinct said it was.

"You think it is him, don't you?" A tear rolled down Arianne's cheek.

"Bambolina," I inhaled a harsh breath, "everything will be fine, I promise."

I regretted the words the second they were out.

Less than one day into married life and I was already making promises I didn't know I could keep.

"Okay, what have we got?" Myself, Enzo, Luis, Maurice, and a couple of our guys were gathered around the club's security camera feeds.

"It's definitely him," Enzo ground out as he glared at a still shot of a guy entering the elevator. "His hair is longer and he's in staff uniform, but I'd know that smirk anywhere."

"He's right." My heart plummeted. "It's Fascini."

"He disappears here." The tech guy pointed to another screen. "It's a blind spot area. But another camera picks him up here and here."

"And then what?" I asked.

"We lose him. It's like he's a ghost."

"Fuck." Enzo slammed his fist into the wall, and I raised a brow.

"Feel better?"

"I'll feel better when that fucker is six-feet in the ground."

The tech guy blanched, but didn't say a word. He knew the score. He knew who we were and what had happened.

"What about the outside cameras?"

"Nothing except this car leaving at," he leaned in, squinting at the screen, "a little after five."

"We have to assume he took her." Luis shot me a concerned look. "Which means he has a five-hour head start."

"Nora is Arianne's best friend," I said. "He knew he wouldn't be able to get to her, so he took the next best thing. He'll use her as leverage to get what he really wants."

"Ari."

I nodded, my stomach twisting violently. "He'll make contact when he's ready."

"So we just wait? That's some bullshit right—"

"Enzo," I warned. "We have to keep our heads. We have no idea where he might be. But it isn't Nora he wants."

It was Arianne.

My Arianne.

"If only I'd have—"

"Don't." I shook my head at Enzo. "You can't blame yourself for this."

"She was right there beside me. I should have felt something. I should have done something. Fuck," he roared.

"We had the place locked down. He was wearing staff uniform and had a keycard to access the elevator," Luis said. "He was prepared."

"Do you need anything else?" the tech guy mumbled, clearly uncomfortable at our presence.

"No, thank you." I flicked my head to the door, and everyone began filing out.

"Anything?" Matteo jogged up to us.

"It's Fascini."

"Fuck."

"Where's Arianne?" I asked.

"She's with her parents and Nora's parents. Mrs. Abato is beside herself."

Enzo kicked the wall before taking off, mumbling something about needing some air.

"Is he okay?"

"He blames himself." I watched him shoulder the door and storm down the hall.

"He was pretty lit when I left them. You know how he can get."

"He says he passed out, but I can't believe he didn't hear anything."

"Maybe Fascini drugged her so she didn't put up a fight. It wouldn't be the first time."

I let out a heavy sigh as I met Matteo's stare. "Did I drop the ball here?"

It had been a month and there had been no sign of Scott.

Not a damn thing.

"We all thought he was gone. You told Enzo not to blame himself, but you can't carry this guilt either, Nic."

"We need to be ready," I said. "When he calls,"—and I knew he would—"we need to be ready."

I was done pussyfooting around where Fascini was concerned.

There was only one way this was going to end.

With a bullet hole through his skull.

THIRTY-TWO

ARIANNE

SCOTT HAD NORA.

It sounded too messed up to possibly be true.

And yet, we'd left the Country Club without her.

She was gone, taken by that psychopath to God only knew where.

Nicco was confident he would call, but it had been almost two hours since we discovered she was gone and still, nothing. Mr. and Mrs. Abato wanted to call the police, but my father and Antonio had talked them down, insisting they would do everything in their power to get Nora back safe and sound.

It had been strange, watching them work together for the common good.

"What's taking so long?" I asked. We were at Antonio's house. Me, Nicco, Matteo, Enzo, and Luis. Maurice was at the apartment with Jay, just in case he showed up, and Tristan was back at my father's estate with mine and Nora's parents.

We all knew he wouldn't show up anywhere familiar though.

He would want to draw me away from everyone.

"He'll call." Nicco squeezed my knee. The two of us sat on the couch while Matteo sat in the chair. Luis stood over by the door, in his usual bodyguard stance, ready to jump into action at any moment; while Enzo paced back and forth like a caged lion.

He'd been quiet.

Too quiet.

I knew he carried guilt over what had happened, but part of me wondered if it was more than that. If he cared because it was Nora.

God, I hoped she was okay.

I didn't know what I would do if she was hurt... because of me.

Because of Scott's depraved infatuation with me.

My phone sat on the coffee table taunting me. We assumed Scott would contact me, but time was ticking.

"Anything?" Alessia came into the room.

"Not yet," I said.

She sat down beside me. "She'll be okay. Nora is a tough cookie."

Enzo made a strangled sound in his throat.

"Maybe you should get some air?" Nicco suggested.

"No," he said. "I need to be here in case—"

The blare of my cell cut through the air. "It's him." I snatched the phone up in my trembling fingers.

"What does it say?" Everyone moved closer as I unlocked the screen and opened the text.

"It's an address."

"Vitelli," Nicco barked.

"On it." Luis glanced over at the screen and began typing something in his own cell phone. "It looks like it's an abandoned industrial unit right on the edge of Romany Square.

"Motherfucker has a death wish," Enzo growled.

Another message came through.

"Come alone, or she dies," someone read it out.

"Oh God," I cried, and Alessia pulled me into her arms.

"Ssh, it's okay. It'll be okay."

"How are we going to play this?" Matteo said. "We can't just send Ari in alone."

"Yes." I pulled away and wiped my eyes. "You can. You have to. I will not let him hurt Nora."

If he hadn't already.

"You can't ask me to do that, Bambolina." The blood had drained from Nicco's face.

"What other choice do we have? He won't hurt me. Not until he gets what he wants. I can placate him while you make your move."

"No." Nicco looked murderous.

"She has a point," Luis said. "He's obsessed with her. If anyone can distract him, it's Ari."

"I will not risk your life." Nicco shot up. "It is *not* an option."

I stood, taking his face in my hands. "Nora is my best friend. I can't stand by and do nothing."

"It's a trap. If we send you in there alone—"

"I won't be alone. I know you'll keep me safe, Nicco."

"Fuck, Bambolina." His eyes shuttered as he swallowed harshly. "Don't ask me to do this."

"We can send her in with a vest," Luis said. "It's not ideal but it's better than nothing."

"A vest.... fuck." Nicco ran a hand down his face.

"I have to do this," I said with more confidence. The longer we sat around and decided what to do, the longer Nora was with him.

"It's our best shot at getting Nora out of there..." Luis swallowed the words.

Words I didn't ever want to hear.

Nora would survive this.

She had to.

We all looked to Nicco, waiting. "Okay," he eventually choked out. "We do it. But you listen to every single word I tell you." I nodded. "I need to speak with my father, and then we head out. Matteo, you stay here with Alessia."

"But, Nic—"

Nicco silenced him with a hard look.

His hands went up. "I'm on babysitting duty, got it."

"Enzo, Luis, you're with us." He moved toward Enzo, lowering his voice so the rest of us couldn't hear.

"Be safe." Alessia pulled my attention from her brother and cousin.

"I will, I promise."

"Arianne," Luis beckoned me over, "we need to get you set up."

I glanced back to Nicco and he gave me a tight smile. "Go. I'll be there soon."

I had no idea where *there* was, but I followed my bodyguard out of the living room and down the hall. He seemed to know his way around the house which surprised me.

"How often have you been here?"

"A few times."

"I see."

He let out a chuckle. "I only ever acted with your safety in mind."

"I know."

I did.

It just seemed weird that a man once so loyal to my father was now on the other side. Although after the wedding, maybe we were all on the same side now.

Luis kept going until we walked right out of the house to his SUV. He popped the trunk and pulled up the interior flooring revealing a hidden compartment. "One bulletproof vest. Put it on under your hoodie."

My hands trembled as I took it from him. "Is this really necess—

He gave me a pointed look. "Scott is unhinged, Arianne. I know you want to do the right thing, and I agree, I think this is our safest bet at saving Nora, but it doesn't change the fact we could be playing right into his hands."

"I know, I just... okay," I let out a weary sigh. "I'll put it on." Slipping out of my hoodie, I let Luis help secure me into the vest. It felt strange, restrictive, and heavy, like a vice around my chest.

"It's not infallible, but it gives you some protection. Knife." He handed me a blade, the one he'd given me before, the one I'd stabbed Scott with.

"I..."

"Take it." He pushed it toward me. "There is no way I'm letting you walk in there unarmed and you know Nicco will agree with me."

My fingers closed around the handle as I stared down at the blade, remembering how it had felt jamming it into Scott's thigh. A shudder rolled through me.

"Ari, look at me. "Luis' hand landed on my shoulder. "You've got this. We'll be there every step of the way."

I nodded, too choked to reply. Earlier I'd been running on adrenaline, on the sheer desperation of saving Nora. But now I was running on fear.

"Arianne," Antonio's deep voice startled me. "Nicco has filled me in on the plan." He came over to us, and Luis gave the two of us some space.

"I have to do this," I said as if I was talking myself into it.

"I know. She is your friend."

"Nora is family. I couldn't live with myself if I didn't do this and she..."

"She will be fine. It is you Scott wants. Just keep him talking and Niccolò will take care of him, okay?"

"Okay." Tears burned the back of my eyes.

In a rare display of affection, Antonio pulled me into his big arms. "You are a part of this family now. We will not let any harm come to you. Do you understand?"

"I do."

"Good." He eased back. "You and my son have your whole future ahead of you. We shall not let Scott Fascini take that from you, either of you."

"All set?" Nicco stalked over to us. He looked deadly, his eyes dark and stormy. He didn't like this, but I had to do it.

"Call me when it's done," Antonio said.

And I realized then, that this was a suicide mission.

But not for me or Nicco.

For Scott.

The industrial unit was a big place on the edge of Romany Square near the border. We rolled to a stop and Nicco went into full protector mode.

"Luis and E, go scope it out." His eyes were narrowed dangerously as he stared out at the warehouse as if it was the enemy.

Maybe in some ways, it was.

Luis and Enzo left, splitting up and sweeping the area.

"It will be okay," I said, breaking the thick silence.

"Bambolina." He exhaled a heavy sigh, fixing his eyes on me. "Why do I feel like this is a bad idea?"

"It's the only option, Nicco. If you go in there, he could hurt Nora, or worse. I won't take that chance."

"So I'm just supposed to take a chance with your life?"

"Scott is a psychopath. I can appeal to his ego."

"You know how this ends, don't you?"

I nodded, swallowing the lump in my throat. "It's okay. I understand."

Scott couldn't walk away from this. No matter how much I didn't want Nicco to kill him, to carry that burden, I knew they would never let him live after this. And I had to make my peace with that.

"I think I understand now. He threatened Nora and I would do anything to save her." I laid my palm on his cheek. "It's okay. Do what you have to, just make sure you come back to me."

Nicco closed the distance between us, sweeping his tongue into my mouth and kissing me. It was a kiss fueled by anger and frustration, desperation and fear. It was a kiss full of promise and reassurance.

A kiss I never wanted to end.

"They're back." Nicco broke away, touching his head to mine. He inhaled a deep breath before sitting up, his cold mask sliding back into place.

Luis yanked open my door and peered inside. "One way in and out. He's backed himself into a corner."

Nervous energy zipped through me, my body vibrating uncontrollably. I took Luis' hand and let him help me out.

Nicco followed. "Okay. I'll walk Arianne to the door," he said. "Once Nora is clear, you wait for my signal." They both nodded as he took my hand and started guiding me toward the building. Every step was like a gunshot to the heart. Blood pounded between my ears, my pulse so fast I felt a little unsteady.

"Wait," Enzo called, jogging over to us.

"What is it?" My voice trembled.

"Just get her back, okay?"

A faint smile lifted the corner of my mouth. "I will." I laid a hand on his arm. His body seemed to relax at my touch, relief seeping into his expression.

"Come on," Nicco urged. "We should..." He flicked his head to the door. The place was locked down, huge steel chains on the front shutters. But there was a door on the side of the building that was ajar.

When we reached it, Nicco tugged me around to face him. "I'm going to be right behind you, okay? Keep him talking but don't get too close."

"Okay." A tear slipped down my face.

"Ssh, Bambolina. This will all soon be over." He cupped the back of my neck and drew me close, kissing my forehead. "I love you more than life, Arianne."

I hesitated, and then, without looking back, I slipped inside.

It was dark and cold, a cloying smell lingering in the dusty air. My sneakers barely made a sound as I moved down the hall, but I could hear my heartbeat. Feel it as it pounded in my chest. The hall opened out into the main warehouse, floor to ceiling steel shelving creating a network of passageways.

"Hello," I called.

"Ari, don't—" Nora's voice became muffled and I heard Scott grunt and grumble.

Picking up my pace, I weaved in and out of the shelving, until I saw them. Scott had Nora tied to a chair, her hands bound behind her back and ankles bound together. "What are you doing, Scott?" I stepped out into the clearing.

In its day it had probably been a sorting bay of some sort, boxes and crates littered around the place. I stepped over some debris, stopping before them. Nora was gagged, thrashing against her restraints, her eyes pleading with me to run.

"Where is he? Where is that fucker, Marchetti?" His voice rose, echoing around the warehouse, sending a violent shiver down my spine.

"Let Nora go, Scott," I said, keeping to the script Luis and Nicco had gone over with me on the ride here. "She isn't a part of this. You wanted me and I'm here. But you have to let Nora go."

"You think I'm stupid?" He whipped out his gun, waving it around maniacally. I slowly lifted my hands into the air and inched closer. "Scott, look at me."

He was jittery, and part of me wondered if he was on something. "Put the gun down and let Nora go, please."

His gaze darted wildly between me and Nora.

"Let her go," I urged. "If you care about me at all, please, you need to let her go."

He stilled; my words finally reaching something deep inside him. "You'll stay?"

I nodded. He was unhinged, utterly deluded. But it worked. Appealing to the part of Scott that was infatuated with me, made him begin to untie Nora.

The second she was free, I beckoned her toward me.

"Wait." He cocked the gun at her.

"Scott." Fear trickled through me, turning my blood to ice. "Let her go and we can talk. Just you and me."

I silently prayed Nicco was somewhere inside the building. Luis and Enzo too. But I daren't look for fear of distracting him.

"Slowly," he ordered Nora to start walking.

She came toward me and I dropped my hand, brushing her fingers. "Go and don't look back, okay?" I whispered and she nodded, tears streaming down her face. Aside from a split in her lip and some bruising around her cheek, she looked to be okay. But I knew better than most, it wasn't the physical scars that stayed with you.

Nora took off toward the maze of huge steel shelving.

"Thank you." I gave Scott my full attention.

"I had to do something... I couldn't get to you, but I knew you'd come for her. You hurt me, baby. You really fucking hurt me." He advanced toward me and I slowly tracked backwards, trying to keep a safe distance between us. The gun was still in his hand, but he wasn't waving it around now. His eyes were locked on mine. Hatred and lust swirling in their depths. He was at war with himself. Scott wanted me. But part of him wanted to hurt me too.

"You were supposed to be mine," he ground out.

"I'm here now." My conscience screamed in protest at the declaration. I would never be his, but he needed to think I was on his side.

I kept moving, turning us so his back was to the only way in and out. He was fixated on me, exactly as I'd known he would be.

"You betrayed me," he spat the words. "All you had to do was love me. *Me*, Arianne. I would have given you everything. I would have made you my queen. But Marchetti swooped in and ruined everything. I'll kill him. I'll fucking kill him. And then I'll finally take what's mine."

The hand holding the gun grew twitchy again as he waved it in my direction. I was paralyzed, rooted to the spot as pain splintered through me. But I forced down the tears, refusing to show him even an ounce of weakness.

"We can talk about this," I said.

"Maybe I don't want to talk." His eyes were black, soulless, as he prowled toward me. "Maybe I'm done talking. You think I'm stupid? You think I don't know he's out there somewhere, waiting for his moment to strike?

"What are you waiting for, Marchetti?" He yelled. "Come save your woman. Come save her before I—"

"Scott..." I was losing him.

"You. Are. Mine." The venom in his words cut my skin like shards of glass. "If I can't have you." He raised the gun higher. "No one ca—"

Nicco came out of nowhere, grabbing Scott and yanking him backward. "Nicco," I screamed as a gunshot rang out. I was thrown backwards, pain ricocheting through me as I hit the ground hard. Stars exploded in my vision.

"Motherfucker," someone grunted, their voices teetering on the edge of my consciousness.

"I should have done this a long time ago."

Nicco.

That was Nicco.

I blinked, bringing a hand to my head as I tried to sit up. Nicco was on top of Scott, the two of them jostling for control. Nicco rained his fists down on Scott, the sickening crunch of bone on bone filling the cavernous room.

"Nicco," I cried, still disorientated. I patted myself down for any signs of blood but there was nothing. The bulletproof vest had done its job.

"She. Is. Mine," Scott roared. "I had her first. Me. You think you can take her from me?"

Another sickening crunch rang out. "She will never be yours," Nicco ground out, his voice cold and deadly. "I should have done this a long time ago." He pressed the barrel of his gun right to Scott's temple. "You will never touch Arianne again. Never look at her. Never breathe the same air as her."

Time seemed to slow down as I watched Nicco whisper something to him.

But Scott didn't look scared, he looked... pleased, his lip curving into a wicked smirk. I saw his hand move, saw the glint of metal.

"Nicco, he has a—"

My scream filled the warehouse as I watched in horror as the knife in Scott's hand sank into Nicco. His body locked with pain, realization washing over him as Scott shoved him away.

Nicco rolled away, landing with a *thud*, a pool of dark red blood seeping between his fingers as he clutched his chest. "Bambolina..." It was a breathy moan as he reached for me.

"No," I cried. "No." Clambering to my feet, I rushed over to his side. There was too much blood. "You're okay," I said, dropping to my knees. "I'm right here."

"I'm sorry, amore mio, I'm… so fucking sorry." His words were cracked, blood trickling from his mouth.

"Ssh, ssh." I leaned down, kissing his head. "You're going to be okay."

"Ari, I need to look at him." Luis gently eased me away. I hadn't even heard him arrive. Hadn't noticed Enzo apprehend Scott, keeping his pistol trained firmly on his head.

"Talk to me, Vitelli," he called over to us.

"There's too much blood." Luis cast me a grim look and then looked at Enzo. "He needs medical attention, now."

"Nicco." I clutched his hand, blood squelching between our fingers. But I didn't care. As long as he was breathing, as long as I felt his fingers still curled around mine, he was alive. "You have to hold on, okay?" Pain ripped through me. "I need you… I need you."

"He's not looking so good. If I can't have you do you really think I would ever let him have you?" The sick and twisted amusement in Scott's voice flipped something inside me, and without thinking, I pulled away from Nicco and stood up. My hand went to the waistband of my jeans.

"Arianne," Luis yelled, but it was too late. I was consumed with hatred, with the overpowering need to hurt Scott the way he had hurt me so many times.

"Anger looks good on you, Principessa." He grinned as I stalked toward him, as if this was all part of his game.

Well, I was done playing.

"Ari," Enzo warned as I creeped closer.

"Relax," Scott chuckled. "She won't hurt me. She doesn't have it in—"

I barely felt the blade pierce the soft tissue of his neck. Barely registered the blood spraying out of his jugular, coating my hand and clothes like a jet spray of red paint. Barely heard his garbled pleas for help as the blood filled his mouth, trickling down his chin like juice from a ripe strawberry.

"Fuck," Enzo holstered his gun and slowly took the bloodied knife from my hand. "Ari, look at me."

My eyes snapped to his as if waking up from a trance. "He's dead." I glanced down at Scott's lifeless body.

"He is," Enzo said. "He can't hurt you anymore."

But when I glanced back at Nicco, at the pool of blood circling him, his shallow breaths and the pallor to his skin, I knew it was too late.

Scott had taken everything from me.

There was no future without Nicco. No life or happiness. There was only pain and grief and hurt.

Nicco was my heart.

The other half of my soul.

I didn't want to live in a world without him.

As I stared at him, the only man I would ever love, and watched the life drain from his eyes, I wanted that too.

I wanted to die.

THIRTY-THREE

ARIANNE

THE DAYS WERE LONG, and my heart was broken.

It had been two weeks since Nicco died in that building.

Two weeks of unimaginable anguish and pain.

I'd wanted to die that day. To follow him into the afterlife. But Enzo and Luis had grounded me, Nora too. They had stood by my side, watching as the EMTs rushed into the warehouse and began working on Nicco, trying to stem the bleeding and find a pulse.

Tears burned my throat just thinking about it. Within less than twenty-four hours I had gone from a bride so full of love and hope for the future, to a murderer with blood on my hands, mourning a loss so inconceivable I didn't think I would survive it.

But I couldn't regret killing Scott.

I could only regret that I didn't do it the first time around, when I'd had the chance.

Maybe then we wouldn't be here now.

"Arianne." Tristan stood as I entered the room. He came over and pulled me into his arms. "How are you?"

"I feel empty inside." My hand fluttered to my chest.

"You can't think like that. He wouldn't want you to."

"I just don't know how I'm supposed to do this without him, Tristan." Tears poured down my cheeks.

My cousin took my face in his hands. "You have hope. The doctors said he's stable. His body just needs time."

Time.

I'd already survived fourteen days without him, I didn't want to survive another.

"Thank you." I wiped my eyes on my sleeves. "For staying with him." Moving over to the bed, I gently brushed the hair from Nicco's eyes. His skin was sallow, and his eyes were sunken. A tube connected him to the machine breathing for him.

He'd died that day, on the cold floor of the warehouse, but the EMT's had brought him back. Twice, in fact. They'd managed to stop the bleeding and save his punctured lung, but Nicco hadn't woken up. They said his body needed to repair itself.

They said he needed time.

But time didn't feel like our friend, it felt like our enemy, closing in around us.

Sitting down, I took his hand in mine. "It's me," I said. "It's day fifteen without you, and I need you to wake up now. Please, Nicco." I kissed his knuckles. "I need you to wake up."

"I'll give the two of you some space." Tristan's hand rested on my shoulders. I glanced up at him, offering him a weak smile.

"Thank you."

After Nicco was moved out of the ICU into his own room, I'd refused to leave his side. For four nights, I had slept curled up on the couch, before Matteo and Enzo practically dragged me out of there. They made Genevieve and Alessia take me back to the house and make sure I got a shower and ate something other than stale sandwiches from the hospital vending machine.

Now we had a schedule. Someone was always with him so that I could try and look after myself too.

A knock on the door startled me and I glanced back to find Enzo standing there. "I know it's your time with him but I—"

"It's fine, you can come in."

Enzo had taken it the hardest. I knew he blamed himself. It was something we had in common.

"How's Nora?" I asked when he dropped into the chair at the other side of Nicco's bed.

"She's... okay." He frowned.

"It's okay that you're spending time with her, you know?"

"It's not like that." He ran a hand through his hair. "She just helps me—"

My hand shot up. "I don't need to know the details."

That made him smile, but it quickly disappeared when he settled his eyes back on Nicco. "Come on, Cous. We need you to wake up."

"Do you think he can hear us?"

"The doc says talking helps. But I always feel like an idiot, sitting here, talking to myself."

Silence enveloped us. Enzo was still as intimidating as ever, but something had changed between us since that day.

"Killing someone changes you," he'd said to me in the hospital as we waited for news about Nicco.

I felt different but not in the way I'd expected.

I'd been so against Nicco and Antonio dealing with Mike Fascini and his deranged son in their way, I hadn't stopped to consider that maybe we all possessed darkness inside us. It just didn't appear until you were pushed to your limits.

I was hardly surprised my limit was Scott hurting Nicco.

I'd let him hurt me, taunt me, and tease me. I'd let him do despicable things to me. But watching him drive that knife into Nicco had ignited a fire inside me, and in that moment, the darkness had shrouded me.

A shudder rolled through me. We'd been through so much.

Too much.

"You'll learn to live with it," Enzo said, as if he could hear my thoughts.

"There's nothing to live with." I looked him dead in the eye. "I did what I had to, and I'd do it again, a thousand times over."

He dragged his bottom lip between his teeth, studying me. "You know, you're kind of scary right now."

"I'm Capizola *and* Marchetti. You should be scared." My lip curved, and laughter rumbled in his chest.

"He won't like it, you know." His eyes flicked to Nicco.

"It doesn't matter," I replied.

All that mattered was that Nicco came back to me.

Three days later, I'd finally got the call I'd been waiting for.

"He's awake," Alessia had squealed down the line.

I'd abandoned Genevieve in the kitchen and asked Luis to drive me straight to the hospital.

"He's going to be disoriented," Luis said. "The doctors said it could still be a long road to recovery."

"I know." My body hummed with trepidation as we rode the elevator to Nicco's floor. "He's awake, Luis. I didn't think—"

"I know." He took my hand, squeezing it gently. "I know."

The second the doors pinged open, I took off running, skidding to a halt when I spotted him through the blinds. Nicco was sitting up, laughing at something Alessia was telling him. He must have felt me watching because his eyes found me, shining with relief.

I'd been so eager to see him, but now the moment had come I couldn't make my legs work.

"He's all yours." Alessia appeared at the door. "Luis can treat me to ice cream in the cafe." She skipped past me and grabbed his hand, dragging him down the hall.

I entered the room, freezing when our eyes collided again.

"Bambolina." His voice was cracked.

"You're awake," I breathed. "You're really awake." The invisible thread between us snapped taut, pulling me toward him. "How are you feeling?" I reached for Nicco's hand, smothering a whimper when his fingers tightened around mine.

"Ssh, don't cry. Please..."

"I thought I'd lost you." My teary gaze dropped to the bed. "I thought you were—"

"Arianne, look at me." Slowly, I lifted my eyes to his. "It's okay. Everything is going to be okay."

"You died, Nicco. I watched you die." All the pain and heartache of the last couple of weeks hit me like a wrecking ball. Big, fat, ugly tears rolled down my cheeks as I tried to process everything.

"Ssh, amore mio." His thumb brushed my cheeks. "I'm here. I'm right here. He can't hurt us anymore."

I stiffened.

"It's okay. I know what happened. I know what you did, Bambolina. And one day, we will need to talk about it. But not today." He gave me a warm smile. "Right now, I just want to enjoy this moment. I love you, Arianne Carmen Lina Marchetti, and I'll never leave you again."

His words sank into me, flooding me with a sense of peace I hadn't felt since our wedding day.

"I love you too," I whispered, kissing the tips of his fingers.

Nicco always said that he would die for me.

What I hadn't realized then, was I would do the same for him.

Love made us strong.

It gave us something to protect.

Something to fight for.

But, most of all, it gave us something to live for.

EPILOGUE

NICCO

THREE WEEKS LATER…

"Nicco, put me down," Arianne's shrieks filled the apartment as I carried her over the threshold.

"Welcome home, Wife." I nuzzled her neck. My body ached like a motherfucker, but I wasn't about to tell her that.

Arianne had been watching me like a hawk since I was released from the hospital. It was cute at first, but now it was starting to test my patience. I wanted to touch her. To strip her naked and make love to her. But Arianne took her job as nursemaid very seriously.

"Tonight, we're going to christen our new bedroom, and maybe the kitchen counter, and shower too."

She pressed her hands to my chest. "You're still healing."

"I'm fine." But I wouldn't be fine if she denied me again.

"Nicco…" She pouted.

"I'm fine. See." I twirled us around, wincing in agony as my muscles contracted. "Fuck."

Arianne wriggled out of my arms, sliding to the floor. "I'll call the doctor." She went to move but I snagged her wrist.

"Bambolina, it's just a little pain. The doctor said I need to take it—"

"Aha, I knew it." She glared at me. "Bed rest for you."

"Will you be in the bed with me?" I smirked.

"Nicco… this is serious. You're still healing. You almost—"

I cut her off with my mouth, kissing Arianne with all the frustration and desperation I felt.

"Wow," she breathed. Her cheeks were flushed, her eyes dilated. "He didn't say anything about no kissing, right?" She dived back in, scraping my jaw with her fingers, dragging me closer.

Laughter rumbled between us and I was about to try my luck at taking things to the next level when a voice boomed, "Nice place."

"You have got to be kidding me?" I dropped my head to Arianne's shoulder.

"Nice to see you too, Cous," Enzo grumbled.

"You guys, this place is so freakin' cute." Nora threw her arms around us both, not caring I was sporting a semi and still had my lips attached to Arianne's neck.

"Isn't it?"

I untangled myself from the girls and leaned against the counter. We'd settled on a place in Romany Square, a stone's throw away from the VCTI. Arianne wanted to continue volunteering there and liked the idea of being able to walk. I hadn't broken it to her yet that the only way I would ever let her walk freely around the neighborhood was if she wore a t-shirt with the words 'Niccolò Marchetti's Wife' stamped across the front, or with at least two bodyguards.

Not that Luis ever let her out of his sight.

"How are you holding up?" Enzo glanced down at where I was holding my side.

"If Arianne asks, I'm fine."

"Hurting like a bitch on the inside?" he whispered.

"Something like that."

"I guess you won't be making an appearance at L'Anello's for a while yet then?"

"Never," Arianne called over. "He'll *never* be making an appearance at L'Anello's again."

"Shit, man. Your girl grew balls."

"Like Nora doesn't have yours firmly in the palm of her hand." My brow quirked up.

"It isn't like—"

"That? Yeah, yeah, keep telling yourself that. Before you know it, you'll be planning how to keep her."

He snorted. "I think you own the market share in being pussy whipped. Have you spoken to your old man this week?"

The question caught me off guard. "Not for a couple of days, why?"

"He seems a little preoccupied. I wondered if you knew what was up with him?"

Dread snaked through me, but I pasted on a smile. "Whatever it is, I'm sure it's fine."

"Yeah, you're probably right." He walked over to Nora and roped his arm around her neck. It was a display of total possessiveness if ever I'd seen one.

Arianne threw Nora a questioning look and she shrugged, but I saw the slight flush to her cheeks. Enzo had surprised her.

And she wasn't the only one.

"So, what's the plan?"

"We have a few more boxes to unpack. Matteo is getting Alessia and Bailey from school and then heading straight here."

"Sounds good. Babe, check the refrigerator and see if Nicco got the beers in." Enzo tapped Nora on the ass before diving over the couch.

"Hmm, what just happened?" She frowned at him and then us.

"I think Enzo grew feelings."

"Heard that," he grumbled.

"Are you two like... *together*?" Arianne whispered. "Because you said it was nothing."

"I thought it was nothing."

"I've known Enzo my entire life," I said. "And that, the way he is with you, isn't nothing. Just be careful, okay?" Enzo was complicated, and the last thing I wanted was for Nora to get hurt. Especially after everything she'd been through.

"Worry less about me and Enzo, and more about when your wife is going to let you get some," she said around a half-smile, moving around us to the refrigerator.

"You told her?" I gawked at Arianne, and guilt filled her expression.

"Well, it's hard not being able to... you know. I had to talk to someone."

"Come here." I snagged her waistband, yanking her closer and dipping my mouth to her ear. "Tonight, when our family and friends leave, I am going to carry you into our bedroom, strip you naked, and spend time reacquainting myself with every single inch of your skin."

Her fingers twisted into my sweater as she suppressed a soft moan. "Any objections?" I asked and she shook her head. "Good, didn't think so."

Arianne turned slightly, brushing my lips with hers. "Until tonight."

"Tonight," I choked out.

Jesus Christ. It was going to be a long fucking day.

The next morning, my father summoned us to the house. We couldn't catch a break. Enzo's words from yesterday lingered in my mind. He was right, something was wrong. I just couldn't put my finger on what.

The arrangement with Roberto was, to my knowledge, going as well as could be expected. Word from our contact down in local PD was that Mike Fascini was looking at serving serious time. Scott was gone, his case open and shut thanks to our friends in the police department. And doctors were confident I would make a full recovery.

"You're nervous," Arianne said as we climbed out of the SUV.

"Thanks." I tipped my chin at Luis. He'd become our personal chauffeur since I was released from hospital. I couldn't ride my bike or drive yet. And Arianne still hadn't gotten her permit. It was on my list of things to do as soon as I was up to it.

"I just don't like surprises."

"I'm sure it's nothing." She leaned into my side.

"Yeah, probably."

We entered the house and headed straight for my father's study. "Niccolò, it's a damn good sight to see you upright, Son."

"Thanks." I accepted his hug but didn't miss the tightness in his expression.

"And Arianne, you look as beautiful as ever."

"Thank you, Antonio. Should I leave the two of you—"

"Actually, this concerns you too. Please, sit."

My senses were working overtime.

"After you and Tommy visited Vermont," my father leaned forward, steepling his fingers, "Luis Vitelli provided Tommy with some information about the failed attempt on Arianne's life."

"I remember," I said, wondering where he could possibly be going with this.

"Tommy did some more digging..." He inhaled a shaky breath, the blood draining from his face.

"He found something?"

"Nothing. He found nothing."

"But that doesn't make any sense." I frowned. "It had to be Fascini."

"I know, Son. Which is why I sent Tommy to see Mike Fascini."

"What?" Now I was really confused.

"Something about the whole thing had been bothering me. Mike would have needed to pin the hit on us. There would have been a paper trail, something." He scrubbed his jaw. "And then, when Fascini moved the wedding date, I started to wonder, what if Fascini didn't orchestrate the hit, but provided the right person with the right information. But I discounted it because it is not possible."

He was talking in riddles... until everything slammed into me.

"You think we have a traitor in our ranks." It wasn't a question.

I'd wondered myself how Fascini could have found out that we visited Elizabeth Monroe, but I'd assumed he was having us watched.

"I don't think, Son." He expression turned grim. "I know."

"Who is it?" Any traitor to the Family knew what it meant.

They knew it was a death sentence.

"Fuck, I don't know how to say this, Niccolò. It is...Vincenzo."

"Vincenzo?" Arianne's voice was small. "Enzo's dad tried to have me killed?"

"According to Fascini, he made contact with Vincenzo under a guise, drip feeding him the information he needed to organize the hit."

"He wanted war," I said flatly.

It made no sense, and yet, it made perfect sense.

My uncle had always spited my father over his soft approach to handling

Roberto Capizola. He preferred to get things done no matter the cost, but my father saw the bigger picture.

"It was Vincenzo who informed Fascini that you and Tommy had been to Vermont, just as it was him who gave them a heads up about the police warrant. But Scott intercepted the call, that's how he managed to evade arrest."

"Figlio di puttana!" My fist clenched. "He betrayed us."

"He did." My father sank back in his chair. "My own brother. I always knew he didn't like the way I ran things, but I never thought..."

"What happens now?" Arianne sounded eerily calm.

"We live by a code, Arianne." My father looked her into the eye, treating her as an equal. Under any other circumstance, it was a moment that would have filled me with pride.

"So he will die for his sins?"

"He will."

She inhaled a shuddering breath. "This will destroy Enzo."

Fuck.

Enzo.

I hadn't even considered my best friend, still trying to wrap my head around the fact my uncle was a traitor.

"Lorenzo is strong. He will survive this."

"When?" I asked through gritted teeth.

"Tonight. It is already set. Me, you, Michele, and Enzo."

"Not Enzo, he doesn't need to witness that."

"You know he must. It is the way things must be done."

I managed a small nod. There would be an interrogation. A chance for Vincenzo to purge his sins and cleanse his soul before death.

"Excuse me." Arianne got up and hurried from the room.

"She needed to know," my father said. "There are some things we cannot protect those we love from."

"I know." Even if my father hadn't asked for her to be here, I would have told her. It just didn't make the reality any easier to process.

"Where?"

"One of the cabins."

I nodded. It wouldn't be the cabin Arianne and I had hidden in, the place I'd proposed. That was sacred now. It would be another one of our places. Somewhere my father had no problem with getting a little dirty.

I stood, desperate to go after Arianne. "What should I tell Enzo?"

"Whatever you need to tell him to get him there."

"You don't have to watch this," I said to my cousin as my father drove his brass knuckles into Vincenzo's face.

"The truth," he roared.

"The truth?" Vincenzo spat, blood oozing from the numerous cuts on his face. "The truth is you don't have what it takes to be the boss..."

Enzo was deathly still beside me, dark energy rolling off him. I didn't want him to be here, to witness this. But my father was right, there was an order to things.

"You know how this ends, Vin," Uncle Michele stepped forward. "Tell us what we need to know, and all of this can stop." Pain glittered in his eyes. He didn't enjoy this. Few men did. He was offering his brother-in-law an out, but Vincenzo always had been a stubborn fool.

"Vaffanculo!"

The crack of Michele's fist against Vincenzo's cheekbone filled the cabin. His head snapped back, rolling on his shoulders like a rag doll.

"Why?" My father hissed. "Why would you betray us? Your famiglia."

"Because it should have been me. He promised me a spot at the table, you know?" Vincenzo was sneering now, rivulets of blood staining his teeth and chin. "Once the Capizola heir was gone and Roberto came for you, I was going to take the Family into a new future. A strong future. You can't trust them. The Capizola are—"

"That is my wife you're talking about." I yanked out my pistol and stormed toward him, jamming it right against his forehead.

"Niccolò," my father warned. This wasn't over until my father said it was over. But I couldn't just stand here and listen to my own flesh and blood talk about hurting Arianne.

"You don't have the balls, kid," he spat. "That Capizola puttana keeps them in her purse."

I cracked the butt of my pistol across the bridge of his nose, blood splattering everywhere. But he didn't look fazed. Instead, his lip curled into a sneer.

"It was me, you know?" he spat. "I did it. I killed Lucia."

A chill rolled through the air as we all realized what he'd just confessed.

"You lie." My father advanced toward us, dark energy rippling off him. "She left." His voice cracked with pain, matching the vise around my heart.

He'd killed her.

My own uncle had taken my mother's life?

What nightmare was this?

"She didn't leave." Vincenzo didn't show even an ounce of remorse. "She found out what I'd done and threatened to tell you. Always so loyal," he said.

"You're telling me you killed my wife?" My father was shaking, anger radiating from him, making the air around us crackle. "I'll fucking gut you and feed you to the fish." My father went to attack, but a gunshot went off and a hole blew right through Vincenzo's skull.

We all looked at Enzo who stood as still as a statue, not even an ounce of emotion in his eyes as he stared at his father's dead body.

"You good, son?" My father walked over and took the pistol from his hands.

"Better than him." His eyes were black. Soulless.

This was bad. Real fucking bad.

"What do you want us to do with the body?" Michele asked.

"Burn him for all I care." Enzo stalked out of the room.

"Go," my father ordered me. "Make sure he doesn't do anything stupid."

I gave him a tight nod and took off. But when I got outside, Enzo was gone.

And so was his car.

ARIANNE

"Do you think he'll be okay?" I asked Nicco as we cuddled in bed. It was two days after Nicco had returned from the cabin, his face pale and hands trembling, and fallen into my arms.

I hadn't asked what had happened.

I hadn't needed to.

Vincenzo was gone.

Enzo was fatherless.

And everyone in Antonio's most inner circle needed to learn how to adjust to life after Vincenzo's betrayal.

But then Nicco had told me about Vincenzo's final confession. He'd killed Nicco and Alessia's mom when she'd discovered her brother-in-law's betrayal. She wasn't gone. She was dead. Nicco had broken in my arms that night and I'd comforted him the only way I knew how—with my body, heart, and soul.

"He just needs some time," Nicco said. "His dad wasn't exactly a doting father growing up but he was still his dad."

"I can't even imagine how he must be feeling. Nora's going out of her mind with worry. He won't answer any of her calls."

"She should probably back off, give him some space."

"This is Nora we're talking about..." And she didn't know the entire story.

Nicco rolled me onto my side so we were face to face. "They're our friends and I know you're worried, I am too, but what I'd really like right now, is to enjoy waking up in bed with my wife." His hand slipped between us, finding my center.

"Oh, God..." I moaned as he rubbed lazy circles over my clit.

"Does that feel good?"

"Hmm-hm," the words got stuck in my throat as he slowly pushed a finger inside me.

"You were already wet for me, Bambolina." Nicco kissed me, his tongue mirroring the way his fingers glided in and out.

"More," I demanded

"Patience." His laughter tickled my face.

"I need you, Nicco. Please..." I wasn't above begging. Besides, it usually paid off.

Nicco dragged one of my legs over his hip, dropping down the bed slightly to position himself at the perfect angle to rock into me.

"Fuck," he hissed. "You feel incredible." Nicco anchored me to his body, doing all of the work. His mouth was everywhere, on my lips, my neck, latched onto my breast. He was like a man starved, feasting on my skin, savoring every inch.

"Ti amo."

"Always," I said, waves of pleasure rising inside me, threatening to pull me under.

But I wanted to fall.

I wanted to lose myself in him. In the way he loved me so completely.

"Jesus, Bambolina. I don't think I will ever get enough of this." He rocked harder, pushing us both closer to the edge.

I was almost there when my cell phone blared.

"Leave it," he growled, sucking and nipping my collarbone.

"I wasn't going to answer it," I panted, barely able to breathe, too overwhelmed with sensation.

Nicco hooked my leg higher, going deeper. So deep it was like he wanted to consume me. "Let go, amore mio." He whispered against my ear and it was my undoing. I shattered around him, my body trembling with ecstasy.

"God, Arianne." He stilled, clutching my body to him as he slowed his movements, drawing out the moment.

"That was nice." I nudged my nose against his.

"Nice—"

My cell phone began to ring again.

"Don't answer it."

"It could be important," I said, fumbling over my head to try and find it. "It's Nora. Hey..."

Her sobs filled the line. "What is it? What's wrong?"

"He kicked me out."

"What do you mean he—"

"I went over there to see if he was okay and he kicked me out. Said he couldn't deal with me right now..." She hiccupped.

"Nora, he's... it's complicated."

"Secret mafia stuff. Yeah, I know. But he was so... cruel, Ari. You didn't see the way he..." Her voice trailed off.

"Why don't you come over to the apartment and we'll figure things out," I suggested.

"No, I'm okay. You told me not to get involved with him, and I didn't listen. But he was different... he was... Do you think I'm stupid?"

"No, I don't think you're stupid. He was changing." We'd all seen it. Enzo cared about Nora. After the warehouse, it was like a switch had been flipped. But Enzo was in a dark place after finding out the truth about his father.

"I'm going to give him some space but then I'm going back over there."

"I'm not sure that is a good idea, Nor."

"He needs me, Ari. I know he does."

"Just be careful, okay?"

"I'm sorry for disturbing you."

"Don't be silly, you can always call me, always." I hung up and turned to Nicco.

"Let me guess, Enzo broke her heart?"

I pressed my lips together and he sat up. "Shit, Enzo did something? I was only joking." He brushed the hair from my face. "What did she say?"

"She went over to his place to check on him and he kicked her out."

"He's not in a good place right now."

"I know that, and you know that, but she doesn't." And we couldn't tell her. "I know he's hurting..." I said. It didn't justify Enzo's behavior, but Nora didn't know everything. "Maybe we should have told her the truth."

"It's not our story to tell." Nicco kissed my shoulder.

"I know but I don't like the idea of them both hurting when they were just getting to a good place."

"You can't fix everyone, Bambolina. Sometimes people have to find their own way."

"You're right." I dropped my head to his. "And look at us, we managed to figure it out despite the odds."

"We did." Nicco's lips lingered on mine. "And I'll be forever thankful you stumbled into my life that night."

Our love was fated.

Written in the stars.

A love so powerful and consuming it should have burned us both into nothing but ash. But we'd defied the odds.

We'd survived to tell the tale.

And all that was left now, was to live our happily-ever-after.

NORA

I wanted to heed Ari's words, I did. But I couldn't just sit in the apartment all day, festering on Enzo's cruel words as he'd all but kicked me out of his place.

"You're nothing to me," he'd gritted out when I'd tried to comfort him.

I knew something bad had happened.

I knew it related to Enzo and Dominion. But no one would tell me. Not even Ari.

It stung.

Over the last few weeks, I'd felt like one of them. Part of the inner circle. But when it came down to it, I wasn't.

Enzo had proved that this morning.

Just when he was finally opening up to me.

After the incident with Scott—and I called it an incident because calling it anything else still paralyzed me with fear—Enzo had been different. Maybe even before then.

We'd had such an amazing night together at the wedding, the sex had been rough and dirty, but the way he worshipped me was beyond my wildest dreams. And then he went and ruined everything.

I shook the thoughts from my head. I wouldn't go there. Not now. Not ever. Scott was gone. Arianne had killed him with her own hand.

"Maurice," I yelled. Despite Scott being gone and the threat of retaliation negligible thanks to Mike Fascini being behind bars, Nicco and Ari had insisted my bodyguard stay with me, for now.

"Yes, Miss Abato?" He rushed into the room, scanning for any sign of danger.

"I'm going out."

"Out? But I thought—" He eyed the pile of candy on the kitchen counter. After leaving Enzo's apartment, I may have gone a little overboard and purchased my body weight in sugar.

But screw that. I wasn't going to sit here wallowing.

I was going to fight.

I knew Enzo was hurting. I knew it had something to do with whatever had happened. If only he'd open up and let me in, I could help him.

I wanted to.

"Change of plans," I said, going over to the wall mirror and checking my reflection. "I'm going to need a ride to Enzo's place."

"Are you sure that's—"

I shot him a terse look. "If I want your opinion, I'll ask."

"Very well." He gave me a small nod. "I'll fetch the car."

"You do that. I'll be five minutes." That gave me enough time to add some gloss to my lips and blush to my cheeks. I didn't bother to change out of my skinny jeans and hoodie. I'd never dressed to impress Enzo before, I wasn't about to start now.

But I would make him hear me out.

Because Nora Hildi Abato didn't take no for an answer.

There was something between us. Something undeniable, something I wasn't about to ignore because he decided he couldn't deal with his feelings.

With a new sense of resolve, I grabbed my purse and keys, and headed for Maurice.

Enzo lived in a small apartment building right where the edge of University Hill met Romany Square. I'd been here a few times before. It was a complete man cave, gray walls with dark gray and black accents. The kitchen was all black hi-gloss cabinets and polished chrome handles. It was sleek and edgy and reminded me of the dangerous guy that lived there.

Matteo stayed there too sometimes, but from what I gathered, he often stayed at home with his family. Not Enzo though. He liked his space.

Maurice let the SUV roll to a stop and climbed out, coming around to open my door. I beat him to it though, leaping out. "I'll be okay, you can wait here."

"Miss Ab—"

"Nora. For the love of God, call me Nora," I mumbled.

It had been weeks, but he still insisted on keeping things strictly professional.

"You can see the door from here. I'll be going to Enzo's apartment. He can protect me."

The words did strange things to my stomach, not that I imagined he would be pleased to see me after this morning.

"I'll see you inside."

"Ugh, fine." I took off toward the building, determination steeling my spine. But my plan was quickly thwarted when Enzo didn't answer his buzzer.

Crap.

What the hell was I going to do now?

Then I spotted a guy coming toward the door. He frowned as he exited the building and I grabbed the door, slipping around him to go inside.

Thankfully, he didn't try to stop me, and I climbed the two flights of stairs to Enzo's apartment. Adrenaline coursed through me. I'd lost it. Completely and utterly lost it. Ari had told me to give him space. Hell, even Maurice tried to tell me not to come. But I never was one to listen. Besides, if you wanted something, you had to fight for it.

And I wanted Enzo in all his dark, brooding glory.

Coming to a stop, I lifted my hand to knock when I noticed the door was ajar.

"Miss Abato, maybe I should—" Maurice's concern rolled off my shoulders as I stepped inside, assaulted with the scent of liquor and weed. The place was a mess, littered with empty bottles and glasses.

"Enzo?" I called, dread slithering through me. It had been a few hours since I last saw him, but still, it looked like he'd had a party.

My heart galloped in my chest as I moved deeper into the apartment, down the hall toward his room. I knew I should call someone. Nicco, maybe. But I didn't want to leave without knowing he was okay.

"Enzo?" I called again, checking the bathroom. Then I heard it. A groan coming from his bedroom.

Relief flooded me. He was okay.

Enzo was okay.

Well he obviously wasn't okay given whatever had gone down here in the middle of the day, but he was alive.

I pressed my palm against his bedroom door, taking a deep breath, and pushed it open. "Enzo? It's me—"

The words died on my tongue.

"What the fuck?" He murmured, pushing up, fixing his bloodshot eyes on me. "Nora?" His brows drew together, his icy cold glare pinning me in place.

But I was too fixed on the person beside him.

The naked girl with her hair fanned out around her as she slept peacefully.

Bile clawed up my throat as realization crashed over me. "You bastard." The words tore from my throat in a rush of air.

"Nora?" He rubbed his eyes as if he didn't know if I was real or not.

"And to think I came here to make sure you were okay. Because I care. I fucking care about you..." Pain flooded me. "And this is the thanks I get. I guess they were right." I laughed bitterly, unable to stop comparing myself to the girl at his side.

She was everything I wasn't

Platinum blonde hair down to her tiny waist.

Big boobs.

Tanned skin.

Curves in all the right places.

I had always had a strong sense of self, but in that moment, I felt worthless.

Enzo finally snapped out of his trance, glancing from me to the girl at his side and back to me. "Fuck," he ground out, pushing the covers off his legs. "Nora, I can explain—"

"Save it." My voice cracked as I backed out of the room, crashing into Maurice.

"Miss Abato?" The pity in his eyes made my stomach sink.

"We're leaving, now." I barged past him and all but ran out of there.

I'd come to fight for Enzo, to show him I was there for him, and he'd betrayed me. He'd taken everything that existed between us and cast it aside like it was nothing.

Like *I* was nothing.

And as I fled from his building, tears streaming down my cheeks, I knew Arianne's warnings about Enzo had all been right.

He wasn't a good guy.

Not like Nicco. He was an anomaly. An outlier.

The hero of her unexpected fairytale.

And Enzo Marchetti...

He was the villain.

VILLAIN OF SECRETS
A VERONA LEGACY STORY

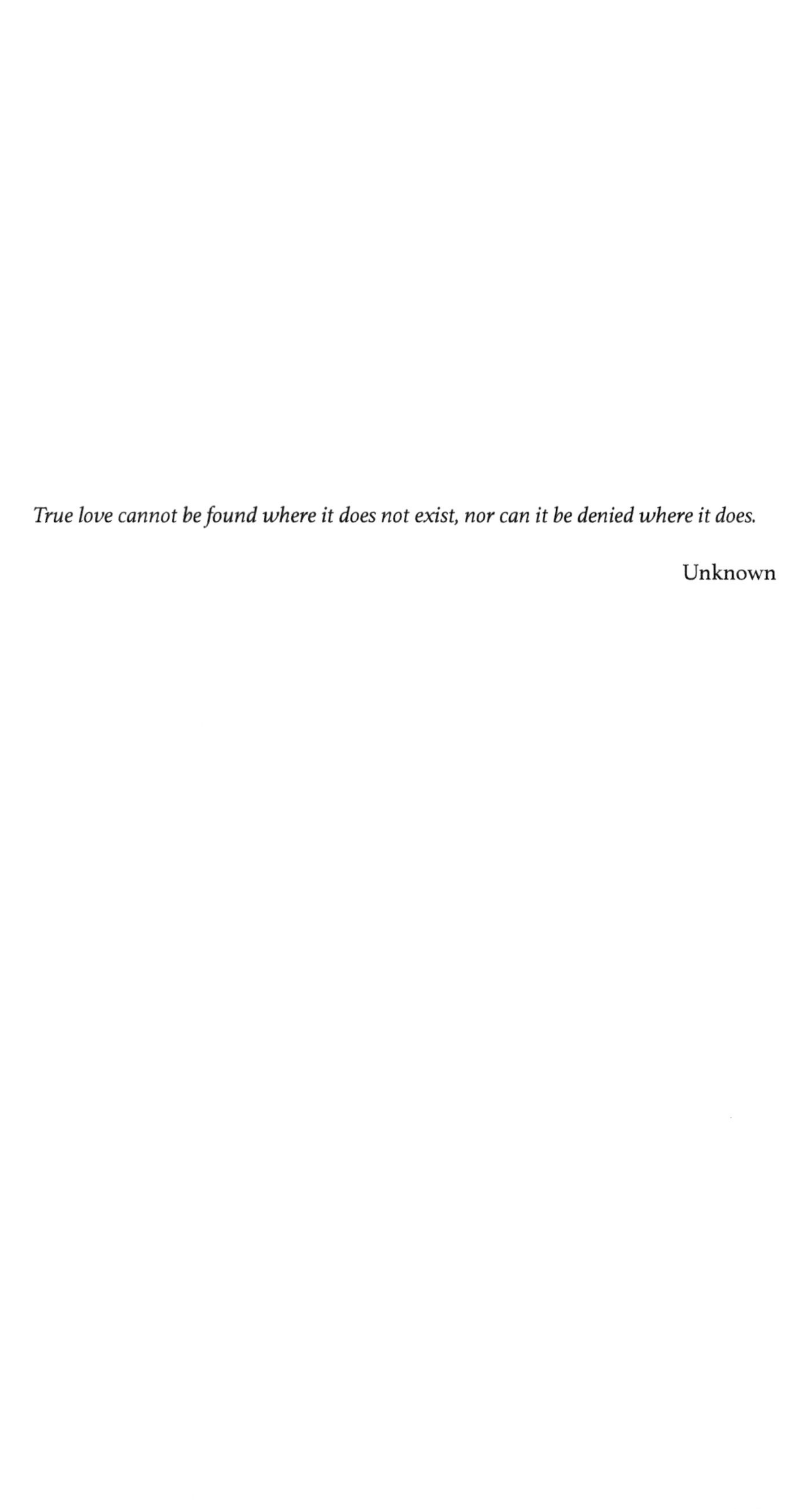

True love cannot be found where it does not exist, nor can it be denied where it does.

Unknown

PROLOGUE

"LORENZO, GET OVER HERE," my dad yelled, waving his hunting knife in the air.

I dropped the ball and jogged over to him and Uncle Toni. "What's up, Papà?"

"You ever skin a rabbit, kid?"

My brows crinkled as I leaned over his shoulder and saw the bloodied fur. "No, I didn't ever skin a rabbit." The words got stuck in my throat. Poor little thing looked like it had been skewered wide open. But there was something fascinating about the way its eyes stared back at me. Empty. Lifeless.

When our Nono died, Aunt Lucia said it was only the physical body that was gone. That the eternal part of a person, their soul, would go on to the afterlife.

Was there an afterlife for rabbits?

"You want to learn?" My father's gruff voice yanked me from my thoughts.

Uncle Toni tsked. "Vin, leave the kid alone. He's nine."

"Ten," I said, proudly. "I'll be ten in a few days."

"Nothing wrong with toughening him up, mio fratello. He might be nine now, but he won't stay that way for long. Here, Son." He thrust the blood-stained knife at me. My hand trembled as it curled around the hilt. Sunlight bounced off the blade, making the drops of blood shimmer.

It was the holidays, and me and my dad were out at one of our family's cabins in the Blackstone Reserve. We came every year—me and my dad, Uncle Toni and Uncle Michele, and my cousins, Nicco, and Matteo—while the women stayed at home and prepared for the holidays.

My dad said shit like that was for women to take care of. He said that it was better to get out of the way while they were doing their thing. Whatever that meant.

He didn't seem to like my aunts very much. My dad didn't really like anyone much. I liked them though. I liked how they always made a fuss over the kids, over me. Growing up without a mom, I'd craved their warm smiles and gentle touch. They were so warm and touchy feely compared to my father. But I was growing now, and I wanted to be tough like him, like my uncles.

I didn't like my girl cousins so much either. They were annoying: always laughing and giggling and talking about stupid girl stuff. I was glad I didn't have a sister like Nicco and Matteo, but a brother would have been nice. Someone to talk to when my dad was out, which was a lot.

My dad didn't like to show his feelings. I often wondered if it was because my mom died when I was born, and he was left with me. Sometimes he acted like I was nothing more than a burden. But then there were other times, like right now, when he looked at me with so much intensity, I knew without doubt that he loved me.

"Come on, figlio mio. Hunting is a rite of passage. It makes you a man. Besides, what's a little blood on your hands." He chuckled darkly, sending a shiver racing down my spine.

Frozen in place, my hand trembled as I stared down at the lifeless animal. I didn't want to skin the poor thing—it sounded messy and disgusting—but I wanted to please my dad. I wanted him to look at me with pride in his eyes, the way Uncle Toni always looked at Nicco.

"What do I have to do?" I asked, trying to disguise the quiver in my voice.

"Vincenzo," Uncle Michele muttered, but my dad ignored him.

I glanced back at my cousins playing in the snow. It was only a thin layer right now, enough to make them slip and slide as they ducked and dodged snowballs.

Sometimes I wondered why their dads didn't want them to learn this stuff. Michele, not so much. He was different to Uncle Toni and my dad. Softer. Calmer. He rarely raised his voice or hand to anyone. But he was always watching. Always taking everything in.

Uncle Toni was the eldest, the head of the family. After our Nono died a few years ago, he had stepped into his role. I was used to being over at Nicco's house. He was my best friend. But something was different about it now.

We weren't supposed to talk about it, but I knew who my family were. I knew what they did. Me, Matteo, and Nicco often snooped on their *business talks* at Nicco's house.

"Lorenzo," my father snapped, jolting me from my thoughts. "We don't got all day, ragazzino."

Ragazzino.

I hated that word. I might have only been ten minus a few days, but I wasn't a kid. I'd practically raised myself. I didn't have a mom around to fuss over me, and Dad's constant string of women never stayed more than one night. We had a housekeeper, Greta, but she barely spoke a word of English. She made good cannoli though.

"What do I do?" I repeated, my stomach a tight ball of nerves.

"Get down here." He grabbed me by the arm and yanked me down onto the overturned log, right at the same time as Uncle Michele got up.

"I'm going to warm up."

"Pussy," my father grumbled, and something passed between them.

"Bloodthirsty coglioni." Uncle Toni got up too, squeezing my father on the shoulder. "Go easy on the boy."

My brows crinkled. I didn't understand what they were talking about. But I still had the knife in my hand and my father's icy stare drilling holes into the side of my head.

"Pinch its hide and cut it near the base of the neck."

My fingers trembled as I reached for the dead animal. The blood was cold and sticky as my hand slid into the wet fur.

"Good, now make the cut," my father barked at my hesitation. I dry heaved as the blade slid into it like butter, but no more blood spilled.

"That's it. Now turn the knife edge facing up and cut from the stomach to the neck." I did as he instructed. "Okay, use your fingers to pry the skin apart. It'll be a little tough, so you'll really need to pull."

Puke rushed up my throat, but I swallowed it down as I began unwrapping the rabbit like a candy sucker. It was all kinds of messed up seeing the flesh and bone underneath, but I couldn't tear my eyes away from the helpless thing.

"Good, Lorenzo, good." My dad gripped my shoulder. "Now we make little cuts around the feet here," he sliced the fur, "and here, see. Then we can pull out the legs."

"Holy crap," I breathed as he helped me.

"What do you think?"

"It's... gross but kinda cool."

Laughter rumbled deep in his chest. "You are more my son than I give you credit for." He stared at me in that intense way of his. I didn't know what he meant, but I liked hearing him say it. All I ever wanted was to make my dad proud. To get him to pay attention to me the way Uncles Toni and Michele doted on my cousins.

"Good, Lorenzo, good. Now we can remove the guts."

"Th-the guts?" I dry heaved, and he chuckled.

"But of course. We can't eat the guts, Son."

"It'll be bloody?" My eyes were fixated on the animal's rounded stomach.

"There will be some blood, but it's small. It won't be as bad as something bigger."

"Like a deer?"

"Exactly." He gently gripped my wrist and guided my hand—and the knife—back toward the rabbit. "You'll have to cut through the membrane and scoop out the entrails with your fingers." He continued forcing my hand until the knife slid into the rabbit's stomach. Blood gurgled around the blade and I squirmed.

"Surely you're not scared of a little blood?"

"N-no," I said, breathing through my nose, hating the way it made my stomach roll. I wanted to be strong like my dad. Like Uncles Toni and Michele.

I didn't want to get all squeamish at a little blood.

Animal blood, no less.

Pushing past the urge to puke all over myself, I pulled the rabbit's insides out. The snow around our feet ran red with the splatters of entrails.

"I did it," I said, puffing out my chest, feeling a lick of satisfaction zip up my spine.

When my father had handed me the hunting knife, I hadn't wanted to do it. Nicco and Matteo weren't expected to do such grim things. They were here enjoying the cabin and the snow and hunting, but then they were left to goof around because their fathers weren't like mine. They didn't push and push and push.

"I'm proud of you, Lorenzo, you did good."

"Yeah?" I grinned. I couldn't help it. Praise from my father was rare. You had to enjoy it while it lasted.

"Yes." He gave me a stiff nod, gripping my jaw, smearing his bloody fingers all over my face. "You have so much to learn about the world, about this life..." he trailed off.

"About what you and my uncles do?" The words spilled out before I could stop them.

His eyes narrowed, a flash of surprise there. "What do you know about what me and your uncles do?"

"I know some things..." My voice wobbled.

"So eager to grow up." He smirked. "There is time. One day soon, Lorenzo. Soon."

I knew we were done here. This rare father-son moment was over, and I'd go back to being nothing more than a pain in his ass.

"Go on. Go clean up and play with your cousins."

"Okay." My head hung low as I moved around him. But at the last second, he snagged my wrist and hope swelled in my chest.

Maybe he wanted to hang out some more. Even if we were skinning rabbits, it was better than him pretending I didn't exist.

I waited, my mouth hanging open like a dog waiting for scraps. "P-Papà?" I said, filling the heavy silence.

And then he said seven little words that would one day mean everything to me.

"Blood is life, Lorenzo. Never forget that."

ONE

ENZO

"E, THAT'S ENOUGH." My cousin Matteo's voice barely penetrated the roar of adrenaline in my ears as I drove my brass knuckles into the guy's face. The skin along his cheekbone split wide open, blood spraying into the air like a fine mist.

"Stop," he whimpered, trying desperately to clutch at my arm. "Please, stop."

"I'll stop when you tell us what we need to know, stronzo."

"I-I already told you... I don't know nothing."

Whack.

I hit him again.

His face was a mangled mess, but I didn't care. The asshole was a rat, the lowest of the low. He could rot in hell for all I cared. I was only here to get answers.

"I'm gonna ask you again, tell me what the fuck you know?"

He trembled like a pussy, a wet patch staining his pants, the smell of piss permeating the already stale air. "I-I... please..." His right eye was swollen shut, his lips puffy and sore.

I raised my fist, ready to lay into him again, but Matteo snagged my wrist. "Enough," he snapped. Our eyes met, and I saw the disapproval shining there.

My cousin never did like getting his hands dirty. He was a lover, not a fighter. But love didn't get you anywhere, especially not in our business.

"I suggest you let me the fuck go, *cousin*," I seethed.

"I'm not going to let you do this, E. Uncle Toni's orders were to feel the guy out, not leave his eyeball hanging out of its socket."

"He knows who pulled that shit at Johnny Morello's."

"Maybe, maybe not." He lowered his voice as if the guy currently tied to the chair could think about anything besides the pain he was in. "But I'm not about to let you kill the guy because you're looking for something to take your anger out on."

"It's not your call to make," I gritted out, feeling a lick of irritation.

Matt didn't get it.

Nobody did.

I needed this.

I needed to feel the crunch of flesh under my brass knuckles. I needed to hear the grunts of pain. I needed the cloying stench of blood.

I needed it all.

"No," he yanked out his cell phone, "but it's not yours either."

Fuck.

Fuck!

"I won't let you do this, E. You want to go into self-destruct mode, fine. I get it. But I won't stand by and watch you lose yourself. So you can either back the fuck up, or I can call for back up." He pinned me with a look that said he wasn't going to give me a choice.

"You never did have the balls for this life, coglioni." I spat the words out, tearing off my brass knuckles and shouldering past him.

I heard his long exhale of relief, but it didn't tamper the anger vibrating inside me.

The guy tied to the chair, bleeding out, was a rat.

A traitor.

He deserved everything he had coming to him and more.

Barreling through the back door of the club where we sometimes handled business, I spilled out into the inky night. It was New Year's Eve, and it was fucking freezing. When I inhaled a ragged breath, it burned my lungs, but no more than the smoke I was about to light up.

Matteo found me a few minutes later, sucking on the cigarette as if my life depended on it. "Those fucking things will kill you," he grumbled, wafting the tendrils of smoke away.

"It's this or I go back in there and finish what I started."

"What the fuck has gotten into you?" His expression softened with concern.

"Like you really have to ask."

He knew.

The entire Family knew.

"Look," he let out a sigh, "I know it was a shock, but it's been weeks. Vincen—"

"Don't. Just don't." I clipped out.

You couldn't put a timeline on discovering your father, the man who raised you, the man who pledged his entire life to the Family was a traitorous piece of shit who had betrayed us.

Betrayed me.

There were days when I still couldn't believe it. Vincenzo Marchetti was the boss' right-hand man. His brother and confidant...

And he'd screwed us over.

But it was worse than that.

So much worse.

My father had killed my aunt. When she'd discovered proof of his betrayal, he'd killed Aunt Lucia, leaving Uncle Toni a widow, and my cousins, Nicco and Alessia, motherless. He'd made it look like she had up and left because she couldn't handle being in this life.

Motherfucker.

I flicked the end of my smoke and dragged my boot across it.

"Better?" Matteo asked.

"What do you think?"

"I think you need to find a better way to relax than with your fists." His eyes dropped to my tender knuckles, but I barely felt the sting. "There's that party at The Diamond. We could swing by and check it out?"

Pushing off the wall, I pulled the collar on my leather jacket up and headed for Matteo's truck. "Let's go," I said.

Liquor *and* pussy?

I didn't need asking twice.

The Diamond was a popular place on the edge of La Riva and Romany Square. One of our guys, Jonah, owned it, and always threw invite-only New Year's Eve parties for the Family's most trusted associates, and a few non-associates if the line of barely-dressed women lining the street was anything to go by.

"Jonah sure knows where to find them." Matteo let out a low whistle.

"See something you like?" I taunted.

"Fuck off." He flipped me off. "I'm just saying, that's a lot of skin on display for winter. I'm pretty sure my balls have crawled back into my body."

He wasn't wrong. The wind had an icy bite that was like a thousand tiny blades over my face as we approached the entrance.

"Enzo, my man," the security guy extended his fist. "Wondered if you'd stop by. Matteo." He nodded at my cousin. "Jonah is inside, already draped in pussy."

"Wouldn't expect anything less." I smirked. Jonah was always down for a good time.

"Hey, you good?" He pressed a hand to my chest, his eyes going to my tender knuckles.

"Nothing I couldn't handle." It came out tight. Giving me a stiff nod, he dropped his hand. "Enjoy your night. Don't do anything I wouldn't." His gruff laughter followed me inside.

The heat instantly hit me, and I shucked out of my jacket and handed it to the attendant in exchange for a ticket. Matteo did the same, rolling up the sleeves on his fitted black shirt.

"It feels weird without Nicco," he said.

"Yeah."

Nicco wasn't only our cousin, he was our best friend, and our capo. Usually where he went, we followed, but we couldn't exactly follow him and his wife—fuck me, we were too young to be wifed up—to New York on their honeymoon.

"Are you... pouting?" Matteo snickered.

"Fuck off. I don't pout."

"Cous, that's a pout if ever I saw one." He grabbed my cheeks and smushed them together. "You're missing him, aren't you?"

"I'm not... oh, fuck off." Shirking him off, I made a beeline for the bar. Sleek, black, and chrome, the counter ran along one length of the room. I dropped onto a stool at the end and rapped my knuckles on the counter.

"Enzo, my man," the bartender said. "What'll it be?"

"The strongest thing you've got."

"Shit, man. Bad day?"

"Try bad fucking year."

"I'll make it a double." He chuckled. "Matteo?"

"I'll take a beer, thanks."

"You should probably wrap those." Matt motioned to my hand.

"Nah, I like the pain."

"Of course you do," he mumbled. "You know, I wasn't trying to be a jerk back there."

"I know." My jaw clenched, remembering how good it had felt to put my fists through that asshole's face. "What did you do with him?"

"Called clean up and told them to turn him over to the cops."

"Shit, Matt, that isn't—"

"He's not going to talk, not to us. But he might if he thinks he's going to spend the next six years getting ass raped in the State Pen. Dante and Craddick will work him over."

Dante and Craddick were two of the local police officers in our pocket.

"Someone tried to move in on our territory, we need to find out who." My hand trembled as I made a tight fist.

Morello's was one of the Family's businesses up in Providence. It had been broken into last week and trashed. They hadn't gotten the contents of the safe, but they had left a nice little message in the way of a barely recognizable Johnny Morello. The guy was lucky to be alive.

It was a bold move, hurting one of our own.

"And we will," Matteo said, eyeing me with caution. "But some decisions aren't our call to make."

The bartender slid our drinks in front of us but didn't hang around. I grabbed mine, taking a big mouthful. As promised, the double measure of scotch was strong, but I welcomed the burn.

"He's a rat, Matt. And you want to just hand him over to the cops?"

The tip-off had come from our friends down in Providence about a guy who had been running his mouth about Johnny Morello's. We'd caught up to him just outside Verona County and lifted his ass to see what we could find out.

"Not me. Uncle Toni. And it's different, you know it is." His expression faltered. "He's not our rat to exterminate."

Silence descended over us, thick and heavy. It was like a fucking noose around my neck. How was I supposed to just accept what my old man had done?

A traitor.

He'd betrayed us right under our noses. I couldn't just let that go.

I wouldn't.

"Hey, Enzo, looking good." A tall blonde approached us, running her hand up my arm. "I was hoping to see you here."

"Yeah?" I tried to place her but came up blank.

"Mari," she reminded me, "we hooked up last month."

"Marielle, right? I remember."

Matteo smothered a snicker, and I shot him a hard look.

"You got any friends for my cousin?" I said around a smirk. "He's going through a bit of a dry spell, if you know what I mean."

"Fuck you," he mouthed, fighting a smile. "I'm going to take a leak." He gripped my shoulder and leaned in, whispering, "Don't do anything I wouldn't."

"What, you mean cuddle and talk about the weather?"

"Don't worry, Matteo, I'll keep him company." Marielle moved closer, tucking her tight little body against mine. She was wearing a sparkly halter top that left nothing to the imagination. Her long hair hung down her back and her pouty lips were painted blood red.

My favorite color.

I could imagine them wrapped around my dick while I fucked her mouth, my hand fisting her silky blonde locks.

"I'm down, if you are." She flashed me a knowing smirk.

"You read minds, hot stuff?" My brow quirked. "What other special skills do you have?"

"Take me around back and I'll refresh your memory."

"Let's go." I nudged her forward so I could climb off the stool. She slipped her hand into mine, and for a second, I wanted to shove her away. I wasn't looking to play games or let some bitch think she had ownership of me. But everyone was too wrapped up in the party to notice me and Marielle slip out the back exit.

Without a word, I pulled her into the wall and gripped her shoulder, forcing her to her knees. Her giggles grated on me, but I tried to block it all out as she popped my belt and the button on my jeans like a pro. Wrapping my hand around her luscious locks, I yanked Mari's head back, forcing her to look at me. She licked her lips, staring up at me with lust-drunk eyes and an overeager smile. "I can't wait to taste you again."

Right. Because we'd danced this dance before... only I had zero recollection of it because I'd been too out of it to remember.

She dipped her hand into my jeans and stroked my dick, pulling it free until it bobbed between us. "Maybe later, I'll get another ride." Her brow lifted.

"Suck me good, and perhaps I'll reward you."

She didn't waste any time, taking me into her mouth and sucking me hard.

"Fuuuuuck," I hissed, my head dropping back against the wall with a *thud*. She felt good, hoovering me down until I hit the back of her throat. I tightened my fist in her hair, forcing her to take me deeper. Her hand went to my hip, trying to steady herself as I fucked her mouth without restraint.

"E-Enzo," she garbled, tearing off me, "what the fuck? I can't breathe."

Her words were like a bucket of ice-cold water and I released her. "I thought you wanted to get me off?" I growled.

"I-I do." She pouted, reaching back for me and jacking me slowly. "But let me take control, yeah?"

"That's not how this works, dolcezza, and you know it."

I didn't want her controlling shit. I wanted to get off, go back to the party, and drown my demons in the strongest liquor Jonah had lining his top shelf.

"Enzo, I can make you feel good. Just relax, let me take care of you."

Her words were like a knife to the fucking stomach.

Let me take care of you.

Only one girl had ever whispered that to me... and I'd almost let her.

I'd almost handed her the power to completely ruin me.

Nora Abato.

Fuck.

Just thinking her name gutted me in a way I hadn't expected.

If my piece of shit father taught me anything, it was that pussy was the enemy. Before you knew what was happening, it lured you in with promises of a good time. You grew attached, you wanted more... you wanted *her*.

But love didn't make you strong, it made you weak.

And I had no desire to find myself wifed up like Nicco, risking everything for something as fickle as love.

"Enzo?" Marielle's shrill voice yanked me back into the moment.

"We're done here." I pulled my dick away and tucked him back inside my jeans.

"Done? But we only just—"

"You should go on back into the party."

"But—"

"Ma sparisci!" I barked and she hurried inside, her gasp of surprise barely thawing the ice around my heart.

I pulled out a smoke and lit it up, dragging in a deep lungful of tobacco. When the back door opened again, I was hardly surprised to find Matteo.

"Thought I'd find you out here," he said. "What did you do? Your little friend looked pissed."

"Told her to fuck off mid-blow job."

"Shit, man," his chuckle came out thin, "that's cold, even for you."

"She was getting clingy."

"And God forbid anyone try to get close to you, right?"

"Don't." I bristled.

"You and Nor—"

"I said don't."

I didn't want to talk about me and Nora, or the way she'd started to soften my hard exterior.

It had been a few good fucks, nothing else.

So what if she was my best friend's wife's best friend? I'd done a pretty good job of avoiding her the past few weeks. I was confident I could keep it up. Especially since I had no plans to return to Montague University next week.

Nicco, Matteo, and I had enrolled eighteen months ago to gather intel about Roberto Capizola, the Family's biggest threat in the last decade. But he was no longer an issue. The job was done, and we didn't need to keep up pretenses anymore.

I no longer had to tolerate college classes or any of the bullshit that came with being a student.

"Whatever, man. I'm heading back inside. Jonah was just about to break out the snacks."

"Snacks? Seriously?"

"What? I'm hungry." He shrugged.

"You're a fucking idiot. It isn't any wonder you can't get regular pussy."

"Hey, I can get regular pussy. I just choose not to."

"Don't tell me you're going to pull a Nicco on me?" It was bad enough I'd lost one best friend to a woman; I didn't need to lose Matteo too.

"Ah, don't worry, cous. Even if I did meet the woman of my dreams, I'd never abandon your cranky ass."

I flipped him off, shouldering past him to go inside. Tension rippled through me and since Marielle had ruined what could have been a perfectly good blow job, I'd have to settle for finding peace at the bottom of a bottle of expensive scotch.

Something strong enough to drown out the demons.

TWO

NORA

THERE WAS something inspiring about the first day of a brand new year. It wasn't so much any one thing, it was the possibilities. The ifs, whats, and maybes.

Being a college freshman, I might have expected to wake up this morning with a killer headache and last night's makeup smeared across my face. As it was, I felt as fresh as a daisy and my skin was silky smooth thanks to the nourishing mask I'd applied last night.

There was something to be said for staying in on New Year's Eve.

"Nora," my mom called. "Breakfast."

My stomach grumbled at the mention of food, and I smiled to myself. Apparently, I wasn't the only one happy that I didn't feel hungover.

Pushing the covers off my body, I sat up and swung my legs over the side of my bed, taming my wild curls out of my face. Hangover or no hangover I never escaped a bad case of bed hair.

A yawn escaped my lips as I leaned over and snatched up my cell phone, checking for messages. I smiled at the two from my best friend Arianne. The first was a picture of her and her husband, Nicco as they posed in front of Times Square. The second was a message.

Happy New Year, Nora. You're the best friend a girl could ever wish for and I love you more than anything. Except Nicco (he made me type that).

. . .

I chuckled, scrolling down the message.

New York is amazing. We have to come one time. Just the two of us. I'll see you when we get back to Verona. Nicco says hi. xo

Smiling, I texted her back.

Enjoy your last couple of days. You deserve it, Ari. xo

After the shitshow that was our first semester at college, my best friend deserved all her dreams to come true. It was hard to believe that she was married to Niccolò Marchetti, son of mafia boss Antonio Marchetti. But having witnessed them fall headfirst in love with one another, who was I to judge?

They were young, yes. But when you knew, you knew. Besides, they had that written-in-the-stars thing working for them.

My heart cinched, but I shook it off, pushing my feet into my fluffy, pink slippers.

"Nora, cucci—"

"I'm coming, Mom," I yelled. Grabbing my Montague University hoodie, I slipped it on and followed the smell of pancakes down the stairs.

"Happy New Year, baby," she sing-songed as I entered the room.

"Happy New Year, Mom." I helped myself to coffee before perching on a stool at the breakfast counter. "Something smells good."

She grinned. "It's almost done."

"Where's Dad?"

"You know your father, Nora, he's out jogging."

My mother and father worked for Arianne's parents, Roberto and Gabriella Capizola, they had for my entire life. We lived on their estate in a separate cottage nestled on the west perimeter. It was modest, but it had the best views of the Blackstone River. I'd grown up here, exploring the grounds, playing with my brother Gio, Ari, and her older cousin Tristan. But as I got older, I dreamed of more. Of life beyond the gated perimeter and guards posted on every way in and out.

"When are you headed back?" Mom placed a stack of pancakes in front of me. I added a handful of blueberries and a drizzle of syrup and dived in.

"I was thinking I might head back later."

Her brows knitted. "I'm not sure I like the idea of you staying there all alone now Ari is—"

"Ari is married, Mom. *Married.* Of course she's going to live with Nicco. I'm safe, I promise. La Stella is one of Roberto's buildings. It has excellent security and Maurice is still around."

He wasn't, not really.

But she didn't need to know that.

I didn't need close protection now. The threat to the Marchetti, to Arianne, was gone. But Maurice, my assigned bodyguard, did show up now and again to check in. I think it was Arianne's way of letting me know she still cared.

I knew she did. But she was married. *Freakin' married.* Our friendship was going to change whether we wanted it to or not.

"What's the matter with your pancakes, cucciola?"

"They're great, Mama, I'm just..." I swallowed the words. It was New Year's Day. I didn't want to be all mopey on the first day of a brand new year.

Giving my head a little shake, I inhaled a deep breath and forked another piece of pancake into my mouth. So what if Arianne no longer lived in our apartment and was married? It didn't mean life was over. She was still going to attend classes at MU. We'd still see each other all the time.

"Love changes people," my mom whispered.

My eyes slid to hers, and a weak smile tugged at the corner of my mouth.

Oh, Mama, you don't know the half of it.

I didn't hang around at the cottage. After eating my mom's famous risotto with my parents, Maurice gave me a ride back to University Hill.

"I'll do a quick sweep," he said, producing his key.

"You still have that?" My brow lifted, and he chuckled.

"I'll just be a second." Hand secured on his gun holster, he slipped inside.

I wasn't even a little bit worried.

The bad guys were gone, and everything was fine. But as I waited for Maurice to do his thing, a shudder ran down my spine as the memories tried to push themselves to the surface.

Less than two months ago, I'd been kidnapped and used as bait to lure Nicco and Arianne to their bloody end. Nicco had been shot, and my best friend had stabbed Scott Fascini, the guy working with his father to bring down the Marchetti with a knife until the life drained from his eyes.

He was gone, and his father was locked away with no chance of parole for a long time.

Nicco and Ari were safe.

I was safe.

Everything was—

"All clear." Maurice yanked the door open and I went inside.

We'd barely had time to make ourselves at home here before Arianne and Nicco got engaged. Swallowing the pinch of loneliness, I walked over to the window and pulled the blinds, letting the winter sun pour into the room.

"You don't have to stay," I said to Maurice when I noticed him hovering.

"Mr. and Mrs. Marchetti—"

"Asked you to stick around?" The words caught over the lump in my throat.

"They thought you might like the company." He gave me a stiff nod.

"Maurice, I'm fine."

Fine.

The word was cotton in my mouth.

I needed to do this—I needed to be here alone, without Maurice standing watch.

"Miss Ab—"

"Maurice," I snapped. "I said I've got this."

His expression softened. "Very well, Miss—"

"And for the love of God, stop calling me Miss Abato. I'm Nora, just Nora."

"Very well, Nora." His mouth quirked. "I'll be right outside."

"That wasn't what I... yeah, okay."

I knew Maurice wasn't going to defy Nicco's orders, so he could stand guard outside for all he liked, and I could go on pretending my life was normal.

I set to unpacking my case. Mom had insisted on doing all my laundry, so all I had to do was hang things back in my closet. Halfway into it, a knock at the door startled me. My brows furrowed wondering what Maurice could possibly want already.

Stomping to the door, I pulled it open. "Yes—you're not Maurice."

"No, I'm Luca." The guy smiled, and I swear my knees went a little weak. He was handsome. Tall with thick dark hair that fell over his eyes a little. Hazel eyes sparkled with humor as he took me in.

"What the hell do you think you're doing?" I snapped, feeling my anger levels rise as he blatantly ogled my chest.

"Uh, your shirt." His gaze lifted to mine.

"My shirt?" I balked.

"Yeah, I like it..."

I looked down, my cheeks burning when I realized I was wearing my boo bees t-shirt.

"Oh my God," I breathed, clapping a hand over my mouth. "I didn't... I wasn't expecting visitors." And humorous shirts were my favorite thing, I had an entire collection.

"Relax, I dig it."

"I... really don't know what to say to that." I forced a smile, slightly mortified that he'd caught me wearing my little ghost-bee motif t-shirt. "What can I do for you, Luca?"

"I just moved in across the hall, and it would seem I forgot all the important things like coffee, cream, and sugar."

"There's a coffee shop right along the street." My brow lifted, and he chuckled.

"Okay, you got me. I'm just trying to introduce myself to the neighbors and asking for some coffee sounds way better than being all creepy."

"Are you... a creep?" A smile played on my lips.

"Depends on your definition, I guess."

Our mutual laughter filled the space between us. "Well, since you're here, do you want to come in for coffee?"

"Yeah?" His whole face lit up. "That would be great... I mean, in a totally non-creepy way."

I glanced down the hall and noticed Maurice trying to make himself inconspicuous. He caught my eye and shook his head.

"Relax, Maurice," I called. "Luca is my new neighbor. I'm sure you know all about him." Nicco's team probably ran background checks on everyone living in the building since Arianne spent time over here.

"Uh, do I need to be worried about the fact you have armed security standing out in the hall?" Luca's brows crinkled as he followed me into the kitchen.

"Who, Maurice? He's nobody. How do you take your coffee?"

"Extra cream, one sugar please."

I switched on the coffee machine, suddenly feeling out of my depth. Here I was, dressed in my lounge pants and my oversized boo bees t-shirt, with a hot guy waiting for me to make coffee.

It wasn't exactly the New Year's Day I'd imagined.

"So Luca from across the hall, what's your story?" I asked as I poured us both a mug of coffee, adding sugar to his and creamer to mine.

"I just moved from Pawtucket. I work for a marketing company and they had a promotion opportunity... and here I am." He pushed his hair out of his eyes, smiling. "What about you?"

"Well, I didn't just move, as you can tell." I glanced around the apartment. "Born and raised in Verona County. I'm a freshman at Montague University."

"A freshman, wow, I thought you were older. Now, I do feel all kinds of creeper for being here."

"How old are you?"

"Twenty-three. I graduated a year ago."

"So old." I rolled my eyes. "Well, you picked a good neighborhood. It's a busy student area so there are plenty of bars and restaurants and good takeout. There's a gym downstairs too, if that's your thing."

From his muscular biceps I assumed it was.

"I work out occasionally, but I prefer to run."

"There's a park one block over that's popular with the jogging crowd."

"Sounds good." He sipped his coffee.

"So didn't anyone else on the floor answer? Or have you been drinking coffee, making small talk with the neighbors all morning?"

"Yours is the first door I tried."

"I see. Well lucky for you I was feeling neighborly then."

"Indeed." His eyes glided down to my chest again, and heat flashed through me.

"Maybe I should change my t-shirt," I suggested with a playful lilt.

"It's very... eye-catching." He chuckled.

"Men," I mumbled to myself as I drained the rest of my coffee and rinsed the mug under the faucet.

"Strange time to move, on New Year's?"

He shrugged. "As good a time as any. Besides, I'm not a fan."

"You're not a fan of New Year's?"

"Bad break up a couple of years ago. Kind of ruined it for me."

"Say no more." My stomach knotted thinking of a certain blue-eyed mafioso who had been avoiding me ever since I'd found him in bed with a busty blonde.

Of course, the first guy I set my sights on after arriving at MU had to be broody and dark and a total asshole.

Enzo Marchetti was as ruthless as he was cold. And now he was my best friend's family. Talk about a stroke of bad luck.

"Nora?" Luca's voice yanked me from memories I'd rather forget.

"Sorry, you were saying?"

"Actually," he stood, "I should be heading out. But thanks for the coffee. It was nice meeting you."

"Oh, okay." His departure seemed a little abrupt, but I wasn't about to beg him to stay. He was a stranger, and I wasn't desperate.

"I'll see myself out," Luca added. "Maybe I can repay the favor soon?"

"Sure." I smiled. Why did things feel awkward all of a sudden?

Luca gave me a small nod and headed for the door. When he reached it, he glanced back. "It really was nice to meet you, Nora. Shirt and all." He smirked.

Then he ducked into the hall and was gone.

"He just invited himself into your apartment?" Arianne shrieked down the line.

"Babe, relax. Maurice was right down the hall. Besides, I thought everyone who moves into La Stella was vetted."

"They are," I heard Nicco grumble in the background.

"*Not* the point," Ari hissed. "He was a total stranger and you let him into our —your home. Sorry." Regret coated her voice.

"Don't be. I could have moved back into dorms, but I didn't want to. Besides, it's nice having my own space." The lie rolled off my tongue. "And now I have a new friend who lives across the hall."

"You met him once," she pointed out.

"And he offered to repay the favor next time." I chuckled, but she didn't join me. "Ari," I added, "I'm going to be okay, you know?"

So she was married now. It wasn't like I didn't have other friends, and we'd still hang out. Nicco would have mafia business to take care of, and me and Ari would have girl's time.

Things wouldn't change that much.

"I know," she finally said, breaking the beat of silence. "I really miss you, Nor. I want you to know that."

"But you're happy, right?"

She hesitated and then let out a dreamy sigh. "I am, I really, really am."

"Well, that's all that matters, babe. Friendship doesn't die just because you went and got yourself a husband." My laughter almost sounded convincing. "When do you get back?"

"Tomorrow. Nicco has to go see his father so I was thinking we could have girl's night at our apartment."

"Sounds good. Just let me know what time."

"I will. I should probably go. Nicco is taking me on a private river cruise to Ellis Island."

"Have fun. I'll speak to you tomorrow."

"And Nora?"

"Yeah, babe?"

"No more inviting strange guys into the apartment."

"Yes, *Mom*," I hung up, smiling.

But it quickly fell when I realized this was my reality now. Arianne was gone. She had a new life, a husband, and a whole new family.

And what did I have?

I had a t-shirt with boo bees on it.

THREE

ENZO

"ARI," I said thinly as she opened the door to her and Nicco's place in Romany Square.

"Hello, Enzo." She smiled and dammit if it didn't soften something inside me. This petite, shy girl had stood up for the Family, she'd stood up for Nicco… I would never forget that. If it ever came to it, I would lay down my life for her. Because like it or not, she was family now, and despite my reservations about their marriage, family was everything to me.

Every-fucking-thing.

"Nic around?"

"He's just in the shower. We only got back an hour ago and we… uh… we were hungry." She flushed from head to toe and I chuckled.

"Hungry, is that what we're calling it these days?"

"Oh God," she murmured, spinning on her heel and disappearing into their apartment.

"This place is really starting to look like home," I said, admiring the living room. It was a big open plan space with a state-of-the-art kitchen set in one corner. They had a huge sectional that was big enough to sleep on, but it was littered in pale pink girly throw cushions.

My cousin was whipped good. It was warm and homey and felt like the kind of place you'd raise kids. Not that I knew anything about that; my childhood wasn't exactly conventional.

I stuffed down that shitshow and perched on one of the stools at the breakfast counter while Ari went to the refrigerator. She didn't even ask if I wanted a beer, just grabbed one, uncapped it, and slid it across the marble to me.

"Thanks," I said. "So how was New York?"

"Amazing." Ari leaned back against the counter and let out a soft sigh. "I never wanted to leave."

"I hope you didn't tell Nic that." He wouldn't ever leave Verona. Not even for his wife. He was bound to this place. It was his legacy, his responsibility. One day, he would be the boss and the Family would look to him for leadership.

You didn't just walk away from that.

But Arianne knew that. She wouldn't be standing here with his ring on her finger if she didn't.

"You don't need to worry, Enzo, home will always be Verona." Her soft laughter made me bristle.

"That's not—"

"Hey." Nicco appeared, towel-drying his hair. "Happy New Year, man."

"Yeah, you too." I got up and we hugged. "Ari was just telling me she didn't want to leave the Big Apple."

He snagged her around the waist and pulled her slender body into his. When I'd first met Arianne, she was this meek girl unsure of her own shadow, but even I couldn't deny she had grown into her role as the Capizola heir… and now the Marchetti princess.

Everyone loved her. Uncle Toni; Matteo; Nicco's sister, Alessia. Ari slotted into our family as if she'd always been there.

And honestly, I still didn't really know how I felt about that.

Nicco loved her, I got it. I did. But he was going to be the boss. Arianne made him weak. He'd almost gone to war for her once. I didn't doubt he'd do it again.

No pussy was worth that, worth losing yourself.

"It was pretty fucking amazing." He tucked her into his chest, resting his chin on the crook of her shoulder. "But we'd never up and leave your cranky ass."

"Have you been talking to Matt?"

"What?" His brows furrowed.

"Nothing," I grumbled. They had a point. It wasn't like I was all rainbows and unicorns lately. But what did they expect after everything I thought I knew was blown to shreds with five little words?

Your father is a traitor.

Even now, weeks later, it was still hard to believe that Vincenzo Marchetti had betrayed his family.

The Family.

He'd broken the most cardinal rule of all, and there was punishment for it.

Death.

I could still hear the echo of the pistol firing, the soft crunch of bone cracking and flesh squelching as the bullet implanted in his head.

The bullet fired from *my* piece.

I'd killed him. My own father. The only parent I'd ever known. The second he'd admitted murdering my aunt, I'd aimed for the kill shot and pulled the trigger.

And I didn't fucking miss.

I didn't regret it, not one fucking bit. You didn't betray the Family and get away with it.

But something like that, it changed you.

"E?" Nicco said, and I jerked out of the memory of my father's brain matter splattering all over the walls.

"You good?" he added, his brow pinched with concern.

"Yeah, nothing a little session at Uncle Mario's gym won't fix."

Arianne's eyes widened. "Not fighting?"

"I might get in the ring and burn off some steam." I wasn't a fighter, not like Nicco, but I wouldn't turn down the chance to go a few rounds with one of Mario's guys.

"Nicco," she whisper-hissed.

"He's a big boy, Bambolina. He can look after himself."

"Well, just so long as *you* don't get in the ring." She leveled him with a hard look.

"I promise."

My brow lifted. That was news to me. I knew Arianne didn't want Nicco fighting at L'Anello's, the club where the underground fight ring happened every weekend, but it was a part of him. You couldn't just switch off the blood thirst, the hunger. I knew that firsthand.

Memories of what I'd done that night didn't diminish over time, they only burrowed their way deeper, infecting my soul like poison.

Just then, the buzzer rang. The way all the blood drained from Arianne's face I knew without asking who it was.

"Crap, she's early." Guilt glittered in her eyes. "Is this going to be a problem?"

"Why the fuck would it be a problem?"

It was Nicco's turn to quirk a brow in my direction. Ari rolled her eyes and left us alone as she went to open the door.

"What?" I snapped.

"Nothing." Nicco searched my face for answers I didn't have.

I felt her before I saw her.

Nora Abato.

The only girl I'd ever let see past my stone-cold exterior.

And the one girl I couldn't ever get close to again.

"The view was amazing." Ari and Nora chatted as they came into the room. "God, Nor, it was perfect."

"Nora." Nicco welcomed her with open arms and they hugged. "It's good to see you."

"I hear you treated my bestie like a Princess."

"Queen," he corrected. "I treated her like a Queen." His eyes found Arianne and the two of them shared a longing look.

"Okay, okay, I know you're newlyweds, but knock it off," Nora let out a strangled laugh, "or I'll need to take a cold shower." Her eyes flicked to mine, but I immediately dropped my gaze, unwilling to acknowledge her.

"Wow, nice to see you too," she said thickly.

"We're going to head out," Nicco filled the beat of awkward silence. "Luis and Alexi will be right outside. Order whatever you want, I left my card on the nightstand." He cupped the back of Arianne's head and pulled her in for a kiss.

Nora's big doe eyes drilled holes into the side of my face, but I didn't look at her.

I couldn't.

If I looked at her, I'd remember, and if I remembered… well, it wouldn't end well for anyone.

My fist clenched against my thigh as I stood up. "I'll wait outside," I grumbled. Nicco was tongue deep in Arianne, and Nora was right there…

I tried to tell myself I didn't care. That the fact she'd found me in bed, hungover with some blonde draped over me like a cheap rug, didn't matter. We weren't anything to one another. I'd made no promises to her. It was just sex. Mind-blowing, hot as sin sex.

That's all it was.

Nora didn't say a word as I stalked out of the apartment and down the hall. I didn't stop until I crashed through the door and pulled out my smokes. It was a nasty habit, but it calmed me a little.

Two minutes later, Nicco found me. "You need to quit that shit," he grumbled.

I inhaled one last hit and dropped the butt, dragging it into the asphalt with my boot. "My car is down the street." He followed me, climbing into my Pontiac GTO without another word.

He was quiet.

Too fucking quiet.

And I knew he was gearing up to rail at me. Sliding into the driver's seat, I ran a hand through my hair.

"Are we going to talk about what happened?"

"Nope." I jammed the key in the ignition.

I wasn't entirely sure which part he wanted to talk about, but either way, it had been weeks. If I'd have wanted to talk, it would have happened by now.

I didn't want to talk. I wanted to forget.

"Enzo," Nicco sighed. My eyes slid to his. "Maybe if you just talked to her—"

"Not going to happen, cous. It is what it is. I would have only disappointed her in the end." Because I wasn't wired right. Because somewhere along the line, I'd got skipped when they were handing out all those happy fucking emotions.

Because deep down, I knew a woman would only bring me drama and distractions I didn't want or need.

"You had your reasons," he said.

"Nic, she found me in bed with some blonde, there's no coming back from that." I didn't even remember what happened that night. But I remembered Nora's face as she stood in the doorway.

My chest squeezed, but I ignored it. It was better this way.

She was too good for this world.

Too fucking good.

Nora believed everyone could be saved, that everyone wanted to be saved.

But I wasn't looking for redemption...

Because my soul already belonged to hell.

"Nicco, figlio mio." Uncle Toni grabbed my cousin and pulled him into a hug. Then he moved to me, gripping my shoulders and searching my face. "Lorenzo."

"What's up, Uncle Toni?"

"You haven't been around lately."

"I've been busy."

"Busy making a mess of our informants?"

Fuck.

"The stronzo deserved it."

"He did, but it wasn't your call to make, son."

I winced at the word.

I was nobody's son now.

I was twenty and my parents were dead. Both killed by me.

Exhaling a long, steady breath, I followed Nicco and his father into Uncle Toni's den. Matteo and his father, Uncle Michele, were already seated at the table.

This wasn't a casual meeting, it was business, and a trickle of anticipation ran through me. I needed something to do. Collecting pizzo, running jobs down in Providence, picking up the dirty work no one else wanted. I needed to keep busy.

"Lorenzo," Uncle Michele tapped the seat beside him, and I went to it. "Sit." He pulled it out, the legs scraping across the hardwood floor.

"What's up, old man?"

"How have you been? Your Aunt Marcella worries."

"I'm good," I said around a tight smile.

"We're here, Enzo." He squeezed my shoulder. "You're not alone."

"I know." Swallowing over the huge fucking lump in my throat, I ran a hand over my face.

"Niccolò," Uncle Toni said. "How was New York? How's that daughter-in-law of mine?"

"Ari is fine. We had a good time."

"A good time," Uncle Michele chuckled. "You think we don't remember being newlyweds, kid? Me and your aunt went at it like—"

"Fuck's sake!" Matteo grumbled. "No one wants to hear about you and Mom, old man."

"It's about time you found yourself a good woman, Son. Your mother wants some grandbabies to fuss over."

Matteo almost choked on nothing. "B-babies? Jesus, Dad, I'm twenty."

"And we're not getting any younger, Matteo."

"Can you believe this shit?" he whispered to Nicco, who chuckled.

"I'm telling you now, Niccolò, don't be coming around to tell me Arianne is knocked up anytime soon. After everything that's happened the last few months, the last thing we need is a baby to contend with."

The mood in the room instantly sobered. Guilt washed over Uncle Toni, and Matteo sank further into his chair.

"Jesus," Nicco breathed, shooting me a wary glance.

"Enzo, I'm sorry, that was—"

"Relax, Uncle T, I'm fine. Shit happens, and he got what was coming to him. I'm only sorry I didn't figure it out sooner."

"No, son. Don't ever think that. What happened, it wasn't your fault, none of it."

All I could manage was a small nod.

"Anyway, I didn't call you all here to shoot the shit. We've got to figure out how to deal with our little problem in Providence." He steepled his fingers, exhaling a long breath.

"What happened with the rat?" Nicco asked. "Did he talk?"

"Ask E," Matteo said, and I pinned him with a hard look.

"Enzo?" Nicco demanded my attention.

"I may have gotten a little carried away when we were squeezing him for intel."

"How bad?" His jaw flexed.

"Broken jaw, smashed eye-socket, three broken ribs, and a couple of missing teeth," Matteo said grimly.

"Fuck, E."

"He's a rat."

"That we needed."

"Fuck that." I kicked my boot against the leg of the table.

"*Basta*!" Uncle Toni slammed his hand down on the table. "I'm changing things up a little. You serious about not going back to MU?"

"As a heart attack," I said.

"You're going to run with Gino and his crew."

"Gino?" Nicco barked. "But Enzo is on my crew."

"You need to focus on things here. On Arianne and your sister. I need you close, Niccolò."

"What does that have to do with moving Enzo to Gino's crew?"

"We're a few men short. Your Uncle Alonso called from Boston. He's dealing with the Diablos and needs some extra hands. I'm sending a few guys. It leaves us short. Things in VC are fairly stable right now. Roberto is playing nice. The shit with Mike Fascini is dead and buried. We can spare a man or two."

"I'm in," I said without hesitation. Gino's crew get their hands dirty. They didn't think first and act later, they handled shit when it needed to be handled.

"Enzo, cous, come on." Nicco's expression wavered. "It's always been the three of us."

"Things change." The second the words were out of my mouth, I regretted them. I didn't want to alienate him. He was my cousin, my best friend, but I needed some space.

I needed to deal with this in my own way, in my own fucking time. I didn't need to be constantly around their concerned pity-filled stares.

"I need this," I grated out, hoping he would drop it.

To my relief, he did.

"You report to Gino now, okay?" Uncle Toni added. "As soon as he gets back from Providence, you're with him."

I nodded at Uncle Toni, feeling a lick of anticipation zip up my spine.

Gino Lupo and his crew were what the Family called enforcers, and I was all too willing to get my hands dirty.

"Good, it's done. You listen to G, follow his guidance, and you come back to us when you've worked through this shit, okay?"

"You got it, Boss."

"You'll be at Bella's birthday party though, right?" Matteo asked. "She'll kick your ass if you don't show."

"Like she could take me." Matteo's sister Arabella was a petite little thing with big blue eyes and a meek personality. "I'll be there." She was family. This wasn't about turning my back on them; it was about dealing with some of the crap running through my head.

The deceit.

The lies.

The betrayal.

Vincenzo Marchetti had been many things: cold, cruel, angry. But he'd always been nothing if not loyal. He'd lived, breathed, and bled for the Family, for Dominion.

Or at least, I'd thought he had.

Fuck.

It was like my head couldn't reconcile what my black dead heart already knew.

The restless energy inside me ignited into a firestorm. I needed a smoke. Some pot or a strong fucking drink. I felt like an addict tweaking for their next hit. I needed something—*anything*—to take the edge off.

"Breathe, son," Uncle Michele said in a hushed voice.

Nicco and his father were arguing about me. Nicco didn't want to let go; he didn't want me to get involved with the likes of Gino and his guys.

"Nic," I barked, my throat dry. "It's okay."

His head snapped up and his narrowed eyes found mine. "I don't like it, E. I don't like it one fucking bit."

"I know."

But it didn't matter because I needed this.

I needed it whether he liked it or not.

The next day I was waiting outside the Verona County Transitions Initiative, a local community center in Romany Square. Nicco had asked me to swing by and pick-up Arianne after she got finished volunteering. I'd wanted to tell him no, I wasn't a fucking babysitting service. But he was my best friend, and after Uncle Toni had dropped the bombshell that I was going to run with Gino and his guys, I figured it was the least I could do.

But when Nora appeared in the doorway, I knew I'd made a huge fucking mistake.

"Enzo?" Her eyes grew to saucers.

"What the fuck are you doing here?"

Hurt flashed in her eyes, but I really hadn't been expecting to find her here too.

"I decided to come help out," she said, pulling her chunky knit cardi closer together. "What are you doing here?"

"Nicco asked me to give Ari a ride home."

"Oh."

The air grew thick around us, energy crackling between us.

"That's nice of you."

I snorted. "Yeah, real nice."

"I know things are... strained between us," she lifted her chin a little, "but you don't have to be such an asshole about it." Her hand went to her mouth. "I'm sorry," sympathy glittered in her eyes, "that was uncalled for. I know you've been through a lot."

She might as well have slapped me upside the head.

Before I knew it, I'd closed the space between us. Nora jerked back, pressing herself against the wall. "Enzo, what are—"

"Hey, oh," Arianne appeared, and I immediately stepped back.

"Nicco couldn't make it and I didn't know..." My eyes flicked to Nora and her breath caught.

"Can you give Nora a ride too?"

"Doesn't look like I have a choice, does it?" I grumbled, taking off toward my car.

"I can call Luis," I heard Ari whisper. "We don't have to—"

"It's fine," Nora said.

Because that was Nora. Stubborn to a fault. Well, she was barking up the wrong fucking tree if she thought there was anything left to salvage between us. Because that shit was done.

The girls climbed into my car, Nora taking the back seat, thank fuck. I quickly realized though it wasn't anything but sweet torture, because every time I looked up, her face was right there. Taunting me. Reminding me of everything I could never have.

Things I didn't even want.

The air had been thick between us outside the VCTI, but it was toxic now.

No one spoke the short distance to Arianne and Nicco's apartment building. It was awkward as fuck, and I was counting the hours until I could get the fuck out of Verona.

When we finally rolled up outside of the building, Arianne turned to me and said, "Thank you. I'll see you at Arabella's party on the weekend?"

I nodded.

She glanced back at Nora, I'll call you later, okay?"

"Actually," Nora's eyes flicked to mine. "I think I'll wait for Luis, after all."

"Of course." Arianne climbed out and lifted the seat for her friend.

"I said I'd give you a ride," I gritted out, irritation vibrating inside me.

"I don't think that's a good idea, do you?" Her brow went up and before I could answer, she slipped out and slammed the door.

And I watched them walk away wondering why I didn't feel as relieved as fuck.

FOUR

NORA

"ARE YOU SURE I LOOK OKAY?" I fluffed my hair for the third time. My wild curls hung around my face, and my eyes were smoky and seductive. I'd even broken out my blood-red lipstick.

"Don't you think you're trying a little too hard?" Arianne eyed me through the mirror, and I frowned.

"I'm not trying to do anything other than look good."

"For Enzo," she quipped.

"No, not for Enzo. For myself." It was Arabella Bellatoni's sweet sixteen party, and it was set to be a big affair. The entire Marchetti family would be there. I wanted to look good. No, I wanted to look like a knockout. It had absolutely nothing to do with the brooding, arrogant guy that was avoiding me at every turn.

My stomach fluttered at the very thought of Enzo. He'd been such a jerk the other day and part of me hated him, hated the way he'd just written us off before we ever really got started... but the other part, the other part still wanted him, mistakes and all.

But I couldn't tell Ari that. She wouldn't understand. Nicco wasn't like his cousin. Nicco was loyal and protective and super possessive. Nicco loved with everything that he was. Fiercely. Deeply. Truly.

Something told me a guy like Enzo didn't know *how* to love.

The thought made my heart ache.

Everyone deserved a chance, a shot at something good. Something pure. Even the darkest of souls.

"Just promise me you'll be careful," Ari said. "After what happened with his father... Enzo is in a bad place. Nicco said—" She stopped herself.

Enzo's father had been killed in a collision right before the holidays. It came as a huge shock to everyone, and I couldn't even begin to imagine how he must be feeling. But he wouldn't even let me get close enough to ask.

"Mafia stuff?" I asked.

"Yeah, sorry." Guilt flashed in her eyes. "He couldn't tell me most of it, but Enzo isn't going to be around much."

"He isn't?" That got my attention.

"Nicco is worried, so whatever it is, must be bad."

"Enzo's a big boy, I'm sure he can handle himself." Except, I didn't really want to think about what handling himself meant. The illusion of a dark brooding bad boy was a hot fantasy, but the last few months had proved that reality and fantasy didn't always match up.

"Mrs. Marchetti, Miss Abato," Luis, Ari's personal bodyguard, appeared. "The car is ready."

"Thank you, Luis. But please, stop calling me that."

"But it's your name, *Mrs. Marchetti.*" I teased.

"It still doesn't feel real."

"Well, it is, babe. Enjoy it. It's not every day an eighteen-year-old girl meets her soul mate, marries him, and moves in together within... four months."

"God, when you say it like that it sounds really bad." Her cheeks pinked, and I fought a smile.

"Ari, who cares what it sounds like? You got your prince, babe. Your very own Prince of Hearts. Own that shit. Hell, I would."

"You know you'll find your prince one day, right?"

"I know." It wasn't like I wanted to settle down right now or anything. I was barely nineteen. I had three-and-a-half years of college left and a whole life to live. But I wanted what Ari and Nicco had. I wanted that special connection with someone, that bond.

"All set?" she asked, steering the subject to safer shores.

"As I'll ever be." I laced my arm through hers and we followed Luis out of the apartment.

"This will be fun," Ari whispered.

I didn't doubt it, but I also knew Enzo would be there... and that would be the sweetest kind of torture.

Antonio Marchetti had hired The Diamond, a high-end bar in Romany Square, for his niece's birthday party. I didn't know what I'd expected, but the pink and black balloons and streamers made it feel every bit a sweet sixteenth. Kids danced on the dance floor, weaving shapes with their arms, singing along to the latest hits while the adults watched on, chatting and drinking.

"Oh my God, look." I grabbed Ari's arm. "He's wearing a Fedora *and* suspenders."

"Nor!"

"What? I'm excited. It isn't everyday a girl gets to attend a mafia—"

She pressed a hand to my mouth. "Just breathe, please." Her eyes pleaded with me and I nodded.

"Sorry, I'm just… wow, okay. I'm chill."

She chuckled, but before she could answer, Nicco intercepted us.

"Bambolina," he breathed, letting his eyes drift slowly down her body. God, the way he looked at Arianne. Hungry. Possessive. As if she was the most beautiful woman on Earth.

She did look stunning though, in a sixties-style black dress with a layered skirt. I'd opted for something fitted and tight, a second skin of glitter and lace.

I felt sexy as hell, but no matter how good I felt, watching Nicco watch my best friend made me feel like I was wearing a burlap sack.

"I'm going to get a drink," I said, leaving them to it.

Ari called after me, but I continued weaving through the big round tables until I arrived at the sleek chrome bar.

"What can I get you?"

"The lady will take a vodka and cranberry," a smooth voice said.

I turned to meet Dane Marchetti's smirk. "Really?" My brow lifted with amusement.

"You look good, Nora."

"So do you." Nicco's cousin might have still been in high school, but there was no denying he had those strong Marchetti genes. Dark eyes and chiseled good looks, the ripped muscles, and tattoos. He was every bit as handsome as his cousins. But he was too young.

Shame. He would have been the perfect distraction from my thoughts tonight.

The bartender served my drink and fetched Dane a beer. He didn't bat an eyelid at his age, just handed it over with a smile.

"You gonna save me a dance later, dolcezza?"

"You're a real smoother talker, you know that?" My lips curved.

"You haven't seen nothing yet, baby."

"God, stop." Laughter bubbled in my chest as I jabbed my finger at his shoulder. "Do these lines actually work on the ladies?"

"Every single time."

"Color me impressed." I tucked a stray curl behind my ear before taking a sip of my drink. The vodka burned, but I liked the way it warmed my insides.

"I didn't know you were coming to town for Arabella's birthday." Dane and his family lived in Boston.

"I didn't know I could until the last minute. My old man has been keeping me on a tight leash after I—"

"Take a walk, kid," Enzo practically growled the words.

"Fuck you, E. I'm almost eighteen. I graduate in five months."

"Which makes you a kid still. I said take a wa—"

"I'll catch you later, Nora. Don't forget to save me a dance." Dane flashed me a wink before leaving me alone… with Enzo.

"Well, that was rude," I scolded him.

"What the fuck are you doing?" He glared down at me.

"Excuse me?"

"You heard me. He's my cousin. Are you really that desperate to snag your very own Marchetti that you'll stoop to Dane's level? He's still in high school."

"Are you done?" My body trembled with rage as I fisted my hands at my sides to stop myself from hitting him and making a scene.

I didn't know how he'd managed to signal the bartender and order a drink, but Enzo picked up his glass and knocked it back in one. Wiping his mouth with the back of his hand, he glowered at me once more. "Stay the fuck away from Dane, Nora. I mean it."

"Or what?" The words tumbled out.

He leaned down into my space, so close I could smell the spicy notes of his cologne. "Or you won't like what happens."

"Fuck you." I slammed my palms against his chest, smiling up at him. "Just because you made it perfectly clear *you* didn't want me, doesn't mean there aren't guys out there who do."

"Like Dane?" He scoffed. "He wouldn't know what to do with a woman like you if he tried."

Not girl.

Not chick.

Woman.

Why did I have to hone in on that, as if it was some kind of code for Enzo's repressed feelings toward me?

It wasn't.

The rational part of my brain knew that. It knew, and yet, the foolish part that believed in romance and fairytales and happily-ever-afters was eagerly waiting for his apology.

"Maybe I can show him the ropes, teach him a trick or two." I don't know who was more surprised at my words, me or Enzo. But the air turned thick around us, making it hard to breathe.

Enzo shook his head, running a hand through his thick dark hair. "Just stay the fuck away from my family," he snapped, and then he walked away.

Taking another small piece of my heart with him.

"What's wrong?" Ari said the second she found me over by the buffet table. I'd made myself scarce after my conversation with Enzo. Not that it could really be called a conversation. No, that would involve actually talking to each other. Instead, he'd barked at me like I was his misbehaving puppy.

Asshole.

The more I stewed on it, the angrier I got. The constant flow of drinks didn't help.

"Nothing," I said, helping myself to another chip. "I'm fine."

"I'm fine usually means you're not fine." She gave me a pointed look. "I'm sorry I abandoned you. Nicco's family can be a little intense."

She said that like it was a bad thing, when I'd spent the last thirty minutes watching how happy she looked moving between Nicco's aunties.

"Please, I'm a big girl, I can take care of myself. Besides, Matteo and Dane keep checking in on me." Dane had repeatedly asked me to dance, but I'd declined. He was like a dog with a bone and I was worried if I threw him some scraps, he'd never leave me alone.

"Did something happen… with Enzo?"

"Like what?"

"I don't know, you tell me."

"Nothing happened." The lie felt all wrong as it rolled off my tongue, but I didn't want Ari to worry, or put her in the middle of Nicco and his cousin.

Besides, nothing had happened. Not really.

Nothing I couldn't handle at least.

"There you are." Alessia appeared, her skin flushed. "What are you both doing hiding over here?"

"Not hiding. Just… observing."

"Well, stop, and come dance with me."

"Don't you want to enjoy the party with your friends?"

"They're not my friends, not really." Her smile fell. "It's different for Bella. Her brother isn't… you know? I mean, kids are still wary, but they don't completely avoid her like they do me."

"Fuck them," I said, draining my drink. "If they don't want to get to know you, that's their loss, Sia."

"You're right." She nodded. "So, you'll come dance?" Hope glittered in her eyes.

"Hell yeah. Ari?"

"You two go, I'm going to say hello to a couple more people."

My brows furrowed. "Sure, okay. But remember, it's a party. You're supposed to have fun."

I tried to ignore the pit in my stomach as Sia and I reached the dance floor. Bella spotted us and rushed over. "Nora, you came." She threw her arms around my neck.

"Uh, hey, birthday girl." I patted her back gently before forcing her to arm's length. "Are you drunk?"

"Ssh, if my dad finds out he'll lose his shit."

"Let me guess, Dane slipped you some drinks?"

"Yeah, right." She scoffed, still dancing. The bubblegum pink dress she wore looked killer with her dark raven hair and stilettos. "He wouldn't risk getting railed at by Matteo and our cousins."

"True story." Sia nodded.

"If your brother asks, I know nothing," I said around a tentative smile. "But please, for the love of God, don't drink anymore."

"Fine. Now dance." Bella grabbed my hand. "Dance!"

Their enthusiasm was infectious and soon the three of us were crowded by Alessia and Arabella's school friends and family, dancing like our lives depended on it.

"Oh my God, I love this one," the birthday girl yelled, pumping her fist in the air. Everyone laughed, watching as she and Sia moved into the middle of the crudely formed circle.

But the DJ slowed it right down on the next song, playing some sappy love song that had everyone pairing off. Nicco and Ari joined us. He scooped Arianne up into his arms while Matteo grabbed Arabella before any of the younger guys could make their move. Sia intercepted Dane and forced him to dance with her. Which left me... all alone.

My heart was heavy as I sank into the shadows and watched them. I liked to think of myself as a strong, independent woman. I was confident in my own skin; loved my curves and lack of filter, and my quirky t-shirt collection. But standing there, watching my best friend laugh and smile with her husband and his family, twisted something inside me.

I was happy for her, so freaking happy. But she was part of something bigger now. Her family was entwined with the Marchetti.

She was one of them.

An insider.

I always knew when Ari found her wings, she would soar, but I'd never anticipated this. I was proud of her, so fucking proud. The way she handled the alpha men around her with nothing but grace and humility. She had them all eating out the palm of her hand, Antonio Marchetti included.

Arianne had this whole other life now, and honestly, I didn't know where I fit into that.

A server waltzed past with another tray of drinks and I snagged one, not bothering to inspect the contents as I drained the glass dry. The liquor coursed through my veins, making everything a little blurry. But I liked the sensation, hovering between being drunk and sober, when the edges of reality began to shimmer and shift into something else.

My eyes scanned the room, landing on Enzo. He stood immediately across from me, the sea of tables and bodies separating us. Our eyes connected and he trapped me there in his icy gaze.

Something had happened to him. Something *before* losing his father in the accident. It had made local news. Vincenzo Marchetti taken too soon from his family and friends. Arianne tried to tell me Enzo was just grieving, but it didn't explain the way he'd betrayed me with that skank.

I didn't know what had happened. I wasn't *allowed* to know. But I knew it was something bad. He wasn't the same Enzo I'd known a few months ago. Sure, he was still the quiet brooding mafioso, but he was different now.

He was cold and cruel.

It didn't stop me from crossing the room to him though. My body hummed with electricity with every step, the thread tethering us pulling taut and reeling me in.

When I finally reached him, he didn't chastise me or taunt me. Enzo grabbed my hand and pulled me away from the party, out of a staff exit and down a long, empty hall. I stumbled behind him, drunk on liquid courage and high on pure lust.

This was a bad idea.

The worst.

But I couldn't stop myself. I was under his thrall, completely at his mercy.

He grabbed a door handle at the end of the hall and pulled me inside. There wasn't even a chance to get my bearings before he was pushing me up against the wall and pinning me there, his big hand wrapped around my throat.

"You're playing with fire, Gattina." Enzo dipped his eyes to mine, searing me to the bone.

But I wasn't scared, not even a little bit.

"Yeah?" I smirked, loving how his eyes danced with torment. "Well, maybe I like the burn."

FIVE

ENZO

SHE WAS UNDER MY SKIN.

I'd watched Nora all night. Watched as Matteo and Dane continually tried to lure her onto the dance floor with the promise of a good time. I knew Matt was probably doing it to piss me off, but Dane... that kid was too fucking self-absorbed to see past his own needs.

I knew she would be here. Arabella loved Nora. Sia too. I knew the root of their obsession with the girl with fire in her eyes and love in her heart.

Nora was good, too fucking good. But she was also strong, and unafraid to speak her mind, determined to go after the things she wanted.

And thank fuck, she still wanted me because the second my eyes landed on her tonight, I knew I had to have her again. I was a selfish bastard, concerned with only one thing, feeling her tight little body beneath me.

It probably meant something different to her. She probably thought it was my way of apologizing. It wasn't.

It was sex.

Nothing more, nothing less.

"Fuck, you're sexy." I clawed at the skirt on her dress, trying to find her pussy.

"And you're moving too slow," she hissed, grabbing my hand and guiding it to her damp panties. "God, yes," she cried as I rubbed her over the lacy material.

Of course, she was wearing lace. I smirked. Nora was good, but she was also as dirty as fuck. It's why I wanted a repeat. The sex had been mind-blowing. I could use that kind of tension reliever tonight.

Dipping my fingers into the lace, I curled two inside her wet heat, rolling my thumb over her clit.

"Enzo, God..." she breathed, her head rolling back against the wall with a *thud*.

"Guardami." I growled, squeezing her throat gently. It would be so easy to snap her neck, to watch the life drain from her hypnotic eyes.

Fuck, what was wrong with me?

I didn't want to kill Nora. I didn't even want to hurt her. But killing my old man, pulling that trigger and watching his brain splatter all over the wall, had flipped something inside me. Unleashed a darkness I wasn't sure I could contain.

"What is it?" she panted. "What's wrong?"

I hadn't even realized I'd pulled away until her voice pulled me from my thoughts. "Enzo?"

"Fuck," I grunted. "*Fuck*! This was a bad idea."

Nora scoffed, the sound so bitter and twisted it was like a punch to the gut. "You don't want me, is that it?"

My eyes narrowed. I needed to leave. I needed to get the hell out of here before I did or said something I couldn't take back.

"Talk to me, E, please." Her expression softened, her bedroom eyes promising me things I had no right wanting. "I've been hoping we can talk. I'm so so sorry about your—"

I froze, red hot fury flooding me. "You shouldn't have come here with me." She flinched at my harsh tone. "Go back to the party, Nora." *Please, I'm begging you.*

"Seriously?" Her voice trembled. "You want me to go back out there and find another guy to keep me company? Dane was more than willing—"

I flew at her, grabbing her around the throat and pinning her to the wall. "Don't push me, Gattina."

"Why, what are you going to do? Hurt me? I'm shaking in my—"

I crashed my mouth down on Nora's, swallowing her sassy words. Stealing the very air from her lungs. She was fucking crazy, always pushing. Acting as if she didn't care about the way I treated her.

Why the fuck didn't she care?

She kissed me back with as much anger and frustration as I was drowning in, the two of us locked in a duel for dominance. Our tongues curled together, teeth nipping and lips sliding together with enough friction to start a wildfire.

"More," Nora rasped, fisting my shirt and erasing every sliver of space between us, until the hard lines of my body were pressed up against every soft curve she had.

Fuck, she felt good.

She wasn't supposed to feel this good.

"Use me," she gripped my jaw, raking her fingers over my scruff. "Use me, E. Take what you need."

She didn't know what she was asking. I wasn't the guy she knew *before*. I was different now. Changed by death.

Changed by *murder.*

Nora's hand went to my jeans and she popped the buttons like a pro. I didn't like to think about how she was so good at this stuff... I didn't like to think about her full stop. But she was there, in the back of my mind like a nightmare that I couldn't escape.

It's just sex, that's all it can ever be.

Her hand found its way into my jeans and she wrapped her fingers around my dick. "You want me," she teased, her lips peppering hot wet kisses all over my neck.

"I want what you can give me," I ground out, my hand flat against the wall as she pumped me harder. But Nora used my precarious position to her advantage and swung us around, so I was pressed up against the wall, completely at her mercy.

"What are you—"

She dropped to her knees and grinned up at me as she freed my dick. Fuck, she was beautiful.

Why did she have to be so fucking beautiful?

"Don't just look it at," I barked, the words rough against my throat. "Suck it."

Nora rolled her eyes at me before running her tongue over the tip. A sharp hiss escaped my lips as she took me into her mouth, hollowing her cheeks.

"Fuuuuck." The word reverberated in my chest as I tried to catch my breath. But she was too damn good at this, at making me forget my own goddamn name.

My fingers slid into her thick, silky curls, guiding her deeper over my length. Not that she needed any encouragement, Nora couldn't get enough of me. And don't even get me started on those little groans of pleasure vibrating from her pouty lips.

"Yeah, just like that." I relaxed against the wall, letting the sensations carry me away to somewhere else.

Her free hand curled around the back of my thigh, pulling me closer.

"Fuck, Gattina, I'm gonna... fuck." My chest heaved as blinding pleasure shot down my spine. Nora didn't miss a beat, swallowing me down like she'd been born to do it.

When she finally released me, her lust-drunk gaze lifted to mine. "Hmm." She grinned, dabbing the corner of her mouth with her thumb.

"Come here." I lifted Nora to her feet and slid my hand along the side of her neck, brushing my thumb over her pulse point. The air crackled between us, taunting me with all the things she wanted to give me that I would never allow myself to take.

Because this right here—stolen touches in the dark—would be all I could offer her. And no girl was cut out for that life.

Not even ones as strong as Nora.

My hand skated down her spine, fitting her body impossibly close to mine. There was something settling about feeling a woman's curves.

"How do you want me, Gattina? Slow and deep, or hard and fast?"

Nora's eyes glittered with desire, her skin flushed and breathing shallow.

"However I can get you," she whispered, her words like a poisoned arrow through my heart.

Because she meant it.

Nora meant every single fucking word.

My hand disappeared under her skirt, finding the soft flesh of her thighs, but Nora snagged my wrist. "No, E. I want you."

She pressed a single kiss to my lips and started walking backward, her fingers slowly hitching her skirt up around her waist. Stopping at a discarded table, Nora perched on the edge and crooked her finger at me. "Come get me," she drawled seductively.

I licked my lips, stalking toward her, imagining all the ways I wanted her. But none stood out more than Nora screaming my name as I fucked her into oblivion.

Loosening my tie, I pulled it free, snapping it between my hands. Nora's breath caught, her eyes wide as saucers.

"Do you trust me?"

"I..." She swallowed her last shred of rationality and nodded.

Looming down over her, I pressed one of my hands against her sternum and pushed her flat onto the table. Taking her hands in mine, I bound her wrists together and stretched them up over her head, securing the end of the tie to the underside of the table,

"Don't. Move," I demanded. "Move, and you won't like what happens."

I grabbed her panties and ripped the scraps of lace clean in two, stuffing them in my pocket. Nora writhed beneath me, and I tapped her thigh. "Behave."

Circling my fingers around my shaft, I pumped a couple of times, before dragging the tip of my dick through her wetness.

A violent shudder rolled through Nora as she cried out, "Condom. We need a condom."

Fuck.

I was two seconds away from slamming inside her and now she wanted to play it safe.

"Yeah," I said. "Okay." Pulling my wallet out, I retrieved a foil packet and ripped it open, rolling the latex over my hard on.

Once it was fully sheathed, I grabbed Nora's legs and slammed inside of her without warning. Her screams of pleasure echoed around the small room, boosting my adrenaline to epic proportions. She was so fucking tight, so fucking good.

I watched myself disappear into her hot little body, over and over, until sweat rolled down my back and her moans became background music.

"Enzo..."

My name on her lips was like music to my ears, and I folded my body over hers, running my nose along her jaw and kissing the corner of her mouth. "Tell me how it feels, Gattina."

"Good... it feels... God..." The words died on a throaty moan.

Nora's tits jiggled inside the cups of her dress as I rode her body fast and hard. I didn't want to stop. Her pussy had magical powers, blocking out all the noise in my head.

"More," she cried, arching her body into mine. My lips trailed down her neck, sucking hard on the skin at the base of her throat. It was a dick move, marking her, but I couldn't resist. Grazing the sensitive skin with my teeth, I reveled in Nora's pleasure-drenched whimpers.

She wanted me to mark her. To brand her and claim her. I would never understand what she saw in me.

My hand found its way back to her throat as I raced toward the edge.

"Let me touch you," she begged, lifting her hands. The tie came loose, and she reached for me. "Please."

I grabbed her wrists, slamming them back to the table. If she touched me, if she held me... I couldn't do it. This couldn't be about more than sex. A release. Two people using each other for a good time.

"No touching," I reminded her, rocking my hips at a slower, deeper pace. I was close, so fucking close.

"Fuck, Nora," I breathed, slipping a hand between our bodies and pinching her clit. Nora shattered, screaming my name into the shadows. It was enough to get me there and I came hard into the condom.

Dropping my head to Nora's collarbone, I dragged in a shaky breath.

"That was... wow." The awe in her voice was like a noose around my neck. But then she anchored her bound hands around the back of my neck, toying with the short hairs at the nape of my neck.

I went rigid, pulling back to look at her. "What the fuck are you doing?"

"What?" Her smile melted away, replaced with confusion.

"I told you not to touch me."

"Yeah, but I thought you meant—"

I yanked her arms back over my head and stood up, ripping off the condom and tying a knot in the end. Slinging it in the trash, I tucked myself back into my jeans and started inching away from her.

"Enzo?" Nora had lost some of her conviction and when I finally looked at her, wearing my kisses... my mark, dread snaked through me.

This was a huge fucking mistake.

"Are you at least going to untie me?" Disappointment glittered in her eyes.

Without a word, I untied Nora, jammed the tie in my pocket, and then made for the door.

"That's it, huh? That's all I'm worth to you. Some rough sex in the storage room?"

"Don't act like you didn't know what this was," I said coolly, my fingers trembling around the handle.

"You think I want more than you're willing to give me. I don't." She let out a resigned sigh, her expression neutral. "But a little respect would have been nice."

Even now, when I was being such an asshole, Nora managed to maintain her composure and grace.

She was a class act.

A strong, confident woman.

Who deserves so much better than you.

Nora ran a hand through her curls, taming them out of her face. Not once did she falter or glance away. She looked right into my eyes and demanded everything I couldn't give her.

Respect.

Apologies.

Love.

Fuck, what did I know about love?

I knew what I was supposed to feel, what I felt for my family and Dominion. I would take a bullet for my cousins, my aunties, and uncles. But I didn't know *how* to love, not the way a woman like Nora deserved.

"I can't do this," I grumbled.

"Do what? What is it you think I'm asking you to do? You ghosted me, Enzo. I was there. I waited for you to find me, to explain… but *you* walked away."

Shame burned through me like wildfire but there was no use dredging up the past. It had happened and although part of me felt like a total asshole for letting Nora find me in bed with that blonde, I knew it was for the best. She was getting too close, trying to soften my jagged edges, but a polished diamond was still sharp.

Nora had moved closer, her big doe eyes unwilling to let me escape. "You can talk to me…" She reached for me.

"Don't." It came out with such ferocity her hand fell away.

"I see." Nora stepped back. "You should go," she said quietly, her hand drifting to her collarbone.

"Yeah, I think you're right." I mentally imprinted the sight of her standing there to my memory. Who knew when I'd see her next. Once I started running for Gino's crew, life wouldn't be as smooth sailing as it was now. And Nora wasn't someone who would give you chance after chance. If I walked away now, there was every chance she would shut me out of her life for good.

But it was better than pulling her into my world, my fucked-up life.

Nora was better off without me.

No matter how much she believed she wanted me.

SIX

NORA

"THERE YOU ARE," Ari said as she reached me. "I've been looking everywhere for you."

"Sorry, I'm feeling a little funny. I think I'm going to call it a night."

"Already? But it's still early."

"Yeah," I replied around a tight smile. "I'm not feeling too great." The lie soured on my tongue, but she didn't need to know what I'd done.

"Do you need me to come—"

"No, I'll be fine." I hugged her. "You stay, enjoy the party. I'll call an Uber."

"Don't be silly, Luis will take you. He's around here somewhere."

He was. I'd spotted him standing watch at the main doors in and out of the room.

"Only if it's okay," I said, knowing she wouldn't let it drop.

"Come on." Ari took my hand and led me toward Luis.

"Mrs.—Arianne," he corrected himself, "Miss Abato, what can I do for you?"

"Can you give Nora a ride home? She's not feeling so good."

"I'm okay, just a little queasy."

"Of course." He nodded. "I'll have one of my men bring the car around front."

"Thanks, Luis, and make sure she gets into her apartment safely." Arianne shot me a bemused smile, and I rolled my eyes.

"I am quite capable of looking after myself."

"I know." She smiled. "But it would make me feel a whole lot better if I know Luis makes sure you're okay."

"What's going on?" Matteo swaggered over to us, beer in hand and collar loose. His smile was easy and his gaze slightly glassy.

Matteo Bellatoni was an adorable drunk.

"Nora is leaving."

"No!" He pouted. "You promised me a dance."

"Raincheck?" I chuckled.

"Everything's okay though, right?" Concern pinched his expression.

"Everything is fine." My smile felt weak, but it was all I could manage. Matteo cocked his head, frowning, and I knew he knew.

Maybe he didn't know everything… but he knew *something*. I needed to escape before the questions started.

"The car is almost ready," Luis announced, touching his hidden earpiece.

"Okay. I'll see you soon." I hugged Ari again. "Matteo, always a pleasure."

"Don't be a stranger," he said.

"You won't get rid of me that easily." I smirked.

Luis stepped aside to let me pass, but just as I was about to leave the room, I felt him.

Glancing over my shoulder, I saw Enzo standing in the shadows, watching me. A shudder rolled through me, remembering our moment in the storage room. I refused to label it as a mistake. How could something be a mistake when you wanted it so badly? And we had—we'd both wanted it.

Enzo just didn't want *me* enough.

With a defeated sigh, I let Luis guide me out of the bar and to the car waiting on the sidewalk. Another one of the Marchetti security detail exited the driver's side and came around to open the back door for me. I slid inside, relieved to be alone, concealed by the security glass and tinted windows.

I didn't cry. I wouldn't. But it hurt. It hurt so fucking much.

I wouldn't let Enzo Marchetti break my spirit though. I was better than that.

Stronger.

All I wanted was to be there for him. What hurt most was knowing I was good enough to fuck, but not good enough to have a conversation with.

Damn you to hell, Enzo.

Inhaling a sharp breath, I pressed my head against the cool glass, watching the city lights roll by until the streets became more familiar. By the time the car rolled to a stop outside La Stella, I wanted nothing more than to wash the night's events off me with a hot shower followed by a hot cocoa and my favorite fluffy pajamas.

Luis came around and opened the door. "Miss Abato."

"Thanks, Luis." I clutched my purse and headed for the door. But he followed.

"You don't need to come up," I said. "It's fine."

"Mrs. Marchetti—"

"Will kick your ass if she knows you're calling her *Mrs.* behind her back."

He cleared his throat. "Arianne."

My lips curved. "Fine. You may escort me inside. But then you're leaving. I'm fine. Everything is fine."

He gave me a pointed look, but I waved him off, going inside.

But when we reached my apartment, I came to an abrupt stop. "Luca?" My brows pinched.

"Oh, hey." He ran a hand through his hair, almost doing a double take when he saw my dress. "Wow, you look... wow."

"Uh, thanks." I flushed around a strangled chuckle. "What are you doing standing outside my apartment?"

"Funny story... I went down to take out the trash and got locked out of my apartment. I rang the super, but he isn't answering."

"You got locked—" I smothered the laughter building in my chest. "Easily done, I guess. Come on, you can come inside until the super answers."

"Miss Abato, I'm not sure that's—"

"You can leave now, Luis." My brow lifted, and he cussed under his breath.

"Very well, I'll be down the hall."

"Fine." I entered my apartment and invited Luca inside.

"Who was that?" he asked, following me to the kitchen.

"My best friend's bodyguard."

"Your best friend has a bodyguard? What is she? A celebrity or something."

Or something.

"My best friend is Arianne Capizola," I said. It was nothing he couldn't find out by Googling me. Ever since the wedding, Arianne's name had popped up in the press. Not to mention the fact she was an active member of Capizola Holdings board of directors now. Something like that got attention.

"Arianne Capizola? The Capizola heir... the same girl who married Niccolò Marchetti and brokered one of the biggest partnerships of Rhode Island's history?"

"That's the one." I offered him a beer.

"Holy shit... makes sense you'd live here I guess then." He took a long pull.

"Why's that?"

"This building belongs to Roberto Capizola." Luca shrugged. "The place is like Fort Knox."

"Especially when you're locking yourself out." I smirked, and he roared with laughter.

"Touché." Luca tipped the neck of his bottle toward me. "So where were you tonight?"

"At a party."

"Some party if you were home early."

"I didn't feel so good."

His expression fell. "Shit, Nora. I can go. Let me try the super one last time and I'll get out of your hair."

"Relax, I'm fine now." I let out a weary sigh. "Can you keep a secret?"

"I'm a closed book."

"I left because of a guy."

"Ah, I see." Sympathy shone in his eyes.

I don't know why I'd told him that, but it felt good getting it off my chest.

"Do you want to talk about him?"

"Not really. But I lied to everyone at the party about why I was leaving, so it feels good to tell someone the truth."

"Your secret's safe with me." A beat of silence followed as we both drank our beers. Then Luca said, "So, do you know them... the Marchetti?"

"Of course I know them, my best friend is married to one."

"And is it true, what they say about them?"

"I don't know, what do they say?"

His eyes crinkled with laughter. "I guess you'd have to kill me if you told me, huh?"

"Yup. So, I'd quit while you're ahead."

"I like you, Nora." The second the words spilled from his lips, the blood drained from Luca's face. "Shit, that came out all wrong. I just mean, it's refreshing to meet someone—a female such as yourself—who can just kick back and shoot the shit."

"Kick back and shoot the shit, huh? You make me sound like one of the guys."

"No, that's not what I mean at all. You just seem like a good person, Nora. Genuine. Funny... Gorgeous."

"Recovery accepted." I flashed him an amused smirk in an attempt to cover how off-guard he'd caught me. I wasn't used to guys being so honest with their feelings.

There had been a couple of guys since I started MU. But they were just sex. Sex and some casual conversation. One guy, Dan, had potential. But in the end, he didn't set my soul alight the way Enzo Marchetti did. So yeah, I'd had sex. Good sex, bad sex, unmemorable sex. But there had only ever been one guy I'd wanted.

Really wanted.

And he was determined to push me away.

Luca's pocket began vibrating, cutting through the silence. "Hopefully that's the super and I can get out of your hair." He stood up and pulled out his cell. "Hello... yeah thanks, I'd appreciate it. Okay... See you in ten." He hung up. "He's on his way. I guess this is goodnight."

"Goodnight." I smiled, walking him to the door.

A strange sensation rolled through me as he slipped into the hall. It was nice talking to Luca. Easy, stimulating... nice. I didn't get any flirty or interested vibes from him. Even when he'd called me gorgeous it had felt more like a genuine compliment than a pickup line.

"I owe you," he said.

"You're new to town, right? Maybe I can show you where they keep the good beer... or coffee..."

"Yeah, I'd like that. I'm not exactly inundated with friends right now."

"Ouch."

"Whoa," guilt flashed in his eyes, "I clearly suck at making conversation tonight. I'd blame it on the beer, but that would only make me seem like a douchebag who can't hold his alcohol."

"It's fine. We can do coffee one day... as friends."

"You got it." He clicked his fingers in a totally dorky way that had me laughing. "Night, Nora."

"Night, Luca."

He took off across the hall, glancing back at the last second. "And Nora?"

"Yeah?"

"Whoever you were running from tonight, he's not worth it."

I closed the door and dropped my head to it with a thud. Luca was right, I knew he was.

But my heart?

My foolish fickle heart still wanted to fix the guy with darkness in his soul and pain in his eyes.

And despite all my better judgment, she was in no hurry to stop.

I didn't expect to see Ari the next day, but there she was standing on my doorstep with a tray of coffee and a brown paper bag from my favorite coffee shop.

"This is a surprise," I said.

"Yeah, well, I felt like a bad friend after you left the party, so consider this a peace offering." She followed me into the kitchen.

"Babe, I already told you, I get it. You're married now. Things are going to change." My smile faltered.

"That's just it though. I don't want them to change. I mean, I love Nicco. God, I love him so much." A dreamy expression washed over her. "But I love you too. You're my best friend."

I snatched the brown paper bag open and pulled out a pastry. "And I'll always be your best friend. Especially, if you keep bringing me treats like this."

That earned me a small chuckle. "What really happened last night?"

My sugar high crashed and burned as I stuttered over the words. "Nothing happened."

"Nor, I'm not stupid. Enzo was extra grouchy after you left, and Matteo said he saw the two of you slip out of—"

"He's such a gossip," I grumbled under my breath.

"Do you want to talk about it?"

"There's nothing to say." My shoulders lifted in a small shrug.

"I don't believe that for a second." A beat passed as Ari searched my face for answers... answers I didn't have.

I couldn't explain why I felt drawn to Enzo, why I wanted to understand him, to fix him. Sure, he had that bad boy appeal, but it wasn't only that. I saw the torment in his eyes, felt his defenses ripple around him like a shield every time we were close. Enzo Marchetti was a complicated guy—layered and complex—and I wanted to strip back each layer and uncover the real him. The guy he didn't let anyone else see.

Even if I didn't like what I found.

"Did he tell you he won't be starting MU on Monday?"

My stomach sank as I tried to school my expression. He'd been inside me, fucking the very soul from my body, and he hadn't mentioned a goddamn thing.

"No," I steeled my spine. "He didn't... You knew?"

"Nicco only confirmed it last night." Sympathy shone in her eyes. "You know there's stuff he can't tell me."

"So that's it? He's just throwing away his entire college career?"

"Nora, you know that's not how it works."

"Nicco and Matteo?" I asked, knowing it was a stupid question. Nicco wouldn't leave Arianne, and Matteo... well, he was different. Something told me he wanted life to be as normal as possible.

But not Enzo.

He'd never really fit in at MU. It didn't make it any easier to hear though.

"What will he do instead? Wait, forget it. You can't answer that either."

She reached over and took my hand. "Because I don't know. If I did, I'd tell you."

"I guess that explains last night then," I murmured, trying hard to erase the images of last night from my head. Enzo's hand around my throat, his body riding mine.

"The two of you—"

I nodded. "It was goodbye." The thought hit me like a wrecking ball. Enzo hadn't dragged me to that storage room because he was jealous, although I didn't doubt that had a little to do with it. He'd done it because he wanted one last time with me.

That cold bastard.

He'd stoked the flames of hope in my chest while knowing he didn't have to see me every day around campus.

A wave of nausea rolled through me.

How foolish I'd been.

Enzo didn't care about me. He cared about what I could give him. A warm, willing body. My stubbornness had refused to accept that, because I felt the threads connecting us. And until this moment, part of me had truly believed that if I pulled hard enough, eventually, I'd find Enzo on the other end.

"Oh, Nor," Ari said, squeezing my hand.

"I'm fine." I shot her a weak smile, surprised to feel the dampness on my cheeks.

I rarely cried.

I was stronger than that.

But I was also only human and being wrong about Enzo cut deep.

"There's someone out there for you, I promise."

But what if I'd already found him?

What if I'd found the guy I was supposed to be with, and he refused to accept it?

What if he rejected me?

I guess I didn't need to wonder anymore.

My heart withered in my chest as reality crashed over me.

"Yeah, well, I think I need to focus on other things for a while." I stuffed the last bite of pastry into my mouth.

"I hate that he hurt you again."

"It's fine." My shoulders lifted in a half-hearted shrug.

"Nora, it's not fine. You deserve so much better. Enzo is... complicated. He doesn't know—"

"I really don't want to talk about this anymore. He's not coming back to school, so it's a moot point." I'd probably still see him occasionally at family events, but I could handle that. "Tell me about the party. Did Arabella enjoy it?"

"She did... until she got caught taking shots with Bailey and Dane. You should have seen Matteo, he lost it."

"Oh wow, I'm sorry I missed it." My lips curved.

"Everyone missed you."

I didn't believe that for a second, but I appreciated the sentiment.

"Bella and Sia made me promise we can all hang out soon, just the four of us."

"We totally should. We could have a girl's night. Face masks, manicures, champagne, a movie..."

"They'll love that. Sia is always talking about you. You're like the older, cooler sister she's never had."

"She loves you too."

"I know. But it's different. I'm her family now."

Her words stung. I knew Ari didn't mean them with any malicious intent, but there it was again. That word.

Family.

I had my mom, my dad, and my brother Gio. It's just the four of us. Three, if you count the fact that Gio was off at UPenn living out his dreams of going all the way to the NFL.

It had always been me and Arianne, the two of us against the world. But she had Nicco now. As the Capizola heir and the newly crowned Marchetti princess, she had a legion of men all willing to lay down their lives for her.

Enzo included.

He would take a bullet for his cousin's wife, protect her no matter what the costs. Because she was family now.

And me?

I was just the best friend worthy of sex...

But not good enough for his heart.

SEVEN

ENZO

"YOU LOOK LIKE SHIT," Matteo said, looking far too breezy for the morning after the night before.

I rubbed a hand over my head and down my face. "Is there juice?"

"Should be." He flicked his head to our refrigerator. Although he didn't stay here a lot anymore. He liked to be around for Arabella, so he usually crashed at their house.

But not last night.

Last night, I had hazy memories of him and Dane carrying me to one of the cars and shoving my drunk ass inside.

Fuck. I'd really hit the liquor hard after Nora left.

I went to open the refrigerator, but groaned in agony when a pain shot through my skull.

"Here," Matteo said. "You sit, and I'll get it."

Slumping onto one of the stools, I buried my face in my hands.

"Want to talk about it?" he asked.

"Nope."

"Good, I'll talk then, and you can listen. What the fuck are you doing, E?"

My head whipped up, another flash of pain ripping through me. Matteo smirked. "Serves you right for drinking your bodyweight in whisky."

"The juice?"

He handed me the carton and I drank straight from the box.

"That is so unhygienic."

"So don't drink it," I grumbled, wiping my mouth with the back of my hand. "Thanks... for getting me home."

"It was that or leave you there. She's really under your skin, huh?"

My eyes narrowed and his smirk only grew. "I don't know what the fuck you're talking about."

"Sure, you don't. So I didn't see the two of you slip out of the staff exit together?"

"Wasn't me."

"You're a terrible fucking liar. What I really want to know though, is what you did to her to make her leave?"

My chest tightened. It had been a dick move. Not the sex, the sex was great. But everything else had been an absolute shitshow.

"Fuck you, man," I hissed. "Fuck you."

"Nora is good people. You know that, right?"

"Seriously," my eyes shuttered as I inhaled a resigned sigh, "I'm not doing this."

"Okay, so you don't want to talk about Nora. Let's talk about the fact you're dropping out of school to run with Gino and his crew. We both know what he and his guys get up to."

"Don't start, Matt, you sound like Nicco."

"He's worried. We both are. This isn't you, cous."

"Do you have any fucking idea what it's like?" A violent storm raged inside me. "I pulled the trigger, Matt. I pointed the gun at my old man's head and I. Pulled. The. Trigger. *Me*." I inhaled a shuddering breath that I felt all the way to my dirty black soul. "So don't stand there and tell me running with Gino isn't me. Because from where I'm standing, I think it's exactly me." I leaped up, and the sound of the stool legs scraping the tiles filled our apartment.

"I'm sorry, okay?" He let out a thin breath. "I know it's hard—"

"Hard?" I sneered. "You don't have any fucking idea what it's like." His world hadn't been blown to shreds that night, not the same way mine had.

"Maybe you should talk—"

"I swear to fucking God, Matt, if you tell me to talk to someone, I'll—"

"Yeah, you're right. That's not the answer." He scrubbed his jaw. "But it's a damn sight better than selling your soul to the likes of Gino and his crew."

"I need this, cous," I said, the anger inside me abating slightly.

Trust Matteo to worm his way under my skin. I knew Nicco didn't approve, but he was less direct than our cousin. He believed in letting people arrive at their own decisions, and I was pretty certain that deep down, he knew what this meant to me.

I needed time away from Verona County. At least until I'd finally slayed the demons that haunted my every waking thought.

"Just promise me you'll be careful. Something's coming. I can feel it." His expression darkened.

"Aunt Marcella giving you too much of that damn tea again?" She was as superstitious as they came.

"Don't you feel it?" He rubbed the back of his neck. "That shit with Johnny Morello… It was a warning."

"Nah," I said. "It's nothing. And even if it was, we'll deal with it."

"I hope you're right."

Matteo wasn't like me. He didn't revel in this life. Tolerated it? Sure, he had to. You didn't escape the Family. If you were born into it, you died in it. It was that simple. *La Famiglia prima di tutto*. The Family came first, always.

Ever since I was a kid, I'd wanted it. I'd wanted to do the Family's bidding. Back then, I'd wanted it so that I could be closer to my old man. I thought it would bond us, make him pleased. I thought if my father saw I was made for this life, he'd be proud.

Looking back, I'm not sure Vincenzo Marchetti was ever cut out to be a father. His parenting skills were lacking at best, but I'd never doubted his ability as a capo.

He was everything I'd ever wanted to be.

Fearless.

Merciless.

Unwavering.

But it was all a lie.

A sham.

He wasn't fearless. He was a fucking coward.

The blare of my cell phone cut through my thoughts and I dug it out of my pocket. "Yeah?" I barked.

"Enzo, son, it's me," Uncle Toni replied.

"What's up, Uncle T?"

"Change of plans. Gino is staying in Providence for a little longer. I want you to ride down there and meet him."

"Today?"

"The sooner the better."

"I'll leave right away."

"Good. I knew I could count on you." A beat passed. "And pack a bag, you could be gone a while."

"On it."

"Good, call me when you get there." He hung up and I pocketed my cell.

"You're leaving?" Matteo let out a long, steady breath.

"Gino needs me in Providence."

"Nicco isn't going to like this."

"Yeah, well, Nicco isn't calling the shots anymore." Not for me, at least.

"You don't have to do this, cous." Matteo smiled weakly. But not even one of his puppy dog smiles was going to change my mind.

"Yeah," I said, grimly. "I do."

Pulling off at a rest stop, I cut the engine and ran a hand down my face. My cell phone had been blowing up since I left Verona less than an hour ago, and I knew the news had got back to my best friend.

I dialed Nicco's number and waited.

"What the fuck, Enzo?" he growled, the hostility in his voice making me bristle.

"I didn't want it to be a big deal. It's not like I'm leaving forever."

"You left without saying a fucking word." Hurt coated his words, making guilt snake through me.

"I need this," I said.

"And I need my best friend to talk to me. But I guess neither of us are getting what we want."

"Shit, Nic, I didn't do it to piss you off..."

"No, you knew if anyone could persuade you to stay, it was me."

"Maybe, yeah." My chest heaved as I expelled a long breath. "If it's any consolation, Matt gave me a pretty good talking to before I left."

"It doesn't," he snorted, "but I would have paid to hear that."

"You're worried, I get it. But you don't need to be. This is who I am."

"E, that's not—"

"We both know you're destined to call the shots and I'm destined to get my hands dirty. I've made my peace with it, you should too."

"Not like this though," he said quietly. "*Never* like this."

"Gino is good people. He'll look out for me."

"Damn right he will, or he'll have me to answer to."

"Hey, this thing with Morello," I said, "do you think we need to be worried?"

It wasn't uncommon for gangs or other organizations to try and make their presence known, especially in and around Providence. But the city had always been Marchetti territory. There was an MC, the Providence Phantoms, who rode out of their compound on the edge of the Woonasquatucket river, but they generally kept to themselves. Then there were the small-time dealers we let fly under the radar so long as they didn't start making waves. The Cruzers controlled all of the heavier narcotics coming in and out of Rhode Island, but we had a good thing going with Santiago Cruze, their top guy. The Family didn't usually get involved in narcotics, but it enjoyed a cut of the profits for letting Santiago and his guys operate out of Providence.

They had been the ones to hand over the rat when they'd gotten word that he'd been whispering Dominion business in a couple of guys ears. Guys no one recognized.

Outsiders.

The rat hadn't talked yet, and poor fucking Morello was lying in a hospital bed pissing through a tube.

"It could be nothing..." he said.

"Or it could be something."

"Yeah." Nicco let out a long sigh. "Just watch your back. Morello is a good guy, no enemies… an innocent."

I knew what he was saying. As far as we were aware, his only vice was being on the Family's books. An attack against him—random or otherwise—was an attack against us.

"Relax, I've got this."

"Yeah, that's what worries me." He scoffed.

"Don't you have husband duties to carry out?"

"Fuck you, cous, fuck you. One day some girl is gonna swoop in and knock you so hard on your ass you're not going to know what's hit you, and I'll be there to enjoy every second."

"I hate to disappoint you," I said, "but you're going to be waiting a long fucking time. I'm not cut out for that life."

"We'll see," Nicco grumbled under his breath.

"I need to get back on the road." I chose to ignore his comment. "I'll text you when I meet up with Gino."

"Make sure you do. I mean it, E. Just because you're running with his crew now, doesn't mean I don't want to be kept in the loop."

"Yeah, yeah, *boss*. I'll talk to you later."

"Stay safe."

"You too." I hung up, gunned the engine, and headed for the city, not stopping until I pulled up outside the address Uncle Toni had sent me.

It was some dive motel just outside the city, and Gino Lupo was leaning against the railing waiting for me.

"Enzo, my man," he said as I climbed out of the car, "long time no see." He approached me, thrusting out his hand.

I accepted it with a firm shake. "Gotta say, I wasn't expecting this. Not after—"

"What's the deal?" I cut him off. I didn't want to shoot the shit or dredge up what happened with my father. Everyone who needed to know the truth, knew about Vincenzo Marchetti's betrayal. And those that didn't, knew about his untimely death thanks to an oncoming truck and bad driving conditions.

Either way, he was gone.

Dead.

I didn't want to keep talking about a ghost.

"We got some intel that some outsiders have been sniffing around. Cruze gave us a name. Dominic Alejandro."

"Never heard of him."

"Tommy did a little digging and Alejandro has ties to a Mexican cartel in Connecticut. Rumor on the street is he's looking for somewhere to put down roots."

Tommy Gabini was the Family's investigator. There wasn't a secret he couldn't uncover, or a ruse he couldn't foil. He was the best, and so compensated heavily for his work.

"You tell Toni all this?"

"Of course. Why do you think he asked us to stay put? He wants us to feel Dominic out, and if necessary, handle him. But enough of that." He came around to my side and slung his arm around my shoulder. "Work can wait. Tonight, we induct you into our crew."

My brows furrowed. "Should I be worried?"

"You like liquor and pussy?" Gino grinned, revealing his gold tooth.

"Does a bear shit in the woods?" My mouth quirked.

"You're gonna fit right in, kid. Let's go."

I'd been here before. DiMarco's was a high-end strip club in the city owned by an arrogant asshole called Zander DiMarco. After he and Nicco almost got into it once last summer, Uncle Toni had given Uncle Michele responsibility over it.

Zander might have been a sleazy asshole known for getting a little handsy with his girls, but his club was a nice earner, one the Family wasn't prepared to lose. The décor was moody and seductive, crushed purple velvet curtains and a lot of chrome and glass. A runway jutted out from the stage, ending in the middle of the room where a pole was situated.

"Well, holy shit, Enzo Marchetti. Gino told me you'd be coming around." Zander swaggered over to us in his crisp white shirt and black slacks. His collar was open at the chest revealing a big gold medallion, and his hair was slicked back in that way guys with too much money and too few morals tended to wear it.

The guy was a grade A asshole, but I wasn't here to start anything. I was here to let off some steam before focusing on the task at hand.

"What'll it be, gentlemen?" He slung his arm over my shoulder, guiding us to a booth in the roped off VIP section. A couple of guys gave us the once over but soon dropped their gazes when they realized who we were.

I dropped down on the plush leather bench.

"I'll have one of my best girls come take your order. First round is on the house. Whatever you want... pussy, blow... dick..." His brow lifted with mild amusement. "I'll provide it." Zander snapped his fingers. "Gisele, get over here and keep my friends company." He glanced back at us. "Enjoy your evening, gentlemen."

The second he was out of earshot, I said, "I really don't like that guy."

"But the whisky is good, and the pussy is tight, my friend." Gino clapped me on the back. "Check out the redhead. Wouldn't mind me a little one on one time with her." He flicked his eyes over to the stage where one of Zander's girls was working the pole. She had legs for miles as she swung herself around it, performing some mesmerizing moves while her ample rack jiggled into the tiny little bra she wore.

"I'm more of a blonde hair, fake tits kind of man," one of Gino's guys said.

"Marc, you wouldn't know good pussy if it landed on your dick primed and ready to go."

"Fuck you, coglioni, fuck you." He flipped Gino off. "Hey, Enzo, back me up... redhead with a small handful, or blonde and busty?"

There had been a time I would have said blonde and busty. But all I saw now was a petite brunette with big doe eyes, pouty lips, and a smile that could bring a guy to his damn knees.

"My bad, man. If you like dick, that's all good—"

"Cazzo si," I tsked. "I like pussy as much as the next guy."

"Shit, bet you still can't believe Nicco went and got himself married?"

Thankfully, Gisele chose that exact moment to come and take our drink order. "What'll it be, gentlemen?" she said.

"Beers all round?" Gino answered.

"Nah, I'll take a whisky on the rocks. The top shelf stuff."

"Anything else?" She batted her eyelashes at me. She was exactly the kind of girl we'd just been discussing. Bottle blonde. Fake tits. Small waist and a pert, round ass. She had a body made for sin and lips made for sucking... and I didn't feel a damn thing.

Fuck.

I was broken. My dick protesting at the fact I'd drawn a line on anymore one on one time with Nora.

"Cat got your tongue or something?" Marc kicked my boot under the table, and I jerked out of my reverie.

"Huh, what?"

The guys chuckled, but I wasn't laughing. I was still stuck on the part where a hot girl was offering me so much more than just top shelf whisky, and I was too busy comparing her to the dark-haired girl I needed to get the fuck out of my system.

EIGHT

NORA

"NORA." Luca flashed me a blinding smile. "Fancy seeing you this morning." His eyes dipped to my chest, and I chuckled.

"No boo bees t-shirt today, sorry to disappoint." Heat flashed through me. Luca's gaze seemed innocent enough, but I was only human, and the guy was a snack.

"You're leaving for work?"

"I am." He nodded. "Walk you out?"

"Sure. Although if I don't get a move on, I'm going to be late."

Of course, the one morning I could have done with Maurice being around, he was taking a personal day. I usually enjoyed the walk to campus, but I was going to be late, on the first day of semester no less.

"I can give you a ride?" Luca said.

"For real? I don't want you to go out of your way."

"It's no problem, I'm going right past the college."

"Oh okay. Well, if you don't mind?"

"Nora," he chuckled, flashing me another blinding smile of his, "I wouldn't have offered if I minded. Come on. If we're quick, we can stop for coffee on the way."

We hurried out of the building and Luca led me to his car.

"A Mustang. Niiiiice."

"You know about cars?" His brow lifted as his hand paused on the door handle.

"I know a little. My dad and brother restored a 1966 Shelby Mustang before my brother left for college."

"My kind of people."

"Really? I didn't have you down as a supercar enthusiast."

"I'm a complex guy." Luca smirked, pulling the door open and motioning for me to get in.

"A gentleman too, it would seem."

"Oh, trust me, you haven't seen anything yet."

The slam of the door startled me as heat trickled through my veins. Luca was flirting with me—at least, I think he was.

When he climbed inside, he ran a hand through his thick, dark hair and flashed me another blinding smile. "Coffee? It'll be a five-minute detour."

"Sure, I have five minutes." I enjoyed his company, the easy banter, and those warm smiles.

Luca—

"What's your surname?" I blurted out, realizing I didn't know.

"Luca Bianco. And you are?"

"Nora." I smiled. "Nora Abato."

"Well, Nora Abato," he fired up the engine, "let's get you coffee and then to class."

Luca insisted on driving me to the parking lot right beside my building. I'd arranged to meet Arianne and sure enough there she stood with Nicco and Matteo.

A deep frown crossed her expression as she made her way over to us.

"That's... the Capizola—"

"Arianne," I corrected Luca who looked a little starstruck.

Dejection flashed through me. It was silly. Arianne was somewhat of a local celebrity and I was no one. But I knew that starry-eyed look Luca was wearing. He was already bewitched by my best friend and they hadn't even officially met yet.

"Thanks for the ride," I said, trying to keep the hurt out of my voice. Shouldering the door, I climbed out, expecting Luca to stay put. Only, he didn't.

"Nora, what's going on?" Ari asked me.

"I was running late, so Luca gave me a ride," I said.

"Luca? The new neighbor."

"Hey," he joined us. "I'm Luca. Luca Bianco."

"And she's married." Nicco wrapped his arm around Arianne, moving her behind him ever so slightly.

"Whoa, man. I know, I was just... okay, that sounded all wrong. I apologize. I'm Luca." He thrust out his hand at Nicco. "Nora's new neighbor."

"You give all your neighbors a ride to class?" Matteo asked, and Nicco ignored his hand.

I shot them both a hard look, Luca let out a strained chuckle. "I can see I've got my work cut out for me. It's okay though, I like a challenge."

"And just what are your intentions for our... Nora".

"Matt," Ari scolded him.

"What? It's not like we aren't all thinking the same thing." He shrugged.

I wanted to be pissed at him, and part of me was. But I couldn't deny it felt nice witnessing his big brother routine. It made me feel like a part of their inner circle.

"You guys know I just moved into La Stella, right?" Luca's gaze flicked to mine and I gave him a weak smile.

"They know."

"So, I've been vetted."

"Okay, okay." I threw up my hands in exasperation. "This is just getting weird now. Luca offered to give me a ride because I was late for class and MU was on his route."

"Where do you work?" Nicco asked, still holding Ari protectively at his side.

"At VC Marketing Solutions."

He frowned. "Isn't that on the other side of the neighborhood?"

"What?" I looked up at Luca, feeling my cheeks heat. "You said it was on your way."

"I... uh, I may have told a tiny white lie."

"But why would you do that?" My brows knitted.

"I—"

The blare of Nicco's cell phone cut the air like a knife and I averted my gaze, feeling stripped bare sharing this strange moment with Luca... in front of my best friend, her overprotective husband, and his best friend.

Nicco barked into the phone before kissing Ari and stalking off to give himself some privacy.

"I should go." Luca touched my arm, startling me.

"Uh, yeah... sorry." My eyes flicked over to where Nicco was shouting into his cell phone. "Thanks for the ride," I said, finally giving Luca attention.

"Anytime." He smiled. "It was nice to meet you all, even if slightly weird."

"You too," Ari said, but Matteo simply frowned.

He was especially grumpy today, which was weird, because the guy was usually a hoot.

I went to walk Luca back to his car, but he held up his hands. "I'll see you around, Nora."

With a wink, he jogged back to his car, climbed inside and drove off.

"I don't like him," Matteo said the second he was gone.

"Funny, I didn't ask." I poked my tongue out at him.

"So what's his deal?"

We began to walk toward the building, leaving Nicco on his call.

"Who Luca? He moved in across the hall."

"So he's interested?"

"Interested?" I balked. "I hardly know him."

"Matt, stop." Ari laced her arm through mine. "He seems… nice."

"But?" My narrowed gaze slid to hers.

"He's…"

"An outsider?" A derisive sigh escaped my lips. "You know, I'm not exactly part of the gang either."

"Nora, that's not—"

Just then, Nicco came back.

"Everything good?" Matteo asked.

"It will be."

The air turned thick with the dark cloud circling Nicco.

"What is it, what's wrong?" Ari asked.

Nicco glanced at me. "It's nothing."

"I see." My expression tightened, my stomach dropping. "How is Enzo by the way?"

"Fuck," Matteo hissed, but I'd already taken off toward the doors.

"Nora, wait." Arianne caught up with me. "He can't…"

"I know. But it doesn't change the fact I'll always be on the outside while you're…" I stopped myself. I wasn't being fair. Arianne hadn't asked to fall in love with a mafioso any more than I'd asked to fall for a guy who couldn't give me what I needed.

Just because she'd got her happy ending and I never would, wasn't reason to push her away.

"I'm sorry. I'm acting crazy," I said around a strained smile.

"You care about him."

"Yeah, well, it doesn't matter, does it? He left and didn't even think to tell me."

"Maybe it's time to move on. Enzo is going through some stuff…"

"You think I don't know that? I might not know everything, but I know…"

"He's gone, Nor. Enzo is gone, and from what I can tell, no one knows when he's coming back." She reached for my hand. "I'm sorry."

"It's fine." The words spilled from my lips with a heavy sigh. "I'm fine."

Ari nodded. "You're one of the strongest people I know."

Yeah. I'd thought so too.

But I wasn't so sure anymore.

After two hours of Intro to Sociology, I met Arianne in the food court for lunch. But as I approached the table where she sat with Nicco, I could tell everything was not fine.

"Hey, guys, what's up?"

"Oh, hey, I didn't see you there." Arianne smiled, but it didn't reach her eyes.

"Is everything okay?" I glanced between them.

"Yeah, it's fine," she said a little too quickly.

"If I interrupted, I can—" I thumbed to the direction I'd just come from.

"No, don't go. Nicco's just worried about Enzo."

"Bambolina." The word vibrated deep in his chest.

"She deserves to know. Besides, I'm not telling her anything, not really."

Sitting down, I inhaled a deep breath. "Where is he?"

"Out of town, on... business."

"I'm not an idiot, Nicco. I know what business means." My lips pursed. "Did something happen?" Fear snaked through me.

"I don't think so, but he hasn't called me in almost three days."

"Okay." My brows crinkled. "He's a big boy, I'm sure he can—"

"He's never gone that long without calling me."

"He's ignoring Nicco's calls." Arianne tucked herself into his side.

"Maybe he wants some space?"

"Yeah, that's what worries me." Nicco's jaw clenched as he stared off into the distance.

"He'll be okay though, right?" The words felt like ash on my tongue. "I mean, it's Enzo."

"Yeah, I'm sure he'll be fine."

"Has Matteo call—"

"Has Matteo what?" He appeared out of nowhere, dropping down on the bench beside me.

"Spoken to Enzo?" I asked.

"Hold up, she knows?" He frowned at Nicco.

"Nice, douchebag, real nice."

"Shit, I'm sorry." He grimaced, running a hand down his face. "I didn't... it came out wrong. I'm just surprised Nicco caved and told you."

"Matteo," Ari sighed, "you're not helping."

"Look, I get it. I'm an outsider. I'm not supposed to know this stuff. But Enzo is my... friend too." God, that word sounded so stupid. Enzo wasn't my friend.

"Friend, really?" Matteo's brow lifted. "Does E know about your *friendship*?"

"Just because he's gone, doesn't mean you have to replace him as the snarky asshole."

"I can see why he likes you."

"Matt!" Nicco snapped.

"Yeah, sorry. I'm just trying to keep things light. E is... he's E. He'll call when he's ready to call. If you're that worried, call Gino."

"Gino?" I asked.

"Shit, sorry." Matteo grimaced, rubbing his jaw. "Just how much are we telling them?"

"I think we're done here." Nicco gently nudged Ari off him and stood. "I'm heading to the gym." He stalked off toward the doors.

"The gym?" Ari said, leaping up, taking off after him.

"He's really that worried?" The knot in my stomach twisted.

"Don't look at me like that, Nora, you know I can't tell you anything."

"Right."

He let out a frustrated breath. "Enzo will be fine. He's just dealing with some stuff. He probably hasn't called because he's ass over elbow drunk and knee deep in pus—" I sucked in a sharp breath and he muttered, "Fuck, I'm sorry."

"For what? Telling me the truth?"

His eyes dropped and he cupped the back of his neck. When Matteo looked up again, his expression softened. "You were good for him, you know? And for what it's worth, I was rooting for you. But Enzo... he isn't like me or Nicco."

"So what you're saying is, he's a lost cause?"

"No, what I'm saying is... maybe you should focus on a guy that is emotionally available, like Luca."

"Luca?" I spluttered. "You think me and Luca—"

"Nora, he gave you a ride to class when he works a five-minute walk away from your building."

"Maybe he's just a nice guy?" I shrugged.

"Yeah, and maybe I'm the Easter Bunny."

"Hmm, I don't see it." My lips curved with amusement.

"Luca is nice... But he doesn't have that dark brooding vibe working for him."

"Oh, shut up. I'm not talking about this with you."

Awkward silence fell over us and then Matteo said, "I know this can't be easy for you. Watching Ari with Nicco. Being on the periphery to... everything."

"It is what it is. She's happy."

"They both are. But still, it sucks to want someone who doesn't feel the same."

His words weren't intended to be malicious, but it didn't stop them from cutting deep. I did want Enzo. I'd wanted him the first time I'd ever laid eyes on him. There was something in his haunted icy gaze that caught my interest. It had pulled me in, shackled me to him whether he wanted me or not.

"What do you know about unrequited feelings?" I teased.

It was a joke, but the second the words came out I saw the flash of hurt in Matteo's eyes.

"Matt?"

"Nothing." He gave me a tight smile. "You're right, I know nothing. But I know something about guys who give their neighbors a ride to class."

Laughter bubbled in my chest. This was the Matteo Bellatoni I knew and loved. Funny and warm. But something bothered me about his earlier mood. Something I realized probably had nothing to do with me, and everything to do with his best friend.

"He'll be okay, right?" I whispered, locking eyes on Matteo.

He let out a steady breath and clucked his tongue. "I hope so, Nora. I really fucking hope so."

"Hey Lucii," I said as I sat down in my Media and Society class.

"Hey, girl." She smiled, her bright blue eyes twinkling under the strip lighting. "Did you enjoy the holidays?"

"It was okay, I guess. I'd forgotten how much parents fuss."

"Tell me about it. My mom was constantly trying to feed me." We shared a chuckle. "I'm relieved to be back. I'd gotten used to the freedom."

"I feel you," I grumbled, thinking how suffocating it had been being back at the house. I loved my parents, loved them something fierce, but being back on the Capizola estate, at the cottage... it had made me realize how small our lives had been there. How sheltered.

"I heard about Arianne. I can't believe she's married... that's... wow."

"Yeah." I managed a weak smile. "But she's happy."

"Must be hard though, losing your best friend freshman year of college."

"It's not like that," I said, even though I could see why Lucii thought that. People were probably expecting to see the baby bump soon.

"Hey, a few of us are heading to Mercutio's tonight for happy hour. You should totally come."

"I..." I hesitated. After everything that had happened last semester, my social life had taken a backseat.

"Come on," she nudged my shoulder, "you know you want to."

"Yeah." A tentative smile spread over my lips. "Okay."

"Yay. It'll be fun. And there's always plenty of hot college guys and graduates hanging out." Her brows waggled suggestively. "I have your number still, so I'll text you with the details later. You're living in La Stella now, right?"

"Yeah."

"Oh my God, I would die to live there. Is it awesome? I bet it's awesome."

"It's pretty awesome." Something inside me twisted. I liked Lucii. We had a couple of classes together and she always made an effort to talk to me, but she didn't *know* me. Maybe it was time to rectify that though. My life was going to be different now Arianne was married. I needed to find my own way, I needed to make new friends and make a life for myself.

Because Enzo wasn't coming for me. He wasn't going to stride into the room and declare his feelings for me. And I was worth fighting for.

I was worth being the center of someone's world.

NINE

ENZO

"TELL me what I need to know." My fist crumpled against the guy's face, his sticky blood coating my hand. I'd left off the brass knuckles this time. I wanted to feel his bones crunch with every punch.

"I-I don't know nothing, Marchetti, I swear."

"That's what they all say until they're bleeding out like a pig, crying for their mama," Gino chuckled darkly. He was leaning against the door, twirling his Tanto blade in his hand.

"Look," I let out an exasperated sigh, clutching the guy by his collar, "we know you rented Dominic Alejandro a storage unit. Word on the street is that the Mexicans are looking to move into town. So just tell me what you know, and we can all be on our way."

"It's... it's not what you think, man. You've got it all wrong. Alejandro doesn't run with the Mexicans anymore, he's—"

I rammed my fist into his face again. He wasn't telling us anything useful. Maybe the fucker didn't know anything or maybe he was just trying to cover his tracks.

If Gino had his way, I knew there was probably zero chance of this coglioni walking out of here alive. Gino and his guys didn't leave loose ends. They cleaned up after themselves, always.

I could do it—I could be the one to drive Gino's blade through the guy's stomach and watch the life drain from his eyes—but a tiny part of me hesitated.

Death changed you.

I knew that from killing my father in cold blood. Every time your knife or pistol or even hands took a life, it took a part of you. And I knew if I walked this slippery slope with Gino's crew, there might not be any pieces of me left to return to Verona with.

But I needed this.

I needed to expel all the anger and betrayal swimming in my veins. I needed to feed the darkness swirling around me like a thundercloud.

I knew it was a slippery slope... but right now, I didn't care.

"Tell. Me. What. I. Need. To. Know." I punched him again, blood spraying into the air as he spat out a couple of teeth. His body slammed back into the chair, his eyes shuttering. Only this time, they didn't open again.

"Okay, Enzo, he's done for now." Gino approached me, laying a firm hand on my shoulder. "Go get cleaned up and get a drink. I'll handle it from here—"

"You don't need to do that, I can—"

"I said go. You've done enough, kid."

I bristled, baring my teeth. Gino noticed, smirking. "You've still got a lot to learn about the world, Lorenzo. Take it from me, give too much of yourself too early, and you'll never get that shit back." Something passed over his mangled face. "Now go. I'll meet you at DiMarco's later."

DiMarco's had become our hangout the last few nights. The liquor flowed as freely as the pussy, and Zander was all too willing to indulge Gino and his men... and now, that invitation extended to myself.

I stormed away and grabbed a towel, wiping the blood off my hands. Then I snatched my jacket off the rack and shucked into it, before shouldering the door and spilling out into the dark alley.

My cell phone vibrated again, and this time, I dug it out of my pocket and checked the screen. It was hardly a surprise to see Nicco's name.

Call me.

Tsking, I texted him back.

You need to relax. I'm fine. Everything is fine. I'll call when the job is done.

My cell started blaring away, my best friend's name lighting up the screen. I hit decline and stuffed it back in my pocket. I didn't want to hear his concerns. I was here and Nicco was back in Verona, and right now, that's the way it needed to be.

My father had killed his mom in cold blood. He'd let Nicco and Alessia and Uncle Toni believe Aunt Lucia left because she couldn't hack being the boss' wife. That wasn't something I could just forget, and knowing Nicco the way I knew Nicco, it wasn't something he could just forget either.

Time and space would be good, for both of us.

Pulling out a smoke, I lit it up and dragged in a deep lungful, relishing the familiar burn. The motel was a stone's throw away from DiMarco's. I figured Gino picked it, so it was easier to fall into bed after a long night of top shelf liquor, high-end pussy, and shooting the shit. But I wondered if he had an ulterior motive.

Zander DiMarco was a showboater. He liked to flash his cash and his relationship with the Family. He was a friend to anyone who entered his bar as long as their wallet was fat, and their tastes expensive. Men wanted to be like Zander DiMarco, to soak up a good time. And when the good times rolled, people got complacent. They started talking about things they shouldn't.

I took off down the street toward the motel. My knuckles burned but I relished the sting. Pain reminded me I was alive, and for a little while, it abated the beast living inside me. I'd tear up the whole of Providence if it led me to whoever thought they could move in on Marchetti territory. Because nothing... *nothing* was more important to me than the Family. And after the shitshow with that traitorous son of a bitch I once called father, I needed to prove it more than ever.

If not to my Uncle Toni and the rest of the family... then to myself.

Gino and the guys met me at DiMarco's a little after eight. Guys crowded the stage, all looking to get a feel of the stripper working the pole. She was a hot little thing, legs for miles and curves in all the right places. But I wasn't feeling it, not tonight.

Not since Matteo had texted me earlier to say he'd bumped into Nora.

I hadn't replied. It wasn't like I had anything to say. Nora was nobody to me. Nothing. Yet, my fucking head hadn't quite got the memo because ever since seeing her name on my screen, I'd been grinding my teeth together like a junkie tweaking for their next hit.

My tight fist rubbed back and forth over my jean-clad thigh as I tried to focus on anything but her.

But it was fucking futile.

Nora Abato was under my skin, no matter how much I tried to claw her out.

"Yo, E," Marc said. "You look tense, my man. Why don't you grab a girl and head to one of the private rooms for a dance?" The sleazy fucker grinned.

"Nah, not tonight."

"That's not what you were saying the other night when you disappeared with Sherri," Dixon added, clapping me on the shoulder.

I shirked him off, barely able to remember the blonde I'd dragged into the restrooms and forced to her knees.

"Fuck you, coglioni."

"Leave the kid alone," Gino said, waving his guys off.

"Come on, boss, we're just goof—"

"Basta!" He slammed his hand down on the table. "Go grab a girl each and get the fuck out of here. Me and Enzo need to have a chat."

"Yeah, boss." Marc shot me an apologetic look. "Whatever you say." They left us alone and Gino ordered another round of drinks.

"You know, Enzo, I was a lot like you once." He relaxed back in the booth, his hard gaze fixed right on my face. "Full of anger and itching for a fight..."

"That's not—"

His hand cut through the air, silencing me. Gino arched a brow. "I get it. What went down with Vincenzo, that was some fucked up shit. But you've got to know, it's not on you."

"I should have known." I jammed my fingers into my hair and tugged the ends, the pit in my stomach carving deeper and deeper.

"The sins of our fathers do not lie on our shoulders. You need to remember that, kid." He smirked.

"Less of the *kid*, old man." I shot back around a wolfish grin of my own.

"Toni told me to take you under my wing, to let you work off some steam, but I won't let you lose yourself, Enzo. Just so we're clear, that's not gonna happen on my watch." His eyes bored into me as if he could see the very depths of my dark, twisted soul.

"I don't know how to let it go."

"You find a way, son. Drink it out of you, fuck it out of you, fight it out of you... you do what you need to do, and then you shake it off and lay that shit to rest, you hear me?"

With a reluctant nod, I downed the rest of my drink and stared out at the club. The rest of the guys were huddled over at the bar, chatting to a busty blonde. Gino and his guys didn't have roots. They didn't have women waiting at home or families wondering where they were and what they were doing. They lived for one thing and one thing only.

The Family.

They found honor and purpose in carrying out Uncle Toni's orders. They drank, fucked, and killed... much like my father had done.

Fuck.

He was infecting my every thought. No matter where my mind went, it all came back to him.

My jaw clenched as I itched for something—*someone*—to take my anger out on. Gino reached across the table, grabbing my wrist. "You need to let it go, son. That shit will eat you up until there's nothing left." He let out a steady breath. "Vincenzo was a traitor, and you took care of him."

My eyes shuttered as the lingering memory of the gunshot went off in my head. It was a sound I couldn't escape; every bang of a door or exhaust backfiring, I was back in that room, standing over my father's dead body.

My fist clenched against my thigh again and I ground out, "I need another drink."

"Sure thing. Then you grab the nearest piece of ass and go fuck some of that anger out of you. Best medicine there is." Gino nodded around a smug smile, as if he had all the fucking answers.

He'd done a lot of fucked up shit in his time. You didn't become the Family's number one enforcer without getting your hands bloody and your soul dirty. But I doubted that he'd killed the man who had given him life.

The waitress brought over another tray of drinks. "Courtesy of Zander," she purred, running a hand over my shoulder. Her thick lashes fluttered in my direction and Gino gave me another nod.

"Thanks," I said thickly, before removing her hand.

Gino tsked under his breath and the girl sauntered away with dejection in her eyes. "If you're not going hit that, then don't mind if I do." He let out a hearty laugh, clambering from the booth.

"No way she'll want a shriveled dick like yours, *old man*."

"You'd be surprised what this shriveled dick can do." He winked, taking off after the waitress.

I leaned back against the booth, letting out a heavy sigh. A bar like this was usually my kind of place. Good liquor and even better pussy. But everything was off.

My cell phone vibrated, and I dug it out of my pocket, half-expecting another text from Nicco.

It wasn't Nicco though.

It was Matteo.

Hope you're staying out of trouble.

Rolling my eyes, I texted him back a quick reply and stuffed my cell phone in my pocket. I knew my cousins meant well, they always did, but this wasn't something a couple of texts and a few nights away from Verona was going to fix.

Downing my drink, I ran a hand over my jaw and stood, making my way to the restrooms. Gino was working his magic on the waitress, whispering into her ear as if she was the most beautiful girl he'd ever seen. Dirty old dog.

With a chuckle, I shouldered the door leading to the restrooms. But the sound of gentle sobs caught my attention, and I went left down the hall inside of the right.

"Hello?" I called, knocking on the door to the female bathroom.

"I, uh… I'll just be a minute."

I heard the faucet run, followed by the whirr of the hand dryer. I should have moved on, doubled back around and gone into the men's bathroom like I'd planned to. But curiosity got the better of me.

A few seconds later, the door creaked open and emerald eyes stared up at me. "Can I help you?"

"You were crying," I stated, backing up to give her room to step out into the hall.

"No, I wasn't." She steeled her expression and rolled out her shoulders.

My eyes narrowed. The faint mascara tracks down her cheeks weren't fooling me. But there was something else, a bruise blossoming along her cheek.

"Who did this to you?" I demanded, reaching for her.

"No one." She jerked back, letting her red hair fall around her face like a shield. "Excuse me, but I have to get back to work."

"You work here?" Anger zipped up my spine. If DiMarco was letting guys put their hands on his girls… fuck, I thought that shit had been dealt with last summer after he and Nicco got into it.

"I-I really have to go." She slipped around me and hurried down the hall.

"Fuck." My fist collided with the wall. I might have been a cold bastard, but I didn't tolerate violence toward women. Back when we were kids, I'd seen how much it had messed with Nicco's head watching his old man lose his temper one too many times with Aunt Lucia. He was a reformed man now, but it didn't change history.

I liked my women submissive, sure. But they were always more than willing to accommodate my rough touch.

My dick twitched behind my jeans, and I shook my head with mild laughter. At least one of us still had our priorities straight.

Because although I'd put space between me and Verona, there were some things you couldn't escape.

TEN

NORA

"WHAT DO YOU THINK?" Lucii yelled over the music.

"It's... loud." I grinned, slurping down my sugary cocktail. I was three drinks in and feeling all kinds of sexy. "Thanks for pushing me to come tonight."

"Anytime. We single girls have to stick together." She ran her tongue over her teeth. "My roommate Allie is already planning her wedding to her new beau. I swear, everyone around me is either going steady or already picking out furniture."

"Tell me about it," I murmured, swaying my hips to the beat.

"Shit, sorry." Lucii grimaced. "I didn't mean to rub salt in the wound."

"Relax, it's fine. Ari is happy, that's all that matters."

"God, of course. But married... wow." She downed the rest of her drink and placed the glass on the nearest table. "It's freshman year of college. I want to live a little first. Sow my wild oats and experiment."

"Experiment?" A deep voice said. "Sign me up."

We both turned to greet the two guys staring at us with hunger in their eyes.

"I'm Isaac and this is my friend Nate."

"Lucii and that's Nora."

Isaac gave me a long, lingering look, letting his eyes fall down my body and back up. "Nice to meet you." The corner of his mouth tipped. He was tall, dark and handsome but looked far too preppy for my tastes.

"Can we get you girls a drink? Our friend Luca is at the bar."

"Luca?" I blurted because what were the chances?

But sure enough, when Isaac pointed at the bar, my new neighbor was standing there with his back to us.

"Wait a second. You're *boo bees Nora*?" A grin split Isaac's face and heat exploded in my cheeks.

"He told you about that?"

"About what?" Lucii asked, brows bunched with confusion.

"Luca, he's uh… he's my neighbor."

"He lives at La Stella too?"

"Sure does," I mumbled, suddenly feeling very overdressed in the skintight little black dress and chunky heeled boots.

I looked hot. I just wasn't entirely sure I wanted Luca to see me like this. Especially not after telling his friends about my boo bees t-shirt.

I noticed Nate whispering to his friend. "I'll be right back," Isaac said, giving me a lingering look. There was something about his eyes that made a shiver skate down my spine. Like he was looking a little too hard. But then he took off, weaving his way through the crowd to Luca.

"We didn't tell him what we're drinking," Lucii added.

"You were drinking a Long Island Iced Tea," Nate arched a brow at her and then settled his dark gaze on mine. "And you're drinking a Strawberry Daiquiri."

"Okay, I don't know whether to be impressed or a little creeped out." She chuckled.

"I worked a semester in a cocktail bar."

"Gotcha." They shared a smile, but his eyes flicked back to mine. I ducked my head, taking another sip of my drink.

Lucii moved closer, chatting to him like they were old friends. But I remained a safe distance, dancing to the music and enjoying my drink. Soon, Luca and Isaac joined us.

"I realize how this looks," Luca said, sliding our tray of drinks onto the nearest table. "But I promise, I'm not stalking you."

"Glad to hear it." I smiled. "So how do you know Isaac and Nate?"

"Funny story, I met them at the gym."

"The gym?"

"Yup, and they took pity on me I guess."

"Lucky you."

"Yeah, I've been pretty lucky since I arrived in Verona." His eyes sparkled with things I wasn't sure I wanted to acknowledge. It had felt safe talking to him at my apartment. But this was different. We were in a bar late on a school night.

"So, wait a second, you told your new friends about my t-shirt?" I shot him a pointed look. "Why do I feel like the brunt of some locker room joke?"

"Nora, I would never…" Genuine hurt flashed over his handsome face. "Actually, I was telling them all about this pretty amazing girl who lives across the hall."

"Oh." My cheeks pinked as I struggled to meet his intense gaze. "I'm not sure what to say to that."

"You don't need to say anything. I get the impression the guy you told me about is still under your skin, so this isn't me making a move." He held up his hands in surrender.

My eyes lifted to his as my breath caught in my throat. "You're not—"

"Hey," Ari appeared out of nowhere.

"Ari? What the hell, babe?" I pulled her into a hug. "I thought you and Nicco had plans?" She'd told me as much when I'd mentioned my plans to her earlier.

"We did." She beamed. "But it feels like so long since we hung out. I hope you don't mind us crashing."

"Us?" My brows furrowed.

"Yeah, Nicco and Matteo are at the bar getting drinks."

"They are?" My stomach sank. I was so excited to have my best friend here, but Nicco and Matteo too… and Luca? Ugh. This was the last thing I'd wanted.

"Hey, Lucii." Arianne greeted her.

"Hey, I love your dress. You look so hot."

"Thanks. Luca, this is a surprise." She finally noticed the quiet guy beside me.

"Hey." He lifted his hand in a small wave. "It's good to see you again."

Ari's eyes flashed to mine, a hundred questions twinkling in her honey brown eyes. But in true Arianne Capizola fashion, she pressed her lips together in a tight smile and swallowed them. No doubt saving them for later, when we were alone.

"There you are." Nicco appeared, slipping his arm possessively around his wife. She smiled up at him in a way only a girl in love with a boy could. To watch them, the way they gravitated to one another, it made my heart soar and ache all at the same time.

They shared a lingering kiss and I heard Lucii let out a little sigh.

"God, I need to get laid," she added.

"I can definitely help with that," Nate said, shooting her a flirty wink.

"Dance with me?"

"It would be my pleasure."

Lucii grabbed his hand and pulled him toward the dance floor.

"Ah, do you want to…" Luca left the question hanging, but a voice chimed in, "If she's dancing with anyone, it'll be me."

I glanced over my shoulder to find Matteo grinning at me. "Behave," I chided.

"You owe me, Abato. Don't even try to deny it."

"Matt!" Nicco warned, but I refused to meet his stare.

Rolling my eyes, I ducked out of Matteo's hold and offered Luca an apologetic smile. This so wasn't how I saw the night going. I wanted to have fun. To relax and forget all about the Marchetti men, and I lumped Matteo in there, because although he was a Bellatoni by name, he was still one of them.

Trading my empty glass for my fresh drink, I slurped down a mouthful of the sugary sweet cocktail hyperaware of the fact they were all watching me: Luca,

Matteo, Isaac, Arianne, and Nicco. I wasn't used to being in the limelight, and I wasn't sure I liked it.

Knocking back the rest of my drink, I inhaled a deep breath and said, "I'm going to dance."

Without waiting for their replies, I melted into the sea of bodies, trying to find Lucii and Nate. They were already pressed close, grinding on each other as they moved to the seductive tones of The Weeknd.

An arm wrapped around my waist from behind and I readied myself to scold Matteo, but when I spun around, I was met with Luca's cheeky grin. "One dance?" He pouted and I found myself grinning back.

"Fine, but just one. Seems like the neighborly thing to do."

Luca grabbed my hands and began weaving shapes in the air. The guy had moves, rolling and popping his hips in a way that had me licking my lips. "See something you like?" he teased.

"Less talking, more dancing, Casanova." I closed my eyes and let the music carry me away. This was what college was all about. Meeting cute guys and dancing in bars. Late nights, and early morning walks of shame back to your dorm room.

I wasn't supposed to be pining after a guy who would never take me out dancing or buy me flowers or make reservations at a fancy restaurant. I bet Luca would do all of those things. I mean, the guy had driven me to class when he worked right around the corner from our building.

My eyes fluttered open to Luca's heated stare as he watched me sway to the music. "You are so fucking beautiful." He grinned.

Just then someone barreled past us, knocking me into Luca. "Watch it, asshole," he shouted over the music, but the guy disappeared into the sea of bodies.

"Relax, I'm fine."

He ran his hands up my shoulders, holding me closer. "You sure?"

"Sure." I nodded. "But answer me this. How drunk are you right now?"

"I think you have me mistaken for someone else." He flashed me a goofy smile.

"You're so wasted." I batted his chest, freezing when I felt his muscles contract beneath my palm.

"Nora, I—"

"Take a walk, new guy." Matteo appeared. "The lady owes me a dance."

"The *lady* is kind of busy." I rolled my eyes and even over the music, I heard the two of them chuckle.

"She's all yours." Luca conceded, and I shot him a questioning look.

"The night's still young." He winked and headed back toward where Ari and Nicco were chatting with Isaac.

"You and me, Abato." Matteo crooked his finger. "Let's go."

He moved with ease, dancing literal circles around me. It wasn't the first time I'd seen Matteo Bellatoni strut his stuff and I soon found myself laughing along with him, letting him spin and twirl me until my feet burned and my cheeks hurt from all the smiling.

Of course, the DJ had to go and ruin it by switching to a slow song, but it didn't deter Matteo. He pulled me into his arms as if we were old friends. "How are you doing really?"

I eased back to meet his eyes. "I'm okay. Have you... have you spoken to him?"

I hated myself for asking, but I couldn't be anyone except the girl desperately concerned about a boy, no matter how hard she tried not to be.

Only Enzo wasn't a boy. He was a complicated, tortured soul. One that would drift into darker seas if he didn't have an anchor to guide him back to safer shores.

"He texted."

"He did?" Hope burrowed itself into my chest. "Is he okay? When will he be coming back? What did he say?"

"Whoa there, Nor. He's okay." His smile fell a little. "The rest... I don't know."

"What do you mean?"

Matteo slid a hand up my spine, holding me tighter as he rocked us to the sultry beat. "Enzo needs to work through some things."

"He lost his father, of course he's going to need time."

He tensed. It was only for a second, but I felt it all the same. "Matt?" My brows pinched. "What is it?"

"Nothing." He shook his head. "Let me enjoy this. It's been a while since I danced with a girl who wasn't my sister or cousin. You know, no one wants E to pull his head out of his ass and see what's right in front of him more than me."

"But?"

"I don't want you to be disappointed when it doesn't happen."

"You think I should move on." The words burned through me.

"I think... ah, fuck, Nor. I don't know what I think. Enzo needs someone like you. Strong willed, beautiful, so fucking smart."

"Easy there, I might start to think this is your attempt at seducing me."

"I know when to hedge my bets, and something tells me you, Nora Abato, would eat me alive in the sack." A playful smirk graced his rugged face.

"Want to know a secret?" He nodded and I added, "You're probably right."

The song faded out, the next one dropping a heavier beat. Matteo released me and ran a hand through his hair. He'd garnered quite the audience, girls standing in the wings, waiting to swoop in and bag themselves a bad boy with so much charm and swagger it practically oozed from his pores. But Matteo was a bad boy with a big heart. And I didn't doubt that one day, he would fall headfirst in love.

But it wasn't like that between us. I saw him as nothing more than a goofy older brother or cousin.

"Luca seems like a good guy. If you want to give him a chance, he gets my seal of approval."

"Didn't know I needed it, but thanks." I chuckled, trying to disguise the flash of hurt lancing my chest. Arianne had told me to move on, to not spend time waiting for Enzo to come around. But hearing it from his cousin, one of his best friends—and a guy I thought was rooting for me—well, it made my stomach sink into my toes.

Matteo thought Enzo was a lost cause too. I wanted to argue the point, but I knew these Marchetti men and it would be pointless.

Everyone had given up on there ever being an 'us.'

"Hey," Matteo added as we walked back to the others. "This is a good thing. Now you can give Luca a chance." He squeezed my shoulder in reassurance, but he might as well have been plunging a dagger in my heart.

Of all the people aware of mine and Enzo's short-lived relationship, I thought I could count on Matteo to fight with me.

But I guess he wasn't a gambling man, after all.

That or the odds were simply too stacked against me, and nobody liked betting on the losing team.

"I had fuuuun tonight." I laid my head on Ari's shoulder as we waited for Luis to bring around their car.

"You're drunk." She eyed me with concern.

"Only a little bit. We should do this again, every month. Or every other weekend. I miss you, babe. I miss you so freakin' much."

"I miss you too." Guilt glittered in her eyes and I realized what a bitch I was being.

Ari deserved this. She deserved the fairytale love story and the happily ever after. She deserved nothing but good things.

"I'm so happy for you." I hugged her tight, pulling her out of Nicco's iron clad hold.

"Luis is here," he said.

"There you are." Lucii's voice pierced the air. If I was drunk, she was toasted. But we'd had fun. Luca, Nate, and Isaac had stuck around, and we'd all spent the night dancing and drinking and dancing some more. I couldn't remember the last time I'd had so much fun. Luca kept his distance, but I was enjoying myself too much to worry.

"We're getting pizza and heading back to my dorm... unless—"

"Afterparty at Luc's," Nate suggested.

"I... I mean I guess we can all go back to mine." His eyes landed on mine, but everything was a little blurry.

"Sounds like fun, but I'll have to bail," Isaac said. "Maybe next time." His eyes lingered on me for a second.

"Your loss, Isaac boy." Nate clapped him on the shoulder. "Let's roll. Nora, you might as well ride with us."

I glanced between Lucii and Ari. My best friend looked concerned, but she had nothing to worry about. I was fine. Better than fine. I was riding a wave of cocktail-induced bliss.

"I'll get a ride with these guys. You two go." I waved them off.

Matteo had left some time ago, something about his sister needing him at home. Ari had insisted on staying, so, of course, Nicco had stayed too.

Luis came around to open the door.

"Go," I said, when Ari hesitated.

"Bambolina, we should—"

"Yes, okay. Be safe," she said, leaning in to press a soft kiss to my cheek. "I'll call you tomorrow. And Nora," she grabbed my hand as I went to move away, "don't do anything you might regret."

Her words rattled inside my skull as I watched Nicco usher her into the car and climb in after her.

"Nora," Lucii's voice startled me and I spun around to greet my new friends. "Are we doing this or what?"

My eyes flicked to Luca and he gave me a timid smile. "We could always go to mine," I said.

"No." His gaze darkened. "I owe you."

ELEVEN

ENZO

I STARED at Matteo's name flashing on the screen. I'd silenced my cell phone a long time ago, sick of his incessant updates. He was at some bar with Nicco and Ari… and Nora. I knew he was trying to get a rise out of me.

"Here you go, gentlemen." A server slid a tray of drinks onto the table. "If you need anything else, just let me know." Her smoky eyes lingered on me, but I stared right through her. The persistent vibration of my cell was like an annoying itch I couldn't scratch.

Or an itch I knew I *shouldn't* scratch.

"You gonna get that?" Gino asked, motioning to my hand covering my cell.

I didn't want to. I needed to keep my distance. It was better… for everyone. *Especially her.*

It started ringing again and Gino chuckled. "If you don't get that, I will. And nobody will like how that ends."

"Yeah, yeah, keep your hair on, old man." I clambered from the booth and headed toward the emergency exit, hitting answer as I shouldered the door. "What?" I barked.

"Nice to hear your voice too," Matteo teased.

"What the fuck do you want?"

"Just to shoot the shit and see how my favorite cousin is doing. Since you've clearly forgotten how to use your cell."

"I texted."

"And I felt your reluctance in every word."

"Matt…"

"Yeah, yeah. I won't keep you. I just thought you'd like to know I left Nora at the bar… with Luca."

"Luca? Who the fuck is Luca?" My spine straightened.

"Luca is the guy who's going to swoop in and make Nora his unless you pull your head out your ass and do something about it."

"Matt, I've told you already—"

"You don't want her. Yeah, yeah, I got the memo when you fucked off to Providence. But you're making a mistake, cous. She cares about you, she cares… you just have to let her—"

"I'm not doing this with you. She's better off forgetting all about me." The words got stuck in my throat. "This Luca? He a good guy?" Because he already sounded like a fucking moron.

"Seems genuine. His rental application didn't flag anything."

"He lives in La Stella?"

"Yep, right across her hall."

Fuck.

"You saw his file?" I tried to keep my voice even.

"Not in person, no. But I had Maurice double check. No one gets an apartment in La Stella without passing all the checks."

"Doesn't mean he's a decent guy though."

"He spent half the night staring at her with that look."

"What look?" My teeth ground together.

"You know, the starry-eyed look Nicco has whenever he's around Arianne."

"Fuck." It spilled out in a ragged breath before I could stop it.

"Exactly why I called," Matteo said.

"What do you want me to say? You know why I'm here. I need to get my head straight, I need to—"

"You need to learn to let people in, E. I know what happened with your old man messed you up, I get it, I do. But pushing us away, pushing her away, isn't the answer."

A loud bang drew my attention, and I dipped my hand into my jacket, feeling my fingers graze the butt of my pistol. I never went anywhere unarmed, an array of weapons strapped to my person. A Wharncliffe knife tucked into my boot, my brass knuckles, my pistol. I loved weapons almost as much as I loved my GTO. There was something comforting about knowing I could protect myself and the people I cared about. Besides, you never knew what enemies were lurking in the shadows.

Fuck.

I was starting to sound like him.

'Our enemies hide in plain sight, Enzo.' My father had once said to me. "They want to destroy what we have built and take it for their own. They want to see the Marchetti fall, to see the Family go up in smoke. Never forget that, figlio mio."

I'd always known my father would die for the Family. I just hadn't anticipated he would die a traitor.

Anger snaked through me, coiling around my chest with its sharp barbs as my fist clenched so tight my knuckles turned white.

He was still in my head… and I didn't know how the fuck to get him out.

"Cous?" Matteo's voice rattled through my skull.

"Yeah, I'm here."

"Just think about it…"

"Yeah."

But as I hung up, we both knew I wouldn't. Because sometimes to exorcise your demons, you had to become them.

"What the—"

An incessant whirring sound pierced my skull, making me groan.

"Hmm, what is that?" A voice said, and I glanced over my shoulder to find a blonde sleeping naked beside me.

Fucking great.

After Matteo's call last night everything was a little hazy. There were drinks, a lot of them. As it neared closing time, Gino and the guys insisted on some of the girls joining us and we'd stayed at the bar getting drunker and hornier.

I had vague memories of the blonde being all over me. Loose lips and wandering hands. Despite the ringing in my ears and bass drum in my head, I felt pretty relaxed, so it wasn't hard to imagine what had happened when we'd eventually got back to my room.

"Are you going to answer that?" she groaned, pulling the sheet over her body.

I swung my legs over the edge and sat up, snatching up my cell. "Yeah?" I barked, not even checking the name.

"It's me," Gino sounded as rough as I felt, "we've got a problem."

"I'm listening."

"It's DiMarco's. There's been a break-in."

"A break-in?" Disbelief coated my words. "But we were only there like… five hours ago." It was barely six thirty.

"I know. Zander got a call from the local PD; they tripped the alarm. They're giving us time to get down there first and take a look."

"Yeah, I'm coming."

"Meet you downstairs in ten."

"Make it five," I said.

"What's wrong?" Blondie stared up at me with tired eyes.

"I've gotta go."

"Go? But it's early—"

"Duty calls." I started pulling on my pants and securing my weapons to my body.

"So it's true what they say about you." She pushed up on one elbow, flicking her hair off one shoulder.

"What do they say?"

"That you're dangerous."

A derisive snort crawled up my throat.

"So it's not... true?"

"What do you think?" I narrowed my eyes, shucking on my jacket. I remembered kissing her, running my hands over her tight little body. But I couldn't remember much after that.

Fuck. I'd been totally wasted.

"I'm thinking you should stay here and finish what you started last night," she damn near purred.

So we hadn't fucked then.

I didn't know whether to be relieved or disappointed.

She must have had her mouth on my dick though because most of the tension I'd felt talking to Matteo last night had dissipated. Even if the jealousy sat heavy in my chest, coiled around my heart like barbed wire.

"No can do, dolcezza, I gotta go. Stay though. Order room service. Take a shower." *But be gone when I get back.*

"You'll come back to me?"

"I don't think so, Blondie. This could take a while."

She pouted. "Well, if you want some company later, I could always leave my number."

"Yeah, you do that." I motioned to the notepad by the telephone. "I gotta go."

She flopped back with an exasperated breath, but I didn't wait around to hear her complaints. I'd stay away long enough to hope she was gone when I got back, and if she wasn't, I'd give it to her straight.

I wasn't interested in anything more than she gave me last night.

Gino was already waiting in reception. The grim expression on his face told me all I needed to know. He suspected Alejandro. Which meant whoever he was working with, or for, they were upping the ante and this time it was personal.

It couldn't have been a coincidence we were drinking at DiMarco's last night, right before it was hit.

They were watching us, taunting us... which changed everything.

"What's the plan?" I asked, noting it was just the two of us.

"We go check it out before the cops arrive. I already spoke with Toni. We keep this between us for now, just you and me, okay?"

My brows furrowed. "What aren't you telling me?"

He gave me a sympathetic look and said, "Let's go."

DiMarco's was a mess. Whoever had been here had caused thousands of dollars worth of damage, smashing the mirrored walls and glass shelves housing Zander's impressive range of liquor. Chairs lay overturned and tables were at strange angles. It looked like a herd of wild animals had stormed right through the place.

"Jesus Christ." Glass crunched under Gino's boots as we made our way toward the back office. "Zander?" he called.

"In here." He sounded pissed.

We found him in his office, standing in the middle of the room with his back to us. "I think it's for you." His eyes caught mine over his shoulder.

"Say what?" I frowned.

"That." He jabbed his finger toward the far wall. I stepped closer, certain my eyes were deceiving me. But sure enough, there scrawled in blood red were the words, 'like father, like son.'

"This is what you wanted me to see?" I pinned Gino with a hard look.

"I wanted you to see it before we scrub it."

"Fuck." I ran a hand down my head and cupped my neck. This was bad, very fucking bad.

"You think this has something to do with my—" I hesitated, glancing at Zander.

"Seriously? My place just got fucking trashed because of yo—"

"Basta!" Gino hissed. "This is not Enzo's doing, and you'd do well to remember who he is."

"Yeah, yeah, my bad." Zander held up his hands in defense. "As long as the insurance covers it, it's all good."

Gino tsked, moving closer. "Give us the room for a second," he said with an air of authority.

"Come on, Gino, this is my fucking—"

"I said, give us the room."

"Yeah, whatever. I'll be out front." He took off, but Gino called after him, "And don't fucking touch anything."

"You good, kid?" He asked, the second Zander was gone.

"They know," I said, disbelief coating my words. "How the fuck do they know?"

Only a handful of people knew about my father's betrayal. In years gone by, if a man betrayed omertà, his death would be broadcast across the Family as a reminder of what happened to traitors. But times were different, and Uncle Toni tried to rule with respect instead of fear.

"They're clearly more connected than we first thought." He clapped me on the shoulder. "That or—"

"No, don't say it." My eyes finally tore away from the scrawl and slid to Gino. "Don't you fucking say it."

"We have to consider it, kid."

"My father." This could all be his doing.

Fuck.

My boot flew out connecting with the leg of the chair. Pain shot through my big toe and skittered up my leg but it barely registered.

"Better?"

"Not in the slightest."

"We'll get them, Enzo. Whoever is behind this, we'll get them. And when we do—"

"I put a bullet between their fucking eyes."

"Rein it in, kid. Harness all that anger and frustration, because something tells me you're gonna need it. Let's get this cleaned up before the cops get here. The last thing we need is them sticking their nose in where it doesn't belong."

Gino scanned the office before strolling toward Zander's drinks cabinet. He grabbed a wad of tissue paper out of the box and poured expensive whisky over it before moving to the mirror and scrubbing away all evidence of the message.

"Get rid of this." He thrust the soggy tissue paper at me. "I'll speak to Zander. You stay cool, okay? We came to assist Zander. That's all. I'm counting on you not to screw this up, kid."

Without a word, I crossed the room and slipped outside. Zander was hovering in the hall. His eyes collided with me and he blanched.

"Problem?" My brow rose. I wasn't afraid of these guys. They might have been older and wiser, but with the amount of anger and thirst for vengeance fueling me, I was deadlier.

"I don't even know where to start." His shady expression gave way to defeat. "This bar is my whole world."

"Let the cops do their job and then we'll send in someone to help you." Because no matter how irritating or shady somebody was, we looked after our own.

"Have you checked in on all the girls? Did everyone get home okay?"

"I can't get hold of Cait." His eyes dropped to the cell in his hand.

"Cait?" I hadn't heard that name in the last few days.

"She's my... she's one of my best girls. If you know what I'm saying." His lip curved with wicked intent.

God, I fucking hated this asshole.

"You want me to go check on her?"

"You'd do that?"

I shrugged. "Beats being here when the cops show up." Even if they sent over someone on our payroll, they still made me antsy.

"She lives on Jefferson Street, Park View Apartments. I just want to know she's okay."

My brows furrowed. "She someone to you?"

"Like I said, she's one of my best girls, and I protect my interests."

I bet you do. Sleazy motherfucker.

Growing up, once Nicco, Matteo, and I were given more responsibility in the Family, I'd always wondered why Uncle Toni aligned himself with guys like DiMarco. He was only out to line his own pocket. But Providence was Marchetti territory and it's just how business went. Plus, guys like DiMarco collected enemies like I collected shiny new sharp-edged toys to play with.

"I'll head over there and make sure she's okay."

Something flashed over his face, and his whole posture shifted. "Actually," he scrubbed his jaw, "I'm sure she's fine. I'll call her ag—"

"It's fine, I got it. I'll call as soon as I get over there and check it out." I regarded him for a second. DiMarco was usually the epitome of cool, calm, and collected, but he seemed a little ruffled and I couldn't work out if it was because of the break-in... or because of Cait.

"What's her full name?"

"Caitlin," he let out a derisive sigh. "Caitlin O'Connell."

"I'm on it. Tell Gino, I'll be back soon."

I didn't wait for his reply, walking straight out of the bar and into the brisk morning air. Dragging in a deep lungful, I gave myself a second before checking my maps app on my cell and taking off in the direction of Caitlin's apartment building.

Gino would probably kick my ass when I got back to DiMarco's, but I needed air. I needed space to fucking think after seeing that message scrawled on the wall. It wasn't done in blood, despite its red coloring. Fresh blood had this smell. A coppery metallic twang that permeated the air.

It was a smell you didn't ever forget.

Pulling out a smoke, I lit it up and inhaled a deep hit. Everyone was right, I needed to kick this habit. It made my skin stink, and my lungs burn... but I needed the routine. I needed to keep myself distracted. Because in the moments of silence, when everything was still, the memory of that night threatened to pull me under so far, I wouldn't ever make it back out in one piece.

I crossed the street and double checked the map. I was close. Caitlin lived around here somewhere. I'd been so desperate to get the fuck out of DiMarco's it hadn't occurred to me how odd it would seem, me turning up at a stranger's door. But I only needed proof she was okay, then I could take a slow walk back to the bar.

Stepping up to the buzzer, I pressed her number and waited. When no one answered, I pressed it again.

Still nothing.

Some guy slipped out of the building, so I waited for him to pass and then stuck my hand out to catch the door, ducking inside. I took two steps at a time until I arrived outside her apartment. I knocked on the door and waited.

Finally, I heard shuffling on the other side, and the door cracked open. "Can I help you?"

It was dark inside, her face cloaked in shadows, but her green eyes glittered up at me.

"DiMarco sent me," I said. "There was an incident at the bar."

"Incident?" She kept the door firmly in place, like a shield between us.

"Are you okay?" I asked. "Zander said you didn't answer his call for you to check-in."

"I… I should go. You can tell him I'm fine." She went to close the door, but my hand shot out, steadying it.

"Wait." There was something familiar about her. Gently, I pushed the door open further, forcing her to sidestep the damn thing.

"You."

Her breath hitched as she met my confused gaze. "Please," she begged. "Just tell him you saw me and that I'm fine."

My hand shot out, capturing her chin. I stared at her, my brows furrowed, and growled, "Tell me what the fuck happened."

TWELVE

NORA

"MORNING," Luca said as I joined him at the breakfast counter.

"Why are you so fresh and awake and I'm... ugh, my head hurts."

He chuckled and shoved a glass of water and a couple of pain pills toward me. "Take these. It'll help."

He leaned back against the counter, watching me with those warm hazel eyes of his.

"Things got a little crazy, huh?"

"You could say that." After we'd gotten back to his apartment, Lucii had challenged the guys to beer pong. Only, Luca had no beer, so it became tequila pong. I'd crashed out after a couple of rounds and vaguely remembered someone carrying me into the guest bedroom.

"Thank you, for putting me to bed," I said.

"You remember that?" His brow arched.

"I remember... bits. I didn't do anything too embarrassing, did I?"

"I never kiss and tell." A faint smirk traced his lips.

"We didn't..." My cheeks burned.

"Relax," he chuckled, "you tried to kiss my face off, but I was the perfect gentleman."

"I did not," I gasped, and Luca's laughter only increased.

"You're teasing me." My brows furrowed, but relief seeped into me.

"I couldn't resist. Nothing happened. I don't take advantage of drunk girls. Even if they're as cute as you."

"Luca..."

"Nora..."

The air crackled with tension. I was ready to change the subject when Lucii breezed into the kitchen looking as fresh as a daisy.

"Why am I sitting here with a nest on my head," my hand went to my hair, trying to take the wild curls from my face, "and you two look like… like *that*."

"Good genes." Lucii shrugged, completely at home in a guy's kitchen. "Is there coffee?"

"I just made a fresh pot and I'm making pancakes."

"My hero." They shared a smile, and something twisted inside of me.

Luca wasn't mine… I had no right to feel jealous of their small interaction.

But did I want him to be mine?

That was the question I'd grappled with all night as we'd sat around until the early hours playing beer pong and listening to Nate regale us with stories of his college days.

"Where is Nate?" I asked her, because the last thing I remembered was the two of them getting up close and personal on Luca's couch.

"He already left."

"Oh. Are you seeing him again?" I teased.

"Maybe." She shrugged.

"Well, before you leave, you can disinfect my couch." Luca gave her a pointed look and the three of us burst into laughter.

"It was a fun night. We should do it again. Although we might have to find a girl for Isaac next time. I kinda got the impression he didn't come because he didn't want to play fifth wheel."

"Fifth wheel?" The words spilled out, even though I knew exactly what she was getting at.

Luca cleared his throat and turned around to tend to the pancakes. Lucii shot me an amused look, but I ducked my head, nursing my glass of water.

"Good thing we don't have classes until late morning," I said. "I'm not sure I could handle it."

"Nothing giant sunglasses, a strong coffee, and some Advil won't fix." She grinned. "I'm going to use the bathroom."

"Can you remember where it is?" Luca asked, and she nodded.

"I think I'm just going to go…" I got up but the room span. My hand shot out to steady myself, but Luca was there, gripping my shoulders as he stared down at me with concern in his eyes.

"You good?"

"I… yeah, thank you."

"You know, I wanted to ask—"

"Your apartment is so—my bad, am I interrupting something?"

We both turned to meet Lucii's suggestive grin.

"Uh, no, I just felt a little lightheaded. I'm going to head back to my apartment though and take a shower. I'll see you in class later?"

"Sure thing."

"But I made pancakes." Luca frowned, but I was already backing away from him.

I smiled weakly. "Maybe another time."

I hurried down the hall into the guest bedroom and gathered up my purse, shoes, and cell phone and slipped out of Luca's apartment.

Last night had been fun… but something had changed between us. The invisible line between us blurring. I was attracted to him, that was a given. He was handsome, and sweet, and good.

But there was just one glaring issue.

He wasn't Enzo.

"You should eat something," Ari said, concern lacing her words.

"I'm fine." I pushed the plate away from me and let out an exhausted sigh. "I'm just tired."

And classes so far today had been killer.

"You're burning the candle at both ends… you can't—"

"It was one night, babe. One night. Besides, it's freshman year. This is exactly what I'm supposed to be doing. Next year is for the hard work. This year is for partying and finding yourself."

"You did a pretty good job of finding yourself last night."

"Hey, what's that supposed to mean?" I didn't like the judgment in her tone.

Ari's expression softened. "I didn't mean it like that. I'm just worried about you. You're all alone in the apartment. Luca is—"

"He's good people, Ari. And he likes me. At least, I think he does. Is that so hard to believe?"

"Of course it isn't." She jerked back as if I'd slapped her. "Why would you even ask that?"

"I'm just grouchy."

"You mean hungover."

"Yeah, that too." My eyes fluttered closed. "Is it so wrong I let my hair down for a night?"

"Not at all. I just hope you're doing it for you and not to escape."

My eyes snapped open. "Say what?"

"I know you Nora. I'm your best friend. What happened with Enzo—"

"I think that ship has sailed, babe. He left."

He freaking left without uttering a word. I didn't ever imagine I was the kind of girl who could make a guy like Enzo stay… but a goodbye? That wasn't too much to ask.

"He did. And honestly, I want to say it's a good thing. But I can see you're hurting, and that makes you vulnerable."

"If you're worried about my honor, you needn't be. I lost my v-card in high school and it was completely unmemorable." I laughed, bitterly.

"Nora." Ari didn't join me. "I'm serious. Luca seems like a good guy. All I'm saying is if you jump into something with him, what happens when Enzo comes back?"

I suspected a whole lot of nothing. Whatever we had, or might have had, was gone. I saw it when he walked away from me at Arabella's party.

"Can we talk about something else? This is hurting my head," I grumbled.

"Here, take this." She slung a box of pills across the table. Luis was watching us from his position at the doors leading in and out of the food court. Students came and went either not noticing him or accepting his presence without question. I guess that's what happened when you went to school with a local celebrity.

But Arianne wasn't a celebrity to me. She was my best friend. My ride or die. The only problem was, now she was Nicco's ride or die too.

"Hey," I said, shaking off my solemn mood. "Do you think the two of—"

"Ladies," Matteo leaped over the back of the couch I was perched on and dropped down beside me. "What's good for lunch?"

"You can have mine." I pushed my plate toward him.

"What's wrong with it?"

"Nothing," Ari said, "she's hungover." Nicco sat down beside her and immediately pulled her into a passionate kiss.

"Do you have to do that in public?" Tristan, Arianne's cousin, also joined us.

"She's my wife, Capizola. If I want to kiss her, I—"

"Okay," he snapped, "I'm sorry I asked. Hungover on a school day, Nor? How rebellious of you." Tristan smirked and I flipped him off.

There had been a time, not so long ago, that I didn't know what side Tristan stood on. He'd been best friends with Scott Fascini, the psychopath responsible for kidnapping me and going after Nicco and Arianne.

It was all water under the bridge now, but I saw the lingering tension between Nicco and Tristan. They had both taken on the role of her protector, and at one point, Tristan had tried to protect her from the one thing she'd needed more than anything.

Nicco.

"Countdown to graduation, Tris," I said. "Are you ready?"

"Is anyone ever ready?" He shrugged, popping a fry into his mouth.

"You still determined to take off for a year and travel?"

"If Mom and Uncle Roberto get their way, I'll be heading up a department at Capizola Holdings. But I feel like I need to spread my wings before I put down roots."

"We need you," Ari said. "I need you."

A low rumble came from Nicco.

"Relax, husband," she teased him, "I need you too."

"Gross, I think I just regurgitated some chili dog." Matteo grabbed my bottle of water. "Mind?"

"Go for it." I motioned for him to continue.

"So how did things go with Captain America?"

"Captain America?" My brows knitted.

"Yeah, Luca. He has that whole Chris Evans vibe working for him."

"Now that you mention it, he kind of does look like Captain America," Nicco added.

I held up my hand. "Can we please stop referring to him as Captain America?"

"They have a point, Nor." Arianne chuckled.

"Oh God, not you too."

"Who's Luca?" Tristan said, watching us with mild confusion.

"Just some guy who wants in Nora's pant—"

"Enough!" I smashed my hand over Matteo's mouth, drowning out his voice. "Luca is my new neighbor."

"Ah gotcha." He smirked.

"I give up. I'm going to hang out somewhere else." I grabbed my bag and got up. "Somewhere where my friends aren't complete assholes."

"Nora, babe, don't be like that," Matteo called after me. "We're only joking."

I flipped him off over my shoulder and kept walking. The truth was, I didn't want to deal with any of this right now. I didn't want to deal with my confusing feelings for Luca or my unrelenting feelings for Enzo.

What I wanted was quiet. My hungover brain couldn't handle much else.

Just as I reached the doors out of the food court, a hand snagged my arm.

"Nora, wait."

"I'm really not in the mood, babe." I stared at my best friend with pleading eyes.

"I know, and I'm sorry. I didn't mean to—"

"No, you did nothing wrong. I'm just... ugh, I'm so confused."

"Why don't we blow off classes this afternoon and have some girl's time?"

"Yeah?" My mood instantly lifted.

"Yeah. It's been too long."

"Ice cream, face masks, and Magic Mike?" I asked, hopeful.

"If that's what you want, then that's what we'll do." She tucked herself into my side and we walked out of the food court like that.

"The guys are sorry too."

"No one needs to be sorry." Any other day, I would have given them some snarky reply. But I wasn't feeling particularly snarky today.

"Everything's different now," I whispered, allowing myself a vulnerable moment.

"I know." Ari let out a soft sigh, gripping my arm tighter. "But you're still my best friend, Nor. Nothing will ever change that. I hope you know that."

"I know," I replied.

Because I did.

Arianne stayed until she could no longer keep her eyes open. We'd gorged ourselves on ice cream and candy, drooling to the sexual revelation that was Channing Tatum and Alex Pettyfer.

Nicco sent Luis to pick her up, and I watched as he carried her down the hall, half-asleep. I closed my door and began cleaning up. This should have been our life together: movie nights and pamper sessions, sitting around gossiping about boys and classes.

But now she was married, and I was… pining after a guy who would never want me for more than what my body could give him.

A frustrated cry spilled from my lips as my chest heaved. I hated feeling like this. Weak and sorry for myself.

I wasn't weak.

I was a freaking firecracker.

I wasn't the kind of girl to sit around and wait for a guy to wake up and realize I was everything he needed.

I made things happen for myself. I took control of my own destiny.

And I refused to sit around and wait for Enzo Marchetti to pull his head out of his ass when there was another guy who saw me.

Luca saw me.

Without thinking, I marched out of my apartment and across the hall, banging on Luca's door.

"N-Nora?" He stared at me, wide-eyed, a towel wrapped firmly around his narrow waist. "Is something wrong?"

I didn't reply. Instead, I threw my arms around his neck and leaned up, crashing my mouth down on his.

"Whoa." His arm went around my waist as we stumbled back into his room, the door clicking shut behind us.

"Kiss me," I urged him, nervous energy zipping through my body. "I need for you to kiss me."

"Slow down…" He broke away, gazing down at me with concern. "Not that I'm complaining, because I'm not…"

"You don't want me?" I batted my eyelashes at him, liquid lust coursing through my veins.

I wanted this.

Needed it.

"Nora, you know I do."

"So, what's the problem?"

Because I could feel the evidence of his desire pressed up against my stomach.

"I don't want to be your rebound guy and I don't want you to do something you'll regret tomorrow."

His words were like a bucket of cold water and I pulled away, turning my back on him.

"You're hurting." It wasn't a question.

Luca stepped up behind me, running his hands up and down my shoulders. "Nora, look at me."

Slowly, I turned around, meeting his intense stare. "You are so fucking beautiful, and strong, and funny... I hate this guy, whoever he is, for making you doubt yourself." He pushed the messy curls from my face. "But if I have you, I'm going to want all of you. And I don't think you're ready for that." His thumb dropped to my mouth, lingering on the pillow of my bottom lip.

Energy pulsed around us, so thick I could almost taste it. I wanted him to kiss me. For the first time since I met Luca, I really *really* wanted him to kiss me.

So why didn't he?

"Luca?" His name fell from my lips in a whispered plea, but he didn't move.

He didn't do anything.

"This was clearly a mistake." Dejection burned through me as I tore out of his arms and retreated back toward the door.

"Nora, wait," he called, but my hand was already on the door handle. "Nora, please."

I spun around and met his apologetic gaze. "What, Luca? What is there left to say?"

He closed the distance between us until his hands gently cupped my face.

"I had a change of heart."

"What do you—"

His mouth captured mine in a bruising kiss.

Luca was kissing me.

He was kissing *me*.

And I was letting him.

THIRTEEN

ENZO

"I GOT A LEAD," Gino said the second I reached him.

It was a little after eight and we were at the restaurant beside the motel getting breakfast. The other patrons gave us a wide berth, but it wasn't anything I hadn't experienced before.

"About fucking time," I grumbled.

It had been six days since I left Verona. Six days of us chasing dead ends.

Whoever was orchestrating this whole thing knew how to stay off the grid.

The server brought over coffee and took our order. The second she turned her back, I said, "Before we get into what the hell we're going to do about this fucker, I need to ask you something."

"Go on."

"You ever seen Zander get violent with his girls?"

Gino's brow pinched. "He gets a bit handsy now and again but hurting them? Nah. He's all talk and no action that one."

I rubbed my jaw. "He asked me to go over and check on one of his girls. Caitlin O'Connell. But when I got over there, I recognized her. Found her crying in the bathroom at the club the other night."

"You think he's hurting her?"

"I don't know. She wouldn't tell me what happened. But if DiMarco is putting his hands on his girls... that shit don't fly with me."

He hissed between his teeth. "Word of advice, kid, don't get involved in another man's business. DiMarco is already a loose cannon. Don't give him a reason to cause a shitstorm we don't need right now. It was probably a John who got a little too enthusiastic."

I didn't like it. I didn't like it at all. But Gino was right. I was here to find out who was coming after the Family, not to get all up in Zander DiMarco's affairs. Besides, Caitlin had been unwilling to even let me inside her apartment, let alone interrogate her about what had happened. I'd left my number with her in case she needed anything, but I didn't expect to hear from her anytime soon.

"What's the plan?" I changed the subject.

"It's an address, an abandoned warehouse out by the river. The guy we worked over. I let him go."

"The fuck?" I gawked at him.

"Relax. Oldest trick in the book. Let a rat free and it'll lead you right back to its nest." He took a sip of his coffee. "I put a tracker on him and followed him out there. He met with another guy, but I didn't get a good look at him. Marc and Dixon have been staking out the place overnight. After our guy left, nobody else came or went."

"You think it's Alejandro?"

Gino nodded, and I clenched my fist against the table.

"When do we go?"

No one was supposed to know the truth about my father, especially not this asshole.

"Relax. Eat." Gino relaxed back in his chair. "It could be a long fucking day."

My skin vibrated with the need to find this motherfucker and get answers: who he was and what the fuck he hoped to achieve coming after the Family.

"Any word about Morello?" I asked Gino, trying to distract myself.

"He's out of the hospital. Won't be running any marathons for a while, but he'll be okay."

"That's good."

"Yeah, but listen, Enzo, we need to do this the right way. We need to find out what this fucker knows and what he plans on doing with it."

I nodded. "How are we doing this?"

"Just you and me initially. We'll stake the place out and bide our time until nightfall."

Which was about seven-and-a-half hours away.

Fuck. Today was going to drag like a bitch. But for as much as I wanted to end this thing, I also didn't want to risk him slipping through our fingers, so I would follow Gino's lead and wait.

"We end this thing tonight," he added. "Then you can get back to Verona and sink deep into your woman and let her absolve you of some of your sins."

"I don't have a woman," I argued.

"Kid, you might tell yourself that, but you ain't foolin' anyone. Seen that look in your eyes one too many times."

"I don't know what you're talking about."

He smirked. "Whatever you say, kid."

Just then, the server brought over our order and Gino dropped all talk of women to dig into his breakfast.

It didn't matter.

He was wrong.

I didn't have a woman.

Didn't want one, didn't need one.

I'd seen what the love of a good woman did to men like me. Made men. It distracted them. Rendered them weak. It blinded them with jealousy, pulling their loyalties in too many directions.

"Eat up, you're going to need your energy." Gino levelled me with a hard look. One that told me all I needed to know…

Tonight, we would finish this.

By the time the sun began to set over the city skyline, I was cold, hungry, and itching for a fight.

"I'm going to take a piss," I said, shouldering the door of my Pontiac.

"Make it quick. This asshole hasn't left the warehouse all day. He's gotta surface eventually."

Marc and Dixon had met us right at the spot this morning, informing us the guy was still inside. There had been no one coming or going all fucking day, which meant he was in there somewhere, biding his time the same way we were.

The brisk air stung my face as I went around the rear end of the car and took a leak behind a tree. We'd survived the day on a few stale chips and cans of soda. Part of me wanted to say, 'fuck it' and storm the warehouse, but as Gino kept reminding me, it wasn't only my ass on the line. Uncle Toni wanted answers. He wanted to know who was messing with us and why. And Gino Lupo had a process.

One that included a lot of sitting around and talking about the fucking weather.

I wiped my hands down my jeans and got back in the car. Gino was peering through his binoculars.

"Anything?" I asked.

"The security light just came on. But I don't think—wait a second. Wait a—fuck, yeah, there's our guy." He shoved the lenses at me.

My heart beat hard in my chest as I focused on the guy in their line of sight. I didn't recognize him, but it was dark, and he was wearing all-black with a skull cap pulled over his head.

"We should move now," I said, eager to get this over with. But Gino's arm shot out in front of me.

"We wait. If he leaves, I want to get a look inside."

"And if he doesn't come back?"

"He will. It's his nest. They always come back."

We watched the guy climb into a beat-up truck and drive off.

"Okay, let's go. Stay behind me and don't fuck this up. This is recon only."

"Recon?" I sneered. "We've been sitting in my car all fucking day."

"What's wrong, kid? The life not as glamorous as you thought it would be?"

I hadn't really given it much thought. But I knew Gino and his guys got their hands dirty and I wanted in on the action.

"Let's go see what this pompinara is hiding." Gino pulled on some gloves before slipping out of the car and disappearing into the night.

I did the same, following him, sticking to the shadows. The warehouse was in a disused industrial area along the river. Its on-site security was long gone, leaving us to explore unnoticed.

Gino ushered me to the side of the building and mouthed, "We'll check for another way in."

I nodded, following him around the outer perimeter until we came across another door. It was secured with a padlock, but Gino produced some small bolt cutters from inside his leather jacket and made quick work of getting it off.

"Bingo," he whispered, gently cracking the door open. "Close it behind you and keep your eyes peeled."

"Got it."

Darkness consumed us as we entered a narrow passageway. Gino pulled out a flashlight and guided us deeper into the abandoned building. At the end there was a doorway leading into a vast open space.

"Anything?" I asked, growing impatient.

"Fuck, you need to see this." He disappeared inside and I followed.

"What the fuck?" My eyes went to the far wall. It was covered in newspaper cuttings, photographs, and string. Like one of those boards from a crime documentary.

"He's been watching us," I said, moving closer to the display. There were pictures of Morello outside his store. DiMarco's and numerous other local businesses in and around Providence that had ties with the Family.

"This doesn't make any sense," I mumbled while Gino took photo after photo on his cell, probably to forward to Uncle Toni.

I reached out, ghosting my fingers over a recent photo of me, Nicco, and Matteo with Alessia. A chill ran down my spine. He wasn't just watching Providence; this fucker had been to Verona. He'd been watching *us*. There were other photos of Uncles Toni and Michele. A newspaper article reporting on Nicco and Arianne's wedding.

"Who the fuck is this asshole?"

Alejandro was supposed to be connected to the Mexican cartel in Connecticut. This didn't seem like their MO.

"Someone who knows too much," Gino said over my shoulder.

"But what's the endgame? It doesn't make any sense."

Morello and DiMarco's were business associates, they weren't legitimate Marchetti businesses. Why mess around with the small timers, when with all this intel, he could come right for the head of the snake?

"We're missing something here..." Gino mused.

But something caught my attention. It wasn't a sound so much as a smell.

"What is that?" I searched the immediate area, tracking the familiar scent. It was the same coppery twang I remembered from my childhood whenever my father and uncles took us hunting.

The unforgettable smell of death.

"We should call for backup," Gino said, but I was transfixed on finding the source of the pungent scent. With little natural light in the warehouse, I pulled out my cell phone to use the flashlight to guide my way. Old shelving was littered around the space, leaning against walls, and toppled over like a haphazard obstacle course. On the far wall there was a row of busted up lockers. I weaved through the mess aware of the sticky, squelchy sound underfoot.

"Gino," I called, and he came running, grinding to a halt when I dropped the beam and illuminated the pool of blood surrounding the lockers.

"Do you want to do the honors?" he asked me, and I leaned over, yanking open the first locker.

"Holy shit." The dead body toppled out, splatting over the floor in a spray of red mist.

"Fuck," Gino hissed. "That's Alejandro."

"Wha—"

Just then the clatter of footsteps sounded from somewhere behind us and we both glanced in that direction.

Someone else was in the warehouse.

Had the guy doubled back? Or had that been his intention all along?

The question evaporated as a figure came out of nowhere, knocking into me and sending me crashing to the bloody ground.

"Enzo," Gino roared as I tried to buck the guy off me. But with the blood acting as a lubricant, it was impossible to get any leverage.

"Surprise." He glared down at me, trapping my body between his and the cold ground beneath me.

"Get the fuck off me." I slammed my forehead into his nose, and he rolled away, grunting in agony. Gino leaned down and grabbed him by his collar, dragging him to his feet. But at the last second, I saw the glint of the blade.

"Gino, watch ou—"

The guy brought his hand high and jabbed it down in one fell swoop, the knife sliding into Gino's jugular like butter. All I could do was stand there and watch as dark-red blood spurted out of his neck.

"H-help me." He gurgled, clutching his neck with both hands, blood oozing down his gloved fingers, as the guy yanked his knife free and stepped away.

Gino staggered backward, swaying a little.

"Fuck, man." I rushed to his side, hardly able to believe what was happening. My hands went to cover his, trying to stem the blood. But it was everywhere seeping through over my gloves like a red river. "Tell me what to do? Tell me..."

"Don't let him e-escape." Gino's eyes went over my shoulder and I glanced back to the guy taking off toward the passageway.

"Go," he breathed with difficulty. The life was draining away from him before my very eyes.

"Fuck, FUCK!" I let out a guttural roar as Gino bled out in my arms.

"G-go." His eyes rolled.

I didn't want to leave him, but when I heard the rumble of an engine, I knew it was now or never.

"I'm sorry, man," I whispered, laying Gino down. He was unconscious now, blood still spurting out of his wound. "I'm so fucking sorry."

I ran out of the warehouse and to my car, ripping the door open and barreling inside. The truck was already on the move, but it was a rusted piece of shit that wouldn't out gun my baby.

Digging my cell from my jeans, I managed to dial Uncle Toni.

"Enzo, son? Thank fuck. Where are you?"

"Gino… he… he's…"

Fuck. There was so much blood.

"I'm sending back up. Just tell me where you are."

"I'm going after him." The words came out icy cold, detached from the bloodbath I'd just left. There would be time to mourn Gino, to raise a glass for him and pay our respects. But that time wasn't now.

"Lorenzo, listen to me. I want you to pull over and take a breath, son. We'll get this fucker, we will. But not tonight. Not like this."

"I can get him. I can—"

"*Vaffanculo!*" Uncle Toni roared. "I am not asking, Enzo. I am giving you a direct order. Pull the fuck over."

Before I could talk myself out of it, I hit disconnect and threw my cell into the center console. I needed to do this—I needed to know why he had all those photographs and newspaper cuttings of my family and friends. The need to know burned through me like acid and was the only thing spurring me on. That and blind rage.

I'd been around death, too much for a twenty-year-old guy. But I'd never watched the life drain, literally drain, right out of a friend before. A guy who had taken me under his wing without question.

I followed the truck, keeping a safe distance. He obviously hadn't noticed I'd given chase, making no effort to speed away. He'd taken the road out of Providence, joining the highway toward Verona. Nicco and Matteo blew up my cell phone, no doubt up to speed from Uncle Toni about what had gone down. I hoped that Marc and Dixon had gotten there in time to get help, but deep down in my gut, I knew Gino was gone.

There was too much blood. I was covered in the stuff. It clung to my clothes like rainwater. The cloying scent only fueling my need for vengeance.

"I'm coming for you," I chanted to myself, driven only by rage. Part of me knew I should heed Uncle Toni's orders to step down, but I couldn't—I couldn't let this motherfucker escape. So I stayed on his ass, keeping the rusty-black truck in my line of sight.

But the guy didn't drive to Verona. He pulled off at a gas station about five miles out.

I made the turn and rolled into the forecourt, hiding between a couple of trucks parked up for the night. The guy climbed out of his truck, pulling on a black jacket over his hoodie. I couldn't see much of his face, hidden under a ball cap he'd obviously pulled on at some point on the drive here.

He disappeared inside and I waited.

My cell phone began blaring again and I finally grabbed it. "Yeah?"

"What the fuck, Enzo?" Nicco growled. "You were told to stand down."

"And let this fucker escape? He knows us, Nic. He fucking knows *us*. And he knows about—" The words died in my throat.

"I know... fuck, I know. But I don't like this. He's clearly dangerous."

I wanted to argue that so was I, but another truck rolled into the forecourt, blocking my line of sight to the store and the guy's truck.

"I need to go." I hung up, cussing the truck driver.

I had no choice now but to drive around the gas pumps to the small parking lot in front of the store if I wanted to keep an eye on his truck. I made the split decision and edged out my spot and slowly crawled the car around the forecourt. But I was too fucking late, the truck already peeling out of the gas station and back onto the highway. I slammed my foot down on the gas and took off, the screech of tires filling the air. I wasn't about to lose this guy for anything.

I just hoped no one called the cops before I got to him.

FOURTEEN

NORA

I'D JUST CLIMBED into bed when a knock at my door rang out through the apartment.

God, I hoped it wasn't Luca. I wasn't ready to see him again yet, not after last night. I'd crept back into my apartment in the early hours of the morning after waking in his bed, his warm body tucked against mine.

My feelings for Luca were confusing. *I* was confused. So I'd taken a day off classes to spend time on some self-love. There wasn't much that a day of slumming around in lounge pants couldn't solve. I'd binge-watched some mindless TV, eaten my bodyweight in snacks, and enjoyed a homemade face mask, manicure, and pedicure. I felt shiny and new, even if my emotional state was still a mess.

Gingerly, I climbed out of bed and pulled an MU hoodie over my pajamas. It barely covered my legs, but it wasn't anything Luca or Maurice hadn't already seen.

But when I checked the peephole, my world imploded.

"Enzo?" I yanked open the door and stared at the guy who had left without so much as a word. "Oh my God, what happened?"

He was covered from head to toe in blood. A dark prince with death on his shoulder.

"Enzo?" I said again when he didn't reply. He just stood there, still and silent, his eyes soulless.

"Come on." I gently pulled him inside, noticing the way he flinched when I touched him. I ignored the pinch of dejection though. He was here and by the looks of him, he needed me.

I checked the hallway, noticing the splatters of blood. Crap.

"Wait right here," I said to Enzo as I went into my bedroom and retrieved my cell phone.

"Who are you—"

I held up my finger at Enzo, silencing him. "Maurice," I said the second he answered. "It's me."

"Miss Abato, what can I—"

"I need you at La Stella now, there's been a… Enzo is here."

"Lorenzo?"

"Yes."

"Is he okay?" Concern laced his words. "Are you safe?"

I smiled at that. If only he knew.

"Yes, I'm quite safe. Enzo won't hurt me." My eyes found Enzo's across the room, but his cloudy expression barely flinched. "You might want to bring some cleaning fluid and a fresh set of clothes."

Maurice sucked in a sharp breath. "I'll be right there. Whatever you do, do not let Enzo leave. Not until I've spoken to Mr. Marchetti."

"Got it and thank you." I hung up, dropping my cell phone onto the sideboard.

Enzo tracked my every move as I slid the safety chain into place and went to the kitchen drawer and grabbed a trash bag.

"You should probably take those off and take a shower," I said. "Maurice is bringing you some clean clothes. There are towels and a robe in the bathroom. You can use whatever you need."

"Why are you doing this for me?" His lip twitched.

"The same reason you ended up on my doorstep and not anyone else's." I smiled weakly. "You know where the bathroom is. I'll give you some space."

Enzo stared at me intently, as if he was seeing me for the first time. I wanted to take that feeling and run with it, but I wasn't some naïve little girl. I knew from the state of him, whatever had gone down tonight wasn't good. And from his detached mood, I knew he was probably in shock.

For as much as I wanted to believe that Enzo being here changed things, I refused to let myself go there.

"You should go get cleaned up, you're a mess."

Blood caked his hands and face, smeared up his neck and soaked through his clothes. The sight was terrifying, but it didn't change the fact Enzo Marchetti was still one of the most beautiful men I'd ever laid eyes on.

He opened his mouth to speak but no words came… and that small flash of hope inside me flickered out.

This doesn't change anything. I had to remember that.

Enzo snatched up the bag and stalked off down the hall, leaving a trail of bloody footprints. I wasn't even sure he was aware of just how blood-soaked he was.

I released a shaky breath and then set about cleaning up. When I was done, I threw the towel in the basin and braced myself against the counter. This was life with a mafioso. Bloodstained clothes and late night clean up jobs. Yet, the second I saw Enzo standing there on my doorstep, the only thing I wanted to do, was protect him. To pull him inside and comfort him.

What did that say about me if I was prepared to act first and ask questions later?

Across the hall was a good guy who wanted me. A good, honest man who could give me a secure, stable future. A man who would be there when I needed him.

Enzo wasn't that guy.

He dealt in dark deeds and secrets.

Yet, my heart beat harder for him than it ever had for another.

There was no explanation for that kind of connection. No rulebook for why some hearts entwined so deeply when others didn't.

It just was.

My cell phone started to vibrate, startling me from my reverie. "Hello?" I whispered.

"Nora, thank God. What happened? I heard Nicco tell Matteo that Enzo is at your place?"

"He just got here like five minutes ago."

"And?"

"It's bad, Ari… really bad. He was covered head to toe in blood and had this look in his eyes…" A violent shiver skated down my spine.

"You said *was* covered in blood?"

"He's taking a shower. I called Maurice, I didn't know what else to do."

"You did the right thing. Nicco is just talking to his father. Are you okay?"

"I guess… I mean, God, Ari…" The threads of my control slowly began to unravel as the weight of what was happening began to sink deep into my bones. "You didn't see how broken he looked."

"Do you want me to come over?"

"No!" I rushed out a little too hastily. "I just mean… it's Enzo. I don't think we should crowd him. I'm sure Nicco will know what to do."

In hindsight, I perhaps should have called him first, but Maurice was my personal bodyguard. He lived a three-minute walk away, and I knew he'd contact Nicco and Antonio Marchetti.

"Okay, text me if you need anything. And Nora…" She hesitated, and I knew I wasn't going to like her next words. "Be careful. It sounds like whatever happened was bad… Enzo will be hurting, he'll be confused. I don't want you to misread anything."

"Remember he doesn't want me, yep, I think I've got it," I said, unable to keep the bitterness out of my voice.

"Nora," she sighed. "That isn't what I meant."

"I'm fine, Ari. You don't have to worry about me. I'll text you later." I hung up before she could impart any more *advice* on me.

I wasn't stupid, I knew Enzo was running on autopilot right now. Trauma did that to people. But he'd still ended up at *my* apartment. I couldn't just completely ignore that.

I made us some hot chocolate while I waited for Maurice. He showed up ten minutes later, armed with a duffel bag full of clothes for Enzo and cleaning fluid.

"Where is he?" he asked.

"Taking a shower."

"Good. When he's done, I want you to give him these and tell him to sit tight. The boss is coming straight here."

"Antonio Marchetti is coming here?"

Maurice ran a hand down his face. "He needs to speak with Enzo. You going to be okay? I can take you somewhere—"

"She stays."

I felt Enzo's deep graveled words all the way to the pit of my stomach.

"Got it." Maurice nodded. "There are fresh clothes in the bag. I'll handle the mess outside."

"Fuck," Enzo gritted out, standing there with just a white towel wrapped around his waist. Heat flowed through me like lava. "I didn't even think," he added.

"Relax, I got it. Just sit tight and wait for Toni to get here."

Enzo nodded, his eyes icy cold as they remained fixed on my face.

"I'll be right outside, Miss Abato."

"It's Nora," I called after him, letting out a sigh of frustration as he closed the door without correcting himself.

Silence echoed through the apartment as my eyes once again found Enzo. "I made us hot chocolate."

It had seemed like a good thing two minutes ago, but now I felt like a child offering the Big Bad Wolf a candy sucker.

"Thanks." Enzo let out a steady breath, his ink-covered abs contracting with the motion. "I should probably—" He picked up the bag.

"Yeah, okay." I swallowed, fire rising in my stomach like a tidal wave.

Enzo took off down the hall and disappeared into the guest bedroom. He'd been here before, but it seemed like a lifetime ago. When things were simpler, and we didn't have so much blood and destruction filling the cracks between us.

I grabbed my mug and got comfy on the couch. But I'd barely settled when there was another knock at the door.

Assuming it was Maurice, I placed down my drink and traipsed to the door, my heart doing another leap when I found Luca standing there.

"You're okay," he breathed, "thank fuck."

"L-Luca." I blinked. "What are you doing here?"

"I heard a commotion out in the hall and saw all the blood… what the hell—"

"You must be Luca."

Every cell in my body fired to life as Enzo stepped up behind me.

"Let me guess, you're the guy." Luca's gaze dropped to mine, a hundred questions there.

"Now is not a good time," I said, forcing my lips into a thin smile.

"Seriously?" Luca dropped his voice an octave. "You're going to do this after what happened last night?"

Enzo bristled behind me and I let out an exasperated breath. "You should go," I said firmly. "I'm okay, I promise. I'll explain everything tomorrow."

Luca's eyes narrowed, hurt flashing there. He lifted his dejected gaze to Enzo and electricity crackled between them.

"Luca, please…" I pulled at his arm. "I need you to go."

"Fine. But I'm right across the hall if you need me."

"I know, thank you," I mouthed, trying to silently convey that everything was okay.

But it wasn't.

I was literally stuck between the two men in my life.

Luca backed up slowly, reluctance etched into his expression. Running a brisk hand over his face, he spun on his heel and disappeared into his apartment. I closed the door with a soft sigh, turning to meet Enzo's hard glare.

"You fuck him?"

"You care?"

He made a clucking sound, pressing his lips into a thin line.

"You want a fight?" I let out a resigned sigh. "You won't find one here, not tonight." Barging past him, I went back to the couch and sat down.

Being around Enzo was always intense. He was like the sun, pulling everything else into its orbit. Except he wasn't the sun, not in the way most of us imagined the sun as a warm, inviting thing that made everything seem better.

He was something much worse.

Fiery, hot destruction.

Enzo grabbed his mug of hot chocolate and joined me, choosing the chair instead of the couch. I tried not to overanalyze why.

"Do you want to talk about what happened?" I asked.

"You know I can't. But for what it's worth, I am sorry I brought this to your door."

"So why did you?" I tucked my feet up onto the couch, noticing Enzo's dark eyes follow the line of my legs. A faint smirk traced his lips when I pulled the blanket off the back of the couch and covered myself.

"The truth?"

I nodded, my heart crashing wildly beneath my rib cage.

"I didn't even think. After I…" He inhaled a sharp breath. "I got in my car and just drove and ended up here. I know I shouldn't have come… fuck." His fist collided with the arm of my chair and I was relieved it was fabric and not wood.

"Antonio will be here soon."

"I'm sorry. I'm so fucking sorry, Gattina."

My breath caught at the pet name. He'd used it as an insult before, but this was different.

"So Luca... he seems nice." His expression darkened even more at the mention of my neighbor.

"He's a good guy."

"Is he treating you right?"

"We're not together, Enzo..."

"But you want to... be with him?"

No, you stubborn asshole, I want to be with you. I silenced the thoughts. If I pushed, Enzo would run. And he was here, talking to me for the first time in what felt like forever.

"It's not that simple."

"No," he let out a soft sigh, "I guess it isn't." Enzo sank into the chair, dropping his head back and closing his eyes. He was crashing. Whatever had happened tonight, the adrenaline was fizzling out.

I sat there, watching him. The clothes Maurice had brought over were dark gray sweats and a t-shirt that fit Enzo's big muscled framed like a second skin. It was rare to see him out of his jeans and black sweaters or shirts, but I wasn't complaining. Enzo could make a burlap sack look hot. He oozed sex appeal. From his electric blue eyes to the tattoos snaking up his arms and around his broad shoulders.

I wanted so badly to go to him, to trace the angles of his jaw with my fingertips and take some of his pain for my own. But a loud knock at the door demanded my attention.

Enzo bolted upright and I smiled. "It's probably your uncle."

"Shit, yeah." He ran a hand through his damp hair.

"I'll get it and then give the two of you some space."

"Thanks."

I got up and went to the door, inhaling a calming breath before welcoming Antonio Marchetti, boss of the Marchetti crime family Dominion, into my apartment.

My home.

Totally not how I saw tonight ever going.

FIFTEEN

ENZO

I WATCHED Nora disappear into her bedroom. I'd heard Maurice suggest she go someplace else, heard Uncle T mutter the same thing when she answered the door and invited him into her home. And I'd told him the same thing as I'd told Maurice. Nora stayed.

I'd already made a colossal fuck up by coming here. I wasn't about to put her at any more risk by sending her off somewhere I didn't have eyes on her.

No, it was better she was here, with me. Where I could keep her safe.

"Gino?" I asked, satisfied Nora was out of earshot.

"He's gone, son. I'm sorry."

"Fuck." I scrubbed my face, feeling the weight of Gino's death heavy on my shoulders.

"Don't do that," Uncle Toni said. "Don't carry this too. Gino knew the risks of the life. We all do. He died for this family and when the time is right, we will honor him into the afterlife. But first I need to know what the hell happened down there?"

"He sent you the photos?" Uncle Toni nodded and I continued. "Gino got a lead on a guy holed up at a warehouse in a disused industrial area along the river. We thought it was Dominic Alejandro. Marc and Dixon staked out the place overnight, we took over and spent the entire day watching. No one came or went." I grabbed one of the bottles of water Nora had left out for us.

She was fucking good at this stuff, so cool and composed. Most girls would have slammed the door in my face or called the cops when they saw all the blood. But not Nora. She was made of different stuff. Strong and sassy and so fucking selfless.

"Enzo, son… I know it's late, but I need to know everything."

Of course he did. There would need to be cleanup, a plan for the next steps. Uncle Toni would have guys out there within minutes of giving the order to look for the asshole toying with us.

"He finally left the warehouse, so Gino wanted to go check out his nest. We watched him drive away, made sure the coast was clear, and broke into the building. That's when we found the photos and the dead body."

"Bodies." Uncle Toni's expression turned grim. "Three in total. All stuffed in lockers."

"Gino said it was Alejandro."

"It looks likely."

"Do we know who the others are yet?"

"No, but I have guys working on it. Michele is already on his way to Providence."

"Is it safe?"

"He's taking precautions."

I nodded.

We were Marchetti. We didn't cower from our enemies. But when they had an inside edge, the rules were different, and everyone felt the pressure.

"He knows us, Uncle T. Like personally. When he attacked us, he said *surprise*." I'd forgotten until now or blocked it out. It had been a crazy couple of hours.

"He knows me. How is that even possible?" I stared at my uncle, hoping he had the answers I'd yet been able to find.

"I don't know, son. But I give you my word, we'll get to the bottom of this. What happened after he attacked Gino?"

"He took off. I gave chase until about five miles out of Verona. I lost him at a gas station." He must have taken the first exit and disappeared on the underpass. By the time I realized I'd lost him, it was too late, and I'd kept on driving.

"You should come home with me and—"

"Actually," my eyes flicked toward the hall, "I think I'm going to stay here."

He gave me a sharp nod and stood. "Niccolò is very fond of Miss Abato. Arianne too…" He left the words hanging. He didn't need to say it. It was only what everyone else thought—that Nora was too fucking good for a guy like me. But I couldn't leave her, not tonight. Not until I knew she was one hundred percent safe.

"I want round the clock security on this place," I said.

"It's already done." Uncle Toni waited for me to stand before pulling me in for a hug. "We have faced worse, Lorenzo. We will get to the bottom of this and Gino will be avenged, I swear to you. La Famiglia prima di tutto." He gripped my shoulder tight in promise. "Now go be with your woman. I have a woman of my own waiting for me at home."

His hearty chuckle filled Nora's apartment. It was good to see him finally admitting his feelings for Genevieve, his long-standing housekeeper.

After the truth came out about Aunt Lucia, we'd all expected him to spiral into a dark hole. But he hadn't.

I guess he was a better man than me.

"Try and get some rest."

Rest was the last thing on my mind. Earlier, on Nora's couch I had almost dropped off, but now... now I had restless energy zipping through me. I needed a drink or to fight or to...

Fuck.

I swallowed hard as I walked my uncle out of Nora's apartment.

"Maurice will be right outside and I'm posting two guys at the door. I'll call you when I know anything."

"Thanks," I said.

He disappeared down the hall and I closed the door, locking it and checking it twice. Then I padded into Nora's bathroom and retrieved all my weapons. My brass knuckles, two knives, and my pistol.

I wanted them all close by in case anything should happen.

Knocking on the bedroom door, I waited, but Nora didn't answer.

"Gattina?" I said, pushing the door open quietly and slipping inside. Nora was asleep, curled up on the bed.

The sight of her was like a lightning bolt to the chest. Without overthinking it, I dropped my weapons on the nightstand and stripped out of my clothes before pulling back the covers and climbing into bed behind her.

It was a bad idea.

The worst one I'd had in a while. But I needed to feel her soft curves against my body. To know she was safe in my arms.

Nora hadn't been in any of the photographs, but I didn't like the idea that this fucker knew about us, about Arianne. Because we all led back to Nora and she'd been through enough already.

When shit had got bad with Scott Fascini and Nora had been kidnapped, I'd been beside myself. He'd taken her right from under my nose. That kind of guilt didn't just evaporate. And I'd vowed to myself, no matter what did or didn't happen between us, that I would never let anything happen to her again.

That's why it had been so easy to walk away.

To protect her.

Not only from myself but also from the darkness of the world I inhabited.

Hooking my arm around her waist, I dragged Nora into the hard lines of my body. She murmured softly, snuggling closer. Wiggling her perfect round ass right against my crotch.

"You stayed," she whispered, her voice thick with sleep.

"Needed you, Gattina." I tucked my chin into the crook of her neck and breathed her in.

"Why do you call me that?"

"Because you're soft right here." My fingers dipped to Nora's navel and stroked her smooth skin.

"And..."

"And you have sharp claws when you need them. You protect those you care about fiercely."

"Keep going..." Her gentle laughter wrapped around me and made some of the tension in my muscles ebb away.

I'd forgotten how easy it was to just *be* with her. No bullshit or pretenses. I don't know how she did it, but Nora disarmed me.

"Enzo?" She turned in my arms, staring up at me through her thick, dark lashes.

"We should get some sleep, it's late." And I'd already woken her once.

"I know there's a lot you can't tell me, and I get it. I do. But if you ever want to talk about anything, I'm here for you. I just want you to know that."

Fuck.

This girl.

This strong, brave, gutsy girl.

"I wish it were that simple," I said, plucking one of her stray curls between my fingers. "But this isn't a fairytale, Gattina."

"You think I don't know that? You think I don't know that you're not the hero of this story, but the villain?"

Her words slayed me. It was as if she'd opened up my chest and looked right into my fucking soul.

"Good and bad aren't two sides of a coin, Enzo. They're two ends of the same piece of string. We all have the capacity to be good just like we all have the capacity to be bad. A thief is a thief until he gives his wares to those less fortunate than himself. Then he becomes the hero of their story."

My lips curved. "It's a nice sentiment but—"

"No buts." She pressed a single kiss to my lips, her touch like fire, branding me to the bone.

"Just because someone makes bad choices doesn't mean they're inherently bad, just as someone who makes good choices isn't always inherently good. We're human, we all have imperfections and flaws.

"You say you're bad for me, but I think you'd go to great lengths to protect me. Even from yourself." She peered up at me, hesitating before she reached for me, gently stroking my jaw.

I snagged her wrist, holding her arm there. "Don't. I didn't stay for this." Although my body always had other ideas whenever she was around.

Nora nodded, withdrawing her hand. I didn't know whether to be disappointed or relieved, but I was bone weary and desperate to close my eyes and find peace.

"Goodnight, Enzo," she whispered, turning away from me. I dragged her body back to me and fitted us together once more.

"Goodnight, Gattina."

I tucked my face against Nora's soft skin and closed my eyes... letting her be my anchor for the night.

"She didn't leave." My father wore a smug smirk as he spoke the words. "She found out what I'd done and threatened to tell you. Always so loyal," he said.

"You're telling me you killed my wife?" Uncle Toni trembled, anger rippling off him like a violent storm.

I couldn't believe what I was hearing. My father—my own fucking father was a traitor... and he'd killed my aunt, the boss' wife. What was this nightmare?

"I'll fucking gut you and feed you to the fish." Uncle Toni stormed toward my father, but I ripped my pistol out of my jeans, pointed and fired the shot, blowing a hole right through the bastard's skull.

Everyone stared at me as if I'd lost my fucking mind. And maybe I had. Maybe this was all a sick, twisted nightmare I would wake up from any second.

"You good, son?" Uncle Toni was in front of me now, trying to peel the pistol from my hands.

"Better than him," I said, but it didn't sound like me.

"What do you want us to do with the body?" Uncle Michele asked.

"Burn him for all I care," I said, before spinning out of the room and stalking out of there. But as I reached the door, my father appeared, a hole right through his skull.

"You think just because I'm dead, I'm gone? I'll haunt you for the rest of your days, SON. You can kill me, burn me, and curse me..." His body began to go up in flames. "But I'm a part of you, Lorenzo. My blood runs through your veins. And you will never—"

"Enzo, wake up. It's just a dream... it's just—"

Something touched me and my eyes snapped open right as my hand flew out and grabbed it.

"Enzo," someone cried. "It's me... it's only me."

"N-Nora?" I blinked, trying to figure out what the fuck was going on. My grip on her throat relaxed a little, but I didn't release her. Slowly, the memories from last night filtered into my mind.

The warehouse...

Gino...

The blood... so much fucking blood...

Finding myself on Nora's doorstep...

"Are you okay?"

"I think that ship has long sailed, Gattina," I ground out.

My thumb stroked her jaw and Nora smothered a moan. She liked a rough touch, being dominated, and in the past I'd been all too willing to oblige her. But something felt different between us now.

Something I didn't want to acknowledge.

"Did you fuck him?"

Luca. I scoffed. He looked like a pussy. Mooning after Nora with those puppy dog eyes. She didn't need an All-American boy next door; she needed a guy who knew how to handle her.

"Enzo, I thought we weren't going—"

"Did. You. Fuck. Him?"

Anger flashed in her eyes as she lifted her chin in defiance. Even with my hand wrapped around her throat, Nora wasn't scared. Turned on maybe, but never scared.

Jesus, this fucking girl.

If I had the capacity to ever love someone, it would be someone exactly like Nora. She was damn near perfect.

"And if I had? You pushed me away, Enzo. You did that. You really expect me to believe you haven't been fucking half of Verona?"

She wasn't angry, just resigned... and it fucking stung.

Because she was right.

Well, maybe not about the fucking part. But I hadn't been a saint. There had been other girls. Faceless girls I'd tried to lose myself in when the voices in my head got too loud.

"See... you're not so innocent. So don't come around here, acting like you care when we both know you don't care enough."

"They're not you." The words were out before I could stop them.

"Excuse me?"

"You heard me, Gattina." My hand slid around the back of her neck and anchored her to me. "They're never fucking you."

I hated it.

Hated the idea another guy had touched her, teased and tasted her. It brought out a primal need to thump my chest and roar her name.

Nora was mine.

Deep down, the caveman instincts buried inside me had claimed her long ago. But my head, my fucking head, knew it couldn't ever be.

This was as good as it got. Stolen touches in the dark. Whispered words in the night.

I didn't know how to love a girl like Nora. Not the way she deserved. I knew how to make her scream, to bring her body pleasure over and over again... but love?

What the fuck did a guy like me know about a thing like that?

"Enzo... we can't keep doing this." Nora touched her head to mine, inhaling a breath so deep I felt it down to the pit of my stomach.

"You make it quiet, Gattina. *You*."

"Sometimes I wish I didn't." Her lips curved into a sad smile, the raw honesty in her words gutting me like a fish.

It wasn't fair to do this to her, not again. But I'd never claimed to be a good guy. I needed her. I needed to sink inside her warm, wet heat and chase away the demons that haunted my every waking thought.

She was strong.

So fucking strong. It would hurt when the sun came up and our masks slid back into place but for now, right here, I wanted to pretend that I wasn't the villain.

"Be with me, Gattina. Make it all go away." I ghosted my mouth over hers, feeling her shudder beneath my touch.

"You already have me," she whispered, and it was all the permission I needed.

In one swift motion, I rolled Nora underneath me, pinning her against the mattress with my hips. Her skin felt like heaven against mine. Soft and smooth and fucking alluring.

"Nemmeno immagini cosa ho intenzione di farti." Her lips parted as her breath caught. "I am going to fuck him right out of you, so you never forget who owns this pussy." My hand slipped between us, cupping her roughly.

But Nora didn't protest, she arched into my touch like the greedy little kitty I knew she was.

"You want this?" I slipped my fingers into her pajama shorts and teased her.

She pressed her lips together, nodding.

"Say it," I demanded. "You want it… say it."

"Y-yes." Nora gasped when I slowly pushed a finger inside her. "Yes, I want it. I want you, Enzo."

"I'm going to make you purr, Gattina." I kissed her jaw, trailing my tongue over the seam of her lips as I worked another finger inside her. "And then I'm going to make you come so hard you see stars."

SIXTEEN

NORA

KISSING ENZO WAS LIKE DROWNING. He stole the breath from my lungs and all thought from my mind. I melted into him as his tongue curled around mine in slow, expert licks. He didn't just kiss me—he devoured me.

I'd known the second I opened the door to him tonight, that this was inevitable. We couldn't be in the same vicinity without something happening between us.

We were magnets.

Drawn together by some invisible force.

But like magnets, we attracted *and* repelled, and I knew come morning, this moment would all be a distant memory. But I could live with that. Enzo needed me *right now*. He needed to lose himself in me. He needed me to chase away his demons and I would.

There wasn't much I wouldn't do for this complicated guy. I knew Arianne wouldn't understand. Later, when the sun rose and she heard it in my voice or saw it in my eyes, I knew she wouldn't understand why I continually let Enzo back in.

Maybe part of myself didn't quite understand it either. But when we were together, in these rare moments of tender touches and desperate kisses, I felt at peace.

So I would give Enzo this, I would give myself this, but I was under no illusion that it meant anything more than this moment.

Enzo couldn't love me, couldn't love anyone, until he chose to a) believe himself worthy of love and b) believe himself capable of love. Whatever had happened in his past—and I'd gleaned snippets from his cousins—had done a real number on him. Nicco and Matteo had their sisters, they had a strong female influence, but not Enzo. He had himself and his father.

And now Vincenzo Marchetti was gone.

I couldn't imagine losing one parent, let alone two. Yet Enzo acted indifferent. I saw the cracks though. The rare moments when he chose to let his guard down, like right now.

Bringing my hands to his face, I took control of the kiss, pouring everything I felt into each brush of my lips, every flick of my tongue. I cared for this man. Deeply, truly, honestly. But I knew you couldn't make someone love you, and I wasn't sure Enzo would ever realize how good we could be together if he'd just open his stone-cold heart to the idea of there being something more between us.

"Fuck, you get me so hot," he drawled, dragging his mouth down the slope of my neck once more. His fingers pressed deep and slow, his thumb circling my clit with steady precision. Enzo knew how to touch me, how to make the waves of pleasure build inside me until I was panting his name.

My legs began to quiver, fire racing through my veins as he pushed me closer to the edge. "God, that feels so good," I breathed, running my nails down his back. A low groan rumbled in his chest and he nipped my bottom lip with his teeth, soothing the sting with his tongue.

"Come for me, Gattina, come all over my fingers."

His dirty words sent me flying off the edge, my body bowing into him as I cried his name.

Enzo crawled off me and stripped out of his boxers. He grabbed his wallet, retrieving a condom, and made quick work of ridding me of my pajamas.

Standing at the foot of the bed, he drank in the sight of me, pumping himself a couple of times. His was rock hard, the piercing in the tip of his dick glinting in the dark. I rubbed my thighs together in eager anticipation, I knew how good that felt rubbing inside me.

Enzo reached forward and wrapped a hand around my ankle, tugging me down the bed. My shriek of surprise filled the room. But then he was there, pressed right against my core, sliding himself through my wetness. It felt divine. Dirty and oh so good.

"Enzo..."

"Patience, Gattina." He pushed my legs wider, hooking them around his waist. Then inch by glorious inch, he rocked inside me. We both moaned, the intensity almost too much to bear.

"Fuck, you feel good." His eyes were blown with desire, dark and dangerous. But I wasn't scared. Enzo would never hurt me, not physically at least.

He pulled out slowly and slammed back inside, eliciting a breathy moan from my lips. His eyes were fixed on where our bodies were joined, and he watched with rapt fascination as he began fucking me hard and fast, as if he was exorcising his demons with every thrust. His thumb found my clit again, mirroring the pace of his hips. I reached for him, needing to feel his lips on mine, and Enzo came willingly, folding his big body over mine and kissing me like I was air, and he was drowning. His hand encircled my throat, pinning me in place to allow him complete control of my mouth, my body.

"So fucking beautiful." He went harder... faster... making the headboard crash against the wall, leaving no mistake as to what we were doing.

But I didn't care.

Nothing, *nothing* had ever felt better than this. Watching—*feeling*—a guy so untouchable as Enzo Marchetti lose control.

"Cazzo, come sei stretta," he purred against my lips, rocking into me with vigor. I could feel him everywhere. But that's what Enzo did whenever he was near—he consumed me. I knew I had it bad for this man. I knew if he asked me to be his, I would say yes in a heartbeat.

I also knew that he would never ask.

Which was why I couldn't keep doing this, not if I wanted to keep my sanity and my self-respect.

"What is it?" he asked, slowing his pace. "What's wrong?"

"Nothing." I forced a smile, curling my fingers in the hair at the nape of his neck and pulling him down to kiss me. "Make me shatter," I whispered.

His lips curved wickedly against mine. "It would be my honor."

No more words were spoken between us as Enzo showed me with his body what he would never tell me in words.

As I came, my body trembling around him, a rogue tear slipped down my cheek, knowing this was probably the last time I would ever be with him.

Our relationship wasn't made for the sunlight. It was nurtured in the dark, made strong only by the shadows and secrets that surrounded it. But come morning, they would turn to ash, and everything would go back to how it was before.

"Fuck, Nora... fuuuuck." Enzo stilled as he reached his own climax. Our bodies were slick with sweat and my lips were sore and swollen.

He pulled out and disappeared into my bathroom to get rid of the condom. I crawled into bed and pulled the covers up around my body. Enzo joined me seconds later, silent as he tucked his big body behind mine and laced his arm around my waist.

"Thank you." He kissed the nape of my neck and heavy silence filled the room.

Thank you.

Those words would forever haunt me.

I'd given Enzo a gift.

Something precious and coveted.

And he was grateful, I didn't doubt that, but that's all it was.

All it would ever be.

But right now, I was happy to let the lie continue.

I fell asleep wrapped in Enzo's arms believing he would never let me go.

The next morning, I was awake first. I slipped out of bed and went to make coffee. After the intensity of last night, I needed some space.

I checked the hall, hardly surprised to find Maurice standing there. "Coffee?" I asked him, opening my door wide.

"I'll take one to go," he said around a thin smile.

"Suit yourself. Give me a minute." I made his coffee in a reusable cup and took it back into the hall.

"Thank you, Miss—" I shot him a hard look and he chuckled. "Nora."

"Better." The corner of my mouth tipped. "If you want another, you know where I am."

Maurice nodded and I went back inside. The apartment was still quiet, so I made myself a coffee and got a couple of biscuits from the tin and made myself comfortable on the couch.

My body ached in the best possible way, but I tried not to relive last night. Instead, I scrolled through my phone. I had a couple of texts from Lucii, inviting me to a party on the weekend. She'd asked Nate and thought I should invite Luca.

Ugh.

I texted her back that I would let her know my plans. I liked Lucii a lot, but I wasn't sure I wanted to make a thing out of going out with her, Nate, and Luca.

Draining my coffee, I went to make a fresh mug. I felt Enzo before I saw him.

"Morning," he said.

Turning slowly, I smiled. "Hey. There's fresh coffee or I have some juice in the refrigerator."

"Thanks." He went over and opened it, and I couldn't resist watching his ass in the snug gray sweatpants.

I got Enzo a glass and he poured himself some juice. "Listen, about last night—"

"Relax," I said, hating how awkward things already felt between us, "we don't have to do this."

"We don't?" He frowned.

"No. I know what last night was and it's fine."

"It is?"

"Yeah." I smiled again. "Do you want some breakfast? I was going to make pancakes."

"I could eat."

"Okay. I have class at ten, so I'll need to leave in like forty minutes."

"Shit, yeah. Maybe I should—"

"Stay. Eat. Something tells me you need it." My eyes dropped to his ridiculously shredded stomach, and it grumbled again.

"I am pretty hungry." His eyes flared, sending a bolt of heat through me. I inhaled a sharp breath.

"Do you miss it?" I asked, as I gathered all the ingredients.

"What's that?"

"School?"

"Nah, I never wanted to enroll at MU, but Uncle Toni thought it would be a good idea."

"So that's it? You'll just... work for your uncle now?" I peeked over at him, surprised to find him smirking at me.

"Yeah, I'll *work* for him."

"But Nicco and Matteo want something different?"

"Nicco won't leave Arianne's side. Especially not after what down with Fascini—"

Everything stopped as I was hit with an overwhelming wave of fear.

"Nora?"

"I'm fine." I brushed him off, forcing myself to take a deep breath. The nightmares had stopped a few weeks ago, but there were still moments when I was back there, tied to that chair with a gun pointed at my head.

"You sure you're—"

"Fine." My lips pursed. "I'm fine."

"You know I'll never forgive myself for what happened back then."

My brows furrowed. "It wasn't your fault. You didn't make Scott Fascini drug and kidnap me."

"I'm not only talking about that, Gattina." Something flashed in Enzo's eyes, but I didn't dare to latch onto it. He was feeling guilty, responsible... it didn't change anything.

"Feel free to use the shower while I make breakfast."

"Are you trying to get rid of me?" His eyes narrowed.

"What? No! I just thought—"

"Relax, Gattina." He stalked toward me and I jerked back.

"I should get moving if I want to make it to class on time."

Enzo stopped dead, letting out a steady breath. "I guess a quick shower couldn't hurt." He spun on his heel and took off down the hall, and I released the breath I'd been holding.

I don't know what I'd expected this morning, but it wasn't this. And it had thrown me for a loop.

Pouring the batter into a heated pan, I focused on the pancakes. By the time I'd made the first stack, Enzo returned, freshly showered and towel drying his hair.

"Smells good," he said, sitting at the breakfast counter.

"I have chocolate sauce or maple syrup." I pushed the plate toward him and retrieved the bottles from the cabinet.

"Thanks."

"Anytime."

Our eyes locked again, the strange current flowing between us. Something was different, but I couldn't quite put my finger on what.

"So how are classes?"

I almost choked on my mouthful of food. Enzo was asking me about classes now? What strange universe had I woken up in?

"Don't look so surprised. It's only a question."

"Classes are good. It feels a little bit like starting over though, now Arianne and Nicco are practically joined at the hip."

"You noticed that, huh?"

"I mean, I get it. But college was supposed to be our adventure, and now it's not." I let out a tiny breath. "God, that sounds so selfish."

"No, it doesn't. You had plans together."

"Yeah. But I made a new friend. Well, not a new friend. I knew her already, but I think she has potential."

"Does this new friend have a name?"

"Lucii. She's in my Media and Society class. We went out the other night to a bar. It was fun." Enzo stiffened and I added, "What?"

"Will you be going out with her again?"

"She invited me to a party tomorrow night."

"Will there be guys at this party?"

"It's a party," I chuckled, "what do you think?"

Enzo didn't return my laughter. In fact, he didn't look pleased at all.

"Will Luca be there?"

"I don't know, maybe." I gave him a dismissive shrug. "I think Lucii has a thing for his friend."

"So you're going to see him again?"

Placing my fork down, I let out a frustrated sigh. "Does it matter if I do?"

"He's not good enough for you."

"You don't even know him. Luca is a good guy, Enzo. I wouldn't have befriended him if he wasn't."

"Oh, come on, Gattina. Don't be so naïve. He doesn't want to be friends. He wants in your panties—"

"How dare you?" My voice shook with anger. "You don't want me, but you don't want anyone else to have me, is that it? Because I'll be honest, Enzo, that's bullshit, and you know it.

"You left. You fucked me and then you just left. Do you have any idea how that made me feel? Finding out from Ari that you were gone? That you thought so highly of me, I didn't even deserve a goodbye?"

"Shit, Nora, that's not..." he rubbed his jaw, "I—"

"No, Enzo. I'm talking, you're listening..." I jabbed my finger in his direction. "You turned up at *my* apartment. You came to me. And I did the only thing I know how when it comes to you, I let you in. But I can't keep doing it, Enzo. I won't. I have too much self-respect to be the girl sitting around waiting for the guy she wants to wake up and see what everyone else sees." I stood up and pushed the curls out of my face.

"One day a guy is going to come along and sweep me off my feet, and do you know what, he'll deserve me. He'll deserve me and when I give him my heart, he won't give it back. He'll keep it, he'll protect it... he'll cherish it. Because my heart is worthy, Enzo. *I'm* worthy."

He stared at me with a blank expression. I knew I'd probably caught him off guard, laying it all out for him, but I felt better.

Even if he had nothing to say to me.

Swallowing the hurt building inside me, I steeled my expression. "I'm going to take a shower. I think it would be a good idea if you're gone when I'm done."

"Nora..."

My fickle heart beat wildly in my chest as I waited....

And waited.

But Enzo's shoulders sank as he swallowed whatever he'd been about to say.

"Well, okay then. I think we're done here." I gave him a tight nod and walked away from him with my head held high...

Even if another part of my heart withered and died.

SEVENTEEN

ENZO

THE URGE TO go after Nora was strong, but she was pissed, and I didn't want to make things any worse.

She hadn't even given me a chance to explain, to try to apologize. Instead, she'd dismissed me. Any other girl, and I would have been relieved to avoid any further awkward conversations. But Nora wasn't any girl.

Fuck, she had felt good under me last night. Chasing away my demons in a way that only she could. I'd come so damn hard, I'd seen stars. Which was pretty ironic considering I'd made a promise to make *her* see stars.

I flinched as her bedroom door slammed. Nora didn't want me here, that much was obvious, so I shoved another pancake in my mouth, drained my juice and set about collecting up my belongings.

Most of my weapons were still in her bedroom, so I slipped inside and grabbed them. I could hear the waterfall from the shower, and couldn't help but picture her in there, naked, water kissing her smooth, olive skin. Fuck, what I wouldn't give to join her and lose myself for another half hour before life came crashing down around me again. But I liked my dick attached to my body and something told me if I even so much as tried to touch her, Nora would cut it right off.

The thought made me smirk. My Gattina could be a little firecracker when she wanted to be.

Get a grip, asshole, she isn't yours.

With one last look at the bathroom door, I hightailed it out of there, running straight into Maurice in the hall.

"Mr. Marchetti," he said in greeting.

"Do not leave her side," I ordered.

"The boss gave me strict orders to stay on her at all times."

Fuck. I didn't like the idea of her going to classes while this fucker was out there, taunting us. But I couldn't exactly tell her that, not before talking to Uncle Toni. And I'd seen nothing so far to suggest Nora was in harm's way. But being associated with the Family had been enough for him to go after Morello's store and DiMarco's bar.

"Change of plan," I said, making a snap decision. "She doesn't leave the apartment. Not until you hear from me."

"Miss Abato won't like that."

"She doesn't have to like it."

"What should I tell her?"

"I'm sure you'll think of something." I clapped him on the shoulder before taking off down the hall. I needed some fresh air and a smoke.

I'd hadn't even reached the front door when my cell started ringing.

"Yeah?"

"Where are you?" Nicco asked.

"Just leaving La Stella, why?"

"Darius got hit."

"Darius? Motherfucker." Darius was good people. A pawnbroker operating right out of Marchetti territory in La Riva, he cleaned money through his books for us occasionally. "What's the damage?"

"It's a mess." Nicco let out a low whistle.

"He's in Verona."

"Yep."

"Which means no one's safe." I was already doubling back around. "I'll bring Nora to your old man's house."

"We're already on our way."

I hung up, jogging up the stairs to Nora's apartment. Maurice was whispering into his earpiece. He gave me a terse nod as I walked straight inside.

"Enzo?" Nora was towel drying her hair as she forked a piece of pancake into her mouth. "What is it? What's wrong?"

"You need to come with me."

"What the hell are you talking about?" She scowled. "I'm not going anywhere with you, I have classes."

"Change of plans, Gattina. It isn't safe for you to be here right now."

"Safe? What the hell, Enzo? You weren't complaining last night when you were fucking me into—" She slammed her lips together and stared me down.

I arched a brow, fighting a smile. I loved this side of her... fucking loved her sass and smart mouth. But it wasn't a social visit, and we didn't have time to stand here and argue.

"Pack a bag. I don't know how long you'll be gone."

Her angry expression melted away. "It's really that serious?"

"We're not sure yet." I ran a hand down my face, letting out a heavy sigh. "But until we figure out how serious the threat is, I need you safe, okay?"

"Okay." She nodded, disappearing down the hall.

I stared after her. That had gone easier than I expected. Just then, there was a knock at the door.

"Yeah?" I called, assuming it was Maurice, but when he opened the door, I didn't expect to see Luca standing there as well.

"You," he said.

"Now's not a good time."

"I'm sorry, do you live here now?" He arched a brow. "I was hoping to talk to Nora."

"She's just—"

"It's fine, Enzo. I've got this." She dropped her bag at my feet and went to Luca pulling him into the hall.

Maurice shot me a bemused look right before he closed the door, and I flipped him off.

Silence echoed around Nora's apartment as she was out there in the hall, talking to him. Jealousy burned through my veins. I didn't like the idea of someone we barely knew out there with his hands on her. But Nora deserved her space and despite all my better judgment, I had to respect that.

Two minutes later, she came back inside.

"How is the lovely Luca?"

"Jealousy looks good on you." Her lips curved into a knowing smirk and I bristled.

"What did you tell him?"

"That I have to go away for a family emergency."

"Good, that'll buy us some time. Do you have everything?"

"I think so."

I nodded. "Let's go."

We didn't take my car. It was too risky. I had Maurice drive us to La Riva, with another security detail tailing behind us.

Nora was quiet on the ride there, texting somebody back and forth. I wanted to ask if it was Luca, to find out what was really going on between them, but I didn't.

It wouldn't change anything.

The most important thing right now was figuring out who this fucker was and bringing him down. Everything else could wait.

When we pulled up at Uncle Toni's house, everyone was already congregated. Arianne rushed over to Nora the second she climbed out of the black SUV.

"Thank God. I've been so worried."

"I'm fine," she said, hugging Ari back. "But I'll be a damn sight better when somebody tells me what the hell is going on." Her eyes went to mine, but Nicco called my name.

"Enzo." He welcomed me with open arms and the two of us hugged. "It's good to see you," he said. "Is she okay?"

"She's Nora," I said with a slight shrug and he chuckled.

"Nora, you're here," Alessia skipped out of the house with Bella in tow, but they both stopped in their tracks when another car rolled into the Marchetti driveway.

"What the fuck is he doing here?" I barked, watching Tristan Capizola climb out of the driver's side.

"I invited him," Nicco said, shooting me a warning look to play nice. "He's family now, and I want as many people looking out for the girls as possible."

He meant Arianne—he wanted as many people as possible looking out for Arianne. I couldn't blame him, but there had been a time when Tristan was the enemy.

I guess a lot had changed.

"I'm glad you called," he said, coming over to us. "Where do you want me?"

"You're with us. Luis," Nicco beckoned Ari's personal bodyguard over. "Take the girls into the living room and stay with them."

"Got it, boss."

My brow arched at that. Nicco wasn't the boss yet. But he sure sounded like the one in control. In fact, Uncle Toni wasn't anywhere to be seen.

"Come on," Nicco said, "let's go inside.

Of course. We needed to meet, to figure out how to deal with the new threat.

"Hey, Uncle T okay?" I asked Matteo as we filed in behind our cousin and Tristan.

"He said something about heartburn. Think Genevieve is trying to find him an antacid. I'm relieved as fuck you're back." He slung his arm around my neck. "Just promise me it's a permanent thing."

"Aww, did you miss me?" I tapped his face, shirking out from under his arm. "Has your old man checked in?"

"Called Uncle Toni right before you got here. He's okay. He's working with our guys in the local PD. But we're pretty sure after the shitshow at Darius' place, that your little friend followed you back to Verona."

Anger skittered down my spine. "Who the fuck is this asshole?"

He grabbed my shoulder. "We'll figure it out, together."

I only hoped he was right…

Before anyone else got hurt.

We left the girls in the living room with Luis and headed for Uncle Toni's office. He was already seated at the head of the table, but he looked a little green around the gills.

"You good, Uncle T?" Matt asked.

"Got this damn acid reflux." He rubbed his chest vigorously. "Driving me up the wall."

"A gallon of milk," Tristan suggested. "Works for my mom every time."

"Well, it ain't working for me, son. Thanks for coming out here."

"Of course, anything to help."

I snorted at that.

"E," Nicco warned and I dropped into a chair, fixing my eyes right on the outsider.

Tristan Capizola wasn't one of us. Sure, he was Arianne's cousin, but being blood related didn't mean shit, my father was evidence of that.

"Enzo, knock it off," Uncle Toni added. "Tristan is our guest, and we will treat him as such. Michele found a bunch of stuff at the warehouse."

"What kind of stuff?"

"More photos, notes, a list of our businesses."

"Fuck," I hissed. "Anything else?"

"Yeah, but you're not going to like it."

"What?" Trepidation coursed through my veins.

"Your name came up a lot."

"It's personal," I said. Call it gut intuition or sixth sense, but I already knew this was somehow linked to me.

"Do you think it's related to Vincenzo?" Matteo asked, immediately realizing his mistake when Tristan said, "Vincenzo? What does he have to do with anything?"

My brow went up and he added, "Shit, man, that sounded insensitive. I was sorry to hear about his death."

I bristled, the temperature cooling in the room.

Nicco looked at me and then to his father. Antonio let out a long, steady breath as he rubbed a hand over his mouth.

"He's a part of this now. He should know the truth."

"What the fuck?" I balked, shooting up out of my seat. "You can't be serious."

"Lorenzo, you need to calm the fuck down."

"Come on, cous," Matteo added. "It sounds like we need all the help we can get right now."

Reluctantly, I sat back down.

"Vincenzo didn't die in a collision, he was killed."

"I see..." Tristan said. "Do I want to know who killed him?"

"Let's just say, he betrayed the Family and got what he deserved."

"No shit. You think the two are connected?"

"It's possible," Nicco replied.

"It's the most likely scenario," I said, conceding to the fact that Tristan was a part of this now, whether I liked it or not. "My father was promised power in return for betraying us. It's possible he might have been working with more people and with Mike Fascini serving jail time, the next in line has decided to try to get some kind of vengeance."

Something about the whole thing still didn't sit right with me. I didn't recognize the guy at all… but the message scrawled across DiMarco's office wall, and then the way he'd said, 'surprise' when he'd knocked me down before attacking Gino… it was almost as if he knew me.

"I think you should lay low for a while," Uncle Toni said. "If this—"

"Fuck that. I want to get to this guy. I can't do that if I'm in hiding."

"Not in hiding. I want the girls with you. At the cabin."

"You're going to stick me on babysitting duty while there's some fucking psycho out there gunning for us? If I'm the target, use me as bait."

I would quite happily walk into the lion's den if it meant getting to look this fucker in the eye before I put a bullet through his skull.

"It isn't permanent. But if you go off the grid, it might smoke him out. He's in Verona County, we know that much. And now he's here, something tells me he won't be leaving until he finishes whatever it is he's started."

"But why hit Providence at all?" Nicco said.

"To lure me there."

"E, come on, that's a stretch. He wouldn't know you—"

"He would if he has been watching me."

I'd seen his display board with my own eyes. He'd been collecting intel, building a picture of our lives. If I was his main target, then it meant everyone around me was at risk.

Everyone including Nora.

"This is fucked up," Matteo breathed.

"I want you all to head up to the cabin for the weekend while we try to get a handle on this. I've locked down our most profitable businesses and given everyone else a warning. They know to keep an eye out. Let's give it twenty-four hours and see if he makes another move."

"And if he doesn't?" I asked, not liking this plan one bit.

"Then we'll cross that bridge when we get there."

Uncle Toni fixed his eyes on Nicco. "Liaise with Luis and his team about getting you all to the cabin and check in the moment you arrive there, okay?"

My cousin nodded. "What do we tell them?"

"It's Sia," Matt teased. "She's probably outside with a glass pressed to the wall as we speak."

"You're not wrong there, son. Just tell them as little as possible, but enough to keep them in line."

"Good luck with that, cous." Matteo clapped Nicco on the back.

"I… uh, where do you want me?" Tristan asked.

"You're with us." Nicco stood.

"This day just keeps getting better and better," I grumbled beneath my breath. Not only was I being exiled to the cabin with my annoying-as-hell cousins, my best friend and his wife, and Nora. But Capizola was also coming.

Fuck my life.

EIGHTEEN

NORA

I'D BEEN to the Marchetti cabin before. It was like a well-kept secret, nestled away in the dense forest of Blackstone Reserve. It was impossible to tell anyone the route given the fact we'd driven for a little over two hours for a journey that should have taken forty minutes tops. But I'd heard Nicco tell Luis they wanted to take the long route to make sure no one was following.

I was riding with Nicco, Arianne, and Enzo, and Arabella and Alessia were in another car with Matteo and Tristan.

That had caused some arguments. Nicco had wanted Tristan to ride with us and Enzo to ride with the girls. But Enzo had refused to budge. It would have been almost sweet if it wasn't for the fact we were being forced to spend the weekend at the cabin while Antonio and his men dealt with the *threat*.

The threat the guys refused to tell us much about. I was pretty certain Nicco had given Arianne the lowdown. She was his wife and she had him wrapped around her little finger. But she was remaining tight-lipped, refusing to tell me anything.

So much for the sacred girl code of sisters before misters.

The SUV finally rolled to a stop. The sun was beginning to sink behind the tree line, the icy blast of wintry air a shock after the toasty warmth of the SUV.

Enzo offered me his hand, but I knocked it away, clambering out myself. I didn't need him suddenly acting like my protector when I'd managed just fine without him the last few weeks.

My cell vibrated and I moved away from the group, to read Luca's text.

. . .

Let me know you're okay, please.

He was concerned when I said I had to go out of town for a family emergency. I wasn't sure he completely bought the lie, but I didn't have time to explain. Not that I could tell him anything.

I'm fine. You don't need to worry.

Too late for that.

I smiled. Luca was one of the good guys. Even after Enzo's sudden appearance in my life, he hadn't done the typical guy thing of getting pissed or jealous or walking away.

But Enzo's reappearance did complicate things because I didn't want to be unfair and lead Luca on. Which is exactly what I'd told him this morning.

"Hey, who is that?" Arianne came over and nudged my shoulder.

"Er, no one." I slipped my cell into my pocket.

"You're a terrible liar." She chuckled, lacing her arm through mine and guiding me toward the cabin. Enzo watched me like a hawk, but I refused to acknowledge him.

I'd been so determined to stand my ground with him this morning and then everything went to shit. Now I was stuck in close confines with him for the weekend.

We followed everyone inside, and Sia and Arabella immediately called dibs on their room.

"Me and Tristan can take the bunks," Matteo said, disappearing after the girls.

I glanced around to see Enzo's reaction, but he hadn't come inside yet.

"How are you holding up?" Tristan asked me.

"Okay, I guess. I'd prefer to be back at MU though."

"You and me both." He grimaced. "Is Enzo always so—"

"So what?"

"Nothing, man." Tristan slipped away with a sheepish expression.

"Where is everyone?" Enzo asked me, barely meeting my gaze.

"Gone to call dibs on their rooms."

His eyes narrowed as he did the math. "Let me guess. Nicco plans on sharing with Arianne?"

"I think they're already christening the bed."

I'd seen Nicco pull her into the first bedroom down the hall.

"But there aren't enough rooms."

"You're on the couch." Matteo appeared.

"The fuck, man?" He gawked. "We always share."

"You heard Uncle Toni, Tristan is our guest." He smirked. "We can't very well have *him* sleeping on the couch."

"It's fine," I said. "You can take the other bed in my room."

"Actually, you got the other king."

"Oh." My cheeks burned. "Well, I guess we can—"

"It's fine," Enzo gritted out, "I'll take the couch."

"Fine." I grabbed my bag off the floor and stomped down the hall. I'd thought that maybe we could be adults and put whatever was or wasn't between us aside, but I guess that was too much to ask. If Enzo wanted to sleep on the couch, then so be it.

Stubborn asshole.

The room was beautiful, just like the rest of the cabin. It was the perfect mix of rustic and modern. An ornately carved closet hugged the wall, beside it a matching dresser. The bed was the focal point on the opposite wall. I slung my bag down and perched on the edge of the bed.

A knock pulled me from my thoughts. "Come in," I called.

"Hey." Sia stuck her head around the door. "We wondered if you wanted to hang out?"

"Sure," I said, tapping the bed. Alessia slipped into the room, Arabella following close behind.

"What's the matter?" she asked.

"Nothing," I said.

"Is it Enzo? I saw the way he was watching you. Did something happen between the two of you?" Alessia's eyes were alight with anticipation.

I chuckled. "Take a breath there, Sia."

"Sorry." She blushed. "I just... Ugh, the two of you would be so good together."

"Right," Arabella agreed. "But Enzo is a total commitment-phobe."

"People change, Bella. Look at Nicco."

"Yeah, but what he and Ari have is rare. Like once in a lifetime."

Ouch.

I knew the youngest Marchetti didn't mean anything, but it didn't stop her words from stinging.

There was another knock and we all looked up at the door.

"Dare I enter?" Matteo appeared around the door, grinning.

"Girls only, get out, scemo." Bella grabbed a pillow and threw it at his head.

"Easy, Bel. I only wanted to let you know me and Enzo are heading out. We'll be back soon."

"Where are you going?" I asked.

"Boys stuff." He winked. "Nicco and Tristan will be here, and Luis and his guys are right outside."

"Be safe," Alessia said.

"Always." Matteo left, closing the door behind him.

"Where do you think they're going?" Bella frowned.

"Probably to check the perimeter."

"Isn't that what we have security for? So the guys don't have to do it?"

"They'll be okay." I offered Bella a reassuring smile.

"Nora's right. Enzo is a hard ass. He'll look out for Matteo."

"You seem awfully okay with all this," I said, and Alessia shrugged.

"It's all part and parcel of being a mafia princess."

"Mafia princess, huh?" My lips curved. "That does have a certain ring to it."

"God, Nora, don't encourage her." Bella rolled her eyes. "This isn't a game, Sia. Besides, you do realize you'll be a princess forever because Nicco and Uncle Antonio are never going to let you date?"

She flipped back against the cushions lined up on the bed. "Don't remind me. Anthony Aielio asked me out last week."

"He did? You never said anything." Hurt flashed across Bella's face.

"There wasn't much point. You're right, they'll never let me date."

"You have time," I said. "I remember guys in high school and—"

"Oh, Anthony isn't in high school. He graduated last year. His brother is in our class. Anthony helps their father run the family auto shop.

"So he's older."

"Only by a couple of years." She shrugged again.

"Trust me when I say, don't rush into something you might regret. Especially not with an older guy."

"How old were you... you know, when you lost your virginity?"

They both stared at me like I held the answers to the universe.

"Oh no you don't. I'm not going to give you sex advice, Nicco and Matteo will kill me."

"We won't tell them, promise."

Bella nodded, agreeing with her cousin. "You can trust us."

"Look, I get it. It's a confusing, scary, exciting time. But if I have one piece of advice, it's to wait and give yourself to someone who deserves you. You can't ever get your first time back."

"Penny Denver said it hurt her so bad she cried the entire time."

"Then he wasn't doing it right," I murmured.

"Have you and Enzo—"

"Nice try," my brow arched, "but I'm not doing this with the two of you. In fact, let's go see if Arianne has managed to detach herself from your brother's mouth. I don't know about you guys but I'm hungry."

I was halfway through making spaghetti when Enzo and Matteo returned.

"Thank God." Bella shot up, making a beeline for her brother. My heart ached watching them. I knew that big brotherly affection firsthand, and although my brother Gio drove me up the wall, I missed him something fierce. But he was always destined for bigger things, for a life outside of Verona. Thanks to a full ride scholarship to UPenn, he was living his dream in Philadelphia, with hopes of going pro next year.

I discreetly glanced at Enzo. Hovering in the doorway, his big body ate up the space. His cheeks were flushed from the cold and it softened the sharp angles of his face. But when his icy gaze found mine, his expression darkened.

He was clearly as pleased to be stuck here as I was.

I turned around to tend to the spaghetti. It was my mom's recipe; the aromatic scent of garlic and herbs filling me with a strange sense of melancholy. I didn't want to worry my parents unnecessarily after what happened before, but the burning need to hear her voice coursed through me.

"Nor?" Arianne laid her hand on my arm, yanking me from my thoughts. "Are you okay?"

"Yeah, I'm fine. Find me some plates?"

"Of course."

I was hardly surprised Arianne knew her way around the kitchen. She had stayed here with Nicco before. Between us, we served the spaghetti, covering it with generous lashings of sauce. I sprinkled each plate with basil before calling everyone to the table. Nicco invited Luis to join us, but he declined, staying outside with the other security men.

"This looks great, Nora," Tristan said, helping me with the bread.

"I'm not just a pretty face, you know."

He chuckled, but it quickly died when Enzo scowled in our direction. "Ignore him," Matteo said. "He's just grouchy because he's gotta take the couch tonight."

"Listen, man, why don't you take my spot, and I can room with Nora. I'm sure she won't—"

Enzo's eyes narrowed to murderous slits as he glared at Tristan.

"I think that's a no, Capizola." Matteo snorted. "You're stuck with me, man, and E is stuck with—"

"*Matt.*" Nicco shot him a hard look and tension rippled around through the air.

"Fuck this," Enzo said, "I need a smoke." He spun around and walked straight out of the cabin, letting the door slam shut behind him.

"Was it something I said?"

Bella grabbed her brother and yanked him down into the empty seat beside her. "You shouldn't push him, you know how he gets."

"He needs to—"

"Basta!" Nicco slammed his hand down on the table, making the silverware rattle. He let out an exasperated breath. "Can we just eat, please?"

"You don't need to tell me twice." Matteo began helping himself to bread and salad. But I wasn't feeling very hungry all of a sudden.

"Matt, you eat like a pig."

"But you love me, pulce." He roped his arm around Bella's neck and began to ruffle her hair.

"Get off of me, you big goofball." She shirked him off. "You are such a dork."

"I think it's cute," Ari said.

"You need me to come over there and ruffle your hair, cous?" Tristan asked her.

"Please don't." Nicco glowered.

"Relax, Marchetti. I'm only busting your balls. This is good, Nor. Just like my Nona used to make it."

"You're not hungry?" Ari caught my eye, and I shook my head, my gaze flicking to the door.

Tempers were bound to be frayed given the circumstances, but Enzo was so volatile, so angry all of the damn time. The fixer in me wanted to excuse myself and go check on him, but I knew he wouldn't thank me for it, so I forced myself to stay put.

"Can someone pass me the cheese, please?" Tristan asked, and in their haste to help, Bella and Alessia knocked over the jug of water.

"Oops." Bella grimaced. "I'll grab some towels."

"Relax," Tristan said. "I've got it."

I wasn't the only one who noticed the girls track his every move as he went and fetched some paper towel.

"What the fuck is happening right now?" Matteo grumbled beneath his breath.

"I think Tristan has a fan club." I fought a smile, but Matteo looked anything but amused.

"Oh hell no." His hand flattened against the table.

"Relax, Matt," Ari said, "you can trust Tristan."

"It's not him I'm worried about." His eyes went to his sister and their cousin. "Don't get any silly ideas."

"God, Matteo, you're so freakin' embarrassing. He's like twenty."

"Twenty-two." Tristan corrected, rejoining us, clearly unaffected by his little fan club. "And Matteo is right. Don't get any ideas. I don't date high schoolers."

"Of course you fucking don't."

"Jesus," Nicco hissed. "Is it too much to ask to have a simple meal?"

"I know Uncle T thought it would be safer to bring the girls out to the cabin, but I'm thinking he didn't consider our safety." Matteo smirked, and Alessia and Bella both grabbed a handful of bread and threw it at him.

Tristan exploded with laughter while me and Ari tried our best not to join him. And Nicco...

Well, he looked like a guy with the weight of the world on his shoulders.

NINETEEN

ENZO

I WALKED the perimeter of the cabin again. We'd been careful, covering our tracks once we left the highway, but it was better than standing still. Because when things were still, I was overcome with so much guilt and anger, I could barely breathe.

Nora made everything quiet. She made everything stop. Losing myself in her last night had been both a blessing and a curse. Every time she let me back in, another piece of me became hers. She'd never own my whole heart—that wasn't possible for something carved out of stone—but she owned enough jagged pieces of my soul for me to notice.

I never wanted this. I never wanted to tie myself to someone knowing that I couldn't ever be who they needed me to be. The Family came first, it would *always* come first. My loyalty, my life… my love, was reserved for Dominion, and Dominion alone.

But there was no denying that Nora Abato had buried herself under my skin. Like a slow acting poison, she was inside me. I cared whether she was safe. I cared who she was seeing and who she was spending time with. And I fucking cared that she was here.

Because of me.

Because this fucker somehow has ties to my old man. There were too many things that didn't quite add up yet, like why he'd started his campaign of destruction in Providence and not Verona. But the end game was the same. And the end game was all that mattered.

As my boots crunched against the ground, made hard from a cold winter, I pulled out my cell and dialed Uncle Michele.

"Enzo, son, what is it?"

"Any more news?" I asked, coming to a stop by a bench on the periphery of the woods.

"All leads ran dry. No prints, no address, no witnesses. This guy is a fucking ghost."

"Ghosts don't weigh two-hundred-and-fifty pounds, and I felt that fucker on top of me." Watched as he sank his blade into Gino's jugular.

Fuck.

He died... because of me.

And now this motherfucker was in Verona County. It was too close... too close to the people I cared about.

Too close to Nora.

Just the thought of him getting anywhere near her had me seething with anger.

"We'll get him, son. You took the girls to the cabin, right? They're safe."

"Yeah, they're here."

"So, let us focus on finding this asshole."

"I can't just sit here, doing nothing." It was fucking killing me.

"Shit, I know, kid. I know. But we'd all feel a helluva lot better knowing our girls have you around."

"Twenty-four hours. I'll stay twenty-four hours, but then I'm joining the hunt."

"You'll have to clear that with Toni, Lorenzo. You know the deal."

"Yeah." The boss's word was final. But I couldn't just stay here doing nothing. It was going to drive me in-fucking-sane.

The girls were inside, acting like this was a girl's weekend away. Not to mention the fact Nora was in there, and she was pissed. At me. At the fact I'd dragged her away from her life... from Luca.

Jesus, the guy was worse than a dog with a bone. Did she really like that good guy routine he had working for him?

"Fuck," I hissed, kicking the hard ground with my boot.

"You need to burn off some steam."

For a second I'd forgotten Uncle Michele was still on the line.

"Go for a run or something," he added.

Or something. I internally grumbled.

My eyes flickered back to the cabin.

"I'll call if there's any news," Uncle Michele said. "Keep our girls safe, Enzo. That's what we need you to do right now," he said. "Your pound of flesh will come."

We said goodbye and hung up.

My uncle was right, of course he was right. But I was never very good at sitting around and waiting for the fight to come to us.

Eventually, I went back inside. I was fucking freezing, not to mention hungry.

"I left you a plate," Nora said. She was curled in one of the chairs, scrolling on her phone.

"Thanks."

Matteo caught my eye and silently asked if I was okay. I nodded, shucking out of my jacket and slinging it over the back of the couch.

"Watch it, asshole," Tristan said.

"Oops, my bad. I didn't see you there." My lips curved with smug satisfaction as I grabbed the plate Nora had left me and put it in the microwave.

"You okay?" Matteo joined me, perching at the breakfast counter.

"I'd rather not be here."

His expression fell and I sucked in a harsh breath. Of course Nora had chosen that exact moment to go to her room, walking straight past the kitchen area.

"Did she—"

"If the look on her face is anything to go by, then yeah, she did."

"Fuck." I scrubbed a hand over my jaw.

"What's happening with you two? I figured after last night you were *working out your differences*, but then today it's like you can't stand to be around one another?"

"We fucked," I said, checking the spaghetti. It was done, so I sat down opposite him and began digging in.

"Yeah, I kinda got that part, asshole. But what I don't understand is, how you even ended up there?"

"Welcome to my world. One minute I was chasing this fucker, the next I was outside her apartment covered in Gino's blood."

"Shit, man. I'm sorry." His teasing expression fell. "That had to be rough."

"It was fucked up, Matt. He just killed him… without a second thought."

"Who is this punk?"

"Whoever he is, we need to find him, and fast." Because my gut told me it was only the beginning.

"Where's Nic?" I shifted the subject to safer shores.

"Where do you think?" Matteo's eyes rolled. "They're still in the honeymoon phase."

"Lucky for him." My eyes flicked down the hall once more. "I met him," I added.

"Met who?"

"Who do you think? Luca." His name soured on my tongue.

"Oooh. And?"

"He's not the right guy for her."

"Is anyone?" His brow arched with amusement.

"Nora deserves…" I swallowed the words. What was I saying? She deserved a lot of things. Things I couldn't give her. So who was I to stand in her way and ruin her shot at happiness?

"Jesus, cous." Matteo got up. "You're a real fucking idiot sometimes." His hand landed on my shoulder as he passed me. "Enjoy the couch."

Matteo disappeared down the hall leaving me with... Tristan.

"What?" I barked at him as he peered over.

"Nothing. Nothing at all." He got up and took off down the hall too, leaving me all alone.

It was barely even nine-thirty, and everyone had fucked off to bed. I grabbed a beer from the refrigerator and finished up the meal Nora had made for everyone. Trust her to play mother hen. I didn't know why she had to do that, be so fucking good all of the time. My fist clenched around the fork.

By the time I was done, my mood had turned pitch black. I rinsed my plate and left it on the side, grabbed a bottle of whisky from the cabinet and the stack of blankets someone had left out, and made my way to the couch. It was a sectional big enough for two people to sleep on, but it wasn't a bed.

Fifteen minutes in, I was beginning to think I should have taken Nora up on her offer. But no good would come from being in the same room as her. She was pissed. And it was only making me even more pissed.

Fucking women.

My old man might have been a traitorous piece of shit, but he wasn't wrong about women. They were nothing but a distraction.

I didn't bother pouring myself a glass of whisky, just drank straight from the bottle. I would have killed for a blunt, but Nicco didn't like us doing that shit around the girls, and I wasn't a total asshole.

The sounds from whatever action movie was playing on the TV became white noise as the burn from the liquor flooded my senses. He was out there, plotting his next move, biding his time. And I was here, hiding like a pussy. Between Nicco, Matteo, Tristan and the security team posted outside, the girls were safe. No one was going to get to them. I could go after him. It was a better use of my skill set being out there, hunting for him, than sitting here drinking my feelings because I couldn't get a hold on all the anger and guilt gnawing at my fucking soul.

I drained the whisky, letting it douse the fire inside me, replacing it with a simmering heat instead. My body slouched further into the couch, my thoughts becoming a jumbled mess of blood and death and destruction.

Until eventually, the darkness consumed me.

I woke with a start, my body caked in sweat.

"Fuck," I rasped, my throat as dry as the Sahara Desert. The open fire roared still, but someone must have turned up the thermostats because the place was like a furnace.

Slowly, I sat up, rubbing my head, trying to ease the pounding in my skull. My eyes landed on the empty bottle of whisky and I groaned. Not my best idea ever. But at least there had been no nightmares. And if there had, I couldn't fucking remember them.

I went in search of water, stripping out of my sweater and jeans as I went. I was half-tempted to go outside and cool off, but I knew if I took one step outside, whoever got the night shift would alert the rest of the team and then everyone would be awake.

So I decided against it, slipping into the bathroom at the end of the hall and splashing some cold water on my face. It wasn't so warm at this end of the cabin which made me think that maybe I had been having a nightmare after all. My skin was feverish, and my heart was racing like I'd just run a marathon.

"Fuck." I slammed my hand down on the counter, making the entire thing shake.

Just then, I heard footsteps in the hall. Shit. Someone was awake and I had no choice but to go out there and face them.

Washing my hands, I dried them on a towel before slipping out into the empty hall. Thank fuck. Whoever it was must have doubled back when they saw the bathroom in use.

I padded down the hall back into the living area, only to realize Nora was up and rummaging in the refrigerator. Staying in the shadows, I watched her for a second. Her hips swayed hypnotically as she leaned in, trying to locate whatever it was she wanted.

"Hungry?" I asked her and she almost jumped out of her skin.

"Oh my God," Nora breathed, clutching her chest, her thin pajama top doing little to conceal her perky tits. "You scared me half to death. What are you doing awake?"

"I could ask you the same thing, Gattina." I smirked.

"Please don't call me that."

My brows furrowed. "Is that how it is between us now?"

"How did you think it was going to be?" Nora lifted her chin in defiance. Usually, her sass turned me the fuck on, but after the night I'd had, it only fanned the flames of anger already raging in my stomach.

"Don't act like you didn't beg for it, la mia puttana."

Her palm collided against my cheek, pain ricocheting through my jaw. Nora gasped, stepping back, and I pressed forward, pinning her to the counter.

"You hit me." I rubbed my cheek, my blood boiling.

"You deserved it," she bit out. "I hate that you're hurting. I do. But I won't be your punching bag, Enzo. I deserve more than that."

I scoffed. "Like Luca?"

"I'm not doing this with you," she said, pressing her lips together and levelling me with a scathing look.

I didn't budge though, too worked up to just let her go. Part of me enjoyed this, craved the push and pull between us. It craved something else too, and before I knew it, I'd leaned in and run my nose along the curve of her neck.

"Fuck, Gattina, you smell delicious." My hips rolled against her, desperately seeking out her heat. Maybe I was still a little drunk or delirious from the nightmare because I couldn't think about anything except getting my hands on her sinful body.

"Enzo, don't do this." Her hands curled against my t-shirt. Even rough, her touch seared me to the bone.

"Are you telling me no, Gattina?" I leaned down, with every intention of letting my mouth ghost over Nora's lips, but she turned away at the last second, giving me her cheek instead.

Bitter laughter rumbled in my chest. I hated that she was defying me, pretending like she wasn't as hot for me as I was her, but Nora's defiance was like a red rag to a bull. I wanted to push her. To push and push until she snapped. Until she succumbed to the tension cracking between us.

"You can pretend I don't affect you, Gattina," I whispered against the shell of her ear, "but we both know if I slipped my hands in your itty-bitty little shorts, I'd find you soaking wet for me."

I heard the hitch of her breath, felt the shiver roll through her body. Nora was as wired as I was. Question was, was she going to give in to her baser instincts or was she going to continue her crusade to keep me out?

My hand slipped to her waist, stroking the sliver of skin there. Nora fought a moan, trying to pull away from me. But there was nowhere to go. I had her caged between the counter. Completely at my mercy. With Nora, nothing else—not the nightmares, or my old man, or the new fucker causing mayhem—could touch me. I was invincible. Untouchable. Nora made me feel like no one else ever had and although I didn't want to admit it, it was addictive.

She was addictive.

"Look at me, Gattina." I took hold of her chin and forced her face to mine. "Tell me you don't want me? Tell me you don't want me to drop to my knees and bury my face between your legs."

"That's all I am to you, isn't it?"

My brows drew together.

"A willing body. A hole to fuck when you need to work off some steam." Nora jabbed her finger in my chest. "You'll fuck me in the middle of the night when everyone's sleeping, but you'd rather sleep on the couch than share a room with me?"

What the fuck was she talking about?

What was happening right now had nothing to do with anything else. I was hungover and horny, and she was—furious.

Fuck.

She was silently seething at me and I'd completely misread the signs... because she was right, I hadn't fucking looked for them. I'd just assumed I could take what I needed from her the way I had before.

My hand dropped from her waist as I backed up and ran my fingers through my hair.

"What?" she sneered. "Nothing to say for yourself. Didn't think so. Now if you don't mind, get the hell out of my way." Shouldering past me, Nora disappeared into the shadows while I watched after her...

Wondering what the fuck had just happened.

TWENTY

NORA

I BARELY SLEPT.

After my run in with Enzo, my body had been too restless. He made me so angry. He'd barely said two words to me all day and then treated me like one of his whores. It hurt.

It hurt so damn much.

But that only amplified my anger because I was frustrated at myself for ever thinking I could reach him. For thinking that cold, cruel Enzo Marchetti would ever let his walls down long enough for me to crawl inside.

I could have let him touch me last night, let him take what he wanted right there up against the kitchen counter, but we weren't alone here. And it was one thing to give into him over and over in private…but in front of our friends and family?

I guess his opinion of me really was that low.

Willing myself out of bed, I pulled on a MU hoodie. It was chilly in the cabin, so I went in search of coffee and the roaring fire.

Enzo was already gone, but I'd expected nothing less. He'd spent most of yesterday gone too, as if he couldn't bear to be in the same room as me, and then, in the cover of darkness, acted as if he couldn't stay away.

I didn't want to live in the shadows. But Enzo was comfortable there. He preferred night over day, more at home in the darkness than the light.

As I turned on the coffee pot, my heart ached for him. But it quickly turned to stone when he appeared in the doorway and didn't even say good morning.

Damn you, Enzo Marchetti.

"Is there coffee?" Matteo appeared, his hair sticking up all in directions.

"Just making a fresh pot."

"You're too good to us," he said, heading straight to the couch and dive-bombing into the huge throw cushions. "How'd you sleep, cous?"

"How do you fucking think?" Enzo growled.

"I figured you'd pull your head out of your ass and go join Nora. But from your good mood this morning, I'm guessing that wasn't the case."

I peeked over at the two of them just in time to see Enzo flip Matteo the bird.

"Can you check if Luis and the guys want coffee?" I asked Enzo.

He narrowed his eyes. "Ask them yourself."

"Children," Matteo whistled. "What's with all this bad energy this morning?"

I stomped across the room and yanked open the door, slipping out onto the porch. The thick layer of ice gave the whole place a winter wonderland vibe. It was so pretty I took a second to appreciate its beauty before calling Luis.

"Coffee?" I asked.

"That would be great, Miss Abato."

I rolled my eyes. No matter how many times I asked him and Maurice to call me Nora they still reverted back to my formal name.

When I went back inside, I found Enzo and Matteo in deep conversation. They both went quiet the second I closed the door and alerted them to my presence. But I ignored them, going straight for the coffee machine.

By the time I'd made enough coffee for Luis and his guys, Nicco and Arianne had joined us.

"You don't have to do all this," she said.

I shrugged. "Someone's gotta do it." Besides, keeping busy was a good distraction from throwing something at Enzo's head.

Asshole.

I stayed in the kitchen area, refusing to join the guys. Ari noticed and came over.

"What's wrong?" she whispered.

"Nothing." I sipped my coffee, letting the liquid warm me inside out.

"Did En—"

"Don't, Ari. Just don't." I let out an exasperated sigh.

Just then, my cell phone vibrated. I plucked it out of my pocket and smiled when I saw Luca's name.

"Your whole face lights up whenever he texts you." She observed.

"It isn't like that."

"But it could be..." Arianne left me with my thoughts while she joined Nicco and the others. He pulled her onto his lap and wrapped a possessive arm around her waist, resting his chin in the crook of her shoulder. They looked so content, so happy.

My gaze collided with Enzo and time stood still. He had issues, I got it. I did. But I didn't really understand why he insisted on pushing everyone away. I didn't understand choosing loneliness.

It wasn't like Nicco had been looking for love either. He had responsibilities, a whole empire resting on his shoulders. Falling in love was the last thing he'd needed. But he couldn't resist destiny's plan. Arianne was made for him, and he for her. There was no escaping that, no matter how much he tried.

And now they were stronger than ever, and one day he would be the boss of the Marchetti Family and Arianne would sit at his side as his queen.

Love didn't make you weak, it made you strong. I truly believed that. It gave you something worth fighting for.

For the right person.

And therein lay the issue. Maybe I had to finally accept that me and Enzo weren't written in the stars. There was no happy ending for us. Because while I wanted all of Enzo, the good, the bad, and the downright ugly, the truth of the matter was, he didn't want all of me.

I felt tears well in my eyes and I averted my gaze, breaking the connection.

No one except him noticed as I slipped away and retreated to my room...

And of course, he let me go.

I'd just pulled on my sweater after a quick shower, when a loud crash boomed through the cabin, followed by raised voices.

I rushed into the living room to find Enzo hunched over, bracing his hand, blood seeping from his knuckles.

"Oh my God, what happened?"

The girls, Sia and Bella, were huddled together on the couch, while Matteo stood between them and Enzo. Nicco was still in the chair, Ari curled in his lap, and Tristan was nowhere to be seen.

"What happened?" I asked, and everyone's head whipped up to me.

"Uncle Toni called," Matteo said. "It wasn't the news Enzo hoped for." His grimace told me all I needed to know.

"Somebody should clean that up." I motioned to Enzo's hand. "I'll find a first aid kit."

"It's nothing." Enzo protested.

Matteo whispered something to him, both of their eyes fixed on me.

"What?" I asked.

"Fuck this, I need some air." Enzo spun around and headed for the door, taking the air with him.

I stuffed down all the hurt and joined the others. "What happened?"

Matteo looked to Nicco and he let out a heavy sigh.

"Girls, go hang out in your room."

"Seriously?" Alessia hissed. "You're going to—"

"Alessia, do as I ask, please."

"Fine." She got up, pulling Bella with her. "But I'm not a kid anymore, Nicco. I know what you and my cousins do. I know what Daddy does. You don't have to protect me from this stuff."

"I will always protect you, sorella. Now go."

They took off down the hall.

"What did I miss?" Tristan appeared.

"I need you to do me a favor. Go keep the girls company."

"The girls?" He frowned. "You want me to babysit them?"

"No, I want you to make sure my sister stays put in her room. There's a difference."

"Fine, whatever." He stalked off after them.

"This is fun," Matteo said. "The whole family together. It's a shame Bailey didn't—"

"Bailey stays out of this," Nicco growled.

"Relax, cous. It was a joke. I was joking."

"Yeah, I know. I just don't want him anywhere near this."

My eyes flicked back and forth to the door Enzo just stormed out of.

"He'll be okay," Nicco said.

"Will he?"

Enzo had lashed out in front of his younger cousins. That seemed out of character, even for him.

"Are you going to tell us what's going on?" I looked at Arianne and she flinched. "You already know," I added, the weight of my words pressing down on my chest.

Nicco wasn't supposed to confide in Ari, not about everything. But she was his wife. The center of his universe.

"If I tell you this, it cannot leave this room."

"You don't trust me." Why did it hurt so much?

Enzo didn't trust me. Nicco didn't trust me. I was beginning to wonder if Arianne, the girl who knew me better than anyone, trusted me.

No, I knew she did. But her loyalties had shifted in the last few months. She was a part of a world I didn't inhabit now. A world I walked the periphery of, crossing in and out but never truly *knowing*.

"Someone is coming after the Family..."

"Okay... but what does that have to do with Enzo?"

Nicco and Matteo shared another look.

"Look, if you don't want to tell me this then—"

"Nor, it's not that," Ari sighed, rubbing her hand over Nicco's thigh. "It's complicated."

"Is Enzo in danger?" My stomach twisted. He wasn't one to shy away from a fight, I knew that. But I couldn't stand the thought of him being in the direct line of fire.

Nicco inhaled a sharp breath. "We think whoever is targeting us, has ties to Vincenzo."

"Enzo's father... but I don't understand." Vincenzo had been Antonio's second, his right-hand man. Why on Earth would—no.

No!

Matteo nodded slowly, his eyes filled with regret. "Vincenzo was a traitor."

"But... that doesn't make any sense. He died. He was in an accident and he—"

"There was no accident," Nicco said, thickly.

"You mean you killed him?" Because that's what the mafia did to traitors. They got rid of them.

An icy shudder rolled through me.

"I didn't kill him, Nora." Nicco looked right through me, and then he said two little words that shattered my heart.

"Enzo did."

"I still can't believe it," I said as me and Ari lay shoulder to shoulder on my bed.

"Yeah... when Nicco told me... I wanted to tell you. But it wasn't my story to tell."

"I understand. It explains so much."

Ari rolled onto her side and leaned on her fist. "Now you know why I've been so worried about you. Enzo isn't... he's in a dark place, Nor. Super dark. I'm not sure I want you around that."

"It doesn't matter now," I said, peering up at her.

"What do you mean?"

"I told him I'm done. I want more, Ari. I *deserve* more." But as I said the words, my heart shattered all over again.

Enzo only had his father growing up. A cold, vicious man by all accounts with a strong sense of loyalty to the Family. A man who shaped his son and his view of the world. A man who molded his son in his image...

"God, I can't imagine what Enzo must be feeling. No wonder he pushed me away."

"No, Nora, don't do that, don't excuse his behavior—"

"I'm not excusing it, but I get it. He killed his father, Ari." My voice cracked. "Enzo shot his father in cold blood. You don't just come back from something like that."

Her expression softened. "I know."

"It's why he left, isn't it?"

She nods. "Antonio wanted to give him time and space to deal with everything. But then this happened, and well, here we are."

"What a mess," I breathed, feeling my chest constrict.

Nicco had explained that the guy targeting them seemed to have a personal vendetta against Enzo, so they assumed it was someone connected to Vincenzo. Maybe a business partner or someone involved with the deal he cut with Mike Fascini to bring down the Marchetti empire.

Just then, male laughter filled the cabin.

"I wonder what they're doing."

"We could always go out there and see?" Ari suggested.

"Sure, okay." It felt like we'd been in here for hours, the sun long set over the tree line.

Matteo and Tristan had taken the girls for a walk earlier, but we'd declined. I wasn't feeling very sociable after Nicco had told me the truth about Enzo and his father.

I couldn't get it out of my head, couldn't even begin to imagine what Enzo was going through. It explained a lot. Why he pulled away suddenly, his deep-seated anger, his cruel words and cold demeanor. Enzo was carrying a burden most of us would never understand.

I followed Arianne into the living room to find the guys crowded around the table, playing poker. Enzo had obviously returned from wherever he'd been all day, but I forced myself not to look at him for fear that he would see the truth in my eyes.

I knew his darkest secrets now, and I knew he'd probably hate me for it.

But it didn't matter, because I didn't plan on telling him. Enzo obviously didn't want me to know... *or he would have told me.*

So I grabbed a chair and tucked myself between Tristan and Matteo so that I wouldn't be in his line of sight.

I was hardly surprised when Nicco pushed his chair back to accommodate Ari on his lap. They couldn't be in the same room without touching.

"Where are the girls?"

"Watching Rivervale or whatever it's called. You know, the one with the guy that wears that stupid hat. Bughead."

"You mean Riverdale?" I snickered. "And it's Jughead."

"Same thing." Matteo shrugged. "Enzo picked them up a bunch of snacks, it should keep them quiet for a while."

At just the mention of his name, my chest tightened.

"Are you playing, Nora?" Tristan asked as he shuffled the deck of cards.

"She doesn't want to play," Enzo said, and I bristled.

"What's the buy in?"

"One hundred dollars."

"Nor," Ari warned.

"Deal me in." I tapped the table.

"We don't have time to explain the rules to you, Abato."

Ouch.

Reducing me to my surname hurt but I refused to let Enzo chase me away. Arianne was my best friend and Tristan, Nicco, and Matteo were my friends by proxy. We had to find a way to be around each other.

"Are we playing Hold 'em, Omaha, or seven card stud?" I asked with a hint of smugness.

"Holy shit, Nora, I think I just came in my pants. You know poker?"

"I know a little bit." I shrugged, graciously accepting a stack of colored chips off Nicco.

"Straight up Texas Hold 'em, yeehaw," Matteo grinned. "But we like to spice things up with a little tequila." He grabbed a bottle off the floor and shook it in front of me. "Lose a hand and you gotta drink."

"Matt, I'm not sure that's a good idea," Arianne protested.

"Don't worry, *bambolina*," he smirked, "Nic won't drink while you're here. But me and Tristan have some unsettled business."

"You do?" Ari asked. "That's news to me."

"Cocky fucker reckons he can drink me under the table."

"I'd put money on it." Tristan snorted.

"I've got twenty on Tristan."

"Seriously, Nora, you wound me." Matteo pouted at me, his huge puppy dog eyes almost too much to resist. But I stuck by my guns. "Sorry, Matt, but I've seen Tristan drink and you're going down."

"Oh, it's on, Capizola." He slapped his hand down on the table. "It's so on."

Matteo uncapped the tequila and poured us each a shot.

"Lose your hand, you drink. Fold, you drink. Go bust... drink. Got it?"

"Just deal the cards, already," Enzo grumbled. I could only just see his big hands from my position which given the stakes had just risen, was probably a good thing.

"Everyone in," Tristan asked, waiting for us to throw our chips in the pot. "Okay, let's play some poker."

TWENTY-ONE

ENZO

NORA WAS KICKING our asses at poker.

I'd sucked in a sharp breath when she and Arianne had emerged from the bedroom and sat with us as if they had any business joining our game. But it had turned out she knew exactly what she was doing.

She'd played it cool to start with, folding on a number of early hands and taking tequila shot after tequila shot like a champ. Part of me wondered if she wanted to end up wasted. I wouldn't blame her if she did. The tension between us was so thick you could cut through it with a knife. Everyone felt it, glancing between us as we went head-to-head in yet another round.

I studied my cards, relieved I could barely see her around Matteo's frame. But as if he felt me staring, the fucker leaned back and gave me a clear view of Nora. Her brows were knitted in deep concentration, the soft lines of her face taut. She was completely invested in the game, and I didn't think I'd ever seen anything so sexy as a girl who knew her way around a game of poker.

"Shit, man, she's going to wipe the floor with you." Matteo cackled, his head rolling slightly. We were almost a bottle and half of tequila in, between the four of us. Matteo and Tristan had lost the most rounds, with me coming in third. But Nora was tiny compared to the three of us, so every shot she took was at least two for us.

"How's it looking, Nor?" Arianne asked her. Nicco had bowed out three rounds in, unable to keep his hands off his wife. But they'd stayed to watch the show.

"It's okay." she pushed a stack of chips into the pot.

"Okay?" Matteo exploded with laughter. "Kick his ass, Nora. Fuck knows he deserves it."

A low growl rumbled in my chest as Tristan waited for me to make my play. "Call," I said confidently, matching her bet.

"Both players call." Tristan discarded the top card and slid off the next card, flipping it over and adding it to the table, followed by two more cards.

Silence echoed through the cabin as we checked our cards. I had a three of a kind. Nora's poker face gave nothing away as she glanced at me to the stack of chips and back to her cards.

"Bet," she said, pushing another stack of chips toward the pot.

I scrubbed a hand down my face. I needed to win this round. It wasn't about the money, it was about her. About not losing to her any more than I already had.

"I'm in," I said.

Tension crackled through the air as Matteo, Nicco, and Arianne watched us duke it out.

Tristan took the next card and flipped it, adding it to the three on the table. "Seven of diamonds."

"Check," Nora said coolly.

"Raise." I called her bluff, trying to force her out of the game. Two-hundred and fifty bucks was a drop in the ocean to me, but to someone like Nora, it was money in her purse.

"Ooof," Matteo grunted.

"Can you shut the fuck up?"

"What? It's tense."

"Nora, the ball's in your court," Tristan said.

She studied her cards closely, her eyes flitting from her hand to the ones lined up on the table.

Fold, I wanted to hiss. *Just fold.*

"Call."

"Nora, are you sure? It's a lot of money." Arianne frowned, but Nora kept quiet, adding the right amount of chips to the pot.

"The turn," Tristan announced adding a fourth card.

Boom. I had four of a kind and the third highest hand a player could have. Logic told me she couldn't have a royal flush, given the lack of picture cards on the table, so she could only beat me with a straight flush. If the river card was a diamond it was a possibility, but what were the chances?

"What'll it be, Abato?" I said without thinking.

Her eyes snapped to mine, filled with an emotion I couldn't decipher. She looked hurt, but she also looked pissed as if I'd just kicked her puppy or something.

My brows furrowed. It was just a name. Shooting the shit over a game of poker. She'd insisted on sitting at the table with us. No one had made her play.

Her eyes narrowed, as she flicked her eyes to her cards and back again.

"Call." The conviction in her voice rattled through my skull. She wasn't going to back down.

"You sure?" My brow lifted, and she craned her neck around Matteo to stare me right in the eyes.

"I said call."

"Have it your way." I matched her bet and waited for Tristan to flip the final card.

A sense of smugness washed over me as I eyed the ten of spades. She couldn't beat me. It was statistically impossible.

But Nora didn't chuck her cards. Instead, she pushed her remaining chips into the pot. "All in." Her eyes held a challenge, only I was no longer sure we were talking about the poker game.

"What's it going to be, Marchetti?" She threw my words back at me, and anger flared inside me.

No way she could beat me.

"Don't come crying to me when you lose, Gattina." I smirked. It shouldn't have felt so good to wipe the table with her, but after last night, the way she'd rejected me, I wanted her to hurt.

Her breath caught. I hadn't meant to say it. Not in front of everyone. But I was enjoying having her at my mercy, even if it wasn't in the way I really wanted.

"E," Nicco warned, but this wasn't between him and me. It was between me and the girl who had buried herself under my skin when I never wanted her there to begin with.

"Okay," Tristan said. "Show your hands."

Nora glanced at me, waiting.

"Four of a kind," I said, laying my cards out.

Her brows knitted for a second but then a slow smile spread over her face. "Looks like you'll be the one paying up, Marchetti." She laid down her cards and I blinked in utter disbelief.

Four tens.

She'd pipped my four sevens. Fuck.

"And that, ladies and gentlemen, is how you play poker." Matteo was enjoying my downfall far too much.

"Fuck off." I grunted, pushing from the table.

"Ah, sore loser, cous?"

I flipped him off over my shoulder as I headed for the door. I needed a smoke. Or another bottle of whisky. Nora had schooled me in front of our friends, and I didn't like the feeling of once again being at her mercy.

Glancing back, I watched the others congratulate her as Tristan exchange the chips for one-hundred-dollar bills.

As if she felt me watching, Nora looked over her shoulder, our eyes colliding. I expected to see smug satisfaction in her big, round, doe eyes, but I found none.

Instead, she looked like the one who'd lost everything.

After walking the perimeter to sober myself up and rein in my anger, I made my way back to the cabin. But right before I reached the door, my cell started vibrating.

"Uncle Toni?"

"How's it going up there?"

"It's... okay."

He chuckled. "The girls giving you a hard time?"

If only he knew.

"Anything?" I asked eagerly. After his call this morning to inform us that there had been no developments overnight, I was hoping they would have something by now.

"Nothing. Not even a sniff."

"Fuck."

"Just hang tight, son. He'll show."

"Maybe he's waiting for me to—"

"Lorenzo." He clucked his tongue. "Listen to me and listen good. I know you want in on this, but until we have no choice, I don't want you here, doing something you might later regret. Stay at the cabin. Leave the hunt to us."

"And if he doesn't show?"

"He will, son. They always do." He inhaled a long, steady breath. "You know, Enzo, your father—"

"Don't."

"You need to hear this, son. Your father, pezzo di merda, lost his way. He was blinded by greed and power. What happened with Vincenzo will haunt me forever because I was his brother. I should have seen the signs. *I* should have noticed. Me. That shit falls on my shoulders, Lorenzo. Not yours."

"It just makes no sense," I confessed. "He would have died for you."

"A wise man once said, 'greed makes a man foolish and blind, and makes him an easy prey for death.' Vincenzo knew what he was doing, and he paid the price. But I refuse to lose you to misplaced guilt, Lorenzo."

I scrubbed a hand over my face. He was right. I didn't want to pay for the sins of my father, but how did you escape his legacy when his DNA flowed through your veins?

"Go be with your cousins. I'll be in touch soon."

"Yeah, okay." I wanted to argue, but I knew there was no point. He was the boss as he'd so aptly pointed out more than once.

But when I stepped back into the cabin, I immediately regretted it.

"What the fuck?" I grumbled, watching as Nora danced with the girls, the three of them falling over each other and giggling hysterically.

"Guess who snuck a bottle of wine into their room." Matteo let out a strained breath. "Next time we need to lock that shit away."

"Oh relax, big brother." Bella poked her tongue out between her lips. "We're having fun. You should try it some time."

"Somebody make it stop." Matteo buried his face in his hands, but Nora strutted over to him and grabbed his hands.

"Bella's right, Matt, don't be such a spoilsport. We're stuck here... we may as well have some fuuuun." She staggered back and he leaped up, steadying her.

"You're halfway to being toasted." His eyes flicked to mine and I ground my teeth together, going to the kitchen. I was going to need something stronger than tequila to get through tonight.

The music went up a notch and the heavy beat of The Weeknd filled the cabin.

"I love this one," Sia yelled.

"Keep an eye on them," Nicco said as he pulled Arianne toward the hall leading to the bedrooms.

"Really? You want me to babysit while you two go fuck like newlyweds?"

Arianne winced at my harsh words.

"Just don't let them drink anymore," he said, cutting me with a hard look, "and make sure they drink a glass of water before bed. Oh, and make sure Tristan stays the fuck away from them."

"Tristan?" I balk. "What the fuck?"

"It would appear the girls have developed quite the crush on my cousin," Arianne explained.

"On *Tristan*?" Disbelief coated my words.

"Stranger things have happened." Nicco shook his head. "Just watch him."

"Nicco, Tristan would never—"

"Fine, watch them then. Just watch them. *All* of them. Nora included. She's drunk and she's hurting."

"Hurting? What the fuck are you—"

"One day you'll realize, E, and it'll probably be too damn late," he said, guiding his wife down the hall.

Nora was hurting?

She was the one who pushed me away last night, not the other way around. If anyone was supposed to feel dejected, it was me.

You called her a whore. I shut down the memory. I didn't mean it; it had just spilled out in the heat of the moment.

I watched her dancing with Matteo, the two of them laughing and joking. He was so fucking different to me. He found it easy; being around girls, charming them with his goofy smile and big heart. It didn't actually get him a lot of pussy. He was too picky when it came to who he let into his bed, but he could have had any girl who laid eyes on him.

Including Nora.

Fuck, they looked good together as he spun her around, reeling her in and then flinging her back out. Tristan watched on, sipping a beer and smiling at the two of them. Alessia and Bella were trying to replicate some girl band dance or something, which made me snort. They looked fucking ridiculous.

"You should come join us," Matteo called, and I flipped him off.

"Oh God," Bella cried suddenly, clutching her stomach. "I don't feel so good." She dashed toward the hall, Alessia hot on her heels.

"Don't throw up in the bedroom," she called after her cousin.

"Fuck's sake," Matteo ground out. "Looks like fun time is over." He stormed after his sister.

"I'm going to call it a night too, I think," Tristan said. He gave me a curt nod as he passed me on the way to the bedrooms.

Nora flopped down on the couch and grabbed her drink.

"Is that a good idea?" I asked, leaning against the wall.

"Do you care?"

My shoulders lifted in a small shrug. "Don't blame me tomorrow when you've got a hangover from hell."

"You're such a fucking hypocrite," she murmured, downing the drink in one.

I flinched at her cold tone.

"What, no comeback?"

My chest heaved as I stalked across the room to go outside for a smoke. She was drunk, and the last thing I wanted to do was get into it with an emotional, drunk girl.

But as I reached the door, she stood up and swayed on her feet.

"Whoa," she breathed.

"You good?" I fought a smirk as I went to go to her.

"I'm fine," she snapped, warding me off with her hand.

She wasn't fine. She was ass over elbow drunk. But I gave her space to pass me. Except she tripped on the corner of the rug and stumbled forward.

"Owwww," she cried, right as I caught her. "I've got it. I've got it." Nora glowered at me, her eyes cloudy and glittering with contempt.

I steadied her and stepped back. "Sure about that?"

She swayed gently on the spot. "I'm fine. At least, I will be when the room stops spinning." Burying her hands in her face, Nora began to topple again.

"Fuck," I grunted as I scooped her up, much to her displeasure.

"Put me down." She batted my chest. "I swear to God, Lorenzo Marchetti, put me down right this—*whoa*!" Her head rolled back as I stalked down the hall toward her room. I could hear Matteo berating Bella for getting drunk and puking everywhere. Thankfully, all was quiet from Nicco and Ari's room. Nobody needed to hear the two of them going at it.

Kicking the door open, I went inside and dropped Nora on the bed.

"Asshole," she hissed.

"I'll get you some water."

"I don't need any—" Her words rolled off my back as I left her to go and get her a glass of water and some Advil.

When I got back to her room, she was curled up in a ball, clutching a pillow.

"Nora?"

No answer.

I leaned over her and stroked the hair from her face. "Gattina?"

She murmured softly, snuggling the pillow tighter.

I lingered for a second, watching the gentle rise and fall of her chest and then I walked out of there...

Wishing I didn't have to.

TWENTY-TWO

NORA

I WOKE with a brass band marching in my head.

"Ugh." Reaching out, I fumbled around to locate my cell phone and dragged it back to me.

It was a little after nine and I felt deathly. My mind was a hazy amateur movie of poker, tequila, and... *dancing*?

Huh?

That seemed a little odd, but I definitely remembered dancing with the girls and Matteo. I'd really hit the tequila hard after beating Enzo and winning the poker game. But it hadn't felt much like winning when he'd called me Gattina in front of everyone and then stormed from the cabin.

Damn him. He was such a stubborn asshole. Everyone could feel the tension between us. They'd spent the entire game glancing from him to me and back again, and it had become so much more than just a friendly game of poker. But in the end, Enzo did what Enzo always did.

He walked away.

And I did something out of the ordinary, I grabbed the half empty bottle of tequila, turned up the music, and decided to make the most of the situation.

Of course it had royally backfired.

My eyes fluttered closed as I tried to remember how I'd gotten to bed. And then it hit.

Enzo.

He'd carried me to bed.

Perfect.

Just perfect.

I clutched the pillow, groaning into the soft material. When I gingerly rolled onto my side, I frowned at the glass of water and box of pain pills. My lips curved a fraction. Maybe he wasn't a cold-hearted bastard after all.

I popped two tabs and swallowed them down. Tomorrow was Monday, and I wanted to go back to my life. To classes and some kind of normal. As far as I was aware, there had been no further attacks, so maybe whoever was targeting the Marchetti had given up. Or maybe they had it wrong. Maybe it wasn't related to Vincenzo at all.

A gentle knock at my door sounded like an explosion in my skull.

"Hello?" I groaned.

"It's me." Arianne slipped inside. "How are you feeling?"

"Like I drank my body weight in tequila."

"I hate to be the one to say it, but you did." She smiled but I found no judgment there. "He's really under your skin, isn't he?"

"What do you think?"

"Honestly?" Her brow lifted. "I think you're too good for him, Nora."

"It doesn't matter now anyway. He made his choice."

And it wasn't me.

"Do you think we can go home soon?"

I didn't want to spend a second longer here than necessary.

"Hopefully. Nicco is on the phone with his father right now."

"How are the girls?" I asked.

"Bella looks as green as you."

"Ouch."

"Matteo is still railing at her."

"At least I don't have to worry about Gio being around to lecture me."

Just then, my cell vibrated.

"Let me guess," Ari said as I checked it. "Luca?"

"Maybe." I smothered a smile as I read his text message.

When are you coming back? Turns out our other neighbors are awfully boring.

Hopefully later today.

Dinner at mine? I still owe you...

"What does he want?" Ari asked, trying to peer over my hands.

"He invited me for dinner."

"Like a date?"

"No, like two friends hanging out," I corrected her.

"Sounds like a date to me."

"He knows I'm not looking for anything serious right now."

"Just be careful, Nora. I know you probably want to get back at Enz—"

"That's not what this is, babe. Luca is a friend." And friends could have dinner, couldn't they?

Only if I can help cook?

I hit send, and his reply came straight back.

Deal. See you around five?

"Tell me you didn't just do what I think you did." Ari frowned, concern shining in her eyes.

"What does it matter?"

"Even if we get to go home, you'll have round the clock security until Antonio is satisfied that the threat is gone."

"So?" I shrugged. "Maurice can protect me from outside Luca's apartment."

"And if Enzo finds out?"

"It's not a secret, babe. It isn't illegal to have dinner with a friend. Besides, he won't care."

"Because Enzo *not* caring has worked out so well for you in the past." She gave me a pointed look.

"What happened to *I'm too good for him*?"

"You are, but love doesn't always follow the rules. All I'm saying is don't push him too hard, because you might not like his response."

"There is nothing that guy can do to hurt me anymore than he already has," I confessed. But the second I said the words, I felt the lie coil around my heart.

There was another knock at the door, and Nicco stuck his head around it.

"What did he say?" Ari got up and went to him.

His eyes moved past her to mine, and just like that we were back to me being on the outside.

I pulled the covers around me and let out a frustrated sigh. "Can we go home or not?"

"Yeah, we're going home. But security will be increased, until we have a handle on this."

"Great, I'd better get used to Maurice following every time I go for a pee again then." In the days after my kidnapping, I'd had someone with me at all times. I couldn't move without Maurice or another security guy leaping into action. It was tiresome, not to mention suffocating. But that's what happened when you were Arianne Capizola's best friend and she was married to the Marchetti crime family's heir.

I didn't get kidnapped because *I* was important, I got taken because I was important to *her*.

It was the same now. No one wanted to hurt me directly, they wanted to hurt people close to the Family.

"We'll leave you to pack." Arianne shot me a sympathetic smile. Life wouldn't change for her. She'd stay at their well-guarded apartment in Romany Square with Nicco by her side. The girls would return home and be protected by their families, and me?

I'd go home to my apartment alone with Maurice for company.

Forty minutes later, after a quick breakfast, we were packed into the SUVs heading back to Verona. Only this time, Tristan was riding with us in place of Enzo. Matteo said it was because tensions were high and Nicco wanted to know Enzo was with his sister should anything happen. But I knew every guy here and they would all take a bullet for Alessia Marchetti. Even Tristan. I'd seen the way he'd watched her this weekend. You couldn't help but be drawn to the Marchetti princess. She was kind and compassionate and she had this warmth that pulled you in whenever you were in her orbit. Tristan would never act on it; he was five years her senior and he knew Nicco would put a bullet through his skull if he so much as looked wrong at her. But I saw it. The longing in his eyes, the hunger. He was a hot-blooded male and in a couple of years she would be every guy's wet dream.

He caught my eye, frowning as if he could hear my thoughts. I smiled meekly and turned my attention to the tinted windows, watching the dense forest fade away in the distance.

My insides still felt a little tender, so I closed my eyes and let the hypnotic whir of the engine lull me to sleep.

It only felt like minutes later when Arianne gently shook my shoulder. "We're here Nora."

"Huh, what?" I blinked, wiping the drool from my mouth.

Tristan snorted and I flipped him off.

"We're at La Stella."

"We are?"

She nodded. "Want me to come—"

"No, Bambolina. Maurice and Alexi will stay with her."

"Fun," I mumbled. "I'll see you soon, okay?"

Arianne pulled me into a tight hug. "Be safe, and please do what Maurice says."

"Relax, I know the drill." I wasn't about to take any unnecessary risks, no matter how much I hated the idea of being under protective custody again.

The door opened and Maurice was there to guide me into the building. "It's good to see you again Miss—Nora." He gave me an apologetic smile.

"I wish I could say the same thing, Maurice, I really do." I trudged ahead of him, glancing around for the second SUV, but it was nowhere to be seen. They probably dropped the girls off at home first before doing whatever Matteo and Enzo planned on doing now they were back.

"Nicco explained that I am to be your full-time security detail again?"

"He did."

"They are happy for you to attend classes on Monday so long as I—"

"Yup, I got it." I waved him off, retrieving my key from my purse and unlocking my apartment. But at the last second, I stepped aside, letting him pass.

He withdrew his pistol and slipped inside. A minute later, he called, "all clear," and I went in.

I was getting another headache, so I went straight to the kitchen cabinet and pulled out a box of Advil and poured myself a glass of water. Dinner with Luca was at five. I had a few hours to recover.

"Maurice," I yelled, and he appeared. "I'm going back to bed. Please don't wake me unless absolutely necessary. This evening I'll be going across the hall to have dinner with Luca."

"Uh, Miss Abato… Nora," he corrected himself, "I'm not sure Mr. Marchetti would allow that."

"Nicco can go fuck himself."

"That's not—"

"Look, Luca was vetted. He's good people. He wouldn't live in the building if he wasn't. You can stand guard right outside or come in for all I care. But Maurice, I am going."

I stormed into my bedroom and slammed the door. I was being petulant, I knew that. But I was so annoyed. Annoyed that I was here alone, annoyed that Enzo lived up to his reputation as a cold-hearted bastard with no remorse, and most of all, I was annoyed at myself for being annoyed when he'd been through so much recently. Gah. My head was a jumble of thoughts and feelings and emotions I couldn't contain. I yanked off my sweater and shimmied out of my jeans, climbing into bed in just my tank top and panties, pulled the cover over my head and closed my eyes.

Maybe when I woke up this time, everything would be a damn sight better.

A girl could dream.

Someone was in the room with me. I felt them watching me, a trickle of awareness making my hair stand on end. But when I finally opened my eyes, it was empty. I sat up and combed my fingers through my unruly curls.

"Maurice?" I called.

Nothing.

Odd.

I'd woken to the strangest sensation of being watched.

"Maurice?" I pushed off the covers and clambered out of bed and went into the living room.

"Nora?" He looked up from his newspaper. "What is it?"

"Were you just in my room?"

"No, why?"

"Huh." My finger found my lips and prodded. "I had the strangest dream. What time is it?"

"A little after three-thirty."

"I slept all day?"

"Hangovers will do that to you." He smirked and I rolled my eyes.

"I'm going to shower and get ready. Make yourself at home." Sarcasm laced my words, and his amused laughter followed me into the bathroom.

I took my time in the shower, washing away the last couple of days. There was no point in dwelling on what would never be. Arianne was right, Enzo was too lost to his demons to pull his head out of his ass long enough to see what was staring him in the face.

We were doomed from the start, and I had to accept it.

No matter how hard it was.

After finishing in the bathroom, I made my way back into my bedroom and checked my cell phone.

I hope you're hungry.

I smiled at Luca's text, my stomach grumbling in appreciation. Now the nausea had passed, I could eat a small cow.

The black turtleneck sweater dress I picked molded to my shapely curves, but I didn't bother with shoes, choosing to go barefoot across the hall. This wasn't a date. It was two friends sharing a good meal and easy conversation. At least, as I knocked on Luca's door, my Maurice-shaped shadow behind me, that's what I hoped it would be.

The door swung open and Luca beamed. "You came."

"I said I would."

"Touché." He motioned for me to enter, but abruptly paused. "Is he joining us or—"

I glanced back at Maurice. "What'll it be, big guy?"

"I'll wait outside."

I nodded, shooting him an appreciative smile. I was safe with Luca. There was one door in and out, so unless the threat was going to scale the building and climb through Luca's balcony door, it was just the two of us.

"I hope everything was okay with your family?"

"It was fine, thank you. Crisis averted." I forced a smile, following him into the living room. The smell of garlic, parsley, and rich tomato sauce hit me, making my stomach growl.

"You're hungry?" An uncertain smirk played on his lips, to which I replied, "ravenous."

"And the bodyguard?"

"Just a precaution."

"Am I a threat now?"

"It isn't you they're worried about," I said, perching on a stool as he tended to the pan of pasta.

"Let me guess, you can't tell me."

"Honestly, I don't know much either." It was a white lie, but it was easier than the truth. "Being best friend's with Arianne Capizola comes with a certain set of complications."

"Is Enzo Marchetti one of them?"

My heart lurched into my throat. "You've been doing your research."

"I wanted to know who I'm up against, yeah."

"Luca, that's not—"

"Yeah, I know." He exhaled out a steady breath. "I was worried, so I did some Googling."

"You shouldn't have done that. If you want to know things about me, you should have asked."

"Would you have told me?" My lips pressed into a thin line and he added, "That's what I thought."'

"I came over here to get away from all that." I sighed.

"You can't blame me for being worried. There's something between us, Nora." His eyes bore into mine with so much intensity, I had to break the connection.

"Luca, don't do this, please. We agreed, friends only."

Silence ticked by, turning the air thick and suffocating. When he didn't answer, I got up. "Maybe this was a mistake."

"Wait," he rushed out. "I'm sorry. I didn't plan to make this awkward, I swear. I was going to play it cool, but then I saw you and everything got messed up in my head."

"Well, can you un-mess it so we can eat, because that smells so good and I'm really hungry." My stomach growled on cue.

"Deal. We eat, we talk, and we leave everything else at the door."

"That sounds perfect," I said. Because it did. Even if it was a temporary truce before Luca started fighting for me again. I knew he would. I saw the fierce determination in his eyes. But what I still didn't know...

Was, did I want him to?

TWENTY-THREE

ENZO

SHE WAS at Luca's eating his food in his fucking apartment. All because I was too fucked up to get my shit together and be the kind of guy she needed.

But I wasn't that guy.

I was never going to be that guy.

So what choice did I have but to let her go?

Grabbing the glass nearest to me, I launched it across the room, watching it smash against the wall, shattering into a thousand pieces.

Everything was a mess.

Nora was with Luca, giving him her smiles and sass and maybe if he was lucky, her sinful body. And I was stuck here, in my apartment, waiting for the call that the fucker toying with us had reared his ugly face again.

I didn't just want to destroy him, I wanted to break every bone in his body and then spend my sweet time putting him back together so I could do it all over again.

I felt the weight of the knife strapped to my ankle, the pistol in its holster around my chest, and the brass knuckles tucked neatly in my inside pocket. I was a fighter primed for a fight... without an opponent. But the time would come, and when it did, that motherfucker was mine. I clenched my fist, feeling a lick of steely determination zip up my spine.

Just then, Matteo's voice rang out through the apartment. "Cous, you here?"

"Where else would I be?" I snapped.

"Thought you might be staking out La Stella. Trying to get a look at Nora and Luca." He strolled over to the refrigerator and grabbed two beers.

"Did you come here to bust my balls or to tell me we have a body to bury?"

"Someone's happy to see me." Matteo handed me a bottle and sat down on the chair opposite. "Actually, I came to stop you from doing something stupid. But I can see that's going well." He eyed the stained wall and pile of glass on the floor.

"I feel like I'm losing my fucking mind," I admitted. "All I can think about is my old man. His wicked fucking smirk as he confessed to killing Aunt Lucia. Then she's there… Nora… tangled up in the memories."

"Just admit it. You want her."

"Yeah, I fucking want her, she's—" Fuck. Nora was like no one else I'd ever met. But it didn't change anything. "I'm not cut out for that life."

"Who says? You? Because I gotta tell you, cous, you're not thinking straight lately."

I flipped him off. "Feel free to leave."

"And miss out on you sitting here like a lost puppy? No fucking chance. Besides, I'm here on official orders."

"You mean Nic's orders."

"Yeah." His expression fell. "He's worried."

My eyes rolled. "Because you're all fucking pussies. Ari has made him soft and you… you've always been soft."

"Seriously though, just go over there and tell her how you really feel. Kills two birds with one stone."

"How do you figure?"

"You get to protect her while boning—"

I grabbed a cushion and threw it at his head.

"What?" He caught it, chuckling. "You know I'm right. If you don't make a move soon, Luca will sweep in and—"

"She's better off without me." I tipped my head back and closed my eyes, swigging my beer.

"Whatever you say, man, but I want it noted that I think you're making a big fucking mistake."

"Noted." My eyes landed on his as I drained the rest of my beer and slammed it down on the table. "I think we're going to need something stronger."

The blare of my cell phone cut through the darkness. I scrambled to find it, tapping the nightstand until my fingers grazed the smooth plastic.

"Yeah?" I grumbled, my head pounding.

"Mr. Marchetti, we've got a problem."

At the sound of Maurice's voice, I bolted upright. "What is it? Is she okay?"

"She's fine. But there's been an incident at La Stella, a package."

"A package?" I was already out of bed, pulling on my clothes, and arming myself with my favorite weapons.

"It was addressed to Nora."

Fuck.

Fuck.

My fist found the nearest wall. Pain exploded along my knuckles, but I barely felt it, red hot anger flooding every inch of me.

"What is it?"

"Well, that's the strange thing, sir." He sucked in a sharp breath. "It appears to be for you."

"I'm on my way."

"What should I tell Miss Abato?"

Shit, Nora. She was going to freak the fuck out.

"Nothing, don't wake her yet."

"That's the other thing, Mr. Marchetti," he hesitated.

"Go on..." My teeth ground together.

"She stayed over at her neighbor's, Mr. Bianco."

My stone heart plummeted into my toes.

She stayed over.

Did she fuck him? Let him touch her sinful curves and kiss her pouty lips?

Jealousy threatened to consume me as I imagined the two of them naked, bodies writhing and slick with sweat.

Rein. It. The. Fuck. In.

Just because she stayed over doesn't mean anything happened.

Who the fuck was I kidding? That's exactly what it meant.

I grabbed my keys. It was a little after midnight. The streets would be clear enough for me to drive, but I knew my cousins would kick my ass if they knew I'd driven over the limit.

"Yo, asshole," I banged on Matteo's door.

"Yeah?" he murmured.

"We need to go."

"Shit, now?" He sounded disoriented, but I knew it was from sleep and not liquor since he'd stopped after two beers while I'd kept going.

The door swung open revealing a half-naked Matteo. "Where?" He ran a hand down his face.

"Nora got a package at La Stella."

"Fuck. What's in it?"

"Maurice didn't give me the details over the phone. Just said he didn't think it was for Nora at all.

"If it's not for Nora then who—*oh shit.*"

"We need to go, now."

"Yeah, okay. Just let me grab some clothes."

Five minutes later, we were climbing into Matt's truck.

My leg bounced uncontrollably as we left Romany Square and made the short journey to University Hill.

"She'll be okay. Maurice and his team are there."

"Nora isn't there," I ground out.

"What do you mean, she isn't there?"

"She stayed over at Luca's."

"Shit, cous, that's rough. I'm sorry."

I felt his eyes on the side of my face, but I didn't meet his sympathetic gaze. "You and Nic were right all along," I muttered.

"I'm not following," he said.

"You told me she'd slip through my fingers."

"So fight for her. You're a Marchetti, E. Fighting's what we do."

My eyes flicked to his in a questioning expression.

"Oh, fuck you," he chuckled. "I can fight."

My brows hit my hairline as I smirked. "You fight like a girl."

"I'm a lover, not a fighter."

"Yeah, you are." But from where I was sitting, it didn't seem like such a bad thing to be. He wasn't harboring all the hate and bitterness I was. Sure, Uncle Michele wasn't a traitorous lying cunt, but I'd been like this *before*.

Angry.

Bitter.

Cold.

I was my father's son, and, deep down, I knew he was the reason I pushed Nora away. Not because of what I did but because of what I *was*.

A killer.

A cold blooded murderer.

A sinner.

She was too good, too fucking pure for this life. She deserved Prince Charming, not the villain.

She deserved someone like Luca. Someone who would be there and show up. Someone who wouldn't bring death and destruction and danger to her doorstep.

I scrubbed a hand down my face, wishing Matteo would step on it.

"So, if the parcel's for you, we have to assume he's watching you, or has, at the very least, done his homework."

"I don't give a shit about me."

"We can protect Nora."

"Not the point, Matt, and you know it." Nora was in this position because of me. Because whoever was fucking with us had some unfinished business all thanks to my father.

After what felt like a lifetime, Matteo finally pulled up outside of La Stella. I leaped from the truck not giving a shit that I was out in the open. I had to get to her. Now.

But Maurice intercepted me before I even reached the stairs. "He left it at the main doors. Security called me when they noticed."

"They get any footage?" I glanced at the security cameras trained on the entrance to the building.

"Alexi is checking now."

"Good, let me know the second you hear. Where's the package?"

"Inside her apartment."

"She still with Luca?"

He nodded. "How do you want to proceed?"

"Show me the package."

I followed Maurice up to Nora's apartment. My eyes narrowed as I passed Luca's door. What I really wanted was to kick the fucking thing down and punish her for ever thinking she could pull that shit on me. But I knew better, and I knew Nora would only dig her heels in all the more if I went off at the deep end all because she'd done what I'd been doing week in and week out.

But those women meant nothing, they were a means to an end. Luca was different. He had boyfriend potential.

I forced myself to take a deep breath and follow Maurice into Nora's apartment.

"It's right over here." He led me to the breakfast counter.

The small box was nondescript except for a hand scrawled label with Nora's address on.

"Here." Maurice handed me a latex glove and I pulled it on, carefully opening the lid.

"What the fuck is that?" I peered inside, paling when I realized what I was staring at. "That's Gino's chain."

Now I could get a better look, I would recognize the heavy gold chain anywhere. The dried blood caked on the chain links confirmed it.

"Who is this motherfucker?" I hissed.

"What shall I do with it, sir?"

"Call our guys at local PD and have them run it for prints. Maybe we'll get lucky."

"I'll make sure it gets into the right hands."

"Thanks."

"And Miss Abato?"

"I'll deal with Nora."

Matteo appeared just then. "Well…"

"He sent me a souvenir."

The blood drained from his face. "Please tell me there were no body parts."

"Gino's blood encrusted gold chain."

"Fuck."

"Yeah. I'll be right back." I stormed past him, but Matteo caught my arm.

"Are you sure this is a good idea?"

"She needs to know."

And I needed her here, where I could keep my eye on her.

"She's going to be pissed." Matt grimaced.

"I can handle it." But as I said the words, I wasn't sure of anything anymore.

I was supposed to want to be out there, hunting him. Not resting until he was six feet under with a bullet hole through his skull. But all I could think about was getting Nora out of Luca's apartment and away from here, to somewhere safe. Somewhere the fucker couldn't walk right up to the door and leave her little packages.

"It's your death sentence," Matteo mumbled as I walked away. It was almost one in the morning. They would be sleeping, hopefully not together because I wasn't ready to see that. It was bad enough collecting her from his apartment as it was.

I rapped my knuckles on the door and waited. When no one answered, I added a little force behind it.

"What the fuck are you doing?" Luca grimaced at the sight of me.

"I need to speak to Nora."

"She's sleeping. It's the middle of the fucking night."

"It's an emergency."

"An emergency? What kind of emergency?" He had the gall to stare me down. "Because from where I'm standing it looks like the guy who continually hurts her wants to hurt her again. Well, I got—"

"Enzo?"

Relief slammed into me, but then I saw what she was wearing and all the anger and jealousy I felt hit me like a tsunami.

"There's something we need to deal with," I said, barely able to look at her. Her long smooth legs peeking out from under a t-shirt.

His fucking t-shirt. Unless all of a sudden, she wore a man's size.

"I'll be across the hall," I said, spinning on my heel.

Luca started trying to comfort her, insisting she didn't need to follow my orders all the time. But I didn't stick around to hear the rest. Visions of her in his clothes were seared into the backs of my eyes.

And I hated it.

I hated it so fucking much.

But it wasn't the hatred that caught me off guard. It was the regret. Thick, sludgy regret that slithered through me like a poisonous snake, coiling around my heart and threatening to squeeze the life right out of it.

I stormed back into her apartment and waited. Matteo didn't say a word, scrolling his phone, no doubt keeping Nicco in the loop.

A minute later, I felt her enter the room.

"What is it, what's wrong?" she asked.

"We've got a problem." I didn't meet her eyes.

"Enzo, look at me." I was powerless against her soft command, turning around to look at her. She was dressed, at least. "What. Happened?"

"Whoever is doing this... he knows you're here."

"*What*?"

"I'll just be..." Matteo left us alone.

"He must have been watching me, watching us." The words were like sandpaper against my throat. "He sent something to you... something for me."

"Oh my God." She wrapped her arms around herself and shivered. "H-he was here?"

"He didn't get inside the building, but he left the package at the front door."

"What was in it?"

"It doesn't matter."

"What was in it, Enzo?" She bit out, and I flinched.

"Gino's gold chain. The guy I was working with in Providence... the guy he... killed."

"Jesus," she breathed, and before I knew what was happening, she marched toward me and threw her arms around me. "I'm so sorry this is happening to you."

I stood there dumbfounded. I'd expected her to be angry, to scream and yell and blame me... I hadn't expected *this*.

"You can hug me back, you know," she chuckled softly, and I gingerly wrapped my arms around her, burying my face in the crook of her neck.

God, she felt good pressed up against me, holding me. I wanted to stay there forever, secreted away from all the shit circling me. But all too soon, she pulled away, tucking her wild curls behind her ear.

"Sorry," a slow blush spread up her neck and into her cheeks, "I just—"

"It's okay."

Something flashed in her eyes, but there was a knock at the door, and Maurice came inside. "We pulled the security footage."

"And?"

He grimaced. "You should probably come and take a look at it."

"Okay. Stay here with Nora. I need to call Nicco and Uncle Toni."

"Already handled."

"Thank you."

"The boss is sending more guys. We'll double security on both exits and put more guys outside Nora's—"

"Whoa, wait a second. You think he'll come back?" The blood drained from her face once more.

I wanted to reach out and touch her, comfort her the way she had comforted me. But I didn't know how. I didn't know...

"We can't take any risks," I said thickly. Glancing away so she wouldn't see the emotion in my eyes.

Jesus, he knew she lived here.

It changed everything.

"Maurice will stay right here with you okay?" I finally went to her and cupped the back of her neck, staring down at her. "I'll be as quick as I can."

"Okay." She swallowed, but I saw the trust glitter in her eyes. After everything, Nora still trusted me to keep her safe.

Yet, it was knowing me, being someone important to me, that had put her in harm's way.

My hand lingered on her neck, the urge to kiss her so fucking overpowering that I immediately released her and stepped away.

She misread the action, hurt flashing in her eyes. “I’m going to get some coffee,” she said. “Looks like it’s going to be a long night.”

I gave her a small nod…

And then I got the hell out of there.

TWENTY-FOUR

NORA

I MADE a fresh pot of coffee while we waited for Enzo to reappear.

Maurice made himself scarce, blending into the shadows in the corner of the living room. But Matteo didn't give me space. He perched at the counter, graciously accepting a mug of coffee from me.

"Nice t-shirt." His brow arched, and I let out a heavy sigh.

"It's not what you think."

"And what do you think I think?"

"Matt..."

"So, you're telling me, you didn't spend the night bumping uglies with your—"

A loud bang at the door startled us.

"What the hell?" Matteo mumbled.

"Stay back." Maurice withdrew his pistol. "I'll get it." But the second he checked the peephole; he holstered his gun. "It's Mr. Bianco."

"Jesus, the guy doesn't know when to quit, does he?"

I shot Matteo a scathing look. "Let him in, Maurice." Maurice glanced at Matteo and I let out an exasperated breath. "It's my apartment and unless I'm mistaken, I am not a prisoner here, so please answer the door for *Mr. Bianco*."

Maurice answered the door and stepped back.

"I'm sorry," Luca rushed out as I approached. "I know you told me to stay away, but I'm over there worrying, dreaming up all these crazy scenarios in my head, and I—"

"Luca, breathe." I chuckled but it came out strained. "I'm okay."

"I can see that." His cheeks burned. "Matteo." He gave him a stiff nod.

"I'd say it's good to see you again, but I'm loyal to my cousin so—"

"*Matt*!"

"What?" He shrugged. "You should probably wrap this up before Enzo comes back."

Fuck my life.

Why did this have to be happening?

All I'd wanted was to have dinner with a friend, and now I was stuck between a rock and a hard place again.

"Matteo's right, you should go," I said. "It's late and the crisis is averted. I'll talk to you tomorrow, okay?" I started to close the door, but Luca's hand flew out, stopping it.

"I suggest you back the fuck up." Enzo growled from down the hall. A shiver ran through me at the sheer anger in his voice. But there was something else there too, under the surface.

Something that sounded a lot like possessiveness.

"*Me*?" Luca balked. "If I recall correctly, it wasn't your apartment Nora spent the night at."

A gasp slipped from my lips, anger flooding. "You should go, Luca. Now!"

"Shit, Nora." He ran a hand down his face. "I didn't mean—"

"Just go. Maurice, please escort Luca back to his apartment." I stepped aside letting my bodyguard usher Luca away. His eyes pleaded with me, but I didn't concede. I was still too shocked he'd said that.

Enzo came closer, anger radiating off him. But he didn't berate me… he didn't say anything. Just stalked past me and disappeared into my apartment.

With a heavy heart, I followed him inside. Everything was such a mess, and this, it was my fault.

Enzo was discussing something with Maurice and Matteo. They looked over, but I disappeared into my bedroom, shedding the t-shirt Luca had let me borrow and pulling on my 'let's avocuddle' t-shirt and some pajama shorts.

When I went back into the living room, Matteo and Maurice were gone.

"Where is everyone?" I asked.

But Enzo didn't hear me, his dark gaze drinking in the sight of me. When his eyes landed on my t-shirt, an amused smirk tipped the corner of his mouth.

"What?"

"You are so fucking weird."

"Gee, thanks." I went over to the coffee machine, needing to distract myself from his intense stare.

I set about making a fresh pot and waited. I didn't feel him move behind me until his hands slid around my waist.

"Is it true?" he whispered, so quietly I almost missed it.

"Is what true?" I sucked in a harsh breath as he pulled me closer to his chest. His mouth dipped to my ear.

"Did you sleep with him, Gattina. Did you let him fuck you?"

"It doesn't matter," I said, my eyes fluttering closed as he breathed against the curve of my neck.

"It matters. You know it does."

"The last time I checked, you didn't want me." The words cut me deep.

"There isn't a single second of the day when I don't want you, Gattina. But it doesn't change the fact I *shouldn't* want you."

"Enzo." I tried to turn in his arms, but he had me caged against the counter.

"Just put me out of my misery and tell me…"

God, I wanted to tell him. I wanted to drive a knife through his heart the way he'd done so many times to me.

But I wasn't cruel and even now, I still didn't want to hurt him. Not when I knew he was dealing with so much.

"Enzo…" My voice cracked.

"It's okay, Gattina." His lips ghosted over my collarbone sending bolts of electricity zipping through me.

"I didn't sleep with him."

"What?"

"I went over to have dinner with him. There was wine. Too much wine. I spilled a glass all over me, so Luca gave me a clean t-shirt. I got embarrassed and a little upset. I didn't want to be alone, so he let me stay. We didn't—"

Enzo spun me in his arms. "You didn't fuck him?"

"I wanted to. I wanted to do it so much. I wanted to get back at you for hurting me. But I couldn't do it because no matter how much you don't want me to care, I do. I care, Lorenzo Marchetti." Tears pooled in the corners of my eyes as I slid my hands up his chest. "I care and I don't know how to stop." The first tear fell right as Enzo splayed his hand around my throat and kissed me. His lips were hard and bruising, every lick of his tongue steady and sure. He didn't just kiss me, he devoured me without hesitation.

"Fuck, Gattina," he rasped against my mouth. "I thought I'd lost you to him." Enzo grabbed my ass and lifted me slightly, grinding into me with impressive restraint.

My heart soared at his words, at the possessive way he held me, as if he would never let me go. I didn't want him to. I'd only ever wanted this. Us. Together.

"Never," I breathed. "He knows I'm yours. Only yours, Enzo."

He hoisted me higher, forcing my legs around his waist and walked me through the apartment until we were in my bedroom.

Liquid lust coursed through my body, I wanted him so much. But Enzo didn't kiss me again. Instead, he placed me on my feet and moved around my bed, pulling back the covers.

"Get in."

"But—"

"Get in the damn bed, Gattina." He smirked before yanking his sweater off.

Heat flooded me as I traced the ink covering Enzo's body, every ridge and muscle. God, he was perfection.

He kicked off his boots and unbuttoned his jeans, pushing them over his hips and letting them pool at his feet. The thick outline of his erection didn't help the firestorm building in my stomach.

He climbed into bed and pulled me into his arms.

"Are you hugging me?"

"No," he said, "I'm avocuddling you."

A wide grin tugged at my mouth as I lifted my face to his. "Is this a dream? Did I bump my head and wake up in some alternate universe where bad boy Enzo Marchetti's got jokes?"

"Don't push it." His fingers attacked my waist, tickling and pinching, making me shriek.

"Okay, okay, I'm sorry… I won't mention it again." My laughter subsided, silence filling the space between us. "Are you okay?" I asked.

"Isn't that supposed to be my line?" Enzo swallowed thickly. "I am so fucking sorry to bring this to your door."

"What can I say, I'm a magnet for deranged murderous psychopaths." It was supposed to be a joke, but the second I said the words, I regretted them. "Enzo, I didn't mean—"

"I know what you meant." His fingers began stroking my skin, sending shivers skating up and down my skin. It was my turn to swallow. "Is this okay?" His voice crackled with lust.

I nodded, mesmerized by the way he looked at me. As if I was a precious stone, fragile and breakable.

His hand dropped to my thigh, hitching my leg over his hip. I leaned in to kiss him, but Enzo moved just out of reach, smirking. "I want to watch you," he said. "I want to see your eyes flutter and your cheeks flush when you come for me."

His hand moved higher along my thigh, stroking the skin there. Back and forth, back and forth, until he slid it between my legs and found my center. Hooking my panties aside, he pushed two fingers inside me, curling them deep while his thumb rolled over my clit in firm, lazy circles.

"God, that feels…" I pressed my lips together, trying to catch my breath. My eyes fluttered, but Enzo growled. "Look at me, Gattina. I need you to look at me."

He worked his fingers deeper… faster… touching some place inside me that made my toes curl and my stomach clench.

"Come sei bagnata. Mi fai impazzire."

My Italian was rusty, but I knew he was talking dirty to me.

"I want you," I breathed, clutching the sheet between my fingers as he took me higher and higher.

"Just let me do this for you." His eyes were almost black as he watched me slowly come undone, stroke by stroke.

"At least kiss me." It was a breathy plea as I arched into his hand, desperate for more.

"So fucking beautiful," he rasped, dipping his head and dragging his tongue along the column of my neck. His teeth nipped my jaw, chased with tiny kisses but Enzo didn't give me what I wanted. Instead, he teased me. Licking and sucking, tasting and touching. He trailed hot, wet kisses over my skin, burning me from the inside out, while his fingers worked me into a boneless, breathless mess.

"God, more..." I chanted like I was praying to some invisible deity. "More... I need—"

Finally, Enzo kissed me, hard and punishing, stealing the air from my lungs, as if he thought I might disappear at any moment and he wanted to imprint the taste of me on his lips forever.

My body began to tremble as intense waves of pleasure crashed over me.

"Come, Gattina," he whispered against my lips. "Come for me."

His name spilled from my lips.

Enzo. Enzo. Enzo.

He kissed me gently, drawing out every last drop of my orgasm. Then he lifted his fingers to his mouth and sucked them clean. "So fucking good."

My tummy clenched.

"I want to return the favor," I said, ready to shimmy down the bed and give him the best blow job of his life. But Enzo pulled me against his big, warm body and said, "Sleep, Gattina."

Sleep?

He wanted me to sleep, nearly naked and wrapped in his arms? It would be almost impossible, my body hyperaware of every place we were joined. Hip to hip, chest to chest, my lips pressed against the hollow of his neck, tasting his salty skin.

How could I possibly sleep when all I wanted to do was jump his bones?

But as he held me tight, a sense of peace washed over me, and I found myself drifting. I didn't want to. I wanted to capture every second of this moment because Enzo had a history of flipping the switch on me once the sun chased away the shadows. And I didn't want this to end.

I *never* wanted it to end.

I woke to an empty bed. My stomach sank as I searched for any signs of Enzo. His clothes no longer littered the floor, and his side of the bed was cold.

He'd been gone a while.

I wanted to be angry at him, but I was only angry at myself. I should have known he would run. He'd been jealous, and jealousy made people act all kinds of crazy.

You foolish, foolish girl.

I let out a weary sigh. Enzo had been so different last night. So warm and tactile. He'd held me most of the night. I knew because I'd woken up at least three times. But the sun was up now, and like a ghost in the night, Enzo was gone.

My cell phone started to ring and I leaned over, snatching it off the nightstand, smiling at my best friend's name.

"Good morning," she said. "How are you?"

"Surprisingly, okay." *All thanks to a certain blue-eyed bad boy.*

"I can't believe it's happening again."

"Whoa, there. It isn't happening again. It was a package, Ari."

"It was a threat, Nor, and you need to take this more seriously. I've been talking to Nicco and we want you to come and stay with us."

"No," I said a little too hastily. "I mean, thank you, it's very kind of you to offer. But I'm not going to run, Ari. I won't do that." I couldn't explain it, but I didn't want to leave. This was my home. It had taken me long enough to feel safe here after what happened before, so I'd be damned if I let some asshole out for revenge chase me off again.

"Nora, just think about it. It isn't safe."

"I'm probably in the safest place I can be right now. Antonio has an army of guys here. No one is going to come or go without them knowing about it."

"When you put it like that... And Enzo is there, that makes me feel a lot better."

"Actually," I hesitated, "he left."

"He did? But Nicco just spoke to him and he said something about breakfast."

"He did?" Hope blossomed in my chest as I climbed out of bed. "Ari, I'm going to have to call you back." I hung up, and quickly pulled on my avocuddle t-shirt.

He left... Enzo left.

Didn't he?

But sure enough, when I opened the bedroom door, I found him cooking shirtless in my freaking kitchen.

Now I know I definitely died and went to heaven. I creeped up behind him, but Enzo sensed me, turning around right as I reached him. "Good morning," I said around the biggest smile.

"Good morning." His eyes dropped to my t-shirt, darting lower to my legs peeking out from under it. "While you eat your breakfast, I'm going to eat you."

His dirty words hit me right in the stomach.

"How long have you been awake?" I asked.

"A while. I don't sleep very well."

"Nightmares?"

He nodded, and I folded myself into his chest. Half of me expected him to pull away or reject me. But it was a morning of many surprises because Enzo wound his arms around my back and held me close.

"You stayed," I whispered.

"Yeah, Gattina," he looked down at me, eyes shining with possession. "I stayed."

TWENTY-FIVE

ENZO

I WATCHED her talking and laughing with Matteo over pancakes. It felt fucking weird, but something had shifted last night. Something I couldn't take back.

Something I didn't want to take back.

The second I'd heard Maurice's voice on the other end of the line, something had slammed into me. Fear that Nora was hurt. Fear that I'd never get to see her again, hold her again... kiss her again. It had ploughed through me like a wrecking ball.

It didn't matter that she was at Luca's, wearing his t-shirt and sleeping in his bed. Nora Abato was mine. Even when I hadn't wanted her to be, she was under my skin and on my mind.

Fuck. Admitting that still felt strange. But I was done fighting it. My number one priority now was finding this motherfucker and making sure he didn't come within an inch of Nora ever again.

The thought he'd been here, at her building, was enough to send me postal. I wanted to tear the fucker limb from limb.

"Are you going to stand there all morning?" Matt asked. "Or join us and eat?"

I pushed off the wall and went to them. Nora smiled up at me and my chest constricted. I guess this was what it felt like to be gone for a girl, all twisted up inside, wanting to make her happy, to see her smile, and soar... while wanting to shield her from anything and anyone who might try to hurt her.

"Are you sweating?" Matteo taunted and I flipped him off.

"It's hot in here."

"I hate to tell you, big guy," Nora shuffled closer, laying her head on my arm, "but it's not that warm." Her soft laughter was like music to my fucking ears.

Jesus, I was turning into a pussy already. I inwardly groaned. Matteo caught my eye and smirked, but I saw no malice there, only understanding.

He'd known. The fucker had known for a while now, and he'd been right.

I'd just been too unwilling to accept it.

"These are really good," Nora said, nibbling a pancake.

"You sound surprised, Gattina?" My brow quirked.

"A little." Her cheeks pinked and she looked so fucking adorable. I wanted to pounce on her and kiss the shit out of her syrupy sweet lips.

"You think just because he's a grumpy fucker with about as much charm as a cardboard cutout that he can't cook?" Matteo chuckled. "Then you would be sorely mistaken. My mom used to teach us. Said the only thing an Italian man needed to know in life was the art of cooking."

"She sounds like a wonderful woman."

"You met her at the wedding, no?" I asked her, immediately regretting it. "Shit, Nora, I didn't—"

"It's okay."

But it wasn't.

She'd been kidnapped after the wedding. Yanked right out of bed beside me and taken by Scott fucking Fascini. My fist clenched against my thigh, anger trickling through me like acid.

"Hey." Her hand covered mine. "I'm okay, Enzo. See." She took my hand and pressed it against her chest, right over her heart.

"You're in so much trouble, cous," Matteo howled with laughter and I flipped him off, keeping my focus on Nora.

"Yeah," I murmured. "I think you're right."

Nora frowned, but a knock at the door interrupted us.

"If that's your neighbor, I swear to God—"

"I'll go." She got up, but I beat her to it.

"Like hell you will." I grabbed my pistol off the counter and marched toward the door.

I heard Matteo mutter something about *letting me get it out of my system*. But disappointment washed over me when I saw Nicco and Arianne standing on the other side of the door.

"Expecting someone else?" he said, eyeing the gun in my hand.

"Don't ask," I grumbled, letting them in.

"You look different," Ari remarked, seeing straight through me.

"Nice to see you too." Closing the door, I followed them inside. Nora jumped up, running to hug Arianne.

"I'm so glad you're okay."

"I feel like we say that too much these days," Nora glanced at me and guilt shredded my insides. But she was in this life now. Whether I stood by her side or not, Nora was inextricably tied to the Family.

I realized that now. I realized why Nicco had refused to let Arianne go. Because whether he claimed her or not, she would forever be a target to his enemies just for the simple fact that she loved him.

The girls went to make everyone coffee while I sat with my cousins.

"Do I need to be worried about that?" His eyes flicked to Nora. She felt him staring and glanced over, smiling when her eyes collided with mine. "She's Arianne's best friend. If you break her heart—"

"It's not like that," I said, feeling myself grow tense. "I—"

"E has a serious case of heart eyes," Matteo said, but there was a strain to his words. "Isn't that right, cous?"

"Fuck off, cretino."

"So it's serious?"

I didn't like the way Nicco's brow furrowed. He doubted me. Probably hated the very idea of me anywhere near his wife's best friend. But at this point, I really didn't give a shit. Some crazy fucker had been within throwing distance of my woman, nothing Nicco did or didn't say would change the fact that I didn't plan on leaving her side unless it was to cut my enemy into tiny pieces.

"It's—"

"What are the three of you talking about?" The girls came over, placing our fresh coffees on the table.

"Nora and Enzo sitting in a tree, k-i-s—"

"If someone hands me my pistol, I can end this now," I joked.

"I think it's cute." Nora hovered since there was no room on the couch. I banded my arm around her waist and pulled her down on my lap. She smiled at me with so much emotion I felt winded.

Fuck, this girl.

My girl.

"So what do we know?" Nicco said.

"Fucker has a death wish," I mumbled, and Nora tensed above me.

"I won't ever pretend with you, Gattina," I whispered the words against the shell of her ear, unable to resist flicking my tongue over her skin. "This is me. I cuss too much, I enjoy making our enemies bleed, and I would die for any one of my family."

She turned into me, cupping my face. "I know who you are, Lorenzo Marchetti. I see you. I've always seen you."

"I really *really* want to fuck you right now."

Matteo snorted and I flipped him off again, while Nicco cleared his throat.

"Relax," I said, tucking her back into my chest. "I'm not going to do it right here."

"Tease," Nora quipped, and everyone laughed. Me included.

"This is nice," Ari said. "All we need now is to find Matteo a girl."

"You can leave me out of your little love fest." He got up and went to clean the breakfast plates. "I can handle my own sex life, thanks."

"You should try using it now and again then," I called after him. "Before it shrivels up and falls off."

Nora batted my chest. "Don't be so cruel."

I wrangled her into my arms and captured her lips in a hard kiss.

"Oh my God," Ari shrieked. "Look at them."

"Ugh." I grunted, dropping my face to Nora's shoulder. She chuckled, stroking her fingers through my hair. It felt so fucking good. My dick jumped to attention, desperate to be alone with her. Especially after last night, watching her come undone. It would have been easy to fuck her into oblivion, but I hadn't wanted to take advantage. The truth was, I needed a second to catch my breath, overwhelmed at all the new and fucking scary feelings I had wrecking me.

"I think it's cute."

I snorted. Cute and me weren't two words ever supposed to be in the same sentence. But that was Nora. Unapologetically honest. She didn't mince her words or hold back what she was feeling. She was the complete opposite of me in every way possible.

I gripped the back of her neck and touched my head to hers. "Why don't you give me and my cousins some space?"

"Anything you have to say, you can say it in front of us." Her brows knitted.

"I know and I'll tell you everything you need to know, I promise. But I really need to talk to them, and I would rather do it where I can keep my eye on you."

"Fine. Have you eaten?" she asked Arianne, who shook her head.

"We came straight here."

"Let's go make you some breakfast then." Nora stood up and bent down to rake her fingers against my jaw, kissing me softly. "You get ten minutes."

"I only need five." I slapped her ass, relishing the little yelping sound she made. I'd have to see how many ways I could make her do that later, when we were alone and she was naked.

Nora led Arianne over to the kitchen and the two of them began getting ingredients out of the refrigerator.

"Matt's right, you've got it bad."

"Seriously, that's what you want to talk about?"

"Just take it slow. She's... and you're..."

"Yeah, I got the memo. She's too good for me." My eyes found her again. I'd never noticed it before—or I'd refused to notice it—but we were like magnets, always searching the other out across a room. Like right now, I felt the pull to her, the invisible thread tethering us.

"Tell me exactly what happened," Nicco's voice pulled me back to reality.

"The package was left outside the main entrance. Security picked it up and alerted Maurice. He called me. I watched the security footage and it's definitely him. He was kitted out in a black hoodie and he didn't make eye contact with the camera, but it was him."

"He didn't leave a note?"

"Nothing but Gino's bloodstained chain."

Nicco let out a thin breath.

"He's toying with me, Nic. Showing me he's got the upper hand. Who the fuck is this guy?"

"I don't know but we've got everyone working on this. You sent the package to the local PD?"

I nodded. "Maurice delivered it to our guys personally. But they won't find any prints. This guy is a professional. He's a fucking ghost."

"We'll get him, I promise."

Something hit me. "Not that I don't appreciate you being here, because I do. But where's Uncle Toni?"

"He's sick." Nicco's expression fell.

Dread snaked through me. "How sick?"

"He says it's a bad case of heartburn, but—"

"You think it's something else."

His lips flattened into a grim line as he nodded. "Listen, I think Nora should move in with us until the worst is over. I can have Luis and Maurice on guard around the clock. The apartment has been modified with a state-of-the-art security system." He wasn't wrong. Their place was like Fort Knox.

But I didn't want Nora out of my sight, and somehow, I didn't think the invitation was for both of us.

"I already told Ari, I'm staying here," Nora called over.

"And I told her we should talk about it." Arianne pinned me with a hard look as if I had any sway over the choices Nora made.

"I can stay here with her," I said.

"Do you think that's a good idea?" Matteo reappeared.

"Where the fuck have you been?"

"To the bathroom, why?"

"Nora wants to stay here. I'm inclined to agree it's probably the safest option right now."

"He has a point, Nic," Matteo agreed. "There's security plus our guys, plus she has the friendly neighbor over the way who would jump in to defend her honor at any given chance."

A low growl rumbled in my chest, and Nicco shot me a strange look. "Do I need to be worried?" he asked.

"Not unless he comes knocking again to stir the pot."

I felt Nora staring at me and when I lifted my eyes to hers, she blushed. I was about two seconds away from telling everyone to get the hell out so I could make her blush all over, when Nicco's cell rang.

"Hello?" The color drained from his face. "Yeah, okay.... No, I understand. I'll be right there."

"What is it?" I asked, the second he hung up.

"It's my father," he exhaled a thin breath, "he collapsed."

Arianne rushed over to his side. "What happened?"

"I'm not sure yet. Genevieve said he was complaining all night of heartburn and this morning he just collapsed. They're on the way to the ER."

"Go," I said without hesitation. "We can handle this."

Nora ran her hand over my shoulder. "Enzo's right. Go be with him."

Before it's too late. I would never say the words, but I knew what losing Antonio would mean to Nicco. What it would mean for him.

For all of us.

"Okay, yeah. Fuck."

"Hey." Arianne pulled him into her arms, whispering softly, "We'll face it together. Always."

Nicco nodded. "Don't leave La Stella. Not until we know more. And be safe. All of you."

"We've got this. Go. And tell Uncle T we expect to see him up and busting balls soon." Matteo struggled to laugh, his face a picture of concern.

Arianne hugged Nora and we walked them to the door. Luis was waiting right outside with a somber expression on his face.

Fuck, this wasn't good. I scrubbed a hand down my face. But then Nora was wrapping her arms around me and just for a second, everything felt okay again.

We spent the morning hanging out at Nora's apartment. She did some studying while Matteo and I watched some gearhead show. It was an episode about restoring vintage Pontiacs, so I was pretty much in mindless TV heaven.

Nicco called to say Uncle Toni had suffered a heart attack, and he was in surgery. Not the phone call you wanted to ever get when the Family was being targeted by someone we couldn't get a hold on.

To say everyone was on edge was an understatement. But Nora took it in stride.

After an hour of studying, she came and sat with us. "Any word?" she asked, sliding her arm around my shoulder.

"Nothing." I planted a kiss on her cheek. "He's still in surgery."

"Surgery is good; it means they can fix him." She gave me a warm smile. "I was thinking, why don't we go out and get some fresh—"

"No." I barked. "No fucking way."

"Just hear me out." Her eyes narrowed with defiance. "We can all go, Maurice too. It's been a long morning and we're all getting a little stir crazy. It's the middle of the day, nothing is going to happen."

"I don't like it. Outside is an unknown factor. I can't control the surroundings. But in here, I can. I know exactly who is coming through that door." My eyes flicked over to the way in and out of her apartment.

"Okay," she let out a soft sigh, "it was just an idea."

I lifted her onto my lap and slid my arms around her waist. "I need to know you're safe, Gattina."

"I understand. But what if you don't find whoever is doing this?" She traced the line of my jaw with her fingers. "You can't keep me locked away in here forever. I have classes. I have a life, Enzo."

Fuck, she was right. But the thought of her stepping foot out of that door terrified me in a way I hadn't ever expected.

"Just give it some more time, please." I couldn't be worrying about her and Uncle Toni.

"Fine, a couple more days." Nora lowered her face to mine, sliding her lips against my mouth. I groaned, pulling her tighter. Matteo grumbled something about needing to check in with Maurice and left us to it.

"Maybe we should stop." She giggled, nudging her nose gently against mine.

I dived back in, kissing her hard. "He'll live. Besides, I've forgotten how good your pussy feels choking my dick."

"Enzo." She batted my chest, my name a breathless sigh on her lips. "You can't say stuff like that to me now I'm your—" Her eyes went wide with panic. "I didn't mean—"

"You're mine, Gattina. Label it, don't label it," I shrugged, "doesn't matter. I own your ass now and there isn't a single thing you can do about it."

TWENTY-SIX

NORA

"ANY NEWS?" I asked Enzo as I made us lunch.

"He's out of surgery, thank fuck." He got up and made his way over to me, snagging me around the waist and pulling me back against his chest.

"Nicco must be going out of his mind." I glanced back at him.

"He'll pull through. Uncle T is made of strong stuff."

"And if he doesn't?" Enzo went rigid and I brushed my nose over his jaw. "Sorry, that was insensitive. I'm sure he'll be fine."

"He has to be, Gattina. Nicco isn't ready to become the boss."

I still couldn't believe Enzo's one-eighty. Not that I was complaining. I loved this side of him. Protective and possessive, it was everything I'd wanted. Everything I'd hoped for. But there was still a little voice in the back of my mind whispering that Enzo was here out of obligation and guilt.

I didn't want to overanalyze, but I couldn't help it. If I'd have never stayed over at Luca's, and if the package had never been left outside La Stella, would I be here now, wrapped in Enzo's arms?

I liked to think we would have found our way back to one another eventually, but a small part of me knew circumstances played a helping hand in things.

"What is it?" Enzo whispered against my neck, his warm breath and the gentle strum of his fingers against my stomach made all my doubts disappear.

"I'm just thinking about Nicco."

"He'll be okay. Ari is with him; she'll keep him sane."

"How long do you think we'll have to stay here for?" I asked him, stirring the pan of boiling pasta.

"Until I know you're one-hundred percent safe."

"Nothing is ever certain," I said.

He stiffened again. "Yeah, well, until this fucker is in the ground, I want you where I can keep you safe."

A thrill went through me at his words. But for as much as I was enjoying having him all to myself, I didn't like the idea of hiding away forever.

I had classes. I had a life to get back to.

My cell vibrated and I slid it across the counter to read the incoming message.

"Is that—"

I quickly shielded it from Enzo, but it was too late.

"He's texting you?" Anger coated his words.

"He just wants to know I'm okay."

"I bet he does," Enzo grumbled, and I turned in his arms.

"Luca is... was a friend. He isn't just going to disappear because we're... doing this."

"It's cute you still can't say it." A slow smirk spread over Enzo's lips.

"No labels, remember?" If I labelled it, it would be real, and if it was real, it would be more painful if it all went wrong.

His eyes darkened as he dropped his head to mine. "I don't know how else to say it, Gattina, but you're mine. I know I don't deserve you. Fuck, I know that. But I have never felt more scared than I did when Maurice called."

Emotion balled in my throat as he pierced me with his icy-blue gaze. "Enzo, I—"

The blare of his cell cut through the room.

"You should get that," I said with a resigned sigh. "It could be Nicco."

He hesitated for a second then pulled away to dig out his cell phone.

"Yeah... thank fuck. Okay, she's fine... yeah, got it. Tell him I'm glad he's okay." He hung up and let out a long, steady breath. "Uncle Toni is okay, he's awake."

"That's great news." I launched myself at him, hugging him tight.

"Fuck, Gattina," he whispered. "I was scared there for a minute that he wasn't going to make it."

"It's okay." My hands slid to his face as I brushed my lips over his. "Everything is going to be okay."

I only hoped it was the truth.

"God, Enzo, more," I breathed as his tongue lapped at my core, taking me higher and higher.

"You taste so fucking good." He speared me with two fingers inside, curling them deep. My fingers tugged his hair, holding him in place as I arched into his mouth, desperate for more.

"My kitty is greedy," he purred, the words vibrating through me, tiny shocks of pleasure drenching my veins.

My 'tea Rex' t-shirt was bunched around my shoulders, giving Enzo the perfect opportunity to tease my breasts. His big hand plucked and squeezed, marking my flesh like he'd already marked my heart.

"Fuck, you taste good. I can't get enough."

His dirty words sent my orgasm crashing over me as I cried his name into the night.

He licked me clean, moaning with appreciation before rocking back on his haunches and gazing down at me.

"My turn?" I smirked, ready to sit up and wrap my lips around his monster dick. But his wicked grin turned my insides to molten lava.

"I'm not done with you yet." He grabbed my hips and flipped me onto my stomach, dragging my ass into the air, barely giving me time to catch my breath before his mouth latched onto me again, lapping at me like a man starved.

My body trembled, my knees buckling, but then he was there, the steel barbell through the tip of his dick brushing my sensitive, swollen skin.

"Fuck," I breathed, burying my head into the pillow.

"You're about to be fucked." His dark chuckle sent chills racing through me.

Enzo teased me a couple more times, sliding himself through my wetness and nudging my clit. But on the third time, he slammed inside me, making my body jolt forward. I pressed my hands into the mattress, steadying myself.

"Fuck, yeah, Gattina. Mi fai impazzire."

"More," I cried, lost to the sensations he stirred inside me.

"Your wish is my command." Enzo gave me everything, rocking into me over and over as his hands held my hips like he couldn't get enough. I'd have bruise marks tomorrow, but I didn't care. All I cared about was him using my body... *loving* my body in the way only he could. Because I was totally gone for this guy. Head over heels in lust with the guy with ice around his heart and hatred in his soul.

I didn't think it was possible to fall anymore, until he banded his arm around my waist and pulled me up, my back to his front. His hand slid to my throat and his lips went to my shoulder, kissing and sucking the damp skin there as he slowed his pace.

"Feel me, Gattina," he rasped. "Feel what you do to me."

"Enzo..." I panted, my body unraveling around him.

"Nothing... *nothing* will ever feel as good as this." His confession splintered me apart. "Yeah, that's it, Nora. Choke my dick... *fuck*." Enzo spilled inside of me, his teeth latching into my flesh as he broke the skin, soothing the sting with his tongue.

"Mine," he whispered. "Il mio."

The word slammed into me with renewed clarity.

I wasn't in lust with this complicated man.

I was head over heels in love with him.

"Nora?" He tilted my face to his and kissed me. "Is something wrong?"

"No." My lips curved with uncertainty as emotion swelled inside me. "Everything is perfect."

We cleaned up and climbed in bed. Enzo immediately dragged me into the curve of his body. "We should get some sleep."

We didn't know what tomorrow would bring. Nobody did. But Antonio was awake, Enzo was here with me, and there had been no more threats. Still, I knew it was only the calm before the storm. But I truly felt like we could face what was coming as long as we stood together.

So when Enzo's cell phone started ringing again, fear trickled down my spine.

"Yeah?" He barked, keeping his arm wrapped firmly around my body. "Fuck, okay. Yeah, I'm coming."

"What is it?" My voice cracked the second he hung up.

"I need to go." He gently released me, climbed out of bed and started pulling on his clothes. "There's been another break-in."

"Where?"

"The VCTI."

"What?" I shot up and climbed out of bed. "But that doesn't make any sense. The VCTI isn't a Marchetti business." It was the center where Arianne volunteered. I'd helped out there a couple of times too.

"Nicco made a large donation to the center for her wedding present."

"Crap." Enzo was right. Arianne had been so excited. There was a press release and everything.

"But the VCTI helps people," I said, still unable to process what was happening. "Why would anyone—"

Enzo's expression darkened. "That's why I need to go, Gattina. This is on me. I should be there."

"But—"

Enzo cupped the back of my neck and smashed his lips to mine. It was a kiss to end all other kisses, a kiss that felt a lot like goodbye... but I refused to believe that. We were in a good place, we were.

"Promise me you'll come back to me," I said, winding my fingers into his t-shirt, my eyes fluttering closed with the weight of my words.

He tilted my face, staring intently at me. "I give you my word." Enzo kissed me again, softer this time, as if he was tracing the shape of my mouth and imprinting it to memory. "Come with me." He guided me into the living room and over to the couch as his fingers flew over his cell phone.

Seconds later, there was a knock at the door and Enzo let Maurice inside.

"You stay right here with her. Move another guy to this floor, but you stay right here until I get back."

"You have my word, Mr. Marchetti."

Enzo nodded. "I'll be back, I promise."

"Be safe." Emotion rushed up my throat, making my eyes sting. I didn't want him to go. I didn't want him to be in harm's way. And I didn't want him to have to hurt anyone, even if they deserved it. But this was what it meant to love a mafioso, to stand by their side. If I wanted to be with Enzo, I had to accept that.

He disappeared into the bedroom to retrieve his weapons, and I watched with strange fascination as he added them to his person. The deadly looking knife strapped to his ankle, a pistol holstered to his chest, and brass knuckles stuffed inside his jacket.

He was an armed soldier and it wasn't supposed to be such a turn on, but I couldn't help the heat pooling in my stomach at the sight of him.

"Promise me that no matter what happens you won't leave this room unless Maurice says it is safe for you to do so."

"I-I promise." I gulped over the lump in my throat.

Another sharp nod and Enzo slipped out of my apartment leaving the room cold…

And my heart empty.

"Anything?" I asked for the hundredth time. Maurice shook his head. "It has only been thirty minutes."

Really?

It felt longer.

It felt like forever.

I hugged myself tighter, staring at the clock of the wall, willing it to move.

It was going to be a long night.

The vibration of my cell phone startled me from my reverie, and relief spread through me as I grabbed it off the coffee table hoping to see Enzo's name.

But it wasn't Enzo at all.

I know this is probably not a good time… but I'm kind of in a bind and I don't have anyone else to call…

"Nora?" Maurice asked and I held up my finger, calling Luca's number.

"Luca, what is it? What's wrong?"

"I… uh…" he sounded a little breathless. "So funny story, I decided to take a shower after drinking my body weight in tequila and I tripped—"

"Oh my God, are you okay?"

"I'll live but my face took the brunt and I have a pretty gruesome cut on my forehead… and I'm not very good with blood…" he trailed off.

"Luca?" I shrieked. "Okay, hold on… I'll—"

"Don't even think about it," Maurice shot up.

Crap. Yeah. Enzo would lose it if he knew I'd stepped foot out of the apartment, even if it was only to go across the hall.

"I'm going to send you help, okay? Maurice, he'll—"

"Need you," he breathed, and I didn't like how out of it he sounded.

"Maurice, go to Luca's, now!"

"Miss Ab—Nora, I had strict orders to stay—"

"I know, which is why I'm asking you to go and check on him." I gave him a pointed look. "If you don't, I will." Maurice hesitated and I let out an exasperated breath. "He's hurt, Maurice. Please just go over there and check on him. I'll lock the door behind you, I swear."

"Fine." He got up and moved to the door. "I'm going to radio downstairs and tell security you're here alone."

"Maurice, I'm not alone, you'll be right across the hall."

"Just stay put." From the furrow of his brows, I knew he wasn't happy about leaving me. But I couldn't just ignore Luca's plea for help. He slipped out of the door and I went and locked it.

What I really wanted was to check in with Enzo and make sure he was okay, but I didn't want to appear clingy.

To distract myself, I made myself a mug of hot cocoa with marshmallows. Despite the way I'd left things with Luca, I really did hope he was okay. I knew he probably felt like I'd led him on, and I guess I had. But I hadn't done it out of malicious intent. Luca was a good guy. He was easy to be around and he made me smile. But he didn't make my heart beat hard the way Enzo did.

A smile played on my lips just thinking about how overprotective and growly Enzo had been today. Some girls would have hated his alpha routine, but I loved it.

By the time I'd finished my hot cocoa I was growing increasingly worried about Luca. Maurice had been gone almost fifteen minutes.

I snatched up my cell phone and called Maurice, but it rang out.

God. What if it was worse than I thought? What if Luca needed medical attention?

I decided to call Luca. It rang out but then right before I hung up, he answered. "Nora?"

"Hey, are you okay?"

"I'm a little embarrassed, but yeah, Maurice fixed me up."

"He's still there?"

"No, he left a couple minutes ago. He isn't back with you?"

"No." Fear slithered up my spine as I went to the peephole and pressed my face to it. "I can't see him."

"Well, he can't have gone far. He was just right here."

"I'm going to call him again. I'll call you back in a second."

I dialed Maurice's number, but he didn't pick up. My heart raced as I mentally went through possibilities. He wouldn't have just up and left me. Not when Enzo had given me strict orders to stay put...

Maybe there was an imminent threat and he'd gone downstairs to deal with it.

Quickly, I called Luca back.

"Anything?" he asked.

"No, but I don't think it's safe here."

"For real? What—"

"I can't explain everything right now. I need to call Enzo."

"He's gone?"

"He had to... he went to deal with something."

"What have you gotten yourself into, Nora?" He trailed off.

"Please, don't. I didn't call to argue with you. I just want to find out where Maurice is."

"Let me help."

Chewing my bottom lip, I weighed up my options. Enzo was at least a twenty-minute ride away across town. Even if he picked up, he couldn't get here straight away. Calling the police wasn't an option, and Nicco was at the hospital with his dad.

"Fine," I said, making a snap decision.

"I'll come to you," he said.

"No, I'll come to you. Then we can figure out what to do." Maurice would probably appear by then, with an explanation for his sudden disappearance.

Changing into some lounge pants and a MU hoodie, I grabbed my keys and cell and made my way across to Luca's apartment.

The door was already open, so I pushed it open and called out, "Luca?" My heart raced in my chest as I slipped inside. "Lu—"

"Hey." He appeared, looking a little flushed.

"Are you okay?"

"I'm fine now. Well, apart from this." He motioned to his forehead. There was a small dressing above his brow.

"You're lucky," I said around a tentative smile. But Luca didn't return it, the air cooling around us.

"Did you call Enzo?" he asked, thinly.

"Not yet. But I should call him." I pulled out my cell phone, but something rang out in the apartment.

"Fuck," Luca muttered under his breath.

"Is something wrong?" I glanced around, drawn to the sound. There was something familiar about it. Something I couldn't quite—

"Is that Maurice's cell phone?" I asked, my blood turning to ice as I crossed Luca's apartment. "What the hell? *Maurice*!" I yelled.

He was crumpled up on the floor of Luca's bedroom floor, blood pouring from a thick gash in his head.

"What did you do?" I spun to face Luca, but he grabbed me from behind, yanking me backward. "What the hell—"

"I'm sorry, Nora." He jabbed me with something sharp. "I'm so fucking sorry." His voice was drowned out by the darkness consuming me.

"No," I screamed, but the words got stuck in my throat.

No!

TWENTY-SEVEN

ENZO

SOMETHING WAS WRONG. Maurice wasn't answering and I couldn't get hold of Nora.

I'd texted and called to reassure her I was okay, but that it was taking longer than planned at the VCTI because somebody had called the police, and they'd sent a rookie.

A rookie who wasn't on our payroll. So me and Matteo had to lie low while they did their thing.

Luckily for us, the center manager was a personal friend of Arianne's and Nicco's and had the foresight to leave out any mention of the package left for me. It was a bloodstained knife that I knew was coated in Gino's blood.

"Anything?" Matteo asked me as I checked my cell again.

"Nothing."

"Nora is probably sleeping," he said.

"Yeah." But it didn't explain why Maurice wasn't returning my calls.

Impatient, I called Alexi instead. But it only rang out.

"What the fuck is happening over there?"

"Try La Stella security." Matteo pulled out his cell and started dialing. "Fuck, it's ringing out."

"I gotta—"

"Yeah, go. I'll handle things here. Just be careful yeah?"

But that was like telling a fighter to take it easy in the ring. Trepidation coursed through me. If Nora was—

No, everything was fine.

It had to be.

The nervous energy zipping through me didn't abate though, as I floored my GTO back toward University Hill.

The second my car rolled to a stop outside the building, I knew what I hadn't wanted to believe.

I pulled out my cell and called Nicco.

"Enzo, what is it?" Sleep thickened his words.

"I'm sorry to call you, cous, but I need you, Nic. I need you at La Stella."

"Shit, yeah, okay. Talk me through what's happened."

Shouldering the door, I slipped inside. I should have passed at least two security guards by now. "Security is gone. I can't reach Maurice or Nora."

"Fuck," he breathed. "Okay, me and Luis are on our way with backup."

Icy cold fear trickled in my veins as I reached Nora's floor. It was silent save for the gentle hum of the strip lighting overhead. I crept close to Nora's apartment, silently praying that she was still inside, sleeping.

I gently tapped my knuckles against the door, waiting. "Come on, Gattina. Where the fuck are you?" I murmured to myself. Scrolling to her name, I hit call, hoping to hear it ring.

Nothing.

Fuck.

I dialed Maurice again. At first, it just rang out. But then I heard it, the faint familiar music of his ringtone. Moving closer to Luca's apartment, anger like I'd never known it swelled inside me.

They were at Bianco's?

What the fuck were they doing over there?

I knocked loudly, my body trembling with fury. If Luca had touched her, touched my Nora, I wouldn't be held responsible for my actions.

But no one answered.

"Yo, asshole, open up," I yelled, uncaring if I woke up the whole building. All kinds of scenarios ran through my head, but I needed to try and stay cool. "Luca!" I banged again. "Fuck this."

I pulled out my knife and wedged in into the door jamb, leveraging the door open enough to crash through the damn thing.

The apartment was empty. But I knew I'd heard Maurice's ringtone. Quickly, I dialed his number again and sure enough the noise rang out. I followed it through the apartment to a closed door.

I didn't want to open it, didn't want this nightmare to be real. Reaching for the handle, I slowly pushed it open. Maurice was laying there with a halo of dark-red blood surrounding his head.

"Fuck," I growled, dropping to my knees to check for his pulse.

He was unconscious, but I detected a faint pulse. Maurice needed medical attention and he needed it now, so I knew I had no choice but to call it in.

"*Fuck!*" I stood up and dragged a hand down my face, trying to figure out what the fuck to do. Luca was gone… Nora too. But I think I'd known the second I couldn't get a hold of her that something bad had happened.

The VCTI wasn't just another break-in, it was a diversion...

But Luca?

It didn't make any sense.

I sent an SOS message to Nicco and Matteo. They would both understand what it meant. If I didn't want another soldier to die right in front of me, I had to call nine-one-one. We'd have to worry about the consequences later.

I called it in, keeping the details as vague as possible. I needed to try to piece together what had happened here.

I needed to find Nora.

Fuck. Nora...

Pain ripped through me, and I staggered back against the wall. If she was hurt again... or worse...

I knew this could happen. I fucking knew and I still left her.

What the fuck was I thinking?

If anything happened to her...

I would never forgive myself.

Nicco and Matteo arrived just as the EMTs were wheeling Maurice out of Luca's apartment.

"Fuck," Matteo breathed, his expression clouded with concern. "Is he going to be okay?"

"He's lost a lot of blood," I said, grimly.

"Mr. Marchetti," Philippi Dante, one of our friends from the local PD approached us. "Do I need to be worried?" he asked quietly.

"We'll handle it."

"I already told them what I know," I said, shooting Dante a warning look.

"I think we've got everything for now. But I won't be able to bury it for long." He glanced around the room before leaning in. "You're going to have to give me something."

"Dante," Nicco said, "walk with me."

The two of them followed the EMTs out of the apartment deep in discussion, and I knew my cousin was probably trying to avoid a scene.

"What do we know?" Matteo asked the second they were gone.

"The security footage was cut about three hours ago. Right after I left."

"So what the hell was that at the VCTI?"

"A decoy."

"Fuck." He scrubbed his jaw. "And we think Luca took her? But he was vetted, man. I double checked his file myself."

"You did?" I jerked back. I knew he'd asked Maurice, but I didn't know he'd pulled Luca's file.

"Figured we should know who was hanging around your woman."

The words made my chest tighten.

"We'll get her back, Enzo," he said, laying a hand on my shoulder. "And our guys?"

"No sign of them."

"No way Bianco did this without help," Matteo said the words I'd been pondering ever since stepping foot into his apartment and finding Maurice bleeding out.

"I should have stayed away," I gritted out, fists clenched painfully at my sides. "I should have fucking stayed away from her."

"Come on, cous, don't do this. You couldn't have known Luca was involved. None of us could."

Before I could stop myself, my fist shot out and collided with the wall. Pain ripped through my knuckles, zipping up my wrist but I welcomed it. I'd welcome a whole lot more than that if it meant getting Nora back in one piece.

I'm sorry, Gattina. I'm so fucking sorry.

"Better?"

"No," I grunted. "But I will be when we find this motherfucker and end him."

"I think we've got to assume he isn't working alone. He had to get Nora and our guys out of here somehow." His brows crinkled but then his eyes widened. "We checked La Stella's security feed, but we didn't check La Luna."

"Shit, you're right." La Luna was Roberto's second building in University Hill, the one across the street with line of sight to its sister building.

Matteo pulled out his cell. "Tristan, yeah, sorry to call so late... We need a favor. Can you call security over at La Luna and tell them we're gonna need to take a look at their security feeds for the last two hours." He gave me a sharp nod. "Appreciate it, man. And yeah, we will."

"He's going to hook us up."

"What's that?" Nicco came back inside, alone this time.

"Tristan is going to call the security guys over at La Luna and have them pull the security footage of the last two hours. Whoever helped Luca had to have a vehicle which means we should be able to see something."

He nodded, his eyes narrowing at me. "You good?"

"What do you think?"

"We'll get her back."

"We have to." Because anything else wasn't an option.

"We will. Nora isn't the target—"

"No, she's the fucking bait." I stormed out of there, needing air.

Crashing through the main doors, I pulled out a smoke, and waited for my cousins to join me, knowing they would be right behind me.

Sure enough, a minute later, they spilled out onto the quiet sidewalk.

"Should we call my dad?" Matteo asked. After my father, Uncle Michele stepped up as Antonio's second. So with Uncle Toni out of action in the hospital, all decisions were supposed to go through Uncle Michele. But time was against us.

"You can update him, but we do this with or without him. I'm not waiting."

The words vibrated deep in the pit of my stomach. “That fucker has Nora, he has my woman.”

And I intended on her getting her back, consequences be damned.

We walked the short distance to La Luna in thick silence. One of Roberto’s guys met us at the door.

“Mr. Capizola called ahead. Please, follow me.”

“Have you pulled the footage?”

“We have, and you’ll want to see this.” He guided us to the security office.

Another guy looked up from the screen. “A black van left the underground parking lot about forty-five minutes ago. Drove right on out. Looked to be in a rush too.”

“Fuck.” My fist slammed against the table, making the computers screens rattle and shake.

“Relax.” Nicco pulled me back, moving around me to get a closer look. He pulled out his phone and scrolled through his contacts. “Tommy, sorry for the late-night call. I need you to run some plates for us. I suspect they’re fake or cloned but see what you can find.” He started reeling off the license plates. When he was done, he hung up. “Where do you lose them?”

“Right here.” The guy pointed to one of the grids on the screen. “The police department might be able to track him on their cameras though.”

“Thanks, we appreciate it.” Nicco went to walk away but I stalled closer to the monitor.

“Wait. When did we see the van arrive?”

“We didn’t run the footage that far back, but we can look.”

“Do it.”

“What are you thinking?” Nicco asked me.

“Something still doesn’t add up.” We’d found nothing. Not even a speck of blood. It was as if they were never there. “We’ve all met Bianco. He might be hiding something but he’s not capable of this. He’s just the puppet.”

I’d met the guy toying with us, been right up close and personal with him. It definitely wasn’t Luca, so what was the connection?

“He’s working with whoever is coming after us,” Nicco said.

“That’s my bet.” I nodded, my jaw working overtime as I tried to piece together the puzzle. We were still missing something.

“Did Luca—Stop,” I yelled, my eyes fixating on Luca and a couple of guys entering the building. “When was that?”

“Yesterday afternoon. A little after one.” My eyes narrowed, watching as security stopped them to interrogate Luca about his friends.

“Wait, freeze it and zoom in. Motherfuck—”

“That’s Nate and Isaac, Luca’s friends,” Matteo cut me off. “We met them the other night at the bar.”

The ground went from under me. “That’s the guy.” I jabbed my finger at the grainy image.

“Who, Isaac? No way! We both met him, he seemed legit.”

"I'm telling you, that's the fucking guy. Fuck." I blew out a steady breath. "I need to know everything you know about that guy, stat." Adrenaline pumped through me, blood roaring in my eyes. I was staring right at him. The guy responsible for killing Gino, the guy who had left the package for me at La Stella and the VCTI. The guy I knew without doubt had taken Nora.

"I don't know anything about him," Matteo said around a tight expression. "His friend Nate hooked up with Nora's friend Lucii."

"Arianne knows her." Nicco pulled his cell out to call his wife. It was the middle of the night, but I had no doubt that Arianne would be glued to her phone waiting for any word from Nicco.

He disappeared out of the room. "I can't believe it. We were right there at the club with him. He seemed... normal."

"This isn't on you, Matt. The fucker is toying with us." It was a game. Some sick, twisted game.

Just then, Nicco came back into the room. "I've got Lucii's name. Tommy is going to do his thing and dig up her number."

"Good, that's good." Matteo shot me a concerned look.

"I'm okay." I lied. Anger had infiltrated every inch of me, coursing through my veins like wildfire. But it wasn't only anger I felt. The bitter sting of regret coiled around my heart.

This was all my fault.

No one could take that away from me.

We left La Luna and walked the short distance back to La Stella, piling into Matteo's truck.

"We need that number," I ground out, my leg bouncing uncontrollably.

"Tommy will come through," Nicco said.

"He'd better."

Because we had nothing else to go on. No clues. No leads. Just a name and a face.

And the hope that my cousins were right—that Nora wasn't the endgame.

I was.

TWENTY-EIGHT

NORA

MY EYES FLICKERED OPEN to faulty strip lighting. It made it difficult to focus, the constant flicker. Dim then glare. Dim then glare. A brass band beat loudly in my skull, making me groan in agony.

Where the hell was I?

And why couldn't I move?

Panic raced up my spine as I slowly found my senses. I couldn't move because my hands were bound behind my back and my ankles bound together, secured to the chair I was seated on.

"What the—" The icy fingers of fear wrapped around my throat, stealing the words. "Hello," I managed to choke out. "Someone help me." Straining against the restraints, another wave of panic crashed over me.

This wasn't happening, not again.

Breathe, I silently urged myself, *just breathe*. Somehow, I managed to calm myself, trying to focus on the things I could control, like my bodily functions. I might have been bound, but I still had my sight and hearing and my sense of smell. A groan sounded over to my right and my eyes strained against the poor lighting.

"Luca?" I gasped. He was slumped in the corner, hands bound in front of his body. "Luca, can you hear me?"

"N-Nora?" His eyes were heavy-lidded. "I'm sorry… so fucking… sorry." He started to fall out of consciousness.

"Luca, stay with me, please… stay with me."

"Hurts… it hurts." His eyes fluttered open.

"What happened?"

The last thing I remembered was Luca jabbing me with a needle... and Maurice—

"Oh God," my voice cracked, "what did you do?"

"I had no choice... he... he—"

"Well, well, you're awake." A figure stepped into the room and confusion welled inside me.

"Isaac?" My eyes grew to saucers.

"Surprise!" He smirked deviously.

"But... I-I don't understand..."

"You're not supposed to, baby. This is between me and your boyfriend."

"My—*what*?"

It didn't make sense. Isaac was Luca's friend. He wasn't the guy doing this.

He couldn't be.

"You... why?"

"Why?" He stalked toward me, crouching to my eye level. "Now there's the million-dollar question, isn't it?" Reaching out, he ran his knuckles down my cheek. Luca groaned to my right, but I didn't look over at him.

"It was all you?"

"The Family's enforcer, the break-ins, and my personal favorite, the VCTI. I've been a busy guy."

"But why?"

"Nah-ah, baby." He beeped my nose. "We'll get to that when your boyfriend arrives. Assuming he figures it out." Isaac winked at me, but my head was too busy swimming with confusion.

What the hell was happening?

Isaac wasn't the guy coming after the Marchetti, he couldn't be. He was just a regular guy who worked out at the same gym as Luca.

Except he wasn't.

Because I was tied to a chair and Luca was on the floor, slumped against the wall and barely conscious.

"What do you want?" I shrieked, fear drenching my words. My hands and feet strained against their bindings, but it was futile. They were too tight, the cable ties cutting into my skin.

"Please, just let us go."

"Aww, now I know you're not one of those girls... a damsel in distress. From what I've seen you like it rough."

Bile crawled up my throat and I swallowed hard, breathing through my nose. He'd been watching me... watching me with Enzo.

Who the hell was this guy?

"Do you like cold-blooded killers, baby?" He pulled a knife out from behind his back. "Do you like a little pain?"

My breath caught in my throat as he pushed the tip of the blade against my clavicle. Featherlight, Isaac traced the knife over my skin, following the hollow of my collarbone.

"Please," it was a ragged plea as I tried not to move even a millimeter.

"How I'd love to slice you open and see what you're really made of." There was a wicked glint in his eye, an honesty that made my stomach wash with fear. "But the fun is only just getting started."

A chill ran down my spine at the threat in his voice.

"Enzo won't let you get away with this," I spat, letting my emotions get the better of me.

"Oh, baby," he flashed me a wolfish grin, before standing, "I'm counting on it."

Isaac left us after that. Left us cold and alone and scared. Luca was in and out of consciousness. I couldn't see any blood or contusions, but the flickering strip lighting made it difficult to see right into the darkened corners of the room.

"Luca, are you awake?" I whispered, every muscle in my body heavy and sore. I had no idea how long we'd been here. It could have been a couple of hours, it could have been an entire day. Time was nothing. But for every minute that passed, my hope faded.

What if Enzo didn't come?

What if he and his family couldn't find us?

Couldn't find me.

What if he did?

I wasn't foolish, I knew this would only affirm Enzo's resistance to be with me. He would take one look at me tied to this chair, dehydrated and confused, and vow to never put me in this situation again.

So as much as I wanted him to appear in the doorway, to come and save us, part of me—the naïve part of me that was just a girl in love with a guy—didn't want it to be him. Because I knew what it meant...

And I knew it was the end of us before we'd even really gotten started.

Emotion rushed up my throat, stinging the backs of my eyes. I was a good person, or at least, I tried to be. I took my vitamins and gave to charity and helped old ladies across the street. I tried to treat people the way I hoped to be treated, kind and with compassion. I often saw past people's walls and didn't judge someone for the lifestyle they chose. But I knew that bad things happened to good people all the time. So even though I was scared and hurting, I didn't have the capacity to blame Enzo or his family for this. The same way I hadn't blamed Nicco and Arianne when Scott Fascini took me.

A strangled laugh spilled from my lips. What were the chances that I would find myself here again? I guess when you kept company with the mafia, anything was possible.

I sucked in a shaky breath. Enzo would find us, he would. I could imagine him now, on a rampage through Verona, burning buildings to the ground and ploughing through anyone who dared to stand in his way. His anger was always there, under the surface, only made worse since his father's death.

God. I'd never gotten the chance to tell him how sorry I was for what he'd had to do. I hadn't wanted him to pull away, not when he was finally letting me in, so I'd kept his secret. I would *always* keep his secret if it meant protecting what we shared. But one day, I'd hoped he would tell me. I'd hoped he would share with me his secrets and pain.

The lights flickered overhead, plunging the room once more into total darkness.

"Luca?" I called, fear sitting heavy in the pit of my stomach. "Luca?"

"H-here…" It was a faint groan. "I'm here."

His voice, although pained, settled something inside me. I knew Luca had a hand in taking me, but I didn't want him to die. I wanted him to survive this thing and then explain to me what the hell had happened.

"Hold on," I croaked, my throat dry and sore. "You have to hold on. Enzo will come."

But as I said the words, all I could think was, he was walking right into a trap.

Time lost all meaning. At some point, Luca had slipped under and hadn't resurfaced. Silent tears rolled down my cheeks. If he didn't get medical help soon, he might never wake up.

"Isaac," I yelled. "ISAAC!"

He appeared in the door like the reaper sent to claim my soul. But he didn't look concerned, he looked… excited.

"Showtime," he rasped, stalking toward me with a knife. He grabbed my hands and slid right through the third cable tie binding the tie around each wrist. Then he worked on setting my ankles free.

"Try anything and I'll gut you like a fish," he snarled. "Your boyfriend is here now, so it makes no difference to me whether you make it out of this alive or in a body bag."

An icy shudder rolled through me. This wasn't the Isaac I'd met at the bar. That guy was cool and aloof, but he wasn't cruel. But then, I remembered I had felt something a little off about him. As if he watched me a little too closely. Honestly, I'd just thought he wanted me.

The idea seemed preposterous now, seeing as he was dragging me down a long hall with a seven-inch blade pressed to the small of my back.

He yanked me into another room, one with windows. Sunlight poured inside, tinged pinkish orange. Sunset. Jesus. I'd been here hours. Enzo would be going out of his mind.

We waited in silence. Isaac was skittish, his eyes darting to and from the window as he kept his knife at my back and his other hand on my shoulder. Then the door in front of me opened and my heart lurched into my throat.

Enzo.

His eyes were wild, anger burning in his icy depths. His jaw was clenched painfully tight and his fists pressed at his sides. He looked murderous. But when his eyes shifted to mine, his whole expression softened.

He was here.

Enzo had come for me.

"Took you long enough," Isaac spat the words, slowly inching us back.

Enzo stepped forward and Isaac whipped the knife around my front, pressing it against my throat. "I wouldn't do that if I were you."

Enzo's hands shot up as he stalled. "This isn't about Nora. It's about you and me, Vinnie."

"Oooh, you're good." He chuckled darkly. "You're really fucking good. How'd you find out?"

"One of our guys is a dab hand at uncovering secrets."

"Tommy Gabini? Should have guessed. He said he was one of the best."

"Who said?" Enzo frowned and I knew my expression matched his. They weren't making any sense.

"Oh, come on, Lorenzo. Surely, you've figured it out by now. Or did the infamous Tommy Gabini fail to uncover the biggest secret of all?"

Enzo started inching closer again, but Isaac moved us deeper into the room. They were dancing around each other with me right in the middle, the sharp edge of the blade so close to my skin I could feel the coolness of it.

I swallowed hard. Enzo caught the small movement, and his eyes went to mine. Dark eyes full of regret and apology. I wanted to tell him to stop, to reassure him that he didn't have to carry this burden alone. But I couldn't speak. I could barely breathe for fear of my skin slicing open against the knife's edge.

My body trembled violently.

"She's shaking," Isaac said. "Trembling like an animal about to meet its bloody end. Do you think he felt it too? The claws of death coming to reap his soul?"

"Vincenzo Marchetti was a traitor and a murderer."

I was still missing something. Something Enzo had apparently figured out.

Isaac wasn't called Isaac at all. His name was Vinnie.

Vinnie.

Vinnie.

Vincenzo...

No.

No!

It wasn't possible... and yet...

"You're wrong, *brother*. Our father was a great man who deserved so much more than being Antonio's right-hand man. Vincenzo had the stomach to get the job done. He—"

"What the fuck did you just say?" The blood had completely drained from Enzo's face.

"You heard me, Lorenzo. Guess you weren't the apple of your father's eye, after all."

Oh God.

Realization flickered across Enzo's face.

A brother.

He had a brother.

A brother Vincenzo had kept from him, kept from everyone if this family reunion was anything to go by.

Oh, Enzo.

"You're lying". Enzo's voice shook with anger.

"Am I? Our father told me all about you, brother. All that rage inside you, the blood thirst, the desire to drown in darkness. He had high, high hopes for you... but like always, you were a bitter disappointment." The temperature cooled in the room as the two brothers faced off against each other.

"And then, you killed him. You chose Antonio, the Family, over your own flesh and blood, you fucking piece of shit."

"What do you want, Vinnie? You want vengeance, is that it? You want your pound of flesh? Then come and get it. I'm right here." Enzo opened his arms to the side, goading my captor.

"You think I want to kill you?" His dark laughter snaked through me, coiled around my heart like barbed wire. "I don't want to kill you... yet. First, I want you to watch as I destroy the thing you love most in the world."

My blood turned to ice at his words, but I couldn't move, I couldn't do anything.

"I'm going to ruin her and you're going to stand here and watch."

"Touch her and I'll—"

"You'll what? Kill me. I'd like to see you try while I have a knife pressed to your girlfriend's throat."

Tears streamed down my face. I wanted to be strong. I wanted to be the kind of woman who laughed in the face of danger. But the reality was, my world was splintering apart right in front of me.

I wanted to live. I wanted to graduate college and decide what to do with my life, maybe travel before settling down. I wanted to get married, a big over the top wedding with all my friends and family, and then I wanted a life with the guy I loved more than anything.

I wanted that... I wanted it so much.

But Vinnie had taken that from me. The second he'd made Luca kidnap me, he'd ruined my future. Because I knew Enzo, and I knew he wouldn't ever forgive himself for this.

My eyes settled on his rugged face. He couldn't even meet my eyes, focused solely on his psychopathic brother.

"This is between me and you, just let her go."

"And give up the opportunity to destroy your world the way you destroyed mine? Our father was everything to me... *everything* and you took him from me."

"She isn't anyone to me," Enzo said with so much sincerity my heart cracked wide open. "She's just good pussy, that's all."

"Ohhh, hear that, baby." Vinnie pressed his mouth to my ear. "He's good. So good I almost believed him."

"It's the truth. If our father taught me anything, it was to never let a woman into my life. Nora isn't my woman, Vinnie, she's just a piece of ass I like to lose myself in occasionally."

His words cut like tiny blades across my heart, ripping open old scars and forming new ones.

"Liar. She's yours... whether you're man enough to admit it or not. She's yours and I'm going to fucking destroy her."

Enzo finally gave me his eyes and what I saw there gutted me. He didn't know how to end this. Not with us both walking away alive.

I screwed my eyes shut, trying to push down the tidal wave of emotion battering my insides.

"Time's up, brother," he sneered. "Say goodbye to your heart."

TWENTY-NINE

ENZO

HE WAS GOING to kill her.

This motherfucker was going to kill the only girl I'd ever loved.

And I did.

I loved Nora.

Maybe not in a conventional way, but she owned my heart... and I think deep down she'd taken mine the first time I'd ever laid eyes on her.

Nora wasn't like most girls. She was strong and selfless and sassy, unapologetic and feisty. She went after what she wanted with zero fucks given.

And she'd wanted me.

Nora Abato had seen past all my darkness and found the sliver of light buried deep inside my soul.

A mistake she was going to die for.

Fuck.

Vinnie yanked her over to a table and folded her over it, dropping his free hand to his belt buckle. My blood turned to molten lava as I watched him claw at her lounge pants, pulling them down enough to reveal her ass.

"Don't," my voice didn't sound like my own as I stepped forward.

"Make a move and I'll end her." He still had the blade pressed right to her throat. Her big brown eyes silently pleaded with me, but I was paralyzed, watching as he grasped his dick and slowly fed it into her.

Nora's cries filled the room, cracking my chest wide open.

"NO!" I yelled. "Please..."

"God, she's tight," Vinnie grinned at me as he thrust into her over and over. "I can see why you fell hard for this pussy. Fuck me, she's squeezing my dick so tight."

His fingers gripped her hips tightly, making pain flare in her eyes, but my strong, brave girl didn't flinch. She took it all while I stood there powerless to do anything else but watch.

Fuck.

FUCK!

A violent storm raged inside of me. I wanted to tear this fucker limb from limb, to rip his heart from his chest and watch the life drain from his eyes. But I was powerless. If I tried to shoot him—and I had a fucking perfect aim—he could still hurt Nora, or worse.

I couldn't take that risk. I had to wait until he was distracted.

His grunts of exertion filled the room as he pounded into her. Bile rushed up my throat, but I forced it down. It was my fault Nora was in this position. The least I could do was be there with her in this living nightmare.

Her eyes remained locked on mine, tears dripping down her face.

"Now," the word formed on her lips and at first, I didn't understand, but then realization slammed into me.

In his vigor to hurt her, to ruin her, Vinnie had let his hand at her throat relax, enough for the knife to drop away from her throat a little.

It was risky, but it was now or never.

"Do it," she mouthed. "Do it."

"Fuck yeah, take it, bitch. Take it like a good little whore."

I slowly reached into my jacket and grasped the butt of my pistol. My heart crashed against my rib cage, blood roaring in my ears, as I whipped it out. "Hey, brother?" I called and Vinnie looked up, fear stunning him. The shot rang out through the room, reverberating through me. "Tell our father to go fuck himself."

Vinnie collapsed in a heap and Nora scrambled away, tripping over his body. I rushed to her side and pulled her into my arms. "I've got you, Gattina. I've got you."

"Oh my God." She clawed at my sweater. "Is he—"

"He's dead." It was a kill shot and I hadn't missed. "It's over..." The words felt like ash on my tongue. Because Nora should never have been in the middle of this in the first place.

"Enzo?" Voices rang out in the building and Nora flinched, pressing herself closer.

"Relax, Gattina, it's just Nicco and Matteo."

"It is?" Her body melted against mine, the adrenaline leaving her and shock kicking in. I gently pulled her to her feet and straightened out her clothes. Nora was like a rag doll in my arms as I picked her up, cradling her against my chest.

"In here," I yelled back.

They burst through the door seconds later, a string of expletives leaving their lips as they took in the sight before me.

"Is she—"

I shook my head. Nora was barely conscious. "I need you to take her," I said to Matteo. "Take her to Arianne and call the doctor."

"How bad?" He gently eased Nora into his arms.

"Bad." My eyes shuttered as anger drenched my veins.

"Fuck. Yeah, okay. Backup is on its way."

I gave my cousin a sharp nod, and he turned to leave, but Nora murmured my name. "Ssh, Gattina." I gently stroked her face. "You're safe now. I promise."

"S-stay with me."

"I've got to take care of some things here, but I'll be there soon. Matteo and Arianne will be with you. Luis too."

"M-Maurice?"

Nicco shook his head and I swallowed the truth. "He's okay." The lie soured on my tongue, but she'd had enough to deal with for one day.

"Go," I said to Matteo, watching as he carried her out and away from me. From this absolute clusterfuck.

"What the fuck happened?" Nicco asked.

"He raped her... he fucking—" I grabbed the nearest chair and launched it across the room, kicking the one next to it. Pain skittered through my foot, but it wasn't enough. I wanted to destroy everything in eyesight.

"E, breathe. You need to bre—"

"He was my *brother*."

"W-what?"

I nodded. "Vincenzo Marchetti's long lost bastard child. By the sounds of it, he and daddy dearest were pretty tight."

"But how—

"Your guess is as good as mine. He knew everything, Nicco. He knew about Nora, about me... what I did. It was all about revenge."

"Fuck." Nicco stalked over to Vinnie's dead body and kicked his leg. "He tell you anything else?"

"Doesn't matter. He's gone now and I hope he rots in hell with our father."

"There's no sign of Bianco."

Just then, a knocking sound filtered down the hall.

"What is that?" I said, drawing my pistol again as we moved through the abandoned building on the outskirts of La Riva. All this time, Vinnie was holed up right on our doorstep.

After Lucii had given us Nate's number. He'd pointed us in the direction of Isaac's apartment. We'd found a copy of a rental agreement for an industrial unit alongside the river. It was almost too easy. Now I was beginning to wonder if it wasn't just another clue, all part of his game.

It didn't matter now, he was gone. And Nora and I were still here.

Fuck. Nora.

"Hey." Nicco gripped my shoulder and then moved ahead of me.

"H-help," a voice said, and we followed the moans into a small room at the back of the building.

"Stay alert," he ordered, and I raised my pistol into the air, taking aim should any more surprises jump out on us.

But when Nicco pushed the door open, I dropped my weapon, my mouth hanging wide open.

Because there in the corner of the room, half-conscious and bound was Luca.

It turned out Luca wasn't an accomplice. Isaac had blackmailed him with threats of going after his ex in Pawtucket. Much like me and my family, he knew things about her. Her address, her place of work. It was enough to spook Luca into doing his bidding, and for as much as I wanted to put a bullet through his brains for ever putting Nora in danger, part of me got it. Because there wasn't much I wouldn't do for the girl I loved either.

Fuck, it felt weird admitting that.

But it was the least of my problems as I pulled up outside Nicco and Arianne's building.

Thanks to mine and Nicco's handiwork, the emergency services were attending to an anonymously reported blaze on the outskirts of La Riva. Soon, there wouldn't be anything left of Vinnie to find. We'd need to figure out a story to tell Lucii and Nate, but that could wait until morning.

Right now, there was only one place I needed to be.

Arianne greeted me at the door.

"Enzo, thank God." She pulled me into her arms and hugged me tight. "I've been so worried." Ari released me with an awkward smile.

"Thanks," I clipped out. "How is she?"

Her expression fell. "She's sleeping right now. Doc checked her over, took some blood, and gave her some pain pills."

I sucked in a harsh breath. "Can I—"

"Of course. She was asking for you the whole time."

My chest squeezed.

Nicco had gone to the hospital with Luca. We needed to get his story straight and he knew I wasn't levelheaded enough to do it.

"Can I get you anything?" Ari asked me as I followed her into the apartment.

"No, I'm good."

I wasn't.

I felt like I'd woken from a nightmare, unsure of what was real and what wasn't.

"I'll give the two of you some space, but if you need anything..."

I nodded. It was all I could manage. As I walked the short distance to their guest bedroom, my heart was in my throat. I'd watched that fucker rape her. Heard his moans of pleasure, witnessed her tears as he broke her.

How the fuck was I supposed to go in there and hold her?

I didn't know how to do this, to be the hero who comes to save the day.

"She'd want you to go to her," Ari said, and I glanced back to find her watching me.

"This is all my fault."

"You know she won't blame you. Isaac... I mean Vinnie," sympathy shone in her eyes, "made his choices. It's the only thing we can control, Enzo. How we choose to respond to something. That's what counts. So you can walk away and prove to her and everyone else that you don't deserve her, or you can be the guy we know you can be, and go in there and just be with her."

"You're different, you know."

"Love changes you," she said with conviction. "I know you think it makes you weak, but it doesn't. Love makes you strong, Enzo. It gives you something worth fighting for."

"I'm glad Nicco has you."

"And I'm glad Nora has you," she said. "I'm trusting you with her heart, don't let me down."

Too stunned for words, I slipped into the bedroom. Nora was curled up on her side, in a fitful sleep. She whimpered and I wanted to go back to that building and kill my brother all over again.

Fuck.

My brother.

It was going to take some time to wrap my head around that. But until Tommy dug around to unearth my father's secrets, I knew answers would have to wait.

"N-no," Nora cried, and I rushed to her side.

"Ssh, Gattina. I'm here. I'm right here."

"E-Enzo?" Her eyes flickered open. "You're here."

"I'm here."

That settled her and she slipped under again. I quickly removed all my weapons and stripped down to my boxer briefs and climbed in beside her. Even in her sleep, Nora gravitated to me, nestling her body in the curve of mine. Slipping an arm around her, I closed my eyes and focused on the sound of her breathing.

And before long, fell into a dreamless sleep.

When I woke up, it was to dark brown eyes staring at me.

"Hey." She smiled weakly. The usual fire in her eyes had dimmed and her skin was pale. And fuck, if it wasn't a stark reminder of what had happened.

"Hey," I replied over the lump in my throat. "How are you feeling?"

"Like I was kidnapped by a psycho... again."

Heavy silence filled the space between us.

"I am so fucking sorry, Gattina. I keep thinking that if I'd have just—"

"Don't." Nora pressed her finger to my lips. "Nothing you say or do will ever make me think any of this was your fault, so I'm asking you... no, I'm telling you, don't." She pinned me with a hard look. "Maurice, is he—"

I couldn't lie to her, not now. Earlier in the building had been different. But Nora was safe now.

She was here, and she was safe.

But it's too late. He already ruined her.

"He didn't make it."

"God, no..." Her pained sobs were like a knife to the heart.

"I'm so sorry, I'm so fucking sorry." My hand curved around the back of Nora's neck, anchoring her to me while she broke apart.

"I can't believe he's gone," she murmured through the deluge of tears.

Panic had me in a chokehold. I didn't know how to do this, to be who she needed. Not when I was the source of her pain and anguish.

Nora cried and cried. She cried until there were no tears left to cry and her breathing slowed. When I was certain she was asleep, I slipped out of the bed and pulled on my clothes.

It was early, a little after six, but I found Nicco sitting at the breakfast counter, nursing a coffee.

"Couldn't sleep?" I asked, joining him.

"Figured someone should keep an eye on you."

"I told her about Maurice. I had to."

"I know."

"How do you do it, Nic? How do you live with yourself knowing that you've pulled her into our world?"

"You just do. Love isn't fair. It doesn't play by the rules, E. It's emotional warfare and Arianne conquered me. She fucking slayed me until I knew I would never be able to let her go." He took a long sip of coffee. "So now I spend my days not worrying about what our love will cost, but how to protect it."

"You're a better man than me," I murmured. "I don't think I'll ever be able to forget watching him—" A lump got stuck in my throat.

"You need to focus on Nora. She's going to need you over the coming days." He levelled me with a dark look. "She needs you, Enzo."

I heard his words, felt them attack my heart like bullets.

Nora needed me.

But it was me who had gotten her into this mess.

Me who had put her in the firing line.

Vinnie wanted to make me pay for killing our father. He wanted to take something from me, the way I'd taken it from him.

I leaped up. "I need to get some air."

Nicco let out a heavy sigh. "I'm begging you, don't do this."

"I'll be back," I said, but I could tell from his grim expression he didn't believe me.

As I grabbed my keys and walked out of his apartment, I wasn't sure I believed me either.

THIRTY

NORA

"NORA," Arianne peeked her face around the door. "I brought you something to eat."

"I'm not hungry," I said.

"Oh, Nor. You've got to eat." She left the plate on the dresser and came over to me.

"I had some crackers this morning."

"It isn't enough."

"I just can't, babe." I felt too sick. It wasn't a physical side effect like a stomach flu, it was something much worse.

It was a symptom of my broken heart.

It was two days since I'd woken up in Nicco and Arianne's guest room, cold and alone.

Enzo had left.

He'd left me.

And although he climbed into bed with me every night after he thought I'd fallen to sleep, I knew he was trying to find the words I didn't know he'd ever manage to say.

We were done.

Tears pooled into the corners of my eyes as I croaked, "How is he?"

"He's... okay."

"You're a terrible liar." A weak smile played on my lips.

"He comes back every night. He just needs time."

Yeah, and I needed him.

I needed him so damn much.

Something inside felt broken, inexplicably altered. Arianne had tried to get me to talk about it, but I wasn't ready.

So I spent my days in bed, watching mindless TV, waiting for Enzo to slide in behind me and draw me into his arms. Because despite the fact he was slowly shredding my heart apart, being close to him was the only time that peace found me.

I could still vividly remember Vinnie rutting into me, his fingers digging into my hips and his dirty words lashing my insides.

"I hate this," I cried. "I fucking hate this."

I wasn't weak.

I was Nora goddamn Abato. I didn't want to let some psychopath like Vinnie break my spirit. But I got it now. I understood what it was like to have your dignity torn to shreds, to have your body used, and your soul stained.

Because that's what it was, a stain on my soul I wasn't sure I would ever forget.

"Nora, you know I—"

"Don't. Please, babe, just don't." I wasn't there yet. I wasn't ready to hear her words of encouragement and reassurance, even though she knew what I was going through.

"Okay. But I just want you to know, whenever you're ready to talk about it, I'm here." She gently squeezed my hand.

"Thanks. I'd feel better if he was here, and not out there doing whatever he's doing," I confessed.

"Nora, you know how he gets. Enzo had a full plate with the stuff with his father but throw in this revelation about Vinnie and you getting hurt..." She let out a small sigh. "It's going to take time."

"I just wish he'd talk to me."

I'd been so sure he would walk away the second he found me, but he hadn't. Sure, he wasn't around during daylight, but he came back to me every night. I knew the fact he came in darkness and left before sunlight wasn't exactly conventional, but nothing about us ever had been.

I pulled the cushion closer, taking comfort in its soft fluffy casing. Arianne leaned over and brushed the stray hairs from my face. "I hate to see you like this. Why don't you come and watch some TV in the living room? It's just the two of us. Nicco is... out."

Code word for Nicco was trying to talk Enzo off a ledge somewhere.

"Maybe later." I closed my eyes and tried to shut it all out. The pain I felt every time I thought of that day, the heartache I felt thinking of Enzo, the utter despair I felt about the future.

"This isn't you, Nora." Concern coated Arianne's words. "I know you're hurting, and I know you need time, but don't let this break you. You're so strong."

"I think I'm going to sleep now," I whispered, refusing to look at her.

"Okay, you know where I am if you need me."

But it wasn't Arianne I needed.

It was Enzo.
And he'd left me.

Cool hands slipped over my hips and dragged my body backward. My eyes fluttered open as Enzo got comfortable behind me. The digital clock on the nightstand read a little after one. His lips hovered against the nape of my neck, whispering Italian words I couldn't quite distinguish, save for one phrase.

Perdonami.

Forgive me.

I don't know how I knew, but I knew this was the last time he would climb into bed with me. Deep down in my soul, I knew this was goodbye.

Tears stung my eyes as my body began to tremble.

"Nora?" It was a whispered slur, a faint trace of liquor on his breath.

Of course he'd been out drinking. Because that's what guys like Enzo did. They drank and fought and fucked their problems away.

Damn you, Enzo.

The silence was deafening, the distance between us cavernous.

His breathing slowed and I knew he was falling to sleep. But I couldn't do it. I couldn't pretend for a second longer.

"Were you even going to tell me?" I whispered. "Or were you going to slip out as if you were never here?"

"You're awake." He tensed behind me.

"You didn't answer my question."

"I... Fuck, I don't know what to say."

I turned in his arms, staring up at him. "You can't even look at me, can you?"

"Fuck, Gattina, that's not what this is." His eyes glittered in the dark, darting around my face, but never fully meeting my eyes.

"So what is it? Because I've spent the last two days in hell, waiting for you to come to me... and you didn't."

"I tried..."

"But you couldn't." I let out a resigned sigh.

"I'm so fucking sorry, Gattina."

"Yeah, me too." The words shattered my heart. But it was only what I already knew.

Enzo had given up.

He was so lost to his own demons that he couldn't see what was staring him in the eyes. I didn't want to beg, I wouldn't.

I had too much self-respect for that.

I wanted to be someone's sun. The center of someone's universe. Instead, I was a burden. And now I was tarnished.

Broken.

"I think you should leave," my voice shook.

"Nora, please don't do this."

"I've given you everything." Tears dripped down my cheeks. "But it still isn't good enough..." *I'm not good enough.*

"It isn't you, Gattina. You have to know that." Enzo cupped my face, running his thumb along the line of my jaw. He touched me like I was fragile glass, about to shatter at any second.

The irony of the sentiment wasn't lost on me.

"You are so fucking good, so fucking strong. You deserve someone who can protect you, someone who will keep you safe. I'm not that guy, Nora." Regret clouded his eyes. "I don't know how to be that guy."

Try, I wanted to scream. *Just try.*

But I didn't want Enzo to try for me, I wanted him to try because *he* wanted to.

Enzo wasn't done though. He closed the distance between us, letting his mouth ghost over mine. "I'm going to go away for a while."

"W-what?" Panic flooded my veins.

He nodded. "I think it's best we get some distance. I need to deal with shit, and it'll be easier on you if I'm not around all the time."

"When will you leave?" He was ripping my heart out of my chest cavity and he was too blinded by anger to see it.

"As soon as Uncle Toni is home, which should be a couple of days."

"I see." Ice began freezing around my heart.

"For what it's worth, I am sorry. The last thing I ever wanted was for you to get hurt. You deserve the world, Gattina, and one day, you'll find someone worthy of you."

Enzo sealed his mouth over mine, kissing me slow and deep, tracing the shape of my lips with his tongue. I kissed him back, imprinting the taste of him, the slight scratch of his stubble against my skin, the way his tongue expertly curled around my own. For as much as I hated him in this moment, I never wanted to forget him.

I never wanted to forget that for a small moment in time, Enzo Marchetti had been mine.

"Go," tears trickled down my lips, "go, before I ask you to stay." I kissed him harder, never wanting to let go.

But eventually I broke away, inhaling a ragged breath. "You know you can keep running from life, Enzo, but one day, you're going to look back and realize you had everything, and you tossed it away, and you'll have to live with that."

He climbed out of bed and pulled on his clothes. Without another word, he went to the door, lingering for a second. In another life he would have declared his undying love for me.

In another life, he would have stayed.

But this wasn't a fairy tale.

And Enzo wasn't the hero.

It took me another four days until I finally left Nicco and Arianne's guest room. My body had finally begun to heal, but my heart... that would take a while longer. You didn't just forget about someone like Enzo. But Ari was right, I couldn't let this—or him—break me.

So I showered, pulled on some clean clothes, and joined Nicco and Arianne for breakfast.

"This is a surprise," my best friend said.

"I figured it's time to enter the real world again." My shoulders lifted in a small shrug.

"I'll get you a plate." Nicco got up.

"I think I'm going to start classes up on Monday."

"I think that sounds like a great idea."

"Here," Nicco offered me a plate. "If you need anything, you only have to ask."

"Actually, I was hoping you might take me to Maurice's grave." I hadn't attended the funeral. I couldn't.

"Of course. Just say when."

"Thank you." A smile traced my lips. "How's your father?"

"He's finding being on bed rest hard. I think Genevieve is ready to throw in the towel."

"She loves him." Ari gazed up at him. "She'll stick by him because that's what you do when you lov—gosh, me and my big mouth."

"You don't need to do that, babe. It's okay. I'm okay."

I didn't ask about Enzo. It was dangerous territory for me. But I knew he had left Verona since Antonio was home.

I locked down my unresolved feelings about him and tried to force down some pancakes.

"If it's okay, I'd like to stay here, just a few more days."

"Actually," Ari said, laying her hand on Nicco's hand. "We've been talking, and we'd like you to move in here."

"Ari, that's kind and all, but I can't—"

"Hear me out," she added. "We don't mean live with us, but there's an apartment up for rent right down the hall."

"There is?"

She nodded. "It's only a one bed but we checked it out and think it would be per—"

"Yes," I rushed out, relief seeping into me. "If you're sure you don't mind, I would actually love that." I wasn't sure I could return to La Stella without Maurice. It would be a permanent reminder of what had happened. Not to mention that I wasn't ready to see Luca. He'd been texting me, but it was still too raw. Part of me was relieved to discover he was moving back to Pawtucket.

Nicco had filled me in on the truth; explained how Vinnie blackmailed Luca to do his bidding. But it didn't diminish the fact that he'd drugged and kidnapped me. I could forgive eventually, but I would never ever forget.

"Of course. We'll take care of everything. You can stay here until it's ready."

"Thank you."

"We just want you to be happy, Nor, and to feel safe."

"I'll get there." Heartache wasn't something you could get over. You had to feel it, embrace it. You had to go through it to get to the other side. But every day, I was beginning to feel a little more of the old me push to the surface. I was a fighter. A survivor. And I would get through this. A sense of resolve washed over me, and I tipped my head to the ceiling, inhaling deeply.

I was going to be okay.

My heart would forever carry the scars of Enzo, but it was slowly piecing itself back together. Because I was resilient.

I was strong.

And I would get through this.

It was Saturday night and Matteo and Alessia had come over to hang out at the apartment. The rental wasn't going to be ready for another week, so I planned to stay with Nicco and Ari until it was.

"Don't start without me," I said, getting up. "I need to pee and then I'm going to make a fresh bowl of popcorn."

We were halfway through a movie marathon, and surprisingly, I was having fun. It was the first day I felt like myself. My cheeks hurt from all the laughter and smiling but it felt so damn good.

It didn't stop the hole in my heart aching, but I was here and I was okay, and that was enough.

It had to be.

After washing my hands, I dried them on the towel and slipped back into the hall, but the low rumble of hushed voices gave me pause.

"Should tell her."

"No, she's been doing better. Knowing will only confuse her," Ari said.

"I think she should know," Alessia added. "She's in love with him. It isn't fair to keep it—"

"Keep what from me?" I stepped into the room taking the air with me.

"Fuck," Matteo grumbled, while Arianne looked as guilty as sin.

"What aren't you telling me?"

"Enzo isn't—"

"*Matt*!" Nicco shook his head. "It doesn't matter, Nora. It won't change anything, and Ari is right, you've been doing so well. Don't let—"

"Will someone please just tell me what's going on?"

"Enzo didn't leave," Sia blurted out.

Nicco buried his face in his hand with a heavy groan.

"Guess the cat's out of the bag." Matteo smiled weakly.

"What do you mean, he didn't leave? He said—"

"We know, Nor." Arianne stood up and came to me. "But he couldn't do it. He couldn't leave."

"W-why couldn't he do it?"

"Why do you think?"

Pain lashed my insides. "Where is he then?" I cried. Because he hadn't been around and no one so much as mentioned him around me.

Nicco made a derisive noise in the back of his throat.

"He's in a bad place, Nor." Ari took my hand. "It's better you don't—"

"He really didn't leave?" It wasn't supposed to matter. Part of me knew it didn't. But the other part clung onto Alessia's words, letting them grow into something else entirely.

He stayed.

He stayed... *for me*?

But he was still punishing himself.

"I need to see him." The words spilled from my lips without thought.

"Nor, I don't think that's a good idea."

"You're probably right, but I need to see him, babe." There was still so much left unsaid between us. Things I should have told him. Things I should have made him hear.

"Arianne is right, now is probably not—"

"Will you help me?" I asked Matteo.

"Oh, come on, Nora, don't put me in this position."

"Weren't you the one who said not to give up?"

"Fuck," he muttered. "I really need to learn not to open my big mouth."

"Will you help me or not?"

He ran a hand down his face and blew out a steady breath. "I will. But I warn you now." His expression dropped, making my chest constrict. "You might not like what you find."

THIRTY-ONE

ENZO

"I'LL HAVE ANOTHER ONE." I slammed my glass down on the bar, and the bartender, a guy named Billy, shook his head.

"I should cut you off."

"But we both know you won't." My brow arched and he shrugged.

"Suit yourself man, but you're going to feel like an ass when I have to call Matteo or Nicco to drag your drunk ass out of here."

Here was L'Anello's. It was Saturday and the bar was crammed full of people looking for a good time. But I wasn't here for anything other than to find solace at the bottom of a glass.

It had been days since I'd seen her.

I couldn't even think about Nora without a huge pit carving through my stomach.

I should have left. I should have gotten in my car and driven far, far away from Verona County. But when it came down to it, I couldn't do it.

I needed to be here, just in case she needed me. Just in case—

Fuck!

My fist curled against the sleek chrome counter. Nora didn't need me. She probably hated me. I didn't blame her. I was a fucking mess.

After the shitshow with Vinnie, I'd spent a couple of nights avoiding her in the day only to sneak into her bed at night to hold her. I think I'd always known she wasn't really sleeping, but I hadn't wanted to talk, and she seemed content in lying there in silence.

I knew it couldn't last though. She would eventually want answers, answers I didn't have. So I'd taken the coward's way out.

And now I felt like a boat adrift without an anchor. Because that's what Nora was to me, my anchor. She was my North fucking Star in dark, dismal skies, and I'd walked away.

Again.

I could imagine my old man and my brother looking down on me, reveling in my misery. I'd killed them both, exterminated them like the vermin they were, but somehow, I was the one still here suffering.

I just needed it to stop. I needed them to get the fuck out of my head.

"Hey, Enzo." A brunette stepped into my line of sight, laying her hand on my thigh. "You're looking good."

For a second, I had to blink through the liquor haze clouding my thoughts. It wasn't Nora, I knew that. But if I squinted a little and didn't focus too hard, she bore some resemblance.

"You look lonely, you should buy me a drink and I'll keep you company." She batted her eyelashes, smirking suggestively.

"Not tonight." I removed her hand from my thigh. "Take a walk."

She pouted, twirling a finger around a lock of hair. It was longer than Nora's, and a lighter shade of brown.

Upon closer inspection she wasn't anything like my Gattina.

Her pet name on my tongue slayed me. I hadn't even spoken the word, but it was right there. Taunting me. Reminding me of everything I wanted and could never have.

"Another." I flagged Billy down, ignoring the girl. Eventually, she took off, moving onto the next available guy.

"Not your type?" he asked.

"Nah."

"More of a blonde and fake tits kinda guy?"

"Something like that."

Or at least, I used to be. Until Nora had swept in and blown everything I thought I knew to shreds.

"I need to piss." I drained my fresh drink in one and wiped my mouth with the back of my hand. The second I stood though, the room spun.

"Whoa, there, Enzo, take it easy."

"I'm good." I waved him off, stalking across the crowded room to the bar. Guys stopped to greet me, and girls tried to get my attention, but I didn't feel like socializing.

In fact, it was a bad fucking idea that I was here in the first place. But it beat being back at my apartment, alone and miserable, wondering what Nora was doing, and whether she missed me as much as I missed her.

Fuck, I missed her.

I missed her smile and sass and those stupid fucking t-shirts she liked to wear.

I just missed *her*.

But I wasn't good for her. I'd proved that one too many times.

I managed to stumble my way to the restrooms, staggering into a stall to do my thing. When I was done, I washed my hands. My reflection stared back at me. The dark circles around my eyes were haunting.

His eyes.

My fist flew out before I could stop it, colliding with the glass. It shattered, slicing open my knuckles.

"Fuck." Blood dripped down my hand and I grabbed a bunch of paper towels out of the dispenser and wrapped it around the cut, trying to stem the flow.

A couple of guys burst into the bathroom, took one look at me and immediately backtracked. Everything was still spinning as I staggered out of there.

"Oh my God, Enzo," the girl from a second ago came rushing over. "What did you do?"

"Doesn't matter," I grunted, trying to shake her off. But she wrapped her hand around my arm in a vice grip and steered me back toward the bar.

"Whisky on the rocks." She signaled Billy. "And a bucket of ice and a first aid kit."

"I'm fine."

"You're getting blood everywhere." Her eyes went to the wet soggy paper towel stained red.

Billy came back with her order. "You might want to do this somewhere a little quieter," he suggested.

"Good thinking. Come on." She tugged me back through the crowd, slipping into a door marked 'private.' A security guy nodded at me, or maybe he was nodding at her. Everything was starting to get really fucked up in my head. But then she was pulling me into a small room with a crushed velvet couch. "Sit," she ordered.

"What's your name?" I slurred as I dropped onto the plush couch.

"Natalia. Now let me look at your hand." Gently unwrapping my hand, she flinched. "You made quite a mess of this."

I could see double. Two of her, two of my hand. Her features blurred together and for a second, I saw Nora.

My Nora.

My Gattina.

"Nora," I mumbled as she cleaned up my cuts, dressing it in a bandage from the first aid kit.

"There," she said. "All better."

"Don't talk," I snapped.

When she talked, I remembered she wasn't Nora. And I really fucking wanted her to be Nora.

"No?" Her eyes darkened as she licked her lips. "What did you want to do then?" Slowly, Natalia lowered herself onto my lap, straddling my hips. She wrapped her slender fingers around my neck and lowered her face to mine. "I can think of a few things that don't involve talking."

Her lips brushed mine, and for a second I was with Nora, kissing Nora.

"Get your slutty hands off him."

"Nora?" I blinked over at the little firecracker in the doorway, glaring at me as if I'd just—

"*Nora*?"

Fuck. I was tripping. Nora wasn't here. She was at Nicco and Ari's apartment.

But then the girl was yanked off my lap, her shrieks filling the air.

"I said get the hell off him." The Nora apparition grabbed a fistful of the girl's hair and started dragging her toward the door while I sat there, barely clinging onto consciousness.

My hand throbbed as blood started seeping through the bandage.

"What the fuck did you do?"

"Matteo?" I balked as he materialized in front of me. I was definitely tripping. Whatever Billy had plied me with was some strong shit.

"You're a fucking mess," he said, throwing a bottle of water at me. "I honestly don't know why she keeps fighting for you." His eyes went to where Nora was standing.

Nora was here too?

What the fuck was going on?

"Give us some space", she said to my cousin who had moved into the room, smirking at me as if he was enjoying the show.

"You sure? Maybe this should wait."

"I don't think it can. Please..."

"Fine, but I'll be right outside." He pinned me with a serious look. "Don't fuck anything else up. This is your last shot."

Last shot?

What the fuck was he talking about? I hadn't asked him to bring Nora here.

Matteo slipped out of the room, closing the door. The door was like a gunshot to my already racing heart.

"You should drink that," she said, eyeing the water in my hand. I uncapped it and guzzled the contents down, letting the ice-cold liquid temper some of the fire inside me.

"Did you fuck her?" Nora approached me. She didn't sound angry, she sounded disappointed... resigned, and it cut deep.

It cut really fucking deep.

She didn't come close, just stood there in front of me. Out of reach. Always fucking out of reach. Contempt rolling off her in thick angry waves.

I swallowed hard. "You think I..."

"Well, did you?"

"No, Gattina, I didn't fuck her." I released a thin breath. Fucking her hadn't even crossed my mind, even when I'd thought she was Nora.

Because deep down, I knew. I knew her face was all wrong and her voice was all shrill. Even if my glassy eyes had betrayed me, my heart knew.

It would always fucking know.

"You're hurt," she said, glancing at my hand.

"It's nothing. Had a little run in with a mirror."

"What are you doing, Enzo? You said you were leaving, you said—"

"Yeah, well, I said a lot of things I didn't mean." My eyes narrowed.

Nora being here was sobering. I felt the liquor coursing through my veins evaporate until I could see every blemish on her skin, the way her lips trembled as she stared me down.

It was her.

It was always fucking her.

I dragged a hand over my face.

"I wanted to kill her."

"E-excuse me?" I spat out.

"For touching you. For *kissing* you," Nora seethed. "I wanted to drag her off you and rip out her heart. But you're not mine anymore," she inhaled a sharp breath, "maybe you never were." Nora took two steps toward me, my heart beating so fucking hard I thought it was going to explode.

"But that doesn't mean you shouldn't hear the words. It doesn't mean that just because you think you're unworthy of love that you should never experience it." She came to a stop in front of me, and gently cupped my face forcing me to look up at her. But she didn't need to force me to do anything, I couldn't take my eyes off her.

Nora was so fucking beautiful it hurt.

"I love you, Enzo Marchetti. I think I've loved you for a while. You think you're a dark soul with a faulty heart. But you're so much more than that. We all need darkness to shine. And you make me light up like no one else ever has. I'm not asking you for anything you don't want to give, but I am asking you to try to at least see what I see. What Nicco and Matteo, and Alessia, and Arianne see.

"You are a good person, Enzo. You care about your family, you would die for them. And I know that your father messed you up. I know he starved you of love until you began to believe you weren't worthy of it. And I know what you had to do to him. But none of it, not a single thing, changes the fact that you are worthy. And I love you, Enzo. I love you."

Speechless.

I was fucking speechless.

It was like she'd taken every insecurity I'd had as a child and plucked it from my soul.

She knew.

She knew about my father, about what I'd done.

I don't know why I was surprised. Nicco couldn't hold his own shit where Arianne was concerned. It went against everything we were to tell outsiders about Family business. But Arianne wasn't an outsider. She was half of his fucking heart, his woman… his Queen.

She was as much a part of this now as he was.

Could it really be that simple?

Could love really conquer all?

"I-I don't know what to say." Dejection flared in her eyes. But everything was coming at me a mile a minute, slamming into me with such force I couldn't sort through the jumbled thoughts to give her a response she deserved.

"That's okay. You have a lot to think about. But you need to know that you don't have to do this anymore. You don't have to escape to bars to try to drown out your feelings. You don't have to fight or fuck your way to peace. I can be that for you. I can be the person you turn to when it gets too much. I can be your shoulder, your willing body… even your punching bag—"

"Gattina, I would never—"

"Ssh, I know." She smiled, pressing a finger to my lips, her touch burning me inside out. "I meant an emotional punching bag. I'll be all of those for you because I love you. I love you so fucking much, Enzo, and I wouldn't be the girl I am if I never told you that."

"I—"

"You have a lot to think on," she cut me off. "But know if you go near another girl again, I won't be held responsible for my actions." Her brow lifted, and laughter rumbled in my chest.

Fuck, this girl.

She was everything.

Every-fucking-thing.

"I love you, Enzo." She gently pulled her finger away, replacing it with her soft lips. "But I won't spend my life chasing you. This is it… your last chance. The question is are you brave enough to take a leap of faith?"

THIRTY-TWO

NORA

FOUR DAYS after I'd stormed into L'Anello's and found Enzo with some whore draped all over him, I still hadn't heard from him.

I'd left him that night with nothing more than a soft kiss and an ultimatum.

A small part of me—the hopeless romantic, the girl who wanted her very own love story—had thought he would chase me down the second I left and declare his endless love for me. But of course, he hadn't. Because this wasn't a fairy tale and Enzo wasn't your average guy.

So I waited.

I didn't let it distract me from pressing forward with my life though. I resumed classes, saw my friends, and threw myself back into life *before* Enzo Marchetti.

As the days went by, so too did the quiet hope that he would eventually show. But I didn't let it crush me this time, I couldn't.

I'd bared my soul to Enzo, confessed every single thing he made me feel. What he chose to do with it... well, that was on him.

I walked the short distance to the main campus parking lot. Nicco and Ari were picking me up as they wanted to show me my new apartment. It was almost ready, and I was looking forward to a fresh start.

They'd both been so supportive. Giving me space when I needed it and keeping me company when I didn't want to be alone. I owed them big time. Only yesterday, they had both accompanied me to visit Maurice's grave. I'd sat at his headstone, in my boo bees t-shirt, talking nonsense, just like old times.

The other five security guards had also been killed at the hands of Vinnie, but I didn't *know* them, not the way I'd known my personal bodyguard.

When I arrived at the parking lot, there was no sign of Nicco's car though. He usually rode his motorbike, but that wasn't practical when you were chauffeuring around your wife and her best friend, so he'd caved and bought a brand new car.

A couple of seconds later, Matteo's truck appeared.

"This is a surprise," I said as he climbed out. "Why aren't you in class?"

"Secret mafia stuff." He winked.

"Haha, very funny." He liked to give me shit about my strange fascination with the Family. But it wasn't every day you got to meet and hang out with real life mafiosi.

"Nicco and Ari got held up. But I was in the area, so I said I'd swing by and give you a ride."

"Well, thank you." I beamed at him, accepting his help into the truck.

Matteo got in and fired up the ignition, the engine rumbling to life. "All set?" he asked and there was something in his eyes.

"What are you up to?" I asked, thinly.

"Who, me? Nothing. Not a damn thing." An amused smirk tipped the corner of his mouth.

It was a look I knew well.

A look that told me Matteo was up to something.

We didn't make it to Nicco and Arianne's apartment. Instead, he pulled up in front of the apartment he shared with Enzo.

"Erm, Matteo, what are we doing here?" My heart picked up speed.

"It's just a pit stop. I need to grab some things."

"Some things?" My brow lifted.

"Yeah, come on, I don't bite. And Enzo is out."

"Oh." I hadn't even noticed his car wasn't in the parking lot.

"I can stay here—"

"Don't be silly. It's my apartment too. Besides, I need you to come and help me with this."

His façade was a lot more convincing than it had been back at MU.

"Fine." I let out a soft sigh. "But I'm not lifting anything heavy."

"Deal."

Matteo came around and got the door. He was such a romantic at heart, so different to his cousin.

My heart lurched into my throat, but I ignored it. It had been four days and there had been no sign of Enzo. I had to accept that maybe my declaration wasn't enough.

"You know," Matteo said as we entered their building. "What you did at the bar, that was pretty badass."

"Yeah, but it didn't change anything." A sigh of resignation escaped my lips.

"Maybe not. But you fought for it, you fought for *him*, Nora. And I think that's a pretty incredible thing."

I nodded over the giant lump in my throat.

I hadn't been here since the morning I'd found Enzo in bed with some busty blonde. The memories gave me pause as we reached the door. But Matteo was right there, to steer me inside.

The second we stepped inside though, I realized Matteo had played me.

Enzo shot up off the couch. "Hi," he said.

"Hi. What is this?" I glanced around at Matteo and guilt twinkled in his eyes.

"Don't hate me." He grinned. "I'm just gonna—" He slipped out of the apartment and closed the door behind him.

"How have you been?" Enzo asked, his eyes darting around mine.

He was nervous.

Big bad Enzo Marchetti was nervous.

"I'm okay. You?"

He rubbed his jaw. "About what happened, at the bar... I swear to God, nothing happened with me and that woman. I was drunk and she was trying to—"

"You don't need to explain. I got a front row seat to what she was trying, remember?"

He flinched, his silence deafening.

"What am I doing here, Enzo?"

"I wanted to talk," he said.

"That would involve actually talking." My lips curved wryly.

"This doesn't come easy for me. I've never had to—"

"I know."

"Fuck. Maybe it'll just be easier if I show you." He offered me his hand, and I took it. Because it was Enzo, and I'd never been able to tell him no.

He pulled me into his arms, staring down at me with such intensity I felt winded.

"After you left L'Anello's, I wanted to come after you. I wanted to chase you so fucking bad. But I knew I needed to figure out what I wanted... I mean, I want you. I've always wanted you, Nora. That isn't the issue here, just so we're clear."

"I know."

"I didn't want to let you down again. Not when you deserve so much..."

Enzo took my hand and led me into his bedroom. At first, I didn't notice anything. But then I saw it.

I saw the perfume on his dresser, the avocuddle t-shirt draped over the back of his chair. I spotted the magazine on the nightstand, and the scarf hanging over the back of his door.

"W-what is this?" Confusion crinkled my brows.

"I know you're supposed to be moving into the apartment in Nicco's building. But what if you moved in... here?"

"You want me to move in? But—"

"I want you, Nora." Enzo snagged a hand around my waist and pulled me into his chest, my back to his front. "I want you in my bed, I want your face to be the first thing I see when I wake up, I want to know you're safe. Always."

"I-I don't know what to say." My heart was a band of wild horses galloping inside my chest.

He wanted me to move in.

Stone-hearted, commitment-phobe Enzo Marchetti wanted to live with me.

I was speechless.

Completely and utterly speechless.

"Nora?" he asked, turning me in his arms, concern glittering in his eyes.

"You'll have to get a mattress. I can't... not after you..."

"Already done."

"You bought me a mattress?"

"And this..." He plucked something out of his back pocket and took my hand, placing the key in my palm.

"You got me a key."

"To *our* apartment. If you want it, that is..."

Tears clung to my lashes as I nodded. "I want it. I really, really want it."

"Thank fuck." He blushed. He actually blushed. "Because I already moved in all your stuff."

"What?" I spluttered.

"I had a little help, but it was my idea." A smug smirk tugged at his mouth.

"I can't believe you did that."

"Well, you see, there's this girl. She's kind of a badass... she's sexy and sassy and so fucking selfless. She taught me some things..."

"Oh yeah, like what?"

"She taught me that it's okay to hurt, that it's okay to live with your pain. But she also taught me that it's okay to accept help, to admit that you can't do it alone. She taught me that just because you've never known the love of a parent doesn't mean you won't ever know love for yourself. Because I do, Gattina. I fucking love you. I love your heart and your strength. I love your body and your pure soul. I even love those fucking ridiculous t-shirts you wear."

"You love me?" My heart was fit to burst at his words. It was everything I'd ever wanted.

"Mi sono innamorato di te."

"I think you should show me," I said around a smug grin.

Enzo scooped me up in his arms and carried me over to the bed. "Your wish is my command il mio cuore."

Our story wasn't perfect.

It was messy and raw and painful, but it was also real. It was ours and nobody could ever take that away from us.

Sometimes you had to go through the darkness to get to the light...

And I wouldn't change a single thing.

Enzo lay me down on the bed and hovered over me. "I can't believe I almost lost you." He stared at me like he was seeing me for the first time.

"I'm right here." I leaned up to kiss him, letting my lips slide softly against his. He buried his hand in my hair, stroking the slope of my neck as he kissed me deeper.

"Is this okay?"

I nodded, locking my hands around his neck and pulling him closer. "I love you," I whispered, and I felt him shiver at my words.

It was a heady feeling, to know that I could bring this man to his knees. But I wouldn't ever take his love for granted or wield it as a weapon.

"I want to touch you, Gattina..." He let the words hang between us. I knew what he was asking me, and the truth was, I didn't know how I felt about being with him so soon after his brother's vicious attack.

I wanted Enzo, that wasn't the problem, but I knew I still hadn't dealt with everything that had happened.

"I... I think I'm ready." My voice cracked, betraying me.

"We'll take it slow." He climbed off me, before shedding his clothes. Then he reached for my hand, tugging me gently.

Enzo handled me softer than he ever had, taking his sweet time to undress me. His fingers followed the curve of my waist, gliding up my spine as he drew me into his warm body. "I need you, Nora. I will always need you. But I need to know that you're safe more."

"Kiss me," I said.

He dipped his head, capturing my lips in a bruising kiss. His tongue curled around mine, slow and unhurried, tasting and teasing while his fingers stroked a blazing path across my skin.

"So fucking beautiful," he hummed against my skin.

"I love this side of you," I murmured overwhelmed with how good he was making me feel.

"Yeah? Well don't tell anyone. I have a rep to protect." Enzo smirked, before guiding me back onto the bed. But this time, he climbed beside me and pulled me close into his body.

"What are you doing?" I asked.

"I figure we should probably talk."

"You want to talk? *Now*? Who are you and what have you done with the Enzo Marchetti I know and love?"

"Gattina," his icy gaze pinned me to the spot. "We need to talk about this."

"I know." I expelled a small breath.

How did you talk about something you wanted to pretend had never happened?

Enzo was there... he watched as his brother—

A garbled sob spilled from my lips.

"I'm here," Enzo said. "I'm right here and I will never let anyone hurt you again. I swear to God, Nora." Fierce possessiveness clung to his words.

My fingers clawed at his chest, needing to get closer as I broke in his arms. Enzo didn't try to shush me or talk to me, he just held me. Held me until the tears subsided and my breathing slowed.

"What happened," he said, gently nudging his nose against mine, "I need you to know it changes nothing for me. Not a damn thing, okay?"

I nodded. "I just hate that you saw it... that it will always be there, between us."

"It doesn't have to be. We can choose to look forward and not back. Someone once said to me, all I needed to do was take a leap of faith. Well, I'm asking you to do the same. Take a leap on me, Gattina... *with* me, and I'll always catch you. I promise."

"You're good at this, you know."

"That's where you're wrong. I'm not good at this... you are. You make me want to try, Nora. You make me want to be a better man." Enzo kissed me, stroking his thumb over my cheek. This, lying here with him, was like a salve to my bruised soul.

"I can't promise I'll always get it right," he went on, "but I promise to spend every second of every day trying to be worthy."

"You don't need to try," I whispered, stealing a chaste kiss. "You already are."

Enzo sucked in a sharp breath and I loved that, again, I'd shocked him with my raw honesty.

But everyone deserved to be loved.

And I would spend every second of every day showing *him* that.

EPILOGUE

NORA

"I SEE IT," I pressed my face against the window of Enzo's GTO as we approached the city. New York's skyline lit up the distance and excitement buzzed inside me.

"I can't wait to explore."

"Explore?" Enzo grumbled, sliding his hand along my knee. "I can't wait to get you naked."

A shiver rolled down my spine. "You were inside me less than six hours ago."

"Six hours too long."

Soft laughter bubbled in my chest.

Enzo was insatiable... and I loved it.

At first, after he finally gave into his feelings for me, I was worried things would be too intense after what happened with his brother. But Enzo had been patient with me. He hadn't pushed or demanded anything of me I couldn't give.

He'd been the perfect gentleman, and then when I was finally ready to be with him, he'd loved me in the way only he could.

His fingers walked higher, disappearing under my skirt. I clapped my hand down on his. "Oh no you don't, you're driving."

"And you're sexy."

I poked my tongue between my teeth. "Patience. Are you going to tell me where we're staying yet?" Enzo had planned our entire weekend from start to finish, and I couldn't wait to enjoy some time away with him, just the two of us.

Since Enzo had given me a key to his apartment, we'd been inseparable. He drove me to classes each morning and picked me up at the end of every day. Antonio was still on strict orders from the doctor to take it easy, so Nicco was taking a more hands-on approach in the Family. I knew Arianne worried, but we'd both made our choice and the Marchetti were part of our lives now, and I wouldn't have wanted it any other way.

My parents and brother hadn't taken the news so well. My father knew all about the hot-headed Marchetti boy with a cold exterior and black soul. But I was an adult, and I was happy. So freaking happy. Besides, I knew Enzo would win them over eventually.

He'd softened somewhat. Not with everyone. But it was there, peeking through the surface. He let Alessia and Arabella come over for girl's night and let me fill his apartment with girly shit, including my array of humorous t-shirts.

Enzo welcomed me into his life as if I was always supposed to be there, and I couldn't explain it, but we just worked.

"It's a shame Arianne and Nicco couldn't come," I said.

Originally, the four of us were going to make the trip to celebrate Ari's birthday. But with Antonio still recovering, they decided to stay behind. Things were quiet since Vinnie, but I knew it wouldn't always be like that. There would be more threats and attacks, more lies and secrets. This was the life I'd chosen though, and I knew without doubt Enzo would always protect me.

"God, it's so beautiful." We were driving right into the thick of the city. I'd never felt more small or insignificant than with New York's high rises looming over us. I cranked the window and stuck my head outside, letting out a shriek of excitement as the cool air rushed over my face. When I ducked back inside, Enzo was frowning over at me.

"You're fucking crazy."

"But you love me."

"Yeah, I do." A smirk played on his lips.

"Are we almost there?"

"Patience, Gattina." He chuckled. It was fast becoming one of my favorite sounds. It didn't happen very often, but whenever it did, it completely melted my insides.

"Can you at least tell me *something*?" I knew he had plans, he'd spent enough time colluding with Nicco and Ari. "Please?" I batted my eyelashes for good measure.

"I can tell you one thing…" It was a heated whisper. "I'm going to fuck you so hard tonight you see stars."

"Enzo, that's not a thing," I tried to sound disappointed. But the truth was… I really hoped he did.

ENZO

"What do you think?" I leaned against the doorjamb, watching Nora's reaction as she took in our suite.

"Are you sure this is our room?"

My bank account was pretty sure. But the fifteen hundred dollar a night price tag was worth every penny to see her speechless.

Pushing off the jamb, I stalked toward her. “It’s ours for three whole nights. Imagine all the ways I can make you scream up here.” My mind was already full of ideas.

I always wanted Nora. The truth was, I couldn’t get enough of her. She’d fast become my newest addiction and she was all too willing to let me indulge.

The guys busted my balls about it all the time. But I didn’t give a fuck. Nora was the better half of my soul and I was so fucking grateful to have her in my life.

Sweeping the hair off her face, I dipped my head and pressed a single kiss to her collarbone.

“Mmm,” a moan slipped from her lips.

“We should check out the view.” I’d specifically booked a room at The NYC Skyline for its amazing view of the city. Nora had been obsessed with coming here ever since Nicco brought Arianne for their honeymoon. She wanted to do the whole tourist thing and visit all the sights.

I just wanted to do her.

My hands clamped on her hips as I guided her over to the enormous window giving us a panoramic view of the iconic skyline.

“Wow,” she murmured, relaxing back into my arms.

Skimming her waist with my hands, I glided them down her back and over the curve of her ass, dipping underneath her sexy as fuck skirt.

“Enzo,” she warned, but she was here, she’d gotten her wish. Now, it was time for me to get mine.

“Hands on the glass, Gattina, and don’t move.” I dropped to my knees and pushed her skirt up her waist to find the waistband on her panties and gently ease them down her hips. I couldn’t resist raking my teeth over the soft curve of her ass, and she moaned again.

“You are so bad.”

It was like being outside, the vast glass panels bringing the city inside. But no one could see us up here. Even if they could, I wouldn’t have stopped.

I needed her.

I needed Nora in a way I couldn’t fully describe.

Deeply.

Wholly.

Viscerally.

She was the calm to my temper, the light to my dark. She was my anchor, my reason, and I was determined to make this weekend memorable, for more than one reason.

Unable to wait a second longer, I dived in, licking her like a man starved. Nora gasped, a string of expletives falling from her lips as I pushed two digits deep inside her and worked her with my tongue while pumping my fingers in and out.

"God… that is… *God*!" Her knees buckled, but I banded my arm around her waist and held her still. She was at my mercy, about to be wrecked by my touch.

"You taste like heaven," I speared my tongue inside her, rolling my thumb over her clit in perfect synchrony.

"Jesus, Lorenzo… it's…" The words died as she moaned over and over, the sounds of her pleasure filling the room.

I wanted the whole fucking place to hear her, to know that this woman belonged to me.

Only ever me.

My love for Nora was borderline obsessive. I drove her to classes every day, returned later to pick her up. If she wanted to hang out with Lucii and her other girlfriends, I usually put one of our guys on them and had him constantly check-in. I'd almost lost her, and I didn't plan on that ever happening again. So yeah, I was a little over the top, but Nora didn't seem to mind. In fact, I think my Gattina secretly liked it.

Her back bowed as she rocked against me, desperate for more, desperate for what only I could give her. "I'm so close…" Raw lust drenched her words. But I had no plans to make her come yet. I wanted her desperate for me.

Boneless.

Breathless.

Mine.

I curved my fingers and rubbed, quickly withdrawing them when I felt her body begin to coil tight.

"Enzo, what the hell?" She glared down at me over her shoulder.

"Patience, Gattina." I smirked.

Standing, I snapped my belt and pushed my jeans open enough to free my dick. I was rock hard and ready to sink deep inside her. "Hands on the glass," I ordered when she tried to turn and reach for me.

Nora giggled. "You're bossy."

"And you're a brat." Stepping up behind her, I wrapped a hand around her throat bringing my mouth to the side of her neck. "Tell me what you want."

"You, Enzo. Only ever you."

"Right answer." I nipped her skin as I folded my body over hers and slammed inside of her. "You're mine, Gattina. Mine."

And I would spend forever showing her.

NORA

We spent the next day sightseeing. Enzo grudgingly let me drag him through Times Square. We took silly selfies in the M&M's store and posed with the Hard Rock Café giant guitar. He was patient and slightly amused by how excited I was. Then we headed to Central Park and Enzo had completely surprised me by suggesting we take one of the horse-drawn carriages. It was so romantic, cuddled up beside my dark and brooding bad boy as we explored the gorgeous landscape.

We had dinner reservations later, but Enzo was keeping quiet about the details.

"Well, do I need to dress up or go casual?" I asked.

"Maybe avoid the t-shirts, yeah?" His eyes dropped to my 'Ah! the element of surprise' shirt.

"There's nothing wrong with my t-shirt." I pouted. It looked killer teamed with my skirt, stockings, boots, and brand-new leather jacket. It had been a gift from Enzo. He said his badass girlfriend needed a badass jacket.

I loved it.

"You'd look better with it tied around your wrists while I—" He leaned in, whispering all the dirty things he wanted to do to me. My soft laughter filled the air as we walked the scenic route back to our hotel.

"You'll need to wear something warm."

I nestled into his side and grinned up at him. "But I have you to keep me warm."

Enzo raked his teeth over my earlobe sending bolts of pleasure rippling through me. "Maybe I should cancel our reservations tonight and eat you instead."

"You are so bad."

His lips curved in a smug smirk. "Oh, you don't know the half of it."

"Holy shit, for real?" I stared up at Edge, the highest outside sky deck in the Western Hemisphere. I'd wanted so badly to get tickets, but when I'd looked into it, it was fully booked.

"But how?"

"I have my ways."

It was late. We'd gotten back to the hotel suite and spent hours wrapped up in each other. Enzo didn't seem in a rush to make our dinner reservations and I was all too happy to enjoy him and our ridiculously swanky suite.

My stomach grumbled. "Maybe we should have grabbed something to eat first."

"Don't you trust me?"

Oh, I did. But I was pretty sure Edge didn't serve food.

We rode the elevator to the hundredth floor. It was so fast there wasn't even time to fool around, but Enzo couldn't resist smacking my ass as I stepped out ahead of him.

"Mr. Marchetti, Miss Abato, welcome to Edge." A host in a three-piece black suit greeted us.

I glanced at Enzo and he smirked.

"We are very honored you chose to dine with us tonight."

"Dine?" I mouthed at my smug looking boyfriend.

"I told you to trust me."

The host led us into the observation room where a server was waiting with a tray of champagne. "Welcome to Edge," she said.

"Thank you." My heart fluttered wildly in my chest. I was used to being with Enzo now. He and his family were well-known all over Rhode Island. But New York? I hadn't expected such treatment.

"We have the place all to ourselves?" I whispered to Enzo, quickly realizing we were the only people not in uniform.

"Just you and me, Gattina. Come on." His hand slipped to the small of my back urging me closer to the huge glass window. The view was incredible; so much so I inhaled a sharp breath.

"It's something, huh?" The host said.

"It really is." I couldn't stop smiling. This was so freaking romantic, and so out of character for my brooding bad boy.

"Dinner will be served shortly. We thought you might like to take in the view first."

"That would be great," I said. "Thank you."

He led us to the doors leading onto the observation deck. Enzo took my hand and moved ahead of me, leading me to the Eastern point. He pulled me around to his front and banded his arms around my waist, dropping his chin on my shoulder as we stared at the city lights. "What do you think?"

"I love it, thank you."

"I knew how badly you wanted to come up here, so I made a few calls."

"I can't believe you did all this for me. It's perfect." A ball of emotion lodged in my throat.

"There isn't much I wouldn't do you for you, Gattina, you know that, right?"

"I know."

"I may not always be able to tell you what I'm feeling or thinking, but I'll always try, Nora. I want you to know that."

Silence drifted over us as we enjoyed the moment.

"What are you thinking right now?" I eventually whispered.

"I'm thinking that one day, I'll bring you back here and ask you to be mine forever."

My heart raced wildly in my chest as I imagined him on one knee before me. I wanted that one day.

God, I wanted it so much.

"What are you thinking?" Enzo ran his lips along my jaw before stealing a kiss.

"I'm thinking that one day," I tilted my face and kissed him back. "I'll say yes."

MATTEO

"So how was the Big Apple? Did you manage to do any sightseeing?"

"Fuck off." Enzo grumbled.

"What? It's a legit question." I chuckled. "Let me guess, you did nothing but sightseeing... Nora was so pumped about the trip."

"She was pumped... a lot." The smug fucker smirked, and I shook my head.

"Did you just make a joke? Fuck, man, I'm going to need to check for your balls because that girl has you all—"

"We saw the sights. I made her come twice on the trip to Ellis Island."

I almost choked on my own breath. "I bet the other passengers loved that."

"Hired a private boat."

"Of course you did."

"If it's good enough for Nic." He shrugged.

"I'm happy for you, man, you two deserved to come out on top." Silence settled between us.

We were in my truck on the way to Providence to see Zander DiMarco. Things were still tense after his bar got hit by Enzo's half-brother. Zander wanted out, but you didn't get out of a deal with the Family. It didn't work like that. And he needed a little reminder of that fact.

Since Enzo had spent time up there with Gino, Nicco had asked us to go try and broker some peace. I wasn't sure Enzo was the man for the job, but he didn't seem to care, all too happy to follow orders and get the job done.

"She's good for you," I said.

He was softer around the edges, we all saw it. He was still Enzo—the love of a good woman didn't change that—but he was different.

My chest tightened, but I stuffed those memories down. It had been months and months since I'd spent one amazing night with a red-haired, green-eyed angel. Caitlin. If that was even her real name.

We'd been in Providence and there had been a bad storm. I'd stumbled across a girl being threatened in a dark alley... and well, one thing led to another and I'd spent the night at her place. It was the best sex I'd ever had. But when I'd finally plucked up the courage to drive back down there and track her down, she was gone.

And I went back to my life without the Irish beauty who had marked my soul.

Enzo's cell phone started ringing, but he took one look at the number and ignored it.

"Who is that?"

"Beats me." He shrugged.

It immediately started ringing again.

"Maybe you should answer it. It could be important."

He plucked the thing out of the center console and barked, "Yeah?"

I smirked. He was such a grumpy asshole still. I guess there were some things the love of a good woman couldn't change.

"What? Yeah, okay. We're on our way." He hung up and grumbled, "Fuck."

"What is it?"

"When I was down here with Gino, I helped one of Zander's girls out. I think that fucker was hurting her."

"What?"

"Yeah, I don't know for sure what went down. But I gave her my number in case she ever needed help."

"That was her?"

"No, that was the hospital."

"Fuck," I breathed. "Is she okay?"

"They didn't say much, but she specifically asked for me."

"She's at Providence General?"

"No, she's at County in Pawtucket. So we're going to have to make a detour."

"Sure, man. Whatever you need." If there was one thing I hated, it was men who beat women.

Thirty minutes later, we arrived at the hospital. A nurse directed us to the correct bay and Enzo went off to chat with another nurse. The place was a hive of activity as staff came and went, treating patients. I'd never much liked these places because they usually ended in bad news.

"She's down here." Enzo beckoned me over and we went down another hall. "Bay five." He grabbed the curtain and slipped inside.

"You came," a voice said.

"Yeah, I brought a friend with me. Is it okay if he—"

"Sure, I guess."

I went inside the small bay and my heart damn near exploded in my chest.

"You."

"I-I don't understand," I croaked, feeling myself grow hot all over.

"Wait, a minute," Enzo frowned. "You two know each other? But how?"

He was drilling holes into my face, but I couldn't take my eyes off the woman lying in bed. Her face was littered with bruises and she had finger marks around her neck.

"Matteo?" Enzo gripped my shoulder as my knees went weak.

"*Caitlin*?" The word barely got out over the lump in my throat.

It was her.

The girl from that night.

She was one of Zander's girls?

A stripper?

It couldn't be.

Yet, Enzo knew her. He'd helped her. And she'd called him.

What the fuck was going on?

SAVIOR OF REGRETS
A VERONA LEGACY STORY

ONE

CAITLIN

HIS EYES FOLLOWED me as I worked the floor, serving drinks and collecting up empties. They never left me, constantly reminding me that my life wasn't my own.

That he owned me.

God, I really hated this gig. The leering men and wandering hands. I didn't work the stage no more; Zander had put a stop to that after he almost killed a guy for getting too handsy with me. Back then, part of me had thought it was charming—him protecting my honor like that—but I soon learned that protection came at a cost.

One I had been unwilling to pay.

Zander DiMarco owned this place. It was one of his high-end strip clubs in and around Providence, its door only open to those with fat wallets and expensive tastes. I'd thought it would be a safe bet.

I was wrong.

"Caitlin," Shaun yelled over to me. "Table four drinks are up."

Nodding, I made my way over, trading my empty tray for the one full of glasses of whisky.

"It's the good stuff," he said with a wink. "So serve it with a smile."

I rolled my eyes, and he stuck his tongue between his teeth, making a tsking noise. "Lover boy can't take his eyes off you tonight."

"Don't call him that." A shudder raced through me.

"Is it so bad to have the boss's attention?"

I forced a false smile.

If only he knew.

Of course, everyone at DiMarco's knew to some extent. They saw the poorly covered bruises, heard me cry in the bathroom. But the number one rule of working here was not to ask questions you might not like the answer to.

And nobody, *nobody* questioned the boss.

I was Zander's favorite girl. Too good to work the stage, but not good enough to avoid floor duty. Because everyone had to pay their dues, even the boss's favorite.

Tray in hand, I headed for the table. One of the guys looked up and gave me a wolfish smile. "Well, hey there, pretty lady."

Oh good, a charmer.

Offering him a fake smile, I gently placed down their drinks. The other two guys barely acknowledged me, too entranced by Gisele as she worked the pole with her lithe, scantily clad body.

"Enjoy your drinks," I said. But the second I stepped away, Charmer's hand shot out and grabbed my wrist.

"What's the rush, sweetheart?"

"I'm sorry, but I have to—"

"Relax," he chuckled, "we're all here to have a good time. Right, Dominic?"

"Oh, I'm sure I could have a real good time with you, darling." Charmer's friend ran his eyes up and down my body, making me feel like a thousand spiders crawled under my skin. "How much for a private dance?" he grunted, pulling out his wallet.

"I'm just a server. You can speak to the boss about a private dance with any one of the dancers." I flicked my head to the stage.

"Thing is though, Red," he said, referring to my thick, auburn curls. "I don't want a dance off any of them. I want one off you."

My eyes darted to Shaun, hoping he would spot me and run interference before Zander realized something was wrong.

Gently yanking my arm out of Charmer's grip, I flashed them both a saccharine smile. "You enjoy the rest of your evening."

Just as I turned to leave, a hand slammed against the table, startling me. "Hang on a minute, you little bit—"

"Gentlemen," Zander appeared at the table at lightning speed. I should have felt relieved, but this never ended well—for anyone.

"Who the fuck are you?" the one called Dominic asked.

"I'm Zander DiMarco, the owner of this fine establishment." He ran a hand through his slicked-back hair before straightening his tie. "Now, what seems to be the problem?"

"Your girl here denied me a dance. My money not good enough for you, DiMarco?"

"Your money is plenty good enough, Cabrioles."

The guy's brows went up. "You know who I am?"

"Dominic Cabrioles." Zander's eyes narrowed. "Clocked you the second you walked into the joint. It's not often we have one of Lombardi's men in here. This is Marchetti territory," Zander added.

The guy snorted. "The Marchetti are a dying breed. Rumor has it Antonio is sick and that son of his has gone all soft since marrying the Capizola heir."

Everyone knew who the Marchetti were; the local crime family who ran most of Rhode Island. They hailed from Verona County but held power across the state. Their men came this way every couple of months to collect pizzo—protection money—and while Zander always paid up, he never did it with a smile.

Tensions between him and the Marchetti were even worse since there had been an incident a few weeks back. DiMarco's got trashed in a series of break-ins targeting Marchetti owned businesses and their associates.

But you didn't just cut ties with them.

"It's all a game," Zander said smoothly. "You just have to know how to play it."

There was something in his smirk. A wicked dark glint that made me bristle.

"I only like playing games if the prize is worthwhile," Dominic drawled, swirling his glass around. "And she..." He pointed at me. "Is a prize worth winning."

Zander stiffened, his entire posture tight with anger. But he managed to rein it in. "Caitlin is one of my best."

"I want to buy a dance. A private dance. I'll make it worth your while." He ran his finger over his thick leather wallet.

"Cait, go get us another round of drinks. It seems like me and my friends have things to discuss."

"Wha—"

"Now, Cait."

I hurried away, my heart in my throat. Surely, Zander wasn't seriously going to make me dance for him?

Bile sloshed in my stomach as I approached the bar.

"What's up?" Shaun asked.

"Table four needs another round please." My voice shook.

He studied me, leaning closer. "Something happen?"

"I... no, I'm fine." I smiled weakly. "Zander knows them. Or they know Zander."

"Just... be careful, Cait. Guys like that," he flicked his head toward them, "they always want something."

Wasn't that the truth.

He set about making their drinks and when they were done, I headed back toward the table on slow, shaky legs.

Zander reached for me, his hand slipping around my waist to steady my approach. "Thank you, Cait." He waited for me to place down the drinks. "Dominic, Jasper, and I were just discussing your... talent."

"Zander was telling us, you're quite the dancer."

"I..." Heat flooded my cheeks as I dipped my gaze.

"Don't hide." Zander's fingers dug into my waist. "I've arranged a special viewing for my new friends. In the Purple Room."

The air left my lungs.

"I-I don't dance anymore." My eyes locked on his, silently pleading with him not to make me do this.

"Well, tonight you'll make an exception. Go and get ready. We'll be there in twenty."

"Zander, please." My voice cracked.

"Run along now, dolcezza. And change into something a little more... enticing." Zander slapped me on the butt, and I stumbled away from the table, hardly able to believe what was happening.

"Cait, what is it?" Mariella intercepted me as I burst into the back room.

"Zander... he..." I gasped, a big greedy lungful of air that did absolutely nothing to ease the fear taking over me. "He wants me to dance in the Purple Room."

"Oh, sweetie." She rested a hand on my shoulder. "It kind of comes with the territory."

It did. But not for me, not anymore.

Zander was too jealous. He'd almost killed a guy for touching me. I couldn't believe he'd just hand me over to that... that sleazeball.

"You know what happened the last time I danced for someone," I said to Mari.

"Maybe he's moving on."

"What is that supposed to mean?" It came out harsh.

"I'm just saying... perhaps you're not his favorite toy anymore and this is his way of letting you know it."

"Wow," I breathed. "Thanks a bunch."

"Shit, Cait, I don't mean it like that. You know I love you, girl. But I thought you wanted out from under his shadow?"

"I do... but..." At least I knew what to expect with him. Zander was the devil in sheep's clothing, yes. But sometimes it was a case of better the devil you knew.

"It's one dance. Do it and you might win his favor. Don't do it and..." Her expression fell.

"Yeah, I know." I rolled my shoulders back and took a deep breath. "Can you help me get ready?"

"Sure thing." She laced her arm through mine. "Let's go see what we can do."

The music thrummed through me, amplifying the wild beat of my heart. It was dark, the mood lighting casting a deep purple hue around the small room. There was a long chaise and a wingback chair, a dark wood coffee table, and then the stage where I stood, my hand poised on the pole.

Mariella had given me one of her outfits to wear, a black lace bralette with matching booty shorts, and six-inch killer stiletto boots.

It was worlds away from the dainty and graceful outfits I used to wear dancing ballet.

I ran my hand up and down the pole, trying to expend some of the nervous energy coursing through me. But it only doubled when the door opened, a ring of light illuminating the profile of Dominic... and Zander?

They sat down. Zander in the chair, Dominic sprawled back on the chaise. Neither of them spoke as the music rose and a spotlight went on over my head. But I heard their intake of breath as I slowly circled the pole, letting muscle memory rise to the surface. It had been a while, months. I hadn't forgotten though, gripping the pole above my head and arching my back to gently dip down. Turning on the rise, I hooked a leg around the cool aluminum and spun myself around with ease, adrenaline drowning out everything else.

I loved to dance.

Loved the freedom that came with giving over to your body's movement. I reveled in how my muscles contracted and expanded to allow me to become one with the music.

The track shifted to something slower, more seductive as I danced my heart out, completely ignoring Zander's possessive stare, and Dominic's dark, hungry gaze. In that moment, it didn't matter that one of them owned me and one of them wanted to own me. Up there on that stage, I was free.

My eyes fluttered as I dipped and rolled, swayed and flew. Dancing wasn't just something you did; it was something you became. The music was my heartbeat, fueling me, pushing me. Breathing life into me.

I didn't dare look at Zander or Dominic. They were mere spectators. For these few moments, I held all the power here.

The closing notes of the song started to fade out and I came to a stop, my chest heaving, my breaths ragged. My muscles zinged and popped but I'd never felt better.

Until Zander stood, calling my name. "Come over here," he demanded. "Come and give Mr. Cabrioles what he's owed."

Owed.

God, I hated that word.

I hated everything about it.

Gingerly, I moved to the steps leading down from the stage. Each one was like a shotgun to my heart, the adrenaline melting away. I didn't want this life. I never wanted this life. But sometimes bad things happened to good people.

"Dance for me, Red." Dominic shuffled on the chaise, letting his legs fall open. He patted his thigh, indicating I should sit on his lap.

"Go to him," Zander demanded.

Steeling myself, I approached him, refusing to acknowledge the obvious bulge in his trousers.

My stomach churned as I began to sway my hips, running my hands up and down my body. Throwing my head back, I dipped low, spreading my legs wide and then I glided back up. Dominic's eyes turned hooded, a wicked glint there. I risked glancing at Zander to gauge his reaction.

Dominic wasn't touching me... yet. But sexual energy radiated from him. Carnal lust and hunger swirling in the air around us.

I wanted to yell at Zander to stop this madness, to get on my knees and beg, but I wouldn't. Not now, not ever. Because my dignity was the only thing I had left. And no matter what Zander did to me, no matter how hard he pushed, I wouldn't give him the satisfaction of believing I needed him anymore than I already did.

"So fucking hot." Dominic's hand shot out and he grasped my hip, dragging me closer. I stumbled a little, my hands going to his shoulders to steady myself. I waited for Zander to lose his cool, to put an end to this game. But he didn't.

"I paid good money for this," he drawled, trailing his fingers over my bare skin. "Make it worth my while."

"Do as the man says," Zander said calmly. Too damn calmly.

What the hell was going on?

My palms were sticky, my heart a runaway train in my chest. I could smell the overbearing scent of his cologne, taste the bitter scent of liquor on his breath. His hands were too big, too wandering as he mapped the curves of my body.

"Ride me, Red." He smirked. "Show me what you can do."

Bile rushed up my throat as I tried to keep my distance. I didn't want to be here, doing this. My life wasn't supposed to turn out this way.

It wasn't supposed to—

Dominic cupped my ass and pulled me closer as he slid forward on the chaise, making all of him press up against all of me. I gulped, trying not to vomit all over him.

"Watch your fucking hands," Zander finally protested.

"Yeah, yeah, keep your hair on, DiMarco. I know the deal."

Deal...

My body began to tremble as I fought the urge to knee him in the balls and make a run for it. I'd stupidly thought this was all over when Zander took a shine to me.

But maybe Mari was right—maybe he was over me.

I didn't know how to feel about that.

I didn't love Zander, not even close. Most of the time, I hated every fiber of his being. And I was definitely scared of him. But at least I knew what to expect with him.

Dominic relaxed back against the chaise again and left me to my own devices. The air turned thick with tension as Zander tracked my every move. I didn't meet his heavy gaze. I couldn't. Just as I refused to make eye contact with Dominic.

After two more songs, Zander finally stood. "You had your money's worth, now get the fuck out."

Dominic chuckled, the epitome of cool, calm, and collected. "I'll give you whatever price you want if you let me fuck her, right here."

I froze, his offer echoing through my skull.

"You couldn't afford her." Zander laughed, but nothing about it sounded amused.

"Try me, DiMarco. I think you'll find I can be very—"

"Not tonight. But stop by again, and perhaps we can do business. Cait, go wait over by the bar." Zander dismissed me as if I was nothing.

Nobody.

Humiliation stained my cheeks as I went to the small bar in the corner of the room. A minute later the door opened. I glanced over just in time to see Dominic disappear into the stream of light.

When the door closed again, Zander was looking right at me. "Come here," he said, crooking a finger at me.

I went to him, hardly surprised when he curved his hand around the back of my neck and held me there. "You did well tonight, dolcezza. Maybe I should consider putting you on the roster again."

"I… I'd prefer not to dance."

"But you're so good at it." His eyes gave nothing away, which unnerved me. "He offered two thousand dollars to feel your tight little pussy wrapped around his cock, dolcezza." Zander leaned in, his warm breath fanning my cheek. "Something tells me he'll come back with a higher offer. Would you like that, Cait? Would you like him to pay all that money to fuck you?"

"You… you know I wouldn't."

"Right answer." Zander's fingers flexed around my neck, yanking my head back to leave me completely at his mercy. He ran his tongue along the seam of my lips before kissing me. Claiming me.

"You're mine, dolcezza. But maybe I'd be a fool if I didn't consider making a buck or two out of you. With Marchetti breathing down my neck, business is harder than ever."

Oh God.

He meant it.

Zander meant every word.

And something told me, if he sold me to Dominic for sex, it would just be the start of a long line of negotiations.

Negotiations that wouldn't end well for me.

TWO

MATTEO

"WHAT'S UP WITH YOU?" My sister nudged my sneaker with hers. "You're moping."

"Am not." I folded my arms over my chest, in a totally non-mopey kind of way.

"You so are." She rolled her eyes. "Is it because Enzo and Nora are in New York, and Nicco and Ari are… doing whatever newlyweds do?"

The humor in her voice made me lift my eyes and glower at her. "Go away, pulce."

"Aww, don't be like that, Matt. I'm only busting your balls."

"Hey. Language."

"Jeez, *Dad*." She poked her tongue out at me. "You know your problem?"

"No," I sighed, "but I'm sure you're going to enlighten me."

"You need to get laid."

"Arabella!" I shot forward, glaring at her. "I swear to God, if you don't—"

"Oh my God." She fell about the chair, laughing. "You should see yourself."

I loved my sister, something fierce, but she was a real pain in my ass sometimes. Even more so since our cousin Nicco got married. Part of me got it. We were young. Too fucking young to be wifed up. But what Nicco and Arianne had… it was something rare. It was that once-in-a-lifetime kind of love.

"Seriously though, Matt. There must be someone you like. Verona County is a big place, and it isn't like you don't get around."

"I just haven't met the right girl yet." I gave her a dismissive shrug, pulling out my cell phone and absently scrolling through my messages.

It was true—I hadn't found the right girl. There had only ever been one woman to catch my eye and she'd forgotten about me the second I walked out of her apartment after the best sex of my life.

Shit. It had been almost a year ago now, and I still couldn't get that night out of my head.

Scrubbing a hand down my face, I stood. "I'm going out."

"Out? But I thought we were going to hang out."

"Change of plans, pulce." I rubbed her head, and she swatted me away like a fly. "I need a drink."

Something strong.

L'Anello's was busy for a Sunday night, but then it was Valentine's Day. Guys were out to impress their girlfriends, and girls were out to try to score the man of their dreams.

Maybe this was a bad fucking idea.

"Matteo, what's up?" Billy, the bartender, headed in my direction. "No hot date tonight?"

"You know how it goes, Bill. Too many fish in the sea."

"A guy like you could have your pick of the bunch."

"If I didn't know better, I'd say you were trying to hit on me," I joked.

"In your dreams, my friend. I'm as straight as they come. Usual?"

"Yeah, make it a double."

"Sure thing."

I turned around and leaned back on the bar, scanning the room. A couple of familiar faces tipped their heads in greeting. Most of the clientele were couples, sitting close together, staring dreamily into their date's eyes.

A pang of jealousy cut through me.

I'd never had that.

Never really considered I could have it. Sure, my name was Matteo Bellatoni, but I was still a Marchetti by blood. My life, my loyalty, and my future belonged to the Family.

Finding a good woman to accept that, to accept everything that came with being a mafioso was no easy feat.

Except, my cousins—my best friends in the entire world—had both managed just that, leaving me to play fifth wheel to their relationships.

It sucked.

Big time.

But it wasn't like I could move on anyway. No, I was still hung up on the Irish beauty who had stolen my heart that night in Providence all those months ago.

"Get a fucking grip," I muttered to myself. I was a twenty-year-old guy for fuck's sake. I had the world at my feet. Good friends, good family, a job that would never see me go without.

"Double whisky on the rocks," Billy said, and I turned around, accepting the glass from him.

"Thanks." I knocked it back, downing it in one. "Hit me with another."

"Shit, man. It must be bad." He smirked and I flipped him off.

"Matteo, that you?" Jimmy, the owner of L'Anello's, strolled over to me, holding his hand out. We shook hands and he flagged down Billy to bring us another round of drinks.

"Alone?"

"Yeah, Nic's having dinner with Arianne, and Enzo is—"

"With his woman in New York. I remember now. Sucks to be us, right?" He clapped me on the back, and I faked a smile. Jimmy was a middle-aged, balding man with a missing tooth and crooked smile. My sex life wasn't exactly happening, but it wasn't that bad, not yet.

"Speak for yourself, Jimmy," I said. "For all you know I could be meeting a hot date here tonight."

"You can't kid a kidder, Matt." He took a sip of his drink, and tsked through the side of his mouth. "How about burning off some excess steam tonight?"

"Come on, man, you know I'm too pretty to get in the ring."

L'Anello's wasn't only a bar in downtown La Riva, it was a front for Verona County's underground fight ring. Before Nicco met Arianne, I'd watched him beat many opponents. They called him the Prince of Hearts, a play on his ruthlessness in the ring, but that all stopped when he fell in love. Enzo dabbled occasionally, but he didn't have the natural talent Nic possessed.

And me?

Well, I was a lover not a fighter.

"Try it on for size. You never know, you might like it."

"I doubt that, Jimmy. Maybe another time."

"Sure thing, Matt. Sure thing." He squeezed my shoulder before clapping me on the back again. "Enjoy your evening, kid."

I snorted at that.

'Kid' was a word the older men liked to use to remind us of our place in the hierarchy of things. But it was steeped in irony considering that as one of Nicco's most trusted men, I outranked nearly every man in here.

My father, Michele Bellatoni was Antonio Marchetti's second. And Nicco his third.

It hadn't always been that way. Enzo's dad had been Antonio's second, but he was gone now. And although the Family was still recovering from shock of Vincenzo Marchetti's betrayal, we were stronger than ever.

"Hey, Matteo," a sultry voice said, and I turned around to find Gina Fabiano smiling at me.

"Gina, you're looking beautiful." I leaned in and kissed her cheek. Left and then right. She placed a perfectly manicured hand on my shoulder and gazed at me through thick lashes. "It's good to see you."

"You too." I returned her smile.

Gina was the daughter of one of the Family's associates. Mario Fabiano owned a string of tailors across Verona County. He was Uncle Toni's first choice every time.

"I didn't realize you were back," I said.

Gina had been studying in Italy.

"Just for a few weeks. My Nonna is sick."

"I'm sorry to hear that."

"Thanks." She tucked her silky dark locks behind one ear. "Are you here alone?"

"I… yeah. Pretty pathetic, right?"

"I'm here with my cousin, her fiancé, and his friend. But between you and me, he's not my type." Gina brazenly checked me out, letting her gaze linger on my mouth.

"You should give the guy a chance," I said, not wanting to get involved.

"Or." She moved closer. "You could pretend to be my ex and we could get out of here."

"Listen, Gina, it's good to see you, it is. But I'm not—"

"Seriously? You're not interested?" She glanced down at herself as if the idea that I would turn her down was preposterous.

I knew most of the male population would agree. Enzo especially. He'd definitely have something to say about me turning down a girl like Gina Fabiano. But I wasn't feeling it. And truth be told, she wasn't my type.

Nowhere close.

"I came to have a quiet drink before I head home."

"Alone…" Her brow lifted.

"You should get back to your date," I said.

"Your loss." She smiled but it had lost some of its sweetness. "Good to see you again, Matteo."

Gina walked away from me, drawing the eye of almost every man in the room. Maybe I was a fool. Maybe I should have taken her up on her offer and tangled with her between the sheets. Sex didn't have to mean anything more than a good time. I knew that.

I knew… and yet, I couldn't do it.

I had no desire to do it.

Fuck. I needed another drink.

Or three.

The next morning, I found myself hungover and alone. After lying in bed for almost an hour, willing myself to get up, I finally dragged my sorry ass into the bathroom and freshened up. I needed extra strong coffee, and something to soak up the liquor.

I'd shared this apartment with Enzo before he'd decided to move out and get a love nest with Nora. It wasn't the same without him, so I didn't stay here a lot, preferring to stay at home with my family. But I couldn't begrudge him. If anyone deserved to be happy, it was E. He had a shitty life at the hands of his old man. Nora was his redemption. His salvation. She was everything he never knew he needed, and I didn't expect him to last long before he made it official and put a ring on her finger.

He was that damn serious about her.

I scrubbed a hand down my face as I padded into the kitchen and turned on the coffee machine. A bang on the door drew my attention. It was barely nine, and I didn't get a lot of visitors.

"Just a minute," I yelled, crossing the room, and opening the door. "Nicco."

"Hey." He grimaced, and I frowned. "What is it? What's wrong?"

"Can I come in?"

"As if you have to ask." I stepped aside and he slipped past me, making a beeline for the breakfast counter.

"I was just making coffee."

"Black, one sugar," he mumbled.

"I know how you take your coffee, Nic. What's up?"

Because this wasn't my best friend. His eyes were ringed with dark circles, and he looked like he'd hardly slept in days.

"Is it Ari? Is she—"

"She's fine. She's back at the apartment, sleeping. We had a late night."

"I bet you did." I smirked, but it melted away when his eyes shuttered with pain.

"Fuck, I don't know what to do."

"Nic, talk to me," I said, feeling like I was missing something huge.

"It's my dad."

"Uncle T?"

He nodded. "He's sick."

"I know. We all do." He had a heart attack earlier on in the year. But he was making a good recovery.

"No, you don't…" He let out a heavy sigh, anguish bleeding from him. "He lied, Matt. He lied to everyone. He isn't okay. He isn't fucking okay at all."

"He's not?"

"It's cancer."

The words echoed in my skull like gunfire.

"C-cancer?"

"Yeah. I found some medical letters."

"He didn't tell you?"

"What do you think?" His expression darkened. Nicco was the levelheaded one out of the three of us. I was the joker, the light-hearted one looking to make people smile. Enzo was the storm. Cold and unforgiving. He didn't trust easily, and his heart was buried under a thick layer of ice.

Then there was Niccolò. He was somewhere in the middle. As the boss's eldest and only son, he knew the responsibility weighing on his shoulders, and he carried it with nothing but strength and honor. He was already a true leader. Men respected him, strangers revered him, and our enemies feared him.

"Shit, Nicco, I'm sorry."

"He said he was fine. He said—" Nicco buried his face in his hands. I gave him a second, waiting. When he eventually lifted his face, what I saw there made my heart squeeze.

"I always knew that one day, I would take his place. But it's too soon. I'm not… ready."

"You've got this, man. Arianne will be right by your side; me and E too. You're not alone in this, cous."

"I thought I had more time."

I got it. If Uncle Toni had to step down, or worse, Nicco would become the boss. That kind of pressure, it left little room to play happy family with your wife. And they were so young.

An idea struck me. "My old man—"

Nicco gave me a weak smile. "We both know Michele isn't cut out to be the boss. Besides, I'm not even sure my father would allow it. No, this falls to me, and me alone."

Silence echoed between us, and then I said, "Whatever you need, cous. I'm here."

"Thank you, Matt. It helps knowing I have you and E in my corner."

"Of course." I nodded. I'd known Nicco since we were babies. He and Enzo were the closest thing to a brother I'd ever have.

"Have you heard from Enzo?" he asked me.

"A couple of texts. He's too busy wooing his girl." I smirked, and Nicco chuckled.

"Who'd have thought it? Lorenzo Marchetti tamed by a female."

"Stranger things have happened."

"You know, it's your turn next. Arianne has some nice friends at—"

"Jesus, does everyone around here think I need help finding a decent girl?"

"Who—"

"Arabella," I scoffed. "She was giving me shit last night."

"She means well." He pinned me with a hard look. "We all do."

"I can handle my own affairs, Nic."

He held up his hands. "I'm shutting up now."

"Good," I grumbled. "I have my whole life ahead of me to think about settling down."

Yet, when I looked at what Nicco and Arianne had, what Enzo had found with Nora… I wanted that. Fuck, I wanted it. But I didn't want it with just any girl. I wanted it with *the* girl.

The one.

All I had to do was find her.

"Listen. When Enzo gets back, I want the two of you to head to Providence.

DiMarco is still making noise and we need to remind him that you don't back out on a deal with the Family."

"You want me to go?" I asked.

Zander DiMarco was one of the Family's business associates in Providence. He owned a string of successful strip clubs that brought in a lot of money. The guy was a grade A asshole, but money talked, and DiMarco knew how to make it in spades.

"Yeah, I'd go myself, but I'm not sure that's wise right now."

Because his old man was sick and that kind of burden... it wreaked havoc with a man's soul. Especially a guy like Nicco.

"Yeah, okay," I said.

"You sure you're okay?"

"Yeah."

It was just a trip to Providence. What was the worst that could happen?

You could try and look up Caitlin again...

I immediately shut down that train of thought. It had been months, and she'd made it perfectly clear she wanted nothing more to do with me. I had to let that shit go—I had to let the idea, the fantasy of her go.

"Who knows, maybe you'll meet the girl of your dreams there." Nicco chuckled, and I flipped him off, adding, "At DiMarco's club? I highly doubt it."

His girls were all beautiful, but I wasn't sure I could handle my woman dancing for other men's enjoyment. And I never wanted to be the kind of man who asked a woman to change for him. I could enjoy the view like every other patron at a strip joint, but I wouldn't find anything more in a place like that.

"How far do we go?" I asked, dreading his answer.

Enzo was our enforcer. He had no problem persuading people—associates, enemies, sometimes even allies—to do our bidding using whatever means necessary. I preferred a softer touch. Negotiation. Coercion. Blackmail if it came down to it. But Zander DiMarco had been pushing against our agreement for a while now. He had warning after warning. If he refused to play ball, then it was likely he'd feel the full wrath of the Family before long.

"Relax, Matt. I'm not asking you to go put a bullet in his head. But DiMarco is becoming a thorn in our side. A thorn my father wants blunting as soon as possible. I'm trusting you can find a way to remind him how things will go if he doesn't play nice. If that fails, I'm sure Enzo can help demonstrate how difficult life will be should he decide to keep disrespecting our arrangement."

"Got it, Boss." My lips curved.

Nicco shook his head, letting out a weary sigh. "I don't think I'll ever get used to that."

"You should probably try."

Because if Uncle Toni was really sick... Nicco could find himself taking charge sooner rather than later.

And I didn't envy my best friend at all.

THREE

CAITLIN

"OH MY GOD, CAIT. WHAT HAPPENED?" Gisele reached for my face, but I swatted her hand away.

"It's nothing, really."

"Girl, that isn't nothing." She scoffed. "You look like you got mauled by a—"

"Gisele, please..." I silently pleaded with her; aware we were drawing an audience.

I'd done my best to conceal the fingermarks around my throat, but the skin along your neck wasn't the easiest place to cover up. I'd even added a scarf, but the bruising was still obvious. And then there was the slight split in my lip.

Maybe I should have stayed at my apartment and feigned a stomach flu. But sometimes it was easier to placate Zander by putting on a brave face and pretending nothing was wrong.

Besides, it could have been worse. He could have actually let Dominic touch me. He hadn't—and for that, I was grateful. Even if he had punished me for exacting his wishes.

Men.

I would never understand their double standards or the games they liked to play.

But I was okay... a few bruises here and there was nothing.

I'd survived much worse.

"I should get ready for my shift," I said, slipping past her to go to my locker.

"Hey, Cait," she called after me.

"Yeah?"

"I'm here, if you ever need someone to talk to."

"Thanks." I smiled, but we both knew I wouldn't take her up on her offer.

I was Zander's favorite toy. If I spoke out against him, I'd find myself living on the streets without a job again. And although he was the devil in an expensive Italian suit, there were still worse things out there than Zander DiMarco.

Ignoring the curious stares of the other girls, I hurried to my locker and dumped my purse and jacket. I was tying my purple-trimmed black apron when Zander called my name.

"Caitlin, my office," he commanded.

My stomach sank. I was hoping he would leave me alone after last night; he usually did. But I guess fate was feeling decidedly cruel.

Gisele shot me a sympathetic look as I passed her and made my way out of the dancers dressing room along the hall to Zander's office.

"Come in," he said, not bothering to look at me, too busy poring over the paperwork on his desk.

"Did you need something?"

"Sit." He motioned to the couch, and I sat down, folding my hands in my lap.

Zander continued checking his papers, murmuring to himself as he punched in numbers on the calculator.

"All done." He threw the stack down and smiled at me. "How are you today?"

"I'm fine, thank you."

"Good, that's good. Last night was... a misjudgment on my part, and for that, I'm sorry."

"It was nothing."

He let out a heavy sigh, rising from his chair to walk over to me. "You're so beautiful, Cait." Sliding his hand along my neck, he gently gripped my jaw and forced me to look up at him. "I was too rough."

I suppressed a shudder. He was always rough. Most men like Zander were. They liked the power, the fear... they liked to possess women to the point of pain.

"I'm sorry."

His apology echoed around my skull. In all the time I'd known Zander, he'd never once apologized.

I didn't know what to make of it.

He ran his thumb over my bottom lip, letting the pillow of flesh pop as he pulled it away.

"I just get so angry when I see other men watch you."

"I thought you wanted me to dance for him?"

"I did, dolcezza. I did. And you did such a good job. But the way I feel about you, Caitlin... it's enough to drive a man to the brink of insanity."

I was his.

Despite the fact we hadn't ever officially gone public or labelled our relationship, I was under no illusion that this was anything but the fact Zander DiMarco had decided I belonged to him.

When he'd first found me and took me off the streets, Zander had given me a safe place to stay, and I'd lapped up his attention. But then he'd started to hint at his true intentions. For so long, I managed to keep him at arm's length. Until one night, Zander had grown tired of waiting for me and had taken what he'd wanted all along.

Me.

"You know I'm not interested in any of those men," I said. There had never been a man to catch my attention. Except one, on a stormy night when I'd found myself in a dark alley with another Zander DiMarco of the world. A man who thought he could just take what he wanted.

I would never forget Matteo. He'd saved my life that night, and then gave me one of the best nights of my almost twenty-one years on Earth.

But that's all it could ever be.

I'd refused to give him my number, locking him away in a little box where Zander couldn't touch him.

If he ever found out about that night... It didn't bear thinking about.

A violent shudder rolled through me, and I took a calming breath, trying to keep my expression neutral.

"So why do you keep stalling, dolcezza? It would be so much easier if you moved in with me. We could play happy family. I could go to sleep every night holding you, wake every morning with you in my arms."

Lies.

It was all lies.

Zander didn't know how to do any of those things. He didn't know how to be soft and tender. Even now, his fingers were gripping me a little too tightly, his jaw clenched with frustration.

"I've told you before, I'm not ready."

He knew why.

I'd given him that much.

But I could see from the flash of anger in his eyes, my excuses weren't enough anymore.

"I've waited," he said. "I've been patient and given you space. But a man will only wait so long, Cait. I can't give you up, dolcezza. I won't."

"I should probably get to work."

Wrong answer.

My neck wrenched as he yanked my face upward, my muscles screaming in protest. Tears pricked the corners of my eyes. "Z-Zander please, I have to go to work."

"You work for me, or have you forgotten that? You. Are. Mine. Caitlin. The sooner you get on board with that, the better. Now be a good girl and kiss me." He practically dragged me to my feet, giving me no time to back out as his lips slammed down on mine. His fingers slid into my hair, clutching me like a rag doll. A puppet. My whole life had been nothing more than a show I had no control over. I came to Providence to start over, but the cycle just continued.

And I hated it.

I hated that I attracted a certain kind of man. I hated that I wasn't strong enough to walk away.

But walking away wasn't that simple.

I had nothing. Nowhere to go, no one to turn to. I was all alone in the world except for the few friends I had at DiMarco's.

I went lax in his arms, knowing that fighting would only stoke the anger rising inside him.

"God, dolcezza, it's like I can't get enough of you." His hands ran over my body, clawing at my modest black skirt.

"Zander," I breathed. "It's the middle of the day, everyone is expecting me."

That snapped him out of his trance, and he backed away slightly. "You're right." He smoothed down his shirt. "Later then."

I nodded, not trusting myself to speak. Slipping around him, I straightened my skirt and headed for the door.

"One day, Cait, you're going to give me what I want."

Pretending not to hear him, I hurried from the room and headed straight to the women's bathroom. I needed a minute to collect my thoughts and stop shaking.

"There you are. I was beginning to wonder—"

"Not now, Shaun," I said, busying myself with polishing glasses. DiMarco's was always quieter in the afternoon, so it gave the floor staff a chance to prepare for the night ahead. Glasses were buffed, tables were cleaned, and the refrigerators and liquor shelves were restocked. It was laborious work, but I didn't mind it. It kept my mind busy.

Zander came and went, sometimes sitting at his usual spot in the corner of the club on the raised platform, giving him a vantage point of the entire room. He liked people to know he was the boss, just like he liked people to know he was always there watching them. It was part of his power play.

But during the day, he had meetings, telephone calls, and paperwork to do, so he wasn't around so much. I took pleasure in those moments, and for a second, I could almost imagine being invisible.

I was busy restocking the tealight votives on each table when I felt him. Zander. He'd barely left me thirty minutes before coming to check up on me.

His behavior toward me was growing more erratic. More possessive. And I knew the thin rope of control I still had would soon snap.

He wanted an answer—an answer I couldn't give him, not willingly.

I glanced over my shoulder, and sure enough, he was across the room watching me. His eyes darkened as he swirled the glass of scotch around in his hand before bringing the rim to his lips. I should have looked away, refused to play his game of cat and mouse. But I wasn't about to cower, not now. Not ever.

"Cait?" Gisele tapped me on the shoulder, and I almost jumped out of my skin. "Sorry, I didn't mean to startle you."

"It's okay." I flashed her a warm smile, still able to feel Zander's eyes drilling holes into the side of my face.

"He's getting more and more obvious," she said between gritted teeth.

"He just enjoys the chase."

"I can try to talk to him? Make him see that—"

"No, no. It's fine. I can handle Zander. But thank you."

"Of course." Her expression was etched with sympathy. "I'd help you get out if I could. But it's—"

"Gisele, I don't expect you or anyone else to fight my battles."

And I would never jeopardize her job like that. Zander wouldn't hesitate to get rid of anyone who tried to get in his way, his best dancers included. Because there were always more girls like Gisele and Marielle... and me. Girls looking to make a quick buck and escape whatever nightmare drove them to a place like DiMarco's in the first place.

A lot of them would argue it wasn't so bad. The club was one of the more high-end joints in Providence, and Zander and his guys afforded them a certain amount of protection—provided they did their job and brought in enough money.

"Ugh, duty calls." Gisele rolled her eyes, and I glanced back again to find Zander glaring at her.

"I'll see you later, okay?" She squeezed my hand before disappearing.

I headed for the bar, trying to keep busy. It was hard with Zander's eyes following me everywhere. Especially so early into my shift.

"Cait, do me a favor and go get some extra napkins, we're short," Shaun said, not looking up from the counter.

"Sure thing." Hurrying into the back, I went straight into the storeroom and grabbed as many packets of napkins as I could find. But when I turned around, Zander was blocking the door.

"Z-Zander, what are you—"

"Relax, dolcezza," he purred. "I just wanted to make sure you're okay. You seemed... tense after our talk this morning."

"I'm fine." I forced a smile. "But I should probably get these back to Shaun before he comes looking for me."

Zander stepped into the room, taking the air with him. "No one's coming back here, Caitlin. It's just you and me." He crowded me into the corner of the storeroom, my back hitting the shelves.

"I... I have to work."

"I'm your boss, and I think you should take a quick break."

"But I..."

"Stop, Cait." His hand shot out, grabbing my jaw. "Just stop."

Tears rushed up my throat as my heart crashed wildly in my chest. I thought I was safe. At least until later.

Fear flooded me, making it hard to breathe.

"I can't stop thinking about fucking Cabrioles with his hands on you. I should never have let him touch you." He brushed his thumb along my cheek. "He wasn't worthy of you, dolcezza."

"It doesn't matter," I said. "It's over. He won't be a problem no more."

Something flashed in Zander's eyes, but he nodded all the same. "Come here." His hand slipped to my neck, curving around my throat. He pulled me closer, forcing me to tilt my face up to look at him.

"The things I want to do to you. The things I want to show you..."

Oh God.

The knot in my stomach twisted. He wasn't going to let me walk away from this untouched. Not this time.

There was a feral look in his eyes. A hunger I'd seen too many times before.

"You're mine, Caitlin. Mine." He lowered his head, pressing his mouth to mine.

Every muscle inside me went rigid as I tried to breathe through the terror. My body trembled at his touch.

"Open up for me," he drawled, licking the seam of my lips, trying to force his way in.

"Zander, not here," I breathed, desperately trying to break out of his hold without seeming too forceful. "I have to—"

He smashed his body into mine, stealing the air from my lungs as he plunged his tongue into my mouth. My head smacked off the edge of the shelves, stars exploding in my vision.

"Zander, no." I tried to fight him, but he was too strong, too heavy, pressing the entire length of his body against mine.

Stars swam in my vision and tears stung my eyes. I heard the familiar clunk of his belt buckle, bile churning in my stomach.

"No," I cried. "Not here, not like—"

He backhanded me so hard my teeth rattled, and pain exploded along my jaw.

"You think you're too good for me? Is that it?" His hands began clawing at my legs, my thighs. My eyes grew heavy, the pounding in my skull making blood roar in my ears.

"I... no... *please*..."

Zander grabbed my face hard, squeezing my cheeks to the point of pain. "I'm going to enjoy this." He grinned, but it was dark and twisted.

That grin was the last thing I saw before oblivion claimed me.

"Stay with me, girl." The voice drifted in and out of my consciousness.

Or maybe that was me.

I couldn't figure it out.

Everything was blurry… like swimming underwater with your eyes open.

"Cait?" The voice sounded panicked. "Cait, hold on… we're almost there."

I wanted to ask where, but when my lips moved nothing but a tiny squeak came out. My mouth felt wrong, swollen and sore, and I could taste the coppery, metallic twang of blood on my tongue.

"Oh God," I murmured, agony shredding my insides. "What…? What…?"

"Shh." Someone reached over and squeezed my hand. "It's going to be okay, Cait."

"Where are you taking me?" Shaun's form shimmered in and out of focus.

"He thinks I'm taking you to Providence General. But fuck that," Shaun spat. "He went too far this time, Cait. Too fucking far. I'm going to drive you to Pawtucket and tell him we stopped for gas and you ran."

"W-what? That's crazy." He was crazy.

I couldn't run.

Where the hell would I go? I could barely keep awake.

"You need to disappear, okay? If he finds you… he'll kill you, Cait. I won't have that on my conscience."

"It hurts," I groaned, touching a shaky finger to my hair. When I pulled it away it was coated with sticky, dried blood. "Oh my God."

What the hell had he done to me?

A shudder went through me as hazy memories assaulted me. Hands grabbing, teeth and tongue, his strong body taking what wasn't his to take.

Oh God.

"We're almost there, just try and keep it together, okay?"

But I couldn't do it. I couldn't fight the agony radiating through my body, my face.

"Shaun," I murmured, barely a whisper. "I'm… I'm scared."

"It's going to be okay, Cait," he said. "It's going to be okay."

It was the last thing I heard.

FOUR

MATTEO

"MORNING, SON," Dad said looking up from his newspaper. "I didn't expect to see you this morning. Nicco said you and Enzo were heading to Providence."

"We are but Enzo and Nora stayed an extra night. They should be back anytime, so I told Arabella I can give her a ride to school."

"You're good to her, Son."

"Of course he is." Mom breezed into the kitchen, swatting me with the towel when she noticed me try to pluck off the freshly made cornetti off the cooling rack. "Later," she chided. "You can have one later."

"I won't be here. I'll be out of town for a couple of nights."

Her shoulders bunched together. "Do I even want to know?"

"It's business, Marcella. They'll be fine."

"That's what they always say," she murmured, making herself busy.

Mom had grown up around my uncles and Nonno. She knew what this life entailed. Part of me sometimes wondered if she'd expected to get out when she married my father. But instead, he'd joined the ranks, swearing his allegiance to the Family. But Michele Bellatoni wasn't like most mafioso. He was quiet and contemplative, and he didn't abuse his power. That wasn't to say he hadn't gotten any blood on his hands—you didn't live this life and never experience death—but he wasn't hungry for it the way some were. He was a good guy.

One of the best.

The kind of man I always hoped to become.

"Just keep your wits about you, Son," he said, his eyes flicking to my mom.

Once he was satisfied she wasn't paying us any attention, he added, "DiMarco is a wily sonofabitch."

"Ain't that the truth," I mumbled, swiping a cornetti while Mom's back was turned.

My old man chuckled, but then his expression soured. "Stay safe, Matteo, and watch your back."

The familiar rumble of Enzo's GTO drew my attention, and I drained my coffee. "Thanks, Mama. I'll see you soon, okay."

She came over to me, taking my face in her dainty hands. "You come back to me in one piece, figlio mio."

"Stop fussing over the boy, woman. He knows the drill by now. Besides, Zander DiMarco is all talk."

Glad he thought so. Because I wasn't so sure. Zander was a showboater. He loved the attention and reputation. In my experience, people like that were dangerous and unpredictable.

But this was my job. My father—the Family—expected me to fall in line and carry out Nicco's and Uncle Toni's orders. You didn't get to argue or shirk your responsibility. Once you swore Omertà, you were all in. *Famiglia prima di tutto.* The Family came first, always.

A heavy knock at the door indicated Enzo was too damn impatient to stay in his car.

"Lorenzo, how was the big city?" Mom greeted him.

"It's the Big Apple, woman," Dad called.

"Big city, big apple, it's all the same." She waved him off, directing Enzo toward the breakfast counter.

"Eat," she said.

"I'm good thanks, Aunt Marcella. I already ate."

"I bet you did." I smirked and he discreetly flipped me off, but I didn't miss the smug look of satisfaction on his face.

Dirty fucker.

But I was happy for him. Him and Nora. After all they'd been through, they deserved to be happy.

"You ready to roll?" He looked at me, and I nodded, snagging another cornetti.

"Let's go."

"Matteo!" Mom called after me, but we were already out of the door.

"So how was the Big Apple? Did you manage to do any sightseeing?" I asked Enzo the second we were in his car.

"Fuck off." Enzo grumbled.

"What? It's a legit question." I chuckled. "Let me guess, you did nothing but sightseeing... Nora was so pumped about the trip."

"She was pumped… a lot." The smug fucker smirked, and I shook my head.

"Did you just make a joke? Fuck, man, I'm going to need to check for your balls because that girl has you all—"

"We saw the sights. I made her come twice on the trip to Ellis Island."

I almost choked on my own breath. "I bet the other passengers loved that."

"Hired a private boat."

"Of course you did."

"If it's good enough for Nic." He shrugged.

"I'm happy for you, man, the two of you deserved to come out on top." Silence settled between us.

I knew Enzo probably wanted to take this trip as much as I did. Things were tense after DiMarco's club got hit in a string of attacks on our businesses a few months back, and since Enzo had been there when it happened… I doubted Zander would be in a hurry to see him either.

But Nicco wanted us to handle it—so here we were. About to handle it.

"She's good for you," I said, glancing over at my cousin.

He was softer around the edges, we all saw it. He was still Enzo—the love of a good woman didn't change that—but he was different.

My chest tightened, but I stuffed those memories down. It had been months since I'd spent one amazing night with a red-haired, green-eyed angel. Caitlin. If that was even her real name.

The three of us—Nicco, Enzo, and myself—had been in Providence and there'd been a bad storm. I'd stumbled across a girl being threatened in a dark alley… and well, one thing led to another, and I'd spent the night at her place. It was the best sex I'd ever had. But she refused to give me her number, and when I'd finally plucked up the courage to drive back down there a few weeks later, to track her down, she was gone.

And I went back to my life without the Irish beauty who had marked my soul.

Enzo's cell phone started ringing, but he took one look at the number and ignored it.

"Who is that?"

"Beats me." He shrugged.

It immediately started ringing again.

"Maybe you should answer it? It could be important."

He plucked the thing out of the center console and barked, "Yeah?"

I smirked. He was such a grumpy asshole still. I guess there were some things not even Nora could change.

"What? Yeah, okay. We're on our way." He hung up and grumbled, "Fuck."

"What is it?"

"When I was down here with Gino, I helped one of Zander's girls out. I think that fucker was hurting her."

"What?"

"Yeah, I don't know for sure what went down. But I gave her my number in case she ever needed help."

"That was her?"

"No, that was the hospital."

"Fuck," I breathed. "Is she okay?"

"They didn't say much, but she specifically asked for me."

"She's at Providence General?"

"No, she's at County in Pawtucket. So, we're going to have to make a detour."

"Sure, man. Whatever you need." If there was one thing I hated, it was men who beat women.

Thirty minutes later, we arrived at the hospital. A nurse directed us to the correct bay and Enzo went off to chat with another nurse. The place was a hive of activity as staff came and went, treating patients. I'd never much liked these places because they usually ended in bad news.

"She's down here." Enzo beckoned me over and we went down another hall. "Bay five." He grabbed the curtain and slipped inside.

"You came," a soft voice said.

"Yeah, I brought a friend with me. Is it okay if he—"

"Sure, I guess."

I went inside the small bay and my heart damn near exploded in my chest.

"You."

"I-I don't understand," I croaked, feeling myself grow hot all over.

"Wait a minute," Enzo frowned. "You two know each other? But how?"

He was drilling holes into my face, but I couldn't take my eyes off the woman lying in bed. Her face was littered with bruises, and she had fingermarks around her neck.

Fucking fingermarks!

"Matteo?" Enzo gripped my shoulder as my knees went weak.

"Caitlin?" The word barely got out over the lump in my throat.

It was her.

The girl from that night.

She was one of Zander's girls?

A stripper?

It couldn't be.

Yet, Enzo knew her. He'd helped her. And she'd called him.

What the fuck was going on?

"Caitlin?" I said again, my heart crashing violently in my chest as I took in her injuries. She was beat up pretty bad. Someone had done this to her... someone had—

The penny dropped as Enzo's words from earlier came back to me.

"DiMarco did this?" My voice didn't sound like my own as red-hot fury exploded inside of me.

"Why is he here?" Caitlin stared at Enzo, her big green eyes pleading with him. I wanted to roar—to tell her not to look at him like he was her savior—but to look at me.

Fuck.

Fuck!

This was totally fucking with my head.

All I could think about was Zander putting his hands on her, hurting her. *Abusing* her.

"Enzo, I said why is he—"

"I'll kill him," the words spilled from my lips. "I'll fucking kill him." My fists clenched by my sides as I plotted all the ways I'd make Zander fucking DiMarco pay for ever laying hands on Caitlin. Something slow and painful, something that would make sure he never laid another hand on Caitlin or any other woman for as long as—

"Matt." Enzo's hand clamped down on my shoulder and I glanced up at him, blinking.

"Yeah?"

"Can you wait outside?"

"The fuck?" I balked, glancing between them.

"You're scaring her, cous."

Scaring her?

I was scaring her?

"Caitlin?" I choked out, but she didn't look at me. She wouldn't.

"Come on, Matt. Let's take a walk." Enzo slung his arm over my shoulder and guided me out of her bay.

"No," I protested, glancing back over my shoulder. "I should stay with her. I should—"

"You need to cool it," he said, the second we were out of earshot.

"Cool it? You want me to cool it? Did you see what he did to her? DiMarco is a dead man walking," I seethed, anger coursing through me like wildfire, burning me inside out.

"You don't get to make that call, and you know it." Enzo scrubbed his jaw, his eyes hardening to slits. He didn't like this anymore than I did, but it wasn't his... whatever the fuck Caitlin was to me, lying in a hospital bed.

"Who is she to you?" he asked.

"Caitlin? She's... Fuck," I murmured, trying to rein in my thoughts. "Remember when we were up in Providence last summer, visiting DiMarco? We... I... I spent the night with her."

"You did?" He frowned.

"Don't look so surprised. Despite what you might think, I do know how to use it."

"I didn't... it doesn't matter." Enzo shook his head. "All that matters is that she's safe."

"She called you. Why the fuck did she call you?"

"I told you, I met her a few weeks ago, and got the impression she was in need of a friend. I don't know why but I gave her my number in case she ever needed help."

Which I was so fucking relieved about. But I couldn't help the stab of jealousy I felt that Caitlin had called Enzo... and yet, she'd refused to give me her number all those months ago.

Was this why?

Was it because she was somehow tangled up with DiMarco?

I couldn't make sense of it all. Because all I could think about was her lying there in that hospital bed, beaten and bruised. He was a... Fucking. Dead. Man.

"You know you need to stay cool about this, right?" Enzo pinned me with a knowing look.

"Like you'd be cool about it if it was Nora lying in that bed?"

His expression darkened. "It's not the same, Matt, and you know it."

"It's—" Shit. He was right. It was a low blow—especially after everything he and Nora had been through.

Besides, it wasn't the same because Caitlin wasn't my... she wasn't my anything.

He exhaled a steady breath. "Look, I get it, the two of you have history. But from the surprise on both of your faces, I'm guessing it's in the past."

Yeah, because she'd ghosted me.

But I'd never stopped thinking about her, not for a second.

Maybe that made me a pussy, but we'd shared something that night. Something that had burrowed deep into my soul.

"Let me go talk to her," he said. "She called me for a reason, let me find out why."

Seemed pretty obvious to me, but I didn't argue. No matter how much I wanted to be the one to go to her.

To protect her.

"Yeah, okay. Tell her... shit, tell her, I only want to help. No pressure."

Enzo's brows knitted together as he scrubbed his jaw. "You really like her, don't you?"

I gave him a weak smile and shook my head, "I don't even know her."

While Enzo went to see Caitlin, I got coffee and tried not to wear a hole in the floor. But I couldn't sit still.

She was here.

Or rather, *we* were here.

Both of us, at the same time, in the same place. If that wasn't some kind of freaky kismet, I don't know what was.

Except, she hadn't looked pleased to see me.

Not even a little bit.

This isn't about you, asshole. It's about the woman lying in a hospital bed hurting because of that fucker.

I could still vividly remember her from that night. Her soft, pale skin. The taste of her lips. How perfectly her body had fit with mine.

I'd been in fucking heaven, ready to make all kinds of promises, and she hadn't even wanted to give me her number.

I wracked my brain for the exact details of our conversations. She'd told me she worked at some diner... but Enzo had said she was one of Zander's girls.

Did that mean she was one of his dancers?

Shit.

How had I not noticed? Although it wasn't like strippers wore a neon sign over their head.

Slumping down in the chair, I drained my coffee and threw the cup in the nearby trash can. I didn't give two shits what Caitlin did for a living. She was still one of the most real, most beautiful women I'd ever met.

And she's here.

I just needed to talk to her. To find out exactly what happened, and who I needed to hurt. My fist clenched against my thigh as I waited. Whatever she and Enzo were talking about was taking a long fucking time.

When he finally appeared, I shot up off the chair. "How is she?"

"She's... a mess. She won't tell me what happened, but it's bad, Matt."

My heart sank as I clenched my fists against my thigh. "Can I see her?"

"I'm not sure that's a good idea."

"What do you mean? I just want to talk to her and reassure—"

"Shit, Matt." Enzo stepped in front of me, cutting off my route to her. "She doesn't want to see you."

"She said that?"

He nodded.

"I see."

Dejection flooded me. It was one thing to be rejected by her all those months ago. But to see her again, find her here of all places, only to have her shut the door in my face again...

"Hey." Enzo gripped my shoulder. "This isn't about you, cous. It's about her."

"Yeah." The word soured on my tongue, my eyes flicking beyond Enzo to the row of curtains offering privacy to each bay.

"The doctor wants to keep her overnight for observations. Then she agreed to come back with us."

"B-back with us?"

"Yeah, to Verona County. She can't go back to Providence, Matt."

"Say it." My teeth ground together, my entire body trembling with rage.

"You need to calm down—"

"Say it, E. Tell me why she can't go back."

He let out a weary sigh, a dark cloud circling him. "Because she's scared of what DiMarco will do if she does."

Motherfucker.

My fist flew out, connecting with the wall before I could stop it. Pain ricocheted through my wrist and into my arm, and I swallowed a grunt of agony.

"Better?" Enzo quirked a brow.

"Fuck off," I muttered.

"Look at you, cous. She's got you all twisted up inside."

"You're telling me you're okay with that piece of shit DiMarco putting his hands on his girls?"

"You know I'm not. But it isn't that simple. He's a trusted associate. And you know we don't get involved with another man's business. Not like this."

I scoffed, cradling my busted hand near my chest. "That's some bullshit and you know it."

"You should get that looked at." His hard gaze dropped to my hand. "You might have broken something."

"I'm fine."

I wasn't, but whatever.

"I'm going to call Nicco. See how he wants us to play this. You going to stay put and refrain from doing anything stupid?"

"Yeah."

"Good," he said, digging his cell out of his pocket. "I'll be five minutes." Enzo took off down the hall.

The minute he was out of sight, I headed for Caitlin's bay.

FIVE

CAITLIN

I WOKE to the sensation of being watched. Slowly, I cracked a tender eye open, silently hoping it was *him*.

Matteo.

I'd dreamed he was watching me, felt his eyes lingering on my face as I dozed in and out of a drug-induced sleep.

I still wasn't over the shock of seeing him, staring at me with a mix of confusion and lust and longing. And rejection.

God, it had been like a physical blow to the heart.

One I wouldn't recover from anytime soon.

Still, it didn't stop the sigh of relief slipping from my lips when my gaze landed on the petite, brown-eyed girl staring at me.

"How are you feeling?" she asked.

"I'm sorry," I said, clearing my throat. "Do I know you?"

The girl approached my bedside, grabbing a cup and pouring me some water. "I'm Arianne, Enzo's friend."

"Arianne..." Her name sounded familiar. "You're his... friend?"

She nodded. "He thought you might prefer some female company."

"That's... very thoughtful."

"How are you feeling?"

"Like I almost got beaten to death."

The joke missed its intended mark, and Arianne's smile fell.

"That's not funny," she breathed.

"No, I suppose it isn't."

Silence descended over us. Thick, oppressive silence.

"Can you remember what happened?"

Fear raced down my spine as I clutched the crisp, white sheet to my body. "I—"

"It's okay. I'm not here to interrogate you. Enzo said you needed somewhere to stay for a while."

I nodded, wondering if I'd done the right thing telling him that. But he'd come through when I'd needed him, hadn't he?

When he'd given me his number, I hadn't ever planned to use it. Then I'd woken up in the hospital, scared and alone, and the doctor was looking at me with so much pity that when he asked me if there was someone he could call, I'd panicked and given him Enzo's number. After all, it wasn't like I could call anyone at the club.

"I can't go back..." Silent tears flowed down my cheeks as I clutched the stiff, white sheet.

Zander would know I was missing by now. He would know I had run.

"You don't have to; you can come back with us."

"With you... or Enzo?" My voice trembled. What the hell was happening here?

"You can stay with Enzo and Nora, or—"

"Nora?"

"His girlfriend. My best friend. You'd like her." Arianne smiled and it was nothing but warm and reassuring.

Despite the strange circumstances in which we were meeting, I liked her. There was just something about her—something comforting.

"Or," she added. "You can stay with me and Nicco."

"Is that your boyfriend?"

"My husband."

"You seem kind of young to be married," I said, clapping a hand over my mouth at my outburst.

Arianne smiled again. "When you know, you know."

That sounded nice.

"We have a place in Romany Square if you wanted to stay with us, until we can figure out your next steps."

Next steps, right, because I needed those. Because I had nowhere to go. Again.

"You'll get to meet Nicco soon. He's outside talking to Enzo and Matteo."

Nicco... Enzo... Matteo.

Why did those names ring a bell?

No.

No!

Everything slammed into me at once.

"What's your husband's surname?" I asked, hoping to God I was wrong.

Arianne let out a steady breath and then said the one little word that changed everything.

"Marchetti."

My savior was a Marchetti.

Both of them.

Well, Matteo wasn't a Marchetti by name, but he was by blood.

If I would've had any idea who Enzo was the day he came to my apartment to check on me, I would never have stored his number in my cell.

Marchetti.

The constant thorn in Zander's side.

I didn't like to listen to backstage gossip or conjecture, but there was no escaping the whispers about the Marchetti crime family.

I should have realized who Enzo was, but I'd been too fragile to pay any attention, assuming he was one of Zander's friends—and he had many—trying to score brownie points.

But a Marchetti.

Jesus.

I might as well have crossed enemy lines because if Zander found out Enzo was helping me—Enzo *and* his family—he wouldn't only be pissed; he'd see it as a declaration of war.

"Caitlin?" Arianne frowned. "You've gone as white as a ghost."

"I'm fine." I forced a smile, swallowing back a fresh wave of tears. "Just a little tired."

"You'll be safe with us," she said, reaching for my hand. "I promise."

I didn't have it in me to tell her that it wasn't me I was worried about. That if they took me back to Verona County and Zander found out, it would be them who needed to worry.

"Maybe this isn't a good idea," I blurted out.

I had nowhere to go. No money, no belongings, nothing. But it wasn't the first time I'd found myself homeless and penniless.

"What?"

"I don't want to be a burden," I said. "I can—"

"But Enzo said you told him you can't go back. Where will you go if you don't come with us?"

"I can call a friend, maybe. She can get some of my stuff and I can get—"

"Don't you have any family you can call?"

"No." It came out harsher than intended.

"We can protect you, Caitlin."

"Cait. You can call me Cait."

She nodded. "If you don't want to stay with me and Nicco or Enzo, I might have another idea. Nicco's family owns some cabins, secluded, off the beaten track. You'd have your own space out there, no one would bother you. It would give you a chance to figure things out."

It sounded too good to be true, but it also sounded safe. And I needed that right now.

"That actually sounds perfect." I hesitated. "But I don't understand why you'd do this for me… I'm no one."

"Everyone needs a helping hand sometimes." She smiled. "Besides, you're not no one, Cait. Not to Matteo."

Oh God, she went there.

She actually went there.

I'd done a good job up until now, pretending that he wasn't out there, in the hall somewhere. He hadn't tried to see me again. But now Arianne had mentioned him, I couldn't stop thinking about him.

He'd looked so shocked, so confused, but it quickly turned to anger. I think it was the agony in his expression that had made me tell Enzo to make Matteo leave.

I didn't want him to see me like this. Not now. Not ever.

"He told you about me?"

"Actually, Enzo filled us in. Matteo is still… trying to process everything."

"It was one night, a long time ago," I whispered, barely able to look her in the eye.

"For you maybe, but for him, I'm not so sure. You know, he told Nicco about you once."

"He did?" My heart fluttered at her words.

Silly, foolish heart.

But I could still remember how nice he'd been to me that night.

Matteo had made a lasting impression—even if I'd known it could never be anything more than one night.

One perfect storm.

"What other options do you have?" Arianne said softly. "You said it yourself, you have no family. You can't go back to Providence, and—"

"Okay," I snapped, embarrassed at her accurate assessment of my situation. "Okay."

"So you'll come back with us?"

I nodded. "I'll come. On one condition," I added.

"I'm listening."

"I don't want Matteo anywhere near me."

I rode with Nicco and Arianne. True to her word, she had kept Matteo away from me—I didn't see so much as a glance of him as we left the hospital.

It was strange. I felt the bitter sting of disappointment at his absence, even though I'd made my position perfectly clear.

What happened between us was history.

Ancient history as far as I was concerned.

It was one night and then we'd gone our separate ways. If I would've known who he was that night, it never would have happened.

So it was a moot point.

He was a Marchetti. And I was... no one.

"How are you holding up?" Arianne asked from upfront of Nicco's sleek, black Range Rover.

"I'm okay, thanks. A little sore but the pain meds help."

The doctor had wanted me to stay in the hospital for another night, but I didn't want that.

I needed to put as much distance between me and Zander as possible, and Arianne was right—they could help me do that.

Shaun had left me with a small amount of cash, since I didn't have my purse with me. Not that I could use my bank cards anymore. Things like that were traceable.

But it was something.

Pain rippled through me. It wasn't only physical, it was emotional. Heart-wrenching, soul deep agony. The kind that didn't just disappear with a hot bath and a mug of hot chocolate.

What Zander had done to me...

A shudder tore through me and Arianne glanced back at me.

"Okay?"

I nodded, breathing through my mouth.

I didn't know these people, not really. Yet, they'd offered me nothing but understanding and compassion. That had to be worth something.

Didn't it?

"So we'll take you back to our place and let you get cleaned up, and then tomorrow, Nicco and I will drive you out to the cabin."

"Are you sure it's okay for me to stay there? I don't want to intrude."

"It's yours for as long as you want it," Nicco said, his eyes catching mine in the rearview mirror.

Niccolò Marchetti was something else. The way he looked at his wife was the kind of adoration documented in the great love stories throughout history. I couldn't deny the stab of jealousy I'd felt when she'd introduced me to him and he'd pulled her straight into his arms, as if she belonged there.

I'd spent my entire childhood wanting that—wanting one person to love me and me alone. Of course, those dreams were quickly replaced with enough nightmares to warn me off men forever.

Until him.

I immediately shut down those thoughts. What Matteo and I had shared last summer was one night of spontaneous passion. It was impulsive and a little bit reckless and for the first time in a long time, I had thrown caution to the wind and trusted a guy to take care of me.

He hadn't disappointed me, at all. But it wasn't real life, and I was under no illusions that the stranger from Verona County would sweep me off my feet and fight my monsters for me.

"Thanks, I really appreciate it. I just need a few days to make a plan and then I'll be out of your hair."

"Take as much time as you need, Cait. Truly."

Gosh, Arianne was too nice. It had been almost impossible to tell her no earlier.

"You're from Providence?" she asked, making small talk.

"I... no." I touched a hand to my face, prodding the tenderness around my cheekbone. "I was born and raised in Rochester, New York."

"You're a long way from home," Nicco added.

"I travelled around a lot when I was younger." The lies came easily. "Decided to settle in Providence."

"How old are you exactly?" His eyes met mine again.

"I turn twenty-one in a couple of months." I stared out of the tinted window, watching the world roll by. I knew there was another SUV following us, but nobody said anything about it, so I played along.

Nicco and Arianne were kind of a big deal in Rhode Island. From the bit of backstage gossip I could remember, he was heir to the Marchetti empire, and Arianne was heir to Capizola Holdings.

Their union had been all anyone had talked about for weeks. People thought it was a power play, aligning two of the most influential families in the state. But they hadn't witnessed Nicco and Arianne together. It had only taken a second for me to see it was the real deal and not some business arrangement.

"We're almost here," Nicco said. He'd been quiet since our introduction. Polite, but quiet, nonetheless. I couldn't help but wonder what he really thought about all of this.

If the rumors were true, he was set to become boss of the Marchetti family one day, so he had to know that taking me to Verona County was a risky move.

My stomach churned and I pressed a hand against it, willing my nerves to calm down. At least here, I was safe for the immediate future. I could go to the cabin, heal, and figure out my next move.

I would be okay.

Because while life had given up on me a long time ago, I refused to stop fighting.

The SUV came to a stop outside a quiet apartment block.

Nicco leaned in, kissing Arianne's head. "I'll be inside."

"Okay."

He didn't spare me a second glance as he climbed out, slamming the door behind him. It reverberated through me, making me flinch.

"Don't mind Nicco," Arianne said. "He's just—"

"Pissed that I'm here." I sunk into the soft leather seat. God, what was I thinking coming here?

"No. No, Cait," Arianne sighed. "That isn't it at all. He has personal experience with..." Her expression softened. "It's not my story to tell. But know that Nicco's issue isn't with you, it's with... the situation."

"If Zander finds out I'm here—"

"He won't. You're safe here, I promise." She smiled. "Why don't we go inside and get you settled? You must be tired."

I wanted to argue—to make her see that Zander wouldn't just give up. He was obsessed with me. Obsessed with the idea of me.

He wouldn't just let me go.

But everything hurt. My face. My muscles and bones. My soul.

I ached in ways I never thought possible, even more than any recital or performance where I'd spent hours twisting and contorting my body into gravity-defying positions.

"Yeah, okay."

Arianne got out of the car and opened the back door, helping me out. I winced, biting back the groan of pain bubbling in my throat.

"The guest room has its own bathroom, so you can take a bath or shower, whatever you want."

"Sleep sounds good."

"Then sleep it is." She smiled, and I couldn't help but smile back.

Their building was fancy. Gold accents and a bellboy outside who opened the door for us.

"Mrs. Marchetti," he greeted Arianne.

"Lowell, this is Ca—"

"Cadence," I blurted out.

"Cadence is going to be staying with us for the night." Arianne didn't miss a beat.

"Very good. Enjoy the rest of your day." His brows knitted slightly, but he didn't comment on the state of my face.

I let out a shaky breath and Arianne grabbed my hand. "It's okay."

"I-I didn't mean to... it's a habit."

"It's okay. Come on, we can take the elevator."

Arianne didn't push. Didn't ask questions or demand answers. She let the silence settle between us. And I was grateful.

So damn grateful.

By the time we reached her apartment, I was ready to crash. She noticed, holding her arm through mine and taking some of my weight.

"Nicco," she called through the open door. He appeared, brows furrowed as he took us in.

"She's crashing."

My head began to swim, thick and sludgy, as I gripped onto Arianne. "I don't feel so good," I murmured, my legs going out from under me.

"Nicco," she yelled.

And I went down, just as strong arms caught me.

SIX

MATTEO

"YOU CAN'T BE HERE," Nicco said, stepping into the hall and pulling the door to his apartment closed.

"Seriously, Nic?" I balked. "He did that. DiMarco fucking—"

"I know, okay. I know." He blew out an exasperated breath. "You think I don't want to drive down there and make that asshole pay? I do. But we have to be smart, and right now, Caitlin needs us."

"You." I scoffed. "She needs you."

She wouldn't even let me get near enough to talk to her.

It stung.

More than that, it fucking hurt.

"She agreed to stay at the cabin," he said. "Maybe once she has some time to figure things out, she'll come around."

My lips pursed. I wouldn't bet on it.

For some reason, she was shutting me out—the same way she'd shut me out all those months ago when she'd refused to give me her number after our amazing night together.

"Yeah, whatever."

"Matt..."

"I get it. She's hurt and she has every right to be wary of me, especially after—"

I couldn't say the words; it made me sick to my stomach just thinking about it. I don't know how but Enzo had managed to sweet talk one of the nurses into giving him a rundown of Cait's injuries. It wasn't good.

He'd raped her.

DiMarco had beaten and raped her and left her barely conscious.

"But shit, Nic, I never thought I'd see her again... and she's here, and I... forget it." Defeat crashed into me. All the times I'd imagined seeing her again, I'd never wanted it to be like this. But we couldn't turn back time.

"I should go," I said, rubbing the back of my neck.

"That's probably a good idea. Maybe go down to Hard Knocks and work it off."

"Yeah."

"I smoothed things over with Uncle Michele," Nicco said. "He thinks Enzo had to rush back here because Nora's sick. He's going to send a couple guys to go see DiMarco. I don't think it's a good idea for you to be anywhere near him right now. Not until we get to the bottom of what really happened."

"You lied..."

"Until we get to the bottom of things, we need to keep her off the radar."

"I think it's pretty obvious what happened. The guy's a fucking woman beater and he—"

"Matt..." His jaw clenched.

Nicco didn't like this. He didn't like lying to my father or the Family. But if anyone hated this kind of thing more than me, it was Nicco.

"If DiMarco finds out we have her—"

"Don't. I'll handle it. For now, we keep this between us. We'll take her out to the cabin tomorrow. She'll be safe there until we can figure out what to do about DiMarco."

"Thank you," I dipped my head, forcing myself to take a breath. Nicco wasn't the enemy here.

"Matt," Nicco pinned me with a hard look, glancing down the hall. He and Ari had the penthouse suite, so access was only via the elevator, but I understood his wariness. You never knew who was around, listening to things they shouldn't be listening to.

One of his security guys gave us a sharp nod.

"Yeah, okay." I relented. "I'm going."

Nicco grabbed my shoulder before I could walk away. "We'll deal with DiMarco, you have my word. But we have to do it the right way."

The way that didn't have any backlash for the Family.

"Okay. Just do me a favor, yeah?"

"Anything."

"Text me later and let me know how she is." I pulled out of his hold and started down the hall.

"She's really under your skin, isn't she?" he called, and I glanced over my shoulder nodding.

He had no idea.

"If this is Nicco's attempt at babysitting me, you're excused," I mumbled to Enzo and Nora as they joined me at my booth in L'Anello's.

"Brooding suits you." Enzo smirked, and I flipped him off.

"E," Nora chided. "Don't be mean. Hey, Matt, how's it going?"

"Oh, you know, the woman I've spent the last eight months trying to forget shows up out of the blue looking like she got into a fist fight with Deontay Wilder and is acting like I'm the bad guy."

She shot Enzo a concerned look before sliding into the booth beside me. "Sounds like you need a strong drink."

"Babe, if the state of him is anything to go by, he already had enough to drink."

"I'm fine," I protested, nursing my empty glass. "But I am out of liquor."

"Get the guy another drink, boyfriend," Nora sassed. "Me and Matt need a little talk."

Oh God.

I loved Nora like a sister, but I didn't want one of her motivational speeches right now.

Enzo's brow quirked and she waved him off with a chuckle.

"The two of you seem happy," I said.

"We are. Blissfully. But I don't want to talk about me and Enzo, I want to talk about you. How are you holding up, really?" She pinned me with her big, brown eyes, and I felt stripped bare. But that was Nora, always seeing right through people's bullshit. It was one of the reasons I'd known from the beginning that she would be good for Enzo. He needed someone with an inner strength and confidence. And Nora Abato had that in spades.

Enzo never stood a chance.

I smiled to myself, and she asked me, "What?"

"Nothing," I replied. "Just thinking how much fun it's going to be watching you domesticate E."

"Don't let him hear you say that." We shared a conspiratorial smile. "Now, back to my question. How are you?"

"I'm... messed up, Nor. Really fucking messed up."

"Oh, Matt. Come here." She slipped her arms around me and hugged me tight. "It must have been a shock seeing her... like that." Nora eased away, offering me a sympathetic smile. "Enzo said it's bad."

"I barely recognized her." But I would've noticed those green eyes and red hair anywhere.

"I can't imagine..." She shuddered.

"She wouldn't even talk to me, Nor."

"Caitlin has been through something traumatic. Her response wasn't about you, Matt, it was about the situation. Trust me, I know."

"I know. Shit, I know." Enzo had said the same thing. But it didn't stop the gnawing pit of despair I felt every time I pictured the horrified look in Cait's eyes when she'd noticed me.

"Tell me about her. About how you two met."

"You mean E didn't give you the CliffsNotes version already?"

"I don't care about his version; I want your version."

I let out a deep sigh, my eyes flicking to where Enzo was chatting with Billy at the bar. He was obviously giving me and Nora a minute.

"It was last summer before the semester started. We were in Providence on... a job."

She rolled her eyes. "I know what you guys do, Matt."

"After we left DiMarco's, I was headed for my truck when I heard a scream. I went to check it out and found some asshole trying to mug Caitlin."

"Holy crap. What did you do?"

"Told him to beat it and offered her a ride home."

"I'm guessing you gave her more than a ride home." Her eyes twinkled.

"Ha-ha, very funny. But yeah, I stayed the night with her. The storm was wild, and she seemed shook up. We played poker and things escalated."

"Then what happened?"

"The next morning, I practically begged for her number, but she wouldn't give it to me."

"You never saw her again?"

"No. I checked out her place once, but she was gone." I'd never told anyone I'd been back to find her. In fact, I'd downright lied when I'd talked to Nicco about her. Told him that she'd blocked my number... when really, she'd up and disappeared as if she had never existed.

"What do you mean gone?"

"She didn't live there anymore."

"That's... weird."

"Right?"

"And she didn't say anything about DiMarco that night?"

"Nope." But I hadn't exactly been upfront about who I was either. "Told me she worked at a diner called Stella's," I added.

"You don't think there's a diner called Stella's?"

"There might be a diner, but I'd put a hundred bucks on her not working there."

"So she lied."

"It would seem so." My jaw clenched.

I still didn't know the truth... because Caitlin wouldn't fucking talk to me.

She didn't owe me anything, I knew that. But damn, I'd thought we'd shared something special that night. Maybe it was one-sided though. Maybe she hadn't felt the connection burning between us.

Maybe I'd spent the last eight months spinning it into something it wasn't. A fantasy.

A dream.

"So what are you going to do?"

"Do?" I blinked at Nora, and she chuckled.

"Don't seriously tell me you're going to stand by and let her slip through your fingers again?"

"You heard the part where she doesn't want to talk to me, right?"

"Yeah, but come on, Matt, this is you."

"What the fuck is that supposed to mean?"

"You're the charmer. The sweet one. The good guy. If anyone can win her over, it's you. After everything she's been through, she'll need reminding that good guys still exist."

"I want to kill him, Nor." My fist clenched against the table. "I want to drive down to Providence and—"

"Matteo, look at me." She covered my hand with her own, prying my fingers open. "That's not you talking."

"Isn't it? You didn't see what he did to her. You didn't—"

"Listen to me and listen good. I know it hurts. I know you want to fix it and try to make it right. But that is not a path you want to walk, Matt, because if you do, you might never come back."

"Everything okay?" Enzo finally returned to our booth.

"Yeah, babe. We're good. Right, Matt?"

"Yeah," I grumbled, accepting my drink from him.

"Jimmy says there's a fight tonight, if you want in." He studied me.

"No, he doesn't want in." Nora balked. "For God's sake, E. Fighting doesn't fix—"

"Tell him I'm in."

"What?" Nora whirled on me. "Have you lost your goddamn mind? You don't fight, Matt. It's not—"

"Relax, babe." Enzo ran a hand down his face. "It'll help him burn off some energy."

"And get his pretty face mangled in the process. This is a bad idea." She glanced between us. "A very bad idea."

Enzo grinned. "But sometimes the bad ideas are the most fun."

Nora was right.

This was a really bad idea.

That's all I could think as the brute of a man circled me. Shirtless, his thick, corded muscles rippled as he held his fists up in front of his face.

"I'm coming for you, kid." He gave me a crooked grin.

"Get him good, Matt," Enzo yelled from somewhere behind me. The two whisky chasers he'd insisted I down before climbing into the ring burned inside me. It had given me a false sense of security before my opponent appeared.

I can do this, I'd thought while I wrapped my fists and let Enzo school me on the softest places on a body to punch.

But looking at him now, I realized two things.

I couldn't do this... and whatever was about to come, was really going to fucking hurt.

In a blur the guy flew at me, his fist crashing into my face. Pain exploded along my jaw, my head snapping back.

"Fucking pussy," the guy hissed, dropping back to let me catch my breath.

"Shake it off, Matt, let's go." Enzo clapped his hands, as I hit myself gently a couple of times trying to focus.

I can do this... I can do it.

I pictured Caitlin, her bruised face and sad eyes. Rage flooded me. Red hot uncontainable rage.

Without thinking, I lunged forward, driving my fist into whatever part of the guy I could find. Bone crunched against bone, blood splattering the air.

"Motherfucker," he grunted, his pained cries drowned out by the bloodthirsty roar of the crowd.

I didn't give him time to come up for air, driving my fists into his face, his ribs, and stomach. Over and over, I punched him, imagining Zander DiMarco's sleazy face.

Fuck, I hated that piece of shit. He'd hurt Caitlin. My Cait.

Deep down, I knew she wasn't mine, but it didn't matter. My heart, my foolish fucking soul had claimed a piece of her that night last summer, or she'd claimed a piece of me. I still couldn't quite process what I felt after seeing her again. But I knew without a doubt, that DiMarco had made a mistake ever laying his hands on her.

Blood coated my knuckles, sweat rolling down my back as I bounced on my feet, sparring with the guy. He gave me a good few hits back, grazing my eye; and catching my jaw a couple of times, once enough to rattle my teeth.

The longer we fought, the more I settled into the bursts of pain. The feel of his soft tissue bowing under my fists. And for a split second, I could understand why my cousin Nicco had once needed this to stave off his own demons.

We both began to tire. I was fit; I liked to workout as much as the next guy, but I'd underestimated how intense going one on one with a guy—almost twice my size—would be.

"Come on, Matt, finish him," Enzo roared, spurring me forward again. We crashed together, jabbing ribs and kidneys.

Pain radiated deep inside my body, but I let it fuel me for one last attack.

"You're mine, pretty boy," the guy spat, slumping away to circle me again.

But I was ready for him.

I was ready to end this.

He came at me, and I ducked his oncoming fist, rolling away enough to counter hit. My knuckles grazed his jaw and I smiled to myself, ready to end this.

But I didn't see his other fist between us.

"Matteo, watch—"

The uppercut sliced into me, rocking my whole body and I began to topple.

"*Matt!*"

I hit the floor, everything inside me cracking, a wave of pain crashing over me.

My eyes shuttered and the last thing I saw was the guy grinning down at me with victory in his eyes.

"Did I win?" I cracked an eye open, wincing in pain.

"You almost had him," Enzo said, fighting a smirk.

"Asshole." Nora slapped him upside the head. "I told you this was a bad idea." She crouched down beside me and pressed a bag of frozen peas to my face. "This will hurt."

I hissed; the pain almost unbearable.

"Ah, don't be such a pussy," Enzo murmured.

I managed to lift my arm and flip him off. He chuckled.

"Tell me it didn't help," he challenged. "Tell me you don't feel even a fraction better for working off some of that anger."

I couldn't.

Because the truth was, for a minute, I had felt better. I didn't feel so great now though.

"How bad is it?" I asked.

"You'll live," Nora said. "Although you might have one or two new scars on your pretty face." Her lip curved with amusement, but I saw the pity in her eyes.

Shaking it off, I said, "Aww, you think I'm pretty."

"I think you're an idiot. What the hell were you thinking?"

"I was thinking I wanted to drive to Providence and put a bullet through DiMarco's eyes, but since you wouldn't let me do that, I had to settle for fighting the Hulk."

"The Hulk?" Enzo snorted. "The guy wasn't that big."

"Fuck you, stronzo, fuck you."

"Hold these." Nora slapped my hand over the peas and stood. "I need to call Ari and tell her you're awake."

"Shit, you called Nic?"

"Don't look at me," Enzo said, his eyes flicking to Nora.

"What?" She shrugged. "She texted and I wasn't going to lie about where we were."

"Ah shit, Nora."

"Should have thought about that before you decided to get in the ring." She walked off, leaving me and Enzo alone.

"How are you holding up really?" he asked.

"I'm messed up." I stared up at the ceiling. "I can't get her out of my head, E. I can't stop thinking about what that fucker did to her."

"You really care about her."

"It's crazy, right?" My eyes slid to his. "I haven't seen her in months. But I can't explain it, that night… something inside me clicked into place."

"You sound like Nicco with all that written-in-the-stars bullshit."

"Yeah, maybe." I let out a weary breath.

"What are you going to do?" he asked quietly.

"There isn't much I can do right now. She doesn't want to talk to me, and I don't want to be another guy who demands things from her. Not after…"

"He'll pay, Matt. One way or another, DiMarco will get his. But we have to be smart, we have to take our lead from Uncle Toni."

"I know."

I did.

But it didn't mean I had to like it.

"And until then, I guess you're just gonna have to be patient."

I glanced over at him. "Nora's changed you, cous."

"Fuck off. I've always been full of useful advice."

My brow arched, and he grumbled something under his breath.

"Oh yeah, you've always been a real Dr. Phil type." I smirked.

"I'll keep my final piece of advice to myself then," he said.

"Nah, go on. It might help." I let out a chuckle but ended up choking on the wave of agony ripping through me.

"You good?"

I nodded, finally catching my breath.

"Well, you know what they say, cous. The best things come to those who wait."

I rolled my eyes at him, shaking my head incredulously. "Who are you and what have you done with Lorenzo Marchetti?" I teased.

"It's regular pussy, Matt. It changes a guy."

"I wouldn't know," I murmured, hating the ache in my chest.

Silently hoping Enzo was right.

That all I needed to do was be patient and wait it out.

After all, I'd waited this long for her to walk back into my life.

SEVEN

CAITLIN

IT TOOK me two days to recover. After passing out in Nicco and Arianne's apartment, I slept... and slept... and slept some more.

They had their family doctor come and check on me, but he said it was to be expected after such a traumatic event.

But this morning, when I woke up in the soft beige sheets, I forced myself out of bed and found Arianne in the kitchen area of their open plan living room.

"Hey, you're up."

"Hi." I smiled weakly, joining her at the breakfast counter.

"How are you feeling?"

"Like I slept for two days."

"The doctor said rest is good."

"You didn't need to do that," I said.

"We were worried. You passed out and—"

"Thank you." I cut her off. I really didn't want to do this... whatever *this* was.

"Coffee?"

I nodded, perching on a stool. My body ached, my muscles tired and weary. Or maybe that was my soul.

"Can I ask you something?" Arianne said as she made our drinks.

"Sure..."

"Before, when we arrived here, with Lowell..."

"The bellhop?"

It was her turn to nod. "You gave him a false name."

"I thought it would be safer." I shrugged.

"No one will hurt you here, Caitlin. I need you to know that."

But I didn't know that.

How could I?

Zander wasn't some two-bit club owner. He was connected. And he was obsessive in a way that terrified me. Not to mention the fact that the Marchetti had direct ties to him. All it would take was for someone to say the wrong thing at the wrong time and word could get back to him...

"Caitlin?"

I blinked over at Arianne. "Sorry, what?"

"I asked if you want sugar and creamer?"

"Oh, yes please."

She pushed the steaming mug of coffee toward me. "I took the liberty of buying you some new things yesterday. I hope that's okay."

"I... you didn't need to do that."

"I know I didn't need to. I wanted to."

"I'll pay you back." I didn't know how, but I would.

"You can take a look at what I got in a bit and if you need anything else before we leave for the cabin, I can get them for you."

"Thank you." The words got stuck on the lump in my throat, tears pricking the corners of my eyes.

"Cait," she said softly, reaching over the counter and resting her hand atop mine. "You're going to be okay."

Another nod. It was all I could manage.

"Are you ready to talk about what happened?"

Pressing my lips together, I shook my head. I wasn't sure I'd ever be ready. Besides, there were too many skeletons in my closet, and if I started down that road... No, I couldn't go there.

Ever.

Sympathy filled her expression, but she didn't push, and heavy silence enveloped us. I loosened a breath when there was a loud knock at the door, but my relief was quickly doused in fear.

"It's okay," Arianne said. "Security only lets up approved guests."

Approved guests? Wow. I didn't know what to say to that, so I sat quietly, watching as she went to open the door.

"Luis." She threw her arms around the immaculately dressed man. "It's good to see you."

"Nicco said you might need me."

"Come in."

She led him over to the kitchen. "Caitlin, this is Luis, our head of security."

I stared at him, unable to speak.

"It's okay," Arianne reassured me. "I trust Luis with my life. He's one of the good guys."

"Hello." It came out weak.

"Miss O'Connell." He gave me a small nod. "How are you feeling?"

I frowned. He knew my name? Interesting.

"I'm okay. Nicco and Arianne have been very kind."

"Coffee?" Arianne asked him.

"That would be great. Where's Nicco?"

"Visiting with his father." Something in her expression tightened.

"How is he?"

"Honestly, I'm not sure."

"Antonio is a fighter." He squeezed her shoulder gently. "If anyone can beat it, he can."

"Thank you."

"I'm to accompany Miss O'Connell to the cabin tomorrow?"

"We'll all go and get her settled. But yes, I'd feel better if you'd stay." She glanced at me. "If that's okay with you?"

"I..."

"I'll keep out of your way. You'll hardly know I'm there."

"O-okay."

The gravity of my situation crashed into me. I was in Niccolò Marchetti's apartment with his young wife, discussing being shipped off to their family's cabin with close protection.

It was too much to process.

And yet, no one had ever gone to such lengths to make me feel safe before.

My entire life had been one big string of disappointments and being let down by the people who were supposed to love and protect you.

"It's going to be okay, Cait."

Arianne kept saying that.

I just didn't know when, or if, I would ever believe it.

"You're sure?"

The voices beyond my room made me stop rising from bed.

After a morning of going through the new things Arianne had bought me, I'd retreated to my room to rest. I must have fallen asleep because it was hours later and already dark outside.

"Our contact at the hospital said DiMarco showed up first thing this morning, sniffing around."

A chill ran down my spine, fear stealing the air from my lungs.

Zander knew—he knew, and he was already looking for me.

"But they didn't tell him anything, right?"

"No, patient confidentiality will protect her to a degree, and we paid off the right people to buy discretion, including wiping the CCTV, but if he manages to get anyone to talk—"

"They could place Enzo and Matteo at the hospital."

"Unlikely, but it's a possibility."

I was up and out of the bed before I knew it. Yanking the door open, I stormed into the living room. Arianne's eyes widened to saucers. "Caitlin, what are—"

"He knows." I looked at Nicco.

He drew in a sharp breath. "It would seem so."

"Shaun?" If anything had happened to him because of me... I wasn't sure I could live with that.

"We don't know yet."

"What do you mean, you don't know yet?"

"We have to tread very carefully. If DiMarco suspects that we're involved—"

"If Zander suspects Shaun lied, do you have any idea what he'll do to him?"

Nicco's eyes darkened. "I have a pretty good idea." He rubbed his jaw. "I know this is hard, but until we figure out how to handle this—"

"Nicco." Arianne inched closer, shooting her husband a scathing look. "I'm sure your friend will be okay and as soon as it's safe to do so, Nicco will send someone to check on him. Won't you?" She pinned him with another hard look.

Hands jammed casually in his pockets, he gave her an imperceptible nod. "We have guys in Providence keeping an eye out, but right now, we have to be discreet."

My gaze bounced between them both as I hugged myself tight.

"Cait," Arianne said softly. "We'll do everything we can to protect you from Zander, I promise."

She kept saying that, but she didn't know what he was capable of, how obsessed he was.

"I need to check in on my father," Nicco said. "I'll be back later." He went to Arianne and cupped her face in his hands. "Ti amo, Bambolina."

Her eyes fluttered as she kissed him back, and I turned away affording them some privacy. Ignoring the ache—the longing—in my chest.

Their love was a living, breathing thing that bled throughout the entire room. It was impossible to be unaffected by it, no matter how much it made my heart squeeze.

Nicco left and Arianne offered to make us both some hot cocoa.

"Are you hungry? There's some leftover lasagna."

"I'm okay, thank you."

"You haven't eaten much since you got here."

"I don't have much of an appetite yet."

She nodded, handing me a mug of frothy, rich hot cocoa topped with marshmallows.

"Is Nicco's father okay?" I blurted out, my cheeks burning at my sudden outburst.

"Actually, no." Grief washed over her. "He's sick."

"I'm sorry. That must be very difficult for Nicco... and you."

"If you have something you want to ask, ask it."

There was no malice in her words, only gentle understanding.

"Will..." I inhaled a sharp breath. "Does that mean Nicco will..." I trailed off, dipping my gaze.

"Will he take over his father's... responsibilities? Yes."

"And you're okay with that?"

"I knew who Nicco was when I married him, Caitlin." Her expression softened. "And my answer would always be the same. I love him. And love knows no bounds."

Spoken with a conviction I myself couldn't understand. I'd never known that kind of love and devotion.

"You seem very happy," I said.

"We are. You know, Matt—"

Panic welled inside me as I rushed out, "Please, don't."

"Very well. But you know, Cait, you can't avoid him forever."

Precisely why I couldn't stop thinking that letting them help me was a huge mistake.

"Cait, we're almost here." Arianne gently shook my shoulders, rousing me from a fitful dream.

I hadn't meant to fall asleep on the way to the cabin—it was only a short ride—but the rumble of the SUV had quickly lulled me into oblivion.

Rubbing my eyes, I peered out of the tinted window, watching the dense trees roll by as Luis drove down the dirt road to the cabin.

"There's only one route in and out," she said. "Luis knows this area like the back of his hand. Nicco and his cousins too. There's hot water, electricity, and plenty of home comforts. Cell service should be okay."

The brand-new iPhone felt heavy in my pocket. I hadn't wanted to accept it, but Arianne wanted me to have a way to contact her should I need to. Plus, it gave me a tether to the real world.

Not that I had anything left in the real world.

"My offer still stands. I can stay—"

"No," I said hastily. "You don't need to do that. I need some time... alone."

Arianne smiled. "I understand. Nora was sorry she couldn't make it."

"That's okay." I didn't need a farewell party. It already felt like they had done too much for me.

"Remember, you can take as much time as you need."

I nodded.

The SUV came to a stop and Luis climbed out, coming around to open my door. "Miss O'Connell," he said.

"Thank you."

God, I seemed to be doing a lot of that. Thanking people. Nodding. Agreeing with them. Zander had turned me into a docile, wounded creature.

And I hated him for it.

But what choice did I have but to acquiesce?

Unless I wanted to go it alone with nothing but the clothes on my back and the few dollars in my purse, I needed the help. At least, until I could figure out a plan.

It wasn't like I had much in my apartment in Providence anyway, and a lot of it came from Zander. Things I didn't ever want to touch or see again.

A shudder ran down my spine as I climbed out of the SUV. The frigid air brushed up against me and I burrowed deeper into the thick sweater Arianne had bought me.

I was grateful, I was. But part of me was angry that I was here. Again. Relying on the charity of others. DiMarco's was supposed to be my way out. When Zander had offered me the job, I'd jumped at the chance to fix my desperate need to earn money. But I'd underestimated his motives, and before it was too late, he'd already set his sights on me.

"Caitlin?" Arianne called, and my head snapped up.

"Coming." I followed them to the cabin. It was impressive on the outside, but the inside was something to behold. There was a large, open plan living space with a kitchen in the back, divided by a gorgeous, soft sectional. The open fire was filled with chopped wood just begging to be lit, and the furniture was all rustic to match the open beams.

It was beautiful.

"There's a heating system," Luis said, stoking the fire. "Though nothing beats an open fire."

"Living room and kitchen," Arianne said. "Then the hall leads to the main bathroom, one master suite, and three guest bedrooms.

"You can have your pick of any of the three, but my favorite is the first door on the left." A warm smile graced her face. "Come on."

She led me down the hall and into the first bedroom.

"Wow, this is... stunning." It rivalled the guest room at their apartment. Decadent décor and ornate, hand-carved furniture. It was rustic and welcoming and everything I'd never had before.

"It's yours," she said. "For as long as you need it."

Emotion welled inside my chest, and I glanced away, trying to hide the moisture clinging to my lashes.

But when Arianne said, "I'll give you a minute." I knew I'd failed.

Silence enveloped me. Thick, oppressive silence. I surveyed the room, my gaze snagging on my reflection in the dresser mirror.

The woman staring back at me looked exhausted, dark circles ringing her dull, lifeless green eyes. Bruises mottled her skin, angry red welts lining her jaw.

She was a mess.

I was a mess.

The tears I'd fought so hard to contain began spilling down my cheeks.

"How did you end up here again? How?" I gripped the edge of the dresser, my eyes shuttering with anguish.

I was a fighter, a survivor, had been since I was just a kid. But over and over, I found myself in these desperate situations. Like a magnet for the broken and bad.

I could hear my mom's raspy voice as clear as day. *"You're nothing but a worthless whore, Cait. That's all you'll ever be."*

But I wasn't that girl. I never had been. She was just too bitter, too angry and high to see it.

"Cait?" Arianne's voice startled me.

"Just a minute." I swiped the tears from my eyes, wincing when I caught the bruising on my cheek. It still hurt, but not nearly as much as my heart.

"Are you okay?"

"I'm coming," I called, forcing myself to take a calming breath.

Checking my reflection one last time, I slipped back into the hall.

"Are you hungry?" she asked. "I thought we could eat before Nicco gets here."

He was picking Arianne up to take her back to Romany Square. Luis would remain here with me as agreed.

I still didn't know how to feel about being here with a man I hardly knew, but I did know it was preferable to being out in the middle of nowhere alone.

My eyes flicked over to where Luis was tending the fire. As if she heard my thoughts, Arianne said, "Luis is practically family. I wouldn't leave him here with you if I didn't trust him."

"We've got company," he announced, peering out of the window.

"It's just Nicco." Arianne moved toward him, frowning at whatever she saw beyond the window.

"I'll be back," she said, glancing over her shoulder at me. With a silent look at Luis, she slipped out of the cabin and a trickle of fear went through me.

"What's wrong?" I asked.

"Nothing. I'm sure it's—"

But I was already moving toward the window, gasping when I saw the figure step out of the car.

"What is he doing here?" My voice quivered as I clutched my throat.

"I'm sure there's a perfectly good explanation," Luis said.

Yeah, like he couldn't stay the hell away.

Anger unfurled in my stomach, heating my blood and without thinking, I yanked open the door, stepped outside, and hissed, "What the hell are you doing here?"

EIGHT

MATTEO

ARIANNE LET OUT a soft sigh as Caitlin glared at me, her anger like a storm raging between us.

"Nicco couldn't come, he—"

"How convenient," she spat the words. "So you figured, what? You'd come and try to force me to talk to you?"

"Caitlin, that isn't what's happening here." Arianne stepped forward, but Caitlin jerked back.

"I trusted you." Hurt flashed over her features. "I trusted you and—"

"Antonio was rushed to the hospital," I blurted out. "Nicco couldn't come because his family needed him."

"Oh." Her expression slipped, some of the anger melting away, replaced with guilt. "I… I didn't know."

"It's okay," Arianne said. "Why don't you go inside, and I'll be right there."

"Yeah, sorry." Caitlin's cool gaze swept over me, leaving me chilled to the bone.

She all but ran back into the cabin.

I let out a frustrated breath. "That went well."

"She needs time, Matt." Sympathy shone in Ari's eyes. "She's… confused and hurting."

"I'm not the enemy," I grumbled, feeling totally out of my depth.

"No, but you are a guy she's been intimate with. It's a lot to confront after everything she's been through."

I glanced up at the cabin and dragged a hand down my face. "I guess I'll wait out here."

"Thank you." Ari squeezed my hand. "I'll just say goodbye and then we can go."

Nicco and Alessia, his sister, were already at the hospital with Enzo and Nora. I'd offered to come get Ari and take her straight there.

I'd almost jumped at the chance to come out here with a valid excuse to see her. Probably not my brightest idea ever, but I'd underestimated just how much Caitlin didn't want to see me.

Way to go, Matt.

Luis stepped out onto the porch. "How's Toni?"

"We don't know yet."

Fuck, if anything happened to him, I didn't want to think about the domino effect that would have.

"Tell Nicco I'll be praying."

I nodded, my eyes flicking beyond him to the door. "How is she?"

"Arianne?"

"No, Caitlin."

He frowned. "She's as well as can be expected given the circumstances."

"You'll watch out for her?"

"Of course. Is she… someone to you?" Luis's brow lifted.

"She's…"

The door opened and Arianne appeared. "I'm going to be a few minutes. Come and wait inside."

"I'm not sure—"

"It's fine."

"I'm going to check the perimeter." Luis took off toward the tree line.

"Come on," Ari beckoned me inside.

There was no sign of Caitlin, and I didn't ask. The sting of dejection weighed heavily on my shoulders.

At least she was here, safe. Out of the clutches of that sick motherfucker.

"Is she—"

Caitlin appeared in the hallway, her lips pulled into a tight line.

"I'll wait in the car," Arianne said to me, before turning her attention on Caitlin. "Remember you can call or text me at any time."

Caitlin gave her an imperceptible nod, hugging herself tight as if she was trying to build a physical wall between us.

This wasn't the same woman I'd met all those months ago. She had fire in her eyes and warmth in her heart that night. But now there was no sparkle in her gaze, only pain and sadness. And it fucking gutted me.

Arianne left, the click of the door like a gunshot in the silence.

"Caitlin, I—"

"Let me," she cut me off. "I'm sorry, about before. You didn't deserve that." Her voice trembled.

"Hey." I stepped forward, but she immediately jerked back. "Caitlin, I'm not going to hurt you. I'm not—"

"I know." She inhaled a shuddering breath. "But I can't… I can't."

"Can't what? I'm not asking you for anything. I just want to help. I want to—"

"You should go." The words tumbled from her lips. "I only wanted to apologize for my behavior. I'm not… that isn't me. But everything is messed up and I need some time."

"I get that." But I didn't want to leave, not with so much left unsaid between us.

Caitlin stared at me, through me, silently begging me to go. I couldn't do it though. Not without doing something.

Glancing around the cabin, my eyes landed on the sideboard. I marched over to it, grabbed the pen and scribbled my cell phone number on the notepad. "Here." I tore it off and held it out to her.

But she just kept staring.

Fine. I didn't need her to take it to know she had it.

Pulling one of the magnets off the refrigerator, I pinned it there. "If you need anything, any time, night or day, you can call me. Text me. Leave me a message. It doesn't matter. I'll pick up. I swear."

Her stone expression gave nothing away, but I at least felt a little better about leaving.

"You're not alone in this, Caitlin. Not one bit."

I made for the door, praying she would call after me.

She didn't.

"Any word from Nicco?" I asked Arianne as we made the ride back into the city.

"Nothing."

"Hey." I reached over and squeezed her arm. "He'll be okay."

"Will he?" She sank back against my leather seats. "If Antonio doesn't pull through… he's too young, Matt."

"Do you ever regret it? Marrying into the Family?"

"No, never. That's not what this is." She let out a weary sigh. "I just worry about the toll it will take on him."

"Nic is one of the best people I know, Ari. He'll find his way. Besides, he has you by his side. Something tells me you'll never let him stray from his path."

"I hope you're right."

"Hey, I am. You're like the Bonnie to his Clyde."

"You did not just say that." Her laughter eased some of the tension in the car. "She's going to be okay, right? Caitlin, I mean?"

"Yeah." It came out strangled. "I mean, she'll lay low at the cabin, we'll deal with DiMarco, and she can go on with her life."

"Matt…"

"What?"

"You sound like a wounded puppy."

"I do not." I shot her a scathing look.

She chuckled. "Do you think she'll text you?"

"No."

"So, why d'you do it?"

"Because..." I shrugged.

"Because... you care about her?"

"Because she's the only woman I've thought about in the last eight months, Ari. And maybe that makes me a fool, but I never thought I'd get to see her again. Now she's here, and I can't believe it's just so I can watch her disappear again."

Arianne's eyes drilled holes into the side of my face, but I couldn't meet her stare.

"You're a good guy, Matt," she said, softly. "One of the best guys I know."

"Yeah."

Maybe that was the problem though.

Maybe I was too nice.

Everyone knew, nice guys usually finished last.

"Bambolina." Nicco was up and out of his chair the second he spotted us. He scooped Ari into his arms, burying his face in the crook of her neck.

"How is he?" I asked Enzo.

"It's not looking good." Pain shone in his eyes as Nora rested her head on his shoulder. "He's in surgery still. But he went into cardiac arrest. Medics managed to stabilize him, but they're worried about swelling to his brain."

I glanced over at Nicco and Ari, my stomach sinking into my boots.

"Matt," Alessia appeared around the corner and ran straight into my arms. "You're here."

"Hey, Sia." I hugged her tight. "How you holding up?"

"I..." She burst into tears, sobbing into my sweater.

"Shh, kid. It's going to be okay." I smoothed my hand down her long golden hair. "Where's Genevieve?" I asked no one in particular.

"She went to visit her mom in Pawtucket last night. She's on her way."

Genevieve was my uncle's housekeeper turned girlfriend. Their relationship was still fairly new and at his request no one made a big deal about it.

But she would want to be here.

I led Alessia over to the row of plastic chairs and sat down. She burrowed into my side, still sobbing.

"We can't lose him," she cried. "We can't."

"Uncle T is a fighter. He's not going anywhere, Sia."

But as I said the words, I felt nothing but dread. Uncle Toni was sick, and who knew what would happen when the doctors opened him up.

I dragged a hand down my face, tipping my head back against the wall. My gaze landed on Nicco and Ari. He was holding her like she was his life raft in an angry sea. He already looked older somehow, as if the burden of what was to come had aged him overnight.

I didn't envy him. Not one bit. He had his beautiful wife and a beautiful home, but his life would never truly be his own.

It'll never be yours either. I let out a weary sigh.

"Niccolò, Alessia." Genevieve burst through the doors, running toward them.

"Gen," Alessia jumped up to greet her, burrowing herself in the woman's arms.

"Oh, sweet girl, shh. I'm here, I'm here." They hugged each other tight, silence falling over the seven of us again.

My mind wandered to Caitlin, to our last conversation. I doubted she would ever call or text me, but I wanted to give her the option. It was just something I needed to do.

"Has the doctor been out?"

"Not since they took him to surgery," Nicco said.

"Okay. I want you all to wait here while I go and speak to a nurse."

"I can come—"

"Stay with your sister," she said to Nicco. "I'll be back as soon as I get some answers."

Genevieve pressed a kiss to Alessia's head and gently nudged her back to me. "Watch her," she mouthed, and I nodded.

"She seems pretty calm," Enzo said.

"The calm before the storm," Nicco replied, his eyes vacant as he looked down the hall where Genevieve had disappeared.

"How did it go?" he asked, glancing between me and Arianne.

"Fine. Don't worry about that right now. This is more important."

Enzo caught my eye, and I knew what he was thinking. It was more important. But if DiMarco found out we were hiding Caitlin…

Then the shit would really hit the fan.

Genevieve returned with the doctor. It was good and bad news. The good news was they had stabilized Uncle Toni, but the bad news was they had put him into a coma to reduce swelling to his brain. The next forty-eight hours would be critical to his recovery.

Nicco and Arianne stayed with Genevieve, but I left with Enzo, Nora, and Alessia. She was going to stay with me and my family until we knew more.

"How is she?" Mom asked me as I joined her in the living room.

"Exhausted, scared… but I think it'll do her good being with Bella." My sister would watch out for her. The two of them were thicker than thieves.

"Poor girl. And Niccolò, mio Dio, such a weight on his shoulder."

"I know, Mama." I took a long pull on my beer.

"I can't imagine..." She let out a heavy sigh. "If we lost your papa."

"Don't think about it."

"It's always there, figlio mio. This life... it takes so much from us."

"Did you ever want to get out?" The words rolled off my tongue before I could stop them.

She tsked. "You think that is a choice?"

"No, Mama, I know it's not... I just..."

"Matteo, what is it?"

"Nothing, Mama."

"Is it a girl?" A knowing smile spread over her face. "You know, you're not getting any younger. Your cousins have both settled down now, perhaps it's time for you to think about meeting someone."

"Because it's that easy," I grumbled.

"There must be someone. Nora and Arianne have plenty of friends at the college. Surely a pretty girl must have caught your eye? You know, if you'd stuck it out there, you could—"

"We're not having this conversation." I'd wanted to finish college, I had. But it had proved too hard splitting my time and keeping up pretenses, and given everything that was happening with Uncle Toni, I'd decided to withdraw.

"Why not?"

"Because..." I shrugged. "It's weird."

"You think I don't know about the birds and the bees? About how young men like yourself like to sow your seeds far and wide before you settle."

"That's not the saying, Mama."

"It's my saying." She tsked again, waving me off. "You are a good man, Matteo. Kind and compassionate. You think with your head. You're not like some of these cogliones."

"Mama!"

"What? I speak the truth."

"I love you, Mama."

"I love you too, figlio mio. And I just know there's a good woman out there somewhere for you."

Oh, Jesus. She was like a dog with a bone. For a second, I'd contemplated telling her about Caitlin, but it would only raise her hopes.

My cell phone had burned a hole in my pocket all afternoon. I knew she wouldn't text or call, but it didn't stop my heart from stuttering every time I got a notification. If I had half a brain, I would forget all about her. But I couldn't do it.

I couldn't get her out of my fucking head.

If I were more like Enzo, I would have gone to the cabin and refused to leave until she agreed to talk to me. Or if I were more like Nicco, I would have made some grand gesture she couldn't ignore.

But I wasn't like them. I was Matteo Bellatoni. Loyal friend. Perpetual joker. Heart on his sleeve kinda guy.

And deep down, all I'd ever wanted was to meet the girl of my dreams.

I didn't think I'd meet her only to lose her...
Twice.

NINE

CAITLIN

MATTEO'S NUMBER pinned to the refrigerator taunted me.

After he and Arianne had left, I'd contemplated throwing it onto the open fire. But I hadn't, yet.

I felt awful after railing at him the way I did, after finding out that Nicco's father was sick. They were clearly all close—Arianne, Nicco, and his cousins—and I'd acted like a complete bitch.

But everything was so messed up. I wasn't the same woman I was last summer when I'd spent the night with Matteo. So much had happened since then. Things I didn't want to ever have to explain to him.

"You can come inside, you know?" I said to Luis as he swept the leaves off the steps leading up to the cabin.

"I'll be in soon. Better to clear these now before the ground frosts."

"I'll make a fresh pot of coffee."

"Perfect." He smiled.

They hadn't been joking when they said Luis would keep to himself. I'd barely seen him in the few hours that had passed since Matteo and Arianne left.

It was hard to believe that less than six days ago, I was at DiMarco's working a regular shift. And now... now my life was in tatters.

All because of him.

Tears burned my throat, but I swallowed them down. I didn't agree to come here to wallow; I wanted to give myself time and space to heal and come back stronger.

But it was easier said than done. Too much time alone with my thoughts was dangerous. Grabbing my phone off the coffee table, I snuggled into the cushions and opened a new browser, typing in Niccolò Marchetti.

Article after article appeared, some documenting the merger between Capizola Holdings and the Marchetti Empire. The reports surrounding Nicco and Arianne's wedding ranged from it being nothing more than a business deal; to an arranged marriage; to the Marchetti calling in payment of a debt from Roberto Capizola, Arianne's father.

But I'd seen their relationship firsthand. There was no denying how much they loved one another.

I scrolled through some more articles before switching to the image search results. Photo after photo appeared of Nicco attending functions, charity events, gala dinners; there were even some photos of him and Arianne working at a community center in Romany Square. Then my eyes landed on him.

Matteo.

Gosh, he looked handsome in the black dinner suit, his dirty-blond hair swept to one side, his charming smile radiating off the screen. He was different to his cousins. They both had the typical dark Italian genes. But Matteo was much fairer. Like sunshine between two storm clouds. The thought made me smile as I ran my finger over his photo.

Guilt sat heavy in my chest at how I'd treated him earlier, and at the hospital. But I'd been so shocked to see him standing there, I hadn't known what else to do. And after what Zander did to me... how could I look Matteo in the eye?

My eyes flicked over to the kitchen, snagging on the note pinned on the refrigerator. Even if I did text him, what the hell would I say?

I'd lied to him that night. Concealed the truth. And I'd do it again if it meant protecting myself.

With a small sigh, I switched off my cell and padded over to the kitchen. I needed to keep busy, which seemed almost impossible in a cabin in the middle of nowhere. But I'd spied a bookshelf full of books and a stack of puzzles, which was better than nothing.

Placing my cell on the counter, I switched on the coffee machine and went over to the puzzles, choosing one. A two-thousand-piece print of the New York skyline.

Satisfied with my choice, I made me and Luis a mug of coffee each and let him know it was ready.

By the time he came inside, I'd already moved to the coffee table and emptied out all the pieces.

"You like puzzles?" Luis asked, leaning back against the counter and sipping his coffee.

"I haven't done a jigsaw puzzle since I was a child," I admitted.

"Want a helping hand?"

"Sure, why not."

Luis brought his coffee over and placed it on the floor out of harm's way. "Okay, what have we got here." He began sorting the pieces.

"Any idea on where we should start?"

"Outside pieces then build on those, preferably in sections."

"Wow, I didn't realize it was so complicated." I chuckled, adding some outside pieces to his pile.

"I used to sit with my nonna and do puzzles. She loved them. But it's been a long time since I did one for fun."

"I'm not sure two-thousand pieces constitutes the word fun. But I figured it would keep my mind occupied."

"You'll be sucked in before you know it. Here you go, look." He slotted a few pieces together like an old pro. "Now you have a point of reference."

Luis stood and I frowned up at him. "What's wrong?"

"You didn't think I was going to do it for you, did you?" A faint smirk traced his mouth.

"Well, no, but a little help wouldn't go amiss."

"You'll figure it out." He winked and walked off.

Well then.

For the next forty minutes, I worked meticulously to sort the pieces into similar groups. Then I began matching them to the section Luis had completed. It was going to take me forever to finish it... if I ever did. But having a focus would be good for me.

Besides, I could kind of relate to the puzzle.

God, how pathetic, relating to a jigsaw puzzle.

I felt fractured though. Shattered into jagged pieces. It wasn't any one thing that had led me to this point, it was an accumulation of events since my childhood.

But unlike this puzzle, which with time and patience I could fix...

I wasn't sure anyone could ever fix me.

I woke with a start, drenched in sweat and clutching the crumpled bed sheets between my fingers.

"It's just a dream," I urged myself, willing my racing heart to calm down.

But it hadn't been a dream at all.

It had been a nightmare.

Zander's wolfish grin taunting me as he and his business associates circled me like predators hunting their prey. No matter how hard I ran, how fast I pumped my legs, I couldn't outrun them. And then their laughter had morphed into voices I'd spent years trying to forget.

A violent shudder rolled through me as I leaned over and snatched my shiny new cell phone off the nightstand and checked the time.

A little after one.

It was going to be a long night.

Luis was down the hall in one of the other guest rooms. For a moment, I'd thought he was going to sleep out in his SUV which was completely unacceptable.

I'd made us both spaghetti and we had eaten in uncomfortable silence. He didn't pry or push me to talk, and I didn't really know what to say to him. I'd quickly excused myself after dinner and retreated to my room.

Pushing back the covers, I climbed out of bed and wandered quietly into the kitchen. I needed a glass of water to temper the lingering fear of my nightmare.

The cabin was steeped in silence, only the silvery hue of moonlight guiding my way. I helped myself to a bottle of water from the refrigerator, my eyes catching on the note pinned there.

Matteo's number.

His words replayed through my mind.

If you need anything, any time, night or day, you can call me.

It was a bad idea, the worst. But it wasn't like I could text Arianne or wake Luis. I barely knew them.

You barely know him.

But I did know him. Or at least, I had known him for one amazing night. And there was something about the way he'd pushed to talk to me... something a small, broken part of me had latched onto.

It was dangerous territory though.

If I gave him the wrong idea...

Before I could stop myself, I tore the note off the refrigerator and hurried back to my bedroom. It practically burned a hole in my hand and the second I was in the safety of my bedroom, I dropped the note on the bed, staring at it.

"Oh for God's sake, Cait, it's just his number," I murmured to myself.

It represented so much more than just his number though.

If I texted or called him, I would be crossing a line I might not be able to come back from.

But being here, alone with my thoughts wasn't as easy as it sounded.

Burrowing back under the sheets, I clutched my cell phone in my hand. Matteo knew me. He knew the intimate parts of my body, my freckles and blemishes; he'd mapped the curves of my skin with his hands and lips.

But he didn't *know* me.

Not really.

I'd given him a piece of me that night, but she was barely a figment of my imagination—the girl I wanted to be if things were different. The girl I could have become if I'd had a normal childhood with normal, loving, supportive parents.

But I didn't have any of those things.

I had a past full of pain and disappointment and heartache. A past that had shaped me into nothing more than a survivor, clinging onto hope, knowing that she was probably never going to escape the ghosts that haunted her.

Punching in Matteo's number, I hit call... and then realized what a foolish mistake I'd made.

He didn't really want me to call him at any hour. He was probably just being polite, offering me an olive branch seeing as we had some shared history.

It started to ring, but before he could answer, I hung up, throwing my phone across the bed.

What the hell was I thinking?

Hopefully he was asleep and wouldn't see the missed call until—

My phone began to vibrate.

"Shit, shit." I snatched it back up and stared at Matteo's number flashing across the screen.

Dragging my bottom lip between my teeth, I waited for it to stop. It did, and relief sank into me. But a couple of seconds later, it vibrated with an incoming text.

I almost didn't open it, but curiosity got the better of me.

Caitlin?

My stomach fluttered. I could text him back. A text was safe, non-committal. A text didn't mean anything. Before I could reply though, another message came through.

Are you okay?

I hit reply and started typing.

I'm fine.

Liar.

So you're calling me in the middle of night to tell me you're fine? I may have a pretty face, but I'm not stupid, Cait.

Gosh, the way he called me Cait. As if we were friends. Intimate. As if we'd known each other forever.

That single word wrapped around my heart and didn't let go.

. . .

I had a nightmare.

Can I call you?

No, please... I can't...

Okay, no phone call. But we can text? This is okay?

I chewed my lip again.

I guess so...

Did you wake Luis?

I didn't want to disturb him. I'm a grown woman. I should be able to handle a bad dream.

We all get scared of the dark sometimes, Cait.

Was he trying to wear me down? Because there, in the dark of night, it was working.

He beat me to a reply again.

How do you like the cabin?

It's very peaceful. I found a two-thousand-piece puzzle to keep me occupied.

A puzzle you say? Sounds... riveting.

A faint smile traced my lips as I got comfortable and settled in to text him back. This was safe, reassuring in a strange way.

It wasn't supposed to be, but there was no denying Matteo made it easy. He had that night all those months ago, and he was doing it again now.

Caitlin?

He texted back when I didn't reply.

I'm still here...

Good. I thought maybe you'd fallen asleep on me.

Not yet.

Oh, it's like that, huh?

I'm sorry I woke you.

Don't be. I was lying here awake anyway.

You were? It's late.

Yeah, I have a lot of things on my mind.

The knot in my stomach tightened, guilt trickling through me.

Well, I feel better about not waking you now.

I'm glad you texted.

Me too.

. . .

It was the truth, I already felt better.

I meant what I said. You can text me anytime and I'll answer.

I know.

Nervous energy vibrated inside me. I'd never had this. Genuine conversation with a guy. There was always something: the expectation of more, veiled threats, or the feeling of something owed. I wasn't used to being... an equal.

In fact, I'd long given up on the idea. In my life, sex and attraction were weapons. Ones that had been used against me too many times.

And then Matteo texted me nine little words that told me exactly how different he was to every man I'd known before him.

DiMarco will pay, Caitlin. I promise you, he'll pay.

I woke up with my phone on the pillow beside me. Matteo and I had texted late into the night. After he'd made his promise to make Zander pay, he'd turned the conversation to safe topics until I'd fallen asleep.

Grabbing my cell, I unlocked the screen and smiled at the message from him.

Good morning. I hope you managed to get some sleep.

I did, thanks to you.

Not exactly how I want to be remembered—for making women fall asleep—but I guess I'll take it.

Laughter bubbled in my chest, but it was quickly dampened by another wave of guilt. He was flirting... and flirting was skirting a line I wasn't sure I wanted to cross.

Not now.
Not ever.

I need coffee then a shower. Thanks again for keeping me company last night.

Things felt different in the harsh light of day. I'd been scared last night. Alone and vulnerable. But I didn't need Matteo to chase off the monsters in my sleep now the sun was up.

"Coffee's brewing," Luis called from the hall. He must have heard me shuffling about.

I grabbed a hoodie and pulled it on over my pajamas and padded into the hall.

"Morning," I said, joining him in the kitchen.

"Sleep well?"

"I... yeah, okay."

"I thought I heard something—"

"I got up to get some water."

"Sorry, I should have checked on you."

I snorted. "I'm a big girl. I can take care of myself."

"Noted." He smiled, pushing a mug of coffee toward me. "What do you want to do today?"

"You mean, I have options?"

"You're not a prisoner here, Caitlin."

"No, I know that. I just... sorry," I shook my head softly, "I'm being rude."

"There's some pretty neat trails in the forest, we could check those out."

"You want to take me trekking through the forest?"

That seemed... weird.

"It sounds stranger than it is. Arianne thought you might like—"

"Ah, Arianne put you up to this." I didn't know why but disappointment welled in my chest.

It was silly. Of course she'd suggested it to him. Or ordered him to ask me. I wasn't entirely sure of the nature of their relationship and how it worked.

They seemed friendly, but what did I know about these things.

Nothing, you know nothing.

I ran my thumb around the edge of my mug, not meeting his heavy gaze.

"She just doesn't want you going stir crazy," he said.

"It's only been a day. I'm sure I'm good for a while yet."

"You do have that epic puzzle to complete."

"Exactly."

I'd only picked it off the shelf on a whim, but it was fast becoming a metaphor for my situation.

"Well, I'm going to take a shower. If you want to venture out, just say the word. I'll be around." He tapped the counter, drained his coffee and then disappeared down the hall.

I considered his suggestion again. It was only a walk. What was the worst that could happen?

Besides, I had to leave here eventually.

TEN

MATTEO

"EXPECTING A CALL?" Enzo asked me with a frown.

"No. Just scrolling." I pocketed my cell and tapped my fingers against the counter.

"Seriously, what's up with you?"

"Nothing. I'm fine."

"You seem—"

My cell vibrated and I whipped it out of my pocket, disappointed when I saw Arabella's name.

"Okay, spit it out."

I hesitated, unsure I wanted to put myself out there like that. But it was Enzo, my cousin, one of my best friends.

"She texted me."

"She—" Realization dawned on his face. "Caitlin? For real?"

"Yeah. Last night."

"And what did she say?"

"She had a nightmare and wanted to talk."

"So you… talked?"

"Yeah." I didn't tell him that I hadn't heard from her since our brief message conversation this morning. Even if it was driving me out of my mind that she hadn't texted me back.

"See, I told you all she needed was some time." My expression fell and he added, "Matt?"

"I want more."

"Shit, yeah, you do. But she made it pretty clear last time—"

"I know. I wasn't planning on doing anything stupid."

Like turning up at the cabin unannounced, hoping she would let me in.

And then what...

I jammed my fingers into my hair and tugged the ends, reveling in the slight pinch.

"Did Lucino call yet?"

"Yeah, they arrived yesterday."

"And?"

"It's been a day, Matt. Give them a chance to feel DiMarco out. You know, your old man is going to lose his shit when he finds out—"

"Don't." My jaw clenched.

It was a risk not telling him what really happened, but Nicco was right—we needed to find out what went down first.

It was more than DiMarco deserved, but it wasn't my call to make.

"What are you thinking?" he asked.

"That I want to break his fucking face." I inhaled a shuddering breath.

"For her?"

My eyes snapped to Enzo's, narrowing. "Why are you pushing me on this?"

"Because I've never seen you like this over a woman. I guess I'm trying to understand how you can feel so strongly for someone you spent one night with. It's even worse than Nicco and Arianne, and I thought that was fast."

"Thanks a bunch," I murmured.

"Surely you can see it from my point of view?"

"It's not something I can explain." Frustration coated my words. "We had this... connection."

"The sex was that good?"

"Oh, fuck off."

"Relax." He chuckled. "I'm joking."

"You're being an asshole."

"I guess I'm just trying to understand. None of that shit comes easy for me."

"You have seen yourself with Nora, right?" My brow lifted.

"She's different."

"I would hope so seeing as she's got you locked down heading straight for wedding town."

"Seriously?" He balked. "We've only been together a few months."

"Like you don't want to put a ring on her at the earliest possible moment."

Enzo was a possessive asshole. No way he didn't want to bind himself to Nora in every way possible, despite his reservations about relationships.

"Fine, you got me there." He smirked. "But it's all her. Only ever her."

"She's good for you, cous," I said. There was silence between us for a moment while we were both lost in our thoughts, before I brought us back to present circumstances. "I still can't believe Uncle Toni is in a coma."

"He'll pull through," Enzo said with arrogant confidence. "He has to."

"Yeah."

But the truth was, I wasn't sure he would.

I didn't think anyone was.

They just didn't want to admit it.

Enzo didn't stick around. Arianne invited Nora over so naturally he went with her. They asked me but I didn't want to play fifth wheel. Not today.

Not when I couldn't get Caitlin out of my head.

How was your day?

I stared at the message I'd sent Caitlin ten minutes ago, willing her to reply. It was borderline desperate the way I clutched my phone, waiting. But I couldn't help it.

The thought of her at the cabin, all alone—Luis hardly counted when he was security—was messing with my head.

When another couple of minutes passed, and she didn't text back, I changed tack.

I'm guessing from your cold shoulder, you're either too wrapped up in your puzzle to reply or Luis decided to take your phone off you.

You got me... this puzzle is addictive.

A smile tugged at my lips.

You know... I heard two hands are better than one.

Good job I have two then, isn't it?

Laughter rumbled in my chest.

You got me there...

. . .

Don't you have better things to be doing than texting me?

Aren't you bored of your own company yet?

I have Luis to keep me company, remember? He's really good at puzzles.

My laughter grew. This felt good. Safe and easy. She wasn't ignoring me or telling me to leave her alone. I wanted to ask if I could go see her, talk in person. But I didn't want to scare her off, no matter how hard it was to stay away.

I guess I should let you get back to your puzzle then.

The buzzer rang and I traipsed over to answer it. "Yeah?"

"It's me," my sister chimed. "I hope you don't mind but I brought Sia with me."

Great. Just what I didn't need—babysitting my sister and cousin.

"Yeah, come up." I pulled the door ajar and padded back to the couch, typing another reply to Caitlin.

Send help. My sister and cousin just turned up to terrorize me.

Sounds like you have your hands full.

You have no idea. Any suggestions on how to keep two teenage girls occupied?

Sounds trickier than my puzzle... trip to the movies? All teenage girls like that, right?

I'm not sure Alessia will want to go out.

Oh... is everything okay?

. . .

It's Sia's and Nicco's father, my uncle. He isn't doing so good.

I remember now. I'm sorry to hear he still isn't doing well. Maybe a home movie night instead?

Their footsteps sounded down the hall, the familiar cadence of Arabella's voice floating into my apartment.

Yeah, maybe. I should probably go see to them. Enjoy your puzzle.

Enjoy your babysitter duties.

"Who's that?" Bella asked the second they came inside. I pocketed my cell and went to greet them.

"No one."

"Yeah, I bet." She smirked.

"How are you feeling?" I asked Alessia. She looked exhausted, dark circles ringing her eyes.

"I… I'm okay. They said he should wake up. That's good, right?"

"Yeah, that's real good, Sia."

"Dad gave you a ride here?"

Bella nodded. "He and Mama are heading to the hospital to sit with Uncle Toni."

"Make yourselves comfortable," I said. "I can order some pizza and we can watch a movie? Might take your mind off everything."

"Sure." The helplessness in Alessia's eyes gutted me. She loved her dad, loved him something fierce. If anything happened to him…

I shook the thoughts away. Uncle Toni would pull through. He had to.

The girls got settled while I grabbed a menu from the noticeboard. I might not have had anyone to lean on, not the way Enzo had Nora and Nicco had Ari, but I could do this for my cousin. I could be her person.

"What movie are you thinking?" I asked, diving onto the couch beside Bella.

"Scemo," she muttered, and I chuckled. "How do you feel about Magic Mike?"

"Oh hell no. I'm not watching a bunch of dudes get naked and dance."

"Insecure about your sexuality, brother?"

"Pulce."

"Fine, we'll pass on Magic Mike. How about the latest Marvel film then?"

"I can get on board with that." I kicked up my feet and set about ordering the pizza.

At least entertaining the girls would keep my mind off Caitlin.

"Matt," Bella's voice trickled through my subconscious. "Matt..."

"Yeah?" I bolted upright. "Huh, what—"

"Your cell phone, it's ringing." She thrust it at me, and I blinked rapidly, trying to get my bearings.

I was half-draped on the couch, my neck stiff and my eyes weary. I must have dozed off during the film.

"What time is it?"

"Late; a little past midnight."

"Shit. Where's Sia?" I glanced around.

"She went to bed hours ago. You fell asleep and I was watching Magic Mike, but it just finished. Who's calling?" She motioned to the phone still in my hand.

It had stopped vibrating, but sure enough, there were two missed calls.

Luis.

"I need to take this." Stumbling off the couch, I went over to the kitchen and dialed his number. The second he answered, I breathed, "What happened?"

"Shit, Matteo. I'm sorry I called. She's awake now. She's—"

"What. Happened?" I ground out, instantly going on high alert.

"She was having a nightmare, a real bad one, and I couldn't wake her. I panicked and I didn't want to disturb Nicco, not since Antonio is... and I tried Enzo, but it rang out. So I called you. But everything is fine, she's fine."

Yeah, fuck that.

I let out a weary breath and glanced over at my sister who watched me intently.

"I'll be there soon," I said.

"Matt, I'm not sure that's a good—"

"I'll be there soon." I hung up and pulled up a new message, texting Alessia's bodyguard. The building had its own security, but I wasn't prepared to leave the girls without someone I trusted watching them.

"You're leaving?" Bella asked.

"Yeah, I need to go check on... a friend."

"A friend, right." Her brow quirked. "What's her name?"

Jesus. Bella always had a way of seeing straight through me.

"You don't need to worry about her."

"She's got you all tied up in knots. Seems like I definitely need to worry, Matt."

"Jay will come watch you while—"

"We don't need babysitting, Matt." She huffed.

"I know you don't, but Nicco would have my balls if I left Alessia unsupervised."

"Fine, whatever. Will you be back?"

"I… I don't know. But I'll text you, okay?"

"Okay." She stood up and came over to me, looping her arms around my waist. "You're a good big brother, Matt."

"I'll always keep you safe, pulce."

"I know."

It was my promise to her. I'd seen what this life could do to people—how it could tear families apart. Arabella was innocent, and she deserved a future. She deserved to chase her dreams.

The idea that she could one day be used as a pawn or collateral against the Family terrified the shit out of me.

A knock at the door pulled me from my thoughts and I eased Bella out of my arms, striding across the apartment to let Jay in.

"Mr. Bellatoni."

"Thanks for coming."

"Of course." He nodded stiffly. "It's what Mr. Marchetti pays me for."

"Hey, Jay." My sister gave him a small wave.

"Miss Bellato—"

"How many times do I have to say it, Jay? Call me Bella."

"Very well, Miss Bellatoni."

She grumbled, throwing her hands up in frustration. A smile curved my lips. Arianne was just the same with our security team. She preferred to keep things on a first name basis, but our men weren't used to it.

"I need to go out for a while," I said. "Bella is about to go to bed, so you won't need to entertain her." I gave her a pointed look.

"Ruin all my fun, why don't you."

"I'll check in with you later." I turned my attention back to Jay.

"I'll handle things here," he said.

"Thanks." I grabbed my jacket and keys.

"I hope she's worth it," Bella called after me, her words hitting me square in the chest.

I didn't look back as I left the apartment with only one thing on my mind.

Getting to Caitlin.

It took me too fucking long to get to the cabin. By the time I pulled up next to Luis's SUV, it was almost one-thirty.

The cabin was steeped in darkness, only a faint, flickering amber glow coming from inside. I padded up the steps and knocked quietly. Nothing. Pulling out my cell phone, I dialed Luis's number.

"Matteo?" He groaned. "Tell me that's not you—"

"Open the door," I said.

"Cait doesn't want—"

"We both know I'm not leaving until I've seen her, Luis. So do yourself a favor and open the fucking door." I hung up and a second later, the lock unlatched and the door swung open.

"Have you lost your goddamn mind?" He glared at me.

"Where is she?"

"In bed… asleep."

Some of the panic coursing through me abated. "I need to see her." I barged past him, but he grabbed my shoulder.

My eyes met his and he blew out an exasperated breath. "Seriously, Matteo, this is a bad idea. I shouldn't have called."

"What happened?"

Relenting, Luis closed the door and ushered me over to the couch. I wanted to go to her, to see with my own eyes that she was okay. But maybe he was right. Maybe I had been too hasty.

Jesus.

I was a mess.

All over a woman who had made it perfectly clear she wanted nothing to do with me.

"Here, you look like you could do with this." He handed me a beer.

"She's okay?"

"She is now." He ran a hand down his face and sat opposite me in the armchair angled toward the open fire.

"I've never seen anything like it, and I've seen a lot in my time," he said. "She was wild… thrashing and fighting some invisible monster. I couldn't wake her…"

"You did the right thing calling me."

"Did I? The second I told her I had, she lost it."

Fuck.

"Did she tell you what it was about?" Although I had a pretty good idea what haunted her dreams. Or rather, *who*.

"No. Wouldn't say a word."

I took a long pull on my beer, stretching my legs out before me. I felt calmer now I was here, knowing she was sleeping in the next room. The urge to storm in there and check on her simmered beneath the surface still, but I could think clearly enough to know that probably wasn't the best idea—not if I ever wanted her to talk to me again.

"What happened to her?" he asked, his eyes narrowed with grim curiosity.

"We still don't know for certain. But we know enough that Zander DiMarco will get what's coming to him." Anger skittered down my spine. I'd never felt so much wrath as I did for him, and the last few months hadn't exactly been a walk in the park for my cousins and our family.

I glanced back at the hall, imagining Caitlin curled up in bed asleep. If I could just see her for a second, see with my own eyes that she was okay.

“A word of advice from someone much older and wiser than you,” Luis said, drawing my attention. “Whatever’s running through your head right now... Don’t do it.”

He was right. Of course he was fucking right.

But I wasn’t sure I could listen.

For once in my life, I wasn’t sure I could be the better man.

Until a small voice startled me.

“Matteo?”

My heart almost lurched into my throat when I turned and met Caitlin’s weary gaze.

“You came,” she choked out.

I got up and strode toward her, only stopping when I was in touching distance. She stared up at me, fear and something I wanted to believe was relief glittering in her eyes.

“Yeah,” I said, curving my hand around the back of her neck and drawing her close. “I came.”

ELEVEN

CAITLIN

MATTEO HELD ME, his big muscular arms cocooning me, shielding me from the world.

My fingers twisted into his jacket as I breathed him in.

"Shh, Tink, I've got you."

My body trembled as I sobbed into his chest. When I'd woken up with a start, and heard his voice, anger had flooded me… but it quickly melted away when I realized he'd come for me.

I tried to make out I didn't care to protect myself, but really it meant more than I could ever put into words.

Luis gave the two of us some space, mumbling something about retiring for the night. Matteo thanked him before guiding me over to the couch and pulling me down beside him.

"How are you feeling?" he asked.

"I can't believe you're here."

His hand rested against my cheek, his thumb brushing a soothing line over my jaw. "I told you, I will always come."

Why, I wanted to ask, but I swallowed the question. Part of me knew why; I just didn't want to admit it.

"Do you want to tell me what happened?"

"It was just a nightmare. I get them sometimes."

"About DiMarco?" His eyes narrowed, searching my face for answers I didn't have.

"Zander DiMarco isn't the only monster I've ever faced, Matteo."

God, why did I say that?

He went rigid. "What does that mean?"

"Nothing," I sighed, glancing away. "Forget I said anything."

Matteo slid his fingers under my jaw and gently tilted my face up to meet his. "Talk to me, Caitlin. That's all I'm asking."

My shoulders sagged a little at his admission. Not that I expected him to try anything—I didn't get those vibes from Matteo. Besides, he was clearly very against hurting women. But still, I'd fallen for that act before.

Even though I wanted to trust him—and I did—I needed to keep my wits about me.

"You know, not a single day has gone by when I haven't thought about you," he said quietly, so quietly I almost missed it.

"Matteo." I breathed out slowly. "You can't say things like that to me." Peeking up at him, I studied his face. Strong jaw and glittering blue eyes. His dirty-blond hair fell over his face, and the smattering of stubble on his jaw sharpened his boy-next-door good looks.

"Just did, Tink, and I don't regret a single word." He gazed down at me, and I felt the strange tug between us. I'd felt it that night all those months ago. I'd felt it again when I saw him standing there in the hospital... and I felt it now.

No one had ever made me feel the way Matteo Bellatoni made me feel. And that was a dangerous thing.

"You can't call me that anymore. I don't have the t-shirt."

My Tinkerbell t-shirt was my favorite thing and I'd worn it the night Matteo and I spent together. But it was with the rest of my things at my apartment—the one I could never return to, all thanks to Zander's temper.

"You'll always be Tink to me." Matteo brushed the hair from my face and smiled, and damn if my heart didn't flutter wildly in my chest.

This man. This determined, gorgeous, honest man.

"What?" he asked, and I realized I was gawking at him.

"Nothing, it's late. You probably need to get back—"

"Cait, stop. I came to make sure you're okay. I'm not going anywhere."

"But—"

"No buts." He pressed his finger against my lips and my breath caught. "I can take one of the guest rooms."

"You're staying?"

"Yeah. In the morning, I'm going to feed you breakfast, and then you're going to show me how much progress you've made on that puzzle."

"You're serious?"

"Do I look like I'm joking? Now, let's go." He got up, pulling me with him.

"Uh, go where?"

"To bed. You just said so yourself, it's late." Hands on my shoulders, Matteo gently nudged me down the hall, stopping at my room. "You'll be okay?"

"I... uh, yeah." I glanced back at him.

"Okay." He nodded. "You need anything, just shout... or text. I'll leave my phone on."

"You're going to go stay in one of the guest rooms, just like that?"

Matteo's brow furrowed. "Yeah, why?"

"I… nothing."

I wasn't used to this. I was used to men taking what they wanted, when they wanted it. The desire in his eyes was obvious. The way the air crackled between us whenever we were near. Matteo wanted me—he just wasn't going to do anything about it without my permission.

He chuckled. "I am quite capable of being around you and controlling myself, you know."

Heat flooded my cheeks. "I wasn't… that's not…" Oh God. He was looking at me with so much yearning, I felt stripped bare.

"I should… it's late and I…"

He leaned in, dropping his mouth to my ear and whispered. "Breathe, Tink. Just breathe." His warm breath tickled my skin, sending a shiver through me.

I felt his lips curve as he said, "Although it's nice to know I affect you too."

Trouble.

I was in so much trouble.

"Goodnight, Matteo." I met his gaze, smiling. "And thank you."

I might not have wanted him to come here, but the truth was…

It was exactly what I needed.

The smell of coffee and bacon lured me from a peaceful sleep. My eyes fluttered open as my stomach rumbled and I smiled.

Until the events of the night before hit me and embarrassment washed over me.

I had a nightmare. A bad one. Luis had eventually shaken me awake, but not before he'd witnessed me lashing out at invisible monsters, screaming and sweating as if they were right there in front of me.

And Matteo…

Oh God. Matteo was here.

It was too early to process what that meant, so I opted for coffee first.

After freshening up in the bathroom, I pulled on some leggings and an off-the-shoulder sweater, tamed my unruly curls into a low ponytail and went in search of breakfast.

"Morning," Matteo said from his position at the cooktop. "I wondered if the smell would wake you."

"You cook?" I asked, surprised.

"Don't get too excited, it's bacon and eggs. Hardly à la carte cuisine. Coffee?"

"Sure. Cream, two sugars."

"Two, huh?" He smiled, and my heart fluttered.

"What?"

"Nothing." His smile morphed to a smirk. "I was just thinking you're already sweet enough."

"Matteo." I rolled my eyes, feeling my cheeks heat under his intense regard. "Where's Luis?" I changed the subject, needing to break the simmering connection between us.

"He's around. Don't worry, you're safe with me."

"I know."

His brow lifted but he didn't comment. "Did you manage to get some sleep?"

"Surprisingly, I did."

"Does that happen a lot... with the nightmares?"

"They come and go. There isn't really a pattern."

"What you said before..."

"Please, don't." I sighed, averting my gaze. I shouldn't have said that last night. But Matteo made it too easy. He made me want things—things I could never have.

"Sorry." He continued cooking the bacon, not looking at me again. My stomach twisted, hating the sudden tension lingering between us.

Matteo plated up the bacon and eggs in silence, pushing a plate toward me.

"Thank you," I said, my stomach growling again.

He fought a smile. "You're hungry."

"Starved, actually."

"Glad I could help."

Matteo didn't eat. He just stood there, watching me devour my breakfast. My body hummed with awareness, his gaze caressing my skin.

"So, about that puzzle," he said. "Are you almost done?"

"You're kidding right? It's like two-thousand pieces."

"Eat up and I'll help you for an hour before I have to get back."

"Why?" I blurted out.

"Do I need a reason other than I want to?"

Pressing my lips together, I shook my head.

"I'm going to make a call. I'll be right back."

"Oh God, your sister," I said, remembering he was supposed to be babysitting her last night.

"Relax. Bella is fine. I left her at my place with our cousin and her bodyguard."

My eyes widened to saucers as I spluttered, "Y-you did what?"

He chuckled. "You're cute when you care."

"I... you didn't have to do that. I would never have—"

"I wanted to come, Cait. I can call you Cait, right?"

"Y-yeah." My chest tightened.

A faint smile traced his lips. Warm. Inviting. Like sunshine on a stormy day.

Matteo was gorgeous and having one hundred percent of his attention was completely disarming.

"Finish your breakfast. I'll be back." He tapped the counter and walked off, and suddenly, I didn't feel so hungry anymore.

"Yes!" Matteo whooped, fist punching the air as he slid in another piece of the puzzle.

He was good. Almost as good as Luis. I'd been too mesmerized watching him to really contribute. He caught me watching him more than once but didn't comment, merely flashed me a knowing smile and went back to the puzzle.

"Are you sure you don't need to go?"

"Do you want me to go?"

"No, I just..."

"Caitlin, I meant what I said before. I don't expect anything. This isn't a transaction where I do you a favor and then you owe me. I came because I care. Because ever since that night, I haven't been able to get you out of my mind."

"Matteo—"

"I know," he let out a heavy sigh, "you don't want to talk about it, and that's okay. I can respect that. But I can't ignore the fact that I thought I'd never see you again, and then here you are, under my family's protection. It might not mean anything to you... but it means something to me."

Without thinking, I leaned over and kissed him. Matteo went rigid beneath my touch. My fingers curled into his t-shirt, but then his hands cupped my face, and he took control.

And I let him.

His tongue gently nudged my lips apart, sliding against my own and coaxing a whimper up my throat. He tasted exquisite, his lips firm yet soft, demanding yet patient as he licked my mouth in slow lazy strokes, as if he was familiarizing himself with the shape of my lips and savoring their taste.

My heart galloped in my chest, my toes curling inside the fluffy slippers Arianne had gifted me.

"Fuck, Tink," he rasped, touching his head to mine and inhaling a ragged breath. "That was..."

"Unexpected."

Our laughter mingled together, finding its own harmony.

"You made a fatal mistake," he said.

My brows furrowed. "I did?"

"Yeah, now whenever I see you, all I'll be able to think about is kissing you again."

My stomach dipped, heat coursing through my veins. Matteo brushed his nose along mine, stealing another kiss. This one was more playful, even a little clumsy. But it was still one of the best kisses I've ever had.

I let out a contented sigh as he pulled away.

"You liked that?"

“It wasn’t awful.” I smiled.

“Good to know.” A faint smirk traced his lips.

His phone began vibrating, but he glanced at the screen and ignored it.

“Don’t you need to take that?” I asked.

“It can wait.”

It stopped vibrating but two seconds later started again.

“I think somebody wants to get a hold of you.”

He muttered something in Italian under his breath and clambered to his feet. “I’ll be right back.”

I watched him answer his cell as he walked toward the window.

“What?” he barked, and I flinched.

It was instinct. An old habit that was hard to break.

Matteo lowered his voice to the point where I couldn’t hear what he was saying, but whatever it was, it didn’t look good. His eyes narrowed, his jaw clenched tight as he listened to whoever was on the other end of the line.

“Yeah, okay.” He hung up and came back over to me.

“Is everything okay?”

“I need to go,” he said, barely meeting my gaze as he loomed over me. A wave of dejection crashed over me.

“Oh, okay.”

“You’ll be okay? Luis is right down the hall. Maybe he can come finish off the puzzle with you.”

“Yeah… I’ll be fine.” Disappointment welled inside me. “I’ll see you out.” I went to get up, but Matteo shook his head.

“Don’t worry about it, I can see myself out.”

By the time I got to my feet he was already at the door. “Matteo,” I called, panic rising inside me. “Are you sure everything’s okay?”

“Yeah, it’s nothing you need to worry about.”

My heart sank at the invisible line he was drawing between us.

It wasn’t supposed to hurt because I was supposed to keep him at arm’s length. But he’d clawed his way inside… and more surprisingly, I’d liked it.

I liked how he made me feel.

Except right now. Now our time together felt tainted, wrong somehow.

It felt like a mistake.

“I’ll see you, Caitlin.”

Not Cait.

Not Tink.

Caitlin.

As if he hadn’t been kissing me only minutes ago.

“Matteo,” I blurted out, but he was already gone, the door slamming closed behind him.

I stood there long after the rumble of his car had faded, wondering what had happened to make him leave in such a hurry.

Without even looking at me.

"Caitlin?" Luis rapped on my door. "I've made some minestrone, if you want to join me?"

"Just a second." I swallowed back the tears burning my eyes and slipped into the bathroom.

It had been hours since Matteo had left, and I'd heard nothing. Not a single text.

It shouldn't have bothered me half as much as it did. After all, I'd been the one who had acted so coolly with him in the beginning.

But something had changed last night when he came for me. At least, I thought it had.

He'd cracked the fortress around my heart and found a way in. And it hadn't panicked me or paralyzed me with fear. Instead, I'd wanted it.

I'd wanted him.

I'd kissed him for God's sake and then he'd gotten that call and left in such a hurry he hadn't even said goodbye, not properly.

I joined Luis at the breakfast counter, smiling weakly when he pushed a bowl of minestrone toward me. "Eat," he said. "And then you can tell me what has you moping around like someone kicked your puppy."

"I am not..." I bit my lip. He was right. I was moping, but with good reason.

"Wouldn't have to do with the way Matteo hauled ass out of here earlier, would it?"

"You saw him leave?"

"Heard him more like." Luis shrugged. "You know, he's a good man, Cait. One of the best people I know. If he left suddenly, he had good reason."

"I wouldn't know, he didn't tell me." My minestrone became mightily interesting as I avoided Luis's questioning gaze.

"This is good," I added.

"It is, but I don't think you'll find any answers at the bottom of the dish."

I peeked up at him. "You're awfully chatty today... and nosey."

"It's my job to know what's going on with my marks." His lips curved with amusement.

"Somehow I find that hard to believe." I smiled back. "Thank you, for the meal."

"You're not alone, Cait. I know it can't be easy, being stuck here with me, but Arianne and Nicco mean well—"

"Oh no, I don't think that at all. What they've done for me..." I swallowed over the lump in my throat. It was more than anyone else had ever done for me. But it didn't change the fact that I couldn't hide out here forever. Eventually, I would have to go back to my life. Wherever that may be.

"They won't let you fight your battles alone. Of that you can be sure."

How could I ask that of them though?

Zander DiMarco was one of their business partners; he wouldn't go quietly. I didn't expect—or want—them to go to war with him.

Only I couldn't see a way out.

Not unless I left...

And never looked back.

TWELVE

MATTEO

"FUCK." I stared down at the dead body, the face barely recognizable. "It's definitely him?"

"Shaun Demetri. Twenty-six years old. Cause of death was blunt force trauma to the head."

"Thanks, Doc," Enzo said, nudging me forward. He waited until we were in the hall to say, "You thinking what I'm thinking?"

"Zander got fed up with chasing her and decided to try and torture it out of him." Acid washed in my stomach.

When Enzo had called me with the news, I'd been so overcome with fear and anger, I had to get out of the cabin before I did something stupid. Looking back, I probably didn't handle it the best way, but I couldn't tell Caitlin, not yet. Not until we confirmed what we already suspected.

DiMarco wasn't going to let her go—he was going to exhaust every possible option available to him to find her. And eventually, he'd hit the jackpot, and someone would give him the vital piece of information he needed.

That we had her.

"We need to deal with him, and soon," I muttered, jamming my fingers into my hair and tugging the ends.

"I know, but it's not that straightforward."

"What do you mean, it's not that straightforward? He's a woman-beating piece of shit. We don't need to be associated with—"

"Word on the street is he made a deal with Lombardi."

"What?" I balked. "Lombardi? But they're not in Rhode Island."

The Lombardi were a crime family operating out of New Haven, Connecticut. Their boss, Massimo Lombardi, was a real nasty piece of work.

"I don't know all the details, but Lucino said he got wind of Dominic Cabrioles and Jasper Peshie being at DiMarco's a few days ago."

Fuck. Dominic Cabrioles was Massimo Lombardi's right-hand man. If he was in Providence sniffing around DiMarco's club, this was bad news.

Bad fucking news.

"When did you find this out?" My teeth ground together.

"Last night."

"And you didn't think to call me? Fuck, E, I went there and you—"

"Whoa, cous. Don't turn this into something it's not. I didn't tell you because I knew you were heading there and I thought... no, I knew, you needed time with her without this shitshow hanging over your heads. This is bigger than just Caitlin, Matt. If the Lombardi are involved... it changes everything."

"What does Nicco say?"

"Nicco's mind is elsewhere right now."

Of course it was. Uncle Toni was still in the hospital.

"Does my old man know they're sniffing around?"

"Lucino told him, yeah."

I went rigid.

"Relax. He doesn't know about Caitlin yet." He released a steady breath. "Uncle Michele is cautious. He doesn't want to start anything that might cause waves. Besides, he doesn't know who she is to you. If you told—"

"No, I'm not ready. I don't even know if she is anything to me."

Enzo gave me a pointed look. "That's bullshit and you know it."

"I don't mean..." I released a heavy sigh. "I like her, E. More than like her, but she's dealing with a lot of stuff, and she still won't talk about what happened."

"Does it matter?"

We exited the county morgue and headed for Enzo's GTO.

"Of course it fucking matters. I don't want to take advantage of her." Just like I didn't want to be her rebound.

When she'd kissed me earlier... fuck, it was like all my dreams come true. It was all I wanted. But then Enzo called, and it was like being doused with a bucket of ice-cold water. A harsh reminder of everything we still had to deal with—things I wasn't sure Caitlin was ready to face. How could I even think about being with her until she came to terms with everything.

And now her co-worker—her friend—was dead.

It would kill her, knowing DiMarco had hurt him.

I climbed inside the car and buckled up. Enzo slid in a second later, running a hand through his hair. "It would be so fucking easy to go settle this right now," he said quietly, a deadly edge to his voice. His hands gripped the steering wheel, the blood draining from his knuckles. "I've never liked that piece of shit... but we have to be smart. Especially if he's in bed with the Lombardi."

"This is a total clusterfuck," I seethed.

Enzo glanced over at me. "We'll figure it out. We need to get out of town before DiMarco gets word that we're sniffing around." He stepped on the gas.

The coroner had agreed to be discreet for a fee, but his silence wouldn't withstand torture.

"DiMarco isn't ballsy enough to start picking off people in positions of authority."

"No?" My brow lifted. I had a feeling we didn't know what he was capable of.

"Any word from Nicco?" Enzo asked as I checked my cell.

"Nothing."

"I keep thinking about what will happen if Uncle T doesn't pull through…"

"Same," I confessed. "Nicco is strong." One of the strongest guys I knew. But losing your father and becoming boss was no easy burden to shoulder.

"I used to dream about the day Nicco stepped up and we became his capos. But I didn't ever want it to happen like this," Enzo said.

I relaxed as we sped out of Providence and hit the highway leading back to Verona County.

"You doing okay?"

"Yeah." I inhaled a deep breath.

"You know why we couldn't go—"

"I know." I snapped, the anger I'd fought so hard to contain spilling over.

We were so close to him… so fucking close, and yet, I had to push my need for vengeance away and focus on the task at hand.

All in the name of the Family.

"I think you should talk to your old man," Enzo said. "If the worst happens and Uncle T… Nicco won't be in any fit state to lead, not straightaway. Which means all decisions will defer to Uncle Michele. He needs to know about her, Matt. About your relationship with her. This is personal and it affects all of us."

I scoffed at that. We didn't have a relationship… did we?

Memories of how good it had felt kissing her invaded my mind, making my body stir to life. She'd been so bold in that moment. I'd caught a glimpse of the girl from last summer. The girl who wasn't afraid to take what she wanted.

When I didn't answer, he added, "You know I'm right."

"Yeah." I dropped my head back against the headrest.

I could already imagine how that conversation would go. My father was a reasonable man. A good man. A family man. But when he found out we had given safe haven to Caitlin, I had no doubt he would have a thing or two to say about the fallout if DiMarco found out. It wasn't that he agreed with hurting women—he didn't, at all—but he would put the Family ahead of emotion. Always.

And when he found out who she was to me—who I wanted her to be—I had no doubt he'd remind me of the Omertà, our code of silence, and what it meant for outsiders.

Caitlin knew who we were. No doubt she had a pretty good idea what we did and how we did it. My father wouldn't look too kindly on a woman who now had valuable information about the Marchetti and at least one of their residences.

Shit.

Maybe I should have told him sooner.

"What?" Enzo broke the thick silence.

"Maybe we shouldn't have brought her back to Verona."

"Do you really believe that? Because I'm not buying it for a second."

"My old man isn't going to like it."

"Then you'd better convince him that you're serious about her."

"What?" My brows pinched.

"If he thinks you're... together, then he can't exactly toss her to the wolves, can he?"

"I can't ask her to play pretend just to pacify my old man." Besides, it would be torture when I wanted the real thing.

"I'll come clean, but I'm not going to ask her to pretend... DiMarco will kill her if she goes back. We had no choice but to offer her a safe haven."

My father wasn't a monster. He would understand, even if he didn't like it.

"Are you going to text her or just stare at your phone the whole ride back?"

"Honestly, I don't know what to say." Her friend was dead. Tortured at the hands of DiMarco or his men.

"He already knew about the hospital, so there isn't much else Shaun could have told him."

"Somehow I don't think she'll see that as any kind of silver lining."

"She deserves to know," he said.

"And I'll tell her, I will." I just didn't know how. I already had to fix things after the way I hightailed it out of there this morning. Now I had to figure out how to tell her about Shaun.

"She was just starting to warm up to me," I said wearily. "But this... this will ruin her."

"You don't know that. She's stronger than she looks, Matt."

"How can you be so sure?"

"It's in her eyes, cous. She's a fighter."

I didn't like to think about what had made her that way, but I couldn't deny the merit in his words. Caitlin had hinted at something similar herself.

"I still can't believe you left Bella and Alessia with Jay last night. I bet he loved that."

"He had it handled."

"Like you gave him any choice." Enzo chuckled.

A pang of guilt went through me. He had a point—I'd just up and left them with Jay. Anything could have happened. But all I'd been able to think about was getting to Caitlin.

She blinded me to everything else, and that was a dangerous thing. Because when you were distracted—as I had been since she appeared in my life again—you dropped your guard.

The scenery turned familiar and the ache in my chest abated slightly. Caitlin was safe here. Not even someone as arrogant as DiMarco would be stupid enough to come into the heart of Marchetti territory and try to take her from us.

From me.

I left Enzo to go check in on Nicco and Arianne, and I headed to my parents' house. He was right—I needed to talk to my father. And then, when I'd ironed things out with him, I needed to go to the cabin and break the news to Caitlin about Shaun.

"Ah, Matteo," Dad said as I entered the kitchen. "I was wondering when you'd show up. Your sister said some interesting things this morning."

"She did?" My chest tightened.

"Something about you leaving late last night to go see a woman." His brow lifted as he shook out his newspaper.

"I... we need to talk."

"Sit," he commanded. "Tell me what's on your mind."

"There's something you should know."

He lowered the newspaper. "Go on."

"When we drove out to see DiMarco, we got... interrupted."

"Yes, Nora was sick, was she not?"

"That's not entirely what happened."

His brows bunched together. "I'm listening."

"Enzo got a call from the hospital down in Pawtucket. He'd given his number to one of DiMarco's girls, he was concerned that DiMarco was hurting her."

"I see. And you went to check in on her?"

I nodded, growing hot all over. "I... I recognized her. She and I... we had a thing last summer."

"A thing—" Realization dawned in his eyes. "And how serious was this thing?"

"It was one night." I rubbed a hand over my face. "But I wanted it to be more."

"And she's one of DiMarco's dancers you say?"

"We suspect she's more than that to him. He... he hurt her, badly, and her friend—a guy that works at the club—got her out. But she said she couldn't go back for fear of what DiMarco would do."

My old man went as stiff as a board. "What did you do, figlio mio?"

"We... fuck." I expelled a long breath. "We brought her back to Verona County with us. She's at the family cabin with Luis."

"Sei proprio un coglione! What the hell were you thinking?" he seethed, palm flat against the table.

"You didn't see her lying there, broken and bruised at the hands of that... that fucker."

"But bringing her here? Do you have any idea what you might have started? And Enzo went along with this?"

"We agreed—"

"Matteo," he tsked. "Did either of you stop to consider what happens if DiMarco finds out we're harboring his—"

"Don't." The word rumbled in my chest. "She is not his."

His eyes flashed with understanding. "You feel for the woman?"

"I do." I lifted my chin in defiance. "And sending her back to DiMarco is not an option."

Tension radiated between us and then I added, "He killed the bartender who helped her."

"Che diavolo!"

"It's where we went earlier. We got a heads up from Lucino that the bartender had been reported missing. He turned up dead."

"You saw the body?"

I nodded. "He was pretty messed up. The official report says he slipped down his stairwell and sustained blunt force trauma to his head."

"Merda!" My father's usual composed façade cracked slightly. "This is the last thing we need right now."

"I know. We should have come to you straightaway, but I—"

"You were too busy thinking with your heart and not your head." He cut me with a scathing look.

"I care about her—"

"A girl you barely know. I take it you didn't know she belonged to DiMarco when you tumbled with her between the sheets?"

Jesus. This was so awkward. I didn't want to discuss the details of that night with him. Not when just thinking about her soft skin pressed up against mine, the taste of her lips, made my body stir to life.

I shifted uncomfortably, clearing my throat. "This isn't about my relationship with Caitlin; it's about doing what's right. She needed help and she called Enzo. What were we supposed to do?"

"You should have called me the second you got to the hospital and realized who she was."

"Well, we didn't. And now she's our responsibility."

He scoffed at that. "Just make sure she doesn't become your doom, Son. Who else knows about this?"

"Nicco, Ari, Enzo and Nora, me, Luis... the bellhop would have seen her at Nicco's place. Maybe security."

"We need to contain this before someone talks and word gets out. DiMarco was a loose cannon before, we don't need to light the fuse on him before we figure out how best to proceed."

"I'll call Nicco and—"

"No, I'll handle it. Niccolò has enough on his plate. What's done is done. We all just have to hope DiMarco doesn't find out before we're ready for him to know."

I went rigid at that. "What do you mean... before we're ready for him to know?"

"Son, be reasonable. We can't just take out DiMarco. He has a string of businesses, a network of employees. He has connections. It wouldn't surprise me if he has a contingency plan should we ever feel the need to sever our ties with him."

"One way or another, this will get out," he said. "Unless she disappears, and something tells me you won't stand by and watch that happen. Anything else you want to tell me..."

Shit. "The Lombardi."

"So you did know." My father let out an exasperated breath.

"About the Lombardi sniffing around his clubs, yes."

"Porca puttana! And when were you going to bring this to my attention?"

"I... I've been kind of distracted."

"By a piece of ass." He snorted. "I thought I raised you better than that."

"No, you raised me to respect women and always do right by them. I learned that from you, Papa."

He studied me, shaking his head slightly. "I take it you're going to break the news to her?"

"Yeah, she needs to know the truth." No matter how much it would gut me to tell her.

"Then go be with her." He stood and gripped my shoulder. "If she has captured your heart, then she must be a good woman."

I swallowed over the giant fucking lump in my throat.

Because he was right.

Caitlin had captured my heart. It had taken precisely one intense night with her for me to fall. And not a single day had gone by where my thoughts hadn't drifted to the redheaded angel who had stolen a piece of me.

I couldn't let her vanish, not again.

But it wasn't my choice to make.

THIRTEEN

CAITLIN

LUIS WAS at the door talking to someone.

Not just anyone.

Matteo.

"Cait," he said, keeping the door half-closed preventing Matteo's access. "There's someone here to see you."

I could have kissed him for giving me the chance to speak up for myself. For giving me the choice. It wasn't something I was used to which only made me appreciate it all the more.

"It's okay," I replied. "You can let him in."

I wanted to hear what he had to say for himself after his stellar performance this morning.

But when Matteo stepped inside, I knew immediately that something was wrong.

"What happened?" I clutched my throat, frozen to the spot.

"Can you give us a minute?" he asked Luis, who glanced at me.

"It's okay." I nodded.

"I'm going for a walk. I won't be far."

"She's safe with me," Matteo said.

Luis gave him a curt nod, but I didn't miss the silent warning in his eyes. It was strange to have someone standing up for me, protecting me. But I liked Luis, I liked him a whole lot. He was easy to be around, if not a little aloof. He didn't probe or push, and he didn't feel the need to fill the silence. It made a difference to be around such a centered male.

He left and the air in the cabin turned thick with tension.

"We should sit," Matteo suggested.

"I'd prefer to stand." I folded my arms around myself, bracing myself for whatever he was about to say.

"The bartender... Shaun..."

"Oh God." Bile rushed up my throat, a wave of nausea battering my insides as I reached out for the counter to steady myself. "He's... dead?"

"I'm so sorry," he started approaching, "I'm so fucking—"

"Don't." I held up my hand. "Just don't."

Shaun.

Kind, funny, big-hearted Shaun. He'd gotten me out of Providence and delivered me to safety... and this was the thanks he got.

"D-did... did he suffer?"

"Cait," Matteo choked out.

"Please. I need to know."

"It would have happened quickly." His expression hardened and I knew he was only pacifying me. But it was probably for the best. I didn't really want to think about what DiMarco and his men had done to Shaun.

Poor Shaun, he didn't deserve this.

It was all my fault.

I should never have let him talk me into running.

"What will happen to him?"

"His family have been notified already."

"And the police?"

Matteo's eyes flared. "As far as the police are concerned, it was an accident. There will be no further investigation."

"But... he was murdered. He was killed by Zander and his..." Tears rolled down my cheeks as reality slammed into me. Zander had done this because of me—to find me.

"Oh no! What if Shaun talked? What if—"

"He didn't know anything past telling you to run. Even if he did talk, he wouldn't have given DiMarco anything more than he already knows."

"He's really gone?" My voice cracked as I stared at Matteo, silently willing him to fix this. To lie and tell me everything was fine.

But everything wasn't fine. And it wouldn't be, so long as Zander was still out there.

An idea popped into my head, and I blurted out, "You can kill him, right? Hire someone to take him out, make it look like an accident or something?"

"It's not that simple—"

"Yes, yes, it is. It solves all our problems."

"Tink." He came closer still, close enough to curve his hand around my arm and gently brace me. "There is nothing more I want than to put a bullet between his eyes, but I can't. Not yet. Not until—"

"Until what?" I shrieked, a tidal wave of emotion crashing over me. "Until he finds me and points a gun at *my* head? You said you cared about me. You said you wouldn't let anything happen to me. You said—"

"Shh." He pulled me into his chest, holding me tight. My fingers clawed at his sweater as I sobbed violently against him.

"I never asked for any of this... I never wanted it."

"Shh, Tink. I've got you. I'm here." He nuzzled my hair, breathing me in.

My heart stuttered in my chest, overwhelmed by all the emotions flowing through me.

"He won't stop," I breathed. "He won't stop until he finds me, Matteo. And when he does—"

"No." He held me at arm's length, forcing me to look at him. "You do not belong to Zander DiMarco, do you hear me? If he wants you, then he'll have to come through me to get you."

My heart swelled but it didn't last. How could I possibly stand here, swooning, while Shaun lay dead on a steel trolley in the morgue.

Slowly, the tears subsided as I grew numb. This was my fault.

My fault.

"You hungry?" Matteo asked, guiding me over to one of the stools.

"Not really."

"Understandable, but you've got to eat something. How about something light?"

"Fine." I stared off into space.

Food was the last thing on my mind, but it had been an intense few days.

Matteo went to the refrigerator and started collecting up ingredients. "I call this, eggs à la Bellatoni."

"If this is your attempt at making me laugh, you might need to try harder." I sucked in a ragged breath, trying not to succumb to the tears again.

"Shit, Tink, I'm sorry. I don't know what I'm supposed to do here." He blanched, running a hand through his messy, dark-blond hair. Without another word, he rounded the breakfast counter and ran his thumb along the line of my jaw before burying his hand deep into my curls. "I wish I could make this all go away. I wish I could fix it."

"Matt," I breathed, fisting his sweater.

We stayed like that, wrapped up in one another until Luis came back into the cabin and cleared his throat.

"A word," he said to Matteo.

Matteo glanced down at me, and I nodded. "Go. I'm okay."

For a second, I thought he might kiss me, but then he pulled away, following Luis back outside.

I waited, wondering what could possibly be happening now. But I was too distracted to worry. My heart, too broken to care.

Shaun was a good guy. He was my friend. And Zander had hurt him because he'd helped me. I still couldn't believe it. But there was no doubt in my mind now that I could never return to Providence, to my friends there.

I wondered what Zander had told them, how he'd covered my disappearance.

I wondered if anyone cared.

Gisele might. Marielle too. But to a lot of the girls, I was merely the competition. The boss's pet. They didn't understand why he'd taken such a shine to me. I didn't either.

All I knew was, once he'd set his sights on me, Zander DiMarco's obsession with me began.

Matteo came back inside, taking the air with him.

"Is everything okay?" I asked.

"Yeah. Luis needs to head back into the city."

"Oh."

"I'll stay until he returns." His eyes narrowed slightly. "You know, I came back for you last summer."

"W-what?"

He nodded. "It drove me out of my mind that I didn't get your number, so a few weeks after, I drove down to Providence and looked you up. Only to find you were gone."

"You came for me?" Disbelief coated my voice. Just when I thought Matteo couldn't do anything more to convince me he was a good guy, he went and said that.

"I felt something that night, Cait." He prowled toward me, with slow, sure steps. In that moment, he reminded me of a predator stalking its prey. But I didn't feel an ounce of fear, only a shiver of anticipation.

"Something I'd never felt before." He laid his hand on the side of my neck, gazing down at me. "But you were his... weren't you?"

The utter defeat in Matteo's eyes gutted me. There was so much he didn't understand, things he didn't know, that I couldn't ever tell him.

But there were some truths I could offer him.

"The lease was up on that apartment. I couldn't afford to renew," I said, grounded by his touch. "He said he knew of an empty apartment in his building."

Matteo went rigid, but I kept going. "I didn't have a choice."

Looking back, part of me wondered if Zander was connected with the sudden rental increase on my apartment; if he'd orchestrated the whole thing to get me to move closer to him. It was his MO to act as savior. When really, he was the villain in an expensive suit.

"Did you and he—"

"Don't," I inhaled a ragged breath. "Don't ask me that."

"I'm just trying to understand... that night, you never said—"

"Because I wanted to pretend, Matteo," I snapped. "I wanted to pretend I was just a girl spending a night with a gorgeous, charming guy. A *good* guy. I haven't had much experience with those," I confessed, averting my gaze. Matteo looked at me too intensely, wearing his emotions for all to see.

It was one of the things I found so attractive about him. He didn't play games or try to hold the upper hand. He was honest and real, and he wasn't scared to show or tell you how he felt. It was so refreshing to meet a guy like that.

But part of me also didn't trust it.

Nobody was that perfect, and I couldn't help but wonder what skeletons he had in his closet.

He slid his fingers under my jaw and tilted my face back up. "You think I'm charming?" A smile tipped the corner of his mouth.

"That's what you're choosing to hear out of all that?" My brows furrowed.

"Made you smile though." He traced the seam of my lips with his thumb, and my tummy clenched. "Your past, whatever did or didn't happen with DiMarco, it means nothing to me, Caitlin. All I care about is that you're safe now."

"You don't even know me, Matteo." If he did—if he knew the truth—he wouldn't feel the same.

"I know enough." His eyes darkened, gazing down at me with reverence. "I know what I felt the night I buried myself deep inside you and heard my name fall from your lips, Tink."

He closed the space between us, ghosting his mouth over the corner of mine. A whimper spilled from my lips.

"We shouldn't," I said, not breaking away.

"Tell me one good reason why?" His fingers glided up my neck and threaded into my hair. The way he held me, with such tenderness and possession, made my heart expand.

He wouldn't hurt me. I knew that without a doubt.

But I wasn't worried about myself.

"Let me in, Tink." He kissed me again, harder this time, sliding his tongue past my lips and tasting me. I was powerless to stop him, melting into his touch. The feel of his hands in my hair and his lips on mine.

In one smooth move, he picked me up and started carrying me down the hall.

"Matteo, what are you doing?" I breathed, twining my arms around his neck.

"What I should have done the second I laid eyes on you again." *Kiss.* "Is that good with you?" *Kiss.*

"I…" My heart crashed so hard inside my chest I couldn't think straight.

"It's okay." He nudged my nose with his. "We don't have to do anything you don't want to. I just want to lie with you, Tink. Kiss you. Hold you in my arms."

Gosh, this man. He knew exactly what to say, exactly what to do to make me acquiesce.

"I am kind of tired." Soft laughter spilled from my lips, but my heart ached. For Shaun. For me.

For us.

Matteo was good. I didn't doubt that. He was mafioso, yes, but he had a code of ethics. Morals. But if he knew the truth… if he knew what monsters haunted my dreams, he wouldn't look at me with such reverence.

He paused on the threshold of my room, sweeping his thumb down my cheek and resting it beneath my bottom lip. "You are the most beautiful thing I've ever laid eyes on. I thought it then... I think it now. If you want to stop... if you want space, or want me to go... just say the word and—"

"I want this," I said, pressing my lips to his thumb. He moved it away, but I caught it in my mouth, sucking the tip.

"Fuck," he rasped. "Keep that up, Tink, and all my good intentions will go out the window."

I chuckled again, snuggling closer to him as he walked me inside the bedroom, kicking the door shut behind him. Matteo lowered me onto the bed and gazed down at me, making my stomach clench with delicious anticipation. I couldn't remember the last time someone looked at me with such hunger and desire. As if I was the center of their universe. The most precious thing to walk the Earth.

The feeling coursed through me, making me feel more confident than I had in a long time. "Come here." I crooked my finger at him.

"Patience, Tink," he said, slipping his hands to the hem of his sweater and yanking it off his body. My eyes went straight to the ink decorating his skin. The Eagle swooping over his shoulder and down his chest, the flowers curving around his biceps and trailing down his arm. The wicked skull sitting on his opposite shoulder. Matteo's body was a work of art, and I was the sculptor who wanted to run my hands over every dip and curve to appreciate something so perfectly formed.

"What?" he asked, looming over me.

"You're... beautiful."

"Beautiful, huh?" A smile tugged at his mouth. "I've been called a lot of things in my time, Tink, but I don't think I've ever been called beautiful."

My cheeks burned. "Maybe we should stop talking now." I scooched back to give him space to lie down, and he did, unfurling his big body beside me so we were lying face to face.

"Hi," he said, tucking a stray curl behind my ear.

"Hi."

"I love your hair. Your eyes... Your smile."

I blushed harder at his words. "It took me a long time to accept my wild curls."

"You know, I've heard redheads tend to have a fiery temper." Matteo's brow lifted.

"Maybe, a long time ago." But it had been long beaten out of me.

I hadn't realized I'd dropped my gaze until Matteo gently gripped my chin and lifted my face back to his. "Right here, right in this moment, the past stays where it belongs. This is about you and me."

It wasn't.

It was about so much more than that. But I wanted to pretend. I wanted to join him in the fantasy. Just like I had that night all those months ago.

"Come here." He buried his hand into my hair and curved it around the nape of my neck, drawing me closer. His lips teased mine, kissing the corner of my mouth, my jaw, pecking the end of my nose.

I began to tremble involuntarily, overwhelmed at his touch, at the emotions coursing through me.

"Caitlin?" Matteo pulled away to look at me. "What's wrong?"

"I... I don't deserve this," I whispered, barely able to look at him.

Anger flashed in his eyes, and I jerked back.

"Shit, Cait, I... I'm not angry at you." He pulled me into his arms, holding me. I relaxed against his chest, breathing in his delicious male scent. Matteo smelled of pinewood and spice and all those things a guy should smell of.

"I'm sorry," I murmured.

I'd ruined it—the moment.

But I couldn't get out of my head. I couldn't stop thinking about what would happen when he found out the truth.

When Matteo discovered I wasn't who he thought I was.

FOURTEEN

MATTEO

CAITLIN SLEPT in my arms for hours. I didn't have the heart to wake her. Besides, laying there with her was everything. Knowing she trusted me enough to be so close to her. It was all I wanted.

When Luis had gotten a call from Arianne to return to the city, I'd wondered if Caitlin would feel comfortable being alone with me. Never in my wildest dreams had I expected this.

But now I had it, I wasn't sure I could ever let it—let her—go.

"No," she murmured, twisting in my arms. "No."

"Shh, Tink, you're dreaming." I stroked a hand down her arm.

"No, no. Please... no!" Fear laced her words as she began thrashing, her hands fighting some invisible monster.

"Cait," I said, shaking her gently. "Wake up. You're dreaming. It's just a—"

"No... *NO*!" She bolted upright and my heart leaped into my throat.

"Cait?" I whispered, reaching for her shoulders. Her body tensed as she let out a pained whimper.

"M-Matteo." She stared up at me with wild, confused eyes.

"Hey, I'm here." I sat up, wrapping my arms around her. "I'm right here."

"I... oh God... I'm sorry. I'm so, so—"

"Hey," I touched the side of her face, coaxing her to look at me. "You have nothing to be sorry for."

"I'm a mess. I didn't..." She sucked in a ragged breath. "I fell asleep?"

I nodded, fighting the urge to ask her what she was dreaming about. Or who.

Red-hot anger zipped through me, but I forced it down. This wasn't about me—it was about her. About what she needed.

"Do you want me to get you a drink, some water?"

"N-no, I—" Her eyes darted to my mouth, and she wet her lips. "I..."

My anger was tamped down by the shift in the air between us.

Caitlin curled into my side as I held her, her body trembling, fear radiating from every pore.

"Tell me what happened, please." My voice cracked.

It was driving me out of my mind not knowing the truth. All I wanted to do was help her, to be by her side when things got too tough.

"Tink," I whispered, hating that she still couldn't tell me.

Caitlin shifted in my arms to look up at me. She smiled, but it didn't reach her eyes and she laid her hand against my chest. "I..."

Time stopped, my heart beating violently in my chest.

"Please, just talk to me." I pushed the hair off her face to look at her. To really look at her.

"Matteo, I..." She pressed her lips together, her gaze dropping.

My heart went with it.

She wasn't going to let me in. Even now, after everything, Caitlin wasn't going to let me in.

I went to roll away, needing some space. But she grabbed my arm. "No, please... just..."

"Just what, Cait?" Our eyes locked, the air between us charged with anticipation. She could feel it too, I knew that. But she was too damaged, too scared to act on it.

"Maybe I should go," I sighed with defeat.

"N-no... I don't want you to leave," she rushed out, panic lacing her words. "I just..."

"You just what, Cait?" Dipping my head, I met her eye-to-eye. "What do you want?"

Her bottom lip wobbled, but then she inhaled a deep breath and whispered, "Make me forget, Matteo. All I want is to forget."

She leaned back, until our noses brushed. I inhaled deeply, my heart galloping in my chest. She was offering me everything I wanted, but part of me knew it was a moment of weakness. A moment that, in the harsh light of day, she might regret.

"Please..." She kissed the corner of my mouth, a featherlight touch I felt all the way down to my soul.

"Shit, Tink, you don't know what you're asking of me."

What was I doing? This was what I wanted... all I wanted. And yet, I didn't want to hurt her.

I didn't want to be something she might regret.

Fuck.

"I need this, Matteo." Her eyes shuttered as she drew in a ragged breath. "I need you."

Those three little words snapped the final shred of my resolve and in one smooth move, I rolled her underneath me.

"Hi," I whispered, brushing my nose over hers.

"Hi." She ran her hands up my chest and over my shoulders. Her eyes glittered so much emotion it was like a punch to the chest. "I'm glad you're here," she said.

Fuck. Why did that mean so much to me?

"You really want this?" *You really want me?* I swallowed the words.

Caitlin nodded, showing me with actions, not words that she was all in. Her lips met mine in a teasing kiss, her hand sliding into the hair at the back of my neck. It felt good, too fucking good, and my hips rocked against her. But there were too many layers between us. My jeans. Her leggings.

I climbed off the bed and shuck out of my jeans, feeling like a fucking god as her eyes drank in every inch of my body. Then I moved to the side of the bed, leaning over Caitlin and slowly pulling down her leggings.

"This okay?" I asked. She nodded.

Thank fuck, she nodded. Because now she'd given me the green light, I couldn't think about anything except feeling her skin pressed up against mine again. Our bodies fused together, moving as one.

When I crawled back over her, she hitched her legs around my hips, pressing her hot center right against my rock-hard dick.

"Fuck, Tink." I gently collared her throat, dragging my tongue up the side of her neck and nipping her ear. "The things I want to do to you."

A violent shudder went through her, and I immediately eased back to look at her.

"Caitlin?"

"It's okay. I'm okay… don't stop." Her pleas were at odds with the fear swimming in her eyes.

Fuck.

Fuck!

I ran a hand down my face, releasing a heavy sigh. "Maybe we should stop."

"No… No!" She locked her hands around the back of my neck and yanked me down. "I want this, I do… it's just…"

DiMarco's attack.

The things DiMarco had done to her had left her mentally scarred.

The thought had my stomach knotting, and I inhaled a sharp breath to try and rein in the anger coursing through my veins.

"I'm not glass, Matteo. I won't shatter if you touch me."

But all I could think about now was his hands on her, taking and hurting. Punishing her. We still hadn't talked about what really happened between them. I wasn't sure I would ever be ready for that conversation, not without doing something reckless. And as my family loved to keep reminding me, I was powerless here.

Caitlin's hand drifted down my abs, her touch burning me inside out as her fingers toyed with the waistband of my boxer briefs.

"Tink," I choked out.

"I trust you, Matteo," she said with renewed confidence. "I trust you."

Lifting her hips slightly, she ground against me, a whimper catching in her throat.

Jesus, she was going to be the death of me.

I was trying to do the right thing...

I was.

But this felt too good—too right. It finally felt like I was exactly where I was supposed to be.

How was that even possible? That a woman I'd met once, could have such an effect on me.

I'd never really considered what spending eight months pining over her meant. I assumed she was just the one who got away. But being here with her, like this, only cemented what I suspected all those months ago.

Caitlin was special.

And she was mine.

"Please." She rubbed on me some more, eliciting a moan from deep inside me.

"No sex," I blurted out, wondering what the fuck was wrong with me. Caitlin frowned, dejection flashing in her green eyes. "We don't have to rush. I want to savor this," I said, trailing my hand up her stomach and gently squeezing her breast, dragging my thumb over her nipple.

"God," she breathed, arching into my touch. "It feels good."

"Just because I'm not going to slide into your warm, wet pussy tonight, doesn't mean I'm not going to make you come so hard you see stars, Tink."

Caitlin shuddered, pressing her lips together and suppressing a moan.

She liked the dirty talk. I'd be storing that little nugget of info for another time. For now, I wanted to give her exactly what she needed.

A distraction.

Dipping my hand between us, I rubbed her over her damp panties. "Already wet for me, Tink?"

"Matteo, God..."

"Not God, baby. Just a guy who really, *really* wants to hear you scream his name." I kissed her, plunging my tongue deep into her mouth as I slid my fingers into her underwear.

"Good?" I checked.

"Yes, don't stop..."

Thank fuck.

I spread her open and found her clit, rolling my thumb in circles until she was panting and writhing beneath me.

"Tell me what you want, Cait."

This had to be on her terms.

She clasped my wrist, pushing my hand south. My fingers grazed her entrance and she moaned.

"Yeah?" I swallowed. "Are you sure? I don't want to hurt you." My brow lifted.

"Please."

Gently, I eased a finger inside her, testing the waters as I curled it deep. Caitlin froze, breathing heavily as I slowly stretched her, letting her adjust to the feel.

"More," she demanded.

I added a second finger, working her in synchrony with my thumb as it strummed her clit. "Fuck, Cait, you're so tight." Twisting my hand a little, I curled my fingers deeper, rubbing her walls.

Caitlin rode my hand, burying her face in my shoulder, drowning out her breathy moans.

"Look at me," I ordered, nudging her gently. Our eyes clashed and I captured her mouth in a bruising kiss. Our tongues tangled together in slow, lazy licks that had my dick straining against my boxers.

I wanted her, more than I'd ever wanted anything in my life.

The connection between us was like an invisible thread, pulling tauter and tauter. Binding us in ways I didn't understand.

"God, Matteo... it's... *God*." Caitlin began to tremble as she clung to me, breathless.

"Come for me, Tink, come for me now."

She shattered, clenching around my fingers as pleasure washed over her. I kissed her harder, swallowing her moans of *more* and *yes* and *oh God*.

Bringing my fingers to my mouth, I sucked them clean, smirking at the flash of surprise in Caitlin's eyes.

"I need to taste the real thing," I declared, dropping a kiss to her lips before I moved down her body.

Her skin was smooth and pale, pinking under my touch. Teeth and tongue and lips. I swirled my tongue around the peak of her breast, sucking gently. Marking her.

Claiming her.

"Ah, that feels..." Her fingers twisted into the sheets as she arched into my mouth.

My fingers slid back and forth through her wetness.

"It's too much." Caitlin slid her fingers into my hair, yanking slightly.

Our eyes clashed over the line of her body, and I smirked. "You don't want my mouth on you?" I blew a stream of air over her clit, and she moaned.

"I... ah, Matteo..."

"Say the word, Tink, and I'll stop."

She pressed her lips together, shaking her head a little. It was all the permission I needed. I dived at her like a man starved, lapping at her pussy with carnal hunger.

She tasted so fucking good as I dipped my tongue inside her.

"God..." She panted. "Matteo, yes..."

I hooked my hand under her thighs and spread her wider, needing more.

I needed everything she was willing to give me.

Caitlin had stolen a piece of my heart all those months ago, but I was pretty sure that right here, in this moment, she stole the rest.

I pulled Caitlin closer, dropping a kiss to her head.

"What?" She peeked up at me.

"Just you... being here with you like this. A guy could get used to it."

"Matteo..."

"It's okay," I said. "I'm not asking you for anything you can't give me."

She relaxed against me. "Thank you, for distracting me."

Hurt crushed my chest.

Is that all this was to her? A distraction?

"It was my pleasure," I laughed off the sting of dejection.

Caitlin pushed up slightly to look me in the eye. "I'm not..."

"It's okay. We don't have to do this."

"Do you regret staying with me?"

"Never," I admitted.

I didn't, but part of me wished things were different. That we'd met under different circumstances.

"You gave me two of the best nights of my life." She whispered the words so quietly I barely heard them.

"I-I did?"

Caitlin nodded. "That night last summer and... right now. I want you to know that, Matteo."

I wanted her to know that I could give her so much more—that I would give her forever if she would let me.

But what kind of person would that make me if I promised her forever when she'd promised me nothing in return.

FIFTEEN

CAITLIN

I WOKE UP AGAINST A WARM, hard body.

Matteo.

My lips curved at the memories of the night before. After he'd made me come apart, touch by touch, kiss by kiss, we'd spent hours talking. He'd shared stories from his childhood. I'd talked about the club. Mostly, I'd listened to him talk about his sister and cousins, about the mischief they used to get into.

Matteo had grown up in a big family, and I could tell from the way he talked about them, that family was everything to him.

Especially his younger sister Arabella.

It couldn't have been further from the truth for me.

Maybe under different circumstances, I would have gotten to meet them all one day—to spend time with them, getting to know them.

"Hey," Matteo murmured, his voice thick with sleep. His hand slid over my hip, dragging me closer into his body. "What time is it?"

"A little after eight," I said, relishing the way it felt to be so close to him, even if it was only temporary.

"I could get used to this," he said, kissing my shoulder. A shiver ran through me at the raw honesty in his words. "How are you feeling?"

"Good," I replied. "I'm good."

I was more relaxed than I had been in weeks. He'd done that.

Matteo had done that with his dirty words, tender touches, and hot kisses. But it was his level of respect for me, and my body, that really got to me. The second I'd recoiled at his touch or flinched when he pressed too far or too hard, he had stopped and checked in with me. It was a revelation to have a guy care like that.

"I was worried you might feel differently this morning." He brushed the hair off my neck and kissed me there.

I rolled over and peeked up at him. "I don't... at all. Last night was... it was perfect. Thank you." I smiled.

"Fuck, Tink, you are so damn beautiful." He leaned in, dusting his mouth over mine.

"I need to brush my teeth," I said, pressing my hands to his chest.

He chuckled. "You think I care about morning breath?"

"You might not, but I do." I kissed his cheek before darting from the bed. "I'll go turn on the coffee machine."

"Stay. We don't have to get up yet." He silently pleaded with me, his eyes hooded with lust and things I didn't want to acknowledge.

But the spell was already broken. I needed some space to think, to clear my head and remember all the reasons why I couldn't allow myself to get swept away in this.

In him.

"I need a girl's minute." I didn't look back as I slipped into the bathroom and closed the door.

At least I hadn't slept with him again. Fooling around was one thing, but sex with Matteo... that would be my undoing. No, I needed to stay strong. I needed to keep some semblance of distance between us. Because if he started asking me for things I couldn't give him, he would start asking me questions I didn't have the answer for.

After taking care of business, I washed my hands and then tamed my curls into a loose ponytail over my shoulder. I felt torn. Part of me was so relieved Matteo was still here, that he had spent the night with me. But the other part knew it would only make things worse when the time came for me to leave.

Shaun was gone.

Zander had killed him... because of me. And I knew it was only the beginning of his rampage to find me. No one was safe around me. Not even Matteo and his family. Because men like Zander didn't play by the rules, they smashed straight through them.

"Tink?" Matteo called, and I smiled to myself. He made everything so simple that it would have been easy to hand over my heart to him right now. But it would only complicate things.

"Cait—"

"Coming," I yelled, unable to keep the frustration out of my voice.

When I slipped back into the bedroom, he was sitting propped up against the headboard, one knee bent.

God, he looked good. Inches upon inches of golden skin stretched over muscle. He could have been something straight out of a sexy magazine shoot.

"Everything okay?"

"Yeah." I smiled a little too enthusiastically. "Why wouldn't it be?" I hesitated, not sure how to do this. It was the morning after. Didn't guys usually make a run for it to avoid this awkward moment?

"Come here." He motioned for me to go to him.

"I should probably—"

"Tink." He dropped his legs over the edge of the bed and sat upright, reaching for me. "Come. Here."

Heat flashed inside me, my stomach clenching. Why did it sound hot when he ordered me around?

I went willingly, like a moth to a flame.

Matteo curved his arm around my waist and pulled me between his legs, staring up at me. "Why do I feel like you're already shutting me out?"

"I... I'm not," I whispered. "It's just... I'm not used to this."

"This?" He frowned, and I nodded.

"The morning after." Heat flooded my cheeks. "In my experience, guys don't usually stick around."

"Maybe you've been picking the wrong guys." He smiled, and it was so playful, so cute, something inside me softened.

Where were you five years ago? I gazed down at him, running my hand through his messy bed hair. He made it look so damn good.

"How are you feeling really?"

"I'll be okay." The lie soured on my tongue. "I just can't believe he's gone." Tears pricked the corners of my eyes, but I blinked them away. If I let myself fall down that dark hole, I wasn't sure I'd ever find a way out.

I didn't kill Shaun—Zander did.

No matter how guilty I felt, I had to remember that.

"What will happen? With Zander?" I asked.

The muscle in Matteo's jaw popped as he released a strained breath. "Honestly, I don't know yet. My family is dealing with a lot right now."

"Because Nicco's father is sick?"

He nodded, pain lingering in his eyes.

"I'm sorry." Without realizing, I scraped my fingers over his skull and a low growl rumbled in his chest. "God, I'm so sorry," I went to pull away, but Matteo grabbed my wrist.

"Don't," he said in a husky voice.

The air crackled around us, thick with anticipation. He wanted to kiss me again. I could see it right there, glittering in his eyes.

"Matteo," I breathed, my heart beating erratically in my chest.

What was happening?

I'd never felt so out of control before.

He pulled me onto his thigh and my arms went around his shoulder to steady myself.

"Hi," he said.

"Hi." A faint smile traced my lips.

"I'm going to kiss you now."

I inhaled a sharp breath, nodding gently. I was under his spell, unable to break through from the all-consuming thoughts of him. Us. Together.

Matteo slid his hand along my clavicle and down to my chest, right where my heart lay. "I can feel your heart racing... so fast." He marveled, closing the distance between us.

The first touch of his lips was like electricity zapping through me. Kissing last night, in the dark, was one thing. But this... this was something else.

His tongue slipped past my lips, gently lapping at my own. Desire swirled inside me, burning me up.

"Matteo," I moaned into his mouth. "I—"

The shrill sound from his cell phone was like a bucket of ice water dousing the flames circling us. Matteo cursed under his breath, and I slipped off his lap and left the room.

I needed some space to think, and I couldn't do that with Matteo breathing down my neck.

But when I went out into the living room, I startled. "Luis," I gasped. "What are you—"

"Coffee?" he asked me with a smile.

"Sure, thanks." I propped myself up on one of the stools. "When did you get back?"

"About an hour ago."

Which means he knew Matteo spent the night with me.

"It isn't what you think," I rushed out, the strange urge to defend my behavior coursing through me.

"Caitlin." He set his mug down and gave me a knowing smile. "I'm not here to judge. I'm here to keep you safe."

"Morning." Matteo appeared, shirtless and completely unaffected by Luis's presence. "Something smells good."

"Grabbed a few freshly baked pastries from the nearest gas station. Luis motioned to the bag on the counter. "Help yourself. Coffee's in the pot."

"My kind of guy." Matteo squeezed Luis's shoulder.

"You good?" He came over to me and curved his hand around the back of my neck, kissing my temple as I stood there, rooted to the spot. My eyes flicked to Luis, and he gave me a discreet smile.

What the hell was that supposed to mean?

"I... yeah," I murmured, certain he would release me. But he didn't, one-handedly making himself a mug of coffee while keeping his hand on my neck. It shouldn't have thrilled me as much as it did. He was acting like I belonged to him... like we were together.

A fact we both knew could never come true. But it didn't stop him from touching me intimately and it didn't make me push him away.

"You want one?" Matteo asked me, nodding toward the coffee machine.

"Sure."

He finally released me, and I sucked in a shaky breath, stepping back to put some more distance between us.

"How's Nicco and Ari?" He asked Luis as he set about making my coffee.

"They're okay. There's been no change with Antonio though."

Matteo went rigid, releasing a steady breath. "He'll pull through. He has to."

Without thinking, I reached for his hand, squeezing gently. The pain in his voice, the glittering in his eyes, was too stark to ignore.

His gaze collided with mine, and my heart hammered in my chest at the intensity in his expression. "Thank you," he mouthed, his eyes shuttering.

When they opened again, his whole expression softened as if just seeing me standing there, by his side, instantly made everything better.

It was a heady feeling; one I wasn't used to.

One I wasn't sure I could ever give up.

"Have you ever been?" Matteo asked me as we worked some more on the puzzle. I thought he would leave once we had breakfast, but he didn't.

And it mattered far more than it should.

This—us—it couldn't go anywhere. It couldn't ever be more than... *this.*

He had a life. A family and future. I didn't care about who he was, about what his family did. It wasn't like I'd grown up in a good, law-abiding family either.

No, I didn't care about any of that. And deep down, I wanted nothing more than for him to make good on his word and take care of Zander. At least then I'd be free of his obsession. But I'd never truly be free.

Not in the way Matteo needed me to be.

"Cait?" He brushed my arm, smiling at me. "Is everything okay?"

"Everything's fine." I smiled back, hoping he didn't notice the pain in my eyes.

"So... have you?"

"Have I what?"

"Ever been to New York?"

"Oh, I... I went a few times as a kid. I don't really remember it." The lie soured on my tongue. The truth was, I remembered every trip. Every single one. I remembered the arguments, my mom and her boyfriend fighting, the sound of his hand cracking against her face. The howl of her sobs echoing through the car.

I remembered it all.

Dropping my gaze to the puzzle, I inhaled a sharp breath.

You escaped.

You got out of there and you never have to look back.

"You were born in New York?"

I frowned. "How do you know...? Oh, your friends."

"They meant no harm."

"You're all very close."

"We are." A look of fondness washed over him. "They're my family. You don't have—"

"Matteo," I let out a heavy sigh. "I can't do this."

"Do what? What are we doing, Cait?" His eyes searched mine for answers.

Answers I didn't have.

"I'm so grateful to you and your friends, I am. But this... us..." I took a deep breath, my heart ready to burst, blood roaring in my ears. "Surely you know we can't—"

"Can't what?" His hand curved around my neck, holding me tenderly. Matteo dropped his head to mine, breathing me in. "It's a sign, Cait. Tell me you know it's a sign."

"I..."

Oh God. Emotion balled in my throat, thick and suffocating. He wasn't going to let this go—he wasn't going to let me go. And I didn't want him to. I wanted Matteo to fight for me. I wanted him to prove that there was good in the world. That I deserved more than the shitty hand I'd been dealt.

But that was fantasy.

And my demons were too big to outrun.

His lips brushed mine. Once. Twice. Until his tongue licked the seam of my lips, silently seeking permission. A soft sigh spilled out of me, and he took it as a yes, sliding his tongue deep into my mouth and tangling it with my own.

God, when he kissed me like this... I felt like the most beautiful girl in the world.

I felt safe and cherished... and loved.

"Matteo—"

"Call me Matt," he breathed against my mouth. "That's what my friends call me."

My lips curved involuntarily. "I'm your friend?"

His fingers threaded into my thick curls, pulling me back slightly so he could look me right in the eye. "No, Cait, you're not my friend." His eyes darkened, and I swallowed, my throat suddenly dry.

"You are so much more than that to me."

Oh my.

Matteo took my face in his hands and captured my mouth in a slow kiss, showing me exactly what I was to him.

A kiss I felt all the way down to my soul.

SIXTEEN

MATTEO

"YOU'RE DIFFERENT." Bella narrowed her eyes at me as we ate Mom's bruschette.

"Just happy to see you." I grinned, and she rolled her eyes.

"No, I think it's the girl. The one you left to go and see the other night."

Rolling my lips together, I swallowed the words on the tip of my tongue.

Truth was, it was Caitlin.

I'd spent the morning at the cabin with her, doing that ridiculously impossible puzzle, laughing and talking. We'd avoided the hard topics. Or at least, she had.

Caitlin was a locked box, and no matter how much I tried to break the chains around her heart, she wouldn't let me in.

But I was so gone for her, I'd take whatever scraps I could get.

"Bella," I warned. "Eat your food."

"Don't change the subject, Matt. I know you like her. It's written all over your face. Who is she? Is she pretty? I bet she's real pretty if you—"

"Take a breath, pulce," I teased.

"Can I meet her? I totally have to meet her. Please."

My heart twisted. "No, you can't meet her. Not yet."

Not until it's safe.

I pushed the words out of my head. Caitlin was safe. As long as she stayed at the cabin, no one knew where she was. Even if DiMarco learned that she'd left the hospital with me and Enzo, he still didn't know *where* she was.

He'd have to come through us to find her, and I had no intentions of ever telling him. I'd rather die than give her up.

Fuck. What was I saying?

I had responsibilities. A family to think about. Arabella.

Anger curled in my stomach.

Nothing made sense anymore, not since Caitlin walked back into my life... and yet, being with her felt right. Like I was exactly where I was supposed to be.

It was a complete mind fuck.

"Seriously, Matt, you suck sometimes. This is the first girl you've liked in... well, forever." Arabella pouted, flashing her best puppy dog eyes at me. "I want to meet her. She must be special if she's caught your eye."

Caitlin was special all right.

My heart beat that much faster whenever I laid eyes on her. All those wild red curls, her alabaster skin, and glittering green eyes. She was stunning and so different compared to the kinds of girls I was used to.

Part of me wondered if I'd pushed her too far last night. Especially after what DiMarco had done to her. But Caitlin had wanted it. I'd felt the need pouring off her. And the fact she'd trusted me enough to touch her and make her come apart meant everything to me.

"*Matt!*" Arabella punched my arm and my eyes snapped up at her.

"What?"

"You didn't hear a word I just said, did you?"

"I..."

"Unbelievable." She rolled her eyes. "Sometimes I don't know why I even bother."

"Relax, drama queen." I leaned over and ruffled her hair, the way I used to when we were kids. "It's... complicated."

"Does she have a boyfriend? A psycho ex? Is it Nicco and Ari all over again? Is she the daughter of a rival—"

"Okay, Bella, that's enough with the crazy talk," I said. "Jeez, you need to get out more."

She scoffed. "Like that's an option."

Guilt flooded me.

"I know things are tough sometimes... but is it really so bad to have a family that cares so much?"

"Matteo." She rolled her eyes. "I'm sixteen and I've never even been kissed."

"What the fuck?" I balked. "Why do you want to be kissed? You have plenty of time—"

"And thank you for proving my point." She threw up her hands. "You think anyone is going to come near me when you act like this?"

"Bella..."

"It's even worse for Alessia. Guys don't look twice at her at school. It's like she has a neon sign above her head saying off-limits. At least guys actually talk to me occasionally."

"What guys?" I snapped.

She shrugged. "Just guys."

"The same guys you want to kiss?"

Jesus, I wasn't ready for this. Arabella was my sister—my baby sister. I still vividly remembered crawling around the yard with her on my back while she pretended to whip me like a horse. She wasn't old enough to date and kiss and... nope, I wasn't going there.

Not until she was at least twenty-one.

"Stop changing the subject. This is about you, not me."

"Caitlin is—"

"Her name's Caitlin?"

Fuck.

Why had I said that?

It just spilled out though because she was always on my fucking mind. Imprinted there with no signs of leaving anytime soon.

Excitement twinkled in my sister's eyes. "Her name is Caitlin? That's pretty. Do you have a photo of her on your phone? Can I see it?"

"No, I don't have a photo of her." But I wished I did.

I laid awake last night for hours, watching her sleep. I couldn't shake the feeling that something bigger was at work here, reuniting us like this. But it was really bad fucking timing.

Uncle Toni was still in a coma. Nicco was barely holding on by a thread. And Lombardi's men were sniffing around DiMarco's.

There wasn't time for me to figure out what Cait and I were to each other. My number one priority had to be keeping her safe. She had already been at the cabin for five days. Eventually, she would want more freedom. Maybe she would even want to leave and go somewhere else, somewhere closer to where she was before.

"So... when can I meet her?" Arabella stared at me with eager eyes, and I chuckled. "What?" she whined.

"Never change, Bella."

My cell phone started ringing and I picked it off the table, checking the caller ID. "I need to take this," I said, trepidation coursing through me. I got up and ruffled her hair again, smiling down at her. "Never change for anything."

"Matteo, Lorenzo." Our Uncle Alonso greeted us the second we stepped into Uncle Toni's study. Genevieve and Alessia were still at the hospital which was the only reason he'd called us to the house instead of meeting somewhere neutral.

"Uncle Al, how's it going?"

"Can't complain."

"Come, sit." He motioned to the table. Nicco; my father; and Stefan, Uncle T and Al's consigliere, were already seated, their expressions grim. Whatever had happened wasn't good.

"We didn't know you were driving down from Boston," Enzo said.

"Didn't know it myself until Michele called me." The two of them shared a knowing look.

"What's going on?" I said, blood roaring in my ears.

"We need to make some hard decisions, son."

"But Uncle Toni isn't—"

"He's not going to get better enough to return."

"W-what?" I blurted out, feeling like the rug had been pulled from under my feet. "Nic?"

"The doctor said that even if he wakes up, the road to recovery will be extensive." He dragged a hand down his face, his eyes vacant and expression haunted. "Given the new intel on DiMarco and Lombardi, Uncle Michele, Stefan, and Uncle Al decided we need to make the change now."

"Fuck," Enzo breathed.

"Effective immediately, Niccolò is now acting boss," Uncle Al said.

Nicco didn't look happy about it. In fact, he looked downright miserable. But I didn't blame him. It was a huge burden to carry.

"Stefan is going to stick around, try to help you figure out this Lombardi thing. It could be something, it could be nothing."

"And DiMarco?" I asked, immediately regretting it.

My father's heavy gaze found me across the table. He leaned back slightly, steepling his fingers, and let out a long, steady breath.

"Tell them."

Shit.

I shifted uncomfortably in my chair. I should have kept my mouth shut. But it was too late now—everyone was watching me and if I didn't tell them, he would.

"We have a problem," I said.

Enzo slouched in his seat, burying his face in his hands.

"Out with it," Uncle Al demanded.

"It was my call," Enzo jumped in.

"No, it was my call. I take full responsibility for this. It ends with me." Nicco addressed his uncle and family advisor. "A little over a week ago, Enzo and Matteo went to visit DiMarco. But they never made it to Providence. Enzo got a call from the hospital over in Pawtucket. When they got there, they found one of DiMarco's girls beaten and raped."

I winced at his harsh assessment, my fist curling against my thigh.

"What was she doing in Pawtucket?" Uncle Al asked. "And why the fuck did she call Enzo?"

Nicco looked to our cousin and nodded.

"A few weeks ago, I was in Providence," Enzo said. "I came across one of DiMarco's girls crying in the bathroom. A couple of days later, he asked me to go check on one of his girls at her apartment. It was the same woman. Something felt off about the whole thing, so I gave her my number and said if she ever needed help to call me."

"It was the same girl?" Stefan asked, and Enzo nodded.

"Let me guess, you brought her back to Verona." Uncle Al shook his head with disbelief.

"I called Nicco, and we decided to bring her with us. She had nowhere else to go."

"Where is she now?"

"She's safe," I bit out.

"Interesting." Uncle Al sat back, studying me. "This woman, she is someone to you, Matteo?"

"She's—"

"She's important to me," I said, cutting Nicco off.

"I see."

"And you understand what you risk… for a woman that is neither your wife nor your family?"

"We couldn't leave her there."

"What's done is done." My father's jaw twitched. "The girl is safe in an undisclosed location. We need to focus on finding out everything we can about what Lombardi wants with DiMarco."

"I might be able to help there." Stefan pulled out a manila envelope. "Rumor has it Lombardi is looking to expand. He's made offers on three local businesses in the last three months. A run-down strip joint on the edge of Providence. And a café and gym downtown."

"He's trying to put down roots?"

"Trying to. My contact down at town planning called with his suspicions. Obviously, Lombardi used an alias, but it was traceable."

"Lombardi has to be a fool if he thinks he can just waltz into our territory and get his feet under the rug."

"Fortune favors the bold, old friend." Uncle Al clapped Stefan on the back and flashed him a grim smile.

"Al's right," Nicco said. "He's making a power play. Lombardi must know we'll have real estate covered. Providence is Marchetti territory. It always has been. If he's sniffing around DiMarco, it means he's been watching us. Learning who might not be happy with current arrangements."

"Fuck." My father expelled a breath. "We need to handle this, sooner rather than later."

Nicco nodded. "Enzo, I want you to go there and meet Lucino. Talk to DiMarco and get a feel for where his head's at."

"Sure thing, boss." Enzo smirked.

"I'm going," I said, pressing my palm into the table. If Enzo was going to see that fucker, I wanted—

"No."

"Excuse me?" I glared at Nicco.

"You're going to stay here. I don't want you anywhere near DiMarco until we know exactly what we're dealing with."

"But I—"

"Dammit, Matteo." He slammed his hand down, making his glass of whisky clatter. "That was an order, not a request. You are already too involved to keep a level head."

My teeth ground together behind my lips. He wasn't telling me anything I didn't already know. But I needed this—I needed to look DiMarco in the eye and see it for myself.

And then I needed to make him fucking hurt for having ever laid a finger on Caitlin.

"He's already looking for her," Nicco added. "We think he killed one of his bartenders; the guy who drove Caitlin to the hospital."

Uncle Al clucked his tongue while my father stared at nothing. This was a clusterfuck, the whole fucking thing.

"How do you want to play this?" Enzo asked, effectively cutting me out from the conversation.

"Sit down with DiMarco and ask him what the fuck he's doing with the Lombardi."

"And if he doesn't tell us what we want to hear?"

"Remind him that his loyalty lies with the Marchetti."

Enzo nodded, tapping the desk. He was different with Nora. Calmer. More settled. But he still had a darkness inside him, a darkness that needed feeding. And Lorenzo Marchetti loved nothing more than getting his hands dirty in the name of business.

"This could cause problems, Niccolò." My father raked a hand through his salt and pepper hair.

"If we give DiMarco even an inch..."

"Sì, you are right. We need to know once and for all what he plans to do. If the Lombardi are in fact trying to make a power grab we need to be prepared."

"And Caitlin?"

I had to ask.

I had to know what they planned on doing with her.

"She can't go back," Nicco said, silently conveying what I so desperately needed to hear.

He had my back.

Regardless.

"Agreed."

Relief slammed into me. I hadn't realized how much I needed to hear my father say those words until they came out.

"But she can't hide forever. You need to talk to her, Matteo. Find out her plans. Either she stands at your side, or she becomes a liability we can't afford right now."

What the fuck?

I swallowed hard.

It wasn't supposed to be like this.

"Michele is right," Nicco said, pinning me with a hard look. "You need to talk to her and find out her next move."

"And if she won't agree to stand at my side… what then?"

Nicco's expression guttered, and I had my answer. Caitlin was either all in on our side, or she wasn't.

Fuck.

"She's a liability, Matt. Until this thing with DiMarco is over, Caitlin cannot be allowed to leave."

"Right, yeah." My throat was dry, my head spinning.

"And if DiMarco is getting into bed with the Lombardi?" Enzo asked the question we all dreaded.

Nicco inhaled a deep breath, his eyes devoid of emotion as he embodied his father and became the boss.

"Then we prepare to go to war."

"Are you sure this is okay?" Bella asked from beside me. She'd barely sat still for the entire ride. It was the morning after the meeting with my cousins and uncles, and I couldn't stay away from the cabin for a second longer.

"I thought you wanted to meet her." I glanced at her.

"I do… I mean, any girl who has managed to catch your eye is a girl I want to meet. I need to make sure she passes the test."

"The test?"

"Yeah." She snickered, keeping her eyes focused on the scenery rolling by. "The 'is she good enough for my brother' test."

"Jesus, Bella," I murmured under my breath.

Maybe this wasn't such a good idea. But when Nicco and my uncles had suggested I talk to Caitlin, to try to find out what her plans were, my mind immediately went to all the reasons she had to leave. To walk away from me and never look back.

They wouldn't allow that though. Caitlin knew too much, making her a risk they couldn't afford. They wanted her to stay to protect our secrets, but I didn't want that. I wanted her to stay because she chose me.

So I'd brought ammunition in the form of my gorgeous, compassionate, slightly over-protective sister.

Arabella charmed everyone she met, and I had no doubt Caitlin wouldn't be able to resist her wiles. But it wasn't only about me. I knew Cait had to be feeling lonely stuck out in the cabin. Having another girl around might help her relax for the conversation we could no longer avoid.

"Ready?" I said, pulling up outside the cabin.

"Hell yes. I want to meet my future sister-in-law."

"What the—"

She exploded with laughter. "Oh God, you should see your face. I'm joking, Matt. But it's good to know just how serious you are about her."

You have no idea.

I ran a hand down my face, letting out a strained breath.

This was totally a bad idea.

But it was too late now.

SEVENTEEN

CAITLIN

LUIS ANSWERED the door and smiled. "Well, this is a surprise."

My brows knitted as I watched him step aside and welcome Matteo, and a young girl who shared his eyes and smile. Her hair was darker though, falling over her shoulders like a waterfall, and she had a vulnerability about her.

Arabella.

This was his sister, Arabella.

"Hey." Matteo dipped his head. "I thought you might appreciate some female company."

"Hello, I'm Arabella, but you can call me Bella. Matteo's told me all about you."

"He has, has he?" I fought a smile.

"No." She chuckled. "It's like getting blood from a stone. But it's really nice to finally meet you."

I glanced between them, surprised at the slight flush to Matteo's cheeks.

He'd told her about me?

"Don't worry," he said as if sensing my sudden discomfort. "I only told her the basics."

Right, and what are those? I wanted to ask. But I rolled my lips together, unsure of what to say. I'd imagined what it would be like to meet his family and get to know those closest to him. But now his sister—his younger sister—was standing there, staring at me, and nothing about this felt right.

I couldn't get to know his sister. What if I liked her? What if we hit it off? It would only be another tether tying me to him. To Verona. I didn't need any more reasons to want to stay here.

Family, love... hope, those things made you weak. And I had no room for weakness, not if I was going to survive the coming weeks.

I'd spent my life running from my past. Trying to escape a family who only ever wanted to hurt me. To use and exploit me. I couldn't risk being found out. No matter how much it meant to me that Matteo was there for me. That he and his family had taken me in and protected me.

"You're very pretty," Arabella said, breaking the tension between me and her brother. "I love your hair."

"Thank you." My fingers went to my curls, pushing them away from my face. "I—"

"What's that?" Her eyes flicked to the puzzle laid out on the coffee table. With Matteo's help, it was well over halfway completed now.

"Just something to pass the time," I said.

"I like puzzles. Can I help?"

"Sure." I motioned for her to go ahead and she sat down and began studying the pieces.

"I'll get us all something to drink."

"I'll help," I blurted out, following Matteo into the kitchen.

"Is this okay?" he asked quietly.

"I... you should have texted first."

"Would you have said yes?" His brow lifted.

He had a point.

I wouldn't have.

"Look. She's harmless. She just wanted to meet the woman I—" Matteo stopped himself and my breath caught.

I didn't think I'd ever wanted to hear words as much as I wanted to hear the ones trapped between his perfect lips.

Heat splashed inside me as I remembered how good it felt to kiss him, to have him kiss me.

"Caitlin?"

Blinking over at him, I shook the unwelcome thoughts out. "Sorry, it's fine. She seems... sweet."

"She is. But don't be fooled by her charm. She has a way of getting under your skin and tricking you into revealing all your deepest, darkest secrets."

I flinched at his words, and Matteo's brow knitted. "What is it? What's wrong?"

"Nothing, I... beer?"

"Sure, one won't hurt. Is there soda or juice for Bella?"

"Yes, I'll be right over." I dismissed him. I needed space. Room to quiet my beating heart.

Being around Matteo was like being close to the sun. You craved the warmth, the seductive feel of its rays, the addictive rush of endorphins. But if you stayed too long, got too close, you risked getting burned.

And I'd been burned one too many times before.

I grabbed their drinks and made my way over to them.

"God, I can't wait until I'm old enough to go to New York."

"You've never been?" I asked Arabella.

"No." Her eyes flicked to Matteo. "But it's not for lack of trying. The men in my family are, how do you say, overprotective."

"How old are you?"

"Sixteen. Yes!" She fitted another piece to the puzzle.

God, I'd been her age when I'd run. Had I seemed so young and naïve back then? Although, Arabella possessed a quiet confidence. And the way Matteo watched her... well, it made my heart ache.

He was a doting brother, determined to protect his family.

It only made him more attractive.

I felt his eyes on me as Arabella and I continued fitting pieces to the puzzle. She quizzed me about my life, about where I was from and what I did for fun, and I dodged her questions with someone with a lifetime of experience of avoiding the truth.

After about an hour, Luis reappeared after leaving the three of us to carry out his daily perimeter walks. He took his job very seriously, but I was relieved to have a friendly face around.

"So, Caitlin, do you have a boyfriend?"

"E-excuse me?" I spluttered, glancing at Matteo for help.

"Bella, that isn't any of your business."

"She can consider it her part of her job interview."

"Job interview... for what exactly?" My eyes narrowed.

An amused smirk tipped the corner of her mouth. "If it makes you feel any better," she added, "I'm rooting for you." Arabella winked at me and went back to the puzzle.

I glanced over at Matteo. He mouthed, "I'm sorry."

Ugh. Did he have to be so gorgeous?

He was making it impossible to forget him.

And even more impossible to leave.

Some hours later, and with the puzzle two-thirds complete, my cheeks ached from all the laughter. Arabella Bellatoni was a breath of fresh air. Unapologetic and with zero filter, she told story after story of Matteo and his cousins, leaving no stone unturned. I'd learned more about him today than in any of our previous encounters.

"This has been fun," she said with a proud smile. "We should do it again sometime."

And just like that, the temporary bubble burst.

I couldn't grow close to these people; it would only make leaving them harder.

"Bella, why don't you go give Luis a hand with the dishes."

Luis had made the four of us spaghetti and had insisted on cleaning up too. Bella got up reluctantly and slid her eyes to me. "This is code for, I want to be alone with Caitlin." Her lips pursed playfully.

"Bella," Matteo warned, and his sister skipped off to find our chef for the evening.

"Sorry about her, she gets—"

"It's no problem. It's been nice..." *Normal.* I swallowed the word.

"We need to talk, Cait."

There it was. The moment I'd known was coming.

All day, I'd felt Matteo's eyes on me. Watching. Waiting. Trying to figure out how to broach the subject with me. I'd been preparing myself from the moment he'd stepped into the cabin.

"It's okay," I said with a weak smile.

"Is it?" His eyes shuttered as he inhaled a deep breath. "Because nothing about this feels okay.

"I'll go. If Luis or someone gives me a ride to the nearest bus station, I can catch—"

"Go?" He balked, staring at me with disbelief. "You think I want you to leave?"

"I... I thought... We both know I can't stay here forever."

"You can, Cait. You just have to..." His voice trailed off right as his gaze dropped.

"Matteo?" I whispered. "What is it?" My heart pounded inside my chest. Whatever he was about to say would change everything. I felt it like the first sign of a storm on the horizon, when the air turns thick and heavy.

"Be mine."

"What?" The air *whooshed* from my lungs. "You can't—"

A knock at the cabin startled me and I pressed my lips together to stop anymore words from spilling out.

Be his?

He didn't know what he was asking.

This wasn't a fairy tale where Prince Charming would swoop in and save the day and get the girl.

Because he doesn't know you.

I shook off the icy fingers of regret, the bitter taste of guilt. I didn't owe Matteo anything except a whole heap of gratitude.

Arabella ran for the door. "I'll get it," she called, yanking it open before either Luis or Matteo could get there and make sure it was safe.

"Sia." She pulled the blonde girl inside. "Wait until you meet Caitlin, she's..."

Her words were drowned out from the roar of blood in my ears as I watched Niccolò Marchetti step into the cabin, his wife Arianne at his side.

"You look well," she said, making a beeline for me.

"I'm much better, thank you."

"Caitlin." Nicco dipped his head in greeting.

"This is Alessia, my cousin. Nicco's sister," Arabella dragged the other girl over to us.

"You knew they were coming?" I asked Arabella, and she bit down on her lip.

"It was a surprise. Sia texted me from the car."

"I see."

"It's nice to meet you, Caitlin." Her eyes glittered with so much warmth and understanding, I almost forgot my manners.

"It's nice to meet you. I'm sorry about your father."

"Thank you. He's strong, a fighter… I still have hope."

"Why don't we all sit," Arianne suggested. "Nicco needs to talk to Matt, and I don't know about anyone else, but I'm parched."

"I think there's a bottle of wine chilling," Luis called from the kitchen.

"Perfect. Bring four glasses."

"Four?" Alessia's eyes grew to the size of saucers.

"Just don't tell your brother." Arianne winked, and the girls giggled.

"How are you, really?" she asked me quietly, while the girls got caught up.

"I'm fine. Is everything okay?" My eyes flicked over to where Nicco and Matteo were talking in hushed voices.

"We visited Antonio in the hospital, but it wasn't good news. Alessia was upset so I suggested we take a trip here. There's something about being out here that soothes the soul. Besides, I wanted to see you."

"Y-you did?"

"Don't look so surprised, Cait. You're one of us now."

I didn't know how to answer that, so I breathed a sigh of relief when Luis arrived with the glasses.

"I hope that's sparkling water." Matteo joined us, eyeing the glass in his sister's hand.

"One glass, please." She pouted.

"One. I don't want a repeat of last time."

"What happened last time?" I asked.

"I spent half the night holding her hair back while she worshipped the porcelain gods."

"*Matt!*"

A smile tipped the corner of my mouth. Their relationship was so easy, so warm and full of love. I envied them. I envied everything about Matteo and his family.

"If it's okay with you," Arianne said, "we're going to stay here for the night."

"I… sure." What could I say?

No, I didn't want them to stay because I didn't want to get dragged any deeper into their world? I couldn't do that; it was their cabin. I was the guest.

"Yes!" Arabella punched the air. "We can have movie night and make the guys watch Magic Mike."

"Porca miseria!" Matteo grumbled. "Should I be worried about your level of obsession with Channing Tatum?"

"What?" She shrugged. "He's hot."

Alessia blushed, gawking at her cousin. "He's… okay."

"Are you blind? He's every girl's wet dream."

"Jesus." Matteo hissed, throwing me a 'help me' look.

"Not your type, Alessia?" I smiled, smothering the laughter bubbling inside me.

"She's too hung up on Trist—"

"Bella!" She snapped.

"Trist who?"

"Tristan, Arianne's cousin. He's tall, dark, and super brooding."

"Oh my God, stop. Nicco is right over there."

"And he can hear you." Nicco's jaw flexed. Arianne's eyes crinkled with amusement as she went over to him and whispered something. He kissed her softly before they both came and joined us.

"So, Cait." Nicco folded one of his legs, resting his ankle on his knee. "How are you finding the cabin?"

"It's very nice, thank you."

He nodded once, not saying whatever was on his mind. Something had changed, but I couldn't put my finger on it. And I didn't miss the silent looks he and Matteo were exchanging.

Did it have something to do with what Matteo had asked me earlier?

Be mine.

Such a loaded question.

"Excuse me," I said, standing. I needed a second, emotion crashing into me from all directions.

"Are you okay?" Arianne asked.

"Fine, I'm fine. Excuse me." Hurrying away from them, I slipped down the hall and into my room.

Except, it wasn't my room. Because I didn't have a place to call my own anymore. Not that Zander's apartment had ever felt like home.

I burst into the small bathroom and clutched the basin, staring at myself in the mirror. It had been almost ten days and I still didn't have a plan.

Deep down, I knew the answer wasn't staying here. Letting these people—letting Matteo—burrow further into my heart.

Heaving a deep breath, my eyes fluttered. I sensed him before I saw him. "What do you want, Matteo?"

"Are you okay?"

"Honestly?" I locked eyes with him in the mirror. "I don't know what I am anymore."

He inched closer, taking the air in the room with him. "About what I said earlier—"

"Don't, please don't. I can't do this." My voice cracked, my agony bleeding out in the space between us. "I can't be who you want me to be. I'm broken, Matt. Don't you see that? I'm broken, and no amount of kind words or gentle touches will fix that. I'm—"

He pulled me into his strong arms, holding me close. My fingers twisted into his sweater as I buried my face in his chest, breathing him in. I was weak, unable to stop myself from taking what he was offering.

"We can help you, Cait. I can help you. You just have to trust me. Let me in, Tink." He held me at arm's length, gazing down at me. "Let me be there for you."

"I..." I can't. The words were on the tip of my tongue, but they didn't come. All I'd ever wanted was this. Someone to care. Someone to lean on. Matteo would never understand what he was offering me, but I knew.

"It's okay, we don't have to do this now." He brushed the tears from my cheeks. "Do you want me to send them away?"

"What? No! I don't... that's not what this is. I just... I have no experience with all of... all of this."

Matteo lowered his head, touching it to mine as his arms banded around my waist. "They're good people, Cait."

I didn't doubt that.

I was a good person, but I still had secrets. Dark, dirty secrets that would send Matteo running for the hills.

What a mess.

I'd never expected to find my hero in all this... but more heartachingly, I'd never expected to become the villain.

When I didn't reply, Matteo brushed his lips over the corner of my mouth. He wasn't playing fair, bewitching me with his touch; his spicy, male scent; and low, raspy voice.

Matteo infiltrated every corner of my mind, hijacking my heart and taking my soul captive.

But it would be our downfall.

I would be his demise.

"Tomorrow," I said, knowing I couldn't put the inevitable off any longer. "We'll talk about it tomorrow."

"We don't have to go back out there. We can stay right here and—"

"No," I said with a small shake of my head. "We should go back out there."

I could pretend for a little while longer.

EIGHTEEN

MATTEO

I WATCHED CAITLIN SLEEP. She was curled up on the end of the couch, a blanket thrown over her as she snored softly.

Everyone except Nicco and I had already gone to bed.

"Is she okay?" he asked.

There hadn't been time to talk earlier. When me and Caitlin had rejoined my family, the girls had picked out the movie and Luis already had snacks.

I only had eyes for Caitlin though.

She hadn't answered me when I'd asked her to be mine. Part of me wondered if she knew my motives and that's why she was hesitant. But the other part suspected it wasn't about me at all. She wanted me; I had no doubts about that. Something was holding her back though.

And I was determined to find out what it was.

"I don't know." I shrugged.

"Do you think she'll agree?"

"Would you?" I laughed dryly. "I didn't want it to be like this. I imagined what it would be like to see her again… but not like this. Fuck." I hissed, running a hand down my face.

"And if she wants to leave?" Nicco studied me, his intense stare almost too much to bear.

I'd churned this over in my head non-stop since bringing Caitlin here. If she wanted to leave, it meant losing her all over again.

"Let's hope she doesn't," I forced out the words past my lips. "I should get her to bed."

"Do you want some help?"

"No, I've got it, thanks."

Nicco stood and nodded. "She watches you too, you know. When you're not looking, she can't take her eyes off you."

His words hit their target and my chest puffed. "Yeah?"

"Yeah." He gave me a sad smile before taking off down the hall.

I stood, looming over Caitlin. She looked so peaceful it seemed a shame to move her.

"M-Matteo?" Her eyes flickered open. "What time is it?"

"Late. Everyone already went to bed."

"They did?"

I nodded, offering her my hand. "Let's get you into bed."

Without argument, Caitlin took my hand and I led her down the hall to her room.

"Where will you sleep?" she asked around a yawn.

I pulled back the covers and flicked my head for her to get in the bed. Pulling off her hoodie, Caitlin slipped into the sheets and nestled down.

"I'll see you tomorrow," I said.

"Stay."

The word echoed through my skull. My eyes found hers in the dark, and she smiled. "Matteo, will you please stay with me?"

Without a word, I yanked off my sweater and shucked out of my jeans, climbing in beside her. Caitlin burrowed into my side and laid her hand on my breastbone. "Thank you," she whispered. "For everything."

I pressed a kiss to her hair, hardly able to wipe the smile off my face. "You're worth it, Tink. I hope you know that."

A beat passed, and another, and Cait still didn't answer.

"Cait?" I gently shook her. Nothing.

She was out for the count, curled into my side like she belonged there.

It was disarming, the deep sense of peace I felt having her close. We didn't know each other, not really, not beyond the surface. Yet, I felt tethered to her in a way I couldn't explain.

I wanted to hold her like this every night and wake every morning to her green eyes and blinding smile.

I wanted her—plain and simple.

But as I closed my eyes, and allowed myself to fall into oblivion, I couldn't help but feel like I was one breath away from losing her.

My eyes flickered open, locking on her face. "Morning," I whispered, fighting a smile.

"It's still early, the sun isn't even up yet," she said. "What happened last night?"

"You don't remember?"

"You carried me to bed?"

I nodded. "You were barely conscious."

"Sorry, I didn't—"

"Shh." I pressed my thumb against her lips, unable to smother the groan that worked its way up my throat when the tip of her tongue darted out and tasted my skin.

"Cait?"

"I don't want to talk, Matt," she said. "I just want to feel... make me feel, please." The sheer desperation in her voice reached inside my chest and grabbed my heart in an iron grip.

"You're sure?"

She nodded, dragging my face down to meet hers. Our lips touched, tentative at first. But the second her tongue found mine, my control dissipated. I rolled onto my back, taking Cait with me so that she straddled my hips. Her hands went to my bare chest as she leaned down and brushed her lips over mine again. A featherlight touch, teasing me. Making my blood heat like lava in my veins.

"Sei bellissima." I pushed her red curls off her shoulder and stroked her collarbone. Caitlin threw back her head, whimpering softly. When our eyes connected again, she said, "What did you just say?"

"I said, you are very beautiful."

Slowly, she rocked her hips, dragging her center along my dick. Even with layers of material separating us, her heat felt incredible.

"What do you want, Tink?" I asked her, curling one hand around her hip to guide her over me harder.

"Y-you," she breathed. "I want you."

My hand grabbed the nape of her neck, pulling her down to me. "You want me, Tink. You want to feel me pushing inside your hot, slick pussy?"

"God, yes... Show me how good it can be..." Her fingers twisted into my chest, clutching and desperate.

Without warning, I held her to me and rolled us, pinning her beneath me. Grinding in slow torturous circles, I brought Caitlin to the edge.

"More?" I quirked a brow.

Mouth hanging open, breathing labored, she nodded.

I chuckled, working my hand inside her panties. "Fuck, you're soaked." Two fingers slid into her with ease.

"No," she wiggled against me, pulling me closer to her body. "I want you inside me. I want to feel you. All of you."

Jesus. She was going to be the death of me. Rocking back on my haunches, I climbed off the bed and pushed my briefs over my hips, kicking out of them. Grabbing my wallet, I retrieved a condom and threw it down on the bed before gently easing off her panties.

A shiver worked through her as I rolled on the condom and crawled up her bed.

"If we do this—"

"Don't," she rushed out, shaking her head. "I don't want to talk about what happens after. I just want to live in the now, Matteo. Can you do that? Can you give me that?"

Jesus, with her staring up at me like that, I would have given her the whole goddamn world.

She had to know that I wouldn't give her up so easily, that I couldn't. Our lives were entwined now, shackled by forces outside of our control.

Caitlin raked her fingers through the hair at the back of my neck, and pulled me down, her lips ghosting mine. "I really need to feel you inside me, Matt."

I filled her with one smooth stroke. Her breath caught as I stilled, just reveling in how tight she felt, how fucking perfect.

Mine.

The word echoed through my skull.

She felt like she was mine.

"I need you to move," she breathed. "Fuck me, Matt. Please..."

I. Lost. Control.

Hitching Caitlin's leg around my waist, I drove her into the mattress with hard, unrelenting thrusts. And she took it. She took everything I gave her, rolling her hips to meet mine, clenching my dick like a fist. It was enough to make me grit my teeth, she felt that damn good.

"Fuck... *fuck*," I panted, straightening my arms to go harder, faster. It wasn't how I wanted to do this; I'd wanted to take my time and go slow. But suddenly, it was like we were on borrowed time. And an urgency to claim her, to take her and make her mine slammed into me. If I marked her, imprinted myself on her, she had to say yes... didn't she?

"Oh God, Matt, yes... *yes*," she choked out, moaning my name into the dark as our bodies rocked in perfect synchrony.

"Shh," I murmured against her lips, kissing her. "You need to be quiet."

"It just feels so... *good*..."

"I know, baby, I know." Pressing my head to hers, I hooked my forearm under one of her thighs and lifted her leg, allowing me to go deeper. Caitlin buried her face in the crook of my shoulder, clinging to my body as I took us higher and higher.

Nothing, nothing would ever feel as good as this. Her skin was soft and warm, and her pussy fit me like a glove. Her curves were a map I wanted to take my time exploring, until I'd learned every hidden treasure.

Whether she knew it or not, Caitlin was made for me. At least, that's all I could think as I raced toward the edge.

"I need you to come for me, Tink," I whispered against her ear, nipping her lobe. She shuddered, clenching around me hard enough that I groaned.

I slowed the pace, circling my hips a couple of times, grinding my pelvis against her clit. Caitlin held her breath, her body coiling tightly until she snapped apart.

"Yes... Yes..."

I kissed her through it, swallowing her moans, the tiny whimpers spilling from her lips.

"Fuck, Cait... you feel so fucking good." One more thrust and I jerked inside her, coming hard.

We stayed like that, wrapped up in one another, breathing each other's air.

"You good?" I asked her.

A faint smile traced her mouth, but it didn't reach her eyes.

I rolled away, quickly disposing of the condom and then climbed back into bed, pulling her into my arms. "That was incredible."

"Matt..." She blushed.

"I know you feel it, Cait."

"It doesn't change anything." Her brows furrowed. "I'm... and you're..."

"What does that even mean? I can protect you. We can protect you. You don't need to worry about DiMarco."

"You promised we wouldn't do this... not now... not after—" She rolled her lips together, refusing to say the words.

Dejection pulsed through me. How the hell could she deny the connection we shared? It was a living, breathing thing, lingering in the space between us. She felt it. I knew she did.

So why the fuck was she still fighting it?

I wanted her—I'd made it more than clear.

Besides DiMarco, what was she running from?

As I pulled her closer and tucked my chin on the top of her head, it was the only question on my mind.

The next time I woke, it was to an empty bed. I let out a frustrated breath and ran a hand over my face. Sunlight poured in through the curtains, a sure sign it was finally morning.

Voices caught my attention beyond the door, and I climbed out of bed and pulled on my jeans and sweater, making a quick stop in the bathroom before I went looking for Caitlin.

I didn't expect to find her laughing and joking with Arabella as they made pancakes. Leaning against the wall, I watched them, my chest constricting.

"I know you're watching," Bella smirked over her shoulder.

"Busted." I held up my hands, going over to the breakfast counter and sitting on one of the stools. "Something smells good."

"Caitlin was making breakfast and I offered to help." She beamed.

That was Bella, she liked to feel helpful.

"So where did you sleep last night, Matt?"

"Bella." I shook my head.

Caitlin didn't look at me, just kept flipping the batter and adding the pancakes to the growing stack.

"What?" My sister grinned. "It's a simple question."

"Stop," I mouthed, right as Cait met my eyes.

"Hey," she said.

"Hey."

"Okay then, I'll just be… over there, making myself scarce." Bella slipped out of the kitchen and down the hall.

"You were gone."

"I didn't want to wake you." My brow lifted and she added, "Fine, I didn't want things to be awkward."

"Why did you think things would be awkward? I don't have a single regret about last night. Do you?"

"Matt, I—"

"Morning." Luis came in through the front door, shaking off his jacket. "It's kicking up a storm out there. Hmm, something smells good."

"I made pancakes," Caitlin smiled at him, and a bolt of jealousy went through me. It was irrational, but I wanted her to look at me the way she looked at him. So comfortable and at ease.

Maybe you should have stayed out here with her.

"Help yourself." She shoved the stack of pancakes into the middle of the counter and started on the bacon. Soon, the smell lured Nicco, Arianne, and Alessia from their bedrooms and we all crammed around the counter.

"So good," Arianne complimented her. "Thank you, you didn't need to cook for us."

"It's no big deal." Caitlin shrugged, remaining over by the cooktop.

"Join us," Arabella added. "You can't cook for us and then not eat."

"I'm not hungry."

I stared at her, willing her to look at me. But she dug in her heels, looking everywhere except in my direction.

Last night had been close to perfect, the way our bodies had moved as one, her soft whimpers and the heat burning between us. The sex was incredible, but it had been so much more than that.

Now, she was acting like it was nothing. Refusing to acknowledge this thing between us. And it pissed me off. I didn't want to force her hand. I wanted her to come to me willingly.

Deep down, I wanted her to want this.

To want me.

"Did Matteo upset you?" Arabella chuckled. "Because I know he isn't the easiest person to—"

"*Bella*!" I snapped, growing tired of her bullshit.

"Jeez, what crawled up your ass and died?" she murmured. "I was only joking."

I swallowed the mouthful of pancake and helped myself to a glass of juice to wash it down. This wasn't quite how I imagined the morning after the night before going. Caitlin deserved more. She deserved hearts and flowers and all that stuff women dreamed of.

The silence stretched out before us as everyone glanced between me and Caitlin. It was awkward as fuck, and I breathed a sigh of relief when Arianne suggested they take their second mugs of coffee into the living area.

"Remind me never to bring Arabella out here again," I muttered to Nicco.

"Did you talk to her?"

"Bella?" I frowned.

His brow quirked and my stomach sank. "No. I tried but she's shutting me out."

"So, you still don't know what she plans to do?"

"She's scared," I whispered.

"Maybe so, but she has to make a choice."

"Is it really a choice?" I stared at him, my best friend. Surely, he had to know what he was asking of me. Of her.

"If she wants to leave, Nic..." I couldn't lose her, not when I'd only just found her again.

"That's her choice, Matt. But if she wants to leave, you need to make it clear what that means."

"I know. Fuck, I know, okay? I just... I need more time."

"We're running out of time. E is heading to Providence soon and then he and Lucino will head straight to see DiMarco."

"One more day. I need one more day."

"Fine. But you need to talk to her, or I will."

"Can you take Bella back with you?"

"Of course." A strained expression washed over him.

"Shit, Nic, I'm sorry," I said. "I know how hard this must be for you."

"He's still alive, there's still hope."

But the emptiness in his eyes told me he'd already given up. He believed Uncle Toni was gone, and it was just a case of his body catching up to what his soul already knew.

"They deserve more." He stared over at the girls, his sharp gaze lingering on Alessia and Arabella.

"Yeah." I swallowed. Nicco knew how I felt about Arabella growing up in this life. I wanted nothing more than to wrap her in cotton wool and protect her at all costs. But it was easier said than done. In this life, people were used as pawns. Collateral. Leverage. If someone—our enemies—wanted to come at us, they would do it through hurting one of our loved ones. Nicco and Enzo had not experienced that firsthand.

It was why my old man was so pissed about Caitlin. We'd brought her here, to one of our safe houses. We'd pulled her into this world, which not only made her a target...

It made her a liability.

NINETEEN

CAITLIN

I WATCHED everyone file out of the cabin. It had been strange, having them all here. I couldn't deny that a part of me had liked it. I liked Arabella's easy way and Alessia's quiet demeanor. I liked Arianne and how kind and compassionate she was. Even Nicco had warmed to our small gathering. And Matteo… I didn't know where to start with him.

Last night had been more than I could've ever dreamed. He wasn't gentle. He didn't handle me like fragile glass. He'd taken what he'd wanted and given me everything I never knew I needed. It had been amazing, being worshipped like that. Every kiss and touch, every roll of his hips, the feel of him moving inside me, was imprinted on my mind—and my soul—and I couldn't imagine forgetting it anytime soon. But the harsh light of day always brought with it a reality neither of us could escape. He was Matteo Bellatoni, a Marchetti by blood. And I was… well, he could never know the truth.

"I'll see you soon, okay?" Bella hurried to my side, hugging me tightly. "You're good for him," she whispered. "And anyone can see that he cares about you a lot."

Emotion balled in my throat.

"See you," I said, the words almost getting stuck.

Arabella regarded me for a second, giving me a warm smile before Matteo called for her. His eyes connected with mine, a bolt of something going through me.

Wasn't he even going to say goodbye?

Disappointment sat heavy in my chest. We hadn't had time to talk—not that

I knew what to say. I knew what he wanted; he'd made that more than clear. But I couldn't do it. I couldn't give him more than right here, right now.

The door banged shut, a gunshot to my heart. I hadn't realized how much I'd missed company until they'd all showed up last night. Luis was nice, and he made me feel comfortable, but it wasn't the same. Back in Providence, I had friends. I had Gisele and Mari and Shaun.

God, Shaun.

I clutched my throat. I'd shut those memories out, but now all I felt was the bitter sting of regret. He'd died because of me, and no one had even mentioned it. As if death was just business as usual. I guess for them, in their line of work, maybe it was.

Everything was such a mess.

Letting out a weary sigh, I hugged myself tight and made my way back to my room. I couldn't stay here for much longer. Every day that I did, Matteo, his family, burrowed their way a little deeper. The door clicked open, and I heard footsteps on the wooden floor. It was probably Luis.

But then his voice washed over me.

"Caitlin?"

I turned slowly, my eyes colliding with Matteo. "What are you—"

"You thought I was leaving?" His brows knitted as he stopped short of me.

"I… I assumed you were going back with your family, yes."

"We need to talk." He ran a hand down his face.

"I know."

I did, and I hated it. I didn't want to talk. I didn't want him to ask me questions I didn't have the answers to.

"Where's Luis?" I glanced over his shoulder.

"He's accompanying them back to Verona. We're alone, for now." His conflicted gaze dropped to my lips, and my tongue darted out, wetting them.

When he looked at me like that, I wanted things. Things I could never have. Not now. Not tomorrow. Not ever.

"Please," I whispered. "Don't look at me like that."

"Like what?" Matteo took a step closer. "How am I looking at you?"

"Like you want things." I craned my neck to look him in the eye, the air thick and heavy around us. "Things I can't give you."

"You are so beautiful, Tink." He tucked my curls behind my ear, cupping my neck as his thumb stroked my jaw, lingering on my bottom lip. "I wish it didn't have to be this way. I wish we'd met under different circumstances. But we didn't…"

"No." My voice cracked, my heart beating wildly in my chest.

"Come, sit." He took my hand, leading me over to the couch. I sat down, barely able to think over my racing pulse. "In a different life, I'd court you, Tink. I'd spend my time getting to know you, getting you to trust me. We'd date and take our time learning about each other. But we don't have that luxury. Not with DiMarco out there looking for you."

A shiver ran down my spine as I sucked in a harsh breath.

Matteo squeezed my hand gently. "I will never let him hurt you, Cait. But by bringing you here, we dragged you into this thing. My elders, they will only protect you if you're—"

"If I'm what?" My lip quivered as I took in his gutted expression.

"If you're my woman."

"W-what are you saying?" I blanched.

"You're either with me, Cait, or you're not."

"I'll go." I shot up. "I'll leave and you won't have to—"

"You think I can just let you walk out of here, out of my life?" Pain etched into his expression. "It doesn't work like that, Tink. I'm not—"

"You're not what, Matteo?" I snapped, feeling indignation burn through me. "Am I a prisoner here? Is that what this is?"

His gaze dropped and I had my answer. He wasn't going to let me go. Either I accepted his proposition of being his woman or I would be kept here until God only knew when.

"It's just until this thing with DiMarco is over." His eyes implored me to understand. But I couldn't... I couldn't make sense of... of this. "If we let you leave and he... finds you... you know things about us, Caitlin. You know where Nicco and Arianne live, you know about my sister and this place.

"For as much as I hate it," Matteo inhaled a ragged breath, "my family are right. It makes you a liability."

"You think I'd tell him anything? I hate him, Matt. I'd rather die than ever tell him a single thing." I shrieked, hot tears rolling down my cheeks.

"And that's exactly what will happen if he finds you." Matteo roared, glowering at me, and I jerked back as if he'd slapped me. "Shit, Cait, that's not... I didn't." He jammed his fingers into his hair, tugging the ends. "I don't want to argue with you. I want us to figure this out. *Together*. You know how I feel about you, Caitlin. I guess I'd hoped—"

"That I'd what? Jump into bed with you straightaway and play happy family? You just said it yourself, I'm a liability. You should never have brought me here." I sneered.

"WE DIDN'T HAVE A FUCKING CHOICE," he bellowed. "You think we could just leave you alone in that hospital, knowing what you'd been through? What he'd done?"

"This is my life, Matteo. My. Fucking. Life. I know how to protect myself. I've been doing it long enough." My chest heaved with the weight of my words.

"Cait, what are you hiding?" He reached for me, but I shook him off. "Just talk to me, please. You think I don't see the shadows in your eyes? You're hiding something. Tell me. Let me help."

"I think you've done enough." I averted my gaze, unable to look at him as I wrapped my arms around my waist, holding myself together.

"This isn't how I wanted it to be. But things are going down that are out of my control. If you leave and DiMarco finds you... the Family won't risk that. They can't."

"I got it," I hissed. "You don't trust me." My eyes locked on his. "Well, you really should have thought about that before bringing me here. I didn't ask to meet your family, Matt. I didn't ask you to bring Arabella here. I didn't ask for anything other than time to figure out what I was going to do next."

"I'm sorry." His eyes bored into mine, stripping me bare. "I just wanted to... fuck," he breathed, "I don't even know what I'm doing."

I wasn't being entirely fair, I knew that. But I'd wanted so much to believe Matteo and his family were different. That I could trust them.

Yet here we were. With an ultimatum hanging between us.

If I didn't fall into line, if I didn't agree to be with Matteo, then I would be a prisoner here until DiMarco was no longer a threat.

However long that would be.

A week.

A month.

Two.

I couldn't stay here for that long. I'd go out of my mind. Especially now that I knew the truth.

Matteo didn't want me, not really.

He just wanted to make this easier on me. He wanted to ease me into the idea of us. Even if it was all for show.

"I need some space." I started backing away.

"Cait, please. We need to talk about this."

"No, we really don't." I sniffled, willing myself not to break in front of him more than I already had. "I think I understand everything perfectly."

"Cait..." he called after me, but I turned on my heel, and didn't look back.

I should have run when I had the chance. Stupidly, I hadn't considered when they first brought me here that Luis was here not for my protection—he was here to make sure I didn't try to escape.

Now, all I could see was him as the guy standing between me and freedom.

I wasn't even sure I wanted to leave. I had nowhere to go. I had no contacts, no friends across the country where I could pitch up and sleep on their couch for a few nights. All I had was the instinct to survive and do whatever it took to stay under the radar.

DiMarco's had been the perfect place to blend in. Until it wasn't. If only I hadn't caught Zander's eyes, I wouldn't be here now. I'd still be working the floor, laughing and joking with Shaun while we watched Gisele and Mari work the crowds of hungry men into a frenzy. It wasn't the dream, but it was something.

It was better than the life I'd spent years running from.

Matteo had left earlier. I'd heard him and Luis talking in hushed voices, only catching the odd word.

Don't let her out of your sight.

Back to Verona.

Call me if she wants to talk.

Watch her.

I hated it. Hated that I'd become such a burden to them. I didn't ask for this—I didn't ask for any of it.

I blamed Enzo. If he had never showed up at my apartment all those weeks ago and given me his number, I never would have ended up here.

No, you probably would have been dead by now.

I inhaled a sharp breath. Like it or not, Enzo and Matteo had saved me that day. They had offered me a lifeline that I couldn't refuse.

So why had I gotten so angry earlier when Matteo had laid out the truth for me?

He wasn't a normal guy. His family were one of the most talked about crime families in New England. Of course they weren't just going to take me in for a couple of weeks, let me find my feet, and then send me on my way with a smile.

They were the mafia for Pete's sake. You didn't graciously accept their help free of charge. You earned it. You became indebted for it.

You *paid* for it.

But I wasn't for sale, and I most certainly wasn't about to pretend to be involved with Matteo to get in their good graces.

"Caitlin?" Luis's gruff voice drifted down the hall. "I made risotto."

"Not hungry," I yelled back.

"You can't stay in there forever." I could almost hear the humor in his voice.

This wasn't funny.

Nothing about this situation warranted laughter. Not a single thing.

"Watch me," I mumbled, throwing myself down on the bed. My cell phone vibrated, and I picked it up.

I'm sorry. M xo

Ugh. It would have hurt less if he was a typical asshole jerk who had broken my heart. But Matteo wasn't a bad guy.

He was just the wrong guy.

Another text came through and I narrowed my eyes.

Is the idea of being with me really that unappealing to you?

. . .

Fueled by rage, I texted back.

That's not the point and you know it...

No, I don't. Because you refused to talk to me. You think I like this? I don't... but my hands are tied.

Another one came straight through.

Regardless of what my family wants, this is about you and me. I know you felt it last night, Cait. You can't deny that we're good together... I was sure of it eight months ago, I'm even more sure of it now. What are you so scared of?

I squeezed my eyes shut.

Everything.

I was scared of everything.

I thought what we had was real. I thought I could trust you.

I hit send, immediately regretting it. But I was hurt and on the defense. Matteo wasn't a bad guy, I knew that. Everything was such a mess though. Just when I was about to truly let him in, to give myself to him, he landed me with the ultimatum, reminding me this wasn't a fairy tale... and he wasn't my white knight.

Sadly, there were no heroes in this story.

And no happy endings.

TWENTY

MATTEO

"THAT BAD, HUH?" Enzo asked me as I lay sprawled on the couch.

"She's pissed."

"Are you surprised?" He chuckled.

"Yes... No... Fuck, I don't know what to think." Dragging a hand down my face, I let out a heavy sigh. "There's something between us, E. Something real. I thought... I thought she might be willing to explore that."

"You blindsided her."

"Did you know it would go this way when we brought her back to Verona?"

"I knew once Uncle Michele and Al got wind of it, they'd want assurances. You know that's how it works."

"Yeah..." I guess I'd just hoped it wouldn't be like this. "What the fuck am I supposed to do now?"

"Give her some space. Caitlin has every right to feel betrayed. Let her cool off."

"I just don't like the idea of her out there all alone."

"So, we'll send the girls. I'm sure Arianne won't mind going out there and Nora is dying to meet her. They can even take Alessia and Bella."

"I guess..."

"What is it?" He paused. "What aren't you telling me?"

Dropping my eyes to the bottle in my hand, I weighed on whether to tell him or not. But I needed to talk to someone.

"I slept with her."

"Of course you did." I could almost hear his eyes roll.

"What the fuck is that supposed to mean?"

"You look at her the way Nicco looks at Arianne. The way I look at Nora. She's yours, Matt. She just hasn't figured it out yet."

"And if I lose her because of this?"

"You won't."

"How can you be so sure?"

"You might be a soft pussy, but you still have Marchetti blood in your veins. We don't give up what's ours without a fight."

His words sank into me. Was he right? Was it only a matter of time before Caitlin realized what I already knew?

We were supposed to find each other again. Even in the dire circumstances, we were both supposed to end up right here. Together. I refused to believe it was anything less than Fate working her will.

"I'll be lucky if she'll ever talk to me again," I huffed, draining my beer.

Enzo chuckled again. "So make her."

It was my turn to roll my eyes. "And how does that go down with Nora?"

"She'd tell you she hates it when I get all bossy, but secretly, she loves it. Gets her all hot for me."

"Okay, that was too much information."

"She especially likes it when I tie her up and—"

"Jesus, what is wrong with you? I don't want to hear your sex stories."

"Did Caitlin already put your balls in her purse? Because you sound like a fucking pussy."

"Fuck off," I grumbled. Just because I didn't want to share all the details about my sex life. I respected women too much to do that.

"What's happening there anyway? Shouldn't you be stalking DiMarco's?"

"Not a lot, not yet. Anyway, I wanted to speak to you first. Make sure you've got your head screwed on right."

"I feel like I'm losing my damn mind."

"Women, cous, they'll do that to a guy."

"You'll call me if you find out anything?"

"You know it."

"And DiMarco?"

"Let's hope he refuses to give us the intel on Lombardi, so I get the pleasure of reminding him of our agreement."

"Make it hurt." I snorted.

"I will. DiMarco will get his, Matt. Whether it's tomorrow or next week or sometime in the future."

I dipped my head in an appreciative nod.

A knock at the door startled me, and I padded over to the door to open it.

"Enzo sent reinforcements."

"Seriously?" I groaned down the line.

"What? I thought she could give you another pep talk."

"Here," I said, handing her the phone. "He wants to talk to you."

"Hi, babe. I'm missing you." Nora moved deeper into the apartment, dropping her purse on the counter. "Yeah, I miss you too."

Her voice lowered and I heard her giggle as they exchanged sweet nothings.

Lucky bastard.

Nora let out a soft whimper as he no doubt let her know exactly how much he was missing her.

"Babe, we have company," she scolded, covering the receiver to mouth, "Sorry, Matt," at me.

"No apology needed." I forced a smile. "I actually need to get off soon. I promised Bella I'd pick her and Alessia up and take them for ice-cream."

"How're things with Caitlin?"

"Don't ask."

"That bad?"

"She'll come around," Enzo shouted down the line, so Nora put him on speaker. "She's been through a lot. Cut her some slack."

"I know."

I did. But that only made it worse. I wanted to help her, to be there for her and support her. I didn't want to be on the sidelines.

"Gattina, how do you feel about going out to the cabin to spend some time with her and the girls?" Enzo asked. "Matt thinks she could use the company."

"Hell yes." She grinned. "Count me in. Some female perspective might help her see things a little differently too."

"No meddling," I warned. "She already doesn't trust me. I don't need you giving her any more ammunition."

Nora gasped. "I'm offended you think I'd mess it up. I can be quite persuasive when I put my mind to it. Ask Enzo." She smirked, and my cousin snorted down the line.

"I think we both know who's in charge around here," he said. "I'm telling you, cous," he added. "If you really think she's the one, fight for her. Fight until she doesn't have any choice but to give in to you."

"Who are you and what have you done with my cousin?" Amusement filled my voice.

"Here," Nora handed me back the cell phone. "I need to pee. Bye babe, video call me later and we can do that thing." She took off down the hall and I turned off the loudspeaker.

"That thing?" I muttered. "Please tell me you're not going to have phone sex while you're supposed to be scoping out DiMarco?"

"I'm telling you cous, one day, I'm going to marry that woman and put my kid in her stomach." He let out a contented sigh.

Jealousy snaked through me.

I wanted that.

I wanted it all...

With a woman who probably hated me now.

"You're not coming inside?" Bella asked as she climbed out of the truck. It was the day after Enzo had suggested the girls visit Caitlin, and I had to admit it wasn't his worst idea ever.

"No, I... No."

"What happened with you two anyway? I heard Nicco and Ari talking and—"

"Just adult stuff."

"Adult stuff. Really, Matt? You're barely four years older than me."

"Listen, Bella, I could use your help a little here. Caitlin is... well, she's pissed at me."

"And you want me to try to smooth the cracks?"

"Something like that." Was this what my life had really come to? Asking my little sister to score me brownie points with the woman I couldn't stop thinking about?

"I only want her safe, Bella. That's all that matters to me."

"She'll come around." Arabella smiled. "No one can resist your charm for long."

"Thanks." I chuckled, but it sounded strained. "Go on, get inside."

"Are you sure you don't want to come inside and see her?"

My eyes went to the cabin. "I don't think that's a good idea."

Sadness crept into my sister's expression. "Okay. But don't worry, I'll work my magic on her." Bella winked before taking off toward the cabin.

This was a good idea, bringing the girls here. I didn't want Caitlin to think she was our captive. And she'd seemed at ease around Ari, Alessia, and Bella. Of course, I had no doubt Nora would insert herself into our fledgling relationship, or whatever was left of it. But I'd take whatever I could get.

Nicco kissed Arianne before watching her disappear inside, then he got into the truck.

"You're not taking the Range Rover?" I asked.

He shrugged. "I figured we could ride together. Then you can bring me back later."

Sneaky.

But I couldn't deny that having an excuse to come back out here was welcomed.

As I pulled onto the dirt road leading back to the highway, I glanced in my rearview mirror and saw Caitlin watching us.

I had to fight the urge to pull a U-turn and go back for her, to demand she heard me out. But she wanted time, and I would give it to her.

"She'll come around," Nicco said as if he heard my thoughts.

"I'm not so sure." I glanced in the mirror again, but she was gone.

Maybe she'd never been there at all.

"I know you… feel something for her. But what do you really know about her, Matt?"

My brows furrowed. "What the hell is that supposed to mean?"

If anyone got it, I thought it would be Nicco. He'd fallen for Arianne in a heartbeat, not realizing who she really was until it was too late.

Theirs had been a case of star-crossed lovers. The tragic kind. The kind that ended in death and heartache. But they had survived. He'd gotten the girl and the life he wanted with her.

So yeah, I thought he might understand how it felt to fall so deeply into someone without ever truly knowing them.

"Don't look at me like that," he rolled his eyes. "I don't have the luxury of being sentimental, not now." Not since his father had been taken sick. "I have to make decisions in the best interests of our business. Decisions that protect everything the Family has built. You know that."

"I know. Fuck, Nic, I know that. But if anyone understood, I thought… it doesn't matter." I released a strained breath, keeping my eyes on the road.

"I get it, I do. I'm just worried. She has you all twisted up in knots and I know that feeling well. It leaves you unable to see straight." It was his turn to sigh. "All I'm saying is, tread carefully. You said it yourself, she's hiding something. I don't want you to be blindsided."

"Yeah." I didn't expand.

His words left a bitter taste in my mouth. So it was okay for him and Enzo to pursue women who they knew deserved more than this life, but the first time I actually showed any interest in a girl, it was deemed irresponsible?

Fuck that.

Caitlin was entitled to her secrets after what she'd survived at the hands of DiMarco.

Nothing she could tell me would change how I felt; of that, I was sure. Because you didn't pick the people you cared about, the people you loved. It wasn't something you could control or switch off. It was something you couldn't fight. Something you couldn't ignore.

"I just keep thinking what happens after, you know? Once this shit with DiMarco is handled. What then? If she doesn't want me, what will you do?"

"I'm not a monster, Matteo. This you know."

"I know. But you are the boss now. I understand that comes with responsibility."

"Once we decide what to do with DiMarco, Caitlin will be safe. I'll see to it personally. You have my word."

"You'll make her disappear," I said, the pit in my stomach stretching.

"It's the only way, Matt, and you know it. Unless—"

"Unless she decides to stay and be with me."

That was it then.

If Caitlin didn't choose me once this was all over, she'd be gone, and I'd never see her again.

Nicco, with the help of our trusted associates, would make her disappear. Give her a new life in exchange for her silence.

I guess I should have felt lucky she wouldn't find herself buried in a ditch somewhere, never to be found again. But I couldn't find it in myself to feel anything but a stab of regret.

Surely the universe wouldn't be so cruel to bring her back into my life and then take her away again?

"I'm sorry," he said. "I'm sorry it has to be this way."

"Me too," I murmured as realization sank deep into my bones.

Everything was changing.

It had always been the three of us—Nicco, Enzo, and me—against the world. Then he met Arianne, and Enzo found Nora. But I was okay with that because seeing them happy was worth being the fifth wheel. I didn't feel like an outsider then. But now, sitting there with Nicco, the guy I'd loved like a brother for my entire life, I couldn't help but feel the power imbalance between us.

He was no longer just my cousin, my best friend, my family. He was the boss. He couldn't let his familiarity or attachment to me get the better of him, and I knew him well enough to know he wouldn't.

Just like I knew if Caitlin refused to give us a chance—refused to give me a chance—after this shit with DiMarco went away, I'd probably never see her again.

What did you do to her?

I stared at Bella's text message, reading the words over and over again.

What's wrong?

She seems… sad.

Fuck.

There's some stuff you don't know…

Arabella's reply came straight through.

. . .

Isn't there always.

Even over a cell phone, I felt the bite to her words.

Is she okay?

I don't know. She seems off, but she won't talk about it. I tried to talk about you, and she completely shut down.

I tipped my head back against the couch and let out a weary sigh. When we'd gotten back to Verona, I'd asked Nicco to drop me off at the apartment. I hadn't officially moved out of my parents' house, but sometimes, I needed the space.

But space from Caitlin was the last thing I wanted. It felt like there was an ocean between us.

Just be there for her. She's had a rough time of it. She needs a friend.

Alessia and Arabella might have been younger, but they were wise beyond their years. I guess that's what happened when you grew up in a family like ours. We tried to protect them as much as we could, but they both had a knack of uncovering the truth.

God help the men who stole their hearts. A shudder went through me. I didn't want to think of my sister falling in love. Not now. Not ever. But I wasn't stupid enough to know it wouldn't happen one day.

My cell vibrated again, and I opened the message, my breath catching at my sister's reply.

Maybe she needs more than a friend.

I screwed my eyes shut, forcing myself to take a deep breath. That's all I wanted—to be Caitlin's guy. To be there for her, to protect her.

To love her.

This was bigger than the both of us though. Bigger than what I wanted, or Caitlin needed.

It was about the Family. The Family I'd sworn my loyalty—*my life*—to.

But it had never felt more of a burden than it did in that moment.

TWENTY-ONE

CAITLIN

"SHE DID NOT," Arabella and Alessia giggled as I told them about the time Marielle had kicked a guy in the balls for getting too handsy with her.

Nicco and Matteo probably didn't want me corrupting their little sisters with stories from the strip club. But it wasn't like I had anything else to tell them. My childhood wasn't normal. There were no cute stories about my high school boyfriend and prom. I didn't have a romantic first-time story or any anecdotes from being on the cheer squad or being student body president.

"What happened to the guy?"

"He had to ice his balls."

Nora stifled a chuckle while Arianne looked a little horrified.

"Sorry," I said. "I didn't mean to—"

"Relax, babe," Nora said. "This is the best thing I've heard all day. Besides, serves the asshole right for touching instead of looking."

I liked Nora. She was feisty in a way I'd always wished I was. She and Arianne had turned up armed with wine and the five of us had spent the last couple of hours sitting around, drinking and talking. It was nice. Normal even.

But I couldn't shake the feeling that it was Matteo's attempt at softening me up to the ultimatum he'd dropped on me.

"Who's that?" Alessia asked Bella who was clutching her cell phone.

"No one." Her eyes flicked to mine but quickly dropped when I frowned.

Matteo.

Even now, he was keeping an eye on me, using his sister to do his bidding.

I didn't know how to feel about that.

But I couldn't deny that part of me liked that he cared so much. Not that it changed anything.

"This is nice," Nora said. "Taking a break from city life."

"You mean from Enzo." Bella snickered.

"I mean, I love the guy, but let a girl breathe." She grinned. "But the sex... holy mother of God, the sex is—"

"Okay, Nor." Arianne leaned over and covered her friend's mouth. "I think that's enough wine for you, and definitely enough share time."

"They're not kids, Ari. They know all about the birds and bees. Hell, I bet they've already—"

"Okay." Arianne grabbed Nora's arm and yanked her up. "We'll just be in the kitchen. Getting Nora a nice, big glass of cold water."

"Yes, *Mom*." Nora rolled her eyes, as she let Arianne pull her away.

"God, I want to be Nora when I'm older," Bella let out a deep sigh. "She's just so... confident, you know? She knows what she wants, and she goes after it. I admire that."

"It's a good quality to have," I murmured, draining my glass. Something told me I was going to need a lot more where that came from if I was going to survive tonight.

"What would you go after, Sia?" Bella mused. "If you could have anything, what would it be?"

"I don't know." Nicco's sister gave a half-shrug. "I've never really thought about it."

"Oh, don't give me that. There must be something... or maybe, someone." Arabella waggled her eyebrows.

"Is there a boy at school you like?" I asked.

"Try man," Bella coughed, smirking.

"Bella!"

"What? I think Tristan is hot too."

"Tristan, who is he... remind me again?" I said.

"Arianne's cousin. The man is fine with a capital F. But he's older. Too old. And he's technically family now. I guess it's weird."

"I don't like Tristan, Bella. You're being ridiculous."

"It's not like Matteo or Nicco will ever let us date anyway." Arabella flopped back into the heap of cushions and looked up at the ceiling. "No one will ever be good enough in their eyes."

"You won't be sixteen forever," I said. "In a couple of years, you'll be your own woman. Old enough to make your own decisions."

Her eyes slid to mine. "You have met the three of them, right?"

"They just care. You should feel very lucky to have them." My chest constricted with every word.

If only I had a big brother or an older cousin to look out for me, things might have gone differently.

But I didn't.

And I couldn't spend my life living in the past, when I was constantly trying to figure out how to live in the present.

"Did you ever dance at the club?" Arabella asked me out of nowhere.

"I… uh, at first, for a little bit. But I didn't like it."

"You didn't?" She leaned up on her elbows.

"No. You see, I used to dance. Before I moved to Providence."

"In a strip club?"

"No, in a dance company."

"What kind of dance?"

"Anything. Ballet. Jazz. Lyrical. Contemporary."

"That's so cool. I always wanted to be a ballerina when I was a kid, but I have the coordination of Bambi."

"I'm sure you don't."

"Oh, she does," Alessia piped up, chuckling.

"You said you *used* to dance?"

"Yeah." My heart cracked. "I had to stop."

"Why?"

"I… I moved here and life got in the way."

The truth was, I hadn't had the extra money for lessons. And then, once Zander found out I loved to dance, he'd put me to *good use*. And I hated him for it. I respected the dancers at DiMarco's, admired them even. They owned their bodies and used them to their full advantage. But dancing was something I never wanted to be used against me, ever again.

Something I would never forgive him for.

"There's an amazing theater in the city. They have an in-house ballet company. One of the best in New England. We should go one time. I'm sure Nicco could get—"

"Bella," Alessia chided, shaking her head.

"That would be nice," I said, wanting to break the sudden tension.

Thankfully, Nora and Arianne chose that moment to rejoin us. "What did we miss?" Nora asked.

"Caitlin is a dancer." Bella beamed. "A ballet dancer."

"No way."

I nodded, tucking my hair behind my ears. "An old hobby I don't get much time for these days."

Sympathy flickered in Nora's gaze. She hadn't pressed me about anything; neither had Arianne. But it was always there, in the space between us. The elephant in the room.

"Hey, we should speak to the guys about a girls' night out sometime. Maybe if—" Nora stopped herself, guilt shining in her eyes. "Shit, my bad."

"What?" Bella asked. "What is it?"

"Nothing." I forced a smile. I didn't want them to worry, and I didn't want her or Alessia to look at me any differently. Because I wasn't sure I could face becoming a victim in the eyes of these innocent pure girls, still full of dreams and hopes and so much goodness it radiated from them like sunshine.

Arianne switched the conversation to a safer topic, telling us about her work at the Verona County Transitions Initiative. But I wasn't paying much attention.

Neither was Arabella, as she discreetly texted someone on her phone.

When she was done, she glanced up at me, her expression wavering for a second. But then an easy smile slid over her face as if she hadn't just been caught red-handed texting her brother.

The next day at lunch, I didn't expect to find Luis waiting for me with a garment bag.

"W-what is that?"

"A surprise." His eyes twinkled. "We leave at six-thirty."

Leave?

"Where are we going?" My stomach fluttered, but I didn't know if it was with excitement or apprehension. Maybe even both.

"Like I said, it's a surprise." He left the bag draped over the back of the couch and slipped out of the cabin, leaving me alone.

I moved closer, plucking the small envelope from the clear pocket in the bag.

Let me make it up to you. M xo

Shivers raced up and down my spine as I slowly pulled the zipper, revealing a gorgeous, deep-green gown. It was fit for a princess, the bodice fitted and woven with delicate lace. The skirt was thick and luscious.

It was beautiful.

Confused, and a little out of my depth, I snatched my cell phone off the counter and texted Matteo.

What happened to house arrest?

His reply came instantly.

Give me a chance to get this right, please...

Why? Why is this so important to you?"

. . .

I glanced back at the gown, hardly able to believe my eyes. No one had ever bought me such a beautiful gift.

I didn't know what to think. Was this Matteo's attempt at buying me or was he merely trying to apologize and do something nice for me? Arabella hadn't mentioned him again last night, and I certainly hadn't brought it up. I was grateful for their company, even if watching them leave was a cold reminder of my situation.

Another reply pulled me from my thoughts.

I care, Caitlin. Let me prove it.

I clutched my cell phone, biting down on my bottom lip. He wasn't going to give up without a fight, and the truth was, I didn't want him to.

I wanted him to fight for me. I wanted Matteo to do what no person had ever done for me.

Before I could talk myself out of it, I texted back.

Okay.

Great, see you later… and Cait, I can't wait to see you in the dress.

I was in trouble.

So much trouble.

Matteo made it so hard to hate him. But could I do it? Could I become his… woman? It would put me in the public eye more. There would be photos and press reports. If I was around Nicco and Arianne, there was every chance I would become noticed.

The smart decision was to reject him and the dress and wait it out.

I wasn't for sale.

Not now, not ever.

But Matteo was different—I knew he was.

It was one night.

One night of freedom. One night to pretend that I was just a girl, and he was just a guy.

I couldn't remember the last time I'd gone on a date, a real honest-to-God date.

It had been too long, that much was certain.

I was pretty sure guys didn't usually forward their dates brand-new dresses. I spied the shoebox on the sideboard... and *shoes*. Oh God, he'd sent shoes.

"You're full of surprises, Matteo Bellatoni," I murmured to myself, lifting the lid and admiring the black kitten heels with a red sole. A red freaking sole.

What was happening?

This morning, I'd been on the verge of making a run for it to escape Matteo and his overbearing ruthless family. This afternoon, I was swooning over a new pair of Louboutins and a dress fit for a princess.

I wanted to tell him he couldn't buy my affection, but the truth was, I wanted it. I wanted one night to play dress up and forget the shitshow that was my life.

Which is why I found myself texting him back.

I'll be waiting.

The knock at the door sent my heart into overdrive. I'd taken my time getting ready. A long soak in a bubble bath, followed by a glass of wine thanks to Luis, while I finished getting myself together. I'd left my hair down, sweeping one side off my face and pinning it into place. My curls were thick and luscious, and my makeup was simple and understated.

I felt beautiful.

I also couldn't shake the feeling that this was a huge mistake.

But when I opened the door to reveal Matteo dressed in dark jeans and a black shirt and dinner jacket, there was no going back.

"For you," he said, holding out a single red rose.

"Thank you." I blushed, inhaling the floral scent before taking it over to the breakfast counter and adding it to a glass of water. "Are you sure this is okay?"

He nodded, his eyes dancing over my body. "Caitlin, you look... wow."

A faint smile tugged at my mouth.

"Tonight, we're just Matteo and Caitlin, okay?" He stepped forward, reaching for my face and brushing the stray hairs away. His eyes glittered with desire and in that moment I felt beautiful. "Nothing else matters," he leaned in and whispered against my cheek, kissing me softly.

"Okay." I gazed up at him, lost in his deep-blue eyes. He looked so good and smelled amazing. It was like a dream. A really good one I didn't want to wake up from.

I didn't have those often.

"Ready?"

It was my turn to nod. Matteo took my hand and led me out of the cabin.

"Miss O'Donnell," Luis smirked as he opened the back door to the sleek black SUV.

"Seriously?" My brow lifted at Matteo, and he chuckled.

"It's just a precaution."

Right. Because I was in hiding so that Zander didn't find me.

My heart ratcheted.

"Maybe this isn't such—"

"Shh." Matteo smoothed his thumb over my hand. "You're safe, I promise. No one will even know we're there."

"And where is there exactly?"

"You'll see. Come on."

He nudged me into the SUV, sliding in beside me. I half-expected for him to keep some distance between us, but Matteo was full of surprises, taking my hand again and keeping it in his lap. As if he needed a physical tether to me.

The thought made me smile. That I could bring this strong, gorgeous mafioso to his knees.

Don't get carried away with yourself, Cait. I ignored the little voice on my shoulder and sank back into the leather seats, determined to follow Matteo's lead tonight.

Thirty minutes later though, when we pulled up outside The Montague Grand Theater, I struggled to keep my composure.

"Matt," I gasped, cupping a hand over my mouth as I stared at the lit-up billboard hanging over the beautiful, imposing building.

"Romeo and Juliet," I murmured, "I-I don't understand." I gawked at him.

"Arabella said you used to dance. In fact, I think her exact words were, 'Matt, she's a ballerina. A real-life ballerina.'"

Soft laughter spilled from my lips.

"I managed to pull some strings." He gave me a shy smile. "I hope it's okay?"

"Okay?" My throat was dry. "It's... it's the nicest thing anyone has ever done for me. I don't know what to say." I glanced back up at the signage, hardly able to believe my eyes. Tickets to these performances didn't come cheap and I knew he'd probably called in some big favors to make this happen.

I couldn't stop smiling.

"Luis, take us around back please. Pascale is meeting us at the stage door."

I frowned and Matteo squeezed my hand. "Precautions. We have a private box that comes with VIP treatment. Besides," his voice dipped, sending a shiver through me. "This way I get you all to myself."

TWENTY-TWO

MATTEO

I COULDN'T TAKE my eyes off Caitlin. The dress clung to her curves as I guided her into our private box. The tickets had cost me a small fortune, but the second Arabella had texted me telling me that Caitlin liked ballet, the idea had taken root.

Nicco had forbidden it at first. I wasn't supposed to be parading Caitlin around the city. So I'd done what any desperate man would do—I begged.

Luis could drive us right to the stage door, and we could slip in and out before anyone was the wiser. Pascale Moretti, the theater director, was a family friend. My mama loved the ballet, but my father only ever brought her for a special occasion: anniversaries or birthdays. I'd only been once, as a child. I remembered being in awe of the opulent building. There was a giant chandelier in the foyer and a split staircase that ran around each side of the entrance. It was all very art nouveau with its gold-plated décor and stylized balconies and railings.

"Right this way, Mr. Bellatoni," Pascale led us up the staircase and down a long hall, pushing open a small door. "You'll find the bottle of Bollinger chilling along with the other items you requested."

"Thank you, Pascale." I took his hand, gripping it firmly. "I appreciate it."

"Of course, Mr. Bellatoni. Enjoy the production.

"Thank you." Caitlin smiled, her eyes glittering with wonder.

I liked that look on her, and wanted to put it there more often.

"Come on, the show is about to start." I ushered her onto the balcony.

"Oh my God, Matteo. This is—" She grasped the rail and looked out over the stage. It was the best seat in the house, a perfect view of the stage and orchestra seated down in the pit below.

I stepped up behind her, sliding my arm around her waist and I dropped my mouth to her ear. "It's beautiful, isn't it?"

"I've never seen anything like it."

I've never seen anything like you. I swallowed the words, leaning closer to breathe her in.

We'd only just arrived, and already, I never wanted this moment to end.

"We should sit," I said, guiding her over to the chairs. I needed a second. Being so close, with her looking like that, it was hard to rein in the storm of emotions raging inside me.

I wanted to kiss her, to take her in my arms and plunge my tongue deep into her mouth and taste her. I wanted to drown in her and never come up for air.

Did she have any idea the effect she had on me?

It was like I wasn't in control of myself. The urge to touch her, move closer, burning through me like wildfire.

"Champagne?" I asked her, trying to get a grip on myself.

"Yes, please." Caitlin handed me a glass and I popped the cork from the bottle, filling her glass. After I filled my own, I lifted it into the air.

"A toast."

"What are we celebrating?" She batted her eyelashes at me, and I almost drowned in her green eyes.

"One night of possibilities."

"Possibilities?" Her brow quirked, a smile touching her lips.

"Yes," I leaned in, ghosting my mouth over hers. "A night of endless possibilities." My eyes held Caitlin's, the air crackling between us the way it did whenever we were close. I wanted to kiss her. Fuck, did I want to kiss her.

The lights dimmed, the opening notes of the violin rising above the eerie silence. Caitlin grabbed my hand, squeezing tightly as the prima ballerina entered centerstage. I turned my palm, threading our fingers together, taking whatever I could get from her.

Her expression was animated as the story unfolded. I felt every emotion that played on her face. Every high and surprise. Every gasp and sigh. Caitlin leaned forward more than once, as if trying to get closer. The first act stole her breath and her heart... and she stole mine.

I wanted this woman. I wanted her in a way I couldn't explain. There was still every chance she would reject me, but I had to try.

The curtain fell and applause filled the theater. Caitlin shot to her feet, clapping and smiling. Silent tears rolled down her cheeks.

"Here," I said, turning into her to wipe them away with the pad of my thumb.

"That was so beautiful. I... I don't know what to say."

"There's still another act to go yet." I chuckled, letting my thumb linger on her skin. "Are you hungry?"

Her eyes went past me to the small table tucked in the shadows.

"Come." I led Caitlin back to her chair and retrieved the plate of chocolate covered strawberries.

"Anyone would think you were trying to seduce me, Matteo Bellatoni."

"Is it working?" I smirked, bringing one of the strawberries to her lips. I didn't consider myself a jealous guy, but in that moment, as Caitlin opened her mouth and took a bite, I was burning with jealousy all over a piece of fruit.

"These are good." She let out a soft moan, and I almost came on the spot. "Here, you try one." Caitlin plucked another strawberry off the plate and fed it to me.

"You're right." I grinned, licking the juice off my lips. "This does taste good. But not as good as you." Sliding my hand along her neck, I pulled her face to mine, kissing her softly.

A whimper bubbled in her throat as she parted her lips for me. Our tongues tangled; deep, lazy strokes that had me wishing we were somewhere a little more private. Not that anyone could see us up here.

"I could kiss you all night and never grow tired of it."

"Matt," she breathed, slipping her hands up my chest.

"Tell me you feel it, Tink. I know you do." I pulled back to stare her in the eye. Caitlin's cheeks were flushed, her eyes bright with desire. She wanted me, there was no denying that.

But did she want me enough?

"Thank you, Matteo. This is beyond my wildest dreams."

"I'm just glad you agreed to come. Despite what you might think about me, about my family, I really do care about you, Cait."

She gave me a small nod before popping another strawberry in her mouth. The conversation was over, the second act about to start.

But there were still so many things left unsaid.

"I think that was the most beautiful thing I've ever seen," Caitlin said as the lights came on. We hadn't kissed again, but I'd held her hand throughout the whole second act. Savoring every second with her that I could.

I didn't want the night to be over.

Because deep down, I knew my grand gesture wasn't enough to convince her to give me—to give us—a shot.

We made our way back down to the SUV in thick silence. Caitlin was lost in her own thoughts, and I was too preoccupied with what came next.

Luis greeted us right at the door, effortlessly guiding Caitlin into the back of the SUV while I followed. "How was it?" he asked, the second he climbed into the driver's seat.

"It was wonderful." Caitlin let out a contented sigh, and I took her hand again, testing the waters.

To my surprise, she didn't pull away. But she refused to look at me, and that alone spoke volumes.

"Tell me about it," I prompted as the SUV's engine purred beneath us.

"About what?" Caitlin finally met my gaze.

"Dancing."

"It was a long time ago." Sadness bled into her expression.

"You were a ballerina?"

"I trained in ballet, along with other disciplines of dancing."

"Why did you stop?"

"Why do we stop doing any of the things we love?" She let out a small sigh.

"Caitlin, you can talk to me." I gently squeezed her hand. "You can trust me."

It was the wrong thing to say.

Caitlin snatched her hand from me and laid it in her lap, staring out of the window. Luis caught my eye in the rearview mirror, frowning.

He'd come to care for Caitlin, anyone could see that. It was him and Arianne all over again.

We rode in silence for the next ten minutes. I didn't want to push her to talk about her past, but I had hoped tonight would be an olive branch. My cell vibrated and I dug it out of my pocket.

So... did she love it?

I smiled. I couldn't help it. My sister was one hundred percent team Matteo and Caitlin. She'd even gone as far as to ship our names. Although I wasn't sure Maitlin or Caitteo had a nice ring to it. But it was nice to know someone was rooting for us.

She did.

I texted back.

That's it? Seriously, Matt. You need to give me something else. Did you kiss her?

Bella!

What? I need to know these things. I like her and she's good for you.

. . .

"Let me guess," Caitlin whispered. "Bella?"

"She's grilling me about my art of seduction." I smiled, hoping to thaw some of the ice between us. "Joke," I quickly added when she didn't reply. "I'm joking."

"What are we doing, Matteo?" Caitlin's eyes shuttered as she inhaled a shaky breath.

"Well, I thought we were watching the ballet, but—"

"Matt, I'm serious. This can't work. You have to know that."

"You're wrong, Cait." I grabbed her hand again, refusing to let her go this time. I didn't care that Luis could hear me, I needed to say this. I needed to make her see.

"What I know is that I can't stop thinking about you. I wake up and the first thing that pops into my head is you. I fall asleep with your face in my mind. Whenever we're near, I want to touch you. It's like my hands get a mind all of their own, needing to be close to you."

"Matt—"

"No, Cait." I pulled her hand to my chest, right over my heart. "Look me in the eye and tell me you don't feel it?" I stared at her, willing her to admit it. "Tell me you don't feel it and I'll walk away. You can stay in the cabin until DiMarco is taken care of and then you can go on your way. You'll never have to see me again. If that's what you want, then—"

"I feel it."

Those three little words should have meant everything to me. But the pain in her eyes made my heart sink.

"Why do I feel like there's a big 'but' in there?"

"You're such a good man, Matteo." Caitlin took my hand in hers. "But I'm..."

"What, Caitlin? Just say it." *Put me out of my misery.*

She sucked in a ragged breath and forced a smile. "It doesn't matter. Tonight was amazing. I'll never forget it." She leaned over and kissed my cheek.

And I let her.

I didn't argue or try to convince her.

Because surely wanting someone to take a chance on you wasn't supposed to be this hard?

By the time we pulled up outside the cabin, Caitlin had fallen asleep on my arm.

"Caitlin," I whispered, gently nudging her. "We're here."

"Huh?" She blinked up at me, confusion glittering in her eyes. "What time is it?"

"A little after midnight. Wait here, okay?" I dropped a kiss on her head and climbed out of the SUV, going around the other side. Pulling the door open, I helped her out.

"I'm sorry I fell asleep."

"Don't be," I said, tucking her into the crook of my arm and guiding her inside. Luis made himself useful by lighting the fire while I walked Caitlin to her room.

"Thank you for tonight," I said.

I'd hoped this night would end differently. That maybe she'd invite me to stay, and I'd get to taste her again. To do all the things I wanted to do to her.

But I wouldn't be that guy. I couldn't.

If she didn't want all of me, then I had to accept that.

"Are you okay getting inside?" I asked, jamming my hands in my pockets to stop myself from reaching for her.

"Matt, I—"

"It's okay, Cait. I get it. You don't want me." At least not the way I wanted her to want me.

"It isn't... I'm sorry. I can't—"

"Shh, Tink." Cupping the back of her neck, I drew her into me. "It's okay." I breathed against her temple. "I'm glad I could give you tonight."

"Matt." Her fingers twisted into my shirt as we stood there, silently saying everything we couldn't say aloud.

"I think Bella wants to come and see you again tomorrow. But if you'd prefer, she doesn't—"

"No, I'd like that." She gazed up at me and I wanted to believe the hunger in her eyes was for me.

"Go. I'll speak to Luis before I leave and let him know to expect Bella tomorrow." I forced myself to take a step backward. "Good night, Caitlin."

"Good night." She watched me back up down the hall before slipping into her room and closing the door.

I let out a strained breath, running a hand over my jaw. I'd really thought tonight would change things for her.

Feeling utterly defeated, I made my way into the living room.

"You're leaving?" Luis asked me.

"Yeah, I think it's best I go." I moved for the door, pausing when I reached it. "Has she told you anything about her past?"

"Not much, why?"

"No reason," I said. "Bella is going to drop by tomorrow. Keep your eye on her."

He nodded. "You have my word."

"Thank you."

"You know, Matteo, I've been around a while, and well, maybe I've learned a thing or two about women."

My hand paused on the door handle. "Really, old man?" I smiled but it was only a polite one.

"Some women are so damaged by their pasts that they can't see when a good thing is standing right in front of them. They'll push you away, make you think they don't want you... when deep down, all they really want is someone to fight for them. To chase them down until they have no choice but to face the truth."

"That's... enlightening, *Dr. Phil*," I teased.

"It's not your job to fix her, Matteo. It's your job to care enough to help her fix herself."

I gave him a small nod before slipping into the inky night.

Help her fix herself.

I wanted nothing more. But in order to help her, she had to trust me enough to open up first.

Not repeatedly shut me out.

TWENTY-THREE

CAITLIN

"WHAT IS ALL THAT?" I gawked at the bags in Arabella's hands.

"I thought we could have a pamper day."

"A pamper day." I blinked as she breezed past me as if we'd been doing this forever.

Part of me wondered if it was weird that Matteo's sister wanted to hang out with me, but the truth was, Bella was a ray of sunshine, and I enjoyed her company.

So much so, I'd jumped at the chance to see her again.

Strangely, being around her also made me feel close to Matteo. It was the sweetest kind of torture, being close to the most important person in his life, knowing that I'd always be on the outside looking in.

But who could tell a bubbly, sweet sixteen-year-old no?

Not me apparently.

"Yeah, you know. Like face packs and manicures, and I got some of those truffles from the Chocolate Boutique in the city. I figured you could sneak me a glass or two of wine." She waggled her brows.

"One. *One* glass. I'm the responsible adult here. I take it Luis won't be joining us?" I peered over her shoulder.

"He's walking the perimeter or polishing his Glock or whatever it is he does."

"Polishing his Glock," I muttered under my breath, stifling the laughter bubbling up my throat.

"You know what I mean." She rolled her eyes, dumping the bags on the chair. "So… how was last night?"

"It was lovely."

"Lovely?" Bella balked. "Matteo bought you the best seats in the theater and you thought it was… lovely?"

It was my turn to roll my eyes. "Okay, it was amazing. I loved every second."

How I'd felt watching the dancers flit across the stage was like no other feeling, and it touched something deep inside that Matteo had done that for me. But it was complicated.

"So what's the problem?"

"What do you—"

"I saw my brother today. He looked… sad."

"Oh." My heart cinched.

"I don't get it. You're perfect for each other." She began unpacking all her pamper supplies while I fetched a bottle of wine from the refrigerator. Luis kept it well stocked thankfully.

"One glass." I slid it across the table to her.

"I can keep a secret, you know."

"I'm sure you can."

"So what's holding you back? I mean, anyone in the same vicinity as the two of you can feel it." I frowned and she added, "The sexual tension."

"I'm not sure you're supposed to be talking about sexual tension at your age."

"*Please*. I know what sex is, Cait."

"Are you… having sex?"

"Oh my God, no! I'm saving myself."

"You are?"

She shrugged. "It's no big deal. I mean, I like guys. I have crushes and I even kissed a few guys at my school. But I've never felt it before."

"It?"

"Yeah, that magical moment where the stars align and everything else fades into nothing and you're the only two people left in the world."

"That's beautiful."

I wish I had that. But my childhood had been filled with nothing but dark, desperate days. There had been no room for magic or stars aligning.

"Some of my school friends think it's silly. But I want what my mom and dad have, and Nicco and Ari, and Enzo and Nora. That once in a lifetime kinda love, you know?"

"Then you should hold out."

Arabella beamed at me. I hadn't really noticed before how much she sought validation. I guess it was a side effect of growing up in a family like theirs.

"Okay, let's do face packs first and then I'll give you a manicure."

"Sounds good." I accepted the packet from her and slid out the cool, refreshing face pack. "Hmm, it smells good enough to eat."

"Wait until you try a truffle. I make Matteo buy me some whenever he's in the city."

Every time she mentioned his name my heart faltered. I'd been unfair to him last night, brushed off his affection after an amazing night together.

It couldn't have been more perfect. Yet, it still wasn't enough for me to shake my fears. It was better this way, it was.

Once the mess with DiMarco was rectified, they would send me on my way and Matteo would move on and find a girl who could meet him halfway. A girl who didn't have copious amounts of baggage and a tragic backstory like me.

Not one that could upend everything he and his family had worked for.

"Caitlin, what is it? What's wrong?"

I didn't realize she could see my expression with the face pack plastered to my skin, but Bella looked concerned.

"I'm fine." I forced my emotions back into their locked box, right where they needed to stay.

She nodded, taking hold of my hand and slathering it in lotion. "I know I'm younger than you and that I'm Matteo's sister, but you can talk to me, Cait. I would never betray your confidence."

"That's very kind of you, but I'm okay. I promise."

For a second, she looked a little hurt at my unwillingness to open up to her. But it quickly melted away as she moved onto color options for my nails.

"My friend Gisele would love you," I mused.

"Your friend from..."

"How very sleuthy of you." Laughter crinkled my eyes. "I worked with Gisele."

"Have you spoken to her? Maybe she can visit and we can—"

My expression fell. "I don't think that'll be possible, Bella."

"I'm sure Matteo would arrange it if you asked. He cares about you, Cait. I know he does."

"It isn't that simple."

Bella hesitated for a second and then she asked me four little words that made my stomach drop. "Are you in danger?"

"I... I'm safe now, that's all that matters."

Bella finished painting the nails on my first hand and placed the bottle of varnish down, sinking back against the chair. "Sometimes I hate this life. I hate that I'll never be normal. I'll never get to be just a normal sixteen-year-old girl. There's always security, or my brother, or my cousins. It's suffocating sometimes.

"But then I feel guilty, because I know that some people have none of that. And I know that although they drive me crazy sometimes, my family would do anything for me."

Emotion balled in my throat as I swallowed down the tears burning the backs of my eyes. "You're very lucky to have so many people who love you, Bella. Don't ever take that for granted."

"I won't." She smiled, grabbed the varnish and started on my other hand.

While I sat there wondering if she knew just how lucky she was.

"Something smells good," I said, joining Bella in the kitchen sometime later. I'd offered to make us something to eat, but she'd said she wanted to cook for us, so I indulged her.

She made everything so easy.

Too easy.

Just like her brother, I could feel myself falling a little bit more in love with her every minute we spent together.

"It's one of my mama's favorite recipes. Simple but delicious." She put on her best Italian accent, laughing at herself.

"Well, it smells good."

"I enjoy cooking. I find it calming."

"And here I would have thought sixteen-year-old girls were into boys and makeup."

She glanced over at me and quirked a brow. "Weren't you listening to anything I said earlier about my brother and cousins."

"It won't be like that forever. Believe me, one day you'll be a force they can't control."

"Damn right I will."

"Although I'm surprised he hasn't been blowing up your cell phone."

"Actually, I told him to give us some space."

"You did, huh?"

"Yeah." She grinned. "I'd like nothing more than to see you and my brother get together, Cait. You're good for him. And I think he could be good for you too. But I also happen to think you're really cool. I meant what I said before... I'd like for us to be friends."

I gave her a tight-lipped smile. "Can I help you do anything?"

"Refill our wine glasses?" A smirk touched her lips.

"Nice try, young lady. But I already let you have two glasses and I'm sure your brother will have something to say if I send you home drunk."

"Fine, I'll have soda. And I think I saw some parmigiana in there. Grate some of that please."

"I can do that." I got to work, topping up our glasses and locating a cheese grater.

"You know, for all my family's faults, I'll always treasure memories of big family meals." She smiled wistfully. "Before she died, my nonna loved to cook for everyone. It was always chaos, too many people and not enough seats. But we made it work."

"You're very lucky, Bella."

"Sorry. I didn't mean to upset you."

"You didn't. You can't be sad over something you never had, right?" I gave her a strained smile.

"You must have some nice memories of growing up?"

"Nothing worth mentioning." My chest grew tight, and I hoped she would change the subject.

To my relief, she did.

"Okay, I think we're done here." Bella tossed the pasta one more time before serving it onto two plates.

"Aglio e Olio."

"This looks great, Bella. Thank you."

"Maybe next time, you can join us at my house for dinner. I know my parents would love to meet you."

I shoved a mouthful of pasta into my mouth and murmured, "Mm-hmm, maybe."

I couldn't lie to her, but I could evade the truth.

We ate and talked, sticking to safer subjects like Bella's school life, and then cleaned the dishes and headed back into the living room and got comfortable on the couch.

"Luis has been gone a while," I checked the time. "What do you think he's doing out there?"

"Probably sitting in the SUV listening to the radio." Bella popped another truffle into her mouth. "Thank you for letting me come by today."

"You don't need to thank me," I said. "I've enjoyed your company very much."

"Even if you and my brother can't figure things out, I'd like to be friends, Caitlin. If you want, I mean."

Guilt snaked through me, coiling around my heart as I choked out, "Sure."

I was a liar.

A liar and a coward.

But I didn't know how to be anything else.

A heavy thud outside the window startled me and I placed the glass down. "Did you hear that?" I stood, moving closer to the window.

"It's probably just Luis clearing the leaves again." Bella grinned.

"Very true." I pulled back the curtains and peered into the night.

"Anything?" Bella asked, and I shook my—

Thud.

My heart lurched into my throat as I let the curtain drop.

"It's just Luis, I bet." Bella made for the door.

"Wait," I called, but it was too late. She yanked it open. "Luis, what the hell are you… oh, you're not Luis."

My blood turned to ice as I went to her. "Bella, what's—" Fear slammed into me as my gaze landed on the guy standing on the porch. "W-what are—"

"You're a very hard woman to track down, *Caitlin.*"

I stared at him, my heart crashing violently in my chest. This couldn't be happening.

It couldn't—

Bella.

Oh God, Arabella was here.

"Please," my voice cracked as I gripped her shoulder to keep myself upright, fear threatening to bring me to my knees.

"Please don't do this."

TWENTY-FOUR

MATTEO

"ANYTHING?" Nicco asked as I tried Luis for the third time.

"Nothing, and neither of the girls are picking up either."

When Bella hadn't replied to my last four text messages, I'd eventually caved and called Luis. He wasn't answering either.

"They're probably busy."

"Busy doing what? They're stranded in a fucking cabin, Nicco." My leg bounced as I watched the scenery roll by.

The cabin was secure. No one except for a handful of people knew the way in or out. Nicco was right—there was probably a perfectly reasonable explanation.

So why couldn't I shake the feeling something was wrong?

"You need to rela—"

"Don't tell me to relax," I snapped. "That's my sister and—" Whatever the hell Caitlin was to me.

"We're almost there," he said.

"If anything has happened to them..."

I couldn't go there.

There had to be a logical explanation, there had to be.

The blare of my cell phone cut through the tension.

"Anything?" Enzo asked, the second I hit answer.

"Nothing yet, we're almost there," I said. "Have you got eyes on DiMarco?"

"Yeah, he's been at the club all day."

"He doesn't leave, understand?" Nicco's voice was deadly calm, a complete contrast to the chaos raging inside me.

"You got it, Boss. The second you get there, call me."

"We will." I hung up and sent my sister and Caitlin another text message.

"Where the fuck are they?" Fear trickled up and down my spine.

"We're almost there." Nicco pulled off the highway and followed the road down to the cabin, his security car following behind. At least we had back up. Four pairs of eyes were better than two.

I slipped my hand in my jacket and felt the pistol strapped there. It was a part of the job I never enjoyed, but it was necessary.

"See," Nicco said the second the cabin came into view. "The SUV is still there. They have to be here."

But I felt zero relief as the Range Rover rolled to a stop and I climbed out. Everything looked normal: the SUV was parked in its usual place, and the cabin door was closed. It didn't stop the hairs along my arms all standing to attention.

Something was wrong.

"Miss Bellatoni and Luis's GPS trackers show her as still here," Nicco's security guard, Dario, said as he stepped out of the car.

Guns drawn, they approached the cabin first. Knocking twice, they waited. When there was no answer, he glanced at Nicco. He nodded and Dario grabbed the handle, testing it.

The door swung open. "Luis?"

Nothing.

"Miss Bellatoni, it's security. Please respond so we know you're okay."

Still nothing.

"We're coming inside." They stepped inside and swept the living room while Nicco and I hung back.

"I have a bad feeling about this," I said, pacing back and forth.

"Clear," someone called, and we went inside.

"Shit, Nic." My eyes immediately found Bella's cell phone. I only knew it was hers because it had one of those pink, glittery cases.

I grabbed it and checked the screen. "She didn't pick up any of my messages."

"Fan out," Nicco ordered his men. "Check every—"

"Mr. Marchetti," Dario called. "You'll want to see this."

We rushed over to the hall, and I froze at the sight of blood smeared over the floor.

"It leads down here." We followed the sticky red trail to the back of the cabin, right to the storage closet.

"Fuck," I cried out at the splatters of blood.

"Looks like there was a struggle." Dario grasped the door handle, gently twisting it open. He gave his partner a nod and checked inside.

"Luis, shit."

He was unconscious, slumped up against the bench, bleeding out of a nasty cut on his forehead.

"He needs medical attention," Dario said, trying to rouse Luis.

Nicco already had his phone out, calling the Family's doctor. "He's on his way. Get him comfortable." He looked to me. "A word outside."

I followed him out of the room, every cell in my body zipping with nervous energy.

Caitlin and Bella were gone. Luis had been hurt. It didn't take much to figure out what had happened here.

"DiMarco found her," I snapped.

"Maybe. Maybe not." Nicco ran a hand through his hair, staring out of the window.

"Come on, Nic. It's fucking obvious that he found her, and he... he fucking took them. My sister and my—" I stopped myself, inhaling a ragged breath.

"I need to call Enzo." Nicco studied me. "You good for a minute?"

Good?

I wanted to break something. Preferably that fucker's neck.

"Promise me we'll get them back, Nic." My voice cracked, fear bleeding into every cell in my body. "Promise me that we'll get them back."

He gave me a small nod, but as he walked out of the cabin, cell phone pressed to his ear, I realized he hadn't answered me.

"Papa," I jumped up and strode toward my father, falling into his open arms.

"Shh, figlio mio. We will find them." He gripped me tightly as the emotion I tried so hard to keep contained, rushed to the surface.

"What do we know?" He held me at arm's length, his hard gaze sliding to Nicco.

"Luis was jumped outside the cabin. He came to and tried to fight off two guys, but one hit him with a tire iron. He's got a nasty contusion to his head, but Doc says he'll be okay."

"Have Enzo and Lucino started interrogating DiMarco?"

"No, they're waiting for us," Nicco said.

"What are we waiting for then? Let's go." I went to barge past my father, but he shouldered me.

"Basta! This isn't helping, Son, you need to calm down."

"Seriously? You're going to tell me to calm down when DiMarco has Arabella? Who knows what he's doing to them. He could be—"

"Shh, Son." My father pulled me into his chest, cupping the back of my neck as a shuddering breath went through me.

If he'd hurt them... I couldn't bear it.

I'd spent my entire life protecting Bella, trying to keep her innocent and out of harm's way.

And now she had been taken... because I'd dropped the ball and allowed her to come here, to be around Caitlin.

"Don't." My father nudged me away to look at me. "Don't do that to yourself.

We all agreed it was safe to let her come here. Security is tight, the location is unknown, and we've been careful. You're not to blame, Son."

Careful… but not careful enough.

Fuck.

My fists clenched, my lips thinning. Nothing, *nothing* anyone said would stop the weight of guilt crushing my chest.

"Make sure Luis is taken care of. We need to head to Providence immediately."

"Thank fuck," I breathed, heading for the door. But my father snagged my wrist, stopping me.

"Cool heads, Matteo. We need to keep cool heads, capisci? With DiMarco in talks with Lombardi, we can't rule out that there is more at play here."

"What are you saying?"

"We talk first. Give DiMarco a chance to tell us what he knows."

"I think that's pretty obvious." I scoffed. "He kidnapped them. He took them and left Luis for dead, and you want to… to talk?"

Un-fucking-believevable.

"Despite what you might think, figlio mio. I want to resolve this with the least bloodshed. For all we know, it could be a trap. Would you so willingly storm in all guns blazing if you thought it might end up with all of us dead?" His gaze cut me to the bone.

"I… I need to do something."

"And you will." He gripped my shoulder. "When we figure out their motives."

"Fine," I grumbled. "But if DiMarco is responsible, he's a dead man."

My father's eyes went over my shoulder to Nicco, something passing between them. But I didn't stick around to ask what; I needed some fresh air before I combusted.

They wanted to talk, to appease that asshole, when he deserved nothing more than a bullet through his skull. But I wasn't the boss and there was protocol.

Fuck.

Fuck!

I slammed my fist against the side of Nicco's Range Rover, pain skittering up my arm. I was about to hit it again, when my phone vibrated.

For a second, hope went through me. But it quickly died when I saw Enzo's name, not Caitlin's.

We'll get them back, cous. You have my word.

I wanted to heed his words; I did. But I'd never felt more helpless than I did in that moment.

By the time we arrived in Providence, it was late, but downtown was alive with activity. The lights and music, the steady hum of cars passing, was all white noise to the blood roaring in my ears.

It had been too long.

At least three hours since Luis last checked in.

A lot could happen in three hours.

"What now?" I asked Nicco, who was white knuckling the steering wheel as we stared at the sign above DiMarco's club.

"We go pay him a visit."

"Thank fuck." I went to climb out, but Nicco grabbed my arm.

"Not you, Matt."

"What the fuck?" I gawked at him in disbelief. He couldn't be serious.

I needed to see him. I needed to look DiMarco in the eye when he confessed his sins.

"You're too close to this. Let me and Michele go in. You stay out here until—"

"That's bullshit and you know it."

"Matt—"

"No, Nic, *no*! Are you telling me that if it was Alessia and Arianne missing you'd just sit by while me and Enzo handled it?"

His jaw clenched as he tipped his head up and let out a strained breath.

"Exactly," I snapped. "I'm coming."

"Fine, fine. But you follow my lead, and you leave your piece here." He motioned to the glove compartment. "I mean it, Matteo. We cannot afford to start something until we know where the girls are."

"Okay," I conceded, unsheathing my pistol and shoving it inside.

He nodded, climbing out of the Range Rover. I followed, meeting him around the front. Nicco motioned to my father and his security guard and the four of us approached the entrance to DiMarco's.

"Mr. Marchetti." The doorman nodded out of respect. "Is the boss expecting you?"

"It's an impromptu visit. We'll make our own way inside, thank you."

"Very well." He stepped aside, letting us enter. My heart pounded in my chest with every step deeper into the club.

We spotted Enzo, Lucino, and Stefan seated in one of the VIP booths. They signaled us over, but Nicco told us to go on ahead.

"Matt." Enzo stood to greet me, pulling me into a hug. "You good?"

I offered him a tight smile. "I will be once we get them back."

"And we will, cous. We will."

It was the only possible solution. Because the alternative… I couldn't even go there.

"Gentlemen." A busty brunette sauntered over to us. "What will it be?"

"A round of Blue Label whisky," Lucino said smoothly, playing the game.

Keeping up appearances. When all I wanted to do was start smashing things up until someone told me where the fuck my sister and Caitlin were.

"Of course." She left us and I pinched my temples as I scanned the club. "Have you spoken to him?"

"He's acting the part. Came to make sure we had everything we wanted and left us to it."

"He didn't seem ruffled?" my father asked.

"Cool as a fucking cucumber." Lucino sucked on his cigar, blowing a plume of smoke into the air.

"He's a fucking snake."

I glanced over at where Nicco was talking to a guy in a sleek black suit. My cousin was the epitome of a leader. Calm. Composed. Head held high and shoulders rolled back. Whether he liked it or not, Nicco had slid into the role of acting boss with total ease, and part of me was relieved that he was the one handling this and not Uncle Toni.

Because despite what he said, Nicco knew what it was like to find yourself torn between duty, family, and the woman you loved.

Did I love Caitlin?

I wasn't sure.

What we had was new, uncertain, and unknown. But part of me felt like I've always known her, that she'd always been a part of me. So maybe it wasn't love right now, in this moment, but I didn't doubt for a second that I could grow to love her.

The second Zander DiMarco appeared, every muscle in my body went taut.

"Easy, cous," Enzo hissed, clamping his hand around my arm. "Let Nicco handle this."

"This was a bad idea," I ground out, curling my fingers into the edge of the table.

Fuck, I wanted to hurt him. The way he'd hurt Caitlin.

"Just breathe," Enzo warned, gripping my arm harder. "If we're going to find them, we need him."

Nicco and Zander were locked in a standoff, the two of them pulled to their full height, staring the other down.

"Should we intervene?" Lucino asked.

"Nicco can handle DiMarco."

Sure enough, DiMarco threw up his hands and walked away. Seconds later, Nicco joined us, sliding into the booth.

"So?" my father asked, rapping his fingers against the table.

"He isn't happy we showed up unannounced."

"Maybe he should have thought about that before getting into bed with Lombardi."

"I didn't tell him we know. I want to feel him out first."

"So we wait?" Enzo said.

"I told him to close the club early."

Lucino let out a low whistle. "Brave move, ki—"

"Kid, really?" Enzo sneered. "He's the fucking boss."

"Perdonami. I meant no offense."

Nicco gave him a nod. "DiMarco needs to realize who's in control here, and it isn't him." Nicco snatched up his glass of whisky and sat back, watching as the place started emptying out.

I couldn't picture Caitlin working here. The men ogling her and objectifying her. Did they touch her? Whisper dark, depraved things in her ear as she served them drinks?

My fists clenched, anger rising inside me.

He didn't deserve this. He'd hurt Caitlin, we were pretty certain he had Shaun killed, and he was aligning himself with the Lombardi crime family.

And we were giving him the benefit of the doubt by talking to him. It was a fucking joke.

I didn't consider myself a violent man. I usually preferred trying to find more amicable ways to end disputes. But this was my family, the woman I wanted to be mine. I couldn't see past DiMarco hurting her, putting his fucking hands on her and making her bleed and bruise. And now he'd taken Caitlin and my sister. My sweet, innocent Arabella.

He didn't deserve the benefit of the doubt—he deserved to die a slow, painful death, begging for mercy down the barrel of a gun.

We waited until the club was empty. Anticipation rippled in the air like an angry storm circling in the distance.

The servers cleaned up around us, casting suspicious looks in our direction. I didn't blame them. They all knew of DiMarco's connections, so they knew what it meant when business was closed down before closing hours.

"Give us the room," Zander barked as he stepped out of a door marked 'private.'

Everyone scuttled out of sight, leaving DiMarco alone save for his two security men who hovered near the entrance.

"Gentleman, let's talk." He helped himself to a glass of Blue Label whisky and swaggered over to us as if he didn't have a care in the world. "I have to say, Niccolò, if I would've known you were coming, I would have rolled out the red carpet."

"Stronzo," Enzo grumbled, lurching forward, but Nicco shot him a warning look.

"We have heard some concerning things, Zander. Things that we want to give you a chance to explain."

"I have no idea what you're talking about." He swept a hand through his hair.

"Let's not play this game." Nicco loosened his collar. "We know all about Lombardi."

"Business is business," Zander shrugged, "and his men came looking to spend good money."

"I noticed Shaun wasn't working tonight," Enzo said. "He's a good man."

"He was," Zander didn't miss a beat. "One of the best. Such a shame what happened."

"Something happened?"

"He was in an accident. Tragic really."

"He died?"

Zander nodded. "It's been hard for us all."

"Condolences," my father said. "It always hurts to lose someone."

"It does."

Jesus, this fucking asshole was good.

"But I'm sure you didn't come here to discuss my employees."

"I'm going to lay it out straight for you," Nicco said, sliding his hand into his jacket. He pulled out his gun and laid it on the table pointed at Zander, keeping his finger on the trigger. "What are your plans with Lombardi?"

"Easy, Niccolò. You don't want to do something you'll later regret." DiMarco smirked, lifting his hands up. "We talked, nothing more. Lombardi is looking to branch out into the strip club business. He asked for my advice."

"That so?" Lucino snorted.

"It's the truth. I know our agreement is irreversible. Just like I told Lombardi, Providence is Marchetti territory."

"Seriously? You buy a single word this sleazeball is telling you?" I sneered.

"Matteo," my father warned.

I ground my teeth together, fighting the urge to leap across the table, grab Zander by the throat, and demand answers about Caitlin and Arabella.

"Where are they, Zander?" my father said.

"They?" His brows pinched. "What are you talking about?"

"Cut the bullshit, figlio di puttana! We know you took them." My father glared at him with enough venom that it rippled around us like a living, breathing thing. "You're playing a very dangerous game, DiMarco. I suggest if you don't want to end up with your brains splattered all over the wall, you pick up your cell phone, call your men, and get them here immediately."

"Listen, Niccolò, Michele, I don't know what you're talking about, but I—"

"Basta!" Nicco slammed his hand down, sending the glasses clattering together. "We wanted to give you the chance to fix this, to—"

His cell phone began blaring, his eyes narrowing on whoever's name was flashing across the screen. "Get him up." He motioned to our security guys, and they approached the booth, manhandling Zander onto his feet.

"Now, now, Niccolò. I don't know what you're—"

"Can it," my father spat as he stood and brushed down his jacket.

"You can't do this," DiMarco kept protesting, thrashing against his man-made restraints. "We have an arrangement. One I've never reneged on."

Nicco picked up his gun and stalked toward him, his eyes cold and deadly.

"N-Niccolò, I swear, man! I don't know what you're talking about."

Quicker than a flash, Nicco had his pistol pressed against Zander's forehead, the safety clicked off. "Let's get one thing straight, *amico*, I don't like liars. And you, Zander DiMarco, are the very worst of them."

"Fuck..." Sweat began beading along his forehead, fear glittering in his eyes. "Fuck, Nicco, I swear, I don't know what—"

The blare of Nicco's cell phone cut through the room again. He dug it out of his pocket and frowned at the name on the screen. "I need to take this," he said. "Watch him."

Enzo stepped into our cousin's place. "Don't move a fucking muscle, stronzo."

"And here I thought we were friends." Zander smirked.

The bastard smirked.

Fucking asshole had a death wish.

"Friends?" Enzo cocked a brow. "I don't associate myself with women beaters."

"What the fuck is that supposed to mean?"

"Oh, I think you know exactly what it means."

"E, back up, son." My father stepped up to his side, whispering something to him.

"It's nothing they don't want." DiMarco laughed darkly. "Nothing they don't beg for."

One second I was standing off to the side, watching Zander sneer at Enzo. The next I was in front of him, my fist flying into his face.

"*Matteo*!" someone yelled, but I was lost to the anger raging inside me. I couldn't see. I couldn't think about anything other than hurting Zander.

"You sick motherfucker," I roared, slamming my fist into his nose. Blood sprayed everywhere, pain radiating through my wrist, splitting open my barely healed knuckles. "Where are they?" I grabbed him by his collar, almost wrenching him out of the guards hold. "You tell me right now where they are or I'll fucking end you, you piece of shit."

Confusion flickered in Zander's eyes, blood pouring from his nose and trickling down his chin. "Who are you... *Caitlin*?" Recognition dawned on his face.

"Don't you say her name. Don't you dare fucking say her—"

"Easy, cous." Strong arms grabbed me from behind, dragging me backwards as DiMarco stared at me.

"You good?" Nicco got in my face. "If Enzo lets you go, are you going to stand down?"

Lips thinned, I nodded. He released me slowly, and I inhaled a ragged breath.

"We need to talk," Nicco said to me. "Alone." He motioned for me to follow him to the opposite side of the club.

"I lost it, Nic, I know. But he's—"

"What do you know about Caitlin, Matt? Really know about her?"

"W-what? How is this important right now?" I gaped at him.

"Just think for a second. What has she told you about her past? About where she comes from?"

"She was raised in Rochester, New York. But that's about all I know. She doesn't like to talk about it. Why?"

Nicco dragged a hand down his face, fixing me with a sympathetic gaze. "I had Tommy run her name."

"What?"

Tommy was the Family's investigator. There wasn't much about anyone or anything that he couldn't dig up.

"Don't act so surprised. I wanted to know who we were taking in, who we were protecting. She's been around Arianne, my sister... Bella. It was the right call, and you know it."

He had a point, but I hadn't considered he would have Tommy look into her past.

"What did you find out?" I asked.

Nicco's eyes dropped to the floor, and when he glanced back at me, I knew.

I knew whatever he'd found changed everything.

"He found something, Matt. Until almost four years ago, Caitlin O'Donnell didn't exist."

"What do you mean, she didn't exist?"

"The trail ends."

"But that's impossible. Unless..."

No.

It couldn't be true.

Until Nicco said eight little words that confirmed my worst fears.

"Unless she isn't who she says she is."

TWENTY-FIVE

CAITLIN

"BELLA?" I whispered into the dark. "Arabella, can you hear me?"

"C-Caitlin?" She sounded woozy. "Where are we? W-what happened?"

I squinted against the darkness, trying to find my bearings. We were in a small room, maybe a large closet or laundry room. I was pressed into the far corner, the wall at my back. A sliver of light trickled under the door, casting dark shadows around the room.

"I'm over here," I called out, my skull rattling with every word.

I winced in agony. The back of my head throbbed from where I'd banged it trying to fight off our captors. Of course, I'd lost. They were big and burly, and I was small and fragile. Still, I'd fought with everything I had, kicking and screaming. I'd even got one of them in the balls, but it made no difference. The other man had thrown me down with such force, I'd slammed my head against the floor and knocked myself out.

At least, I assumed that's what happened, given that when I came to, we were no longer in the cabin and in this cold, dark room instead.

"C-Cait, I'm scared."

My heart cracked.

Bella didn't deserve this—she didn't deserve any of it. It was all my fault she was here. I should never have accepted help from Enzo and Matteo. I should have refused to let them bring me back to Verona. But I'd let myself believe in the fairy tale. I'd let myself believe they could protect me.

A hand grazed mine and I strained to see Bella crawling toward me. "Thank God." I grabbed her, pulling her into my arms. "Are you hurt?"

"My... my face. One of them hit me when I bit his hand."

"You bit him?"

"Well, yeah. I wasn't about to let them take us without a fight. H-he hurt you. You were lying there, and I didn't know if you were dead or—"

"Shh." I pulled her closer, whispering soothing things against her matted hair. "It's okay. It's going to be okay." The lie soured on my tongue.

Because I didn't know that. I had no idea where we were.

"I-I don't understand what's happening." Bella sobbed into my shoulder, clinging to me.

"Shh. Shh." Silent tears rolled down my cheeks.

I needed to figure out where we were, and who had taken us.

If it was Zander, I could negotiate with him. Offer him what he wanted in exchange for Bella's freedom. Surely, he had to know that Matteo and his family would find out Arabella was missing, and when he realized who she was, the smart thing would be to hand her over if they wanted to avoid the Marchetti's wrath.

But if it wasn't Zander...

No.

It wasn't possible.

There was no way he had found me. I'd been careful. I'd covered my tracks and left my old life behind.

It was Zander.

It had to be Zander.

I inhaled a sharp breath, pain radiating through my skull again.

"They'll know, right?" Bella's voice trembled. "Matteo will know we're missing, and they'll be looking for us and... oh God, Cait. What if they don't find us? What if..." She choked over a huge sob, her body wracking under the power of her tears.

"Try and calm down, okay?" I said softly, smoothing my hand down her back. "We need to try and stay strong."

Heavy footsteps outside the door sent all my bravado crumbling though.

"Who is that?" Bella whispered.

"Shh, okay. Just try to be quiet."

There was a rattle of a lock and a heavy clunk and then light poured into the room. I threw my arm up, trying to give my eyes time to adjust to the stark brightness.

"Water and something to eat," a gruff voice said, his dark shadow filling the door. I didn't recognize him, but I wasn't surprised.

Zander had a lot of friends I didn't know. Bad men who worked for him in the shadows, doing despicable things.

"Where are we?" I asked, trying to keep the fear out of my voice. But he started to close the door. "No, wait, please. I'm hurt. My head—"

"Not my problem," he grunted, yanking the door closed.

"Bella, ease up a second." I gently pushed her off me. "We need to drink." I managed to shuffle over to the tray and retrieve the two small bottles of water.

"Here, take one." I held it out for her.

"It's so dark, I can barely see." She fumbled, her fingers brushing mine.

"There, you got it. Now drink. Small sips, okay?"

"Why is this happening? I-I don't understand."

"I... I'm sorry." My heart broke in two at the pain and confusion in her voice.

"I'm here... because of you?" She gasped as if she hadn't realized until now. "No, that's not possible."

"I'm so, so sorry. If I would've known... I didn't mean for this to happen, Bella. You have to know that. I didn't... I wasn't..." My breaths came in ragged pants.

"Who are you, Caitlin?" she whispered, scooting away from me.

Tears streaked down my face as I tipped my head back against the wall and let out a pained whimper.

Someone you're better off not knowing.

"Firefly, wake up." A finger stroked down my cheek. "I've got a job for you."

Fear paralyzed me as I clutched the blanket to my changing body. I was only fifteen, but I had the curves of a young woman. I hated them. Hated how my mom's boyfriend and his friends looked at me.

"I don't want to," I cried, refusing to open my eyes.

"I need you to do this for me, firefly. You want to make me happy, don't you? After all I've done for you and your mom." He grabbed my arm, wrenching me up.

"Stop, you're hurting me."

He tsked, the bitter scent of cigars and liquor wafting over my face. I fought down the urge to gag. He didn't like that, didn't like me acting repulsed by him.

"Stop acting like a spoiled brat then. I have a job for you, and you'll be a good fucking girl, and do it unless you want me to cut your momma off. And we both know how she gets without her fix."

A shiver went through me. He was right, of course. If Mom didn't get her fix, she was insufferable.

Pushing my wild curls out of my face, I looked up at the man who had raised me. Raised me... and ruined me.

Pain coiled through my chest as I choked out, "Fine. I'll do it."

What other choice did I have?

If I didn't, it would only be me who suffered. And no matter how cruel my mom could be, no matter how much her barbed words hurt, she was still my mom.

My family.

He cupped my face, dragging his thumb down my cheek, the glint of his gold ring standing out against the darkness surrounding him.

"That's my good girl. Now get dressed. It's showtime."

. . .

I bolted upright, sucking in fresh lungfuls of air. My head felt strange, like it might roll off my shoulders at any given moment.

"Caitlin?" a voice called from somewhere in the darkness.

"B-Bella?" Her name was like ash on my tongue. "I... I don't feel so good."

"You've been sleeping. I thought... I thought—"

"I'm here. I'm right here."

"Caitlin?"

"Yeah?" I sank back against the wall again, my muscles screaming in protest. I felt stiff, groggy, and sore.

"Who's firefly?

The icy fingers of fear wrapped around my throat. "What did you just say?"

"I said who's firefly? You were crying out in your sleep. Murmuring it over and over."

"I was?" A violent shudder rolled through me. It had been a long time since I had that dream.

"It's nothing," I said, refusing to let those thoughts penetrate my mind.

"It didn't sound like nothing."

"How long was I out?"

"I don't know. One, maybe two hours."

Shit.

"Did anyone come back?"

"No one. Although I heard voices beyond the door. It sounded like they were arguing."

"Did you hear any names?"

"None, why?"

"It doesn't matter." Defeat coated my words.

I'd never felt more powerless than I did in this moment, and I'd experienced some dire circumstances in the past. But Arabella was innocent. She didn't deserve to know this terror or fear. And I hated myself for ever dragging her into my life.

"I want you to know something," I said, biting back the tears threatening to fall. "Whatever happens, I'm going to do everything I can to make sure you make it out of this safely, okay?"

"W-what does that mean, Cait? What things? What are you going to do?"

I squeezed my eyes shut, tears dripping down my face. When they opened, a new sense of resolve washed over me.

Zander wanted me.

Bella was just collateral. I would make sure he had no reason to hurt her. I would do whatever it took to see to it that she walked out of here alive and unharmed.

But if I was going to negotiate, I needed to speak to him. I needed to look him in the eye and give him what he wanted.

"Whatever happens," I said to Bella, as I staggered to my feet, "I need you to keep quiet, okay?"

"What are you going to do?"

"What needs to be done. Just keep quiet and promise me you won't antagonize them."

"Cait, I'm not—"

"Promise me, Arabella."

"Okay, okay. I promise."

Before I could second guess myself, I grabbed the tray off the floor and smacked it against the door. "Hey, hey," I yelled, "I need to speak with the boss. I need to talk to him."

"Caitlin, are you mad?" Bella cried. What are you—"

"Shh," I hissed. "I need to attract their attention. I can fix this, Bella. I can make it all okay." I banged the tray against the door again. "Hey, come on, let me out. I need to—"

"What the fuck?" someone grunted from the other side of the door. I stepped back as it flung open.

"Do you have a fucking death wish?" He cocked a thick brow at me.

"I'm ready to talk."

"Oh, you're ready to talk, are you?" A sly smile tugged at his mouth. "That's not how things work around—"

"We both know the boss wants me to cooperate, so tell him. Tell him I'm ready to do whatever he wants. All I ask is that she's released. She isn't any part of this."

He studied me, muttering something about women under his breath. "Come with me." He grabbed my shoulder and yanked me out of the room.

"Caitlin!" Bella screamed as the guy dragged me down the hall.

"Grayson, grab the other one," the guy barked at a guy standing at the end of the hall.

"No, no, she's no part of this. You have to let her go," I shrieked.

"Not my call, darlin'."

We reached another door and he banged it once.

"Enter," a voice boomed, and the guy shouldered it open, dragging me inside. He pushed me hard and I crashed to my knees, pain slicing through me.

Inhaling a couple of breaths, I slowly lifted my head. "You," I gasped, hardly able to believe my eyes. "But it's not possible."

"It's been a long time, firefly."

That single word sent a bolt of fear straight into my heart, and in that moment, I knew... I knew I couldn't protect Arabella. My mom's boyfriend didn't care about right or wrong, or morals, or girls with their whole lives ahead of them. He only cared about business and keeping his associates happy.

I glanced over at Bella as she huddled in the corner of the room and my heart broke as I silently begged for forgiveness I knew would never come.

"I'm sorry," I cried. "I'm so sorry."

TWENTY-SIX

MATTEO

"WHAT'S TAKING SO LONG?" I tapped my foot against the floor, draining another whisky.

"That isn't going to help anything." My father eyed me with concern.

"Well, it's either this or I go beat some answers out of DiMarco. Take your pick."

After Nicco had delivered the blow that Caitlin wasn't really Caitlin O'Donnell at all, our men had dragged Zander away to his office, where they had secured him until we could figure out what the hell to do.

But if he didn't have Caitlin and Bella… who the hell did?

Nicco appeared with Enzo trailing behind him.

"Anything?" I leaped up.

"Nothing that makes sense." Nicco motioned to the booth, and we all sat down. "Tommy was able to pull her cell phone number from DiMarco's staff records."

"He hacked his system?"

Nicco nodded.

"Okay," I frowned, not really following.

"There was nothing unusual at first. But then when he pulled her cell phone records, he noticed she called the same number on the same day of every month, for the last couple of years."

"Did he get a name?" my father asked.

"Yeah. Olivia Walsh. Born and raised in Rochester, New York until she moved to New Haven, Connecticut in the nineties. He's running a more extensive search as we speak."

"I don't understand." I raked a hand through my hair. "What is she running from?"

"That's what we need to find out. I want you to talk to DiMarco," Nicco said.

"Hang on a minute, Boss. You really think that's a good idea?" Enzo glanced between the two of us.

"In his own way, I think DiMarco cares about her. Or, in the very least, he's infatuated with her. Matt can appeal to that side of him."

Enzo snorted. "Or it'll send DiMarco straight off the deep end."

"He's the only tangible connection we have to Caitlin right now, and if he didn't take them, maybe he knows something that might help us find out who did."

"What about the girls that work here? They knew her, someone might know something," I said.

"Already got Lucino and Stefan on it."

Good. That was good.

"Do you think you can talk to him?" Nicco levelled me with a sympathetic look.

What choice did I have?

If Zander had information that could help us, I had to put my anger aside and reach out to him. Man to man.

"Yeah," I breathed, hoping to God I was right. "I can do it."

"Good, come on." Nicco got up and waited for me. "Michele." He glanced back at my father. "Keep in touch with Tommy. I want to know what he finds out as he finds it."

He nodded. In the short time we'd been here, my father had already aged. Arabella was the apple of his eye. It would kill him if anything happened to her.

It would kill all of us.

I followed Nicco through the door marked 'private' and down the hall to Zander's office. Nicco went in first and then beckoned me inside.

"Matteo wants to talk to you," he said.

"*Matteo* can go fuck himself." Zander was nursing his broken nose with a bag of ice.

"Caitlin is missing," I said.

His eyes went wide. "You know Caitlin?"

"I... yes." I pulled a chair closer to him and sat down.

"I'm not sure I follow."

I looked to Nicco, and he nodded, silently giving me permission. "Last year, I met Caitlin when we were here in Providence. I had no idea she was one of your girls, or even knew you. She told me she worked at a diner called Stella's. We... we spent the night together."

I gauged Zander's reaction, but his stone-cold mask gave nothing away.

"It was one night. I went home to Verona and never saw her again... until a couple of weeks ago, when the hospital over in Pawtucket called Enzo. We were on our way to see you but detoured to the hospital where we found Caitlin..."

As I remembered what it was like to see her lying there, in that hospital bed, it took everything inside me not to pounce on him. But I had to keep myself in check if we were going to get the information we needed. Caitlin and my sister came first; they trumped my burning need for vengeance.

The bastard didn't even flinch.

"We took her back to Verona County with us," I went on. "Gave her a safe place to stay."

That got a reaction. Jealousy and anger blazed in his eyes. Yeah, the fucker didn't like the idea of someone else looking after his girl.

It sent a sick thrill of satisfaction through me. Especially knowing he would never get to lay a hand on her again.

"Earlier today, Caitlin and my sister went missing."

"What?" he spat.

"Now you can see why we suspected it was you."

"I didn't... I swear to you, Bellatoni, this wasn't my doing."

"Strangely, I believe you. But you need to tell us everything you know about Cait so we can try to piece together who might have taken them."

"I... fuck," he heaved a deep sigh. "I don't know what to say. I found her on the streets about four years ago. She was cold and hungry and needed a place to stay."

"So you took her in?" It came out harsher than I intended, and I felt the weight of Nicco's stare burning into the side of my face.

"She was new to the area; I was a girl down at the club. It was a win-win."

Yeah, right.

"At first, she worked the floor, taking orders and serving drinks, that kind of thing. Until one night after closing I saw her fooling around backstage with a couple of my dancers."

My spine went rigid as I listened to him recall those early days with Caitlin. The day he'd discovered her love of dancing.

"She was good," he said. "Really fucking good. So I offered her a spot, told her she could make a decent wage dancing for me. But I quickly realized the error of my ways. Caitlin was a little too good. Men queued up for her and it drove me in-fucking-sane." He looked me dead in the eye as he said the words. "I almost killed a guy for touching her. I was completely bewitched by her. But she fought me at every turn, determined to keep things strictly professional between us."

"So you took what you wanted instead." My voice was low, deadly. Rage like I'd never known it coursing through my veins.

"Matt," Nicco hissed.

I forced myself to take a deep, calming breath. I could do this—I could do it for her.

"None of this is helping us," I said. "We need to know about her life. Friends? Family? Did she ever talk about anyone important in her life? Or her past?"

"Never. And I never asked. Most of the girls who end up working for me are running from something."

Wasn't that the truth.

But it didn't help us.

"So there's nothing?"

Zander shrugged, but I caught the glimpse of regret in his eyes. "I can't think of anything."

My patience began to wane, frustration bleeding into my voice. "You've known her all this time and you can't think of anything that might help us?"

"I... Wait, there was something. I didn't think much of it at the time, but when Dominic Cabrioles and his men first visited the club, he took an immediate interest in Caitlin. Offered me a lot of cash for a private audience with her."

"I thought you said she didn't dance no more."

"She didn't, but business is business." He shrugged again, as if dealing in sins of the flesh was a normal occurrence.

And maybe it was for assholes like DiMarco, but I couldn't stand the thought of Caitlin being forced to dance to line his pockets.

Nicco stepped forward. "Did Cabrioles say anything else?"

"He backed off pretty quickly when I made it clear she belonged to me. But now that I think about it, he was unusually interested in her."

"I'll be back." Nicco got straight on his phone and strolled out of the room, sending in one of his guards to no doubt make sure I didn't overstep my orders.

"You love her?"

DiMarco's question caught me off guard.

"I... I care for her very much."

He gave me a small nod, but I still couldn't gauge where his head was at. This wasn't the sleazy, cocksure asshole I was used to. But then, he was tied to a chair with a broken nose and no hope of being released.

"You killed Shaun to find her."

"He took something from me," he quietly seethed. "He betrayed me."

"He protected her, and you had him murdered in cold blood."

"Tell me, Matteo. What lengths would you go to, to get her back?"

I rolled my lips together. He was right. There wasn't much I couldn't imagine doing if it meant having her back safe in my arms.

But I still had honor and integrity. I wanted her to stand at my side, not cower at my feet.

"We're not the same."

"Maybe. Maybe not. But it doesn't matter now."

"No?" My brow arched.

"I am many things, Matteo. A fool is not one of them. You think I don't know how this goes? You think I don't know the second you get the chance, you'll put a bullet between my eyes? I can see it written all over your face."

I stood, taking a couple of steps closer to him. The guard moved with me, ready to intervene. Looming down over Zander, I said, "I pity you. You had her. You had her and you let her slip through your fingers because you're not a man, DiMarco, you're a coward. And I hope you rot in hell." I spat at his feet, turned on my heel and walked out of there without looking back.

The second I exited the room, Nicco glanced over at me. "You good?" he asked, pocketing his cell phone.

"Unless you want me to end him, I suggest you don't ask me to go back in there." I stalked off down the hall, needing some fresh air and a strong drink.

Enzo found me outside the back of the club. I'd grabbed a bottle of whisky off the shelf and took off in search of some quiet.

"I'm not sure that's gonna help, cous," he said, eyeing the bottle in my hand.

"Like I told Nic, it's either this or I go put a bullet in his head."

"DiMarco will get his, you know he will. But first we need to find the girls and figure out this thing with Lombardi."

"You think it's connected?"

"Yes, no... maybe," he let out a frustrated sigh. "I don't know. But you heard what he said, Cabrioles took a liking to Caitlin. Maybe they were watching her. Maybe they thought she was the way to DiMarco and when we swooped in and saved her, it got the wires all crossed."

"We were careful, E. We would have noticed if someone was watching her."

Wouldn't we?

"She came to us with no cell phone, no bank cards, nothing that was traceable."

"Maybe they were already watching us, getting ready to make their move, and it was sheer coincidence that our paths crossed when they did."

"Yeah, maybe." I took another swig from the bottle, but Enzo snatched it off me and threw it against the wall.

"Hey, that was good whisky." I watched it sluice down the wall.

"I know you're hurting, cous, but we need you sober. Caitlin and Bella need you sober, okay?"

"Fuck. *Fuck*!" I punched the brick, relishing in the bite of pain.

"Better?"

"Fuck you," I grunted, clutching my busted hand to my chest. It was a mess, but I barely felt it over the anger residing in me.

"Channel it into finding them." He gripped my shoulder. "Because we will find them, Matt. And when we do, they'll need you."

I nodded, too choked up to reply. If anything had happened to them... I couldn't bear it.

Bella was my sister. My little sister for fuck's sake. And Caitlin... she was my heart.

The door swung open revealing my father. "There you two are," he said. "Come on, Tommy's got something."

"About time," Enzo grumbled, nudging me forward.

We followed my father back into the club, congregating with the rest of our men near the bar.

"Tommy just called," Nicco said. "He ran Olivia Walsh through the system, and it pinged numerous hits." He scanned his cell phone. "Married to Darragh Walsh, they had one daughter, Erin Walsh. Born May twentieth, two thousand."

My brain was already doing the math when Nicco locked his eyes on me. "He managed to pull a photo of Olivia." Holding up his phone to me, he said, "Look like anyone we know?"

No. Fucking. Way.

It was Caitlin. Well, her eyes and red hair, at least. The woman in the photo was at least twenty years older.

"So wait a second," Enzo said. "You're saying Caitlin O'Donnell is really Erin Walsh?"

"It looks that way."

"Where's Olivia now?" I asked, my heart crashing against my chest.

"Well, that's where it gets interesting. Officially, she's divorced and has lived alone in New Haven for years."

"And unofficially?"

"Tommy found numerous police reports for breach of the peace and countless overdoses."

"The mom's a junkie?" Lucino asked.

"Looks like it."

"Any record of who bailed her out?"

"That's where things get really interesting." Nicco fixed his eyes on me again. "It looks like Olivia Walsh has had an on-off relationship with Massimo Lombardi for the best part of thirteen years."

"Lombardi?" I balked, the ground going from under me. "No. No way."

We'd all heard the stories about Massimo Lombardi's predilection for the seedier things in life. Drugs. Trafficking. Brothels. Lombardi's empire was built of the underbelly of society. He couldn't be connected so personally to Caitlin.

It made no sense.

Yet, I couldn't deny the photo of Olivia had been like looking at an older version of Caitlin.

Erin.

Whatever the hell she was called.

No wonder she'd been cagey about her past. Her mom's boyfriend was the lowest of the low. And definitely not the kind of guy we were looking to do business with.

Lucino let out a low whistle. "If the rumors about Lombardi and his preference for young girls are true, it makes sense why she ran."

My blood ran cold. Lombardi wasn't just immoral; he was sick and twisted and definitely the kind of man you wouldn't want your daughter or sister around.

"Bella." My knees buckled as I slumped against the counter.

"Shh, figlio mio." My father squeezed my shoulder. "We'll get her back. Both of them." There was a fierceness in his eyes I hadn't seen in a long time.

"Do we have any idea where he might have taken them?" Enzo asked, the silent consensus being that Lombardi had taken them.

It was the only lead we had, and despite not wanting to believe it, it made the most sense.

"We can assume Lombardi has been watching Caitlin for some time. Hence why he sent his men here, to scope out DiMarco."

"If she hadn't ended up in the hospital, it's likely he would have grabbed her before now."

"So you're saying we should be thankful DiMarco roughed her up?" Sarcasm clung to my every word.

"Matt, that's not what anyone is saying," Nicco said. "But Lucino has a point. We have to assume Zander changed their course of action."

"What do we do now? What's the plan?" Enzo said.

"Tommy is pulling up a list of possible locations. They took Bella, so I'm inclined to think there's a bigger picture here."

"You think they'll use her as leverage?"

"Most likely. She's one of our capo's daughters. Which makes her a strong bargaining chip."

"We can't negotiate with a man like Lombardi."

"No, but we need him to believe we're willing." Nicco began texting someone.

Just then my cell phone started ringing. I dug it out of my pocket and frowned.

"Who is it?" my father asked.

"It's an unknown number."

"Answer it on loudspeaker. Everyone quiet." Nicco gave me a nod, and I hit answer.

"Hello?"

"Mr. Bellatoni?"

"Yes. Who's this?"

"I believe I have something that belongs to you."

"Is she okay?" I choked out.

"She's fine. They both are. But their remaining so will depend on your actions over the next hour. I'm going to text you coordinates. You are to come with Niccolò and no one else."

"How do we know we can trust you?"

"You don't. One hour. The clock is ticking." He hung up, and a text message came straight through.

"Forward those to me," Nicco said, pulling out his cell. "Tommy, yeah, I'm about to forward you some coordinates. Pull everything you can find about the location. I also want to know everything you can find on Dominic Cabrioles."

"What are you thinking, Nicco?" My father's brows knitted.

"We need to know what we're walking into. We also need allies."

"Cabrioles will never betray his boss." Lucino huffed as if the idea was preposterous.

"Everyone has a price, Luc. We have less than an hour to find out Dominic's."

TWENTY-SEVEN

CAITLIN

"PLEASE, LET HER GO," I said for the twentieth time. After being dragged into this room and discovering that it wasn't Zander who had taken us at all, it was the man who had raised me for the best part of eight years, I'd been forced to sit here and talk.

Of course, Massimo Lombardi didn't talk in the conventional sense. He preferred to gloat. And for thirty minutes, I'd been made to sit here while he filled in the missing pieces about how he found me hiding in Providence.

I should have known she would sell me out. But she was my mother and I'd left her.

I'd left and never looked back.

That kind of guilt, it did something to you. Festered inside of you like poison. In hindsight, I should have used a burner phone or called from a pay phone. But she was my mom. The woman who had given birth to me. Part of me was just a scared child still, desperate for the attention and love of her mother.

And it had cost me dearly.

"So, you see, firefly." The nickname made me shudder. "This presented itself as an opportunity too good to miss."

Massimo sat back in his chair, steepling his fingers.

"You need to let her go," I said again, glancing at Arabella who was curled up on a worn leather couch. She sniffled and I mouthed, "Be strong."

"Let her go?" Massimo chuckled darkly. "And why, pray tell, would I do that? She is worth more to me than you."

Ouch.

His words cut deep, but he wasn't wrong.

"When the Marchetti find out what you've done, how do you think they'll react?"

He leaned forward, palms flat on the desk. There was an entire table between us, yet it still wasn't enough. Fear raced down my spine, the familiar bitter scent of his breath like a punch to the stomach.

My fingers curled into the arm of the chair, nails gouging the wood as I desperately tried to maintain some semblance of control. If I fell apart, Bella had no one.

And she was the important one here, the one who deserved to walk out of this alive.

I had to be strong—for her.

"I think, firefly." His lips twisted. "They'll give me whatever I desire."

"She's just a kid." My voice cracked. "She doesn't deserve this. I'll do whatever you want. Please just let her go."

Massimo's brow lifted with curiosity, and he dragged a hand down his face. "Was life that hard with me, no? I gave you and your momma everything. I made sure she had her fix, I made sure you had nice things. And all I asked in return was that you helped me keep my associates... happy."

My eyes shuttered, memories I'd fought hard to contain rushing to the surface.

When they opened again, I locked eyes with him, the man I'd spent four years running from, and inhaled a sharp breath.

"I was just a child and you made... you made me—"

"I remember it well, firefly. So young and supple and pretty."

Bile washed in my stomach at the affection in his tone, the longing.

"There have been others of course, but none as good as you."

Massimo Lombardi was a sick man. He treated his girls—his dancers and prostitutes—like dogs. Usually, he got them hooked on meth or crack, and then he made them do his bidding.

I guess I should have been grateful he'd never forced drugs on me. But I was special, he'd said. And besides, he had other leverage to use against me.

"Where is my mom, Massimo?" I changed tack.

"You know Liv." He waved his hand through the air. "She'll be out somewhere trying to score her next high."

She was alive.

Thank God, she was alive.

I'd always suspected that when I fled, she would fall apart, or that Massimo would kill her. It's why eventually, I'd caved and called her. I'd needed to know she was safe. I'd needed to know she was still alive. When she stopped answering a couple of months ago, I feared the worst.

She's alive.

I hadn't realized how much I needed to know that until this moment. She was my family—the only family I had. No matter how hard things had been between us, I didn't wish her dead.

Massimo checked his wristwatch and tapped the table. "It's time."

"Time?" I cried. "Time for what?"

"Secure Erin," he ordered one of his men.

"No, *no*!" I yelled, leaping up to my feet. But a rough hand snaked around my neck and clamped down over my mouth. I could hear Bella crying out behind me and then everything went quiet.

Massimo lifted his cell phone to his ear and with his eyes locked on mine he said, "Mr. Bellatoni? I believe I have something that belongs to you."

Matteo.

My heart almost burst out of my chest. I didn't want this; I didn't ever want this.

Oh God.

What had I done?

"She's fine," Massimo said. "They both are. But they're remaining so will depend on your actions over the next hour. I'm going to text you coordinates. You are to come with Niccolò and no one else."

Another long pause while he listened.

"You don't. One hour. The clock is ticking." Massimo hung up, and then typed something out on a text message.

"It's done. Lock them back up until I say it's time."

"I-I don't understand," Bella said as we sat huddled in the small room again. It was dark and stuffy, the air heavy with fear.

"Who is he?"

"Massimo Lombardi was... is my mom's boyfriend."

"So he's like what, your stepdad?"

"I guess you could say that. Although they never married, and we didn't live together in the traditional sense." I wrung my hands in my lap, my stomach a tight ball of nerves.

"He's..."

"A monster." My eyes shuttered as eight years of bad memories flooded my mind.

"What happened?"

"You don't want to know," I breathed.

"This... this is what haunts you," Bella said.

"He's why I ran, yes."

"Tell me. I want to understand."

"Why?" I searched for her in the darkness, but Bella found me, her hand twining with mine.

"Because I think my brother loves you, Cait—I mean, Erin."

"You can call me Cait. I left Erin behind when I left New Haven. And don't you see, this is why I held back. Because I knew. Deep down, I knew I would never truly escape my past. But I never wanted to put you in harm's way, Bella. I never thought—"

"Shh." She shifted closer, laying her head on my arm. "We're your family now. And I know my brother and cousins will do whatever they need to do to get us back safely. Both of us."

It was the nicest thing she could have said to me, even if it was but a fantasy.

There was no happy ending for me in all of this. Now he'd found me again, Massimo would never give me up. And I wouldn't risk Bella or Matteo or any of their family getting hurt... for me.

Not anymore than they had been already.

"Can I ask you something?" she whispered, and I smiled. Bella had the innocence of youth. She might have been raised in the Marchetti family, but she was still young and idealistic.

"Sure," I sighed, too exhausted to argue.

"Do you love my brother?"

"I barely know him."

The lie wrapped around my heart like thorns, shredding me wide open. Because while I didn't know his favorite color, band, or food, I knew Matteo's soul. I knew his heart and his loyalty and devotion to his family.

I knew all the things that mattered.

The things about a person you could fall in love with.

"Your brother is a very easy person to love, Bella."

"That isn't really an answer," she mumbled.

"Well, it's all I have right now."

Silence enveloped us. This was always the worst part, the waiting. The calm before the inevitable storm. When Massimo would demand I *performed* for his associates, there was always that moment before I went on where I would silently pray for someone to come and take me away.

Of course, no one ever came. And, like a puppet on strings, I was forced to dance at his will. I guess in some ways, I was lucky he never let any of them touch me. In those few minutes, I was able to completely detach myself and get lost in the music.

Dancing was my salvation then. But eventually, Zander stole that from me. Two men. Both obsessed with me in their own ways, using the thing I loved most in the world against me.

"Caitlin?" Bella's voice pulled me back to the moment.

"Yes?"

"I'm scared."

"Bella?" I whispered.

"Yeah?"

"I am too."

I don't know how much time passed before anyone came back for us. We dozed in and out of sleep, too cold and uncomfortable and scared to really succumb to oblivion. My arm was stiff from Bella's weight, but I didn't have the heart to tell her to move. She needed me, and I would do everything I could to make her feel as safe as possible.

When the door handle finally rattled, part of me was relieved that this would all be over soon. I only hoped that Bella, Matteo, and their family got to walk away without any casualties.

But I knew Massimo and although he was a monster, he didn't like unnecessary risk, and hurting Bella would rain down a whole heap of destruction on his empire.

Light poured into the room, and two men entered, dragging us to our feet.

"Caitlin," Bella shrieked as one guy carried her from the room, kicking and screaming.

"It'll be okay," I called after them. "It'll be okay, Bella."

The guy smirked at me, and I narrowed my eyes.

"What?" I snapped.

"I can see why Massimo was upset when he lost you." His eyes brazenly checked out my body. I had to swallow my repulsion. I knew men like this, and they didn't care to be emasculated.

"He didn't lose me, asshole. I left."

"Well, he found you now, and I think we both know he isn't going to let you go again."

My stomach sank.

Of course I knew that.

But it didn't make it any easier to hear.

He yanked me from the room, shoving me down the opposite hall, away from the office where I'd seen Massimo.

"Where are you taking me?" I said, fear bleeding into my voice.

"It's showtime, sweetheart," he chuckled darkly, shouldering open another door. This one led to a vast space, some kind of abandoned storage warehouse.

Bella was already tied to a chair, her big eyes pleading with me to do something.

"It's okay," I mouthed.

I had to believe it would all be okay.

Matteo and his family were smart. After all, you didn't get to be one of the biggest crime families in New England without some intelligence. So long as they got Bella out safe and unharmed, I could live with that.

I had to. Because I'd known all along there was no happy ending for me.

I just hadn't expected it to end like this.

TWENTY-EIGHT

MATTEO

THE COORDINATES WERE for an abandoned warehouse on the state border separating Rhode Island and Connecticut. Nicco and I rode in his Range Rover, tailed by Lucino, Enzo, and my father. Stefan had remained at the club with Zander and a couple of our guys. Another SUV was trailing behind with the rest of our men in it.

Lombardi had requested that only Nicco and I show up, but it didn't mean we would come unprepared.

"How are you holding up?" Nicco asked me.

"How do you think?"

Everything I thought about Caitlin was a lie.

It wasn't even her name, for fuck's sake. And yet, I'd known—I'd known she was hiding something. I'd never expected this though.

So much made sense now, even if nothing seemed to make much sense at all.

"I'm sorry," he said.

"Yeah, me too." I stared out of the window, watching the scenery roll by. The GPS indicated we were almost there. There was nothing around for miles but a desolate stretch of land and a series of derelict warehouses.

"Lovely," I murmured as Nicco drove through the busted open security gates.

We pulled over at the first warehouse and the other two vehicles followed.

"Remember the plan," Nicco said, checking his pistol.

"You don't have to worry about me." I just wanted this over with.

We climbed out of the Range Rover and made our way back to my father's vehicle. He already had the window lowered.

"You good?" he asked. I nodded. "Save her, Son. Bring my daughter home."

"I will." The words were raw against my throat.

"Stay here," Nicco ordered. "We'll signal if we're in trouble."

Until Bella was in safe hands, we couldn't risk open gunfire. Not that we hoped it would come to that.

Lombardi was a monster, but he wasn't bloodthirsty. He ran New Haven with an iron fist through fear, not mindless killing. Besides, if he didn't honor his word, Uncle Al knew what to do.

"Jay, you're with us." Nicco beckoned for him to follow us back to the Range Rover. He'd joined us at Nicco's insistence. Bella knew Jay; if me and Nic couldn't get out of there, he could get her to safety.

"As soon as we negotiate Bella's release, you move. Don't stop for anyone or anything. You get her to my car, and you drive."

"Got it, Mr. Marchetti."

"Please, it's Nicco." He gave Jay a sharp nod.

We climbed back in the Range Rover and Nicco put it into drive. "You'll wait outside the building. Once Lombardi gives us the green light, I'll text you."

"Got it. I still think we should consider placing two more men—"

"No. He'll be watching. We already risked enough by bringing two more cars."

But my father wouldn't stay behind, and we needed backup nearby, just in case things went south.

The coordinates led us to the furthest warehouse. There was a single black SUV parked outside, with one armed guard by the door.

"We need to be cool," Nicco said to me. "Follow my lead. No matter what happens in there, I need you to keep your head. Capisci?"

I nodded, too wound up to speak.

So much could go wrong. And my sister was in there. Caitlin too.

Her name isn't Caitlin.

I shut the little voice down. None of that mattered right now. All that mattered was getting them out in one piece.

The rest could wait.

"Okay," Nicco said, checking his gun. "Let's go."

Jay climbed out and opened Nicco's door. I rounded the hood and met them, and the three of us approached the armed guard together.

"Stop right there," the man called, his pistol trained right on Nicco.

Jay inched forward, ready to shield him, but Nicco threw out his arm and stepped forward. "Lombardi requested a meeting with us," he said calmly.

"He specified two of you."

"Jay is going to wait right out here. He's my cousin's bodyguard. She trusts him and I want someone she's familiar with waiting for her."

"You stay right there," the guy ordered, shifting his pistol to Jay.

"No problem, amico." Jay held up his hands and took a step back.

I didn't like the idea of leaving Jay alone with this asshole, but it wasn't like we had a choice. Lombardi held all the cards. Or at least, he thought he did.

"Wait for my signal," Nicco said to him, and Jay nodded, not taking his eyes off our less than friendly greeter.

"I need to check you for weapons."

"Hang on a—"

"Matt, it's fine."

Like hell it was.

But sure enough, Nicco let the guy pat him down and remove his gun.

"Your turn, sweetheart." He smirked.

I hesitated, but Nicco urged me to comply. "Fine," I hissed, unclipping it from its sheath and handing it over.

"Inside. Follow the hall."

"I don't like this," I said, following Nicco inside.

"Lombardi is protecting himself. He knows he's playing with fire taking Bella. If I were him, I would have demanded the same."

"Or he's one very brave coglione," I murmured.

We walked the long hall in thick silence. My heart beat against my chest like a runaway train, blood pounding in my ears.

Eventually, we reached another door. Nicco opened it and stepped inside the large room.

"Ah, Mr. Marchetti, Mr. Bellatoni, you made it."

My eyes landed on Massimo Lombardi sitting in a chair, smoking a cigar. Over in the corner of the room, Bella and Caitlin were seated on a bench, their wrists bound and mouths duct taped. They were guarded by two guys.

Anger swelled inside me so rapidly, I struggled to catch my breath.

"Easy," Nicco whispered, keeping his eyes on Lombardi. "I don't appreciate your method of business, Mr. Lombardi."

"I needed to capture your attention. It was an opportunity too good to pass up. I'm sure you can appreciate that." Lombardi snapped his fingers, and two chairs were brought in for us. "Please, sit."

We did, the air rippling with tension. I surveyed the room again. Including the two men guarding the girls, I counted three more men. One standing directly behind Massimo, and two over by another door.

Dominic Cabrioles was nowhere to be seen.

I cast Nicco a sideways glance, but he didn't take his eyes off Lombardi.

"Now," Massimo said. "Let's discuss business."

"That's not how this works," Nicco said. "You came into my territory and kidnapped my cousin, and you want to talk business? You have some big balls, my friend."

Lombardi chuckled, darkly. "Excuse my brashness. Your cousin was but an incentive."

"That's my sister you're talking about," I growled.

"Matt," Nicco warned. "I'm sure Mr. Lombardi realizes what a mistake he made by dragging an innocent into this. I'm sure he wouldn't want to find the full wrath of the Family at his doorstep all because he didn't do the right thing when he had the chance."

Nicco was like another person, sitting there, issuing veiled threats to Lombardi. This wasn't my best friend, my cousin, the guy I'd grown up with. This was Niccolò Marchetti, the boss of the Marchetti crime family.

The Boss of Dominion.

Lombardi regarded him, narrowing his eyes slightly, no doubt trying to assess the young man seated before him.

"I'm sure you can understand, I didn't expect to get your attention without making a grand gesture as it were."

Grand gesture?

The guy was fucking delusional.

"Drago," he snapped his fingers. "Release the girl."

He dragged Bella up by her arm, and I was up and out of my seat, running to catch my sister as she stumbled forward. "Shh, Bella. Shh." I hugged her tightly, my eyes finding Caitlin over her shoulder.

Her gaze was full of apologies, regrets, and explanations. None of which I had time for right now, given the terrified girl clutching my sweater.

"I have someone waiting outside to return Arabella to our family," Nicco said.

"Fine, bring them in."

Nicco sent the text and seconds later, Jay appeared. Gently, I pulled the duct tape off Bella's mouth and cupped her face. "I need you to go with Jay, okay?"

"N-no, Matt, I want to stay with you. I want—"

"Shh, Bella. I need you to listen to me. Go with Jay and do whatever he says. I'll be right behind you, I promise."

I hated myself at that moment, but she needed to hear the words and I needed to say them, even if it was a promise I wasn't sure I could keep.

"I don't understand," she cried. "What about Caitlin? We need to—"

"Go," I nudged her into Jay's waiting arms. "I'll see you soon."

I dipped my head, silently indicating for him to take her. Her shrieks pierced the air but slowly tapered out as they moved further out of the room.

Seconds ticked by, each longer than the last. Until Nicco's cell phone eventually pinged, and he let out a long breath. "They're safe."

"Despite what you might think, Mr. Marchetti. I am no monster."

My eyes involuntarily flicked to Caitlin. I was sure she would have something to say about that, but I managed to swallow the words.

Bella was safe. Jay would be taking her far away from here and Lombardi's grip.

I could finally breathe a little easier.

Nicco wasted no time getting down to business. "You had your men approach Zander DiMarco, but I can't work out your true motivation. Was it only to get to Erin, or was it to make inroads into our territory?"

All while he spoke, I watched Caitlin, gauging her reaction. But she gave nothing away, her green eyes devoid of emotion.

Fuck, Tink, what did he do to you?

"I'll admit, I have searched a long time for Erin. It wasn't until a few months ago her mother finally confessed that she had the means to contact her." Lombardi sat back in his chair, crossing one ankle over his knee. "Of course, I didn't expect to find her under the protection of someone like DiMarco. But I quickly realized that I could use that to my advantage. For weeks, I watched that spineless creature obsess over her. It was pathetic really. But love is a man's only weakness, and I knew that in his own way, DiMarco loved my firefly."

My firefly.

He had a pet name for her.

I was going to puke.

Staring straight ahead, I tried to rein in the storm of emotions battering my insides.

"My plan was to use his feelings for Erin to leverage my organization's foothold in Providence. But then he almost killed her."

Lombardi's whole demeanor shifted. Gone was the amiable businessman, replaced with a deadly monster. His hand curved around the arm of the chair, gripping it so tightly the blood drained from his knuckles.

"I couldn't believe it when we lost her again. Gone, from right under our noses. Until we picked up security footage of you." He pinned me with a hard look. "Leaving the hospital with her."

Fuck.

All this time we were worried that Zander would discover the truth, but we had been worrying about the wrong person.

"You're not an easy bunch to track down," Lombardi shifted on his chair. "But nothing is impossible to find, you just have to know where to look. And I have always been intrigued by the Marchetti and their stronghold in Verona County."

"And here we are," Nicco said.

"Here we are indeed."

"What do you want, Lombardi?"

"I want what you have, Niccolò. Power. Legitimate business revenue. We both know you're going to put a bullet between DiMarco's eyes for trying to cross you." His eyes locked on mine again. "And for... hurting her. The way I see it, you'll need a new partner to run things in Providence and I want to be considered for the job."

"And what makes you think I would ever consider doing business with the man who kidnapped my cousin?"

"You're a reasonable man, Niccolò. I took a risk with Arabella, yes. But I needed to get your attention. Would you have considered sitting down with me otherwise?"

No, he wouldn't.

Because Massimo Lombardi was scum. His lack of morals and values made him a dangerous man to work with. And he knew it.

The faint smile touching his mouth told us as much.

"My reputation leaves little to be desired." I snorted at that, and he added, "Okay, very little to be desired, which is why I'm looking to clean things up. Times are changing and we have to change with them."

"What's in it for us?" Nicco asked.

I shot forward in my chair. "You cannot be serious," I shrieked. "He's a sleazeball. You can't trust him as far—"

"Matt." Nicco glared at me. "If you can't keep your opinion to yourself, you'll have to leave."

I slumped down with defeat, flicking my eyes to Caitlin again.

Erin. Her name is Erin.

She stared at me, but I didn't attempt to decipher any of what I saw there, dropping my gaze instead.

"One of my top guys, Dominic Cabrioles, knows a thing or two about business, especially running a successful string of clubs. We can provide security, a high caliber of girls, and investment. You help me clean up my reputation, and he'll make your family a lot of money. I can also take care of DiMarco."

"He's mine," I snarled.

"Easy there, Bellatoni. That kind of rage isn't healthy for a guy like you. But I can't blame you for wanting to defend Erin's honor." He glanced over at her. "She really is something special."

This asshole made my skin crawl and I wanted nothing more than to lunge for him and wipe that smirk off his face.

"It would seem we have much to discuss," Nicco said.

"I'm glad you think so." Lombardi exhaled a steady breath, his eyes flicking to the door. "Once Dominic arrives, we can iron out the details."

"And what of... Erin?" Nicco asked.

"She'll remain under my protection, of course. I'm sure since discovering her true identity, you don't want her to remain with you?"

Me.

He was asking *me* that question.

"I..." Nicco shot me a hard look, and I choked out, "you're welcome to her. Whatever I thought we had, it's over."

"Excellent." Lombardi clapped his hands on his knees. "I think this relationship could be very lucrative for both of us."

"Indeed." Nicco nodded, while I sat there, numb.

TWENTY-NINE

CAITLIN

IT'S OVER.

The words echoed through my skull, over and over.

Matteo couldn't even look at me. And I didn't blame him. Everything he thought he knew about me was a lie. I'd lied. I'd led him down a path that didn't exist, because the woman he fell for, the woman he met all those months ago, she didn't exist.

I was Erin Walsh. Daughter of an abusive drug addict and pawn in her boyfriend's sick games.

I'd spent most of high school doing Massimo's bidding, entertaining his friends. He'd drag me around New Haven, to bars and clubs and seedy back rooms, and have me *perform*. My life wasn't my own, my body wasn't my own.

One night, things had gotten out of control. One of his associates had tried to touch me. I'd managed to fight him off, but he'd roughed me up pretty bad.

I was sixteen. Ostracized by my classmates at school for being Liv Walsh's daughter and Massimo Lombardi's pet. That's what they'd called me. *His pet*. Teachers were too scared to report it to child protective services, and no one cared enough to ask me if I was okay.

I was all alone.

So I ran.

I had a small amount of cash saved up, so I used it to buy a bus ticket out of New Haven. I had nothing but the clothes on my back, some extra supplies crammed into a rucksack, and the instinct to survive.

For the first year, I'd moved from town to town, never staying in one place too long. I slept in store doorways, on park benches, and in shelters. Once I knew Lombardi's men weren't following me, I started staying put for longer. I'd bus tables, collect empties; anything to make a few bucks. It's surprising how little you can live off when you have to.

Then one day, right before my eighteenth birthday, Zander found me.

I knew his offer was probably too good to be true, but the sad fact was, I needed a steady job if I was ever going to get an apartment. And he wasn't concerned about my lack of social security number or ID.

The door opened, pulling me back to the present, and Dominic Cabrioles stepped inside. He smoothed his suit jacket and dipped his head. "My apologies," he said. "I was taking care of some things."

"Dom, join us," Massimo had someone bring in another chair. "We have much to discuss."

I risked glancing over at Matteo again. He seemed agitated, unlike Nicco, who was a picture of calm.

"The girl?" Dominic asked, sitting.

"Has been safely returned to them."

He gave Nicco a small nod, running a hand over his head.

He was new. Or at least, he hadn't been with Massimo when I'd known him. I'd never laid eyes on Dominic before that night at DiMarco's. Part of me wondered if Massimo knew how he'd acted that night or if it was all part of his ruse to test Zander. Either way, being in the same room as him again made my skin crawl.

"Do they understand why we had to take the girl as well?" he asked Massimo.

"Sì, they do. And hopefully we can all move forward and discuss business."

"I'll need to discuss this with my uncles," Nicco said. "I'm sure you can understand they will have concerns about aligning ourselves with the Lombardi, especially after you took Arabella."

"Of course, of course. We should sit down in a week, when tempers have cooled. Dominic, take Erin straight back to New Haven. I'm sure she's eager to be reacquainted with her momma. Take Carrick and Thiago with you. I'll follow with Drago, Grayson, and Miller."

"Very well. Gentleman." He addressed Nicco and Matteo. "We shall talk soon."

Nicco stood, clasping Dominic's hand. "To new allies."

My heart withered in my chest. They were going to let them take me. Just like that.

Deep down I'd known it would happen, but part of me clung to the hope that Matteo would fight for me.

You lied to him. What did you expect?

I stared at him, pleading with him to look at me. If this was the last time I ever saw him, I at least wanted to try to tell him everything I was feeling.

But he didn't glance my way. In fact, he very obviously, very purposefully avoided looking anywhere near my direction.

Defeat slammed into me, making me choke on a whimper. Luckily, it couldn't escape my duct taped lips. Neither could the yelp of pain as Dominic grabbed my arm and wrenched me to my feet.

"We meet again, Red." He smirked, and bile washed in my stomach.

I didn't take my eyes off Matteo, desperately hoping to get one final look at him.

Look at me. Please just look at me.

We finally reached the door and Matteo looked over, our eyes connecting for the briefest moment.

Then he was gone, and I was being led out of the building toward a black SUV with my heart in tatters and my pride in disarray.

"Mr. Cabrioles," one of the guards said.

"Get her in the trunk."

Trunk?

"Are you sure that's—"

"Do you have a problem following orders?" he growled.

"N-no, sir. We shall secure her immediately."

"See to it that you do."

Without a second glance at me, Dominic climbed in the SUV.

"Let's go, sweetheart." The guy snorted. "Guess you've got a long way to go to get back into the boss's good graces."

Another guy popped the trunk and I stared at the dark, small space before glancing back at the building.

"No one's coming to help you," the guy barked. "In you go."

Oh God.

He was right.

No one was coming to save me.

Least of all Matteo.

Curled up on my side, I focused on the purr of the engine instead of the erratic beat of my heart. We'd been travelling for what felt like forever, but realistically, it couldn't have been more than thirty minutes. Every minute slower and more drawn out than the last.

My heart was broken. Shattered by the only guy who had the power to mend it.

But I'd expected nothing less. The Marchetti were criminals, yes. But they had a code. They had principles. Family was everything to them.

Once Matteo found out the truth about me, I'd known everything would change.

The things I'd done—the things I'd been forced to do at the hands of the man who had raised me for all those years. Like it or not, I was tainted. First by Massimo, and then by Zander.

Matteo needed a woman by his side who was strong, not one who had enough emotional baggage to fill a plane.

It didn't matter now; he'd let me go. He and Nicco weren't prepared to go to war for me, and I couldn't blame them.

I wasn't worth it, I knew that.

But I wasn't sure I could go back to this life, not after all I'd done to leave it behind. Once I'd seen my mom one last time, I would find a way to end it. Maybe I should have done that in the beginning. But I was young and naïve back then. I thought that maybe, just maybe, the universe had other plans for me.

I was all out of hope now.

Matteo had given me a glimpse of how good things could be. He'd shown me what it could feel like to be loved and adored and treated with respect. And it was everything.

But it wasn't my story.

Tears pricked the corners of my eyes, emotion balled in my throat. But I would not cry.

The SUV slowed to a stop, and I strained to listen. We couldn't already be back in New Haven, could we?

Fear snaked through me. Had I missed something? Had Massimo been lying when he ordered Dominic to bring me back to New Haven? Was that code for get rid of her?

Oh God. Was Dominic going to kill me?

I swallowed down the rush of bile up my throat. Doors opened and slammed shut, heavy footsteps hitting the asphalt. I could just make out the rumble of voices, but they were too far away to decipher the conversation.

A heavy thud rocked the SUV and I screamed; the sound trapped behind my sealed lips. There was another thud and then eerie silence.

What the hell was going on?

The trunk popped open, light spilling inside. Dominic's face came into view, and he said, "Come on, we need to move if we're going to make the drop."

Drop?

He helped me out of the trunk, and I scanned our surroundings, my eyes almost bugging out of my head at the two dead bodies.

I stared up at his, my eyes wide with fear.

"I'm going to remove the tape. But you have to promise not to scream, okay?"

I nodded slowly, confusion saturating every cell in my body.

He tried to be gentle, but my lips smarted against the strong adhesive.

"W-what is—"

"Shh. I need you to be quiet, okay? We don't have long, and I need to deal with this... mess." He gently took my arm and led me around to the front passenger door. "Get in and wait for me."

Dominic opened the door and helped me inside, not offering to cut the restraints binding my wrists and ankles. Did he think I was a flight risk, or was I still a prisoner?

My head was spinning as I slumped against the cool leather seats.

"I'll be right back."

"W-wait," I said as he went to shut the door. "Why are you doing this?"

His eyes narrowed. "I'll explain everything soon."

I nodded, watching through the rearview as he rounded up the dead bodies of his men, and loaded them into the trunk.

When he came around to the driver's door, I caught the glint of his pistol as he climbed inside. "Who are you?" I breathed, my body trembling.

Dominic looked at me and gave me a strained smile. "A friend."

We rode in silence. Every time I went to ask a question, the words died on my lips. Exhaustion anchored me to the seat, my limbs heavy and sore.

It was the middle of the night, the rest of the world sleeping while Dominic Cabrioles was driving me to some undisclosed location.

When we eventually pulled off the highway and the car stopped, I twisted around to face him. "Where are we?"

"I need to make a call," he said, slipping from the SUV.

Glancing around, I tried to find a landmark or something, but it was futile. There was nothing but miles and miles of highway flanked by dense trees. We could have been anywhere.

Headlights flashed up ahead and my body went rigid. The vehicle slowed, making the same turn as us until a black SUV much like this one, slowed to a stop.

Dominic walked over to the driver's window, and it lowered. I couldn't see inside though. Fear skittered up and down my spine, making me shiver.

But then, the back door opened, and a figure climbed out. He stepped into the stream of moonlight and my heart almost burst out of my chest.

Matteo.

Matteo was here.

I tried to open the door only to realize I was still bound. Our eyes collided through the glass, and I saw it then. I saw what I hadn't been able to see back at the warehouse.

He cared.

Matteo cared.

With big sure strides, he approached the SUV and opened my door. "You're here," I choked out as he reached for me. "You came."

"Shh, I got you. I got you." Gingerly, he lifted me out of the SUV, lowering me to my feet. "Really, Cabrioles?" He hissed, noticing my restraints.

"What?" Dominic shrugged. "I couldn't trust that she wouldn't try to gut me like a fish. Fuck knows I deserved it for what I put her through." His eyes glittered with apology.

"I-I don't understand." Silent tears streaked down my cheeks.

Nicco appeared, dipping his head slightly toward me. "Sorry for the theatrics. We needed Lombardi to believe everything was okay."

"Wait a minute," I swung my head between them. "All that back there... you were acting?"

Relief slammed into me. Matteo hadn't meant it; he hadn't meant any of it.

It had all been for show.

A wave of emotion crashed over me, and I swayed on my legs.

"Easy there," Matteo caught me.

I realized now; he would always catch me.

"Lombardi?" Dominic asked.

"He's secure. We need to get Cait... Erin—"

"No," I blurted out. "I'm not Erin, not anymore."

That girl was dead to me. Everything she was, everything she'd survived. I didn't want to shackle her past to my future. I couldn't.

Matteo's expression softened and he nodded with understanding. "We need to get Cait somewhere safe. We'll deal with DiMarco and Lombardi tomorrow."

"Very well. I'll lay low until I get the call." Dominic settled his hard gaze on me. "For what it's worth, I am sorry for how things went down at the club. I'm ambitious, but I'm no monster."

Matteo pulled me closer, and I drew strength from being in his arms. I still didn't understand all that had transpired to get us to this point, but one thing was certain, Dominic had betrayed Massimo to deliver me safely to Matteo and Nicco.

And for that I would always be grateful.

"Come on, let's get you somewhere warm," Matteo led me back to their SUV, climbing into the back with me.

"Are you hurt?" he asked, running his eyes over me.

"I'm okay."

"Cait, I am so sor—"

"Don't." I slid my finger against his lips. "Not yet. I know we need to talk. I know we both have things we need to explain, but right now, I just want to be here with you."

"I can do that." He slipped his arm around my shoulder and pulled me into his side. "I love you, Cait. I need you to know that. I think I've loved you since that night I saw you standing in that alley."

"Matt, I—"

"Don't. Not yet. I just needed you to know."

My eyes fluttered closed as I finally let myself relax. Matteo was here.

He came for me.

And he loved me.

I woke up in soft sheets in a bedroom I didn't recognize. It reminded me of my room at the cabin, but the décor was different, and it was smaller.

Sitting up, I ran a hand over my wild curls, trying to tame them. I could hardly remember getting here. But I remembered Matteo. The way he'd carried me to bed, whispering promises in my ear that had carried me off into a deep sleep.

Smiling to myself, I touched my lips. He'd kissed me. *That* I could remember.

Voices beyond the door caught my attention, and I pushed back the sheet and padded over to it. I was in a brand new, oversized Tinkerbell t-shirt.

I was desperate to go and find him, but I needed a girl's minute, so I went into the bathroom and cleaned up a little.

When I was done, I took a deep breath and went in search of the man who had saved me.

I found Matteo in the kitchen area, making a fresh pot of coffee. "Good morning," I said.

"Cait?" His head whipped around, his expression softening the minute he laid eyes on me. "You're awake." He smiled.

"I am. Sorry for crashing on you like that."

He abandoned the coffee, taking big strides until he was in front of me. "You have nothing to be sorry for, not a damn thing." He slid his hand into my hair and leaned down, touching his head to mine. "How are you feeling?"

"Weary. A little confused. But I'm okay."

I'm here with you. It's more than I could have ever asked for.

"You must have some questions." He searched my eyes.

"I do. But no more than you, I imagine."

"Go get comfortable and I'll make us both a mug of coffee."

"Okay." I went to walk away, but Matteo snagged my wrist, whirling me around to him. His hands cupped my face as he stared at me with a heady mix of relief and longing.

"I meant what I said last night. Every word. I love you, Caitlin. I'm in love with you."

"Matteo, I..."

He kissed me, stealing whatever words I'd been about to say. And the truth was, I didn't know. I had so much going around in my head, it was very confusing.

But the second his lips touched mine, everything quieted. My soul rejoicing at being reunited with its other half. I wound my arms around Matteo's neck, kissing him back with the same desperation and ferocity. Our tongues tangled, his hand drifting down my spine, forcing us closer.

But it wasn't enough. I needed all of him. More than that, I needed him to need all of me.

"Cait," he breathed, tearing his mouth from mine. Matteo inhaled a ragged breath, gazing down at me with such reverence I felt winded. "We should talk."

I nodded, not trusting myself to speak.

"Go. I'll be right there."

On shaky legs, I managed to get to the couch, and sat down. Matteo made quick work of making the coffee and joined me.

"Thank you." I accepted the mug from him, grateful for something to hold, to stop me from reaching for him. He was right, we needed to talk first. The rest, I hoped, would come later.

"What do you want to know?" I asked.

Matteo drew in a sharp breath and said, "Everything."

THIRTY

MATTEO

CAITLIN TOLD ME EVERYTHING. She told me about her life growing up with Massimo. She told me about what he used to make her do, the way he'd make her dance and perform for his associates; sick men who got their kicks off watching a child dress up and play stripper. Then she told me how one day it went too far so she ran. Escaped Massimo, her junkie mom, and fucked up life and ran.

By the time she was done, I could barely contain my anger. My body trembled with rage as I stared at her, imagining what life had been like for her. How she'd escaped one monster, only to end up right in the arms of another.

It was almost too much to bear.

"Matt?" she whispered, blinking away the silent tears clinging to her lashes.

"Come here, Tink." I pulled her into my arms, needing to feel her.

Caitlin was safe. She was safe and she was here. Nothing else mattered.

"I thought... when you said all those things, I thought I'd lost you..." Her walls shattered and she cried into my chest, violent sobs wracking her body.

"Shh, I got you."

But it wasn't only her I was worried about. A vortex of anger spiraled inside me, sucking my soul dry. What Massimo and DiMarco had done to her... what she had survived.

Caitlin wasn't only strong; she was a fucking warrior, and she deserved so much more than the hand she'd been dealt.

"Gosh, look at me." She pulled away, drying her eyes on the back of her hand. "I'm a mess."

"You're beautiful." I pulled her hands away, using the pad of my thumb to swipe the remaining moisture away.

"What happened last night, Matt?" she asked.

"We thought DiMarco had taken you. But when we interrogated him, it became clear he didn't know what we were talking about. Nicco had asked our investigator to look into you—"

"He had?" Her eyes went wide.

"Yes. I wasn't happy about it, but I understood his motivations. I need you to know I trusted you, Cait. I have always trusted you."

"It's okay," she said. "I'm okay. I take it he found something?"

"Your mom… he managed to track her down after finding her number on your old cell phone records."

"That's how Massimo found me. He was watching me for a while."

"Yes. He saw an opportunity to use you as leverage against DiMarco. But that plan went to shit when Zander hurt you and we found you in the hospital."

I still couldn't believe how many things had fallen into place to lead us to this moment. It was fate that had brought Caitlin back into my life, there was no other explanation.

"When we talked to Zander, he mentioned that Cabrioles had taken a shine to you at the club, so Nicco reached out to him in hopes that we could use him in negotiations with Lombardi. Luck was on our side, because he jumped at the chance to remove Lombardi from power. Turns out, he's a very ambitious man who is keen to align himself with powerful players."

"You mean the Marchetti," she said, and a faint smile traced my lips.

"He agreed to double-cross his boss in exchange for control of DiMarco's empire."

"I… wow. I don't know what to say."

"You don't have to say anything, Tink. It's over. Cabrioles proved himself and I think he was telling you the truth. He isn't a bad guy, he's just a guy caught up with bad people."

"I'm so sorry, Matt. I never wanted to put you or your family in harm's way. But I'd been running for almost five years, and I knew if I told you—"

"Hey, hey." I ran my hand over her shoulder and squeezed gently. "It's okay. Arabella is safe. You're safe. Everything's going to be okay now."

Things could have ended very differently, I knew that. But they hadn't, and I wasn't about to punish Caitlin for something out of her control.

"Bella loves you," I said. "She's been blowing up my cell phone all morning desperate to see you."

"S-she has?"

I nodded. "But I thought you'd want space."

And I needed some time alone with you.

"I don't know what to say. Everything you've done for me; the fact that I'm sitting here now. I owe you my life."

I slid my palm along her cheek. "All I'm asking for is your heart."

"It's yours," she breathed, leaning into my touch. "It's been yours since that night eight months ago."

Cautiously, I leaned in, ghosting my lips over Caitlin's. Electricity sparked between us, the way it did whenever we were close. And I soaked it up, relished in the feel of her, her warmth and soft skin.

I loved this woman and I would spend my life showing her.

"What will happen to them?" Caitlin whispered against my lips. And I hated that these people were still between us. But she deserved closure. We both did.

Cupping her face, I stared her straight in the eyes as I said, "They die."

"Are you sure about this?" I asked Caitlin as we pulled up outside one of the Family's other cabins. This one wasn't used for family getaways or laying low though. This was where we disposed of our problems.

"I am." She gave me a weak smile. Neither of us were particularly looking forward to this, but we knew we needed to put the past behind us and move on.

Nicco, Enzo, and Luis were already waiting for us.

"Luis?" Caitlin leaped out of the car and straight into his arms. "Thank God you're okay."

"I'm sorry I failed you." He dipped his head in apology.

"Never," Caitlin said, squeezing his arm. "Tell him, Matt. Tell him it wasn't his fault."

"Luis knows," Nicco reassured her. "Are you ready, Cait?"

She nodded.

"You're looking good, cous." Enzo pulled me in for a hug, clapping me on the back. "How is she?"

"Good," I said quietly. "She's... good."

We'd spent two days off the grid at the other cabin. Two days sharing stories about our pasts and hopes for the future. Then I'd loved her, more times than I could count. I'd loved her not with words but my body.

We'd finally surfaced for air after Nicco called to inform me that everything was set.

"I'm happy for you, Matt."

"Thanks." I squeezed Enzo's shoulder before rejoining my woman. She stepped into my body with easy familiarity, as if she belonged there.

And she did. Without a shadow of a doubt, Caitlin belonged with me.

"Let's get this over with," I said, adrenaline coursing through my veins.

"It doesn't have to be you," Nicco said, grimly.

"Yes, it does." I needed to look them both in the eyes one last time.

"You should be aware that Lombardi is... a mess," Nicco told Cait, and I gauged her reaction.

She didn't even flinch.

"Good. I hope it hurt."

Enzo let out a low whistle as he followed us inside.

The cabin was cold, bare of furniture or décor. Fitting really for a man's last few hours on Earth before he was forced to atone for his sins.

Caitlin stuck close to me as we moved deeper into the cabin, down the hall to the last bedroom. Inside, Lombardi and DiMarco were each tied to a chair, their mouths taped and ankles bound.

Nicco was right, Lombardi was a mess. One of his eyes was swollen shut and his lip was busted open. He'd obviously put up a fight... and lost. And a sick sense of satisfaction went through me. He deserved more, so much more, but it would have to do.

"Wake them," I said. "I want to look them both in the eyes when I do it."

Caitlin tugged on my hand, and I glanced down at her. "Wait over by the door with E, okay?"

"No, I want to be at your side when you..." She inhaled a sharp breath.

"Okay," I said, withdrawing my pistol.

Luis roughly grabbed Lombardi's head and the fucker cracked his eyes open. The second he saw the gun in my hand, he began thrashing against his restraints. Luis moved to DiMarco next, slapping his face. He woke with a start, his eyes immediately finding Caitlin and filling with relief.

He'd made his peace with this. But it still didn't change the fact he'd hurt her.

"Caitlin, do you have anything you wish to say to them?" Nicco asked her.

"I..."

"It's okay," I said. "I'm right here. They can't hurt you anymore."

She stepped forward, steeling herself. "I will not let you define my future. After today, I won't even give you a second thought. But today, today I hope you rot in hell." Her eyes found mine and she nodded. "Do it."

Two gunshots rang out in the small room, reverberating inside me as I watched their lifeless bodies slump in the chair.

It was done.

And Caitlin was right.

Once we walked out of here, I would never spare them a second thought.

"Cait!" Bella was on us the second we walked through the door, wrapping her slim arms around Caitlin's waist. "I'm so happy you're here."

"Hey, Bella." Cait hugged her back. "It's good to see you."

My sister jabbed me in my arm, and I frowned. "What the hell was that for?"

"That's for making me wait to see her. Do you have any idea how hard it's been?"

"Sorry, pulce. But I needed some time alone with her."

"Whatever." Bella rolled her eyes, lacing her arm through Cait's. "I'm just glad you're here now. Mama is making—"

"Sorry," Cait mouthed over her shoulder as I watched Bella drag her toward the kitchen. I chuckled, my heart fit to burst at the sight of two of the most important women in my life all wrapped up in each other.

"Son." My father came to greet me. "How is she?"

"Good, she's good."

"And you?"

"I'm getting there."

He gave me an understanding nod. "I'm eager to meet the woman who has captured your heart, figlio mio."

"You're not angry?"

"Arabella is safe. You have your woman at your side. And Cabrioles will make a better business partner than DiMarco ever did. Things seemed to work themselves out for the best." He clapped me on the shoulder. "Now come, let us eat. Your mama is cooking up a storm."

Why was I not surprised?

We found Caitlin, Bella, and Mom in the kitchen. Talking like old friends. Cait glanced up and smiled, and it was like a fist around my heart.

"I love you," I mouthed.

"I love you too." Her cheeks burned as Mom caught us.

"Oh, Michele, would you look at that." She clutched her chest. "Our Matteo is all grown up and in love."

"Okay, woman, let's not embarrass the boy." He got us both a beer and handed me one. "It's nice to finally meet you, mia cara."

"You too, Mr. Bellatoni."

"Please, it's Michele. I can't be having my future daughter-in-law calling me Mr. Bellatoni, can I now?"

"Dibs on being bridesmaid."

Caitlin's eyes were the size of saucers as she gawked at my family.

"Welcome to the family," I said around a knowing smile as I approached her.

"They're very... welcoming." Caitlin buried her face in my shoulder, laughing nervously.

"Hey." I gently grabbed the back of her neck and steered her face to mine. "They might be joking, but I'm serious. I want that. One day, I want it all... with you."

"Matt," she let out a soft sigh, gazing up at me while my family continued planning our entire future around us.

"What do you say, Tink? Want to spend the rest of your life with me?"

"I... yes. Yes, I want it. So much."

"Good." I brushed my mouth against hers. "Because you're mine now, Caitlin. And I don't plan on ever letting you go."

EPILOGUE

MATTEO

SOMETHING FLUTTERED over my hip bone, stirring me to life. "What the—"

Holy shit.

I must have died and gone to heaven because Caitlin's mouth was on me, sucking me down like a popsicle she couldn't get enough of.

"This is one hell of a wakeup call." My hand slid into her hair as I thrust gently into her mouth, loving the way it felt.

"Good morning." She grinned before flattening her tongue against my shaft and licking from root to tip.

"Fuck, Cait," I breathed when she did some little tongue flick at the end.

"You like that?"

"I don't like that, I fucking love that. But I'd love you riding my dick even more." I pulled Cait up my body, and her legs fell to either side of my hips as she sat above me.

"Hi." She smiled again.

It was a sight I would never grow tired of. Her green eyes alight with love, laughter, and happiness. Over the last month, our relationship had only gotten stronger. Everyone loved her: my family, my friends, me. God, I loved her so fucking much. She was everything I'd ever wanted, and I couldn't wait for the rest of our lives together.

"Matt." Cait rolled her hips, teasing me.

"Ride me, Tink. Show me how much you want me." Grasping myself, I steadied one hand on her hip as she rose up on her knees slightly to work me inside her.

"Fuuuuck, that feels good."

"Move, I need you to move," she panted.

I gently thrust forward, finding the perfect pace while Caitlin circled her hips. She leaned down, kissing me. Hot, wet, dirty kisses that drove me wild.

"It's official," I murmured against her mouth. "You have permission to wake me up like this every morning."

"More..." she cried. "Harder."

Placing my feet flat on the bed, I really let her have it, fucking her faster, until our collective moans filled our apartment.

"Yes... *yes*!" Cait threw her head back, her thick red curls spilling down over her shoulders.

Sometimes I could hardly believe this woman was mine.

"Are you ready to come for me, Tink?" I sat up, sliding my hands under her arms and up over her shoulders, anchoring us together.

"Yes... God, *yes*..."

"Together." I kissed her, plunging my tongue deep into her mouth as I guided her up and down on me, over and over. "Clench for me, Cait," I urged, and she squeezed around me, milking me.

"Fuck... *fuck*!" The familiar tingling started at the bottom of my spine as I slipped a hand between us and rubbed her clit.

"Matt... I love you," she cried, falling over the edge. I buried my face in her neck as my own release slammed into me.

"I love you, so fucking much." Winding my hand into her hair, I gently tugged, forcing her to look at me.

"Hi."

"Hi."

"That was—"

"Incredible."

"It was." I smirked. "Give me five minutes and I might be good to go again."

"We have to pick Bella up soon."

"Ugh, that's today?" I flopped back on the bed, taking Caitlin with me. She rolled off me and ran her nose along my shoulder.

"We promised her. It's junior prom. She needs a dress."

"Junior prom," I grumbled. "She's sixteen."

"And you need to face up to the fact she's no longer a kid."

"She'll always be my kid sister."

"You're impossible," Cait muttered, pecking my lips. "I'm going to clean up and then make breakfast."

"I could always eat you." My brows waggled and she batted my chest.

"Behave."

"With you?" I captured her lips again. "'Never."

Caitlin finally untangled herself from my arms and climbed off the bed, smiling back at me. "I'm really happy, Matteo. I hope you know that."

She slipped out of our bedroom, and I stared up at the ceiling wondering how the hell I got so lucky.

Sure, we'd been through hell and back to get to this point. But she was worth it.

And I would spend my whole life showing her.

CAITLIN

"What about this one?" Bella darted from rack to rack, pulling out dresses. Pink ones and black ones, one with sleeves and strapless ones. Her excitement was infectious, and I couldn't help but get swept up in it.

"I could do your hair," I said, observing her latest favorite gown. "Something intricate and sexy."

"Sexy?" Matteo appeared out of nowhere. "I thought we agreed on innocent and demure?"

"No, you agreed to that. We overruled you and decided with sassy and sexy." I threw Bella a conspiratorial glance and she smothered a giggle.

"Something low cut and short," she added. "Like mid-thigh."

"What?" Matteo's eyes practically bugged out of his head. "No! No way is she wearing something mid-thigh with her... her breasts falling out all over the place."

"Did you just say... breasts?" Bella exploded with laughter; so loud that we drew the attention of the store assistants.

"Is everything okay?" one of them called, and I smiled.

"We're fine, thank you. But I think we're ready to try on a few dresses."

Bella clapped. "I want to do this one, and the two we chose earlier."

"Good choice. Then we'll think about shoes and accessories."

"Accessories? Nobody said anything about accessories."

"God, Matt, you're such a drag." Bella followed the assistant to the dressing room while Matt and I took a seat on the plush velvet couch.

"It's nice that you're doing this with her."

"Let's be honest, Tink. I'm just here to pick up the bill."

"So dramatic," I rolled my eyes. "Bella looks up to you. She loves you and this is important to her."

"And I love you." He swooped in kissing me deeply.

"Matt, we're in public."

"What's the problem, Tink? Scared you can't control yourself around me?" He winked playfully.

I liked this side of Matteo. Oh who was I kidding? I liked all sides of him. The last month had been the best few weeks of my life.

I'd moved into Matteo's apartment immediately after everything happened. He'd offered to get me my own place, but I didn't want to waste another second without him.

We'd spent an entire week barely coming up for air. But life had to keep moving. Matteo had responsibilities to his family, and I found a part-time job helping with children's dance classes at the VCTI where Arianne volunteered.

Nicco and Arianne had arranged for my mom to go into a drug treatment program and surprisingly she was doing well. Whether things would stay that way remained to be seen, but I could only hope she saw this was a real chance for change, now that she was away from Massimo. Things would never be the same between us, too much had happened. But it was a start.

Life was good.

Better than good, it was perfect.

And I thanked God every day that Matteo found me in that alley all those months ago and saved me.

"Okay you two, stop with the highly embarrassing displays of PDA," Bella called through the stall door. "I'm ready to show you the first dress."

"We can't wait," I said, elbowing Matteo in the ribs when he rolled his eyes.

"What do you think?" Bella stepped out and Matteo almost stumbled off the couch.

"Holy shit, pulce. Is that you?"

"Asshole," she muttered.

"I'm being serious, Bella. You look beautiful."

"I do?" She glanced down at herself, twirling slowly. "Caitlin, what do you think?"

"Matt is right, sweetheart. You look stunning."

"I want this one. I feel… like a princess. Connor is going to die."

"*Connor*. Who the hell is Connor?" Matteo stood up, frowning at his sister.

"Didn't Cait tell you? I have a date."

I jumped up, lacing my arm through Matteo's.

"Isn't that nice, Matt. She has a date." I dug my nails into his arm, and he stuttered, "Nice, yeah, real nice."

Bella snorted. "I already cleared it with Daddy, so you don't get to sabotage this for me." She stormed off toward the stall.

"A date?" He whirled on me.

"It's junior prom. Of course she has a date."

"Over my dead body."

"Maybe we can find a compromise." I pushed my body into his, running my hands up his chest.

"A compromise, you say. I'm listening."

"I'll go buy a set of that lingerie I caught you eyeing earlier, if you promise to play it cool about her date."

"The black and gold set with the suspender belt?" he whispered, eyes hooded with desire.

"And the crotchless panties."

"Fuck, Cait," he groaned, running a hand down his face. "You're killing me here."

"Do we have a deal?" I cocked my brow, waiting.

"Get it in the pink as well and I think we can come to an arrangement."

I smirked. "Men. So predictable."

He leaned in, brushing his lips along the shell of my ear. "You won't be saying that when you're bent over the back of the couch with my mouth on your pussy."

"Matt," I breathed, shivers skittering down my spine.

He stepped back, winking. "Don't start games you can't finish, Tink."

Bastard.

Bella appeared a second later, glancing between the two of us. "What's wrong with you?" she asked me. "Why are you all flushed like that?"

"Me? I'm fine."

Matteo caught my eye over her shoulder and shook his head with silent laughter.

"Your dress is beautiful," I tried to change the subject, ignoring the ache deep inside me.

"Are you sure you're okay?"

"It's hot," I said. "Don't you think it's hot in here?"

"I'm okay. Maybe you're coming down with something?"

"Maybe." I gave her a tight smile before suggesting we look for accessories. Bella was all too happy making a beeline for the rows and rows of purses.

"You okay there, Tink?" It was Matteo's turn to smirk.

"I'm fine," I said indignantly, brushing past him.

"We could always sneak off to a stall and I'll help you with your little problem."

"You're a bad, bad man, Matteo Bellatoni." Heat burned my cheeks, and he chuckled.

"Only for you, Tink. Only ever for you."

After torturing Matteo with another couple hours of accessory shopping, we gave Bella a ride home and returned to our apartment to get ready for dinner with Arianne and Nicco, and Nora and Enzo.

We tried to get together as a group at least once a week. It wasn't always easy, but family was important to all of them, and we tried our best to make it work.

"Wow, this place is—"

"Very exclusive." Matteo kissed my cheek, his hand pressed to the small of my back as he guided me to the front of the opulent looking building. He threw his truck keys to the valet and jabbed a finger in the young man's direction. "Look after her like she's your own."

"Y-yes, Mr. Bellatoni."

"Seriously, for a truck?" I rolled my eyes.

"She's not just any truck." He leaned closer. "If you play your cards right, she's the truck you might get lucky in on the drive home."

"Do you ever stop?" My lips curved.

"Never."

"Good evening," the maître d' greeted us.

"Hello, we're joining Mr. Marchetti," Matteo said.

"Ah yes, they are already at your table. This way please."

The restaurant was beautiful. It had a curved window with panoramic views of the river. Everything was gold and black, giving the whole place an elegant feel. And everyone was dressed to the nines, Verona's elite socializing.

It was world's away from anything I'd ever experienced, but I loved it.

"Caitlin." Arianne stood to greet us, pulling me in for a hug. "You look beautiful."

"Thank you, so do you."

"Cait." Nicco kissed my cheek.

"This place is amazing."

"Isn't it?" Arianne patted the seat beside her. "We don't come here often. Nicco doesn't like all the fuss. But since we're celebrating, I persuaded him."

"Celebrating?" Matteo said. "Nicco didn't mention we were celebrating." He sat on my other side, resting his hand on my knee. I loved that he always insisted on having some part of him touching some part of me.

"So… what are we celebrating?" Matteo prompted, but Arianne glanced over his shoulder.

"Oh look, here's Enzo and Nora."

The two of them joined us and we all did another round of hugs and compliments.

Nora picked up her menu and let out a low whistle. "I hope you brought your wallet, babe."

"Nicco invited us," Enzo grumbled. "I figured he'd pick up the tab."

"Classy, E, really classy." Matteo snorted, taking a long pull of his beer.

I was used to being with them in public by now. The constant stares and whispers. Matteo and his cousins were well-known around Verona County. Even more so since Antonio had stepped down.

He had made a surprising recovery and finally been released from hospital a couple of weeks ago. But health complications had deemed him unfit to continue his duties, so he'd officially handed Nicco full responsibility.

Matteo didn't go into much detail about it all, and I knew there would always be things he couldn't tell me, but I didn't resent him for it.

I loved and trusted him implicitly. His family were nothing like the monsters of my past. A past I rarely gave a second thought to now my life was full of people who genuinely cared.

"How is the job?" Nora asked me.

"It's great. The kids are just the sweetest, and Debra, the dance teacher, is talking about handing me more responsibility soon."

"That's amazing. I keep thinking that maybe college isn't for me, you know? I'm restless."

"E not keeping you satisfied, Nor?" Matteo chuckled, and Enzo flipped him off.

"Says the guy who didn't use his dick for eight months after he got ghosted by Caitlin."

"What?" I gawked at Matt, certain Enzo was busting his balls.

"It wasn't that bad, but it's absolutely not something we're discussing right now at dinner."

I smothered the laughter bubbling in my chest.

"Anyway, what's going on with you two?" Matteo changed the subject. "You said we're celebrating?"

Nicco took Arianne's hand in his and she nodded. "We have something to tell you," he said.

"We're pregnant." Arianne beamed.

"Oh my God, babe, that is… oh my God." Tears filled Nora's eyes. "What… how… tell us everything."

"Not everything, Boss. I don't need to hear your sex stories." Enzo smirked, adding, "Congratulations."

"It wasn't planned, so it was quite a shock," Ari said. "But we've taken some time to think about it and after everything that happened with Antonio, we've decided we want this." She gazed up at her husband as if he was the only man in the room.

"That's amazing news, congratulations." I hugged Arianne, emotion welling in my chest.

Matteo slipped his arm around my shoulder and pulled me into his side, dropping a kiss on my head. "One day," he whispered. "One day that'll be us."

I wanted it.

More than anything.

I wanted the big white wedding, and two or three little olive-skinned, dirty-blond haired babies running around. But we had all the time in the world, and I didn't want to rush a single second of it.

"Congratulations, guys. It's amazing news." Matteo lifted his beer in the air. "To baby Marchetti. May his—or her—life be filled with love, happiness, and super cool uncles."

"To baby Marchetti." We all toasted.

"Thank you," Nicco said. "You're the best friends a guy could have, and I'm lucky to call you family too." He lifted his drink in the air and smiled. "To family."

Matteo dropped his mouth to my ear again. "To family. My heart. My home. My everything. I love you, Caitlin."

With tears in my eyes, I smiled up at the man who had saved me in more ways than he would ever know.

"I love you, Matteo Bellatoni, and I can't wait to spend forever with you. No regrets?"

His lips brushed my cheek as he whispered. "No regrets."

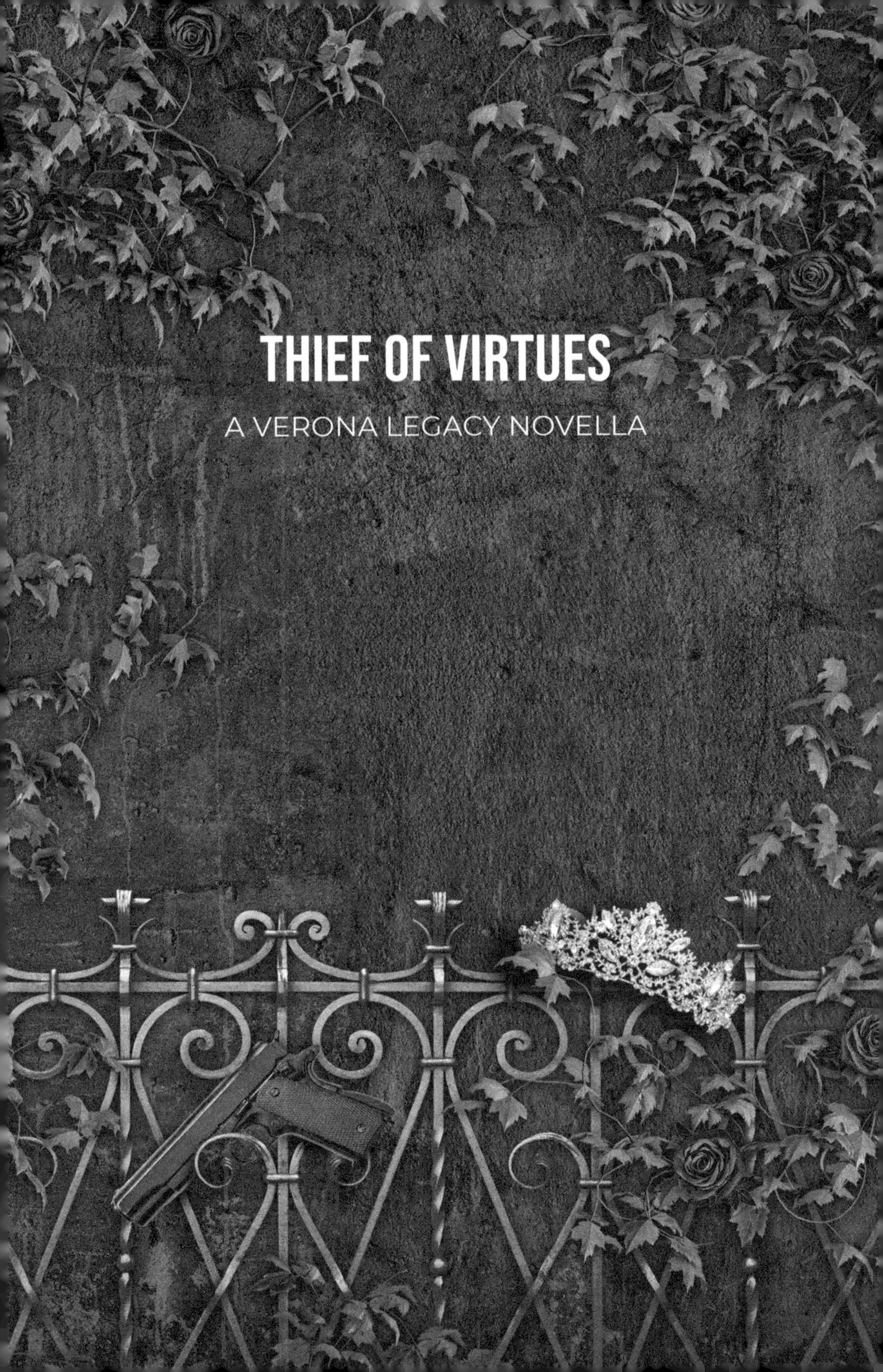
THIEF OF VIRTUES
A VERONA LEGACY NOVELLA

ONE

ALESSIA

"LOOK AT YOU, PICCOLA." I held out my arms, offering my niece Lucia a safe place to waddle to. She was headstrong though, scrunching her nose up at my offer of support and batting my arm away.

"Ucia, do. Ucia, do."

"I know sweet girl, you can do it." Soft laughter spilled out of me.

"How's my little princess?" Arianne came into the room with a tray of cookies and milk for Lucia.

"She's stubborn, just like her father." I smiled.

"Don't let Nicco hear you say that." Ari placed the tray down and Lucia dropped to her knees, crawling like a rocket toward the cookies.

"That's cheating," her mamma scolded, scooping her up and sitting her on her knee. "One. You can have one." Ari pressed a kiss to Lucia's dark curls.

"She's getting so big. I can't believe she'll be two in a few months."

"Tell me about it. I miss the baby stage. At least when she couldn't crawl or walk, I didn't need eyes in the back of my head."

"Is Nicco—"

"Working." There was a hint of pride in Arianne's eyes, which I found a little strange considering what my brother did. But since taking over, the Family had gone from strength to strength. Nicco was keen to make sure we had as many legitimate businesses as the not so legitimate ones. While a few of the older men weren't happy with some of the changes, a lot of them did appreciate his attempts at diversifying.

Nicco might have been the boss but he had a family now, a daughter, and he wanted her to have a legacy she could be proud of.

"Are you looking forward to the party?" Ari asked me.

"I guess." I picked up some of Lucia's toys and dropped them in the toy box. "Bella is so excited, she has like three dresses picked out."

"Three?" Ari gawked, and I nodded.

"There could be outfit changes."

We both laughed and Lucia joined in, her little forced belly laughs so freaking adorable.

"I still can't believe you graduated. We're very proud of you Sia."

I blushed at her compliment. Arianne had been in my life less than three years, but she was the sister I never had, and I loved her dearly. Even if I was slightly jealous of the love she and my brother shared. It was the kind of love that shone; the kind of love that people immortalized in songs and poems and romance novels.

They had both endured so much, they deserved a lifetime of happiness together.

"Sia?" I glanced up at the sound of my name on Ari's lips. "Is everything okay?"

"Fine." My smile didn't reach my eyes.

But the truth was, I was restless.

School was over. I was supposed to be on the precipice of the best time of my life. College. Moving into an apartment with Bella. Discovering what I wanted to do with my life. But when I looked at Nicco, at Arianne, and their beautiful daughter, I knew in my heart of hearts what I wanted.

I wanted a family.

I wanted someone to love me.

I wanted the fairy tale.

There was just one small problem.

I was desperately, hopelessly in love with a man who would never be mine.

"Oh my God, Sia, you look amazing." Bella peeked around the bathroom door and grinned.

"I told you to wait."

"I know but you were taking too long." She came further inside. "What's the matter?"

"Is it… too much?"

"Too much? Have you seen yourself, you look beautiful, Sia."

I studied myself in the mirror. The jade green dress complimented my tan skin. Cinched tight at the waist, the silk fell over my hips and down my legs like a glistening waterfall. But the slit that ran up one thigh was a little risqué, more so than I was used to.

"I love the sweetheart neckline. So pretty." Bella fingered the thin straps. The back dipped low, revealing the expanse of my spine, another feature I wasn't so sure about.

"Don't look so worried," Bella said, swishing her own dress.

In typical Bella fashion, it was a bright pink princess gown. Over the top, bold, and of course, it looked like it was made for her.

"You look amazing."

"So do you. Now come on, we don't want to be late for our own party." Her brows knitted and then a slow grin spread over her face. "Actually, we should totally be late. Just enough to make a grand entrance."

The thought irked me.

I didn't like being in the spotlight, preferring to stay back and let Bella shine.

She was my best friend, my cousin, the one person who knew me better than anyone. We'd grown up together in a world dominated by men. Our brothers. Our fathers. Their associates. The Family. In a place like Verona County, when your father, brother, uncles, and cousins were all mafioso, true freedom was a luxury I had little experience of.

If I wanted to go to the movies or on a date—not that I dated—or to the gym, Jay, my bodyguard had to come along. I understood the need for precaution, the family had enemies a plenty, and we'd been through too much over the last few years to become complacent. But it was... exhausting. I had everything I could ever want, and yet the thing I craved the most would always be out of reach.

Because I was Alessia Marchetti, the only daughter to Antonio Marchetti and sister to Niccolò Marchetti.

A mafia princess.

I suppose I was lucky that my brother and father didn't want to marry me off to the son of some influential family to strengthen their position in Rhode Island. They would never use me like that. But that didn't mean being a female in the Marchetti family didn't come with responsibilities.

When—*if*—I ever met someone, I would be faced with the dilemma of either lying to them about my family and our history, or entrusting them with the truth. It was a burden I didn't care to carry, which is probably why I had very little experience with men.

I wasn't like Bella who could compartmentalize the different parts of her life. Besides, it was easier for her. Her father, my uncle Michele, had married into the Family. He was one of my father's captains but he and my aunt Marcella still retained some level of normalcy.

She made sure of it.

"Come on, babe. It's time."

"Yeah." Another weak smile tugged at my lips.

I wanted to be excited about the party. Genevieve, my father's fiancée, had gone to a lot of trouble planning the perfect celebration with Nora and Caitlin, my cousins' girlfriends. Nora was six months pregnant and already on maternity leave due to some complications, so she'd jumped at the chance to help plan the party. Much to her boyfriend Enzo's annoyance. If he had his way, he'd tie her to their bed and never let her leave. But if anyone had a right to be extra protective, it was Enzo. A couple of years ago, Nora had been kidnapped. Twice. My cousin had always been a brooding hothead but something changed after Nora was hurt. He changed. Girls dreamed of having a guy who would burn down the world for them—Enzo Marchetti was that guy.

I couldn't imagine ever knowing that kind of love.

Pushing the loose curls out of my face, I grabbed my purse, following Bella out of her room. Aunt Marcella was at the hotel helping Genevieve put the final touches on everything, and Uncle Michele was doing whatever he and my dad liked to do when the women were fussing.

Bella checked her cell phone and grinned. "Jay and Tristan are waiting downstairs in the car."

Just the mention of *his* name sent a thrill through me. But it was quickly chased away by an icy cold blast of jealousy.

Jay was my bodyguard. But Tristan, he was Bella's, after refusing to work on my security detail. Of course, he didn't know that I knew. That I'd overheard him and Nicco arguing about it at the beginning of senior year.

There had been a threat. Nothing too serious, but we hadn't known that at the time. Nicco closed ranks, putting the family under tighter surveillance. He wanted Tristan to be my bodyguard but he flat out refused. I hadn't waited around to hear his reasons. It was more than apparent he didn't want to be around the girl who'd tried and failed over the years to hide her silly little crush.

When we were younger, it had been a well-documented joke, the way me and Bella trailed around after Tristan. No one made a big deal about it because we were just teenage girls with a crush on Arianne's older and insanely hot cousin.

But as I got older, the feelings didn't go away. If anything, they only intensified. And now here I was, an eighteen year old girl desperately in love with a guy who would never see me as anything more than his cousin's husband's little sister.

"Tonight is going to be so good, Sia." Bella checked her reflection one last time. "Who knows, maybe you'll even get your first kiss."

Strangled laughter spilled out of me. "With our entire family right there? It's not exactly how I imagined it."

She rolled her eyes. "Because you overthink everything. It's just a kiss, Sia. Better to get the first one out of the way. It's usually a disappointment." With a little shrug, she headed for the door.

I followed, my brows crinkled. I'd always imagined my first kiss to be worth remembering. Butterflies in my stomach, toes curling in my shoes. Maybe she was right, maybe I had worked it up to be something unattainable. But it was my downfall.

I was a dreamer.

A hopeless romantic.

I saw the couples around me—Nicco and Arianne, my cousins and their girlfriends, even my father and Genevieve—and I didn't see their struggles, I only saw people who overcame the odds and fought for love despite living in a world where love was often perceived as a weakness.

And I wanted that.

I deserved it, dammit.

But the guy, the only guy I saw, the only guy I dreamed of being with...

Well, he didn't see me.

"Miss Marchetti." Jay gave me a curt nod as he opened the door to the black SUV.

"Jay, you've been with me what, almost two years... I think we can skip the Miss. Please, I'm begging you, just call me Alessia."

"Very well, Miss Marchetti."

Bella shot me a bemused look and ducked around me to climb into the car. "Hey Jay, looking hot as usual."

He flinched, the way he always did when Bella teased him.

Bella was the opposite of me in every way. Confident. Determined. One hundred and ten percent unafraid to go after what she wanted.

Arabella Bellatoni liked to ruffle feathers and shake up the status quo. I, on the other hand, was all too happy to go with the flow, blending in with the shadows. It wasn't that I was insecure in my own skin, I wasn't. I liked how I looked. I liked my long wavy blonde hair and my dark brown eyes and slim figure. But I just didn't feel comfortable being in the spotlight.

After all, some stars shined brighter than others.

And I was okay with that.

I gave Jay a warm smile and slid into the SUV. He slammed the door behind me and my heart did a little somersault. But it wasn't just the door banging closed that startled me, it was the trickle of awareness that came from being close to Tristan.

He didn't even acknowledge me, staring straight, away from me. Aloof but focused. Aware of his surroundings, aware of his charges, and any potential threats in a way only my brother's security team could be.

"A little something to get the party started." Bella slipped open her purse and pulled out a small pink hip flask.

"*Bella!*"

"What? It's only a spritzer. Besides, what they don't know won't hurt them," she said, referring to our brothers and fathers.

"Here." She thrust the flask at me and I peeked up to where Jay was driving and Tristan was sitting silently beside him.

His eyes caught mine for the briefest second in the mirror, a tiny zap of electricity pulsing through me. I didn't know why my body had always responded to him in such a visceral way. Part of me thought it was the fact he was one of the most gorgeous men I'd ever laid eyes on. Tall with dark hair, shaved closer on the sides and longer on the top. It was perfect for running your fingers through. At least, I imagined it to be. Thick lashes framed his dark brown eyes, eyes that penetrated my soul whenever they fixed in my direction. And he had big strong hands, hands I imagined him doing all kinds of dirty things with.

I had it bad. I'd lusted over Tristan since I was a fifteen-year-old girl who barely understood the havoc he wreaked on my body. Now I was a young woman, in tune with my wants and needs and desires. I'd filled out, proud of my shapely curves, aware of how men's heads turned whenever I entered a room, even if I didn't appreciate their hungry gazes.

Because they weren't him.

Bella was constantly trying to talk me into dipping my toe in the dating pool. But I couldn't do it. I couldn't betray my emotions. Because it felt like I was betraying *him*.

Which was ridiculous.

Tristan didn't care.

It had gotten to the point with Bella where I had to pretend I just wasn't interested in men. I had enough valid reasons. An overbearing brother and father. The fact I was Alessia Marchetti. I told her I wanted to wait until college, until we had some freedom. That I wasn't in any hurry to experiment. But it didn't stop her from pushing, trying to get me to give someone a chance.

The truth was though, I didn't see the point trying to force a connection with some random guy.

Not when my heart already belonged to another.

TWO

TRISTAN

"THANK FUCK," I muttered under my breath as Jay pulled up outside of the hotel.

Shouldering the door open, I climbed out and opened the back door while Jay talked to the valet.

"Thanks, Tris," Bella said, climbing out. There had been a time her gaze would have lingered, and would have brazenly checked me out. But she was too busy checking out every other guy in the vicinity to worry about me now.

Unlike her cousin, who tried, and failed, to look anywhere but at me.

"Alessia," I said with a curt nod, waiting for her to exit the car.

"Thank you." Her voice was quiet, hesitant even as she brushed past me and joined Bella.

I inhaled a sharp breath, slamming the door a little harder than I intended.

Get a fucking grip, Capizola.

Jay shot me a strange look as he rounded the car, ready to escort the girls inside. "Luis has eyes on all entrances and exits. No one gets in or out without us knowing," he said.

"Sounds good. Let's do this."

"You know, you didn't have to work tonight. They're family, you could have been off the clock."

"I'm here, aren't I?"

"Yeah, but come on, Tris, it's—"

"There you two are, we've been waiting." Nora waddled over to the girls. She was six months pregnant and glowing. It was still hard to believe Nora Abato was all grown up, engaged to Lorenzo Marchetti and about to give birth to his kid. Part of me—the part that had grown up thinking the Marchetti were the enemy—still couldn't reconcile it. But she was happy, and things between our two families were different now.

All thanks to my cousin Arianne and her husband Nicco.

There had been a day where I'd wanted more from my life than... this. Working for Nicco's security detail. But I liked the work. I liked being able to have a hands-on role in protecting Arianne and my niece and their family.

My eyes landed on Alessia again.

Fuck. She had been just a kid when I'd first met her. Fifteen with stars in her eyes.

She wasn't a kid anymore though. Tonight she looked like a woman.

And that was a fucking problem.

"Tristan." Nora moved in front of me and leaned in for a hug. "You had to work tonight, really?"

"Don't start, Nor."

"Spoilsport." She rolled her eyes. "We need to get the girls inside. The party can't start properly without them." Ushering Alessia and Bella toward the big ornate double doors, Nora snapped a couple of photos with her phone. "Ready?"

"Hell yeah." Bella grinned.

Jay got the door, and the girls slipped inside leaving me to trail after them. Music spilled out of the darkened room but everyone cheered. It looked more like a wedding reception than a graduation party. Black stemmed vases filled with pink candles adorned each round table and there was a black and hot pink balloon arch framing the stage. It suited Bella down to a tee. She'd even managed to color coordinate her dress.

But that was Arabella Bellatoni. Life and soul of the party. I didn't envy Matteo, her big brother, that was for sure. She was going to stir up all kinds of trouble at Montague University in the fall.

Alessia, however, she seemed to shrink into the shadows. It was always the same. Bella shone whereas Alessia did everything in her power to disappear.

"Tristan," Nicco beckoned me over and I joined him and his father at the bar. "Any problems on the ride over?"

"Nothing," I said. He and Antonio shared a look, and I added, "Is something wrong?"

"Hopefully, it's nothing." Toni rubbed his jaw, his hard gaze settled on his daughter and niece as they greeted some of their guests.

"Nic?" My brows furrowed.

"We got word that Jericho Mahoney is making waves. A couple of our guys down in Cranston have got their ears to the ground."

"The Irish guy?"

"That's the one." Nicco nodded, a dark storm swirling in his eyes as he drank his whiskey.

"Do the rest of the guys know?"

"Luis is sending someone to meet our guys in Cranston. If there's anything to worry about, we'll know soon enough."

"Okay."

I'd been around the Marchetti long enough to know that threats weren't unusual. Hell, my own cousin and Nora had been caught in the crossfire more than once.

When you were as powerful as Nicco and his father, there was always someone waiting to take your empire out from under you. But tonight was Alessia and Bella's night, and the idea that someone might seek to ruin that, to use it to further their cause, well, it made my blood boil.

"Relax, amico," Nicco said, gripping my shoulder. "Security is tight. We're good, for now. Let the girls enjoy their night."

"Niccolò is right, Tristan." Antonio turned his attention to me. "Nothing will happen here. You should enjoy the party. Take the night off. There are enough men here who would lay down their lives for figlia mia and Bella. Have a drink, relax. You always look so tense."

My spine snapped straight. His words were so on the mark it wasn't even funny. Yet, he couldn't know. Couldn't have even the slightest idea about the thoughts which consumed my mind.

Don't look at her. Don't you dare fucking looking at her while you're standing with her father and brother.

"I'm going to check in with Luis," I said.

Nicco grabbed my arm. "Stay close tonight."

I wanted to ask him if we needed to be more concerned than he was letting on. Because there was something in his grip, a warning that made a shiver run down my spine. "Are you—"

"There you are." Arianne appeared. "Tristan." She leaned up and pressed a kiss to my cheek. "I hope you're not working too hard."

"Never. But I do need to go talk to Luis. Excuse me."

"You should take the night off," she called after me. "Relax. Celebrate with us."

I kept walking. It was easier this way. Easier if I kept things professional, a clear line in the sand.

It hadn't always been like this. When Nicco and Arianne first got together, after we buried the hatchet, for a while there, I was one of them. A trusted member of their innocent circle.

Family.

But last year, things changed.

She changed.

And I could no longer be around her. Not when she was so far off-limits we might as well have been on different continents.

Alessia Marchetti was the Marchetti family's crown jewel. She was pure and good and she deserved a life better than the one she'd been born into.

Safely out of sight of my cousin and her husband, I allowed myself a second to look at her.

Really look at her.

The emerald green dress clung to her slender curves, taunting me. Taunting every fucking guy in the room. Her dark blonde curls were pulled into a messy ponytail, a few loose tendrils falling around face. Her makeup was light but enough to make her blue eyes pop. She was a fucking vision. A goddess among men.

And she didn't even realize the effect she had on them.

As if she felt me watching, Alessia's head turned and our eyes collided. A bolt of awareness went through me. Powerful and a little unnerving. Her lips parted and even from across the room, I saw her breath hitch.

Look away, asshole. Look. The. Fuck. Away.

I forced myself to break the connection and walked in the opposite direction, not sparing her a second glance.

Even though I felt her eyes on me the whole way.

I found Luis in the hotel's security room, running a keen eye over each of the camera feeds.

"Everything good?" I asked, slipping inside and closing the door.

"Nothing out of the ordinary. Everything okay inside?" His brow went up.

"Fine."

He snorted at that. Luis was Arianne's bodyguard long before he became Nicco's head of security. They trusted him implicitly, and so did I. I wouldn't want anyone else guarding my cousin and niece but sometimes, it stung knowing that she no longer needed me.

She hadn't for a long time.

There had been a time when Arianne was poised to take over our family's empire. Capizola Holdings. With me by her side, we would have taken the reins of her father's company and watched it soar to new heights. Until she fell in love with Nicco and that dream went up in flames. I couldn't resent her for it, not after everything she'd been through, but I hadn't only lost my cousin to Nicco. I'd lost my purpose, my future.

No matter what role Nicco offered me within his family, I would always be a Capizola.

"You know, you didn't have to work—"

I leveled Luis with a dark look.

He chuckled, holding up his hands. "Message received loud and clear. The girls give you any trouble on the way over?"

"When doesn't Bella give me trouble?" It was her middle fucking name. "Caught her drinking out of a hot pink hip flask."

"Did you tell Michele?"

"What do you think?"

I'd learned quickly with Bella what battles to fight. And her sneaking a drink or two at her own party wasn't something I wanted to start a war over.

Besides, even if I told on her, she would find a way to make sure she got a nice buzz tonight.

"And Sia?"

"What about her?"

Fuck. My voice was too telling. Too tight and rough against my throat.

Luis arched a brow again. "It's hard to believe she's no longer in high school, isn't it? Another three months and she'll be off to college, out in the big wide world, getting into all kinds of tro—"

The pound of my fist against the desk sent a mug clattering to the floor. Thankfully, it landed on the soft rug and didn't crack.

"You are in so much trouble, my friend." Luis chuckled, and I chose silence.

And denial.

"Nicco said Mahoney is making waves. What do we know?" I changed the subject.

"Not a lot. I sent Harvey and Sal out there to keep an eye on things."

"You think they would make a move?"

"They would be signing their own death certificate."

He had a point. Nicco gave the illusion of a calm, composed mob boss, but he didn't beat around the bush where his family's safety was concerned. And now he had Lucia to consider, he was even more ruthless.

Luis went back to the monitors, studying them. Looking for any signs of something being wrong. I grabbed his arm, and his head snapped over to me.

"Are you worried?"

"I'm always worried." He let out a weary sigh. "Arianne is... like a daughter to me. And Lucia, that little girl deserves to know peace."

I bristled. Because he was right. Like Alessia, Lucia was innocent. She had been born into this world, this *life*, and now she would have to suffer the consequences. I didn't doubt Nicco would do everything in his power to make sure the dark side of his life never touched the bright side of hers. But she was a target simply for being his.

For being a Marchetti.

"You should go enjoy the party," Luis said. "They are your family. We've got enough men here."

"It's fine." I didn't meet his questioning gaze.

I couldn't.

Luis had this knack of seeing past someone's bullshit, straight to the truth.

"She watches you, you know," he said, quietly. "For the last two years, I have watched her watch you."

"Don't." My hands gripped the edge of the desk, the blood draining from my knuckles. I didn't want to hear this. Not now, never ever.

"It isn't a crush, Tristan. It isn't going away. She's a woman now, she will—"

"STOP," I barked, narrowing my eyes at him. Forcing myself to take a deep breath, I considered my next words. "This isn't helping."

"I apologize." Luis held up his hands. "All I'm saying is, perhaps you should talk to her. At least try to clear the air… Set her free."

Something inside me twisted. I couldn't talk to her, what would I possibly say?

No, avoidance was the best course of action. Soon she would be going off to college. Somebody else could guard Bella. And I could finally be free of her.

Luis gripped my shoulder again. "You are a good man, Tristan. One of the best. The fact you have stayed away all this time only proves that."

"I am not having this conversation."

"Whatever you say, amico." He chuckled. "Whatever you say."

"I'll be in there if you need me." I tipped my head to the monitor displaying the main room where the party was being held.

Slipping out into the hall, I inhaled a sharp breath. I felt… restless. It wasn't just seeing Alessia in that sinful green dress, it was Nicco and Antonio's strange behavior, Luis's knowing remarks.

I needed a drink. A strong one. But I couldn't do that here so it would have to wait until I was home, back in the sanctuary of my apartment.

The party was in full swing when I went back inside. People were already dancing; Bella lapping up the attention as she stood in the middle of the circle. Her smile was big and bright, her eyes twinkling with laughter as she and her friends let loose.

A prickle of unease went through me as I scanned the dancefloor for Alessia. She wasn't there so I searched the room, half-expecting to find her sitting with Arianne and Nora or Genevieve.

But I couldn't find her anywhere.

My movements became more insistent, my heart rate kicking up a notch as I tried to remain discreet. "Does anyone have eyes on Alessia?" I asked through my wrist mic.

"Relax, Cap," Jay answered. "She's in the bathroom."

Relief washed over me as I took up a position in the corner of the room.

She was safe.

She was—

"Excuse me," her voice came from behind me.

I turned slowly to find her gazing up at me, and then I realized. I'd positioned myself right outside the door leading to the bathrooms.

What were the fucking chances?

"Alessia." I nodded curtly, dragging my eyes away from her face.

She let out a small sigh and moved around me. Her floral perfume hit me like a wrecking ball to the stomach. That smell. It slayed me every single time.

Keep walking, Principessa, just keep walking.

But she stopped, turning to me enough that her profile was illuminated by the disco lights behind her. “Why do you hate me so much, Tristan?” Her voice quivered softly but there was fire in her eyes.

The Marchetti princess was pissed but it wasn’t her demeanor that shocked me, it was her words.

Why do you hate me?

“Alessia, I don’t—”

“Please. I know you didn’t want to be on my security detail. I heard you tell Nicco you wouldn’t do it. But what I can’t work out is why.” Dejection etched in the lines of her face. “I haven’t done anything to warrant your distance. I’ve always been polite, I’ve always—”

“You think I hate you?”

She gave a little shrug. “It’s the only thing that makes sense.”

“Principessa, I don’t—”

“There you are.” Bella flounced over to us, grabbing Alessia’s arm. “You have to come dance with us. It’s our party. Come on.”

She didn’t look at me again, letting Bella lead her away while I stood there, dumbfounded.

She thought I hated her.

She couldn’t be more wrong.

I didn’t hate her.

I wanted her.

Fuck, I wanted her so badly.

And I hated myself for it.

THREE

ALESSIA

I TRIED.

Tried and failed to forget about my embarrassing moment with Tristan.

I don't know what came over me, what part of me thought it was a good idea to challenge him. But I was tired of always being on the receiving end of his cold shoulder. When I'd seen him standing there, as I came out of the bathroom, the words had just broken free.

Why do you hate me?

It wasn't my finest moment, and Bella would tease me until the end of time if she knew what I'd said to him, but it was done now.

I glanced over at him, still in position over by the door leading to the bathrooms. He didn't look at me though, keeping his hard gaze on his surroundings.

The knot in my stomach tightened.

"Alessia, you remember Joe," Bella shoved a guy in front of me. He smiled down at me, his sandy blond hair flopping over his eyes. "

"I'm Joe," he yelled. "You look really pretty."

"Uh, thanks." I flashed Bella a desperate look but she simply smothered her laughter and continued dancing with our friends.

Traitor.

"This is some party," he went on. "Guess it's true what they say about your family."

I bristled at that.

"What is it they say?" My lips pursed.

"Come on, you know." Joe waggled his brows. "I mean, I didn't really believe it before... but this is insane. The security is so tight."

My heart sank a little.

This is exactly what I tried to avoid. The awkward conversation about my family. About *who* my family were.

Marchetti was synonymous with the very birth of Verona County, and anyone born and raised here, knew the stories. Sure, a lot of it was conjecture, exaggerated stories told to friends over drinks, but there was never smoke without fire. And it didn't take much of a dig into Verona's history to discover that the Marchetti were the real deal.

Joe tried to wrap his hand around my waist but I politely batted him away, keeping a safe distance. Dejection flashed in his eyes but he quickly shrugged it off.

"Sorry, I just—"

"Hey, no hard feelings." He moved swiftly onto a new target, and Bella immediately marched over to me.

"What the hell, Sia. Joe is a good guy."

"I didn't say he wasn't."

"So, what's the problem?" She scowled.

"I'm not like you, Bella."

"Like me? What the hell is that supposed to mean?"

"Forget it." I didn't want confrontation, least of all here, in front of everyone.

"Yeah, whatever." She flounced off and grabbed a guy from our class, pressing her body up close to his.

She didn't even care that her parents were sitting right there, watching their daughter flirt and dirty dance with a boy.

But that was Bella.

She was as unapologetic and fearless as they came.

All danced out, I made my way over to the buffet table and plucked up a couple of hors d'oeuvres.

"Enjoying the party?" My brother appeared, snagging a tiramisu cup.

"Yeah," I said, nibbling the mini bruschetta.

"So why are you over here when you could be on the dancefloor with your friends?"

"Come on, Nic, you know this isn't me."

I wasn't a party girl. I preferred quiet nights in with a good book or curled up in front of the television.

He gave me a thin smile. "You know, we're so proud of you, Sia. All we want is for you to be happy. I know it isn't easy being—"

"Don't." A lump clogged my throat. "I love my family, Nicco. More than anything."

Family was everything to me, even if being the Marchetti princess made things difficult at times.

"I know. But I also know you're not a child anymore. In a few weeks, you'll be leaving for college—"

"I'm hardly leaving." I chuckled but it came out strained.

"You know what I mean. It's a big deal. You and Bella will be living it up in University Hill. That kind of freedom can be overwhelming."

I turned my attention back to the buffet table and let out a little indignant huff. "I think I can handle it."

"Sia, that's not..." Nicco drew in a sharp breath. "I'm just saying, college is your chance to spread your wings. Meet new people. Meet a nice young—"

My eyes snapped up to his. "So help me God, if you're about to start giving me dating advice, stop. Stop right now."

"We can talk about this stuff," he insisted.

"No, we really can't."

"There isn't... someone you like, is there?"

"What?" My heart catapulted into my throat. "No, why would you say that?"

Nicco jerked back, frowning. "Relax, Sia. I'm joking. It's a joke."

I pressed my lips together, trying to get a grip on my racing pulse.

"Although," he added, studying me. "From how cagey you're acting, I might be inclined to think there is a guy." Nicco's brow went up and I scowled.

"You are such a pain in the ass."

"I tell him that almost every day." Arianne joined us, pressing herself into my brother's side. He looped his arm around her waist and pressed a kiss to her hair.

"Alessia likes a boy."

"I do not."

"Don't tease her." Ari reprimanded, offering me an apologetic smile. But then she added, "You know Bailey's friend Kye seems nice."

"Ugh, go away. Both of you."

"What? I'm just saying he's a nice guy. He's going to be at Montague too in the fall.

You could show him—"

"I'm going to get some air." I didn't stop to hear their pleas and apologies as I hurried out of the room and down the hall toward the back exit that led to the hotel's courtyard.

Moving a distance away from the building, I climbed the stairs to a small gazebo and gripped the railing, looking out over the stunning gardens.

I was hardly surprised to hear footsteps behind me. It was Jay's job to follow my every move. Unless I was at home or at Nicco and Arianne's apartment, he was my permanent shadow. Most of the time, I could forget he was there. But times like right now, when I craved a moment alone with my thoughts, it was impossible.

"You know, you didn't have to follow me out here. It's quite safe." I let out an exasperated sigh, not sparing him a backward glance.

"You know that's not now it works, Principessa."

"Tristan?" My heart galloped in my chest like a band of wild horses as I turned to meet his cool gaze. "What are you doing out here?"

"I wanted to clear the air after our conversation earlier."

"Conversation?" A bitter laugh spilled from my lips. "We didn't have a conversation, Tristan."

His lips pulled into a flat line as he approached me. Slow, sure steps, his legs ate up the distance. He was tall, towering over me. I'd always liked that about him. The way he made me feel small and safe and protected. At least, until I overheard that conversation between him and my brother.

Everything changed after that.

Like some invisible line had been drawn in the sand between us.

Before, I'd been Nicco's younger sister with an innocent crush on my brother's girlfriend's cousin. It was harmless. Cute. Unthreatening.

Until it wasn't.

Until he decided that he'd rather guard Bella than be around me and my silly little crush.

A sticky trail of embarrassment snaked through me.

It wasn't like I actually thought anything would ever happen between us. He was Tristan Capizola, not to mention incredibly good looking, he could have any woman he wanted.

"I should get back to the party," I said, moving around him. I didn't want to be out here, listening to his forced apologies.

But his hand shot out, grabbing me. "Wait, Principessa."

"Why do you keep calling me that?" I bristled.

His eyes darkened, glinting under the moonlight. It was a beautiful night, a blanket of stars twinkling like diamonds across the clear, inky sky.

"I… fuck," he breathed, releasing me as if I'd burned him.

My brows knitted with frustration. "Why did you follow me out here, Tristan?"

"I told you, I wanted to clear the air."

"Why?" I implored.

"Because…" He stopped himself, torment swirling in his stormy gaze.

"I need to go." I spun on my heel and started marching toward the veranda leading back inside.

"I don't hate you, Alessia. Not by a long shot."

Something in his voice gave me pause. He sounded… sad.

I glanced back, overwhelmed by his haunted expression. "Tristan?" His name quivered on my tongue.

He moved toward me, every step like a shot to my heart, until he was looming over me. "Do you have any idea how insane you drive me?"

"W-what?" I blinked. And blinked again, trying to swallow and drag air into my lungs.

I drove him insane?

It didn't make any sense.

He hated me.

He hated—

Realization dawned and I gasped. "No," I whispered, clutching my throat.

Because it was too impossible. Too far out of the realms of possibility to even comprehend.

Tristan didn't... like me. He couldn't.

I was Nicco's sister.

I was family, albeit not by blood.

He worked for the Family. My brother.

Not to mention he was a man—a twenty-four year old man—and I was just a young woman barely out of high school.

His hand wrapped around my shoulder as he stared down at me.

What was happening?

Tristan, the guy I'd lusted after since I was a fifteen-year-old girl, was looking at me with hunger in his eyes.

"T-Tristan," I choked out. "You're hurting me."

That seemed to snap him out of his trance and he released my arm, only to stroke along my shoulder with his thumb.

"This dress is... it's a test I'm having to fight real damn hard to pass." His gaze trailed over my skin, leaving a blazing path in its wake. "Dio dammi la forza."

"I don't understand." My throat was dry, parched as I stared up at Tristan. The air shifted and crackled around us, butterflies fluttering in my stomach.

He reached for me, curving his hand along my cheek and sliding his fingers deep into my hair. "I could never hate you, Principessa."

"But I don't—"

"Sia." A voice rang out and Tristan stepped away from me, putting distance between us.

Too much distance.

A cold shiver went through me.

"There you are." Bella appeared. "I've been looking everywhere for you. I'm sorry for being—Tristan?"

"Bella." He gave her a curt nod. "Enjoying the party?"

"What are the two of you doing out here?"

She glanced between us, eyes narrowed in accusation.

"I needed some fresh air." I forced a smile. "Tristan followed to make sure I was okay."

"Oh okay, well, you have to come back inside. Joe is looking for you. He wants to dance. And I think Uncle Toni is going to make a speech."

I looked over at Tristan, not wanting to leave. Wanting to continue our conversation. Desperate to know what he was going to say.

But his silent gaze seemed to say, 'you need to go with her.'

Reluctantly, I did. Bella laced her arm through mine, pulling me back inside the hotel.

But this time, Tristan didn't follow.

Tristan didn't seek me out again. For the rest of the party—while trying to dodge Joe and Kye's advances—I searched for him, trying to get a glimpse. But Tristan remained out of sight, and the knot in my stomach only intensified.

For two years, I'd believed he avoided me because he couldn't stand being the object of my affections. That he was distancing himself in hopes I would realize the truth—that nothing would ever become of my infatuation.

But what if...

What if he was avoiding me because he also felt something for me?

A dark thrill zipped down my spine as Bella draped herself over me, forcing me to dance to some popular song.

"I love you, Sia," she slurred, thanks to all the covertly acquired glasses of champagne she'd drank.

"I love you too, drunken girl."

"I am not!" She grinned, waggling her brows. "You know it wouldn't hurt you to let loose and have some fun. High school is over, baby."

Yanking my arm, Bella flung herself out and twirled back into me. I glanced around, shaking my head at her antics.

The party was winding down though. Nicco and Ari had left earlier with Nora and Enzo. Nora was exhausted and Lucia was refusing to settle for Janelle, Luis's partner who sometimes babysat for my brother.

"Oh God, Matt is coming over here. Hide me." Bella ducked behind me and I frowned.

"Seriously, Bel? I can still see you standing right there."

"Oh, hey, big brother." She stepped around me. "You're looking very handsome tonight."

He narrowed his eyes. "And you've been drinking."

"I had one, maybe two glasses of champagne."

"I won't tell, if you don't." He grinned. "Just came to say goodnight. Me and Caitlin are heading out."

"Okay, I'll see you tomorrow?"

"You bet." He pulled her in and kissed her head. "I'm proud of you, Bel."

"Yeah, yeah, I'm wonderful. Now get out of here." Bella gave him a playful shove.

"Night, Sia."

"Night." I offered Matteo a smile.

"Make sure this one gets home okay."

"I will."

Technically, Jay and Tristan would but I wasn't going to get into the semantics.

"Tonight has been a good night," Bella hugged me again, although part of me wondered if she was using me as a leaning post.

"It has." I smiled.

"You didn't get your first kiss though."

"There's always next time." Strained laughter bubbled out of me.

For a second, outside under the gazebo, I'd thought Tristan might kiss me. I'd imagined it enough times, his lips touching mine, his hands in my hair, his strong body pressed up against me.

Did he think of me?

Is that why he avoided me?

"Sia?" Bella tugged on my arm and I slid my gaze back to her.

"I think I'm going to puke." Bella tore away from me and all but ran toward the restrooms.

I went after her, hardly surprised when Tristan caught up to me, gently grasping my arm. "What's wrong with her?"

"She drank too much."

"Fuck," he breathed, scrubbing the hint of his five o'clock shadow. "Okay, I'll tell Jay to fetch the car around and we'll get her home. Then Jay can take you—"

"I'm staying at her house tonight."

His jaw clenched.

"If it's a problem, Jay can take us," I snapped, surprising us both. But his hot and cold mood swings were giving me whiplash.

"I'm quite capable of doing my job, Principessa."

My eyes narrowed, as I yanked my arm away from him. "Good, we shouldn't have a problem then. Should we?" I stormed off after Bella, ignoring Tristan as he called after me.

FOUR

TRISTAN

ALESSIA MARCHETTI WAS GOING to be the slow tortured death of me.

That dress.

Her unblemished skin.

Her surprisingly sassy mouth tonight.

It had all gone to shit the second I'd followed her out into the courtyard.

Luis was right. I was screwed. So fucking screwed.

Two years ago, it had been easy to ignore the longing in her eyes, the way her gaze followed me whenever I walked into a room. She was a kid. My boss's little sister. Once the daughter of my family's most hated enemy.

But things were different now.

She wasn't a kid anymore, she hadn't been for a while. And although I'd fought it, fought the way my body responded every time she walked into the room, the tightly spun lines of my restraint were beginning to fray.

It hadn't helped watching her dance with Bella and their friends. That fucking goofy beanpole that kept trying to hit on her. Alessia was polite, trying to avoid hurting the guy's feelings no doubt, but it had only made my jealousy levels rise to the point where I had to physically stop myself from storming over there and telling him to keep his fucking hands to himself.

I needed to get a grip.

Needed to think about something—*anything*—other than the fact that she was sitting in the back of the SUV in that dress made of sin and silk, refusing to even look in my direction.

Women.

This is exactly why I didn't get involved past tangling in the sheets when the need arose. Women complicated things. In this life, they were a distraction—a weakness—I didn't want or need.

But Alessia... fuck, she was like the sun in a world that was too often dark.

And now I'd let myself get close, too fucking close, I couldn't undo it.

Jay glanced over and raised a brow as if to say, 'you good.' I answered with a curt nod, scanning the road ahead and behind us, for any signs of trouble.

The sooner we got the girls home, the better. After Nicco and Antonio's warning earlier, I couldn't shake the feeling that things were about to go to shit. But maybe that was because I felt restless. Disarmed by the fact I'd almost crossed a line tonight.

A line I'd vowed never to cross.

Alessia wasn't mine.

She was never going to be mine.

No matter how much I wanted her.

Michele Bellatoni's house came into view and relief flowed through me. Alessia was quiet in the back, Bella asleep on her shoulder.

Our eyes caught in the rearview mirror only this time, I didn't look away.

I couldn't.

Alessia seemed... different.

A quiet storm raged in her thin gaze as if tonight hadn't only opened my eyes but hers as well. And from the death stare she was giving me, she was clearly pissed at whatever she'd discovered.

Jay pulled into the driveway and parked beside Michele's car. He and his wife Marcella had left the party earlier, but I didn't doubt he would be up and waiting inside to see that his daughter and niece made it safely home.

"I'll get the door. You get Bella," Jay said, and I nodded.

It wasn't the first time we'd carried Bella home drunk and asleep. She was quite the party girl. A fact that Michele said had started turning him gray long before his time.

Gently, I eased Bella out of the car and into my arms. Alessia climbed out behind us, saying nothing. Jay went ahead, almost at the door when the screech of tires pierced the night.

"Shit, shit," he withdrew his pistol and jogged toward me and the girls.

"Oh God," Alessia breathed. "Are they—"

Shots rang out around us, a kick of adrenaline blasting through me as I started barking orders at Jay. "Radio for backup," I yelled, lowering a rousing Bella to her feet.

"What is—oh my God, is that gunfire?"

"Go, to the house, now."

Unsheathing my weapon, I shoved her toward the house, grabbing Alessia as she stood there paralyzed with fear.

The van pulled to a stop and three masked men jumped out.

"Fuck, fuck," I glanced back to Alessia. "Go," I urged, the icy cold fingers of fear dragging down my spine.

"Take cover behind the SUV," Jay yelled, firing back at the shooters as they approached the house. Bullets whizzed past my head, lodging themselves in the brick behind me.

"Draw their fire," I hissed at Jay. He immediately fired another round of shots, and they answered.

Pressed close to the side of the SUV, I crept along the body, lifting my pistol, readying myself to—

Bang.

One of the guys went down but not before he fired off a shot that found its mark inside my shoulder.

Pain exploded through me as I grunted, the air sucked clean from my lungs.

"Tristan!" Alessia screamed, and I glanced back just in time to see another attacker grab her.

Fear like I'd never known slammed into me and I didn't think, didn't consider the consequences or the fact it might be a trap as I turned and ran toward them. Alessia's eyes widened, her body going deathly still in the attacker's grasp, as he raised the barrel of his gun pressed to her temple.

I ground to a halt, dropping my arm, my hand holding my gun. "Don't—"

Something slammed into the back of my head and darkness embraced me.

I woke to a heavy bass drum in my skull.

"What the—"

Images flooded me. The masked gunmen jumping out of the speeding van. Alessia wide eyed and trembling as that fucker pressed his gun to her head.

"Tristan?"

Her voice sank into me, filling me with bittersweet relief. She was okay. Alessia was safe and okay…

But where the fuck was here?

Bracing my hand against my head, I attempted to sit up, groaning in agony as pain ripped through my shoulder.

"Shh." Soft hands touched my face. "Try not to move."

"Principessa?"

"I'm here," she breathed from somewhere in the dark. "I'm here and I'm okay."

My eyes shuttered as I inhaled a sharp breath. My body felt wrecked, fiery pain lancing my shoulder and radiating down my arm.

"How long was out?"

"An hour, maybe two."

Fuck.

"Any idea where we are?"

"No. They covered my eyes in the van."

Anger rippled through me but I managed to croak out, "Jay? Bella?"

"I... I don't know."

"Did they take your cell phone?"

"Yeah. Yours too. And your weapons. Then they brought us here. I think it's a warehouse."

"Okay, okay." I forced myself to sit up, shuffling backward until the wall came up behind me.

"Tristan?"

"Yeah?"

"I'm scared."

My heart cracked. They knew, Nicco and Antonio knew there was a threat but to come into Marchetti territory, to Michele's home, and attack...

It was a declaration of war.

"Come here." I reached blindly for her, following her small whimpers. Alessia found my hand, threading her fingers with mine, and I managed through gritted teeth, to pull her into my side. "We'll figure this out," I said.

"You need medical attention. Your shoulder—"

"It'll be okay." It hurt like a bitch but I was pretty sure it was a clean shot. In and out. So long as I didn't catch an infection, I'd live.

"What are we going to do?" Alessia whispered. "What if Bella and Uncle Michele are..." A pained sob caught in her throat and I pulled her closer, dropping a kiss to her head. "We'll figure it out, I promise."

But it was one promise I wasn't sure I would be able to keep.

Footsteps sounded out beyond the wall, heavy boots. Two men. Maybe three. Alessia went stiff in my arms, her breathing shallow, fear radiating from her.

"Don't say anything, okay?" I whispered. "Let me do the talking."

A door creaked open, light streaming into what I now realized was a small room, nothing distinguishing about it.

"Ah, the Marchetti princess in the flesh. It is a pleasure, truly."

Alessia trembled beside me and I ran a soothing hand up and down her spine.

I'm here, and I will not let anything hurt you.

"And you must be the guard dog. Jay Toretti."

One of the man's seconds leaned in and whispered something to him. His eyes flared in recognition and then quickly guttered.

"Tristan Capizola, what an interesting turn of events." He stroked his proud jaw. "Sorry for the... theatrics. But Niccolò has refused to parley with us for some time so we had no choice but to force his hand."

"W-what do you want?" Alessia asked.

"Ahhh, such a young innocent girl to be caught up in this dark, dangerous world." The man's—who I assumed was Jericho Mahoney—gaze hardened. "Let's hope your brother and his men come to their senses."

The idea of Alessia being used as a pawn was like a knife to the heart. He was right. She was too young, too innocent to be caught up in this.

Yet here we were.

And I knew without a shadow of a doubt, I had to find a way to get her out of this.

Or I'd die trying.

Mahoney and his men left, but not before one of them threw a bottle of water at us and some bandages.

So they didn't want us dead. At least, not yet.

They also had the decency to leave the flickering light on.

"Here," Alessia tugged at the hem of her dress, tearing a strip of silk off. Soaking it in water she reached for my shoulder but I grabbed her hand. "Tristan, let me do this, please." I gave her a gentle nod, letting my hand drop away. "This might hurt."

Her touch was gentle but it didn't stop the hiss of agony that spilled out of me.

"Crap, I'm sorry. I just want to clean it out and then I can—"

"Just... hurry," I gritted out.

"Alcohol would be better."

"It's fine."

It wasn't, but her trembling hands and shaky breaths forced me to steady my own breath, to fight against the urge to roar at the fiery pain consuming me.

"Sorry, I'm so sorry." She worked quickly, binding my shoulder with the bandage as best she could. "I'm not sure it's enough, but it'll have to do."

"Thank you." My lips curved into a faint smile.

"Now what?"

"I... fuck, I don't know." I dragged my good hand down my face.

Alessia's eyes filled with tears. "We're not going to get out of this al—"

"Hey, hey, don't talk like that. If they wanted us dead, we'd already be dead." The lie was like ash on my tongue but I couldn't not lie to her. She didn't deserve this.

She didn't deserve any of it.

And if I could make her feel better, even by lying to her, I would.

"You're their leverage."

"You mean a hostage." She gave me a pointed look, a tear slipping free.

I reached for her cheek, brushing it away with the pad of my thumb. Alessia turned into my touch, covering my hand with her own. "There's so much I haven't done... so much I want to experience." More tears ran down her cheeks, shredding my insides like jagged pieces of glass.

"Shh." I pulled her into me, sliding my hand along her collarbone. "I promise you, Principessa, I will do whatever it takes to get you out of here."

I just needed a plan and a moment to catch my breath.

Fuck.

Hours passed as I tried desperately to fight the exhaustion, the bone-deep pain ravaging my body. Alessia was curled up beside me, her head in my lap as she slept fitfully. I ran my hand over her hair, trying to soothe her nightmares.

No one had visited us again. I was thirsty, tired, and there wasn't a part of my body that didn't ache—maybe from the bullet wound in my shoulder or maybe from the concussion I was sure I'd received. Either way, the fight to remain conscious had been a brutal one I was surprised to have won. Although, I couldn't be sure that I hadn't dozed off a couple of times.

Earlier, I'd been grateful for the light but now, my eyes were strained and bleary.

I'd mentally scanned every inch of the room for something that might help me get us out of here. But there was nothing.

There was one option... but just the idea of using Alessia as bait made me want to vomit.

As if she heard my dark thoughts, she began to stir.

"Tristan?" Panic saturated her voice as she sat up, blinking at me.

"I'm here, Principessa, I'm right here."

A faint smile graced her lips. "What's wrong?" Her brows pinched, and I huffed out a little sigh of resignation.

"I have a plan, but you're not going to like it."

"We've got to do something," she said. "Whatever it is, I can handle it."

Conviction clung to her features and I don't think I'd ever seen Alessia look more determined.

"Okay," I said. "This is what I need you to do."

FIVE

ALESSIA

MY HEART BEAT FURIOUSLY in my chest as I inhaled a deep breath.

I could do this.

I could totally do this.

Tristan gave me a small nod and I bellowed, "Help, help. Somebody help me. Oh God."

I glanced back at Tristan who was now lying prone, his eyes closed and expression lax. It was a convincing act, so convincing that I wanted to tell him to wake up.

"Help me, oh God, help—"

The door swung open and two men appeared. I didn't recognize them as the men from earlier.

"Help him," I shrieked. "Somebody help him."

"Shit," one of the guy's murmured. "Grab the girl while you see to him."

"Nah, leave him. He's—"

"Fuck."

Tristan started convulsing on the floor.

"Help him, please. You have to help him." I tried to go to him but the guy banded his arm around my waist, pulling me into him.

"Easy, easy," he said as I kicked and screamed, thrashing in his arms.

"Seriously Grant, just put a bullet through his head and be done with it. The boss wants us—"

"He's a Capizola," The man said, slowly approaching Tristan. "Her cousin. Do you have any idea the shit that will rain down on us if we don't return them in one piece?"

Fear clung to his every word but my captor chuckled darkly. "You actually think Mahoney plans to let them go? You really are a—"

It happened so fast, I could hardly process what I was witnessing.

One minute Tristan was lying on the floor, gasping for breath, his body jerking violently. The next, he had tackled the guy to the floor, dispatched his gun and shot him point blank through the skull.

"Back the fuck up." The guy behind me pressed his own gun to my temple and fear turned my blood to ice.

Not again.

Not like this.

I blinked away the tears, trying to remain strong—trying desperately to focus on Tristan and not the cool metal licking my skin.

"Think about this Capizola, you take another step and I will end her."

"You need her. If the Marchetti don't get proof she is alive, they will rain down all kinds of hell on you. You have to know that." He inched closer, keeping his gun trained on us.

Not me, I realized. But the man holding me.

"Let her go," Tristan said. "And I'll consider letting you live."

His eyes flicked to mine, just for a second.

Just long enough for me to understand.

He seemed to let loose a long, steady breath, his finger flexing around the trigger. And then he barked, "Now."

I ducked, the crack of gunfire ringing in my ears and the man behind began to fall backwards, pulling me with him.

"Shit, Alessia." Tristan rushed over to me, yanking me off the dead, lifeless body. A single bullet hole through his skull.

"Y-you killed them." Bile rushed up my throat and I swallowed it down.

Tristan held me for a second. But all too soon, he gently pushed me away. "We need to move, now." He left me to check the bodies for weapons, retrieving another pistol and a radio.

"No cell phone. Shit." He rubbed his temple. "Okay, I'm getting you out of here."

I nodded, not trusting myself to speak. The radio crackled, a gruff voice coming over the speaker.

"Grant, the fuck's going on down there? I thought I heard shots."

Tristan messed with the button and whispered. "Now, we need to move now." He grabbed my hand and pulled me toward the door, pausing to poke his head out into the hall. "When I say run," he whispered. "You run straight down the hall and don't stop. For anything."

I managed a mindless nod, a violent shiver going through me. My eyes fluttered as I tried to catch my breath.

"Alessia, look at me," Tristan snapped. "I need you to stay focused, okay? You've got this." He cupped my face. "I'm not going to let anything happen to you, but we need to go now."

"O-okay."

Without another word, we slipped into the hall and he tilted his head to the left, mouthing, "Go."

I moved around him, silently pleading with him not to leave me.

"I'll be right behind you," he said. "Now run."

Something inside me snapped and I hurtled down the hall, Tristan's footsteps a steady beat behind me. The long narrow hall whizzed past me, a door appearing in the distance. Not just any door, a fire exit.

"Keep going," he urged.

"What the fuck," someone yelled from behind us.

"Go, go," Tristan yelled, shoving me toward the door. I hit the bar and crashed through it, spilling into fresh air.

Gunfire rang out behind us, and Tristan fired back, every crack of the gun making me startle.

It was a noise I would never get used to hearing.

Ever.

"Where?" I sucked in a sharp breath, certain my lungs had stopped working. That maybe even my heart had too. "I can't—"

Tristan grabbed my arm and yanked me toward the tree line and didn't stop until we were swamped by the overgrowth.

"We have to keep moving."

He kept peering over his shoulder. As if he expected an enemy to jump out at us at any moment.

Voices filled the air, their shouts rippling through the trees like angry wind.

"We need to find somewhere to hide," Tristan whispered, concern etched in the lines of his face.

It was apparent we were in the middle of nowhere, nothing but trees and wilderness in every direction.

I stumbled forward, trying to keep up with Tristan as he cut through branches and bushes like a knife. But he caught me, hoisting me against his side, keeping his arm wrapped tightly around my waist as we moved deeper into the woods.

It was still dawn, the sun barely peeking out from behind the tree line.

"What are we going to do?" I didn't even try to disguise the tremor in my voice.

We'd escaped, yes. Only to be cast into another nightmare. If we didn't find shelter or help, we would be hunted down like cattle.

"Keep moving," Tristan rasped. "We have to keep moving."

His grip on my hand tightened and the brush swallowed us whole. Even the shouts of our captors seemed to grow quieter.

I glanced over my shoulder, shuddering.

"Come on, Principessa." His eyes met mine, his expression possessive and fierce, at odds with the sheer terror in his voice. "We need to go."

We ran for what felt like an eternity. Every time I slowed my pace, Tristan tugged my hand and motioned for me to speed up. My body ached, my muscles burning with exertion. My dress was torn, shredded as if I'd had a fight with a vicious clawed beast, and my skin was marred with cuts and scrapes. But adrenaline kept me moving. Fear kept me putting one foot in front of the other and pushing.

Suddenly, Tristan stopped, pulling me into his side, and raising a finger to his lips. I nodded, pressing my lips together. Then I saw what he had spotted. A derelict cabin, buried deep in the scrub.

"Stick close to me," he said quietly. "Any sign of trouble and you run and don't look back."

We approached slowly, quietly treading through the overgrowth. Gun drawn, Tristan tucked me behind him as he pressed against the weathered paneling.

The windows were cracked, thick with mildew and moss. Tristan tapped the barrel of his gun against it and waited.

Nothing.

Nothing but the sound of my beating heart and the sounds of the forest.

"Come on, I think it's safe."

We moved around the cabin until we came to the door. It was intact, which couldn't be said for the rest of the place.

"Careful," Tristan said, glancing back at me. "The steps don't feel very secure." He tested a couple and then offered me his hand, helping me up.

The door opened without protest, and Tristan ordered me to wait outside while he checked inside. When it was clear, he beckoned me in, shutting the door behind me.

"Now what?" I said, scanning the ramshackle room. Nature had taken over, moss and creeping vines growing up through the floorboards. The remnants of a kitchen were caked in years of muck and storm debris.

"We take a breather," he said, sliding the gun into the waistband of his black slacks. "Here." He shucked off his jacket and helped me into it, wincing with pain.

"How is it?" I asked.

"I'll live."

Those words. God, those words.

Things didn't feel as bleak as when we were holed up in the warehouse but now we were stranded in a derelict cabin in the middle of nowhere with no food or water, and without a way of contacting anybody.

Tristan started scanning the cabin, checking behind the two other doors. He quickly closed one, retching. "Don't go in there."

My stomach churned.

"In here," he called from inside the second room. I peeked in, surprised to find a small bedroom with its furniture mostly intact. "I need you to stay here while I go scout the area."

"W-what? No... *No.*" Panic rose inside of me. "We should stay together, we should—"

"Alessia. Principessa." He pulled me into his arms, letting his hand run down my spine. "It's okay, it's going to be okay."

"You don't know that," I cried out, fisting his shirt as the reality of our situation crashed over me. "We're in the middle of nowhere, Tristan. You were shot for God's sake. What are we going to do?"

"Alessia, look at me." His fingers slid under my jaw, coaxing my eyes to his. "We're safe for now but I need to find some supplies, okay. I need to scout the area."

"Then I'll come with you, I'll—"

"I need you to stay here, Principessa." He inhaled deeply, pressing a kiss to my forehead. My eyes fluttered closed. All I'd ever wanted was for Tristan to kiss me. But not here, not like this.

"Stay in this room, don't come out until I return. I'm going to leave you this." He stepped back and unsheathed the second gun he had taken off one of the dead bodies earlier.

"N-no, I can't."

"Yes," he pressed the gun into my hand, "you can. You know how to use this?"

I nodded, despite silently roaring at him that I didn't want this. I didn't want to ever have to use it. But I would. I'd have to. If it was a choice between life or death, I would have to point the gun and pull the trigger.

I was going to puke.

But I steeled my spine, forcing air into my lungs.

"I'll be as quick as I can, okay? I'll tap the window twice when I return so you know it's me." He turned to leave but I blurted out his name.

"Yeah?" he asked.

"Just... be careful."

"Always." He slipped out of the room and closed the door behind him, and I sank on to the floor, the wall to my back, and pointed the gun at the door.

Praying that the next person to walk through it would be Tristan returning.

He had been gone for hours. At least, that's what it felt like.

In reality, it couldn't have been more than thirty minutes. I was tightly strung, my stomach hollow and aching.

It had been hours since we were taken from outside of Uncle Michele's house. But I didn't allow myself to think on that too much. On what might have happened to him or Aunt Marcella or Bella or the rest of my family.

God, what if—

No, Alessia, don't go there.

I couldn't accept that I would never see my brother again. Arianne and Lucia. My cousins and their partners who I'd come to consider family.

Tristan would find us a way out of this. He would figure something out and—

Tap. Tap.

I went deathly still, my fingers curled into the hem of my dress as I listened.

Tap. Tap.

Tristan. It had to be Tristan. But I couldn't move, paralyzed by the fear coiled around my heart, my chest and lungs. It had me in its chokehold, refusing to let go.

"Sia, it's me." Tristan's voice filled the cabin and I sagged with relief, a garbled cry spilling from my lips.

He appeared in the doorway, his brows pulled tight. "What is it? What happened?" He rushed to my side and crouched down, and I leaped into his arms, holding on tight. Breathing him in and letting his familiar scent comfort me.

"I-I thought..."

"Shh, it's okay. I'm here, I'm here. And I found supplies."

"You did?" I eased away to look at him.

"Yeah, there's an old truck out back, there were a few things we can make use of. Wait here." He pressed a kiss to my forehead, lingering for a second. The air crackled between us as I peered up at him, trying to verbalize the words on the tip of my tongue.

It wasn't time to tell him how I felt, to confess what was in my heart, but what if all we had was this moment?

What if we both didn't make it out alive?

A violent shudder went through me, my eyes fluttering closed.

"Wait here," he said, running his knuckles down my cheek.

His touch felt different. Tender and possessive but I wasn't thinking straight, how could I with everything that was going on?

What if I was misreading things?

Imagining signs that weren't really there?

He'd said things last night, things I so desperately wanted to believe, but what if that was just a spur of the moment thing? What if he didn't really mean it or had no plans to act on it?

My heart careened against my chest, a wild band of horses inside of me.

I curled up against the old bed, hugging Tristan's jacket to my body, praying to a God I didn't believe in for mercy.

SIX

TRISTAN

I WATCHED her from the door, folded in on herself. Holding herself together.

She didn't deserve this—she didn't deserve any of it. But there was no escaping this life for her. Not now.

Not ever.

Alessia was the Marchetti princess. Whether she wanted it or not.

In another life, I could have protected her, loved and cherished her above all else. But Nicco and Antonio would never accept it.

They would never accept me.

The thought was like a punch to the gut.

"What do you have over there?" she asked, finally noticing me.

"Some blankets, water, a flashlight and some candles, and an emergency kit."

"It's like someone knew to expect us." Her smile didn't reach her eyes but I drank it in, all the same.

She was so fucking beautiful it hurt.

Not like the pain the bullet hole in my shoulder created but something deeper. A wound on my soul.

"What?" she whispered, looking up at me through thick lashes and those dark eyes. Eyes I could get lost in. Eyes that I wanted to fucking drown in.

Shit, I needed to focus. Needed to concentrate on getting us the hell out of here and to safety before Mahoney's men found us.

When I'd gone in search of supplies, I hadn't heard them. But we couldn't have run that far, so there was every chance they would find us eventually. And I was only one man against many.

Fuck.

Fuck!

"Nothing." I forced my lips into a smile. "I think we should hole up here for the day and then try and find a route out under the cover of darkness."

"And if they find us."

It wasn't a question, more like a forgone conclusion.

My jaw clenched. "Let's hope they don't."

Nicco and his men would be working on finding us. Even if they played Mahoney's game, I didn't doubt for a second that they would be working behind the scenes to locate us.

By the way the sun was cresting over the tree line, it had to be about seven am. Which meant we'd been gone for approximately seven hours.

My thoughts started to turn to Jay and Bella, Michele and Marcella, but I slammed the door shut on them. I couldn't go there, not yet. Not until I'd gotten Alessia the hell out of here.

"We're going to be here for a while," I said. "You should try and get some rest."

Alessia's gaze flickered to the bed beside her and she shook her head. "I-I can't..."

"Sure you can," I said, dropping the pile of supplies down on a rickety old chair. A plume of dust filled the air and I wafted it away. "We'll put a couple of these blankets down and it'll be as good as new."

She didn't look convinced but I needed to do something. Anything to try and ease the sheer panic in her eyes.

"If you come over here for a second, I have an idea."

Alessia got up and moved aside, worrying her lip as she watched me push the bed up against the wall with no window. I pulled off the threadbare sheet and flipped the mattress surprised by how sturdy it still felt and laid out two blankets.

"See as good as new." I winked, trying to lighten the mood. Alessia grimaced but sat on the edge, running her hands over the thick woolen blanket.

"Thank you."

I leaned over to grab a bottle of water but overstretched. "Fuck," I hissed, cradling my shoulder. "I could really use some pain pills."

"Did you check the first aid kit?"

"Yeah, nothing. It's fine. I'll be okay."

"What about a sling? Maybe I can—"

"Principessa, I said I'll be fine." Moving to the bed, I dropped down and uncapped a bottle of water, taking a sip. "Here."

She took it from me, our fingers brushing, sending a shudder through me.

"You should lie down, get some rest."

"I'm not sure I can sleep."

Alessia scooched back into the middle of the bed and tucked her hand underneath her head. "I'm glad you're here, Tristan."

"Me too." I swallowed thickly. Because the idea of not being here... I couldn't deal with that.

I reached her, pushing the stray hairs from her face. "We'll make it out of this, I promise."

Eyes closed, she nodded. "Talk to me so I know you're here."

"What do you want me to talk about?"

"Anything. Tell me about your childhood. About what it was like growing up with the Capizola."

So I did.

I told her about my time spent on the Capizola estate, playing with Arianne and Nora and her brother Gio. I told her about the mischief we caused, the trouble me and Gio got into. The summers were spent exploring the far perimeters of the land. The stream and woods. I told her how I grew up wanting nothing more than to one day help Arianne run the Capizola empire.

I told her everything.

And when I finally stopped, finally came back from the memories, I realized she was fast asleep.

"Hey."

I bolted upright at the sound of Alessia's voice.

After she'd fallen asleep, I'd kicked up my legs and stretched out of the bed beside her, the gun in my hand, my other draped over her shoulder, stroking up and down her arm.

I didn't know how much time had passed but I needed to piss and find us something to eat.

I was fucking starving.

"Hey," I pulled my arm away, wincing at the movement. But I swallowed down the pain, masking it. The last thing I wanted was for Alessia to worry any more than she already was.

Sitting up, she smoothed a hand down her hair. "I must look like such a mess."

"You're beautiful, Principessa. Always." I brushed her cheek with my thumb, letting it linger at the corner of her mouth.

"Tristan," she asked quietly, hesitating. "Why do you keep calling me that?"

"I... it's just a silly nickname, Sia."

Fuck, why did I say that?

The hope in her eyes guttered out, the tension around us ratcheting up a notch.

"I see." She glanced away and guilt washed over me.

"Principessa, look at me." I gently gripped her chin, forcing her eyes back to mine. "I lied. It isn't just a silly nickname."

"Because you... like me?"

"It doesn't matter, Alessia. All that matters is that I get you out of this, safe and unharmed. Okay?"

"It matters to me." Defiance burned in her eyes.

"Don't do this. Whatever you feel... whatever I might feel, it can never be." I let out a heavy sigh, wishing things could be different. Silently wishing that she wasn't the Marchetti princess and I wasn't one of her father's grunts.

"Because I'm just a silly naïve girl—"

"No. Never. But Nicco, your father, they wouldn't understand."

Hell, I wasn't sure I understood it.

"And what about what I want? Doesn't that count for something? We could die out here, Tristan. They could hunt us down like animals and I'll never have known..." Alessia slammed her lips together, trapping whatever words she'd been about to say.

"We need to eat," I said, needing a distraction. Needing a reason to get out of the cabin for a minute and catch my fucking breath.

I couldn't stand it. The pain and terror in her eyes. The dejection.

"We're in the middle of nowhere, Tristan." She let out a bitter laugh that made me flinch. "What are you going to do, forage for berries?"

My eyes narrowed and I clicked my tongue. "Stay here. Don't move, I'll tap twice. I'll be back as soon as I find something we can eat."

"We don't need something to eat," she snapped. "We need to get out of here, we need—"

"What would you have me do? Risk running into those... those stronzos again? They'll kill me, Principessa. And then they'll..."

"Don't. Don't say it." She inhaled a sharp ragged breath, the blood drained from her face.

"Shit, I'm sorry. I'm sorry." I dropped to my knees beside the bed and reached for her, grabbing the back of her neck and pulling her into me.

"I shouldn't have said that... I shouldn't have—"

"It's okay."

Alessia touched her head to mine, looking up at me with those haunting eyes of hers.

"Nothing about this is okay, Principessa."

Not a damn thing.

"I'm okay."

"Okay. I won't be long. Don't hesitate to use this." I pressed the pistol into her hand. My hand brushed along her jaw, my eyes dropping to her mouth.

"Tristan..." Half-whisper, half-plea, the desperation in her voice almost snapped my restraint. It would have been so easy to kiss her, to take what she was so obviously offering.

But I couldn't do it.

I couldn't be the man who took advantage of her. Not when we'd been thrust into this nightmare.

Her eyes closed as she leaned in, closer, her soft lips almost brushing mine. I pulled back and cleared my throat. "I should go see what I can find."

It was a lame excuse but I got the hell out of there as fast as I could, not sparing her a second glance. Because if I looked back, if I saw the wanting in her eyes, I would break every vow I'd ever made to the Family.

And to myself.

I stayed out in the forest longer than I intended. But I couldn't go back there, not until I knew I had myself under control.

Fuck.

The way she'd looked at me, the way my name had sounded rolling off her tongue. She didn't know what she was asking for.

What she was asking me to do.

I had every intention of getting out of this, of saving her. How could I ever look Nicco and my cousin in the eye if I kissed her? If I touched her the way I was so desperate to.

It couldn't happen.

Forcing myself to rein in my emotions, I climbed the steps to the cabin. Alessia had been right, I hadn't managed to find much in the way of food. But so long as we had water, we would be okay for a while.

It was still light out, but the thick blanket of clouds made it a little hard to guesstimate the time.

What I really needed was some kind of plan. But I'd been over every option and none of them were good. When darkness fell, I could try and retrace my steps back to the warehouse, try and locate a cell phone or steal a car. But that left Alessia alone and vulnerable. And even if I found a car, I couldn't drive it through the dense brush. No, she'd either have to come with me or we'd need to wander the forest and hope to find another way out.

It was hopeless.

We were in the middle of nowhere, surrounded by nothing but trees. There had been nothing distinguishing about the warehouse. No markers or landmarks and I hadn't stopped to search for a way in or out.

Maybe I'd been too hasty making a run for it. But the alternative had been too unthinkable, all I'd wanted was to get Alessia the hell out of there.

Slipping into the cabin, I found Alessia curled up in a ball, sleeping. The floorboards groaned and she startled, her head snapping up. "You're back."

"Sorry, I—"

"It's fine," she clipped out. "Did you find anything?"

"No."

She shrugged. "At least we have water. How's your shoulder?"

"Fine."

"Good."

Awkward silence filled the room, thick and suffocating.

"Alessia, I—"

"Don't. Just… don't." She pulled the end of the blanket over her and I wondered if it was an attempt to create a physical shield between us.

Why did the idea of that hurt so fucking much?

"What's the plan?" she demanded. "I can help. I know how to use the gun. Maybe if we double back, we can—"

"No, absolutely not." Over my dead fucking body.

Yet, I'd thought of the same idea only minutes earlier.

"Tristan, be reasonable. We don't know how many of them there are. Your shoulder—"

"I said no." I ran a hand over my jaw, trying to tamp down the anger rising inside of me. "When it gets dark, I'll retrace our steps back—"

The radio crackled.

"Shit, shit." I grabbed it and tried to get a clearer signal.

"Keep looking… can't… gone far." The words were choppy as the signal dropped in and out.

"They're still out there." Alessia's voice trembled. "They're not going to stop looking. Oh God."

"Hey, hey." I sat down on the edge of the bed and pulled her into my arms. "It's just a standard two-way radio so the range could be anywhere between two and six miles. We're okay. We're safe."

God, I wanted to believe it.

I wanted to believe that they wouldn't wander in this direction and come across the cabin hidden in the overgrowth.

Alessia shook violently in my arms as she sobbed, her tears soaking my blood-stained shirt.

"I've got you, Principessa. I've got you."

Her grip on me tightened as she moved her face to the crook of my neck. Her warm breath danced over my skin, making my groin ache.

Fuck.

This was dangerous territory. But I wanted to comfort her, I wanted to hold her and reassure her and keep her safe.

I wanted her.

More than I had ever wanted anything.

And she was right there, pressed up against me. He fingers curled into the hair at the nape of my neck and she was—

Kissing me.

Alessia was kissing me.

Her lips trailed up my neck, her body trembling not with fear, I realized. But inexperience.

"Alessia, Principessa, stop." I gently pushed her shoulders, forcing us apart. "You have to stop."

"Y-you don't want me?" Hurt flashed in her eyes.

"It doesn't matter what I want, we can't do this."

"We could die out here, Tristan. We could die and I'll never have known the kiss of a man. His touch. I'll never have known what it's like to give myself to another."

"You're a—"

I couldn't even say the word.

Virgin.

She was a virgin, and she was staring at me like I was all her goddamn dreams come true.

I was screwed.

So fucking screwed.

SEVEN

ALESSIA

"TRISTAN, SAY SOMETHING," I whispered, my cheeks burning with shame. And other things.

Dark, desperate things.

I hadn't meant to kiss him, to press my lips to his neck. But he was my anchor in such stormy unpredictable seas, and I didn't want to let go.

Everything I'd said was true.

I didn't want to die a virgin. To take my last breath without ever knowing what it felt like to be worshipped and adored, even if only for a moment.

"Principessa, you don't know what you're asking of me." He dropped his head to mine, inhaling a ragged breath.

His torment was a living breathing thing, an icy wall between us. But I would not be deterred, not this time.

"I want this, Tristan." I laid my hand against his cheek. "I want you... so much. I always have."

"Fuck," he breathed, easing away to look at me. "It's wrong. So fucking wrong."

"Nothing about this situation is right, but I choose this. I choose you. Please. Show me what it is like, Tristan. Give me this, just once, I beg you."

His hand buried deep in my hair, tilting my face up so he could brush his lips over mine. Once. Twice. Letting his tongue dart out and taste me, parting my lips softly and plunging deep inside.

A whimper caught in my throat. Needy and breathless. He felt so good, kissing me, holding me right where he wanted me. I'd dreamed of this so many times before but it didn't come close to the real thing. His mouth was unyielding, giving me everything I wanted and taking all that he demanded in return. Our tongues tangled, with slow, sure strokes that made me burn inside.

"We should stop," he breathed the words on my lips.

I shook my head, pulling him closer, locking my fingers together behind his neck. "Give me this... please."

"You don't know what you're asking."

"I want to feel you, *all* of you."

Tristan murmured something under his breath, his eyes shuttering. But when they opened again, they were dark and full of hunger. He dragged me onto his lap, letting my legs fall open so that I straddled him.

"I shouldn't want—"

"Shh." I pressed a finger to his lips. "Touch me, Tristan. Feel how much I want this."

It was messed up. We were in the middle of nowhere, being hunted. But all I could think about was this. Him. Us. Being with him before we went back out there, into that... that nightmare.

"Please..." I rolled my hips above him, desperate to feel him. He gripped my hips, stilling me.

"Hold on," he breathed the words against my mouth as his other hand dipped between our bodies and found my core. "Fuck, Principessa. You are so wet for me."

Heat flooded my cheeks, and I nodded.

Tristan cupped me, sliding his fingers over my damp underwear, hissing his approval. "Something tells me once I do this, I'll never be able to stop."

His words sent a dark thrill through me as I slid my fingers through his hair, brushing my nose against his and peppering tiny kisses over his face.

He took his time, teasing me, rubbing me in slow, torturous circles before hooking his fingers into the lace and touching me. Skin on skin, he opened me to him and pressed two fingers inside me.

"Oh God." My forehead dropped to his shoulder as I lifted my hips slightly, trying to guide him deeper.

"Patience, Principessa." He scolded, curling them deeper, stretching me to the point where pain and pleasure blurred together.

"You're so fucking tight." Tristan grazed my neck with his teeth, soothing the sting with his tongue. "Look at me, Alessia. Let me see your eyes as you fall apart."

It was too much. His long fingers moving inside me, his teeth and tongue at my throat, his stormy gaze promising me things I had no right to want.

"Tristan... *God*," I moaned, writhing against his hand.

His thumb began to circle my clit, taking me higher and higher. Carrying me away to another world, another moment. One where the threat of death wasn't circling.

"It feels good... so good. Don't stop... don't ever stop."

He whispered words of encouragement in my ear. Strings of Italian phrases I could barely decipher between the moans and whimpers he was eliciting from my throat.

"Come for me, Principessa. Give it to me."

Something inside me coiled tight. Tighter… tighter… tighter…

Then snapped.

I clung to Tristan, crying out his name over and over as an intense wave of pleasure crashed over me. "W-what was that?" I peeked up at him through hooded eyes, and he smirked.

"That… was just the beginning."

Tristan lifted me off him like a rag doll and stood, lying me down on the bed. "You want this, Principessa?" His hand paused on his belt buckle. "You want me?"

"More than anything," I whispered. Shivered as I watched him slowly undress. His body was a work of art, inches upon inches of tan skin stretched taut over muscles that rippled and contracted with every breath he took. Dark swirls of ink snaked up one side of his waist, curling around his pecs. I wanted to trace the pattern, mark it with my fingertips and my lips and tongue.

"Tristan…" I breathed as he climbed over me, pushing my thighs apart to accommodate his body.

"If things were different, I would take my time, acquaint myself with every inch of your skin. But—"

"Shh." I touched his mouth again. "None of that matters."

All that mattered was he kissed me, touched and loved me the way I so desperately needed.

With the skill of a man far more experienced than I, he managed to bend and move my body until he was right there, pressed up against me. Thick and long and as hard as steel.

"Will it hurt?" I asked, my voice not my own.

"Only for a second." His jaw clenched, teeth bared as if he was fighting some internal battle.

"Tristan." I laid my hand against his cheek. "I want this. I want you."

"Mi fai impazzire," he rasped and then pushed forward, breaking through the final barrier of my innocence.

Emotion surged inside my chest as he sang my name over and over like a prayer. I cried out, too overwhelmed, too everything. Tristan was like a storm I couldn't escape, sweeping me up in its intensity. Its strength and unforgiving power.

He hitched my leg around his waist, grinding his pelvis against me in slow rolls like a wave ebbing and flowing against the shore.

"Okay?" he asked, and I nodded.

Sliding my hand around the back of his neck, I pulled his face down to kiss him.

At first, it wasn't particularly comfortable as he filled me, stretched me around him. But soon, the lingering ache gave way to a warm current of pleasure.

My hips began to lift to meet his every thrust, desperate to feel him deeper, harder.

"Fuck, Principessa. You feel... *fuck.*" He buried his face into the crook of my neck, licking and sucking the skin there while his hands mapped my curves.

"Ah," I cried as he picked up the pace, hitting some place deep inside me. "Tristan..."

He lifted his head and gazed down at me, holding my eyes, trapping me there. "Shh, I got you," he whispered.

Sweat beaded between my breasts, rolled down my back as he lowered his head to mine and circled his hips, changing the angle. A whimper tore from my throat, needy and wanton as pleasure blasted through me.

It was too intense, too much but I wanted more.

I wanted everything.

"I'm not going to last much longer," he muttered. "Do you think you can get there?"

"Touch me," I said, taking one of his hands in mine and guiding it to my clit. "Touch me like before."

Raw lust glittered in his dark eyes as he pressed his thumb there and began working me.

"Yes... God, yes..." I held on to his forearm, chanting his name like a vigil as my body began to tremble. "Tristan... *Tristan*... I'm..."

"Let go, Principessa. Come for me."

His words were my undoing and I splintered apart. Soaring higher than I ever had before.

He grabbed my hips and lifted me slightly, thrusting into me with vigor. "Fuck... *fuuuuck.*" He came hard, jerking inside me.

Breathless we held onto one another as if we never wanted to let go. And part of me didn't. Because when we did, this perfect moment would dissipate...

Leaving nothing but the nightmare we were trapped in.

"How do you feel?" Tristan asked me as he checked the weapons for the third time.

There had been no post-sex cuddles, no romantic talks. Tristan had held me for a few minutes, found me something to clean up with, then informed me we needed to get ready.

Part of me knew he was trying to avoid talking about what had happened. He'd taken my virginity after I'd begged him to do it. It had been the single most intense experience of my life and he was acting like it was nothing.

"I'm fine," I clipped out, hating how quickly things had gone to crap.

But what did I really expect?

Tristan had made it clear we couldn't be together and I'd pushed him anyway.

Tears stung my eyes but I swallowed them down.

"Alessia, look at me."

I was Alessia now.

That stung.

I met his eyes and gave him a tight smile that didn't reach my eyes. "I said I'm fine."

He let out an exasperated breath. "We need to talk about this, but now isn't the right time."

"There's nothing to talk about."

He clicked his tongue, murmuring something in Italian.

"We don't—"

The radio crackled to life and fear flooded me. Tristan messed with the dials and lowered the volume, holding it to his ear.

"What are they—"

He silenced me with a hard look and finger to his mouth.

Avoiding me and treating me like a child.

My heart sank.

He regretted what had happened between us, that much was obvious. And I didn't for a second doubt that when—*if*—we made it out of this, he would order me to never speak about it again.

But regardless of how he felt about it, it would always mean something to me.

Even if I meant nothing to him.

When I glanced back, he wore a grim expression. "We need to move. Now."

"They've found us."

"Not yet but they're getting closer. We can circle around them and beat them back to the warehouse. I can find somewhere to leave you and—"

"I'm coming."

"Alessia, be reasonable. I need to find a cell phone and some transport. I can't do that if I'm worrying about you."

"Fine."

"Please, don't make this any harder than it needs to be. This is our chance. Unless you want to spend the night out here like sitting ducks."

"I'll follow your instructions." I conceded.

He was right, I didn't want to stay here a second longer. And I certainly didn't want to spend the night here.

But I didn't want to go out there either.

"I'm scared," I admitted.

Tristan lifted his hand and I thought he might reach for me but he didn't.

And it spoke volumes.

He was building a wall around his heart and whatever had been building between us was gone. He would protect me, kill our enemy without hesitation; he would die for me if it came down to it. But Tristan wouldn't fight for me.

He wouldn't fight for us.

"Put this in your pocket." He handed me a bottle of water, and I slipped it into one of his jacket pockets.

"We move quickly and silently. You stay behind me at all times, unless I say run, in which case, you run. Do you understand?"

I nodded.

"We're going to get as close to the warehouse as we can and try and scope out how many of them there are."

Another nod.

"I need you to stay light on your feet, watching where you're treading, and keep your eyes and ears open. First sign of gunfire you take cover, okay?"

"Okay."

"I know it's scary, I know we don't have a better plan but we can do this. You can do this."

It was on the tip of my tongue to ask him to kiss me, to hold me and tell me we would make it out of this alive. But I trapped the words behind pursed lips, refusing to beg any more than I already had.

"I'm ready."

It was Tristan's turn to nod. He grabbed the radio and I followed him outside. The sun had already sunk behind the tree line, casting the forest in a murky haze. It would be dark within the hour.

I tried not to think about that as we made our way through the dense brush.

Tristan repeatedly glanced back, checking that I was behind him. But he barely met my eyes. With every step, I felt the distance between us grow. By the time we got out of here, *if* we got out of here, I knew we'd go back to pretending we were nothing to one another.

It hurt.

More than I anticipated. But I guess that was the consequence of knowing what I'd lost. Not that I'd ever really had it.

Tristan made it perfectly clear last night, before everything went to crap, that he had no intention of exploring things between us.

In his head, I was untouchable. Off-limits. Forbidden fruit.

"I see it," he whispered into the night, sweeping his arm out for me to stop.

Adrenaline and fear pumped through me, my heart a constant drum in my chest. I was cold and tired and so hungry. I just wanted it to be over.

I wanted to go back home and sleep for a week, nursing my broken heart and wounded pride. I wanted to see my brother and Arianne and my gorgeous little niece.

Clapping a hand over my mouth, I smothered the sob trying to escape. Tristan glanced back, narrowing his eyes but I didn't meet his gaze.

"Follow me," he instructed.

Slowly, we made our way around the outer perimeter of the warehouse. I could vaguely see the structure through the trees. My heart was beating so hard I felt light-headed.

Suddenly, he grabbed my hand and picked up the pace. Stumbling forward, I tried to keep up with him. Until we arrived at a small shed, secreted away in the scrub.

Tristan whirled on me and cupped my cheek. "Listen to me, I want you to stay here until I come back. No matter what you hear, don't leave, okay?"

"N-no, I can't… you can't leave me. What if… oh God, what if—"

"Shh, Principessa." His eyes shuttered. "I need to get a cell phone. Or at least find a way out of here. But I need you to be safe."

He pulled the door open and tipped his head inside. "Here, take the flashlight."

My trembling fingers closed around it, tears streaking down my cheeks.

"I'll come back for you, I promise. Just sit tight."

He inhaled a ragged breath, pressed a kiss to my forehead and ushered me inside. With one last lingering look, he closed the door.

And left me alone in the dark.

EIGHT

TRISTAN

IT TOOK everything inside me to leave Alessia. My heart roared at me with every step I took away from her, but I had to know she was safe.

I had to—

The radio crackled to life again, barely audible voices coming through. I lifted it to my ear and tried to distinguish what they were saying. The fact the reception was so poor suggested they were at the farthest end of the range. Which could work in my favor, assuming Mahoney hadn't left a small army to guard the warehouse.

I scanned the area and slipped out under the cover of darkness. My white shirt was like a beacon under the pale moonlight, but I didn't have the heart to take my jacket back from Alessia. So I would have to make do, and hope I found a phone before they found me.

Get a grip, Capizola. She's depending on you.

Alessia Marchetti, the girl who now held my heart in the palm of her hands.

I knew it the second I pushed inside her and claimed her first time. But it could never work. The Marchetti princess and… me. I was a soldier for the Family. I was family.

Nicco and Antonio wouldn't want me anywhere near their precious, sweet Alessia. If they ever found out what I'd done… Not even Arianne's protection could save me from their wrath.

I shoved down those thoughts, I needed to focus. If I didn't get lucky and find a cell phone or a way out of this place, Nicco's wrath would be the least of my concerns.

Darting across the gravel, I pressed myself flat across the side of the building and began inching my way toward the door. It wasn't the door Alessia and I had fled from, which meant there was more than one way in and out. But without schematics of the place, I'd have to make do.

The door was unlocked, and I slipped inside, surprised to find myself in the main warehouse space. The rows and rows of pallets gave me plenty of cover as I worked my way across the room. I'd almost made it to the other side, when approaching footsteps halted me.

I lifted my gun, aiming in the direction of the footsteps. My pulse quickened, the air around me growing thick.

"This is total bullshit," somebody said. "No one said nothing about—"

"Quit your bitchin' Monroe. You're getting paid, doesn't matter what for."

Two of them. I could take two of them. The gunfire would draw attention, but if I was fast, I could be in and out and back to Alessia before anyone got back here.

Inhaling a calming breath, I checked the safety on the gun and emerged from out behind the pallet. One of the guys saw me, drawing his weapon.

"Shit, shit!" he yelled. But before he could get another word out, I pulled the trigger and fired.

His body went down like a ton of bricks, hitting the concrete with a thud, blood trickling out of the single bullet hole in his forehead.

"Motherfucker," the other guy grunted, fumbling with the assault rifle on his back.

A fucking assault rifle.

I didn't think about it as I dove for another stack of pallets, ducking out of sight.

"You're a dead man, Capizola," he shouted.

Shit. I hadn't seen if he had a radio. If he did...

I jumped up and fired. Once. Twice. The crack of gunfire, making my heart falter. But I didn't hesitate, didn't stop as I raced toward him and slammed into him. We went down. Hard. The air whooshing from my lungs as I rolled to the side and unsheathed my second weapon. I swung around, aiming it at the guy who was grappling with his rifle, trying to get a grip on the weapon strewn at an odd angle across his body.

"You're gonna die for that," he spat.

Bang.

I shot him point blank, the spray of blood a red mist in the air.

Rushing over to them, I searched their bodies for a cell phone or keys. Relief slammed into me the second I discovered a cell phone tucked into one of their pockets. But before I could dial Nicco's number, voices rang out around me.

"He's in the warehouse," someone yelled. "I heard gunshots."

Shit.

Shit.

I pocketed the cell phone, grabbed the assault rifle, and slung it over my shoulder, doubling back around to the side door.

Gunfire ricocheted off the wall beside my head, catapulting my heart into my fucking throat. But adrenaline spurred me forward. Adrenaline and the desperate need to get back to Alessia and get the fuck out of here so we could call for help.

I careened into the door, slamming my hands down on the bar and barreling into the night.

"Get the fucker." The words pierced the air but I kept running, kept moving. Ducking and dodging bullets. One clipped my thigh and I went down for a second, grunting in agony.

The shed was right through the trees, I could see it. I couldn't give in now. Not until I had Alessia safe in my arms.

Swinging the assault rifle around, I let it rip, spraying bullets toward my pursuers. I didn't stop to see if I'd hit anyone, planting my feet under me, I made a dash toward the tree line.

The wet trickle of blood saturated my slacks but I kept running.

I had to reach Alessia and get us out of here.

I had to—

Pain blasted through my side and I started to fall. "No," I yelled. "No." I was so close. So fucking close. "Alessia."

My vision started to flicker as I dragged my body toward the trees. So close...

I was so close.

"Alessia," I choked out, clawing at the gravel, the earth beneath me. "*Principessa*."

But the pain was too much, the blinding agony like a dark cloud swarming me. Consuming me.

Dragging me down to the pits of hell until there was nothing but oblivion.

"Tristan, stay with me... stay with me," the voice of an angel called out to me somewhere in the darkness. "Don't leave, please don't leave me."

Her voice.

Alessia.

My Principessa.

I tried to speak, to force out the words lodged into my throat. But I couldn't.

"No, no..." Her voice wrapped around me, the pain in it squeezing my heart like a vise. "Don't leave me, please..."

"Sia, Principessa," the words formed on my lips, barely a whisper. Something brushed my hand, soft and warm.

Was this the end?

"I love you," she whispered. "I think I have always loved you."

No.

No.

That wasn't right.

She didn't...

She couldn't.

"Come back to me, please." Her voice grew quiet. Distant. Cold sweeping in and through me.

I gasped for air, trying to clutch my throat but my arms were like lead.

What was happening?

A weight pressed down on me. Suffocating and unyielding, forcing the air from my lungs. I couldn't breathe... I couldn't...

Don't leave me, Principessa. Don't leave me.

But she was gone.

And the dream—the nightmare—swallowed me whole.

My eyes peeled open only to be met with stark white light. I blinked, pain radiating through my body. My shoulder. Thigh. Torso. Fuck. It took my breath away.

"Tristan?" Someone gasped, emotion clinging to every syllable.

"A-Arianne?"

"Thank God." She rushed to my side, taking my hand in hers. "I thought... God, you scared me."

"Where am I? What happened?"

Her brows, knitted with concern glittering in her eyes. "You don't remember?"

"I—"

One after another the memories slammed into me.

"Alessia, is she—"

"Okay, she's okay. Thanks to you. God, when we realized you'd both been taken..."

Relief sank into me.

Safe.

She was safe.

I wasn't a religious man by any means, but I said a silent prayer to God, thanking him for watching over her. For saving her.

"What—"

The door opened and Nicco appeared. "You're awake."

I gauged his expression. Did he know?

Know of my betrayal?

I swallowed, wincing at how sore and dry my throat was.

"Here." Arianne offered me a cup of water. "Little sips."

When I'd quenched my unbearable thirst, I looked to Nicco and asked, "What happened?"

"We got there just in time by all accounts." His jaw clenched, a distant look in his eyes.

"Mahoney and his men?"

"Bambolina, give us a second..."

"Nicco, no, I—"

"Please."

"Fine." Irritation coated her voice. "I'll go update everyone." She kissed my head. "I'll be back soon."

She left, taking the air with her.

"They're dead?" I asked, and Nicco nodded.

"We were too complacent and it almost cost us..." His eyes guttered.

"She's okay, she's safe," I said, trying to keep my voice even.

"She won't talk to me about what happened. Won't breathe a word of it. Did... did they hurt her?"

"Not any more than they did me," I said, guilt swarming my chest.

I was a bastard.

A liar and a thief.

I'd stolen her innocence when I should have been strong enough to resist. To say no.

"When that bullet hit me..." My eyes shuttered as I inhaled a ragged breath. "I thought it was the end."

"We got there just in time."

"How?"

"We picked up one of Mahoney's men. Enzo tortured the location out of him."

"Of course he did." I snorted but the humor died the second I took in Nicco's gaunt expression.

"It's my fault," he said quietly, his voice so full of pain and despair it tainted the air around us.

"You can't blame yourself. That's a road you can't travel down, you know that. This life is..."

"Fucked up." He let out a heavy sigh, dropping into the chair beside my bed. "When I got the call, I almost lost it. Arianne had to calm me down. She's my sister. My baby sister and they thought to use her against me."

"Love, family, is weakness. You know that." His eyes narrowed dangerously, and I added, "But it's also strength, Nicco," I added. "It gives you something to fight for. Something to strive to be better for."

"I just keep asking myself if I made the wrong call, dragging Arianne into this life. And now Lucia.

"I love them more than life," he said. "But I want more for Alessia. I want her to know more than... than this."

He might as well have driven a knife through my heart and finished the job Mahoney's men started.

"I'm sure she'll flourish at college." The words soured on my tongue.

"I'm considering asking her to go away to college."

"W-what?"

He nodded, rubbing a hand over his jaw. "I think it would do her good… after everything."

"But what about Bella? They have everything planned."

"Maybe they should both consider it. I don't want her to feel trapped by this life, Tris. I don't ever want that for her."

I got it, I did.

Family meant everything to Nicco. But asking her to leave Verona…

I couldn't wrap my head around that.

Didn't want to.

"I should let you rest." He stood. "Thank you, for everything."

I wanted to argue, to tell him he couldn't possibly send Alessia away, not when I—

Fuck.

I couldn't even say the words.

Because saying them wouldn't change anything.

She was young, she had her entire life ahead of her. Nicco was right, she could do anything, be anything. Maybe this life was a shackle she shouldn't have to bear.

I gave him a small nod, not trusting myself to reply, and closed my eyes.

At least in my dreams, I could allow myself to think about her.

Ten days.

That's how long it took until the doctors finally relented and agreed to discharge me.

The bullet wounds in my shoulder and thigh were mostly superficial and just needed time to heal. But the bullet that had hit me in the back had almost perforated my left kidney, and the doctors wanted to monitor me closely. But after a week, I was climbing the walls.

Arianne stopped by as much as she could. She even brought Lucia a couple of times. Jay and Luis came by too. Thankfully Bella had been unharmed in the attack but Jay had taken a bullet to arm and managed to knock himself out when he smashed his head against the asphalt. Thankfully Michele and Marcella were also unharmed. Enzo and Matteo even stopped by with Antonio.

The only person who didn't come was Alessia.

Not that I truly expected her to. Not after how things had ended between us. But maybe it was better this way. She needed to move on, to prepare for college, figure out what she wanted to do with life, and date guys her own age.

Yet, I couldn't shake the feeling that I was missing something. Fragments of a hazy dream where Alessia was crying over my dying body, whispering three little words I didn't deserve to hear, lingered in my mind, taunting me.

I love you.

But it wasn't real. It was just my pain-addled brain playing tricks on me.

Alessia didn't love me.

How could she?

"You look like you've seen better days." Enzo walked into the room, pushing a wheelchair.

"Nice to see you too."

"The boss sent me. He and Ari are having some kind of teething drama. Lucia hasn't stopped crying all morning. You know Nicco, he's one tear away from taking her to the ER. Ready to get out of here?"

"Fuck yes." I pushed up off the bed, wincing as a dull pain shot through me.

"You good?"

"Hurts like a bitch, but I'll live."

"If it's any consolation, we made Mahoney suffer." Enzo didn't miss a beat as he said the words, his blood lust obvious.

"Good." I gave him a curt nod, lowering myself into the wheelchair. "Have you seen Alessia? How is she?"

"She won't admit it, but everyone's worried about her. She's... distant."

"She went through something traumatic."

"Yeah, but this feels... more than that. Nicco tried to broach transferring colleges with her and by all accounts, she lost it. He had to send in reinforcements to calm her down. Nora's worried. We all are."

Fuck.

That hollow ache inside me had me rubbing my chest, trying to ease the phantom pain. Because it wasn't something physical I could heal from. It was bone deep guilt.

Soul deep regret.

But more than that, it was a mark on my heart I wasn't sure I would ever recover from.

I'd hurt her.

And in doing so, I'd hurt myself.

Enzo wheeled me toward the door and chuckled. "I hope you're ready to be fussed over. I don't know who will be worse. Ari, Nora, or Caitlin."

But it didn't matter because the only girl I cared about visiting me, wouldn't be there.

NINE

ALESSIA

I WASN'T TALKING to Nicco.

I wasn't really talking to anyone. He'd stopped by a couple of days ago and suggested I transfer to a college out of state, and I'd been ignoring him ever since.

After everything I'd been through, he wanted to ship me away to a new town, a new place where I didn't know anyone.

"It'll give you a chance to spread your wings," he'd said.

I didn't want to spread my wings. I wanted to see Tristan. I wanted to see for myself that he was okay.

No one had kept me away from the hospital, but I hadn't been brave enough to visit. To see the rejection I knew I'd find in his eyes. Whatever happened between us in the cabin was fleeting. A moment of madness fueled by fear and desperation.

Yet, it had been so much more to me.

When I'd heard the gunshots, heard him scream my name, and I'd run from the shed and found him bleeding out on the gravel, my heart had fractured.

Irrevocably and unequivocally broken.

Because in that moment, I realized two things.

One, I truly was desperately and hopelessly in love with Tristan Capizola, and two, I was going to watch the man I loved die. I didn't remember falling to my knees or crawling toward him, reaching for him before strong arms hoisted me off the ground.

Matteo.

Matteo found me first. Then Enzo, Luis, and Nicco had appeared. I couldn't remember much about what happened after. The dead bodies and hushed conversations. The smell of burning.

They said I went into shock. I'm not sure I snapped out of it until I heard those two little words.

He's alive.

Tears burned the backs of my eyes but I blinked them away. I was done crying, my eyes bleary and sore from all the tears that had fallen these past few days. Tears for myself, for what might have been and what would never be.

I was angry and frustrated and empty. But more than anything, I was heartbroken.

Being with Tristan was all I'd ever wanted since I was just a young naïve girl, lusting after a man she thought she could never have.

But that was the problem—I'd had him. For a single moment, I'd had everything I'd ever wanted. I knew what he tasted like, how good he felt pressed up against me. How it felt when he moved inside me.

"Sia?" Bella called out and I sat up, waiting for her to come bounding into my room.

Ever since what happened, she'd been fiercely protective of me, visiting daily. Some nights she even stayed with me. It was nice, but it was starting to get a little suffocating.

"Hey," I said as she poked her head inside.

"How are you feeling?"

"Same as I did when you called this morning." A faint smile traced my lips.

"Is that your way of saying I'm fussing?"

"You know you are. But I love you for it."

"Damn right you do. Anyway, I'm not here to stay, I'm here to take you out."

"W-what? No!"

I didn't want to go out.

"Don't look so worried. Jay is downstairs. He's taking me to visit Tristan. Mom made him a batch of cornetti and I offered to deliver them. You should come."

"Oh, I don't think so." Panic flooded me. "He probably doesn't want visitors, he just got out of the hospital."

"He's been home two days, Sia, and according to Caitlin who told Matt, he's going out of his mind. I'm sure he'd like to see you."

I very much doubted that.

But I couldn't exactly tell her anything.

Bella's brow furrowed. "Sia, what aren't you telling me?"

"What? Nothing. I just don't think Tristan will want the two of us bothering him."

She chuckled. "We're not the annoying girls we were back then, babe. It's just a nice gesture. Nora and Caitlin were there practically all day yesterday and he didn't kick them out." She shrugged as if it was nothing.

I guess to her, it wasn't.

Tristan was as good as family. And our family looked after its own.

"You go, I don't feel like—"

"Alessia, you're coming. I won't take no for an answer. Besides, you need to get out of the house for a bit. I know you're scared—"

"I'm not.

At least, I wasn't scared because of what had happened.

I wasn't an idiot. I knew my brother and cousins had taken care of the men who took us. They hadn't said it, not in so many words, but I knew.

You didn't cross the Marchetti and live to tell the tale. And I was the boss's sister, his blood. Those men had signed their death certificate the second they jumped out of that van and opened fire on us.

But no, I didn't care about any of that.

I cared about the man they'd hurt. The man who had almost died.

The man I'd given my heart and body to, only for him to give me my heart back.

"You have five minutes," Arabella said. "I'll wait downstairs so you can fix... that." She waved her hand in my general direction.

"What's wrong with me?"

She grimaced. "I know your silly little crush on Tristan ended a long time ago, but it won't hurt to make an effort, babe. After all, you're not the young innocent girl you were back then."

It was a harmless comment, meant to make me feel better about the whole thing, no doubt. But I still bit down on the inside of my cheek to stop my secrets from tumbling out.

If only she knew.

By the time we pulled up outside Tristan's apartment block, my stomach was a tight ball of nerves.

I shouldn't have come, that was apparent from the way my body trembled as Jay opened the door and helped me climb out of the SUV.

"I'm sure seeing you will cheer him up," he said.

I gave him a tight-lipped smile, following him and Bella up to Tristan's apartment. My stomach churned as Jay let himself in.

"Yo, Cap, I brought company."

"And cornetti." Bella chuckled, so at ease with the whole situation while I felt like I might vomit all over the hardwood floors.

"Sia." Bella glanced back. "What is it? You've gone as white as a sheet."

"Nothing." I swallowed the acid in my throat. "I'm fine. Let's go."

The quicker we get this over with, the quicker I can leave.

Bella laced her arm through mine and guided me deeper into Tristan's apartment. The hall opened up into a big open plan living room with amazing views of the river.

"How are you feeling, Tris?" Bella dropped my arm and skipped over to him. He was sprawled out on the couch, a thin blanket pulled up over his naked torso. His gaze went right past Bella and landed on me, widening with surprise.

"Alessia," he said in that deep, gravelly voice of his.

I inhaled a sharp breath, too stunned to move.

"Mom sent cornetti," Bella interrupted the sudden tension between us and I dropped my gaze.

"She shouldn't have."

"Yeah, well, you know Italian women, food fixes everything." She plopped down on the end of his couch.

I sat on the smaller couch with Jay, putting as much distance between us. Tristan couldn't easily look at me from this angle. Couldn't see the hurt in my eyes.

The three of them chatted about his recovery, and Bella told them all about her plans for the summer. Plans she'd made for the both of us. Plans I wanted no part of.

Nothing felt the same now.

I didn't feel the same.

And maybe I wasn't.

Maybe I'd left the old me there in that cabin, and now I had to figure out who I was in the aftermath of everything that had happened.

"Alessia."

"Uh, yes?" I blinked over at her. "Jay asked you if you wanted a drink."

"Oh no, thank you."

He went over to the kitchen area and I realized Tristan now had a direct line of sight to me. His eyes burned into the side of my face but I refused to look at him.

I couldn't.

Not without risking my emotions betraying me. It was taking everything in me not to rush to his side and touch him, to make sure he was really here and okay.

Instead, I pressed my hands into the couch beneath my thighs, physically restraining myself.

Bella cast me a funny look, mouthing, 'Are you okay?'

Lips pursed, I nodded.

Thankfully, Jay returned with drinks and the three of them fell back into easy conversation. While I sat there…

Wishing the couch would swallow me whole.

After sixty painful minutes, Tristan announced he needed to rest. I'd never been more grateful to hear those words.

We got up to leave, and Bella, in true Bella fashion, leaned down to give him a kiss on the cheek. "Get better soon," she said. "Jay's good company but he's not you, Tris." She flashed my bodyguard a playful wink.

"I'll stop by soon, Cap." Jay held out his fist and Tristan bumped it.

"Goodbye," I managed to force out over the lump in my throat as I followed Jay toward the door.

"Alessia, can we talk for a second?"

No.

No!

I smothered the whimper caught in my throat. I didn't want to do this, not here, not now.

"Go ahead." Bella gave me a reassuring smile. "Me and Jay will wait in the car."

They left without another word.

"Please," he said.

Slowly, I turned, my heart crashing violently against my chest, my palms sweating.

"How are you?"

"I... I'm okay."

"Look at me, please," he urged.

My eyes lifted and I immediately wished I hadn't. Regret shone in his eyes. Regret and guilt.

"I am so sorry, for everything."

"S-sorry?"

"Yes, for what happened. For... what I did. I... fuck, Sia." He exhaled a pained breath. "I had no right to do that. To take that from you. You were confused, scared and—"

"Please, don't. Don't treat me like a child who didn't know what she was doing."

How could he even think that?

I began to tremble, indignation burning in the hollow pit of my stomach.

"Sia, I meant no offense. But you have to know how sorry I am." He scrubbed his jaw and the moment struck me as strange. There he was, laid out on his couch, completely immobile and I was the one looming over him as if I held the power.

Yet, he was the one breaking my heart all over again.

Silence stretched out before us.

Then he said, "Thank you, for not telling Nicco."

"I should go."

I needed to get far, far away from here.

From him.

But he couldn't let me do it. Tristan couldn't let me walk away with the tiny shred of dignity I still possessed.

"You should do it, you know."

"Excuse me?" I turned and met his conflicted gaze.

"Transfer schools. Get out of Verona. Experience life away from the family."

"You want me to leave?"

His brows pinched. "That's not—"

"I thought you were dying. I watched you bleeding out on the gravel and all I could think was I'd never gotten to tell you how I really felt. That I… I love you. I'm in love with you. And you're telling me to leave? God, I am such an idiot." My chest heaved with the weight of my words. "I've spent the last year falling deeper and deeper and then at the party, out there in the cabin, I thought you felt it too. For a second, I thought you felt it."

Tears streamed down my cheeks but I wiped them away with the back of my hand.

"Alessia." He tried to sit up. "I'm—"

Before he could say another word, I rushed out, "I'm glad you're okay, I am. But stay away from me Tristan. If you care about me at all, you'll stay away from me."

Then I ran out of there.

With my heart in tatters.

And only myself to blame.

The next day, Genevieve made me join her, Dad, Nicco, Arianne, and Lucia for dinner. I'd tried to get out of it, feigning a headache, but she wouldn't take no for an answer.

I'd barely slept. Replaying Tristan's words over and over in my head. In between all the tears, of course.

Heartbreak sucked.

And now, I had to endure a family meal and pretend everything was okay.

"See-ah, See-ah." Lucia clapped her pudgy little hands as I sat down beside her.

"Hi, precious girl." I ruffled her brown curls, feeling lighter than I had all day.

"How are you feeling?" Arianne asked.

"Fine."

"It's the only answer we get out of her," my father grumbled.

"Antonio," Genevieve scolded him.

"I'm fine, Papa, I promise."

I served myself a heap of salad to avoid any further questions. At least if I pretended to eat, they wouldn't all add that to their list of concerns.

Genevieve had just started serving the spaghetti when the doorbell rang.

"Are you expecting someone?" She glanced at Nicco and then my father.

"No. Stay here." Nicco leaped up.

But Luis beat him to it.

"Tristan," he said, "this is a surprise."

Tristan?

Despite being seated, the ground went from under me and I grabbed the edge of the table.

"He shouldn't be here," Arianne hissed. "He's supposed to be on bed rest." She went storming off.

"Invite him in," Genevieve called after her. "There's plenty of food."

But when they returned, Nicco fixed his eyes on me, frowning. "He wants to talk to you."

"Me?"

"Isn't he coming in?" My father frowned.

"He can barely stand." Nicco watched me. Studying me. Trying to see past the façade I'd worn ever since they found me at that warehouse.

"I should probably go and see what he wants." I threw my napkin on the table and hurried out of the room and down the hall. "You can't be here," I hissed, the second I reached him.

"We need to talk," he said, holding his stomach.

"You shouldn't be up and out of bed. You'll pull your stitches."

"I needed to see you. I haven't been able to stop thinking about what you said."

"Well, you didn't listen very clearly, Tristan. I told you to stay away from me."

"Yeah, about that..." He rubbed the back of his neck. "I don't think that's going to be possible."

"What?"

He moved a step closer. "Say it," he breathed, reaching for my face, cupping my cheek. "Say it, Principessa."

"Tristan, you should go before—"

"Say it, Alessia. Please."

"I-I can't." Because I'd said it twice now. And neither time he said it back.

"Okay then, I'll say it." He gazed down at me. "You love me."

"Don't tease me." I tried to glance away from him, but he kept me there. Anchored in place so I had no choice but to stare up at him.

"I'm not teasing you. I'm here because... because I—"

"Tristan?" The sound Arianne's voice made cut through the air. "What's going on?" Confusion clouded her eyes as she watched us.

"That's something I'd also like to know the answer to." Nicco stepped up behind his wife and glared at me.

No, not me, I realized.

Tristan.

"Why are you touching my sister like that, Capizola?"

Crap.

This was bad. So very bad.

"Nicco, I can explain," I rushed out. "It's not what you think."

"Actually, Nic," Tristan stepped around me, tucking me into his side. "It's exactly what it looks like."

"The two of you..." Arianne wagged a casual finger between us but her expression was anything but casual.

"It's always been Tristan," I said, finding my voice. What happened in the cabin had only confirmed it.

"And you, when did you decide you had a thing for my baby sister?" Nicco cut Tristan with a seething glare.

"Nicco." I stepped forward, putting myself between them. "Don't do this. I'm begging you. Tristan saved my life. He saved me, Nic. Doesn't that count for something?"

"Go inside, Alessia. Me and Tristan are going to have a little chat."

"No." I lifted my chin in defiance. "I will always be your little sister. But I am not a child. I can choose who I love, who I give my heart to." I took Tristan's hand in mine and gazed up at him. "And I choose him. I choose Tristan."

"Tristan?" Arianne said softly.

He let out a heavy sigh, his breath skittering over my neck. "I didn't mean for it to happen, but she's right. Something changed between us out there. And I'm done fighting it."

"Please, Nicco." I silently implored my brother. "It's time to let somebody else protect me."

"You know I will," Tristan added, squeezing my hand. "I would die before I ever let anything hurt her."

The muscle in Nicco's jaw flexed, but then he exhaled a steady breath, and said, "You should come inside. It seems we have a lot to talk about, and Genevieve made enough to feed the whole neighborhood."

"Thank you." I threw my arms around him and hugged him tight. "Thank you."

"It doesn't mean I'm okay with this. Whatever this is. But I'm prepared to hear him out."

I nodded, unable to fight the grin tugging at the corner of my mouth. "We'll be right in," I said, hoping they would give me and Tristan a moment's privacy.

"One minute, and not a second longer," Nicco said, spinning on his heel and heading back into the kitchen.

Arianne gave me a small tentative smile. "I can't pretend to understand this. But if I know anything, it's that love works in mysterious ways." She took off after Nicco but paused at the last second and glanced back. "Tristan, I know I don't need to tell you that if you hurt Alessia, I won't be able to stop the hell that Nicco will rain down on you."

Tristan stiffened behind me but I saw the playful glint in her eyes. It was a warning but one laced with amusement.

"Make it quick. The food is getting cold." She disappeared, leaving us alone at last.

I inhaled a shaky breath, hardly able to believe what was happening. Tristan brushed the hair off my shoulder and pressed his lips there before whispering, "Look at me, Principessa, give me your eyes."

Slowly, I turned in his arms, gazing up at him. "Is this real?"

"Does this feel real?" He pressed his lips to mine. Slow, uncertain, but full of passion.

"Tristan, we shouldn't..."

"I know." He touched his head to mine and inhaled deeply. "Later, when we're alone."

"You want this? You really want me?"

"Principessa, it's not a case of what I do or don't want anymore. The second you ran out of my apartment yesterday, I knew I'd fucked up. I've tried to fight it. Tried to tell myself that you deserve more. Deserve better... but I'm done fighting it. I'm done." He swept his fingers along my neck and buried his fingers in my hair, inhaling a sharp breath. "We should probably go inside."

"We should," I whispered, my heart fluttering wildly.

"How do you think your father will handle the news?"

"Don't worry," I said with a tiny smirk, my heart so full that it felt ready to explode. "I'll protect you."

After all, it was my turn to save him.

EPILOGUE

ALESSIA

I NEEDED TO GET UP.

We were meeting my brother and his friends in less than two hours, but I was too comfortable to move.

"Hmm, this is nice," Tristan nuzzled my neck, kissing and nipping the skin there, sending delicious shivers through me.

I ran my fingers through his hair, smiling to myself. Sometimes, I couldn't believe we'd made it here.

It had been almost six weeks since we were taken by Jericho Mahoney's men. A month since Tristan had turned up on my doorstep and announced to Nicco and Arianne, and then my father and Genevieve, that we were *involved*.

Involved. I smirked again.

Such a mundane word to describe what I felt for this man.

"I already want you again," he whispered against my ear. "How is that possible?" Tristan sucked my lobe, grazing the delicate skin with his teeth.

"We should probably get up and get ready," I said. "I don't want to be late."

"We have time, plenty of time, Principessa." He dragged me back into his chest, curving his strong powerful body around me.

Tristan was almost healed. But he hadn't let that stop him from making love to me every opportunity he got. Which was more than I'd anticipated once news of our relationship reached my cousins.

Like Nicco, they were wary about it at first. Tristan was older than me. He worked for the Family—*was* family—but despite his loyalty, there was still a messy history between his family and ours.

I didn't care though. Even without their blessing, I wouldn't have been able to walk away.

"I love you," I purred, leaning back to find his mouth. Tristan captured my lips in a slow, passionate kiss, his hand slipping down my body and between my legs.

"Ti amo anch'io." His fingers curled inside me and I smothered a moan. "You are always so ready for me," he whispered, lifting my leg slightly and hooking it behind his thigh. His fingers were replaced with his thick, hard length. He rocked forward, inch by inch until he was seated inside me. "Fuck, Principessa, you feel... made for me."

"Move," I whispered, grinding back onto him. "I need you to move."

Tristan kept the pace slow, going as deep as he could. Sex with him was always breathtaking but the thing I loved most was his patience as we learned each other's bodies, our likes and dislikes, all of the ways to make each other come undone.

And this intimate, intense position... *this* I liked.

One of his hands gripped my hip, anchoring me in place as he rode my body, while the other glided up my stomach, gently squeezing my breasts before dipping between my thighs and rubbing my clit.

"God, Tristan," I cried. "It feels... ah..."

"That's it, Principessa, give it to me. Give me everything."

Heat pooled low in my stomach, a tight ball of tension ready to snap. "More... *God*, more..."

He circled his hips, changing the angle. "Feel how deep I am," he breathed the words against my cheek. "Feel how deep you pull me into your body."

I looped my arm around the back of his neck and held on, giving into the sensations crashing over me.

"You're mine, Alessia. Mine." The possession in Tristan's voice was enough to tip me over the edge. I cried out, riding the waves of pleasure crashing over me.

Tristan followed me over, thrust deep one last time and held himself there as he came hard. "You are amazing." He kissed my shoulder.

"That was some wake up call," I said around a smile.

I couldn't stop smiling lately.

I think it was one of the reason's Nicco had been so calm about everything—that and the fact Tristan had played a role in saving my life.

"But now I really need to pee," I said, wiggling out of his arms.

Climbing out of bed, I grabbed his t-shirt and pulled it over my head. I liked wearing his clothes, being in his space. We hadn't talked much beyond the here and now, but I knew without a doubt that I wanted it all with him.

"What?" he asked as I glanced back at him, my gaze lingering.

"I'm happy, Tristan," I said. "You make me happy."

TRISTAN

Alessia looked radiant as we sat crammed into a booth at Arianne's favorite diner. I was hardly surprised that Nicco insisted we meet here. Boss or no boss, my cousin had Niccolò Marchetti wrapped around her finger.

Matteo and Caitlin were already here. The girls were chatting about nothing and everything and I could have spent a lifetime watching Alessia's expressions. The small uncertain smiles to the big wide grins. The way her eyes danced with excitement or how her brows furrowed tightly whenever she was confused or concerned about something.

There wasn't a single thing I didn't know—or love—about her. Much to the disapproval of her cousins and Nicco. Not that I'd ever tell her that.

"How is everything?" Matt asked me.

"Good. It's good."

"I take it she stayed at your place last night?"

I nodded, my collar growing tighter. "How did you—"

"You have that look, man." His expression darkened.

"What look?" I played along but I had a feeling where he was going with this.

"You know," he said tightly. "And I gotta say it, Tris. Makes me feel fucking uncomfortable thinking about you and her. Shit, she's still just a kid in my head."

"She's eighteen."

"I know, I know. But she'll always be Nicco's baby sister. The little girl who followed us around, calling us out on our shit. Just do me a favor and promise me whatever happens or wherever this goes between the two of you, you'll try your best not to break her heart."

"You have my word, I have no plans on ever hurting her."

He gawked at me. "Ever?" His brow lifted. "That is a big claim to make."

"You know what I mean." I shrugged, and his eyes flicked to Caitlin.

"Yeah, I know exactly what you mean. But that's what worries me. I know how wild Caitlin drives me. I want inside her every second of every day. Even after two years, that feeling still hasn't diminished. Sia is young, she's—"

"Sitting right here." She gave Matt an irritated look. "I appreciate the big brotherly concern, Matteo, I do. But I'm a big girl, I can handle my own dating life."

Dating.

The word clanged through me.

Is that what we were doing? Dating?

Because it sure as hell felt like a lot more than just dating to me.

She was in my bed almost every night. Which meant I was inside her almost double that amount. I couldn't get enough. Couldn't believe I'd denied myself this for so long.

Caitlin shot me a knowing look as if she could hear my very thoughts. But before she could comment, the others arrived and the booth became a flurry of hugs and kisses and the girls all cooing over Nora's ever growing baby bump.

"I need a drink," Enzo grumbled.

"But it isn't even lunch—"

"I'll be at the bar." He stalked off and Nora scowled.

"Anyone would think he's carrying the small human jumping on my bladder every freaking minute of the day."

"How long do you have left now?" I asked.

"Too freaking long.

"Six weeks at the most," Arianne said. "You can do it, babe."

"Yeah well, what I really need right now is a burger. The biggest greasiest burger they make. Yo, baby daddy," she hollered across the bar to Enzo. "I'll have a club soda."

I smothered a chuckle. But then she went completely still, the blood drained from her face.

"Nor?" Arianne asked, touching her arm.

"I think I just... peed myself."

"Ew, gross. That's just—babe, what the hell?" Matteo doubled over from where Caitlin had jabbed him in the ribs.

"Are you having any pains?"

"Just Braxton Hicks, the OB-GYN said it's completely normal this far in. Why?"

"Because I don't think you peed yourself, Nor." Arianne blanched. "I think your water just broke."

"My... *what*? Lorenzo Marchetti get your ass over here right now." She started hyperventilating.

"Shit, what can we do?" I asked.

"We need to get her to the hospital." Arianne was in full crisis mode. "Nicco make sure Enzo is in one piece. We can take her in our SUV."

"The baby's coming... now?" Nora started crying. "But it isn't time, it isn't—"

"Shh. We're all right here, and everything is going to be fine."

Alessia burrowed deeper into my side as we watched Arianne and Matteo help Nora out of the booth. "We'll meet you there," she said, glancing up at me.

I nodded like the pussy-whipped fool I already was. But I'd follow her anywhere. Pretty sure there wasn't a single thing I wouldn't do for her.

Because Alessia Marchetti owned me.

Heart. Body. And... Soul.

ALESSIA

Three hours later, we were all sitting in the hospital, waiting for an update on Nora's delivery.

Nicco had tried to persuade Tristan to take me home, but I wanted to be here. Nora was my friend too; more than that, she was family.

Besides, much to his disapproval, I was done letting Nicco dictate my life.

"I can't believe she's giving birth right now," Caitlin said.

"What do you think, Tink?" Matteo hooked his arm around her neck and drew her close. "Ready to make some babies with me?"

"Babies, plural?" She arched a brow. "Because I'm pretty sure you would freak the hell out if we ever had twins. Besides—"

The door swung open and Enzo burst into the corridor, tears streaming down his face. "It's a girl."

In all my years of knowing him, I don't think I'd ever seen Lorenzo Marchetti cry.

"Fuck, she's perfect. So tiny but so fucking perfect."

"Congratulations, cous." Tristan pulled him in for a hug. Nicco too. Then I went and Caitlin and Arianne.

"Get back in there, Daddy." Arianne sniffled. "We'll visit when you're all settled. Give Nora and the baby a big kiss from all of us."

He nodded, then ran a hand down his face, completely awestruck, and slipped back into the room.

"I can't believe he's a father," Tristan murmured.

"That little girl is going to have him wrapped around her finger."

We all moved back to our seats, and Tristan pulled me into his side. "One day, Principessa. One day that will be you and me." He hugged me tighter, and I gazed up at him.

"I think I'd like that," I whispered.

I think I'd like that a lot.

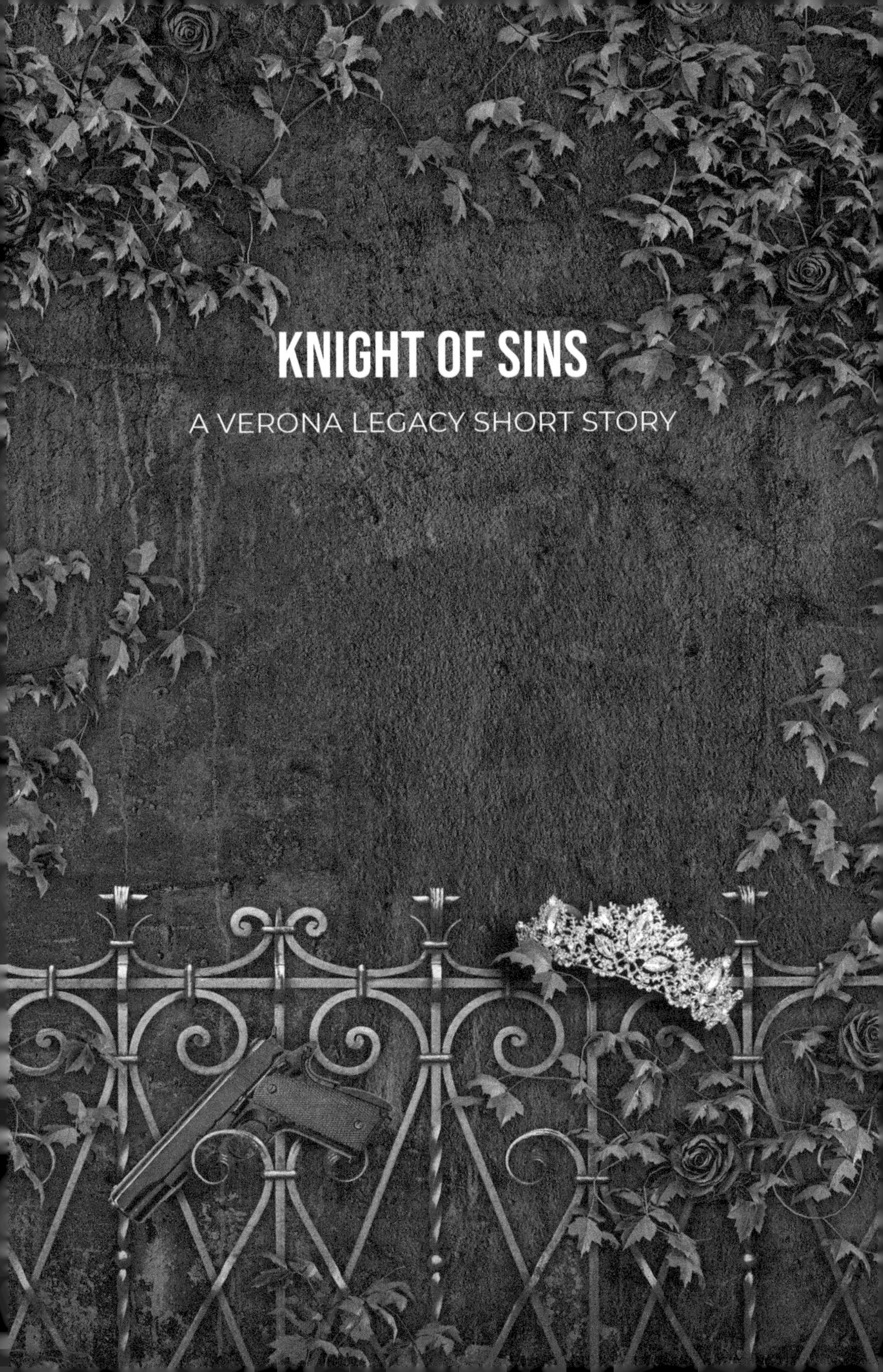
KNIGHT OF SINS
A VERONA LEGACY SHORT STORY

ONE

ARABELLA

"OH MY GOD, it's so beautiful." I beamed, letting my eyes run over the idyllic winter wonderland sprawled out in front of us.

"It's fucking freezing," my brother Matteo grumbled, burrowing deeper into his ski jacket.

"Bella's right. It's magical." His fiancée, Cait, commented while pressed into his side, and I watched as the frown melted off his face, replaced by sheer adoration.

Jesus, my brother had it bad.

"You should have waited to propose," I said. "This would have been amazing."

"Oh, I don't know"—Cait grinned up at him—"It was pretty special."

"Okay, lovebirds, let's do this." I readjusted my wooly pom-pom hat and took off toward the row of private cabins.

This was exactly what I needed—a long weekend away from everything.

I thought college would be fun. It was supposed to be fun. But so far, it had been nothing more than a string of bad dates, endless deadlines, and killer hangovers.

"Last on the left," my cousin Nicco said from behind me.

"Wow, it's... huge."

The two-story Swiss chalet sat proudly against the snowy backdrop. Complete with a first-floor wraparound porch and an overhanging wooden roof. It was the perfect winter getaway.

"I'm so excited." His sister—and my best friend—Alessia, laced her arm through mine. "This is just what we need."

A strange pang went through me. She made it sound like it was what *we* needed, but I suspected she was talking about her and her boyfriend. They were still in that annoying honeymoon phase where they couldn't keep their hands off each other.

Thankfully, Nicco would be around for the weekend, so I wouldn't have to endure too much PDA.

Nicco went ahead and let us in, the smell of pine and berries greeting us.

"You did good, cous." I flashed him a smile. "This place is—"

"Too fucking cold." My brother stomped inside, shaking off the snow all over me.

"Matt!" I shrieked, and everyone laughed.

It was a real family affair. Me, my brother, and his fiancée Caitlin. Nicco, his wife, and their daughter—my gorgeous niece Lucia. Alessia and her partner Tristan. And our cousin Enzo, his fiancée Nora, their daughter Chiara, and Nora's brother Gio.

After the recent passing of Nicco and Alessia's father, Uncle Antonio, Nicco had arranged the long weekend in Gstaad, Switzerland, for the twelve of us. Family time, he said. But really, we all knew it was his way of escaping the responsibilities and pressure that lay on his shoulders now as the boss of the Marchetti family.

"What's the room situation?" Tristan asked, and Nicco threw him a murderous look.

"Nic," Alessia sighed. "I thought we were past this."

"Past the part where the stronzo is sleeping with his little sister? Good luck with that, Sia," Enzo chuckled, squeezing her shoulder as he moved further into the cabin.

"Niccolò." Arianne handed him Lucia. "You promised."

"I know, Bambolina." He kissed them both, making Lucia chuckle, the soft sound cutting through the heavy tension and making everyone smile.

That little girl had everyone wrapped around her little finger, and there was nothing more amusing than watching four brooding mafioso dote on her and baby Chiara.

Gio didn't count—he wasn't one of them. Not really.

He'd left Verona County years ago to go to college in Philadelphia and bought an apartment there with his fiancée after they graduated.

Ex-fiancée.

I glanced over at him, noting the sadness in his eyes. After returning home, he'd put on a brave face, but we all saw the cracks. And it was the holidays—the worst time of the year to be alone.

His tortured gaze snagged on mine, and I smiled. But he didn't return it.

Okay then.

With a little sigh, I announced, "I'm going to check out the bedrooms."

"You take a twin," someone called after me, and I waved them off.

I knew the deal. I was used to playing the spare wheel around them all. At least Gio was here this time, and maybe we could cause some trouble together if I could only convince him to turn his frown upside down.

But it was the holidays, and we were at a gorgeous ski resort with nothing to do but enjoy the festivities and take in the sights.

He couldn't stay miserable for long.

Surely.

After showering the eleven-hour journey off me, I joined my friends and family downstairs for dinner.

"Holy cow, something smells good." My stomach growled as I snagged a cookie off the plate on the counter.

"Bella, this is Jacques, our chef for the weekend."

A young man currently at the stove glanced back at me and grinned. "Bonjour," he said with a smile.

"Bonjour, Jacques, and what is that divine smell?"

"Älplermagronen or, as it's sometimes known, Alpine macaroni."

"Sounds incredible." I helped myself to a glass of champagne and hopped on the counter beside him. "Do you mind if I—"

"Come on, pulce, leave the poor kid alone," Matteo called, and I flipped him off.

"You are trouble, no?" Jacques chuckled, and I frowned.

"What—"

A high-pitched toddler shriek filled the room, and I watched with mild amusement as Enzo and Tristan chased Lucia around the sectional. She was the cutest toddler I'd ever seen in her tulle-fairy dress and little ringlets.

"So, Jacques, are you—"

"I'm sorry," he said in a thick French accent. "But I must concentrate."

"Oh, okay." I slid off the counter, dejection sitting heavy in my stomach.

I wasn't used to being dismissed by a guy. Usually, guys waited until after they got what they wanted—or until they realized who my brother and cousins were.

It was easier for me to disguise my true identity being a Bellatoni and not a Marchetti. But the truth usually came out... and sent my guy of the moment running for the hills.

Eight dates.

I'd been on eight dates since starting at Montague University. And not one of them made it past date number four. But I didn't let that deter me because my prince was out there somewhere. Maybe I just had to kiss a whole lot of frogs before I found him.

"Bella, what's wrong?" Alessia touched my arm, and I startled.

"N-nothing."

"Did he say something to you?" She tilted her head toward our chef.

"Who, Jacques? No. I'm fine. Just a little tired. Isn't this place great?"

"It's something, although I'm not looking forward to tomorrow when they all want to try the snow sports."

"You're not going to join us?"

"Us? Please tell me you're not going to try—"

"Hell, yes, I am. I haven't come all the way to Switzerland to watch the guys have all the fun. You don't have to do anything too risky; they have beginner slopes," I said.

"I think I'll stick to watching."

"Your loss." I shrugged.

"Have you spoken to Gio at all? He seems so... sad." Alessia glanced around the cabin, but Gio was nowhere to be seen.

"Not really. I tried to make small talk on the plane, but he basically told me to go to hell."

"He's hurting."

"Yeah, I know. But it's been four months." His fiancée had ended things over the summer, and he'd moved back to Verona County. Nicco had given him an apartment in one of his buildings until Gio could get back on his feet. But it was taking time.

He rarely attended family gatherings, and when he did, he sucked the joy from the room like a black hole.

"He had their whole lives planned out"—Alessia grimaced—"that's got to hurt."

"Yeah."

Not that I would know. I had yet to meet Mr. Right. But I was only eighteen. Life was for living, experiencing things, and having fun.

So why did I feel so empty all of the time?

As if something was missing?

Part of me knew why. It was hard watching everyone around you fall hopelessly in love—my cousins Nicco, Enzo, and then Matteo. And now Alessia was completely smitten with Tristan. I might have been young, but family was everything to me, and I wanted that—I wanted what they all had.

I forced the negative thoughts out of my mind and pasted on a bright smile. "I'm going to find him," I said.

"Are you sure that's a good idea?"

"Relax. Sia, I'm not going to torment the poor guy. But he's single, and I'm single; we can bond over being the odd ones out."

"You're not the odd ones out." She frowned.

"You know what I mean. I know I'm a catch," I chuckled, but it came out strangled.

"Bella, what is—"

"There she is." Tristan hooked his arm around Alessia's waist and pulled her back into his chest, nuzzling her shoulder.

A dreamy look washed over her, and I gagged. "That's my cue to leave."

"No, Bella, you don't—"

But I was already gone, leaving the lovebirds to it.

I loved my family more than anything, but the constant PDA was enough to send any single gal crazy.

"Dinner is almost ready," Jacques announced. "If you would like to be seated."

"I suppose I'll go and drag Gio out of his room." Nora glanced toward the stairs, but I intercepted her.

"I'll go."

"I'm not sure he—"

"Relax." I waved her off. "I got it."

"Fine. But don't blame me if he bites your head off."

I climbed the stairs, humming a little tune to myself. Gio had chosen the second room on the third floor. The room right opposite mine. I guess he'd wanted to avoid the couples too.

I got it. It wasn't easy always being around them, but for him, it must have been ten times worse.

He'd had that. His person. His whole future was mapped out before him. But it had been months since they split. The guy needed to get back on the horse and have a little fun. Or at least, distract himself from all the misery.

I walked up to his door and gently knocked. "Gio, dinner's almost ready."

"Not hungry," he replied flatly.

"Come on. You can't hide in there all evening. We're in Switzerland. And when in Switz—"

"I said I'm not hungry."

Irritation rolled through me, but I breathed it out. I was used to dealing with stubborn men—my family was full of them.

Gripping the door handle, I turned it and walked inside.

"Bella, what the fuck?" Gio reached for the towel on the bed, banding it around his waist to cover his very hard, very thick—

"Oh, God. God, sorry." I clapped a hand over my face. "I'm—" I spun around, embarrassment burning my cheeks. "I didn't realize you were..."

"Naked?" I caught a slight hint of amusement in his voice. But it quickly diminished when he grumbled, "Do you make a habit of walking into bedrooms without warning?"

"Habit, no. But the occasional error in judgment, yes. I'm sorry, I should go." I went to hurry from the room.

"It's okay. You can look now."

I realized my mistake the second I turned and found him standing in a pair of fitted black boxer briefs. They hugged his muscular thighs, sitting snugly on his tapered waist.

Sweet baby Jesus, Gio had the kind of body artists only dreamed of painting.

"I..."

"You're staring," he ground out, not even a flicker of amusement this time.

"I... crap, sorry. I just didn't expect... never mind." I was completely tongue-tied, and he was looking at me like I was nothing more than dirt on his shoe. "Dinner," I rushed out. "You should come down for dinner."

Then I ran out of his room, silently praying that I could erase the image of him naked from my head.

Because Gio Abato was the most beautiful man I'd ever seen naked.

And that was a problem.

TWO

GIO

DRAGGING A HAND DOWN MY FACE, I watched Bella flee from the room.

We weren't friends, not really. None of us were. The Marchetti and Bellatoni were my sister's friends—her future family. I'd left Verona County eight years ago for college and settled in Philadelphia after graduating from UPenn. I had my whole life planned out.

A life with Jordan.

My heart squeezed, pain radiating through me. I'd never much believed in heartbreak before. I guess I hadn't had to give it any thought because I was in love. I was one hundred percent secure in my relationship. I was ready to go whole hog—house, wedding, a family.

I'd wanted it all with her, but it wasn't enough.

I wasn't enough.

Fuck.

This weekend was going to be the worst kind of torture. I knew Nora was only trying to do a good thing by inviting me on the trip.

"You need to get away for a bit," she'd said.

Mom and Dad had obviously felt the same because they'd practically packed my suitcase for me.

How fucking pathetic. A twenty-six-year-old man is being forced on a family vacation by his sister and parents. All because I couldn't get my shit together.

But how do you get over losing everything?

"Gio, let's go," Enzo's gruff voice filtered down the hall. "Nora wants you at dinner. Don't disappoint her."

I winced.

The fucker knew how to tug on my heartstrings—the ones still intact, anyway.

I pulled on a pair of jeans and a cable-knit sweater, ran some wax through my hair, and made my way downstairs. Nora would only come looking if I didn't make an appearance. She was worse than Mamma.

Part of me got it; I was her big brother. The one who was supposed to have his shit together, but I felt lost ever since Jordan had ended things.

The sound of laughter settled in the pit of my stomach, and I sucked in a sharp breath when I hit the bottom step and found them all around the table, about to eat.

"You're here." Nora leapt up, making her way over to me. "I was getting worried." She kissed my cheeks. Left and then right.

"Sorry, I took a shower."

"It's fine. You're here now. We saved you a seat next to Bella."

My eyes immediately found her at the end of the table. She looked like a deer caught in headlights as she ducked her head and pretended to inspect something on her plate.

My mouth twitched a little. Little Bellatoni sure embarrassed easily, which was surprising given how much of a notorious flirt she was.

"Come," Nicco said, "let's eat."

I made my way over to the far end of the long table and sat down beside Arabella, hyper-aware of my thigh brushing hers as I tucked myself in.

"Sorry," she whispered, and I met her wide-eyed stare again.

"Sorry, you burst into my room uninvited?" I shot back through gritted teeth. "Or sorry you saw my dick?"

I hadn't anticipated saying that, but it was too late now. Her breath caught, and she started choking on air.

"Bella, what's wrong?" Alessia said, leaning over to pass her the jug of water.

"I'm okay." She flashed me an irritated look. But I saw the slight stain on her cheeks.

"Jacques, this looks incredible." Arianne smiled warmly at him as he began to serve.

When he reached our end of the table, I didn't miss the way his eyes lingered on Bella for a little too long. Not that I blamed him. She looked good.

She always did.

The pale green sweater dress hugged her curves, long brown hair spilling over her shoulders in loose waves, framing her heart-shaped face. Her eyes—

Fuck, what was I saying?

Four months without sex was seriously screwing with my common sense. I wasn't attracted to Arabella Bellatoni. She was eighteen, for fuck's sake. Barely an adult. She went through guys the way kids went through candy. I'd heard enough of the stories. She was a party girl who enjoyed the attention.

Sure, she looked good. In a way that any hot-blooded male would find a pretty brunette with a slim curvy figure and big brown come-to-bed eyes attractive.

Shit, Abato. You cannot lust after Matteo's little sister. A) She's too young, and B) Matteo will have your balls if you so much as look in her direction.

I hitched my chair further to the right, putting some space between us. Bella stared up at me, frowning. "Problem?" she mouthed.

"It's your perfume," I mumbled.

"My... perfume. There's nothing wrong with my—"

"They say less is more for a reason."

It was a douchebag thing to say. But I needed her to stop looking at me like that—looking at me, period.

"Oh." Her expression fell, and I felt like an asshole. But it was better this way. Better than her trying to make me her vacation project.

I didn't need her help.

I didn't need anyone's help.

Because no one could fix me.

No one could ever replace Jordan.

"Here"—the man slid a drink my way—"you look like you could use this."

"Thanks." I dipped my head in appreciation.

"I'm Felix," he said.

"Gio."

"Why the long face?"

"Family vacation." The lie rolled off my tongue as I nursed the drink. I wasn't looking to open up to a stranger. But I had been quick to bail on dinner.

"Enough said."

He leaned back against the bar, the sleeves of his plaid shirt rolled up to the elbow. He had that unkempt cool artist vibe going for him.

"This place is something else, isn't it?"

"It's something alright." I scanned the room.

"Do you ski or board?" he asked, and I shook my head.

"Neither. I'm here for the whisky."

He chuckled at that. "I can't fault you there."

"There you are." A petite blonde sidled up to him, scraping her nails along his bearded jaw.

"Mmm, you look good enough to eat." He kissed her deeply, uncaring that they had an audience of one.

I cleared my throat, shifting uncomfortably on my stool. I hadn't fled the cabin to come here and have another relationship shoved down my throat.

Felix chuckled again, running his hand down her skintight wholly-inappropriate-for-a-ski-resort black dress. "Sorry, she loves to tease me, and I can't resist. This is Gio, my new friend." He winked.

"Hello, I'm Sapphire."

"Nice to meet you." I downed the rest of my drink, aware of the chemistry crackling between them.

I'd had that once. Desire so strong it made you giddy inside. Love so pure you wanted that shit injected into your veins. Now I had nothing but memories and a fuck ton of resentment and anger.

Sapphire moved her mouth to Felix's ear and whispered something. I caught the words strawberries and champagne.

"You'll have to excuse us," he said, his eyes brimming with desire. "We have some business to attend to."

It didn't take a genius to figure out what business that might be.

Jealousy surged through me as I gave them a polite nod and watched them walk away. They only had eyes for each other, the two lost in their own little bubble.

Fuck.

It was a bad idea coming here. But I'd needed to escape the cabin. I'd needed to get out of there so I could just breathe.

"Another one." I pushed my empty glass across the bar, and the bartender picked it up.

"Coming right up," he said in a thick French accent.

"Actually," I blurted, "better make it a double."

The room spun. Round and round. But at least there wasn't any room to think when you couldn't see straight.

After the guy I'd met at the bar and his woman had disappeared, I'd drained another three double whiskys. No one else approached me. No one even looked my way, too busy enjoying the festivities. The soft flutter of music from the pretty pianist playing on a grand piano in the corner of the room. The elegant and subtle décor. Good conversation and laughter.

I didn't want to laugh. I wasn't sure I even could laugh anymore. Hearing Jordan saying she didn't want me, that she didn't want the future we'd planned, killed something inside me. It ripped out my heart and left me hollow and hurting.

Fuck.

I needed another drink. I needed to forget. I just need the constant pain to stop.

Lifting my glass, I waved it at the bartender and mouthed, "another." His brows pinched, but he got me the drink anyway.

I shouldn't have got on the fucking plane. This weekend was going to be nothing more than a painful reminder of everything I'd lost.

"There you are." A small hand landed on my shoulder, and I glanced back through glassy eyes to find Arabella smiling sadly at me.

"What the fuck do you want?"

"I came to make sure you were okay. After—"

"Don't do that." I knocked her hand away as I whirled around on her. "Don't pretend to know what I'm going through or how hard it is. You're a kid, Bella. A fucking kid, and I'm—"

"An asshole?" Her brow arched as she scowled at me.

"Whatever, you should go."

"I'll take a Long Island iced tea, please," she said to the bartender over my shoulder.

"She won't. She's only eighteen," I spat.

"Newsflash, Gio, the drinking age is sixteen here." She grabbed the glass and brought the straw to her lips, making a show of taking a long drink. Her big brown eyes didn't leave mine, and I tumbled into their bottomless depths.

Fuck.

She was stunning.

And I was trashed.

It was the whisky talking.

"What?" she asked.

"N-nothing. I came to drink alone. So you should go find somewhere else to sit."

A flicker of hurt moved across her face, but she steeled herself. "Fine. I'm sure I can find some young, hot guys to talk to. Enjoy the rest of your evening." She turned her back on me and started to walk away, but my hand shot out, snagging her wrist.

Arabella's eyes flashed to mine. "Yes?"

"Stay," I sighed. "You can stay."

Her lips curved a fraction. "You need to switch to water," she said. "I'll never be able to carry you back to the cabin."

"I'm not that drunk," I huffed.

She leaned in a little, narrowing her eyes right at me. "You look drunk."

"You look..." I stopped myself, panic rising inside me like a tidal wave. Shit, what had I been about to say?

Get a grip, Abato. Get a fucking grip.

But she was so beautiful and here—Arabella was here. Unlike Jordan, who had left me at the first taste of something better—someone better.

A sharp stab of pain went through me.

"Gio, what is it?" Bella asked.

"I need another drink," I groaned, turning away from her.

This was a mistake.

All of it.

But at least in about three more drinks' time, I wouldn't even be able to remember my own name.

THREE

ARABELLA

GIO IGNORED ME.

For a second, I'd thought he might actually let me in and talk to me. But after the strange moment between us, he turned his back on me and continued drinking whisky like it was his life source.

He was hurting. That much was obvious. And for some strange reason, I wanted to help him.

I wanted to make him smile.

It was my biggest flaw, trying to fix people. Trying to be what they needed. Sometimes, at my own expense. But I had an innate desire to be close to people. To feel needed. Wanted.

It made something light up inside me. So sitting here for the best part of an hour, watching Gio drown his sorrows in whisky while not sparing me a second glance, hurt a little.

Okay, it hurt a lot.

Nobody else had bothered to come after him, happy to let him wallow. But then, everyone else had somebody. They weren't alone, always wondering when it would be their turn.

I let out a soft sigh, but still, Gio ignored me. "Maybe we should head back," I said, reaching for his arm. "It's getting late."

"You go," he slurred, barely meeting my gaze.

Jesus, he was wasted.

"Come on, Gio, I'm not leaving you here."

"The lady is right," the bartender interjected. "You've had enough, friend."

"My money is as good as anyone's." Gio pulled out his wallet and slammed it down on the counter, making the glasses rattle. "I want another—"

"Gio, please," I whisper-hissed, aware that he was drawing attention.

"Just go home, Bambina. I don't want you here."

Well then.

With a heavy sigh, I grabbed his arm and yanked sharply. "We're leaving. Now. Or I'll call my brother and Enzo."

His eyes widened, swirling with anger and disbelief. "You wouldn't..."

"Try me. You're causing a scene, and people are staring."

"Let them—"

"Gio," I implored, "please."

His hard gaze faltered, a streak of something going through his expression. He blinked at me. "God, you're beautiful, Bambina." He reached out and stroked his thumb down my cheek, sparking a shiver down my spine.

"Gio," I breathed, gently pushing his hand away.

"I just want it to stop, Bella. In here." He grabbed my hand and pressed it to his chest, right over his heart.

"I—"

"Shit." He hiccoughed, clapping a hand over his mouth.

Gio bolted from the stool and staggered toward the door. I gave the bartender an apologetic smile, prattled off our cabin number for the tab, and hurried after him.

I found him hidden in the shadows, puking up top-shelf whisky around the corner of the bar.

"I'll get you some water," I said.

"N-no." He thrust out a hand. "I'm okay. I'm... okay now." Wiping his mouth with the back of his hand, he stood, inhaling a shuddering breath. "Sorry, you had to see that."

"I've seen worse." I shrugged. "Ready to go home?"

Pain flashed in his eyes again. "Home?" A bitter laugh spilled from his lips. "I don't know where the fuck home is anymore."

By the time we returned to the cabin, I was breathless and sweating under my thick, padded jacket.

Gio hung over my shoulder, weighing me down, but I stood firm, taking his weight under my petite frame. The powdery snow crunched under my boots as I dug out the keycard and hauled him up the three steps to the door.

"Think you can manage to stand?"

"Yeah," he murmured, grabbing the wooden railing while I opened the door.

"It's late. Try and be quiet in case everyone is sleeping."

I very much doubted Matteo and Cait were asleep. They'd mentioned checking out the hot tub on the deck out back. It was a gorgeous space with a wooden gazebo, a built-in fire pit, and an outside bar. They were probably having their own little party for two while Nicco, Arianne, Nora, and Enzo slept upstairs with the children. Tristan had whisked Alessia away earlier on a romantic moonlit sleigh ride, and we all knew he had plans for her. I'd overheard Nicco warning him to look out for her more than once.

The smart lights came on the second I entered the cabin, casting an amber glow around the place.

"Come on." I helped Gio inside, but he lost his footing, sending us both careening across the room.

"Fuck," he breathed, wrapping his arms around me and spinning, so that his body broke our fall.

I braced myself and had my eyes screwed shut as we landed with a resounding thud.

"Gio?" I whispered, panic flooding me at the muted groan he made followed by deathly silence. "Gio." I pushed up on his chest, trying to get my bearings. "Are you—"

"Fuck, that hurt," he murmured.

Laughter pealed out of me. We were a mess, me half strewn over him, our legs tangled, and faces pressed close. He frowned up at me, his dark eyes glinting under the dim lighting, and the air crackled around us.

"Gio, I just wanted to say—"

He exhaled, and the bitter scent of vomit hit me, and I reared back.

"What... oh." He gently nudged me off him, and I rolled to the side, clambering to my hands and knees so I could stand.

"I need to take a shower," he said, barely looking at me.

We were back to that then.

A strange pang of disappointment went through me, which was ridiculous. It wasn't like we had bonded tonight—he ignored me most of the time. But I couldn't help feeling sorry for him. He looked so... sad.

"Do you want me to help?"

"No," he rushed out. "You've done enough. I'll be fine."

Gio staggered toward the staircase, leaving me all alone.

Wondering what I'd done that was so wrong.

The next morning, Gio didn't surface for breakfast.

"Where the fuck is he?" Enzo grumbled. "I thought he wanted to hit the slopes."

"Cut him a little slack." Nora dropped a kiss on his cheek as she got up from the table. "He's still wallowing."

"He needs to get back on the horse," Matteo added. "Fuck Jordan right out of his psyche."

"Babe." Caitlin glowered. "Children present."

Lucia cooed at that, clapping her pudgy little hands together while Chiara slept peacefully in her mom's arms.

"Here, let me take her while you eat." Alessia scooped up our niece from Arianne and started pacing the living room, bouncing Lucia in her arms.

"What do you want to do today?" somebody said.

It took me a moment to realize my brother was talking to me.

"Sorry, what?"

"Are you okay? You're acting strange."

"No, I'm not."

"You were completely zoned out just now, staring at the..."—he twisted around to see what had my attention—"the stairs."

"Nope. Just staring because I didn't get much sleep."

Lying in bed opposite Gio's room, wondering what he was doing, and what he was thinking. Questioning whether or not I should go check on him.

I didn't.

He'd made it pretty obvious he didn't appreciate me sticking my nose into his business. Still, it didn't stop me from staring at the door, wondering.

"I'm going to check on Gio." Nora put her mug next to the sink and headed upstairs.

Not one of them knew what had happened last night, and I was all too happy for it to stay that way.

"We're hitting the slopes if you want to come," Matteo added.

"I think I'm going to walk into town and check out the shops. But thanks."

"Alessia and I are heading to the spa if you want to join us." Caitlin smiled, but it was at odds with the dejection swimming in my stomach.

"You're going to the spa?" I asked. It was the first I'd heard about it.

"Yeah, they have all these different treatments," Alessia said. "Hot stones and Swedish massage. It looks amazing."

"Sounds great."

"You should come. The guys are going to meet us afterward and get a massage."

"Oh, it's a couples thing?"

"What, no? It's not like that. We want you to come."

So much so that this was the first time I'd heard about their spa plans.

"I think I'm going to check out the shops. But you guys have fun."

"Are you sure?" Alessia followed me away from everyone else. "I feel bad now, but Cait asked me if I wanted to—"

"Hey, it's fine. The two of you can bond. And I can... shop." I shrugged. "It's all good."

"You're sure? We can do something together tonight or tomorrow."

I nodded, not trusting myself to reply. Because we both knew it wouldn't happen. She was too wrapped up in her new relationship. And I got it. I did. She and Tristan were head over heels in love. But losing my best friend to a guy and their new life together was hard.

"Actually, I think I'm going to head out now and explore. I'll see you all later."

"Bella, hold up." Matteo jogged over to the door; concern etched into his face. "You good, pulce?"

"I'm fine." I forced a smile. "I promise."

"Cait didn't mean to exclude you. That's not—"

"It's fine, really," I chuckled, hoping it didn't sound as fake as it felt. "It's everyone's vacation, and besides, I really do want to check out the stores."

"We can hang out tomorrow. Just the two of us."

Sweet baby Jesus. There was nothing more embarrassing than a pity offer from my big brother.

Maybe I should have stayed at home after all. But usually, I didn't mind hanging out with my brother and our family. I did love them all so much. Even if being around four couples was a constant reminder that I was the odd one out.

I was only eighteen, sure. But when you grew up in a tight Italian family who lived by a strict code of loyalty and love, it was hard not to want to follow in their footsteps.

To meet *my* knight in shining armor.

"We have a reservation at Élégance tonight. You can dress up and play princess." He winked, and I smiled.

"Who knows, maybe I'll even meet my prince."

His smile dropped, and he rubbed his jaw. "Not until you're at least twenty-one, Bella. I'm not ready for you to date."

"Alessia is with Tristan," I countered.

"That's different. He... saved her life."

"So what you're saying is, I need to get myself into a precarious situation and hope a dashing young man will rescue me? And then he'll be worthy in your eyes?"

"Bella..." He warned.

"Have fun on the slopes, dear brother. I intend to shop my heart out."

And my worries away.

FOUR

GIO

I HAD the cabin to myself. Even Jacques had disappeared. But I appreciated the silence.

After dragging myself into the ridiculously huge walk-in shower, I threw on some clean clothes and went in search of food to soak up my killer hangover.

I'd overdone it last night. Tried—and failed—to drown my sorrows in the bottom of a glass of whisky.

Then, to top it all off, I'd been a total asshole to Arabella when all she'd tried to do was help me.

Fuck. I still remember how it felt when we landed on the floor in a heap of limbs. Feeling her tight little body pressed up against mine. The zing of desire blasted through me, rocking me to my broken core.

Four months.

Four months, and I hadn't so much as touched another woman. Still consumed by the devastation and loss of Jordan. The life I had planned for us. And now I was thinking highly inappropriate things about my future brother-in-law's cousin—his eighteen-year-old bratty cousin.

When had life gotten so fucking complicated?

Right about the time, Jordan dumped your sorry ass and moved on to bigger and better things.

But maybe there was a silver lining in all this. Maybe my weird and inappropriate moment with Arabella was a sign it was time to get back on the horse. Fuck Jordan and her betrayal right out of my system.

Gstaad was probably full of beautiful women looking for a night of no string's passion. All I had to do was get out there and find a willing volunteer.

Yeah, this was a good thing.

I needed sex—hot, dirty, sweaty sex without the emotional attachment. Once my dick got with the program and realized we could enjoy sex again, maybe I'd shake the feeling of hopelessness that seemed to follow me wherever I went.

Feeling a lick of determination I hadn't felt in a long time, I made myself something to eat and downed two cups of coffee to chase away the lingering headache.

Enzo had texted earlier to say they were hitting the snow park first, but I'd replied that I wasn't feeling up to it. The last thing I wanted was to listen to him, Matteo, Tristan, and Nicco talk about their women and how wonderful their lives were.

But meaningless, casual sex—that I could do.

At least, that was the plan as I tidied up the kitchen, pulled on my thick padded jacket, and left the cabin. The snowfall was light but had already filled over mine and Bella's footsteps from the night before.

I shoved those thoughts away. I didn't need to be thinking about her or her smart mouth and luscious curves.

I needed a woman who knew what they wanted and understood that I was looking for a transaction, not a holiday fling.

No feelings. If this was going to work, that was the rule. I didn't have the capacity to let someone in again.

Not after how broken Jordan had left me.

I ended up at the main hotel bar, perched on a stool, watching people come and go. I started on soda, my stomach still a little queasy. But after forty minutes, I grew restless and switched to beer. Some European ale that went down a little too easily.

"Good, yah?" The bartender asked me, and I nodded.

"Very."

He smiled and moved on to his next patron, a sexy redhead in a black all-in-one outfit and fur-lined heeled boots. She noticed me looking in her direction and gave me a coquettish smile. "I'm Liesel."

"Gio. I'll get this." I indicated to the bartender.

"Thank you." She moved closer, dragging her perfectly manicured nails along the bar, and scanned my hand. "No ring?" Her brow arched.

"I'm single."

She held up her left hand and wiggled her fingers. "What a coincidence."

Hardly.

I resisted the urge to roll my eyes, instead forcing a smile. "How long are you here?"

"Until Monday. We flew in for the weekend."

"We?" I asked.

"Oh, I'm traveling with my sister and her family. I just got out of a bad relationship, so they thought a trip to Gstaad might help me heal." She raked her gaze over my body, not bothering to hide the lust in her eyes.

"Shall we get a table?"

Her whole face lit up. "That sounds like an excellent idea."

We made our way over to one of the booths at the back of the room near the large open fire. It crackled and hissed, throwing out a wall of heat. But Liesel didn't seem to mind, using it as an excuse to strip out of her all-in-one, revealing a skintight tank top underneath. She flicked her long red hair over one shoulder and smirked. "That's better."

I couldn't have planned this more perfectly. It was obvious she was up for it. Bad breakup. Check. On vacation with her family. Check. Ready to get back on the horse. Check. Beautiful face and a banging body. Check. At least in her mid-twenties. Check.

"So, Gio, what do you do?"

"I recently moved home, so I'm kind of between jobs. I'm helping my dad out a little with the family business. Doing some work with my sister's fiancé.

"And where is home? I detect an American accent."

"I hail from Verona County, Rhode Island. You?"

"I'm from Austria."

"Well, it's nice to meet you." I lifted my drink, and she clinked her glass against mine.

"Likewise. Something tells me we're going to be very good friends, Gio from Rhode Island."

I couldn't do it.

Fuck.

What a fucking shitshow.

Liesel had been perfect. Funny and sweet and willing—so fucking willing. But after almost two hours of talking and drinking, when she invited me back to her room, I couldn't do it.

My head was in the game, but my dick wasn't on board.

Not even a little bit.

Not when she pressed against me and kissed my jaw or ran her fingers down my chest.

Nothing.

So I'd made my excuses and gotten the hell out of there, shame biting at my heels as I trudged down the cobbled path. It was already dusk, the sun sinking behind the quaint snow-dusted rooftops.

I'd spent almost three hours with her, only to flake out at the final hurdle.

I needed a drink—something much stronger than the ale I'd been drinking.

I quickly texted my sister, saying I wouldn't be back yet, and turned off my phone.

I didn't want to deal with her or anyone else yet.

The street was lined with boutiques and bars. I ducked inside the nearest building and headed for the bar, drawing short, when I spotted Arabella at a table with some blond-haired guy I didn't recognize. She was laughing at something he said, eyes dancing with amusement as she hung on his every word.

Before I knew what I was doing, I marched toward them. "Who the fuck is this?" I demanded.

"G-Gio?" She blinked up at me, cheeks heating at my harsh words. "What are you—"

"The name's Benni. Benni with an I."

"Well, Benni with an I, fuck off. I'm here now, but thanks for keeping my girl company."

The fuck?

The words just came out, and I knew from the look of utter shock on her face I couldn't take them back.

"Uh, sorry, dude, but who are you?"

"I'm—"

"My cousin," Bella rushed out. "He's my older, much grumpier, and overprotective cousin." She flashed him a warm smile before pinning me with a death stare. "And he was just leaving."

I folded my arms over my chest and cocked a brow. "Yeah, not happening."

"Whoa, everyone, just take a chill pill." Benni with an I held up his hands. "We were just hanging, bro. No need to get—"

"Leave. Now."

"Y-yeah, okay. Catch you around, Bell."

"It's Bella," I corrected, anger rolling through me.

He took off, and Arabella shot up out of her seat too. "What the hell was that?" she seethed. "You completely embarrassed me."

"You're too good for a snowboarding hippy like Benni with an I."

"Gio! You're being ridiculous. You—"

"Get a drink with me?"

"What?" She balked. "Last night, you basically ignored me all night, and now you want to get a drink?"

"It's been a shitty day."

"What happened?" Concern flitted across her expression.

"Get that drink with me, and I'll tell you all about it."

"Fine. One drink. But I'd better text my brother and tell him I'm not going to make dinner."

"Maybe leave out the part where you say we're together."

Shit. Why did that sound so loaded?

"I didn't mean—"

"I know what you meant, Gio." Her lips twitched, and my dick stood to attention.

Motherfucker.

It responded to Arabella—the one girl I had no business going after—but it had wanted nothing to do with Liesel and her seductive smile and fiery red hair.

"What?" Her brows pinched.

"The bar," I blurted out. "We should move this to the bar."

If we sat at the bar, it would be less intimate. More like two friends shooting the shit after a long day on the slopes. Not that I'd been anywhere near the slopes yet.

Maybe tomorrow. If I didn't end up trashed again. Which was entirely possible, given the way Arabella was looking at me.

"What's your poison of choice?" I asked, pulling out a stool for her. She hopped up and smiled.

"I'll have a cocktail. Nothing too sweet."

"Let me guess because you're sweet enough."

She laughed at that.

"What's funny?"

"That's not typically a word people use to describe me."

"Oh?"

"No." Her gaze dropped, but I slid my fingers under her jaw and tilted her face up.

"Don't hide from me, Bambina."

The air turned thick around us, crackling with electricity.

"Bella, I—"

"What can I get you, sir?"

I snatched my hand away from Arabella and focused on the bartender, ignoring the way my heart crashed in my chest.

Nervous.

She made me nervous. Which was fucking ridiculous.

"A beer and a cocktail for the lady. Nothing too sweet." I glanced at Bella, and she smiled.

"So Benni with an I."

"Stop," she groaned, burying her face in her hands. "It was just a drink... well, at least it was until you ambushed us."

"I was looking out for you. We're a long way from home, Bambina."

"I'm eighteen, Gio. I grew up in a house full of overbearing men who always made it perfectly clear what would happen if anyone ever laid an unwanted hand on me. I know how to look out for myself."

Her words struck me deep in the chest. It was true. I'd never met three guys as fierce as Matteo, Nicco, and Enzo. But it was hardly any surprise given the world they grew up in. Given who they were.

It was the very reason I shouldn't be here with Arabella now. Noticing things.

Noticing her.

Matteo and his cousins would string me up and cut off my balls if they knew the dirty things running through my mind.

"Why do you keep looking at me like that?" Bella's lashes fluttered as she inhaled a small breath, tucking a strand of hair behind her ear.

"No reason," I lied to her.

But most of all, to myself.

FIVE

ARABELLA

SOMETHING WAS DIFFERENT ABOUT GIO. When he'd stormed up to the table and dismissed Benni like it was his God-given right to decide who I talked to or got a drink with, I'd almost kneed him in the balls.

I'd never been so embarrassed in all of my life—and Matteo Bellatoni was my older brother. But something had simmered in his dark gaze—torment and desire and... jealousy.

Gio was jealous, and I didn't know what that meant or if it could ever mean anything, but I was willing to find out.

"How is it?" he asked, watching me intently as I sipped my cocktail.

"It's good."

He gave a small nod, his throat bobbing.

"So... you were saying something about a shitty day?" I asked.

"Forget it. We don't need to talk about that," he said dismissively. "I'd rather hear all about Benni with an I."

"There's nothing to say. He saw me drinking alone and invited me to sit with him. It was innocent enough." Gio tsked at that, and I frowned. "What?"

"It's never innocent, Bambina. You know better than that."

"Jesus, *Dad*. It wasn't like I was going to sleep with him." He wasn't really my type, and despite what people thought, I wasn't a put-out-on-the-first-date kind of girl.

"Maybe not. But he definitely wanted to sleep with you."

"You don't know that."

"Single guy spots a woman all alone in a bar dressed like that"—his eyes raked over my body, sending a shiver down my spine—"and invited her to sit with him? He isn't looking for conversation, Bambina."

"You sound like you're speaking from experience."

"I..." Something flashed over his expression, and he ran a hand down the back of his neck.

"Oh my God, are you out looking to pick up a woman?"

"We're not talking about me. We're talking about you."

"You were, weren't you?" My stomach sank. I thought... Dammit, I don't know what I thought when he spotted me with Benni. But I didn't stop to consider that maybe he was out looking for a hookup.

"I just thought..." Gio glanced away from me, pain radiating from him. When he finally gave me his eyes again, all the disappointment I felt melted away. "I thought sex might help me move on," he admitted. "Get back on the horse. Put all the shit with Jordan behind me."

He heaved a heavy sigh, downing the rest of his drink and indicating to the bartender to bring him another.

"What happened?"

I wasn't sure I wanted to know the answer, but I needed to know.

"I... there was a woman. A redhead."

"Oh." My gaze dropped right along with my heart.

He'd hooked up with someone. Gio had... God, I was an idiot.

The last thing I wanted was to sit here and listen to him tell me all about some other woman, but he was clearly confused and hurting over it. And I wasn't a heartless bitch.

Besides, it was my own fault for imagining things that weren't there.

Gio didn't like me.

Why would he?

He'd been engaged, for God's sake. To Jordan, who was as stunning as she was kind—at least before she shredded his heart in two.

"Well, good for you." I fixed a smile on my face, refusing to let him see how much his confession had hurt me.

It was silly. Gio didn't owe me anything. He could hook up with whoever he wanted.

"I hope you got what you were—"

"I couldn't go through with it."

"What do you mean?"

"I mean... she invited me to her room, and I— fuck, I couldn't do it."

"Maybe you're not ready."

"Oh, I'm ready. It's been almost five months. I'm ready." He grabbed his new drink and took a long pull.

"I'm not following," I said. "If you're ready, and she was offering... What was the problem?"

"My dick."

"Your dick?" I spluttered over the word, flushing all over.

"He wasn't into her."

"Oh. So maybe you need to find another woman."

Jesus, was I his wing woman now? Because it sure felt like it.

"Nope. Pretty sure that won't help."

"It won't?" I frowned.

"It would seem my dick doesn't want just any woman, Bambina."

"It... it doesn't?"

He shook his head, a faint smirk tracing his lips. "No." Gio leaned in, ghosting his lips over the shell of my ear. "There's only one woman my dick is interested in..."

"Mm-hmm," I murmured, gulping a mouthful of air.

"You, Bambina." His hand glided along the side of my neck, burying deep in my hair. "It wants you."

"Oh."

"Oh?" He chuckled. "That's all you've got to say?"

"I... what do you want me to say?"

"How do you feel about one night of sin?"

"One night..."

He wanted one night with me.

I didn't know how to feel about that.

"I need it to stop, Bella." He inhaled a sharp breath. "I just need it to fucking stop. In here." Grabbing my hand, he pressed it to his chest and looked me in the eye. "Please."

God. How could I tell him no when he looked so sad, so vulnerable.

I didn't know Jordan, not really. But I'd crossed paths with them both a few times, and witnessed their love story from afar. She had owned his heart and cruelly gave it back in tatters. And now he was looking at me like I could somehow piece him back together.

One night.

He only wants one night.

"Yes," the word spilled from my lips before I could stop it.

Because that was who I was destined to be.

The friend. The confidante. The one-night stand.

But never the forever girl.

"Bella? Where are you?" Alessia asked.

"In some bar with a bunch of people." The lie came easily, too easily. "It's fine, Sia. I'm having fun."

"But what about dinner?"

"I already ate. You guys go and have fun. I'll see you back at the cabin later."

"Arabella?" My brother's voice came over the line. "Where the fuck—"

"Relax, Matt. I'm fine. I made a bunch of friends. We're dancing."

Gio grinned, waggling his brows as he leaned up against the side of one of the cabins. A smile looked good on him.

Too good.

We were both drunk. Not wasted or anything but enough to give us the courage to sneak back to the cabin and wait for everyone to leave for dinner.

"I swear to God, Bel—"

"Hi, it's me." Alessia came back on. "Sorry about Matt, he's—"

"An overprotective ass?"

"He only cares," she sighed.

"Sure. Well, I'm eighteen, and it's my vacation too. So I'm going to enjoy it. See you later."

"Bel—"

But I hung up. I didn't want to hear her apologies or excuses. She was on their side now—the couples' side.

"They're just about to leave," Gio said, pulling me into him. We hadn't kissed yet.

We hadn't really done anything except drink, talk, and watch each other.

It was the best kind of foreplay.

He looked at me like he didn't know what to do with me first. And it had butterflies fluttering wildly in my stomach.

We were doing this.

One night.

No promises.

Maybe I'd regret it come morning. But I didn't ever want to live life wondering what if.

Growing up in the Marchetti family, I'd seen firsthand how short life could be. How precious. I'd witnessed how one decision or moment could change everything. I'd watched Nicco and Arianne fight for their love. Watched Enzo risk it all for Nora. I'd seen my own brother do whatever it took to save the woman he loved.

Life—*love*—was never guaranteed in our world. So despite wanting what they'd all found, I still couldn't tell Gio no.

Because sometimes all you had were moments. Small snapshots in time that you had to make the most of.

The door to the cabin swung open, and our family and friends appeared, their laughter filling the air. Enzo carried a sleeping Chiara in his arms while Ari bounced Lucia on her hip. They looked so freaking adorable.

Gio was tense behind me while we waited for them to leave, piling into a sleek black SUV. The second it disappeared down the private driveway, he moved his mouth to my ear again and whispered, "Shall we?"

A nervous shiver ran through me, but I nodded.

Because there was no backing down now.

Gio wanted one night of sin, and I intended to give it to him.

"So..." I said, watching Gio as he unzipped his jacket and hung it on the rack.

"Come here." He crooked his finger toward me, and like a moth to a flame, I went willingly, falling into his arms.

He gripped my shoulders as nervous energy danced in my stomach, heat licking my insides. My mouth was dry, and my head was swimming with lust.

This was happening. It was really—

He kissed me. A light brush of his lips over mine while his hands slid deep into my hair, holding me there.

"Fuck, I have wanted to do that all night, la mia bellezza."

My heart fluttered wildly at his words.

My beauty.

Except, I wasn't his.

I never would be.

I shoved those thoughts out, wanting only to live in the moment. To take whatever pieces Gio was willing to give me.

Maybe this wasn't the start of my fairy tale—my happy ending—but it was still a chapter in my story.

He touched his head to mine, breathing me in, the significance of what we were about to do settling over us both.

"My room or yours?" he asked.

"Mine."

He nodded thickly, kissing me again. Deeper this time—running his tongue along the seam of my mouth, coaxing me to open for him. A whimper bubbled out of me at the taste of him. The feel of his tongue tangling with mine.

"Come on. I need to get my hands on you." He banded his arm around my waist with a possession that startled me.

Blood pounded between my ears as we climbed the staircase to our floor. His hands were all over me, mapping my curves like he wanted to learn every hidden dip and swell.

We didn't even make it to my room before he pushed me up against the wall and attacked my mouth with deep, drugging kisses that made lust swim in my mind.

"Gio," I breathed, clutching onto his shoulders.

"Shh, Bambina, I got you." He grabbed my thigh, hitching my leg around his waist as he rolled his hips into me.

"Oh God," I cried as his hard length pressed against my stomach.

"You feel that? Feel what you do to me?"

Yes, I wanted to cry. But I trapped the words, refusing to give them a voice.

Because it was one night.

That was all.

Even if I already knew I wanted more.

SIX

GIO

Fuck, she was perfect. Soft and curvy under my palms, Arabella's skin was smooth and warm. And I needed a taste.

I dropped my lips to the crook of her neck, licking and nipping.

"Gio." She raised up, clutching onto my shoulders tighter as I pressed into her, desperately seeking the heat of her pussy.

"My room," she breathed. "We should go into my room."

"Shit, yeah, okay."

I fumbled for the door handle, pushing it open. We stumbled inside, all hands touching and mouths kissing.

"Clothes off, now," I demanded. I needed to see her, to imprint the sight of her naked and wanting in my mind.

Because we only had this.

One night.

And I intended to make the most of it.

Arabella pulled away, smiling at me as if I hung the fucking moon.

Her hands went to her sweater as she walked backward, swaying her hips a little, mischief dancing in her eyes.

"Mmm," I purred, dropping into the chair in the corner of the room, lust crackling in my veins.

She got me something fierce. And I needed that. I needed to remember how it could be, needed to remember that my body liked sex.

That I fucking liked sex.

Pulling the dress up her body, she ripped it off in one smooth, seductive move. Her hands traced over her tits and down her stomach as she continued watching me.

"All of it," I said, leaning back in the chair, palming my rock-hard dick.

"So bossy." She rolled her eyes, slipping her hands into her pants and pushing them slowly down her hips.

My breath caught in my throat as I drank in the sight of her standing there in nothing more than her skimpy black underwear.

"Fuck," I hissed, pure lust running through my veins. "You are stunning, Bambina. Come here."

Arabella approached me, surprising the shit out of me when she dropped to her knees and crawled between my legs. I pushed my hand into her hair, cupping the side of her neck and brushing my thumb over her jaw. "The things I want to do to you."

"So do them. I'm right here, Gio. Tonight, I'm yours."

"I want to feel your mouth." My eyes dropped to my crotch as I rubbed the obvious bulge in my jeans.

"Take off your sweater first," she said. "I want to see you."

I hesitated.

Fuck, I hesitated.

Here she was—beautiful, bold Arabella offering herself to me for the night.

And I fucking hesitated.

"Gio?" Confusion danced in her eyes. "What's wrong?"

The silence stretched out between us, the confusion in her eyes turning to dejection.

"Maybe this was a bad idea." She got to her feet, refusing to meet my eyes as she went to leave.

"Wait." I grabbed Bella's wrist, tugging her back to me.

The second her eyes landed on mine. I was done. She might as well have torn right through my defenses and burrowed her way inside me.

"Gio, it's okay. We don't—"

"Yeah, we do." I pulled her closer, gliding my hands up her body. "I want this, Bambina. I want you. So fucking much."

"Show me," she whispered, running her fingers through my hair.

The tender intimate action sent shivers running down my spine.

My lips brushed her navel, and I dragged my tongue along her hip bone. Arabella moaned a soft whimper that hit me right in the stomach.

Fuck, she was sexy. Confident and soft under my hands. My mouth.

"Gio," she breathed again as I skimmed a palm over her bra, fumbling with the front clasp to get it open. The shells fell apart, and she slipped them off her body, revealing her pert tits. Anchoring my hands on her waist, I trailed my tongue up her stomach until my mouth closed over one of her peaks.

"God, yes," she moaned, fisting my hair tighter as I teased her, sucking and licking. Switching from one breast to the other.

One of my hands dipped between her thighs, trailing higher until my fingers grazed her damp panties. Working the material to one side, I pressed two fingers inside, curling them deeply, reveling in the way she gasped my name.

"You're so wet for me, Bambina."

"I... God, more. More..." she whimpered.

I worked her faster. Pumping my fingers in and out as my mouth continued feasting on her skin.

"I want you to come all over my fingers."

"Yes, God, yes." Bella started riding my hand, crying out when I hit that spot deep inside her. "Gio, God.... *God.*"

"That's it, Bambina. Give it to me."

My spare hand went to my jeans, popping the button. I managed to pull out my dick and fist myself while I got her off. She was so fucking sexy. I needed more. I needed to feel her wrapped around me.

"You almost there?" I asked.

Lips parted on a moan, she nodded. "So good... it's so damn good."

I pulled her closer, forcing her onto my lap. It made it a little harder to touch her like this, but Bella was too far gone to care, riding the waves of pleasure crashing over her.

I replaced my fingers with the tip of my dick, sliding it through her wetness, nudging her clit.

"Oh God," she cried, anchoring her hands over my shoulders.

"You like that, Bambina?"

"Yes... *yes.*" Bella shifted closer, impaling herself on my dick as her orgasm slammed into her. Our eyes locked as she trembled around me, tightening down on my dick.

Jesus, she felt good. Too good.

I wasn't going to last long at this rate.

"I can feel you coming." I smirked, feeling the shackles of the past few months slowly unravel.

I'd forgotten how good this could be—watching a woman fall. Seeing her come apart, *feeling* it.

"Move, Gio. I really need you to—"

I bucked upward, groaning at how fucking good it felt. My hand slid over the curve of Arabella's hips as I began to fuck her. She met me thrust for thrust, though, rolling her hips in a way that had me seeing stars.

"Fuck, you feel good." I wound my hand into the back of her hair to grip her nape and kiss her.

All teeth and tongue and sweet desperation.

"You take me so well, Bambina," I crooned, brushing my lips up her neck to the soft skin beneath her ear as she rode me. Perfectly circling her hips as I thrust up over and over.

"God, Gio... God..."

Her words made my chest swell. Fuck, I needed this. I needed to know I wasn't broken. That I could enjoy sex again. And Arabella ... well, she was perfect.

But I needed more.

Grabbing her hips, I managed to stand, carrying her over to the bed and laying her down. My knees hit the mattress as I fell on top of her, lifting her legs around my hips and slamming home, making her scream my name.

"Take it, Bambina. Take it all," I rasped, fucking her harder. Faster. Focused on nothing except the need to make her come first. Before I exploded.

Dipping a hand between us, I toyed with her clit, rubbing and pinching. Until Bella writhed beneath me, a breathless, boneless mess.

"Yes... yes... yes," she cried over and over.

"Come, Bambina. I need you to come."

"More... just a little—"

I pressed her knee higher and went as deep as I could until her body shuddered around me.

Arabella grabbed my face, kissing me as the orgasm crashed over her. I went harder, chasing my own release, the bottom of my spine tingling as I came with a deep groan.

"Fuck, Bambina," I breathed. "Fuck."

Silence settled over us as we both fought to catch our breath.

I'd done it.

I'd finally had sex after losing the love of my life.

I'd had sex with Arabella Bellatoni.

A freshman in college.

My future brother-in-law's cousin.

Fuck.

Fuck.

"Gio?" Bella gazed up at me, a dreamy look on her face. The kind girls got after sex.

"We should probably wrap this up and—fuck. We didn't use a condom."

"I'm on birth control, and I figured since you haven't been with anyone since..." She trailed off, the moment between us well and truly over.

"That's good," I said, rolling off her, panic creeping in, blotting out the post-sex glow I'd felt. "I should probably get to my own room before they get back."

"Oh, yeah." Disappointment flashed in her eyes. "Okay." She pulled the sheet over her body as I climbed off the bed and grabbed my clothes.

I hadn't even taken my jeans off all the way. Because this wasn't anything more than a quick fuck. One night of sin. A way to break the curse I'd been under ever since Jordan left me.

Making a beeline for the door, I glanced back at her. "So I guess I'll see you tomorrow?"

"Sure." She barely met my gaze, and a sticky trail of guilt snaked through me.

But we'd agreed this could only be one night.

So the second I walked out of her room, why did I feel like I'd just made a giant mistake?

I barely slept.

I heard everyone return, their laughter drifting up the stairs and down the hall.

Arabella didn't join them, and I didn't hear anyone check in on her. But I couldn't stop thinking about her. How good she'd felt riding me. How easy and right it had felt kissing her. Touching her.

But she was off-limits. Not to mention too young for me.

I wasn't ready to jump into a new relationship, and Matteo would never approve of his sister having a friends-with-benefits type of arrangement with me.

It was one night—that was all it could ever be.

But it didn't stop me from imagining waking her up and kissing her senselessly. Feeling her soft and pliant beneath me.

Fuck, she had blown my mind. The sex was that damn good. And I'd all but run out of there like a coward.

Because there was something between us, something more than lust and great sex. Arabella was funny and beautiful, and for some reason, she'd made it her business this trip to ensure I was okay.

Get her out of your head, Abato. It was one night. It can never happen again.

Noise down the hall informed me everyone was up and at it. I could hear Lucia and Chiara's little cries and murmurs as Nicco and Enzo no doubt carried them downstairs. They were good fathers. Doting, protective, involved. I'd wanted that. Fuck, I'd wanted it all with Jordan.

But she was gone, and with it, my dreams of a future together.

The thought didn't hit me like a wrecking ball this morning, though. I didn't get the same pang of hurt and betrayal I usually did. I was sad about everything I'd lost, sure. But I didn't feel devastated. Instead, I felt renewed. Strong. For the first time in what felt like forever, I felt like I could do this.

I could live.

There was only one person to thank for that.

And she was the one person I should have never gone near in the first place.

Shit.

I was in trouble.

SEVEN

ARABELLA

What's wrong with you, pulce?" Matteo slid into the seat next to me as I nursed my coffee.

"Nothing." I gave him a tight smile.

"Something happen last night?" he earnestly askeds, in full protective big brother mode.

"What? No! I'm fine. Just tired."

Like I was ever going to tell him I'd barely slept a wink, too confused over Gio's quick exit last night.

We'd agreed on one night. I knew that. But I hadn't expected him to come and then disappear like it had never happened.

Unless he really was just using me to move on.

God, what had I done?

I trapped a groan of frustration behind my lips, hoping Matteo wouldn't look too closely at my expression. Thankfully, Enzo plopped down beside him with Chiara in his arms.

"Hey, pretty girl." My brother took her pudgy little hand and blew raspberries on her cheek.

"Don't get her all riled up, Matt. She had us up half the night."

"Like you sleep anyway. You probably sit vigil on the side of her crib all night. Protecting her from the big bad, evil of the world."

"Fuck off," Enzo mouthed, humor crinkling his eyes.

I chuckled, "Like you won't be exactly the same when you and Cait have a baby."

"Nah, I'll be the laid-back, cool dad."

"Keep telling yourself that, asshole."

"Shh, E. You can't swear in front of the tiny human."

Enzo rolled his eyes before turning his attention to me. "Where did you get to last night anyway?"

"I was at some bar."

"With a guy?"

"With a group of people." The lie came easily.

"Yeah, but what people? You dropped us for a bunch of—"

Gio appeared, and Enzo said, "And where the fuck did you get to?"

"Leave it, man. I feel like shit." He stalked over to the coffee machine and made himself a strong coffee.

My stomach dipped. Had he been that drunk? Had I completely misread the signs? I'd been tipsy too, but I'd been fully aware of what I was doing.

Gio's eyes flashed to mine but moved right past me, sending a trickle of dejection down my spine.

This was awkward.

So awkward that I stood abruptly. "I'm going to take a shower."

I hurried out of there, not sparing Gio a second glance. But not quick enough to avoid hearing my brother say, "She's acting weird. Maybe it's shark week."

Their laughter chased me down the hall and up the stairs.

I'd agreed to one night.

I'd said that.

Seeing him this morning, though, replaying last night over in my mind... it was crystal clear I'd been fooling myself.

One night wasn't enough.

But it was all he was willing to give to me.

A knock at the door startled me as I towel-dried my hair.

"Just a minute," I called, half expecting to see Alessia or my brother standing at the door as I yanked it open. "Gio."

The air thinned around us as he stared at me. "I..." His eyes dropped down my body, heat flaring in his dark depths. When his gaze settled on my face again, I felt it down to my soul. "Can we talk?"

"Sure." I invited him inside, closing the door behind us. "Let me just grab a robe."

His heated stare followed me all the way to my small en suite. I grabbed the fluffy robe and pulled it over my body, throwing the towel over a hook.

"What's up?" I asked, trying to remain casual.

"I... fuck." He ran a hand through his hair and down the back of his neck.

"Gio," I snapped.

"Shit, sorry. It's just I didn't expect to find you like this."

"This?" My brows knitted.

"Yeah, fresh out of the shower, looking… like this."

"This?"

"Fuckable. You look fuckable, Bella."

"Oh." My stomach clenched.

"What's wrong?" He stepped into me, and my breath caught as I craned my neck to look up at him.

"I… what do you want, Gio?"

"I came to apologize about how I left things last night. It was a dick move. But I panicked."

"It's fine. It was one night, right? You didn't want to turn it into something it wasn't. I get it." I shrugged, dropping my gaze a little. Because looking at him was dangerous. Losing myself in his eyes was dangerous.

Wanting things I couldn't have… was dangerous.

"You get it? Good, that's…" He swallowed. "Good."

"So we're cool?"

"Yeah, we're cool, Bambina."

"Okay, so you should probably go."

"Go, yeah. Right." He started backing up toward the door, his eyes still fixated on me.

"Gio, what—"

"Fuck it," he murmured before striding toward me and taking my face in his hands, kissing me.

My hands went to his sweater, fisting the material as he ravaged my mouth. Plunging his tongue past my lips and licking. Dominating.

All I could do was cling to him, my head swimming with confusion and lust. Desire and uncertainty.

"W-what was that?" I breathed when he pulled away.

"I… fuck, I don't know. But you were standing there looking like that and saying all that shit about it being one night, and I… shit, Bella. What have you done to me?"

"Me?" I gasped. "What have I done?"

"You are so fucking beautiful." He trailed his finger along my jaw and down my throat. "I laid awake most of the night thinking of you. Of how I left things."

"You panicked."

"I did." His hand curved around my neck, holding me there.

"I like you, Gio."

There. I'd said it. What he chose to do with those three words was on him.

"I know, I like you too, Bambina. But it's not that simple. You deserve more than me. I'm broken. And your brother—"

"This is not about my brother or our families. This is about us." I ran my hands up his chest. "About what we want. What do you want, Gio Abato?"

My heart crashed violently against my chest as I waited for his answer. The words that could change everything.

A beat passed. Two… Three.

Until the hope inside me began to wither. Because he wasn't saying anything, and with every second that passed, I realized that maybe whatever existed between us wasn't enough to mend his broken heart.

That I wasn't enough.

Finally, he cleared his throat, "Bella, I…"

"Don't. Don't say it." My eyes shuttered, but I forced myself to take a deep, calming breath. "It's okay. I get it. You're not ready. Just let's promise each other not to make this weird. We only have another couple of days, and then we can go our separate ways and pretend this never happened."

I went to walk away, but his grip on me tightened. "Wait," he said. "You think I want to forget about last night?"

"Don't you?" I frowned up at him.

"Are you kidding me? Last night was… it was amazing. You were amazing. I'm just a little rusty, and honestly, I feel out of my depth here. You're… perfect, Bella. But your family, they kind of scare me a little." Gio touched his head to mine, breathing me in.

"I'm not asking for anything more than you're willing to give me," I said, and it was the truth.

He'd had his heart broken. Healing took time. Moving on took time. But I wanted to be the one to help him do it.

"We can spend some time together, and see where this goes. We don't have to tell anyone yet."

"You'd do that? Keep this thing between us a secret?"

"For now, until we figure out things, yes."

"Your brother will cut off my balls if he finds out about this."

"I can handle Matteo, Gio." My lips curved. "Besides, he has his hands full with Caitlin and our nieces."

Lucia especially loved her Uncle Matt.

But Gio wasn't smiling. "I can't promise you anything, Bella. Not yet. Not so soon after Jordan."

"The only thing I want you to promise me is full transparency. If you want to bail on whatever this is. Tell me. If you need space. Tell me. If things move too quickly. Tell me. Despite what my brother and cousins might think, I'm not a child, Gio. We can spend time together, get to know each other, and see where things go."

He gazed at me with awe. "You're pretty fucking amazing. You know that, right?"

"Hmm, I'm not sure. You should probably show me."

"Yeah?" He smirked, his eyes darting to the door behind me.

I gripped his jaw and pressed a kiss to his mouth. "We have time. You'll just have to be quick."

Gio picked me up and carried me into the bathroom, kicking the door shut behind me, my quiet laughter filling the small room.

"If I'm going to be quick, Bambina"—a wicked glint flashed in his eyes —"then you have to promise not to scream."

But I refused to answer...

Because that was one promise, I wasn't sure I could keep.

EPILOGUE

GIO

I'd never met anyone like Arabella Bellatoni.

She was confident and kind and one hundred percent unapologetic. And the sex was fucking amazing.

But it was more than that. There was something real between us. Something I was dying to explore.

We spent the rest of the weekend sneaking around behind our families' backs, making up excuses to stay behind when they ventured out onto the slopes or staying up late after everyone had gone to bed to steal some time together.

I wasn't complaining. I felt lighter than I had in months. And I was smiling again.

Smiling.

Who'd have thought?

But we avoided the heavy topics for now. Bella didn't ask about Jordan, and I didn't ask about any of her exes. Not that there had been many, according to Matteo and the guys.

I knew when they found out—and they would eventually because I wasn't in any hurry to give her up—that shit would hit the fan. But I couldn't find it in myself to care, not when it meant I got her sweet kisses and downright sinful body.

But tonight was our final night in Gstaad, and Nicco had insisted we sit down and eat as a family. So here I was, sitting opposite Arabella, trying to keep my dick in line and not imagine her on her knees for me, gazing up at me like I was all she wanted.

"Before we eat," Nicco said, standing at the head of the table. "I'd like to say a few words. Family is everything to me: my beautiful wife and daughter, my sister, my cousins, and their partners. I couldn't ask for a better group of people to do this thing called life with. I know things will be slightly different when we return to Verona County. The responsibilities I must shoulder, the footsteps I must walk, but this—all of you—will always be the most important thing in my life. To family. La famiglia e tutto.

"Family," everyone echoed back at him.

Arabella flashed me a secretive smile as she sipped her champagne.

"Now, let's eat."

"Actually." Matteo stood. "I have a few words I'd like to say."

Fuck.

My heart jumped into my chest.

"Nicco's right. Family means everything. And having the opportunity to spend this long weekend with you all has been amazing. I love my life. My family. My beautiful fiancée. Caitlin, you make me a better man, and I can't wait until the day I call you my wife." He winked at her. "And my sister. My beautiful Arabella. You wear your heart on your sleeve and deserve the world. You deserve to meet someone who will treat you like a princess. Someone who is proud to stand by your side."

Fuck.

Fuck.

Sweat beaded along my forehead and the back of my neck.

"Gio," he set his knowing gaze on mine, "something you'd like to tell me?"

"Matt," Caitlin hissed. "Not now. Not like this."

"Fuck that, Cait. He's been—"

"Spending time with her." I shot up out of my seat. "We've been spending time together."

"Sneaking around, you mean. You've been—"

"Matt!" Bella cried. "Please, don't do this. Not like this."

"State your intentions with my sister, Abato. My baby fucking sister."

"I like her." I looked him right in the eye. "I like her a lot. But it's new, and we didn't want it to become a thing before we know if it's a thing."

"Gio, you don't have to do this," she rushed out. "Sit down, Matt, and stop making a scene."

"Gio?" Nora said, a hint of disappointment in her eyes. Unlike Enzo, who looked amused by the whole thing.

Asshole.

"I'm sorry, okay. It kind of caught me off guard, too. But Bella is... well, she's kind of amazing. And I enjoy hanging out with her."

Matt stared me down, anger and betrayal swirling in his eyes. But Arabella was eighteen; she was her own person with her own mind.

"Matt, please," she said. "You always do this."

"That's not fair—"

"You'll never think anyone is good enough for me."

"Because they aren't, pulce."

"But that's for me to decide. You can't protect me forever."

"Watch me," he grumbled, but he did sit. "And you, keep your fucking hands to yourself until she's at least twenty-one."

"Matt," Cait whispered, squeezing his hand. His expression softened a fraction, and I found myself looking back at Arabella.

"Sorry," she mouthed.

The silence was deafening as everyone processed Matteo's revelation.

"Well, if that isn't a holly jolly Christmas, I don't know what is," Enzo chuckled, thrusting his glass in the air. "But be warned, Abato," he said ominously. "Break her heart, and Matt isn't the only one you need to worry about because I'll break your fucking legs."

"Welcome to the family," Nicco added with a smirk. "I hope you know what you're getting yourself into."

But oddly, their words didn't scare me. Not even a little bit.

Because Arabella was worth it.

And that one night we'd promised each other...

It would never be enough.

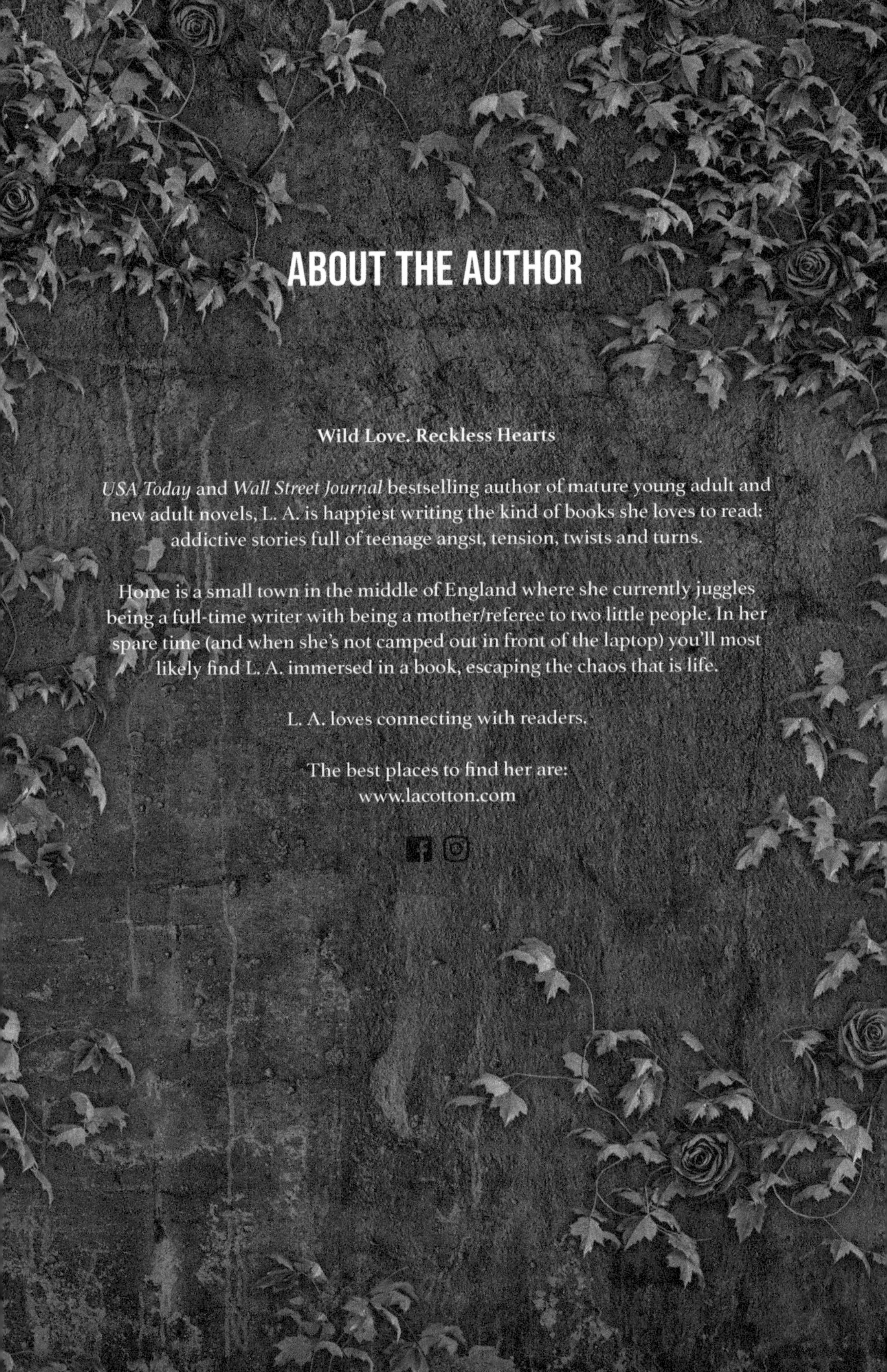

ABOUT THE AUTHOR

Wild Love. Reckless Hearts

USA Today and *Wall Street Journal* bestselling author of mature young adult and new adult novels, L. A. is happiest writing the kind of books she loves to read: addictive stories full of teenage angst, tension, twists and turns.

Home is a small town in the middle of England where she currently juggles being a full-time writer with being a mother/referee to two little people. In her spare time (and when she's not camped out in front of the laptop) you'll most likely find L. A. immersed in a book, escaping the chaos that is life.

L. A. loves connecting with readers.

The best places to find her are:
www.lacotton.com

www.ingramcontent.com/pod-product-compliance
Lightning Source LLC
Chambersburg PA
CBHW071335020826
48982CB00023B/461

9781738439829